Tom Clancy

Since the phenomenal worldwide success of *The Hunt for Red October*, his controversial, ground-breaking first novel, Tom Clancy has become the world's fastest-selling author. Three of his novels have been made into highly successful films: *The Hunt for Red October*, *Patriot Games* and *Clear and Present Danger*. He is also the author of the non-fiction books *Submarine*, *Armoured Warfare*, *Fighter Wing* and *Marine*, and co-creator of the *Op-Centre* series. Tom Clancy lives in Maryland, USA.

Executive Orders has become his most successful book ever, a record-breaking *Sunday Times* and *New York Times* #1 bestseller.

EXECUTIVE ORDERS

'Ryan is back, and not just for an encore. The pace is frantic, the detail, as ever, exhaustive . . . a relentless, plot-packed blockbuster.'
The Times

'Clancy is the supreme exponent of the technothriller: readers who want to know how to incubate a deadly virus, or what air, sea and land warfare in the near future is like, can find out here. All this is excellent and, combined with his unsurpassed ability to co-ordinate complex and multiple plot strands, make *Executive Orders* another good and gripping read.'
Sunday Times

'The ultimate disaster scenario . . . for those who like thrillers with patriotic fervour and every sort of twist from germ warfare to personal revenge.'
Daily Mail

TOM CLANCY

EXECUTIVE ORDERS

1) Haycroft Gardens
Nw 10 3BJ
London

HarperCollins*Publishers*

HarperCollins*Publishers*
77–85 Fulham Palace Road,
Hammersmith, London W6 8JB

Special overseas edition 1997
This paperback edition 1998
1 3 5 7 9 8 6 4 2

First published in Great Britain by
HarperCollins*Publishers* 1996

First published in the USA by
G. P. Putnam's Sons 1996

Copyright © Jack Ryan Limited Partnership 1996

The Author asserts the moral right to
be identified as the author of this work

ISBN 0 00 647975 8

Set in Trump Mediaeval

Printed and bound in Great Britain by
Caledonian International Book Manufacturing Ltd, Glasgow

TO

RONALD WILSON REAGAN,

FORTIETH PRESIDENT OF THE UNITED STATES:
THE MAN WHO WON THE WAR

Yenbirdeska? How are you?
Goengki?

Tanoshikata? Do you have a good time?

Sayonara

Ryoko → journy

Ryokowadodata? How about your journey?

In the original hardcover edition of *Without Remorse* are the words of a poem which I found by accident and whose title and author I was unable to identify. I found in them the perfect remembrance for my 'little buddy,' Kyle Haydock, who succumbed to cancer at the age of eight years and twenty-six days – to me he will never really be gone.

Later I learned that the title of this poem is 'Ascension,' and that the author who penned these magnificent words is Colleen Hitchcock, a poet of rare talent living in Minnesota. I wish to take this opportunity to commend her work to all students of the lyric phrase. As her words caught and excited my attention, I hope they will have the same effect on others.

The poem reads as follows:

ASCENSION

And if I go,
while you're still here. . .
Know that I live on,
vibrating to a different measure
—behind a thin veil you cannot see through.
You will not see me,
so you must have faith.
I wait for the time when we can soar together again,
—both aware of each other.
Until then, live your life to its fullest.
And when you need me,
Just whisper my name in your heart,
. . . I will be there.

I pray Heaven to bestow the best of blessings on this house and on all that shall hereafter inhabit it. May none but honest and wise men ever rule under this roof.

JOHN ADAMS,
second President of the United States,
letter to Abigail, November 2, 1800,
on moving into the White House

ACKNOWLEDGMENTS

Again, I needed a lot of help:

Peggy, for some valued insights;
Mike, Dave, John, Janet, Curt and Pat at
the Johns Hopkins Hospital;
Fred and his pals at the USSS;
Pat, Darrell and Bill, all repeat offenders at the FBI;
Fred and Sam, men who've honored the
uniform with their service;
H. R., Joe, Dan and Doug, who still do.

America is because of people like this.

EXECUTIVE

ORDERS

PROLOGUE

STARTING HERE

It had to be the shock of the moment, Ryan thought. He seemed to be two people at the same time. One part of him looked out the window of the lunchroom of CNN's Washington bureau and saw the fires that grew from the remains of the Capitol building – yellow points springing up from an orange glow like some sort of ghastly floral arrangement, representing over a thousand lives that had been snuffed out not an hour earlier. Numbness suppressed grief for the moment, though he knew that would come, too, as pain always followed a hard blow to the face, but not right away. Once more, Death in all its horrid majesty had reached out for him. He'd seen it come, and stop, and withdraw, and the best thing to be said about it was that his children didn't know how close their young lives had come to an early conclusion. To them, it had simply been an accident they didn't understand. They were with their mother now, and they'd feel safe in her company while their father was away somewhere. It was a situation to which both they and he long since had unhappily become accustomed. And so John Patrick Ryan looked at the residue of Death, and one part of him as yet felt nothing.

The other part of him looked at the same sight and knew that he had to *do* something, and though he struggled to be logical, logic wasn't winning, because logic didn't *know* what to do or where to start.

'Mr President.' It was the voice of Special Agent Andrea Price.

'Yes?' Ryan said without turning away from the window. Behind him – he could see the reflections in the window glass – six other Secret Service agents stood with weapons out to keep the others away. There had to be a score of CNN employees outside the door, gathered together partly from professional interest – they were newspeople, after all – but mostly from simple human curiosity at being face-to-face with a moment in history. They were wondering what it looked like to be there, and didn't quite get the fact that such events were the same for everyone. Whether presented with an auto accident or a sudden grave illness, the unprepared human mind just stopped and tried to make sense of the senseless – and the graver the test, the harder the recovery period. But at least people trained in crisis had procedures to fall back upon.

'Sir, we have to get you to –'

'Where? A place of safety? Where's that?' Jack asked, then quietly reproached himself for the cruelty of the question. At least twenty agents were part of the pyre a mile away, all of them friends of the men and women standing in the lunchroom with their new President. He had no right to transfer his discomfort to them. 'My family?' he asked after a moment.

'The Marine Barracks, Eighth and I Streets, as you ordered, sir.'

Yes, it was good for them to be able to report that they'd carried out orders, Ryan thought with a slow nod. It was also good for him to know that his orders had been carried out. He had done one thing right, anyway. Was that something to build on?

'Sir, if this was part of an organized –'

'It wasn't. They never are, Andrea, are they?' President Ryan asked. He was surprised how tired his voice sounded, and reminded himself that shock and stress were more tiring than the most strenuous exercise. He didn't even seem to have the energy to shake his head and clear it.

'They can be,' Special Agent Price pointed out.

Yes, I suppose she's right. 'So what's the drill for this?'

'Kneecap,' Price replied, meaning the National Emergency Airborne Command Post, a converted 747 kept at Andrews Air Force Base. Jack thought about the suggestion for a moment, then frowned.

'No, I can't run away. I think I have to go back there.' President Ryan pointed to the glow. *Yes, that is where I belong, isn't it?*

'No, sir, that's too dangerous.'

'That's my place, Andrea.'

4

He's already thinking like a politician, Price thought, disappointed.

Ryan saw the look on her face and knew he'd have to explain. He'd learned something once, perhaps the only thing that applied at this moment, and the thought had appeared in his mind like a flashing highway sign. 'It's a leadership function. They taught me that at Quantico. The troops have to see you doing the job. They have to know you're there for them.' *And I have to be sure that it's all real, that I actually am the President.*

Was he?

The Secret Service thought so. He'd sworn the oath, spoken the words, invoked the name of God to bless his effort, but it had all been too soon and too fast. Hardly for the first time in his life, John Patrick Ryan closed his eyes and willed himself to awaken from this dream that was just too improbable to be real, and yet when he opened his eyes again the orange glow was still there, and the leaping yellow flames. He knew he'd spoken the words – he'd even given a little speech, hadn't he? But he could not remember a single word of it now.

Let's get to work, he'd said a minute earlier. He did remember that. An automatic thing to say. Did it mean anything?

Jack Ryan shook his head – it seemed a major accomplishment to do even that – then turned away from the window to look directly at the agents in the room.

'Okay. What's left?'

'Secretaries of Commerce and Interior,' Special Agent Price responded, having been updated by her personal radio. 'Commerce is in San Francisco. Interior is in New Mexico. They've already been summoned; the Air Force will bring them in. We've lost all the other Cabinet secretaries: Director Shaw, all nine Supreme Court justices, the Joint Chiefs. We're not sure how many members of Congress were absent when it happened.'

'Mrs Durling?'

Price shook her head. 'She didn't get out, sir. The kids are at the White House.'

Jack nodded bleakly at the additional tragedy, compressed his lips, and closed his eyes at the thought of one more thing he had to do personally. For the children of Roger and Anne

Durling, it wasn't a public event. For them it was immediately and tragically simple: Mom and Dad had died, and they were now orphans. Jack had seen them, spoken with them – really nothing more than the smile and the 'Hi' that one gave to another man's kids, but they were real children with faces and names – except their surnames were all that was left, and the faces would be contorted with shock and disbelief. They'd be like Jack, trying to blink away a nightmare that would not depart, but for them it'd be all the harder because of their age and vulnerability. 'Do they know?'

'Yes, Mr President,' Andrea said. 'They were watching TV, and the agents had to tell them. They have grandparents still alive, other family members. We're bringing them in, too.' She didn't add that there was a drill for this, that at the Secret Service's operations center a few blocks west of the White House was a security file cabinet with sealed envelopes in which were contingency plans for all manner of obscene possibilities; this was merely one of them.

However, there were hundreds – no, thousands – of children without parents now, not just two. Jack had to set the Durling children aside for the moment. Hard as it was, it was also a relief to close the door on that task for the moment. He looked down at Agent Price again.

'You're telling me I'm the whole government right now?'

'It would seem that way, Mr President. That's why we –'

'That's why *I* have to do the things I have to do.' Jack headed to the door, startling the Secret Service agents into action by his impulse. There were cameras in the corridor. Ryan walked right past them, the leading wave of two agents clearing the rows of newspeople too shocked themselves to do much more than operate their cameras. Not a single question. That, Jack thought without a smile, was a singular event. It didn't occur to him to wonder what his face looked like. An elevator was waiting, and thirty seconds later, he emerged into the capacious lobby. It had been cleared of people, except for agents, more than half of whom had submachine guns out, and pointed up at the ceiling. They must have come from elsewhere – there were more than he remembered from twenty minutes earlier. Then he saw that

6

Marines stood outside, most of them improperly uniformed, some shivering in their red T-shirts over camouflaged 'utility' trousers.

'We wanted the additional security,' Price explained. 'I asked for the assistance from the barracks.'

'Yeah.' Ryan nodded. Nobody would think it unseemly for the President of the United States to be surrounded by US Marines at a time like this. They were kids, most of them, their smooth young faces showing no emotion at all – a dangerous state for people carrying weapons – their eyes surveying the parking lot like watchdogs, while tight hands gripped their rifles. A captain stood just outside the door, talking to an agent. When Ryan walked out, the Marine officer braced stiffly and saluted. *So, he thinks it's real, too.* Ryan nodded his acknowledgment and gestured to the nearest HMMWV.

'The Hill,' President John Patrick Ryan ordered curtly.

The ride was quicker than he'd expected. Police had cordoned off all the main streets, and the fire trucks were already there, probably a general alarm, for whatever good it might do. The Secret Service Suburban – a cross between a stationwagon and a light truck – led off, its lights flashing and siren screaming, while the protective detail sweated and probably swore under its collective breath at the foolishness of their new 'Boss,' the in-house term for the President.

The tail of the 747 was remarkably intact – at least the rudder fin was, recognizable, like the fletching of an arrow buried in the side of a dead animal. The surprising part for Ryan was that the fire still burned. The Capitol had been a building of stone, after all, but inside were wooden desks and vast quantities of paper, and God only knew what else that surrendered its substance to heat and oxygen. Aloft were military helicopters, circling like moths, their rotors reflecting the orange light back down at the ground. The red-and-white fire trucks were everywhere, their lights flashing red and white as well, giving additional color to the rising smoke and steam. Firefighters were racing about, and the ground was covered in hoses snaking to every hydrant in sight, bringing water to the pumpers. Many of the couplings leaked, producing little sprays of water that quickly froze in the cold night air.

The south end of the Capitol building was devastated. One could recognize the steps, but the columns and roof were gone, and the House chamber itself was a crater hidden by the rectangular lip of stones, their white color scorched and blackened with soot. To the north, the dome was down, sections of it recognizable, for it had been built of wrought iron during the Civil War, and several of the pie-slice sections had somehow retained their shape. A majority of the fire-fighting activity was there, where the center of the building had been. Countless hoses, some on the ground, some directed from the tips of aerial ladders and cherry-picker water towers, sprayed water in the hope of stopping the fire from spreading further, though from Ryan's vantage point there was no telling how successful the effort might be.

But the real story of the scene was the collection of ambulances, several knots of them, their paramedic crews standing with bitter idleness, folding stretchers before them, empty, the skilled crews with nothing to do but look at the white rudder fin with the red crane painted on it, also blackened from the fire, but still hatefully recognizable. Japan Airlines. The war with Japan had ended, everyone thought. But had it? Was this one lone, last act of defiance or revenge? Or just some hideously ironic accident? It hit Jack that the scene was very much like an auto accident, at least in kind if vastly different in scale, and for the trained men and women who'd responded, it was the same story as with so many other calls – too late. Too late to stop the fire in time. Too late to save the lives they were sworn to rescue. Too late to make much of a difference at all.

The HMMWV pulled in close to the southeast corner of the building, just outside the gaggle of fire trucks, and before Ryan could step out, a full squad of Marines had him surrounded again. One of them, the captain, opened the door for the new President.

'So, who's in charge?' Jack asked Agent Price. For the first time he noticed how bitterly cold the night was.

'I guess one of the firemen.'

'Let's find him.' Jack started walking toward a collection of pumpers. He was already starting to shiver in his light wool suit. The chiefs would be the ones with the white hats, right? And the regular cars, he remembered from his youth in Baltimore. Chiefs didn't ride in trucks. He spotted three red-painted sedans and angled that way.

'Damn it, Mr President!' Andrea Price fairly screamed at him. Other agents ran to get in front, and the Marines couldn't decide whether to lead the group or to follow. There wasn't an entry in anyone's manual for this, and what rules the Secret Service had, their Boss had just invalidated. Then one of them had a thought and sprinted off to the nearest ladder truck. He returned with a rubberized turnout coat.

'This'll keep you warm, sir,' Special Agent Raman promised, helping Ryan into it, and disguising him as one of the several hundred firefighters roaming around. Special Agent Price gave him an approving wink and nod, the first moment of almost-levity since the 747 had arrived at Capitol Hill. All the better that President Ryan didn't grasp the real reason for the heavy coat, she thought. This moment would be remembered by the protective Detail as the beginning of the management race, the Secret Service vs. the President of the United States, generally a contest of ego against cajolery.

The first chief that Ryan found was talking into a hand-held radio and trying to direct his firefighters closer into the flames. A person in civilian clothes was close by, holding a large paper roll flat on the car's hood. Probably plans of the building, Jack thought. Ryan waited a few feet away, while the two men moved hands left and right over the plans and the chief spoke staccato instructions into his radio.

'And, for Christ's sake, be careful with all those loose stones,' Chief Paul Magill finished his last command. Then he turned around and rubbed his eyes. 'Who the hell are you?'

'This is the President,' Price informed him.

Magill's eyes blinked. He took a quick look at the people with guns, then back at Ryan. 'This is pretty damned bad,' the chief said first.

'Anyone get out?'

Magill shook his head. 'Not from this side. Three people on the other side, all beat up. We think they were in the Speaker's cloak room, someplace around there, probably the explosion just shot them through the windows. Two pages and a Secret Service guy, all burned and busted up. We're conducting a search – well, we're trying to, but so far even the people who weren't roasted – they had the oxygen sucked right out of them, asphyxia, you're just as dead.' Paul Magill was Ryan's height, but a barrel-chested black man. His hands were mottled with large pale areas that gave testament to a very intimate battle with fire sometime in his professional past. His rugged face showed only sadness now, for fire wasn't a human enemy, just a mindless thing that scarred the fortunate and killed the rest. 'We might get lucky. Some people in small rooms, doors closed, like that, sir. There's a million damned rooms in this place, 'cording to these here plans. We might get a couple people out alive. I seen it happen before. But most of 'em . . .' Magill just shook his head for a moment. 'The line's holding, ought not to spread much more.'

'Nobody from the chamber?' Agent Raman asked. He really wanted to know the name of the agent who'd been blown clear, but it would not have been professional to ask. Magill just shook his head in any case.

'No.' He stared off at the diminishing glow, and added, 'It would have been real quick.' Magill shook his head again.

'I want to see,' Jack said impulsively.

'No,' Magill replied at once. 'Too dangerous. Sir, it's my fire, and my rules, okay?'

'I *have* to see,' Ryan said, more quietly. The two pairs of eyes met and communicated. Magill still didn't like it. He saw the people with guns again, and decided, wrongly, that they would support this new President, if that's what he was. Magill hadn't been watching TV when the call had come.

'Ain't gonna be pretty, sir.'

It was just after sundown in Hawaii. Rear Admiral Robert Jackson was landing at Barbers Point Naval Air Station. His peripheral vision took note of the well-lit hotels on Oahu's south shore, and a passing thought wondered what it cost to stay in one of them now. He hadn't done it since his early twenties, when two or three naval aviators would share accommodations in order to save money for hitting the bars and impressing the local women with their worldly panache. His Tomcat touched down gently, despite the lengthy ride and three aerial refuelings, because Robby still thought of himself as a fighter pilot, and therefore an artist of sorts. The fighter slowed down properly during its run-out, then turned right onto the taxiway.

'Tomcat Five-Zero-Zero, continue down to the end –'

'I've been here before, miss,' Jackson replied with a smile, breaking the rules. But he was an admiral, wasn't he? Fighter pilot *and* admiral. Who cared about rules?

'Five-Zero-Zero, there's a car waiting.'

'Thank you.' Robby could see it, there by the farthest hangar, along with a sailor waving the usual lighted wands.

'Not bad for an old guy,' the backseater noted as he folded up his maps and other unnecessary but gravely important papers.

'Your vote of approval is noted.' *I was never this stiff before*, Jackson admitted to himself. He shifted himself in the seat. His butt felt like painful lead. How could all feeling be gone, yet there still be pain? he asked himself with a rueful smile. *Too old*, was how his mind answered the question. Then his leg made its presence known. *Arthritis, damn it*. He'd had to make it an order to get Sanchez to release the fighter to him. It was too far for a COD to take him from USS *John C. Stennis* back to Pearl, and the orders had been specific enough: *Expedite return*. On that basis he'd borrowed a Tom whose fire-control system was down, and therefore was non-mission-capable anyway. The Air Force had supplied the tankers. So after seven hours of blessed silence, he'd flown half the Pacific in a fighter – doubtless for the last time. Jackson moved again as he turned the fighter toward the parking spot, and was rewarded with a back spasm.

'Is that CinCPac?' Jackson asked, spotting the white-clad figure by the blue Navy car.

Admiral David Seaton it was, and not standing erect, but leaning against the car and flipping through messages as Robby cut the engines and opened the canopy. A sailor rolled up a stepladder, the sort used by mechanics, to make Robby's descent easier. Another enlisted man – woman, actually – extracted the arriving admiral's bag from the storage compartment underneath. Somebody was in a hurry.

'Trouble,' Seaton said the moment Robby had both boots on the ground.

'I thought we won,' Jackson replied, stopping dead still on the hot concrete of the ramp. His brain was tired, too. It would be a few minutes before his thinking ran at the customary speed, though his instincts were telling him that something unusual was afoot.

'The President's dead – and we got a new one.' Seaton handed over the clipboard. 'Friend of yours. We're back to DEFCON Three for the time being.'

'What the hell . . .' Admiral Jackson said, reading the first page of dispatches. Then he looked up. 'Jack's the new . . . ?'

'Didn't you know about him becoming VP?'

Jackson shook his head. 'I was tied up with other things before I got off the boat this morning. Holy God,' Robby concluded with another shake of the head.

Seaton nodded. Ed Kealty resigned because of that sex scandal, the President persuaded Ryan to take the vice presidency until the elections next year, the Congress confirmed him, but before he could enter the chamber well, you can see what happened. Plane hit down center. 'The JCSs are all gone. The deputies are stepping in. Mickey Moore' – Army General Michael Moore, the Deputy Chairman of the Joint Chiefs – 'has put in a call for all the CINCs to come into DC, ASAP. We have a KC-10 waiting for us at Hickam.'

'Threat board?' Jackson asked. His permanent job insofar as any uniformed posting was permanent, was Deputy J-3, the number-two planning officer for the Joint Chiefs.

Seaton shrugged. 'Theoretically, it's blank. The IO's calmed down. The Japanese are out of the war business –'

Jackson finished the statement: 'But America's never been hit like this before.'

'The plane's waiting. You can change aboard. Neatness doesn't count at the moment, Robby.'

As always, the world was divided by time and space, especially time, she would have thought had she a moment to think, but she rarely did. She was over sixty, her small frame bowed down by years of selfless work, made all the worse because there were so few young ones to give her rest. That wasn't fair, really. She'd spelled others in her time, and those of generations past had done the same in their time, but not now, not for her. She did her best to put that thought aside. It was unworthy of her, unworthy of her place in the world, and certainly unworthy of her promises, made to God more than forty years before. She now had doubts about those promises, but she'd admitted them to no one, not even her confessor. Her failure to discuss them was more troubling to her conscience even than the doubts were, though she vaguely knew that her priest would speak gently to her about her sin, if that's what it was – was it? she wondered. Even if it were, yes, he'd speak gently about it. He always did, probably because he had such doubts himself, and both of them were of the age when one looks back and wonders what might have been, despite all the accomplishments of a productive and useful life.

Her sister, every bit as religious as she, had chosen the most common of the vocations and was now a grandmother, and Sister M. Jean Baptiste wondered what that was like. She'd made her choice a long time ago, in a youth she could still remember, and like all such decisions it had been made with poor reflection, however correct the choice itself had been. It had seemed simple enough at the time. They were respected, the ladies in black. In her distant youth she could recall seeing the German occupation troops nod politely to their passing, for even though it was widely suspected that the nuns aided Allied airmen, and maybe even Jews trying to escape, it was also known that the nursing order treated everyone equally and fairly, because God required it. Besides even the Germans wanted their hospital when they were wounded, because you had a better chance there than anywhere else. It was a proud tradition, and even though Pride was a sin, it was one the dark ladies had committed after a fashion, telling themselves that perhaps God didn't mind, because the tradition was in His Holy Name. And so when the time had been right, she'd made the decision, and that was that. Some had left, but the critical time for her to make such a choice had been difficult, what with the condition of the country after the war, and the need for her skills, and a world that had not yet changed enough for her to see her options for what they were. So she had thought about leaving, briefly, and put the idea aside, and stayed with her work.

Sister Jean Baptiste was a skilled and experienced nurse. She'd come to this place when it had still belonged to her parent country, and stayed after its status had changed. In that time she'd done her job the same way, with the same skill, despite the tornadic political changes that had gone on around her, no matter that her patients were African or European. But forty years, more than thirty of that in this same place, had taken their toll.

It wasn't that she didn't care anymore. Certainly it wasn't that. It was just that she was almost sixty-five, and that was just too old to be a nurse with too few aides, often as not working fourteen-hour days, with a few hours for prayer tossed in, good for her soul but tiring for everything else. In younger years her body had been robust – not to say rugged – and healthy, and more than one of the physicians had called her Sister Rock, but the physicians had gone their way, and she had stayed and stayed and stayed, and even rocks can be worn down. And with fatigue came mistakes.

She knew what to be wary of. You could not be a health-care professional in Africa and not be careful if you wanted to live. Christianity had been trying to establish itself here for centuries, but while it had made some inroads, it might never make others. One of those problems was sexual prom-iscuity, a local proclivity that had horrified her on her arrival nearly two generations earlier, but was now just . . . normal. But all too often lethally so. Fully a third of the patients in the hospital had what was known locally as 'the thin disease' and elsewhere as AIDS. The precautions for that ailment were set in stone, and Sister Jean Baptiste had taught them in courses. The sad truth was that, as with the plagues of old, all that the medical professionals could really do with this modern curse was to protect themselves.

Fortunately with this patient, that was not a concern. The boy was only eight, too young to be sexually active. A hand-some boy, well formed and bright, he'd been an honor student at the nearby Catholic school, and an acolyte. Perhaps he'd hear the call someday and become a priest – that was easier for the Africans than the Europeans, since the Church, in quiet deference to African customs, allowed priests down here to marry, a secret that was not widely known through the rest of the world. But the boy was ill. He'd come in only a few hours earlier, at midnight, driven in by his father, a fine man who was a senior official in the local government and had a car of his own. The doctor on call had diagnosed the boy with cerebral malaria, but the entry on the chart wasn't confirmed by the usual laboratory test. Perhaps the blood sample had gotten lost. Violent headaches, vomiting, shaking of the limbs, disorientation, spiking fever. Cerebral malaria. She hoped *that* wasn't going to break out again. It was <u>treatable</u>, but the problem was getting people *to* treatment.

The rest of the ward was quiet this late at – no, early in the morning, actually – a pleasant time in this part of the world. The air was as cool as it would get in any twenty-four-hour period, and still, and quiet – and so were the patients. The boy's biggest problem at the moment was the fever, and so she pulled back the sheet and sponged him down. It seemed to calm his restless young body, and she took the time to examine him for other symptoms. The doctors were doctors, and she but a nurse – even so, she'd been here for a very long time, and knew what to look for. There wasn't much really, except for an old bandage on his left hand. How had the doctor overlooked that? Sister Jean Baptiste walked back to the nurses' station, where her two aides were dozing. What she was about to do was properly their job, but there was no sense in waking them. She returned to the patient with fresh dressings and disinfectant. You had to be careful with infections down here. Carefully, slowly, she peeled off the bandage, herself blinking with fatigue. A bite, she saw, like one from a small dog . . . or a monkey. That made her blink hard. Those could be dangerous. She ought to have walked back to the station and gotten rubber gloves, but it was forty meters away, and her legs were tired, and the patient was resting, the hand unmoving. She uncapped the disinfectant, then rotated the hand slowly and gently to fully expose the injury. When she shook the bottle with her other hand, a little escaped from around her thumb and it sprinkled on the patient's face. The head came up, and he sneezed in his sleep, the usual cloud of droplets ejected into the air. Sister Jean Baptiste was startled, but didn't stop; she poured the disinfectant on a cotton ball, and carefully swabbed the wound. Next she capped the bottle and set it down, applied the new bandage, and only then did she wipe her face with the back of her hand, without realizing that when her patient had sneezed, his wounded hand in hers had jerked, depositing blood there, and that it had been on her hand as it had swept across her eyes. The gloves, therefore, might not have mattered at all, a fact that would have been of scant comfort even if she had remembered it, three days hence.

Should have stayed put, Jack told himself. Two paramedics had guided him up a clear corridor on the east steps, along with the gaggle of Marines and agents, all moving upward with guns still out in a scene of grimly obscene humor, no one knowing quite what to do. They then had encountered a nearly solid line of firefighters and hoses, spraying their water, much of which blew back in everyone's faces in the sort of chill that ran straight into the bones. Here the fire had been smothered by the water fog, and though the hoses continued to wet things down, it was safe for rescue personnel from the ladder companies to creep into the remains of the chamber. One didn't have to be an expert to understand what they found. No lifted heads, no urgent gestures, no shouts. The men – and women, though one couldn't tell at this distance – picked their way carefully, more mindful of their own safety than anything else, because there was plainly no reason to risk one's life on behalf of the dead.

Dear God, he thought. People he knew were here. Not just Americans. Jack could see where a whole section of gallery had fallen down to the well of the chamber. The diplomatic gallery, if he remembered correctly. Various dignitaries and their families, many of whom he'd known, who had come to the Hill for the purpose of seeing him sworn. Did that make their deaths his fault?

He'd left the CNN building because of the need to do something, or that was what he'd told himself. Ryan wasn't so sure now. Just a change of scenery, perhaps? Or was he merely drawn to the scene the same way the people at the perimeter of the Capitol grounds were, standing silently as he was, just looking, as he was, and not doing anything, as he was. The numbness hadn't gone away. He'd come here expecting to find something to see and feel and then to do, but only discovered something else for his soul to shrink from.

'It's cold here, Mr President. At least get out of this damned spray,' Price urged.

'Okay.' Ryan nodded and headed back down the steps. The

coat, he found, wasn't all that warm. Ryan was shivering again, and he hoped it was merely from the cold.

The cameras had been slow setting up, but they were there now, Ryan saw. The little portable ones – Japanese made, all of them, he noted with a grunt – with their small, powerful lights. Somehow they'd managed to get past the police lines and the fire chiefs. Before each of them stood a reporter – the three he could see were all men – holding a microphone and trying to sound as though he knew more than anyone else did. Several lights were trained his own way, Jack noted. People all over the country and the world were watching him, expecting him to know what to do. How did such people ever adopt the illusion that senior government officials were any brighter than their family physician, or lawyer, or accountant? His mind trekked back to his first week as a second lieutenant in the Marine Corps, when the institution which he'd served then had similarly assumed that he knew how to command and lead a platoon – and when a sergeant ten years his senior had come to him with a family problem, expecting the 'ell-tee,' who lacked both a wife and children, to know what to say to a man who had trouble with both. Today, Jack reminded himself, such a situation was called a 'leadership challenge,' meaning that you didn't have a clue about what to do next. But there were the cameras, and he had to do something.

Except he still didn't have a clue. He'd come here hoping to find a catalyst for action, only to find increased feelings of helplessness. And maybe a question.

'Arnie van Damm?' He'd need Arnie, sure as hell.

'At the House, sir,' Price replied, meaning the White House.

'Okay, let's head over there,' Ryan ordered.

'Sir,' Price said, after a moment's hesitation, 'that's probably not safe. If there was –'

'I can't run away, damn it. I can't fly away on Kneecap. I can't sneak off to Camp David. I can't crawl into some damned hole. Can't you see that?' He was frustrated rather than angry. His right arm pointed to the remains of the Capitol building. 'Those people are dead, and I *am* the government for now, God help me, and the government doesn't run away.'

*   *   *

17

'That looks like President Ryan there,' an anchorman said in his warm, dry studio. 'Probably trying to get a handle on rescue operations. Ryan is a man not unaccustomed to crisis, as we all know.'

'I've known Ryan for six years,' a more senior network analyst opined, studiously not looking at the camera, so as to give the appearance of instructing the more highly paid anchorman who was trying to report on the event. Both had been in the studio to provide commentary for President Durling's speech, and had read all the briefing material on Ryan, whom the analyst didn't really know, though they'd bumped into each other at various dinners during the past few years. 'He's a remarkably low-key gentleman, but without question one of the brightest people in government service.' Such a statement could not go unchallenged. Tom the anchor leaned forward, half-looking at his colleague, and half at the cameras.

'But, John, he's not a politician. He has no political background or experience. He's a national-security specialist in an age when national security is not the issue it once was,' he pontificated.

John the analyst managed to stifle the reply that the statement so richly deserved. Someone else did not.

'Yeah,' Chavez grumbled. 'And that airplane that took the building out was really a Delta flight that got lost. Jesus!' he concluded.

'It's a great country we serve, Ding, my boy. Where else do people get paid five mill' a year to be stupid?' John Clark decided to finish his beer. There was no sense in driving back to Washington until Mary Pat called. He was a worker bee, after all, and only the top-floor CIA types would be racing around now. And racing around they would be. They wouldn't be accomplishing much, but at times like this you *didn't* really accomplish much of anything, except to look harried and important ... and to the worker bees, ineffective.

With little to show the public, the network reran tape of President Durling's speech. The C-SPAN cameras in the chamber had been remotely controlled, and control-room technicians froze various frames to show the front row of senior government officials, and, again, the roll of the dead was cataloged: All but two of the Cabinet secretaries, the Joint Chiefs of Staff, senior agency directors, the Chairman of the Federal Reserve Board, Director Bill Shaw of the FBI, the Director of the Office of Management and Budget, the Administrator of NASA, all nine Justices of the Supreme Court. The anchorman's voice listed the names and the positions they'd held, and the tape advanced frame by frame until the moment when the Secret Service agents were shown racing into the chamber, startling President Durling and causing some brief confusion. Heads turned, looking for danger, and perhaps the quicker-minded among them had wondered about the presence of a gunman in the galleries, but then came three frames from a wide-shot camera that showed the blurred displacement of the back wall, followed by blackness. Anchor and commentator were then back on-screen, staring down at their desktop monitors, then back up at each other, and perhaps only now the full enormity of the event finally began to hit them, as it was hitting the new President.

'President Ryan's principal task will be to rebuild the government, if he can,' John the analyst said, after a long moment's pause. 'My God, so many good men and women . . . dead . . .' It had also occurred to him that a few years earlier, before becoming the senior network commentator, he would have been in that chamber, along with so many of his professional friends; and for him, also, the event finally broke past the shock, and his hands started quivering below the top of the desk. An experienced pro who did not allow his voice to shake, he nonetheless could not totally control the look on his face, which sagged with sudden, awful grief, and on the screen his face went ashen under the makeup.

'God's judgment,' Mahmoud Haji Daryaei muttered over six thousand miles away, lifting the controller and muting the sound to eliminate extraneous twaddle.

God's judgment. That made sense, didn't it? America. The colossus that had thwarted so many, a godless land of godless people, at the pinnacle of her power, winner of yet another contest – now, grievously harmed. How else but by God's will could such a thing happen? And what else could it mean

19

but God's own judgment, and God's own blessing? Blessing on what? he wondered. Well, perhaps that would be clear with reflection.

He'd met Ryan once before, found him spiteful and arrogant – typically American – but not now. The cameras momentarily zoomed in to show a man clutching at his coat, his head turning left and right, mouth slightly open. No, not arrogant now. Stunned, not even aware enough to be frightened. It was a look he'd seen on men's faces before. How interesting.

The same words and the same images were flooding the world now, delivered by satellites to over a billion pairs of eyes that'd been watching the news coverage, or been alerted to the event and had changed channels from morning shows in some countries, lunch and evening shows in others. History had been made, and there was an imperative to watch.

This was particularly true of the powerful, for whom information was the raw material of power. Another man in another place looked at the electronic clock that sat next to the television on his desk and did some simple arithmetic. A horrid day was ending in America, while a morning was well begun where he sat. The window behind his desk showed a wide expanse of paving stones, a huge square, in fact, criss-crossed by people mainly traveling by bicycle, though the number of cars he saw was now substantial, having grown by a factor of ten over the past few years. But still bicycles were the main mode of transportation, and that wasn't fair, was it?

He'd planned to change that, quickly and decisively in historical terms – and he was a serious student of history – only to have his carefully laid plan killed aborning by the Americans. He didn't believe in God, never had and never would, but he did believe in Fate, and Fate was what he saw before his eyes on the phosphor screen of a television set manufactured in Japan. A fickle woman, Fate was, he told himself as he reached for a handleless cup of green tea. Only days before she had favored the Americans with luck, and now, this . . . So what was the intention of the Lady Fate? His own intentions and needs and will mattered more, the man decided. He reached for his phone, then thought better of it. It would ring soon enough, and others would ask his opinion, and he would have to answer with something, and so it was time to think. He sipped his tea. The heated water stung his mouth, and that was good. He would have to be alert, and the pain focused his mind inward, where important thoughts always began.

Undone or not, his plan hadn't been a bad one. Poorly executed by his unwitting agents, largely because of the Lady Fate and her momentary largesse to America – but it had been a fine plan, he told himself yet again. He'd have another chance to prove that. Because of the Lady Fate. The thought occasioned a thin smile, and a distant look, as his mind probed the future and liked what it saw. He hoped the phone would not ring for a while, because he had to look further still, and that was best done without interference. It came to him after a moment's further thought that the real objective of his plan had been accomplished, hadn't it? He'd wished America to be crippled, and crippled America now was. Not in the manner he'd chosen, but crippled even so. *Even better!* he asked himself.

Yes.

And so, the game could go on, couldn't it?

It *was* the Lady Fate, toying as she did with the ebb and flow of history. She wasn't a friend or enemy of any man, really – or was she? The man snorted. Maybe she just had a sense of humor.

For another person, the emotion was anger. Days before had come the humiliation, the bitter humiliation of being told by a foreigner – nothing more than a former provincial governor! – what her sovereign nation must do. She'd been very careful, of course. Everything had been done with great skill. The government itself had not been implicated in anything more than extensive naval exercises on the open sea, which was, of course, free for the passage of all. No threatening notes had been dispatched, no official démarche issued, no position taken, and for their part the Americans hadn't done anything more than – what was their arrogant phrase, 'rattle their cage'? – and call for a meeting of the Security Council, at which there was nothing to be said, really, since nothing official had taken place, and her country had made no announcement. What they had done was nothing more than *exercises*, weren't they? *Peaceful* exercises. Of course, those exercises had helped split the American capability against Japan – but she couldn't have known ahead of time, could she? Of course not.

She had the document on her desk at this very moment: the time required to restore the fleet to full capability. But, no, she shook her head, it wouldn't be enough. Neither she nor her country could act alone now. It would take time and friends, and plans, but her country had needs, and it was her job to see to those needs. It was not her job to accept commands from others, was it?

No.

She also drank tea, from a fine china cup, with sugar and a little milk in the English way, a product of her birth and station and education, all of which, along with patience, had brought her to this office. Of all the people around the world watching the same picture from the same satellite network, she probably understood the best what the opportunity was, how vast and appealing it had to be, all the sweeter that it had come so soon after she'd been dictated to in this very office. By a man who was now dead. It was too good to pass up, wasn't it?

Yes.

'This is scary, Mr C.' Domingo Chavez rubbed his eyes – he'd been awake for more hours than his jet-lagged brain could compute – and tried to organize his thoughts. He was sprawled back on the living-room couch, shoeless feet up on the coffee table. The womenfolk in the house were off to bed, one in anticipation of work the next day, and the other with a college exam to face. The latter hadn't figured that there might not be any school tomorrow.

'Tell me why, Ding,' John Clark commanded. The time for worrying himself about the relative skills of various TV personalities had passed, and his young partner *was*, after all, pursuing his master's degree in international relations.

Chavez spoke without opening his eyes. 'I don't think anything like this has ever happened in peacetime before. The world ain't all that different from what it was last week, John. Last week, it was real complicated. We kinda won that little war we were in, but the world ain't changed much, and we're not any stronger than we were then, are we?'

'Nature abhors a vacuum?' John asked quietly.

'Sum'tim like that.' Chávez yawned. 'Damned if we ain't got one here and now.'

'Not accomplishing very much, am I?' Jack asked, in a voice both quiet and bleak. It was hitting him full force now. There was still a glow, though most of what rose into the sky now was steam rather than smoke. What went into the building was the most depressing sight. Body bags. Rubberized fabric with loop handles at the ends, and some sort of zipper in the middle. Lots of them, and some were coming out now, carried by pairs of firefighters, snaking down the wide steps around the fragments of broken masonry. It had just started, and would not end soon. He hadn't actually seen a body during his few minutes up top. Somehow, seeing the first few bags was worse.

'No, sir,' Agent Price said, her face looking the same as his. 'This isn't good for you.'

'I know.' Ryan nodded and looked away.

I don't know what to do, he told himself. *Where's the manual, the training course for this job? Whom do I ask? Where do I go?*

I don't want this job! his mind screamed at itself. Ryan reproached himself for the venality of the thought, but he'd come to this newly dreadful place as some sort of leadership demonstration, parading himself before the TV cameras as though he knew what he was about – and that was a lie. Perhaps not a malicious one. Just stupid. *Walk up to the fire chief and ask how it's going, as though anyone with eyes and a second-grade education couldn't figure that one out!*

'I'm open to ideas,' Ryan said at last.

Special Agent Andrea Price took a deep breath and fulfilled the fantasy of every special agent of the United States Secret Service all the way back to Pinkerton: 'Mr President, you really need to get your, er, stuff' – she couldn't go *that* far – 'together. Some things you can do and some things you can't. You have people working for you. For starters, sir, figure out who they are and let them do their jobs. Then, maybe, you can start doing yours.'

'Back to the House?'

'That's where the phones are, Mr President.'

'Who's head of the Detail?'

'It was Andy Walker.' Price didn't have to say where he was now. Ryan looked down at her and made his first presidential decision.

'You just got promoted.'

Price nodded. 'Follow me, sir.' It pleased the agent to see that this President, like all the others, could learn to follow orders. Some of the time, anyway. They'd made it all of ten feet before Ryan slipped on a patch of ice and went down, to be picked back up by two agents. It only made him look all the more vulnerable. A still photographer captured the moment, giving *Newsweek* its cover photo for the following week.

'As you see, President Ryan is now leaving the Hill in what looks like a military vehicle instead of a Secret Service car. What do you suppose he's up to?' the anchor asked.

'In all fairness to the man,' John the commentator said, 'it's unlikely that he knows at the moment.'

That opinion rang across the globe a third of a second later, to the general agreement of all manner of persons, friends and enemies alike.

Some things have to be done fast. He didn't know if they were the right things – well, he did, and they weren't – but at a certain level of importance the rules got a little muddled, didn't they? The scion of a political family whose public service went back a couple of generations, he'd been in public life practically since leaving law school, which was another way of saying that he hadn't held a real job in his entire life. Perhaps he had little practical experience in the economy except as its beneficiary – his family's financial managers ran the various trusts and portfolios with sufficient skill that he almost never bothered meeting with them except at tax time. Perhaps he had never practiced law – though he'd had a hand in passing literally thousands of them. Perhaps he had never served his country in uniform – though he deemed himself an expert in national security. Perhaps a lot of things militated against doing anything. But he knew government,

24

for that had been his profession for all of his active – not to say 'working' – life, and at a time like this, the country needed someone who really knew government. The country needed healing, Ed Kealty thought, and he knew about that.

So, he lifted his phone and made a call. 'Cliff, this is Ed . . .'

1

STARTING NOW

The FBI's emergency command center on the fifth floor of the Hoover building is an odd-shaped room, roughly triangular and surprisingly small, with room for only fifteen or so people to bump shoulders. Number sixteen to arrive, tieless and wearing casual clothes, was Deputy Assistant Director Daniel E. Murray. The senior watch officer was his old friend, Inspector Pat O'Day. A large-framed, rugged man who raised beef cattle as a hobby at his northern Virginia home – this 'cowboy' had been born and educated in New Hampshire, but his boots were custom-made – O'Day had a phone to his ear, and the room was surprisingly quiet for a crisis room during a real crisis. A curt nod and raised hand acknowledged Murray's entry. The senior agent waited for O'Day to conclude the call.

'What's going on, Pat?'

'I was just on the phone with Andrews. They have tapes of the radar and stuff. I have agents from the Washington Field Office heading there to interview the tower people. National Transportation Safety Board will have people there, too, to assist. Initial word, looks like a Japan Airlines 747 kamikaze'd in. The Andrews people say the pilot declared an emergency as an unscheduled KLM flight and drove straight over their runways, hung a little left, and . . . well . . .' O'Day shrugged. 'WFO has people on the Hill now to commence the investigation. I'm assuming this one goes on the books as a terrorist incident, and that gives us jurisdiction.'

'Where's the ADIC?' Murray asked, meaning the Assistant Director in Charge of the Bureau's Washington office, quartered at Buzzard's Point on the Potomac River.

'St Lucia with Angie, taking a vacation. Tough luck for Tony.' The inspector grunted. Tony Caruso had gotten away only three days earlier. 'Tough day for a lot of people. The body count's going to be huge, Dan, lots worse'n Oklahoma.

I've sent out a general alert for forensics experts. Mess like this, we'll have to identify a lot of bodies from DNA. Oh, the TV guys are asking how it's possible for the Air Force to let this happen.' A shake of the head accompanied the conclusion. O'Day needed somebody to dump on, and the TV commentators were the most attractive target of opportunity. There would be others in due course; both hoped the FBI would not be one of them.

'Anything else we know?'

Pat shook his head. 'Nope. It's going to take time, Dan.'

'Ryan?'

'Was on the Hill, should be on his way to the White House. They caught him on TV. He looks kinda rocky. Our brothers and sisters at USSS are having a really bad night, too. The guy I talked to ten minutes ago almost lost it. We might end up having a jurisdictional conflict over who runs the investigation.'

'Great.' Murray snorted. 'We'll let the AG sort that one –' But there wasn't an Attorney General, and there wasn't a Secretary of the Treasury for him to call.

Inspector O'Day didn't have to run through it. A federal statute empowered the United States Secret Service as lead agency to investigate any attack on the President. But another federal statute gave FBI jurisdiction over terrorism. A local statute for murder also brought the Washington Metropolitan Police in, of course. Toss in the National Transportation Safety Board – until proven otherwise, it could merely be a horrible aircraft accident – and that was just the beginning. Every agency had authority and expertise. The Secret Service, smaller than the FBI, and with fewer resources, did have some superb investigators, and some of the finest technical experts around. NTSB knew more about airplane crashes than anyone in the world. But the Bureau had to be the lead agency for this investigation, didn't it? Murray thought. Except that Director Shaw was dead, and without him to swing the clout club . . .

Jesus, Murray thought. He and Bill went back to the Academy together. They'd worked in the same squad as rookie street agents in riverside Philadelphia, chasing bank robbers . . .

Pat read his face and nodded. 'Yeah, Dan, takes time to

catch up, doesn't it? We've been gutted like a fish, man.' He handed over a sheet from a legal pad with a handwritten list of known dead.

A nuclear strike wouldn't have hurt us this badly, Murray realized as he scanned the names. A developing crisis would have given ample strategic warning, and slowly, quietly, senior people would have left Washington for various places of safety, many of them would have survived – or so the planners went – and after the strike there would have been some sort of functioning government to pick up the pieces. But not now.

Ryan had come to the White House a thousand times, to visit, to deliver briefings, for meetings important and otherwise, and most recently to work in his own office as National Security Advisor. This was the first time he hadn't had to show ID and walk through the metal detectors – more properly, he did walk straight through one from force of habit, but this time, when the buzzer went off, he just kept walking without even reaching for his keys. The difference in demeanor of the Secret Service agents was striking. Like anyone else, they were comforted by familiar surroundings, and though the entire country had just had another lesson in how illusory 'safety' was, the illusion was real enough for trained professionals to feel more at ease within the substance of a lie. Guns were holstered, coats buttoned, and long breaths taken as the entourage came in through the East Entrance.

An inner voice told Jack that this was now his house, but he had no wish to believe it. Presidents liked to call it the People's House, to use the political voice of false modesty to describe a place for which some of them would have willingly run over the bodies of their own children, then say that it wasn't really all that big a thing. If lies could stain the walls, Jack reflected, then this building would have a very different name. But there was greatness here, too, and that was more intimidating than the pettiness of politics. Here James Monroe had promulgated the Monroe Doctrine and propelled his country into the strategic world for the first time. Here Lincoln had held his country together through the sheer force of his own will. Here Teddy Roosevelt had made America a real global player, and sent his Great White Fleet around the world to announce American. Here Teddy's distant cousin had saved his country from internal chaos and despair, with little more than a nasal voice and an up-angled cigarette holder. Here Eisenhower had exercised power so skillfully that hardly anyone had noticed his doing anything at all. Here Kennedy had faced down Khrushchev, and nobody had cared that doing so had covered a multitude of blunders. Here Reagan had plotted the destruction of America's most dangerous enemy, only to be accused of sleeping most of the time. What ultimately counted more – the achievements or the dirty little secrets committed by imperfect men who only briefly stepped beyond their weaknesses? But those brief and halting steps made up the sort of history that lived, while the rest was, mainly, forgotten – except by revisionist historians who just didn't get the fact that people weren't supposed to be perfect.

But it still wasn't his house.

The entrance was a tunnel of sorts, which headed under the East Wing, where the First Lady – until ninety minutes earlier Anne Durling – had her offices. By law the First Lady was a private citizen – an odd fiction for someone with a paid staff – but in reality her functions were often hugely important, however unofficial they might be. The walls here were those of a museum, not a home, as they walked past the small White House theater, where the President could watch movies with a hundred or so close personal friends. There were several sculptures, many by Frederic Remington, and the general motif was supposed to be 'pure' American. The paintings were of past presidents, and Ryan's eyes caught them – their lifeless eyes seemed to look down at him with suspicion and doubt. All the men who had gone before, good and bad, whether judged well or poorly by historians, they looked at him –

I'm an historian, Ryan told himself. *I've written a few books. I've judged the actions of others from a safe distance of both time and space. Why didn't he see this? Why didn't he do that?* Now, too late, he knew better. He was *here* now, and from the inside it looked very different. From the outside you could see in, looking around first to catch all the information and analyze it as it passed by, stopping it when you had to, even making it go backward, the better to understand it all, taking your time to get things exactly right.

But from the inside it wasn't that way at all. Here everything came directly at you like a series of onrushing trains, from all directions at once, moving by their own time schedules, leaving you little room to maneuver or reflect. Ryan could sense that already. And the people in the paintings had mainly come to this place with the luxury of time to think about their ascension, with the luxury of trusted advisers, and of good will. Those were benefits he didn't have. To historians, however, they wouldn't matter for much more than a cursory paragraph, or maybe even a whole page, before the writer moved on with pitiless analysis.

Everything he said or did, Jack knew, would be subjected to the 20/20 vision of hindsight – and not just from this moment forward. People would now look into his past for information on his character, his beliefs, his actions good and bad. From the moment the aircraft had struck the Capitol building, he was President, and *every* breath he'd drawn since would be examined in a new and unforgiving light for generations to come. His daily life would have no privacy, and even in death he would not be safe from scrutiny by people who had no idea what it was like merely to walk into this oversized dwelling-office-museum and know that it was your prison into all eternity. The bars were invisible, perhaps, but even more real because of it.

So many men had lusted for this job, only to find how horrid and frustrating it was. Jack knew *that* from his own historical readings, and from seeing three men at close quarters who'd occupied the Oval Office. At least they had come here with eyes supposedly open, and perhaps they could be blamed for having minds smaller than their egos. How much the worse for someone who'd never wished for it? And would history judge Ryan more kindly for it? That was worth an ironic snort. No, he'd come to this House at a time when his country *needed*, and if he didn't meet that need, then he'd be cursed for all future time as a failure, even though he'd come to the job only by accident – condemned by a man now dead to do the job which the other man had craved.

For the Secret Service, this was a time to relax a little. Lucky them, Ryan thought, allowing bitterness to creep into his mind, unfair or not. It was their job to protect him and his family. It was his job now to protect them and theirs, and those of millions of others.

'This way, Mr President.' Price turned left into the ground-floor corridor. Here Ryan first saw the White House staff people, standing there to see their new charge, the man whom they would serve to the best of their abilities. Like everyone else, they just stood and looked, without knowing what to say, their eyes evaluating the man and without revealing what they thought, though they would surely exchange views in the privacy of their locker or lunchrooms at the first possible moment. Jack's tie was still crooked in his collar, and he still wore the turnout coat. The water spray that had frozen in his hair and given him an undeserved gray look was melting now. One of the staff members raced out of sight as the entourage continued west. He reappeared a minute later, darting through the security detail and handing Ryan a towel.

'Thank you,' Jack said in surprise. He stood still for a moment and started drying his hair. There he saw a photographer running backward and aiming his camera, snapping merrily away. The Secret Service didn't impede him in any way. That, Ryan thought, made him a member of the staff, the official White House photographer whose job it was to memorialize everything. *Great, my own people spy on me!* But it wasn't time to interfere with anything, was it?

'Where are we going, Andrea?' Jack asked as they passed yet more portraits of Presidents and First Ladies, all staring at him . . .

'The Oval Office. I thought . . .'

'Situation Room.' Ryan stopped dead, still toweling off. 'I'm not ready for that room yet, okay?'

'Of course, Mr President.' At the end of the wide corridor they turned left into a small foyer walled with cheap-looking wood latticework, and then right to go outside again, because there wasn't a corridor from the White House into the West Wing. That's why no one had taken his coat, Jack realized.

'Coffee,' Jack ordered. At least the food service would be good here. The White House Mess was run by Navy stewards, and his first presidential cup of coffee was poured into an exquisite cup from a silver pot, by a sailor whose smile was both professional and genuine, and who, like everyone else, was curious about the new Boss. It occurred to Ryan that he was like a creature in the zoo. Interesting, even fascinating – and how would he adapt to the new cage?

Same room, different seat. The President sat in the middle of the table so that aides could assemble on both sides. Ryan picked his place and sat in it naturally enough. It was only a chair, after all. The so-called trappings of power were merely things, and the power itself was an illusion, because such power was always accompanied by obligations that were greater still. You could see and exercise the former. The latter could only be felt. Those obligations came with the air, which suddenly seemed heavy in this windowless room. Jack sipped at his coffee briefly, looking around. The wall clock said 11:14 PM He'd been President for ... what? Ninety minutes? About the time for the drive from his home to ... his new home ... depending on traffic.

'Where's Arnie?'

'Right here, Mr President,' Arnold van Damm said as he came through the door. Chief of staff to two Presidents, he would now set an all-time record as chief of staff to a third. His first President had resigned in disgrace. His second was dead. Would the third one be the charm – or did bad things always come in threes? Two adages, equally quoted, and mutually exclusive. Ryan's eyes just bored in on him, asking the question that he couldn't voice: *What do I do now?*

'Good statement on TV, just about right.' The chief of staff sat down on the other side of the table. He appeared quiet and competent, as always, and Ryan didn't reflect on the effort such an appearance required of a man who'd lost more friends than Ryan had.

'I'm not even sure what the hell I said,' Jack replied, searching his mind for memories that had vanished.

'That's about normal for an ad-lib,' van Damm allowed. 'It was still pretty good. I always thought your instincts were okay. You're going to need 'em.'

'First thing?' Jack asked.

'Banks, stock markets, all federal offices are closed, call it 'til the end of the week – maybe beyond that. We have a state funeral to plan for Roger and Anne. National week of mourning, probably a month for the flags to be at half-staff.

We had a bunch of ambassadors in the chamber, too. That means a ton of diplomatic activity on top of everything else. We'll call that housekeeping stuff – I know,' van Damm said with a raised hand. 'Sorry. You have to call it something.'

'Who –'

'We have a Protocol Office here, Jack,' van Damm pointed out. 'They're already in their cubbyholes and working on this for you. We have a team of speechwriters; they'll prepare your official statements. The media people will want to see you – what I mean by that is, you have to appear in public. You have to reassure people. You have to instill confidence –'

'When?'

'In time for the morning TV shows at the latest, CNN, all the networks. I'd prefer that we go on camera within the hour, but we don't have to. We can cover that by saying you're busy. You will be,' Arnie promised. 'You'll have to be briefed on what you can say and what you can't before you go on TV. We'll lay the law down to the newsies on what they may and may not ask, and in a case like this they'll cooperate. Figure you have a week of kind treatment to lean on. That's your press honeymoon, and that's as long as it'll last.'

'And then?' Jack asked.

'And then you're the by-God President and you'll have to act like it, Jack,' van Damm said bluntly. 'You didn't have to take the oath, remember?'

That statement made Ryan's head jerk back as his peripheral vision caught the stony looks on the others in the room – all of them Secret Service at the moment. He was the new Boss, and their eyes weren't so very different now from those in the portraits on the walk in from the East Wing. They *expected* him to do the right thing. They'd support him, protect him from others and from himself, but he had to do the job. They wouldn't let him run away, either. The Secret Service was empowered to protect him from physical danger. Arnie van Damm would try to protect him from political danger. Other staffers would serve and protect, too. The housekeeping staff would feed him, iron his shirts, and fetch coffee. But none of them would allow Ryan to run away, either from his place or his duties.

It *was* a prison.

But what Arnie had just said was true. He could have refused to take the oath, couldn't – no, Ryan thought, looking down at the polished oak tabletop. Then he would have been damned for all eternity as a coward – worse, he would have been damned in his own mind as the same thing, for he had a conscience that was more harmful an enemy than any outsider. It was his nature to look in the mirror and see not enough there. As good a man as he knew himself to be, he was never good enough, driven by – what? The values he'd learned from his parents, his educators, the Marine Corps, the many people he'd met, the dangers he'd faced? All those abstract values, did he use them, or did they use him? What had brought him to this point? What had made him what he was – and what, really, was John Patrick Ryan? He looked up, around the room, wondering what *they* thought he was, but they didn't know, either. He was the President now, the giver of orders, which they would carry out; the man who made speeches which others would analyze for nuance and correctness; the man who decided what the United States of America would do, then to be judged and criticized by others who never really knew how to do the thing to which they objected. But that wasn't a person; that was a job description. Inside of that had to be a man – or someday soon, a woman – who thought it through and tried to do the right thing. And for Ryan, less than an hour and a half before, the right thing had been to take the oath. And to try to do his best. The judgment of history was ultimately less important than what he'd judge of himself, looking in the mirror every morning at not enough. The real prison was, and would always be, himself.

Damn.

The fire was out now, Chief Magill saw. His people would have to be careful. There were always hot spots, places where the fire had died, not from the cooling water but rather from lack of oxygen, and waited for the chance to flare back up, to surprise and kill the unwary. But his people were wary, and those little flares of malevolent life would not be important in the greater scheme of things for this fire site. Hoses were already being rolled, and some of his people were taking their trucks back to their houses. He'd stripped the entire city of apparatus for this fire, and he had to send much of it back, lest a new fire go unanswered, and more people die unnecessarily.

He was surrounded by others now, all wearing one-layer vinyl jackets with large yellow letters to proclaim who they were. There was an FBI contingent, another from Secret Service, the DC Metropolitan Police, NTSB, The Treasury Department's Bureau of Alcohol, Tobacco, and Firearms, and his own fire investigators, all looking for someone to be in charge so that they could claim command themselves. Instead of holding an informal meeting and establishing their own chain of command, they stood mostly in homogeneous little knots, probably waiting for someone else to tell them who was running things. Magill shook his head. He'd seen it before.

The bodies were coming out faster now. For the moment they were being taken to the DC Armory, about a mile north of the Hill just off the railroad tracks. Magill didn't envy the identification teams, though he hadn't yet troubled himself to descend into the crater – that's how he thought of it at the moment – to see how badly destroyed things were.

'Chief?' a voice asked behind him. Magill turned.

'Yeah?'

'NTSB. Can we start looking for the flight recorder?' The man pointed to the rudder fin. Though the tail assembly of the aircraft was anything but intact, you could tell what it had once been, and the so-called black box – actually painted Day-Glo orange – would be somewhere in there. The area was actually fairly clean. The rubble had been catapulted westward for the most part, and they might actually have a chance of recovering it quickly.

'Okay.' Magill nodded and pointed to a pair of firefighters to accompany the crash team.

'Could you also tell your people as much as possible not to move the aircraft parts around? We need to reconstruct the event, and it helps to leave things pretty much in place.'

'The people – the bodies come first,' Magill pointed out. The federal official nodded with a grimace. This wasn't fun for anyone.

'I understand.' He paused. 'If you find the flight crew,

please don't move them at all. Call us, and we'll handle it. Okay?'

'How will we know?'

'White shirts, shoulder boards with stripes on them, and they'll be Japanese, probably.'

It should have sounded crazy, but it didn't. Magill knew that bodies often did survive airplane crashes in the most incredible outward condition, so intact that only a trained eye could see the signs of fatal injury on first inspection. It often unnerved the civilians who were usually the first to arrive at a scene. It was so strange that the human body seemed more robust than the life it contained. There was a mercy to it, for the survivors were spared the hellish ordeal of identifying a piece of burned, torn meat, but that mercy was balanced by the cruelty of recognizing someone that could not talk back. Magill shook his head and had one of his senior people relay the special order.

The firefighters down below had enough of them already. The first special order, of course, had been to locate and remove the body of President Roger Durling. Everything was secondary to that, and a special ambulance was standing by for his body alone. Even the First Lady, Anne Durling, would have to wait a little for her husband, one last time. A contractor's mobile crane was maneuvering into the far side of the building to lift out the stone cubes that covered the podium area like a battered pile of children's hardwood blocks; in the harsh light it seemed that only the letters and numbers painted on their sides were lacking to make the illusion complete.

People were streaming in to all the government departments, especially the senior officials. It was hardly the usual thing for the VIP parking slots to fill up at midnight, but this night they did, and the Department of State was no exception. Security personnel were called in as well, for an attack on one government agency was an attack on all, and even though the nature of the attack on the government devalued the advantage of calling in people armed with handguns, it didn't really matter. When A happened, B resulted, because it was written down somewhere that B was what you did. The people with the handguns looked at one another and shook their heads, knowing that they'd be getting overtime pay, which put them one up on the big shots who'd storm in from their places in Chevy Chase and suburban Virginia, race upstairs, and then just chat with one another.

One such person found his parking place in the basement and used his key-card to activate the VIP elevator to the seventh floor. What made him different was that he had a real mission for the evening, albeit one he'd wondered about all the way in from his Great Falls home. It was what he thought of as a gut check, though that term hardly applied here. Yet what else could he do? He owed Ed Kealty everything, his place in Washington society, his career at State, so many other things. The country needed someone like Ed right now. So Ed had told him, making a strong case for the proposition, and what he himself was doing was ... what? A small voice in the car had called it treason, but, no, that wasn't so, because 'treason' was the only crime defined in the Constitution, cited there as giving 'aid and comfort' to the enemies of his country, and whatever Ed Kealty was doing, he wasn't doing *that*, was he?

It came down to loyalty. He was Ed Kealty's man, as were many others. The relationship had started at Harvard, with beers and double dates and weekends at his family's house on the water, the good times of a lively youth. He'd been the working-class guest of one of America's great families – why? Because he'd caught Ed's youthful eye. But why that? He didn't know, had never asked, and probably would never find out. That was the way of friendship. It just happened, and only in America could a working-class kid who'd scratched into Harvard on a scholarship get befriended by the great son of a great family. He would have done well on his own, probably. No one but God had given him his native intelligence. No one but his parents had encouraged his development of that gift and taught him manners and ... values. The thought caused his eyes to close as the elevator doors opened. Values. Well, loyalty was one of those values, wasn't it? Without Ed's patronage he would have topped out, maybe, as a DAS, a *Deputy* Assistant Secretary of State. The first word had long since been expunged from the title painted in gold letters on his office door. In a just world, he would have been in the running for the removal of the next word from the title as well, for wasn't he as good with foreign policy as anyone else on the seventh floor? Yes, he surely was, and that would not have come to be without his having been Ed Kealty's man. Without the parties where he'd met the other mover-shakers, and talked his way to the top. And the money. He'd never taken a bribe of any sort, but his friend had advised him wisely (the advice having come from his own advisers, but that didn't matter) on investments, allowing him to build up his own financial independence and, by the way, buy a five-thousand-square-foot home in Great Falls, and to put his own son into Harvard, *not* on a scholarship, for Clifton Rutledge III was the son of *somebody* now, not merely the issue of a worker's loins. All the work he might have done entirely on his own would not have brought him to this place, and loyalty was owed, wasn't it?

That made it a little easier for Clifton Rutledge II (actually his birth certificate said Clifton Rutledge, *Junior*, but 'Jr.' wasn't quite the suffix for a man of his station), Under Secretary of State for Political Affairs.

The rest was mere timing. The seventh floor was always guarded, all the more so now. But the guards all knew him, and it was merely a matter of looking like he knew what he was doing. Hell, Rutledge told himself, he might just fail, and that could well be the best possible outcome – 'Sorry, Ed, it wasn't there . . .' He wondered if that was an unworthy thought as he stood there by his office door, listening for footsteps that would match in speed the beating of his heart. There would be two guards on the floor now, walking about separately. Security didn't have to be all that tight at a place like this. Nobody got into State without a reason. Even in daytime, when visitors came in, they needed escorts to wherever they were going. At this time of night, things were tighter still. The number of elevators in service was reduced. Key-card access was needed to get all the way to the top floor, and a third guard was always at the elevator banks. So it was just timing. Rutledge checked his watch for several cycles of footsteps, and found that the intervals were regular to within ten seconds. Good. He just had to wait for the next one.

'Hi, Wally.'

'Good evening, sir,' the guard replied. 'Bad night.'

'Do us a favor?'

'What's that, sir?'

'Coffee. No secretaries to get the machines going. Could you skip down to the cafeteria and have one of their people bring an urn up here? Have them set it up in the conference room up the hall. We'll be having a meeting in a few minutes.'

'Fair enough. Right away?'

'If you could, Wally.'

'Be back in five, Mr Rutledge.' The guard strode off with purpose, turned right twenty yards away and disappeared from view.

Rutledge counted to ten and headed the other way. The double doors to the Secretary of State's office were not locked. Rutledge walked right in through the first set, then through the second, turning on the lights as he did so. He had three minutes. Half of him hoped that the document would be locked away in Brett Hanson's office vault. In that case he would surely fail, since only Brett, two of his assistants, and the chief of security had the combination, and *that* did have an anti-tamper alarm on it. But Brett had been a gentleman, and a careless one at that, always so trusting on the one hand and forgetful on the other, the sort who never locked his car or even his house, unless his wife made him. If it were in the open, it would be in one of two places. Rutledge pulled open the center drawer of the desk and found the usual array of pencils and cheap pens (he was always losing them) and paper clips. One minute gone, as Rutledge carefully shuffled through the desk. Nothing. It was almost a relief, until he examined the desktop, and then he nearly laughed. Right there on the blotter, tucked into the leather edging, a plain white envelope addressed to the Secretary of State, but without a stamp. Rutledge took it from its place, holding the envelope by the edges. Unsealed. He moved the flap and extracted the contents. A single sheet of paper, two typed paragraphs. It was at this point that Cliff Rutledge got a chill. The exercise had been theoretical to this point. He could just replace it, forget he'd been here, forget about the phone call, forget about everything. Two minutes.

Would Brett have receipted it? Probably not. Again, he'd been a gentleman about everything. He would not have

40

humiliated Ed that way. Ed had done the honorable thing by resigning, and Brett would have responded honorably, undoubtedly shaken his hand with a sorrowful look, and that would have been that. Two minutes fifteen.

Decision. Rutledge tucked the letter in his jacket pocket, headed for the door, switched off the lights, and returned to the corridor, stopping short of his own office door. There he waited half a minute.

'Hi, George.'

'Hello, Mr Rutledge.'

'I just sent Wally down to get coffee for the floor.'

'Good idea, sir. Bad night. Is it true that –'

'Yeah, afraid so. Brett was probably killed with all the rest.'

'Damn.'

'Might be a good idea to lock his office up. I just checked the door and –'

'Yes, sir.' George Armitage pulled out his key ring and found the proper one. 'He's always so –'

'I know.' Rutledge nodded.

'You know, two weeks ago I found his vault unlocked. Like, he turned the handle but forgot to spin the dial.' A shake of the head. 'I guess he never got hisself robbed, eh?'

'That's the problem with security,' the Under Secretary of State for Political Affairs sympathized. 'The big boys never seem to pay attention, right?'

How beautiful it was. Who had done it? The question had a cursory answer. The TV reporters, with little else to do, kept telling their cameras to look at the tail fin. He remembered the logo well enough, having long ago participated in an operation that had blown up an aircraft with the red crane on its rudder fin. He almost regretted it now, but envy prevented that. It was a matter of propriety. As one of the world's foremost terrorists – he used the word within his own mind, and in that private place relished the term, though he couldn't use it elsewhere – such an event ought to have been his doing, not the work of some amateur. For that's who it had been. An amateur whose name he would learn in due course, along with everyone else on earth – from television coverage. The irony was striking enough. Since puberty he'd devoted himself to the study and practice of political violence, learning, thinking, planning – and executing such acts, first as a participant, then as a leader/commander. And now what? Some *amateur* had outstripped him, had outstripped the entire clandestine world to which he belonged. It would have been embarrassing except for the beauty of the event.

His trained mind ran over the possibilities, and the analysis came rapidly. A single man. Perhaps two. More likely one. As always, he thought with a tight-lipped nod, one man willing to die, to sacrifice himself for the Cause – whatever Cause he might have served – could be more formidable than an army: In the case at hand, the man in question had possessed special skills and access to special means, both of which had served his purpose well.

That was luck, as was the single-actor aspect to the feat. It was easy for a single man to keep a secret. He grunted. That was the problem he'd always faced. The really hard part was finding the right people, people whom he could trust, who wouldn't boast to or confide in others, who shared his own sense of mission, who had his own discipline, and who were truly willing to risk their lives. That last criterion was the price of entry, once easy enough to establish, but now it was becoming so much harder in a changing world. The well into which he dipped was running dry, and it did no good to deny it. He was running out of the truly devoted.

Always smarter and farther-seeing than his contemporaries, he himself had faced the necessity of participating in three real operations, and though he'd had the steel in his soul to do what had to be done, he didn't crave to repeat it. It was too dangerous, after all. It wasn't that he feared the consequences of his action – it was that a dead terrorist was as dead as his victims, and dead men carried out no more missions. Martyrdom was something he'd been prepared to risk, but nothing he'd ever really sought. He wanted to *win*, after all, to reap the benefits of his action, to be recognized as a winner, liberator, conqueror, to be in the books which future generations would read as something other than a footnote. The successful mission on the TV in his bedroom would be remembered as an awful *thing* by most. Not the act of a man, but something akin to a natural disaster, because, elegant as it was, it served no political purpose. And that was the problem with the mad act of one dedicated martyr. Luck wasn't enough. There had to be a reason, a result. Such a successful act was only so if it led to something else. This manifestly had not. And that was too bad. It wasn't often that –

No, the man reached for his orange juice and sipped it before he allowed his mind to proceed. Wasn't *often*? This had never happened, had it? That was a largely philosophical question. He could say, harkening back to history, that the Assassins had been able to topple or at least decapitate governments, but back then such a task had meant the elimination of a single man, and for all the bravura shown by emissaries of that hill-top fortress, the modern world was far too complex. Kill a president or prime minister – even one of the lingering kings some nations clung to – and there was another to step into the vacant place. As had evidently happened in this case. But this one was different. There was no Cabinet to stand behind the new man, to show solidarity and determination and continuity on their angry faces. If only something else, something larger and more important had been ready when the aircraft had made its fall, then this thing of beauty would have been more beautiful still. That it hadn't could not be changed, but as with all such events, there was much to learn from both its success and failure, and its aftermath, planned or not, was very, very real.

In that sense it was tragic. An opportunity had been wasted. If only he'd known. If only the man who'd flown that airplane to its final destination had let someone know what was planned. But that wasn't the way of martyrs, was it? The fools had to think alone, act alone, and die alone; and in their personal success lay ultimate failure. Or perhaps not. The aftermath was still there . . .

'Mr President?' A Secret Service agent had picked up the phone. Ordinarily it would have been a Navy yeoman, but the Detail was still a little too shell-shocked to allow just anyone into the Sit Room. 'FBI, sir.'

Ryan pulled the phone from its holder under the desktop. 'Yes?'

'Dan Murray here.' Jack nearly smiled to hear a familiar voice, and a friendly one at that. He and Murray went back a very long way indeed. At the other end, Murray must have wanted to say *Hi, Jack*, but he wouldn't – couldn't be so familiar without being so bidden – and even if Jack had encouraged him, the man would have felt uncomfortable to do so, and would have run the further risk of being thought an ass-kisser within his own organization. One more obstacle to being normal, Jack reflected. Even his friends were now distancing themselves.

'What is it, Dan?'

'Sorry to bother you, but we need guidance on who's running the investigation. There's a bunch of people running around on the Hill right now, and –'

'Unity of command,' Jack observed sourly. He didn't have to ask why Murray was calling him. All those who could have decided this issue at a lower level were dead. 'What's the law say for this?'

'It doesn't, really,' Murray replied. The discomfort in his voice was clear. He didn't wish to bother the man who had once been his friend, and might still be, in less official circumstances. But this was business, and business had to be carried out.

'Multiple jurisdictions?'

'To a fare-thee-well,' Murray confirmed with an unseen nod.

'I guess we call it a terrorist incident. We have a tradition of that, you and I, don't we?' Jack asked.

'That we do, sir.'

Sir, Ryan thought. *Damn it*. But he had another decision to make. Jack scanned the room before replying.

'The Bureau is the lead agency on this. Everybody reports to you. Pick a good man to run things.'

'Yes, sir.'

'Dan?'

'Yes, Mr President?'

'Who's senior over at FBI?'

'The Associate Director is Chuck Floyd. He's down at Atlanta to give a speech and –' Then there would be the Assistant Directors, all senior to Murray . . .

'I don't know him. I do know you. You're acting Director until I say otherwise.' That shook the other side of the connection, Ryan immediately sensed.

44

'Uh, Jack, I –'

'I liked Shaw, too, Dan. You've got the job.'

'Yes, Mr President.'

Ryan replaced the phone and explained what he'd just done.

Price objected first: 'Sir, any attack on the President is under the jurisdiction of –' Ryan cut her off.

'They have more resources, and somebody has to be in command. I want this one settled as quickly as possible.'

'We need a special commission.' This was Arnie van Damm.

'Headed by whom?' President Ryan asked. 'A member of the Supreme Court? Couple of senators and congressmen? Murray's a pro from way back. Pick a good – whoever's the senior career member of the Department of Justice's Criminal Division will oversee the investigation. Andrea, find me the best investigator in the Service to be Murray's chief assistant. We don't have outsiders to use, do we? We run this from the inside. Let's pick the best people and let them run with it. Like, we act as though we trust the agencies who're supposed to do the work.' He paused. 'I want this investigation to run fast, okay?'

'Yes, Mr President.' Agent Price bobbed her head, and Ryan caught an approving nod from Arnie van Damm. Maybe he was doing something right, Jack allowed himself to think. The satisfaction was short-lived enough. Against the wall in the far corner was a bank of television sets. All showed essentially the same picture now, and the flash of a photographer's strobe on all four sets caught the President's eyes. He turned to see four iterations of a body bag being carried down the steps of the Capitol building's west wing. It was one more cadaver to identify – large or small, male or female, important or not, one couldn't tell from the rubberized fabric of the bag. There were only the strained, cold, sad faces of the firefighters carrying the damned thing, and that had attracted the attention of a nameless newspaper photographer and his camera and his flash, and so brought their President back to a reality he now, again, shrank from. The TV cameras followed the trio, two living, one dead, down the steps to an ambulance whose open doors revealed a pile of such bags. The one they were carrying was passed across

45

gently, the professionals showing mercy and solicitude to the body which the living world had forsaken. Then they headed back up the steps to get the next one. The Situation Room fell silent as all eyes took in the same picture. A few deep breaths were taken, and eyes were too steely or too shocked as yet for tears as, two by two, they turned away to stare down at the polished oak of the table. A coffee cup scraped and rattled its way from a saucer. The slight noise only made the silence worse, for no one had the words to fill the void.

'What else has to be done now?' Jack asked. It hit him so hard, the fatigue of the moment. The earlier racing of his heart in the face of death and in fear for his family and in agony at the loss was taking its toll on him now. His chest seemed empty, his arms weighed down, as though the sleeves of his coat were made of lead, and suddenly it was an effort just to hold up his head. It was 11:35, after a day that had begun at 4:10 in the morning, filled with interviews about a job he'd held for all of eight minutes before his abrupt promotion. The adrenaline rush which had sustained him was gone, its two-hour duration making him all the more exhausted for its length. He looked around with what seemed an important question:

'Where do I sleep tonight?' Not here, Ryan decided instantly. Not in a dead man's bed on dead man's sheets a few feet from a dead man's kids. He needed to be with his own family. He needed to look at his own children, probably asleep by now, because children slept through anything; then to feel his wife's arms around him, because that was the one constant in Ryan's world, the single thing that he would never allow to change despite the cyclonic events that had assailed a life he had neither courted nor expected.

The Secret Service agents shared a look of mutual puzzlement, before Andrea Price spoke, taking command as was her nature and now her job.

'Marine Barracks? Eighth and I?'

Ryan nodded. 'That'll do for now.'

Price spoke into her radio microphone, which was pinned to the collar of her suit jacket. 'SWORDSMAN is moving. Bring the cars to the West Entrance.'

The agents of the Detail rose. As one person they

unbuttoned their coats, and as they passed out the door, hands reached for their pistols.

'We'll shake you loose at five,' van Damm promised, adding, 'Make sure you get the sleep you need.' His answer was a brief, empty stare, as Ryan left the room. There a White House usher put a coat on him – whose it was or where it might have come from, Jack didn't think to ask. He climbed into the Chevy Suburban backseat, and it moved off at once, with an identical vehicle in front, and three more behind. Jack could have avoided the sights, but not the sounds, for sirens were still wailing beyond the armored glass, and it would have been cowardice to look away in any case. The fire glow was gone, replaced by the sparkling of lights from scores of emergency vehicles, some moving, most not, on or around the Hill. The police were keeping downtown streets clear, and the presidential motorcade headed rapidly east, ten minutes later arriving at the Marine Barracks. Here everyone was awake now, properly uniformed, and every Marine in sight had a rifle or pistol in evidence. The salutes were crisp.

The home of the commandant of the Marine Corps dated back to the early nineteenth century, one of the few official buildings that hadn't been burned by the British during their visit in 1814. But the commandant was dead. A widower with grown children, he'd lived here alone until this last night. Now a full colonel stood on the porch in pressed utilities with a pistol belt around his waist and a full platoon spread around the house.

'Mr President, your family is topside and all secure,' Colonel Mark Porter reported immediately. 'We have a full rifle company deployed on perimeter security, and another one is on the way.'

'Media?' Price asked.

'I didn't have any orders about that. My orders were to protect our guests. The only people within two hundred meters are the ones who belong here.'

'Thank you, Colonel,' Ryan said, not caring about the media, and heading for the door. A sergeant held it open, saluting as a Marine ought, and without thinking, Ryan returned it. Inside, a more senior NCO pointed him up the stairs – this one also saluted, as he was under arms. It was clear to Ryan now that he couldn't go anywhere alone. Price, another agent, and two Marines followed him up the stairs. The second-floor corridor had two Secret Service agents and five more Marines. Finally, at 11:54, he walked into a bedroom to find his wife sitting.

'Hi.'

'Jack.' Her head turned. 'It's all true?'

He nodded, then he hesitated before coming to sit next to Cathy. 'The kids?'

'Asleep.' A pause. 'They don't really know what's going on. I guess that makes four of us,' she added.

'Five.'

'The President's dead?' Cathy turned to see her husband nod. 'I hardly got to know him.'

'Good guy. Their kids are at the House. Asleep. I didn't know if I was supposed to do anything. So I came here.' Ryan reached for his collar and pulled the tie loose. It seemed to take a considerable effort to do so. Better not to disturb the kids, he decided. It would have been hard to walk that far anyway.

'And now?'

'I have to sleep. They get me up at five.'

'What are we going to do?'

'I don't know.' Jack managed to get out of his clothes, hoping that the new day would contain some of the answers that the night merely concealed.

2

PRE-DAWN

It was to be expected that they'd be as exactly punctual as their electronic watches could make them. It seemed to Ryan that he'd hardly closed his eyes when the gentlest of taps at the door startled him off the pillow. There came the brief moment of confusion normal to the moment of awakening in any place other than one's own bed: *Where am I?* The first organized thought told him that he'd dreamed a lot of things, and maybe – But hard on the heels of that thought was the internal announcement that the worst of the dream was still real. He was in a strange place, and there was no other explanation for it. The tornado had swept him up into a whirling mass of terror and confusion, and then deposited him here, and *here* was neither Kansas nor Oz. About the best thing he could say, after five or ten seconds of orientation, was that he didn't have the expected headache from sleep-deprivation, and that he wasn't quite so tired. He slid out from under the covers. His feet found the floor, and he made his way to the door.

'Okay, I'm up,' he told the wooden door. Then he realized that his room didn't have an attached bathroom, and he'd have to open the door. That he did.

'Good morning, Mr President.' A young and rather earnest-looking agent handed him a bathrobe. Again, it was the job of an orderly, but the only Marine he saw in the corridor was wearing a pistol belt. Jack wondered if there had been another turf fight the night before between the Marine Corps and the Secret Service to see who had primacy of place in the protection of their new Commander-in-Chief. Then he realized with a start that the bathrobe was his own.

'We got some things for you last night,' the agent explained in a whisper. A second agent handed over Cathy's rather tattered maroon housecoat. So, someone had broken into their home last night – must have, Jack realized, as he hadn't

49

handed over his keys to anyone; *and* defeated the burglar alarm he'd installed a few years earlier. He padded back to the bed and deposited the housecoat there before heading back out. Yet a third agent pointed him down the hall to an unoccupied bedroom. Four suits were hanging on a poster bed, along with four shirts, all newly pressed by the look of them, along with half a score of ties and everything else. It wasn't so much pathos as desperation, Jack realized. The staff knew, or at least had an idea of what he was going through, and every single thing they could do to make things easier for him was being done with frantic perfection. Someone had even spit-shined his three pair of black shoes to Marine specifications. They'd never looked so good before, Ryan thought, heading for the bathroom – where, of course, he found all of his things, even his usual bar of Zest soap. Next to *that* was the skin-friendly stuff Cathy used. Nobody thought that being President was easy, but he was now surrounded by people who were grimly determined to eliminate every *small* worry he might have.

A warm shower helped loosen his muscles, and clouded the mirror with mist, which made things even better when he shaved. The usual morning mechanics were finished by 5:20, and Ryan made his way down the stairs. Outside, he saw through a window, a phalanx of camouflage-clad Marines stood guard on the quad, their breathing marked by little white puffs. Those inside braced to attention as he passed. Perhaps he and his family had gotten a few hours of sleep, but no one else had. That was something he needed to remember, Jack told himself as the smells drew him to the kitchen.

'Attention on deck!' The voice of the sergeant-major of the Marine Corps was muted in deference to the sleeping children upstairs, and for the first time since dinner the previous night, Ryan managed a smile.

'Settle down, Marines.' President Ryan headed toward the coffeepot, but a corporal beat him there. The correct proportions of cream and sugar were added to the mug – again, someone had done some homework – before she handed it across.

'The staff is in the dining room, sir,' the sergeant-major told him.

'Thank you.' President Ryan headed that way.

They looked the worse for wear, making Jack feel briefly guilty for his shower-fresh face. Then he saw the pile of documents they'd prepared.

'Good morning, Mr President,' Andrea Price said. People started to rise from their chairs. Ryan waved them back down and pointed to Murray.

'Dan,' the President began. 'What do we know?'

'We found the body of the pilot about two hours ago. Good ID. His name was Sato, as expected. Very experienced airplane driver. We're still looking for the co-pilot.' Murray paused. 'The pilot's body is being checked for drugs, but finding that would be a surprise. NTSB has the flight recorder – they got that around four, and it's being checked out right now. We've recovered just over two hundred bodies –'

'President Durling?'

Price handled that one with a shake of the head. 'Not yet. That part of the building – well, it's a mess, and they decided to wait for daylight to do the hard stuff.'

'Survivors?'

'Just the three people who we know to have been inside that part of the building at the time of the crash.'

'Okay.' Ryan shook his head as well. That information was important, but irrelevant. 'Anything important that we know?'

Murray consulted his notes. 'The aircraft flew out of Vancouver International, BC. They filed a false flight-plan for London Heathrow, headed east, departed Canadian airspace at 7:51 local time. All very routine stuff. We assume that he headed out a little while, reversed course, and headed southeast toward DC. After that he bluffed his way through air-traffic control.'

'How?'

Murray nodded to someone Ryan didn't know. 'Mr President, I'm Ed Hutchins, NTSB. It's not hard. He claimed to be a KLM charter inbound to Orlando. Then he declared an emergency. When there's an in-flight emergency, our people are trained to get the airplane on the ground ASAP. We were up against a guy who knew all the right buttons to push. There's no way anyone could have prevented this,' he concluded defensively.

'Only one voice on the tapes,' Murray noted.

'Anyway,' Hutchins continued, 'we have tapes of the radar tracks. He simulated an aircraft with control difficulties, asked for an emergency vector to Andrews, and got what he wanted. From Andrews to the Hill is barely a minute's flying time.'

'One of our people got a Stinger off,' Price said, with somewhat forlorn pride.

Hutchins just shook his head. It was the gesture for this morning in Washington. 'Against something that big, might as well have been a spitball.'

'Anything from Japan?'

'They're in a national state of shock.' This came from Scott Adler, the senior career official in the State Department, and one of Ryan's friends. 'Right after you turned in, we got a call from the Prime Minister. It's not as though he hasn't had a bad week himself, though he sounds happy to be back in charge. He wants to come over to apologize personally to us. I told him we'd get back –'

'Tell him yes.'

'You sure, Jack?' Arnie van Damm asked.

'Does anybody think this was a deliberate act?' Ryan countered.

'We don't know,' Price responded first.

'No explosives aboard the aircraft,' Dan Murray pointed out. 'If there had been –'

'I wouldn't be here.' Ryan finished his coffee. The corporal refilled it at once. 'This is going to come down to one or two nuts, just like they all do.'

Hutchins nodded tentative agreement. 'Explosives are fairly light. Even a few tons, given the carrying capacity of the 747–400, would not have compromised the mission at all, and the payoff would have been enormous. What we have here is a fairly straight-forward crash. The residual damage was done by about half a load of jet fuel – upwards of eighty tons. That was plenty,' he concluded. Hutchins had been investigating airplane accidents for almost thirty years.

'It's much too early to draw conclusions,' Price warned.

'Scott?'

'If this was – hell,' Adler shook his head. 'This was not an act by their government. They're frantic over there. The newspapers are calling for the heads of the people who sub-orned the government in the first place, and Prime Minister Koga was nearly in tears over the phone. Put it this way, if somebody over there planned this, they'll find out for us.'

'Their idea of due process isn't quite as stringent as ours,' Murray added. 'Andrea is right. It is too early to draw con-clusions, but all of the indications so far point to a random act, not a planned one.' Murray paused for a moment. 'For that matter, we know the other side developed nuclear weapons, remember?' Even the coffee turned cold with that remark.

This one he found under a bush while moving a ladder from one part of the west face to another. The firefighter had been on duty for seven straight hours. He was numb by now. You can take only so much horror before the mind starts regarding the bodies and pieces as mere things. The remains of a child might have shaken him, or even a particularly pretty female, since this fireman was still young and single, but the body he'd accidentally stepped on wasn't one of those. The torso was headless, and parts of both legs were missing, but it was clearly the body of a man, wearing the shredded remains of a white shirt, with epaulets at the shoulders. Three stripes on each of them, he saw. He wondered what that meant, too tired to do much in the way of thinking. The fireman turned and waved to his lieutenant, who in turn tapped the arm of a woman wearing a vinyl FBI windbreaker.

This agent walked over, sipping at a plastic cup and wish-ing she could light a cigarette – still too many lingering fumes for that, she grumbled.

'Just found this one. Funny place, but –'

'Yeah, funny.' The agent lifted her camera and snapped a couple of pictures which would have the exact time elec-tronically preserved on the frame. Next she took a pad from her pocket and noted the placement for body number four on her personal list. She hadn't seen many for her particular area of responsibility. Some plastic stakes and yellow tape would further mark the site; she started writing the tag for it. 'You can turn him over.'

Under the body, they saw, was an irregularly shaped piece of flat glass – or glass-like plastic. The agent snapped another photo, and through the viewfinder things somehow looked more interesting than with the naked eye. A glance up showed a gap in the marble balustrade. Another look around revealed a lot of small metallic objects, which an hour earlier she'd decided were aircraft parts, and which had attracted the attention of an NTSB investigator, who was now conferring with the same fire-department officer with whom she'd been conferring a minute earlier. The agent had to wave three times to get his attention.

'What is it?' The NTSB investigator was cleaning his glasses with a handkerchief.

The agent pointed. 'Check the shirt out.'

'Crew,' the man said, after putting them back on. 'Maybe a driver. What's this?' It was his turn to point.

There was a strange delicacy to it. The white uniform shirt had a hole in it just to the right of the pocket. The hole was surrounded by a red-rust stain. The FBI agent held her flashlight close, and that showed that the stain was dried. The current temperature was just under twenty degrees. The body had been thrown into this harsh environment virtually at the moment of impact, and the blood about the severed neck was frozen, the purple-red color of some horrid plum sherbet. The blood on the shirt, she saw, had dried before having the chance to freeze.

'Don't move the body anymore,' she told the fireman. Like most FBI agents, she'd been a local police officer before applying to the federal agency. It was the cold that made her face pale.

'First crash investigation?' the NTSB man asked, seeing her face, and mistaking her pallor.

She nodded. 'Yes, it is, but it's not my first murder.' With that she switched on her portable radio to call her supervisor. For this body she wanted a crime-scene team and full forensics.

The telegrams came from every government in the world. Most were long, and all had to be read – well, at least the ones from important countries. Togo could wait.

'Interior and Commerce are in town and standing by for a Cabinet meeting along with all the deputies,' van Damm said while Ryan flipped through the messages, trying to read and listen at the same time. 'The Joint Chiefs, all the vices, are assembled, along with all the command CINCs to go over national security –'

'Threat Board?' Jack asked without looking up. Until the previous day he'd been President Durling's National Security Advisor, and it didn't seem likely that the world had changed too much in twenty-four hours.

Scott Adler handled the answer: 'Clear.'

'Washington is pretty much shut down,' Murray said. 'Radio and TV announcements for people to stay home, except for essential services. The DC National Guard is out. We need the warm bodies for the Hill, and the DC Guard is a military-police brigade. They might actually be useful. Besides, the firemen must be about worn out by now.'

'How long before the investigation gives us hard information?' the President asked.

'There's no telling that, Ja – Mister –'

Ryan looked up from the official Belgian telegram. 'How long since we've known each other, Dan? I'm not God, okay? If you use my name once in a while, nobody's going to shoot you for it.'

It was Murray's turn to smile. 'Okay. You can't predict with any major investigation. The breaks just come, sooner or later, but they do come,' Dan promised. 'We have a good team of investigators out there.'

'What do I tell the media?' Jack rubbed his eyes, already tired from reading. Maybe Cathy was right. Maybe he did need glasses, finally. Before him was a printed sheet for his morning TV appearances, which had been selected by lot. CNN at 7:08, CBS at 7:20, NBC at 7:37, ABC at 7:50, Fox at 8:08, all from the Roosevelt Room of the White House, where the cameras were already set up. Someone had decided that a formal speech was too much for him, and not really appropriate to the situation until he had something substantive to deliver. Just a quiet, dignified, and above all, intimate introduction of himself to people reading their papers and drinking their morning coffee.

'Softball questions. That's already taken care of,' van Damm assured him. 'Answer them. Speak slowly, clearly. Look as relaxed as you can. Nothing dramatic. The people don't expect that. They want to know that somebody's in charge, answering the phones, whatever. They know it's too soon for you to say or do anything decisive.'

'Roger's kids?'

'Still asleep, I expect. We have the family members in town. They're at the White House now.'

President Ryan nodded without looking up. It was hard to meet the eyes of the people sitting around the breakfast table, especially on things like that. There was a plan for this, too. Movers were already on the way, probably. The Durling family – what was left of it – would be removed from the White House kindly but quickly, because it wasn't their house anymore. The country needed someone else in there, and that someone needed to be as comfortable as possible, and *that* meant eliminating all visible reminders of the previous occupant. It wasn't brutal, Jack realized. It was business. They doubtless had a psychologist standing by to assist the family members with their grief, to 'process' them through it as best as medical science allowed. But the country came first. In the unforgiving calculus of life, even so sentimental a nation as the United States of America had to move on. When it came time for Ryan to leave the White House, one way or another, the same thing would happen. There had been a time when an ex-President had walked down the hill to Union Station from his successor's inauguration to get a train ticket home. Now they used movers, and doubtless the family would fly out on Air Force transport, but go the children would, leaving behind schools and such friends as they had made, returning to California and whatever life their family members could reconstruct for them. Business or not, it *was* cold, Ryan thought while staring mindlessly at the Belgian telegram. How much the better for everyone if the aircraft had not fallen on the Capitol building . . .

On top of all that, Jack had rarely been called upon to console the children of a man he knew, and damned sure hadn't ever taken their home away. He shook his head. It wasn't his fault, but it was his job.

The telegram, he saw on returning to it, noted that America had twice helped to save that small country within a space of less than thirty years, then protected it through the NATO alliance, that there was a bond of blood and friendship between America and a nation which most American citizens would have been taxed to locate on a globe. And that was true. Whatever the faults of his country, whatever her imperfections, however unfeeling some of her actions might seem to be, the United States of America had done the right thing more often than not. The world was far the better for it, and that was why business had to be carried out.

Inspector Patrick O'Day was grateful for the cold. His investigative career had stretched over almost thirty years, and this was not his first time in the presence of multiple bodies and their separated parts. His first had been in Mississippi one May, a Sunday school bombed by the Ku Klux Klan, with eleven victims. At least here the cold eliminated the ghastly odor of dead human bodies. He'd never really wanted a high rank in the Bureau – 'inspector' was a title with variable importance in the sense of seniority. In his case, much like Dan Murray, O'Day worked as a troubleshooter, often dispatched from Washington to assist on touchy ones. Widely recognized as a superb street agent, he'd been able to stick to real cases, large and small, instead of high-level supervision, which he found boring.

Assistant Director Tony Caruso had gone along another track. He'd been special agent-in-charge of two field offices, risen to head the Bureau's Training Division, then taken over the Washington Field Office, which was sufficiently large to merit 'AD' rank for its commander, along with one of the worst office locations in North America. Caruso enjoyed the power, prestige, higher pay, and reserved parking place which his status accorded him, but part of him envied his old friend, Pat, for his often dirty hands.

'What do you figure?' Caruso asked, staring down at the body. They still needed artificial light. The sun was rising, but on the far side of the building.

'You can't take it to court yet, but this guy was dead hours before the bird came down.'

Both men watched a gray-haired expert from Headquarters Laboratory Division hover over the body. There were all manner of tests to be carried out. Internal body temperature was one – a computer model allowed for environmental conditions, and while the data would be far less reliable than either senior official would want, anything prior to 9:46 PM the previous evening would tell them what they needed to know.

'Knifed in the heart,' Caruso said, shivering at the thought. You never really got over the brutality of murder. Whether a single person or a thousand, wrongful death was wrongful death, and the number just told you how many individual records had been tied. 'We got the pilot.'

O'Day nodded. 'I heard. Three stripes, makes him the co-pilot, and he was murdered. So maybe it was just one guy.'

'What's the crew on one of these?' Caruso asked the NTSB supervisor.

'Two. The earlier ones had a flight engineer, but the new ones don't bother with it. For really long flights they might have a backup pilot, but these birds are pretty automated now, and the engines hardly ever break.'

The lab tech stood and waved in the people with the body bag before joining the others. 'You want the early version?'

'You bet,' Caruso replied.

'Definitely dead before the crash took place. No bruising from the crash trauma. The chest wound is relatively old. There should be contusions from the seat belts, but there aren't, just scrapes and gouges, with damn little blood there. Not enough blood from the severed head. In fact, not enough blood anywhere in the remains right here. Let's say he was murdered in his seat in the aircraft. The belts hold him in a sitting position. Postmortem lividity drains all the blood down to the lower extremities, and the legs are torn off when the bird hits the building – that's why there's so little blood. I got a lot of homework to do, but quick-and-dirty, he was dead three hours at least before the plane got here.' Will Gettys handed over the wallet. 'Here's the guy's ID. Poor bastard. I guess he wasn't a part of this at all.'

'What chance you could be wrong on any of that?' O'Day had to ask.

'I'd be real surprised, Pat. An hour or two on time of death – earlier rather than later – yeah, that's possible. But there's nowhere near enough blood for this guy to have been alive at time of impact. He was dead before the crash. You can take that to the bank,' Gettys told the other agents, knowing that his career rode on that one, and comfortable with the wager.

58

'Thank God for that,' Caruso breathed. It did more than make things easier for the investigation. There would be conspiracy theories for the next twenty years, and the Bureau would proceed on its business, checking out every possibility, aided, they were sure, by the Japanese police, but one guy alone had driven this aircraft into the ground, and that made it extremely likely that this _grand mal_ assassination, like most of the others, was the work of a single man, demented or not, skilled or not, but in any case alone. Not that everyone would *ever* believe that.

'Get the information to Murray,' Caruso ordered. 'He's with the President.'

'Yes, sir.' O'Day walked over toward where his diesel pickup was parked. He probably had the only one in town, the inspector thought, with a police light plugged into the cigarette lighter. You didn't put something like this over a radio, encrypted or not.

Rear Admiral Jackson changed into his blue mess jacket about ninety minutes out from Andrews, having managed about six hours of needed sleep after being briefed on things that didn't really matter very much. The uniform was the worse for having been packed in his travel bag, not that it would matter all that much, and the navy blue wool hid wrinkles fairly well anyway. His five rows of ribbons and wings of gold attracted the eye, anyway. There must have been an easterly wind this morning, for the KC-10 flew in from Virginia, and a muttered, 'Jesus, look at that!' from a few rows aft commanded all in the forward part of the aircraft to crowd at the windows like the tourists they were not. Between the beginnings of dawn and the huge collection of lights on the ground it was plain that the Capitol building, the centerpiece of their country's first city, wasn't the same as it had been. Somehow this was more immediate and real than the pictures many of them had seen on TV before boarding the plane in Hawaii. Five minutes later, the aircraft touched down at Andrews Air Force Base. The senior officers found an aircraft of the Air Force's First Heli Squadron waiting to take them to the Pentagon's pad. This flight, lower and slower, gave them a better look still at the damage to the building.

'Jesus,' Dave Seaton said over the intercom. 'Did anybody get out of there alive?' Robby took his time before responding. 'I wonder where Jack was when it happened . . .' He remembered a British Army toast – 'Here's to bloody wars and sickly seasons!' – which referred to a couple of sure ways for officers to be promoted into vacant slots. Surely quite a few people would fleet up from this incident, but none really wanted advancement this way, least of all his closest friend, somewhere down there in the wounded city.

The Marines looked very twitchy, Inspector O'Day saw. He parked his truck on Eighth Street, S.E. The Marine Barracks were thoroughly barricaded. The curbs were fully blocked with parked cars, the gaps in the buildings doubly so. He dismounted his truck and walked toward an NCO; he was wearing his FBI windbreaker, and carrying his ID in his right hand.

'I have business inside, Sergeant.'

'Who with, sir?' the Marine asked, checking the photo against the face.

'Mr Murray.'

'You mind leaving your side arm here with us, sir? Orders,' the sergeant explained.

'Sure.' O'Day handed over his fanny pack, inside of which was his Smith & Wesson 1076 and two spare magazines. He didn't bother with a backup piece on headquarters duty. 'How many people you have around now?'

'Two companies, near enough. There's another one setting up at the White House.' There was no better time to lock the barn door than after the horse got out, Pat knew. It was all the more grim since he was delivering the news that it was all unnecessary, but nobody would really care about that. The sergeant waved to a lieutenant who had nothing better to do – the NCOs ran things like this – than to conduct visitors across the quad. The lieutenant saluted for no more reason than being a Marine.

'Here to see Daniel Murray. He's expecting me.'

'Please follow me, sir.'

The inner corners of the buildings on the quad had yet another line of Marines, with a third on the quad itself, complete with a heavy machine gun. Two companies amounted to upwards of three hundred rifles. Yeah, President Ryan was fairly safe here, Inspector O'Day thought, unless some other maniac driving an airplane was around. Along the way, a captain wanted to compare the photo on his ID with the face again. It was being overdone. Somebody had to point that out before they started parking tanks on the street.

Murray came out to meet him on the porch. 'How good is it?'

'Pretty good,' the inspector replied.

'Come on.' Murray waved him in, and led his friend into the breakfast room. 'This is Inspector O'Day. Pat, I think you know who these people are.'

'Good morning. I've been on the Hill, and we found something a little while ago that you need to know,' he began, going on for another couple of minutes.

'How solid is it?' Andrea Price asked.

'You know how this works,' O'Day responded. 'It's preliminary, but it looks pretty solid to me, and we'll have good test data after lunch. The ID's already being run. That may be a little shaky, because we don't have a head to work with, and the hands are all ripped up. We're not saying that we've closed the case. We're saying that we have a preliminary indication that supports other data.'

'Can I mention this on TV?' Ryan asked everyone around the table.

'Definitely not,' van Damm said. 'First, it's not confirmed. Second, it's too soon for anyone to believe it.'

Murray and O'Day traded a look. Neither of them was a politician. Arnie van Damm was. For them, information control was about protecting evidence so that a jury saw it clean. For Arnie, information control was about protecting people from things he didn't think they could understand until it was spin-controlled and spoonfed, one little gulp at a time. Both wondered if Arnie had ever been a father, and if his infant had starved to death waiting for his strained carrots. Both noted next that Ryan gave his chief of staff a long look.

The well known black box really wasn't much more than a tape recorder whose leads trailed off to the cockpit. There they collected data from engine and other flight controls, plus, in this case, the microphones for the flight crew. Japan

Airlines was a government-run carrier, and its aircraft had the latest of everything. The flight-data recorder was fully digitized. That made for rapid and clear transcription of the data. First of all, a senior technician made a clean, high-speed copy of the original metallic tape, which was then removed to a vault while he worked on the copy. Someone had thought to have a Japanese speaker standing by.

'This flight data looks like pure vanilla on first inspection. Nothing was broken on the aircraft,' an analyst reported, scanning the data on a computer screen. 'Nice easy turns, steady on the engines. Textbook flight profile . . . until here' – he tapped the screen – 'here he made a radical turn from zero-six-seven to one-niner-six . . . and settles right back down again until his penetration.'

'No chatter in the cockpit at all.' Another tech ran the voice segment of the tape back and forth, finding only routine traffic between the aircraft and various ground-control stations. 'I'm going to back it up to the beginning.' The tape didn't really have a beginning. Rather it ran on a continuous loop, on this machine, because the 747 routinely engaged in long, over-water flights, forty hours long. It took several minutes for him to locate the end of the immediately preceding flight, and here he found the normal exchange of information and commands between two crewmen, and also between the aircraft and the ground, the former in Japanese and the latter in English, the language of international aviation.

That stopped soon after the aircraft had halted at its assigned jetway. There was a full two minutes of blank tape, and then the recording cycle began again when the flight-deck instruments were powered up during the preflight procedures. The Japanese speaker – an Army officer in civilian clothes – was from the National Security Agency.

The sound pickup was excellent. They could hear the *clicks* of switches being thrown, and the background *whirs* of various instruments, but the loudest sound was the breathing of the co-pilot, whose identity was specified by the track on the recording tape.

'Stop,' the Army officer said. 'Back it up a little. There's another voice, can't quite . . . Oh, okay. "All ready, question mark." Must be the pilot. Yeah, that was a door closing, pilot just came in. "Preflight checklist complete . . . standing by for before-start checklist . . ." Oh . . . oh, God. He killed him. Back it up again.' The officer, a major, didn't see the FBI agent don a second pair of headphones.

It was a first for both of them. The FBI agent had seen a murder on a bank video system, but neither he nor the intelligence officer had ever heard one, a grunt from an impact, a gasp of breath that conveyed surprise and pain, a gurgle, maybe an attempt at speech, followed by another voice.

'What's that?' the agent asked.

'Run it again.' The officer's face stared at the wall. ' "I am very sorry to do this." ' That was followed by a few more labored breaths, then a long sigh. 'Jesus.' The second voice came on a different vox channel less than a minute later, to notify the tower that the 747 was starting its engines.

'That's the pilot, Sato,' the NTSB analyst said. 'The other voice must be the co-pilot.'

'Not anymore.' The only remaining noise over the co-pilot's channel was spill-over and background sounds.

'Killed him,' the FBI agent agreed. They'd have to run the tape a hundred more times, for themselves and for others, but the conclusion would be the same. Even though the formal investigation would last for several months, the case was effectively closed less than nine hours after it had begun.

The streets of Washington were eerily empty. Normally at this time of day, Ryan knew all too well from his own experience, the nation's capital was gridlocked with the automobiles of federal employees, lobbyists, members of Congress and their staffers, fifty thousand lawyers and their secretaries, and all the private-industry service workers who supported them all. Not today. With every intersection manned by a radio car of the Metropolitan Police or a camouflage-painted National Guard vehicle, it was more like a holiday weekend, and there was actually more traffic heading away from the Hill than toward it, the curious turned away from their place of interest ten blocks from their intended destination.

The presidential procession headed up Pennsylvania. Jack

was back in the Chevy Suburban, and there were still Marines leading and following the collection of Secret Service vehicles. The sun was up now. The sky was mainly clear, and it took a moment to realize that the skyline was wrong.

The 747 hadn't even harmed the trees, Ryan saw. It hadn't wasted its energy on anything but the target. Half a dozen cranes were working now, lifting stone blocks from the crater that had been the House chamber, depositing them onto trucks that were taking them off somewhere. Only a few fire trucks remained. The dramatic part was over for now. The grim part remained.

The rest of the city seemed intact enough at 6:40 AM Ryan gave the Hill a final sideways look through the darkened windows as his vehicle headed downhill on Constitution Avenue. If cars were being turned away, the usual morning collection of joggers was not. Perhaps they'd run to the Mall as part of the normal morning ritual, but there they stopped. Ryan watched their faces, some of which turned to see his vehicle pass before returning their gaze eastward, talking in little knots, pointing and shaking their heads. Jack noticed that the Secret Service agents in the Suburban with him turned to watch them, perhaps expecting one to pull a bazooka from under his sweats.

It was novel to drive so fast in Washington. Partly it was because a rapidly moving target was harder to hit, and partly because Ryan's time was far more valuable now, and not to be wasted. More than anything else it meant that he was speeding toward something he would just as soon have avoided. Only a few days before, he'd accepted Roger Durling's invitation for the vice-presidency, but he'd done so mainly as a means of relieving himself from government service once and for all. That thought evoked a pained look behind closed eyes. Why was it that he'd never been able to run away from anything? Certainly it didn't seem like courage. It actually seemed the reverse. He'd so often been afraid, afraid to say no and have people think him a coward. Afraid to do anything but what his conscience told him, and so often what it had told him had been something he hated to do or was afraid to do, but there wasn't ever an honorable alternative that he could exercise.

'It'll be okay,' van Damm told him, seeing the look, and knowing what the new President had to be thinking.

No, it won't, Jack could not reply.

3

SCRUTINY

The Roosevelt Room is named for Teddy, and on the east
wall was his Nobel Peace Prize for his 'successful' mediation
of the Russo-Japanese War. Historians could now say that
the effort had only encouraged Japan's imperial ambitions,
and so wounded the Russian soul that Stalin – hardly a friend
of the Romanov dynasty! – had felt the need to avenge his
country's humiliation, but that particular bequest of Alfred
Nobel had always been more political than real. The room
was used for medium-sized lunches and meetings, and was
conveniently close to the Oval Office. Getting there proved
to be harder than Jack had expected. The corridors of the
White House are narrow for such an important building, and
the Secret Service was out in force, though here their firearms
were not in evidence. That was a welcome relief. Ryan
walked past ten new agents over and above those who had
formed his mobile guard force, which evoked a sigh of
exasperation from SWORDSMAN. Everything was new and
different now, and the protective Detail that in former
times had seemed businesslike, sometimes even amusing,
was just one more reminder that his life had been traumatically changed.

'Now what?' Jack asked.

'This way.' An agent opened a door, and Ryan found the
presidential makeup artist. It was an informal arrangement,
and the artist, a woman in her fifties, had everything in a
large fake-leather case. As often as he'd done TV – rather a
lot in his former capacity as National Security Advisor – it
was something Jack had never come to love, and it required
all of his self-control not to fidget as the liquid base was
applied with a foam sponge, followed by powder and hair
spray and fussing, all of which was done without a word by
a woman who looked as though she might burst into tears
at any moment.

'I liked him, too,' Jack told her. Her hands stopped, and their eyes met.

'He was always so nice. He hated this, just like you do, but he never complained, and he usually had a joke to tell. Sometimes I'd do the children just for fun. They liked it, even the boy. They'd play in front of the TV, and the crews would give them tapes and . . .'

'It's okay.' Ryan took her hand. Finally he'd met someone on the staff who wasn't all business, and who didn't make him feel like an animal in the zoo. 'What's your name?'

'Mary Abbot.' Her eyes were running, and she wanted to apologize.

'How long have you been here?'

'Since right before Mr Carter left.' Mrs Abbot wiped her eyes and steadied down.

'Well, maybe I should ask you for advice,' he said gently.

'Oh, no, I don't know anything about that.' She managed an embarrassed smile.

'Neither do I. I guess I'll just have to find out.' Ryan looked in the mirror. 'Finished?'

'Yes, Mr President.'

'Thank you, Mrs Abbot.'

They sat him in an armed wooden chair. The lights were already set up, which brought the room temperature into the low eighties, or so it felt. A technician clipped a two-headed microphone to his tie with movements as delicate as Mrs Abbot's, all because there was a Secret Service agent hovering over every member of the crew, with Andrea Price hovering over them all from the doorway. Her eyes were narrow and suspicious, despite the fact that every single piece of gear in the room had been inspected, every visitor scanned continuously by eyes as casually intense and thorough as a surgeon's. One really could make a pistol out of non-metallic composites – the movie was right about that – but pistols were still bulky. The palpable tension of the Detail carried over to the TV crew, who kept their hands in the open, and only moved them slowly. The scrutiny of the Secret Service could rattle almost anyone.

'Two minutes,' the producer said, cued by his earpiece. 'Just went into commercial.'

'Get any sleep last night?' CNN's chief White House

correspondent asked. Like everyone else, he wanted a quick and clear read on the new President.

'Not enough,' Jack replied, suddenly tense. There were two cameras. He crossed his legs and clasped his hands in his lap in order to avoid nervous movements. How, exactly, was he supposed to appear? Grave? Grief-stricken? Quietly confident? Overwhelmed? It was a little late for that now. Why hadn't he asked Arnie before?

'Thirty seconds,' the producer said.

Jack tried to compose himself. His physical posture would keep his body still. *Just answer the questions. You've been doing that long enough.*

'Eight minutes after the hour,' the correspondent said directly into the camera behind Jack. 'We're here in the White House with President John Ryan.

'Mr President, it's been a long night, hasn't it?'

'I'm afraid it has,' Ryan agreed.

'What can you tell us?'

'Recovery operations are under way, as you know. President Durling's body has not yet been found. The investigation is going on under the coordination of the FBI.'

'Have they discovered anything?'

'We'll probably have a few things to say later today, but it's too early right now.' Despite the fact that the correspondent had been fully briefed on that issue, Ryan saw the disappointment in his eyes.

'Why the FBI? Isn't the Secret Service empowered to –'

'This is no time for a turf fight. An investigation like this has to go on at once. Therefore, I decided that the FBI would be the lead agency – under the Department of Justice, and with the assistance of other federal agencies. We want answers, we want them fast, and this seems the best way to make that happen.'

'It's been reported that you've appointed a new FBI Director.'

Jack nodded. 'Yes, Barry, I have. For the moment I've asked Daniel E. Murray to step in as acting Director. Dan is a career FBI agent whose last job was special assistant to Director Shaw. We've known each other for many years. Mr Murray is one of the best cops in government service.'

* * *

68

'Murray?'

'A policeman, supposed to be an expert on terrorism and espionage,' the intelligence officer replied.

'Hmm.' He went back to sipping his bittersweet coffee.

'What can you tell us about preparation for – I mean, for the next several days?' the correspondent asked next.

'Barry, those plans are still being made. First and foremost, we have to let the FBI and other law-enforcement agencies do their job. There will be more information coming out later today, but it's been a long and difficult night for a lot of people.' The correspondent nodded at that, and decided it was time for a human-interest question.

'Where did you and your family sleep? I know it wasn't here.'

'The Marine Barracks, at Eighth and I,' Ryan answered.

'Oh, *shit*, Boss,' Andrea Price muttered, just outside the room. Some media people had found out, but the Service hadn't confirmed it to anyone, and most news organizations had reported that the Ryan family was at 'an undisclosed location.' Well, they'd be sleeping somewhere else tonight. And the location would not be disclosed this time. Damn.

'Why there?'

'Well, it had to be somewhere, and that seemed convenient. I was a Marine myself once, Barry,' Jack said quietly.

'Remember when we blew them up?'

'A fine night.' The intelligence officer remembered watching through binoculars from the top of the Beirut Holiday Inn. He'd helped set that mission up. The only hard part, really, had been selecting the driver. There was an odd cachet about the American Marines, something seemingly mystical about them that this Ryan's nation clung to. But they died just like any other infidel. He wondered with amusement if there might be a large truck in Washington that one of his people might buy or lease . . . He set the amusing thought aside. There was work to be done. It wasn't practical, anyway. He'd been to Washington more than once, and the Marine Barracks was one of the places he'd examined. It was too easily defended. Too bad, really. The political significance of the target made it highly attractive.

'Not smart,' Ding observed over his morning coffee.

'Expect him to hide?' Clark asked.

'You know him, Daddy?' Patricia asked.

'Yes, as a matter of fact. Ding and I used to look after him back when we were SPOs. I knew his father, once . . . ,' John added without thinking, which was very unusual for him.

'What's he like, Ding?' Patsy asked her fiancé, the ring still fresh on her finger.

'Pretty smart,' Chavez allowed. 'Kinda quiet. Nice guy, always has a kind word. Well, usually.'

'He's been tough when he had to be,' John observed with an eye to his partner and soon-to-be son-in-law, which thought almost occasioned a chill. Then he saw the look in his daughter's eyes, and the chill became quite real. Damn.

'That's a fact,' the junior man agreed.

The lights made him sweat under his makeup, and Ryan fought the urge to scratch the itches on his face. He managed to keep his hands still, but his facial muscles began a series of minor twitches that he hoped the camera didn't catch.

'I'm afraid I can't say, Barry,' he went on, holding his hands tightly together. 'It's just too soon to respond substantively to a lot of questions right now. When we're able to give hard answers, we will. Until then, we won't.'

'You have a big day ahead,' the CNN reporter said sympathetically.

'Barry, we all do.'

'Thank you, Mr President.' He waited until the light went off and he heard a voice-over from the Atlanta headquarters before speaking again. 'Good one. Thank you.'

Van Damm came in then, pushing Andrea Price aside as he did so. Few could touch a Secret Service agent without seriously adverse consequences, much less bustle one, but Arnie was one who could.

'Pretty good. Don't do anything different. Answer the questions. Keep your answers short.'

Mrs Abbot came in next to check Ryan's makeup. A gentle hand touched his forehead while the other adjusted his hair with a small brush. Even for his high-school prom – what *was* her name? Ryan asked himself irrelevantly – neither he nor anyone else had been so fussy about his coarse black hair. Under other circumstances it would have been something to laugh about.

The CBS anchor was a woman in her middle thirties, and proof positive that brains and looks were not mutually exclusive.

'Mr President, what is left of the government?' she asked after a couple of conventional get-acquainted questions.

'Maria' – Ryan had been instructed to address each reporter by the given name; he didn't know why, but it seemed reasonable enough – 'as horrid as the last twelve hours have been for all of us, I want to remind you of a speech President Durling gave a few weeks ago: America is still America. All of the federal executive agencies will be operating today under the leadership of the sitting deputy secretaries, and –'

'But Washington –'

'For reasons of public safety, Washington is pretty well shut down, that is true –' She cut him off again, less from ill manners than from the fact that she only had four minutes to use, and she wanted to use them.

'The troops in the street . . . ?'

'Maria, the DC police and fire departments had the roughest night of all. It's been a long, cold night for those people. The Washington, DC National Guard has been called out to assist the civilian agencies. That also happens after hurricanes and tornadoes. In fact, that's really a municipal function. The FBI is working with the mayor to get the job done.' It was Ryan's longest statement of the morning, and almost left him breathless, he was wound so tightly. That was when he realized that he was squeezing his hands to the point that his fingers were turning white, and Jack had to make a conscious effort to relax them.

'Look at his arms,' the Prime Minister observed. 'What do we know of this Ryan?'

The chief of her country's intelligence service had a file folder in his lap which he had already memorized, having had the luxury of a working day to familiarize himself with the new chief of state.

'He's a career intelligence officer. You know about the incident in London, and later in the States some years ago –'

'Oh, yes,' she noted, sipping her tea and dismissing that bit of history. 'So, a spy . . .'

'A well-regarded one. Our Russian friends think very highly of him indeed. So does Century House,' said the army general, whose training went back to the British tradition. Like his Prime Minister, he'd been educated at Oxford, and, in his case, Sandhurst. 'He is highly intelligent. We have reason to believe that in his capacity as Durling's National Security Advisor he was instrumental in controlling American operations against Japan –'

'And us?' she asked, her eyes locked on the screen. How convenient it was to have communications satellites – and the American networks were all global now. Now you didn't have to spend a whole day in an aircraft to go and see a rival chief of state – and then under controlled circumstances. Now she could see the man under pressure and gauge how he responded to it. Career intelligence officer or not, he didn't look terribly comfortable. Every man had his limitations.

'Undoubtedly, Prime Minister.'

'He is less formidable than your information would suggest,' she told her adviser. *Tentative, uncomfortable, rattled . . . out of his depth.*

'When do you expect to be able to tell us more about what happened?' Maria asked.

'I really can't say right now. It's just too soon. Some things can't be rushed, I'm afraid,' Ryan said. He vaguely grasped that he'd lost control of this interview, short as it was, and wasn't sure why. It never occurred to him that the TV reporters were lined up outside the Roosevelt Room like shoppers in a checkout line, that each one wanted to ask something new and different – after the first question or two – and that each wanted to make an impression, not on the new President, but on the viewers, the unseen people behind the cameras who watched each morning show out of loyalty which the reporters had to strengthen whenever possible. As gravely wounded as the country was, reporting the news was the business which put food on their family tables, and Ryan was just one more subject of that business. That was why

Arnie's earlier advice on how they'd been instructed on what questions to ask had been overly optimistic, even coming from an experienced political pro. The only really good news was that the interviews were all time-limited – in this case by local news delivered by the various network affiliates at twenty-five minutes after the hour. Whatever tragedy had struck Washington, people *needed* to know about local weather and traffic in the pursuit of their daily lives, a fact perhaps lost on those inside the DC Beltway, though not lost on the local stations across the country. Maria was more gracious than she felt when the director cut her off. She smiled at the camera –

'We'll be back.'

– and Ryan had twelve minutes until NBC had at him. The coffee he'd had at breakfast was working on him now, and he needed to find a bathroom, but when he stood, the microphone wire nearly tripped him.

'This way, Mr President,' Price pointed to the left, down the corridor, then right toward the Oval Office, Jack realized too late. He stopped cold on entering the room. It was still someone else's in his mind, but a bathroom was a bathroom, and in this case, it was actually part of a sitting room off the office itself. Here, at least, there was privacy, even from the Praetorian Guard, which followed him like a pack of collies protecting a particularly valuable sheep. Jack didn't know that when there was someone in this particular head, a light on the upper door frame lit up, and that a peephole in the office door allowed the Secret Service to know even that aspect of their President's daily life.

Washing his hands, Ryan looked in the mirror, always a mistake at times like this. The makeup made him appear more youthful than he was, which wasn't so bad, but also phony, the false ruddiness which his skin had never had. He had to fight off the urge to wipe it all off before coming back out to face NBC. This anchor was a black male, and on shaking hands with him, back in the Roosevelt Room, it was of some consolation that his makeup was even more grotesque than his own. Jack was oblivious to the fact that the TV lights so affected the human complexion that to appear normal on a television screen, one had to appear the clown to non-electronic eyes.

'What will you be doing today, Mr President?' Nathan asked as his fourth question.

'I have another meeting with acting FBI Director Murray – actually we'll be meeting twice a day for a while. I also have a scheduled session with the national security staff, then with some of the surviving members of Congress. This afternoon, we have a Cabinet meeting.'

'Funeral arrangements?' The reporter checked off another question from the list in his lap.

Ryan shook his head. 'Too soon. I know it's frustrating for all of us, but these things do take time.' He didn't say that the White House Protocol Office had fifteen minutes of his afternoon to brief him on what was being planned.

'It was a Japanese airliner, and in fact a government-owned carrier. Do we have any reason to suspect –'

Ryan leaned forward at that one: 'No, Nathan, we don't. We've had communications with the Japanese government. Prime Minister Koga has promised full cooperation, and we are taking him at his word. I want to emphasize that hostilities with Japan are completely over. What happened was a horrible mistake. That country is working to bring to justice the people who caused that conflict to take place. We don't yet know how everything happened – last night, I mean – but "don't know" means *don't know*. Until we do, I want to discourage speculation. That can't help anything, but it can hurt, and there's been enough hurt for a while. We have to think about healing now.'

'Domo Arigato,' muttered the Japanese Prime Minister. It was the first time he'd seen Ryan's face or heard his voice. Both were younger than he'd expected, though he'd been informed of Ryan's particulars earlier in the day. Koga noted the man's tension and unease, but when he had something to say other than an obvious answer to an inane question – why did the Americans tolerate the insolence of their media? – the voice changed somewhat, as did the eyes. The difference was subtle, but Koga was a man accustomed to noting the smallest of nuance. It was one advantage of growing up in Japan, and all the more so for having spent his adult life in politics.

'He was a formidable enemy,' a Foreign Ministry official

noted quietly. 'And in the past he showed himself to be a man of courage.'

Koga thought about the papers he'd read two hours earlier. This Ryan had used violence, which the Japanese Prime Minister abhorred. But he had learned from two shadowy Americans who had probably saved his life from his own countrymen that violence had a place, just as surgery did, and Ryan had taken violent action to protect others, suffered in the process, then done so again before returning to peaceful pursuits. Yet again he'd displayed the same dichotomy, against Koga's country, fighting with skill and ruthlessness, then showing mercy and consideration. A man of courage . . .

'And honor, I think.' Koga paused for a moment. So strange that there should already be friendship between two men who had never met, and who had only a week before been at war. 'He is samurai.'

The ABC correspondent, female and blond, had the name of Joy, which for some reason struck Ryan as utterly inappropriate to the day, but it was probably the name her parents had given her, and that was that. If Maria from CBS has been pretty, Joy was stunning, and perhaps a reason ABC had the top-rated morning show. Her hello handshake was warm and friendly – and something else that almost made Jack's heart stop.

'Good morning, Mr President,' she said softly, in a voice better suited to a dinner party than a morning TV news show.

'Please.' Ryan waved her to the chair opposite his.

'Ten minutes before the hour. We're here in the Roosevelt Room of the White House to speak with President John Patrick Ryan,' her voice cooed to the camera. 'Mr President, it's been a long and difficult night for our country. What can you tell us?'

Ryan had it down sufficiently pat that the answer came out devoid of conscious thought. His voice was calm and slightly mechanical, and his eyes locked on hers, as he'd been told to do. In this case it wasn't hard to concentrate on her liquid brown eyes, though looking so deeply into them this early in the morning was disconcerting. He hoped it didn't show too much.

'Mr President, the last few months have been very

traumatic for all of us, and last night was only more so. You will be meeting with your national security staff in a few minutes. What are your greatest concerns?'

'Joy, a long time ago an American President said that the only thing we have to fear is fear itself. Our country is as strong today as yesterday –'

'Yes, that is true.' Daryaei had met Ryan once before. He'd been arrogant and defiant then, in the way of a dog standing before his master, snarling and brave – or seemingly so. But now the master was gone, and here was the dog, eyes fixed on a beautiful but sluttish woman, and it surprised Daryaei that his tongue wasn't out and drooling. Fatigue had something to do with it. Ryan was tired; that was plain to see. What else was he? He was like his country, the Ayatollah decided. Outwardly strong, perhaps. Ryan was a young man still, broad of shoulder, erect of posture. His eyes were clear, and his voice firm, but when asked of his country's strength, he spoke of fear and the fear of fear. Interesting.

Daryaei knew well enough that strength and power were things of the mind more than the body, a fact as true of nations as of men. America was a mystery to him, as were America's leaders. But how much did he have to know? America was a godless country. That was why this Ryan boy talked of fear. Without God, both the country and the man lacked direction. Some had said that the same was true of Daryaei's country, but if that were true at all, it was for a different reason, he told himself.

Like people all over the world, Daryaei concentrated on Ryan's face and voice. The answer to the first question was obviously mechanical. Whatever America knew about this glorious incident, they weren't telling. Probably they didn't know very much, but that was to be understood. His had been a long day, and Daryaei had used it profitably. He'd called his Foreign Ministry and had the chief of the America desk (actually a whole department in the official building in Tehran) order a paper on the working of the American government. The situation was even better than Daryaei had hoped. They could make no new laws, could levy no new taxes, could spend no new money until such time as their Congress was reconstituted, and that would require time.

Almost all of their ministries were headless. This Ryan boy – Daryaei was seventy-two – *was* the American government, and he was not impressed with what he saw.

The United States of America had thwarted him for years. So much power. Even after reducing its might following the downfall of the Soviet Union – the 'lesser Satan' – America could do things possible for no other nation. All it needed was political resolve, and though that was rare enough, the threat of it was ever daunting. Every so often the country would rally behind a single purpose, as had happened not so long before against Iraq, with consequences so startlingly decisive as compared with what little his own country had managed in a shooting war that had lasted nearly a full decade. That was the danger of America. But America was a thinner reed now – or rather, America was, if not quite headless, then nearly so. The strongest body was rendered crippled and useless by an injury to its neck, the more so from one to its head . . .

Just one man, Daryaei thought, not hearing the words from the television now. The words didn't matter now. Ryan wasn't saying anything of substance, but telling the man half a world away much with his demeanor. The new head of that country had a neck that became the focus of Daryaei's gaze. Its symbolism was clear. The technical issue, after all, was to complete the separation of head from body, and all that stood between the two was the neck.

'Ten minutes to the next one,' Arnie said after Joy left to catch her car to the airport. The Fox reporter was in makeup.

'How am I doing?' Jack disconnected the mike wire before standing this time. He needed to stretch his legs.

'Not bad,' van Damm judged, charitably. He might have said something else to a career politician, but a real politico would have had to field really tough questions. It was as though a golfer were playing against his handicap instead of a tour-pro partner, and that was fair, as far as it went. Most important, Ryan needed to have his confidence built up if he were to function at all. The presidency was hard enough at the best of times, and while every holder of that office had wished more than once to be rid of Congress and other agencies and departments as well, it was Ryan who would have to learn how indispensable the whole system of government was – and he'd learn the hard way.

'I have to get used to a lot, don't I?' Jack leaned against the wall outside the Roosevelt Room, looking up and down the corridor.

'You'll learn,' the chief of staff promised him.

'Maybe so.' Jack smiled, not realizing that the activity of the morning – the recent activity – had given his mind something to shunt aside the other circumstances of the day. Then a Secret Service agent handed him a slip of paper.

However unfair it was to the other families, it was to be understood that the first priority had to be the body of President Durling. No fewer than four mobile cranes had been set up on the west side of the building, operating under the direction of hard-hatted construction foremen standing with a team of skilled workers on the floor of the chamber, much too close for safety, but OSHA wasn't around this morning. The only government inspectors who mattered were Secret Service – the FBI might have had overall jurisdiction, but no one would have stood between them and their own mournful quest. There was a doctor and a team of paramedics standing by as well, on the unlikely chance that someone might have survived despite everything to the contrary. The real trick was coordinating the actions of the cranes, which dipped into the crater – that's how it looked – like a quartet of giraffes drinking from the same water hole, never quite banging together due to the skill of the operators.

'Look here!' The construction supervisor pointed. In the blackened claw of a dead hand was an automatic pistol. It had to be Andy Walker, principal agent of Roger Durling's Detail. The last frame of TV had shown him within feet of his President, racing to spirit him off the podium, but too late to accomplish anything more than his own death in the line of duty.

The next dip of the next crane. A cable was affixed around a block of sandstone, which rose slowly, twirling somewhat with the torsion of the steel cable. The remainder of Walker's body was now visible, along with the trousered legs of someone else. All around both were the splintered and discolored remains of the oak podium, even a few sheets of charred paper. The fire hadn't really reached through the pile of stones in this part of the ruined building. It had burned too rapidly for that.

'Hold it!' The construction man grabbed the arm of the Secret Service agent and wouldn't let him move. 'They're not going anywhere. It's not worth getting killed for. Couple of more minutes.' He waited for one crane to clear the path for the next, and waved his arms, telling the operator how to come in, where to dip, and when to stop. Two workers slipped a pair of cables around the next stone block, and the foreman twirled his hand in the air. The stone lifted.

'We have JUMPER,' the agent said into his microphone. The medical team moved in at once, over the warning shouts of several construction men, but it was plain from twenty feet away that their time was wasted. His left hand held the binder containing his last speech. The falling stones had probably killed him before the fire had reached in far enough to singe his hair. Much of the body was misshapen from crushing, but the suit and the presidential tie-clasp and the gold watch on his wrist positively identified President Roger Durling. Everything stopped. The cranes stood still, their diesel engines idling while their operators sipped their coffee or lit up smokes. A team of forensic photographers came in to snap their rolls of film from every possible angle.

They took their time. Elsewhere on the floor of the chamber, National Guardsmen were bagging bodies and carrying them off – they'd taken over this task from the firefighters two hours before – but for a fifty-foot circle, there were only Secret Service, performing their last official duty to JUMPER, as they had called the President in honor of his service as a lieutenant in the 82nd Airborne. It had gone on too long for tears, though for all of the assembled agents those would come again, more than once. When the medics withdrew, when the photographers were satisfied, four agents in SECRET SERVICE windbreakers made their way down over the remaining stone blocks. First they lifted the body of Andy Walker, whose last conscious act had been to protect his 'principal,' and lowered it gently into the rubberized bag. The agents held it up so that another pair of their fellows could lift it clear and take it on its way. The next task was President Durling. This proved difficult. The body was askew in death, and the cold had frozen it. One arm was at a right angle to the rest of the body and would not fit into the bag. The agents looked at one another, not knowing what to do about it. The body was evidence and could not be tampered with. Perhaps more important was their horror at hurting a body already dead, and so President Durling went into the bag with the arm outstretched like Captain Ahab's. The four agents carried it out, making their way out of the chamber, around all of the fallen blocks, and then down toward an ambulance waiting for this single purpose. That tipped off the press photographers near and far, who snapped away, or zoomed in their TV cameras to capture the moment.

The moment cut into Ryan's Fox interview, and he watched the scene on the monitor that sat on the table. Somehow in his mind that made it official. Durling really was dead, and now he really was the President, and that was that. The camera in the room caught Ryan's face as it changed, as he remembered how Durling had brought him in, trusted him, leaned on him, guided him . . .

That was it, Jack realized. He'd always had someone to lean on before. Sure, others had leaned on him, asked his opinion, given him his head in a crisis, but there was always someone to come back to, to tell him he'd done the right thing. He could do that now, but what he'd receive in return would be just opinions, not judgments. The judgments were his now. He'd hear all manner of things. His advisers would be like lawyers, some arguing one way, some arguing another, to tell him how he was both right and wrong at the same time, but when it was all over, the decision was his alone.

President Ryan's hand rubbed his face, heedless of the makeup, which he smeared. He didn't know that what Fox and the other networks were sending out was splitscreened now, since all had access to the pool feed from the Roosevelt Room. His head shook slightly from side to side in the way of a man who had to accept something he didn't like, his face too blank now for sadness. Behind the Capitol steps, the cranes started dipping again.

'Where do we go from here?' the Fox reporter asked. That question wasn't on his list. It was just a human reaction to a human scene. The cut to the Hill had bitten deep into the allotted time for the interview, and for another subject they would have carried over into the next segment, but the rules in the White House were adamantine.

'Quite a lot of work to be done,' Ryan answered.

'Thank you, Mr President. Fourteen minutes after the hour.'

Jack watched the light on the TV camera blink off. The originating producer waited a few seconds before waving his hand, and the President detached his microphone and cable. His first press marathon was over. Before leaving the room, he looked more carefully at the cameras. Earlier in his life he'd taught classes in history, and more recently he'd delivered briefings, but all of those had gone to a live audience whose eyes he could see and read, and from their reaction he would adjust his delivery somewhat, speeding up or slowing down, maybe tossing in a little humor if circumstances allowed, or repeating something to make his point clearer. Now his intimate chats would be directed to a *thing*. Something else not to like. Ryan left the room, while all over the world, people evaluated what they'd seen of the new American President. Television commentators would discuss him in fifty or more countries while he found the bathroom again.

'This is the best thing that's happened to our country since Jefferson.' The older man rated himself a serious student of history. He liked Thomas Jefferson for his statement about how a country governed least was governed best, which was about all he knew of the adages from the Sage of Monticello.

'And it took a Jap to do it, looks like.' The statement was trailed by an ironic snort. Such an event could even invalidate his closely held racism. Couldn't have that, could he?

They'd been up all night – it was 5:20 local time – watching the TV news coverage, which hadn't stopped. The newsies, they noted, looked even more wasted than this Ryan guy. Time zones did have an advantage. Both had stopped drinking beer around midnight, and had switched to coffee two hours later when they'd both started dozing. Couldn't have that. What they saw, switching through channels downloaded on a large satellite dish outside the cabin, was like some sort of fantastic telethon, except this one wasn't about raising money for crippled children or AIDS victims or nigger schools. This one was fun. All those Washington bastards, must have been burned to a crisp, most of them.

'Bureaucrat barbecue,' Peter Holbrook said for the seventeenth time since 11:30, when he'd come up with his summation of the event. He'd always been the creative one in the movement.

'Aw, *shit*, Pete!' gasped Ernest Brown, spilling some of his coffee into his lap. It was *still* funny, enough so that he didn't leap immediately to his feet from the uncomfortable feeling that resulted from his slip.

'Has been a long night,' Holbrook allowed, laughing himself. They'd watched President Durling's speech for a couple of reasons. For one, all of the networks had pre-empted normal programs, as was usually the case for an important event; but the truth of the matter was that their satellite downlink gave them access to a total of 117 channels, and they didn't even have to switch the set off to avoid input from the government they and their friends despised. The deeper reason was that they cultivated their anger at their government, and usually watched such speeches – both men caught at least an hour a day of C-SPAN-1 and -2 – to fuel those feelings, trading barbed comments back and forth every minute of a presidential speech.

'So, who is this Ryan guy, really?' Brown asked, yawning.

'Another 'crat, looks like. A bureaucrat talking bureaucrap.'

'Yeah,' judged Brown. 'With nothing to back him up, Pete.'

Holbrook turned and looked at his friend. 'It's really som'thin', isn't it?' With that observation he got up and walked to the bookshelves that walled the south side of his den. His copy of the Constitution was a well-thumbed pamphlet edition which he read as often as he could, so as to improve his understanding of the *intent* of the drafters. 'You know, Pete, there's nothing in here to cover a situation like this.'

'Really?'

Holbrook nodded. 'Really.'

'No shit.' That required some thought, didn't it?

*   *   *

'Murdered?' President Ryan asked, still wiping the makeup off his face with wet <u>towelettes</u> of the same sort he'd used to clean off baby bottoms. At least it made his face feel clean when he'd finished.

'That's the preliminary indication, both from a cursory examination of the body and from a quick-and-dirty examination of the cockpit tapes.' Murray flipped through the notes faxed to him only twenty minutes before.

Ryan leaned back in his chair. Like much else in the Oval Office, it was new. On the credenza behind him, all of Durling's family and personal photos had been removed. The papers on the desk had been taken away for examination by the presidential secretarial staff. What remained or what had been substituted were accoutrements from White House stores. The chair at least was a good one, expensively designed to protect the back of its occupant, and it would soon be substituted for a custom-designed chair fitted to his own back by a manufacturer who performed the service for free and – remarkably – without public fanfare. Sooner or later he'd have to work in this place, Jack had decided a few minutes earlier. The secretaries were here, and it wasn't fair to make them trek across the building, up and down stairs. Sleeping in this place was another issue entirely – for the moment; that, too had to change, didn't it? *So*, he thought, staring across the desk at Murray, *murder*.

'Shot?'

Dan shook his head. 'Knife right in the heart, only one penetration. The wound looked to our agent to be from a thin blade, like a steak knife. From the cockpit tapes, it appears that it was done prior to takeoff. Looks like we can time-stamp that pretty exactly. From just prior to engine start-up to the moment of impact, the only voice on the tapes is the pilot. His name was Sato, a very experienced command pilot. The Japanese police have gotten a pile of data to us. It would seem that he lost a brother and a son in the war. The brother commanded a destroyer that got sunk with all hands. The son was a fighter pilot who cracked up on landing after a mission. Both on the same day or near enough. So, it was personal. Motive and opportunity, Jack,' Murray allowed himself to say, for they were almost alone in the office. Andrea Price was there, too. She didn't quite approve; she had not yet been told exactly how far back the two men went.

'That's pretty fast on the ID,' Price observed.

'It has to be firmed up,' Murray agreed. 'We'll do that with DNA testing just to be sure. The cockpit tape is good enough for voice-print analysis, or so they told our agent. The Canadians have radar tapes tracking the aircraft out of their airspace, so confirming the timing of the event is simple. We have the aircraft firmly ID'd from Guam to Japan to Vancouver, and into the Capitol building. Like they say, it's all over but the shouting. There *will* be a lot of shouting. Mr President' – Andrea Price felt better this time – 'it will be at least two months before we have every lead and tidbit of information nailed down, and I suppose it's possible that we could be wrong, but for all practical purposes, in my opinion and that of our senior agents at the scene, this case is well on its way to being closed.'

'What could make you wrong?' Ryan asked.

'Potentially quite a few things, but there are practical considerations. For this to be anything other than the act of a single fanatic – no, that's not fair, is it? One very angry man. Anyway, for this to be a conspiracy, we have to assume detailed planning, and that's hard to support. How would they know the war was going to be lost, how did they know about the joint session – and if it were planned as a war operation, like the NTSB guy said, hell, ten tons of high explosives would have been simple to load aboard.'

'Or a nuke,' Jack interjected.

'Or a nuke.' Murray nodded. 'That reminds me: the Air Force attaché is going to see their nuclear-weapons-fabrication facility today. It took the Japanese a couple of days to figure out where it was. We're having a guy who knows the things flying over there right now.' Murray checked his notes. 'Dr Woodrow Lowell – oh, I know him. He runs the shop at Lawrence Livermore. Prime Minister Koga told our ambassador that he wants to hand over the damned things PDQ and get them the hell out of his country.'

Ryan turned his chair around. The windows behind him faced the Washington Monument. That obelisk was surrounded by a circle of flagpoles, all of whose flags were at half-staff. But he could see that people were lined up for the elevator ride to the top. Tourists who'd come to DC to see the sights. Well, they were getting a bargain of sorts, weren't they? The Oval Office windows, he saw, were incredibly thick, just in case one of those tourists had a sniper rifle tucked under his coat . . .

'How much of this can we release?' President Ryan asked.

'I'm comfortable with releasing a few things,' Murray responded.

'You sure?' Price asked.

'It's not as though we have to protect evidence for a criminal trial. The subject in the case is dead. We'll chase down all the possibilities of co-conspirators, but the evidence we let go today will not compromise that in any way. I'm not exactly a fan of publicizing criminal evidence, but the people out there want to know something, and in a case like this one, you let them have it.'

Besides, Price thought, *it makes the Bureau look good.* With that silent observation, at least one government agency started returning to normal.

'Who's running this one at Justice?' she asked instead.

'Pat Martin.'

'Oh? Who picked him?' she asked. Ryan turned to see the discourse on this one.

Murray almost blushed. 'I guess I did. The President said to pick the best career prosecutor, and that's Pat. He's been head of the Criminal Division for nine months. Before that he ran Espionage. Ex-Bureau. He's a particularly good lawyer, been there almost thirty years. Bill Shaw wanted him to become a judge. He was talking to the AG about it only last week.'

'You sure he's good enough?' Jack asked. Price decided to answer.

'We've worked with him, too. He's a real pro, and Dan's right, he's real judge material, tough as hell, but also extremely fair. He handled a mob counterfeiting case my old partner ramrodded in New Orleans.'

'Okay, let him decide what to let out. He can start talking to the press right after lunch.' Ryan checked his watch. He'd been President for exactly twelve hours.

* * *

Colonel Pierre Alexandre, US Army, retired, still looked like a soldier, tall and thin and fit, and that didn't bother the dean at all. Dave James immediately liked what he saw as his visitor took his seat, liked him even more for what he'd read in the man's cv, and more still for what he'd learned over the phone. Colonel Alexandre – 'Alex' to his friends, of which he had many – was an expert in infectious disease who'd spent twenty productive years in the employ of his government, divided mainly between Walter Reed Army Hospital in Washington and Fort Detrick in Maryland, with numerous field trips sprinkled in. Graduate of West Point and the University of Chicago Medical School, Dr James saw. Good, his eyes again sweeping over the residency and other professional-experience entries. The list of published articles ran to eight single-spaced pages. Nominated for a couple of important prizes, but not lucky yet. Well, maybe Hopkins could change that. His dark eyes were not especially intense at the moment. By no means an arrogant man, Alexandre knew who and what he was – better yet, knew that Dean James knew.

'I know Gus Lorenz,' Dean James said with a smile. 'We interned together at Peter Brent Brigham.' Which Harvard had since consolidated into Brigham and Women's.

'Brilliant guy,' Alexandre agreed in his best Creole drawl. It was generally thought that Gus's work on Lassa and Q fever put him in the running for a Nobel Prize. 'And a great doc.'

'So, why don't you want to work with him in Atlanta? Gus tells me he wants you pretty bad.'

'Dean James –'

'Dave,' the Dean said.

'Alex,' the colonel responded. There was something to be said for civilian life, after all. Alexandre thought of the dean as a three-star equivalent. Maybe four stars. Johns Hopkins carried a lot of prestige. 'Dave, I've worked in a lab damned near all my life. I want to treat patients again. CDC would just be more of the same. Much as I like Gus – we did a lot of work together in Brazil back in 1987; we get along just fine,' he assured the dean. 'I am *tired* of looking at slides and printouts all the time.' And for the same reason he'd turned down one hell of an offer from Pfizer Pharmaceuticals, to head up one of their new labs. Infectious diseases were a coming thing in medicine, and both men hoped that it wasn't too late. Why the *hell*, James wondered, hadn't this guy made general-officer rank? Maybe politics, the dean thought. The Army had that problem, too, just as Hopkins did. But their loss . . .

'I talked about you with Gus last night.'

'Oh?' Not that it was surprising. At this level of medicine everyone knew everyone else.

'He says just hire you on the spot –'

'Good of him,' Alexandre chuckled.

'– before Harry Tuttle at Yale gets you for his lab.'

'You know Harry?' Yep, and everybody knew what everybody else was doing, too.

'Classmates here,' the dean explained. 'We both dated Wendy. He won. You know, Alex, there isn't much for me to ask you.'

'I hope that's good.'

'It is. We can start you off as an associate professor working under Ralph Forster. You'll have a lot of lab work – good team to work with. Ralph has put a good shop together in the last ten years. But we're starting to get a lot of clinical referrals. Ralph's getting a little old to travel so much, so you can expect to get around the world some. You'll also be in charge of the clinical side in, oh, six months to get your feet good and wet . . .?'

The retired colonel nodded thoughtfully. 'That's just about right. I need to relearn a few things. Hell, when does learning ever stop?'

'When you become an administrator, if you're not careful.'

'Yeah, well, now you know why I hung up the green suit. They wanted me to command up a hospital, you know, punch the ticket. Damn it, I know I'm good in a lab, okay? I'm *very* good in a lab. But I signed on to treat people once in a while – and to teach some, naturally, but I like to see sick people and send them home healthy. Once upon a time somebody in Chicago told me that's what the job was.'

If this was a selling job, Dean James thought, then he'd taken lessons from Olivier. Yale could offer him about the same post, but this one would keep Alexandre close to Fort Detrick, and ninety minutes' flying time to Atlanta, and close to the Chesapeake Bay – in the résumé, it said

Alexandre liked to fish. Well, that figured, growing up in the Louisiana bayous. In sum total, that was Yale's bad luck. Professor Harold Tuttle was as good as they came, maybe a shade better than Ralph Forster, but in five years or so Ralph would retire, and Alexandre here had the look of a star. More than anything else, Dean James was in the business of recruiting future stars. In another reality, he would have been the GM for a winning baseball team. So, that was settled. James closed the folder on his desk.

'Doctor, welcome to the Johns Hopkins University School of Medicine.'

'Thank you, sir.'

4

OJT

The rest of the day was a blur. Even while living through it, Ryan knew that he'd never really remember more than snippets. His first experience with computers had been as a student at Boston College. Before the age of personal computing, he'd used the dumbest of dumb terminals – a teletype – to communicate with a mainframe somewhere, along with other BC students, and more still from other local schools. That had been called 'time-sharing,' just one more term from a bygone age when computers had cost a million or so dollars for performance that now could be duplicated in the average man's watch. But the term still applied to the American presidency, Jack learned, where the ability to pursue a single thought through from beginning to end was the rarest of luxuries, and work consisted of following various intellectual threads from one separate meeting to the next, like keeping track of a whole group of continuing TV series from episode to episode, trying not to confuse one with another, and knowing that avoiding that error was totally impossible.

After dismissing Murray and Price, it had begun in earnest.

Ryan's introduction began with a national-security briefing delivered by one of the national intelligence officers assigned to the White House staff. Here, over a period of twenty-six minutes, he learned what he already knew because of the job he'd held until the previous day. But he had to sit through it anyway, if for no other reason than to get a feel for the man who would be one of his daily briefing team. They were all different. Each one had an individual perspective, and Ryan had to understand the nuances peculiar to the separate voices he'd be hearing.

'So, nothing on the horizon for now?' Jack asked.

'Nothing we see at the National Security Council, Mr President. You know the potential trouble spots as well as I do, of course, and those change on a day-to-day basis.' The man hedged with the grace of someone who'd been dancing to this particular brand of music for years. Ryan's face didn't change, only because he'd seen it before. A real intelligence officer didn't fear death, didn't fear finding his wife in bed with his best friend, didn't fear any of the normal vicissitudes of life. A national intelligence officer *did* fear being found wrong on anything he said in his official capacity. To avoid that was simple, however: you never took a real stand on any single thing. It was a disease not limited to elected officials, after all. Only the President *had* to take a stand, and it was his good fortune to have such trained experts to supply him with the information he needed, wasn't it?

'Let me tell you something,' Ryan said after a few seconds of reflection.

'What is that, sir?' the NIO asked cautiously.

'I don't just want to hear what you know. I also want to hear what you and your people *think*. You are responsible for what you know, but I'll take the heat for acting on what you think. I've been there and done that, okay?'

'Of course, Mr President.' The man allowed himself a smile that masked his terror at the prospect. 'I'll pass that along to my people.'

'Thank you.' Ryan dismissed the man, knowing then and there that he needed a National Security Advisor he could trust, and wondering where he'd get one.

The door opened as though by magic to let the NIO out – a Secret Service agent had done that, having watched through the spy hole for most of the briefing. The next in was a DOD briefing team.

The senior man was a two-star who handed over a plastic card.

'Mr President, you need to put this in your wallet.'

Jack nodded, knowing what it was before his hands touched the orange plastic. It looked like a credit card, but on it was a series of number groups . . .

'Which one?' Ryan asked.

'You decide, sir.'

Ryan did so, reading off the third such group twice. There were two commissioned officers with the general, a colonel and a major, both of whom wrote down the number group he'd selected and read it back to him twice. President Ryan now had the ability to order the release of strategic nuclear weapons.

'Why is this necessary?' he asked. 'We trashed the last ballistic weapons last year.'

'Mr President, we still have cruise missiles which can be armed with W-80 war-heads, plus B-61 gravity bombs assigned to our bomber fleet. We need your authorization to enable the Permissible Action Links – the PALs – and the idea is that we enable them as early as possible, just in case –'

Ryan completed the sentence: 'I get taken out early.'

You're really important now, Jack, a nasty little voice told him. *Now you can initiate a nuclear attack.* 'I hate those goddamned things. Always have.'

'You aren't supposed to like them, sir,' the general sympathized. 'Now, as you know, the Marines have the VMH-1 helicopter squadron that's always ready to get you out of here and to a place of safety at a moment's notice, and . . .'

Ryan listened to the rest while his mind wondered if he should do what Jimmy Carter had done at this point: *Okay, let's see, then. Tell them I want them to pick me up* NOW. Which presidential command had turned into a major embarrassment for a lot of Marines. But he couldn't do that now, could he? It would get out that Ryan was a paranoid fool, not someone who wanted to see if the system really worked the way people said it would. Besides, today VMH-1 would definitely be spun up, wouldn't it?

The fourth member of the briefing team was an Army warrant officer in civilian clothes who carried a quite ordinary-looking briefcase known as 'the football,' inside of which was a binder, inside of which was the attack plan – actually a whole set of them . . .

'Let me see it.' Ryan pointed. The warrant hesitated, then unlocked the case and handed over the navy blue binder, which Ryan flipped open.

'Sir, we haven't changed it since –'

The first section, Jack saw, was labeled MAJOR ATTACK OPTION. It showed a map of Japan, many of whose cities were marked with multicolored dots. The legend at the bottom showed what the dots meant in terms of delivered megatonnage; probably another page would quantify the predicted deaths. Ryan opened the binder rings and removed the whole section. 'I want these pages burned. I want this MAO eliminated immediately.' That merely meant that it would be filed away in some drawer in Pentagon War Plans, and also in Omaha. Things like this never died.

'Sir, we have not yet confirmed that the Japanese have destroyed all of their launchers, nor have we confirmed the neutralization of their weapons. You see –'

'General, that's an order,' Ryan said quietly. 'I can give them, you know.'

The man's back braced to attention. 'Yes, Mr President.'

Ryan flipped through the rest of the binder. Despite his previous job, what he found was a revelation. Jack had always avoided too-intimate knowledge of the damned things. He'd never expected them to be used. After the terrorist incident in Denver and all the horror that had swept the surface of the planet in its aftermath, statesmen across continents and political beliefs had indulged themselves in a collective think about the weapons under their control. Even during the shooting war with Japan just ended, Ryan had known that somewhere, some team of experts had concocted a plan for a nuclear retaliatory strike, but he'd concentrated his efforts at making it unnecessary, and it was a source of considerable pride to the new President that he'd never even contemplated implementing the plan whose summary was still in his left hand. LONG RIFLE, he saw, was the code name. Why did the names have to be like that, virile and exciting, as though for something that one could be proud of?

'What's this one? LIGHT SWITCH . . . ?'

'Mr President,' the general answered, 'that's a method of using an EMP attack. Electromagnetic pulse. If you explode a device at very high altitude, there's nothing – no air, actually – to absorb the initial energy of the detonation and convert it into mechanical energy – no shock wave, that is. As a result all the energy goes out in its original electromagnetic form. The resulting energy surge is murder on power and telephone lines. We always had a bunch of weapons fused for high-altitude burst in our SIOPs for the Soviet Union. Their telephone system was so primitive that it would have been easy to destroy. It's a cheap mission-kill, won't really hurt anybody on the ground.'

'I see.' Ryan closed the binder and handed it back to the

warrant officer, who immediately locked the now-lighter document away. 'I take it there's nothing going on which is likely to require a nuclear strike of any kind?'

'Correct, Mr President.'

'So, what's the point of having this man sitting outside my office all the time?'

'You can't predict all possible contingencies, can you, sir?' the general asked. It must have been difficult for him to deliver the line with a straight face, Ryan realized, as soon as the shock went away.

'I guess not,' a chastised President replied.

The White House Protocol Office was headed by a lady named Judy Simmons, who'd been seconded to the White House staff from the State Department four months earlier. Her office in the basement of the building had been busy since just after midnight, when she'd arrived from her home in Burke, Virginia. Her thankless job was to prepare arrangements for what would be the largest state funeral in American history, a task on which over a hundred staff members had already kibitzed, and it was not yet lunchtime.

The list of all the dead still had to be compiled, but from careful examination of the videotapes it was largely known who was in the chamber, and there was biographical information on all of them – married or single, religion, etc. – from which to make the necessary, if preliminary, plans. Whatever was finally decided, Jack would be the master of the grim ceremony, and had to be kept informed of every step of the planning. A funeral for thousands, Ryan thought, most of whom he hadn't known, for most of whose as yet unrecovered bodies waited wives and husbands and children.

'National Cathedral,' he saw, turning the page. The approximate numbers of religious affiliations had been compiled. That would determine the clergy to take the various functions in the ecumenical religious service.

'That's where such ceremonies are usually carried out, Mr President,' a very harried official confirmed. 'There will not be room for all of the remains' – she didn't say that one White House staffer had suggested an outdoor memorial service at RFK Stadium in order to accommodate all the victims – 'but there will be room for the President and Mrs Durling, plus a representative sampling of the congressional victims. We've contacted eleven foreign governments on the question of the diplomats who were present. We also have a preliminary list of foreign-government representatives who will be coming in to attend the ceremony.' She handed over that sheet as well.

Ryan scanned it briefly. It meant that after the memorial service he'd be meeting 'informally' with numerous chiefs of state to conduct 'informal' business. He'd need a briefing page for each meeting, and in addition to whatever they all might ask or want, every one would be checking him out. Jack knew how that worked. All over the world, presidents, prime ministers, and a few lingering dictators would now be reading briefing documents of their own – who was this John Patrick Ryan, and what can we expect of him? He wondered if they had a better idea of the answer than he did. Probably not. Their NIOs wouldn't be all that different from his, after all. And so a raft of them would come over on government jets, partly to show respect for President Durling and the American government, partly to eyeball the new American President, partly for domestic political consumption at home, and partly because it was expected that they should do so. And so this event, horrific as it was for uncounted thousands, was just one more mechanical exercise in the world of politics. Jack wanted to cry out in rage, but what else was there to do? The dead were dead, and all his grief could not bring them back, and the business of his country and others would go on.

'Have Scott Adler go over this, will you?' Somebody would have to determine how much time he should spend with the official visitors, and Ryan wasn't qualified to do that.

'Yes, Mr President.'

'What sort of speeches will I have to deliver?' Jack asked.

'We have our people working on that for you. You should have preliminary drafts by tomorrow afternoon,' Mrs Simmons replied.

President Ryan nodded and slid the papers into his out-pile. When the Chief of Protocol left, a secretary came in – he didn't know this lady's name – with a pile of telegrams, the leftovers from Eighth and I that he hadn't gotten to, plus another sheet of paper that showed his activities for the day, prepared without his input or assistance. He was about to grumble about that when she spoke.

'We have over ten thousand telegrams and e-mails from – well, from citizens,' she told him.

'Saying what?'

'Mainly that they're praying for you.'

'Oh.' Somehow that came as a surprise, and a humbling one at that. But would God listen?

Jack went back to reading the official messages, and the first day went on.

The country had essentially come to a halt, even as its new President struggled to come to terms with his new job. Banks and financial markets were closed, as were schools and many businesses. All the television networks had moved their broadcast headquarters to the various Washington bureaus in a haphazard process that had them all working together. A gang of cameras sited around the Hill kept up a continuous feed of recovery operations, while reporters had to keep talking, lest the airwaves be filled with silence. Around eleven that morning, a crane removed the remains of the 747's tail, which was deposited on a large flatbed trailer for transport to a hangar at Andrews Air Force Base. That would be the site for what was called the 'crash investigation,' for want of a better term, and cameras tracked the vehicle as it threaded its way along the streets. Two of the engines went out shortly thereafter in much the same way.

Various 'experts' helped fill the silence, speculating on what had happened and how. This was difficult for everyone involved, as there had been few leaks as yet – those who were trying to find out what had happened were too busy to talk with reporters on or off the record, and though the journalists couldn't say it, their most fertile source of leaks lay in ruin before thirty-four cameras. That gave the experts little to say. Witnesses were interviewed for their recollections – there was no tape of the inbound aircraft at all, much to the surprise of everyone. The tail number of the aircraft was known – it could hardly be missed, painted as it was on the wreckage of the aircraft, and that was as easily checked by reporters as by federal authorities. The ownership of the aircraft by Japan Airlines was immediately confirmed, along with the very day the aircraft had rolled out of the Boeing plant near Seattle. Officials of that company submitted to interviews, and along the way it was determined that the 747–400 (PIP) aircraft weighed just over two hundred tons empty, a number doubled with the mass of fuel, passengers, and baggage it could pull into the air. A pilot with United Airlines who was familiar with the aircraft explained to two of the networks how a pilot could approach Washington and then execute the death dive, while a Delta colleague did the same with the others. Both airmen were mistaken in some of the particulars, none of them important.

'But the Secret Service is armed with antiaircraft missiles, isn't it?' one anchor asked.

'If you've got an eighteen-wheeler heading for you at sixty miles an hour, and you shoot out one of the tires on the trailer, that doesn't stop the truck, does it?' the pilot answered, noting the look of concentrated intelligence on the face of a highly paid journalist who understood little more than what appeared on his TelePrompTer. 'Three hundred tons of aircraft doesn't just *stop*, okay?'

'So, there was no way to stop it?' the anchor asked with a twisted face.

'None at all.' The pilot could see that the reporter didn't understand, but he couldn't come up with anything to clarify matters further.

The director, in his control room off of Nebraska Avenue, changed cameras to follow a pair of Guardsmen bringing another body down the steps. An assistant director was keeping an eye on that set of cameras, trying to maintain a running tally of the number of bodies removed. It was now known that the bodies of President and Mrs Durling had been recovered and were at Walter Reed Army Medical Center for autopsy – required by law for wrongful death – and disposition. At network headquarters in New York, every foot of videotape of or about Durling was being organized and spliced for presentation throughout the day. Political colleagues were being sought out and interviewed. Psychologists were taken on to explain how the Durling children could deal with the trauma, and then expanded their horizons to talk about the impact of the event on the country as a whole, and how people could deal with it. About the only thing not examined on the television news was the spiritual aspect; that many of the victims had believed in God and attended church from time to time was not worthy of air time, though the presence of many people in churches was deemed newsworthy enough for three minutes on one network – and then, because each was constantly monitoring the others for ideas, that segment was copied by the others over the next few hours.

It all came down to this, really, Jack knew. The numbers only added individual examples, identical to this one in magnitude and horror. He'd avoided it for as much of the day as had been possible, but finally his cowardice had run out.

The Durling kids hovered between the numbness of denial, and terror of a world destroyed before their eyes as they'd watched their father on TV. They'd never see Mom and Dad again. The bodies were far too damaged for the caskets to be open. No last good-byes, no words, just the traumatic removal of the foundation that held up their young lives. And how were children supposed to understand that Mom and Dad weren't just Mom and Dad, but were – had been – something else to someone else, and for that reason, their deaths had been necessary to someone who hadn't known or cared about the kids?

Family members had descended on Washington, most of them flown in by the Air Force from California. Equally shocked, they nevertheless, in the presence of children, had to summon from within themselves the strength to make things somewhat easier for the young. And it gave them something to do. The Secret Service agents assigned to JUNIPER and JUNIOR were probably the most traumatized of all. Trained to be ferociously protective of any 'principal,' the agents who looked after the Durling kids – more than half were women – carried the additional burden of the normal solicitude any human held for any child, and none of them would have hesitated a microsecond to give his or her life to protect the youngsters – in the knowledge that the rest of the Detail would have weapons out and blazing. The men and women of this sub-detail had played with the kids, had bought them Christmas and birthday presents, had helped with homework. Now they were saying good-bye, to the kids, to the parents, and to colleagues. Ryan saw the looks on their faces, and made a mental note to ask Andrea if the Service would assign a psychologist to them.

'No, it didn't hurt.' Jack was sitting down so that the kids could look level into his eyes. 'It didn't hurt at all.'

'Okay,' Mark Durling said. The kids were immaculately dressed. One of the family members had thought it important that they be properly turned out to meet their father's successor. Jack heard a gasp of breath, and his peripheral vision caught the face of an agent – this one a man – who was on the edge of losing it. Price grabbed his arm and moved him toward the door, before the kids could take note of it.

'Do we stay here?'

'Yes,' Jack assured him. It was a lie, but not the sort to hurt anyone. 'And if you need anything, anything at all, you can come and see me, okay?'

The boy nodded, doing his best to be brave, and it was time to leave him to his family. Ryan squeezed his hand, treating him like the man he ought not to have become for years, for whom the duties of manhood were arriving all too soon. The boy needed to cry, and Ryan thought he needed to do that alone, for now.

Jack walked out the door into the oversized hall of the bedroom level. The agent who'd left, a tall, rugged-looking black man, was sobbing ten feet away. Ryan went over to him.

'You okay?'

'*Fuck* – sorry – I mean – shit!' the agent shook his head, ashamed at the display of emotion. His father had been lost in an Army training accident at Fort Rucker, Price knew, when he was twelve years old, and Special Agent Tony Wills, who'd played tight end at Grambling before joining the Service, was unusually good with kids. At times like this, strengths often became weaknesses.

'Don't apologize for being human. I lost my mom and dad, too. Same time,' Ryan went on, his voice dreamy and uneven with fatigue. 'Midway Airport, 737 landed short in snow. But I was all grown up when it happened.'

'I know, sir.' The agent wiped his eyes and stood erect with a shudder. 'I'll be okay.'

Ryan patted him on the shoulder and headed for the elevator. To Andrea Price: 'Get me the hell out of here.'

The Suburban headed north, turning left onto Massachusetts Avenue, which led to the Naval Observatory and the oversized Victorian-gingerbread barn which the country provided for the sitting Vice President. Again, it was guarded by Marines, who let the convoy through. Jack walked into the house. Cathy was waiting at the entry. She only needed one look.

'Tough one?'

All Ryan could do was nod. He held her tight, knowing that his tears would start soon. His eyes caught the knot of agents around the periphery of the entry hall of the house, and it occurred to him that he'd have to get used to them, standing like impassive statues, present in the most private of moments.

I hate this job.

But Brigadier General Marion Diggs loved his. Not everyone had stood down. As the Marine Barracks in Washington had gone to a high level of activity, then to be augmented from the sprawling base at Quantico, Virginia, so other organizations remained busy or became busier, for they were people who were not really allowed to sleep anyway – at least not all of them at once. One of these organizations was at Fort Irwin, California. Located in the high Mojave Desert, the base really did sprawl, over an area larger than the state of Rhode Island. The landscape was bleak enough that ecologists had to struggle to find an ecology there among the scrawny creosote bushes, and over drinks even the most dedicated of that profession would confess to finding the surface of the moon far more interesting. Not that they hadn't made his life miserable, Diggs thought, fingering his binoculars. There was a species of desert tortoise, which was distinguished from a turtle somehow or other (the general didn't have a clue), and which soldiers had to protect. To take care of that, his soldiers had collected all the tortoises they could find and then relocated them to an enclosure large enough that the reptiles probably didn't notice the fence at all. It was known locally as the world's largest turtle bordello. With that out of the way, whatever other wildlife existed at Fort

Irwin seemed quite able to look after itself. The occasional coyote appeared and disappeared, and that was that. Besides, coyotes were not endangered.

The visitors were. Fort Irwin was home to the Army's National Training Center. The permanent residents of that establishment were the OpFor, 'the opposing force.' Originally two battalions, one of armor and the other of mechanized infantry, the OpFor had once styled itself the '32nd Guards Motor Rifle Regiment,' a *Soviet* designation, because at its opening in the 1980s, the NTC had been designed to teach the US Army how to fight, survive, and prevail in a battle against the Red Army on the plains of Europe. The soldiers of the '32nd' dressed in Russian-style uniforms, drove Soviet-like equipment (the real Russian vehicles had proved too difficult to maintain, and American gear had been modified to Soviet shapes), employed Russian tactics, and took pride in kicking the hell out of the units that came to play on their turf. It wasn't strictly fair. The OpFor lived here and trained here, and hosted regular units up to fourteen times per year, whereas the visiting team might be lucky to come here once in four years. But nobody had ever said war was fair.

Times had changed with the demise of the Soviet Union, but the mission of the NTC had not. The OpFor had recently been enlarged to three battalions – now called 'squadrons,' because the unit had assumed the identity of the 11th Armored Cavalry Regiment, the Blackhorse Cav – and simulated brigade or larger enemy formations. The only real concession to the new political world was that they didn't call themselves Russians anymore. Now they were 'Krasnovians,' a word, however, derived from *krasny*, Russian for 'red.'

General-Lieutenant Gennady Iosefovich Bondarenko knew most of this – the turtle bordello was something on which he'd not been briefed; his initial tour of the base had taken care of that, however – and was as excited as he had ever been.

'You started in Signal Corps?' Diggs asked. The base commander was terse of speech and efficient of movement, dressed in desert-camouflage fatigues called 'chocolate chip' from their pattern. He, too, had been fully briefed, though, like his visitor, he had to pretend that he hadn't been.

'Correct.' Bondarenko nodded. 'But I kept getting into

trouble. First Afghanistan, then when the Mudje raided into Soviet Union. They attacked a defense-research facility in Tadzhik when I was visitor there. Brave fighters, but unevenly led. We managed to hold them off,' the Russian reported in a studied monotone. Diggs could see the decorations that had resulted; he had commanded a cavalry squadron leading Barry McCaffrey's 24th Mechanized Infantry Division in a wild ride on the American left during Desert Storm, then gone on to command the 10th 'Buffalo' ACR, still based in the Negev Desert, as part of America's commitment to Israeli security. Both men were forty-nine. Both had smelled the smoke. Both were on the way up.

'You have country like this at home?' Diggs asked.

'We have every sort of terrain you can imagine. It makes training a challenge, especially today. There,' he said. 'It's started.'

The first group of tanks was rolling now, down a broad, U-shaped pass called the Valley of Death. The sun was setting behind the brown-colored mountains, and darkness came rapidly here. Scuttling around also were the HMMWVs of the observer-controllers, the gods of the NTC, who watched everything and graded what they saw as coldly as Death himself. The NTC was the world's most exciting school. The two generals could have observed the battle back at base headquarters in a place called the Star Wars Room. Every vehicle was wired, transmitting its location, direction of movement, and when the time came, where it was shooting and whether it scored a hit or not. From that data, the computers at Star Wars sent out signals, telling people when they had died, though rarely why. That fact they learned later from the observer-controllers. The generals didn't want to watch computer screens, however – Bondarenko's staff officers were doing that, but the place for their general was here. Every battlefield had a smell, and generals had to have the nose for it.

'Your instrumentation is like something from a science novel.'

Diggs shrugged. 'Not much changed from fifteen years ago. We have more TV cameras on the hilltops now, though.' America would be selling much of that technology to the Russians. That was a little hard for Diggs to accept. He'd been too young for Vietnam. His was the first generation of flag officers to have avoided that entanglement. But Diggs had grown up with one reality in his life: fighting the Russians in Germany. A cavalry officer for his entire career, he'd trained to be in one of the forward-deployed regiments – really, augmented brigades – to make first contact. Diggs could remember a few times when it had seemed pretty damned likely that he'd find his death in the Fulda Gap, facing somebody like the man standing next to him, with whom he'd killed a six-pack the night before over stories of how turtles reproduced.

'In,' Bondarenko said with a sly grin. Somehow the Americans thought Russians were humorless. He *had* to correct that misimpression before he left.

Diggs counted ten before his deadpan reply: 'Out.'

Ten more seconds: 'In.' Then both started laughing. When first introduced to the favorite base joke, it had taken half a minute for Bondarenko to get it. But the resulting laughter had ended up causing abdominal pain. He recovered control and pointed. 'This is the way war should be.'

'It gets pretty tense. Wait and see.'

'You use *our* tactics!' That was plain from the way the reconnaissance screen deployed across the valley.

Diggs turned. 'Why not? They worked for me in Iraq.'

The scenario for this night – the first engagement for the training rotation – was a tough one: Red Force in the attack, advance-to-contact, and eliminate the Blue Force reconnaissance screen. The Blue Force in this case was a brigade of the 5th Mechanized Division conducting hasty defense. The overall idea was that this was a very fluid tactical situation. The 11th ACR was simulating a division attack on a newly arrived force one third its theoretical size. It was, really, the best way to welcome people to the desert. Let them eat dirt.

'Let's get moving.' Diggs hopped back into his HMMWV, and the driver moved off to a piece of high ground called the Iron Triangle. A short radio message from his senior OC made the American general growl. 'God damn it!'

'Problem?'

General Diggs help up a map. 'That hill is the most important piece of real estate in the valley, but they didn't see it.

Well, they're going to pay for that little misjudgment. Happens every time.' Already, the OpFor had people racing for the unoccupied summit.

'To push that far that fast, is it prudent for Blue?'

'General, it sure as hell ain't prudent not to, as you will see.'

'Why hasn't he spoken more, appeared in public more?'

The intelligence chief could have said many things. President Ryan was undoubtedly busy. So many things to do. The government of his country was in shambles, and before he could speak, he had to organize it. He had a state funeral to plan. He had to speak to numerous foreign governments, to give them the usual assurances. He had to secure things, not the least of which was his own personal safety. The American Cabinet, the President's principal advisers, was gone and had to be reconstituted . . . but that was not what he wanted to hear.

'We have been researching this Ryan,' was the answer given. Mainly from newspaper stories – a lot of them – faxed from his government's UN mission. 'He has made few public speeches before this day, and then only to present the thoughts of his masters. He was an intelligence officer – actually an "inside" man, an analyst. Evidently a good one, but an inside person.'

'So, why did Durling elevate him so?'

'That was in the American papers yesterday. Their government requires a vice-presidential presence. Durling also wanted someone to firm up his international-affairs team, and in this Ryan had some experience. He performed well, remember, in their conflict with Japan.'

'An assistant then, not a leader.'

'Correct. He has never aspired to high office. Our information is that he agreed to the second post as a caretaker, for less than a year.'

'I am not surprised.' Daryaei looked at the notes: *assistant* to Vice Admiral James Greer, the DDI/CIA; briefly the *acting* DDI; then *Deputy* Director of Central Intelligence; then National Security *Advisor* to President Durling; finally he'd accepted the *temporary* post of *Vice* President. His impressions of this Ryan person had been correct from the very beginning: a helper. Probably a skilled one, as he himself had skilled assistants, none of whom, however, could assume his own duties. He was not dealing with an equal. Good. 'What else?'

'As an intelligence specialist, he will be unusually well informed of foreign affairs. In fact, his knowledge of such things may be the best America has had in recent years, but at the cost of near-ignorance of domestic issues,' the briefing officer went on. This tidbit had come from the *New York Times*.

'Ah.' And with that bit of information, the planning started. At this point it was merely a mental exercise, but that would soon change.

'So, how are things in your army?' Diggs asked. The two generals stood alone atop the principal terrain feature, watching the battle play out below them with low-light viewing gear. As predicted, the 32nd – Bondarenko *had* to think of them that way – had overwhelmed the Blue Force reconnaissance screen, maneuvered to the left, and was now rolling up the 'enemy' brigade. With the lack of real casualties, it was a lovely thing to watch as the blinking yellow 'dead' lights lit up one by one. Then he had to answer the question.

'Dreadful. We face the task of rebuilding everything from the ground up.'

Diggs turned. 'Well, sir, that's where I came in at.' *At least you don't have to deal with drugs*, the American thought. He could remember being a new second lieutenant, and afraid to enter barracks without sidearms. If the Russians had made their move in the early 1970s . . . 'You really want to use our model?'

'Perhaps.' The only thing the Americans got wrong – and right – was that the Red Force allowed tactical initiative for its sub-unit commanders, something the Soviet Army would never have done. But, combined with doctrine developed by the Voroshilov Academy, the results were plain to see. That was something to remember, and Bondarenko had broken rules in his own tactical encounters, which was one reason why he was a living three-star instead of a dead colonel. He was also the newly appointed chief of operations for the Russian Army. 'The problem is money, of course.'

'I've heard that song before, General.' Diggs allowed himself a rueful chuckle.

Bondarenko had a plan for that. He wanted to cut the size of his army by fifty percent, and the money saved would go directly into training the remaining half. The results of such a plan he could see before him. Traditionally, the Soviet Army had depended on mass, but the Americans had proven both here and in Iraq that training was master of the battlefield. As good as their equipment was – he'd get his matériel briefing tomorrow – he envied Diggs his personnel more than anything. Proof of that arrived the moment he formed the thought.

'General?' The new arrival saluted. 'Blackhorse! We stripped their knickers right off.'

'This is Colonel Al Hamm. He's CO of the 11th. His second tour here. He used to be OpFor operations officer. Don't play cards with him,' Diggs warned.

'The general is too kind. Welcome to the desert, General Bondarenko.' Hamm extended a large hand.

'Your attack was well executed, Colonel.' The Russian examined him.

'Thank you, sir. I have some great kids working for me. Blue Force was overly tentative. We caught them between two chairs,' Hamm explained. He looked like a Russian, Bondarenko thought, tall and meaty with a pale, florid complexion surrounding twinkling blue eyes. For this occasion, Hamm was dressed in his old 'Russian'-style uniform, complete with a red star on the tanker's beret, and his pistol belt outside the over-long blouse. It didn't quite make the Russian feel at home, but he appreciated the respect the Americans showed him.

'Diggs, you were right. Blue should have done everything to get here first. But you made them start too far back to make that option seem attractive.'

'That's the problem with battlefields,' Hamm answered for his boss. 'Too much of the time they choose you instead of the other way around. That's lesson number one for the boys of the 5th Mech. If you let anybody else define the terms of the battle, well, it isn't much fun.'

ARRANGEMENTS

It turned out that both Sato and his co-pilot had donated blood for purposes of helping casualties in the abortive war with America, and the blessedly small numbers of wounded had never called that blood into use. Located by computer search by the Japanese Red Cross, samples had been obtained by the police and dispatched by messenger to Washington, via Vancouver – Japanese commercial aircraft were, understandably, still not permitted to fly into the United States, even Alaska – and an Air Force VC-20 from there to Washington. The courier was a senior police officer, with the aluminum case handcuffed to his left wrist. A trio of FBI agents met him at Andrews and drove him to the Hoover building at Tenth and Pennsylvania. The FBI's DNA lab took the samples and went to work to compare them with blood and other tissue specimens from the bodies. They already had matches for the blood types, and the results of the tests seemed a foregone conclusion, which would, nonetheless, be treated as though they were the only tenuous clue in a baffling case. Dan Murray, the acting Director, wasn't exactly a slave to 'the book' in criminal investigations, but for the purposes of this case, the book was Holy Writ. Backing him up were Tony Caruso, back from his vacation and working around the clock to head up the Bureau's side of the investigation, Pat O'Day in his capacity as roving inspector, and a cast of hundreds, if not quite thousands yet. Murray met the Japanese representative in the Director's conference room. He, too, found it hard to move into Bill Shaw's office right away.

'We are performing our own tests,' Chief Inspector Jisaburo Tanaka said, checking his watches – he had decided to wear two, one each for Tokyo and Washington time. 'They will be faxed here as soon as they are completed.' Then he opened his briefcase again. 'Here is our reconstruction of Captain

Sato's schedule for the last week, notes of interviews with family members and colleagues, background on his life.'

'Fast work. Thank you.' Murray took the pages, not quite sure what to do next. It was clear that his visitor wanted to say more. Murray and Tanaka had never met, but the word on his guest was impressive enough. A skilled and experienced investigator, Tanaka had specialized in political-corruption violations, a specialty that had kept him very busy. Tanaka had the Cromwellian look of such a policeman. His professional life had turned him into a priest of the sort used by the Spanish to burn people at the stake. That made him perfect for this case.

'You will have our total cooperation. In fact, if you wish to send a senior official from your agency to oversee our investigation, I am authorized to tell you that we will welcome it.' He paused for a few seconds, looking down before proceeding. 'This is a disgrace for my country. The way those people *used* us all . . .' For a representative of a country incorrectly known for its lack of emotional display, Tanaka was a surprise. His hands balled tightly, and his dark eyes burned with anger. From the conference room, both men could look down Pennsylvania Avenue to a Capitol Hill scarred by the crash, still lit in the pre-dawn darkness by the hundreds of work lights.

'The co-pilot was murdered,' Murray said. Maybe that would help a little.

'Oh?'

Dan nodded. 'Stabbed, and it appears as though that took place prior to the takeoff. It appears at the moment that Sato acted alone – at least as far as flying the airplane was concerned.' The lab had already determined that the weapon used was a thin-bladed steak knife with a serrated edge, of the sort used on the airline. As long as he'd been in the investigative business, it still amazed Murray what the lab techs could discern.

'I see. That makes sense,' Tanaka observed. 'The co-pilot's wife is pregnant, with twins, in fact. She is in the hospital now under close observation. What we have learned to date makes him appear to be a devoted husband and a man of no special political interests. My people thought it unlikely that he would end his life in this way.'

'Did Sato have any connections with –'

A shake of the head. 'None that we have found. He flew one of the conspirators to Saipan, and they spoke briefly. Aside from that, Sato was an international pilot. His friends were his colleagues. He lived quietly in a modest house near Narita International Airport. But his brother was a senior officer in the Maritime Self-Defense Force, and his son was a fighter pilot. Both died during the hostilities.'

Murray already knew that. *Motive and opportunity*. He scribbled a note to have the legal attaché in Tokyo take up the offer to participate in the Japanese investigation – but he'd have to get approval from Justice and/or State about that. For damned sure the offer seemed sincere enough. Good.

'Love the traffic,' Chavez observed. They were coming up I-95, passing the Springfield Mall. Normally at this time of day – it was still dark – the highway was wall-to-wall with bureaucrats and lobbyists. Not today, though John and Ding had been called in, confirming their 'essential' status to any who might have doubted it. Clark didn't respond, and the junior officer continued, 'How do you suppose Dr Ryan is doing?'

John grunted and shrugged. 'Probably rolling with the punches. Better him than me.'

'Roge-o, Mr C. All my friends at George Mason are going to have a fine old time.'

'Think so?'

'John, he's got a government to rebuild. This will be a textbook case in real life. Ain't nobody ever done that before, *mano*. You know what we're going to find out?'

A nod. 'Yeah, if this place really works or not.' *Better him than me*, John thought again. They'd been called in for their mission debriefing on operations in Japan. That was ticklish enough. Clark had been in the business for quite a while, but not long enough to be especially happy about telling others the things he'd done. He and Ding had killed – not for the first time – and now they'd get to describe it in detail to people, most of whom had never even held a gun, much less fired one in anger. Secrecy oaths or not, some of them might talk someday, the least consequence of which would be embarrassing revelations in the press. Somewhere in the middle came sworn testimony before a congressional committee – well, not anytime soon on that, John corrected himself – questioning under oath and the necessity of answering questions from people who didn't understand any better than the CIA weenies who sat at desks and judged people in the field for a living. The worst case was an actual prosecution, because while the things he had done weren't exactly illegal, they weren't exactly legal, either. Somehow the Constitution and the United States Code, Annotated, had never quite reconciled themselves with the activities the government carried out but did not wish to admit in open fora. Though his conscience was clear on that and many other things, his views on tactical morality wouldn't strike everyone as reasonable. Probably Ryan would understand, though. That was something.

'What's new this morning?' Jack asked.

'We expect recovery operations to be completed by this evening, sir.' It was Pat O'Day doing the morning FBI brief. He'd explained that Murray was busy. The inspector passed over a folder with the numbers of bodies recovered. Ryan gave it a quick scan. How the hell was he supposed to eat breakfast with such facts before him? the President wondered. Fortunately, there was just coffee at the moment.

'What else?'

'Things seem to be dropping into place. We've recovered what we think is the body of the co-pilot. He was murdered hours before the crash, leading us to believe that the pilot acted alone. We'll be doing DNA tests on the remains to confirm identities.' The inspector flipped through his notes, not trusting to memory to get things right. 'Drug and alcohol tests on both bodies proved negative. Analysis of the flight-data recorder, tapes of radio traffic, radar tapes, everything we've managed to pull together, it all leads to the same picture, one guy acting alone. Dan's meeting with a senior Japanese cop right now.'

'Next step?'

'It will be a textbook investigation process. We reconstruct everything Sato – that's the pilot's name – did over the last month or so, and take it back from there. Phone records, where he went, whom he saw, friends and associates, diary if any, everything we can get our hands on. The idea is to rebuild the guy completely and determine if he was part of any possible conspiracy. It will take time. It's a fairly exhaustive process.'

'Best guess for now?' Jack asked.

'One guy acting alone,' O'Day said again, rather more positively this time.

'It's too damned early for any conclusion,' Andrea Price objected. O'Day turned. 'It's not a conclusion. Mr Ryan asked for a best guess. I've been in the investigation business for quite a while. This looks like a fairly elaborate impulse crime. The method of the co-pilot's murder, for example. He didn't even move the body out of the cockpit. He *apologized* to the guy right after he stabbed him, according to the tapes.'

'*Elaborate* impulse crime?' Andrea objected.

'Airline pilots are highly organized people,' O'Day replied. 'Things that would be highly complex for the layman are as natural to them as pulling up your zipper. Most assassinations are carried out by dysfunctional individuals who get lucky. In this case, unfortunately, we had a very capable subject who largely made his own luck. In any event, that's what we have at the moment.'

'For this to have been a conspiracy, what would you look for?' Jack asked.

'Sir, successful criminal conspiracies are difficult to achieve under the best of circumstances.' Price bristled again, but Inspector O'Day went on: 'The problem is human nature. The most normal of us are boastful; we like to share secrets to show how bright we are. Most criminals talk their way right into prison one way or another. Okay, in a case like this we're not talking about your average robber, but the principle holds. To build any sort of conspiracy takes time and talk, and as a result, things leak. Then there's the problem of selecting the . . . "shooter," for want of a better term. Such time did not exist. The joint session was set up too late for much in the way of discussions to have taken place. The nature of the co-pilot's murder is very suggestive of a spur-of-the-moment method. A knife is less sure than a gun, and a steak knife isn't a good weapon, too easily bent or broken on a rib.'

'How many murders have you handled?' Price asked.

'Enough. I've assisted on plenty of local police cases, especially here in DC. The Washington Field Office has backed up the DC police for years. Anyway, for Sato to have been the "shooter" in a conspiracy, he would have had to meet with people. We can track his free time, and we'll do that with the Japanese. But to this point there is not a single indicator that way. Quite the contrary, all circumstances point to someone who saw a unique opportunity and made use of it on an impulse.'

'What if the pilot wasn't –'

'Ms Price, the cockpit tapes go back before the takeoff from Vancouver. We've voice-printed everything in our own lab – it's a digital tape and the sound quality is beautiful. The same guy who took off from Narita flew the airplane into the ground here. Now, if it wasn't Sato, then why didn't the co-pilot – they flew together as a team – notice? Conversely, if the pilot and co-pilot were show-ups, then both were part of the conspiracy from the beginning, then why was the co-pilot murdered prior to takeoff from Vancouver? The Canadians are interviewing the rest of the crew for us, and all the service personnel say that the flight crew was just who they were supposed to be. The DNA-ID process will prove that beyond doubt.'

'Inspector, you are very persuasive,' Ryan observed.

'Sir, this investigation will be rather involved, what with all the facts that have to be checked out, but the meat of the issue is fairly simple. It's damned hard to fake a crime scene. There's just too many things we can do. Is it theoretically possible to set things up in such a way as to fool our people?' O'Day asked rhetorically. 'Yes, sir, maybe it is, but to do that would take months of preparation, and they didn't have months. It really comes down to one thing: the decision to call the joint session happened while that aircraft was over mid-Pacific.'

Much as she wanted to, Price couldn't counter that argument. She'd run her own quick investigation on Patrick O'Day. Emil Jacobs had reinstituted the post of roving inspector years before, and collected people who preferred investigation to management. O'Day was an agent for whom running a field division had little appeal. He was part of a small team of experienced investigators who worked out of the Director's office, an unofficial inspectorate which went into the field to keep an eye on things, mainly sensitive cases. He was a good cop who hated desk work, and Price had to concede that he knew how to run an investigation, better yet was someone outside the chain of command who wouldn't ham things up in order to get a promotion. The inspector had driven to the House in a four-by-four pickup – he wore cowboy boots! she noticed – and probably wanted publicity about as much as he wanted the pox. So Assistant Director Tony Caruso, titularly in charge of the investigation, would report to the Department of Justice, but Patrick O'Day would short-circuit the chain to report directly to Murray – who would, in turn, farm O'Day to the President so as to garner personal favor. She'd figured Murray for a sharp operator. Bill Shaw, after all, had used him as personal troubleshooter. And Murray's loyalty would be to the institution of the FBI. A man could have a worse agenda, she admitted to herself. For O'Day it was simpler still. He investigated crimes for a living, and while he appeared to jump too quickly to conclusions, this transplanted cowboy was doing it all by the book. You had to watch the good ol' boys. They were so good at hiding their smarts. But he would never have made the Detail, she consoled herself.

'Enjoy your vacation?' Mary Pat Foley was either in very early or in very late, Clark saw. It came to him again that of all the senior people in government, President Ryan was probably getting the most sleep, little though that might be. It was a hell of a way to run a railroad. People simply didn't perform well when denied rest for an extended period of time, something he'd learned the hard way in the field, but put a guy into high office, and he immediately forgot that – such pedestrian items as human factors faded into the mist. And then a month later, they wondered how they'd screwed up so bad. But that was usually after they got some poor line-animal killed in the field.

'MP, when the hell is the last time you slept?' Not many people could talk to her that way, but John had been her training officer, once upon a time.

A wan smile. 'John, you're not Jewish, and you're not my mother.'

Clark looked around. 'Where's Ed?'

'On his way back from the Gulf. Conference with the Saudis,' she explained. Though Mrs Foley technically ranked Mr Foley, Saudi culture wasn't quite ready to deal with a female King Spook – Queen Spook, John corrected himself with a smile – and Ed was probably better on the conferences anyway.

'Anything I need to know about?'

She shook her head. 'Routine. So, Domingo, did you drop the question?'

'You are playing rough this morning,' Clark observed before his partner could speak.

Chavez just grinned. The country might be in turmoil, but some things were more important. 'Could be worse, Mr C. I'm not a lawyer, am I?'

'There goes the neighborhood,' John grumbled. Then it was time for business. 'How's Jack doing?'

'I'm scheduled to see him after lunch, but it wouldn't surprise me if they canceled out. The poor bastard must be buried alive.'

'What I saw about how he got roped into this, is what the papers said true?'

'Yes, it is. So, we have a Kelly Girl for President,' the Deputy Director (Operations) posed as a multifaceted inside joke. 'We're going to do a comprehensive threat assessment. I want you two in on it.'

'Why us?' Chavez asked.

'Because I'm tired of having all that done by the Intelligence Directorate. I tell you one thing that's going to happen: we have a President now who understands what we do here. We're going to beef up Operations to the point where I can pick up a phone, ask a question, and get an answer I can understand.'

'PLAN BLUE?' Clark asked, and received a welcome nod. 'Blue' had been his last function before leaving the CIA's training facility, known as 'the Farm,' down near the Navy's nuclear-weapons locker at Yorktown, Virginia. Instead of hiring a bunch of Ivy League intellectuals – at least they didn't smoke pipes anymore – he had proposed that the Agency recruit cops, police officers right off the street. Cops, he reasoned, knew about using informants, didn't have to be taught street smarts, and knew about surviving in dangerous areas. All of that would save training dollars, and probably produce better field officers. The proposal had been File-13'd by two successive DDOs, but Mary Pat had known about it from the beginning, and approved the concept. 'Can you sell it?'

'John, you're going to help me sell it. Look how well Domingo here has turned out.'

'You mean I'm not affirmative action?' Chavez asked.

'No, Ding, that's only with his daughter,' Mrs Foley suggested. 'Ryan will go for it. He isn't very keen on the Director. Anyway, for now I want you two to do your de-brief on SANDALWOOD.'

'What about our cover?' Clark asked. He didn't have to explain what he meant. Mary Pat had never got her hands dirty in the field – she was espionage, not the paramilitary side of the Operations Directorate – but she understood just fine.

'John, you were acting under presidential orders. That's written down and in the book. Nobody's going to second-guess anything you did, especially with saving Koga. You both have an Intelligence Star coming for that. President Durling wanted to see you and present the medals himself up at Camp David. I suppose Jack will, too.'

Whoa, Chavez thought behind unblinking eyes, but nice as that thought was, he'd been thinking about something else on the three-hour drive up from Yorktown. 'When's the threat-assessment start?'

'Tomorrow for our side of it. Why?' MP asked.

'Ma'am, I think we're going to be busy.'

'I hope you're wrong,' she replied, after nodding.

'I have two procedures scheduled for today,' Cathy said, surveying the breakfast buffet. Since they didn't know what the Ryans liked to have in the morning, the staff had prepared some – actually quite a lot – of everything. Sally and Little Jack thought that was just great – even better, schools were closed. Katie, a recent graduate to real foods, gnawed at a piece of bacon in her hand while contemplating some buttered toast. For children, the immediate has the greatest importance. Sally, now fifteen (going on thirty, her father sometimes lamented), took the longest view of the three, but at the moment that was limited to how her social life would be affected. For all of them, Daddy was still Daddy, whatever job he might hold at the moment. They'd learn different, Jack knew, but one thing at a time.

'We haven't figured that out,' her husband replied, selecting scrambled eggs and bacon for his plate. He'd need his energy today.

'Jack, the deal was that I could still do my work, remember?'

'Mrs Ryan?' It was Andrea Price, still hovering around like a guardian angel, albeit with an automatic pistol. 'We're still figuring out the security issues and –'

'My patients need me. Jack, Bernie Katz and Hal Marsh can backstop me on a lot of things, but one of my patients today needs *me*. I have teaching rounds to prep for, too.' She checked her watch. 'In four hours.' Which was true, Ryan didn't have to ask. Professor Caroline Ryan, MD, FACS, was top-gun for driving a laser around a retina. People came from all over the world to watch her work.

'But schools are –' Price stopped, reminding herself that she knew better.

'Not medical schools. We can't send patients home. I'm sorry. I know how complicated things are for everybody, but I have people who depend on me, too, and I have to be there for them.' Cathy looked at the adult faces in the kitchen for a decision that would go her way. The kitchen staff – all sailors – moved in and out like mobile statues, pretending not to hear anything. The Secret Service people adopted a different blank expression, one with more discomfort in it.

The First Lady was supposed to be an unpaid adjunct to her husband. That was a rule which needed changing at some point. Sooner or later, after all, there would be a female President, and *that* would really upset the applecart, a fact well known but studiously ignored to this point in American history. The usual political wife was a woman who appeared at her husband's side with an adoring smile and a few carefully picked words, who endured the tedium of a campaign, and the surprisingly brutal handshakes – certainly Cathy Ryan would not subject her surgeon's hands to *that*, Price thought suddenly. But *this* First Lady actually had a job. More than that, she was a physician with a Lasker Memorial Public Service Award shortly to sit on her mantel (the awards dinner had yet to be held), and if she had learned anything about Cathy Ryan, Price knew that she was dedicated to her profession, not merely to her husband. However admirable that might be, it would be a royal pain in the ass to the Service, Price was sure. Worse yet, the principal agent assigned to *Mrs* Dr Ryan was Roy Altman, a tall bruiser of a former paratrooper whom she'd not yet met. That decision had been made for Roy's size as well as his savvy. It never hurt to have one obvious bodyguard close aboard, and since the First Lady appeared to many as a soft target, one of Roy's functions was to make the casual troublemaker think twice on that basis alone. Other members of her Detail would be virtually invisible. One of Altman's other functions was to use his bulk to block bullets, something the agents trained for but didn't dwell on.

Each of the Ryan kids would have to be protected as well, in a sub-detail that routinely split into segments. Katie's had been the hardest to select – because agents had fought for the job. The boss there would be the oldest member of the team, a grandfather named Don Russell. Little Jack would get a youngish male principal who was a serious sports fan, while Sally Ryan drew a female agent just over thirty, single, and hip (Price's term rather than the agent's), wise in the ways of young men and mall-shopping. The idea was to make the family as comfortable as was possible with the necessity of being followed everywhere except the bathroom by people with loaded firearms and radios. It was, in the end, a hopeless task, of course. President Ryan had the background to accept the need for all of this. His family would learn to endure it.

'Dr Ryan, when will you have to leave?' Price asked.

'About forty minutes. It depends on traf –'

'Not anymore,' Price corrected the First Lady. The day would be bad enough. The idea had been to use the previous day to brief the *Vice* President's family in on all the things that had to be done, but that plan had been shot completely to hell, along with so many other things. Altman was in another room, going over maps. There were three viable land routes to Baltimore: Interstate-95, the Baltimore-Washington Parkway, and US Route 1, all of them packed every morning with rush-hour traffic which a Secret Service convoy would disrupt to a fare-thee-well; worse, for any potential assassin, the routes were too predictable, narrowing down as they did on nearing Baltimore. Johns Hopkins Hospital had a helicopter pad atop its pediatrics building, but nobody had yet considered the political fallout that could result from hopping the First Lady to work every day in a Marine Corps VH-60. Maybe that was a viable option now, Price decided. She left the room to confer with Altman, and suddenly the Ryan family was alone, having breakfast as though they were still a normal family.

'My God, Jack,' Cathy breathed.

'I know.' Instead of talking, they enjoyed the silence for a full minute, both of them looking down at their breakfast, poking things around with forks instead of eating.

'The kids need clothes for the funeral,' Cathy said finally.

'Tell Andrea?'

'Okay. Do you know when it'll be?'

'I should find out today.'

'I'll still be able to work, right?' With Price gone she could allow her concern to show.

Jack looked up. 'Yes. Look, I'm going to try my best to keep us as normal as we can, and I know how important your work is. Matter of fact, I haven't had much chance to tell you what I think of that prize you just bagged.' He smiled. 'I'm damned proud of you, babe.'

Price came back in. 'Dr Ryan?' she said. And, of course, both heads turned. They could see it on her face. The most basic of issues hadn't been discussed yet. Did they call her *Doctor* Ryan, *Missus* Ryan, or –

'Make it easier on everyone, okay? Call me Cathy.'

Price couldn't do *that*, but she let it slide for the moment. 'Until we figure things out, we'll fly you there. The Marines have a helicopter on the way here.'

'Isn't that expensive?' Cathy asked.

'Yes, it is, but we have to figure out procedures and things, and for the moment this is the easiest thing to do. Also' – a very large man came into the room – 'this is Roy Altman. He'll be your principal agent for a while.'

'Oh,' was all Cathy was able to say at the moment. Six feet three and 220 pounds of Roy Altman came into the room. He had thinning blond hair, pale skin, and a sheepish expression that made him seem embarrassed by his bulk. Like all Secret Service agents, his suit coat was cut a little big to help conceal his service automatic, and in his particular case hiding a machine gun would have been fairly easy. Altman came over to shake her hand, which he did with considerable delicacy.

'Ma'am, you know what my job is. I'll try to keep as much out of the way as possible.' Two more people came into the room. Altman introduced them as the rest of her Detail for the day. All of them were temporary. They all had to get along with their principal, and that wasn't all so easy to predict, even with amiable principals, as all the Ryans seemed thus far to be.

Cathy was tempted to ask if all this was really necessary, but she knew better. On the other hand, how would she shepherd this mob around the Maumenee Building? She traded a look with her husband, and reminded herself that they would not be in this unhappy predicament had she not agreed to Jack's elevation to the vice presidency, which had lasted all of – what? Five minutes? Maybe not even that long. Just then came the roar of the Sikorsky Black Hawk helicopter, landing up the hill from the house and creating a mini-blizzard on what had once been the site of a small astronomical observatory. Her husband looked at his watch and realized that the Marines of VMH-1 were indeed operating off a short fuse. How long, he wondered, before the smothering attention drove them all mad?

'This shot is *live* from the grounds of the Naval Observatory on Massachusetts Avenue,' the NBC reporter said, cued by the director. 'That looks like one of the Marine helicopters. I suppose the President is going somewhere.' The camera zoomed in as the snow cloud settled down somewhat.

'An American Black Hawk, extensively modified,' the intelligence officer said. 'See there? That's a "Black Hole" infrared suppression system to protect against ground-to-air missiles that track engine heat.'

'How effective?'

'Very, but not against laser-guided weapons,' he added. 'Nor is it useful against guns.' No sooner had the aircraft's main rotor stopped turning than a squad of Marines surrounded it. 'I need a map of the area. Wherever that camera is, a mortar would also be effective. The same is true of the White House grounds, of course.' And anybody, they knew, could use a mortar, all the more so with the new laser-guided rounds first developed by the British and soon thereafter copied by the rest of the world. In a way it was the Americans who showed the way. It was their aphorism, after all: *If you can see it, you can hit it. If you can hit it, you can kill it.* And everyone inside of it, whatever 'it' might be.

With that thought, a plan began to form. He checked his watch, which had a stop-watch function button, placing his finger there and waiting. The TV director, six thousand miles away, had nothing better to do than keep on that long-lens camera. Presently, a large vehicle approached the helicopter, and four people got out. They walked right to the aircraft, whose crewman held the sliding door open.

'That's Mrs Ryan,' the commentator said. 'She's a surgeon at Johns Hopkins Hospital in Baltimore.'

'You suppose she's flying to work?' the reporter asked.

'We'll know in a minute.'

Which was about right. The intelligence officer pushed the watch button the moment the door closed. The rotor started turning a few seconds later, building power from the two turbine engines, and then the helicopter lifted off, nose-down as they all did, gaining altitude as it headed off, probably to the north. He checked his watch to see the elapsed time from door-close to liftoff. This aircraft had a military crew, and they would take pride in doing everything the same way every time. More than enough time for a mortar round to travel three times the necessary distance, he judged.

It was her first time in a helicopter. They had Cathy sit in the jump seat behind and between the two pilots. They didn't tell her why. The Black Hawk's rugged air-frame was designed to absorb fully fourteen g's in the event of a crash, and this seat was statistically the safest in the bird. The four-bladed rotor made for a smooth ride, and about the only objection she had to the experience was the cold. No one had yet designed a military aircraft with an efficient heating system. It would have been enjoyable but for the lingering embarrassment, and the fact that the Secret Service agents were scanning out the doors, obviously looking for some sort of danger or other. It was becoming clear that they could take the fun out of anything.

'I guess she's commuting to work,' the reporter decided. The camera had tracked the VH-60 until it disappeared into the tree line. It was a rare moment of levity. All of the networks were doing the same thing they'd done after the assassination of John Kennedy. Every single regular show was off the air while the networks devoted every waking hour – twenty-four hours per day now, which had not been the case in 1963 – to coverage of the disaster and its aftermath. What that really meant was a bonanza for the cable channels, as had been proven by tracking information through the various ratings services, but the networks had to be responsible, and doing *this* was responsible journalism.

'Well, she *is* a physician, isn't she? It's easy to forget that, despite the disaster that has overtaken our government, outside the Beltway, there are still people who do real work. Babies are being born. Life goes on,' the commentator observed pontifically, as was his job.

'And so does the country.' The reporter looked directly at the camera for the transition to commercial. He didn't hear the voice from so far away.

'For now.'

The kids were shepherded away by their bodyguards, and the real work of the day began. Arnie van Damm looked like hell. He was about to hit the wall, Jack decided; the combination of grueling work and grief was about to destroy the man. All well and good that the President should be spared as much as possible, Ryan knew, but not at the cost of wrecking the people upon whom he depended so much.

'Say your piece, Arnie, then disappear for a while and get some rest.'

'You know I can't do that –'

'Andrea?'

'Yes, Mr President?'

'When we've finished here, have somebody drive Arnie home. You will not allow him back in the House until four this afternoon.' Ryan shifted his gaze. 'Arnie, you will *not* burn out on me. I need you too much.'

The chief of staff was too tired to show any gratitude. He handed over a folder. 'Here are the plans for the funeral, day after tomorrow.'

Ryan flipped open the folder, his demeanor deflated as suddenly as he had exercised another dollop of presidential authority.

Whoever had put the plan together had been clever and sensitive about it. Maybe somewhere there had been a contingency plan for this sort of thing, a question Ryan would never bring himself to ask, but whatever the truth was, someone had done well. Roger and Anne Durling would lie in state in the White House, since the Capitol Rotunda was not available, and for twenty-four hours people would be allowed to walk through, entering through the front, and exiting from the East Wing. The sadness of the event would be muted for the mourners by later exposure to the Americana and presidential portraits. The Durlings would be taken by hearse to National Cathedral the next morning, along with three members of the Congress, a Jew, a Protestant, and a Catholic, for the interdenominational memorial service. Ryan had two major speeches to give. The text of both was in the back of the folder.

'What's that for?' Cathy was wearing a crash helmet with full connections into the helicopter's intercom. She pointed at another aircraft fifty yards to their right rear.

'We always fly with a backup aircraft, ma'am. In case something breaks and we have to land,' the pilot explained from the right-front seat, 'we don't want to delay you unnecessarily.' He didn't say that in the back-up helicopter were four more Secret Service agents with heavier weapons.

'How often does that happen, Colonel?'

'Not since I've been around, ma'am.' Nor did he say that one of the Marine Black Hawks had crashed into the Potomac in 1993, killing all hands. Well, it had been a long time. The pilot's eyes were scanning the air constantly. Part of VMH-1's institutional memory was what had seemed to be an attempted ramming over the California home of President Reagan. In fact it had been a screwup by a careless private pilot. After his interview with the Secret Service, the poor bastard had probably given up flying entirely. They were the most humorless people, Colonel Hank Goodman knew from long experience. The air was clear and cold, but pretty smooth. He controlled the stick with his fingertips as they followed I-95 northeast. Baltimore was already in view, and he knew the approach into Hopkins well enough from previous duty at Naval Air Station Patuxent River, whose Navy and Marine helos occasionally helped fly accident victims. Hopkins, he remembered, got the pediatric trauma cases for the state's critical-care system.

The same sobering thought hit Cathy when they flew past the University of Maryland's Shock-Trauma building. This *wasn't* her first flight in a helicopter, was it? It was just that for the other one she'd been unconscious. People had tried to kill her and Sally, and all the people around her were in jeopardy if somebody else made another try – why? Because of who her husband was.

'Mr Altman?' Cathy heard over the intercom.

'Yeah, Colonel?'

'You called ahead, right?'

'Yes, they know we're coming, Colonel,' Altman assured him.

'No, I mean, is the roof checked out for a -60?'

'What do you mean?'

'I mean this bird is heavier than the one the state troopers use. Is the pad certified for us?' Silence provided the answer. Colonel Goodman looked over at his co-pilot and grimaced. 'Okay, we can handle that this one time.'

'Clear left.'

'Clear right,' Goodman replied. He circled once, checking the wind sock on the roof of the building below. Just puffs of wind from the northwest. The descent was gentle, and the colonel kept a close eye on the radio whips to his right. He touched down soft, keeping his rotor turning to prevent the full weight of the aircraft from resting on the reinforced-concrete roof. It probably wasn't necessary, of course. Civil engineers always put more strength into buildings than they actually needed. But Goodman hadn't made the rank of bird-colonel by taking chances for the fun of it. His crew chief moved to pull the door open. The Secret Service agents went first, scanning the building while Goodman kept his hand on the collective, ready to yank up and rocket from the building. Then they helped Mrs Ryan out, and he could get on with his day.

'When we get back, call this place yourself and get the rating on the roof. Then ask for plans for our files.'

'Yes, sir. It just went too fast, sir.'

'Tell me about it.' He switched to the radio link. 'Marine Three, Marine Two.'

'Two,' the orbiting backup aircraft responded at once.

'On the go.' Goodman pulled the collective and angled south off the roof. 'She seems nice enough.'

'Got nervous just before we landed,' the crew chief observed.

'So was I,' Goodman said. '*I'll* call them when we get back.'

The secret service *had* called ahead to Dr Katz, who was waiting inside, along with three Hopkins security officers. Introductions were exchanged. Nametags were passed out, making the three agents ostensible staff members of the medical school, and the day of Associate Professor Caroline M. Ryan, MD, FACS, began.

'How's Mrs Hart doing?'

'I saw her twenty minutes ago, Cathy. She's actually rather pleased to have the First Lady operating on her.' Professor Katz was surprised at Professor Ryan's reaction.

6

EVALUATION

It took a lot to crowd Andrews Air Force Base, whose expansive concrete ramps looked to be the approximate size of Nebraska, but the security police force there was now patrolling a collection of aircraft as dense and as diverse as the place in Arizona where they kept out-of-work airliners. Moreover, each bird had its own security Detail, all of whom had to be co-ordinated with the Americans in an atmosphere of institutional distrust, since the security people were all trained to regard everyone in sight with suspicion. There were two Concordes, one British and one French, for sex appeal. The rest were mainly wide-bodies of one sort or another, and most of them liveried in the colors of the nation-flag carrier of their country of origin. Sabena, KLM, and Lufthansa led off the NATO row. SAS handled each of the three Scandinavian countries, each with its own 747. Chiefs of state traveled in style, and not one of the aircraft, large or small, had flown as much as a third full. Greeting them was a task to tax the skills and patience of the combined White House and State Department offices of protocol, and word was sent through the embassies that President Ryan simply didn't have the time to give everyone the attention he or she deserved. But the Air Force honor guard got to meet them all, forming, dismissing, and reforming more than once an hour while the red VIP carpet stayed in place, and one world leader followed another – at times as quickly as one aircraft could be rolled to its parking place and another could taxi to the specified arrival point with band and podium. Speeches were kept brief and somber for the ranks of cameras, and then they were moved off briskly to the waiting ranks of cars.

Moving them into Washington was yet another headache. Every car belonging to the Diplomatic Protection Service was tied up, forming four sets of escorts that hustled in and out of town, convoying the embassy limousines and tying up Suitland Parkway and Interstate 395. The most amazing part, perhaps, was that every president, prime minister, and even the kings and serene princes managed to get delivered to the proper embassy – most of them, fortunately, on Massachusetts Avenue. It proved to be a triumph of improvised organization in the end.

The embassies themselves handled the quiet private receptions. The statesmen, all in one place, had to meet, of course, to do business or merely to chat. The British Ambassador, the most senior of both the NATO countries and his nation's Commonwealth, would this night host an 'informal' dinner for twenty-two national leaders.

'Okay, his gear *is* down this time,' the Air Force captain said, as darkness fell on the base.

The tower crew at Andrews was, perversely, the same one which had been on duty on That Night, as people had taken to call it. They watched as the JAL 747 floated in on runway Zero-One Right. The flight crew might have noticed that the remains of a sister aircraft were to be found in a large hangar on the east side of the base – at this moment a truck was delivering the distorted remains of a jet engine, recently extracted from the basement of the Capitol building, but the jetliner completed its rollout, following directions to turn left and taxi behind a vehicle to the proper place for deplaning its passengers. The pilot did notice the cameras, and the crewmen walking from the relative warmth of a building to their equipment for the latest and most interesting arrival. He thought to say something to his co-pilot, but decided not to. Captain Torajiro Sato had been, well, if not a close friend, then a colleague, and a cordial one at that, and the disgrace to his country, his airline, and his profession would be a difficult thing to bear for years. It could only have been worse had Sato been carrying passengers, for protecting them was the first rule of their lives, but even though his culture respected suicide for a purpose as an honorable exercise, and beyond that awarded status to the more dramatic exits from corporeal life, this example of it had shocked and distressed his country more than anything in living memory. The pilot had always worn his uniform with pride. Now he would change out of it at the earliest opportunity, both abroad and at home. The pilot shook off the thought, applied the brakes smoothly, and halted the airliner so that the old-fashioned wheeled stairway was exactly even with the forward door of the Boeing airliner. It was then that he and his co-pilot turned inward to share a look of irony and shame at having performed their job with skill. Instead of sleeping over at the usual mid-level Washington hotel, they would be quartered in officers' accommodations on the base, and, probably, with someone to watch over them. With a gun.

The door of the airliner opened under the gentle ministrations of the senior stewardess. Prime Minister Mogataru Koga, his coat buttoned, and his tie straightened in his collar by a flustered aide, stood in the door briefly, assaulted by a blast of cold February air, and headed down the steps. The Air Force band struck up 'Ruffles and Flourishes.'

Acting Secretary of State Scott Adler was waiting at the bottom. The two had never met, but both had been fully briefed, Adler rather more quickly, as this was his fourth and most important arrival of the day. Koga looked just like his pictures. The man was grossly ordinary, about five feet six inches in height, of middle age, with a full head of black hair. His dark eyes were neutral – or tried to be, Adler thought on closer examination. There was sadness there. Hardly a surprise, the diplomat thought as he extended his hand.

'Welcome, Mr Prime Minister.'

'Thank you, Mr Adler.' The two men walked to the podium. Adler spoke a few muted words of welcome – this speech, drafted at Foggy Bottom, had taken an hour to get right, which amounted to about a minute to the world. Then Koga came to the microphone.

'First of all, I must thank you, Mr Adler, and thank your country, for allowing me to come today. As surprising as this gesture is, I have come to understand that such things are a tradition in your vast and generous country. I come to represent my country today on a sad but necessary mission. I hope it will be a mission of healing for your country and for mine. I hope that your citizens and ours can see in this tragedy a bridge to a peaceful future.' Koga stepped back, and Adler led him off down the red carpet, as the assembled band played *Kimagayo*, the brief anthem of Japan which had actually been written by an English composer a hundred years earlier. The Prime Minister looked at the honor guard and tried to read the young faces, looking for hatred or disgust in them, but finding only impassivity on the way to the waiting car. Adler got in behind him.

'How are you feeling, sir?' SecState asked.

'Well, thank you. I slept on the flight.' Koga assumed that the question was a mere pleasantry, then learned that it was not. It had been Ryan's idea, not Adler's, oddly enough, made somewhat more convenient by the time of day. The sun was down below the horizon now, and the sunset would be a brief one, as clouds rolled in from the northwest.

'If you wish, we can see President Ryan on the way to your embassy. The President instructed me to say that if you would prefer not to do so, because of the lengthy flight or other reasons, he will not be offended.' Scott was surprised that Koga didn't hesitate an instant.

'I gladly accept this honor.'

The acting Secretary of State pulled a portable radio from his coat pocket. 'EAGLE to SWORDBASE. Affirmative.' Adler had chuckled a few days earlier to learn his Secret Service codename. 'EAGLE' was the English counterpart to his German-Jewish surname.

'SWORDBASE copies affirmative,' the encrypted radio crackled back.

'EAGLE, out.'

The motorcade speeded up Suitland Parkway. Under other circumstances a news helicopter might have tracked them with a live camera, but Washington airspace was effectively shut down for the moment. Even National Airport was closed, with its flights shunted to Dulles or Baltimore-Washington International. Koga hadn't noticed the driver, who was American. The car turned right off the parkway, then hopped a block to the ramp for I-295, which turned almost immediately into I-395, a bumpy thoroughfare that led across the Anacostia River toward downtown Washington. As it merged with the main roadway, the stretch Lexus in which he was sitting veered to the right. Another identical car took its place as his formed up with three Secret Service Suburbans in a maneuver that took a mere five seconds. The empty streets made the rest of the trip easy, and in but a few minutes, his car turned onto West Executive Drive.

'Here they come, sir,' Price said, notified by the uniformed guard at the gatehouse.

Jack walked outside just as the car halted, not sure of the protocol for this – one more thing he'd yet to figure out about his new job. He almost moved to pull open the door himself, but a Marine corporal got there first, yanking the door and saluting like a robot.

'Mr President,' Koga said on standing up.

'Mr Prime Minister. Please come this way.' Ryan gestured with his hand.

Koga had never been to the White House before, and it struck him that had he flown over – what? three months earlier – to discuss the trade problems that had led to a shooting war ... yet another shameful failure. Then Ryan's demeanor came through the haze. He'd read once that the full ceremonies of a state arrival were not the sign of importance here – well, that was not possible or appropriate in any case, Koga told himself. But Ryan had stood alone at the door, and that must have meant something, the Japanese Prime Minister told himself on the way up the stairs. A minute later, whizzed through the West Wing, he and Ryan were alone in the Oval Office, separated only by a low table and a coffee tray.

'Thank you for this,' Koga said simply.

'We had to meet,' President Ryan said. 'Any other time and we'd have people watching and timing us and trying to read our lips.' He poured a cup for his guest and then himself.

'*Hai*, the press in Tokyo have become much more forward in the past few days.' Koga made to lift his cup, but stopped. 'Whom do I thank for rescuing me from Yamata?'

Jack looked up. 'The decision was made here. The two officers are in the area, if you want to see them again personally.'

'If it is convenient.' Koga sipped at his cup. He would have preferred tea, but Ryan was doing his best to be a host, and the quality of the gesture impressed his guest. 'Thank you for letting me come, President Ryan.'

'I tried to talk to Roger about the trade problem, but ... but I wasn't persuasive enough. Then I worried that something might be happening with Goto, but I didn't move quickly enough, what with the Russian trip and everything.

It was all a great big accident, but I suppose war usually is. In any case, it is up to the two of us to heal that wound. I want it done as rapidly as possible.'

'The conspirators are all under arrest. They will appear in court for treason,' Koga promised.

'That is your affair,' the President replied. Which wasn't really true. Japan's legal system was a curious one in which courts often enough violated the country's constitution in favor of broader but unwritten cultural mores, something unthinkable to Americans. Ryan and America expected that the trials would go by the book with no such variations. Koga understood that fully. A reconciliation between America and Japan depended absolutely on that, along with a multitude of other understandings which could not be spoken, at least not at this level. For his own part, Koga had already made sure that the judges selected for the various trials understood what the rules were.

'I never thought it possible that such a thing could happen, and then, that madman Sato . . . My country and my people are shamed by it. I have so much to do, Mr Ryan.'

Jack nodded. 'We both do. But it will be done.' He paused. 'The technical issues can be handled at the ministerial level. Between ourselves, I only wanted to be sure that we understood each other. I will trust your goodwill.'

'Thank you, Mr President.' Koga set his cup down to examine the man on the opposite sofa. He was young for such a job, though not the youngest American president. Theodore Roosevelt would probably hold that distinction into eternity. On the lengthy flight from Tokyo he'd read up on John Patrick Ryan. The man had killed with his own hand more than once, had been threatened with his own death and that of his family, and had done other things which his intelligence advisers only speculated about. Examining his face over a brief span of seconds, he tried to understand how such a person could also be a man of peace, but the clues were not there to be seen, and Koga wondered if there was something in the American character that he'd never quite understood. He saw the intelligence and the curiosity, one to measure and the other to probe. He saw fatigue and sadness. His recent days must have been the purest form of hell, Koga was sure. Somewhere still in this building, probably, were the children of Roger and Anne Durling, and that would be like a physical weight for the man to carry about. It struck the Prime Minister that Ryan, like most Westerners, was not very skilled at concealing his inner thoughts, but that wasn't true, was it? There had to be other things happening behind those blue eyes, and those things were not being advertised. They were not in any way threatening, but they were there. This Ryan *was* samurai, as he'd said in his office a few days earlier, but there was an additional layer of complexity as well. Koga set that aside. It wasn't all that important, and there was something that he had to ask, a personal decision he'd made over mid-Pacific.

'I have a request, if that is permitted.'

'What is that, sir?'

'Mr President, this is not a good idea,' Price objected a few minutes later.

'Good or not, we're going to do it. Get it organized,' Ryan told her.

'Yes, sir.' Andrea Price withdrew from the room.

Koga watched the exercise and learned something else. Ryan was a man capable of making decisions and giving orders entirely without histrionics.

The cars were still at the West Entrance, and it was simply a matter of donning coats and getting into them. A total of four Suburbans U-turned in the parking area, heading south, then east toward the Hill. The motorcade this time didn't use sirens and lights, instead proceeding almost in accord with the traffic laws – but not quite. The empty streets made it easy for them to jump lights, and soon enough they turned left onto Capitol Street, and left again toward the building. There were fewer lights now in evidence. The steps had been cleared, allowing an easy climb up once the cars had parked and the Secret Service agents deployed. Ryan led Koga upwards, and presently they were both looking down into the now-empty bowl that had been the House chamber.

The Japanese Prime Minister stood erect at first. He clapped his hands loudly, once, to garner the attention of the spirits who, his religious beliefs told him, would still be here. Then he bowed formally, and said his prayers for them. Ryan was moved to do the same. There were no TV cameras present to record the moment – actually there were still a few network cameras about, but the evening news broadcasts were over, and the instruments stood idle, their crews in the control vans drinking coffee and unaware of what was taking place a hundred yards away. It took only a minute or two in any case. When it was over, an American hand was extended, and a Japanese hand took it, and two pairs of eyes came to an understanding that ministers and treaties could never really have achieved, and in the harsh February wind, peace was finally and completely made between two countries. Standing ten feet away, Andrea Price was glad that the White House photographer had come along, and the tears she blinked away from her eyes were not from the wind. Then she conducted the two men back down the steps and into separate cars.

'Why did they overreact so?' the Prime Minister asked, before sipping her sherry.

'Well, as you know I have not been fully briefed,' the Prince of Wales replied, first qualifying himself, since he didn't really speak for Her Majesty's Government. 'But your naval exercises did have the appearance of a threatening act.'

'Sri Lanka must come to terms with the Tamils. They've shown a regrettable reluctance to enter into substantive negotiations, and we were trying to influence them. After all, we have our own troops deployed as peacekeepers, and we don't want them to be held hostage to the overall situation.'

'Quite so, but then, why don't you withdraw your peacekeepers as the government requested?'

The Indian Prime Minister sighed tiredly – it had been a long flight for her, too, and under the circumstances a little exasperation was permissible. 'Your Royal Highness, if we withdraw our troops and then the situation flares up yet again, we will face difficulties with our own Tamil citizens. This is truly a most unhappy situation. We attempted to help assuage a difficult political impasse, entirely at our own expense, but then the Sri Lankan government finds itself unable to take the remedial action necessary to prevent an embarrassment to my country, and a continuing rebellion in their own. *Then* the Americans interfere without any real cause, and only bolster the intransigence of the Sri Lankans.'

'When does their Prime Minister arrive?' the Prince asked.

The substantive reply was a shrug, followed by verbiage. 'We offered the chance to fly over together so that we might discuss the situation, but he regrettably declined. Tomorrow, I think. If his aircraft doesn't malfunction,' she added. That national-flag carrier had all manner of technical problems, not to mention a long-lived security threat.

'If you wish, the ambassador can probably arrange a quiet meeting.'

'Perhaps that would not be entirely useless,' the Prime Minister allowed. 'I also wish the Americans would get the proper spin on things. They've always been so hopeless on our part of the world.'

Which was the point of the exercise, the Prince understood. He and President Ryan had been friends for years, and India wanted him to be the intercessor. It would hardly have been the first time for such a mission on his part, but in all such cases the Heir Apparent was constrained to seek guidance from the government, which, in this case, meant the ambassador. Someone in Whitehall had decided that His Royal Highness's friendship with the new American President was more important than a government-to-government contact, and besides, it would make the monarchy look good at a time when such appearances were both useful and necessary. It also gave His Highness an excuse to visit some land in Wyoming which was quietly owned by the Royal Family, or 'the Firm,' as it was sometimes called by insiders.

'I see,' was as substantive a reply as he could make, but Britain had to take a request from India seriously. Once the brightest diadem in a world-spanning crown, that country was still an important trading partner, bloody nuisance though it might frequently be. A direct contact between the two heads of government might be embarrassing. The American harassment of the Indian fleet was not widely publicized, falling as it had toward the end of hostilities between America and Japan, and it was in everyone's interest that things should remain that way. President Ryan had enough on his plate, his old friend knew. The Prince hoped that Jack was getting some rest. For the people in the reception room, sleep was just a defense against jet lag. For Ryan it was necessary fuel, and he'd need plenty for the next two days.

*   *   *

The line was endless, the typical cliché. It stretched well beyond the Treasury building, and the far end of it was like the ragged end of a rope, with new people forming up and tightening into the line so that it appeared to generate itself out of air, constantly replenishing as its members moved slowly forward in the cold air. They entered the building in groups of fifty or so, and the opening-closing cycle of the doors was regulated by someone with a watch, or maybe just counting slowly. There was an honor guard, an enlisted member of each uniformed service. The Detail was commanded by an Air Force captain at the moment. They and the caskets stood still while the people shuffled past.

Ryan examined their faces on his office TV just after he came in, again before sunrise, wondering what they thought and why they'd come. Few had actually voted for Roger Durling. He'd been the number-two man on the ticket, after all, and he'd taken over the job only with the resignation of Bob Fowler. But America embraced her presidents, and in death Roger was the recipient of love and respect that had never seemed all that close to him in life. Some of the mourners turned away from the coffins to look around at the entry hall of a building which many had probably never seen before, using their few seconds of time there strangely to look away from the reason for their having come, then to go down the steps and out the East Entrance, no longer a line, but in groups of friends or family members, or even alone, to leave the city and do their business. Then it was time for him to do the same – more properly, to head back to his family, and study up for the tasks of the following day.

Why not? they'd decided on arriving at Dulles. Lucky enough to find a cheap motel at the end of the Metro's Yellow Line, they'd ridden the subway into town, and gotten off at the Farragut Square station, only a few blocks from the White House so that they could take a look. It would be a first for both of them – many firsts, in fact, since neither had ever visited Washington, the cursed city on a minor river that polluted the entire country from which it sucked blood and treasure – these were favored lines of the Mountain Men. Finding the end of the line had taken time, and they'd shuffled along for several hours, with the only good news being that they knew how to dress for cold, which was more than they could say for the East Coast idiots in the line with them, with their thin coats and bare heads. It was all Pete Holbrook and Ernest Brown could do to keep from cracking their jokes about what had happened. Instead they listened to what other people in line said. That turned out to be disappointing. Maybe a lot of them were federal employees, both men thought. There were a few whimpers about how sad it all was, how Roger Durling had been a very nice man, and how attractive his wife had been, and how cute the children were, and how awful it must be for them.

Well, the two members of the Mountain Men had to agree between themselves, yeah, sure enough it was tough on the kids – and who didn't like kids? – but scrambling eggs was probably something mama chicken didn't like to see, right? And how much suffering had their father inflicted on honest citizens who only wanted to have their constitutional right to be left alone by all these useless Washington jerks? But they didn't say that. They kept their mouths mostly shut as the line wended its way along the street. Both knew the story of the Treasury building, which sheltered them from the wind for a while, how Andy Jackson had decided to move it so that he couldn't see the Capitol building from the White House (it was still too dark for them to make out very much), causing the famous and annoying jog in Pennsylvania Avenue – not that *that* mattered anymore, since the street had been closed in front of the White House. And why? To protect the President from the *citizens*! Couldn't trust the citizens to get too close to the Grand Pooh-Bah. They couldn't say that, of course. It was something the two had discussed on the flight in. There was no telling how many government spy types might be around, especially in the line to the White House, a name for the structure they'd accepted only since it had allegedly been selected by Davy Crockett. Holbrook had recalled that from a movie he'd seen on TV, though he couldn't remember which movie, and ol' Davy was without a doubt their kind of American, a man who'd named his favorite rifle. Yeah.

It wasn't really a bad-looking house, and some good men had lived there. Andy Jackson, who'd told the Supreme Court where to get off. Lincoln, a tough old son of a bitch. What a shame he'd been killed before implementing his plan to ship the niggers back to Africa or Latin America . . . (Both rather liked James Monroe as well for starting that idea by helping to establish Liberia as a place to ship the slaves back to; a pity that nobody had followed up on it.) Teddy Roosevelt, who had a lot of good things going for him, a hunter and outdoorsman and soldier who'd gone a little far in 'reforming' the government. Not many since, though, both men judged, but it wasn't the building's fault that it had more recently been occupied by people they didn't like. That was the problem with Washington buildings. The Capitol had once been home to Henry Clay and Dan'l Webster, after all. Patriots, unlike the bunch who'd been roasted by that Jap pilot.

Things got a little bit tense when they turned into the White House grounds, like entering enemy territory. There were guards at the gatehouse of the Secret Service's uniformed division, and inside were Marines. Wasn't that a shame? Marines. Real Americans, even the colored ones, probably, 'cause they went through the training same as the white ones, and probably some of them were patriots, too. Too bad they were niggers, but it couldn't be helped. And all the Marines did what they were told by the 'crats. That made the looks a little hard to take. They were just kids, though, and maybe they'd learn. After all, the Mountain Men had a few ex-military in it. The Marines were shivering in their long coats and white fairy gloves, and finally one of them, a buck sergeant by the stripes, opened the door.

Some house, Holbook and Brown thought, looking up and around the towering foyer. It was easy to see how somebody who lived here might think himself king-shit. You had to watch out for stuff like that. Lincoln had grown up in a log cabin, and Teddy had known life in a tent, hunting up in the mountains, but nowadays whoever lived here was just another damned 'crat. Inside were more Marines, and the honor guard around the two boxes, and most disquieting of all, people in civilian clothes with little plastic curly things that led from their suit collars to their ears. Secret Service. Federal cops. The face of the enemy, members of the same government department that held the Bureau of Alcohol, Tobacco, and Firearms. That figured. The first instance of citizens' objecting to the government had been about alcohol, the Whiskey Rebellion – which was why the Mountain Men were equivocal in their admiration for George Washington. The more liberal of them remarked that even a good man can have a bad day, and George wasn't a guy to fuck with. Brown and Holbrook didn't look directly at the Secret Service pukes. You had to be careful fucking with them, too.

Special Agent Price walked into the foyer then. Her principal was safe in his office, and her responsibilities as Detail commander extended throughout the entire building. The procession wasn't a security threat to the House. In terms of security it was just a nuisance. Even if a gang of gunmen had secreted itself in the line, behind the closed doors all around this area were twenty armed agents, many of them with Uzi submachine guns in their fast-action-gun bags, unkindly known as FAG bags. A metal detector hidden in the doorway told a crew from the Technical Security Division whom to look at, and other agents concealed in their hands photos stacked together like a deck of cards, which they shuffled through constantly until every face coming through the door could be compared with known or suspected troublemakers. For the rest they depended on instincts and training, and that came down to people who looked 'funny,' the usual Americanism for inappropriate demeanor. The problem with that was the cold weather outside. People came in, and a lot of them looked funny. Some stamped their feet a little. Others shoved hands into pockets, or adjusted coats, or shivered, or just looked around oddly – all of which was calculated to attract the attention of somebody on the Detail. On those occasions when the gestures came from one who had pinged the metal detector, an agent would raise his or her hand as though scratching one's nose and speak into a microphone. 'Blue coat, male, six feet,' for example, would cause four or five heads to turn for a closer look at, in that case, a dentist from Richmond who had just switched his pocket hand warmer from one side to the other. His physical dimensions were checked against threat photos of similarly sized subjects and found not to match – but they watched him anyway, and a hidden TV camera zoomed in to record his face. In a few more extreme cases, an agent would join up with the exiting mourners and follow a subject to a car to catch the tag number. The long-since-deestablished Strategic Air Command had taken as its official motto PEACE IS OUR PROFESSION. For the Secret Service the business was paranoia, the necessity for which was made plain by the two caskets in the White House foyer.

Brown and Holbrook had their five seconds of direct viewing. Two expensive boxes, doubtless purchased at government expense, and blasphemously, they thought, draped with the Stars and Stripes. Well, maybe not for the wife. After all, the womenfolk were supposed to be loyal to their men, and that couldn't be helped. The flow of the crowd took them to the left, and velvet ropes guided them down the steps. They could feel the change in the others. A collective deep breath, and some sniffles of people wiping their eyes of tears – mainly the womenfolk. The two Mountain Men stayed impassive, as most of the men did. The Remington sculptures on the way out caused both to stop and admire briefly, and then it was back into the open, and the fresh air was a welcome cleansing after the few minutes of federal steam heat. They didn't speak until they were off the grounds and away from others.

'Nice boxes we bought them,' Holbrook managed to say first.

'Shame they weren't open.' Brown looked around. Nobody was close enough to hear his indiscretion. 'They do have kids,' Pete pointed out. He headed south so that they could see down Pennsylvania Avenue.

'Yeah, yeah, yeah. And they'll grow up to be 'crats, too.' They walked a few more yards. 'Damn!'

There was nothing else one could say, except maybe, 'Fuck!' Holbrook thought, and he didn't like repeating things Ernie said.

The sun was coming up, and the absence of tall buildings to the east of the Hill meant that the white building was beautifully silhouetted. Though it was the first trip to Washington for both, either man could have done a reasonably accurate sketch of the building from memory, and the *wrongness* of the horizon could not have been more obvious. Pete was glad that Ernie had talked him into coming. Just the sight made all the travel hassles worth it. This time he managed the first collective thought: 'Ernie,' Holbrook said in awe, 'it's inspirational.'

'Yeah.'

One problem with the disease was that the warning signs were equivocal, and her main concern was one of her patients. He was such a nice boy, but – but he was gravely ill, Sister Jean Baptiste saw now that his fever had spiked to 40.4 degrees Celsius, and that was deadly enough, but the other signs were worse. The disorientation had gotten worse. The vomiting had increased, and now there was blood in it. There were indications of internal bleeding. All that, she knew, could mean one of several things – but the one she worried about was called Ebola Zaire. There were many diseases in the jungle of this country – she still thought of it occasionally as the Belgian Congo – and while the competition for the absolute worst was stiffer than one might imagine, Ebola was at the bottom of that particular pit. She had to draw blood for another test, and this she did with great care, the first sample having been lost somehow or other. The younger staff here weren't as thorough as they ought . . . His parents held the arm while she drew the blood, her hands fully protected with latex gloves. It went smoothly – the boy was not even semiconscious at the moment. She withdrew the needle and placed it immediately in a plastic box for disposal. The blood vial was safe, but that, too, went into another container. Her immediate concern was the needle. Too many people on staff tried to save money for the hospital by reusing instruments, this despite AIDS and other diseases communicated by blood products. She'd handle this one herself, just to make sure.

She didn't have time to look more at the patient. Leaving the ward, she walked through the breezeway to the next building. The hospital had a long and honorable history, and had been built to allow for local conditions. The many low frame buildings were connected by covered walkways. The laboratory building was only fifty meters away. This facility was blessed; recently the World Health Organization had established a presence here, along with which had come modern equipment and six young physicians – but, alas, no nurses. All were British- or American-trained.

Dr Mohammed Moudi was at the lab bench. Tall, thin, swarthy, he was somewhat cold in his demeanor, but he was proficient. He turned as he saw her approach, and took note of the way she disposed of the needle.

'What is it, Sister?'

'Patient Mkusa. Benedict Mkusa, African male, age eight.' She handed the paper-work over. Moudi opened the folder and scanned it. For the nurse – Christian or not, she was a holy woman, and a fine nurse – the symptoms had occurred one at a time. The paper presentation to the physician was far more efficient. Headache, chills, fever, disorientation, agitation, and now signs of an internal bleed. When he looked up his eyes were guarded. If petechiae appeared on his skin next . . .

'He's in the general ward?'

'Yes, Doctor.'

'Move him to the isolation building at once. I'll be over there in half an hour.'

'Yes, Doctor.' On the way out she rubbed her forehead. It must have been the heat. You never really got used to it, not if you came from northern Europe. Maybe an aspirin after she saw to her patient.

7

PUBLIC IMAGE

It started early, when two E-3B Sentry aircraft which had deployed from Tinker Air Force Base in Oklahoma to Pope Air Force Base in North Carolina took off from the latter at 0800 local time and headed north. It had been decided that closing down all the local airports would have been too much. Washington National remained closed – and with no congressmen to race there for a flight to their districts (their special parking lot was well known), it even appeared that the facility might remain that way – and at the other two, Dulles and Baltimore-Washington International, controllers were under very precise instructions. Flights in and out were to avoid a 'bubble' more than twenty miles in diameter and centered on the White House. Should any aircraft head toward the 'bubble' it would instantly be challenged. If the challenge were ignored, it would soon find a fighter aircraft off its wingtip. If that didn't work, the third stage would be obvious and spectacular. Two flights, each of four F-16 fighters, were orbiting the city in relays at an altitude of eighteen and twenty thousand feet, respectively. The altitude kept the noise down (it also would enable them to tip over and reach supersonic speed almost immediately), but the white contrails made patterns in the blue sky as obvious as those the 8th Air Force had once traced over Germany.

About the same time, the 260th Military Police Brigade of the Washington, DC, National Guard redeployed to maintain 'traffic control.' More than a hundred HMMWVs were in side streets, each with a police or FBI vehicle in close attendance, controlling traffic by blocking the streets. An honor guard assembled from all the services lined the streets to be used. There was no telling which of the rifles might be equipped with a full magazine.

Some people had actually expected the security precautions to be kept quiet because armored vehicles had been dispensed with.

There was a total of sixty-one chiefs of state in the city; the day would be security hell for everyone, and the media made sure that everyone would share the experience.

For the last one of these, Jacqueline Kennedy had decided on morning clothes, but thirty-five years had passed, and dark business suits would now suffice, except for those foreign government officials who wore uniforms of various sorts (the Prince of Wales *was* a commissioned officer), or visitors from tropical countries. Some of them would wear their national garb, and would suffer the consequences in the name of national dignity. Just getting them around town and into the White House was a nightmare. Then came the problem of how to line them up in the procession. Alphabetically by country? Alphabetically by name? By seniority in office would have given undue primacy of place to a few dictators who had come to find for themselves some legitimacy in the diplomatic major leagues – bolstering the status of countries and governments with which America had friendly relations but for which America had little love. They all came to the White House, marching past the coffins after the last of the line of American citizens had been cut off, pausing to pay personal respects, and from there into the East Room, where a platoon of State Department officials struggled to get things organized over coffee and Danish.

Ryan and his family were upstairs, putting the finishing touches on their dark clothes, attended by White House staff members. The children handled it the best, accustomed to having Mom and Dad brush their hair on the way out the door, and amused to see Mom and Dad being treated the same way. Jack was holding a copy of his first speech. It was past time for him to close his eyes and wish everything away. Now he felt like a boxer, overmatched by his opponent but unable to take a dive, taking every punch as best he could and trying not to disgrace himself. Mary Abbot applied the final touches to his hair and locked everything in place with spray, something Ryan had never used voluntarily in his life.

'They're waiting, Mr President,' Arnie said.

'Yeah.' Jack handed the speech binder to one of the Secret Service agents. He headed out of the room, followed by

Cathy, who held Katie. Sally took Little Jack's hand to follow them into the corridor and down the stairs. President Ryan walked slowly down the square spiral of steps, then turned left to the East Room. As he entered the room, heads turned. Every eye in the room looked at him, but these looks were in no way casual, and few of them were sympathetic. Almost every pair belonged to a chief of state. Those that did not belonged to an ambassador, each of whom would this night draft a report on the new American President. It was Ryan's good fortune that the first to approach him was one who would not need to do anything of the sort.

'Mr President,' said the man in the Royal Navy mess jacket. His ambassador had positioned things nicely. On the whole, London rather liked the new arrangement. The 'special relationship' would become more special, as President Ryan was an (honorary) Knight Commander of the Victorian Order.

'Your Highness.' Jack paused, and allowed himself a smile as he shook the offered hand. 'Long time since that day in London, pal.'

'Indeed.'

The sun wasn't as warm as it should have been – the wind saw to that – its hard-cast shadows merely making things appear colder. The DC police led off with a rank of motorcycles, then three drummers followed by marching soldiers – they were a squad from 3rd Platoon, Bravo Company, First Battalion, 501st Infantry Regiment, 82nd Airborne, which had once been Roger Durling's own – then the riderless horse, boots reversed in the stirrups, and the gun carriages, side by side for this funeral, husband and wife. Then the lines of cars. The cold air did one other thing. The drums' brutal thunder echoed sharply up and down the man-made canyons. As the procession headed northwest, the soldiers, sailors, and Marines came to present arms, first for the old President, then for the new. Men mainly removed whatever hats they might be wearing (some forgot) for the former.

Brown and Holbrook didn't forget. Durling may just have been another 'crat, but the Flag was the Flag, and it wasn't the Flag's fault that it was draped there. The soldiers strutted up the street, incongruously wearing battle-dress uniforms with red berets and bloused jump boots because, the radio commentator said, Roger Durling had been one of their own. Before the gun carriage walked two more soldiers, the first carrying the presidential flag, and the second with a framed plaque which contained Durling's combat decorations. The deceased President had won a medal for rescuing a soldier under fire. That former soldier was somewhere in the procession, and had already been interviewed about a dozen times, soberly recounting the day on which a President-to-be had saved his life. A shame he'd gone wrong, the Mountain Men reflected, but more likely he'd been a politician the whole time.

The new President appeared presently, his automobile identifiable by the four Secret Service agents pacing alongside it. This new one was a mystery to the two Mountain Men. They knew what they'd seen on TV and read in the papers. A shooter. He'd actually killed two people, one with a pistol and one with an Uzi. Ex-Marine, even. That excited a little admiration. Other TV coverage, repeated again and again, mainly showed him doing Sunday talk shows and briefings. In most of the former he looked competent. In the latter he often appeared uncomfortable.

Most of the car windows in the procession had the dark plastic coating that prevented people from seeing who rode inside, but not the President's car, of course. His three children sitting ahead of him and facing back from the jump seat, with his wife at his side, President John Ryan was easy to see from the sidewalk.

'What do we really know about Mr Ryan?'

'Not much,' the commentator admitted. 'His government service has been almost exclusively in CIA. He has the respect of Congress, on both sides of the aisle. He's worked with Alan Trent and Sam Fellows for years – that's one of the reasons both members are still alive. We've all heard the story of the terrorists who attacked him –'

'Like something out of the Wild West,' the anchor interjected. 'What do you think about having a President who's –'

'Killed people?' the commentator returned the favor. He was tired from days of long duty, and just a little tired of this coiffeured airhead. 'Let's see. George Washington was a general. So was Andy Jackson. William Henry Harrison was a soldier. Grant, and most of the post-Civil War presidents. Teddy Roosevelt, of course. Truman was a soldier. Eisenhower. Jack Kennedy was in the Navy, as were Nixon, and Jimmy Carter, *and* George Bush . . .' The impromptu history lesson had the visual effect of a cattle prod.

'But he was selected as Vice President really in a caretaker status, wasn't he, and as payback for his handling of the conflict' – nobody really called it a 'war' – 'with what turned out to be Japanese business interests.' There, the anchor thought, that would put this overaged foreign correspondent in his place. Who ever said that a President was entitled to any honeymoon at all, anyway?

Ryan wanted to look over his speech, but he found that he couldn't. It was pretty cold out there. It wasn't exactly warm in the car, but thousands of people stood out there in twenty-nine-degree air, five to ten deep on the sidewalks, and their faces tracked his car as it passed by. They were close enough that he could see their expressions. Many pointed and said things to the people standing next to them – *there he is, there's the new one.* Some waved, small embarrassed gestures from people who were unsure if it was okay to do so, but wanting to do something to show that they cared. More nodded respect, with the tight smile that you saw in a funeral home – *hope you'll be okay.* Jack wondered if it was proper to wave back, but decided that it wasn't, bound by some unwritten rule that applied to funerals. And so he just looked at them, his face, he thought, in a neutral mien, without saying anything because he didn't know what to say, either. Well, he had a speech to handle that, Ryan thought, frustrated with himself.

'Not a happy camper,' Brown whispered to Holbrook. They waited a few minutes for the crowd to loosen up. Not all of the spectators were interested in the procession of foreign dignitaries. You couldn't see into the cars anyway, and keeping track of all the flags that flew on the front bumpers merely started various versions of 'Which one is that one?' – often with an incorrect answer. So, like many others, the two Mountain Men shouldered their way back from the curb into a park.

'He ain't got it,' Holbrook replied, finally.

'He's just a 'crat. Remember the Peter Principle?' It was a book which, both thought, had been written to explain government workers. In any hierarchy, people tended to rise to their level of incompetence. 'I think I like this.'

His comrade looked back at the street and the cars and the fluttering little flags. 'I think you may be right.'

Security at the National Cathedral was airtight. In their hearts the Secret Service agents knew that, and knew that no assassin – the idea of professional assassins was largely a creation of Hollywood anyway – would risk his life under these circumstances. Every building with a direct line of sight to the Gothic-style church had several policemen, or soldiers, or USSS special agents atop it, many of them armed with rifles, and their own Counter-Sniper Team armed with the finest of all, $10,000 hand-made instruments that could reach more than half a mile and touch someone in the head – the team, which won competition shoots with the regularity of the tides, was probably the best collection of marksmen the world had ever seen, and practiced every day to keep that way. Anyone who wanted to do mischief would either know all these things and stay away, or, in the case of an amateur madman, would see the massive defensive arrangements and decide this wasn't a good day to die.

But things were tense anyway, and even as the procession appeared in the distance, agents were hustling around. One of them, exhausted from thirty hours of continuous duty, was drinking coffee when he tripped on the stone steps and spilled the cup. Grumbling, he crushed the plastic foam in his hand, stuffed it in his pocket, and told his lapel-mounted radio microphone that everything was clear at his post. The coffee froze almost instantly on the shaded granite.

Inside the cathedral, yet another team of agents checked out every shadowed nook one more time before taking their places, allowing protocol officers to make final preparations, referring to seating instructions faxed to them only minutes before and wondering what would go wrong.

The gun carriages came to a halt in front of the building,

and the cars came up one at a time to discharge their passengers. Ryan got out, followed by his family, moving to join the Durlings. The kids were still in shock, and maybe that was good, or maybe it was not. Jack didn't know. At times like this, what did a man do? He placed his hand on the son's shoulder while the cars came, dropped off their passengers, and pulled rapidly away. The other official mourners – the senior ones – would form up behind him. Less senior ones would be entering the church now from side entrances, passing through portable metal detectors, while the churchmen and choir, having already done the same, would be taking their places.

Roger must have remembered his service in the 82nd with pride, Jack thought. The soldiers who'd led the procession stacked arms and prepared to do their duty under the supervision of a young captain, assisted by two serious-looking sergeants. They all looked so young, even the sergeants, all with their heads shaved nearly down to stubble under their berets. Then he remembered that his father had served in the rival 101st Airborne more than fifty years before, and had looked just like these kids, though probably with a little more hair, since the bald look hadn't been fashionable in the 1940s. But the same toughness, the same fierce pride, and the same determination to get the job done, whatever it might be. It seemed to take forever. Ryan, like the soldiers, couldn't turn his head. He had to stand at attention as he'd done during his own service in the Marine Corps, though allowing his eyes to scan around. His children turned their heads and shifted on their feet with the cold, while Cathy kept her eyes on them, worrying as her husband did about the exposure to the cold, but caught in a situation where even parental concerns were subordinated to something else. What was it, she wondered, this thing called duty that even orphaned children knew that they had to stand there and just take it?

Finally the last of the official procession alighted from their cars and took their places. Someone gave it a five-count, and the soldiers moved to the gun carriages, seven to each. The officer in charge of them unscrewed one clamp, then the other, and the caskets were lifted and moved off in robotic side-steps. The soldier holding the presidential flag started up the steps, followed by the caskets. The President's was in front, led by the captain and followed by the sergeant in charge of the sub-detail.

It wasn't anybody's fault. There were three soldiers on either side, marching to the slow cadence called by the sergeant. They were stiff from standing fifteen minutes at parade rest after a healthy morning walk up Massachusetts Avenue. The middle one on the right slipped on the frozen coffee just as all were taking a step. He slid inward, not outward, and in going down his legs swept away the soldier behind him. The total load was over four hundred pounds of wood, metal, and body, and it all came down on the soldier who'd been first to slip, breaking both his legs in an instant on the granite steps.

A collective gasp came up from the thousands of people watching. Secret Service agents raced in, fearing that a shot might have felled the soldiers. Andrea Price moved in front of Ryan, her hand inside her coat and obviously holding her service automatic, ready to draw it out, while other agents poised to drag the Ryans and the Durlings clear of the area. The soldiers were already moving the casket off their fallen comrade, his face suddenly white with pain.

'Ice,' he told the sergeant through clenched teeth. 'Slipped.' The soldier even had enough self-control to refrain from the profanity that echoed through his mind at the shame and embarrassment of the moment. An agent looked at the step and saw it there, a white-brown mound that reflected light. He made a gesture that told Price she could stand down, which command was instantly radioed out to all the agents in sight:

'Just a slip, just a slip.'

Ryan winced to see what had happened. Roger Durling would not have felt it, his mind thought, but the insult to him was an insult to his children, who cringed and snapped their heads away when their father bounced on the stone steps. The son turned back first, taking it all in, the child part of him wondering why the fall hadn't awakened his father. Only hours before he'd risen during the night and walked to the door of his room, wanting to open it, wanting to cross the hall and knock on his parents' door to see if they might be back.

*　　*　　*

'Oh, God,' the commentator groaned.

The cameras zoomed in as two of the 3rd Regiment soldiers pulled the injured paratrooper clear. The sergeant took his place. The casket was lifted back up in seconds, its polished oak clearly gouged and defaced by the fall.

'Okay, soldiers,' the sergeant said from his new place. 'By the left.'

'Daddy,' whimpered Mark Durling, age nine. 'Daddy.' Everyone close by heard it in the silence that had followed the accident. The soldiers bit their lips. The Secret Service agents, already shamed and wounded by the loss of a President, took a second to look down or at one another. Jack instinctively wrapped his arms around the boy, but still didn't know what the hell he was supposed to say. What else could possibly go wrong? the new President wondered as Mrs Durling followed her husband up the steps and inside.

'Okay, Mark.' Ryan placed his arm around the youngster's shoulder and guided him to the door, without thinking about it taking the place of a favored uncle for a few yards. If there were only a way to take away their sorrow, even for a few seconds. The thought was an impossible one, and all it did for Jack was to give him another layer of sadness, as what he added to himself didn't detract a whit from what the children felt.

It was warmer inside, which was noticed by those less caught up in the emotion of the moment. Fluttering protocol officers took their places. Ryan and his family went to the first pew on the right. The Durling party went opposite them. The caskets sat side by side on catafalques in the sacristy, and beyond them were three more, those of a senator and two members of the House, 'representing' one last time. The organ played something Ryan had heard before but didn't recognize. At least it wasn't Mozart's grim Masonic procession with its repeating, brutal chant, about as uplifting as a film of the Holocaust. The clergymen were lined up in front, their faces professionally composed. In front of Ryan, in the slot usually occupied by hymnals, was another copy of his speech.

The scene on the TV screen was such to make anyone in his chosen profession either ill or excited in a manner beyond sex. If only . . . but such opportunities as this one only happened by accident, never allowing the time to prepare anything. Preparation was everything for a mission like this. Not that it would have been technically hard, and he allowed his mind to consider the method. A mortar, perhaps. You could mount one of those in the back of an ordinary delivery truck such as one might find in any city in the known world. Walk the rounds down the roof of the building, dropping it on the targets. You'd get off at least ten, maybe fifteen or twenty, and though the selection would be random, a target was a target, and terror was terror, and that was his profession.

'Look at them all,' he breathed. The cameras traced along the pews. Mostly men, some women, sitting in no order that he could discern, some chatting in whispers, most not, with blank expressions as their eyes surveyed the inside of the church. Then the children of the dead American President, a son and a daughter with the beaten look of those who'd been touched by the harsh reality of life. Children bore the burden surprisingly well, didn't they? They'd survive, all the more so that they were no longer of any political significance, and so his interest in them was as clinical as it was pitiless. Then the camera was on Ryan again, closing in on his face and allowing some careful examination.

He hadn't said good-bye to Roger Durling yet. There hadn't been time for Jack to compose his mind and concentrate on the thought, the week had been so busy, but now he found his eyes staring at just that one coffin. He'd hardly known Anne, and the three others in the sacristy were strangers to him, actually chosen at random for their religious affiliations. But Roger had been a friend. Roger had brought him back from private life, given him an important job, and trusted him to run it, taking Jack's advice most of the time, confiding in him, chiding and disciplining on occasion, but always as a friend. It had been a tough job, all the harder with the conflict that had developed with Japan – even for Jack, now that it was over, it was no longer a 'war,' because war was a thing of the past. No longer a part of the real world that was progressing beyond such barbarism. Durling and Ryan had gotten through that, and while the former had wanted to move on to finish the job in other ways, he had also recognized that for Ryan the race had ended. And so, as a friend, he'd given Jack a golden bridge back to private life, a capstone on a career of public service that had turned into a trap.

But if he'd offered the job to someone else, where would I have been that night? Jack asked himself. The answer was simple. He would have been in the front row of the House chamber, and now he would have been dead. President Ryan blinked hard at the realization. *Roger had saved his life.* Probably not just his own. Cathy – and maybe the kids – would have been in the gallery, along with Anne Durling . . . Was life really that fragile as to turn on such small events? Throughout the city at this moment, other bodies lay in other caskets for other ceremonies, most for adults but some for the children of other victims who'd chosen that night to bring their families to the joint session.

Mark Durling was whimpering now. His elder sister, Amy, pulled his head inward to her. Jack turned his head slightly, allowing his peripheral vision to take it in. *They're just* kids, *dear God, why do* kids *have to go through this?* The thought hammered home in an instant. Jack bit his lip and looked down at the floor. There was no one to be a target for his anger. The perpetrator of this crime was dead himself, his body in yet another box in the Washington, DC, morgue, and some thousands of miles away, such family as the man had left behind bore the additional burden of shame and guilt placed on them. This was why people called all violence senseless. There was nothing to learn from any of this, only the lingering harm of lives lost and lives wrecked – and lives spared for no particular reason other than mere chance. Like cancer or other serious illness, this sort of violence struck with no discernible plan, and no real defense, just one dead man who had decided not to enter alone such afterlife as he believed in. What the hell was anyone supposed to learn from this? Ryan, long a student of human behavior, grimaced and continued to look down, his ears focusing on the sounds of an orphaned child in the hollow echoes of a stone church.

He's weak. It was obvious on his face. This supposed man, this *President*, was struggling to hold back tears. Didn't he know that death was part of life? He'd caused death, hadn't he? Didn't he know what death was? Was he only learning now? The other faces did know. One could see that. They were somber, because at a funeral it was expected that one had to be somber, but all life came to an end. Ryan ought to know. He'd faced danger – but that was long ago, he reminded himself, and over time men forget such things. Ryan had had ample cause to forget life's vulnerabilities, protected as he'd been as a government official. It amazed the man how much one could learn from a few seconds' examination of a human face.

That made things easier, didn't it?

She was five rows back, but was on the aisle, and though the Prime Minister of India could see only the back of President Ryan's head, she, too, was a student of human behavior. A chief of state couldn't act like this. A chief of state was, after all, an actor on the world's most important stage, and you had to learn what to do and how to behave. She'd been going to funerals of various sorts all of her life, because political leaders had associates – not always friends – young and old, and one had to show respect by appearing, even for those one had detested. In the latter case, it could be amusing. In her country the dead were so often burned, and then she could tell herself that, perhaps, the body was still alive as it burned. Her eyebrows flickered up and down in private amusement at the thought. *Especially for the ones you detested.* It was such good practice. To appear saddened. *Yes, we had our differences, but he was always someone to be respected, someone you could work with, someone whose ideas were always worth serious attention.* With practice over the years, you got good enough that the survivors believed the lies – partly because they wanted to believe. You learned to smile just so, and to show grief just so, and to speak just so. You had to. A political leader could rarely allow true feelings to show. True feelings told others what your weaknesses were, and there were always those to use them against you – and so over the years you hid them more and more, until eventually you had few, if any, true feelings left. And that was good, because politics wasn't about feelings.

Clearly this Ryan fellow didn't know that, the Prime Minister of 'the world's largest democracy' told herself. As a result, he was showing what he really was, and worse still, for him, he was doing so in front of a third of the world's highest political leaders, people who would see and learn and file their thoughts away for future use. Just as she was doing. Marvelous, she thought, keeping her face somber and sad in honor of someone she'd thoroughly detested. When the organist began the first hymn, she lifted her book, turned the page to the proper number, and sang along with everyone else.

The rabbi went first. Each clergyman was given ten minutes, and each of them was an expert – more properly, each was a genuine scholar in addition to his calling as a man of God. Rabbi Benjamin Fleischman spoke from the Talmud and the Torah. He spoke of duty and honor and faith, of a merciful God. Next came the Reverend Frederick Ralston, the Senate Chaplain – he'd been out of town that night, and so spared of a more restrained participation in the events of the day. A Southern Baptist and distinguished authority on the New Testament, Ralston spoke of Christ's Passion in the garden, of his friend Senator Richard Eastman of Oregon, who lay in the sacristy, universally respected as an honorable member of the Congress, segueing then into praise of the fallen President, a devoted family man, as all knew . . .

There was no 'right' way to handle such things, Ryan thought. Maybe it would be easier if the minister/priest/rabbi had time to sit with the grieving, but that hadn't happened in this case, and he wondered –

No, this isn't right! Jack told himself. This was theater. It wasn't supposed to be that. There were *kids* sitting a few feet across the aisle to his left, and for them this wasn't theater at all. This was a lot simpler for them. It was *Mom* and *Dad*, ripped out of their lives by a senseless act, denying them the future that life was supposed to guarantee them, love and guidance, a chance to grow in a normal way into normal people. Mark and Amy were the important ones here, but the lessons of this service, which were supposed to help them, were instead aimed at others. This whole event was a *political* exercise, something to reassure the country, renew people's faith in God and the world and their country, and maybe the people out there behind the twenty-three cameras in the church needed that, but there were people in greater need, the children of Roger and Anne Durling, the grown sons of Dick Eastman, the widow of David Kohn of Rhode Island, and the surviving family of Marissa Henrik of Texas. Those were real people, and their personal grief was being subordinated to the needs of the country. *Well, the country be damned!* Jack thought, suddenly angry at what was happening, and at himself for not grasping it early enough to change things around. The country had needs, but those needs could not be so great as to overshadow the horror fate had inflicted on kids. Who spoke for them? Who spoke *to* them?

Worst of all for Ryan, a Catholic, Michael Cardinal O'Leary, Archbishop of Washington, was no better. 'Blessed are the peacemakers, for they will be called . . .' For Mark and Amy, Jack's mind raged, their father wasn't a peacemaker. He was Dad, and Dad was gone, and that wasn't an abstraction. Three distinguished, learned, and very decent members of the clergy were preaching to a nation, but right before them were children who got a few kind words of lip service, and that was all. Somebody had to speak to them, for them, about their parents. Somebody had to try to make things better. It wasn't possible, but someone had to try, damn it! Maybe he was President of the United States. Maybe he had a duty to the millions behind the cameras, but Jack remembered the time his wife and daughter had been in Baltimore's Shock-Trauma Center, hovering between life and death, and that hadn't been a damned abstraction, either. *That* was the problem. *That* was why his family had been attacked. *That* was why all these people had died – because some misguided fanatic had seen them all as abstractions instead of human beings with lives and hopes and dreams – and kids. It was Jack's job to protect a nation. He'd sworn to preserve, protect, and defend the Constitution of the United States, and he would do that to the best of his ability. But the purpose of the *Constitution* was pretty simple – to secure the blessings of liberty for *people*, and that included kids. The country he served and the government he was trying to lead were nothing more or less than a mechanism to protect individual people. *That* duty was not an abstraction. The reality of that duty sat ten feet to his left, holding back tears as best they could, and probably failing, because there was no feeling lonelier than what those kids were suffering right now, while Mike O'Leary spoke to a country instead of a family. The theater had lasted long enough. There came another hymn, and then it was Ryan's turn to rise and walk to the pulpit.

Secret Service agents turned around, again sweeping the nave, because now SWORDSMAN was an ideal target. Getting to the lectern, he saw that Cardinal O'Leary had done as instructed and set the presidential binder on the wooden top. No, Jack decided. No. His hands grasped the sides of the lectern to steady himself. His eyes swept briefly across the assembly, and then looked down on the children of Roger and Anne Durling. The pain in their eyes broke his heart. They'd borne all the burdens placed on them by duties never theirs to carry. They'd been told by some unnamed 'friends' to be braver than would have been asked of any Marine at such a time, probably because, 'Mom and Dad would want you to.' But bearing pain in quiet dignity was not the business of children. That was what adults were supposed to do, as best they could. *Enough*, Jack told himself, *my duty starts here*. The first duty of the strong was ever to protect the weak. His hands squeezed on the polished oak, and the self-inflicted pain helped compose his thoughts.

'Mark, Amy, your father was my friend,' he said gently. 'It was my honor to work for him and help him as best I could – but you know, he was probably even more help for me. I know you always had to understand that Dad and Mom had important jobs, and didn't always have time for the really important things, but I can tell you that your father did everything he could to spend time with you, because he loved you more than anything in the world, more than being President, more than all the things that came along with that, more than anything – except maybe your Mom. He loved her a lot, too . . .'

What rubbish! Yes, one cared for children. Daryaei did, but children grew to adulthood no matter what. Their place was to learn, and to serve, and someday to do the deeds of adults. Until then, they were children, and the world told them what must be. Fate did. Allah did. Allah was merciful, even though life was hard. He had to admit that the Jew had spoken well, citing scripture quoted exactly the same way in their Torah and his Holy Koran. He would have chosen a different passage, but that was a matter of taste, wasn't it? Theology allowed such things. It had all been a wasted exercise, but formal occasions such as this usually were. This Ryan fool was wasting his chance to rally his nation, to appear strong and sure, thus to consolidate his hold on his government. Talking to children at such a time!

His political handlers must be having a collective heart attack, the Prime Minister thought, and it required all of the self-control learned over a political lifetime to keep her face composed. Then she decided to change her expression to sympathy. After all, he might be watching her, and she was a woman and a mother, after all, and she would be meeting with him later today. She tilted her head slightly to the right, so as to give herself a better view of the scene and the man. He might like that, too. In another minute or so, she'd pull a tissue from her purse to wipe her eyes.

'I wish I'd had the chance to get to know your mom better. Cathy and I were looking forward to that. I wanted Sally and Jack and Katie and you to become friends. Your dad and I talked a little about that. I guess that won't be happening the way we wanted it to.' That impromptu thought made Jack's stomach do a flip. They were crying now, because he'd told them without words that now it was okay to cry. Jack couldn't let himself do that. Not for the others. He had to be strong now for them, and so he gripped the lectern harder still until his hands really hurt, and he welcomed the pain for the discipline it imposed on him.

'You probably want to know why this had to happen. I don't know, kids. I wish I did. I wish *somebody* did, so that I could go to that person for the answers. But I've never found that person,' Jack went on.

'Jesus,' Clark managed to say in the <u>grumbly</u> voice that men used to prevent a sob. In his CIA office, as with all senior officials, was a TV set, and every channel was covering this. 'Yeah, I've looked once or twice myself, man.'

'You know something, John?' Chavez was under more control. It was a man's place to be calm at such times, so that the women and kids could cling to him. Or so his culture told him. Mr C., on the other hand, was just full of surprises. As always.

'What's that, Domingo?'

'He gets it. We're working for somebody who gets it.'

John turned at that. Who'd believe it? Two CIA paramilitary officers, thinking the same thoughts as their President. It was nice to know that he'd read Ryan correctly from the first moment. *Damn, just like his dad*. A pity Fate had denied him the chance to know that Ryan. He next wondered if Jack would succeed as President. He wasn't acting like one of the others. He was acting like a real person. But why was that so bad? Clark asked himself.

'I want you to know that you can come to Cathy and me whenever you want. You're not alone. You will *never* be alone. You have your family with you, and now you have my family, too,' he promised them from the pulpit. It just got harder. He had to say what he'd just said. Roger was a friend, and you looked after their kids when you had to. He'd done it for Buck Zimmer's family, and now he'd do it for Roger's.

'I want you to be proud of Mom and Dad. Your father was a fine man, a good friend. He worked very hard to make things better for people. It was a big job, and it denied him a lot of time with you, but your father was a big man, and big men do big things. Your mother was always there, too, and she also did big things. Kids, you will always have them in your heart. Remember all the things they told you, all the little things, and the games, and the tricks, and the jokes, all the ways moms and dads show love for their children. You will never lose that. Never,' Jack assured them, stretching and hoping for something that could soften the blow Fate had dealt them. He couldn't find anything better. It was time to end it.

'Mark, Amy, God decided He wanted your mom and dad back. He doesn't explain why in ways that are easy for us to understand, and we can't ... we can't fight it when that happens. We just can't –' Ryan's voice finally cracked.

* * *

How courageous of the man, Koga thought, to allow his emotions to show. Anyone could have stood up there and spoken the usual political drivel, and most would have – in or from any country – but this Ryan wasn't like that at all. Speaking to the children in this way was brilliant – or so he'd thought at the outset. But it wasn't that at all. Inside the President was a *man*. He wasn't an actor. He didn't care about showing strength and resolve. And Koga knew why. More than anyone else in this church, Koga knew what Ryan was made of. He'd guessed right in his own office a few days before. Ryan was samurai, and even more. He did what he did, not caring what others thought. The Japanese Prime Minister hoped that wasn't a mistake as he watched the President of the United States come down the steps, then approach the Durling children. He embraced them, and the audience watched tears well up on Ryan's face. There were sobs around him in the chiefs-of-state seating, but he knew that most of those were forced or feigned – or at most brief, fleeting moments of residual humanity, soon to be forgotten. He regretted that he couldn't join in that, but the rules of his culture were stern, all the more so as he bore the shame of one of his citizens having caused this monstrous tragedy. He *had* to play the political game, much as he would have preferred otherwise, and it wasn't so much that Ryan didn't have to play the game as that he didn't care. He wondered if America realized her good fortune.

'He didn't use his prepared speech at all,' the anchorman objected. The speech had been distributed to all the news networks, and all the copies had been highlighted and excerpted already so that the reporters could repeat favored passages, so to reinforce the important things the President had to say for the viewing public. Instead the anchor had been forced to take notes, which he did badly, long past his time as a working reporter.

'You're right,' the commentator reluctantly agreed. Things just weren't done this way. On his monitor, Ryan was still holding the Durling children, and that was going too long as well. 'I guess the President decided that this was an important personal moment for them –'

'And it surely is,' the anchorman inserted.

'But Mr Ryan's job is to govern a nation.' The commentator shook his head, clearly thinking something he couldn't say quite yet: *not presidential*.

Jack had to let go, finally. There was only hurt in their eyes now. The objective part of his mind thought that was probably good – they had to let it out – but that made it no easier to see, for children of that age weren't supposed to have such things at all. But these children did, and there was nothing to be done for it but to try, somehow, to ease the pain. He looked over at the uncles and aunts who'd accompanied them. They were weeping also, but through their tears he saw a grateful look, and that, at least, told him that he'd done something. Nodding, he turned to return to his seat. Cathy looked at him, and there were tears in her eyes, too, and though she couldn't speak, she gripped his hand. Jack saw one more example of his wife's intelligence. She'd worn no eye makeup to run from her tears. Inwardly, he smiled. He didn't like makeup, and his wife didn't really need it.

'What do we know of her?'
'She's a physician, an eye surgeon, actually, supposed to be a good one.' He checked his notes. 'The American news media say that she is continuing to work at her profession despite her official duties.'
'And their children?'
'There's nothing on that, though ... I should be able to find out what school they attend.' He saw the quizzical look and went on. 'If the wife will continue to do her medical work, then I would guess that the children will continue to attend the same schools.'
'How do you find that out?'
'Easily. All American news stories can be accessed by computer. Ryan has been the subject of numerous news pieces. I can find out anything I want.' In fact he already had, but not information about his family. The modern age had made the life of an intelligence officer so much easier. He already knew Ryan's age, height, weight, color of hair and eyes, and much of his personal habits, favorite food and drink, the golf clubs he belonged to, all manner of trivia, none of which was trivial to a man in his line of work. He didn't have to ask

what his boss was thinking. The opportunity which both had missed with all of the chiefs of state at the National Cathedral was gone forever, but it would not be the only one.

With one final hymn, it was over. The soldiers returned to collect the caskets, and the procession began again in reverse. Mark and Amy collected themselves well, aided by their relatives, and followed their parents. Jack led his family just after them. Katie was mainly bored and glad to be moving. Jack Jr. was sad for the Durling kids. Sally looked worried. He'd have to talk to her about that. Down the aisle he looked closely into a number of faces, distantly surprised that the first four or five rows of them looked not at the caskets, but at him. They never turned it off, did they? His fellow chiefs of state, Jack thought, wondering just what sort of club he'd just entered. A few faces were friendly. The Prince of Wales, who was not a chief of state and therefore placed by protocol behind the others – some of whom were outright thugs, but that could not be helped – gave a friendly nod. Yeah, he would understand, Jack thought. The new President wanted to check his watch, so tired he felt from the events of a day yet young, but he'd been sternly lectured about looking at one's watch, to the point of being advised to take it off. A President didn't need a watch. There were always people to tell him what came next, just as there were now people searching coat racks, ready to hand Ryan and his family what they needed before going back outside. There was Andrea Price, and other members of the Detail. Outside would be more: a not-so-small army of people with guns and fears, and a car to take him to his next destination, where he would perform more official duties, then be whisked off to the next set, and on, and on.

He couldn't let all this take control of his life. Ryan frowned at the thought. He'd do the work, but he couldn't make the mistake Roger and Anne had made. He thought of the faces he'd seen walking out of the church and knew that it was a club he might be forced to enter but which he would never join. Or so he told himself.

8

CHANGE OF COMMAND

The part at Andrews was mercifully short. From the Cathedral, the caskets had traveled in hearses, with the large official party left behind to disperse throughout Embassy Row. Air Force One was waiting on the ramp to take the Durlings back to California one last time. It seemed far more desultory now. There was yet another honor guard to salute the flag-draped coffins, but this was different. The crowd was smaller, composed mostly of Air Force and some other military personnel who had worked directly with the presidential party in one way or another. At the family's request, the actual burial ceremony would be smaller, and limited to relatives only, which was probably better for everybody. And so here at Andrews came the last 'Ruffles and Flourishes' and the last 'Hail to the Chief.' Mark stood at attention, holding his hand over his heart in a gesture sure to be on the cover of all the news magazines. A good kid, doing his best, and being more manly than he would ever know. A scissors lift took the caskets to the cargo door, for at this point that's what the bodies were; mercifully, that part of the transfer was hidden from view. Then it was time. The family walked up the steps into the VC-25 for their last ride. It wouldn't even have the Air Force One call sign anymore, because that label went with the President, and the President wasn't aboard. Ryan watched the aircraft taxi off, then rumble down the runway. TV cameras tracked it until it was a mere dot in the sky. Ryan's eyes did the same. By that time, a flight of F-16s, relieved of their guard duty over Washington, landed one by one. When that was done, Ryan and his family climbed aboard a Marine helicopter to return to the White House. The flight crew smiled and fussed over his children. Little Jack got a unit patch after he buckled in. The mood of the day changed with that. The Marines of VMH-1 had a new family to take care of, and life for them moved on.

Already the White House staff was at work, moving their things in (they'd labored throughout the morning moving the Durlings' things out), changing some furniture, and tonight his family would sleep in the same house first occupied by John Adams. The kids, being kids, looked out the windows as the helicopter began its descent. The parents, being parents, looked at each other.

Things changed at this point. At a private family funeral, this would have been the wake. The sadness was supposed to be left behind, and the mourners would remember what a great guy Roger was, and then talk about what new things were going on in their lives, how the kids were doing at school, discussions of the baseball off-season trades. It was a way for things to return to normal after a sad and stressful day. And so it was in this case, if on a somewhat broader scale. The White House photographer was waiting there on the South Lawn as the helicopter touched down. The stairs were lowered, and a Marine corporal stood at the bottom of them. President Ryan came out first, getting a salute from the corporal in dress blues, which he automatically returned, so ingrained were the lessons from Quantico, Virginia, more than twenty years before. Cathy came down behind, and then the kids. The Secret Service agents formed a loose corridor which told them where to head. News cameras were off to the west, their left, but no questions were shouted – this time, that would change very quickly, too. Inside the White House, the Ryans were directed to the elevators for a rapid trip to the second, bedroom floor. Van Damm was waiting there.

'Mr President.'

'Do I change, Arnie?' Jack asked, handing his coat to a valet. Ryan stopped cold, if only for a second or two, in surprise at how easy that simple activity was. He was President now, and in small ways he had automatically started to act like one. Somehow that was more remarkable than the duties he'd already undertaken.

'No. Here.' The chief of staff handed over a list of the guests already downstairs in the East Room. Jack scanned it, standing there in the middle of the hall. The names weren't so much people as countries, many friendly, many acquaintances, some genuine strangers, and some . . . Even as a former

National Security Advisor, he didn't know everything he ought to have known about them. While he read, Cathy hustled the kids off to the bathroom – or started to. An agent from the Detail had to assist in locating them. Ryan walked into his own, checking his hair in the mirror. He managed to comb it himself, without the ministrations of Mrs Abbot, under van Damm's scrutiny. *Not even safe in here*, the President told himself.

'How long will this go, Arnie?'

'No telling, sir.'

Ryan turned. 'When we're alone, the name's still Jack, remember? I've been afflicted, not anointed.'

'Okay, Jack.'

'Kids, too?'

'That'll be a nice touch . . . Jack, so far, you've been doing well.'

'Do I have my speechwriter mad at me?' he asked, checking his tie and leaving the bathroom.

'Your instincts weren't so bad, but next time we can have a speech prepared for that.'

Ryan thought about that, handing the list back to van Damm. 'You know, just because I'm President doesn't mean I stopped being a person.'

'Jack, get used to it, okay? You're not allowed to be "just a person" anymore. Okay, you've had a few days to get used to the idea. When you walk downstairs, you are the United States of America, *not* just a person. That goes for you, that goes for your wife, and to some degree that goes for your kids.' For his revelation, the chief of staff got a poisonous look that may have lasted a second or two. Arnie ignored it. It was just personal, not business. 'Ready, Mr President?'

Jack nodded, wondering if Arnie was right or not, and wondering why the observation had angered him so much. And then wondering again how true it was. You couldn't tell with Arnie. He was and would continue to be a teacher, and as with most skilled teachers, he would occasionally tell lies as harsh exemplars of a deeper truth.

Don Russell appeared in the corridor, leading Katie by the hand. She had a red ribbon in her hair as she broke free and ran to her mother. 'Look what Uncle Don did!' At least one member of the Detail was already a member of the family.

'You may want to get them all into the bathroom now, Mrs Ryan. There are no restrooms on the State Floor.'

'None?'

Russell shook his head. 'No, ma'am, they sort of forgot when they built the place.'

Caroline Ryan grabbed the two youngest and led them off, doing her motherly duty. She returned in a couple of minutes.

'Want me to carry her downstairs for you, ma'am?' Russell asked with a grandfatherly smile. 'The stairs are a little tricky in heels. I'll hand her off at the bottom.'

'Sure.' People started heading for the stairwell, and Andrea Price keyed her microphone.

'SWORDSMAN and party are moving from the residence to the State Floor.'

'Roger,' another agent responded from downstairs.

They could hear the noise even before making the last turn on the marble steps. Russell set Katie Ryan on the floor next to her mother. The agents faded away, becoming strangely invisible as the Ryans, the First Family, walked into the East Room.

'Ladies and gentlemen,' a staff member announced, 'the President of the United States, Dr Ryan, and family.' Heads turned. There was a brief wave of applause which quickly faded, but the looks continued. They appeared friendly enough, Jack thought, knowing that not all were. He and Cathy moved a little to the left, and formed the receiving line.

They came mainly one by one, though some of the visiting chiefs of state had brought wives. A protocol officer at Ryan's left whispered the name of each into his ear, making Jack wonder how she knew all of these people by sight. The procession to him wasn't quite as haphazard as it appeared. The ambassadors representing countries whose heads had chosen not to make the trip held back, but even those, standing about in little knots of associates and sipping at their Perrier-with-a-twist, didn't hide their professional curiosity, checking out the new President *and* the way he greeted the men and women who came up to him.

'The Prime Minister of Belgium, M Arnaud,' the protocol officer whispered. The official photographer started clicking away to record every official greeting, and two TV cameras were doing the same, albeit more quietly.

'Your telegram was very gracious, Mr Prime Minister, and it came at a sensitive moment,' Ryan said, wondering if the truth sounded good enough, wondering if Arnaud had even read it – well, of course he had, though he probably hadn't drafted it.

'Your talk to the children was very moving. I'm sure everyone here thinks the same,' the PM replied, gripping Ryan's hand, testing it for firmness, looking hard and deep into his eyes, and rather pleased with himself for the very skilled mendacity of his greeting. For all that, he had read the telegram and pronounced it fitting, and was gratified at hearing Ryan's reaction to it. Belgium was an ally, and Arnaud had been well briefed by the chief of his country's military-intelligence service, who'd worked with Ryan at several NATO conferences, and always liked the American's read on the Soviets – and now, the Russians. An unknown quantity as a political leader, the gist of the briefing had been, but a bright and capable analyst. Arnaud did his own reading now, first in line mainly by accident, by grip and look and many years of experience in such things. Then he moved on.

'Dr Ryan, I have heard so much about you.' He kissed her hand in a very graceful Continental way. He hadn't been told how attractive the new First Lady was, and how dainty her hands were. Well, she was a surgeon, wasn't she? New to the game and uncomfortable with it, but playing along as she had to.

'Thank you, Prime Minister Arnaud,' Cathy replied, informed by her own protocol officer (this one was just behind her) who this gentleman was. The hand business, she thought, was very theatrical . . . but nice.

'Your children are angels.'

'How nice of you to say that.' And he moved on, to be replaced by the President of Mexico.

News cameras floated around the room, along with fifteen reporters, because this was a working function of sorts. The piano in the room's northeast corner played some light classical – not quite what on the radio was called 'easy listening,' but close.

'And how long have you known the President?' The question came from the Prime Minister of Kenya, pleased to find a black admiral in the room.

'We go back quite a ways, sir,' Robby Jackson replied.

'Robby! Excuse me, *Admiral* Jackson,' the Prince of Wales corrected himself.

'Captain.' Jackson shook his hand warmly. 'It's been a while, sir.'

'You two know – ah! Yes!' the Kenyan realized. Then he saw his counterpart from Tanzania and moved off to conduct business, leaving the two alone.

'How is he doing – really, I mean,' the Prince asked, vaguely saddening Jackson. But this man had a job. Sent over as a friend in what Robby knew to have been a political decision, he would, on his return to Her Britannic Majesty's embassy, dictate a contact report. It was business. On the other hand, the question deserved an answer. The three of them had 'served' together briefly one hot, stormy summer night.

'We had a short meeting with the acting chiefs a couple of days ago. There'll be a working session tomorrow. Jack'll be okay,' the J-3 decided he would say. He put some conviction behind it. He had to. Jack was now NCA – National Command Authority – and Jackson's loyalty to him was a matter of law and honor, not mere humanity.

'And your wife?' He looked over to where Sissy Jackson was talking with Sally Ryan.

'Still number two piano for the National Symphony.'

'Who's the lead?'

'Miklos Dimitri. Bigger hands,' Jackson explained. He decided it would be impolitic to ask any family questions of his own.

'You did well in the Pacific.'

'Yeah, well, fortunately we didn't have to kill all that many people.' Jackson looked his almost-friend in the eye. 'That really stopped being fun, y'know?'

'Can he handle the job, Robby? You know him better than I do.'

'Captain, he *has* to handle the job,' Jackson answered, looking over at his Commander-in-Chief–friend, and knowing how much Jack detested formal occasions. Watching his new President endure the circulating line, it was impossible to avoid thinking back. 'Long way from teaching history at the Trade School, Your Highness,' the admiral observed in a whisper.

For Cathy Ryan, it was more than anything else an exercise in protecting her hand. Oddly she knew the formal occasion drill better than her husband. As a senior physician at Johns Hopkins's Wilmer Ophthalmological Institute, she'd had to deal with numerous formal fund-raisers over the years, essentially a high-class version of begging – most of which occasions Jack had missed, often to her displeasure. So, here she was, again, meeting people she didn't know, would never have the chance to like, and not one of whom would support her research programs.

'The Prime Minister of India,' her protocol officer said quietly.

'Hello.' The First Lady smiled her greeting, shook the hand, which was blessedly light.

'You must be very proud of your husband.'

'I've always been proud of Jack.' They were of the same height. The Prime Minister's skin was swarthy, and she squinted her eyes behind her glasses, Cathy saw. She probably needed a prescription change, and she probably got headaches from her out-of-date one. Strange. They had some pretty good doctors in India. Not all of them came to America.

'And such lovely children,' she added.

'How nice of you to say that.' Cathy smiled again, in an automatic sort of way, to an observation that was as perfunctory as a comment on the clouds in the sky. A closer look at the woman's eyes told Cathy something she didn't like. *She thinks she's better than me.* But why? Because she was a politician and Caroline Ryan a mere surgeon? Would it be different had she chosen to become a lawyer? No, probably not, her mind went on, racing as it sometimes did when a surgical procedure went bad unexpectedly. No, it wasn't that at all. Cathy remembered a night right here in the East Room, facing off with Elizabeth Elliot. It was the same supercilious mind-set: *I'm better than you because of who I am and what I do.* SURGEON – that was her Secret Service code name, which had not displeased her at all, really – looked more deeply into the dark eyes before hers. There was even more to it than that. Cathy let go of her hand as the next big shot came through the mill.

The Prime Minister departed the line and headed for a circulating waiter, from whom she took a glass of juice. It would have been too obvious to do what she really wanted to do. That would come the next day, in New York. For now she looked at one of her fellow Prime Ministers, this one representing the People's Republic of China. She raised her glass a centimeter or so, and nodded without smiling. A smile was unnecessary. Her eyes conveyed the necessary message.

'Is it true they call you SWORDSMAN?' Prince Ali bin Sheik asked with a twinkle in his eye.

'Yes, and, yes, it is because of what you gave me,' Jack told him. 'Thank you for flying over.'

'My friend, there is a bond between us.' His Royal Highness was not quite a chief of state, but with the current illness of his sovereign, Ali was taking over more and more of the Kingdom's duties. He was now in charge of foreign relations *and* intelligence, the former schooled by Whitehall, the latter by Israel's Mossad, in one of the most ironic and least-known contradictions in a part of the world known for its inter-locking non sequiturs. On the whole, Ryan was pleased by that. Though he had much on his plate, Ali was capable.

'You've never met Cathy, have you?'

The Prince shifted his gaze. 'No, but I have met your col-league, Dr Katz. He trained my own eye doctor. Indeed, your husband is a fortunate man, Dr Ryan.'

And the Arabs were supposed to be cold, humorless, and disrespectful of women? Cathy asked herself. Not this guy. Prince Ali took her hand gently.

'Oh, you must have met Bernie when he went over in 1994.' Wilmer had helped establish the eye institute in Riyadh, and Bernie had stayed five months to do some clini-cal instruction.

'He performed surgery on a cousin who was injured in a plane crash. He's back flying. And those are your children over there?'

'Yes, Your Highness.' This one went into the card file as a good guy.

'Would you mind if I spoke with them?'

167

'Please.' The Prince nodded and moved off.

Caroline Ryan, he thought, making his mental notes. *Highly intelligent, highly perceptive. Proud. Will be an asset to her husband if he has the wit to make use of her.* What a pity, he thought, that his own culture utilized its women so inefficiently – but he wasn't King yet, might never be, and even if he were to become so, there were limits to the changes he could make under the best of circumstances. His nation still had far to go, though many forgot how breathtakingly far the Kingdom had come in two generations. Even so, there *was* a bond between him and Ryan, and because of that, a bond between America and the Kingdom. He walked over to the Ryan family, but before he got there he saw what he needed. The children were slightly overwhelmed by everything. The smallest daughter was having the easiest time of it, sipping at a soft drink under the watchful eye of a Secret Service agent, while a few diplomatic wives attempted to talk to her. She was accustomed to being doted on, as so small a child ought to be. The son, older, was the most disoriented, but that was normal for a lad of his age, no longer a child but not yet a man. The eldest, Olivia to the briefing documents but Sally to her father, was dealing well with the most awkward age of all. What struck Prince Ali was that they were *not* used to all this. Their parents had protected them from Jack's official life. Spoiled as they undoubtedly were in some ways, they did not have the bored, haughty look of other such kids. You could tell much of a man and woman by examining their children. A moment later, he bent down over Katie. Initially she was taken aback by his unusual clothing – Ali had feared frostbite only two hours before – but in a moment his warm smile had her reaching up to touch his beard while Don Russell stood a meter away like a watch-bear. He took the time to catch the agent's eye, and the two traded a quick look. He knew that Cathy Ryan would be watching, too. What better way to befriend people than to show solicitude to their children? But it was more than that, and in his written report to his ministers, he would warn them not to judge Ryan by his somewhat awkward funeral speech. That he was not the usual sort to lead a country didn't mean that he was unfit to do so.

But some were.

Many of them were in this room.

Sister Jean Baptiste had done her best to ignore it, working through the heat of the day to sunset, trying to deny the discomfort that soon grew into genuine pain, hoping it would fade away, as minor ailments did – always did. She'd come down with malaria virtually her first week in this country, and that disease had never really gone away. At first she'd thought that's what it was, but it wasn't. The fever she'd written off to a typically hot Congo day wasn't that, either. It surprised her that she was afraid. For as often as she'd treated and consoled others, she'd never really understood the fear they had. She knew they were afraid, understood the fact that fear existed, but her response to it was succor and kindness, and prayer. Now for the first time, she was beginning to understand. Because she thought she knew what it was. She'd seen it before. Not often. Most of them never got this far. But Benedict Mkusa had gotten here, for what little good it had done. He would surely be dead by the end of the day, Sister Maria Magdalena had told her after morning mass. As little as three days before she would have sighed – but consoled herself with the thought that there would be another angel in heaven. Not this time. Now she feared that there might be two. Sister Jean Baptiste leaned against the door frame. What had she done wrong? She was a careful nurse. She didn't *make* mistakes. Well.

She had to leave the ward. She did so, walking down the breezeway to the next building, directly into the lab. Dr Moudi was, as usual, at his workbench, concentrating as he always did, and didn't hear her walk in. When he turned, rubbing his eyes after twenty minutes on the microscope, he was surprised to see the holy woman with her left sleeve rolled up, a rubber strip tight around her upper arm, and a needle in her antecubital vein. She was on her third 5cc test tube, and discarding that, expertly drew a fourth.

'What is the matter, Sister?'

'Doctor, I think these need to be tested at once. Please, you will wish to put on a fresh pair of gloves.'

Moudi walked over to her, staying a meter away while she withdrew the needle from her arm. He looked at her face and eyes – like the women in his home city of Qom, she dressed in a very chaste and proper manner. There was much to admire about these nuns: cheerful, hardworking, and very devoutly in service to their false god – that wasn't strictly true. They were People of the Book, respected by the Prophet, but the Shi'a branch of Islam was somewhat less respectful of such people than . . . no, he would save those thoughts for another time. He could see it in her eyes, even more clearly than the overt symptoms which his trained senses were beginning to discern, he saw what she already knew.

'Please sit down, Sister.'

'No – I must –'

'Sister,' the physician said more insistently. 'You are a patient now. You will please do as I ask, yes?'

'Doctor, I –'

His voice softened. There was no purpose in being harsh, and truly this woman did not deserve such treatment before God. 'Sister, with all the care and devotion you have shown to others in this hospital, please, allow this humble visitor to show some of it to you.'

Jean Baptiste did as she was told. Dr Moudi first donned a fresh pair of latex gloves. Then he checked her pulse, 88, her blood pressure, 138/90, and took her temperature, 39 – all the numbers were high, the first two because of the third, and because of what she thought it was. It could have been any of a number of ailments, from trivial to fatal, but she'd treated the Mkusa boy, and that luckless child was dying. He left her there, carefully picking up the test tubes and moving them to his laboratory bench.

Moudi had wanted to become a surgeon. The youngest of four sons, all nephews of his country's leader, he'd waited impatiently to grow up, watching his elder brothers march off to war against Iraq. Two of them had died, and the other had come back maimed, later to die by his own despairing hand, and he'd thought to be a surgeon, the better to save the lives of Allah's warriors, so that they could fight another day in His Holy Cause. That desire had changed, and instead he'd learned about infectious diseases, because there was more than one way to fight for the Cause, and after years of patience, his way was finally appearing.

Minutes later, he walked to the isolation ward. There is

an aura to death, Moudi knew. Perhaps the image before him was something of the imagination, but the fact of it was not. As soon as the sister had brought the blood sample, he'd divided it in two, sending one carefully packed test tube by air express to the Centers for Disease Control in Atlanta, Georgia, USA, the global center for the analysis of exotic and dangerous agents. The other he'd kept in cold storage to await developments. CDC was as efficient as ever. The telex had arrived hours earlier: Ebola Zaire was the identification, followed by a lengthy set of warnings and instructions which were entirely unnecessary. As was the diagnosis, really. Few things killed like this, and none of them so fast.

It was as if Benedict Mkusa had been cursed by Allah Himself, something Moudi knew not to be true, for Allah was a God of Mercy, who did not deliberately afflict the young and innocent. To say 'it was written' was more accurate, but hardly more merciful for the patient or his parents. They sat by the bedside, dressed in protective garb, watching their world die before their eyes. The boy was in pain – horrid agony, really. Parts of his body were already dead and rotting while his heart still tried to pump and his brain to reason. The only other thing that could do this to a human body was a massive exposure to ionizing radiation. The effects were grossly similar. One by one at first, then in pairs, then in groups, then all at once, the internal organs became necrotic. The boy was too weak to vomit now, but blood issued from the other end of his GI tract. Only the eyes were something close to normal, though blood was there as well. Dark, young eyes, sad and not understanding, not comprehending that a life so recently begun was surely ending now, looking to his parents to make things right, as they always had during his eight years. The room stank of blood and sweat and other bodily fluids, and the look on the boy's face became more distant. Even as he lay still he seemed to draw away, and truly Dr Moudi closed his eyes and whispered a prayer for the boy, who was just a boy, after all, and though not a Muslim, still a religious lad, and a person of the Book unfairly denied access to the words of the Prophet. Allah was merciful above all things, and surely He would show mercy to this boy, taking him safely into Paradise. And better it were done quickly.

If an aura could be black, then this one was. Death enveloped the young patient one centimeter at a time. The painful breaths grew more shallow, the eyes, turned to his parents, stopped moving, and the agonized twitches of the limbs traveled down the extremities until just the fingers moved, ever so slightly, and presently that stopped.

Sister Maria Magdalena, standing behind and between mother and father, placed a hand on the shoulder of each, and Dr Moudi moved in closer, setting his stethoscope on the patient's chest. There was some noise, gurgles and faint tears as the necrosis destroyed tissue – a dreadful yet dynamic process, but of the heart there was nothing. He moved the ancient instrument about to be sure, then he looked up.

'He is gone. I am very sorry.' He might have added that for Ebola this death had been merciful, or so the books and articles said. This was his first direct experience with the virus, and it had been quite dreadful enough.

The parents took it well. They'd known for more than a day, long enough to accept, short enough that the shock hadn't worn off. They would go and pray, which was entirely proper.

The body of Benedict Mkusa would be burned, and the virus with it. The telex from Atlanta had been very clear on that. Too bad.

Ryan flexed his hand when the line finally ended. He turned to see his wife massaging hers and taking a deep breath. 'Get you something?' Jack asked.

'Something soft. Two procedures tomorrow morning.' And they still hadn't come up with a convenient way of getting Cathy to work. 'How many of these things will we have to do?' his wife asked.

'I don't know,' the President admitted, though he knew that the schedule was set months in advance, and that most of the program would have to be adhered to regardless of his wishes. As each day passed, it amazed him more and more that people sought after this job – the job had so many extraneous duties that it could scarcely be done. But the extraneous duties in a real sense *were* the job. It just went round and round. Then a staffer appeared with soft drinks for the President and First Lady, summoned by another who'd heard what Cathy had said. The paper napkins were mono-grammed – stamped, whatever the process was called – with the image of the White House, and under it the words, THE PRESIDENT'S HOUSE. Husband and wife both noticed that at the same moment, then allowed their eyes to meet.

'Remember the first time we took Sally to Disney World?' Cathy asked.

Jack knew what his wife meant. Just after their daughter's third birthday, not long before their trip to England . . . and the beginning of a journey which, it seemed, would never end. Sally had fixed on the castle in the center of the Magic Kingdom, always looking to see it no matter where they were at the time. She'd called it Mickey's House. Well, they had their own castle now. For a while, anyway. But the rent was pretty high. Cathy wandered over to where Robby and Sissy Jackson were speaking with the Prince of Wales. Jack found his chief of staff.

'How's the hand?' Arnie asked.

'No complaints.'

'You're lucky you're not campaigning. Lots of people think a friendly handshake is a knuckle-buster – man-to-man and all that. At least these people know better.' Van Damm sipped at his Perrier and surveyed the room. The reception was going well. Various chiefs of state and ambassadors and others were engaged in friendly conversation. There were a few discreet laughs at the exchange of jokes and pleasantries. The mood of the day had changed.

'So, how many exams did I pass and fail?' Ryan asked quietly.

'Honest answer? No telling. They all looked for something different. Remember that.' And some of them really didn't give a damn, having come for their own domestic political reasons, but even under these circumstances it was impolitic to say so.

'Kinda figured that out on my own, Arnie. Now I circulate, right?'

'Hit India,' van Damm advised. 'Adler thinks it's important.'

'Roger.' At least he remembered what she looked like. So many of the faces in the line had turned immediately into blurs, just as happened at an over-large party of any sort. It made Ryan feel like a fraud. Politicians were supposed to have a photographic memory for names and faces. He did not, and wondered if there were some sort of training method to acquire one. Jack handed his glass off to an attendant, wiped his hands with one of the special napkins, and headed off to see India. Russia stopped him first.

'Mr Ambassador,' Jack said. Valeriy Bogdanovich Lermonsov had been through the receiving line, but there hadn't been time then for whatever he wanted to say. They shook hands again anyway. Lermonsov was a career diplomat, popular in the local community of his peers. There was talk that he'd been KGB for years, but that was hardly something Ryan could hold against him.

'My government wishes to ask if an invitation to Moscow could be entertained.'

'I have no objection to it, Mr Ambassador, but we were just over a few months ago and my time has many demands on it right now.'

'I have no doubt of that, but my government wishes to discuss several questions of mutual interest.' That code phrase made Ryan turn his body fully to face the Russian.

'Oh?'

'I feared that your schedule would be a problem, Mr President. Might you then receive a personal representative for a quiet discussion of issues?'

That could only be one person, Jack knew. 'Sergey Nikolay'ch?'

'Would you receive him?' the Ambassador persisted.

Ryan had a brief moment of, if not panic, then disquiet. Sergey Golovko was the chairman of the RVS – the reborn, downsized, but still formidable KGB. He also was one of the few people in the Russian government who had both brains and the trust of the current Russian president, Eduard Petravich Grushavoy, himself one of the few men in the world with more problems than Ryan had. Moreover, Grushavoy was keeping Golovko as close as Stalin had kept Beriya, needing a counselor with brains, experience, and muscle. The comparison wasn't strictly fair, but Golovko would not be coming over to deliver a recipe for borscht. 'Items of mutual interest' usually meant serious business; coming directly to the President and not working through the State Department was another such indicator, and Lermonsov's persistence made things seem more serious still.

'Sergey's an old friend,' Jack said with a friendly smile. *All the way back to when he had a pistol in my face.* 'He's always welcome in my house. Let Arnie know about the scheduling?'

'I will do that, Mr President.'

Ryan nodded and moved off. The Prince of Wales had the Indian Prime Minister in a holding pattern, awaiting Ryan's appearance.

'Prime Minister, Your Highness,' Ryan said with a nod.

'We thought it important that some matters be clarified.'

'What might those be?' the President asked. He had an electrical twitch under his skin, from knowing what had to be coming now.

'The unfortunate incident in the Indian Ocean,' the Prime Minister said. 'Such misunderstandings.'

'I'm – glad to hear that . . .'

Even the Army takes days off, and the funeral of a President was one such day. Both Blue Force and OpFor had taken a day to stand down. That included the commanders. General Diggs's house was on a hilltop overlooking a singularly bleak valley, but for all that it was a magnificent sight, and the desert was warm that day from Mexican winds, which allowed a barbecue on his walled and hedged back yard.

'Have you met President Ryan?' Bondarenko asked, sipping an early-afternoon beer.

Diggs shook his head as he flipped the burgers and reached for his special sauce. 'Never. Evidently he had a piece of getting the 10th ACR deployed to Israel, but, no. I know Robby Jackson, though. He's J-3 now. Robby speaks very well of him.'

'This is American custom, what you do?' The Russian gestured to the charcoal burner.

Diggs looked up. 'Learned it from my daddy. Could you pass my beer over, Gennady?' The Russian handed the glass to his host. 'I do hate missing training days, but . . .' But he liked a day off as much as the next guy.

'This place you have here is amazing, Marion.' Bondarenko turned to survey the valley. The immediate base area looked typically American, with its grid of roads and structures, but beyond that was something else. Scarcely anything grew, just what the Americans called creosote bushes, and they were like some sort of flora from a distant planet. The land here was brown, even the mountains looked lifeless. Yet there was something magnificent about the desert – and it reminded him of a mountaintop in Tajikistan. Maybe that was it.

'So, exactly how did you get those ribbons, General?' Diggs didn't know all the story. His guest shrugged.

'The Mudjeheddin decided to visit my country. It was a secret research facility, since closed down – it's a separate country now, as you know.'

Diggs nodded. 'I'm a cavalryman, not a high-energy physicist. You can save the secret stuff.'

'I defended an apartment building – the home for the scientists and their families. I had a platoon of KGB border guards. The Mudje attacked us in company strength under cover of night and a snowstorm. It was rather exciting for an hour or so,' Gennady admitted.

Diggs had seen some of the scars – he'd caught his visitor in the shower the previous day. 'How good were they?'

'The Afghans?' Bondarenko grunted. 'You did not wish to be captured by them. They were absolutely fearless, but sometimes that worked against them. You could tell which bands had competent leadership and which did not. That one did. They wiped out the other half of the facility, and on my side' – a shrug – 'we were bloody lucky. At the end we were fighting on the ground floor of the building. The enemy commander led his people bravely – but I proved to be a better shot.'

'Hero of the Soviet Union,' Diggs remarked, checking his burgers again. Colonel Hamm was listening, quietly. This was how members of that community measured one another, not so much by what they had done as by how they told the story.

The Russian smiled. 'Marion, I had no choice. There was no place to run away, and I knew what they did to captured Russian officers. So, they give me medal and promotion, and then my country – how you say? Evaporate?' There was more to it, of course. Bondarenko had been in Moscow during the coup, and for the first time in his life faced with making a moral decision, he'd made the right one, attracting the notice of several people who were now highly placed in the government of a new and smaller country.

'How about a country reborn?' Colonel Hamm suggested. 'How about, we can be friends now?'

'*Da*. You speak well, Colonel. And you command well.'

'Thank you, sir. Mainly I just sit back and let the regiment run itself.' That was a lie that any really good officer understood as a special sort of truth.

'Using Sov – Russian tactical doctrine!' It just seemed so outrageous to the Russian general.

'It works, doesn't it?' Hamm finished his beer.

It would work, Bondarenko promised himself. It would work for his army as it had worked for the American, once he got back and got the political support he needed to rebuild the Russian Army into something it had never been. Even at its fighting peak, driving the Germans back to Berlin, the Red Army had been a heavy, blunt instrument, depending on the shock value of mass more than anything else. He also knew what a role luck had played. His former country had fielded the world's finest tank, the T-34, blessed with a diesel engine designed in France to power dirigibles, a suspension system designed by an American named J. Walter Christie, and a handful of brilliant design innovations from young Russian engineers. That was one of the few instances in the history of the Union of Soviet Socialist Republics in which his countrymen had managed to turn out a world-class product – and in this case it had been the right one at the right time – without which his country would surely have died. But the time was past for his country to depend on luck and mass. In the early 1980s the Americans had come up with the right formula: a small, professional army, carefully selected, exquisitely trained, and lavishly equipped. Colonel Hamm's OpFor, this 11th Cavalry Regiment, was like nothing he'd ever seen. His pre-travel brief had told him what to expect, but that was different from believing it. You had to see it to believe. In the right terrain, that one regiment could take on a division and destroy it in hours. The Blue Force was hardly incompetent, though its commander had declined the chance to come and eat here in order to work with his sub-unit leaders this day, so badly had they been mauled.

So much to learn here, but the most important lesson of

all was how the Americans faced their lessons. Senior officers were humiliated regularly, both in the mock battles and afterward in what they called the AAR, 'after-action review,' during which the observer-controller officers analyzed everything that had taken place, reading their notes off multicolored file cards like hospital pathologists.

'I tell you,' Bondarenko said after a few seconds of reflection, 'in my army, people would be start fistfights during –'

'Oh, we came close to that in the beginning,' Diggs assured him. 'When they started this place up, commanders got relieved for losing battles, until everybody took a deep breath and realized that it was supposed to be tough here. Pete Taylor is the guy who really got the NTC running right. The OCs had to learn diplomacy, and the Blue Force people had to learn that they were *here* to learn, but I'll tell you, Gennady, there isn't another army in the world that inflicts humiliation on its commanders the way we do.'

'That's a fact, sir. I was talking with Sean Connolly the other day – he's CO of the 10th ACR in the Negev Desert,' Hamm explained to the Russian. 'The Israelis still haven't got it all the way figured out. They still bitch about what the OCs tell 'em.'

'We keep installing more cameras over there.' Diggs laughed as he started shoveling burgers onto the plate. 'And sometimes the Israelis don't believe what happened even after we show them the videotapes.'

'Still too much *hoo-uh* over there,' Hamm agreed. 'Hey, I came here as a squadron commander, and I got my ass handed to me more'n once.'

'Gennady, after the Persian Gulf War, 3rd ACR came here for their regular rotation. Now, you remember, they led Barry McCaffrey's 24th Mech –'

'Kicked ass and took names for two hundred twenty miles in four days,' Hamm confirmed. Bondarenko nodded. He'd studied that campaign in detail.

'Couple months later, they came here and got the shit kicked outa them. That's the point, General. The training here is *tougher* than combat. There's no unit in the world as smart and fast and tough as Al's Blackhorse Cav –'

'Except your old Buffalo Soldiers, General,' Hamm interjected.

Diggs smiled at the reference to the 10th. He was used to Hamm's interruptions anyway. 'That's a fact, Al. Anyway, if you can just break even against the OpFor, you're ready to take on anybody in the world, on the wrong side of three-to-one odds, and kick their ass into the next time zone.'

Bondarenko nodded, smiling. He was learning fast. The small staff that had come with him was still prowling the base, talking with counterpart officers, and learning, learning, learning. Being on the wrong side of three-to-one odds wasn't the tradition of Russian armies, but that might soon change. The threat to his country was China, and if that battle were ever fought, it would be at the far end of a lengthy supply line, against a huge conscript army. The only answer to that threat was to duplicate what the Americans had done. Bondarenko's mission was to change the entire military policy of his country. Well, he told himself, he'd come to the right place to learn how.

Bullshit, the President thought behind an understanding smile. It was hard to like India. They called themselves the world's largest democracy, but that wasn't especially true. They talked about the most high-minded principles, but had, when convenient, muscled neighbors, developed nuclear weapons, and in asking America to depart the Indian Ocean – 'It is, after all, called the *Indian* Ocean,' a former PM had told a former American Ambassador – decided that the doctrine of Freedom of the Seas was variably applicable. And for damned sure, they'd been ready to make a move on Sri Lanka. It was just that now, the move having been foiled, they were saying that no such move had ever been planned. But you couldn't look in the eyes of a chief of state and smile, and say, 'Bullshit.'

It just wasn't done.

Jack listened patiently, sipping at another glass of Perrier fetched for him by a nameless aide. The situation in Sri Lanka was complex, and did, unfortunately, lend itself to misunderstanding, and India regretted that, and there were no hard feelings at all, but wouldn't it be better if both sides stood down. The Indian fleet was withdrawing back to its bases, training complete, and a few ships damaged by the American demonstration, which, the Prime Minister said without so many words, wasn't exactly cricket. Such bullies.

And what does Sri Lanka think of you? Ryan could have asked, but didn't.

'If only you and Ambassador Williams had communicated more clearly on the issue,' Ryan observed sadly.

'Such things happen,' the Prime Minister replied. 'David – frankly, pleasant man though he is, I fear the climate is too hot for one of his age.' Which was as close as she could come to telling Ryan to fire the man. Declaring Ambassador Williams persona non grata was far too drastic a step. Ryan tried not to change his expression, but failed. He needed Scott Adler over here, but the acting SecState was somewhere else at the moment.

'I hope you can appreciate the fact that I am really not in a position to make serious changes in the government at the moment.' *Drop dead.*

'Please, I wasn't suggesting that. I fully appreciate your situation. My hope was to allay at least one supposed problem, to make your task easier.' *Or I could make it harder.*

'Thank you for that, Prime Minister. Perhaps your Ambassador here could discuss things with Scott?'

'I'll be sure to speak to him on the matter.' She shook Ryan's hand again and walked away. Jack waited for several seconds before looking at the Prince.

'Your Highness, what do you call it when a high-ranking person lies right in your face?' the President asked with a wry smile.

'Diplomacy.'

9

DISTANT HOWLS

Golovko read over Ambassador Lermonsov's report without sympathy for its subject. Ryan looked 'harried and uncomfortable,' 'somewhat overwhelmed,' and 'physically tired.' Well, that was to be expected. His speech at President Durling's funeral, the diplomatic community agreed – along with the American media, which was straining its capacity for politeness – was not presidential. Well, anyone who knew Ryan knew him to be sentimental, especially when it came to the welfare of children. Golovko could easily forgive that. Russians were much the same. He ought to have done otherwise – Golovko had read over the official, undelivered oration; it was a good one, full of assurances for all listeners – but Ryan had always been what the Americans called a maverick (he'd had to look up the word, discovering that it denoted a wild, untamed horse, which was not far off the mark). That made Ryan both easy and impossible for the Russian to analyze. Ryan was an American, and Americans *were* and had always been devilishly unpredictable from Golovko's perspective. He'd spent a professional lifetime, first as a field intelligence officer, then as a rapidly climbing staff officer in Moscow, trying to predict what America would do in all manner of situations, and only avoiding failure because he'd never failed to present three possible courses of action in his reports to his superiors.

But at least Ivan Emmetovich Ryan was predictably unpredictable, and Golovko flattered himself to think of Ryan as a friend – perhaps that was going a bit far, but the two men had played the game, most of the time from opposite sides of the field, and for the most part both had played it skillfully and well, Golovko the more experienced professional, Ryan the gifted amateur, blessed by a system more tolerant of mavericks. There was respect between them.

'What are you thinking now, Jack?' Sergey whispered to

himself. Right now the new American President was sleeping, of course, fully eight hours behind Moscow, where the sun was only beginning to rise for a short winter day.

Ambassador Lermonsov had not been overly impressed, and Golovko would have to append his own notes to the report lest his government give *that* evaluation too much credence. Ryan had been far too skilled an enemy to the USSR to be taken lightly under any circumstances. The problem was that Lermonsov had expected Ryan to fit into one mold, and Ivan Emmetovich was not so easily classified. It wasn't so much complexity as a different variety of complexity. Russia didn't have a Ryan – it was not likely that he could have survived in the Soviet environment which still pervaded the Russian Republic, especially in its official bureaucracies. He was easily bored, and his temper, though kept under tight control at most times, was always there. Golovko had seen it bubbling more than once, but only heard of times when it had broken loose. Those stories had percolated out of CIA to ears which reported to Dzerzhinskiy Square. God help him as a head of government.

But that wasn't Golovko's problem.

He had enough of his own. He hadn't entirely relinquished control of the Foreign Intelligence Service – President Grushavoy had little reason to trust the agency which had once been the 'Sword and Shield of the Party,' and wanted someone he could rely upon to keep an eye on that tethered predator; Golovko, of course – and at the same time, Sergey was the principal foreign-policy adviser to the beleaguered Russian President. Russia's internal problems were so manifest as to deny the President the ability to evaluate foreign problems, and *that* meant that for all practical purposes the former spy gave advice that his President almost invariably followed. The chief minister – that's what he was, with or without the title – took the burden seriously. Grushavoy had a domestic hydra to deal with – like the mythical beast of old, every head cut off just gave room for another to grow into its place. Golovko had fewer to deal with, but they made up for it in size. And part of him wished for a return to the old KGB. Only a few years before, it would have been child's play. Lift a phone, speak a few words, and the criminals would have been picked up, and that would have been that

– not really, but it would have made things more . . . peaceful. More predictable. More orderly. And his country needed order. But the Second Chief Directorate, the 'secret police' division of the agency, was gone, spun off into an independent bureau, its powers diminished, and its public respect – fear bordering on outright terror in the not-so-old days – had evaporated. His country had never been under the degree of control expected by the West, but now it was worse. The Russian Republic teetered on the edge of anarchy as her citizens groped for something called democracy. Anarchy was what had brought Lenin to power, for the Russians craved strong rule, scarcely having known anything else, and while Golovko didn't want that – as a senior KGB officer he knew better than any what damage Marxism-Leninism had done to his nation – he desperately needed an organized country behind him, because the problems within attracted problems without. And so it was that his unofficial post as chief minister for national security was hostage to all manner of difficulties. His were the arms of an injured body, trying to fend off the wolves while it tried to heal.

And so he had little pity for Ryan, whose nation may have taken a severe blow to the head, but was otherwise healthy. However differently it might appear to others, Golovko knew better, and because he did, he would be asking Ryan for help.

China. The Americans had defeated Japan, but the real enemy hadn't *been* Japan. He had a desk covered with overhead photographs just brought down from a reconnaissance satellite. Too many divisions of the People's Liberation Army were exercising in the field. Chinese nuclear-rocket regiments were still at a somewhat increased alert status. His own country had discarded its ballistic weapons – despite the threat from China, the huge resulting development loans from American and European banks had made the gamble look attractive only a few months before. Besides, his country, like America, still had bombers and cruise missiles which could be armed with atomic warheads, and so the disadvantage was far more theoretical than real. If one assumed that the Chinese subscribed to the same theories, that is. The Chinese were in any case maintaining their armed forces at a high state of readiness, and Russia's Far Eastern group of forces was at a historic low. He consoled himself that with Japan taken out of play, the Chinese would not move. Probably not move, he corrected himself. If the Americans were hard to understand, the Chinese might as easily have been aliens from another planet. It was enough to remember that the Chinese had been as far as the Baltic once before. Like most Russians, Golovko had a deep respect for history. There he was, Sergey thought, lying on the snow, a stick in his hand to fight off the wolf while he tried to heal. His arm was still strong enough, and the stick still long enough to keep the fangs away. But what if there came another wolf? A document to the left of the satellite photographs was the first harbinger of that, like a distant howl on the horizon, the sort to make blood chill. Golovko didn't reflect far enough. Lying down on the ground, the horizon could be surprisingly close.

The amazing thing was that it had taken so long. Protecting an important person against assassination is a complex exercise at best, all the more so when that person went out of his way to create enemies. Ruthlessness helps. The ability to snatch people off the street, to make them disappear, was a deterrent of no small value. The further willingness to take away not just a single person, but an entire family – sometimes an entire extended family – and do the same was more effective still. One selected the people to be 'disappeared,' an unhappy pseudo-verb that had originated in Argentina, through intelligence. That was a polite term for informers, paid in the coin of the realm or in power, which was better still. They would report conversations for their seditious content, to the point that a mere joke about someone's mustache could entail the sentence of death for its raconteur; and soon enough, because institutions were institutions, informers had quotas to fill, and since the informers were themselves human beings with likes and dislikes, their reports as often as not reflected personal slights or jealousy, because the delegated power of life and death was as corrupting to the small as to the great. Eventually a corrupt system was itself corrupted, and the logic of terror reached its logical conclusion: a humble rabbit, cornered by a fox, has nothing to lose by striking out, and rabbits have teeth, and sometimes the rabbit gets lucky.

Because terror was not enough, there were passive measures as well. The task of assassinating an important man can be made difficult by the simplest of procedures, especially in a despotic state. A few lines of guards to limit approach. Multiple identical cars in which the target might travel – often as many as twenty in this case – denied one the ability to know which car to engage. The life of such a person was busy, and so it was both a convenience and a protective measure to have a double or two, to appear, and give a speech, and take the risk in return for a comfortable life as the staked goat on the public stage.

Next came the selection of the protectors – how did one pick truly reliable fish from a sea of hatred? The obvious answer here was to pick people from one's extended family, then to give them a lifestyle that depended absolutely upon the survival of their leader, and finally to link them so closely with his protection and its necessary ramifications that his death would mean far more than the loss of a highly paid government job. That the guards' lives depended on the guarded one was an effective incentive toward efficiency.

But really it all came down to one thing. A person was invincible only because people thought him to be so, and therefore that person's security was, like all of the important aspects of life, a thing of the mind.

But human motivation is also a thing of the mind, and fear has never been the strongest emotion. Throughout history, people have risked their lives for love, for patriotism, for principle, and for God far more often than fear has made them run away. Upon that fact depends progress.

The colonel had risked his life in so many ways that he could scarcely remember them all, and done that just to be noticed, just to be asked to be a small part in a larger machine, then to rise within it. He'd taken a long time to get this close to the Mustache. Eight years, in fact. In that time he'd tortured and killed men, women, and children from behind blank and pitiless eyes. He'd raped daughters before their fathers' eyes, mothers before their sons'. He'd committed crimes to damn the souls of a hundred men, because there was no other way. He'd drunk liquor in quantities to impress an infidel in order to defile that law of his religion. All of this he had done in God's name, praying for forgiveness, desperately telling himself that it was written that his life should be so, that, no, he didn't enjoy any of it, that the lives he took were sacrifices necessary to some greater plan, that they would have died in any case, and that in this way their deaths by his hand could serve a Holy Cause. He had to believe in all of that lest he go mad – he'd come close enough in any case, until his fixed purpose passed far beyond the meaning of 'obsession,' and he became that which he did in every possible way, all with one objective, that he would get close enough and trusted enough for a single second's work, to be followed instantly by his own death.

He knew he had become that which he and everyone around him were trained to fear above all things. All the lectures and the drinking sessions with his peers always came back to the same thing. They spoke of their mission and the dangers of that mission. And *that* always came down to one subject. The lone dedicated assassin, the man willing to throw away his own life like a gambling chip, the patient man who waited his chance, *that* was the enemy whom every protective officer in the world feared, drunk or sober, on duty or off, even in his dreams. And that was the reason for all the tests required to protect the Mustache. To get here, you had to be damned before God and men, because when you got here, you saw what really was.

The Mustache was what he called his target. Not a man at all, an apostate before Allah who desecrated Islam without a thought, a criminal of such magnitude as to deserve a newly designed room in Perdition. From afar the Mustache looked powerful and invincible, but not up close. His bodyguards knew better because they knew all. They saw the doubts and the fears, the petty cruelties inflicted on the undeserving. He'd seen the Mustache murder for amusement, maybe just to see if his Browning pistol worked today. He'd seen him look out the window of one of his white Mercedes autos, spot a young woman, point, give a command, then use the hapless girl for one night. The lucky ones returned home with money and disgrace. The unlucky floated down the Euphrates with their throats cut, not a few by the Mustache himself, if they'd resisted a little too well in the protection of their virtue. But powerful as he was, clever and cunning as he was, heartlessly cruel as he was, no, he was not invincible. And it was now his time to see Allah.

The Mustache emerged from the building onto the expansive porch, his bodyguards behind him, his right arm outstretched to salute the assembled multitude. The people in the square, hastily assembled, roared their adoration, which fed the Mustache as surely as sunlight fed the flower. And then, from three meters away, the colonel drew his automatic pistol from its leather holster, brought it up in one hand, and fired a single aimed round straight into the back of his target's head. Those in the front of the crowd saw the bullet erupt from their dictator's left eye, and there followed one of those moments in history, the sort when the entire earth seemed to stop its spin, hearts paused, and even the people who'd been screaming their loyalty to a man already dead would remember only silence.

The colonel didn't bother with another shot. He was an expert marksman who practiced with his comrades almost every day, and his open, blank eyes had seen the impact of his round. He didn't turn, and didn't waste time in fruitless efforts at self-defense. There was no point in killing the comrades with whom he'd drunk liquor and raped children. Others would see to that soon enough. He didn't even smile, though it was very funny indeed, wasn't it, that the Mustache had one instant looked at the square full of the people whom he despised for their adoration of himself – then to look Allah in the face and wonder what had happened. That thought had perhaps two seconds to form itself before he felt his body jerk with the impact of the first bullet. There was no pain. He was too focused on his target, now on the flat paving stones of the porch, already a pool of blood draining rapidly from the ruined head. More bullets hit, and it seemed briefly strange that he could feel them yet not the pain of their passage, and in his last seconds he prayed to Allah for forgiveness and understanding, that all his crimes had been committed in the name of God and His Justice. To the last, his ears reported not the sound of the shots, but the lingering cries of the mob, not yet grasping that their leader was dead.

'Who is it?' Ryan checked his clock. *Damn, the extra forty minutes of sleep would have been nice.*

'Mr President, my name is Major Canon, Marine Corps,' the unknown voice announced.

'That's nice, Major, who are you?' Jack blinked his eyes and forgot to be polite, but probably the officer understood.

'Sir, I'm the watch officer in Signals. We have a report with high confidence that the President of Iraq was assassinated about ten minutes ago.'

'Source?' Jack asked at once.

'Kuwait and Saudi both, sir. It was on Iraqi TV live, some sort of event, and we have people over there to monitor their TV. We have a tape being uplinked to us right now. The initial word is a pistol right in the head, at close range.' The tone of the officer's voice wasn't exactly regretful. *Well, they finally popped that fucker!* Of course, you couldn't exactly say that to the President.

And you needed to figure who 'they' was.

'Okay, Major, what's the drill?' The answer came quickly enough. Ryan replaced the phone.

'Now what?' Cathy asked. Jack swung his feet out of bed before answering.

'The President of Iraq was just killed.'

His wife almost said, *Good*, but stopped. The death of such a person was not as distant a concept as it had once been. How odd to feel that way about someone who could best serve the world by leaving it.

'Is that important?'

'In about twenty minutes, they'll tell me.' Ryan coughed before going on. 'What the hell, I used to be competent in those areas. Yeah, it's potentially very important.' With that he did what every man in America did in the morning. He headed to the bathroom ahead of his wife. For her part, Cathy lifted the remote and performed the other ordinarily male function of clicking on the bedroom TV, surprised to find that CNN didn't have anything on but reports on which airports were operating behind schedule. Jack had told her a few times just how good the White House Signals Office was.

'Anything?' her husband asked, coming back out.

'Not yet.' Then it was her turn.

Jack had to think about where his clothes were, wondering how a President was supposed to dress. He found his robe –

moved in from the Naval Observatory after having been moved there from Eighth and I, after having been removed from their home . . . damn – and opened the bedroom door. An agent in the hall handed him three morning papers. 'Thanks.'

Cathy saw that and stopped cold in her tracks, belatedly realizing that there had been people just outside her bedroom door all night. Her face turned away, forming the sort of smile generated by finding an unexpected mess in the kitchen.

'Jack?'

'Yes, honey?'

'If I kill you in bed some night, will those people with guns get me right away, or will it wait until morning?'

The real work was being done at Fort Meade. The video had traveled from one monitoring station on the Kuwait-Iraq border and another in Saudi Arabia, known as PALM BOWL and STORM TRACK, respectively, the latter set up to record all signals out of Baghdad, and the former watching the southeastern part of the country, around Basra. From both places the information traveled by fiber-optic cable to the National Security Agency's deceptively small building in King Khalid Military City (KKMC) and uplinked to a communications satellite, which then shot it back to NSA headquarters. There in the watch room, ten people summoned by one of the junior watch officers huddled around a TV monitor to catch the tape, while the more senior troops, in a separate glass-walled office, sipped their coffee soberly.

'Yes!' an Air Force sergeant observed on seeing the shot, 'Nothin' but net!' Several high fives were exchanged. The senior watch officer, who'd already called White House Signals, nodded his more restrained approval and relayed the original signal along the way, and ordered a digital enhancement, which would take a few minutes – only a few frames were all that important, and they had a massive Cray supercomputer to handle that.

Ryan remarked quietly that while Cathy was getting the kids ready for school, and herself ready to operate on people's eyes, here he was in Signals watching the instant replay of a murder. His designated national intelligence officer was still at CIA, finishing his morning intake of information, which he would then regurgitate to the President by way of the morning intelligence briefing. The post of National Security Advisor was currently vacant – one more thing to address today.

'Whoa!' Major Canon breathed.

The President nodded, then reverted to his former life as an intelligence officer. 'Okay, tell me what we know.'

'Sir, we know that somebody got killed, probably the Iraqi President.'

'Double?'

Canon nodded, 'Could be, but STORM TRACK is now reporting a *lot* of VHF signals that started all of a sudden, police and military nets, and the activity is radiating out from Baghdad.' The Marine officer pointed to his computer monitor, which displayed real-time 'take' from the NSA's many outposts. 'Translations will take a little time, but I do traffic analysis for a living. It looks pretty real, sir. I suppose it could be faked, but I wouldn't – there!'

A translation was coming up, identified as emanating from a military command net. *He's dead, he's dead, stsnd your regiment to and be prepared to move into the city imediately – recipient is Replican Gurds Special Operations regiment at Salman Pak – reply is: Yes I will yes I will, who is giving the oders, what are my orders –*

'Typos and all,' Ryan noted.

'Sir, it's hard for our people to translate and type it at the same time. Usually we clean it up before –'

'Relax, Major. I only use three fingers myself. Tell me what you think.'

'Sir, I'm only a junior officer here, that's why I draw the midwatch and –'

'If you were stupid, you wouldn't be here.'

Canon nodded. 'He's deader 'n hell, sir. Iraq needs a new dictator. We have the imagery, we have unusual signal traffic that fits the pattern of an unusual event. That's my estimate.' He paused and went on to cover himself, like a good spook. 'Unless it's a deliberate exercise to smoke out disloyal people inside his government. That's possible, but unlikely. Not in public like this.'

'Kamikaze play?'

'Yes, Mr President. Something you can only do once, and dangerous the first time.'

'Agreed.' Ryan walked to the coffee urn – the White House Office of Signals was mainly a military operation, and they made their own. Jack got two cups and came back, handing one to Major Canon, rather to the horror of everyone else in the room. 'Fast work. Send a "thanks" to the guys working this, okay?'

'Aye aye, sir.'

'Who do I talk to to get things happening around here?'

'We got the phones right here, Mr President.'

'I want Adler in here ASAP, the DCI . . . who else? State and CIA desks for Iraq. DIA estimate of the state of their military. Find out if Prince Ali is still in town. If he is, ask him to please stand by. I want to talk to him this morning if possible. I wonder what else . . . ?' Ryan's voice trailed off.

'CentCom, sir. He'll have the best military-intelligence troops down at Tampa, most familiar with the area, I mean.'

'Get him up here – no, we'll do that by landline, and we give him time to get briefed in.'

'We'll get it all going for you, sir.' Ryan patted the officer on the shoulder and headed out of the room. The heavy door closed behind him before Major Charles Canon spoke again. 'Hey, NCA knows his shit.'

'Is it what I heard?' Price asked, coming up the corridor.

'Do you ever sleep?' Then he thought about it. 'I want you in on this.'

'Why me, sir, I'm not –'

'You're supposed to know about assassinations, right?'

'Yes, Mr President.'

'Then right now you're more valuable to me than a spook.'

The timing could have been better. Daryaei had been surprised by the information just delivered. Not in the least bit displeased by it – except maybe the timing. He paused for a moment, whispering a prayer first of thanks to Allah, then for the soul of the unknown assassin – assassin? he asked himself. Perhaps 'judge' would be a better term for the man, one of many who'd been infiltrated into Iraq ages ago, while the war had still been going on. Most had merely disappeared, probably shot one way or another. The overall mission had been his idea, not nearly dramatic enough for the 'professionals' working in his intelligence service. Largely leftovers from the Shah's Savak – trained by the Israelis in the 1960s and 1970s – they were effective, but they were mercenaries at heart however much they might protest their religious fervor and their loyalty to the new regime. They'd proceeded along 'conventional' lines for the unconventional mission, trying bribes of various sorts or testing the waters for dissidents, only to fail at every turn, and for years Daryaei had wondered if the target of all that attention might have Allah's perverse blessings somehow or other – but that had been the counsel of despair, not of reason and faith, and even Daryaei was subject to human weakness. Surely the Americans had tried for him also, and probably in the same way, trying to identify military commanders who might like to try out the seat of power, trying to initiate a coup d'état such as they had done often enough in other parts of the world. But, no, this target was too skilled for that, and at every turn he'd become more skilled, and so the Americans had failed, and the Israelis, and all the others. *All but me.*

It was tradition, after all, all the way back to antiquity. One man, operating alone, one faithful man who would do whatever was necessary to accomplish his mission. Eleven such men had been dispatched into Iraq for this specific purpose, told to go deep under cover, trained to forget everything they had ever been, entirely without contact or control officers, and all records of their existence destroyed so that even an Iraqi spy in his own agencies could not discover the mission without a name. Within an hour, some of his own cronies would come into this office, praising God and lauding their leader for his wisdom. Perhaps so, but even they didn't know all the things he had done, or all the people he'd dispatched.

The digitized rendition of the event didn't change much, though now he had a more professional opinion of the options:

'Mr President, a guy with a Silicon Graphics workstation could fake this,' the NIO told him. 'You've seen movies, and movie film has much higher resolution than a TV set. You can fake almost anything now.'

'Fine, but your job is to tell me what did happen,' Ryan pointed out. He'd seen the same few seconds of tape eight times now, and was growing tired of instant replay.

'We can't say with absolute certainty.'

Maybe it was the week's sleep deprivation. Maybe it was the stress of the job. Maybe it was the stress of having to face his *second* crisis. Maybe it was the fact that Ryan was himself still a carded national intelligence officer. 'Look, I'm going to say this once: Your job isn't to cover your ass. Your job is to cover *mine!*'

'I know that, Mr President. That's why I'm giving you all the information I have . . .' Ryan didn't have to listen to the rest of the speech. He'd heard it all before, a couple of hundred times. There had even been cases when he'd said similar things himself, but in Jack's case, he'd always hung his hat on one of the options.

'Scott?' Jack asked the acting SecStatc.

'The son of a bitch is dead as yesterday's fish,' Adler replied.

'Disagreement?' President Ryan asked the others in the room. Nobody contradicted the assessment, giving it a sort of blessing. Even the NIO would not *disagree* with the collective opinion. He'd delivered his assessments, after all. Any mistakes now were the Secretary of State's problem. Perfect.

'Who was the shooter?' Andrea Price asked. The answer came from CIA's Iraq-desk officer.

'Unknown. I have people running tapes of previous appearances just to make sure that he's been around before. Look, from all appearances it was a senior member of his protection detail, with the rank of an army colonel, and – '

'And I damned well know everybody on my detail,' Price concluded the statement. 'So, whoever it was, he belonged there, and that means whoever pulled this off managed to get somebody all the way inside, close enough to make the hit, and committed enough to pay the price for it. It must have taken years.' The continuation of the tape – they'd watched that only five times – showed the man crumble after a fusillade of pistol shots at point-blank range. That struck Agent Price as odd. You damned well wanted to bag such people alive. Dead men still didn't tell any tales, and executions could always be arranged. Unless he'd been killed by other members of a conspiracy. But how likely was it that more than one assassin had made it that far? Price reflected that she could ask Indira Gandhi that someday. Her whole detail had turned on her one afternoon in a garden. For Price that was the final infamy, killing the person you were sworn to defend. But, then, she hadn't sworn to defend such people as that. One other thing on the tape got her attention: 'Did you notice the body language?'

'What do you mean?' Ryan asked.

'The way the gun came up, the way he took the shot, the way he just stood there and watched. Like a golfer, it's called follow-through. He must have waited a long time for the chance. He damned sure thought about it for a long, long time. He must have dreamed about it. He wanted the moment to be perfect. He wanted to see it and enjoy it before he went down.' She shook her head slowly. 'That was one focused, dedicated killer.' Price was actually enjoying herself, chilling though the subject of the meeting was. More than one President had treated the Secret Service agents as if they were furniture, or at best nice pets. It wasn't often that big shots asked their opinion of much more than narrow professional areas, like where a bad guy might be in a particular crowd.

'Keep going,' CIA said.

'He must have been from outside, a guy with a totally clean record, no connection at all with anybody who made noise in Baghdad. This wasn't a guy getting even for somebody taking his mother out, okay? It was somebody who worked his way up the system, slow and careful all the way.'

'Iran,' CIA said. 'Best guess, anyway. Religious motivation. No way he'd walk away from the hit, so it had to be somebody who didn't care. That could also mean straight revenge, but Ms Price is correct: his people were clean in that respect. Anyway, it wasn't the Israelis, wasn't the French. The Brits don't do this anymore. The domestic angle is probably taken out by their vetting procedures. So it wasn't for money. It wasn't for personal or family motives. I think we can discount political ideology. That leaves religion, and *that* means Iran.'

'I can't say I'm familiar with all the intelligence side, but from looking at the tape, yeah,' Andrea Price agreed. 'It's like he was saying a prayer, the way he killed the guy. He just wanted the moment to be perfect. He didn't care about anything else.'

'Somebody else to check that out?' Ryan asked.

'FBI, their Behavioral Sciences people are pretty good at reading minds. We work with them all the time,' Price responded.

'Good idea,' CIA agreed. 'We'll rattle the bushes to ID the shooter, but even if we can get good information, it might not mean anything.'

'What about the timing?'

'If we can stipulate that the shooter was there for a while – we have enough tapes of public appearances to determine that – then timing is an issue,' CIA thought.

'Oh, that's just great,' the President opined. 'Scott, now what?'

'Bert?' SecState said to his desk officer. Bert Vasco was the State Department senior desk officer for that country. Rather like a specialist in the trading industry, he concentrated his efforts on learning everything he could about one particular country.

'Mr President, as we all know, Iraq is a majority Shi'a Muslim country ruled by a Sunni minority through the Ba'ath political party. It has always been a concern that the elimination of our friend over there could topple –'

'Tell me what I don't know,' Ryan interrupted.

'Mr President, we simply do not know the strength of any opposition group that may or may not exist. The current regime has been very effective at cutting the weeds down early. A handful of Iraqi political figures has defected to Iran. None are top-quality people, and none ever had the chance to develop a firm political base. There are two radio stations that broadcast from Iran into Iraq. We know the names of the defectors who use those transmitters to talk to their countrymen. But there's no telling how many people listen and pay attention. The regime isn't exactly popular, we know that. We do not know the strength of the opposition, or what sort of organization exists to make use of an opportunity such as this one.'

CIA nodded. 'Bert's right. Our friend was awfully good at identifying potential enemies and taking them out of play.

We tried to help during and after the Persian Gulf War, but all we really managed to do was get people killed. For sure nobody over there trusts us.'

Ryan sipped at his coffee and nodded. He'd made his own recommendations back in 1991, and they hadn't been exercised. Well, he'd still been a junior executive then.

'Do we have any options to play?' the President asked next.

'Honestly, no,' Vasco answered.

CIA agreed: 'No assets in place. What few people we have operating in that country are tasked to coverage of weapons development: nuclear, chemical, and so forth. Nobody on the political side. We actually have more people in Iran looking at the political side. We can rattle those bushes some, but not in Iraq.'

Fabulous, Jack thought, a country may or may not go down in one of the most sensitive areas of the world, and the world's most powerful nation could do nothing more than watch television coverage of the event. So much for the power of the American presidency.

'Arnie?'

'Yes, Mr President,' the chief of staff replied.

'We bumped Mary Pat off the schedule a couple days ago. I want her in today if we can work the schedule.'

'I'll see what we can do on that, but –'

'*But* when something like this happens, the President of the United States is supposed to have more than his dick in his hand.' Ryan paused. 'Is Iran going to make a move?'

10

POLITICS

Prince Ali bin Sheik had been ready to fly home on his personal aircraft, an aging but beautifully appointed Lockheed L-1011, when the call came in from the White House. The Saudi embassy was located close to the Kennedy Center, and the ride correspondingly short in his official limousine, accompanied by a security force almost as large as Ryan's and made up of American Diplomatic Protection Service personnel, plus the Prince's own detail, composed of former members of Britain's Special Air Service. The Saudis, as always, spent a lot of money and bought quality with it. Ali was no stranger to the White House, or to Scott Adler, who met him at the door and conducted him upstairs and east into the Oval Office.

'Mr President,' His Royal Highness said, walking in from the secretaries' room.

'Thank you for coming over on such short notice.' Jack shook his hand and waved him to one of the room's two sofas. Some thoughtful person had started a fire in the fireplace. The White House photographer snapped a few shots, and was dismissed. 'I imagine you've seen the news this morning.'

Ali managed a worried smile. 'What does one say? We will not mourn his passing, but the Kingdom has serious concerns.'

'Do you know anything we don't?' Ryan asked.

The Prince shook his head. 'I was as surprised as everyone else.'

The President grimaced. 'You know, with all the money we spend on –' His visitor raised a tired hand.

'Yes, I know. I will have the same conversation with my own ministers as soon as my airplane lands back home.'

'Iran.'

'Undoubtedly.'

'Will they move?'

The Oval Office got quiet then, just the crackling of the seasoned oak in the fireplace as the three men, Ryan, Ali, and Adler, traded looks across the coffee table, the tray and cups on it untouched. The issue was, of course, oil. The Persian – sometimes called the *Arabian* – Gulf was a finger of water surrounded by, and in some places sitting atop, a sea of oil. Most of the world's known supply was there, divided mainly among the Kingdom of Saudi Arabia, Kuwait, Iraq, and Iran, along with the smaller United Arab Emirates, Bahrain, and Qatar. Of these countries, Iran was by far the largest in terms of population. Next came Iraq. The nations of the Arabian Peninsula were richer, but the land atop their liquid wealth had never supported a large population, and there was the rub, first exposed in 1991, when Iraq had invaded Kuwait with all the grace of a schoolyard bully's attack on a smaller child. Ryan had more than once said that aggressive war was little more than an armed robbery writ large, and such had been the case in the Persian Gulf War. Seizing upon a minor territorial dispute and some equally trivial economic issues as an excuse, Saddam Hussein had attempted at a stroke to double his country's inherent wealth, and then threatened to double down his bets yet again by attacking Saudi Arabia – the reason he'd stopped at the Kuwait-Saudi border would now remain forever unexplained. At the most easily understood level, it was about oil and oil's resulting wealth.

But there was more to it than that. Hussein, like a Mafia don, had thought about little more than money and the political power that money generated. Iran was somewhat more farsighted.

All the nations around the Gulf were Islamic, most of them very strictly so. There were the exceptions of Bahrain and Iraq. In the former case, the oil had essentially run out, and that country – really a city-state separated from the Kingdom by a causeway – had evolved into the same function that Nevada exercised for the western United States, a place where the normal rules were set aside, where drinking, gambling, and other pleasures could be indulged a convenient distance from a more restrictive home. In the latter case, Iraq was a secular state which paid scant lip service to the state religion, which largely explained its President's demise after a long and lively career.

But the key to the region was and would always be religion. The Saudi Kingdom was the living heart of Islam. The Prophet had been born there. The holy cities of Mecca and Medina were there, and from that point of origin had grown one of the world's great religious movements. The issue was less about oil than about faith. Saudi Arabia was of the Sunni branch, and Iran of the Shi'a. Ryan had once been briefed in on the differences, which had at the time seemed so marginal that he'd made no effort to remember them. That, the President told himself now, was foolish. The differences were large enough to make two important countries into enemies, and that was as large as any difference needed to be. It wasn't about wealth <u>per se.</u> It was about a different sort of power, the sort that grew from the mind and the heart – and from there into something else. Oil and money just made the struggle more interesting to outsiders.

A lot more interesting. The industrial world depended on that oil. Every state on the Gulf feared Iran for its size, for its large population, and for the religious fervor of its citizens. For the Sunni religious, the fear was about a perceived departure from the true course of Islam. For everyone else, it was about what would happen to them when 'heretics' assumed control of the region, because Islam is a comprehensive system of beliefs, spreading out into civil law and politics and every other form of human activity. For Muslims the Word of God was Law Itself. For the West it was continuing their economies. For the Arabs – Iran is *not* an Arab country – it was the most fundamental question of all, a man's place before his God.

'Yes, Mr President,' Prince Ali bin Sheik replied after a moment. 'They will move.'

His voice was admirably calm, though Ryan knew that inwardly he must be anything but. The Saudis had never wanted Iraq's President to fall. Enemy though he was, apostate though he was, aggressor though he was, he had fulfilled a useful strategic purpose for his neighbors. Iraq had long been a buffer between the Gulf states and Iran. It was a case in which religion played second fiddle to politics, which thereby served religious purposes. By rejecting the Word of

Allah, Iraq's majority Shi'a population was taken out of play, and the dual border with Kuwait and the Kingdom was one of mere politics, not religion. But if the Ba'ath Party fell along with its leader, then Iraq might revert to majority religious rule. That would put a Shi'a country on the two borders, and the leader of the Shi'a branch of Islam was Iran.

Iran would move, because Iran had been moving for years. The religion systematized by Mohammed had spread from the Arabian Peninsula to Morocco in the west and the Philippines in the east, and with the evolution of the modern world was represented in every nation on earth. Iran had used its wealth and its large population to become the world's leading Islamic nation, by bringing in Muslim clergy to its own holy city of Qom to study, by financing political movements throughout the Islamic world, and by funneling weapons to Islamic peoples who needed help – the Bosnian Muslims were a case in point, and not the only one.

'*Anschluss,*' Scott Adler thought aloud. Prince Ali just looked over and nodded.

'Do we have any sort of plan to help prevent it?' Jack asked. He knew the answer. No, nobody did. That was the reason the Persian Gulf War had been fought for limited military objectives, and not to overthrow the aggressor. The Saudis, who had from the beginning charted the war's strategic objectives, had never allowed America or her allies even to consider a drive to Baghdad, and this despite the fact that with Iraq's army deployed in and around Kuwait, the Iraqi capital had been as exposed as a nudist on a beach. Ryan had remarked at the time, watching the talking heads on various TV news shows, that not a single one of the commentators remarked that a textbook campaign would have totally ignored Kuwait, seized Baghdad, and then waited for the Iraqi army to stack arms and surrender. Well, not everyone could read a map.

'Your Highness, what influence can you exercise there?' Ryan inquired next.

'In practical terms? Very little. We will extend the hand of friendship, offer loans – by the end of the week we will ask America and the UN to lift sanctions with an eye to improving economic conditions, but . . .'

'Yeah, but,' Ryan agreed. 'Your Highness, please let us

know what information you can develop. America's commitment to the Kingdom's security is unchanged.'

Ali nodded. 'I will convey that to my government.'

'Nice, professional job,' Ding observed, catching the enhanced instant replay. "Cept for one little thing.'

'Yeah, it is nice to collect the paycheck before your will is probated.' Clark had once been young enough and angry enough to think in such terms as the shooter whose death he'd just seen repeated, but with age had come circumspection. Now, he'd heard, Mary Pat wanted him to try again for a White House appearance, and he was reading over a few documents. Trying to, anyway.

'John, ever read up on the Assassins?' Chavez asked, killing the TV with the remote.

'I saw the movie,' Clark replied without looking up.

'They were pretty serious boys. They had to be. Using swords and knives, well, you have to get pretty close to do the job. Decisively engaged, like we used to say in the 7th Light.' Chavez was still short of his master's degree in international relations, but he blessed all the books that Professor Alpher had forced him to read. He waved at the TV. 'This guy was like one of them, a two-legged smart bomb – you self-destruct, but you take out the target first. The Assassins were the first terrorist state. I guess the world wasn't ready for the concept back then, but that one little city-state manipulated a whole region just 'cuz they could get one of their troops in close enough to do the job on anybody.'

'Thanks for the history lesson, Domingo, but –'

'Think, John. If they could get close to him, they can get close to anybody. Ain't no pension plan in the dictator business, y'know? The security around him is, like, real, real tight – but somebody got a shooter in close and blew him into the next dimension. That's scary, Mr C.'

John Clark continually had to remind himself that Domingo Chavez was no dummy. He might still speak with an accent – not because he had to, but because it was natural for him to; Chavez, like Clark, had a gift for language – and he might still interlace his speech with terms and grammar remembered from his days as an Army sergeant, but God damn if he wasn't the quickest learner John had ever met.

He was even learning to control his temper and passion. When it suited him to, John corrected himself.

'So? Different culture, different motivation, different –'

'John, I'm talking about a capability. The political will to use it, 'mano. And patience. It must have taken years. Sleeper agents I know about. First time I saw a sleeper shooter.'

'Could have been a regular guy who just got pissed and –'

'Who was willing to die? I don't think so, John. Why not pop the guy on the way to the latrine at midnight and try to get the hell out of Dodge? No way, Mr C. Gomer there was making a statement. Wasn't just his, either. He was delivering a message for his boss, too.'

Clark looked up from his briefing papers and thought about that one. Another government employee might have dismissed the observation as something out of his purview, but Clark had been suborned into government service as a result of his inability to see limits on his activities. Besides that, he could remember being in Iran, being part of a crowd shouting 'Death to America!' at blindfolded captives from the US embassy. More than that, he remembered what members of that crowd had said after Operation Blue Light had gone to shit, and how close it had been – how near the Khomeini government had been to taking out its wrath on Americans and turning an already nasty dispute into a shooting war. Even then, Iranian fingerprints were on all manner of terrorist operations worldwide, and America's failure to address the fact hadn't helped matters.

'Well, Domingo, that's why we need more field officers.'

SURGEON had one more reason not to like her husband's presidency. She couldn't see him on the way out the door, for one thing. He was in with somebody – well, it had to do with what she'd seen on the morning news, and that was business, and sometimes she'd had to scoot out of the house unexpectedly for a case at Hopkins. But she didn't like the precedent.

She looked at the motorcade. Nothing else to call it, a total of six Chevy Suburbans. Three were tasked to getting Sally (now code-named SHADOW) and Little Jack (SHORTSTOP) to school. The other three would conduct Katie (SANDBOX) to her day-care center. Partly, Cathy Ryan admitted, that was her fault. She didn't want the children's lives disrupted. She wouldn't countenance changing their schools and friends because of the misfortune that had dropped on their lives. None of this was the kids' fault. She'd been dumb enough to agree to Jack's new post, which had lasted all of five minutes, and as with many things in life, you had to accept the consequences. One consequence was increased travel time to their classes and finger-painting, just to keep friends, but, damn it . . . there was no right answer.

'Good morning, Katie!' It was Don Russell, squatting down for a hug and a kiss from SANDBOX. Cathy had to smile at that. This agent was a godsend. A man with grandchildren of his own, he truly loved kids, especially little ones. He and Katie had hit it right off. Cathy kissed her youngest good-bye, and her bodyguard – it was just outrageous, a child needed a bodyguard! But Cathy remembered her own experiences with terrorists, and she had to accept that, too. Russell lifted SANDBOX into her car seat, strapped her in, and the first set of three vehicles pulled away.

'Bye, Mom.' Sally was going through a phase in which she and Mom were friends, and didn't kiss. Cathy accepted that without liking it. It was the same with Little Jack: 'See ya, Mom.' But John Patrick Ryan Jr was boy enough to demand a front seat, which he'd get this one time. Both sub-details were augmented due to the manner in which the Ryan family had come to the White House, with a total of twenty agents assigned to protect the children for the time being. That number would come down in a month or so, they'd told her. The kids would ride in normal cars instead of the armored Suburbans. In the case of SURGEON, her helicopter was waiting.

Damn. It was all happening again. She'd been pregnant with Little Jack, then to learn that terrorists were . . . why the *hell* had she ever agreed to this? The greatest indignity of all, she was married to supposedly the world's most powerful man, but he and his family both had to take orders from other people.

'I know, Doc.' It was the voice of Roy Altman, *her* principal agent. 'Hell of a way to live, isn't it?'

Cathy turned. 'You read minds?'

'Part of the job, ma'am, I know –'

'Please, my name is Cathy. Jack and I are both "Doctor Ryan."'

Altman nearly blushed. More than one First Lady had taken on royal airs with the accession of her husband to POTUS, and the children of politicians weren't always fun to guard, but the Ryan family, the Detail members had already agreed, were not at all like the people they usually had to guard. In some ways that was bad news, but it was hard not to like them.

'Here.' He handed over a manila folder. It was her caseload for the day.

'Two procedures, then follow-ups,' she told him. Well, at least she could do paperwork on the flight. That was convenient, wasn't it?

'I know. We've arranged with Professor Katz to keep us posted – so we can keep up with your schedule,' Altman explained.

'Do you do background checks on my patients, too?' Cathy asked, thinking it a joke.

It wasn't. 'Yes. Hospital records provide names, birthdays, and Social Security numbers. We run NCIC checks, and checks against our own file of – uh, of people we keep an eye on.'

The look that pronouncement generated wasn't exactly friendly, but Altman didn't take it personally. They walked back into the building, then back out a few minutes later to the waiting helicopter. There were news cameras, Cathy saw, to record the event, as Colonel Hank Goodman lit up his engines.

In the operations room for the US Secret Service, a few blocks away, the status board changed. POTUS (President of the United States) was shown by the red LED display as in the White House. FLOTUS (First Lady of the United States) was shown as in transit. SHADOW, SHORTSTOP, and SANDBOX were covered on a different board. The same information was relayed by secure digital radio link to Andrea Price, sitting and reading the paper outside the Oval Office. Other agents were already at St Mary's Catholic School and the Giant Steps Day Care Center, both near Annapolis, and at Johns Hopkins Hospital. The Maryland State Police knew that the Ryan children were rolling along US Route 50, and had additional cars posted along the travel route for an obvious police presence. At the moment, yet another Marine helicopter was following SURGEON's, and a third, with a team of heavily armed agents aboard, was pacing the three children. Were there a serious assassin out there, then he would see the overt display of force. The agents in the moving vehicles would be at their usual alert state, scanning for cars, filing them away for the chance that the same one would show up a little too much. Unmarked Secret Service cars would maneuver around independently, doing much the same thing while being disguised as ordinary commuters. The Ryans would never really know how much security was arrayed around them, unless they asked, and few ever wanted to know.

A normal day was under way.

There was no denying it now. She didn't need Dr Moudi to tell her. The headaches had worsened, the fatigue had gotten worse. As with young Benedict Mkusa, she'd thought, then hoped it might be a recurrence of her old malaria, the first time she'd ever entertained that sort of thought. But then the pains had come, not in the joints, but in the stomach first of all, and that had been like watching an advancing weather front, the tall white clouds that led a massive, violent storm, and there was nothing for her to do but wait and dread what was approaching, for she knew everything that was to be. Part of her mind still denied it, and another part tried to hide away in prayer and faith, but as with a person at a horror movie, face covered by denying hands, her eyes still peeked sideways to see what was coming, the horror all the worse because of her useless retreat from it.

The nausea was worse, and soon she'd be unable to control it with her will, strong as that was.

She was in one of the hospital's few private rooms. The sun was still bright outside, the sky clear, a beautiful day in the unending African spring-summer season. An IV tree was next to her bed, running sterile saline into her arm, along with some mild analgesics and nutrients to fortify her body, but really it was a waiting game. Sister Jean Baptiste could do little else but wait. Her body was limp with fatigue, and so pained that turning her head to look at the flowers out the window required a minute of effort. The first massive surge of nausea came almost as a surprise, and somehow she managed to grasp the <u>emesis</u> tray. She was still nurse enough and detached enough to see the blood there, even as Maria Magdalena took the tray away from her, to empty it into a special container. Fellow nurse, and fellow nun, she was dressed in sterile garb, wearing rubber gloves and a mask as well, her eyes unable to conceal her sorrow.

'Hello, Sister.' It was Dr Moudi, dressed much the same way, his darker eyes more guarded above the green mask. He checked the chart hanging at the foot of the bed. The temperature reading was only ten minutes old, and still rising. The telex from Atlanta concerning her blood had arrived even more recently, inspiring his immediate walk to the isolation building. Her fair skin had been pale only a few hours earlier. Now it appeared slightly flushed, and dry. Moudi thought they'd work to cool the patient down with alcohol, maybe ice later, to fight the fever. That would be bad for the Sister's dignity. They did indeed dress chastely, as women should, and the hospital gown she now wore was ever demeaning to that virtue. Worse still, however, was the look in her eyes. She knew. But he still had to say it.

'Sister,' the physician told her, 'your blood has tested positive for Ebola antibodies.'

A nod. 'I see.'

'Then you also know,' he added gently, 'that twenty percent of the patients survive this disease. You are not without hope. I am a good doctor. Sister Magdalena here is a superb nurse. We will support you as best we can. I am also in contact with some of my colleagues. We will not give up on you. I require that you do not give up on yourself. Talk to your God, good lady. He will surely listen to someone of your virtue.' The words came easily, for Moudi was after all a physician, and a good one. He surprised himself by half wishing for her survival.

'Thank you, Doctor.'

Moudi turned to the other nun before leaving. 'Please keep me informed.'

'Of course, Doctor.'

Moudi walked out of the room, turning left toward the door, removing his protective garb as he went, and dumping the articles into the proper container. He made a mental note to speak to the administrator to be sure that the necessary precautions were strictly enforced. He wanted this nun to be the last Ebola case in this hospital. Even as he spoke, part of the WHO team was on its way to the Mkusa family, where they would interview the grief-stricken parents, along with neighbors and friends, to learn where and how Benedict might have encountered the infection. The best guess was a monkey bite.

But only a guess. There was little known about Ebola Zaire, and most of the unknowns were important. Doubtless it had been around for centuries, or even longer than that, just one more lethal malady in an area replete with them, not recognized as anything more than 'jungle fever' by physicians as recently as thirty years before. The focal center of the virus was still a matter of speculation. Many *thought* a monkey carried it, but which monkey no one knew – literally thousands had been trapped or shot in the effort to determine that, with no result. They weren't even sure that it was really a tropical disease – the first properly documented outbreak of this class of fever had actually taken place in Germany. There was a very similar disease in the Philippines.

Ebola appeared and disappeared, like some sort of malignant spirit. There was an apparent periodicity to it. The recognized outbreaks had occurred at eight- to ten-year intervals – again, unexplained and slightly suspect, because Africa was still primitive, and there was ample reason to believe that victims could contract the disease and die from it in but a few days, without the time to seek medical help. The structure of the virus was somewhat understood and its symptoms recognized, but its mechanism was still a mystery. That was troubling to the medical community, because Ebola Zaire had a mortality rate of roughly eighty percent. Only one in five of its victims survived, and why that happened was just one more entry in the 'unknown' column. For all of those reasons, Ebola was perfect.

So perfect that it was one of the most feared organisms known to man. Minute quantities of the virus were in Atlanta, the Pasteur Institute in Paris, and a handful of other institutions, where it was studied under conditions resembling those of a science-fiction novel, the doctors and technicians in virtual space suits. There wasn't even enough known about Ebola to do work on a vaccine. The four known varieties – the fourth had been discovered in a bizarre incident in America; but *that* strain, while uniformly lethal to monkeys, incomprehensibly had *no* serious effects on humans – were too different. Even now scientists in Atlanta, some of whom he knew, were peering into electron microscopes to map the structure of this new version, later to compare it with samples of other known strains. That process could take weeks and, probably, as with all previous efforts, would yield only equivocal results.

Until the true focal center of the disease was discovered, it remained an alien virus, something almost from another planet, deadly and mysterious. Perfect.

Patient Zero, Benedict Mkusa was dead, his body incinerated by gasoline, and the virus dead with him. Moudi had a small blood sample, but that wasn't really good enough. Sister Jean Baptiste was something else, however. Moudi thought about it for a moment, then lifted the phone to call the Iranian embassy in Kinshasa. There was work to be done, and more work to prepare. His hand hesitated, the receiver halfway from the desk to his ear. What if God did listen to her prayers? He might, Moudi thought, He just might. She was a woman of great virtue who spent as much of her day in prayer as any Believer in his home city of Qom, whose faith in her God was firm, and who had devoted her life to service of those in need. Those were three of Islam's Five Pillars, to which he could add a fourth – the Christian Lent wasn't so terribly different from the Islamic Ramadan. These were dangerous thoughts, but if Allah heard her prayers, then what he intended to do was not written, and would not happen, and if her prayers were not heard . . . ? Moudi cradled the phone between his ear and shoulder and made the call.

'Mr President, we can't ignore it anymore.'

'Yeah, I know, Arnie.'

It came down to a technical issue, oddly enough. The bodies had to be identified positively, because a person wasn't dead until there was a piece of paper that said so, and until that person was declared dead, if that person had been a senator or congressperson, then his or her post wasn't vacant, and no new person could be selected for it, and Congress was an empty shell. The certificates would be going out today, and within an hour, governors of 'the several states' would be calling Ryan for advice or to advise what they would be doing unbidden. At least one governor would today resign his post and be appointed to the United States Senate by his succeeding lieutenant governor in an elegant, if obvious, political payoff, or so the rumors said.

The volume of information was stunning, even to someone familiar with the sources. It went back over fourteen years. The timing could scarcely have been better, however, since that was about the time the major newspapers and magazines had gone to electronic media, which was easily cross-loaded to the World Wide Web, and for which the media empires could charge a modest fee for material which otherwise would have been stored in their own musty basements or at most sold to college libraries for practically nothing. The WWW was still a fairly new and untested source of income, but the media had seized it by the throat, since now for the first time news was less volatile than it had been in the past. It was now a ready source for its own reporters, for students, for those with individual curiosity, and for those whose curiosity was more strictly professional. Best of all, the huge number of people doing a keyword search would make it impossible for anyone to check all the inquiries.

He was careful anyway – rather, his people were. The inquiries being made on the Web were all happening in Europe, mainly in London, through brand-new Internet-access accounts which would last no longer than the time required to download the data, or which came from academic accounts to which numerous people had access. Keywords RYAN JOHN PATRICK, RYAN JACK, RYAN CAROLINE, RYAN CATHY, RYAN CHILDREN, RYAN FAMILY, and a multitude of others were inputted, and literally thousands of 'hits' had resulted. Many were spurious because 'Ryan' was not that uncommon a name, but the vetting process was not all that difficult.

The first really interesting clips came when Ryan had been thirty-one and had first come into the public spotlight in London. Even the photos were there, and though they took time to download, they were worth waiting for. Especially the first. That one showed a young man sitting on a street, covered with blood. Well, wasn't that inspirational? The subject of the photograph actually looked quite dead in it, but he knew that wounded people often appeared that way. Then had come another set of photos of a wrecked automobile and a small helicopter. In the intervening years the data on Ryan was surprisingly scarce, mainly squibs about his testifying before the American Congress behind closed doors. There were additional hits concerning the end of the Fowler presidency – immediately after the initial confusion it had been reported that Ryan himself had prevented a nuclear-missile launch . . . and Ryan himself had hinted at it to Daryaei . . . but that story had never been officially confirmed, and Ryan himself had never discussed the matter with anyone. That was important. That said something about the man. But that could also be set aside.

His wife. There was ample press coverage on her, too, including in one article the number of her office at her hospital. A skilled surgeon. That was nice – a recent piece said that she'd continue that. Excellent. They knew where to look for her.

The children. The youngest – yes, the youngest used the same day-care center that the oldest had used. There was a photo of that, too. A feature article on Ryan's first White House job had even identified the school the older ones attended . . .

This was all quite amazing. He'd initiated the research effort in the knowledge that he'd get all or most of this information, but even so, here was in a single day more information than ten people in the field could have gathered – at considerable risk of exposure – in a week. The Americans were so foolish. They practically invited attack. They had no idea of secrecy or security. It was one thing for a leader to appear in public with his family from time to time – everyone did that. It was quite another to let everyone know things that nobody really needed to know.

The document package – it came to over 2,500 pages – would be collated and cross-referenced by his staff. There were no plans to take action on any of it. It was just data. But that could change.

*   *   *

'You know, I think I like flying in,' Cathy Ryan observed to Roy Altman.

'Oh?'

'Less wear and tear on the nerves than driving myself. I don't suppose that'll last,' she added, moving into the food line.

'Probably not.' Altman was constantly looking around, but there were two other agents in the room, doing their best to look invisible and failing badly at it. Though Johns Hopkins was an institution with fully 2,400 physicians, it was still a professional village of sorts where nearly everyone knew nearly everyone else, and doctors didn't carry guns. Altman was staying close, the better to learn his principal's routine, and she didn't seem to mind. He'd been in with her for the two morning procedures, and teacher that she was, Cathy had explained every step of the process in minute detail. This afternoon she'd be doing teaching rounds with a half dozen or so students. It was Altman's first educational experience on the job – at least in something that had value in an area other than politics, a field he'd learned to detest. His next observation was that SURGEON ate like the proverbial bird. She got to the end of the line and paid for her lunch and Altman's, over his brief protest.

'This is my turf, Roy.' She looked around, and spotted the man she wanted to lunch with, heading that way with Altman in tow. 'Hey, Dave.'

Dean James and his guest stood up. 'Hi, Cathy! Let me introduce a new faculty member, Pierre Alexandre. Alex, this is Cathy Ryan –'

'The same one who –'

'Please, I'm still a doctor, and –'

'You're the one on the Lasker list, right?' Alexandre stopped her cold with that one. Cathy's smile lit up the room.

'Yes.'

'Congratulations, Doctor.' He held out his hand. Cathy had to set her tray down to take it. Altman watched with eyes that tried to be neutral, but conveyed something else. 'You must be with the Service.'

'Yes, sir. Roy Altman.'

'Excellent. A lady this lovely and this bright deserves proper protection,' Alexandre pronounced. 'I just got out of the Army, Mr Altman. I've seen you guys at Walter Reed. Back when President Fowler's daughter came back from Brazil with a tropical bug, I managed the case.'

'Alex is working with Ralph Forster,' the dean explained as everyone sat down.

'Infectious diseases,' Cathy told her bodyguard.

Alexandre nodded. 'Just learning the ropes at the moment. But I have a parking pass, so I guess I really belong.'

'I hope you're as good a teacher as Ralph is.'

'A great doc,' Alexandre agreed. Cathy decided she'd like the newbie. She next wondered about the accent and the southern manners. 'Ralph flew down to Atlanta this morning.'

'Anything special happening?'

'A possible Ebola case in Zaire, African male, age eight. The e-mail came through this morning.'

Cathy's eyes narrowed at that. Though she was in a completely different field of medicine, like all physicians she got *Morbidity and Mortality Report*, and she kept current on everything she could. Medicine is a field in which education never stops. 'Just one?'

'Yep.' Alexandre nodded. 'Seems the kid had a monkey bite on his arm. I've been over there. I deployed out of Detrick for the last mini-outbreak in 1990.'

'With Gus Lorenz?' Dean James asked. Alexandre shook his head.

'No, Gus was doing something else then. The team leader was George Westphal.'

'Oh, yeah, he –'

'Died,' Alex confirmed. 'We, uh, kept it quiet, but he got it. I attended him. It wasn't real great to watch.'

'What did he do wrong? I didn't know him well,' James said, 'but Gus told me he was a rising star. UCLA, as I recall.'

'George was brilliant, best man on structures I ever met, and he was as careful as any of us, but he got it anyway, and we never figured out how that happened. Anyway, that mini-outbreak killed sixteen people. We had two survivors, both females, both in their early twenties, and nothing remarkable about them that we could ever find. Maybe they were just lucky,' Alexandre said, not really believing it. Things like this happened for some reason or other. It was just that he hadn't found it, though it was his job to find it. 'In any case, only eighteen total victims, and that *was* lucky. We were over there for six or seven weeks. I took a shotgun into the woods and blew up about a hundred monkeys, trying to find a carrier. No dice. That strain is called Ebola Zaire Mayinga. I imagine right now they're comparing it to what this little kid contracted. Ebola's a slippery little bastard.'

'Just one?' Cathy asked.

'That's the word. Method of exposure unknown, as usual.'

'Monkey bite?'

'Yeah, but we'll never find the monkey. We never do.'

'It's that deadly?' Altman asked, unable to hold back from joining the conversation.

'Sir, the official guess is eighty percent mortality. Put it this way. If you pull your pistol out and shoot me in the chest, right here, right now, my odds are better than beating this little bug.' Alexandre buttered his roll and remembered visiting Westphal's widow. It was bad for the appetite. 'Probably a lot better, what with the surgeons we have working over in Halstead. You have much better odds with leukemia, much better odds with lymphoma. Somewhat worse odds with AIDS, but that agent gives you ten years. Ebola gives you maybe ten days. That's about as deadly as it gets.'

MONKEYS

Ryan had done all of his own writing. He'd published two books on naval history – that now seemed like a previous lifetime summoned to memory on a hypnotist's couch – and uncounted papers for CIA. Each of these he had done himself, once on a typewriter and later on a series of personal computers. He had never enjoyed the writing – it was ever difficult work – but he had enjoyed the solitude of it, alone in his own little intellectual world and safe from any sort of interruption as he formed his thoughts and adjusted their method of presentation until they were as close to perfect as he could achieve. In that way, they were always his thoughts, and there was integrity in the process.

No longer.

The chief speechwriter was Callie Weston, short, petite, dirty blond, and a wizard with words who, like many of the enormous White House staff, had come aboard with President Fowler and never managed to leave.

'You didn't like my speech for the church?' She was also irreverent.

'Honestly, I just decided that I had to say something else.' Then Jack realized he was defending himself to someone he scarcely knew.

'I cried.' She paused for effect, staring into his eyes with the unblinking gaze of a poisonous snake for several seconds, manifestly sizing him up. 'You're different.'

'What do you mean?'

'I mean – you have to understand, Mr President. President Fowler kept me around because I made him sound compassionate – he's rather a cold fish in most things, poor guy. President Durling kept me around because he didn't have anybody better. I bump heads all the time with staffers across the street. They like to edit my work. I don't like being edited by drones. We fight. Arnie protects me a lot because I went to school with his favorite niece – and I'm the best around at what I do – but I'm probably the biggest pain in the ass on your staff. You need to know that.' It was a good explanation, but not to the point.

'Why am I different?' Jack asked.

'You say what you really think instead of saying what you think people think they want to hear. It's going to be hard writing for you. I can't dip into the usual well. I have to learn to write the way I used to like to write, not the way I'm paid to write, and I have to learn to write like you talk. It's going to be tough,' she told him, already girding herself for the challenge.

'I see.' Since Ms Weston was not an inner-circle staff member, Andrea Price was leaning against the wall (it would have been in a corner, except the Oval Office didn't have one) and observing everything with a poker face – or trying to. Ryan was learning to read her body language. Clearly Price didn't much care for Weston. He wondered why. 'Well, what can you turn out in a couple of hours?'

'Sir, that depends on what you want to say,' the speechwriter pointed out. Ryan told her in a few brief sentences. She didn't take notes. She merely absorbed it, smiled, and spoke again.

'They're going to destroy you. You know that. Maybe Arnie hasn't told you yet, maybe nobody on the staff has, or ever will, but it's going to happen.' That remark jolted Agent Price from her spot on the wall, just enough that her body was standing instead of leaning.

'What makes you think I want to stay here?'

She blinked. 'Excuse me. I'm not really used to this.'

'This could be an interesting conversation, but I –'

'I read one of your books day before yesterday. You're not very good with words – not very elegant, that's a technical judgment – but you do say things clearly. So I have to dial back my rhetoric style to make it sound like you. Short sentences. Your grammar is good. Catholic schools, I guess. You don't bullshit people. You say it straight.' She smiled. 'How long for the speech?'

'Call it fifteen minutes.'

'I'll be back in three hours,' Weston promised, and stood. Ryan nodded, and she walked out of the room. Then the President looked at Agent Price.

'Spit it out,' he ordered.

'She's the biggest pain in the ass over there. Last year she *attacked* some junior staffer over something. A guard had to pull her off him.'

'Over what?'

'The staffer said some nasty things about one of her speeches, and speculated that her family background was irregular. He left the next day. No loss,' Price concluded. 'But she's an arrogant prima donna. She shouldn't have said what she did.'

'What if she's right?'

'Sir, that's not my business, but any –'

'*Is* she right?'

'You are different, Mr President.' Price didn't say whether she thought that was a good or bad thing, and Ryan didn't ask.

The President had other things to do in any case. He lifted his desk phone, and a secretary answered.

'Could you get me George Winston at the Columbus Group?'

'Yes, Mr President, I'll get him for you.' She didn't have that number immediately to mind, and so she lifted another phone for the Signals Office. Down there a Navy petty officer had the number on a Post-It note, and read it off. A moment later he handed the Post-It to the Marine in the next chair over. The Marine fished in her purse, found four quarters, and handed them over to the smirking squid.

'Mr President, I have Mr Winston,' the intercom phone said.

'George?'

'Yes, sir.'

'How fast can you get down here?'

'Jack – Mr President, I'm trying to put my business back together and –'

'How fast?' Ryan asked more pointedly.

Winston had to think for a second. His Gulfstream crew wasn't standing by for anything today. Getting to Newark Airport . . . 'I can catch the next train.'

'Let me know which one you're on. I'll have someone waiting for you.'

'Okay, but you need to know that I can't –'

'Yes, you can. See you in a few hours.' Ryan hung up, then looked up to Price. 'Andrea, have an agent and a car meet him at the station.'

'Yes, Mr President.'

Ryan decided that it was nice to give orders and have them carried out. A man could get used to this.

'I don't like guns!' She said it loudly enough that a few heads turned, though the kids immediately turned back to their blocks and crayons. There was an unusual number of adults around, three of whom had spiraling cords leading to ear-pieces. Those heads all turned to see a 'concerned' (that was the word everyone used in such a case) mother. As head of this detail, Don Russell walked over.

'Hello.' He held up his Secret Service ID. 'Can I help you?'

'Do you have to be here!'

'Yes, ma'am, we do. Could I have your name, please?'

'Why?' Sheila Walker demanded.

'Well, ma'am, it's nice to know who you're talking to, isn't it?' Russell asked reasonably. It was also nice to get background checks on such people.

'This is Mrs Walker,' said Mrs Marlene Daggett, owner-operator of Giant Steps Day Care Center.

'Oh, that's your little boy over there, Justin, right?' Russell smiled. The four-year-old was building a tower with hard-wood blocks, which he would then tip over, to the general amusement of the room.

'I just don't like guns, and I don't like them around children.'

'Mrs Walker, first of all, we're cops. We know how to carry our firearms safely. Second, our regulations require us to be armed at all times. Third, I wish you would look at it this way: your son is as safe here with us as he's ever going to be. You'll never have to worry about having somebody come over and steal a kid off the playground outside, for example.'

'Why does she have to be here?'

Russell smiled reasonably. 'Mrs Walker, Katie over there didn't become President. Her father did. Isn't she entitled to a normal kid's life, just like your Justin?'

'But it's dangerous and –'

'Not while we're around, it isn't,' he assured her. She just turned away.

'Justin!' Her son turned to see his mother holding his jacket. He paused for a second, and with one finger pushed the blocks a fraction of an inch, waiting for the four-foot pile to teeter over like a falling tree.

'Budding engineer,' Russell heard through his earpiece. 'I'll check her tag number.' He nodded to the female agent in the doorway. In twenty minutes they'd have a new dossier to look over. Probably it would just say that Mrs Walker was a New Age pain in the ass, but if she had a history of mental problems (possible), or a criminal record (unlikely), it would be something to remember. He scanned the room automatically, then shook his head. SANDBOX was a normal kid surrounded by normal kids. At the moment she was crayoning a blank sheet of paper, her face screwed into a look of intense concentration. She'd been through a normal day, a normal lunch, a normal nap, and soon would have an abnormal trip back to a decidedly abnormal home. She hadn't noticed the discussion he'd just had with Justin's mother. Well, kids were smart enough to be kids, which was more than one could say for a lot of their parents.

Mrs Walker guided her son to the family car, a Volvo wagon to no one's surprise, where she dutifully strapped him into the safety seat in the back. The agent memorized the tag number for processing, knowing that it would turn nothing of real importance, and knowing that they'd run it anyway, because there was always the off chance that ...

It all came back just then, the reason why they had to be careful. Here they were, at Giant Steps, the same day-care center the Ryans had used since SHADOW was a munchkin, just off Ritchie Highway above Annapolis. The bad guys had used the 7-Eleven just across the road to stake out the location, then followed SURGEON in her old Porsche, using a custom van, and on the Route 50 bridge they'd pulled off a sweet little ambush, and later killed a state trooper in their escape. Dr Ryan had been pregnant with SHORTSTOP then. SANDBOX had been far off into a future yet undreamed of at the time. All of this had a strange effect on Special Agent Marcella Hilton. Unmarried, again – she was twice divorced, with no kids of her own – being around kids had made her heart flutter a little, tough professional that she was. She figured it was part of her hormones, or the way the female brain was wired, or maybe she just liked kids and wished she had one of her own. Whatever it was, the thought that people would deliberately hurt little kids made her blood chill for a brief moment, like a blast of cold wind that came and went.

This place was too vulnerable. And there really were people out there who didn't care a rat's ass about hurting kids. And that 7-Eleven was still there. There were six agents on the SANDBOX detail now. That would be down to three or four in a couple of weeks. The Service wasn't the all-powerful agency people thought it was. Oh, sure, it had a lot of muscle, and investigative clout which few suspected. Alone of the federal police forces, the United States Secret Service could knock on somebody's door and walk in and conduct a 'friendly' interview with someone who might represent a threat – an assumption based on evidence which might or might not be usable in a court of law. The purpose of such an interview would be to let the person know that he or she had an eye fixed firmly on him or her, and though that wasn't strictly true – the Service had only about 1,200 agents nationwide – the mere thought of it was enough to scare the hell out of people who'd said the wrong thing into the wrong ear.

But those people weren't the threat. As long as the agents did their job correctly, the casual threat wasn't a deadly one. Those people almost always tipped their hand, and people like her knew what to look for. It was the ones their intelligence division didn't hear about who constituted the real threat. Those *could* be deterred somewhat through a massive show of force, but the massive show was too expensive, too oppressive, too obvious not to attract notice and adverse comment. Even then – she remembered another event, months after the near death of SURGEON, SHADOW, and the yet unborn SHORTSTOP. *A whole squad*, she thought. It was a case study at the Secret Service Academy at Beltsville. The Ryan house had been used to film a re-creation of the event. Chuck Avery – a good, experienced supervisory agent – and his whole squad taken out. As a rookie she'd watched the taped analysis of what had gone wrong, and even then she'd chilled at how easy it had been for that team to make a small mistake, that to be compounded by bad luck and bad timing . . .

'Yeah, I know.' She turned to see Don Russell, sipping from a plastic coffee cup while he got some fresh air. Another agent was on post inside.

'Did you know Avery?'

'He was two years ahead of me at the academy. He was smart, and careful, and a damned good shot. He dropped one of the bad guys then, in the dark from thirty yards, two rounds in the chest.' A shake of the head. 'You don't make little mistakes in this business, Marci.'

That is when the second chill came, the one that made you want to reach for your weapon, just to be sure that it was there, to tell yourself that you were ready to get the job done. That's when you remembered, in this case, how cute a little kid could be, and how even if you took the hits you'd make damned sure your last conscious act on the planet would be to put every round through the bastard's X-ring. Then you blinked, and the image went away.

'She's a beautiful little girl, Don.'

'I've rarely seen an ugly one,' Russell agreed. This was the time when one was supposed to say, *Don't worry, we'll take good care of her*. But they didn't say that. They didn't even think it. Instead they looked around at the highway and the trees and the 7-Eleven across Ritchie Highway, wondering what they'd missed, and wondering how much money they could spend on surveillance cameras.

George Winston was used to being met. It was the ultimate perk, really. You got off the airplane – almost always an airplane in his case – and there was somebody to meet you and take you to the car whose driver knew the quickest way to where you were going. No hassles with Hertz and figuring the useless little maps out, and getting lost. It cost a lot of money, but it was worth it, because time was the ultimate commodity, and you were born with only so much to spend, and there was no passbook to tell you the exact amount. The Metroliner pulled into Union Station's track 6. He'd gotten some reading done, and had himself a nice nap between Trenton and Baltimore. A pity the railroad couldn't make money carrying passengers, but you didn't have to buy air to fly in, while it was necessary to build a right-of-way for ground transport. Too bad. He collected his coat and briefcase and headed for the door, tipping the first-class attendant on the way out.

'Mr Winston?' a man asked.

'That's right.' The man held up a leather ID holder, identifying himself as a federal agent. He had a partner, Winston noted, standing thirty feet away with his topcoat unbuttoned.

'Follow me, please, sir.' With that they were merely three more busy people heading off to an important meeting.

There were many such dossiers, each of them so large that the data had to be edited so as not to overflow the file cabinets, and it was still more convenient to do it with paper than a computer, because it was hard to get a computer that worked well in his native language. Checking up on the data would not be difficult. For one thing, there would be more press coverage to confirm or alter what he had. For another, he could confirm a lot very simply, merely by having a car drive past a few places once or twice, or by observing roads. There was little danger in that. However careful and thorough the American Secret Service might be, they were not omnipotent. This Ryan fellow had a family, a wife who worked, children who went to school; and Ryan himself had a schedule he had to keep. In their official home they were safe – reasonably so, he corrected himself, since no fixed place was ever truly safe – but that safety did not follow them everywhere, did it?

It was more than anything else a matter of financing and planning. He needed a sponsor.

'How many do you need?' the dealer asked.

'How many do you have?' the prospective buyer asked.

'I can get eighty, certainly. Perhaps a hundred,' the dealer thought aloud, sipping at his beer.

'When?'

'A week will suffice?' They were in Nairobi, capital of Kenya, and a major center for this particular trade. 'Biological research?'

'Yes, my client's scientists have a rather interesting project under way.'

'What project might that be?' the dealer asked.

'That I am not at liberty to say,' was the not unexpected answer. Nor would he say who his client was. The dealer didn't react, and didn't particularly care. His curiosity was human, not professional. 'If your services are satisfactory, we may be back for more.' The usual enticement. The dealer nodded and commenced the substantive bargaining.

'You must understand that this is not an inexpensive undertaking. I must assemble my people. They must find a small population of the creature you desire. There are the problems of capture and transport, export licenses, the usual bureaucratic difficulties.' By which he meant bribes. Trade in African green monkeys had picked up in the last few years. Quite a few companies used them for various experimental purposes. That was generally bad for the monkeys, but there were a lot of monkeys. The African green was in no way endangered, and even if they were, the dealer didn't especially care. Animals were a national resource for his country, as oil was for the Arabs, to be marketed for hard currency. He didn't get sentimental about them. They bit and spat, and were generally unpleasant little beggars, 'cute' though they might appear to the tourists at Treetops. They also ate the crops tended by the numerous small farmers in the country, and were thoroughly detested for that reason, whatever the game wardens might say.

'These problems are not strictly our concern. Speed is. You will find that we are willing to reward you handsomely in return for reliable service.'

'Ah.' The dealer finished his beer, and, lifting his hand, snapped his fingers for a refill. He named his price. It included his overhead, pay to the gatherers, the customs people, a policeman or two, and a mid-level government bureaucrat, plus his own net profit, which in the terms of the local economy was actually quite fair, he thought. Not everyone did.

'Agreed,' the buyer said without so much as a sip of his soft drink.

It was almost a disappointment. The dealer enjoyed haggling, so much a part of the African marketplace. He'd scarcely begun to depose on how difficult and involved his business was.

'A pleasure doing business with you, sir. Call me in . . . five days?'

The buyer nodded. He finished his drink and took his leave. Ten minutes after that, he made a call, the third such communication to the embassy in the day, and all for the same purpose. Though he didn't know it, yet more such calls had been made in Uganda, Zaire, Tanzania, and Mali.

Jack remembered his first time in the Oval Office, the way you shuffled left to right from the secretaries' room through what turned out to be a molded door set in a curved wall, much in the manner of an eighteenth-century palace, which the White House actually was, if a modest one in the context of the times. You tended to notice the windows first of all, especially on a sunny day. Their thickness made them look green, rather like the glass walls of an aquarium designed for a very special fish. Next you saw the desk, a large wooden one. It was always intimidating, all the more so if the President was standing there, waiting for you. All this was good, the President thought. It made his current job all the easier.

'George,' Ryan said, extending his hand.

'Mr President,' Winston responded pleasantly, ignoring the two Secret Service agents standing immediately behind him, there to grab him if he did something untoward. You didn't have to hear them. The visitor could feel their eyes on the back of his neck, rather like laser beams. He shook Ryan's hand anyway, and managed a crooked smile. Winston didn't know Ryan very well. They'd worked together well during the Japanese conflict. Previously they'd bumped into each other at a handful of minor social functions, and he knew of Ryan's work in the market, discreet but effective. All that time in the intelligence business hadn't been entirely wasted.

'Sit down.' Jack waved to one of the couches. 'Relax. How was the trip down?'

'The usual.' A Navy mess steward appeared seemingly from nowhere and poured two cups of coffee, because it was that time of the day. The coffee, he found, was excellent, and the china exquisite with its gold trim.

'I need you,' Ryan said next.

'Sir, look, there was a lot of damage done to my –'

'Country.'

'I've never wanted a government job, Jack,' Winston replied at once, speaking rapidly.

Ryan didn't even touch his cup. 'Why do you think I want you? George, I've been there and done that, okay? More than once. I have to put a team together. I'm going to give a speech tonight. You might like what I'm going to say. Okay, first, I need somebody to run Treasury. Defense is okay for the moment. State's in good hands with Adler. Treasury is first on my list of things that have to be filled with somebody new. I need somebody good. You're it. Are you clean?' Ryan asked abruptly.

'What – bet your ass I am! I made all my money within the rules. Everybody knows that.' Winston bristled until he realized that he was expected to.

'Good. I need somebody who has the confidence of the financial community. You do. I need somebody who knows how the system really works. You do. I need somebody who knows what's broke and needs fixing, and what isn't and doesn't. You do. I need somebody who isn't political. You aren't. I need a dispassionate pro – most of all, George, I need somebody who's going to hate his job as much as I hate mine.'

'What exactly do you mean by that, Mr President?'

Ryan leaned back for a second and closed his eyes before going on. 'I started working inside when I was thirty-one. I got out once, and I did okay on the Street, but I got sucked back, and here I am.' The eyes opened. 'Ever since I started with the Agency, I've had to watch how things work on the inside, and guess what? I never did like it. I started on the Street, remember, and I did okay then, too, remember? I figured I'd become an academic after I made my pile. History's my first love, and I thought I'd teach and study and write, figure out how things worked and pass my knowledge along. I almost made it, and maybe things didn't work out that way, exactly, but I've done a lot of studying and learning. So, George, I'm going to put a team together.'

'To do what?'

'Your job is to clean up Treasury. You've got monetary and fiscal policy.'

'You mean –'

'Yes.'

'No political bullshit?' He had to ask that.

'Look, George, I don't know *how* to be a politician, and I don't have time to learn. I never liked the game. I never liked most of the people in it. I just kept trying to serve my country as best I could. Sometimes it worked, sometimes it didn't. I didn't have a choice. You remember how it started. People tried to kill me and my family. I didn't want to get sucked in, but God damn it, I learned that *somebody* has to try to get the job done. I'm not going to do it alone anymore, George, and I'm not going to fill all the vacant posts with ticket-punchers who know how to work "the system," okay? I want people with *ideas* in here, not politicians with agendas.'

Winston set his cup down, managing not to rattle the saucer as he did so. He was a little surprised that his hand wasn't shaking. The length and breadth of what Ryan proposed was quite a bit more than the job which he'd had every intention of declining. It would mean more than was obvious. He'd have to cut himself off from his friends – well, not really, but it meant that he would not make executive decisions based on what campaign contributions the Street would give the President as a result of the nice things that Treasury did for the trading houses up there. That's the way the game had always been played, and though he'd never been a player, he'd talked often enough with those who were, working the system in the same old way, because that was how things were.

'Shit,' he whispered half to himself. 'You're serious, aren't you?'

As founder of the Columbus Group, he'd assumed a duty so basic that few ever thought about it, beyond those who actually undertook it – and not always enough of them. Literally millions of people, directly or indirectly, entrusted their money to him, and that gave him the theoretical ability to be a thief on the cosmic scale. But you couldn't do that. For one thing, it was illegal, and you ran the risk of rather substandard federal housing as a result of it, with very substandard neighbors to boot. But that wasn't the reason you didn't. The reason was that those were people out there, and they trusted you to be honest *and* smart, and so you treated their money the same as you treated your own, or maybe even a little better, because they couldn't gamble the way a rich man did. Every so often you'd get a nice letter from some widow, and that was nice, but it really came from inside. Either you were a man of honor or you were not, and honor, some movie writer had once said, was a man's gift to himself. Not a bad aphorism, Winston told himself. It was also profitable, of course. You did the job in the right way, and chances were that people would reward you for it, but the real satisfaction was playing the game well. The money was merely a result of something more important, because money was transitory, but honor wasn't.

'Tax policy?' Winston asked.

'We need Congress put back together first, remember?' Ryan pointed out. 'But, yes.'

Winston took a deep breath. 'That's a very big job, Ryan.'

'You're telling *me* that?' the President demanded . . . then grinned.

'It won't make me any friends.'

'You also become head of the Secret Service. They'll protect you, won't they, Andrea?'

Agent Price was not used to being pulled into these conversations, but she feared she'd have to get used to it. 'Uh, yes, Mr President.'

'Things are just so damned inefficient,' Winston observed.

'So fix it,' Ryan told him.

'It might be bloody.'

'Buy a mop. I want your department cleaned up, streamlined, and run like you want it to make a profit someday. How you do that is your problem. For Defense, I want the same thing. The biggest problem over there is administrative. I need somebody who can run a business and make a profit to cull the bureaucracy out. That's the biggest problem of all, for all the agencies.'

'You know Tony Bretano?'

'The TRW guy? He used to run their satellite division . . .' Ryan remembered his name as a former candidate for a senior Pentagon post, which offer he'd turned down flat. A lot of good people declined such offers. That was the paradigm he had to break.

'Lockheed-Martin is going to steal him away in a couple weeks, at least that's what my sources tell me. That's why

Lockheed's stock is nudging up. We have a buy-advisory on it. He gave TRW a fifty-percent profit increase in two years, not bad for an engineer who isn't supposed to know beans about management. I play golf with him sometimes. You should hear him scream about doing business with the government.'

'Tell him I want to see him.'

'Lockheed's board is giving him a free hand to –'

'That's the idea, George.'

'What about my job, I mean, what you want me to do. The rule is –'

'I know. You'll be acting Secretary until we get things put back together.'

Winston nodded. 'Okay. I need to bring a few people down with me.'

'I'm not going to tell you how to do it. I'm not even going to tell you all the things you have to do. I just want it to get done, George. You just have to tell me ahead of time. I don't want to read about it in the papers first.'

'When would I start?'

'The office is empty right now,' Ryan told him.

A final hedge: 'I have to talk to my family about it.'

'You know, George, these government offices have phones and everything.' Jack paused. 'Look, I know what you are. I know what you do. I might have turned out the same way, but I just never found it . . . satisfactory, I guess, just to make money. Getting start-ups off the ground, that was something different. Okay, managing money is important work. I didn't like it myself, but I never wanted to be a doctor, either. Fine, different strokes and all that. But I *know* you've sat around a lot of tables with beer and pretzels talking about how screwed up this town is. Here's your chance. It will never come again, George. Nobody will ever have a opportunity to be SecTreas without political considerations. Never. You can't turn it down, because you'd never forgive yourself if you did.'

Winston wondered how one could be so adroitly cornered in a room with curved walls. 'You're learning the political stuff, Jack.'

'Andrea, you have a new boss,' the President told his principal agent.

For her part, Special Agent Price decided that Callie Weston might be wrong after all.

The notice that there would be a presidential address tonight upset a carefully considered timetable, but only by a day. More of concern was the coordination of that event with another. Timing was everything in politics, as much as in any other field, and they'd spent a week working on this. It wasn't the usual illusion of experts moving with practiced skill. There had never been practice in this particular exercise. It was all guesses, but they'd all made guesses before, and mostly good ones, else Edward J. Kealty would never have risen as far as he had, but like compulsive gamblers, they never really trusted the table or the other players, and every decision carried with it a lot of ifs.

They even wondered about right and wrong on this one – not the 'right and wrong' of a political decision, the considered calculation of who would be pleased and who offended by a sudden stand on the principle du jour, but whether or not the action they were contemplating was objectively correct – honest, *moral!* – and that was a rare moment for the seasoned political operatives. It helped that they'd been lied to, of course. They knew they'd been told lies. They knew *he* knew that *they* knew that he'd lied to them, but that was an understood part of the exercise. To have done otherwise would have violated the rules of the game. They had to be protected so long as they did not break faith with their principal, and being protected from adverse knowledge was part of that covenant.

'So you never really resigned, Ed?' his chief of staff asked. He wanted the lie to be clear, so that he could tell everyone that it was the Lord's truth, to the best of his knowledge.

'I still have the letter,' the former Senator and former Vice President, and that was the rub, replied, tapping his jacket pocket. 'Brett and I talked things over and we decided that the wording of the letter had to be just so, and what I had with me wasn't quite right. I was going to come back the next day with a new one, dated properly, of course, and it would have been handled quietly – but who would have thought . . . ?'

228

'You could just, well, forget about it.' This part of the dance had to be stepped out in accordance with the music.

'I wish I could,' Kealty said after a moment's sincere pause, followed by a concerned, passionate voice. This was good practice for him, too. 'But, dear God, the shape the country's in. Ryan's not a bad guy, known him for years. He doesn't know crap about running a government, though.'

'There's no law on this, Ed. None. No constitutional guidance at all, and even if there were, no Supreme Court to rule on it.' This came from Kealty's chief legal adviser, formerly his senior legislative aide. 'It's strictly political. It won't look good,' he had to say next. 'It won't look –'

'That's the point,' the chief of staff noted. 'We're doing this for apolitical reasons, to serve the interests of the country. Ed knows he's committing political suicide.' To be followed by instant and glorious resurrection, live on CNN.

Kealty stood and started walking around the room, gesturing as he spoke. 'Take politics out of this, damn it! The government's been *destroyed!* Who's going to put it back together? Ryan's a goddamned CIA spook. He knows *nothing* about government operations. We have a Supreme Court to appoint, policy to carry out. We have to get Congress put back together. The country needs leadership, and he doesn't have a clue on how to do that. I may be digging my own political grave, but somebody has to step up and protect our country.'

Nobody laughed. The odd thing was that it never occurred to them to do so. The staffers, both of whom had been with EJK for twenty years or more, had so lashed themselves to this particular political mast that they had no choice in the matter. This bit of theater was as necessary as the passage of the chorus in Sophocles, or Homer's invocation of the Muse. The *poetics* of politics had to be observed. It was about the country, and the country's needs, and Ed's duty to the country over a generation and a half, because he'd been there and done it for all that time, knew how the system worked, and when it all came down, only a person like he could save it. The government *was* the country, after all. He'd spent his professional lifetime devoted to that proposition.

They actually believed all that, and no less than the two staffers, Kealty was lashed to the same mast. How much he was responding to his own ambition even he could no longer say, because belief becomes fact after a lifetime of professing it. The country occasionally showed signs of drifting away from his beliefs, but as an evangelist has no choice but to entreat people back to the True Faith, so Kealty had a duty to bring the country back to its philosophical roots, which he'd espoused for five terms in the Senate, and a briefer time as Vice President. He'd been called the Conscience of the Senate for more than fifteen years, so named by the media, which loved him for his views and his faith and his political family.

It would have been well for him to consult the media on this call, as he'd done often enough in the past, briefing them on a bill or amendment, asking their views – the media *loved* for people to ask their opinion on things – or just making sure they came to all the right parties. But not in this case. No, he couldn't do that. He had to play everything straight. The appearance of currying favor could not be risked, whereas the deliberate avoidance of that maneuver would give the patina of legitimacy to his actions. High-minded. That was the image to project. He'd forgo all of the political tapestry for the first time in his life, and in so doing embroider a new segment. The only thing to consider now was timing. And *that* was something his media contacts could help with.

'What time?' Ryan asked.

'Eight-thirty Eastern,' van Damm replied. 'There are a couple of specials tonight, sweeps week, and they've asked us to accommodate them.'

Ryan might have growled about that, but didn't. His thoughts showed clearly on his face anyway.

'It means you get a lot of West Coast people on their car radios,' Arnie explained. 'We have all five networks, plus CNN and C-SPAN. That's not a given, you know. It's a courtesy. They don't have to let you on at all. They play that card for political speeches –'

'Damn it, Arnie, this *isn't* political, it's –'

'Mr President, get used to it, okay? Every time you take a leak, it's political. You can't escape that. Even the absence of politics is a political statement.' Arnie was working very hard to educate his new boss. He listened well, but he didn't always hear.

'Okay. The FBI says I can release all of this?'

'I talked to Murray twenty minutes ago. It's okay with him. I have Callie incorporating that in the speech right now.'

She could have had a better office. As the number-one presidential speech-writer, she could have asked for and gotten a gold-plated personal computer sitting on a desk of Carrara marble. Instead she used a ten-year-old Apple Macintosh Classic, because it was lucky and she didn't mind the small screen. Her office might have been a closet or storeroom once upon a time, back when the Indian Treaty Room had really been used for Indian treaties. The desk had been made at a federal prison, and while the chair was comfortable, it was thirty years old. The room had high ceilings. That made it easier for her to smoke, in violation of federal and White House rules, which were in her case not enforced. The last time someone had tried to muscle her, a Secret Service agent really had been forced to pull her off the male staffer lest she scratch his eyes out. That she had not been terminated at once was a sign to the rest of the personnel in the Old Executive Office Building. Some staff people could not be touched. Callie Weston was one of those.

There were no windows in her room. She didn't want them. For her, reality was her computer and the photographs on her walls. One was of her dog, an aging English sheepdog named Holmes (Oliver Wendell, not Sherlock; she admired the prose of the Yankee from Olympus, an accolade she accorded few others). The rest were of political figures, friends and enemies, and she studied them constantly. Behind her was a small TV and VCR, the former usually tuned to C-SPAN-1 and -2 or CNN, and the latter used to review tapes of speeches written by others and delivered in all manner of places. The political speech, she thought, was the highest form of communication. Shakespeare might have had two or three hours in one of his plays to get his idea across. Hollywood tried the same thing in much the same time. Not her. She had fifteen minutes at the bottom end, and maybe forty-five at the top, and her ideas had to count.

231

They had to sway the average citizen, the seasoned pol, and the most cynical reporter. She studied her subject, and she was studying Ryan now, playing and replaying the few words he'd said on the night of his accession, then the TV spots the next morning. She watched his eyes and his gestures, his tension and intensity, his posture and body language. She liked what she saw in the abstract sense. Ryan was a man she'd trust as an investment adviser, for example. But he had a lot to learn about being a politician, and somebody had to teach him – or maybe not? She wondered. Maybe . . . by *not* being a politician . . .

Win or lose, it would be fun. For the first time, fun, not work.

Nobody wanted to admit it, but she was one of the most perceptive of the people working here. Fowler had known that, and so had Durling, which was why they put up with her eccentricities. The senior political staff hated her, treated her as a useful but minor functionary, and seethed at how she could stroll across the street and go right into the Oval Office, because the President trusted her as he trusted few others. That had finally occasioned a comment suggesting that the President had a rather special reason for calling her over, and, after all, people from her part of the country were known to be a little loose when it came to . . . She wondered if he'd managed to get it up lately. The agent had pulled her hands off the little prick's face, but he'd been too slow to contain her knee. It hadn't even made the papers. Arnie had explained to him that a return to the Center of Power would be impeded by a charge of sexual misconduct – and then blacklisted him anyway. She liked Arnie.

She liked the speech, too. Four hours instead of the three she'd promised, a lot of effort for twelve minutes and thirty seconds – she tended to write them a little short because presidents had a way of speaking slowly. Most did. Ryan would have to learn that. She typed CONTROL P to print up the speech in Helvetica 14-point, three copies. Some political pukes would look things over and try to make corrections. That wasn't as much a problem now as it had been. When the printer stopped, she collated the pages, stapled them together, and lifted her phone. The topmost speed-dial button went to the proper desk across the street.

'Weston to see the Boss,' she told the appointments secretary.

'Come right over.'

And with that everything was as it should be.

God had not heard her prayers, Moudi saw. Well, the odds had been against that. Mixing his Islamic faith with scientific knowledge was as much a problem for the doctor as for his Christian and pagan colleagues – the Congo had been exposed to Christianity for over a hundred years, but the old, animistic beliefs still prospered, and that made it easier for Moudi to despise them. It was the old question, if God were a God of mercy, then why did injustice happen? That might have been a good question to discuss with his imam, but for now it was enough that such things did happen, even to the just.

They were called petechiae, a scientific name for blotches of subcutaneous bleeding, which showed up very plainly on her pale north European skin. Just as well that these nuns didn't use mirrors – thought a vanity in their religious universe, and one more thing for Moudi to admire, though he didn't quite understand that particular fixation. Better that she should not see the red blotches on her face. They were unsightly all by themselves, but worse than that, they were the harbingers of death.

Her fever was 40.2 now, and would have been higher still but for the ice in her armpits and behind her neck. Her eyes were listless, her body pulled down with induced fatigue. Those were symptoms of many ailments, but the petechiae told him that she was bleeding internally. Ebola was a hemorrhagic fever, one of a group of diseases that broke down tissue at a very basic level, allowing blood to escape everywhere within the body, which could only lead to cardiac arrest from insufficient blood volume. That was the killing mechanism, though how it came about, the medical world had yet to learn. There was no stopping it now. Roughly twenty percent of the victims did survive; somehow their immune systems managed to rally and defeat the viral invader – how that happened was one more unanswered question. That it would not happen in this case was a question asked and answered.

He touched her wrist to take the pulse, and even through

his gloves the skin was hot and dry and ... slack. It was starting already. The technical term was systemic necrosis. The body had already started to die. The liver first, probably. For some reason – not understood – Ebola had a lethal affinity for that organ. Even the survivors had to deal with lingering liver damage. But one didn't live long enough to die from that, because all the organs were dying, some more rapidly than others, but soon all at once.

The pain was as ghastly as it was invisible. Moudi wrote an order to increase the morphine drip. At least they could attenuate the pain, which was good for the patient and a safety measure for the staff. A tortured patient would thrash about, and that was a risk for those around a fever victim with a blood-borne disease and widespread bleeding. As it was, her left arm was restrained to protect the IV needle. Even with that precaution, the IV looked iffy at the moment, and starting another would be both dangerous and difficult to achieve, so degraded was her arterial tissue.

Sister Maria Magdalena was attending her friend, her face covered, but her eyes sad. Moudi looked at her and she at him, surprised to see the sympathy on his face. Moudi had a reputation for coldness.

'Pray with her, Sister. There are things I must do now.' And swiftly. He left the room, stripping off his protective garb as he did so and depositing it in the proper containers. All needles used in this building went into special 'sharps' containers for certain destruction – the casual African attitude toward those precautions had resulted in the first major Ebola outbreak in 1976. That strain was called Ebola Mayinga, after a nurse who had contracted the virus, probably through carelessness. They'd learned better since, but Africa was still Africa.

Back in his office, he made another call. Things would begin to happen now. He wasn't sure what, exactly, though he'd help determine whatever they were, and he did that by commencing an immediate literature search for something useless.

'I'm going to save you.' The remark made Ryan laugh and Price wince. Arnie just turned his head to look at her. The chief of staff took note of the fact that she still didn't dress the part. That was actually a plus-point for the Secret Service, who called the sartorially endowed staffers 'peacocks,' which was more polite than other things they might have said. Even the secretaries spent more on clothes than Callie Weston did. Arnie just held his hand out. 'Here you go.'

President Ryan was quietly grateful for the large type. He wouldn't have to wear his glasses, or disgrace himself by telling somebody to increase the size of the printing. Normally a fast reader, he took his time on this document.

'One change?' he said after a moment.

'What's that?' Weston asked suspiciously.

'We have a new SecTreas. George Winston.'

'The zillionaire?'

Ryan flipped the first page. 'Well, I could have picked a bum off a park bench, but I thought somebody with knowledge of the financial markets might be a good idea.'

'We call them "homeless people," Jack,' Arnie pointed out.

'Or I could have chosen an academic, but Buzz Fiedler would have been the only one I'd trust,' Jack went on soberly, remembering again. A rare academic, Fiedler, a man who knew what he didn't know. Damn. 'This is good, Ms Weston.'

Van Damm got to page three. 'Callie . . .'

'Arnie, baby, you don't write Olivier for George C. Scott. You write Olivier for Olivier, and Scott for Scott.' In her heart, Callie Weston knew that she could hop a flight from Dulles to LAX, rent a car, go to Paramount, and in six months she'd have a house in the Hollywood Hills, a Porsche to drive to her reserved parking place off Melrose Boulevard, *and* that gold-plated computer. But no. All the world might be a stage, but the part she wrote for was the biggest and the brightest. The public might not know who she was, but she knew that her words changed the world.

'So, what am I, exactly?' the President asked, looking up.

'You're different. I told you that.'

12

PRESENTATION

There were few aspects of life more predictable, Ryan thought. He'd had a light dinner so that his stomach flutters would not be too painful, and largely ignored his family as he read and reread the speech. He'd made a few penciled changes, almost all of them minor linguistic things to which Callie had not objected, and which she herself modified further. The speech had been transmitted electronically to the secretaries' room off the Oval Office. Callie was a writer, not a typist, and the presidential secretaries could type at a speed that made Ryan gasp to watch. When the final draft was complete, it was printed on paper for the President to hold, while another version was electronically uploaded onto the TelePrompTer. Callie Weston was there to be sure that both versions were exactly the same. It was not unknown for someone to change one from the other at the last minute, but Weston knew about that and guarded her work like a lioness over new-born cubs.

But the predictably awful part came from van Damm: *Jack, this is the most important speech you will ever give. Just relax and do it.*

Gee, thanks, Arnie. The chief of staff was a coach who'd never really played the game, and expert as he was, he just didn't know what it was like to go out on the mound and face the batters.

The cameras were being set up: a primary and a backup, the latter almost never used, both of them with TelePrompTers. The blazing TV lights were in place, and for the period of the speech the President would be silhouetted in his office windows like a deer on a ridgeline, one more thing for the Secret Service to worry about, though they had confidence in the windows, which were spec'd to stop a .50-caliber machine-gun round. The TV crews were all known to the Detail, who checked them out anyway, along with the equipment. Everyone knew it was coming. The evening TV shows had made the necessary announcements, then moved on to other news items. It was all a routine exercise, except to the President, of course, for whom it was all new and vaguely horrifying.

He'd expected the phone to ring, but not at this hour. Only a few had the number of his cellular. It was too dangerous to have a real number for a real, hard-wired phone. The Mossad was still in the business of making people disappear. The newly found peace in the Middle East hadn't changed that, and truly they had reason to dislike him. They'd been particularly clever in killing a colleague through his cellular phone, first disabling it via electronic signal, and then arranging for him to get a substitute ... with ten grams of high explosive tucked into the plastic. The man's last phone message, or so the story went, had come from the head of the Mossad: 'Hello, this is Avi ben Jakob. Listen closely, my friend.' At which point the Jew had thumbed the # key. A clever ploy, but good only for a single play.

The trilling note caused his eyes to open with a curse. He'd gone to bed only an hour earlier.

'Yes.'

'Call Yousif.' And the circuit went dead. As a further security measure, the call had come through several cutouts, and the message itself was too short to give much opportunity to the electronic-intelligence wizards in the employ of his numerous enemies. The final measure was more clever still. He immediately dialed yet another cellular number and repeated the message he'd just heard. A clever enemy who might have tracked the message through the cellular frequencies would probably have deemed him just another cutout. Or maybe not. The security games one had to play in this modern age were a genuine drag on day-to-day life, and one could never know what worked and what did not – until one died of natural causes, which was hardly worth waiting for.

Grumbling all the more, he rose and dressed and walked outside. His car was waiting. The third cutout had been his driver. Together with two guards, they drove to a secure location, a safe house in a safe place. Israel might be at peace, and even the PLO might have become part of a democratically elected regime – was the world totally mad? – but Beirut was still a place where all manner of people could operate. The proper signal was displayed there – it was the pattern of lighted and unlighted windows – showing that it was safe for him to exit the car and enter the building. Or so he'd find out in thirty seconds or so. He was too drowsy to care. Fear became boring after a lifetime of it.

There was the expected cup of coffee, bittersweet and strong, on the plain wooden table. Greetings were exchanged, seats taken, and conversation begun.

'It is late.'

'My flight was delayed,' his host explained. 'We require your services.'

'For what purpose?'

'One might call it diplomacy,' was the surprising answer. He went on to explain.

'Ten minutes,' the President heard.

More makeup. It was 8:20. Ryan was in place. Mary Abbot applied the finishing touches to his hair, which merely increased the feeling that Ryan was an actor instead of a . . . politician? No, not that. He refused to accept the label, no matter what Arnie or any of the others might say. Through the open door to his right, Callie Weston stood by the secretary's desk, giving him a smile and a nod to mask her own unease. She had written a masterpiece – she always felt that way – and now it would be delivered by a rookie. Mrs Abbot walked around to the front of the desk, occulting some of the TV lights to look at her work from the perspective of the viewer, and pronounced it good. Ryan merely sat there and tried not to fidget, knowing that soon he'd start sweating under the makeup again, and that it would itch like a son of a bitch, and that he couldn't scratch at it no matter what, because Presidents didn't itch or scratch. There were probably people out there who didn't think that Presidents had to use the toilet or shave or maybe even tie their shoes.

'Five minutes, sir. Mike check.'

'One, two, three, four, five,' Ryan said dutifully.

'Thank you, Mr President,' the director called from the next room.

Ryan had occasionally wondered about this sort of thing. Presidents delivering these official statements – a tradition going back at least as far as FDR and his 'fireside chats,' which he'd first heard about from his mother – always seemed confident and at ease, and he'd always wondered how they ever managed to bring that off. He felt neither. One more layer of tension for him. The cameras were probably on now, so that the directors could be sure they were working, and somewhere a tape machine was recording the look on his face and the way his hands were playing with the papers in front of him. He wondered if the Secret Service had control of that tape, or whether they trusted the TV people to be honorable about such things ... surely their own anchorpeople occasionally tipped over their coffee cups or sneezed or snarled at an assistant who messed up right before airtime ... oh, yes, those taped segments were called bloopers, weren't they ... ? He was willing to bet, right there, right then, that the Service had a lengthy tape of presidential miscues.

'Two minutes.'

Both cameras had TelePrompTers. These were odd contraptions. A TV set actually hung from the front of each camera, but on those small sets the picture was inverted left-to-right because just above it was a tilted mirror. The camera lens was behind the mirror, shooting through it, while on it the President saw the text of his speech reflected. It was an otherworldly feeling talking to a camera you couldn't really see to millions of people who weren't really there. He'd actually be talking *to* his speech, as it were. Ryan shook his head as the speech text was fast-tracked, to make sure the scrolling system worked.

'One minute, stand by.'

Okay. Ryan adjusted himself in the seat. His posture worried him. Did he plant his arms on the desktop? Did he hold his hands in his lap? He'd been told not to lean back in the chair, because it was both too casual and too arrogant-looking, but Ryan tended to move around a lot, and holding still made his back hurt – or was it something he just imagined? A little late for that now. He noted the fear, the twisting heat in his stomach. He tried to belch, and then stifled it.

'Fifteen seconds.'

Fear almost became panic. He couldn't run away now. He had to do the job. This was important. People depended on him. Behind each camera was an operator. There were three Secret Service agents to watch over them. A director-assistant was there as well. They were his only audience, but he could barely make them out, hidden as they were in the glare of the lights, and they wouldn't react anyway. How would he know what his real audience thought?

Oh, shit.

A minute earlier, network anchors had come on to tell people what they already knew. Their evening TV shows would be put back a time for a presidential address. Across the country an indeterminate number of people lifted their controllers to switch to a cable channel as soon as they saw the Great Seal of the President of the United States of America. Ryan took a deep breath, compressed his lips, and looked into the nearer of the two cameras. The red light went on. He counted to two and began.

'Good evening.

'My fellow Americans, I'm taking this time to report to you on what has been happening in Washington for the past week, and to tell you about what will be happening over the next few days.

'First of all, the Federal Bureau of Investigation and the Department of Justice, assisted by the Secret Service, the National Transportation Safety Board, and other federal agencies, have taken the lead in investigating the circumstances surrounding the tragic deaths of so many of our friends, with praiseworthy assistance from the Japanese national police and the Royal Canadian Mounted Police. Full information will be released this evening, and will be in your morning papers. For now I will give you the results of the investigation to date.

'The crash of the Japan Airlines 747 into the Capitol building was the deliberate act of one man. His name was Torajiro Sato. He was a senior captain with that airline. We've learned quite a lot about Captain Sato. We know that he lost both a brother and a son during our conflict with his country. Evidently he was unbalanced by this, and decided, on his own, to take his revenge.

'After flying his airliner to Vancouver, Canada, Captain Sato faked a flight order to London, ostensibly to replace a disabled aircraft with his own. Prior to takeoff, Captain Sato murdered his co-pilot in cold blood, a man with whom he had worked for several years. He then continued on entirely alone, the whole time with a dead man strapped in the seat next to him.' Ryan paused, his eyes tracking the words on the mirror. His mouth felt like raw cotton as a cue on the TelePrompTer told him to turn the page.

'Okay, how can we be sure of this?

'First, the identities of both Captain Sato and his co-pilot have been verified by the FBI, using DNA testing. Separate tests conducted by the Japanese national police have produced identical results. An independent laboratory checked these tests with their own, and again the results were the same. The possibility of a mistake in these tests is virtually zero.

'The other flight-crew members who remained in Vancouver have been interviewed both by the FBI and the Royal Canadian Mounted Police, and they are certain that Captain Sato was aboard the aircraft. We have similar eyewitness reports from local officials of the Canadian Ministry of Transport, and from American passengers on the flight – more than fifty people have positively identified him. We have Captain Sato's fingerprints on the bogus flight plan. Voice-print analysis of the cockpit tapes also confirms the pilot's identity. There is, therefore, no question of the identity of the flight crew of the aircraft.

'Second, the cockpit tapes from the aircraft's flight recorder give us an exact time for the first murder. We even have the voice of Captain Sato on the tape, apologizing to the man as he killed him. After that time, the only voice on the tapes is that of the pilot. The cockpit tapes have been checked against other recordings of Captain Sato's voice, and also have positively established his identity.

'Third, forensic tests have proven that the co-pilot was dead at least four hours before the crash. This unfortunate man was killed with a knife in the heart. There is no reason to believe that he had anything at all to do with what came later. He was merely the first innocent victim in a monstrous act. He left behind a pregnant wife, and I would ask all of you to think about her loss and remember her and her children in your prayers.

'The Japanese police have cooperated fully with the FBI, even allowing us full access to their investigation and to conduct our own interviews of witnesses and others. We now have a full record of everything Captain Sato did during the last two weeks of his life, where he ate, when he slept, with whom he talked. We have found no evidence to suggest even the possibility of a criminal conspiracy, or that what this demented man did was part of some larger plan on the part of his government or anyone else. Those investigations will continue until every leaf and stone has been turned, until every possibility, however remote, has been fully checked, but the information we have now would be more than sufficient to convince a jury, and that is why I can give it to you now.' Jack paused, allowing himself to lean forward a few inches.

'Ladies and gentlemen, the conflict between our country and Japan is over. Those who caused it will face justice. Prime Minister Koga has personally assured me of that.

'Mr Koga is a man of honor and courage. I can tell you now for the first time that he was himself kidnapped and nearly murdered by the same criminals who started the conflict between his country and ours. He was rescued from his kidnappers by Americans, assisted by Japanese officials, in a special operation right in downtown Tokyo, and after his rescue he worked at great personal risk to bring an early end to the conflict, and so save his country and ours from further damage. Without his work, many more lives might have been lost, on both sides. I am proud to call Minoru Koga my friend.

'Just a few days ago, minutes after he arrived in our country, the Prime Minister and I met privately, right here in the Oval Office. From here we drove to the Capitol building, and together we prayed there. That's a moment I will never forget.

'I was there, too, when the aircraft struck. I was in the tunnel between the House Office Building and the Capitol, with my wife and children. I saw a wall of flame race toward us, and stop, and pull back. I'll probably never forget that. I wish I could. But I have put those memories aside as best I can.

'Peace between America and Japan is now fully restored. We do not now have, nor did we ever have a dispute with the citizens of that country. I call on all of you to set aside whatever ill feelings you might have toward the Japanese now and for all time to come.'

He paused again and watched as the text stopped scrolling. He turned the page on his printed text again.

'Next, we all have a major task before us.

'Ladies and gentlemen, one man, one disturbed and demented individual, thought that he could do fatal damage to our country. He was wrong. We have buried our dead. We will mourn their loss for a long time to come. But our country lives, and the friends we lost on that horrible night would have it no other way.

'Thomas Jefferson said that the Tree of Liberty often requires blood to grow. Well, the blood has been shed, and now it's time for the tree to grow again. America is a country that looks forward, not backward. None of us can change history. But we can learn from it, building on our past successes, and correcting our mistakes.

'For the moment, I can tell you that our country is safe and secure. Our military is on duty around the world, and our potential enemies know that. Our economy has taken a nasty shock, but survived, and is still the strongest in the world. This is still America. We are still Americans, and our future starts with every new day.

'I have today selected George Winston to be acting Secretary of the Treasury. George heads up a large New York mutual-fund company which he founded. He was instrumental in repairing the damage done to our financial markets. He's a self-made man – as America is a self-made country. I will soon be making other Cabinet appointments, and I will report each of those to you as they are made.

'George cannot become a full Cabinet secretary, however, until we restore the United States Senate, whose members are charged by the Constitution to advise and consent to such appointments. Selecting new senators is the job of the governors of the several states. Starting next week, the governors will pick individuals to fill the posts left vacant.' Next came the tricky part. He leaned forward again.

'My fellow Americans – wait, that's a phrase I don't like

243

very much. I never have.' Jack shook his head slightly, hoping that it didn't look overly theatrical.

'My name is Jack Ryan. My dad was a cop. I started in government service as a Marine, right after I graduated from Boston College. That didn't last very long. I got hurt in a helicopter crash, and my back didn't get better for years. When I was thirty-one, I got in the way of some terrorists. You've all heard the story, and how it ended, but what you don't know is, that incident is why I reentered government service. I enjoyed my life until that point. I'd made a little money as a stock trader, and then left that business to go back to history, my first love. I taught history – I loved teaching – at the Naval Academy, and I think I would have been content to stay there forever, just as my wife, Cathy, likes nothing more than to practice medicine and look after me and our kids. We would have been perfectly content to live in our house and do our jobs and raise our children. I know I would have.

'But I couldn't do that. When those terrorists attacked my family, I decided that I had to do something to protect my wife and children. I soon learned that it wasn't just us who needed protecting, and that I had a talent for some things, and so I joined the government and left behind my love for teaching.

'I've served my country – you – for quite a few years now, but I've never been a politician, and as I told George Winston today in this office, I do not have time to learn how to become one. But I have been inside the government for most of my working life, and I have learned a few things about how government is supposed to work.

'Ladies and gentlemen, this is not a time for us to do the usual things in the usual way. We need to do better. We can do better.

'John Kennedy once told us, "Ask not what your country can do for you. Ask what you can do for your country." Those are good words, but we've forgotten them. We need to bring them back. Our country needs all of us.

'I need your help to do my job. If you think I can do it alone, you're wrong. If you think the government can fix itself by itself, you're wrong. If you think the government, fixed or not, can take care of you in every way, you're wrong.

It's not supposed to be like that. You men and women out there, you *are* the United States of America. I work for you. My job is to preserve, protect, and defend the Constitution of the United States, and I will do that to the best of my ability, but each one of you is on the team as well.

'We need our government to do for us the things we cannot do for ourselves, like providing for the common defense, enforcing the law, responding to disaster. That's what the Constitution says. That document, the one I swore to protect and defend, is a set of rules written by a small group of fairly ordinary men. They weren't even all lawyers, and yet they wrote the most important political document in human history. I want you to think about that. They were fairly ordinary people who did something extraordinary. There's no magic to being in government.

'I need a new Congress to work with me. The Senate will arrive first, because the governors will appoint replacements for the ninety-one men and women we lost last week. The House of Representatives, however, has always been the People's House, and it's *your* job to pick those, in a voting booth, exercising your rights.' *Here we go, Jack.*

'Therefore, to you, and to the fifty governors, I have a request. Please, do not send me politicians. We do not have the time to do the things that must be done through that process. I need people who do real things in the real world. I need people who do not want to live in Washington. I need people who will not try to work the system. I need people who will come here at great personal sacrifice to do an important job, and then return home to their normal lives.

'I want engineers who know how things are built. I want physicians who know how to make sick people well. I want cops who know what it means when your civil rights are violated by a criminal. I want farmers who grow real food on real farms. I want people who know what it's like to have dirty hands, and pay a mortgage bill, and raise kids, and worry about the future. I want people who know they're working for you and not themselves. That's what I want. That's what I need. I think that's what a lot of you want, too.

'Once those people get here, it's your job to keep an eye on them, to make sure they keep their word, to make sure they keep faith with you. This is *your* government. A lot of people have told you that, but I mean it. Tell your governors what you expect of them when they make their appointments to the Senate, and then *you* select the right people for the House. These are the people who decide how much of your money the government takes, and then how it is spent. It's your money, not mine. It's your country. We all work for you.

'For my part, I will pick the best Cabinet people I can find, people who know their business, people who have done real work and produced real results. Each of them will have the same orders from this office: to take charge of his or her department, to establish priorities, and to make every government agency run efficiently. That's a big order, and one which you've all heard before. But this President didn't run an election campaign to get here. I have no one to pay off, no rewards to deliver, no secret promises to keep. I will do my damnedest to execute my duties to the best of my ability. I may not always be right, but when I'm not, it's your job, and that of the people you select to represent you, to tell me about it, and I'll listen to them and to you.

'I will report to you regularly on what is going on, and what your government is doing.

'I want to thank you for listening to me. I will do my job. I need you to do yours.

'Thank you, and good night.'

Jack waited and counted to ten before he was sure the cameras were dead. Then he lifted the water glass and tried to drink from it, but his hand was shaking so badly that he nearly spilled it. Ryan stared at it in quiet rage. Why was he shaking now? The tense part was over, wasn't it?

'Hey, you didn't puke or anything,' Callie Weston said, suddenly standing next to him.

'Is that good?'

'Oh, yes, Mr President. Vomiting on national television tends to upset people,' the speechwriter answered with a hooting laugh.

Andrea Price fantasized about drawing her automatic at that moment.

Arnie van Damm merely looked worried. He knew that he couldn't turn Ryan away from his course. The usual strictures that Presidents listened to – *if you want to get reelected, pay attention!* – simply didn't apply. How could he protect someone who didn't care about the only thing that mattered?

'Remember *The Gong Show*?' Ed Kealty asked.

'Who wrote this abortion manual?' his legal aide chimed in. Then all three men in the room returned their attention to the TV set. The picture changed from an external shot of the White House to the network studio.

'Well, that was a most interesting political statement,' Tom the anchor observed with the expressionless voice of a poker player. 'I see that this time the President stayed with his prepared speech.'

'Interesting and dramatic,' John the commentator agreed. 'This was not your usual presidential speech.'

'Why, John, does President Ryan insist so strongly on inexperienced people to assist him in running the government? Don't we need experienced hands to put the system back together?' Tom asked.

'That's a question many will ask, especially in this town –'

'You bet we will,' Kealty's chief of staff observed.

'– and what's most interesting about it is that he must know that, and even if he didn't, Chief of Staff Arnold van Damm, as canny a political operator as this city has ever seen, must have made that very clear to Mr Ryan.'

'What about his first Cabinet appointment, George Winston?'

'Winston heads the Columbus Group, a mutual-fund company which he founded. He's enormously wealthy, as President Ryan told us, a self-made man. Well, we want a Treasury Secretary who knows money and the financial markets, and surely Mr Winston does, but many will complain –'

'That he's an insider.' Kealty smirked.

'– with too many contacts in the system,' John went on.

'How do you think official Washington will react to this speech?' Tom asked.

'*What* official Washington?' Ryan growled. This was a first. The two books he'd published had been treated generally well by reviewers, but back then you had to wait a few weeks for people to make comments. It was probably a mistake to watch the instant analysis, but it was also impossible to avoid. The hardest part was keeping track of all the TVs that were running at the same time.

'Jack, "official Washington" is fifty thousand lawyers and lobbyists,' Arnie pointed out. 'They may not be elected or appointed, but they're official as hell. So is the media.'

'So I see,' Ryan replied.

' – and we need experienced professionals to get the system put back together. That's what they'll say, and a lot of people in this town will agree.'

'What did you think of his revelation on the war and the crash?'

'What interested me the most was his "revelation" that Prime Minister Koga was first kidnapped by his own countrymen and then rescued – by Americans. It would be interesting to learn more about that. The President is to be commended for his clear desire to settle things between our country and Japan, and I'd give him high marks for it. A photograph came to us along with the President's speech.' The network picture changed, showing Ryan and Koga at the Capitol. 'This is a truly moving moment captured by the White House photographer –'

'But the Capitol building is still ruined, John, and just as we need good architects and skilled workers to rebuild it, so, I think, we need something other than amateurs to restore the government.' Tom turned to stare right into the camera. 'So that was the first official speech from President Ryan. We'll have more news as it develops. Now we return you to our regularly scheduled programming.'

'That's our theme, Ed.' The chief of staff rose and stretched. 'That's what we need to say, and *that*'s why you've decided to come back into the political arena, however damaging to your reputation it may be.'

'Start making your calls,' Edward J. Kealty ordered.

'Mr President.' The chief usher presented a silver tray with a drink on it. Ryan took it and sipped his sherry.

'Thanks.'

'Mr President, finally –'

'Mary Pat, how long have we known each other?' It seemed to Ryan that he was always saying this.

'At least ten years,' Mrs Foley replied.

'New presidential rule, executive order, even: after hours, when we're serving drinks, my name is Jack.'

'*Muy bien, jefe,*' Chavez observed, humorously but with a guarded look.

'Iraq?' Ryan asked curtly.

'Quiet but very tense,' Mary Pat replied. 'We're not hearing much, but what we are getting is that the country's under lock-down. The army is in the streets, and the people are in their homes watching TV. The funeral for our friend will be tomorrow. After that, we don't know yet. We have one fairly well placed agent in Iran, he's on the political beat. The assassination came as a total surprise, and he's not hearing anything, aside from the expected praise to Allah for taking our friend back.'

'Assuming God wants him. It was a beautiful job,' Clark said next, speaking from authority. 'Fairly typical in a cultural sense. One martyr, sacrificing himself and all that. Getting him inside must have taken years, but our friend Daryaei is a patient sort. Well, you've met him. You tell us, Jack.'

'Angriest eyes I ever saw,' Ryan said quietly, sipping his drink. 'That man knows how to hate.'

'He's going to make a move, sure as hell.' Clark had a Wild Turkey and water. 'The Saudis must be a little tense about this.'

'That's putting it mildly,' Mary Pat said. 'Ed's staying over for a few days, and that's what he's getting. They've increased the readiness state of their military.'

'And that's all we've got,' President Ryan summarized.

'For all practical purposes, yes. We're getting a lot of SigInt out of Iraq, and what we're getting is predictable. The lid is screwed down tight, but the pot's boiling underneath. It has to be. We've increased coverage with the satellites, of course –'

'Okay, Mary Pat, give me your speech,' Jack ordered. He didn't want to hear about satellite photos right now.

'I want to increase my directorate.'

'How much?' Then he watched her take a deep breath. It was unusual to see Mary Patricia Foley tense about anything.

'Triple. We have a total of six hundred fifty-seven field officers. I want to jack that number up to two thousand over the next three years.' She delivered the words in a rush, watching Ryan's face for a reaction.

'Approved, *if* you can figure a payroll-neutral way to bring it off.'

'That's easy, Jack,' Clark observed with a chuckle. 'Fire two thousand desk weenies, and you still save money.'

'They're people with families, John,' the President told him.

'The Directorates of Intelligence and Administration are featherbedded all to hell and gone. You've been there. You know that. It's worth doing just to ease the parking situation. Early retirement will handle most of it.'

Ryan thought that one over for a second. 'I need somebody to swing the axe. MP, can you handle being under Ed again?'

'It's the usual position, Jack,' Mrs Foley replied with a twinkle in her fey blue eyes. 'Ed's better at administration than I am, but I was always better in the street.'

'Plan Blue?'

Clark answered that. 'Yes, sir. I want us to go after cops, young detectives, regular blue-suits. You know why. They're largely pre-trained. They have street smarts.'

Ryan nodded. 'Okay. Mary Pat, next week I'm going to accept with regret the resignation letter of the DCI and appoint Ed in his place. Have him present me with a plan for increasing the DO and decreasing the DI and DA. I will approve that in due course.'

'Great!' Mrs Foley toasted her Commander-in-Chief with her wineglass.

'There's one other thing. John?'

'Yes, sir?'

'When Roger asked me to step up, I had a request for him.'

'What's that?'

'I'm going to issue a presidential pardon for a gentleman named John T. Kelly. That will be done this year. You should have told me that Dad worked your case.'

For the first time in a very long time, Clark went pale as a ghost. 'How did you know?'

'It was in Jim Greer's personal files. They were sort of conveyed to me a few years ago. My father worked the case,

I remember it well. All those women who were murdered. I remember how twisted he was about it, and how happy he was to put it behind him. He never really talked about that one, but I knew how he felt about it.' Jack looked down into his drink, swirling the ice around the glass. 'If you want a good guess, I think he'd be happy about this, and I think he'd be happy to know you didn't go down with the ship.'

'Jesus, Jack . . . I mean . . . Jesus.'

'You deserve to have your name back. I can't condone the things you did. I'm not allowed to think that way now, am I? Maybe as a private citizen I could – but you deserve your name back, Mr Kelly.'

'Thank you, sir.'

Chavez wondered what it was all about. He remembered that guy on Saipan, the retired Coast Guard chief, and a few words about killing people. Well, he knew Mr C. didn't faint at the thought, but this story must be a good one.

'Anything else?' Jack asked. 'I'd like to get back to my family before all the kids go to bed.'

'Plan Blue is approved, then?'

'Yes, it is, MP. As soon as Ed writes up a plan for implementing it.'

'I'll have him heading back as soon as they can light up his airplane,' MP promised.

'Fine.' Jack rose and headed for the door. His guests did the same.

'Mr President?' It was Ding Chavez.

Ryan turned. 'Yeah?'

'What's going to happen with the primaries?'

'What do you mean?'

'I stopped over at school today, and Dr Alpher told me that all of the serious candidates in both parties were killed last week, *and* the filing deadlines for all the primaries have passed. Nobody new can file. We have an election year, and nobody's running. The press hasn't said much about that yet.'

Even Agent Price blinked at that, but an instant later they all knew that it was true.

'Paris?'

'Professor Rousseau at the Pasteur Institute thinks he's

developed a treatment. It's experimental, but it's the only chance she has.'

They spoke in the corridor outside Sister Jean Baptiste's room, both wearing blue-plastic 'space suits' and sweating inside of them despite the environmental-control packs that hung on the belts. Their patient was dying, and while that was bad enough, the manner of her protracted death would be horrid beyond words. Benedict Mkusa had been fortunate. For some reason or other, the Ebola had attacked his heart earlier than usual; it had been a rare act of mercy, which allowed the boy to expire much more quickly than usual. This patient wasn't quite so lucky. Blood tests showed that her liver was being attacked, but slowly. Heart enzymes were actually normal. Ebola was advancing within her body at a rapid but uniform rate. Her gastrointestinal system was quite literally coming apart. The resulting bleeding, both from vomiting and diarrhea, was serious, and the pain from it was intense, but the woman's body was fighting back as best it could in a valiant but doomed effort to save itself. The only reward for that struggle would be increasing pain, and already the morphine was losing its battle to stay ahead of the agony.

'But how would we –' She didn't have to go on. Air Afrique had the only regular service to Paris, but neither that carrier nor any other would transport an Ebola patient, for the obvious reasons. All of this suited Dr Moudi just fine.

'I can arrange transport. I come from a wealthy family. I can have a private jet come in and fly us to Paris. It's easier to take all of the necessary precautions that way.'

'I don't know. I'll have to –' Maria Magdalena hesitated.

'I will not lie to you, Sister. She will probably die in any case, but if there is any chance, it is with Professor Rousseau. I studied under him, and if he says he has something, then he does. Let me call for the aircraft,' he insisted.

'I cannot say no to that, but I must –'

'I understand.'

The aircraft in question was a Gulfstream G-IV, and it was just landing at Rashid Airfield, located to the east of a wide meandering loop of the River Tigris, known locally as the Nahr Dulah. The registration code near the aircraft's tail denoted Swiss registry, where it was owned by a corporation that traded in various things and paid its taxes on time, which ended official interest on the part of the Swiss government. The flight in had been short and unremarkable, except perhaps for the time of day, and the routing, Beirut to Tehran to Baghdad.

His real name was Ali Badrayn, and while he'd lived and worked under several other names, he'd finally returned to his own because it was Iraqi in origin. His family had left Iraq for the supposed economic opportunity in Jordan, but then been caught up like everyone else in the region's turmoil, a situation not exactly helped by their son's decision to become part of the movement which would put an end to Israel. The threat perceived by the Jordanian king, and his subsequent expulsion of the threatening elements, had ruined Badrayn's family, not that he'd especially cared at the time.

Badrayn cared now, somewhat. The life of a terrorist paled with the accumulating years, and though he was one of the best in that line of work, especially at gathering information, he had little to show for it beyond the undying enmity of the world's most ruthless intelligence service. A little comfort and security would have been welcome. Perhaps this mission would allow that. His Iraqi identity and the activities of his life had garnered him contacts throughout the region. He'd provided information for Iraqi intelligence, and helped finger two people they had wished to eliminate, both successfully. That had given him entree, and that was why he'd come.

The aircraft finished its rollout, and the co-pilot came aft to lower the steps. A car pulled up. He entered it, and it pulled off.

'Peace be with you,' he told the other man in the back of the Mercedes.

'Peace?' The general snorted. 'The whole world cries out that we have little enough of that.' Clearly the man hadn't slept since the death of his president, Badrayn saw. His hands shook from all the coffee he'd drunk, or perhaps from the alcohol he'd used to counteract it. It would not be a pleasant thing to look into the coming week and wonder if one would live to see the end of it. On the one hand one needed to stay awake. On the other, one needed to escape. This general had a family and children in addition to his mistress. Well, they probably all did. Good.

'Not a happy situation, but things are under control, yes?' The look this question generated was answer enough. About the only good thing that could be said was that had the President merely been wounded, this man would now be dead for failing to detect the assassin. It was a dangerous job, being intelligence chief for a dictator, and one which made many enemies. He'd sold his soul to the devil, and told himself that the debt would never be collected. How could a bright man be such a fool?

'Why are you here?' the general asked.

'To offer you a golden bridge.'

13

TO THE MANNER BORN

There were tanks in the streets, and tanks were 'sexy' things for the 'overhead imagery' people to look at and count. There were three KH-11-class reconnaissance satellites in orbit. One of them, eleven years old, was dying slowly. Long since out of maneuvering fuel, and with one of its solar panels degraded to the point that it could barely power a flashlight, it could still take photos through three of its cameras and relay them to the geosynchronous communications bird over the Indian Ocean. Less than a second later they were down-linked and forwarded to various interpretation offices, one of them at CIA.

'That ought to cut down on pursesnatchings.' The analyst checked his watch and added eight hours. Okay, approaching ten AM 'Lima,' or local time. People should have been out on the streets, working, moving around, socializing at the many sidewalk restaurants, drinking the awful local version of coffee. But not today. Not with tanks in the streets. A few individuals were moving around, mainly women by the look of them, probably shopping. A main battle tank was parked about every four blocks on the main thoroughfares – and one at every traffic circle, of which there were many – supported by lighter vehicles on the side streets. Little knots of soldiers stood at every intersection. The photos showed that all of them carried rifles, but couldn't determine rank or discern unit patches.

'Get a count,' his supervisor instructed.

'Yes, sir.' The analyst didn't grumble. Counting the tanks was something they always did. He'd even type them, mainly by checking the main gun. By doing this they'd be able to determine how many of the tanks regularly counted in their regimental laagers had turned their engines over and moved from one place to another. The information had importance to someone or other, though for the past ten years they'd been doing the same thing, generally to learn that whatever the faults and flaws of the Iraqi military, it did its maintenance well enough to keep the engines running. It was rather less diligent about its gunnery, which they'd learned in the Persian Gulf War, but as the analyst had already noted, you look at a tank and assume that it works. It was the only prudent course. He hunched down over the viewer and saw that a white car, probably a Mercedes from the shape, was driving up National Route 7. A more detailed look at the photos would have showed it heading towards the Sibaq' al Mansur racetrack, where he would have seen more automobiles of the same type, but he'd been told to count the tanks.

Iraq's climatic variations are more striking than in most places in the world. This February morning, with the sun high in the sky, it was barely above freezing, though in the summer 115 degrees Fahrenheit attracted little in the way of notice. The assembled officers, Badrayn saw, were in their winter wool uniforms, with high collars and voluminous gold braid; most of them were smoking, and all of them were worried. His host introduced the visitor to those who didn't know him. He didn't bother wishing peace unto them. They weren't in the mood for the traditional Islamic greeting. These men were surprisingly Western and totally secular in their outlook and demeanor. Like their departed leader, they gave mere lip service to their religion, though at the moment they all wondered if the teachings of eternal damnation for a sinful life were true or not, knowing that some of them would probably find out soon enough. That possibility worried them enough that they had left their offices and come to the racetrack to hear him speak.

The message Badrayn had to deliver was a simple one. This he did.

'How can we believe you?' the army chief asked when he'd finished.

'It is better for everyone this way, is it not?'

'You expect us to abandon our motherland to ... *him!*' a corps commander demanded, disguising frustration as anger.

'What you decide to do is your concern, General. If you desire to stand and fight for what is yours, the decision is clearly yours as well. I was asked to come here and deliver a message as an honest broker. This I have done,' Badrayn replied evenly. There was no sense getting excited about things like this, after all.

'With whom are we supposed to negotiate?' This was the chief of the Iraqi air force.

'You may make your reply to me, but as I have already told you, there really is nothing to negotiate. The offer is a fair one, is it not?' *Generous* would be a better term. In addition to saving their own skins, and the skins of those close to them, they would all emerge from their country wealthy. Their president had salted away huge sums of money, little of which had ever actually been detected and seized. They all had access to travel documents and passports from any country in the known world. In that particular area the Iraqi intelligence service, assisted by the engraving bureau of its treasury, had long since established its expertise. 'You have his word before God that you will not be harassed, wherever you may go.' And that was something they had to take seriously. Badrayn's sponsor was their enemy. He was as bitter and spiteful as any man on earth. But he was also a man of God, and not one to invoke His name lightly.

'When do you need your reply?' the army chief asked, more politely than the others.

'Tomorrow would be sufficient, or even the day after. Beyond that, I cannot say. My instructions,' Badrayn went on, 'go only that far.'

'And the arrangements?'

'You may set them yourselves, within reason.' Badrayn wondered how much more they could possibly expect from him, or his sponsor.

But the decision he demanded was harder than one might imagine. The patriotism of the assembled general officers was not of the usual sort. They loved their country, largely because they controlled it. They had power, genuine life-and-death power, a far greater narcotic than money, and one of the things for which a man would risk his life and his soul. One of their number, many of them thought – hoped – just might pull it off. One of them just might assume the presidency of their country successfully, and together they just might calm things down and continue as before. They'd have to open their nation up somewhat, of course. They'd have to allow UN and other inspectors to see everything, but with the death of their leader they'd have the chance to start anew, even though everyone would know that nothing new at all was happening. Such were the rules of the world. A promise here or there, a few remarks about democracy and elections, and their former enemies would fall all over themselves giving them and their nation a chance. A further incentive was the sheer opportunity of it. Not one of them had felt truly secure in years. Everyone knew of colleagues who had died, either at the hands of their dead leader, or under circumstances euphemistically called 'mysterious' – helicopter crashes had been a favorite ploy of their fallen and beloved President. Now they had a chance to live lives of power with much greater confidence, and against that was a life of indolence in some foreign place. Each of them already had a life of every luxury a man could imagine – *plus* power. Each could snap his fingers and the people who jumped were not servants but soldiers . . .

Except for one thing. To stay would be the greatest and most dangerous gamble of their lives. Their country was now under the strictest control they could remember, and there was a reason for it. The people who'd roared their love and affection for the dead one – what did they really think? It hadn't mattered a week before, but it mattered now. The soldiers they commanded came from the same human sea. Which of them had the charisma to assume the leadership of the country? Which of them had the keys to the Ba'ath Party? Which of them could rule by the force of will? Because only then could they look into the future, if not without fear, then with a small enough quantity of it that their experience and courage could deal with the chances they would be taking. Each of them, standing at the racetrack, looked around the assembly of brother officers and wondered the same question: *Which one?*

That was the problem, because if there had been one of their number to do it, he would already have been dead, probably in a tragic helicopter mishap. And a dictatorship was not operated by a committee. Strong as they all felt themselves to be, each looked at the others and saw potential weakness. Private jealousies would destroy them. Jockeying and rivalries would, probably, cause such internal turmoil that the iron hand needed to control the people would weaken. And in a few months, probably, it would come apart. They had all seen it happen before, and the ultimate result was foretold in their deaths, standing before a line of their own soldiers, and a wall to their backs.

There was no ethos for these men other than power and its exercise. That sufficed for one man, but not for many. *Many* needed to be unified around something, whether it be the rule imposed by one superior, or a commonly held idea, but it had to be something that imposed a common outlook. No one of them could do the former, and collectively they lacked the latter. Powerful as they each might be, they were also weak in a fundamental way, and as the officers stood there, looking around at one another, they all knew it. At base, they believed in nothing. What they enforced with weapons they could not impose with will. They could command from behind, but not lead from the front. At least most of them were intelligent enough to know it. That was why Badrayn had flown to Baghdad.

He watched their eyes and knew what they were thinking, however impassive their faces might have been. A bold man would have spoken up with confidence, and thus assumed leadership of the group. But the bold ones were long since dead, cut down by one bolder and more ruthless, only to be cut down by the unseen hand of someone more patient and more ruthless still – enough so that he could now make a generous offer. Badrayn knew what the answer had to be, and so did they. The dead Iraqi President had left nothing behind to replace himself, but that was the way of men who believed in nothing except themselves.

The phone rang at 6:05 this time. Ryan didn't mind awakening before 7:00. It had been his custom for years, but back then he'd had to drive in to work. Now the job was an elevator ride away, and he'd expected that the time previously spent in a car could now be spent in bed. At least he'd been able to doze in the back of his official car.

'Yes?'

'Mr President?' Jack was surprised to hear Arnie's voice.

Even so, he was tempted to demand who the hell else would pick the phone up.

'What is it?'

'Trouble.'

Vice President Edward J. Kealty had not slept all night, but one would not have known it from looking at him. Shaved pink, clear of eye, and straight of back, he strode into the CNN building with his wife and his aides, there to be met by a producer who whisked him into an elevator for the trip upstairs. Only the usual pleasantries were exchanged. The career politician just stared forward, as though trying to convince the stainless-steel doors that he knew what he was about. And succeeding.

The preparatory calls had been made over the previous three hours, starting with the head of the network. An old friend, the TV executive had been thunderstruck for the first time in his career. One halfway expected airplane crashes, train wrecks, violent crimes – the routine disasters and sorrows from which the media made its living – but something like this was the occurrence of a lifetime. Two hours earlier, he'd called Arnie van Damm, another old friend, because one had to cover one's bases as a reporter; besides, there was also a love of country in him that he rarely expressed but it was there nonetheless, and the CNN president didn't have a clue where this story would go. He'd called on the network's legal correspondent, a failed trial attorney, who in turn was now on the phone with a professor friend at Georgetown University Law School. Even now, the CNN president called into the green room.

'Are you really sure, Ed?' was all he had to ask.

'I don't have a choice. I wish I didn't have to.' Which was the expected answer.

'Your funeral. I'll be watching.' And the line went dead. At the far end there was a form of rejoicing. It would be a *hell* of a story, and it was CNN's job to report the news, and that was that.

'Arnie, is this totally crazy or am I still dreaming?' They were in an upstairs sitting room. Jack had thrown on some casual clothes. Van Damm didn't have his tie on yet, and his socks were mismatched, Ryan noticed. Worst of all, van Damm looked rattled, and he'd never seen that before.

'I guess we'll just have to wait and see.' Both men turned when the door opened.

'Mr President?' A fiftyish man came in, properly dressed in a business suit. He was tall and harried-looking. Andrea followed him in. She, too, had been briefed, insofar as that was possible.

'This is Patrick Martin,' Arnie said.

'Criminal Division at Justice, right?' Jack rose to shake hands and waved him to the coffee tray.

'Yes, sir. I've been working with Dan Murray on the crash investigation.'

'Pat's one of our better trial lawyers. He also lectures at George Washington on constitutional law,' the chief of staff explained.

'So, what do you think of all this?' the President asked, his voice still somewhere between whimsy and outright disbelief.

'I think we need to see what he has to say.' The quintessential lawyer's reply.

'How long at Justice?' Jack asked next, returning to his seat.

'Twenty-three years. Four years in the FBI before that.' Martin poured a cup and decided to stand.

'Here we go,' van Damm observed, unmuting the TV.

'Ladies and gentlemen, with us here in our Washington bureau is Vice President Edward J. Kealty.' CNN's chief political correspondent also looked as though he'd been dragged from his bed and genuinely shaken. Ryan noted that, of all the people he'd seen that day, Kealty looked the most normal. 'Sir, you have something unusual to say.'

'Yes, I do, Barry. I probably need to start by saying that this is the most difficult thing I've ever had to do in over thirty years of public life.' Kealty's voice was quiet and restrained, speaking in the tone of an essay by Emerson, slow and clear, and painfully earnest. 'As you know, President Durling asked me to resign from my post. The reason for this was a question of my conduct while a senator. Barry, it's no secret that my personal conduct has not always been as exemplary as it should have been. That's true of many people in public life, but it's no excuse, and I do not claim that it is. When Roger and I discussed the situation, we agreed that it would be best for me to resign my office, allowing him to select a new running mate for the elections later this year. It was his further intention to have John Ryan fill my post as interim Vice President.

'Barry, I was content with that. I've been in public life for a very long time, and the idea of retiring to play with my grandchildren and maybe teach a little bit actually looked pretty attractive. And so I agreed to Roger's request in the interests of – well, really for the good of the country.

'But I never actually resigned.'

'Okay,' the correspondent said, holding his hands up as though to catch a baseball. 'I think we need to be really clear on this, sir. What exactly did happen?'

'Barry, I drove over to the State Department. You see, the Constitution specifies that when the President or Vice President resigns, the resignation is presented to the Secretary of State. I met with Secretary Hanson privately to discuss the issue. I actually had a letter of resignation prepared, but it was in the wrong form, and Brett asked me to redraft it. So I drove back, thinking that I could have it done and resubmitted the following day.

'None of us expected the events of that evening. I was badly shaken by them, as were many. In my case, as you know, well, so many of the friends with whom I'd worked for years were just snuffed out by that brutal and cowardly act. But I never actually resigned my office.' Kealty looked down for a moment, biting his lip before going on. 'Barry, I would have been content even with that. I gave my word to President Durling, and I had every intention of keeping it.

'But I can't. I just can't,' Kealty went on. 'Let me explain. 'I've known Jack Ryan for ten years. He's a fine man, a courageous man, and he's served our country honorably, but he is, unfortunately, not the man to heal our country. What he said last night, trying to speak to the American people, proves it. How can we possibly expect our government to work under these circumstances without experienced, capable people to fill the offices left vacant?'

'But he is the President – isn't he?' Barry asked, scarcely believing what he was doing and what he was hearing.

'Barry, he doesn't even know how to do a proper investigation. Look at what he said last night about the plane crash. Hardly a week has passed and already he says he knows what happened. Can anyone believe that?' Kealty asked plaintively. 'Can anyone really believe that? Who has oversight over this investigation? Who's actually running it? To whom are they reporting? And to have conclusions in a *week*? How can the American people have confidence in that? When President Kennedy was assassinated, it took months. The investigation was run by the Chief Justice of the Supreme Court. Why? Because we had to be sure, that's why.'

'Excuse me, Mr Vice President, but that really doesn't answer my question.'

'Barry, Ryan was never Vice President, because I never resigned. The post was never vacant, and the Constitution allows only one Vice President. He never even took the oath associated with the office.'

'But –'

'You think I want to do this? I don't have a choice. How can we rebuild the Congress and the executive branch with amateurs? Last night Mr Ryan told the governors of the states to send him people with no experience in government. How can laws be drafted by people who don't know how?'

'Barry, I've never committed public suicide before. It's like being one of the people, one of the senators at the impeachment trial of Andrew Johnson. I'm looking down into my open political grave, but I have to place the country first. I have to.' The camera zoomed in on his face, and the anguish there was manifest. One could almost see tears in his eyes as his voice proclaimed his selfless patriotism.

'He always was good on TV,' van Damm noted.

'I do have trouble believing all this,' Ryan said after a moment.

'Believe it,' Arnie told him. 'Mr Martin? We could use some legal guidance.'

'First of all, get someone over to State and check the Secretary's office out.'

'FBI?' van Damm asked.

'Yes.' Martin nodded. 'You won't find anything, but that's how it has to start. Next, check phone logs and notes. Next, we start interviewing people. That's going to be a problem.

Secretary Hanson's dead, along with his wife, and President and Mrs Durling, of course. Those are the people most likely to have knowledge on the facts of the issue. I would expect that we will develop very little hard evidence, and not very much useful circumstantial evidence.'

'Roger told me that –' Martin cut him off.

'Hearsay. You're telling me that someone said to you what he was told by somebody else – not much use in any court of law.'

'Go on,' Arnie said.

'Sir, there really is no constitutional or statutory law on this question.'

'And there's no Supreme Court to rule on the issue,' Ryan pointed out. To that pregnant pause, he added: 'What if he's telling the truth?'

'Mr President, whether or not he's telling the truth is really beside the point,' Martin replied. 'Unless we can prove that he's lying, which is unlikely, then he has a case of sorts. By the way, on the issue of the Supreme Court, assuming that you get a new Senate and make your nominations, all of the new Justices would ordinarily have to recuse themselves because you selected them. That probably leaves no legal solution possible.'

'But if there's no law on this issue?' the President – was he? – asked.

'Exactly. This is a beauty,' Martin said quietly, trying to think. 'Okay, a President or Vice President stops holding office when he or she resigns. Resignation happens when the office holder conveys the instrument of resignation – a letter suffices – to the proper official. But the man who accepted the instrument is dead, and we will doubtless find that the instrument is missing. Secretary Hanson probably called the President to inform him of the resignation –'

'He did,' van Damm confirmed.

'But President Durling is also dead. His testimony would have had evidentiary value, but that isn't going to happen, either. That puts us back to square one.' Martin didn't like what he was doing, and he was having enough trouble trying to talk and think about the law at the same time. This was like a chessboard with no squares, just the pieces arrayed at random.

'But –'

'The phone logs will show there was a call, fine. Secretary Hanson might have said that the letter was poorly worded and would be fixed the following day. This is politics, not law. So long as Durling was President, Kealty had to leave, because –'

'Of the sexual harassment investigation.' Arnie was getting it now.

'You got it. His TV statement even covered that, and he did a nice job of neutralizing the issue, didn't he?'

'We're back to where we started,' Ryan observed.

'Yes, Mr President.' That elicited a wry smile.

'Nice to know that somebody believes.'

Inspector O'Day and three other agents from Headquarters Division left their car right in front of the building. When a uniformed guard came over to object, O'Day just flashed his ID and kept on going. He stopped at the main security desk and did the same.

'I want your chief to meet me on the seventh floor in one minute,' he told the guard. 'I don't care what he's doing. Tell him to come up right now.' Then he and his team walked to the elevator bank.

'Uh, Pat, what the hell –'

The other three had been picked more or less at random from the Bureau's Office of Professional Responsibility. That was the FBI's own internal-affairs department. All experienced investigators with supervisory rank, their job was to keep the Bureau clean. One of them had even investigated a former Director. OPR's charter was to respect nothing but the law, and the surprising thing was that, unlike similar organizations in city police forces, it retained, for the most part, the respect of the street agents.

The lobby guard had called ahead to the guard post on the top floor. It was George Armitage this morning, working a different shift from the previous week.

'FBI,' O'Day announced as the elevator door opened. 'Where's the Secretary's office?'

'This way, sir.' Armitage led them down the corridor.

'Who's been using the office?' the inspector asked.

'We're getting ready to move Mr Adler in. We've just about got Mr Hanson's things out and –'

'So people have been going in and out?'

'Yes, sir.'

O'Day hadn't expected that it would be much use bringing in the forensics team, but that would be done anyway. If there had ever been an investigation that had to go strictly by the book, this was the one.

'Okay, we need to talk to everyone who's been in or out of the office since the moment Secretary Hanson left it. Every single one, secretaries, janitors, everybody.'

'The secretarial staff won't be in for another half hour or so.'

'Okay. You want to unlock the door?'

Armitage did so, letting them into the secretaries' room, and then through the next set of doors into the office itself. The FBI agents stopped cold there, the four of them just looking at first. Then one of them took post at the door to the main corridor.

'Thank you, Mr Armitage,' O'Day said, reading the name tag. 'Okay, for the moment, we're treating this as a crime scene. Nobody in or out without our permission. We need a room where we can interview people. I'd like you to make a written list of everyone you know to have been in here, with date and time if that's possible.'

'Their secretaries will have that.'

'We want yours, too.' O'Day looked up the corridor and was annoyed. 'We asked for your department chief to join us. Where do you suppose he is?'

'He usually doesn't get in until eight or so.'

'Could you call him, please? We need to talk to him right now.'

'You got it, sir.' Armitage wondered what the hell this was all about. He hadn't seen the TV this morning, nor heard what was going on yet. In any case, he didn't care all that much. Fifty-five and looking forward to retirement after thirty-two years of government service, he just wanted to do his job and leave.

'Good move, Dan,' Martin said into the phone. They were in the Oval Office now. 'Back to you.' The attorney hung up and turned.

'Murray sent one of his roving inspectors over, Pat O'Day.

266

Good man, troubleshooter. He's being backed up by OPR guys' – Martin explained briefly what that meant – 'another smart move. They're apolitical. With that done, Murray has to back away from things.'

'Why?' Jack asked, still trying to catch up.

'You appointed him acting Director. I can't be involved much with this, either. You need to select someone to run the investigation. He has to be smart, clean, and not the least bit political. Probably a judge,' Martin thought. 'Like a Chief Judge of a US Circuit Court of Appeals. There's lots of good ones.'

'Any ideas?' Arnie asked.

'You have to get that name from somebody else. I can't emphasize enough, this has to be clean in every possible respect. Gentlemen, we're talking about the Constitution of the United States here.' Martin paused. He had to explain things. 'That's like the Bible for me, okay? For you, too, sure, but I started off as an FBI agent. I worked mainly civil-rights stuff, all those sheet-heads in the South. Civil rights are important, I learned that looking at the bodies of people who died trying to secure those rights for other people they didn't even know. Okay, I left the Bureau, entered the bar, did a little private practice, but I guess I never stopped being a cop, and so I came back in. At Justice, I've worked OC, I've worked espionage, and now I just started running the Criminal Division. This is important stuff to me. You have to do it the right way.'

'We will,' Ryan told him. 'But it would be nice to know how.'

That evoked a snort. 'Damned if I know. On the substance of the issue, anyway. On the form, it has to appear totally clean, no questions at all. That's impossible, but you have to try anyway. That's the legal side. The political side I leave to you.'

'Okay. And the crash investigation?' Ryan was slightly amazed with himself. He'd actually turned away from the investigation to something else. Damn.

This time Martin smiled. 'That pissed me off, Mr President. I don't like having people to tell me how to run a case. If Sato were alive, I could take him into court today. There won't be any surprises. The thing Kealty said about the JFK investigation was pretty disingenuous. You handle one of

these cases by running a thorough investigation, not by turning it into a bureaucratic circus. I've been doing that my
whole life. This case is pretty simple – big, but simple – and
for all practical purposes it's already closed. The real help
came from the Mounties. They did a nice job for us, a ton
of corroborative evidence, time, place, fingerprints, catching
people from the plane to interview. And the Japanese police
– Christ, they're ready to eat nails, they're so angry about
what happened. They're talking to all of the surviving conspirators. You, and we, don't want to know their interrogation methods. But their due process is not our problem. I'm
ready to defend what you said last night. I'm ready to walk
through everything we know.'

'Do that, this afternoon,' van Damm told him. 'I'll make
sure you get the press coverage.'

'Yes, sir.'

'So you can't be part of the Kealty thing?' Jack asked.

'No, sir. You cannot allow the process to be polluted in
any way.'

'But you can advise me on it?' President Ryan went on. 'I
need legal counsel of some sort.'

'That you do, and, yes, Mr President, I can do that.'

'You know, Martin, at the end of this –'

Ryan cut his chief of staff off cold, even before the attorney
could react. 'No, Arnie, none of that. God damn it! I will not
play that game. Mr Martin, I like your instincts. We play
this one absolutely straight. We get professionals to run it,
and we trust them to be pros. I am sick and fucking tired of
special prosecutors and special this and special that. If you
don't have people you can trust to do the job right, then what
the hell are they doing there in the first place?'

Van Damm shifted in his seat. 'You're a naïf, Jack.'

'Fine, Arnie, and we've been running the government with
politically aware people since before I was born, and look
where it's gotten us!' Ryan stood to pace around the room.
It was a presidential prerogative. 'I'm tired of all this. What
ever happened to honesty, Arnie? What ever happened to
telling the goddamned truth? It's all a fucking game here,
and the object of the game isn't to do the right thing, the
object of the game is to *stay* here. It's not supposed to be
that way! And I'll be *damned* if I'll perpetuate a game I don't

like.' Jack turned to Pat Martin. 'Tell me about that FBI case.'

Martin blinked, not knowing why that had come up, but he told the story anyway. 'They even made a bad movie about it. Some civil-rights workers got popped by the local Klukkers. Two of them were local cops, too, and the case wasn't going anywhere, so the Bureau got involved under interstate commerce and civil rights statutes. Dan Murray and I were rookies back then. I was in Buffalo at the time. He was in Philly. They brought us down to work with Big Joe Fitzgerald. He was one of Hoover's roving inspectors. I was there when they found the bodies. Nasty,' Martin said, remembering the sight and the horrid smell. 'All they wanted to do was to get citizens registered to vote, and they got killed for it, and the local cops weren't doing anything about it. It's funny, but when you see that sort of thing, it isn't abstract anymore. It isn't a document or a case study or a form to fill out. It just gets real as hell when you look at bodies that've been in the ground for two weeks. Those Klukker bastards broke the law and killed fellow citizens who were doing something the Constitution says isn't just okay – it's a *right*. So, we got 'em, and put 'em all away.'

'Why, Mr Martin?' Jack asked. The response was exactly what he expected.

'Because I swore an oath, Mr President. That's why.'

'So did I, Mr Martin.' *And it wasn't to any goddamned game.*

The cueing was somewhat equivocal. The Iraqi military used hundreds of radio frequencies, mainly FM VHF bands, and the traffic, while unusual for the overall situation, was routine in its content. There were thousands of messages, as many as fifty going at any given moment, and STORM TRACK didn't begin to have enough linguists to keep track of them all, though it had to do just that. The command circuits for senior officers were well known, but these were encrypted, meaning that computers in KKMC had to play with the signals in order to make sense of what sounded like static. Fortunately a number of defectors had come across with examples of the encryption hardware, and others trickled over various borders with daily keying sequences, all to be handsomely rewarded by the Saudis.

The use of radios was more now rather than less. The senior Iraqi officers were probably less concerned with electronic intercepts than with who might be listening in on a telephone line. That simple fact told the senior watch officers a lot, and a document was even now being prepared to go up the ladder to the DCI for delivery to the President.

STORM TRACK looked like most such stations. One huge antenna array, called an Elephant Cage for its circular configuration, both detected and localized signals, while other towering whip antennas handled other tasks. The listening station had been hastily built during the buildup for DESERT STORM as a means of gathering tactical intelligence for allied military units, then to be expanded for continuing interest in the region. The Kuwaitis had funded the sister station, PALM BOWL, for which they were rewarded with a good deal of the 'take.'

'That's three,' a technician said at the latter station, reading off his screen. 'Three senior officers heading to the racetrack. A little early in the day to play the ponies, isn't it?'

'A meet?' his lieutenant asked. This was a military station, and the technician, a fifteen-year sergeant, knew quite a bit more about the job than his new boss. At least the elltee was smart enough to ask questions.

'Sure looks like it, ma'am.'

'Why there?'

'Middle of town, not in an official building. If you're out to meet your honey, you don't do it at home, do you?' The screen changed. 'Okay, we cracked another one. The Air Force chief is there, too – was, probably. Traffic analysis seems to show that the meet broke up an hour or so ago. I wish we could crack their crypto gear faster . . .'

'Content?'

'Just where to go and when, ma'am, nothing substantive, nothing about what they're meeting for.'

'When's the funeral, Sergeant?'

'Sunset.'

'Yes?' Ryan lifted the phone. You could pretty much tell how important the call was from the line that was lit. This one was Signals.

'Major Canon, sir. We're getting feed from Saudi. The intel

community is trying to make sense of it now. They told me to cue you on that.'

'Thank you.' Ryan replaced the phone. 'You know, it would be nice to have 'em come in one at a time. Something happening in Iraq, but they're not sure what yet,' he told his guests. 'I guess I have to start paying attention. Anything else I have to do now?'

'Put Secret Service protection on Vice President Kealty,' Martin suggested. 'He's entitled to it anyway under the law as a former VP – for six months?' the attorney asked Price.

'That's correct.'

Martin thought about that. 'Did you have any discussions on that issue?'

'No, sir.'

'Pity,' Martin thought.

14

BLOOD IN THE WATER

Ed Foley's executive aircraft was big and ugly, a Lockheed C-141B cargo carrier, known to the fighter community as a 'trash hauler,' in whose cargo area was a large trailer. The trailer's history was interesting. It had originally been built by the Airstream company as a receiving facility for the Apollo astronauts, though this one was a backup and had never actually been used for that purpose. It allowed senior officials to travel with homelike amenities and was used almost exclusively by senior intelligence officers. This way they could travel in both anonymity and comfort. There were lots of Air Force Starlifters, and from the outside Foley's looked like any other – big, green, and ugly.

It touched down at Andrews just before noon, after an exhausting flight of almost seven thousand miles, seventeen hours, and two aerial refuelings. Foley had traveled with a staff of three, two of them security and protection officers, called SPOs. The ability to shower had improved the attitude of each, and their night's sleep hadn't been interrupted by the signals that had started to arrive a few hours earlier. By the time the cargo lifter stopped rolling and the doors opened, he was refreshed and informed. That didn't happen often enough for the ADDO to regard it as anything short of a miracle. So much the better that his wife was there to greet him with a kiss. It was enough that the Air Force ground crew wondered what the hell this was all about. The flight crew was too tired to care.

'Hi, honey.'

'We really need to fly together this way once,' her husband observed with a twinkle in his eye. Then he shifted gears in a heartbeat. 'What's the word on Iraq?'

'Something's happening. At least nine, probably twenty or so senior officers got together for a quiet little meeting. We don't know what about, but it wasn't to pick the menu for the wake.' They got in the back of the car, and she handed over a folder. 'You're getting promoted, by the way.'

'What?' Ed's head came up from the document package.

'DCI. We're moving with Plan Blue, and Ryan wants you to front it for the Hill. I stay DDO, and I get to run my shop the way I want to, don't I, honey?' She smiled sweetly. Then she explained the other problem of the day.

Clark had his own office at Langley, and his seniority guaranteed him a view of the parking lot and the trees beyond, which beat a windowless cubby. He even shared a pool secretary with four other senior field officers. In many ways Langley was alien country for him. His official job title was that of a training officer down at the Farm. He came to headquarters to deliver reports and get briefed in on new jobs, but he didn't like it here. There was a smell to any headquarters facility. The desk weenies wanted things their way. They didn't want irregularities. They didn't care to work overtime, and miss favorite TV shows as a result. They didn't much like surprises and data that made them rethink stuff. They were the bureaucratic tail in an intelligence agency, but at CIA the tail had become so massive that it wagged the dog without ever moving itself. The phenomenon wasn't exactly unusual, but when things went bad, his was the life at risk in the field, and if he were ever killed out there, he'd turn into one residual memo, to be quickly filed and forgotten by people who did National Intelligence Estimatcs based often as not on newspaper stories.

'Catch the news this morning, Mr C.?' Chavez asked lightly on entering the room.

'I got in at five.' He held up a folder with PLAN BLUE printed on it. Because he so hated paperwork, when he did it he worked with supreme intensity, the more quickly to be rid of it.

'Then turn your set to CNN.' John did, expecting a news story that would surprise his Agency. And that's what he got, but not quite what he'd expected.

'Ladies and gentlemen, the President.'

He had to get out in public fast. Everyone agreed on that. Ryan walked into the press room, stood behind the podium, and looked down at his notes. It was easier than looking out at the room, smaller and shabbier than most parts of the building, built atop the former swimming pool. There were eight rows of six seats each. Every one, he'd seen on the way in, was full.

'Thank you for coming in so early,' Jack said in as relaxed a voice as he could manage.

'Recent events in Iraq affect the security of a region which is of vital interest to America and her allies. We note without grief the death of the Iraqi President. As you know, this individual was responsible for the instigation of two wars of aggression, the brutal suppression of that country's Kurdish minority, and the denial of the most fundamental human rights to his own citizens.

'Iraq is a nation which should be prosperous. It has a sizable fraction of the world's petroleum reserves, a respectable industrial base, and a substantial population. All that is lacking in that country is a government which looks after the needs of its citizens. We would hope that the passing of the former leader offers an opportunity for just this.' Jack looked up from his notes.

'America therefore extends the hand of friendship to Iraq. We hope that there will be an opportunity to normalize relations, and to put an end once and for all to the hostility between Iraq and its Gulf neighbors. I have directed acting Secretary of State Scott Adler to make contact with the Iraqi government, and to offer the chance of a meeting to discuss matters of mutual interest. In the event that the new regime is willing to address the question of human rights, and to commit to free and fair elections, America is willing to address the question of the removal of economic sanctions, and the rapid restoration of normal diplomatic relations.

'There has been enough enmity. It is unseemly for a region of such natural wealth to be the site of discord, and America is willing to do her part as an honest broker to assist in bringing peace and stability, along with our friends among the Gulf states. We await a favorable reply from Baghdad so that initial contacts might be established.' President Ryan folded the paper away.

'That's the end of my official statement. Any questions?' That took about a microsecond.

'Sir, this morning, as you know,' the *New York Times* shouted first, 'Vice President Edward Kealty claimed that he is the President and you are not. What do you have to say about that?'

'The allegation by Mr Kealty is groundless and totally without value,' Jack replied coldly. 'Next question.'

Having forsworn the game, Ryan was now condemned to playing it. Nobody in the room was the least bit fooled by his appearance. The announcement he'd just made could as easily have been delivered by his press secretary or the official State Department spokesman. Instead, he was here in front of the lights, looking at the assembled faces, and feeling rather like a lone Christian in a Colosseum full of lions. Well, that's what the Secret Service was for.

'A follow-up – what if he actually didn't resign?' the *Times* insisted over the shouts of others.

'He *did* actually resign. Otherwise, I could not have been appointed. Therefore your question has no meaning.'

'But, sir, what if he is telling the truth?'

'He isn't.' Ryan took a breath, as Arnie had told him to do, and then went on, saying what Arnie had told him to say. 'Mr Kealty resigned his position at the request of President Durling. You all know the reason. He was under investigation by the FBI for sexual misconduct while he was a senator. The investigation was in the matter of a sexual assault – not to say' – which Ryan then said – 'rape of one of his Senate aides. His resignation was part of a . . . deal, a plea bargain, I guess, to avoid criminal prosecution.' Ryan paused just then, somewhat surprised to see the assembled faces go a little pale. He'd just hurled down a gauntlet, and it made a loud noise on the floor. The next one was even louder. 'You know who the President is. Now, shall we get on with the business of the country?'

'What are you doing about this?' ABC asked.

'You mean Kealty or Iraq?' Ryan asked. His tone indicated what the subject ought to be.

'The Kealty question, sir.'

'I've asked the FBI to check into it. I expect them to report back to me later today. Aside from that, we have enough things to be done.'

'Follow-up – what about what you said to the governors

in your speech last night, and what Vice President Kealty said this morning? Do you really want inexperienced people to –'

'Yes, I do. First of all, what people do we have who are experienced in the workings of Congress? The answer is, not very many. We have the few survivors, people fortunate enough to have been elsewhere that night. Aside from that – what? People defeated in the last election? Do you want them back? I want, and I think the country needs, people who know how to do things. The plain truth is that government is by nature inefficient. We can't make it more efficient by selecting people who've always worked in government. The idea the Founding Fathers had was for citizen legislators, not for a permanent ruling class. In that I think I am in agreement with the intentions of the framers of our Constitution. Next?'

'But who will decide the question?' the *Los Angeles Times* asked. It wasn't necessary to say which question.

'The question is decided,' Ryan told him. 'Thanks for coming. If you will excuse me, I have a lot of work to do today.' He picked up his opening statement and walked off to his right.

'Mr Ryan!' The shout came from a good dozen voices. Ryan walked through the door and around the corner. Arnie was waiting.

'Not bad under the circumstances.'

'Except for one thing. Not one of them said "Mr President."'

Moudi took the call, which required only a few seconds. With that he walked over to the isolation ward. Outside, he donned protective gear, carefully checking the plastic fabric for leaks. The suit was made by a European company, modeled on the American Racal. The thick plastic was an incongruous powder blue, reinforced with Kevlar fiber. At the back on the web belt hung the ventilation unit. This pumped filtered air into the suit, and did so with a slight overpressure so that a tear would not suck environmental air inside. It wasn't known if Ebola was airborne or not, and nobody wanted to be the first to prove that it was. He opened the door to go inside. Sister Maria Magdalena was there, attending her friend, dressed the same way. Both knew all too well what it meant for a patient to see her attendants dressed in a way that so clearly denoted their fear of what she carried within her.

'Good afternoon, Sister,' he said, his gloved hands lifting the chart off the foot of the bed. Temperature 41.4, despite the ice. Pulse rapid at 115. Respiration 24 and shallow. Blood pressure was starting to fall from the internal bleeding. The patient had received a further four units of whole blood – and probably lost at least that much, most of it internally. Her blood chemistry was starting to go berserk. The morphine was as high as he could prescribe without risking respiratory failure. Sister Jean Baptiste was semiconscious – she should have been virtually comatose from the drugs, but the pain was too severe for that.

Maria Magdalena just looked over at him through the plastic of her mask, her eyes beyond sadness into a despair that her religion forbade. Moudi and she had seen all manner of deaths, from malaria, from cancer, from AIDS. But there was nothing so brutally cruel as this. It hit so fast that the patient didn't have the time to prepare, to steel the mind, to fortify the soul with prayer and faith. It was like some sort of traffic accident, shocking but just long enough in duration for the suffering to – if there were a devil in creation, then this was his gift to the world. Physician or not, Moudi put that thought aside. Even the devil had a use.

'The airplane is on the way,' he told her.

'What will happen?'

'Professor Rousseau has suggested a dramatic treatment method. We will do a complete blood-replacement procedure. First the blood supply will be removed completely, and the vascular system flushed out with oxygenated saline. Then he proposes to replace the blood supply completely with whole blood in which he has Ebola antibodies. Theoretically, in this way the antibodies will attack the virus systemically and simultaneously.'

The nun thought about that. It wasn't quite as radical as many would imagine. The total replacement of a body's blood supply was a procedure dating back to the late 1960s, having been used in the treatment of advanced meningitis. It wasn't a treatment that could be used routinely. It required a heart-lung-bypass machine. But this was her friend, and she was well past thinking of other patients and practicality.

Just then, Jean Baptiste's eyes opened wide. They looked at nothing, unfocused, and the very slackness of the face proclaimed her agony. She might not even have been conscious. It was just that the eyes could not remain closed in severe pain. Moudi looked over at the morphine drip. If pain had been the only consideration, he might well have increased it and taken the risk of killing the patient in the name of mercy. But he couldn't chance it. He had to deliver her alive, and though her fate might be a cruel one, he hadn't chosen it for her.

'I must travel with her,' Maria Magdalena said quietly.

Moudi shook his head. 'I cannot allow that.'

'It is a rule of our order. I cannot allow her to travel unaccompanied by one of us.'

'There is a danger, Sister. Moving her is a risk. In the aircraft we will be breathing recirculated air. There is no need to expose you to the risk as well. Her virtue is not in question here.' And one death was quite enough for his purposes.

'I have no choice.'

Moudi nodded. He hadn't chosen her destiny either, had he? 'As you wish.'

The aircraft landed at Jomo Kenyatta International Airport ten miles outside Nairobi and taxied to the cargo terminal. It was an old 707, once part of the Shah's personal fleet, the internal furnishings long since ripped out to reveal a metal deck. The trucks were waiting. The first of them backed up to the rear door, located on the right side, which opened a minute after the chocks secured the wheels in place on the ramp.

There were a hundred fifty cages, in each of them an African green monkey. The black workers all wore protective gloves. The monkeys, as if sensing their fate, were in an evil mode, using every opportunity to bite and scratch at the handlers. They screeched, urinated, and defecated as well, but to little avail.

Inside, the flight crew watched, keeping their distance. They wanted no part of the transfer. These noisy, small, nasty little creatures might not have been designated as unclean by the Koran, but they were clearly unpleasant enough, and after this job was over, they'd have the aircraft thoroughly washed and disinfected. The transfer took half an hour. The cages were stacked and tied down in place, and the handlers moved off, paid in cash and pleased to be done with the job, and their truck was replaced by a low-slung fuel bowser.

'Excellent,' the buyer told the dealer.

'We were lucky. A friend had a large supply ready to go, and his buyer was slow getting the money. In view of this . . .'

'Yes, an extra ten percent?'

'That would be sufficient,' the dealer said.

'Gladly. You will have the additional check tomorrow morning. Or would you prefer cash?'

Both men turned as the 707 lit off its engines. In minutes it would take off, this flight a short hop to Entebbe, Uganda.

'I don't like the smell of this,' Bert Vasco said, handing the folder back.

'Explain,' Mary Pat commanded.

'I was born in Cuba. Once my dad told me about the night Batista bugged out. The senior generals had a little meeting and started boarding airplanes, quick and quiet, off to where their bank accounts were, and left everybody else holding the bag.' Vasco was one of the State Department people who enjoyed working with CIA, probably as a result of his Cuban birth. He understood that diplomacy and intelligence each worked better when working together. Not everyone at Foggy Bottom agreed. That was their problem. They'd never been chased out of their homelands.

'You think that's what's happening here?' Mary Pat asked, beating Ed by half a second.

'That's the morning line from where I sit.'

'You feel confident enough to tell the President that?' Ed Foley asked.

'Which one?' Vasco asked. 'You should hear what they're saying over at the office. The FBI just took over the seventh floor. That has things a little shook up. Anyway, yes. It's just a guess, but it's a good guess. What we need to know is, who, if anyone, has been talking to them. Nobody on the ground, eh?'

The Foleys both looked down, which answered the question.

'Mr Ryan's allegations show that he's learned the shabby part of politics faster than the proper ones,' Kealty said, in a voice more hurt than angry. 'I had honestly expected better of him.'

'So, you deny the allegations?' ABC asked.

'Of course I do. It's no secret that I once had an alcohol problem, but I overcame it. And it's no secret that my personal conduct has at times been questionable, but I've changed that, too, with help from my church, and the love of my wife,' he added, squeezing her hand as she looked on with soft compassion and ironclad support. 'That really has nothing to do with the issue here. We have to place the interests of our country first. Personal animosity has no place in this, Sam. We're supposed to rise above that.'

'You bastard,' Ryan breathed.

'This is not going to be pleasant,' van Damm said.

'How can he win, Arnie?'

'Depends. I'm not sure what game he's playing.'

'– could say things about Mr Ryan, too, but that isn't the sort of thing we need to do now. The country needs stability, not discord. The American people are looking for leadership – experienced, seasoned leadership.'

'Arnie, how much has this –'

'I remember when he'd fuck a snake, if somebody held it straight for him. Jack, we can't think about that sort of thing. Remember what Allen Drury said, this is a town in which we deal with people not as they are, but as they are reputed to be. The press likes Ed, always has. They like him. They like his family. They like his social conscience –'

'My ass!' Ryan nearly shouted.

'You listen to me right now. You want to be the President? You're not *allowed* to have a temper. You hold on to that thought, Jack. When the President loses his temper, people die. You've seen how that happens, and the people out there want to know that you are calm and cool and collected *at all times*, got it?'

Ryan swallowed and nodded. Every so often it was good to lose one's temper, and Presidents *were* allowed. But you had to know when, and that was a lesson as yet unlearned. 'So what are you telling me?'

'You *are* the President. Act like it. Do your job. Look presidential. What you said at the press conference was okay. Kealty's claim is groundless. You're having the FBI check out his claim, but the claim doesn't matter. You swore the oath, you live here, and that's that. Make him irrelevant and he'll go away. Focus on this thing and you give him legitimacy.'

'And the media?'

'Give them a chance, and they'll get things right.'

'Flying home today, Ralph?'

Augustus Lorenz and Ralph Forster were of an age, and a profession. Both men had begun their medical careers in the United States Army, one a general surgeon, the other an internist. Assigned to the Military Assistance Command, Vietnam (MAC-V), in the time of President Kennedy, long before the war had heated up, both men had at the same time discovered things in the real world that they'd studied and passed over in *Principles of Internal Medicine*. There were diseases out in the remote sections of the world that killed people. Brought up in urban America, they were old enough to remember the conquest of pneumonia, tuberculosis, and poliomyelitis. Like most men of their generation, they'd thought that infectious diseases were a defeated enemy. In the jungles of a relatively peaceful Vietnam, they'd learned different, occasionally seeing healthy, fit young men, American and Vietnamese soldiers, die before their eyes from bugs they had never learned about and which they could not combat. It wasn't supposed to be that way, they both had decided one night in the Caravelle Bar, and like the idealists and scientists they were, both went back to school and started relearning their profession, and in that process beginning yet another process that would not end in their lifetimes. Forster had wound up at Johns Hopkins, Lorenz at Atlanta, head of the Special Pathogens Branch of the Centers for Disease Control. Along the way they'd flown more miles than some airline captains, and to more exotic places than any photographer for *National Geographic*, almost always in pursuit of something too small to see, and too deadly to ignore.

'I'd better, before the new kid takes my department over.'

The Nobel candidate chuckled. 'Alex is pretty good. I'm glad he got out of the Army. We did some fishing together down in Brazil, back when they had the . . .' In the hot lab, a technician made a final adjustment on the electron microscope. 'There,' Lorenz said. 'There's our friend.'

Some called it the Shepherd's Crook. Lorenz thought it more like an ankh, but that wasn't right, either. It was in any case not a thing of beauty. To both men it was evil incarnate. The vertical, curved strand was called RNA, ribonucleic acid. That contained the genetic code of the virus. At the top was a series of curled protein structures whose function wasn't yet understood, but which probably, both thought, determined how the disease acted. Probably. They didn't know, despite fully twenty years of intensive study.

The damned thing wasn't even alive, but it killed even so. A true living organism had both RNA and DNA, but a virus had only one or the other. It lived, somehow, in a dormant state until it came in contact with a living cell. Once there, it came to murderous life, like some sort of alien monster waiting its chance, able to live and grow and reproduce only with the help of something else, which it would destroy, and from which it would try to escape, then to find another victim.

Ebola was elegantly simple and microscopically tiny. A hundred thousand of them, lined up head to tail, would scarcely fill out an inch on a ruler. Theoretically one could kill and grow and migrate and kill again. And again. And again.

Medicine's collective memory wasn't as long as either physician would have liked. In 1918, the 'Spanish flu,' probably a form of pneumonia, had swept the globe in nine months, killing at least twenty million people – probably quite a few more – and some so rapidly that there had been victims who went to sleep healthy and failed to wake up the next day. But while the symptoms of the disease had been fully documented, the state of medical science hadn't yet progressed to the point of understanding the disease itself, as a result of which nobody knew what that outbreak had actually been about – to the point that in the 1970s suspected victims buried in permafrost in Alaska had been exhumed in the hope of finding samples of the organism for study; a good idea that hadn't worked. For the medical community, that disease was largely forgotten, and most assumed that should it reappear, it would be defeated with modern treatment.

Specialists in infectious disease weren't so sure. That disease, like AIDS, like Ebola, was probably a virus, and medicine's success in dealing with viral disease was precisely –

Zero.

Viral diseases could be prevented with vaccines, but once infected, a patient's immune system either won or lost, with the best of physicians standing by and watching. Doctors, as with any other profession, frequently preferred to ignore that which they didn't see and didn't understand. That was the only explanation for the medical community's inexplicably slow recognition of AIDS and its lethal implications. AIDS was another exotic pathogen which Lorenz and Forster studied, and another gift from the jungles of Africa.

'Gus, sometimes I wonder if we'll ever figure these bastards out.'

'Sooner or later, Ralph.' Lorenz backed away from the microscope – it was, actually, a computer monitor – and wished he could smoke his pipe, a vice he didn't really want to break, though working in a government building made it hard for him to indulge. He thought better with a pipe, Gus told himself. Both men stared at the screen, looking at the curlicue protein structures. 'This one is from the kid.'

They walked in the footsteps of a handful of giants. Lorenz had written a paper on Walter Reed and William Gorgas, the two Army doctors who had defeated Yellow fever with a combination of systematic investigation and ruthless application of what they had learned. But learning in this business came so slow and so dear.

'Put up the other one, Kenny.'

'Yes, Doctor,' the intercom replied. A moment later, a second image came up alongside the first.

'Yep,' Forster said. 'Looks pretty much the same.'

'That's from the nurse. Watch this.' Lorenz hit the button on the phone. 'Okay, Kenny, now hit the computer.' Before their eyes a computer image of both examples appeared. The computer rotated one to match the other, then overlaid them. They matched exactly.

'At least it hasn't mutated.'

'Hasn't had much of a chance. Two patients. They've done a good job of isolating. Maybe we were lucky. The kid's parents have been tested. They seem to be clean, or so the telex says. Nothing else from his neighborhood. The WHO team is checking around the area. The usual, monkeys, bats, bugs. So far, nothing. Could just be an anomaly.' It was as much a hope as a judgment.

'I'm going to play with this one a little. I've ordered some monkeys. I want to grow this one, get it into some cells, and then, Ralph, I'm going to examine what it does on a minute-by-minute basis. Get the infected cells, and pull a sample out every minute, slice it down, burn it with UV, freeze it in liquid nitrogen, and put it under the scope. I want to look at how the virus RNA gets going. There's a sequencing issue here . . . can't quite say what I'm thinking. The thought's kind of lurking out there on me. Damn.' Gus opened his desk drawer, pulled out his pipe, and lit it with a kitchen match. It *was* his office, after all, and he *did* think better with a pipe, in his mouth. In the field he said that the smoke kept the bugs away, and besides, he didn't inhale. Out of politeness, he cracked open the window.

The idea for which he had just received funding was more complicated than his brief expression, and both men knew it. The same experimental procedure would have to be repeated a thousand times or more to get a correct read on how the process took place, and that was just the baseline data. Every single sample would have to be examined and mapped. It could take years, but if Lorenz were right, at the end of it, for the first time, would be a blueprint of what a virus did, how its RNA chain affected a living cell.

'We're playing with a similar idea up in Baltimore.'

'Oh?'

'Part of the genome project. We're trying to read the complex interactions. The process – how this little bastard attacks the cells down at the molecular level. How Ebola replicates without a proper editing function in the genome. There's something to be learned there. But the complexity of the issue is a killer. We have to figure out the questions to ask before we can start looking for answers. And then we need a computer genius to tell a machine how to analyze it.'

Lorenz's eyebrows went up. 'How far along are you?'

Forster shrugged. 'Chalk on a blackboard.'

'Well, when I get my monkeys, I'll let you know what we develop here. If nothing else, the tissue samples ought to shed a little light.'

The funeral was epic, with a ready cast of thousands, howling their loyalty to a dead man and concealing their real thoughts; you could almost feel them looking around and wondering what came next. There was the gun carriage, the soldiers with reversed rifles, the riderless horse, the marching soldiers, all captured off Iraqi TV by STORM TRACK and uplinked to Washington.

'I wish we could see more faces,' Vasco said quietly.

'Yeah,' the President agreed. Ryan didn't smile but wanted to. He'd never really stop being an intelligence officer. Jack was sure of that. He wanted the data fresh, not massaged and presented to him by others. In this case he got to watch it live, with his color commentators at his side.

In America, a generation earlier, it would have been called a happening. People showed up and acted out because it was an expected thing. A literal sea of people filled the square – it had a name, but nobody seemed to know it – and even those who couldn't see . . . oh, a new camera gave the answer to the question. Big-screen TVs showed everyone what was happening. Jack wondered if they'd do an instant replay. Two lines of generals marched behind the gun carriage, and were keeping step, Ryan saw.

'How much farther you think they'll walk?'

'Hard to say, Mr President.'

'It's Bert, right?' the President asked.

'Yes, sir.'

'Bert, I can call in one of my NIOs to tell me he doesn't know.'

Vasco blinked, as expected. Then he decided, what the hell? 'Eight out of ten, they bug out.'

'Those are betting odds. Tell me why.'

'Iraq has nothing to fall back on. You don't run a dictatorship by committee, at least not for long. Not one of those people has the stones to take over on his own. If they stay put and the government changes, it won't change into something nice for them. They'll end up like the Shah's general staff did, backs to a wall, looking at guns. Maybe they'll try to fight it out, but I doubt it. They must have money salted away somewhere. Drinking daiquiris on a beach may not be as much fun as being a general, but it beats the hell out of looking at flowers from the wrong side. They have families to worry about, too.'

'So we should plan on a completely new regime in Iraq?' Jack asked.

Vasco nodded. 'Yes, sir.'

'Iran?'

'I wouldn't bet against it,' Vasco answered, 'but we just don't have good enough information to make any kind of prediction. I wish I could tell you more, sir, but you don't pay me to speculate.'

'That's good enough for now.' Actually it wasn't, but Vasco had given Ryan the best he had. 'There's not a thing we can do, is there?' This one was for the Foleys.

'Not really,' Ed replied. 'I suppose we could get someone over there, maybe fly one of our people up from the Kingdom, but the problem then is, whom does he try to meet? We have no way of knowing who's in command there.'

'If anyone,' Mary Pat added, looking at the marching men. None of them took the lead.

'What do you mean?' the buyer asked.

'You didn't pay me on time,' the dealer explained with a belch after draining his first beer. 'I had another buyer.'

'I was only two days late,' the buyer protested. 'There was an administrative problem getting the funds transferred.'

'You have the money now?'

'Yes!'

'Then I will find you some monkeys.' The dealer lifted his hand, snapped his fingers, and caught the attention of the bar boy. An English planter could not have done it better, in this same bar, fifty years earlier. 'It isn't all *that* hard, you know. A week? Less?'

'But CDC wants them at once. The aircraft is already on the way.'

'I will do my best. Please explain to your client that if they want their consignment on time, then they should pay their bills on time as well. Thank you,' he added for the bar boy. 'One for my friend, too, if you please.' He could afford that, what with the payment he'd just accepted.

'How long?'

'I told you. A week. Perhaps less.' Why was the chap so excited over a few days?

The buyer had no choice, at least not in Kenya. He decided to drink his beer down and speak of other things. Then he'd make a telephone call to Tanzania. After all, the African green monkey was 'abundant' throughout Africa. It wasn't as though there were a shortage of the things, he told himself. Two hours later, he learned something different. There *was* a shortage, though it would last only a few days, as long as it took for the trappers to find a few more troops of the long-tailed pests.

Vasco handled the translation in addition to his commentary duties. ' "Our wise and beloved leader who has given our country so much . . ." '

'Like population control the hard way,' Ed Foley snorted.

The soldiers, all guardsmen, moved the coffin into the prepared tomb, and with that, two decades of Iraqi history passed into the books. More likely a loose-leaf binder, Ryan thought. The big question was, who would write the next chapter?

15

DELIVERIES

'So?' President Ryan asked, after dismissing his latest set of guests.

'The letter, if there ever was one, is missing, sir,' Inspector O'Day replied. 'The most important bit of information developed to the moment is that Secretary Hanson wasn't all that scrupulous in his document-security procedures. That comes from the State's security chief. He says he counseled the Secretary on several occasions. The people I took over with me are interviewing various people to determine who went in and out of the office. It will go on from there.'

'Who's running it?' Ryan remembered that Hanson, good diplomatic technician though he might have been, had never listened all that well to anybody.

'Mr Murray had designated OPR to continue the investigation independently of his office. That means I'm out, too, because I have reported directly to you in the past. This will be my last direct involvement with the case.'

'Strictly by the book?'

'Mr President, it has to be that way,' the inspector said with a nod. 'They'll have additional help from the Legal Counsel Division. Those are agents with law degrees who act as in-house legal beagles. They're good troops.' O'Day thought for a moment. 'Who's been in and out of the Vice President's office?'

'Here, you mean?'

'Yes, sir.'

Andrea Price answered that one: 'Nobody lately. It's been unused since he left. His secretary went with him and –'

'You might want to have someone check the typewriter. If it uses a carbon-tape ribbon –'

'Right!' She almost moved right out of the Oval Office. 'Wait. Have your people –'

I'll make the call,' O'Day assured her. 'Sorry, Mr President.

I should have thought of that sooner. Please seal the office for us?'

'Done,' Price assured him.

The noise was unbearable. The monkeys were social animals, who customarily lived in 'troops' of up to eighty individuals that populated mainly the margins of forests on the edge of the broad savannas, the easier to come down from their trees and raid the surrounding open land for food. They had learned in the past hundred years to raid farms, which was easier and safer than what Nature had programmed into their behavior, because the humans who operated the farms typically controlled the predators which ate the monkeys. An African green was a tasty morsel for a leopard or hyena, but so was a calf, and farmers had to protect those. What resulted was a curious bit of ecological chaos. To protect livestock, the farmers, legally or not, eliminated the predators. That allowed the monkey population to expand rapidly, and the hungry African greens would then attack the cereal and other crops which fed both the farmers and their livestock. As a complication, the monkeys also ate insects which preyed on the crops as well, leading local ecologists to suggest that eliminating the monkeys was bad for the ecology. For the farmers it was much simpler. If it ate their livestock, it was killed. If it ate their crops, it was killed also. Bugs might not be large enough to see, but monkeys were, and so few farmers objected when the trappers came.

Of the family *cercopithecus*, the African green has yellow whiskers and a gold-green back. It can live to thirty years of age – more likely in comfortable captivity than in the predator-infested wild – and has a lively social life. The troops are made of female families, with male monkeys joining the troops individually for periods of a few weeks or months before moving on. An abundance of females in mating season allows a number of males cooperatively to enjoy the situation, but that was not the case in the aircraft. Rather, the cages were stacked like a truckload of chicken coops on the way to market. Some females *were* in season but totally inaccessible, frustrating the would-be suitors. Males stacked next to the cages of other males hissed, clawed, and spat at their unwilling neighbors, all the more unhappy that their captors had not noted the simple fact that same-sized cages were used to imprison different-sized monkeys – the male African green is fully double the size of the female – and cramping males who could smell that most welcome of natural signals, so near and yet so far. Added to the unfamiliar smells of the aircraft and the absence of food and water, the crowding caused nothing short of a simian riot, and since the issue could not be resolved by combat, all that resulted was a collective screech of rage from hundreds of individuals which far outstripped the sound of the JT-8 engines driving the aircraft east over the Indian Ocean.

Forward, the flight crew had their cabin door firmly shut and their headphones clamped tightly over their ears. That attenuated the sound, but not the fetid smell which the aircraft's recirculation systems cycled back and forth, both further enraging the cargo and sickening the crew.

The pilot, normally an eloquent man with his invective, had run out of curses and had tired of entreating Allah to expunge these horrid little creatures from the face of the earth. In a zoo, perhaps, he would have pointed to the long-tailed creatures, and his twin sons would have smiled and perhaps tossed some peanuts to their amusing captives. No more. With his tolerance gone, the pilot reached for the emergency oxygen mask and switched the flow on, wishing then he might blow open the cargo doors, depressurize the aircraft and thus both extinguish the monkeys and vent the dreadful smell. He would have felt better had he known what the monkeys knew. Something evil was afoot for them.

Badrayn met them again in a communications bunker. It didn't give him the sense of security that all the massed concrete might have. The only reason this one still stood was that it was concealed under the falsework of an industrial building – a bookbindery, in fact, which actually turned out a few books. This one and a handful of others had survived the war with America only because the Americans' intelligence had been faulty. Two 'smart bombs' had targeted a building directly across the road. You could still see the crater where the Americans had thought this structure to be. There was a lesson in that, Badrayn thought, still waiting. You had to see it, really, to believe it. It wasn't the same to look at a

TV screen or hear about it. There were five meters of rebarred concrete over his head. Five meters. It was solid, built under the supervision of well-paid German engineers. You could still see the impression of the plywood sheets which had held the wet concrete in place. Not a crack to be seen – and yet the only reason this place still stood was because the Americans had bombed the wrong side of the street. Such was the power of modern weapons, and though Ali Badrayn had existed in the world of arms and struggle for all of his life, this was the first time he fully appreciated that fact.

They were good hosts. He had a full colonel to look after him. Two sergeants fetched snacks and drinks. He'd watched the funeral on the TV. It was as predictable as one of the American police programs that blanketed the world. You always knew how it would end. The Iraqis, like most people in the region, were a passionate race, particularly when assembled in large numbers and encouraged to make the proper noises. They were easily led and easily moved, and Badrayn knew that it didn't always matter by whom. Besides, how much of it had been genuine? The informers were still out there to note who didn't cheer or grieve. The security apparatus which had failed the dead President still operated, and everyone knew it. And so little of the emotion which had flowed so freely on the screen and across the broad plazas was real. He chuckled to himself. Like a woman, Badrayn told himself, feigning her moment of supreme pleasure. The question was, would the men who so often took their pleasure without giving it notice the difference?

They arrived singly, lest a pair or small group travel together and discuss things which the entire assembly needed to hear as one. A fine wooden cabinet was opened to reveal bottles and glasses, and the laws of Islam were violated. Badrayn didn't mind. He had a glass of vodka, for which he'd acquired the taste twenty years earlier in Moscow, then the capital of a country now vanished.

They were surprisingly quiet for such powerful men, all the more so for people attending the wake of a man they'd never loved. They sipped their drinks – mainly scotch – and again they mainly looked at one another. On the television, still switched on, the local station was replaying the funeral procession, the announcer extolling the surpassing virtue of the fallen leader. The generals looked on and listened, but the look on their faces was not one of sadness, but fear. Their world had come to an end. They were not moved by the shouts of the citizens or the words of the news commentator. They all knew better.

The last of them arrived. He was the intelligence chief who'd met Badrayn earlier in the day, fresh from having stopped in at his headquarters. The others looked to him, and he answered without the necessity of hearing the question.

'Everything is quiet, my friends.'

For now. That terse observation didn't have to be spoken either.

Badrayn could have spoken, but didn't. His was an eloquent voice. Over the years he'd had to motivate many persons, and he knew how, but this was a time when silence was the most powerful statement of all. He merely looked at them, and waited, knowing that his eyes spoke far more loudly than any voice could have done.

'I don't like this,' one of them said finally. Not a single face changed. Hardly surprising. None of them liked it. The one who spoke merely affirmed what all thought, and showed himself in doing so to be the weakest of the group.

'How do we know we can trust your master?' the head of the Guards asked.

'He gives you his word in the name of God,' Badrayn replied, setting down his glass. 'If you wish, a delegation of your number may fly to see him. In that case, I will remain here as your hostage. But if you wish that, it must be done quickly.'

They all knew that, too. The thing they feared was as likely to happen before their possible departure as after. There followed another period of silence. They were scarcely even sipping at their drinks now. Badrayn could read their faces. They all wanted someone else to make a stand, and then that stand could be agreed to or disputed, and in the process the group would reach a collective position with which all would probably abide, though there might be a faction of two or three to consider an alternative course of action. That depended on which of them placed his life on the scales and tried to weigh it against an unknown future. He waited vainly to see who would do that. Finally, one of them spoke.

'I was late marrying,' the air force chief said. His twenties and thirties had been the life of a fighter pilot – on the ground if not quite in the air. 'I have young children.' He paused and looked around. 'I think we all know the possible – the *likely* – outcome for our families should things . . . develop unfavorably.' It was a dignified gambit, Badrayn thought. They could not be cowardly. They were soldiers, after all.

Daryaei's promise in God's name was not overly convincing to them. It had been a very long time since any of them had visited a mosque for any purpose other than to be photographed there in his simulated devotions, and though it was very different for their enemy, trust in another's religion begins in one's own heart.

'I presume that finances are not at issue here,' Badrayn said, both to be sure that it was not, and to make them examine that option themselves. A few heads turned with looks that were close to amusement, and the question was answered. Though official Iraqi accounts had long been frozen, there were other such accounts which had not. The nationality of a bank account was, after all, fungible, all the more so with the size of the account. Each of these men, Badrayn thought, had personal access to nine figures of some hard currency, probably dollars or pounds, and this was not the time to worry about whose money it should have been.

The next question was, Where could they go, and how could they get there safely? Badrayn could see that in their faces, and yet he could do nothing at the moment. The irony of the situation, which only he was in a position to appreciate, was that the enemy whom they feared and whose word they distrusted wished nothing more than to allay their fear and keep his word. But Ali knew him to be a surpassingly patient man. Else he would not have been here at all.

'You're quite sure?'

'The situation is nearly ideal,' Daryaei's visitor told him, explaining further.

Even for a religious man who believed in the Will of God, the confluence of events was just too good to be true, and yet it was – or appeared to be so.

'And?'

'And we are proceeding according to the plan.'

'Excellent.' It wasn't. Daryaei would have much preferred to deal with each in turn, the better to concentrate his formidable intellect on the three developing situations one at a time, but this was not always possible, and perhaps that was the sign. In any case, he had no choice. How strange that he should feel trapped by events resulting from plans he himself had set in motion.

The hardest part was dealing with his World Health Organization colleagues. That was only possible because the news was good so far. Benedict Mkusa, the 'Index Patient' or 'Patient Zero,' depending on one's favored terminology, was dead, and his body was destroyed. A team of fifteen had scoured the family's neighborhood and found nothing as yet. The critical period had yet to run out – Ebola Zaire had a normal incubation period of four to ten days, though there were extreme cases as brief as two days and as long as nineteen – but the only other case was before his eyes. It turned out that Mkusa was a budding naturalist, who spent much of his free time in the bush, and so now there was a search team in the tropical forest, catching rodents and bats and monkeys to make yet another attempt to discover the 'host,' or carrier of the deadly virus. But above all they hoped that, for once, fortune had smiled on them. The Index Patient had come directly to hospital because of his family status. His parents, educated and affluent, had let health-care professionals treat the boy instead of doing so themselves, and in that they had probably saved their own lives, though even now they were waiting out the incubation period with what had to be stark terror that surpassed even their grief at the loss of a son. Every day they had their blood drawn for the standard IFA and antigen tests, but the tests could be misleading, as some insensitive medico had foolishly told them. Regardless, the WHO team was allowing itself to hope that this outbreak would stop at two patient-victims, and because of that, they were willing to consider what Dr Moudi proposed to do.

There were objections, of course. The local Zairean physicians wanted to treat her here. There was merit to that. They had more experience with Ebola than anybody, though it had done little good to anyone, and the WHO team was reluctant for political reasons to insult their colleagues. There had been some unfortunate incidents before, with the natural hauteur of the Europeans resented by the local doctors. There was justice on both sides. The quality of the African doctors was uneven. Some were excellent, some terrible, and some ordinary. The telling argument was that Rousseau in Paris was a genuine hero to the international community, a gifted scientist and a ferociously dedicated clinician who refused to accept the fact that viral diseases could not be treated effectively. Rousseau, in the tradition of Pasteur before him, was determined to break that rule. He'd tried ribavirin and interferon as treatments for Ebola, without positive result. His latest theoretical gambit was dramatic and likely to be ineffective, but it had shown some small promise in monkey studies, and he wanted to try it on a human patient under carefully controlled conditions. Though his proposed method of treatment was anything but practical for real clinical application, you had to start somewhere.

The deciding factor, predictably, was the identity of the patient. Many of the WHO team knew her from the last Ebola outbreak at Kikwit. Sister Jean Baptiste had flown to that town to supervise the local nurses, and doctors no less than others could be moved by familiarity with those under their care. Finally, it was agreed that, yes, Dr Moudi could transport the patient.

The mechanics of the transfer were difficult enough. They used a truck rather than an ambulance, because a truck would be easier to scrub down afterward. The patient was lifted on a plastic sheet onto a gurney and wheeled out into the corridor. That was cleared of other people, and as Moudi and Sister Maria Magdalena wheeled the patient toward the far door, a group of technicians dressed in plastic 'space suits' sprayed the floor and walls, the very air itself, with disinfectant in a smelly man-made chemical fog that trailed the procession like exhaust from an overaged car.

The patient was heavily sedated and firmly restrained. Her body was cocooned to prevent the release of virus-rich bleeding. The plastic sheet under her had been sprayed with the same neutralizing chemicals, so that leaks would immediately find a very adverse environment for the virus particles they carried. As Moudi pushed the gurney from behind, he marveled at his own madness, taking such chances with something as deadly as this. Jean Baptiste's face, at least, was placid from the dangerously high dosage of narcotics, marked though it was with the growing petechiae.

They moved outdoors onto the loading dock where supplies arrived at the hospital. The truck was there, its driver seated firmly behind the wheel and not even looking backward at them, except perhaps in the mirror. The interior of the van body had likewise been sprayed, and with the door closed and the gurney firmly locked in place, it drove off with a police escort, never exceeding thirty kilometers per hour for the short trip to the local airport. That was just as well. The sun was still high, and its heat rapidly turned the truck into a mobile oven, boiling off the protective chemicals into the enclosed space. The smell of the disinfectant came through the suit's filtration system. Fortunately, the doctor was used to it.

The aircraft was waiting. The G-IV had arrived only two hours earlier after a direct flight from Tehran. The interior had been stripped of everything but two seats and a cot. Moudi felt the truck stop and turn and back up. Then the cargo door opened, dazzling them with the sun. Still the nurse, and still a compassionate one, Sister Maria Magdalena used her hand to shield the eyes of her colleague.

There were others there, of course. Two more nuns in protective garb were close by, and a priest, with yet more farther away. All were praying as some other lifted the patient by the plastic sheet and carried her slowly aboard the white-painted business jet. It took five careful minutes before she was firmly strapped in place, and the ground crewmen withdrew. Moudi gave his patient a careful look, checking pulse and blood pressure, the former rapid and the latter still dropping. That worried him. He needed her alive as long as possible. With that done, he waved to the flight crew and strapped into his own seat.

Sitting down, he took the time to look out his window, and Moudi was alarmed to see a TV camera pointed at the aircraft. At least they kept their distance, the doctor thought, as he heard the first engine spool up. Out the other window, he saw the cleanup crew respraying the truck. That was overly theatrical. Ebola, deadly as it was, appeared to be a delicate organism, soon killed by the ultraviolet of direct sunlight, vulnerable also to heat. That was why the search for the host was so frustrating. *Something* carried this dreadful 'bug.' Ebola could not exist on its own, but whatever it was that provided a comfortable home to the virus, whatever it was that Ebola rewarded for the service by not harming it, whatever the living creature was that haunted the African continent like a shadow, was as yet undiscovered. The physician grunted. Once he'd hoped to discover that host and so make use of it, but that hope had always been in vain. Instead he had something almost as good. He had a living patient whose body was now breeding the pathogen, and while all previous victims of Ebola had been burned, or buried in soil soaked with chemicals, this one would have a very different fate. The aircraft started moving. Moudi checked his seat belt again and wished he could have something to drink.

Forward, the two pilots were wearing flight suits of protective nomex previously sprayed. Their face masks muffled their words, forcing repetition of their request for clearance, but finally the tower got things right, and the Gulfstream began its takeoff roll, rotating swiftly into the clean African sky, and heading north. The first leg of their trip would be 2,551 miles, and would last just over six hours.

Another, nearly identical G-IV had already landed at Benghazi, and now its crew was being briefed on emergency procedures.

'Cannibals.' Holbrook shook his head in temporary disbelief. He'd slept very late, having been up late the night before, watching all manner of talking heads on C-SPAN discuss the confusing situation with Congress after this Ryan guy's speech. Not a bad speech, considering. He'd seen worse. All lies, of course, kind of like a TV show. Even the ones you liked, well, you just knew that they weren't real, funny though they might be in ways intended and not. Some talented man had written the speech, with the purpose of getting just the right points across. The skill of those people was impressive. The Mountain Men had worked for years to develop a speech they could use to get people mobilized to their point of view. Tried and tried, but they just couldn't ever get it right. It wasn't that their beliefs had anything wrong with them, of course. They all knew that. The problem was packaging, and only the government and its ally, Hollywood, could afford the right people to develop the ideas that twisted the minds of the poor dumb bastards who didn't really get it – that was the only possible conclusion.

But now there was discord in the enemy camp.

Ernie Brown, who'd driven over to wake his friend up, muted the TV. 'I guess there just isn't enough room for both of them in that there town, Pete.'

'You think one will be gone by sundown?' Holbrook asked.

'I wish.' The legal commentary they'd just watched on the CNN political hour had been as muddled as a nigger march on Washington to increase welfare. 'Well, uh, gee, the Constitution doesn't say what to do in a case like this. I suppose they *could* settle it with forty-fours on Pennsylvania Avenue at sundown,' Ernie added with a chuckle.

Pete turned his head and grinned. 'Wouldn't that be a sight?'

'Too American.' Brown might have added that Ryan *had* actually been in a position like that once, or so the papers and TV said. Well, yeah, it was true. Both vaguely remembered the thing in London, and truth be told, they'd both been proud to see an American showing the Europeans how a gun is used – foreigners didn't know dick about guns, did they? They were as bad as Hollywood. It was a shame Ryan had gone bad. What he'd said in his speech, that was why he'd entered the government – that's what they *all* said. At least with that Kealty puke, he could fall back on family and stuff. They were all crooks and thieves, and that's just how the guy was brought up, after all. At least he wasn't a hypocrite about it. A high-class gypsy or ... coyote? Yeah, that was right. Kealty was a lifetime political crook, and he was just being what he was. You couldn't blame a coyote for crooning at the moon; he was just being himself, too. Of course, coyotes were pests. Local ranchers could kill all they wanted ... Brown tilted his head. 'Pete?'

'Yeah, Ernie?' Holbrook reached for the TV controller and was about to unmute it.

'We got a constitutional crisis, right?'

It was Holbrook's turn to look. 'Yeah, that's what all the talking heads say.'

'And it just got worse, right?'

'The Kealty thing? Sure looks that way.' Pete set the controller down. Ernie was having another idea attack.

'What if, um . . .' Brown started and stopped, staring at the silent TV. It took time for his thoughts to form, Holbrook knew, though they were often worth waiting for.

The 707 landed, finally, at Tehran-Mehrabad International Airport, well after midnight. The crew were zombies, having flown almost continuously for the past thirty-six hours, well over the cautious limits of civil aviation, abused all the more by the nature of their cargo, and in so foul a mood from it all that angry words had been traded during the long descent. But the aircraft touched down with a heavy thump, and with that came relief and embarrassment, which each of the three felt as they took a collective sigh. The pilot shook his head and rubbed his face with a tired hand, taxiing south, steering between the blue lights. This airport is also the site of Iranian military and air force headquarters. The aircraft completed its turn, reversing directions and heading for the spacious air force ramp area – though its markings were civil, the 707 actually belonged to the Iranian air force. Trucks were waiting there, the flight crew was glad to see. The aircraft stopped. The engineer switched off the engines. The pilot set the parking brakes. The three men turned inward.

'A long day, my friends,' the pilot said by way of apology.

'God willing, a long sleep to follow it,' the engineer – he'd been the main target of his captain's temper – replied, accepting it. They were all too weary to sustain an argument in any case, and after a proper rest they wouldn't remember the reasons for it anyway.

They removed their oxygen masks, to be greeted by the thick fetid smell of their cargo, and it was everything they could do not to vomit as the cargo door was opened in the rear. They couldn't leave just yet. The aircraft was well and truly stuffed with cages, and short of climbing out the windows – which was too undignified – they'd have to await their freedom, rather like passengers at any international terminal.

Soldiers did the unloading, a process made all the more difficult by the fact that no one had warned their commander to issue gloves, as the Africans had done. Every cage had a wire handle at the top, but the African greens were every bit as testy as the men up front, clawing and scratching at the hands trying to lift them. Reactions differed among the soldiers. Some slapped at the cages, hoping to cow the monkeys into passivity. The smart ones removed their field jackets and used them as a buffer when they handled the cages. Soon a chain of men was established, and the cages were transferred, one at a time, to a series of trucks.

The procedure was noisy. It was barely fifty degrees in Tehran that night, far below what the monkeys were accustomed to, and that didn't help their collective mood any more than anything else that had happened to them over the past few days. They responded to the newest trauma with screeches and howls that echoed across the ramp. Even people who'd never heard monkeys before would not mistake it for anything else, but that could not be helped. Finally it was done. The cabin door opened, and the crew had a chance to look at what had become of their once-spotless aircraft. It would be weeks before they got the smell out, they were sure, and just scrubbing it down would be an onerous task best not considered at the moment. Together they walked aft, then down the stairs and off to where their cars were parked.

The monkeys headed north in what for them was their third or fourth – and last – journey by truck. It was a short one, up a divided highway, over a cloverleaf interchange built under the reign of the Shah, then west to Hasanabad. Here there was a farm, long since set aside for the same purpose which had occasioned the transport of the monkeys from Africa to Asia. The farm was state-owned, used as an experimental station to test new crops and fertilizers, and it had been hoped that the produce grown here would feed the new arrivals, but it was still winter and nothing was growing at the moment. Instead, several truckloads of dates from the southeastern region of the country had just arrived. The monkeys smelled them as their transport pulled up to the new three-story concrete building that would be their final home. It only agitated them all the more, since they'd had neither food nor water since leaving the continent of their birth, but at least it gave them the hope of a meal, and a tasty one at that, as a last meal is supposed to be.

The Gulfstream G-IV touched down at Benghazi exactly on its flight plan. It had actually been as pleasant a journey as was possible under the circumstances. Even the normally roiled air over the central Sahara had been calm, making for a smooth ride. Sister Jean Baptiste had remained unconscious for most of the flight, drifting into semi-awareness only a few times, and soon drifting back out again, actually more comfortable than the other four people aboard, whose protective garb prevented even a sip of water.

The doors never opened on the aircraft. Instead fuel trucks pulled up and their drivers dismounted to attach hoses to the caps in the long white wings. Dr Moudi was still tensely awake. Sister Maria Magdalena was dozing. She was as old as the patient, and had scarcely slept in days, devoted as she was to her colleague. It was too bad, Moudi thought, frowning as he looked out the window. It was unjust. He didn't have it in his heart to hate these people anymore. He'd felt that way once. He'd thought all Westerners were enemies of his country, but these two were not. Their home country was essentially neutral towards his. They were not the animistic pagans of Africa, ignorant and uncaring of the true God. They'd devoted their lives to service in His name, and both had surprised him by showing respect for his personal prayers and devotions. More than anything, he respected their belief that faith was a path to progress rather than acceptance of preordained destiny, an idea not totally congruent with his Islamic beliefs, but not exactly contrary to them either. Maria Magdalena had a rosary in her hands – disinfected – which she used to organize her prayers to Mary, mother of Jesus the prophet, venerated as thoroughly in the Koran as in her own abbreviated scriptures, and as fine a model for women to follow as any woman who had ever lived . . .

Moudi snapped his head away from them to look outside. He couldn't allow such thoughts. He had a task, and here were the instruments of that task, one's fate assigned by Allah, and the other's chosen by herself – and that was that. The task was without, not within, not one of his making, a fact made clear when the fuel trucks pulled away and the engines started up again. The flight crew was in a hurry, and so was he, the better to get the troublesome part of his mission behind, and the mechanical part begun. There was reason to rejoice. All those years among pagans, living in tropical heat, not a mosque within miles of his abode. Miserable, often tainted food, always wondering if it was clean or unclean, and never really being sure. That was behind him. What lay before was service to his God and his country.

Two aircraft, not one, taxied off to the main north-south runway, jostling as they did so on concrete slabs made uneven by the murderous desert heat of summer and the surprising cold of winter nights. The first of them was not Moudi's. That G-IV, outwardly identical in every way but a single digit's difference on the tail code, streaked down the runway and lifted off due north. His aircraft duplicated the takeoff roll, but as soon as the wheels were up, this G-IV turned right for a southeasterly heading toward Sudan, a lonely aircraft in a lonely desert night.

The first turned slightly west, and entered the normal international air corridor for the French coast. In due course, it would pass near the island of Malta, where a radar station existed to serve the needs of the airport at Valetta and also to perform traffic-control duties for the central Mediterranean. The crew of this aircraft were all air force types who customarily flew political and business luminaries from point to point, which was safe, well paid, and boring. Tonight would be different. The co-pilot had his eyes fixed jointly on his knee chart and the GPS navigation system. Two hundred miles short of Malta, at a cruising altitude of 39,000 feet, he took the nod from the pilot and flipped the radar transponder setting to 7711.

'Valetta Approach, Valetta Approach, this is November-Juliet-Alpha, Mayday, Mayday, Mayday.'

The controller at Valetta immediately noted the triple-bogie signature on his scope. It was a quiet watch at the traffic-control center, the normally sparse air traffic to monitor, and this night was as routine as any other – he keyed his microphone at once as his other hand waved for his supervisor.

'Juliet-Alpha, Valetta, are you declaring an emergency, sir?'

'Valetta, Juliet-Alpha, affirmative. We are medical evacuation flight inbound Paris from Zaire. We just lost number-two engine and we have electrical problems, stand by –'

'Juliet-Alpha, Valetta, standing by, sir.' The scope showed the aircraft's altitude as 390, then 380, then 370. 'Juliet-Alpha, Valetta, I show you losing altitude.'

The voice in his headphones changed. 'Mayday, Mayday, Mayday! Both engines out, both engines out. Attempting restart. This is Juliet-Alpha.'

'Your direct penetration course Valetta is three-four-three, say again, direct vector Valetta three-four-three. We are standing by, sir.'

A terse, clipped 'Roger' was all the controller got back. The altitude readout was 330 now.

'What's happening?' the supervisor asked.

'He says both engines out, he's dropping rapidly.' A computer screen showed the aircraft to be a Gulfstream, and the flight plan was confirmed.

'It glides well,' the supervisor offered optimistically; 310, they both saw. The G-IV didn't glide all that well, however.

'Juliet-Alpha, Valetta.'

Nothing.

'Juliet-Alpha, this is Valetta Approach.'

'What else is –' The supervisor checked the screen himself. No other aircraft in the area, and all one could do was watch anyway.

The better to simulate the in-flight emergency, the pilot throttled his engines back to idle. The tendency was to ham things up, but they wouldn't. In fact, they'd say nothing else at all. He pushed the yoke farther forward to increase his rate of descent, then turned to port as though angling towards Malta. That should make the tower people feel good, he thought, passing through 25,000 feet. It actually felt good. He'd been a fighter pilot for his country once, and missed the delightful feelings you got from yanking and banking an airplane around the sky. A descent of this speed would have his passengers white-faced and panicking. For the pilot it just felt like what flying was supposed to be.

*　　*　　*

'He must be very heavy,' the supervisor said.

'Cleared into Paris De Gaulle.' The controller shrugged and grimaced. 'Just topped off in Benghazi.'

'Bad fuel?' The answer was merely another shrug.

It was like watching death on television, all the more horrible that the alpha-numeric blip's altitude digits were clicking down like the symbols on a slot machine.

The supervisor lifted a phone. 'Call the Libyans. Ask if they can get a rescue aircraft up. We have an aircraft about to go down in the Gulf of Sidra.'

'Valetta Approach, this is USS *Radford*, do you copy, over.'

'*Radford*, Valetta.'

'We have your contact on radar. Looks like he's coming down hard.' The voice was that of a junior-grade lieutenant who had the CIC duty this night. *Radford* was an aging Spruance-class destroyer heading for Naples after an exercise with the Egyptian navy. Along the way she had orders to enter the Gulf of Sidra to proclaim freedom-of-navigation rights, an exercise which was almost as old as the ship herself. Once the source of considerable excitement, and two pitched air-sea battles in the 1980s, it was now boringly routine, else *Radford* wouldn't be going it alone. Boring enough that the CIC crewmen were monitoring civilian radio freqs to relieve their torpor. 'Contact is eight-zero miles west of us. We are tracking.'

'Can you respond to a rescue request?'

'Valetta, I just woke the captain up. Give us a few to get organized here, but we can make a try for it, over.'

'Dropping like a rock,' the petty officer on the main scope reported. 'Better pull out soon, fella.'

'Target is a Gulf-Four business jet. We show him one-six-thousand and descending rapidly,' Valetta advised.

'Thank you, that's about what we have. We are standing by.'

'What gives?' the captain asked, dressed in khaki pants and a T-shirt. The report didn't take long. 'Okay, get the rotor heads woke up.' Next the commander lifted a growler phone. 'Bridge, CIC, captain speaking. All ahead full, come right to new course –'

'Two-seven-five, sir,' the radar man advised. 'Target is two-seven-five and eighty-three miles.'

'New course two-seven-five.'

'Aye, sir. Coming right to two-seven-five, all ahead full, aye,' the officer of the deck acknowledged. On the bridge the quartermaster of the watch pushed down the direct engine-control handles, dumping additional fuel into the big GE jet-turbines. *Radford* shuddered a bit, then settled at the stern as she began to accelerate up from eighteen knots. The captain looked around the capacious combat information center. The crewmen were alert, a few shaking their heads to come fully awake. The radarmen were adjusting their instruments. On the main scope, the display changed, the better to lock in the descending aircraft.

'Let's go to general quarters,' the skipper said next. Might as well get some good training time out of this. In thirty seconds, everyone aboard was startled into consciousness and running to stations.

You have to be careful descending to the ocean surface at night. The pilot of the G-IV kept a close eye on his altitude and rate of descent. The lack of good visual references made it all too easy to slam into the surface, and while that might have made their evening's mission perfect, it wasn't supposed to be *that* perfect. In another few seconds they'd drop off the Valetta radar scope, and then they could start pulling out of the dive. The only thing that concerned him now was the possible presence of a ship down there, but no wakes were visible before him in the light of a quarter moon.

'I have it,' he announced when the aircraft dropped through five thousand feet. He eased back on the yoke. Valetta might note the change in descent rate from his transponder, if they were still getting a signal, but even if they did, they'd assume that after diving to get airflow into his engines, the better to achieve a restart, he was now trying to level out for a controlled landing on the calm sea.

'Losing him,' the controller said. The display on the screen blinked a few times, came back, then went dark.

The supervisor nodded and keyed his microphone. '*Radford*, this is Valetta. Juliet-Alpha has dropped off our screen.

Last altitude reading was six thousand and descending, course three-four-three.'

'Valetta, Roger, we still have him, now at four thousand, five hundred, rate of descent has slowed down some, course three-four-three,' the CIC officer replied. Just six feet away from him, the captain was talking with the commander of *Radford*'s air detachment. It would take more than twenty minutes to get the destroyer's single SH-60B Seahawk helicopter launched. The aircraft was now being pre-flighted prior to being pulled out onto the flight deck. The helicopter pilot turned to look at the radar display.

'Calm seas. If he has half a brain, somebody might just walk away from this. You try to splash down parallel to the ground swells and ride it out. Okay, we're on it, sir.' With that, he left the CIC and headed aft.

'Losing him under the horizon,' the radar man reported. 'Just passed through fifteen hundred. Looks like he's going in.'

'Tell Valetta,' the captain ordered.

The G-IV leveled out at five hundred feet by the radar altimeter. It was as low as the pilot cared to risk. With that done, he powered the engines back up to cruising power and turned left, south, back toward Libya. He was fully alert now. Flying low was demanding under the best circumstances, and far more so over water at night, but his orders were clear, though their purpose was not. It went rapidly in any case. At just over three hundred knots, he had forty minutes to the military airfield, at which he'd refuel one more time for a flight out of the area.

Radford went to flight quarters five minutes later, altering course slightly to put the wind over the deck from the proper direction. The Seahawk's tactical navigation system copied the needed data from the ship's CIC. It would search a circle of water fifteen miles in diameter in a procedure that would be tedious, time-consuming, and frantic. There were people in the water, and rendering assistance to those in need was the first and oldest law of the sea. As soon as the helicopter lifted off, the destroyer came back left and raced off with all four main engines turning full power, driving the ship at thirty-four knots. By this time the captain had radioed his situation to Naples, requesting additional assistance from any nearby fleet units – there were no American ships in the immediate vicinity, but an Italian frigate was heading south for their area, and even the Libyan air force asked for information.

The 'lost' G-IV landed just as the US Navy helicopter reached the search area. The crew left the aircraft for refreshments while their business jet was fueled. As they watched, a Russian-made AN-10 'Cub' four-engine transport fired up its engines to participate in the search-and-rescue mission. The Libyans were cooperating now with such things, trying to rejoin the world community, and even their commanders didn't know very much – indeed, hardly anything at all – of what had gone on. Just a few phone calls had made the arrangements, and whoever had taken the call and cooperated knew only that two aircraft would be landing to fuel and move on. An hour later, they lifted off again for the three-hour flight to Damascus, Syria. It had been originally thought that they would fly right back to their home base in Switzerland, but the pilot had pointed out that two aircraft of the same ownership flying over the same spot at nearly the same time would cause questions. He turned the aircraft east during the climb-out.

Below to his left, in the Gulf of Sidra, they saw the flashing lights of aircraft, one of them a helicopter, they were surprised to note. People were burning fuel and spending time and all for nothing. That thought amused the pilot as he reached his cruising altitude and relaxed, letting the autopilot do the work for the remainder of a long day's flying.

'Are we there yet?'

Moudi turned his head. He'd just changed the IV bottle for their patient. Inside his plastic helmet his face itched from his growing beard. He saw that Sister Maria Magdalena had the same crawly, unwashed feeling he had. Her first action on waking was to move her hands to her face, stopped short by the clear plastic.

'No, Sister, but soon. Please, rest yourself. I can do this.'

'No, no, you must be very tired, Dr Moudi.' She started to rise.

'I am younger and better rested,' the physician replied with a raised hand. Next he replaced the morphine bottle with a fresh one. Jean Baptiste was, thankfully, still too heavily drugged to be a problem.

'What time is it?'

'Time for you to rest. You will attend your friend when we arrive, but then other doctors will be able to relieve me. Please, conserve your strength. You will need it.' Which was true enough.

The nun didn't reply. Accustomed to following the orders of doctors, she turned her head, probably whispered a prayer, and allowed her eyes to close. When he was sure that she was back asleep, he moved forward.

'How much longer?'

'Forty minutes. We'll land a little early. The winds have been good to us,' the co-pilot answered.

'So, before dawn?'

'Yes.'

'What is her problem?' the pilot asked, not turning, but sufficiently bored that he wanted to hear something new.

'You do not wish to know,' Moudi assured him.

'She will die, this woman?'

'Yes, and the aircraft must be completely disinfected before it is used again.'

'That's what they told us.' The pilot shrugged, not knowing how frightened he should be of what he was carrying. Moudi did. The plastic sheet under his patient would now contain a pool of infected blood. They'd have to be extremely careful unloading her.

Badrayn was grateful that he'd avoided alcohol. He was the most conscious man in the room. Ten hours, he thought, looking at his watch. Ten hours they'd talked and disputed like a bunch of old women in a market.

'He will agree to this?' the Guards commander asked.

'It is not unreasonable in the least,' Ali replied. Five senior mullahs would fly to Baghdad, offering themselves as hostage to – if not the goodwill, then the good word of their leader. It actually worked out better than the assembled generals knew, not that they really cared. With that settled, the general officers looked at one another, and one by one they nodded.

'We accept,' the same general said, speaking for the group. That hundreds of lesser officers would be left behind to face whatever music was in store for them was, after all, a small thing. The lengthy discussion hadn't touched on that subject very much.

'I require a telephone,' Badrayn told them next. The intelligence chief led him to a side room. There had always been a direct line to Tehran. Even during hostilities there had been a communications link – that one via microwave tower. The next one was a fiber-optic cable whose transmissions could not be intercepted. Under the watchful eyes of the Iraqi officer he punched the numbers he'd memorized several days earlier.

'This is Yousif. I have news,' he told the voice which answered.

'Please wait,' was the reply.

Daryaei didn't enjoy being awakened early any more than a normal person, the less so that he'd slept poorly over the last few days. When his bedside phone rang, he blinked his eyes for several rings before reaching to lift it.

'Yes?'

'This is Yousif. It is agreed. Five friends are required.'

All praise to Allah, for He is beneficent, Daryaei thought to himself. All the years of war and peace had come to fruition in this moment. No, no, that was premature. There was much yet to be done. But the most difficult thing *was* done now.

'When shall we begin?'

'As quickly as possible.'

'Thank you. I will not forget.' With that he came fully awake. This morning, the first in many years, he forgot his morning prayers. God would understand that His work must be done quickly.

How weary she must have been, Moudi thought. Both nuns started to wakefulness when the aircraft touched down. There came the usual jolting as the aircraft slowed, and a watery sound announced the fact that Jean Baptiste had indeed bled out as he'd expected. So, he'd gotten her here alive at least. Her eyes were open, though confused as an infant's as she stared at the curving ceiling of the cabin. Maria Magdalena took a moment to look out the windows, but all she saw was an airport, and those appeared the same all over the world, particularly at night. In due course the aircraft stopped, and the door dropped open.

Again they would travel in a truck. Four people came into the aircraft, all of them dressed in protective plastic. Moudi loosened the straps on his patient, waving the other nun to stay in place. Carefully, the four army medics lifted the sturdy plastic sheet by the corners and moved towards the door. As they did so, Moudi saw something drip onto the flat-folded seat which had served their patient as a bed. He shook it off. The flight crew had their orders, and the orders had been repeated often enough. When the patient was safely on the truck, Moudi and Maria Magdalena walked down the steps as well. Both removed their headgear, allowing themselves to breathe fresh, cool air. He took a canteen from one of the armed party around the aircraft and offered it to her, as he fetched another for himself. Both drained a full liter of water before entering the truck. Both were disoriented by the long flight, she the more so for not knowing where she really was. Moudi saw the 707 which had arrived shortly before with the monkeys, though he didn't know that was the cargo.

'I've never seen Paris – well, except flying through, all these years,' she said, looking around before the back flap was dropped, cutting off the view.

A pity you never will.

16

THE IRAQI TRANSFER

'A whole lot of nothing here,' the pilot observed. The Sea-hawk was circling at a thousand feet, scanning the surface with a search radar acute enough to detect wreckage – it was designed to spot a submarine's periscope – but finding not so much as a floating bottle of Perrier. Both also wore low-light goggles, and they should have turned up a slick of jet fuel from the oily shine, but that also was negative.

'Must have hit pretty hard not to leave anything,' the co-pilot replied over the intercom.

'Unless we're looking in the wrong spot.' The pilot looked down at his tactical navigation system. They were in the right place. They were down to an hour's fuel. Time to start thinking about landing back on *Radford*, which was now combing the search area herself. The searchlights looked theatrical in the pre-dawn darkness, like something out of a World War II movie. A Libyan Cub was circling around, too, trying to be helpful but mainly being a pain in the ass.

'Anything at all?' the controller on *Radford* asked.

'Negative. Nothing, say again nothing, down there that we can see. One hour's worth of gas here, over.'

'Copy one hour gas,' *Radford* acknowledged.

'Sir, the target's last course was three-four-three, speed two-nine-zero knots, rate of descent three thousand foot per minute. If he ain't in this footprint, I don't know why,' a chief operations specialist said, tapping the chart. The captain sipped at his coffee and shrugged. Topside, the fire-and-rescue party was standing by. Two swimmers were in wetsuits, with a boat crew standing by the launch. There was a lookout posted for every set of binoculars aboard, look-ing for strobe lights or anything else, and sonar was listening for the high-frequency ping of the aircraft's emergency loca-tor. Those instruments were designed to survive a severe impact, were automatically activated when exposed to seawater, and had battery power to operate for several days. *Radford*'s sonar was sensitive enough to detect the damned thing from thirty miles away, and they were right over the impact zone predicted by the radar crew. Neither the ship nor her crew had ever done a rescue like this, but it was something for which they regularly drilled, and every procedure had been executed as perfectly as the CO could wish.

'USS *Radford*, USS *Radford*, this is Valetta Approach, over.'

The captain lifted the microphone. 'Valetta, this is *Radford*.'

'Have you located anything, over?'

'Negative, Valetta. Our helo's been all over the area, nothing to report yet.' They'd already queried Malta for corrected data on the aircraft's last speed and heading, but it had dropped off the civilian radar even before departing the destroyer's more precise coverage. On both ends of the radio link, men sighed. They all knew how this would play out now. The search would continue for a day, no more, no less, and nothing would be found, and that was that. A telex had already gone to the manufacturer, informing them that one of their aircraft was lost at sea. Gulfstream representatives would fly to Bern to go over maintenance records and other printed data on the aircraft, hoping to garner a clue, and probably finding nothing, and this whole case would go into the 'unknown' column in somebody's ledger book. But the game had to be played out, and, hell, it was still good training time for the crew of USS *Radford*. The crew would shrug it off. It wasn't anyone they knew, however desirable and uplifting a successful rescue would have been.

It was probably the smell that told her what was wrong. The drive from the airport had been brief. It was dark outside still, and when the truck stopped, both doctor and nurse were still suffering from the lengthy time in movement. They arrived, and the first business was to get Sister Jean Baptiste inside. Only then did both of them remove their plastic garb for the last time. Maria Magdalena smoothed her short hair and breathed heavily, finally taking the time to look around, then was surprised at what she saw. Moudi saw the confusion, and led her inside before she could comment on it.

That was when the smell hit them, a familiar African smell from the entry of the monkeys a few hours earlier, decidedly not something one would associate with Paris or a place as clean and orderly as the Pasteur Institute had to be. Next, Maria Magdalena looked around and realized that the signs on the walls were not in French. There was no way she could know what the situation was, there were merely grounds for confusion, to be followed by questions – and then, just as well, it was time, before the questions could be asked. A soldier appeared and took her arm and led her away, too uncomprehending still to say anything. She merely looked over her shoulder at an unshaven man in surgical greens, a sad look on his face giving greater substance to her confusion.

'What is this? Who is she?' the director of the project asked.

'It is a rule of their religion that they cannot travel alone. To protect their chastity,' Moudi explained. 'Otherwise I could not have come here with our patient.'

'She is still alive?' He hadn't been there for the arrival.

Moudi nodded. 'Yes, we should be able to keep her going another three days, maybe four,' he thought.

'And the other?'

Moudi dodged: 'That is not for me to say.'

'We could always have another –'

'No! That would be barbaric,' Moudi protested. 'Such things are hateful to God.'

'And what we plan to do is not?' the director asked. Clearly Moudi had been in the bush for too long. But it wasn't worth fighting over. One fully infected Ebola patient was all they needed. 'Get cleaned up and we will go up to see her.'

Moudi headed off to the doctors' lounge on the second floor. The facility was actually more private than its Western counterparts, as people in this part of the world had higher standards of body modesty. The plastic suit, he saw with some surprise, had survived the trip without a single tear. He dumped it in a large plastic bin before heading into a shower whose hot water was supplemented with chemicals – he hardly noticed the smell anymore – and there he enjoyed five minutes of sanitary bliss. On the flight he'd wondered if he would ever be clean again. In the shower now, his mind asked a similar question, but more quietly. He emerged to don fresh greens – fresh everything, in fact – and to complete his normally fastidious routine. A medical orderly had placed a brand-new suit in the lounge for him, this one a blue American Racal fresh out of its box, which he put on before heading out into the corridor. The director, similarly dressed, was waiting for him, and together they walked down toward the suite of treatment rooms.

There were only four of them, behind sealed, guarded doors. The Iranian army ran this facility. The doctors were military physicians, and the orderlies all men with battlefield experience. Security was tight, as one would expect. Moudi and the director had cleared security on the first floor, however, and the guard at the post touched the buttons to open the doors into the air lock. These opened with a hiss of hydraulics to reveal a second set, and they could see that smoke from the soldier's cigarette was sucked into the secure area. Good. The air system was working properly. Both men had a strange prejudice against their own countrymen. It would have been preferable for this entire facility to have been built by foreign engineers – Germans were popular in the Middle East for such things – but Iraq had made that mistake to its sorrow. The orderly Germans kept plans of everything they built, as a result of which so many of their projects had been bombed to dust. And so while a lot of the building's hardware had been bought elsewhere, the facility had been constructed locally. Their very lives depended on the exact performance of every subsystem here, but that could not be helped now. The inner doors would not open unless the outer ones were locked tight. That worked. The director activated them, and they proceeded.

Sister Jean Baptiste was in the last room on the right. Three medical orderlies were in with her. They'd already cut off all her clothing, revealing a death in progress. The soldiers were repulsed by what they saw, her condition more terrible than any battlefield injury. Quickly, they cleaned off her body, then covered it, respectful of the woman's modesty as their culture insisted. The director looked at the morphine drip and immediately turned it back by a third.

'We want to keep her alive as long as possible,' he explained.

'The pain from this –'

314

'Cannot be helped,' he responded coldly. He thought to reproach Moudi, but stopped himself. He was a physician, too, and knew that it was hard to regard one's patient with harshness. Elderly Caucasian female, he saw, stuporous from the morphine, respiration too slow for his liking. The orderlies attached leads for the electrocardiograph, and he was surprised at how well her heart was working. Good. Blood pressure was low, as expected, and he ordered two units of whole blood to be hung on the IV tree. The more blood the better.

The orderlies were well drilled. Everything that had come in with the patient had already been bagged, then double-bagged. One of their number carried the bundle out of the room and off to the gas-fired incinerator which would leave behind nothing but sterilized ashes. The main issue here was management of the virus. The patient was their culture dish. Previously, such victims had had a few cc's of blood drawn for analysis, and the patient in due course would die, and the body was either burned or sprayed and buried in chemically treated ground. Not this time. He would have in his control, in due course, the largest quantity of the virus ever seen, and from that he would grow more, all virulent, all powerful. He turned.

'So, Moudi, how did she contract it?'

'She was treating the Index Patient.'

'The Negro boy?' the director asked, standing in the corner. Moudi nodded. 'Yes.'

'What did she do wrong?'

'We never found out. I asked her when she was still lucid. She never gave the boy an injection, and Sister was always very careful with "sharps." She's an experienced nurse,' Moudi reported mechanically. He really was too tired to do much of anything but report what he knew, and that, the director thought, was just fine. 'She worked with Ebola before, at Kikwit and other places. She taught procedures to staff.'

'Aerosol transmission?' the director asked. It was too much to hope for.

'CDC believes that this is the Ebola Mayinga sub-type. You will recall that this strain is named for a nurse who contracted the disease through unknown means.'

That statement made the director look hard into Moudi's eyes. 'You're quite sure of what you said?'

'I'm not sure of anything at the moment, but I also interviewed staff at the hospital, and all injections were given to the Index Patient by others, not Sister here. So, yes, this may be a case of aerosol transmission.'

It was a classic case of good news and bad news. So little was known of Ebola Zaire. It *was* known that the disease could be passed on by blood and other bodily fluids, even by sexual contact – that was almost entirely theoretical, since an Ebola victim was hardly in a position to engage in such practices. It was further believed that the virus fared poorly out of a living host, quick to die in the open. For that reason it was not believed that the disease could be spread through the air in the manner of pneumonia or other common ailments. But at the same time every outbreak of the virus produced cases which could not be explained. The unfortunate nurse Mayinga had given her name to a strain of the disease which had reached out to claim her life through an unknown means. Had she lied about something, or forgotten something, or had she searched her mind and reported the truth, and thus memorialized a sub-type of Ebola which *did* survive in the air long enough to be transmitted as readily as the common cold? If so, that would make the patient before them the carrier of a biological weapon of such power as to make the entire world shake.

Such a possibility also meant that they were quite literally dicing with Death himself. The smallest mistake could be lethal. Without conscious thought, the director looked upward at the air-conditioning vent. The building had been designed with that very contingency in mind. The incoming air was all clean, sucked in through a vent located at the end of two hundred meters of piping. The air exiting from the 'hot' areas passed through a single plenum chamber before leaving the building. There it was subjected to blazingly powerful ultraviolet lights, since that frequency of radiation destroyed viruses with total reliability. The air filters were soaked with chemicals – phenol was one of them – to achieve the same end. Only then was it ejected to the outside, where other environmental factors also could be depended upon to deny the disease a chance to survive. The filters – three separate banks of them – were changed with religious precision every twelve hours. The UV lights, five times the number required for the task, were constantly monitored. The Hot Lab was kept at intentionally low ambient air pressure to prevent a leak, and that fact enabled the building to be evaluated for structural integrity. For the rest, he thought, well, that was why they'd all trained so carefully in suit-safety and sharps procedures.

The director, too, was a physician, trained in Paris and London, but it had been years since he'd treated a human patient. Mainly he'd devoted the last decade to molecular biology, most particularly to the study of viruses. He knew as much as any man about them, though that was little enough. He knew how to make them grow, for example, and before him now was a perfect medium, a human being converted by fate into a factory for the deadliest organism known to man. He'd never known her healthy, had never spoken with her, never seen her at work. That was good. Perhaps she had been an effective nurse, as Moudi said, but that was all in the past, and there was little point in getting overly attached to someone who would be dead in three days, four at the most. The longer the better, though, for the factory to do its work, using this human body for its raw material as it turned out its product, turning Allah's finest creation into His most deadly curse.

For the other question, he'd given the order while Moudi had been showering. Sister Maria Magdalena was taken to another cleanup area, issued clothing, and left to herself. There she had showered in privacy, wondering as she did so what was going on – where was she? She was still too confused to be truly afraid, too disoriented to understand. Like Moudi, she showered long, and the procedure did clear her head somewhat, as she tried to form the right questions to pose. She'd find the doctor in a few minutes to ask what was happening. Yes, that's what she would do, Maria Magdalena thought as she dressed. There was a comfortable familiarity to the medical garb, and she still had her rosary, taken into the shower with her. It was a metal one rather than the formal rosary that went along with her religious habit, the same one given to her when she'd taken her final vows more than forty years before. But the metal one was more easily disinfected, and she'd taken the time in the shower to clean it. Outside, dressed, she decided that prayer would be the best preparation for her quest for information, and so she knelt, blessed herself, and began her prayers. She didn't hear the door open behind her.

The soldier from the security force had his orders. He could have done it a few minutes earlier, but to invade a woman's privacy while nude and bathing would have been a hateful act, and she wasn't going anywhere. It pleased him to see that she was praying, her back to him, plainly comfortable and well practiced with her devotions. This was proper. A condemned criminal was invariably given the chance to speak to Allah; to deny that chance was a grave sin. So much the better, he thought, raising his 9mm automatic. She was speaking to her God now . . .

. . . and now she was doing so more directly. He decocked the hammer, holstered his weapon, and called for the two orderlies outside to clean up the mess. He'd killed people before, had participated in firing parties for enemies of the state, and that was duty, sometimes distasteful, but duty nonetheless. This one made him shake his head. This time, he was sure, he'd sent a soul to Allah. How strange to feel good about an execution.

Tony Bretano had flown in on a TRW-owned business jet. It turned out that he hadn't yet decided to accept the offer from the Lockheed-Martin board, and it was pleasing to Ryan that George Winston's information was incorrect. It showed that he wasn't privy to this particular piece of insider information, at least.

'I've said "no" before, Mr President.'

'Twice.' Ryan nodded. 'To head ARPA and to be Deputy Secretary for Technology. Your name came up for NRO also, but they never called you about it.'

'So I heard,' Bretano acknowledged. He was a short man, evidently with short-man complex, judging by his combativeness. He spoke with the accent of someone from Manhattan's Little Italy, despite many years on the West Coast, and that also told Ryan something. He liked to proclaim who and what he was, this despite a pair of degrees from MIT, where he might as easily have adopted a Cambridge accent.

'And you turned the jobs down because it's a great big clusterfuck over there across the river, right?'

'Too much tail and not enough teeth. If I ran my business that way, the stockholders would lynch me. The Defense bureaucracy –'

'So fix it for me,' Jack suggested.

'Can't be done.'

'Don't give me that, Bretano. Anything man can make, he can unmake. If you don't think you have the stuff to get the job done, fine, tell me that, and you can head back to the coast.'

'Wait a minute –'

Ryan cut him off again.

'No, you wait a minute. You saw what I said on TV, and I'm not going to repeat it. I need to clean up a few things, and I need the right people to do it, and if you don't have it, fine, I'll find somebody tough enough to –'

'Tough?' Bretano nearly came off his seat. '*Tough*? I got news for you, *Mister* President, my papa sold fruit from a cart on the corner. The world didn't give me shit!' Then he stopped short when Ryan laughed, and thought a moment before going on. 'Not bad,' he said more sedately, in the manner of the corporate chairman he was.

'George Winston says you're feisty. We haven't had a halfway decent SecDef in ten years. Good. When I'm wrong, I need people to tell me so. But I don't think I'm wrong about you.'

'What do you want done?'

'When I pick up the phone, I want things to happen. I want to know that if I have to send kids into harm's way, they're properly equipped, properly trained, and properly supported. I want people to be afraid of what we can do. It makes life a lot easier for the State Department,' the President explained. 'When I was a little kid in east Baltimore and I saw a cop walking up Monument Street, I knew two things. I knew it wasn't a good idea to mess with him, and I also knew I could trust him to help me if I needed it.'

'In other words, you want a product that we can deliver whenever we have to.'

'Correct.'

'We've drawn down a long way,' Bretano said warily.

'I want you to work with a good team – you pick it – to draw up a force structure that meets our needs. Then I want you to rebuild the Pentagon to deliver it.'

'How much time do I have?'

'I'll give you two weeks on the first part.'

'Not long enough.'

'Don't give me that. We study things so much I'm surprised the paper all those things are printed on hasn't consumed every tree in the country. Hell, *I* know what the threats are out there, remember? That used to be *my* business. A month ago we were in a shooting war, sucking air because we were out of assets to use. We got lucky. I don't want to depend on luck anymore. I want you to clear out the bureaucracy, so if we need to do something it gets done. In fact, I want things done before we have to do them. If we do the job right, nobody'll be crazy enough to take us on. Question is, are you willing to take it on, Dr Bretano?'

'It'll be bloody.'

'My wife's a doc,' Jack told him.

'Half the job's getting good intelligence,' Bretano pointed out.

'I know that, too. We've already started on CIA. George ought to be okay at Treasury. I'm checking out a list of judges to head Justice. I said it all on TV. I'm putting a team together. I want you on it. I made my way on my own, too. You think two people like us would have got this far anywhere else? Payback time, Bretano.' Ryan leaned back, pleased with himself for the delivery.

There was no fighting it, the executive knew. 'When do I start?'

Ryan checked his watch. 'Tomorrow morning suit you?'

The maintenance crew showed up just after dawn. The aircraft had a military guard arrayed around it to keep the curious away, though this airport was already more secure than most of its international counterparts because of the Iranian air force presence. The crew foreman's clipboard told him what had to be done, and the long list of procedures had him curious, but little else. Aircraft of this type always got special treatment, because the people who flew in them deemed themselves the elect of God, or something even higher still. Not that it mattered. He had his procedures, and the advice for extra caution was hardly necessary. His people were always thorough. The aircraft maintenance sheet said that it was time to replace two cockpit instruments, and two replacements were ready, still in the manufacturer's boxes; those would have to be calibrated after installation. Two other members of his crew would refuel the aircraft and change the engine oil. The rest would work on the cabin under the foreman's supervision.

They'd scarcely begun when a captain showed up with fresh orders, predictably ones which contradicted the first set. The seats had to be replaced quickly. The G-IV would be taking off in a few hours for another flight. The officer didn't say where to, and the foreman didn't care to ask. He told his instrument mechanic to hurry with his assigned task. That was fairly easy in the G-IV with its modular instrument arrangement. A truck appeared with the seats that had been taken out two days earlier, and the cleanup crewmen assisted, manhandling them into place before they could properly begin. The foreman wondered why they'd been removed in the first place, but it wasn't his place to ask, and the answer would not have made much sense anyway. A pity everyone was in a hurry. It would have been easier to do the cleaning with so much open space. Instead, the fourteen-seat configuration was quickly reestablished, making the aircraft back into a mini-airliner, albeit a very comfortable one. The replacement seating had been dry-cleaned in the hangar as it always was, the ashtrays emptied and swabbed out. The caterer showed up next with food for the galley, and soon the aircraft was overcrowded with workers, each getting in the other's way, and in the resulting confusion, work was not done properly, but that was not the foreman's fault. Things just accelerated from there. The new flight crew showed up with their charts and flight plans. They found a mechanic lying half on the pilot's seat and half on the cabin floor, finishing his work on the digital engine instruments. Never patient with mechanics, the pilot merely stood and glared as the man did his work – for his part, the mechanic didn't care at all what pilots thought. He attached the last connector, wriggled his way free, and ran a test program to make sure it was working properly, without so much as a look at the aviators who would be sure to curse him all the louder if he failed to install the electronics properly. He'd not yet left the area when the co-pilot took his place and ran the same test program again. Leaving the aircraft to get out of the way, the mechanic saw the reason for the rush.

Five of them, standing there on the ramp, looking impatient and important as they stared at the white-painted executive jet, excited about something. The mechanic and everyone else on the crew knew them all by name, they appeared so often on TV. All of them nodded deference to the mullahs and speeded their efforts, as a result of which not everything got done. The cleanup crew was called off the aircraft, and limited their efforts to wiping a few surfaces down after getting all the seats reinstalled. The VIP passengers boarded at once, heading to the after portion of the cabin so that they could confer. The flight crew started up, and the Guards force and the trucks hardly had a chance to withdraw before the G-IV taxied off to the end of the runway.

In Damascus, the second member of that small executive fleet touched down, to discover that it had orders to return to Tehran at once. The crew swore, but did as they were told, limiting their time on the ground to a scant forty minutes before lifting off again in their turn for the short hop into Iran.

It was a busy time at PALM BOWL. Something was going on. You could tell that by what wasn't going on. Traffic on the encrypted channels used by senior Iraqi generals had peaked and zeroed, then peaked again, and zeroed again. At the moment it was back at zero. Back at KKMC in Saudi Arabia, the computers were grinding through solutions to the chip-controlled scrambling systems used on Iraqi tactical radios. It took time in every case. Encryption technology, once the province only of affluent countries, had, with the advent of personal computers, become readily available to the humblest citizen in America and other technically advanced countries, and an unexpected spin-off of that fact was the current availability of highly advanced communications-security apparatus to the humblest nations. Now Malaysia had codes nearly as hard to break as Russia's – and so did Iraq, courtesy of Americans who worried about having the FBI read their fictitious e-mail adulteries. The encryption systems on tactical radios were necessarily somewhat simpler, and still breakable, but even that required a Cray computer that had been flown to the Saudi Kingdom years earlier. Another factor was that PALM BOWL was in Kuwait, and had indeed been fully financed by the local government, for which courtesy a return courtesy was required. They got to see the 'take' from the NSA station. That was only fair, but the NSA and military-intelligence personnel hadn't been trained to consider what 'fair' was. They had their orders, even so.

'They're talking about their families?' a USAF sergeant asked himself aloud. That was new. PALM BOWL had tapped into intimate information on this network before, and learned more than a few things about the personal habits of senior Iraqi generals, along with some crude jokes which alternately did and did not translate well into English, but this was a first.

'Evac,' the Chief Master Sergeant next to him observed. 'It's a bug-out. Lieutenant!' he called. 'Something happening here.'

The junior watch officer was working on something else. The radar at Kuwait International Airport was an unusually powerful one, installed since the war, and it operated in two modes, one for the aircraft controllers, and another for the Kuwaiti air force. It could see a good, long way. For the second time in as many days, there was a business jet heading toward Baghdad from Iran. The flight path was identical with the previous trip, and the transponder code was the same. The distance between the two capitals was a mere four hundred miles, just enough distance to make it worthwhile for a business jet to climb up to cruising altitude and so make efficient use of its fuel – and, by the way, touch the fringe of their radar coverage. There would be a circling E-3B AWACS around, too, but that reported directly to KKMC and not to PALM BOWL. It was a matter of professional pride for the uniformed spooks at the ground station to beat the airborne people at their own game, all the more so since most of them were themselves USAF personnel. The lieutenant made a mental note of that information, then walked across the room to where the sergeants were.

'What is it, Chief?' she asked.

The chief master sergeant scrolled his computer screen, showing the translated content of several 'cracked' conversations, tapping his finger on the screen to call attention to the times. 'We have some folks getting the hell outa Dodge City, ma'am.' A moment later, a Kuwaiti major slid alongside. Ismael Sabah was distantly related to the royal family, Dartmouth-educated, and rather liked by the American personnel. During the war he'd stayed behind and worked with a resistance group – one of the smart ones. He'd laid low, gathered information on the movement and disposition of Iraqi military units, and gotten it out, mainly using cellular phones which were able to reach into a Saudi civilian network just across the border, and which the Iraqis had been unable to track. Along the way, he'd lost three close family members to the Iraqi terror. He'd learned all manner of lessons from the experience, the least of which was a hatred for the country to his north. A quiet, insightful man in his middle thirties now, he seemed to get smarter every day. Sabah leaned in to scan the translations on the computer screen.

'How do you say, the rats are leaving the ship?'

'You think so, too, sir?' the chief asked, before his lieutenant could.

'To *Iran*?' the American officer asked. 'I know it looks that way, but it doesn't make sense, does it?'

Major Sabah grimaced. 'Sending their air force to Iran didn't make sense either, but the Iranians kept the fighter planes and let the pilots go home. You need to learn more of the local culture, Lieutenant.'

I've learned that nothing here makes much sense, she couldn't say.

'What else do we have?' Sabah asked the sergeant.

'They talk and go quiet and then they talk some more and go quiet. There's traffic under way now, but KKMC is still trying to crack it.'

'Radar surveillance reports an inbound from Mehrabad to Baghdad, coded as a business jet.'

'Oh? Same one as before?' Sabah asked the American lieutenant.

'Yes, Major.'

'What else? Anything?' The chief master sergeant handled the answer.

'Major, that's probably what the computers are cooking on right now. Maybe in thirty minutes.'

Sabah lit a cigarette. PALM BOWL was technically a Kuwaiti-owned facility, and smoking was permitted, to the relief of some and the outrage of others. His relatively junior rank did not prevent him from being a fairly senior member of his country's intelligence service, all the more so that he was modest and businesslike in manner, a useful contrast with his war record, on which he'd lectured in Britain and America.

'Opinions?' he asked, already having formed his own.

'You said it, sir. They're bugging out,' the chief master sergeant replied.

Major Sabah completed the thought. 'In hours or days, Iraq will not have a government, and Iran is assisting in the transition to anarchy.'

'Not good,' the chief breathed.

'The word "catastrophe" comes to mind,' Sabah observed mildly. He shook his head and smiled in a grim sort of way, earning additional admiration from the American spooks.

The Gulfstream landed in calm air after the sixty-five-minute flight in from Tehran, timed by Badrayn's watch. As punctual as Swissair, he noted. Well, that was to be expected. As soon as it stopped, the door dropped open and the five passengers deplaned, to be met with elaborately false courtesy, which they returned in kind. A small convoy of Mercedes sedans spirited them off at once to regal accommodations awaiting them in the city center, where they would, of course, be murdered if things went poorly. Scarcely had their cars pulled off when two generals, their wives, their children, and one bodyguard each emerged from the VIP terminal and walked to the aircraft. They quickly boarded the G-IV. The co-pilot lifted the door back into place, and the engines started up, all in less than ten additional minutes by Badrayn's Seiko. Just that fast, it taxied off to make the return flight to

Mehrabad International. It was something too obvious for the tower personnel to miss. That was the problem with security, Badrayn knew. You really couldn't keep some things secret, at least not something like this. Better to use a commercial flight, and treat the departing generals as normal passengers on a normal trip, but there were no regular flights between the two countries, and the generals would not have submitted themselves to such plebeian treatment in any case. And so the tower people would know that a special flight had come in and out under unusual circumstances, and so would the terminal employees who'd been required to fawn on the generals and their retinues. For one such flight, that might not be important. But it would matter for the next.

Perhaps that was not overly important in the Great Scheme of Things. There was now no stopping the events he had helped to set in motion, but it offended Ali Badrayn in a professional sense. Better to keep everything he did secret. He shrugged as he walked back to the VIP terminal. No, it didn't matter, and through his actions he'd won the gratitude of a very powerful man in charge of a very powerful country, and for doing no more than talking, telling people what they already knew, and helping them to make a decision which could not have been avoided, whatever their efforts to the contrary. How curious life was.

'Same one. Jeez, he wasn't on the ground very long.' Through a little effort, the radio traffic for that particular aircraft was isolated and playing in the ear-phones of an Army spec-6 language expert. Though the language of international aviation was English, this aircraft was speaking in Farsi. Probably thought a security measure, it merely highlighted that aircraft, tracked by radar and radio-direction finders. The voice traffic was wholly ordinary except for that, and for the fact that the aircraft hadn't even been on the ground long enough to refuel. That meant the whole thing was pre-planned, which was hardly a surprise under the circumstances, but enlightening even so. Aloft, over the far northwest end of the Persian Gulf, an AWACS was now tracking the aircraft as well. Interest, cued by PALM BOWL, had perked up enough to move the E-3B off its normal patrol station, now escorted by four Saudi F-15 Eagle fighters. Iranian and Iraqi electronic-intelligence troops would take note of this and know that someone was interested in what was going on – and wonder why, because *they* didn't know. The game was ever a fascinating one, neither side knowing all it wished, and assuming the other side – at the moment there were actually *three* sides in the game – knew too much, when in fact none of the three knew much of anything.

Aboard the G-IV, the language was Arabic. The two generals chatted quietly and nervously in the rear, their conversation masked by engine sounds. Their wives just sat, more nervous still, while the various children read books or napped. It was hardest on the bodyguards, who knew that if anything went wrong in Iran they could do nothing but die uselessly. One of these sat in the middle of the cabin and found that his seat was wet, with what he didn't know, but it was sticky and . . . red? Tomato juice or something, probably. Annoyed, he went to the lavatory and washed his hands off, taking a towel back to wipe the seat off. He returned the towel to the lav before he reseated himself, then looked down at the mountains and wondered if he'd live to see another sunrise, not knowing that he'd just limited the number to twenty.

'Here we go,' the chief master sergeant said. 'That was the vice-chief of their air force, and the commanding general of Second Iraqi Army Corps – *plus* families,' he added. The decryption had required just over two hours from the time the scrambled signal had been copied down.

'Expendables?' the USAF lieutenant asked. She was learning, the other spooks thought.

'Relatively so,' Major Sabah agreed with a nod. 'We need to look for another aircraft lifting off from Mehrabad soon after this one lands.'

'Where to, sir?'

'Ah. Lieutenant, that is the question, is it not?'

'Sudan,' the chief thought. He'd been in-country for two years, and it was his second tour at PALM BOWL.

'I would not wager against you on that, Sergeant,' Sabah observed with a wink. 'We should confirm that through the time cycle of the flights out of Baghdad.' And he really couldn't make a judgment call on the entire exercise until then, though he already had flagged his own superiors that something unusual was afoot. Soon it would be time for the Americans to do the same.

Twenty minutes later, a preliminary report was on its way from KKMC to Fort Meade, Maryland, where the vagaries of time landed it in the watch center just after midnight. From the National Security Agency it was cross-decked by fiber-optic cable to Langley, Virginia, into Mercury, the CIA's communications-watch facility, then upstairs to the CIA's Operations Center, room 7-F-27 in the old headquarters building. At every stop, the information was handed over raw, sometimes with the local assessment, but more often without, or if it were, placed at the bottom so that the national intelligence officers in charge of the various watches could make their own assessments, and duplicate the work of others. Mostly this made sense, but in fast-breaking situations it very often did not. The problem was that one couldn't tell the difference in a crisis.

The national intelligence officer in charge of the watch at CIA was Ben Goodley, a fast-riser in the Directorate of Intelligence, recently awarded his NIO card, along with the worst duty schedule because of his lack of seniority. As usual, he showed his good sense by turning to his area-specialist and handing over the printout just as fast he could read the pages and tear the sheets away from the staple.

'Meltdown,' the area-specialist said by the end of page three. Which was not unexpected, but neither was it pleasant.

'Doubts?'

'My boy' – the area specialist had twenty years on his boss – 'they ain't going to Tehran to shop.'

'SNIE?' Goodley asked, meaning a Special National Intelligence Estimate, an important official document meant for unusual situations.

'I think so. The Iraqi government is coming down.' It wasn't all that much of a surprise.

'Three days?'

'If that much.'

Goodley stood. 'Okay, let's get it drafted.'

17

THE REVIVAL

It is to be expected that important things never happen at convenient times. Whether the birth of a baby or a national emergency, all such events seem to find the appropriate people asleep or otherwise indisposed. In this case, there was nothing to be done. Ben Goodley determined that CIA had no assets in place to confirm the signal-intelligence take, and interested though his country was in the region, there was no action that could be taken. The public news organizations hadn't twigged to this development, and as was often the case, CIA would play dumb until they did. In doing so, the Central Intelligence Agency would give greater substance to the public belief that the news organizations were as efficient as the government in finding things out. It wasn't always the case, but was more frequently so than Goodley would have preferred.

This SNIE would be a short one. The substance of it didn't require a great deal of pontificating, and the fact of it didn't take long to present. Goodley and his area specialist took half an hour to draft it. A computer printer generated the hard copy for in-house use, and a modem transmitted it via secure lines to interested government agencies. With that done, the men returned to the Operations Center.

Golovko was doing his best to sleep. Aeroflot had just purchased ten new Boeing 777 jetliners for use in its international service to New York, Chicago, and Washington. They were far more comfortable, and reliable, than the Soviet airliners in which he'd traveled for so many years, but he was less than enthralled with the idea of flying so far on two engines, American-made or not, rather than the usual four. The seats, at least, were comfortable here in first class, and the vodka he'd had soon after takeoff was a premium Russian label. The combination had given him five and a half hours of sleep until the usual disorientation of travel clicked in, waking him up over Greenland, while his bodyguard next to him managed to remain in whatever dreamland his profession allowed. Somewhere aft, the stewardesses were probably sleeping as well as they could in their folding seats.

In previous times, Sergey Nikolayevich knew, it wouldn't have been like this. He would have flown on a special charter with full communications gear, and if something had taken place in the world, he'd be informed just as quickly as the transmission towers outside of Moscow could dot-dash the information out. All the more frustrating was the fact that something was happening. Something had to be. It was always this way, he thought in the noisy darkness. You traveled for an important meeting because you expected something to take place, and then it happened while you were on the move and, if not totally out of touch, then at least denied the chance to confer with your senior aides. Iraq *and* China. Thankfully, there was a wide separation between the two hot spots. Then Golovko reminded himself that there was a wider separation still between Washington and Moscow, one which lasted about as long as an overnight flight on a twin-engine aircraft. With that pleasant realization, he turned slightly and told himself that he'd need all the sleep he could get.

The hard part wasn't getting them out of Iraq. The hard part would be getting them from Iran to Sudan. It had been a long while since flights from Iran had been allowed to overfly the Saudi Kingdom, and the only exceptions were the pilgrimage flights into Mecca during the annual hajj. Instead, the business jet had to skirt around the Arabian Peninsula, then up the Red Sea before turning west to Khartoum, tripling both time and distance on the delivery leg of the process, and the next short flight couldn't begin until the first long one had arrived in Africa, *and* the VIPs had arrived at their hastily prepared quarters, *and* found them satisfactory, *and* made a phone call with the inevitable code word confirming that all was well. It would have been so much easier had it been possible to load them all onto a single airliner for a single Baghdad-Tehran-Khartoum cycle, but that wasn't possible. Neither was it possible to take the far shorter air routing directly from Baghdad to Khartoum through the simple expedient of overflying Jordan. But that meant passing close to Israel, not a prospect to make the Iraqi generals happy. And then there was the secrecy issue, too, to make things inconvenient.

A lesser man than Daryaei would have found it enraging. Instead he stood alone at the window of a closed portion of the main terminal, watching the G-IV stop alongside another, watching the doors open, watching the people scurry down one staircase and immediately onto another, while baggage handlers transferred what few belongings they'd brought along – doubtless jewels and other items of high value and portability, the holy man thought without a smile. It took only a few minutes, and then the waiting aircraft started moving.

It was foolish, really, to have come down just to see something so pedestrian and tedious as this, but it represented fully two decades of effort, and man of God though he was, Mahmoud Haji Daryaei was still human enough to want to see the fruits of his labor. A lifetime had gone into this, and even so it was a task not even half done. And his time was running out . . .

As it was for every man, Daryaei reminded himself, one second, one minute, one hour, one day at a time, the same for all, but somehow it seemed to run faster when one was over seventy years of age. He looked down at his hands, the lines and scars of a lifetime there, some natural, some not. Two of his fingers had been broken while a guest of Savak, the Shah's Israeli-trained security service. He remembered the pain of it. He remembered even better the reckoning with the two men who'd interrogated him. Daryaei hadn't spoken a word. He'd just looked at them, stood there like a statue, as they were taken off to the firing squad. Not very much satisfaction in it, really. They'd been functionaries, doing a job assigned to them by others, without really caring who he was or why they were supposed to hate him. Another mullah had sat with each in turn to pray with them, because to deny anyone a chance to reconcile himself with Allah was a crime – and what did it hurt? They died just as quickly that way as any other. One small step in a lifetime's journey, though theirs had ultimately been far shorter than his.

All the years spent for his single-minded purpose. Khomeini had taken his exile in France, but not Daryaei. He'd remained in the background, coordinating and directing for his leader. Picked up that one time, he'd been let go because he hadn't talked, nor had anyone close to him. That had been the Shah's mistake, one of many. The man had ultimately succumbed to indecision. Too liberal in his policies to make the Islamic clergy happy, too reactionary to please his Western sponsors, trying vainly to find a middle ground in a part of the world where a man had only two choices. Only one, really, Daryaei corrected himself as the Gulfstream jet lifted off. Iraq had tried the other path, away from the Word of God, and what had it profited them? Hussein had started his war with Iran, thinking the latter country weak and leaderless, and achieved nothing. Then he had struck out to the south and accomplished even less, all in the sole quest for temporal power.

It was different for Daryaei. He'd never lost sight of his goal, as Khomeini had not, and though the latter was dead, his task lived on. His objective lay behind him as he faced north, too far to see, but there even so, in the holy cities of Mecca and Medina . . . and Jerusalem. He'd been to the first two, but not the third. As a boy, young and pious, he'd wanted to see the Rock of Abraham, but something, he didn't remember what, had prevented his merchant father from taking him there. Perhaps in time. He'd seen the city of the Prophet's birth, however, and of course made the pilgrimage to Mecca, the hajj, more than once despite the political and religious differences between Iran and Saudi Arabia. He wished to do so again, to pray before the veiled Kaaba. But there was more to it than that, even.

Titular chief of state, he wanted more. Not so much for himself. No, he had a larger task at the bottom of his humble life. Islam stretched from the extreme west of Africa to the extreme east of Asia, not counting the small pockets of the Faith's adherents in the Western Hemisphere, but the religion had not had a single leader and a single purpose for over a thousand years. It caused Daryaei pain that this should be so. There was but one God and one Word, and it must have saddened Allah that His Word was so tragically misunderstood. That was the only possible reason for the failure of all men to grasp the True Faith, and if he could change that, then he could change the world and bring all of mankind to God. But to do that –

The world was the world, an imperfect instrument with imperfect rules for imperfect men, but Allah had made it so, and that was that. Worse, there were those who would oppose everything he did, Believers and un-Believers both, another cause more for sadness than for anger. Daryaei didn't hate the Saudis and the others on the far side of the Persian Gulf. They were not evil men. They *were* Believers, and despite their differences with him and his country, they'd never be denied access to Mecca. But their way wasn't *the* Way, and that couldn't be helped. They'd grown fat and rich and corrupt, and that had to be changed. Daryaei had to control Mecca in order to reform Islam. To do that meant acquiring worldly power. It meant making enemies. But that wasn't new, and he'd just won his first major battle.

If only it didn't take so long. Daryaei often spoke of patience, but his was the work of a lifetime, and he was seventy-two, and he didn't want to die as his mentor had, with the work not even half done. When there came his moment to face Allah, he wanted to speak of accomplishment, of successfully fulfilling the noblest task any man could have, the reunification of the True Faith. And Daryaei was willing to do much for that goal. He himself didn't even know how much it was that he was willing to undertake, because not all the questions had yet been asked. And because his goal was so pure and bright, and his remaining time so short, he'd never asked himself how deeply he would cross into darkness in order to get there.

Well. He turned away from the window and walked off with his driver to the car. The process had begun.

People in the intelligence community are not paid to believe in coincidences, and these particular people had maps and watches to predict them. The unrefueled range of the G-IV was well known, and the distances to be covered were easily computed. The circling AWACS aircraft established a track heading south from Tehran. Transponder settings told them the type of aircraft, along with speed, heading, and altitude, the last being 45,000 feet for maximum fuel efficiency.

Timing was checked between one such flight and another. The course told them even more.

'Sudan,' Major Sabah confirmed. It could have gone elsewhere. He almost thought that Brunei was a possible option, but, no, that would be too far from Switzerland, and Switzerland was where the money was – had to be.

With that judgment, a satellite signal was sent to America, again to CIA, and this one occasioned waking a senior DO official up merely to say yes to a brief question. The answer was relayed back to PALM BOWL out of courtesy to the Kuwaitis. Then it was just a matter of waiting.

The CIA had a small presence in Khartoum, really just a station chief and a couple of field officers and a secretary whom they shared with the NSA-run signals section. The station chief was a good one, however, who had recruited a number of local citizens to act as agents. It helped that the Sudanese government had little to hide, most of the time, too poor to be of interest as much of anything. In previous times the government had used its geographic location as a ploy to play East against West, garnering cash and weapons and favor out of the bargain, but the USSR had fallen and with it the Great Power Game which had sustained the Third World for two generations. Now the Sudanese had to depend on their own resources, which were slim, and the few crumbs tossed their way by whichever country had transitory need for what little they had. The country's leaders were Islamic, and in proclaiming it as loudly as they could lie – they were no more devout than their Western counterparts – they managed to get aid from Libya and Iran and others, in return for which they were expected to make life hard on the pagan animists in the southern part of the country, plus risk a rising Islamic political tide in their own capital, people who knew the real level of devotion of the country's leaders, and wanted to replace them with people who truly believed. On the whole the political leaders of that impoverished nation thought it was easier to be religious and rich than religious and poor.

What that meant to the American embassy personnel was great unpredictability. Sometimes Khartoum was safe, when the fundamentalist troublemakers were under control. Sometimes it was not, because they were not. At the moment, the former seemed to be the case, and all the American foreign service officers had to worry about were the environmental conditions, which were vile enough to place this post in the bottom ten of global embassy assignments even without a terrorist threat. For the station chief it meant early advancement, though his wife and two children remained home in Virginia, because most of the official American residents didn't feel safe enough to set up their families here. Almost as bad, AIDS was becoming a threat sufficient to deny much in the way of nightlife to them, not to mention the question of getting safe blood in the event of an injury. The embassy had an Army doctor to handle those issues. He worried a lot.

The station chief shook that off. He'd jumped a whole pay grade on taking this assignment. He'd performed well, with one especially well-placed agent in the Sudanese foreign ministry to inform America about everything that country did. That his country didn't do all that much was not important to the desk-sitters at Langley. Better to know everything about nothing than nothing about everything.

He'd handle this one himself. Checking time and distance against his own maps, the station chief had an early lunch and drove off to the airport, only a few miles out of town. Security there was African-casual, and he found a shady spot outside. It was easier to cover the private terminal than the public one, especially with a 500mm lens on his camera. He even had time to make sure he had the aperture right. A buzz on his cellular phone from the NSA people at the embassy confirmed that the inbound aircraft was on final, a fact further verified by the arrival of some official-looking cars. He'd already memorized two photographs faxed to him from Langley. Two senior Iraqi generals, eh? he thought. Well, with the death of their boss, it wasn't all that surprising. The problem with the dictatorship business was that there wasn't much of a retirement plan for any of those near the top of it.

The white business jet floated in with the customary puffs of rubber smoke. He locked the camera on it and shot a few frames of high-speed black-and-white to make sure the motor drive worked. The only worry now was whether the bird would stop in such a way that he could cover the exit with the camera – the bastards could always face the wrong way and spoil the whole thing for him. In that he had little choice. The Gulfstream stopped. The door dropped open, and the station chief started shooting frames. There was a middle-level official there to do the semi-official greeting. You could tell who was important by who got the hugs and kisses – and from the sweep-around look they gave the area. *Click. Click.* He recognized one face for sure, and the other was a probable hit. The transfer took only a minute or two. The official cars pulled off, and the station chief didn't much care where they were heading at the moment. His agent in the foreign ministry would fill that one in. He shot the remaining eight frames of the aircraft, already being refueled, and decided to wait to see what it would do. Thirty minutes later, it lifted off yet again, and he headed back to the embassy. While one of his junior people handled the developing, he made a call to Langley.

'Confirmation,' Goodley said, approaching the end of his watch. 'Two Iraqi generals touched down at Khartoum fifty minutes ago. It's a bug-out.'

'Makes the SNIE look pretty good, Ben,' the area specialist observed, with a raised eyebrow. 'I hope they pay attention to the time stamp on it.'

The national intelligence officer managed a smile. 'Yeah, well, the next one has to say what it means.' The regular analysts, just starting to arrive for a day's work, would fiddle around with that.

'Nothing good.' But you didn't need to be a spook to figure that one out.

'Photos coming in,' a communications officer called.

The first call had to go to Tehran. Daryaei had told his ambassador to make things as clear as possible. Iran would assume responsibility for all expenses. The best possible accommodations were to be provided, with every level of comfort that the country could arrange. The overall operation would not cost a great amount of money, but the savages in that country were impressed by small sums, and ten million American dollars – a pittance – had already been transferred electronically to ensure that everything went well. A call from the Iranian ambassador confirmed that the first pickup had gone properly and that the aircraft was on its way back.

Good. Now perhaps the Iraqis would begin to trust him. It would have been personally satisfying to have these swine eliminated, and that would not have been difficult to arrange under the circumstances, but he'd given his word, and besides, this wasn't about personal satisfaction. Even as he set the phone down, his air minister was calling in additional aircraft to expedite the transfer. This was better done quickly.

Badrayn was trying to make the same point. The word was going to get out, probably in one day, certainly no more than two. They were leaving people behind who were too senior to survive the coming upheaval, and too junior to merit the solicitude the Iranians were willing to show the generals. Those officers, colonels and brigadiers, would not be overly happy at the prospect of becoming the sacrificial goats necessary to assuage the awakening rage of the mob. This fact was becoming clear, but instead of making them more eager to leave, it emerged as a non-specific fear that made all the other fears loom larger in the unknown darkness ahead. They stood on the deck of a burning ship off an unfriendly shore, and they didn't know how to swim all that well. But the ship was still afire. He had to make them grasp that.

It was routine enough by now that Ryan was becoming used to it, at home with it, even comfortable with the discreet knock on the door, more startling in its way than the clock-radio which had begun his days for twenty years. Instead his eyes opened at the muted knock, and he rose, put on his robe, walked the twenty feet from the bed to the door, and got his paper, along with a few sheets of his daily schedule. Next, he headed to the bathroom, and then to the sitting room adjoining the presidential bedroom, while his wife, a few minutes behind him, started her wake-up routine.

Jack missed the normality of merely reading the paper. Though it wasn't nearly as good – usually – as the intelligence documents waiting on the table for him, the *Washington Post* also covered things whose interest was not strictly governmental, and so was fuel for his normal desire to keep abreast of things. But the first order of business was a SNIE, an urgent official document stapled inside a manila folder. Ryan rubbed his eyes before reading it.

Damn. Well, it could have been worse, the President told himself. At least this time they hadn't awakened him to let him know about something he couldn't change. He checked the schedule. Okay, Scott Adler would be in to discuss that one, along with that Vasco guy. Good. Vasco seemed to know his stuff. Who else today? He skimmed down the page. Sergey Golovko? Was that today? Good luck for a change. Brief press conference to announce Tony Bretano's appointment as Sec-Def, with a list of possible questions to worry about, and instructions from Arnie – ignore the Kealty question as much as possible. Let Kealty and his allegations die from apathy – *oh, yeah,* that's *a good one-liner!* Jack coughed as he poured some coffee – getting himself the right to do that alone had entailed direct orders; he hoped the Navy mess stewards didn't take it as a personal insult, but Ryan was used to doing *some* things for himself. Under the current arrangement, the stewards set up breakfast in the room and let the Ryans serve themselves, while others hovered in the corridor outside.

'Morning, Jack.' Cathy's head appeared in his view. He kissed her lips and smiled.

'Morning, honey.'

'Is the world still out there?' she asked, getting her own coffee. That told the President that the First Lady wasn't operating today. She never touched coffee on a surgery day, saying that she couldn't risk the slight tremor that caffeine might impart to her hands when she was carving up some-body's eyeball. The image always made him shudder, even though she mainly operated with lasers now.

'Looks like the Iraqi government is falling.'

A female snort. 'Didn't that happen last week?'

'That was act one. This is act three.' *Or maybe act four.* He wondered what act five would be.

'Important?' Jack also heard the toast go down.

'Could be. What's your day like?'

'Clinic and follow-ups, budget meeting with Bernie.'

'Hmph.' Jack next started looking at the *Early Bird,* a col-lection of government-edited clippings from the major papers. Cathy appeared again in his peripheral vision, as she looked at his office schedule.

'Golovko . . . ? Didn't I meet him in Moscow – he's the one who joked about having a gun on you!'

'Wasn't a joke,' Ryan told his wife. 'It really happened.'

'Come on!'

'He said later that the gun wasn't loaded.' Jack wondered if that was true. Probably, he thought.

'But he was telling the truth?' she asked incredulously.

The President looked up and smiled. Amazing, he thought, that it seemed funny now. 'He was very pissed with me at the time. That's when I helped with the defection of the KGB chairman.'

She lifted her morning paper. 'Jack, I never know when you're kidding or not.'

Jack thought about that. The First Lady was, technically, a private citizen. Certainly in Cathy's case, since she was not a political wife but a working physician who had about as much interest in politics as she did in group sex. She was also, therefore, *not* technically the holder of a security clearance, but it was assumed that the President would confide in his spouse just as any normal person did. Besides, it made sense. Her judgment was every bit as good as his, and unschooled as she might be in international relations, every day she made decisions that directly affected the lives of real people in the most immediate way. If she goofed, they went blind.

'Cathy, I think it's about time to tell you some of the things I've been stuck with over the years, but for now, yeah, Golovko had a pistol to my head once, on one of the runways at Moscow airport, because I helped two very senior Russians skip the country. One of them was his boss at KGB.'

That made her look up, and wonder again about the nightmares that had plagued her husband for months, a few years ago. 'So where is he now?'

'In the DC area, I forget exactly where, Virginia horse country, I think.' Jack vaguely remembered hearing that the daughter, Katryn Gerasimov, was engaged to some old-money fox-killer out around Winchester, having changed from one form of nobility to another. Well, the stipend CIA had paid to the family was enough to maintain a very comfortable lifestyle.

Cathy was used to her husband's jokes. Like most men, he would tell amusing little stories whose humor was in their exaggeration – and besides, his ancestry was Irish – but now she marked the fact that his revelation was as casual as a report of the baseball scores. He didn't see her stare at the back of his head. *Yes*, she decided, as the kids entered the room, *I'd like to hear the stories*.

'Daddy!' Katie said, seeing Jack first. 'Mommy!' With that the morning routine stopped, or rather changed over to something more immediately important than world news and events. Katie was already in her school clothes, like most small children, able to awaken in a good mood.

'Hi,' Sally said, coming next, clearly vexed.

'What's the matter?' Cathy asked her elder daughter.

'All those people out there! You can't even walk around here without people seeing you everywhere!' she grumped, getting a glass of juice off the tray. And she didn't feel like Frosted Flakes this morning. She'd rather have Just Right. But that box was all the way down on the ground floor in the capacious White House kitchen. 'It's like living in a hotel, but not as private.'

'What exam is it today?' Cathy asked, reading the signals for what they were.

'Math,' Sally admitted.

'Did you study?'

'Yes, *Mom*.'

Jack ignored that problem, and instead fixed cereal for Katie, who liked Frosted Flakes. Little Jack arrived next and turned on the TV, selecting the Cartoon Channel for his morning ration of Road Runner and Coyote, which Katie also approved.

Outside, the day was starting for everyone else. Ryan's personal NIO was putting the finishing touches on his dreaded morning intelligence brief. This President was far too hard to please. The chief usher was in early to supervise some maintenance on the State Floor. In the President's bedroom, the valet was setting out clothes for POTUS and FLOTUS. Cars were waiting to take the children off to school. Maryland State Police officers were already checking out the route to Annapolis. The Marines were warming up their helicopter for the trip to Baltimore – *that* problem had still not been worked out. The entire machine was already in motion.

Gus Lorenz was in his office early because of a telephone call from Africa returning his call from Atlanta. Where, he demanded, were his monkeys? His purchasing agent explained from eight time zones away that, because CDC had fumbled getting the money cleared, somebody else had bought up the shipment, and that a new batch had to be obtained from out in the bush. A week, perhaps, he told the American doctor.

Lorenz grumbled. He'd hoped to start his new study this week. He made a note on his desk pad, wondering who the hell would have bought so many African greens just like that. Was Rousseau starting something new in Paris? He'd call the guy a little later, after his morning staff conference. The good news, he saw, was that – oh, that was too bad. The second patient, killed in a plane crash, the telex from WHO said. But there were no new cases reported, and it had been long enough from Number Two that they could say now, rather than hope, that this micro-outbreak was over – probably, maybe, hopefully, Lorenz added with his thoughts. That was good news. It looked like the Ebola Zaire Mayinga strain under the electron microscope, and that was the worst of the sub-types of the virus. It could still be that the host was out there, waiting to infect someone else, but the Ebola host was the most bafflingly elusive quarry since malaria – 'bad air,' in Italian, which was what people had thought caused it. Maybe, he thought, the host was some rodent that had gotten run over by a truck. He shrugged. It was possible, after all.

With the reduction in her morphine drip, Patient Two was semiconscious at the Hasanabad facility. She was aware enough to know, and to feel, the pain, but not to understand what was really happening. The pain would have taken over in any case, all the worse because Jean Baptiste knew what every twinge meant. The abdominal pain was the worst, as the disease was destroying her gastrointestinal tract throughout its ten-meter length, quite literally *eating* the delicate tissues designed to convert food into nutrients, and dumping infected blood down toward her rectum.

It felt as though her entire body were being twisted and crushed and burned at the same time. She needed to move, to do *something* to make things different, just to make the pain come briefly from a new direction, and so briefly relieve that which tormented her, but when she tried to move she found that every limb was restrained with Velcro-coated straps. The insult of that was somehow worse than the pain, but when she tried to object it only caused violent nausea that started her gagging. At that indication the blue-coated spaceman rotated the bed – what sort of bed was this? she wondered – which allowed her to vomit into a bucket, and what she saw there was black, dead blood. It distracted her from the pain for a second, but all the distraction told her was that she could not survive, that the disease had gone too far, that her body was dying, and then Sister Jean Baptiste started praying for death, because this could have only one end, and the pain was such that the end needed to come soon, lest she lose her faith in the process. The prospect sprang out into her diminished consciousness like a jack-in-the-box. But this childhood toy had horns and hooves. She needed a priest at hand. She needed – where was Maria Magdalena? Was she doomed to die alone? The dying nurse looked at the space suits, hoping to find familiar eyes behind the plastic shields, but though the eyes she saw were sympathetic, they were not familiar. Nor was their language, as two of them came close.

The medic was very careful drawing blood. First he checked to see that the arm was fully restrained, unable to move more than a centimeter. Then he had a comrade hold the arm in his two strong hands, careful himself to keep those hands well away from the needle. With a nod of agreement, the first selected the proper vein and stabbed the needle in. He was lucky this time. The needle went right in on the first try. To the back of the needle-holder he attached a 5cc vacuum tube, which took in blood that was darker than the usual purple. When it was full, he withdrew it, and set it carefully in a plastic box, to be followed by three more. He withdrew the needle next, and placed gauze on the puncture, which wouldn't stop bleeding. The medic released the arm, noting that their brief grasp had discolored the skin badly. A cover was placed on the box, and the first medic walked it out of the room, while the second went to the corner to spray his gloves and arms with dilute iodine. They'd been fully briefed on how dangerous this duty was, but in the way of normal men they hadn't really believed it, despite all the repetitions and the films and the slides. Both men believed it now, every cursed word, and to a man the army medics wished and prayed for Death to come and spirit this woman off to whatever destination Allah had planned for her. Watching her body disintegrate was bad enough. The thought of following her in this horrid journey was enough to quail the stoutest heart. It was like nothing they'd ever seen. This woman was *melting* from the inside out. As the medic finished cleaning the outside of his suit, he turned, startled by her cry of pain, as if from an infant tortured by the hands of the devil himself. Eyes open, mouth wide, a rasping, liquid cry escaped into the air and penetrated the plastic of his suit.

The blood samples were handled quickly, but under the greatest care, in the Hot Lab up the corridor. Moudi and the project director were in their offices. It wasn't strictly necessary for them to be in the lab for this, and it was easier for them to view the tests without the hindrance of the protective garb.

'So fast, so remarkably fast.' The director shook his head in awe.

Moudi nodded. 'Yes, it overwhelms the immune system like a tidal wave.' The display on the computer screen came off an electron microscope, which showed the field full of the shepherd-staff-configured viruses. A few antibodies were visible on the screen, but they might as well have been individual sheep in a pride of lions for all the good they might do. The blood cells were being attacked and destroyed. Had they been able to take tissue samples of the major organs, they could have found that the spleen was turning into something as hard as a rubber ball, full of little crystals which were like transport capsules for the Ebola virus particles. It would, in fact, have been interesting, and maybe even scientifically useful, to do laparoscopic examination of the abdomen, to see exactly what the disease did to a human patient over measured time intervals, but there was the danger of accelerating the patient's death, which they didn't want to risk.

Samples of her vomitus showed tissue fragments from her upper GI, and those were interesting because they were not merely torn loose, but dead. Large sections of the patient's still-living body had already died, come loose from the living remainder, and been ejected as the corporate organism fought vainly to survive. The infected blood would be centrifuged and deep-frozen for later use. Every drop that came out was useful, and because of that, more blood was dripped into her via rubber IV tubes. A routine heart-enzyme test showed that her heart, unlike that of the Index Patient, was still normal and healthy.

'Strange how the disease varies in its mode of attack,' the director observed, reading the printout.

Moudi just looked away, imagining that he could hear her cries of anguish through the multiple concrete walls of the building. It would have been an act of supreme mercy to walk into the room and push in 20ccs of potassium, or just to turn the morphine drip all the way open and so kill her with respiratory arrest.

'Do you suppose the African boy had a preexisting cardio-vascular problem?' his boss asked.

'Perhaps. It wasn't diagnosed if he did.'

'Liver function is failing rapidly, as expected.' The director scanned the blood-chemistry data slowly. All the numbers were well out of normal ranges, except the heart indicators, and those but barely. 'It's a textbook case, Moudi.'

'Indeed it is.'

'This strain of the virus is even more robust than I'd imagined.' He looked up. 'You've done well.'

Oh, yes.

'. . . Anthony Bretano has two doctorates from MIT, Mathematics and Optical Physics. He has an impressive personal record in industry and engineering, and I expect him to be a uniquely effective Secretary of Defense,' Ryan said, concluding his statement. 'Questions?'

'Sir, Vice President Kealty –'

344

'*Former* Vice President,' Ryan interrupted. 'He resigned. Let's get that right.'

'But he says he didn't,' the *Chicago Tribune* pointed out.

'If he said he had a talk with Elvis, would you believe that?' Ryan asked, hoping that he'd delivered the prepared line properly. He scanned faces for the reaction. Again, all forty-eight seats were filled, with twenty more reporters standing. Jack's scornful remark made them all blink, and a few even allowed themselves a smile. 'Go ahead, ask your question.'

'*Mister* Kealty has requested a judicial commission to ascertain the facts of the matter. How do you respond to that?'

'The question is being investigated by the FBI, which is the government's principal investigative agency. Whatever the facts are, they have to be established before anyone can make a judgment. But I think we all know what is going to happen. Ed Kealty resigned, and you all know why. Out of respect for the constitutional process, I have directed the FBI to look into the matter, but my own legal advice is absolutely clear. Mr Kealty can talk all he wants. I have a job to do here. Next question?' Jack asked confidently.

'Mr President' – Ryan nodded fractionally at hearing the *Miami Herald* say that – 'In your speech the other night, you said that you're not a politician, but you are in a political job. The American people want to know your views on a lot of issues.'

'That makes good sense. Like what?' Jack asked.

'Abortion, for one,' the *Herald* reporter, a very liberated woman, asked. 'What exactly is your position?'

'I don't like it,' Ryan answered, speaking the truth before thinking about it. 'I'm Catholic, as you probably know, and on that moral issue I think my Church is correct. However, *Roe v. Wade* is the law of the land until such time as the Supreme Court might reconsider the ruling, and the President isn't allowed to ignore the rulings of the federal courts. That puts me in a somewhat uncomfortable position, but as President I have to execute my office in accordance with the law. I swore an oath to do that.' *Not bad, Jack*, Ryan thought.

'So you do not support the right of a woman to choose?' the *Herald* asked, smelling the blood.

345

'Choose what?' Ryan asked, still comfortable. 'You know, somebody once tried to kill my wife while she was pregnant with our son, and soon thereafter I watched my oldest child lying near death in a hospital. I think life is a very precious commodity. I've learned that lesson the hard way. I'd hope that people would think about that before deciding to have an abortion.'

'That doesn't answer the question, sir.'

'I can't stop people from doing it. Like it or not, it's the law. The President may not break the law.' Wasn't this obvious?

'But in your appointments for the Supreme Court, will you use abortion as a litmus-test issue? Would you like to have *Roe v. Wade* overturned?' Ryan scarcely noticed the cameras changing focus, and the reporters concentrating on their scribbled notes.

'I don't like *Roe v. Wade*, as I said. I think it was a mistake. I'll tell you why. The Supreme Court interjected itself into what should have been a legislative matter. The Constitution doesn't address this issue, and on issues where the Constitution is mute, we have state and federal legislatures to write our laws.' This civics lesson was going well. 'Now, for the nominations I have to make to the Supreme Court, I will look for the best judges I can find. That's something we will be addressing shortly. The Constitution is sort of the Bible for the United States of America, and the justices of the Supreme Court are the – theologians, I guess, who decide what it means. They aren't supposed to write a new one. They're supposed to figure out what it means. When a change in the Constitution is needed, we have a mechanism to change it, which we've used more than twenty times.'

'So, you will select only strict-constructionists who are likely to overturn *Roe.*'

It was like hitting a wall. Ryan paused noticeably before answering. 'I hope to pick the best judges I can find. I will not interrogate them on single issues.'

The *Boston Globe* leaped to his feet. 'Mr President, what about where the life of the mother is in danger, the Catholic Church –'

'The answer to that is obvious. The life of the mother is the paramount consideration.'

'But the Church used to say –'

346

'I don't speak for the Catholic Church. As I said earlier, I cannot violate the law.'

'But you want the law changed,' the *Globe* pointed out.

'Yes, I think it would be better for everybody if the matter was returned to the state legislatures. In that way the people's elected representatives can write the laws in accordance with the will of their electorates.'

'But then,' the *San Francisco Examiner* pointed out, 'we'd have a hodgepodge of laws across the country, and in some areas abortion would be illegal.'

'Only if the electorate wants it that way. That's how democracy works.'

'But what about poor women?'

'It's not for me to say,' Ryan replied, feeling the beginnings of anger, and wondering how he'd ever gotten into this mess.

'So, do you support a constitutional amendment against abortion?' the *Atlanta Constitution* demanded.

'No, I don't think that's a constitutional question. I think it is properly a legislative question.'

'So,' the *New York Times* summarized, 'you are personally against abortion on moral and religious grounds, but you will not interfere with women's rights; you plan to appoint conservative justices to the new Supreme Court who will probably overturn *Roe*, but you don't support a constitutional amendment to outlaw freedom of choice.' The reporter smiled. 'Exactly what *do* you believe in on this issue, sir?'

Ryan shook his head, pursed his lips, and bit off his first version of an answer to the impertinence. 'I thought I just made that clear. Shall we go on to something else?'

'Thank you, Mr President!' a senior reporter called loudly, so advised by the frantic gestures of Arnold van Damm. Ryan left the podium puzzled, walked around the corner, then another until he was out of sight. The chief of staff grabbed the President by the arm, and nearly pushed him against the wall, and this time the Secret Service didn't move a muscle.

'Way to go, Jack, you just pissed off the entire country!'

'What do you mean?' the President replied, thinking, *Huh?*

'I mean you don't pump gas in your car when you're smoking a cigarette, God damn it! Jesus! Don't you know what you just did?' Arnie could see that he didn't. 'The pro-choice people now think you're going to take their rights away. The pro-life people think you don't care about their issue. It was just perfect, Jack. You alienated the whole fucking country in five minutes!' Van Damm stormed off, leaving his President outside the Cabinet Room, afraid that he'd really lose his temper if he said anything more.

'What's he talking about?' Ryan asked. The Secret Service agents around him didn't say anything. It wasn't their place – politics – and besides, they were split on the issue as much as the country was.

It was like taking candy from a baby. And after the initial shock, the baby cried pretty loud.

'BUFFALO SIX, this is GUIDON SIX, over.' Lieutenant Colonel Herbert Masterman – 'Duke' to his peers – stood atop 'Mad Max II,' his MIA2 Abrams command tank, microphone in one hand, and binoculars in the other. Before him, spread over about ten square miles in the Negev Training Area, were the Merkava tanks and infantry carriers of the Israeli army's 7th Armored Brigade, all with yellow lights blinking and purple smoke rising from their turrets. The smoke was an Israeli innovation. When tanks were hit in battle, they burned, and when the MILES gear receptors recorded a laser 'hit' they set off the marker. But the idea had been for the Israelis to count coup that way on the OpFor. Only four of Masterman's tanks and six of his M3 Bradley Scout tracks were similarly 'dead.'

'GUIDON, BUFFALO,' came the return call from Colonel Sean Magruder, commander of the 10th 'Buffalo' Armored Cavalry Regiment.

'I think this one's about concluded, Colonel, over. The fire sack is full.'

'Roger that, Duke. Come on down for the AAR. We're going to have one really pissed Israeli in a few minutes.' Just as well the radio link was encrypted.

'On the way, sir.' Masterman stepped down off the turret as his HMMVW pulled up. His tank crew started back up, heading down toward the squadron lager.

It didn't get much better than this. Masterman felt like a football player allowed to play every day. He commanded 1st 'Guidon' Squadron of the 10th ACR. It would have been called a battalion, but the Cav was different, to the yellow facings on their shoulder straps and the red-and-white unit guidons, and if you weren't Cav, you weren't shit.

'Kickin' some more ass, sir?' his driver asked as his boss lit up a Cuban cigar.

'Lambs to the slaughter, Perkins.' Masterman sipped some water from a plastic bottle. A hundred feet over his head, some Israeli F-16 fighters roared past, showing outrage at what had happened below them. Probably a few of them had run afoul of the administrative SAM 'launches.' Masterman had been especially careful today siting his Stinger-Avenger vehicles, and sure enough, they'd come in just as he'd expected. Tough.

The local 'Star Wars Room' was a virtual twin to the original one at Fort Irwin. A somewhat smaller main display screen, and nicer seats, and you could smoke in this one. He entered the building, shaking the dust off his chocolate-chip cammies and striding like Patton into Bastogne. The Israelis were waiting.

Intellectually, they had to know how useful the exercise had been to them. Emotionally, it was something else. The Israeli 7th Armored was as proud an outfit as any in the world. Practically alone, it had stopped an entire Syrian tank corps on the Golan Heights back in 1973, and their current CO had been a lieutenant then who'd taken command of a headless company and fought brilliantly. Not accustomed to failure, he'd just seen the brigade in which he'd practically grown up annihilated, in thirty brutal minutes.

'General,' Masterman said, extending his hand to the chastened brigadier. The Israeli hesitated before taking it.

'Not personal, sir, just business,' said Lieutenant Colonel Nick Sarto, who commanded the 2nd 'Bighorn' Squadron, and who had just played hammer to Masterman's anvil. With the Israeli 7th in the middle.

'Gentlemen, shall we begin?' called the senior observer-controller. As a sop to the Israeli Army, the OC team here was a fifty-fifty mix of experienced American and Israeli officers, and it was hard to determine which group was the more embarrassed.

There was, first, a quick-time replay of the theoretical engagement. The Israeli vehicles in blue marched into the shallow valley to meet GUIDON's reconnaissance screen, which leapfrogged back rapidly, but not toward the prepared defense positions of the rest of the squadron, instead leading them away at an angle. Thinking it a trap, the Israeli 7th had maneuvered west, so as to loop around and envelop their enemies, only to walk into a solid wall of dug-in tanks, and then to have Bighorn come in from the east much faster than expected – so fast that Doug Mills's 3rd 'Dakota' Squadron, the regimental reserve, never had a chance to come into play for the pursuit phase. It was the same old lesson. The Israeli commander had guessed at his enemy's positions instead of sending his reconnaissance screen to find out.

The Israeli brigadier watched the replay, and it seemed that he deflated like a balloon. The Americans didn't laugh. They'd all been there before, though it was far nicer to be on the winning side.

'Your reconnaissance screen wasn't far forward enough, Benny,' the senior Israeli OC said diplomatically.

'Arabs don't fight that way!' Benjamin Eitan replied.

'They're supposed to, sir,' Masterman pointed out. 'This is standard Soviet doctrine, and that's who trained 'em all, remember. Pull 'em into the fire sack and slam the back door. Hell, General, that's exactly what you did with your Centurions back in '73. I read your book on the engagement,' the American added. It defused the mood at once. One of the other things the American officers had to exercise here was diplomacy. General Eitan looked sideways and managed something approaching a smile.

'I did, didn't I?'

'Sure as hell. You clobbered that Syrian regiment in forty minutes, as I recall.'

'And you, at 73 Easting?' Eitan responded, grateful for the compliment, even though he knew it was a deliberate effort to calm his temper.

It was no accident that Magruder, Masterman, Sarto, and Mills were here. All four had participated in a vicious combat action in the Persian Gulf War, where three troops of the 2nd 'Dragoon' Cav had stumbled into an elite Iraqi brigade force under very adverse weather conditions – too bad for the regimental aircraft to participate, even to warn of the enemy's presence – and wiped it out over a period of a few hours. The Israelis knew it, and therefore couldn't complain that the Americans were book soldiers playing theoretical games.

Nor was the result of this 'battle' unusual. Eitan was new, only a month in command, and he would learn, as other Israeli officers had learned, that the American training model was more unforgiving than real combat. It was a hard lesson for the Israelis, so hard that nobody really learned it until he'd visited the Negev Training Area, the NTA, and had his head handed to him. If the Israelis had a weakness, it was pride, Colonel Magruder knew. The OpFor's job here, as in California, was to strip that away. A commander's pride got his soldiers dead.

'Okay,' the senior American OC said. 'What can we learn from this?'

Don't fuck with the Buffalo Soldiers, all three squadron commanders thought, but didn't say. Marion Diggs had re-established the regiment's gritty reputation in his command tour before moving on to command Fort Irwin. Though the word was still percolating down through the Israeli Defense Forces, the troopers of the 10th had adopted a confident strut when they went out shopping, and for all the grief they caused the Israeli military on the playing fields of the NTA, they were immensely popular. The 10th ACR, along with two squadrons of F-16 fighters, was America's commitment to Israeli security, all the more so that they trained the Jewish state's ground forces to a level of readiness they hadn't known since the Israeli army had nearly lost its soul in the hills and towns of Lebanon. Eitan would learn, and learn fast. By the end of the training rotation he'd give them trouble. Maybe, the three squadron commanders thought. They weren't in the business of giving freebies.

'I remember when you told me how delightful democracy was, Mr President,' Golovko said chirpily, as he walked through the door.

'You must have caught me on TV this morning,' Ryan managed to reply.

'I remember when such comments would have gotten such people shot.' Behind the Russian, Andrea Price heard the comment and wondered how this guy had the chutzpah to twist the President's tail.

'Well, we don't do that here,' Jack responded, taking his seat. 'That will be all for now, Andrea. Sergey and I are old friends.' This was to be a private conversation, not even a secretary present to take notes, though hidden microphones would copy down every word for later transcription. The Russian knew that. The American knew that he knew that, but the symbolism of no other people in the room was a compliment to the visitor, another fact which the American knew the Russian to know as well. Jack wondered how many sets of interlocking wheels he was supposed to keep track of, just for an informal meeting with a foreign representative.

When the door closed behind the agent, Golovko spoke on. 'Thank you.'

'Hell, we are old friends, aren't we?'

Golovko smiled. 'What a superb enemy you were.'

'And now . . . ?'

'How is your family adjusting?'

'About as well as I am,' Jack admitted, then shifted gears. 'You had three hours at the embassy to get caught up.'

Golovko nodded; as usual, Ryan was well briefed for this meeting, covert though it was. The Russian embassy was only a few blocks up Sixteenth Street, and he'd walked down to the White House, a simple way to avoid notice in a town where official people traveled in official cars. 'I didn't expect things in Iraq to fall so quickly.'

'Neither did we. But that's not why you came over, Sergey Nikolay'ch. China?'

'I presume your satellite photos are as clear as ours on the issue. Their military is at an unusually high state of readiness.'

'Our people are divided on that,' Ryan said. 'They might be building up to put some more pressure on Taiwan. They've been building their navy up.'

'Their navy isn't ready for combat operations yet. Their army still is, and their rocket forces. Neither is going to cross the Formosa Strait, Mr President.'

That made the reason for his trip clear enough. Jack paused to look out the window at the Washington Monument, surrounded as it was by a circle of flagpoles, rather like a garland. What was it George had said about avoiding entangling foreign alliances? But it had been a far simpler world back then, two months to cross the Atlantic, not six or seven hours . . .

'If you are asking what I think you are, yes – or should I say, no.'

'Could you clarify?'

'America would not look kindly upon an attack by China against Russia. Such a conflict would have very adverse effects upon world stability, and would also impede your progress to full democratic status. America wants to see Russia become a prosperous democracy. We were enemies long enough. We should be friends, and America wants her friends safe and peaceful.'

'They hate us, they covet what we have,' Golovko went on, not satisfied with America's statement.

'Sergey, the time for nations to steal what they cannot earn is past. It's history, and not to be repeated.'

'And if they move on us anyway?'

'We'll cross that bridge when we get to it, Sergey,' the President answered. 'The idea is to prevent such actions. If it appears that they are really thinking about a move, we'll counsel them to reconsider. We are keeping an eye on things.'

'I don't think you understand them.' Another push, Ryan saw. They really were worked up about this.

'Do you think anyone does? Do you think they themselves know what they want?' The two intelligence officers – that was how both men would always think of themselves – shared a look of professional amusement.

'That is the problem,' Golovko admitted. 'I try to explain to my President that it is difficult to predict the behavior of undecided people. They have capabilities, but so do we, and the calculus of the matter appears different from both sides – and then the personalities come into play. Ivan Emmetovich, those are old men with old ideas. Their personalities are the major consideration here.'

'And history, and culture, and economics, and trade – and I haven't had the chance to look them in the eye yet. I'm weak on that part of the world,' Jack reminded his guest. 'I spent most of my life trying to figure you people out.'

'So you will stand with us?'

Ryan shook his head. 'It's too early and too speculative to go that far. We will do everything in our power, however, to prevent a possible conflict between the PRC and Russia. If it happens, you'll go nuclear. I know it. You know it. I think they know it.'

'They don't believe it.'

'Sergey, nobody's that stupid.' Ryan made a mental note to discuss this with Scott Adler, who knew the region far better than he did. It was time to close the book on that issue for the moment, and open another. 'Iraq. What are your people saying?'

Golovko grimaced. 'We had a network go down three months ago. Twenty people, all shot or hanged – after interrogation, that is. What we have left doesn't tell us much, but it appears that senior generals are preparing to do something.'

'Two of them just showed up in the Sudan this morning,' Ryan told him. It wasn't often he caught Golovko by surprise.

'So fast?'

Ryan nodded, handing over the photographs from the Khartoum airport. 'Yep.'

Golovko scanned them, not knowing the faces, but not really needing to. Information passed along at this level was never, ever faked. Even with enemies and former enemies, a nation had to keep its word on some things. He handed the photos back. 'Iran, then. We have some people there, but we've heard nothing in the last few days. It's a dangerous environment in which to operate, as you know. We expect that Daryaei had something to do with the assassination, but we have no evidence to support it.' He paused. 'The implications of this are serious.'

'You're telling me that you can't do anything about it, either, then?'

'No, Ivan Emmetovich, we cannot. We have no influence there, and neither do you.'

18

LAST PLANE OUT

The next shuttle flight got off early. The shell corporation's third and last business jet was recalled from Europe, and with a change of flight crews, was ready three hours early. That meant that the first of the G-IVs could fly to Baghdad, pick up two more generals, and return. Badrayn felt rather like a travel agent or dispatcher in addition to his unusual role as diplomat. He just hoped it wouldn't take too long. It might be dangerous to be a passenger on the last plane, because the last one – well, there was no telling *which* would be the last, was there? The generals didn't grasp that yet. The last one might well be pursued by tracer fire, leaving people on the ground to face the music, and Badrayn knew he would be with them . . . in a region where selectivity wasn't an integral part of the justice system. Well, he shrugged, life had risks, and he was being well paid. They'd told him, at least, that there would be another pickup flight in less than three hours, and a fourth five hours beyond that one. But the sum total would be ten or eleven, and that would go for another three days on the current schedule, and three days could be a lifetime.

Beyond the confines of this airport, the Iraqi army was still in the streets, but there would be a change now. Those conscript soldiers, and even the elite guardsmen, would have been out there for several days, settled into a dull and purposeless routine, and *that* was something destructive to soldiers. They'd be shuffling around on their feet, smoking cigarettes, starting to ask questions amongst themselves: *What exactly is going on?* Initially there would be no answers. Their sergeants would tell them to mind their duties, so advised by their company officers, so advised in turn from battalion staffs, and so on all the way up the line . . . until somewhere that same question would be repeated, and there would *be* no one farther up the chain of command to tell the questioner to sit down and shut up. At that point the question would rebound back *down* the line. It was something an army could sense, as a thorn in the foot instantly told the brain that something was amiss. And if the thorn was dirty, then an infection would follow that could spread and kill the entire body. The generals were supposed to know such things – but, no, they didn't anymore. Something very foolish happened to generals, especially in this part of the world. They forgot. It was that simple. They just forgot that the villas and the servants and the cars were not a divine bequest, but a temporal convenience that could disappear as quickly as morning fog. They were still more afraid of Daryaei than of their own people, and that was foolish. It would have merely been annoying to Badrayn, except that his life now depended on theirs.

The seat on the right side of the cabin was still damp. This time it was occupied by the youngest daughter of the general who had, until minutes before, commanded the 4th Guards Division (Motorized), and who was now conferring with an air force colleague. The child felt the lingering damp on her hand and, puzzled, licked at it, until her mother saw it and sent her off to wash her hands. Then the mother complained to the Iranian steward who rode in the back with this group. He had the child moved, and made a note to have the seat cleaned or replaced at Mehrabad. There was less tension now. The first pair of officers had reported in from Khartoum that all was well. A Sudanese army platoon guarded the large house which they shared, and all appeared to be secure. The generals had already determined that they would make a sizable 'contribution' to that country's treasury, to ensure their own safety for the time – hopefully brief – they'd spend in that country before moving on. Their intelligence chief, still back in Baghdad, was on the phone now, calling around to various contacts in various countries to find secure permanent housing for them. Switzerland? They wondered. A cold country in terms of both climate and culture, but a safe one, and for those with money to invest, an anonymous one.

'Who owns three G-IVs over there?'

'The registration of the aircraft is Swiss, Lieutenant,' Major

Sabah reported, having just learned the fact. From the photos shot at Khartoum he'd gotten the tail number, and that was easily checked on a computer database. He flipped the page to determine the ownership. 'A corporately owned jet. They have three of them, and a few smaller turboprops for flying around Europe. We'll have to check further to learn more about the corporation.' But somebody would be working on that, and they'd find the obvious. Probably some import-export concern, more a letter-drop than anything else, perhaps with a small storefront that conducted real, if negligible, business for appearance's sake. The corporation would have a medium-sized account in a commercial bank; it would have a law firm to make sure that it scrupulously obeyed every local rule; its employees would be fully briefed on how to behave – Switzerland was a law-abiding country – and how to keep everything in order; the corporation would vanish into the woodwork, because the Swiss didn't trouble people who deposited money in their banks and kept within their laws. Those who broke the rules severely could find the country as inhospitable as the one the generals were leaving. That was well understood, too.

The pity of it, Sabah thought, was that he knew the first two faces, and probably also knew the faces now in transit. It would have been pleasing to get them before the bar of justice, especially a Kuwaiti bar. They'd been more junior, most of them, when Iraq had invaded his country. They would have participated in the pillaging. Major Sabah remembered prowling the streets, trying to look as inconspicuous and harmless as possible while other Kuwaiti subjects had resisted more actively, which had been brave, but dangerous. Most of them had been caught and killed, along with family members, and though the survivors were now famous and well rewarded, those few had operated on information he'd gathered. The major didn't mind. His family was wealthy enough, and he *liked* being a spook. Even more, he was damned sure his country would never be surprised like that again. He would see to that personally.

In any case, the generals who were leaving were less a concern than the ones who would replace them. That had the major worried.

* * *

'Well, I'm afraid it was a pretty weak performance in all respects for Mr Ryan,' Ed Kealty said on the noon news-interview show. 'Dr Bretano is, first of all, an industry official who has long since opted out of public service. I was there when his name came up before, and I was there when he refused to consider a high government position – so that he could stay where he was to make money, I suppose. He's a talented man, evidently a good engineer,' Kealty allowed with a tolerant smile, 'but a Secretary of Defense, no.' A shake of the head emphasized it.

'What did you think of President Ryan's position on abortion, sir?' Barry asked on CNN.

'Barry, that's the problem. He's *not* really the President,' Kealty replied in a mild, businesslike tone. 'And we need to correct that. His lack of understanding for the public showed clearly in that contradictory and ill-considered statement in the Press Room. *Roe v. Wade* is the law of the land. That's all he had to say. It's not necessary that the President should like the laws, but he has to enforce them. Of course, for any public official not to understand how the American people think on this issue doesn't so much show insensitivity to the rights of women to choose, as simple incompetence. All Ryan had to do was listen to his briefers on what to say, but he didn't even do that. He's a loose cannon,' Kealty concluded. 'We don't need one of those in the White House.'

'But your claim –' A raised hand stopped the correspondent cold.

'It's not a claim, Barry. It's a fact. I never resigned. I never actually left the vice-presidency. Because of that, when Roger Durling died, I became President. What we have to do right now, and Mr Ryan will do this if he cares about his country, is to form a judicial panel to examine the constitutional issues and decide who the President really is. If Ryan does not do that – well, he's putting himself before the good of the country. Now, I must add that I fully believe that Jack Ryan is acting in good conscience. He's an honorable man, and in the past he's shown himself to be a courageous man. Unfortunately, right now, he's confused, as we saw at the press conference this morning.'

'A pat of butter would not melt in his mouth, Jack,' van

Damm observed, turning the sound down. 'You see how good he is at this?'

Ryan nearly came out of his chair. 'God damn it, Arnie, that's what I said! I must have said it three or four times – that's the law, and I can't break the law. *That's what I said!*'

'Remember what I told you about keeping your temper under control?' The chief of staff waited for Ryan's color to go back down. He turned the sound back up.

'What's most disturbing, however,' Kealty was saying now, 'is what Ryan said about his appointments to the Supreme Court. It's pretty clear he wants to turn the clock back on a lot of things. Litmus tests on issues like abortion, appointing only strict-constructionists. It makes you wonder if he wants to overturn affirmative action, and heaven knows what else. Unfortunately, we find ourselves in a situation where the sitting President will exercise immense power, particularly in the courts. And Ryan just doesn't know how, Barry. He doesn't, and what we learned today about what he wants to do – well, it's just plain frightening, isn't it?'

'Am I on a different planet, Arnie?' Jack demanded. 'I didn't say "litmus test." A reporter did. I didn't say "strict-constructionist." A reporter did.'

'Jack, it isn't what you say. It's what people hear.'

'Just how much damage do you think President Ryan could do, then?' Barry asked on the TV. Arnie shook his head in admiration. Kealty had seduced him right out of his shorts, right on live television, and Barry had responded perfectly, framing the question to show that he still called Ryan the President, but then asking the question in a form that would shake people's faith in him. It was no wonder that Ed was so good with the ladies, was it? And the average viewer would never grasp the subtlety with which he'd pulled Barry's drawers off. What a pro.

'In a situation like this, with the government decapitated? It could take years to fix what he might break,' Kealty said with the grave concern of a trusted family physician. 'Not because he's an evil person. He certainly is not. But because he simply doesn't know how to execute the office of President of the United States. He just doesn't, Barry.'

'We'll be back after these messages from our cable operators,' Barry told the camera. Arnie had heard enough, and didn't need to see the commercials. He lifted the controller and clicked the TV off.

'Mr President, I wasn't worried before, but I'm worried now.' He paused for a moment. 'Tomorrow you will see some editorials in a few of the major papers agreeing that a judicial commission is necessary, and you'll have no choice but to let it go forward.'

'Wait a minute. The law doesn't say that – '

'The law doesn't say anything, remember? And even if it did, there's no Supreme Court to decide. We're in a democracy, Jack. The will of the people will decide who's the President. The will of the people will be swayed by what the media says, and you'll never be as good at working the media as Ed is.'

'Look, Arnie, *he* resigned. *I* got confirmed by the Congress as VP, Roger got killed, and *I* became President, and that's the fucking law! And *I* have to abide by the law. I swore an oath to do that, and I will. I never wanted this fucking job, but I've never run away from anything in my life, either, and I'll be damned if I'll run away from this!' There was one other thing. Ryan despised Edward Kealty. Didn't like his political views, didn't like his Harvard hauteur, didn't like his private life, damned sure didn't like his treatment of women. 'You know what he is, Arnie?' Ryan snarled.

'Yes, I do. He's a pimp, a hustler, a con man. He has no convictions at all. He's never even practiced law, but he's helped write thousands of them. He's not a doctor, but he's established national health policy. He's been a professional politician his whole life, always on the public payroll. He's never generated a product or a service in the private sector of the economy, but he's spent his life deciding how high the taxes should be, and how that money should be spent. The only black people he ever met as a kid were the maids who picked up his bedroom, but he's a champion of minority rights. He's a hypocrite. He's a charlatan. And he's going to win unless you get your shit together, Mr President,' Arnie said, pouring dry ice over Ryan's fiery temper. 'Because he knows how to play the game, and you don't.'

The patient, the records said, had taken a trip to the Far East back in October, and in Bangkok had indulged himself in the sexual services for which that country was well known. Pierre Alexandre, then a captain assigned to a military hospital in the tropical country, had once indulged in them himself. His conscience didn't trouble him about it. He'd been young and foolish, as people of that age were supposed to be. But that had been before AIDS. He'd been the guy to tell the patient, male, Caucasian, thirty-six, that he had HIV antibodies in his blood, that he could not have unprotected sex with his wife, and that his wife should have her blood tested at once. Oh, she was pregnant? Immediately, right away. Tomorrow if possible.

Alexandre felt rather like a judge. It wasn't the first time he'd delivered news like this, and damned sure it wouldn't be the last, but at least when a judge pronounced a sentence of death it was for a serious crime, and there was an appeals process. This poor bastard was guilty of nothing more than being a man twelve time-zones from home, probably drunk and lonely. Maybe he'd had an argument over the phone with his wife. Maybe she'd been pregnant then, and he wasn't getting any. Maybe it had just been the exotic locations, and Alex remembered well how seductive those childlike Thai girls could be, and what the hell, who'd ever know? Now a lot of people would, and there was no appeals process. That could change, Dr Alexandre thought. He had just told the patient that. You couldn't take their hope away. That's what oncologists had told their patients for two generations. That hope was real, was true, wasn't it? There were some smart people working on this one – Alexandre was one of them – and the breakthrough could happen tomorrow, for all he knew. Or it could take a hundred years. The patient, on the form card, had ten.

'You don't look very happy.'

He looked up. 'Dr Ryan.'

'Dr Alexandre, and I think you know Roy.' She gestured at the table with her tray. The dining area was packed today. 'Mind?'

He got halfway to his feet. 'Please.'

'Bad day?'

'E-Strain case,' was all he had to say.

'HIV, Thailand? Over here now?'

'You *do* read *M&M*.' He managed a smile.

'I have to keep up with my residents. E-Strain? You're sure?' Cathy asked.

'I reran the test myself. He got it in Thailand, business trip, he said. Pregnant wife,' Alex added. Professor Ryan grimaced at the addition.

'Not good.'

'AIDS?' Roy Altman asked. The rest of SURGEON's detail was spread around the room. They would have preferred that she ate in her office, but Dr Ryan had explained that this was one of the ways in which Hopkins docs kept up with one another, and was for her a regular routine. Today it was infectious disease. Tomorrow pediatrics.

'E-Strain,' Alexandre explained with a nod. 'America is mostly B-Strain. Same thing in Africa.'

'What's the difference?'

Cathy answered. 'B-Strain is pretty hard to get. It mainly requires direct contact of blood products. That happens with IV drug users who share needles or through sexual contact, but mainly it's still homosexuals who have tissue lesions either from tearing or more conventional venereal diseases.'

'You forgot bad luck, but that's only one percent or so.' Alexandre picked up the thread. 'It's starting to look as though E-Strain – that cropped up in Thailand – well, that it makes the heterosexual jump a lot more easily than B. It's evidently a heartier version of our old friend.'

'Has CDC quantified that yet?' Cathy asked.

'No, they need a few more months, least that's what I heard a couple weeks ago.'

'How bad?' Altman asked. Working with SURGEON was turning into an educational experience.

'Ralph Forster went over five years ago to see how bad things were. Know the story, Alex?'

'Not all of it, just the bottom line.'

'Ralph flew over on a government ticket, official trip and all that, and first thing happens off the plane, the Thai official meets him at customs, walks him to the car and says, "Want some girls for tonight?" That's when he knew there was a real problem.'

'I believe it,' Alex said, remembering when he would have smiled and nodded. This time he managed not to shudder.

'The numbers are grim. Mr Altman, right now, nearly a third of the kids inducted into the Thai army are HIV positive. Mainly E-Strain.' The implications of that number were unmistakable.

'A third? A *third* of them?'

'Up from twenty-five percent when Ralph flew over. That's a hard number, okay?'

'But that means –'

'It might mean in fifty years, no more Thailand,' Cathy announced in a matter-of-fact voice that masked her inner horror. 'When I was going to school here, I thought oncology was the place to be for the supersmart ones' – she pointed for Altman's benefit – 'Marty, Bert, Curt, and Louise, those guys in the corner over there. I didn't think I could take it, take the stress, so I cut up eyeballs and fix 'em. I was wrong. We're going to beat cancer. But these damned viruses, I don't know.'

'The solution, Cathy, is in understanding the precise inter-actions between the gene strings in the virus and the host cell, and it shouldn't be all *that* hard. Viruses are such tiny little sunzabitches. They can only do so many things, not like the interaction of the entire human genome at concep-tion. Once we figure that one out, we can defeat all the little bastards.' Alexandre, like most research docs, was an optimist.

'So, researching the human cell?' Altman asked, interested in learning this. Alexandre shook his head.

'A lot smaller than that. We're into the genome now. It's like taking a strange machine apart, every step you're trying to figure what the individual parts do, and sooner or later you got all the parts loose, and you know where they all go, and then you figure out what they all do in a systematic way. That's what we're doing now.'

'You know what it's going to come down to?' Cathy sug-gested with a question, then answered it: 'Mathematics.'

'That's what Gus says down at Atlanta.'

'Math? Wait a minute,' Altman objected.

'At the most basic level, the human genetic code is composed of four amino acids, labeled A, C, G and T. How those letters – the acids, I mean – are strung together deter-mines everything,' Alex explained. 'Different character sequences mean different things and interact in different ways, and probably Gus is right: the interactions are mathematically defined. The genetic code really is a code. It *can* be cracked, and it *can* be understood.' *Probably someone will assign a mathematical value to them. . . complex polynomials. . .* he thought. Was that important?

'Just nobody smart enough to do it has come along yet,' Cathy Ryan observed. 'That's the home-run ball, Roy. Someday, somebody is going to step up to the plate, and put that one over the fence, and it will give us the key to defeating all human diseases. All of them. Every single one. The pot of gold at the end of that rainbow is medical immortality – and who knows, maybe human immortality.'

'Put us all out of business, especially you, Cathy. One of the first things they'll edit out of the human genome is myopia, and diabetes and that –'

'It'll unemploy you before it unemploys me, Professor,' Cathy said with an impish smile. 'I'm a surgeon, remember? I'll still have trauma to fix. But sooner or later, you're going to win your battle.'

But would it be in time for this morning's E-Strain patient? Alex wondered. Probably not. Probably not.

She was cursing them now, mainly in French, but Flemish also. The army medics didn't understand either language. Moudi spoke the former well enough to know that, vile as the imprecations were, they were not the product of a lucid mind. The brain was now being affected, and Jean Baptiste was unable to converse even with her God. Her heart was under attack, finally, and that gave the doctor hope that Death would come for her and show some belated mercy for a woman who deserved far more than she had received from life. Maybe delirium was a blessing for her. Maybe her soul was detached from her body. Maybe in not knowing where she was, who she was, what was wrong, the pain didn't touch her anymore, not in the places that mattered. It was an illusion the doctor needed, but if what he saw was mercy, it was a ghastly variety of it.

The patient's face was a mass of rashes now, almost as though she'd been brutally beaten, her pale skin like an opaque window onto misplaced blood. He couldn't decide if her eyes were still working. There was bleeding both on the surface and the interior of each, and if she could still see, it wouldn't last much longer. They'd almost lost her half an hour earlier, occasioning his rush to the treatment room to see her choking on aspirated vomit and the medics trying both to clear her airway and keep their gloves intact. The restraints that held her in place, coated though they were with smooth plastic, had abraded away her skin, causing more bleeding and more pain. The tissues of her vascular system were breaking down as well, and the IV leaked as much out on the bed as went into the arms and legs, all of the fluids as deadly as the most toxic poison. Now the medical corpsmen were truly frightened even of touching the patient, gloves or not, suits or not. Moudi saw they they'd gotten a plastic bucket and filled it with dilute iodine, and as he watched, one of them dipped his gloves into it, shaking them off but not drying them, so that if he touched her there would be a chemical barrier against the pathogens that might leap at him from her body. Such precautions weren't necessary – the gloves were thick – but he could hardly blame the men for their fear. At the turning of the hour, the new shift arrived, and the old one left. One of them looked back on his way out the door, praying with silent lips that Allah would take the woman before he had to come back in eight hours. Outside the room, an Iranian army doctor similarly dressed in plastic would lead the men to the disinfection area, where their suits would be sprayed before they took them off, and then their bodies, while the suits were burned to ashes in the downstairs incinerator. Moudi had no doubts that the procedures would be followed to the letter – no, they would be exceeded in every detail, and even then the medics would be afraid for days to come.

Had he possessed a deadly weapon right then and there, he might have used it on her, and to hell with the consequences. A large injection of air might have worked a few hours before, causing a fatal embolism, but the breakdown of her vascular system was such that he couldn't even be sure of that. It was her strength that made the ordeal so terrible. Small though she was, she'd worked forty years of long hours, and earned surprisingly good health as a result. The body which had sustained her courageous soul for so long would not give up the battle, futile as it was.

'Come, Moudi, you know better than this,' the director said behind him.

'What do you mean?' he asked without turning.

'If she were back in the hospital in Africa, what would be different? Would they not treat her the same way, taking the same measures to sustain her? The blood, and the IV fluids, and everything else. It would be exactly the same. Her religion does not allow euthanasia. If anything, the care here is better,' he pointed out, correctly, if coldly, then turned away to check the chart. 'Five liters. Excellent.'

'We could start –'

'No.' The director shook his head. 'When her heart stops, we will drain all her blood. We will remove the liver, kidneys and spleen, and then our real work begins.'

'Someone should at least pray for her soul.'

'You will, Moudi. You are a fine doctor. You care even for an infidel. You may be proud of that. If it were possible to save her, you would have done so. I know that. You know that. She knows that.'

'What we are doing, to inflict this on –'

'On unbelievers,' the director reminded him. 'On those who hate our country and our Faith, who spit upon the words of the Prophet. I will even agree that this is a woman of virtue. Allah will be merciful with her, I am sure. You did not choose her fate. Neither did I.' He had to keep Moudi going. The younger man *was* a brilliant physician. If anything, too good. The director for his part thanked Allah that he'd spent the last decade in laboratories, else he might have succumbed to the same human weaknesses.

Badrayn insisted. This time, three generals. Every seat full, and one of them with two small children strapped in together. They understood now. They had to. He'd explained it to them, pointing to the tower, whose controllers had watched every flight in and out, and who *had to know* what was going on by now, and arresting them would do little good, as their families would miss them, and if their families were picked up, the neighbors would know, wouldn't they?

Well, yes, they had agreed.

Just send a damned airliner next time, he wanted to tell Tehran, but no, someone would have objected, here or there, it didn't matter, because no matter what you said, no matter how sensible it was, somebody would object to it. Whether on the Iranian side or the Iraqi, that didn't matter, either. Either way it would get people killed. It certainly would. There was nothing for him to do but wait now, wait and worry. He could have had a few drinks, but he decided against it. He'd had alcohol more than once. All those years in Lebanon. As Bahrain still was, Lebanon had been, and probably would be again, a place where the strict Islamic rules could be violated, and there he had indulged in Western vice along with everyone else. But not now. He might be close to death and, sinner or not, he was a Muslim, and he would face death in the proper way. And so he drank coffee for the most part, staring out the windows from his seat, next to the phone, telling himself that the caffeine was making his hands shake, and nothing else.

'You're Jackson?' Tony Bretano asked. He'd spent the morning with the acting chiefs. Now it was time for the worker bees.

'Yes, sir, J-3. I guess I'm your operations officer,' Robby replied, taking his seat and not, for once, carrying a bundle of papers and scurrying around like the White Rabbit.

'How bad is it?'

'Well, we're spread pretty thin. We still have two carrier battle-groups in the IO looking after India and Sri Lanka. We're flying a couple battalions of light infantry to the Marianas to reassert control there and supervise the withdrawal of Japanese personnel. That's mainly political, we don't expect any problems. Our forward-deployed air assets have been recalled to CONUS to refit. That aspect of operations against Japan went well.'

'You will want me to speed production of the F-22 and restart B-2 production, then? That's what the Air Force said.'

'We just proved that Stealth is one hell of a force-multiplier, Mr Secretary, and that's a fact. We need all of those we can get.'

'I agree. What about the rest of the force structure?' Bretano asked.

'We're too damned thin for all the commitments we have. If we had to go to Kuwait again, for example, like we did in 1991, we can't do it. We literally do not have all that force to project anymore. You know what my job is, sir. I have to figure out how to do the things we have to do. Okay, operations against Japan took us as far as we could go, and –'

'Mickey Moore said a lot of nice things about the plan you put together and executed,' the SecDef pointed out.

'General Moore is very kind. Yes, sir, it worked, but we were on a shoestring the whole time, and that's not the way American forces are supposed to go out into harm's way, Mr Secretary. We're supposed to scare the bejeebers out of people the moment the first private steps off the airplane. I *can* improvise if I have to, but that's not supposed to be my job. Sooner or later, I goof, or somebody goofs, and we end up with dead people in uniform.'

'I agree with that, too.' Bretano took a bite of his sandwich. 'The President's given me a free hand to clean this department out, do things my way. I have two weeks to put the new force requirements together.'

'Two weeks, sir?' If Jackson were able to go pale, that would have done it to him.

'Jackson, how long you been in uniform?' the SecDef asked.

'Counting time at the Trade School? Call it thirty years.'

'If you can't do it by tomorrow, you're the wrong guy. But I'll give you ten days,' Bretano said generously.

'Mr Secretary, I'm Operations, not Manpower, and –'

'Exactly. In my way of looking at things, Manpower fills the needs that Operations defines. Decisions in a place like this are supposed to be made by the shooters, not the accountants. That's what was wrong at TRW when I moved in. Accountants were telling engineers what they could have to be engineers. No.' Bretano shook his head. 'That didn't work. If you build things, your engineers decide how the company runs. For a place like this, the shooters decide what they need, and the accountants figure out how to shoehorn it into the budget. There's always a struggle, but the product end of the business makes the decisions.'

Well, damn. Jackson managed not to smile. 'Parameters?'

'Figure the largest credible threat, the most serious crisis that's likely, not possible, and design me a force structure

368

that can handle it.' Even that wasn't good enough, and both men knew it. In the old days there had been the guideline of two and a half wars, that America could deploy to fight two major conflicts, plus a little brush fire somewhere else. Few had ever admitted that this 'rule' had always been a fantasy, all the way back to the Eisenhower presidency. Today, as Jackson had just admitted, America lacked the wherewithal to conduct a single major military deployment. The fleet was down to half of what it had been ten years earlier. The Army was down further. The Air Force, ever sheltering behind its high-tech, was formidable, but had still retired nearly half its total strength. The Marines were still tough and ready, but the Marine Corps was an expeditionary force, able to deploy in the expectation that reinforcements would arrive behind them, and dangerously light in its weapons. The cupboard wasn't exactly bare, but the enforced diet hadn't really done anyone much good.

'Ten days?'

'You've got what I need sitting in a desk drawer right now, don't you?' Planning officers always did, Bretano knew.

'Give me a couple days to polish it up, sir, but, yes, we do.'

'Jackson?'

'Yes, Mr Secretary?'

'I kept track of our operations in the Pacific. One of my people at TRW, Skip Tyler, used to be pretty good at this stuff, and we looked over maps and things every day. The operations you put together, they were impressive. War isn't just physical. It's psychological, too, like all life is. You win because you have the best people. Guns and planes count, but brains count more. I'm a good manager, and one hell of a good engineer. I'm not a fighter. I'll listen to what you say, 'cause you and your colleagues know how to fight. I'll stand up for you wherever and whenever I have to. In return for that, I want what you really need, not what you'd like to have. We can't afford that. We can cut bureaucracy. That's Manpower's job, civilian and uniform. I'll lean this place out. At TRW I got rid of a lot of useless bodies. That's an engineering company, and now it's run by engineers. This is a company that does operations, and it ought to be run by operators, people with notches cut in their gun grips. Lean. Mean. Tough. Smart. You get what I'm saying?'

'I think so, sir.'

'Ten days. Less if you can. Call me when you're ready.'

'Clark,' John said, picking up his direct line.

'Holtzman,' the voice said. The name made John's eyes go a little wide.

'I suppose I could ask how you got this number, but you'd never reveal your source.'

'Good guess,' the reporter agreed. 'Remember that dinner we had a while back at Esteban's?'

'Vaguely,' Clark lied. 'It's been a long time.' It hadn't actually been a dinner, but the tape machine that had to be on the phone didn't know that.

'I owe you one. How about tonight?'

'I'll get back to you.' Clark hung up and stared down at his desk. What the hell was this about?

'Come on, that's not what Jack said,' van Damm told the *New York Times*.

'That's what he meant, Arnie,' the reporter responded. 'You know it. I know it.'

'I wish you'd go easy on the guy. He's not a politician,' the chief of staff pointed out.

'Not my fault, Arnie. He's in the job. He has to follow the rules.'

Arnold van Damm nodded agreement, concealing the anger that had risen in an instant at the correspondent's casual remark. Inwardly he knew that the reporter was right. That's how the game was played. But he also knew that the reporter was wrong. Maybe he'd grown too attached to President Ryan, enough so that he'd actually absorbed some of his flaky ideas. The media, exclusively composed of the employees of private businesses – most of them corporations with publicly traded stock – had grown in power to the point that they *decided* what people said. That was bad enough. What was worse, they enjoyed their jobs too much. They could make or break anyone in this town. They made the rules. He who broke them could himself be broken.

Ryan *was* a naïf. There was no denying it. In his defense, he'd never sought his current job. He'd come here by accident, having sought nothing more than a final opportunity to serve, and then to leave once and for all, to return to private life. He'd not been elected to his post. But neither had the media, and at least Ryan had the Constitution to define his duties. The media was crossing the line. They were taking sides in a constitutional matter, and they were taking the wrong side.

'Who makes the rules?' Arnie asked.

'They just are,' the *Times* answered.

'Well, the President isn't going to attack *Roe*. He never said that he would. And he's not going to pick Justices off park benches, either. He isn't going to pick liberal activists, and he isn't going to pick conservative activists, and I think you know that.'

'So Ryan misspoke himself?' The reporter's casual grin said it all. He'd report this as spin control by a senior administration official, ' "clarifying," which means correcting, what the President said,' the article would read.

'Not at all. You misunderstood him.'

'It sounded pretty clear to me, Arnie.'

'That's because you're used to listening to professional politicians. The President we have now says things straight. Actually I kind of like that,' van Damm went on, lying; it was driving him crazy. 'And it might even make life easier for you. You don't have to check the tea leaves anymore. All you have to do is take proper notes. Or maybe just judge him by a fair set of rules. We've agreed that he's not a politician, but you're treating him as if he were. Listen to what he's really saying, will you?' Or maybe even look at the videotape, he didn't add. He was skating on the edge now. Talking to the media was like petting a new cat. You never knew when they'd reach up and scratch.

'Come on, Arnie. You're the most loyal guy in this town. Damn, you would have been a great family doctor. We all know that. But Ryan doesn't have a clue. The speech at National Cathedral, that loony speech from the Oval Office. He's about as presidential as the chairman of the Rotary in Bumfuck, Iowa.'

'But who decides what's presidential and what isn't?'

'In New York, I do.' The reporter smiled again. 'For Chicago, you have to ask somebody else.'

'He *is* the President of the United States.'

'That's not what Ed Kealty says, and at least Ed *acts* presidential.'

'Ed's out. He resigned. Roger took the call from Secretary Hanson, and told me about it. Damn it, *you* reported that yourself.'

'But what possible motive could he have for –'

'What motive could he have for boffing every skirt that crossed his bow?' the chief of staff demanded. *Great*, he thought, *now I'm losing control of the media!*

'Ed's always been a ladies' man. He's gotten better since he got off the booze. It never affected his duties,' the White House correspondent made clear. Like his paper, he was a strong proponent of women's rights. 'This one will have to play out.'

'What position will the *Times* take?'

'I'll get you a copy of the editorial,' the reporter promised.

He couldn't stand it anymore. He lifted the phone and dialed the six digits while staring out at the darkness. The sun was down now, and clouds were rolling in. It would be a cold, rainy night, leading to a dawn which might or might not take place before his eyes.

'Yes?' a voice said halfway through the first ring.

'Badrayn here. It would be more convenient if the next aircraft were larger.'

'We have a 737 standing by, but I need authorization to have it sent.'

'I will work on this end.'

It was the TV news which had gotten him moving. Even more muted than usual, there had not been a single political story. Not one, in a nation where political commentary often as not displaced the weather forecasts. Most ominously of all, there was a story about a mosque, an old Shi'a mosque, one that had fallen into disrepair. The story lamented that fact, citing the building's long and honorable history, and ignoring the fact that it had fallen into disrepair because it had once been a meeting place for a group charged, perhaps truthfully, with plotting the demise of Iraq's fallen, belovéd, great, and evidently soon-to-be-forgotten political leader. Worst of all, the taped footage had shown five mullahs standing outside the mosque, not even looking directly at the camera, merely gesturing at the faded blue tile on the wall and probably discussing what needed to be done. The five were the same ones who'd flown in to be hostages. But not a single soldier was in sight on the TV screen, and the faces of at least two of the mullahs were well known to Iraqi audiences. Somebody had gotten to the TV station, more precisely to the people who worked there. If the reporters and others wanted to retain their jobs and their heads, it was time to face a new reality. Were the brief few moments on the screen enough for the common folk to see and recognize the visitors' faces – and get the message? Finding out the answer to that question could be dangerous.

But the common people didn't matter. Colonels and majors did. Generals not on the proper list did. Quite soon they'd know. Probably some already did. They'd be on the phone, first calling up the line to see what was going on. Some would hear lies. Some would hear nothing. They'd start thinking. They'd start making contacts. Over the next twelve hours they'd talk among themselves and have to make hard decisions. These were the men who were identified with the dying regime. The ones who couldn't run, who had no place to run to and no money to run with, the ones who had to stay. Their identification with the past regime could be a death sentence – for many, certainly would be so. For others, there was a chance. To survive, they would have to do what criminals all over the world did. They would save their own lives by offering up a larger fish. So it always was. The colonels would overthrow the generals.

Finally, the generals understood.

'There is a 737 standing by. Enough room for all. It can be here in ninety minutes,' he told them.

'And they will not kill us at Mehrabad Airport?' the deputy chief of staff of the Iraqi army demanded.

'Would you prefer to die here?' Badrayn asked in reply.

'What if it's all a trap?

'There is that risk. In that case, the five television personalities will die.' Of course they wouldn't. That would have to be the act of troops loyal to generals already dead. That sort of loyalty didn't exist here. They all knew that. The mere act of taking hostages had been an instinctive gesture, and one already invalidated by someone, perhaps in the media, but maybe the colonel who'd headed the guard force over the Iranian clerics. *He* was supposed to be a trusted intelligence specialist, Badrayn remembered on reflection, a loyal Sunni officer, son of a Ba'ath Party member. That could mean that the Ba'ath Party was already being suborned. It was going too fast now. The mullahs would not have concealed the nature of their mission, would they? But none of that mattered. Killing the hostages would accomplish nothing. The generals were doomed if they stayed here, and martyrdom wasn't exactly offensive to Iranian clerics. It was an integral part of the Shi'a tradition.

No, the decision had already been irreversibly made. These senior commanders hadn't grasped that. They hadn't thought it all the way through.

Well, had they been truly competent officers, they would have been killed ages ago, by their belovéd leader.

'Yes,' the most senior of them said.

'Thank you.' Badrayn lifted the phone and punched the buttons again.

The dimensions of the constitutional crisis in which America has found itself were not apparent until yesterday. Although the issue may seem to be technical, the substance of it is not.

John Patrick Ryan is a man of ability, but whether or not he has the necessary talent to perform his presidential duties has yet to be established. The initial indications are less than promising. Government service is not a job for amateurs. Our country has often enough turned to such people, but always in the past they have been in the minority, able to grow into their duties in an orderly way.

There is nothing orderly about the crisis facing the country. To this point Mr Ryan has done a proper and careful job of stabilizing the government. His interim appointment to head the FBI, for example, Daniel Murray, is an acceptable choice. Similarly, George Winston is probably a fair interim choice for the Department of the Treasury, though he is politically unschooled. Scott Adler, a highly talented,

*lifelong foreign service officer, may be the best member of
the current cabinet. . .* Ryan skipped the next two paragraphs.

*Vice President Edward Kealty, whatever his personal fail-
ings, knows government, and his middle-of-the-road position on most national issues offers a steady course until
elections can select a new administration. But are his claims
true?*

'Do you care?' Ryan asked the lead editorial for the next
day's *Times*.

'They know him. They don't know you,' Arnie answered.
Then the phone rang.

'Yes?'

'Mr Foley for you, Mr President. He says it's important.'

'Okay . . . Ed? Putting you on speaker.' Jack pushed the
proper button and replaced the receiver. 'Arnie's listening
in.'

'It's definite. Iran's making a move, big and fast. I have a
TV feed for you if you have the time.'

'Roll it.' Jack knew how to do that. In this office and others
were televisions fed off secure fiber-optic cables to the Pentagon and elsewhere. He pulled the controller from a drawer
and turned the set on. The 'show' lasted only fifteen seconds,
was re-run again, then freeze-framed.

'Who are they?' Jack asked.

Foley read off the names. Ryan had heard two of them
before. 'Mid- and top-level advisers to Daryaei. They're in
Baghdad, and somebody decided to get the word out. Okay,
we know senior generals are flying out. Now we have five
mullahs talking about rebuilding an important mosque on
national TV. Tomorrow they'll be talking louder,' the DCI-
designate promised.

'Anything from people on the ground?'

'Negative,' Ed admitted. 'I was talking to station chief
Riyadh about sneaking up there for a sit-down, but by the
time he gets there, there won't be anyone to sit down with.'

'That's a little big,' an officer said aboard the duty AWACS.
He read off the alpha-numeric display. 'Colonel,' the lieutenant called over the command line, 'I have what appears to
be a 737 charter inbound Mehrabad to Baghdad, course two-
two-zero, speed four-five-zero knots, twenty thousand feet.

PALM BOWL reports encrypted voice traffic to Baghdad from that track.'

Farther aft, the senior officer commanding the aircraft checked his display. The elltee in front was right. The colonel lit up his radio to report to KKMC.

The rest of them arrived together. They should have waited longer, Badrayn thought. Better to show up with the aircraft already here, the quicker to – but, no.

It was amusing to see them this way, these powerful men. A week earlier they'd strutted everywhere, sure of their place and their power, their khaki shirts decorated with various ribbons denoting some heroic service or other. That was unfair. Some *had* led men into battle, once or twice. Maybe one or two of them had actually killed an enemy. Iranian enemies. The same people to whom they would now entrust their safety, because they feared their own countrymen more. So now they stood about in little worried knots, unable to trust even their own bodyguards. Especially them. They had guns and were close, and they would not have been in this fix had bodyguards been trustworthy.

Despite the danger to his own life, Badrayn could not help but be amused by it. He'd spent his entire adult life dedicated to bringing about a moment such as this. How long had he dreamed of seeing senior Israeli officials standing about an airport like this – leaving their own people to an uncertain fate, defeated by his . . . *that* irony was not amusing, was it? Over thirty years, and all he'd accomplished was the destruction of an *Arab* country? Israel still stood. America still protected her, and all he was doing was adjusting the chairs of power around the Persian Gulf.

He was running away no less than they were, Badrayn admitted. Having failed in the mission of his life, he had done this one mercenary job, and then what? At least these generals had money and comfort before them. He had nothing ahead, and only failure behind. With that thought, Ali Badrayn swore, and sat back in his seat, just in time to see a dark shape race across the near runway in its rollout. A bodyguard at the door gestured at the people in the room. Two minutes later, the 737 came back into view. Additional fuel was not needed. The truck-borne stairway headed off, stopping only when the aircraft did. The stairs were in place before the door opened, and the generals, and their families, and one bodyguard each, and for most of them a mistress, hurried out the door into the cold drizzle that had just begun. Badrayn walked out last. Even then he had to wait. The Iraqis had all arrived at the bottom of the stairs in a tight little knot of jostling humanity, forgetting their importance and their dignity as they elbowed their way onto the steps. At the top was a uniformed crew member, smiling a mechanical greeting to people he had every reason to hate. Ali waited until the stairs were clear before heading up, arriving at the small platform and turning to look back. There hadn't really been all that much reason to rush. There were as yet no green trucks approaching with their confused soldiers. Another hour, it turned out, would have been fine. In due course they'd come here and find nothing but an empty lounge. He shook his head and entered the aircraft. The crewman closed the door behind him.

Forward, the flight crew radioed the tower for clearance to taxi, and that came automatically. The tower controllers had made their calls and passed along their information, but without instructions, they just did their jobs. As they watched, the aircraft made its way to the end of the runway, increased power, and lifted off into the darkness about to descend on their country.

19

RECIPES

'It's been a while, Mr Clark.'

'Yes, Mr Holtzman, it has,' John agreed. They were in the same booth as before, all the way in the back, close to the jukebox. Esteban's was still a nice family place off Wisconsin Avenue, and still well patronized by nearby Georgetown University. But Clark remembered that he'd never told the reporter what his name was.

'Where's your friend?'

'Busy tonight,' Clark replied. Actually Ding had left work early and driven down to Yorktown, and was taking Patsy out to dinner, but the reporter didn't need to know that. It was clear from his face that he already knew too much. 'So, what can I do for you?' the field officer asked.

'We had a little deal, you'll recall.'

Clark nodded. 'I haven't forgotten. That was for five years. Time isn't up yet.' The reply wasn't much of a surprise.

'Times change.' Holtzman lifted the menu and scanned it. He liked Mexican food, though of late the food didn't seem to like him very much.

'A deal's a deal.' Clark didn't look at his menu. He stared straight across the table. His stare was something people often had trouble dealing with.

'The word's out. Katryn is engaged to be married to some fox-chaser out in Winchester.'

'I didn't know,' Clark admitted. Nor did he especially care.

'Didn't think you would. You're not an SPO anymore. Like it back in the field?'

'If you want me to talk about that, you know I can't–'

'More's the pity. I've been checking up on you for a couple of years now,' the reporter told his guest. 'You have one *hell* of a service reputation, and the word is that your partner is a comer. You were the guy in Japan,' Holtzman said with a smile. 'You rescued Koga.'

A scornful look concealed John's real feelings of alarm. 'What the hell would give you that idea?'

'I talked with Koga when he was over. Two-man rescue team, he said. Big guy, little guy. Koga described your eyes – blue, hard, intense, he said, but he also said that you were a reasonable man in your speech. How smart do I have to be to figure that one out?' Holtzman smiled. 'Last time we talked, you said I would have made a good spook.' The waiter showed up with two beers. 'Ever have this before? Pride of Maryland, a new local micro on the Eastern Shore.' Then the waiter went away. Clark leaned across the table.

'Look, I respect your ability, and the last time we talked, you played ball, kept your word, and I respect that, too, but I would like you to remember that when I go out in the field, my life rides on–'

'I won't reveal your identity. I don't do that. Three reasons, it's wrong, it's against the law, and I don't want to piss off somebody like you.' The reporter sipped his beer. 'Someday I'd sure as hell like to do a book about you. If half the stories are true–'

'Fine, get Val Kilmer to play me in the movies.'

'Too pretty.' Holtzman shook his head with a grin. 'Nick Cage has a better stare. Anyway, what this meet is about . . .' He paused. 'It was Ryan who got her father out, but I'm not clear on how. You went on the beach and got Katryn and her mother out, took them out by boat to a submarine. I don't know which one, but I know it was one of our nuclear subs. But that's not the story.'

'What is?'

'Ryan, like you, the Quiet Hero.' Robert Holtzman enjoyed seeing the surprise in Clark's eyes. 'I like the guy. I want to help him.'

'Why?' John asked, wondering if he could believe his host.

'My wife, Libby, got the goods on Kealty. Published it too soon, and we can't go back to it now. He's scum, even worse than most of the people down there. Not everybody in the business feels that way, but Libby's talked to a couple of his victims. Once upon a time a guy could get away with that, especially if his politics were "progressive." Not anymore. Not supposed to, anyway,' he corrected himself. 'I'm not so sure Ryan's the right guy, either, okay? But he's honest. He'll try to do the right thing, for the right reasons. As Roger Durling liked to say, he's a good man in a storm. I have to sell my editors on that idea.'

'How do you do that?'

'I do a story about how he did something really important for his country. Something old enough that it isn't sensitive anymore, and recent enough that people know it's the same guy. Jesus Christ, Clark, he *saved* the Russians! He prevented an internal power play that could have dialed the Cold War back in for another decade. That's a big *fucking* deal – and he *never* told anybody about it. We'll make it clear that Ryan didn't leak this. We'll even approach him before we run it, and you know what he'll say–'

'He'd tell you not to run it,' Clark agreed. Then he wondered whom Holtzman might have talked with. Judge Arthur Moore? Bob Ritter? Would they have talked? Ordinarily he'd be sure the answer to that one was an emphatic *no*, but now? Now he wasn't so sure. You got to a certain level and people figured breaking the rules was part of some higher duty to the country. John knew about 'higher duty' stuff. It had landed him in all manner of trouble, more than once.

'But it's too good a story not to run. It took me years to figure it all out. The public has a right to know what kind of man is sitting in the Oval Office, especially if he's the right man,' the reporter went on. Holtzman clearly was a man who could talk a nun right out of her habit.

'Bob, you don't know the half of it.' Clark stopped talking an instant later, annoyed with himself for saying that much. This was deep water, and he was trying to swim with a weight belt on. Oh, what the hell . . . 'Okay, tell me what you know about Jack.'

It was agreed that they'd use the same aircraft, and somewhat to the relief of both sides, that they wouldn't stay one unnecessary minute in Iran. There was the problem that the 737 didn't have the range of the smaller G-IVs, however, and it was agreed that the airliner would land in Yemen to refuel. The Iraqis never left the plane at Mehrabad, but when the stairs pulled up, Badrayn did, without a single word of thanks from the people he'd saved. A car was waiting. He didn't look back. The generals were part of his past, and he part of theirs.

The car took him into town. There was just a driver, who took his time negotiating the streets. Traffic wasn't all that dense at this time of night, and the going was easy. Forty minutes later, the car stopped in front of a three-story building. Here there was security. So, Badrayn thought, he was living in Tehran now? He got out of the car on his own. A uniformed security guard compared a photograph with his face and gestured him toward the door. Inside another guard, this one a captain by the three pips at his shoulders, patted him down politely. From there it was upstairs to a conference room. By now it was three in the morning, local time.

He found Daryaei sitting in a comfortable chair reading some papers stapled together at the corner, the quintessential government briefing document instead of the Holy Koran. Well, Daryaei must have had it memorized by now, so long had he studied it.

'Peace be unto you,' Ali said.

'And unto you, peace,' Daryaei replied, not so mechanically as Badrayn had expected. The older man rose and came to him for the expected embrace. The face was far more relaxed than he'd expected. Tired, certainly, since it had been a long day or two for the cleric, but old or not, the man was buoyed by the events. 'You are well?' he asked solicitously, waving his guest to a chair.

Ali allowed himself a long breath as he took his seat. 'I am now. I'd wondered how long the situation in Baghdad would remain stable.'

'There was nothing to be gained from discord. My friends tell me that the old mosque is in need of repair.'

Badrayn might have said that he didn't know – he didn't – but the reason was that he hadn't seen the inside of a mosque in rather a long time, a fact not calculated to please Daryaei. 'There is much to do,' he decided to respond.

'Yes, there is.' Mahmoud Haji Daryaei returned to his chair, setting the papers aside. 'Your services were very valuable. Were there any difficulties?'

Badrayn shook his head. 'Not really, no. It's surprising how fearful such men can be, but I was prepared for that. Your proposal was generous. They had no choice but to take it. You will not . . . ?' Ali allowed himself to ask.

He shook his head. 'No, they shall go in peace.'

And that, if true, was something of a surprise, though Ali didn't allow his face to show it. Daryaei had little reason to love those men. All had played a role in the Iran-Iraq war, and been responsible for the deaths of thousands, a wound still raw on this nation. So many young men had died. The war was one of the reasons why Iran had played no major role in the world for years. But that was about to change, wasn't it?

'So, may I ask what you will do next?'

'Iraq has been a sick country for so long, kept away from the True Faith, wandering in the darkness.'

'And strangled by the embargo,' Badrayn added, wondering what information this observation would elicit.

'It is time for that to end,' Daryaei agreed. Something in his eyes congratulated Ali for the observation. Yes, that was the obvious play, wasn't it? A sop to the West. The embargo would be lifted. Food would then flood the country, and the population would be delighted with the new regime. He would please everybody at once, all the while planning to please no one but himself. And Allah, of course. But Daryaei was one of those who was sure that his policies were inspired by Allah, an idea Badrayn had long since disposed of.

'America will be a problem, as will others closer to you.'

'We are examining those issues.' This statement was delivered comfortably. Well, that made sense. He must have been thinking about this move for years, and at a moment like this one he must have felt invincible. That also made sense, Badrayn knew. Daryaei always thought Allah was on his side – *at* his side was more accurate. And perhaps He was, but there was much more to it than that. There had to be if you wanted success. Miracles most often appeared when summoned by preparation. Why not a play to see if he might take a hand in the next miracle, Ali thought.

'I've been looking at the new American leader.'

'Oh?' Daryaei's eyes focused a little more tightly.

'It's not difficult, gathering information in the modern age. The American media publishes so much, and it can all be easily accessed now. I have some of my people working on it even now, building a careful dossier.' Badrayn kept his voice casual. It wasn't hard. He was bone-tired. 'It really is quite remarkable how vulnerable they are now.'

'Indeed. Tell me more.'

'The key to America is this Ryan fellow. Is that not obvious?'

'The key to changing America is a constitutional convention,' Ernie Brown said, after long days of silent contemplation. Pete Holbrook was flipping the controller on his slide projector. He'd shot three rolls of film of the Capitol building, and a few more of other buildings like the White House, unable completely to avoid being the tourist. He grumbled, seeing that one of the slides was in the caddie upside-down. This idea had gestated long enough, and the result wasn't all that impressive.

'We've talked about that for a long time,' Holbrook agreed as he lifted the caddie off the projector. 'But how do you–'

'Force it? Easy. If there's no President and no way to select one within the Constitution, then *something* has to happen, doesn't it?'

'Kill the President?' Pete snorted. '*Which* one?'

There was the problem. You didn't have to be a rocket scientist to figure that one out. Take out Ryan, and Kealty would step in. Take out Kealty, and Ryan was in like Flynn. It would be tough enough now. Both men remembered all the security they'd seen at the White House. Kill either one, and the American SS would put a wall around the one who was left that you'd need a nuke to breach. The Mountain Men didn't have any of those. They preferred traditional American weapons, like rifles. Even those had their limitations. The South Lawn of the White House was thoroughly forested with trees, and, they'd noticed, also shielded by skillfully concealed earthen berms. Just seeing the White House was possible down only one visual avenue, past the fountain at the building itself. The surrounding buildings were all government-owned, and atop them would always be people with binoculars – and rifles. The American SS were determined to keep the people away from 'their' President, the servant of the people, whose guards didn't trust the people at all. But if the man who lived in that house was really one of the people, there would have been no need, would there? Once Teddy Roosevelt had thrown open the doors and shaken hands with ordinary citizens for four whole hours. No way *that* would happen anymore!

'Both at once. The way I figure, Ryan will be the hard target, right?' Brown asked. 'I mean, he's *there* where most of the protection is. Kealty has to move around a lot, talking to the newspaper pukes, and he won't be as well protected, will he?'

Holbook replaced the slide caddie. 'Okay, that makes sense.'

'So, if we figure a way to do Ryan, taking Kealty out will be much easier to do on the fly.' Brown took the cellular phone out of his pocket. 'Easy to coordinate.'

'Keep going.'

'It means getting a fix on his schedule, learning his routine, and picking our time.'

'Expensive,' Holbrook observed, flipping to the next slide. It was one so often taken by so many people, from the top of the Washington Monument, the tiny north window, looking down on the White House. Ernie Brown had taken one, too, and had the print blown up to poster size in the local photo shop. Then he'd stared at it for hours. Then he'd gotten a map and checked the scale. Then he'd done some rough calculations.

'The expensive part's buying the cement truck, and renting a place not too far out of town.'

'What?'

'I know what the spot is, Pete. And I know how to bring it off. Just a matter of picking the time.'

She wouldn't live through the night, Moudi decided. Her eyes were open now. What they saw was anyone's guess. Finally, mercifully, she was beyond pain. That happened. He'd seen it before, with cancer patients, mostly, and it was always the harbinger of death. His knowledge of neurology was insufficient to understand the reason for it. Maybe the electro-chemical pathways got overloaded, or maybe there was some editing function in the brain. The body knew what was happening, that the time for battle had ended, and since

384

the nervous system reported pain mainly as a warning system, when the time for warning was past, so was the time for pain. Or maybe it was all his imagination. Possible her body was simply too damaged to react to anything. Certainly the intra-ocular bleeding had her blind. The last blood line had fallen out, so damaged were her veins now, and she was bleeding from that point in addition to so many others. Only the morphine drip remained, held in place with tape. The heart was being starved of blood, and trying ever harder to pump what diminished supply it had left, it was exhausting itself.

Jean Baptiste still made noises – difficult to hear through the Racal suit – the occasional whimper, and the timing of them made the physician wonder if they might be prayers. They probably were, he decided. Robbed of sanity along with her life, the one thing that remained in her would be the endless hours of prayer, the discipline which had ruled her life, and she'd return to that in her madness because her mind had nowhere else to go. The patient cleared her throat, choking, really, but then murmuring more clearly, and Moudi leaned his head down to listen.

'. . . – ther of God, pray for us sinners . . .'

Oh, that one. Yes, it would have to be her favorite prayer.

'Fight no more, lady,' Moudi told her. 'It is your time. Fight no more.'

The eyes changed. Even though she could not see, the head turned and she stared at him. It was a mechanical reflex, the physician knew. Blind or not, years of practice told the muscles what to do. The face instinctively turned to a source of noise, and the eyes – the muscles still worked – focused in the direction of interest.

'Dr Moudi? Are you there?' The words came slowly, and not all that clearly, but understandable even so.

'Yes, Sister. I am here.' He touched her hand automatically, then was dumbfounded. *She was* still *lucid*?

'Thank you for . . . helping me. I will pray for you.'

She would. He knew that. He patted her hand again, and with the other increased the morphine drip. Enough was enough. They could put no more blood into her to be polluted with the virus strands. He looked around the room. Both army medics were sitting in the corner, quite content to let the doctor stand with the patient. He walked over to them and pointed to one.

'Tell the director – soon.'

'At once.' The man was very pleased to leave the room. Moudi counted to ten before speaking to the other.

'Fresh gloves, please.' He held up his hands to show that he didn't like touching her either. That medic left, too. Moudi figured he had a minute or so.

The medication tray in the corner had what he needed. He took a 20cc needle from its holder and stuck it into the vial of morphine, pulling in enough to fill the plastic cylinder completely. Then he returned to the bedside, pulled the plastic sheet back and looked for . . . there. The back of her left hand. He took it in his and slid the needle in, immediately pushing down the plunger.

'To help you sleep,' he told her, moving back across the room. He didn't look to see if she responded to his words or not. The needle went into the red-plastic sharps container, and by the time the medic came back with new gloves, everything was as before.

'Here.'

Moudi nodded and stripped the overgloves off into their disposal container, replacing them with a new set. Back at the bedside, he watched the blue eyes close for the last time. The EKG display showed her heart rate at just over one-forty, the spiky lines shorter than they should have been, and irregularly spaced. Just a matter of time now. She was probably praying in her sleep, he thought, dreaming prayers. Well, at least he could be sure now that she was in no pain. The morphine would be well into her diminishing blood supply now, the chemical molecules finding their way to the brain, fitting into the receptors, and there releasing dopamine, which would tell the nervous system . . . yes.

Her chest rose and fell with the labored respiration. There was a pause, almost like a hiccup, and the breathing restarted, but irregularly now, and the flow of oxygen to the bloodstream was now diminishing. The heart rate changed, becoming yet more rapid. Then respiration ceased. The heart still didn't stop at once, so strong it was, so valiant, the doctor thought sadly, admiring this undying part of a person already dead, but that couldn't last long, and with a few final traces on the screen, it, too, ceased to function. The EKG machine began making a steady alarm tone. Moudi reached up and shut it off. He turned to see the medics sharing a look of relief.

'So soon?' the director asked, coming into the room and seeing the flat, silent line on the EKG readout.

'The heart. Internal bleeding.' Moudi didn't have to say anything else.

'I see. We are ready, then?'

'Correct, Doctor.'

The director motioned to the medics, who had one last job to do. One of them bundled up the plastic sheeting to contain drips. The other disconnected the last IV and the electronic EKG leads. This was done expeditiously, and when the former patient was wrapped like a piece of slaughtered meat, the locks on the wheels were kicked loose, and the two soldiers wheeled her out the door. They would return to clean the room so thoroughly as to make sure that nothing could live on the walls, floor, or ceiling.

Moudi and the director followed them to 'Post,' a room in the same confined area behind the double doors. Here was an autopsy table made of smooth, cold stainless steel. They wheeled the treatment bed beside it, uncovering the body and rolling it to a facedown position on the steel, while the doctors observed from the corner, each donning surgical gowns over his protective suit – more from habit than necessity; some habits are just that. Next the plastic sheets were lifted, held by the edges to form a U shape that allowed the accumulated blood to be poured into a container. About half a liter, the doctors estimated. The sheets were carefully carried to a large bin. The medics stuffed them in and left the room, wheeling the bin with them, off to the incinerator. Nervous as they were, it didn't appear that they'd spilled a drop anywhere.

'Very well.' The director pressed a button and the table elevated from the far end. Out of long-standing professionalism, he touched his fingertips to the left carotid artery to make sure there was no pulse, then to the right, where again there was none. When the body was at a twenty-degree angle, he took a large scalpel and cut both arteries, along with the parallel jugular veins. Blood poured out onto the table, pulled by gravity out of the body, channeled into grooves leading in turn to a drain, and over the next several minutes four liters of blood were captured in a plastic container. The body went pale so quickly, Moudi saw. Moments earlier, the skin had been mottled red and purple. It seemed to fade before his eyes, or perhaps it was just imagination. A laboratory technician came to collect the blood container, which he placed on a small wheeled cart. Nobody wanted to carry something like that, even for a short distance.

'I've never posted an Ebola victim,' the director observed. Not that this was a proper postmortem examination. For all the care the director had just shown for the patient's departed humanity, bleeding her out like that, he might have slaughtered a lamb.

They still had to be careful, however. In cases like this, only one pair of hands worked within the surgical field, and Moudi let the director do that, as he made rough, wide incisions. Stainless-steel retractors pulled back the flaps of skin and muscle. Moudi handled those, his eyes locked on the scalpel in the director's gloved hands. In another minute, the left kidney was fully exposed. They waited for the medical corpsmen to return. One of them set a tray on the table next to the cadaver. Moudi was revolted by what he saw next. One effect of the Ebola virus and its disease process was to break down tissue. The exposed kidney was half liquefied, and when the director reached in to remove it, the organ actually broke – pulled itself apart into two pieces like a horrid red-brown pudding. The director clucked at himself with annoyance. He'd known what to expect, but forgotten even so.

'Remarkable what happens to the organs, isn't it?'

'Expect the same from the liver, but the spleen–'

'Yes, I know. The spleen will be like a brick. Watch your hands, Moudi,' the director warned. He lifted a fresh retractor – the instrument was shaped rather like a scoop – to remove the remaining kidney fragment. This went onto the tray. He nodded, and the medic took it off to the lab. The right kidney went more smoothly. At the director's insistence, after all the muscle and blood vessels were disconnected, both doctors used their hands to remove it, and this one stayed reasonably intact – until it landed on the tray. There the organ deformed and split open. The only good thing about it was that the softness of the tissue would not compromise the integrity of their doubled gloves. That fact didn't prevent both doctors from cringing.

'Here!' The director flicked his hand for the orderlies to approach. 'Turn it over.'

The medics did so, one grasping the shoulders, and the other the knees, flipping the body over as briskly as they could. That caused blood and some tissue to spatter on their cloth gowns. The orderlies pulled back, keeping as far away as possible.

'I want the liver and spleen, that's all,' the director told Moudi, looking up. He turned to the orderlies. 'Then you will wrap the body and remove it to the incinerator. This room will then be disinfected thoroughly.'

Sister Jean Baptiste's eyes were open, as sightless now as they had been thirty minutes earlier. The doctor took a cloth and covered the face, murmuring a prayer for her soul which the director heard.

'Yes, Moudi, she is doubtless in Paradise. Now, shall we continue?' he asked brusquely. He made the usual Y-shaped incision to open the thorax, deep and crude as before, peeling back the layers quickly, more like a meat-cutter than a physician. What they saw there even shocked the director. 'How did she live so long like this . . . ?' the man breathed.

Moudi thought back to his medical-school days, remembering a life-sized plastic model of the human body in his first anatomy class. It was as though someone had taken the model and poured in a bucket of powerful solvent. Every exposed organ was misshapen. The surface tissue layer on most of them was . . . dissolved. The abdomen was a sea of black blood. All they'd put in, Moudi thought . . . not even half of it had leaked out. Amazing.

'Suction!' the director commanded. An orderly appeared at his side with a plastic tube leading to a vacuum bottle, and the sound of it was obscene. The process lasted fully ten minutes, with the doctors standing back while the orderly moved the suction tube around, like a maid cleaning a house. Another three liters of contaminated, virus-rich blood for the lab.

The body was supposed to be a Temple of Life, the Holy

Koran taught. Moudi looked down to see one transformed into – what? A factory of death, more surely than the building in which he stood. The director moved back in, and Moudi watched his hands uncover the liver, more carefully than before. Perhaps he'd been spooked by the blood in the abdominal cavity. Again the blood vessels were cut, the connective tissue cut away. The director set his instruments down, and without being so bidden, Moudi reached in to lift out the organ and set it on the tray which, again, an orderly removed.

'I wonder why the spleen behaves so differently?'

Downstairs, other medical orderlies were at work. One by one, the monkey cages were lifted from the orderly piles in the storage room. The African greens had been fed, and they were still recovering from the shock of their travel. That somewhat reduced their ability to scratch and bite and fight the gloved hands moving the cages. But the panic of the animals returned soon enough when they arrived in another room. This part of the operation was being handled ten at a time. Once in the killing room, when the doors were all tightly closed, the monkeys knew. The unlucky ones got to watch as one cage at a time was set on a table. The door to each was opened, and into the cage went a stick with a metal-band loop on the end. The loop went over the head of each monkey and was yanked tight, usually to the faint crackling sound of the broken neck. In every case the animal went taut, then fell limp, usually with the eyes open and outraged at the murder. The same instrument pulled the dead animal out. And when the loop was loosened, the body was tossed to a soldier, who carried it to the next room. The others saw and screeched their rage at the soldiers, but the cages were too small to give them room to dodge. At best one might interpose an arm in the loop, only to have that broken as well. Intelligent enough to see and know and understand what was happening to them, the African greens found it not unlike sitting in a lone tree on the savanna, watching a leopard climb up, and up, and up . . . and there was nothing they could do but screech. The noise was troublesome to the soldiers, but not that troublesome.

In the next room, five teams of medical corpsmen worked at five separate tables. Clamps affixed at the neck and at the base of the tail helped keep the bodies in place. One soldier, using a curved knife, would slice open the back, tracing up the backbone, and then the other would make a perpendicular cut, pulling the hide apart to expose the inner back. The first would then remove the kidneys and hand them to the second, and while the small organs went into a special container, he would remove the body, tossing it into a plastic trash barrel for later incineration. By the time he returned to pick up his knife, the other team member would have the next monkey corpse fixed in place. It took about four minutes per iteration of the procedure. In ninety minutes, all the African green monkeys were dead. There was some urgency to this. All the raw material for their task was biological, and all subject to biological processes. The slaughtering crew handed off their product through double-doored openings cut into the walls, leading to the Hot Lab.

There things were different. Every man in the large room wore the blue plastic suit. Every motion was slow and careful. They'd been well drilled and well briefed, and what little might have been overlooked in their training had recently been recounted by the medical corpsmen selected by lot to treat the Western woman upstairs, in every dreadful detail. When something was carried from one place to another, an announcement was made, and people made a path.

The blood was in a warming tank, and air bubbled through it. The simian kidneys, two large buckets of them, were taken to a grinding machine – actually not terribly different from the kind of food processor found in gourmet kitchens. This reduced the kidneys to mush, which was moved from one table to another and layered onto trays, along with some liquid nutrients. It struck more than one of the people in the lab that what they were doing was not at all unlike baking a cake or other confection. The blood was poured generously into the trays. About half was used in that way. The rest, divided into plastic containers, went into a deep-freezer cooled by liquid nitrogen. The Hot Lab was kept warm and moist, not at all unlike the jungle. The lights were not overly bright, and shielded to contain whatever ultra-violet radiation the fluorescent might emit. Viruses didn't like UV. They needed the right environment in which to grow, and the kidneys of the African green monkey were just that, along with nutrients, proper temperature, correct humidity, and just a pinch of hate.

'You've learned so much?' Daryaei asked.

'It's their media, their newspeople,' Badrayn explained.

'They're all spies!' the mullah objected.

'Many think so,' Ali said with a smile. 'But they aren't, really. They are – how does one explain them? Like medieval heralds. They see what they see and they tell what they see. They are loyal to no one except themselves and their profession. Yes, it is true that they spy, but they spy on *everyone*, their own people most of all. It's mad, I admit, but it's true even so.'

'Do they believe in anything?' That was a hard one for his host to grasp.

Another smile. 'Nothing that I've ever identified. Oh, yes, the American ones are devoted to Israel, but even that is an exaggeration. It took me years to understand that. Like dogs, they will turn on anyone, bite any hand, no matter how kind. They search and they see and they tell. And so, on this Ryan fellow, I've been able to learn everything – his home, his family, the schools his children attend, the number of the office his wife works in, everything.'

'What if some of the information is lies?' Daryaei asked suspiciously. As long as he'd dealt with the West, the nature of their reporters was just too foreign to him to be fully understood.

'It's all easily verified. His wife's workplace, for example. I'm sure there must be some of the faithful on staff at that hospital. It's simply a matter of approaching one and asking a few harmless questions. Their home, well, that will be guarded. The same is true of the children. It's a conundrum for all such people. They must have some protection to move about, but the protection can be *seen*, and that tells one where they are, and who they are. Given the information I've developed, we even know where to start looking.' Badrayn kept his remarks short and simple. It wasn't that Daryaei was a fool – he most assuredly was not – just that he was insular. One advantage to all his years in Lebanon was that Ali had been exposed to much and had learned much. Most of all, he'd learned that he needed a sponsor, and in

Mahmoud Haji Daryaei he had a prospective one. This man had plans. He needed people. And for one reason or another, he didn't fully trust his own. Badrayn didn't wonder why. Whatever the reason was, it was good fortune, and not to be questioned.

'How well protected are such people?' the mullah asked, his hand playing with his beard. The man hadn't shaved in nearly twenty-four hours.

'Very well indeed,' Badrayn replied, noting something odd about the question and filing that fact away. 'American police agencies are quite effective. The crime problem in America has nothing to do with their police. They simply don't know what to do after the criminals are caught. As applied to their President . . . ?' Ali leaned back for a stretch. 'He will be surrounded by a highly trained group of expert marksmen, well motivated, and utterly faithful.' Badrayn added these words to his presentation to see if his interlocutor's eyes changed. Daryaei was weary, and there was such a change. 'Otherwise, protection is protection. The procedures are straightforward. You do not need my instruction on that.'

'America's vulnerability?'

'It's severe. Their government is in chaos. Again, you know this.'

'They are difficult to measure, these Americans . . . ,' Daryaei mused.

'Their military might is formidable. Their political will is unpredictable, as someone we both . . . *knew* found out to his misfortune. It is a mistake to underestimate them. America is like a sleeping lion, to be treated with care and respect.'

'How does one defeat a lion?'

That one caught Badrayn short for a second or two. Once on a trip to Tanzania – he'd been advising the government on how to deal with insurgents – he'd gone into the bush for a day, driving with a colonel in that country's intelligence service. There he'd spotted a lion, an old one which had nonetheless managed a kill all by himself. Perhaps the wildebeest had been crippled. Then there came into view a troop of hyenas, and seeing that, the Tanzanian colonel had stopped the Soviet-made Zil jeep and handed binoculars to

Badrayn, and told him to observe and so learn a lesson about insurgents and their capacities. It was something he'd never forgotten. The lion, he remembered, was a large one, perhaps old, perhaps slowed down from his prime, but still powerful and forbidding to behold, even from two hundred meters away, a creature of undeniable magnificence. The hyenas were smaller, doglike creatures, with their broken-back gait, an odd canter that must have been very efficient. They gathered first in a little group, twenty meters from the lion, which was trying to feed on his kill. And then the hyenas had moved, forming a circle around the lion, and whichever one was directly behind the powerful cat would move in to nip at the hindquarters, and the lion would turn and roar and dart a few meters, and that hyena would withdraw quickly – but even as that happened, another one would advance behind the lion for another nip. Individually, the hyenas would have had no more chance against this king of the grasslands than a man with a knife would have against a soldier armed with a machine gun, but try though he might, the lion could not protect his kill – nor even himself – and in just five minutes the lion was on the defensive, unable even to run properly, because there was always a hyena behind him, nipping at his balls, forcing the lion to run in a way that was pathetically comical, dragging his bottom on the grass as he tried to maneuver. And finally the lion just went away, without a roar, without a backward glance, while the hyenas took the kill, cackling in their odd, laughing barks, as though finding amusement in their usurpation of the greater animal's labor. And so the mighty had been vanquished by the lesser. The lion would get older, and weaker, and someday would be unable to defeat a real hyena attack aimed at his own flesh. Sooner or later, his Tanzanian friend had told him, the hyenas got them all. Badrayn looked at his host's eyes again.

'It can be done.'

20

NEW ADMINISTRATIONS

There were thirty of them in the East Room – all men, much to his surprise – with their wives. As Jack walked into the reception his eyes scanned the faces. Some pleased him. Some did not. Those who did were as scared as he was. It was the confident, smiling ones who worried the President.

What was the right thing to do with them? Even Arnie didn't know the answer, though he had run through several approaches. Be very strong and intimidate them? Sure, Ryan thought, and tomorrow the papers would say he was trying to be King Jack I. Take it easy? Then he'd be called a wimp who was unable to take his proper leadership position. Ryan was learning to fear the media. It hadn't been all that bad before. As a worker bee, he'd been largely ignored. Even as Durling's National Security Advisor, he'd been thought of as a ventriloquist's dummy. But now the situation was very different, and there was not a single thing he could say that could not, and *would* not, be twisted into whatever the particular listener wanted to say himself. Washington had long since lost the capacity for objectivity. Everything was politics, and politics was ideology, and ideology came down to personal prejudices rather than the quest for truth. Where had all these people been educated that the truth didn't matter to them?

Ryan's problem was that he really didn't *have* a political philosophy per se. He believed in things that worked, that produced the promised results and fixed whatever was broken. Whether those things adhered to one political slant or another was less important than the effects they had. Good ideas worked, even though some of them might seem crazy. Bad ideas didn't, even though some of them seemed sensible as hell. But Washington didn't think that way. Ideologies *were* facts in this city, and if the ideologies didn't work, people would deny it; and if the ones with which they

…isagreed *did* work, those who'd been opposed would never admit it, because admitting error was more hateful to them than any form of personal misconduct. They'd sooner deny God than deny their ideas. Politics had to be the only arena known to man in which people took great action without caring much for the real-world consequences, and to which the real world was far less important than whatever fantasy, right, left, or center, they'd brought to this city of marble and lawyers.

Jack looked at the faces, wondering what political baggage they'd brought along with their hanging bags. Maybe it was a weakness that he didn't understand how that all worked, but for his part, he had lived a life in which mistakes got real people killed – and in Cathy's case, made people blind. For Jack, the victims were people with real names and faces. For Cathy, they were those whose faces she had *touched* in an operating room. For political figures, they were abstractions far more distant than their closely held ideas.

'Like being in a zoo,' Caroline Ryan, FLOTUS, Surgeon, observed to her husband, behind a charming smile. She'd raced home – the helicopter helped – just in time to change into a new white slinky dress and a gold necklace that Jack had bought her for Christmas … a few weeks, he remembered, before the terrorists had tried to kill her on the Route 50 bridge in Annapolis.

'With golden bars,' her husband, POTUS, Swordsman, replied, fronting a smile of his own that was as fake as a three-dollar bill.

'So what are we?' she asked as the assembled senators-designate applauded their entrance. 'Lion and lioness? Bull and cow? Peacock and peahen? Or two lab bunnies waiting to have shampoo poured in our eyes?'

'Depends on who's doing the beholding, baby.' Ryan was holding his wife's hand, and together they walked to the microphone.

'Ladies and gentlemen, welcome to Washington.' Ryan had to pause for another round of applause. That was something else he'd have to learn. People applauded the President for damned near anything. Just as well that his bathroom had a door. He reached into his pocket and pulled out some three-by-five cards, the way Presidents always kept their speaking points. The cards had been prepared by Callie Weston, ar. the hand-printing was large enough that he didn't need his reading glasses. Even so he'd come to expect a headache. He had one every day from all the reading.

'Our country has needs, and they're not small ones. You're here for the same reason I am. You've been appointed to fill in. You have jobs which many of you never expected, and which some of you may not have wanted.' This was vain flattery, but the sort they wanted to hear – more accurately, which they wanted to be *seen* to hear on the C-SPAN cameras in the corners of the room. There were perhaps three people in the room who were not career politicians, and one of those was a governor who'd done the me-you dance with his lieutenant governor and so come to Washington to fill out the term of a senator from another party. That was a curveball which the papers had only started writing about. The polarity of the Senate would change as a result of the 747 crash, because the control of thirty-two of America's state houses hadn't quite been in line with the makeup of the Congress.

'That's good,' Ryan told them. 'There is a long and honorable tradition of citizens in service to their nation that goes back at least as far as Cincinnatus, the Roman citizen who more than once answered his country's call, then returned to his farm and his family and his work. One of our great cities is named in memory of that gentleman,' Jack added, nodding to a new senator from Ohio – his home was in Dayton, which was close enough.

'You would not be here if you didn't understand what many of those needs are. But my real message for you, today, is that we must work together. We do not have the time and our *country* does not have the time for us to bicker and fight.' He had to pause for applause again. Annoyed by the delay, Ryan managed to look up with an appreciative smile and nod.

'Senators, you will find me an easy man to work with. My door is always open, I know how to answer a phone, and the street goes both ways. I will discuss any issue. I will listen to any point of view. There are no rules other than the Con-stitution which I have sworn to preserve, protect, and defend.

'The people out where you come from, out there beyond

...terstate 495, expect all of us to get the job done. They don't expect us to get reelected. They expect us to work for them to the best of our ability. We work for them. They don't work for us. We have the duty to perform for them. Robert E. Lee once said that "duty" is the most sublime word in our language. It's even more sublime and even more important now, because none of us has been elected to our offices. We represent the people of a democracy, but in every case we have come here in a way that simply wasn't supposed to happen. How much greater, then, is our personal duty to fulfill our roles in the best possible manner?' More applause.

'There is no higher trust than that which fate has conferred on us. We are not medieval noblemen blessed by birth with high station and great power. We are the servants, not the masters, to those whose consent gives us what power we have. We live in the tradition of giants. Henry Clay, Daniel Webster, John Calhoun, and so many other members of your house of the Congress must be your models. "How stands the Union?" Webster is said to ask from his grave. We will determine that. The Union is in our hands. Lincoln called America the last and best hope of mankind, and in the past twenty years America has given truth to that judgment by our sixteenth President. America is still an experiment, a collective idea, a set of rules called the Constitution to which all of us, within and without the Beltway, give allegiance. What makes us special is that brief document. America isn't a strip of dirt and rock between two oceans. America is an idea and a set of rules we all follow. That's what makes us different, and in holding true to that, we in this room can make sure that the country we pass on to our successors will be the same one entrusted to us, maybe even a little bit improved. And now' – Ryan turned to the Chief Judge of the United States Court of Appeals for the Fourth Judicial Circuit, the nation's most senior appellate judge, up from Richmond – 'it's time for you to join the team.'

Judge William Staunton came to the microphone. Every senatorial spouse held a Bible, and every senatorial appointee placed his left hand on it, raising the other.

'I – state your name . . .'

As Ryan watched, the new senators were duly sworn. At least it looked solemn enough. The oaths were spoken. A few

of the new legislators kissed the Bibles, either from perso
religious conviction or because they were close to th
cameras. Then they kissed their wives, most of whom
beamed. There was a collective intake of breath, and then
they all looked around at one another, and the White House
staff came into the room with drinks just after the cameras
were turned off, because now the real work started. Ryan got
himself a glass of Perrier and walked into the middle of the
room, smiling despite his fatigue and his unease at performing political duties.

The photos came in one more time. Security at Khartoum
airport had not improved, and this time three American intelligence officers were snapping photos of the people walking
down the stairs. Everyone around was surprised that no
newspeople had yet twigged to the story. A stream of official
cars – probably the entire complement for this poor nation
– ferried the visitors away. When the process was complete,
the 737 airliner went back east, and the spooks drove off to
the embassy. Two others of their number were camped out
at the dwellings assigned to the Iraqi generals – this tidbit
had come from the station chief's contact in the Sudanese
Foreign Ministry. When those photos had been taken, the
additional officers also drove back, and in the embassy dark-
room the frames were processed, blown up, and faxed off via
satellite. At Langley, Bert Vasco identified every face,
assisted by a pair of CIA desk officers and a set of mug shots
in the CIA files.

'That's it,' the State Department officer pronounced.
'That's the whole military leadership. But not one civilian
out of the Ba'ath Party.'

'So we know who the sacrificial goats are.' That observation came from Ed Foley.

'Yep,' Mary Pat answered with a nod. 'And it gives a chance
for the senior surviving officers to arrest them, "process"
them, and show loyalty to the new regime. Shit,' she concluded. 'Too fast.' Her station chief in Riyadh was all dressed
up with no place to go. The same was true of some Saudi
diplomats who'd hastily put together a program of fiscal
incentives for the notional new Iraqi regime. It would now
be unnecessary.

d Foley, the new DCI-designate, shook his head in admir-
.on. 'I didn't think they had it in 'em. Killing our friend,
.ure, but coaxing the leadership out this fast and this smooth,
who would've thunk it?'

'You got me there, Mr Foley,' Vasco agreed. 'Somebody
must have brokered the deal – but who?'

'Get buzzin', worker bees,' Ed Foley told the desk officers,
with a wry smile. 'Everything you can develop, ASAP.'

It looked like some sort of awful stew, the darkened human
blood and the red-brown nephritic mush of monkey kidneys,
just sitting there, marinating in flat, shallow glass trays under
dim lights shielded to keep ultraviolet light from harming
the viruses. There wasn't much to do at this point except to
monitor the environmental conditions, and simple analog
instruments did that. Moudi and the director walked in,
wearing their protective garb, to check the sealed culturing
chambers for themselves. Two-thirds of Jean Baptiste's blood
was now deep-frozen in case something went wrong with
their first effort at reproducing the Ebola Mayinga virus. They
also checked the room's multi-stage ventilation systems,
because now the building was truly a factory of death. The
precautions were double-sided. As in this room they strove
to give the virus a healthy place to multiply, just outside the
door the army medical corpsmen were spraying every square
millimeter to make sure that it was the only such place –
and so the virus had to be isolated and protected from the
disinfectant as well. Thus the air drawn into the culture
chambers had to be carefully filtered, lest in their effort to
stay alive the people in the building killed that which might
kill them if they made another sort of mistake.

'So you really think this version might be airborne?'

'As you know, the Ebola Zaire Mayinga strain is named
for a nurse who became infected despite all conventional
protective measures. Patient Two' – he had decided it was
easier not to speak her name – 'was a skilled nurse with
Ebola experience; she did not give any injections; and she
didn't know how she might have contracted the virus. Therefore, yes, I believe this is possible.'

'That would be very useful, Moudi,' the director whispered,
so faintly that the junior physician had trouble hearing it.

He heard it even so. The thought alone was loud enough. 'We can test for it,' the older man added.

That would be easier on him, Moudi thought. At least he wouldn't know those people by name. He wondered if he was right about the virus. Might Patient Two have made a mistake and forgotten it? But, no, he *had* examined her body for punctures, as had Sister Maria Magdalena, and it wasn't as though she might have licked secretions from the young Benedict Mkusa, was it? So what did that have to mean? It meant that the Mayinga strain survived for a brief period of time in air, and that meant they had a potential weapon such as man had never before encountered, worse than nuclear weapons, worse than chemical weapons. They had a weapon which could reproduce itself and be spread by its own victims, one to another and another until the disease outbreak burned out in due course. It *would* burn out. All the outbreaks did. It had to burn out, didn't it?

Didn't it?

Moudi's hand came up to rub his chin, a contemplative gesture stopped short by the plastic mask. He didn't know the answer to that one. In Zaire and the few other African countries afflicted by this odious disease, the outbreaks, frightening though they were, all did burn out – despite the ideal environmental conditions which protected and sustained the virus strands. But on the other side of that equation was the primitive nature of Zaire, the horrible roads and the absence of efficient transport. The disease killed people before they could get far. Ebola wiped out villages, but did little more. But nobody really knew what would happen in an advanced country. Theoretically, one could infect an aircraft, say an international flight into Kennedy. The travelers would leave one aircraft and fan out into others. Maybe they'd be able to spread the disease through coughs and sneezes immediately, or maybe not. It didn't matter, really. Many of them would fly again in a few days, wondering if they had the flu, and then they'd be able to communicate the virus, and so infect more.

The question of how an epidemic spread was one of time and opportunity more than anything else. The more rapidly it got out from the focal center, and the more rapid the instrumentalies of travel, the farther a disease could spread laterally through a population. There were mathematical models, but they were all theoretical, dependent on a multitude of individual variables, each of which could affect the entire threat equation by at least one order of magnitude. To say the epidemic would die out in time was correct. The question was *how fast?* That would determine the number of people infected before protective measures took effect. One percent invasion of a society, or ten percent, or fifty percent? America wasn't a provincial society. Everyone interacted with everyone else. A truly airborne virus with a three-day incubation period ... there was no model for that known to Moudi. The deadliest recent Zaireian outbreak in Kikwit had claimed fewer than three hundred lives, but it had started with one unfortunate woodcutter, then his family, then their neighbors. The trick, then, if you wanted to create a much wider outbreak, was to increase the number of index cases. If you could do that, the initial blossoming of Ebola Zaire Mayinga *America* could be so large as to invalidate conventional control measures. It would spread not from one man and one family, but from hundreds of individuals and families – or thousands? Then the next generational leap could involve hundreds of thousands. About this time, the Americans would realize that something evil was afoot, but there would be time for one more generational leap, and that would be an order of magnitude greater still, perhaps into the millions. At that point, medical facilities would be overwhelmed...

... and there might be no stopping it at all. Nobody knew the possible consequences of a deliberate mass infection in a highly mobile society. The implications might be truly global. But probably not. Almost certainly not, Moudi judged, looking down at the glass culture trays behind thick wire-glass panels, through the plastic of his mask. The first generation of this disease had come from an unknown host and killed a young boy. The second generation had claimed but a single victim, due to fate and luck and his own competence as a physician. The third generation would grow before his eyes. How far that might spread was undetermined, but it was generations Four, Five, Six, and perhaps even Seven which would determine the fate of an entire country – which happened to be the enemy of his own.

It was easier now. Jean Baptiste had had a face and a voice and a life which had touched his own. He could not make that mistake again. She'd been an infidel, but a righteous one, and she was now with Allah, because Allah was truly merciful. He'd prayed for her soul, and surely Allah would hear his prayers. Few in America or elsewhere could possibly be as righteous as she had been, and he knew well that Americans hated his country and distrusted his religious faith. They might have names and faces, but he didn't see them here and he never would, and they were all ten thousand kilometers away, and it was easy to switch the television off.

'Yes,' Moudi agreed. 'Testing for it will be easy enough.'

'Look,' George Winston was telling a knot of three new senators, 'if the federal government made cars, a Chevy pickup would cost eighty thousand dollars and have to stop every ten blocks to fill up the tank. You guys know business. So do I. We can do better.'

'It is really that bad?' the (alphabetically) senior senator from Connecticut asked.

'I can show you the comparative-productivity numbers. If Detroit ran this way, we'd all be driving Japanese cars,' Winston replied, jabbing his finger into the man's chest, and reminding himself to get rid of his Mercedes 500SEL, or at least garage it for a while.

'It's like having one cop car to cover East LA,' Tony Bretano was saying to five more, two of them from California. 'I don't have the forces I need to cover one MRC. That's major regional conflict,' he explained to the new people and their spouses. 'And we're supposed to – on paper, I mean – we're supposed to be able to cover two of them at the same time, plus a peacekeeping mission somewhere else. Okay? Now, what I need at Defense is a chance to reconfigure our forces so that the shooters are the most important, and the rest of the outfit supports them, not the other way around. Accountants and lawyers are useful, but we have enough of them at Treasury and Justice. My side of the government, we're the cops, and I don't have enough cops on the street.'

'But how do we pay for that?' Colorado the younger asked. The senior senator from the Rocky Mountain State had been at a fund-raiser in Golden that night.

'The Pentagon isn't a jobs program. We have to remember that. Now, next week I'll have a full assessment of what we need, and then I'm going to come to the Hill, and together we'll figure how to make that happen at the least possible cost.'

'See, what did I tell you?' Arnie van Damm said quietly, passing behind Ryan's back. 'Let them do it for you. You just stay pleasant.'

'What you said was right, Mr President,' the new senator from Ohio professed to believe, sipping a bourbon and water now that the cameras were off. 'You know, once in school, I did a little history paper on Cincinnatus, and . . .'

'Well, all we have to do is remember to put the country first,' Jack told him.

'How do you manage to do your job and – I mean,' the wife of the senior senator from Wisconsin explained, 'you still do your surgery?'

'And teaching, which is even more important,' Cathy said with a nod, wishing she were upstairs and doing her patient notes. Well, there was the helicopter ride in tomorrow. 'I will *never* stop doing my work. I give blind people their sight back. Sometimes I take the bandages off myself, and the look on their faces is the best thing in the world. The best,' she repeated.

'Even better than me, honey?' Jack asked, placing his arm around her shoulder. This might even be working, he thought. Charm them, Arnie and Callie had told him.

The process had already started. The colonel assigned to guard the five mullahs had followed them into the mosque, where, moved by the moment, he'd worshiped with them. At the conclusion of the devotions, the senior of their number had spoken to him, quietly and politely, touching on a favored passage in the Holy Koran, so as to establish some common ground. It brought to the colonel a memory of his youth and his own father, a devout and honorable man. It was the usual thing in dealing with people, no matter the place or the culture. You got them talking, read their words, and chose the proper path for continuing the conversation. The mullah, a member of the Iranian clergy for over forty years, had counseled people on their faith and on their troubles for all that time, and so it was not hard for him to establish a rapport with his captor, a man supposedly sworn to kill him and his four colleagues should those orders arrive from his superiors. But in picking a man deemed faithful, the departing generals had chosen a little too wisely, because men who display true loyalty are men of thoughts and principles, and such men are ever vulnerable to ideas demonstrably better than those to which they adhere. There could be no real contest. Islam was a religion with a long and honorable history, neither of which attribute attached to the dying regime which the colonel had sworn to uphold.

'It must have been a hard thing, fighting in the swamps,' the mullah told him a few minutes later, as the conversation turned to relations between the two Islamic countries.

'War is evil. I never took pleasure in killing,' the colonel admitted. It was rather like being a Catholic in the confessional, and all at once the man's eyes teared up, and he related some of the things he'd done over the years. He could see now that while he'd never taken such pleasure, he had hardened his heart to it, finally not distinguishing the innocent from the guilty, the just from the corrupt, and done what he'd been told – *because* he'd been told, not because it had been in any way the right thing to do. He saw that now.

'Man falls often, but through the words of the Prophet we may always find our way back to a merciful God. Men are forgetful of their duties, but Allah is never forgetful of His.' The mullah touched the officer's arm. 'I think your prayers are not finished this day. Together we will pray to Allah, and together we will find peace for your soul.'

After that, it had been very easy indeed. On learning that the generals were even now leaving the country, the colonel had two good reasons for cooperating. He had no wish to die. He was quite willing to follow the will of his God in order to stay alive and serve. In demonstration of his devotion, he assembled two companies of soldiers to meet with the mullahs and get their orders. It was very easy for the soldiers. All they had to do was follow the orders of their officers. To do anything else was a thought that never occurred to any of them.

It was now dawn in Baghdad, and at a score of large houses, doors were kicked in. Some occupants they found awake.

Some were drunkenly asleep. Some were packed to leave and trying to figure a place to go and a way to get there. All were a little too late in their understanding of what was going on around them, in a place where a minute's error was the difference between prosperous life and violent death. Few resisted, and the one man who came closest to doing so successfully was cut nearly in half by a twenty-round burst from an AK-47, along with his wife. Mostly they were led barefoot from their homes into waiting trucks, heads down to the sidewalk, knowing the way this particular drama would end for them.

These tactical radio nets were not encrypted, and the faint VHF signals were monitored, this time at STORM TRACK, which was closer to Baghdad. Names were spoken, more than once in every case as the pickup teams reported back to their dispatchers, which made life easy for the ELINT teams close to the border and at King Khalid Military City. The watch officers called in their supervisors, and CRITIC-priority dispatches were shot off via satellite.

Ryan had just walked the last of the new senators to the door when Andrea Price walked up.

'My shoes are killing me, and I have a procedure at –' Cathy stopped talking.

'FLASH Traffic coming in now, sir.'

'Iraq?' Jack asked.

'Yes, Mr President.'

The President kissed his wife. 'I'll be up in a little while.'

Cathy had no choice but to nod and head to the elevator, where one of the ushers was waiting to take the First Couple upstairs. The kids would already be in bed. Their homework was all done, probably in some cases with the help of their bodyguards. Jack turned right, trotted down the stairs, then right again, left to get outside of the building, then back inside the West Wing and the Situation Room.

'Talk to me,' the President commanded.

'It's started,' Ed Foley's face said on the wall-mounted TV. And all they could do was watch.

* * *

Iraqi national television greeted a new day and a new reality. This was clear when the newsreaders commenced their daily presentation with an invocation of Allah's name, not for the first time, but never with this degree of fervor. 'Gimme that ol' time religion, it's good enough for me – now,' observed the chief master sergeant at PALM BOWL, because the transmission was national, and repeated from the transmitters in nearby Basra. He turned and waved. 'Major Sabah?'

'Yes, Chief, yes,' the Kuwaiti officer replied with a nod as he came over. He hadn't had much in the way of doubt before. His superiors had expressed reservations. They always did, they were never quite as close to the pulse of their enemy as the major was, thinking politics instead of ideas. He checked his watch. They'd be in their offices in two hours after the normal morning routine, and that didn't matter now. Hurrying wouldn't change anything. The dam had broken, and the water would spill out. The time to stop it had passed, assuming that such a chance had ever existed.

The Iraqi military had taken over, the TV news broadcast said. This was announced as though the situation were unique. A council of revolutionary justice had been formed. Those guilty of crimes against the people (a good catchall term which meant very little but was understood by all) were being arrested, and would face the judgment of their countrymen. The nation needed calm most of all, the TV told them. Today would be a national holiday. Only those in essential public-service jobs were expected to go to work. For the rest of the country's citizens, it was advised that they consider this a day of prayer and reconciliation. For the rest of the world, the new regime promised peace. The rest of the world would have all day to think about that.

Daryaei had already done a good deal of thinking about it. He'd managed three hours of sleep before awakening for morning prayers. He found that as he aged he needed less and less. Perhaps the body understood that, with little time remaining, there was no longer time for rest, though there was for dreams, and he'd dreamed of lions in the early hours of this day. Dead lions. The lion had also been the symbol of the Shah's regime, and truly Badrayn had been correct. Lions could be killed. The real ones had once been native to

Iran – Persia, in the old style – and had been hunted down to extinction in classical times. The symbolic ones, the Pahlavi dynasty, had similarly been eradicated with a combination of patience and ruthlessness. He'd played a role in that. It hadn't always been pretty. He'd ordered and supervised an atrocity, the fire-bombing of a crowded theater filled with people more interested in Western decadence than their Islamic faith. Hundreds had died horribly, but – but it had been necessary, a needed part of the campaign to bring his country and his people back to the True Path, and while he regretted that particular incident, and regularly prayed in atonement for the lives taken, no, he didn't regret it. He was an instrument of the Faith, and the Holy Koran itself told of the need for war, Holy War, in defense of the Faith.

Another gift of Persia (some said India) to the world was the game of chess, which he had learned as a child. The very word for the end of the game, *checkmate*, came from the Persian *shah mat* – 'the king is dead' – something he had himself helped to achieve in real life, and while Daryaei had long since stopped playing mere games, he remembered that a good player thought not move by move, but four, or even more, moves ahead. One problem with chess, as with life, was that the next move could sometimes be seen, especially when the other player was skilled – to assume him to be anything else could be dangerous. But by playing ahead, it was far more difficult to see what was coming, until the very end, at which point the opponent could see clearly but, maneuvered out of position, depleted of his players, power, and options, he had no choice but to resign the game. Such had been the case in Iraq until this morning. The other player – actually, many of them – had resigned and run away, and Daryaei had been pleased to allow it. It was even more delicious when the other player could not run, but the point was winning, not satisfaction, and winning meant thinking farther and faster than the other player, so that the next move *was* a surprise, so that the other player was harried and confused, would be forced to take time to react, and in a chess match, as in life, time was limited. It was all a thing of the mind, not the body.

So it was with lions, it would seem. Even one so powerful could be outmaneuvered by lesser creatures if the time and the setting were right, and that was both the lesson and the task of the day. Finished with his prayers, Daryaei called for Badrayn. The younger man was a skilled tactician and gatherer of information. He needed the direction of one schooled in strategy, but with that guidance he would be very useful indeed.

It had been conclusively decided in an hour's conversation with his country's leading experts that the President could do absolutely nothing at all. The next move was simply to wait and watch and see. Any citizen could do it, but America's leading experts could wait and watch and see a little faster than anyone else, or so they told themselves. That would all be done for the President, of course, and so Ryan walked out of the Situation Room, up the steps, and outside to see wet, cold rain falling on the South Lawn beyond the overhang of the walkway. The coming day promised to be blustery, with March arriving, typically, like a lion, then to be replaced by a lamb. Or so the aphorism went. At the moment it just looked gloomy, however nurturing the rain might be to ground recovering from a cold, bitter winter.

'This will finish off the last of the snow,' Andrea Price said, surprising herself by speaking unbidden to her principal.

Ryan turned and smiled. 'You work harder than I do, Agent Price, and you're a –'

'Girl?' she asked with a weary smile.

'My chauvinism must be showing. I beg your pardon, ma'am. Sorry, I was just wishing for a cigarette. Quit years ago – Cathy bullied me into it. More than once,' Jack admitted with good humor. 'It can be tough, being married to a doctor.'

'It can be tough, being married.' Price was wedded to her job, with two failed relationships to prove it. Her problem, if one could call it that, was in possessing the same devotion to duty that only men were supposed to have. It was a simple enough fact, but one which first a lawyer and then an advertising executive had failed to grasp.

'Why do we do it, Andrea?' Ryan asked.

Special Agent Price didn't know, either. The President necessarily was a father figure to her. He was the man supposed to have the answers, but after years on the Detail, she knew better. Her father had always had such answers, or so it had seemed in her youth. Then she'd grown, finished her education, joined the Service, worked her way rapidly up a steep and slippery ladder, and in the process lost her way in life somehow. Now she was at the pinnacle of her profession, alongside the nation's 'father,' only to learn that life didn't allow people to know what they wanted and needed to know. Her job was hard enough. His was infinitely worse, and maybe it was better for the President to be something other than the decent and honorable gentleman John Patrick Ryan was. Maybe a son of a bitch could survive better here . . .

'No answer?' Ryan smiled at the rain. 'I think you're supposed to say that *somebody* has to do it. Jesus, I just tried to seduce thirty new senators. You know that? Seduce,' Jack repeated. 'Like they were girls or something, and like I was that kind of guy – and I don't have a fucking clue.' The voice stopped cold and the head shook in surprise at what he'd said. 'Sorry, excuse me.'

'That's okay, Mr President. I've heard the word before, even from other presidents.'

'Who do you talk to?' Jack asked. 'Once upon a time, I'd talk to my father, my priest, to James Greer when I worked for him, or Roger, until a few weeks ago. Now they all ask *me*. You know, they told me at Quantico, at the Basic Officers' School, that command could be lonely. Boy, they weren't kidding. They really weren't kidding.'

'You have one hell of a good wife, sir,' Price pointed out, envying both of them for that.

'There's always supposed to be somebody smarter than you. The person you go to when you're just not sure. Now they come to me. I'm not smart enough for that.' Ryan paused, just then hearing what Price had told him. 'You're right, but she's busy enough, and I'm not supposed to burden her with my problems.'

Price decided to laugh. 'You *are* a chauvinist, Boss.'

That snapped his head around. 'I beg your pardon, Ms Price!' Ryan said in a voice that sounded cross until a presidential laugh followed it. 'Please don't tell the media I said that.'

'Sir, I don't tell reporters where the bathroom is.'

The President yawned. 'What's tomorrow look like?'

'Well, you're in the office all day. I imagine this Iraq business will wreck your morning. I'll be out early, back in the afternoon. I'm going to do a walk-around tomorrow, to check security arrangements for all the kids. We have a meeting to see if there's a way to get SURGEON to work and back without the helicopter –'

'That is funny, isn't it?' Ryan observed.

'A FLOTUS with a real job is something the system never really allowed for.'

'Real job, hell! She makes more money than *I* do, has for ten years, except for when I was back in the market. The papers haven't picked up on that, either. She's a great doc.'

His words were meandering, Price saw. He was too tired to think straight. Well, that happened to Presidents, too. Which was why she was around.

'Her patients love her, that's what Roy says. Anyway, I'm going to look over arrangements for all your children – routine, sir, I'm responsible for all of the arrangements for your family. Agent Raman will stand post with you for most of the day. We're moving him up. He's coming along very nicely,' Special Agent Price reported.

'The one who got the fire coat to disguise me back on the first night?' Jack asked.

'You knew?' Price asked in return. The President turned to enter the White House proper. The grin was one of exhaustion, but for all that the blue eyes twinkled at his principal agent.

'I'm not *that* dumb, Andrea.'

No, she decided, it wasn't better to have a son of a bitch as POTUS.

21

RELATIONSHIPS

Patrick O'Day was a widower whose life had changed in a particularly cruel and abrupt way after a late-life marriage. His wife, Deborah, had been a fellow agent in the Laboratory Division, an expert on forensic investigation, which had occasioned a great deal of travel out of headquarters, until one afternoon, flying into Colorado Springs, her aircraft had crashed into the ground for reasons still undetermined. It had been her first field assignment after maternity leave, and she'd left behind a daughter, Megan, aged fourteen weeks.

Megan was two and a half now, and Inspector O'Day was still wrestling with how he should introduce Megan to her mother. He had videotapes and photographs, but were he to point to dyed paper or a phosphor screen and tell his daughter, 'That's Mommy,' might it make her think that all life was artificial? What effect would it have on her development? It was one more question in the life of a man supposed to find answers. The single fatherhood enforced on him by fate had made him all the more devoted as a father, and this on top of a professional career in which he'd worked no less than six kidnappings all the way to conclusion. Six four, two hundred wiry pounds, he had sacrificed his Zapata mustache to the requirements of Headquarters Division, but tough guy among tough guys, his attention to his daughter would have made his colleagues chuckle. Her hair was blondish and long, and each morning he brushed it to silky smoothness after dressing her in colorful toddler clothes and helping her with her tiny sneaks. For Megan, Daddy was a great big protective bear who towered into the blue sky, and snatched her off the ground like a rocket so that she could wrap her arms around his neck.

'Oof!' Daddy said. 'You hug too hard!'

'Did I hurt?' Megan asked in mock alarm. It was part of the morning routine.

A smile. 'No, not this time.' With that, he walked out of the house and opened the door to his muddy pickup, carefully strapped her into her car seat, and set her lunch box and blanky between them. It was six-thirty, and they were on their way to a new day-care center. O'Day could not start his truck without looking down at Megan, the image of her mother, a daily realization that always made him bite his lip and close his eyes and shake his head, wondering again why the 737 had rolled and plunged straight into the ground with his wife of sixteen months in seat 18-F.

The new day-care center was more convenient to his route to work, and the people next door loved it for their twin boys. He turned left onto Ritchie Highway, and found the place right across from a 7-Eleven where he could get a pint of coffee for the commute in on US 50. Giant Steps, nice name.

Hell of a way to make a living, Pat thought, parking his truck. Marlene Daggett was always there at six, tending to the children of the bureaucrats who trekked to DC every morning. She even came out to meet them for the first arrival.

'Mr O'Day! And this is Megan!' the teacher announced with stunning enthusiasm for so early an hour. Megan had her doubts, and looked up at her daddy. She turned back in surprise to see something special. 'Her name is Megan, too. She's *your* bear, and she's been waiting all day for you.'

'Oh.' The little girl seized the brown-furred creature and hugged it, name tag and all. 'Hello.'

Mrs Daggett looked up in a way that told the FBI agent, *it works every time*. 'You have your blanky?'

'Right here, ma'am,' O'Day told her, also handing over the forms he'd completed the night before. Megan had no medical problems, no allergies to medicine, milk, or food; yes, in case of a real emergency you can take her to the local hospital; and the inspector's work and pager numbers, and his parents' number, and the number of Deborah's parents, who were damned good grandparents. Giant Steps was well organized. O'Day didn't know how well organized only because there was something Mrs Daggett wasn't supposed to talk casually about. His identity was being checked out by the Secret Service.

'Well, Miss Megan, I think it's time for us to play and make some new friends.' She looked up. 'We'll take good care of her.'

O'Day got back into his truck with the usual minor pain that attended leaving his daughter behind – anywhere, no matter the time or place – and jumped across the street to the 7-Eleven for his commute coffee. He had a conference scheduled at nine o'clock to go over further developments on the crash investigation – they were down to T-crossing and I-dotting now – followed by a day of administrative garbage which would at least not prevent him from picking his little girl up on time. Forty minutes later, he pulled into FBI Headquarters at Tenth and Pennsylvania. His post as roving inspector gave him a reserved parking place. From there he walked, this morning, to the indoor pistol range.

An expert marksman since Boy Scouts, Pat O'Day had also been a 'principal firearms instructor' at several FBI field offices, which meant that he'd been selected by the SAC to supervise weapons training for the other agents – always an important part of a cop's life, even though few ever fired their side arms in anger.

The range was rarely busy this time of day – he got in at 7:25 – and the inspector selected two boxes of Federal 10mm hollow-points for his big stainless Smith & Wesson 1076 automatic, along with a couple of standard 'Q' targets and a set of ear protectors. The target was a simple white cardboard panel with an outline of the vital parts of a human body. The shape resolved itself into the rough size and configuration of a farmer's steel milk can, with the letter 'Q' in the center, about where the heart would be. He attached the target to the spring-clip on the traveler, set the distance for thirty feet, and hit the travel switch. As it moved downrange, he let his thoughts idle, contemplating the sports page and the new Orioles lineup in spring-training camp. The range hardware was programmable. On arriving at its destination, the target turned sideways, and became nearly invisible. Without looking, O'Day dialed the timer to a random setting and continued to look downrange, his hands at his side. Now his thinking changed. There was a Bad Guy there. A serious Bad Guy. Convicted felon, now cornered. A Bad Guy who had told informants that he'd *never* go back inside, never be taken alive. In his long career, Inspector O'Day had heard that one many times, and whenever possible he'd given the subject the opportunity to keep his word – but they all folded, dropped their gun, wet their pants, or even broke down into tears when confronted by real danger instead of the kind more easily considered over beers or a joint. But not this time. This Bad Guy was serious. He had a hostage. A child, perhaps. Maybe even his own little Megan. The thought made his eyes narrow. A gun to her head. In the movies, the Bad Guy would tell you to drop your weapon, but if you did that, all you were guaranteed was a dead cop *and* a dead hostage, and so you talked to your Bad Guy. You made yourself sound calm and reasonable and conciliatory, and you waited for him to relax, just a little, just enough to move the gun away from the hostage's head. It might take hours, but sooner or later –

– the timer clicked, and the target card turned to face the agent. O'Day's right hand moved in a blur, snatching the pistol from its holster. Simultaneously, his right foot moved backward, his body pivoted and crouched slightly, and the left hand joined the right on the rubber grips when the gun was halfway up. His eyes acquired the gunsights at the bottom of his peripheral vision, and the moment they were aligned with the head of the 'Q' target, his finger depressed the trigger twice, firing so fast that both ejected cartridge cases were in the air at the same time. It was called a double-tap, and O'Day had practiced it for so many years that the sounds almost blended in the air, and the two-shot echo was just returning from the steel backstop when the empty cases pinged off the concrete floor, but by then there were two holes in the head of the target, less than an inch apart, between and just above where the eyes would be. The target flipped side-on, less than a second after it had turned, rather nicely simulating the fall of the subject to the ground.

Yes.

'I think you got 'em there, Tex.'

O'Day turned, startled from his fantasy by a familiar voice. 'Morning, Director.'

'Hey, Pat.' Murray yawned, a set of ear protectors dangling in his left hand. 'You're pretty fast. Hostage scenario?'

'I try to train for the worst possible situation.'

'Your little girl.' Murray nodded. They all did that, because the hostage had to be important enough in your mind. 'Well, you got him. Show me again,' the Director ordered. He wanted to watch O'Day's technique. There was always something to learn. After the second iteration, there was one ragged hole in the target's notional forehead. It was actually rather intimidating for Murray, though he considered himself an expert marksman. 'I need to practice more.'

O'Day relaxed his routine now. If you could do it with your first shot of the day – and he'd done it with all four – you still had it figured out. Two minutes and twenty shots later, the target's head was an annulus. Murray, in the next lane, was busy in the standard Jeff Cooper technique, two rapid shots into the chest, followed by a slower aimed round into the head. When both were satisfied that their targets were dead, it was time to contemplate the day.

'Anything new?' the Director asked.

'No, sir. More follow-up interviews on the JAL case are coming in, but nothing startling.'

'What about Kealty?'

O'Day shrugged. He was not allowed to interfere with the OPR investigation, but he did get daily summaries. A case of this magnitude had to be reported to somebody, and though supervision of the case was entirely under the purview of OPR, the information developed also went to the Director's office, filtered through his lead roving inspector. 'Dan, enough people went in and out of Secretary Hanson's office that anybody could have walked off with the letter, assuming there was one, which, our people think, there probably was. At least Hanson talked to enough people about it – or so those people tell us.'

'I think that one will just blow over,' Murray observed.

'Good morning, Mr President.'

Another day in the routine. The kids were off. Cathy was off. Ryan emerged from his quarters suited and tied – his jacket was buttoned, which was unusual for him, or had been until moving in here – and his shoes shined by one of the valet staff. Except that Jack still couldn't think of this place as a home. More like a hotel, or the VIP quarters he'd had while traveling on Agency business, albeit far more ornate and with much better service.

'You're Raman?' the President asked.

'Yes, sir,' Special Agent Aref Raman replied. He was six feet and solidly built, more a weight lifter than a runner, Jack thought, though that might come from the body armor that many of the Detail members wore. Ryan judged his age at middle thirties. Good-looking in a Mediterranean sort of way, with a shy smile and eyes as blue as SURGEON's. 'SWORDSMAN is moving,' he said into his microphone. 'To the office.'

'Raman, where's that from?' Jack asked, on the way to the elevator.

'Mother Lebanese, father Iranian, came over in '79, when the Shah had his problems. Dad was close to the regime.'

'So what do you think of the Iraq situation?' the President asked.

'Sir, I hardly even speak the language anymore.' The agent smiled. 'Now, if you want to ask me about who's lookin' good in the NCAA finals, I'm your man.'

'Kentucky,' Ryan said decisively. The White House elevator was old, pre-Art Deco in the interior finishings, with worn black buttons, which the President wasn't allowed to push. Raman did that for him.

'Oregon's going all the way. I'm never wrong, sir. Ask the guys. I won the last three pools. Nobody'll bet against me anymore. The finals will be Oregon and Duke – my school – and Oregon will win by six or eight. Well, maybe less if Maceo Rawlings has a good night,' Raman added.

'What did you study at Duke?'

'Pre-law, but I decided I didn't want to be a lawyer. Actually I decided that criminals shouldn't have any rights, and so I figured I'd rather be a cop, and I joined the Service.'

'Married?' Ryan wanted to know the people around him. At one level, it was mere good manners. At another, these people were sworn to defend his life, and he couldn't treat them like employees.

'Never found the right girl – at least not yet.'

'Muslim?'

'My parents were, but after I saw all the trouble religion

caused them, well' – he grinned – 'if you ask around, they'll tell you my religion is ACC basketball. I never miss a Duke game on the TV. Damned shame Oregon's so tough this year. But that's one thing you can't change.'

The President chuckled at the truth of that statement. 'Aref, you said, your first name?'

'Actually, they call me Jeff. Easier to pronounce,' Raman explained as the door opened. The agent positioned himself in the center of the doors, blocking a direct line of sight to POTUS. A member of the Uniform Division was standing there, along with two more of the Detail, all of them known by sight to Raman. With a nod, he walked out, with Ryan in tow, and the group turned west, past the side corridor that led to the bowling alley and the carpenter shops.

'Okay, Jeff, an easy day planned,' Ryan told him unnecessarily. The Secret Service knew his daily schedule before he did.

'Easy for us, maybe.'

They were waiting for him in the Oval Office. The Foleys, Bert Vasco, Scott Adler, and one other person stood when the President walked in. They'd already been scanned for weapons and nuclear material.

'Ben!' Jack said. He paused to set his early morning papers on the desk, and joined his guests.

'Mr President,' Dr Ben Goodley replied with a smile.

'Ben's prepared the morning brief,' Ed Foley explained.

Since not all of the morning visitors were part of the inner circle, Raman would stay in the room, lest somebody leap across the coffee table and try to strangle the President. A person didn't need a firearm to be lethal. A few weeks of study and practice could turn any reasonably fit person into enough of a martial-arts expert to kill an unwary victim. For that reason, members of the Detail carried not only pistols, but also Asps, police batons made of telescoping steel segments. Raman watched as this Goodley – a carded national intelligence officer – handed out the briefing sheets. Like many members of the Secret Service, he got to hear nearly everything. The 'EYES-ONLY PRESIDENT' sticker on a particularly sensitive folder didn't really mean that. There was almost always someone else in the room, and while the Detail members professed even among themselves not to pay any attention to such things, what that really meant was that they didn't discuss them very much. Not hearing and not remembering were something else. Cops were not trained or paid to forget things, much less to ignore them.

In that sense, Raman thought, he was the perfect spy. Trained by the United States of America to be a law enforcement officer, he had performed brilliantly in the field, mainly in counterfeiting cases. He was a proficient marksman, and a very organized thinker – a trait revealed all the way back in his schooling; he'd graduated from Duke summa cum laude, with nothing less than an A grade on his transcript, plus he'd been a varsity wrestler. It was useful for an investigator to have a good memory, and he did. Photographic, in fact, a talent which had attracted the Detail leadership to him early on, because the agents protecting the President needed to be able to recognize a particular face instantly from the scores of photographs which they carried when the Boss was out pressing flesh. During the Fowler administration, as a junior agent gazetted to the Detail from the St Louis field office to cover a fund-raising dinner, he'd ID'd and detained a suspected presidential stalker who'd turned out to have a .22 automatic in his pocket. Raman had pulled the man from the crowd so quietly and skillfully that the subject's processing into the Missouri state mental-health system had never made the papers, which was just what they tried to achieve. The young agent had 'Detail' written all over him, the then-Director of the United States Secret Service had decided on reviewing the case, and so Raman had been transferred over soon after Roger Durling's ascension to the Presidency. As a junior member of the Detail he'd stood boring hours on post, run alongside the Presidential limousine, and gradually worked his way up rather rapidly for a young man. He'd worked the punishing hours without complaints, only commenting from time to time that, as an immigrant, he knew how important America was, and as his distant ancestors might have served Darius the Great as one of the 'Immortals,' so he relished doing the same for his new country. It was so easy, really, much easier than the task his brother – ethnic, not biological – had performed in Baghdad a short time earlier. Americans, whatever they might say to pollsters, truly loved immigrants in their large and foolish hearts.

They knew much, and they were always learning, but one thing they had yet to learn was that you could never look into *another* human heart.

'No assets we can use on the ground,' Mary Pat was saying.

'Good intercepts, though,' Goodley went on. 'NSA is really coming through for us. The whole Ba'ath leadership is in the jug, and I don't think they're going to be coming out, at least not standing up.'

'So Iraq is fully decapitated?'

'A military ruling council, colonels and junior generals. Afternoon TV showed them with an Iranian mullah. No accident,' Bert Vasco said positively. 'The least that comes out of this is a rapprochement with Iran. At most, the two countries merge. We'll know that in a couple of days – two weeks at the outside.'

'The Saudis?' Ryan asked.

'They're having kittens, Jack,' Ed Foley replied at once. 'I talked with Prince Ali less than an hour ago. They cobbled together an aid package that would just about have paid off *our* national debt in an effort to buy the new Iraqi regime – did it overnight, biggest goddamned letter of credit ever drafted – but nobody's answering the phone. That has 'em shook in Riyadh. Iraq's always been willing to talk business. Not now.'

And that would be what frightened all the states on the Arabian Peninsula, Ryan knew. It wasn't well appreciated in the West that the Arabs were businessmen. Not ideologues, not fanatics, not lunatics, but businessmen. Theirs was a maritime trading culture that predated Islam, a fact remembered in America only in remakes of Sinbad the Sailor movies. In that sense they were very like Americans, despite the difference in language, clothing, and religion, and just like Americans they had trouble understanding people who were not willing to do business, to reach an accommodation, to make some sort of exchange. Iran was such a country, changed from the previous state of affairs under the Shah by the Ayatollah Khomeini into a theocracy. *They're not like us* was the universal point of concern for any culture. *They're not like us ANYMORE* would be a very frightening development for Gulf States who'd always known that, despite political differences, there had always been an avenue of commonality and communication.

'Tehran?' Jack asked next. Ben Goodley took the question unto himself.

'Official news broadcasts welcome the development – the routine offers of peace and renewed friendship, but nothing beyond that at this point,' Goodley said. 'Officially, that is. Unofficially, we're getting all sorts of intercept traffic. People in Baghdad are asking for instructions, and people in Tehran are giving them. For the moment they're saying to let the situation develop apace. The revolutionary courts come next. We're seeing a lot of Islamic clergy on TV, preaching love and freedom and all that nice stuff. When the trials start, and people start backing into walls to pose for rifle-fire, then there's going to be a total vacuum.'

'Then Iran takes over, probably, or maybe runs Iraq like a puppet on a string,' Vasco said, flipping through the latest set of intercepts. 'Goodley may be right. I'm reading this SigInt stuff for the first time. Excuse me, Mr President, but I've been concentrating on the political side. This stuff is more revealing than I expected it to be.'

'You're saying it means *more* than I think it does?' the NIO asked.

Vasco nodded without looking up. 'I think it might. This is not good,' the desk officer opined darkly.

'Later today, the Saudis are going to ask us to hold their hand,' Secretary Adler pointed out. 'What do I tell them?'

Ryan's reply was so automatic that it startled him. 'Our commitment to the Kingdom is unchanged. If they need us, we're there, now and forever.' And with two sentences, Jack thought a second later, he had committed the full power and credibility of the United States of America to a non-democratic country seven thousand miles away. Fortunately, Adler made it easier for him.

'I fully agree, Mr President. We can't do anything else.' Everyone else nodded agreement, even Ben Goodley. 'We can do that quietly. Prince Ali understands, and he can make the King understand that we're not kidding.'

'Next stop,' Ed Foley said, 'we have to brief Tony Bretano in. He's pretty good, by the way. Knows how to listen,' the DCI-designate informed the President. 'You plan to do a cabinet meeting about this?'

Ryan shook his head. 'No. I think we should play this

one cool. America is observing regional developments with interest, but there's nothing for us to get excited about. Scott, you handle the press briefing through your people.'

'Right,' SecState replied.

'Ben, what do they have you doing at Langley now?'

'Mr President, they went and made me a senior watch officer for the Operations Center.'

'Good briefing,' Ryan told the younger man, then turned to the DCI. 'Ed, he works for me now. I need an NIO who speaks my language.'

'Gee, do I at least get a decent relief pitcher back?' Foley replied with a laugh. 'This kid's a good prospect, and I expect to be in the pennant race this fall.'

'Nice try, Ed. Ben, your hours just got worse. For now, you can have my old office around the corner. The food's a lot better here,' the President promised.

Throughout it all, Aref Raman stood still, leaning against the white-painted walls while his eyes flickered automatically from one visitor to another. He was trained not to trust anyone, with the possible exceptions of the President's wife and kids. No one else. Of course, they all trusted him, including the ones who had trained him not to trust anyone, because everybody had to trust somebody.

It was just a matter of timing, really, and one of the things his American education and professional training had conferred upon him was the patience to wait for the chance to make the proper move. But other events on the other side of the globe were bringing that moment closer. Behind expressionless eyes Raman thought that maybe he needed guidance. His mission was no longer the random event he'd promised to fulfill twenty years earlier. That he could do almost any time, but he was *here* now, and while anyone could kill, and while a dedicated person could kill almost anyone, only a truly skilled assassin could kill the proper person at the proper moment in pursuit of a larger goal. So deliciously ironic, he thought, that while his mission came from God, every factor in its accomplishment had come directly from the Great Satan himself, embodied in the life of one man who could best serve Allah by departing this life at just the proper moment. Picking the moment would be the hard part, and so after twenty years, Raman decided that he might just have to break cover after all. There was a danger in that, but, he judged, a slight one.

'Your objective is a bold one,' Badrayn said calmly. Inwardly he was anything but calm. It was breathtaking.

'The meek do not inherit the earth,' Daryaei replied, having for the first time explained his mission in life to someone outside his own inner circle of clerics.

It was a struggle for both of them to act like gamblers around a poker table, while they discussed a plan that would change the shape of the world. For Daryaei it was a concept toward which he'd labored and thought and planned for more than a generation, the culmination of everything he'd ever done in life, the fulfillment of a dream, and such a goal as to put his name aside that of the Prophet himself – if he achieved it. The unification of Islam. That was how he typically expressed it in his inner circle.

Badrayn merely saw the power. The creation of a new superstate centered on the Persian Gulf, a state with immense economic power, a huge population, self-sustaining in every detail and able to expand across Asia and Africa, perhaps fulfilling the wishes of the Prophet Mohammed, though he didn't pretend to know what the founder of his religion would or would not have wished. He left that to men like Daryaei. For Badrayn the game was simply power, and religion or ideology merely defined the team identities. His team was this one because of where he'd been born, and because he'd once looked closely at Marxism and decided it was insufficient to the task.

'It is possible,' Badrayn said after a few more seconds of contemplation.

'The historical moment is unique. The Great Satan' – he didn't really like to fall into ideological cant in discussions of statecraft, but sometimes there was no avoiding it – 'is weak. The Lesser Satan is destroyed, with its Islamic republics ready to fall into our laps. They need an identity, and what better identity could there be than the Holy Faith?'

And that was entirely true, Badrayn agreed with a silent nod. The collapse of the Soviet Union and its replacement with the so-called Confederation of Independent States had merely generated a vacuum not yet filled. The southern tier of 'republics' were still economically tied to Moscow, rather like a series of carts hitched to a dying horse. They'd always been rebellious, unsettled mini-nations whose religion had set them apart from the atheist empire, and now they were all struggling to establish their own economic identity so that they could once and for all separate themselves from the center of a dead country to which they'd never truly belonged. But they couldn't sustain themselves economically, not in the modern age. They all needed another patron, another guide into the new century. That new leadership had to mean money, and lots of it, plus the unifying banner of religion and culture long denied them by Marxism-Leninism. In return, the republics would provide land and people. And resources.

'The obstacle is America, but you do not need me to tell you that,' Badrayn observed unnecessarily. 'And America is too large and powerful to destroy.'

'I've met this Ryan. But first, you tell me what you think of him.'

'He's no fool, and no coward,' Badrayn said judiciously. 'He has shown physical bravery, and he is well versed in intelligence operations. He is well educated. The Saudis trust him, as do the Israelis.' Those two countries mattered at this moment. So did a third: 'The Russians know and respect him.'

'What else?'

'Do not underestimate him. Do not underestimate America. We have both seen what happens to those who do,' Badrayn said.

'But America's current state?'

'What I have seen tells me that President Ryan is working hard to reconstitute the government of his country. It is a huge task, but America is a fundamentally stable country.'

'What about the problem in the succession?'

'This I do not understand,' Badrayn admitted. 'I haven't seen enough news reports to understand the issues.'

'I have met Ryan,' Daryaei said, finally revealing his own thoughts. 'He is an assistant, nothing more. He appears strong, but is not. Were he a man of strength, he would deal with this Kealty directly. The man commits treason, does he not? But this is not important. Ryan is one man. America is one country. Both can be attacked, at the same time, from more than one direction.'

'Lion and hyenas,' Badrayn noted, then explained himself. Daryaei was so pleased with the idea that he didn't object to his own place in the metaphor.

'Not one great attack, but many small ones?' the cleric asked.

'It has worked before.'

'And what of many large ones? Against America, and against Ryan. For that matter, what if Ryan were to fall? What would happen then, my young friend?'

'Within their system of government, chaos would result. But I would counsel caution. I would also recommend allies. The more hyenas and the more directions, the better to harry the lion. As for attacking Ryan personally,' Badrayn went on, wondering why his host had said *that*, and wondering if it was an error, 'the President of the United States is a difficult target, well protected and well informed.'

'So I am told,' Daryaei replied, behind dark eyes devoid of expression. 'What other countries would you recommend as our allies?'

'Have you paid close attention to the conflict between Japan and America?' Badrayn asked. 'Did you ever wonder why some large dogs did not bark at all?' It was a funny thing about large dogs. They were always hungry. More than once now, however, Daryaei had talked about Ryan and his protection. One dog was the hungriest of all. It would make for an interesting pack.

'Maybe it just malfunctioned.'

The Gulfstream representatives were sitting in a room with Swiss civil-aviation officials, along with the chief of flight operations of the corporation which owned the jets. His written records showed that the aircraft had been properly maintained by a local firm. All parts had come from the approved suppliers. The Swiss corporation which did the maintenance had ten years of accident-free history behind it, regulated in turn by the same government agency which oversaw the investigation.

'It wouldn't be the first time,' the Gulfstream rep agreed. The flight-data recorder was a robust piece of hardware, but they didn't always survive crashes, because every crash was different. A careful search by USS *Radford* had failed to turn up the locator pings. Absent that, the bottom was too deep for an undirected search, and then there was the issue of the Libyans, who didn't want ships poking around their waters. Had the missing aircraft been an airliner, the issue might have been pushed, but a business jet with a crew of two and three reported passengers – one of them with a deadly plague – wasn't important enough. 'Without the data, there isn't much to be said. Engine failure was reported, and that could mean bad fuel, bad maintenance –'

'Please!' the maintenance contractor objected.

'I'm speaking theoretically,' Gulfstream pointed out. 'Or even pilot error of some sort or other. Without hard data, our hands are pretty well tied.'

'The pilot had four thousand hours in type. The co-pilot had over two thousand,' the owner's representative said for the fifth time this afternoon.

They were all thinking the same thing. The aircraft manufacturer had a superb safety record to defend. There were relatively few airliner manufacturers for the big carriers to choose from, and as important as safety was for them, it was even more so for the builders of business jets, for whom competition was stiffer. The buyers of such corporate toys had long memories, and without hard information to hang their hats on about the few crashes which took place, all they remembered was a missing aircraft with missing passengers.

The maintenance contractor had no wish to be firmly associated with a fatal accident, either. Switzerland had a lot of airfields, and a lot of business aircraft. A bad maintainer could lose business as well, not to mention the trouble from the Swiss government for violating its stringent civil-aviation rules.

The corporate owner had the least to lose in terms of reputation, but *amour propre* would not allow him to assume responsibility without real cause.

And there was no real cause for any of them to take the blame, not without the flight-data recorder. The men looked at one another around the table, thinking the same thought: good people *did* make mistakes, but rarely did they wish to admit them, and never when they didn't have to. The government representative had gone over the written records and been satisfied that the paperwork was all correct. Beyond that there was nothing any of them could do except talk to the engine manufacturer and try to get a sample of the fuel. The former was easy. The latter was not. In the end, they'd know little more than they knew now. Gulfstream might lose a plane or two in sales. The maintenance contractor would undergo increased government scrutiny. The corporation would have to buy a new jet. To show loyalty, it would be another G-class business jet and with the same maintenance contractor. That would please everybody, even the Swiss government.

Being a roving inspector paid more than being a street agent, and it was more fun than sitting behind a desk all the time, but Pat O'Day still chafed at spending most of his day reading over written reports generated by agents or their secretaries. More junior people cross-checked the data for inconsistencies, though he did the same, keeping careful penciled notes on his own yellow pad, which *his* secretary would collate for his summary reports to Director Murray. Real agents, O'Day believed implicitly, didn't type. Well, that's what his instructors at Quantico would have said, probably. He finished his meetings early down at Buzzard's Point and decided that his office in the Hoover Building didn't need him. The investigation was indeed at the point of diminishing returns. The 'new' information was all interviews, every single one of which confirmed information already developed and already verified by voluminous cross-referenced documents.

'I've always hated this part,' ADIC Tony Caruso said. It was the point when the United States Attorney had everything he needed to get a conviction, but, being a lawyer, never had enough – as though the best way to convict a hood were to bore the jury to death.

'Not even a sniff of contrary data. This one's in the bag, Tony.' The two men had long been friends. 'Time for me to get something new and exciting.'

'Lucky you. How's Megan?'

'New day-care center, started today. Giant Steps, on Ritchie Highway.'

427

'Same one,' Caruso observed. 'Yeah, I guess it would be.'

'Huh?'

'The Ryan kids – oh, you weren't here back then when those ULA bastards hit it.'

'She didn't – the owner of the place didn't say anything about . . . well, I guess she wouldn't, would she?'

'Our brethren are a little tight-assed about that. I imagine the Service gave her a long brief on what she can and cannot say.'

'Probably an agent or two helping with the finger painting.' O'Day thought for a second. There was a new clerk at the 7-Eleven across the street. He'd remembered thinking when he'd gotten his coffee that the guy was a little too clean-cut for that early in the morning. Hmph. Tomorrow he'd eyeball the guy for a weapon, as the clerk had surely done with him already, and out of professional courtesy he'd show his ID, along with a wink and a nod.

'Kinda overqualified,' Caruso agreed. 'But what the hell, can't hurt to know there's coverage where your kid is.'

'You bet, Tony.' O'Day stood. 'Anyway, I think I'll go and pick her up.'

'Headquarters puke. Eight-hour day,' the Assistant Director in Charge of the Washington Field Office grumped.

'You're the one wanted to be a bigshot, Don Antonio.'

It was always liberating to leave work. The air smelled fresher on the way out than on the way in. He walked out to his truck, noting that it hadn't been touched or stolen. There was an advantage to dirt and mud. He shed his suit jacket – O'Day rarely bothered with an overcoat – and slipped into his ten-year-old leather one, a Navy-type flight jacket worn just enough to be comfortable. The tie was disposed of next. Ten minutes later, he was outbound on Route 50 toward Annapolis, just ahead of the bow wave of government commuters, and listening to C&W on the radio. Traffic was especially favorable today, and just before the hourly news he pulled into the Giant Steps parking lot, this time looking for official cars. The Secret Service was fairly clever about that. Like the Bureau, its automobiles were randomly tagged, and they'd even learned not to go with the obvious cheap-body, neutral-paint motif that fingered so many unmarked cop cars. He spotted two even so, and confirmed his suspicions by parking next to one and looking down inside see the radio. That done, he wondered about his own disguis and decided to see how good *they* were, then realized that i they were halfway competent, they'd already checked out his ID through the documents he'd handed over to Mrs Daggett that very morning, or more likely even before. There was a considerable professional rivalry between the FBI and the USSS. In fact, the former had been started with a handful of Secret Service agents. But the FBI had also grown much larger, and along the way accumulated far more corporate experience in criminal investigation. Which was not to say the Service wasn't damned good, though as Tony Caruso had truthfully observed, very tight-assed. Well, they were probably the world's foremost baby-sitters.

He walked across the parking lot with his jacket zipped up, and spotted a big guy just inside the door. Would he stay covert? O'Day walked right past him, just another father in to pick up his munchkin. Inside, it was just a matter of checking out the clothes and the earpieces. Yep, two female agents wearing long smocks, and under them would be Sig-Sauer 9mm automatics.

'Daddy!' Megan hooted, leaping to her feet. Next to her was another child of similar age and looks. The inspector headed over, bending down to look at the day's crayoning.

'Excuse me.' And he felt light hand pressure through the jacket, on his service automatic.

'You know who I am,' he said without turning.

'Oh! I do now.' And then O'Day recognized the voice. He turned to see Andrea Price.

'Demoted?' He stood to look her in the face. The two female agents mingled with the kids were also watching him closely, alerted by the bulge under the leather jacket. Not bad, O'Day thought. They'd had to look closely; the bulk of the leather was good concealment. Both had their gun hands off whatever educational task they'd been performing, and the looks in their eyes would appear casual only to the unschooled.

'Sweep. Checking out arrangements for all the kids,' she explained.

'This is Katie,' Megan said, introducing her new friend. 'And that's my daddy.'

Well, hello, Katie.' He bent down again to shake her hand, then stood again. 'Is she . . . ?'

'SANDBOX, First Toddler of the United States,' Price confirmed.

'And one across the street?' Business first.

'Two, relays.'

'She looks like her mom,' Pat said of Katie Ryan. And just to be polite he pulled out his official ID and tossed it to the nearest female agent, Marcella Hilton.

'You want to be a little careful testing us, okay?' Price asked.

'Your man at the door knew who I was coming in. He looks like he's been around the block.'

'Don Russell, and he has, but –'

'But ain't no such thing as "too careful," ' Inspector O'Day agreed. 'Yeah, okay, I admit it, I wanted to see how careful you were. Hey, my little girl's here, too. I guess this place is a target now.' *Damn*, he didn't say aloud.

'So do we pass?'

'One across the street, three I can see here. I bet you have three more camped out within a hundred yards, want me to look for the Suburban and the long guns?'

'Look hard. We've got them well concealed.' She didn't mention the one in the building he hadn't spotted.

'I bet you do, Agent Price,' O'Day agreed, catching the clue and looking around some more. There were two disguised TV cameras that must have gone in recently. That also explained the faint smell of paint, which in turn explained the lack of little hand-prints on the walls. The building was probably wired like a pinball machine. 'I must admit, you guys are pretty smooth. Good,' he concluded.

'Anything new on the crash?'

Pat shook his head. 'Not really. We went over some additional interviews at WFO today. The only inconsistencies are too minor to count for much of anything. The Mounties are doing a hell of a job for us, by the way. So are the Japs. I think they've talked to everybody from Sato's kindergarten teacher on up. They even turned two stewardesses he was playing with on the side. This one's in the bag, Price.'

'Andrea,' she replied.

'Pat.' And they both smiled.

'What do you carry?'

'Smith 1076. Better than that 9mm mouse gun you guys pack.' This was delivered with a somewhat superior attitude. O'Day believed in making big holes, to date only in targets, but in people if necessary. The Secret Service had its own weapons policy, and in that area he was sure the Bureau had better ideas. She didn't bite.

'Do us a favor? Next time you come in, show your ID to the agent out front. Might not always be the same one.' She didn't even ask him to leave it in his truck. Damn, there was professional courtesy.

'So, how's he doing?'

'SWORDSMAN?'

'Dan – Director Murray – thinks the world of him. They go back a ways. So do Dan and I.'

'Tough job, but you know – Murray's right. I've met worse men. He's smarter than he lets on, too.'

'The times I've been around him, he listens well.'

'Better than that, he asks questions.' They both turned when a kid yelled, swept the room at the same time and in the same way, then turned back to the two little girls, who were sharing crayons for their respective works of art. 'Yours and ours seem to get along.'

Ours, Pat thought. That said it all. The big old bruiser at the door, Russell, she'd said. He'd be the chief of the sub-detail, and sure as hell that was one experienced agent. They'd have selected younger ones, both women, for inside work, the better to blend in. They'd be good, but not as good as he was. *Ours* was the key word, though. Like lions around their cubs, or just one cub in this case. O'Day wondered how he'd handle this job. It would be boring, just standing post like that, but you couldn't allow yourself to get bored. That would be a fight. He'd done his share of 'discreet surveillance' assignments, quite a feat for one of his size, but this would be far worse. Even so, a cop's eye saw the difference between them and the other preschool teachers in the room.

'Andrea, looks to me like your people know their job. Why so many?'

'I know we have this one overmanned.' Price tilted her head. 'We're still figuring this one out. Hey, we took a big

431

hit on the Hill, y'know? Ain't gonna be any more, not on my watch, not while I run the Detail, and if the press makes noise about it, fuck 'em.' She even talked like a real cop.

'Ma'am, that's just fine with me. Well, with your permission, I have to go home and make cheese and macaronis.' He looked down. Megan was about finished with her masterpiece. The two little girls were difficult to tell apart, at least for the casual observer. That was distantly worrisome, but that was also the reason the Service was here.

'Where do you practice?' He didn't have to say practice *what*.

'There's a range in the old Post Office building, convenient to the White House. Every week,' she told him. 'There's not an agent here who's short of "expert," and I'll put Don up against anybody in the world.'

'Really.' O'Day's eyes sparkled. 'One day we'll have to see.'

'Your place or mine?' Price asked, with a twinkle of her own.

'Mr President, Mr Golovko on three.' That was the direct line. Sergey Nikolayevich was showing off again.

Jack pushed the button. 'Yes, Sergey?'

'Iran.'

'I know,' the President said.

'How much?' the Russian asked, his bags already packed to go home.

'We'll know in ten days or so for sure.'

'Agreed. I offer cooperation.'

This was getting to be habit forming, Jack thought, but it was always something to think over first. 'I will discuss that with Ed Foley. When will you be back home?'

'Tomorrow.'

'Call me then.' Amazing that he could speak so efficiently with a former enemy. He'd have to get Congress trained that way, the President thought with a smile. Ryan stood from his desk and headed into the secretaries' room. 'How about some munchies before my next appointment –'

'Hello, Mr President,' Price said. 'Have a minute?'

Ryan waved her in while his number-two secretary called the mess. 'Yes?'

'Just wanted to tell you, I looked over the security arrange-

ments for your children. It's pretty tight.' If this was suppo~~se~~
to please POTUS, he didn't show it, Andrea thought. B~~ut~~
that was understandable. *Hey, we have enough bodyguards*
on your children. What a world it was. Two minutes later,
she was talking with Raman, who was ready to head off duty,
having arrived in the White House at 5:00 AM There was, as
usual, nothing to report. It had been a quiet day in the House.

The younger agent walked out to his car and drove off
the compound, first showing his pass to the gate guards and
waiting for the fortified gate to open – a nine-inch-square
post held the leaves in place, and looked strong enough to
stop a dump truck. From there he made his way through the
concrete barricades on Pennsylvania Avenue – which until
fairly recently had been a public street. He turned west and
headed toward Georgetown, where he had a loft apartment,
but this time he didn't go all the way home. Instead he turned
onto Wisconsin Avenue, then right again to park.

It was vaguely amusing that the man should be a rug merchant. So many Americans thought that Iranians became
either terrorists, rug merchants, or impolite physicians. This
one had left Persia – but most Americans didn't connect
Persian rugs with Iran, as though they were two distinct
nations – more than fifteen years before. On his wall was a
photograph of his son who, he told those who asked, had
been killed in the Iran-Iraq war. That was quite true. He also
told those who expressed interest that he hated the government of his former country. That was not true. He was a
sleeper agent. He'd never had a single contact with anyone
even connected at third hand with Tehran. Maybe he'd been
checked out. More likely he had not. He belonged to no
association, didn't march, speak out, or otherwise do anything but conduct a properous business – like Raman, he
didn't even attend a mosque. He had, in fact, never met
Raman, and so when the man walked in the front door, his
interest only concerned which of his wide selection of handmade rugs the man might want. Instead, after determining
that there was no one else in the shop at the moment, his
visitor went directly to the counter.

'The picture on the wall. He looks like you. Your son?'

'Yes,' the man replied with a sadness which had never left
him, promises of Paradise or not. 'He was killed in the war.'

Many lost sons in that conflict. Was he a religious boy?'

Does it matter now?' the merchant asked, blinking hard.

'It always matters,' Raman said, in a voice that was totally casual.

With that, both men went over to the nearer of two rug piles. The dealer flipped a few corners.

'I am in position. I require instructions on timing.' Raman didn't have a code name, and the code phrase he'd just exchanged was only known to three men. The dealer didn't know anything beyond that, except to repeat the nine words he'd just heard to someone else, then wait for a reply, and pass that along.

'Would you mind filling out a card for my client list?'

That Raman did, putting down the name and address of a real person. He'd picked the name in the phone book – actually a crisscross directory right in the White House, which had made it easy to select a number that was one digit off his own. A tick mark over the sixth digit told the dealer where to add 1 to 3 to get 4 and so complete the call. It was excellent tradecraft, taught to his Savak instructor by an Israeli more than two decades earlier and not forgotten, just as neither man from the holy city of Qom had forgotten much of anything.

22

TIME ZONES

The size of the earth and the location of the trouble spots made for great inconvenience. America was going to sleep when other parts of the world were just waking up to a new day, a situation made even more difficult by the fact that the people eight or nine hours ahead were also the ones making decisions to which the rest of the world had to react. Added to that was the fact that America's vaunted CIA had little in the way of agents or officers to predict what was happening. That left to STORM TRACK and PALM BOWL the duty of reporting mainly what the local press and TV were saying. And so while the US President slept, people struggled to collect and analyze information which, when he saw it, would be late by a working day, and the analysis of which might or might not be accurate. Even then, the best of the spooks in Washington were in the main too senior to be stuck with night duty – they had families, after all – and so they also had to be brought up to speed before they could make their own pronouncements, which involved discussion and debate, further delaying presentation of vital national-security information. In military terms it was called 'having the initiative' – making the first move, physical, political, or psychological. How much the better if the other side in the race started off a third of a day behind.

Things were slightly better in Moscow, which was only an hour off Tehran time, and in the same time zone with Baghdad, but here for once the RVS, successor to the KGB, was in the same unhappy position as CIA, with nearly all of its networks wiped out in both countries. But for Moscow the problems were also somewhat closer to home, as Sergey Golovko would find out when his aircraft landed at Sheremetyevo.

The largest problem at the moment would be reconciliation. Morning TV in Iraq announced that the new government in Baghdad had informed the United Nations that all international inspection teams were to be given full freedom to visit any facility in the country, entirely without interference – in fact, Iraq requested that the inspections be carried out as rapidly as possible – that full cooperation with any requests would be instantly provided; that the new Baghdad government was desirous of removing any obstacle to full restoration of their country's international trade. For the moment, the neighboring country of Iran, the announcement said, would begin trucking in foodstuffs in accordance with Islamic ancient guidelines on charity for those in need; this in anticipation of the former nation's willingness to reenter the community of nations. Video copied at PALM BOWL from Basra TV showed the first convoy of trucks carrying wheat down the twisting Shahabad Highway and crossing into Iraqi territory at the foot of the mountains which separated the two countries. Further pictures showed Iraqi border guards removing their obstacles and waving the trucks through, while their Iranian counterparts stood peacefully aside on their side of the border, no weapons in evidence.

At Langley, people ran calculations on the number of trucks, the tonnage of their cargo, and the number of loaves of bread which would result. They concluded that shiploads of wheat would have to be delivered to make more than a symbolic difference. But symbols *were* important, and the ships were even now being loaded, a set of satellite overheads determined. United Nations officials in Geneva, only three hours behind the time, received the Baghdad requests with pleasure and sent immediate orders to their inspection teams, which found Mercedes automobiles waiting for them, to be escorted to the first entries on their inspection lists by wailing police cars. Here they also found TV crews to follow them around, and friendly installation staffs, who professed delight at their newfound ability to tell all they knew and to offer suggestions on how to dismantle, first, a chemical-weapons facility disguised as an insecticide plant. Finally, *Iran* requested a special meeting of the Security Council to consider the lifting of the remaining trade sanctions, something as certain as the rising of the sun, even late, over the American East Coast. Within two weeks, the average Iraqi's diet would increase by at least five hundred calories. The

psychological impact wasn't difficult to figure, and the le̱
country in restoring normality to the oil-rich but isolate̱
nation was its former enemy, Iran – as always, citing religion
as the motivating factor in offering aid.

'Tomorrow we will see pictures of bread being distributed
for free from mosques,' Major Sabah predicted. He could have
added the passages from the Koran which would accompany
the event, but his American colleagues were not Islamic
scholars and would not have grasped the irony terribly well.

'Your estimate, sir?' the senior American officer asked.

'The two countries will unite,' Sabah replied soberly. 'And
soon.'

There was no particular need to ask why the surviving
Iraqi weapons plants were being exposed. Iran had all it
needed.

There is no such thing as magic. That was merely the word
people used to explain something so cleverly done that there
was no ready explanation for it, and the simplest technique
employed by its practitioners was to distract the audience
with one moving and obvious hand (usually in a white glove)
while the other was doing something else. So it was with
nations as well. While the trucks rolled, and the ships were
loaded, and the diplomats were summoned, and America was
waking up to figure out what was going on, it was, after all,
evening in Tehran.

Badrayn's contacts were as useful as ever, and what he
could not do, Daryaei could. The civilian-marked business
jet lifted off from Mehrabad and turned east, heading first
over Afghanistan, then Pakistan, in a two-hour flight that
ended at the obscure city of Rutog near the Pakistani-Indian-
Kashmiri border. The city was in the former country's Kun-
lun Mountains, and home to some of China's Muslim
population. The border town had an air force base with some
locally manufactured MiG fighters, and a single landing strip,
all separate from the city's small regional airport. The location was ideal for everyone's purpose, as it was a bare 600
miles from New Delhi, though perversely the longest flight
came from Beijing, nearly two thousand miles away, even
though the real estate was Chinese-owned. The three aircraft
landed a few minutes apart, soon after local sunset, taxied

the far end of the ramp, and parked. Military vehicles took their occupants to the ready room for the local MiG contingent. The Ayatollah Mahmoud Haji Daryaei was accustomed to cleaner accommodations and, worse, he could smell the odor of cooked pork, always a part of the Chinese diet but quite nauseating to him. This he put aside. He wasn't the first of the faithful who'd had to treat with pagans and unbelievers.

The Indian Prime Minister was cordial. She'd met Daryaei before at a regional trade conference and found him withdrawn and misanthropic. That, she saw, had not changed very much.

Last to arrive was Zhang Han San, whom the Indian had met as well. He was a rotund, seemingly jolly man – until one watched his eyes closely. Even his jokes were told with an aim to learn something of his companions. Of the three, he was the only one whose job was not really known to the others. It was clear, however, that he spoke with authority, and since his country was the most powerful of the three, it was not regarded as an insult that a mere minister-without-portfolio was treating with chiefs of state. The meeting was conducted in English, except for Zhang's dismissal of the general officer who'd handled the greetings.

'Please forgive me for not being here when you arrived. The ... irregularity in protocol is sincerely regretted.' Tea was served, along with some light snacks. There hadn't been time to prepare a proper meal, either.

'Not at all,' Daryaei responded. 'Speed makes for inconvenience. For myself, I am most grateful for your willingness to meet under such special circumstances.' He turned. 'And to you, Madam Prime Minister, for joining us. God's blessing on this meeting,' he concluded.

'My congratulations on developments in Iraq,' Zhang said, wondering if the agenda was now entirely in Daryaei's hands, so skillfully had he posed the fact that he'd convened the assembly. 'It must be very satisfying after so many years of discord between your two nations.'

Yes, India thought, sipping her tea. So clever of you to murder the man in such a timely fashion. 'So how may we be of service?' she asked, thus giving Daryaei and Iran the floor, to the impassive annoyance of China.

'You've met this Ryan recently. I am interest▓
impressions.'

'A small man in a large job,' she replied at onc▓
speech he gave at the funeral, for example. It would▓
been better suited to a private family ceremony. For a Pr▓
dent, bigger things are expected. At the reception later, h▓
seemed nervous and uneasy, and his wife is arrogant – a▓
physician, you see. They often are.'

'I found him the same when we met, some years ago,'
Daryaei agreed.

'And yet he controls a great country,' Zhang observed.

'Does he?' Iran asked. 'Is America still great? For where
comes the greatness of a nation, except in the strengths of
its leaders?' And that, the other two knew at once, was the
agenda.

'Jesus,' Ryan whispered to himself, 'this is a lonely place.'
The thought kept returning to him, all the more so when
alone in this office with its curving walls and molded three-
inch doors. He was using his reading glasses all the time now
– Cathy's recommendation – but that merely slowed down
the headaches. It wasn't as though he were a stranger to
reading. Every job he'd held in the past fifteen years had
required it, but the continual headaches were something
new. Maybe he should talk to Cathy or another doc about
it? No. Ryan shook his head. It was just job stress, and he
just had to learn to deal with it.

Sure, it's just stress. And cancer is just a disease.

The current task was politics. He was reading over a position paper prepared by the political staffers across the street
in the OEOB. It was a source of amusement, if not consolation, that they didn't know what to advise him. Ryan had
never belonged to a political party. He'd always registered
himself as an independent, and that had managed to keep him
from getting solicitation letters from the organized parties,
though he and Cathy had always ticked the box on their tax
returns to contribute their one dollar to the government
slush fund. But the President was not only supposed to be a
member of a party – but also the *leader* of that party. The
parties were even more thoroughly decapitated than the
three branches of government were. Each of them still had

..n, neither of whom knew what to do at the
.. For a few days, it had been assumed that Ryan was
..ber of the same party as Roger Durling, and the truth
..only been discovered by the press a few days before, to
.. collective *oh, shit!* of the Washington establishment. For
..he ideological mavens of the federal city, it was rather
like asking what 2 + 2 equaled, and finding out that the
answer was, 'Chartreuse.' His position paper was predictably chaotic, the product of four or so professional
political analysts, and you could tell who had written the
different paragraphs, which resolved into a multi-path tug
of war. Even his intelligence staff did better than this,
Jack told himself, tossing the paper into the out basket and
wishing, again, for a cigarette. That was stress talking, too,
he knew.

But he still had to go out to the *hustings*, a word whose
meaning he'd never learned, and *campaign* for people, or
at least give speeches. Or something. The position paper's
guidance hadn't exactly been clear on that. Having already
shot himself in the foot on the issue of abortion – higher up
and more to the centerline, Arnie van Damm had remarked
acidly the previous day, to reinforce his earlier lesson – now
Ryan would have to make his political stance clear on a
multitude of issues: affirmative action at one end of the
alphabet, and welfare at the other, with taxes, the environment, and God only knew what else in between. Once he'd
decided where he stood on such things, Callie Weston would
write a series of speeches for him to deliver from Seattle to
Miami and God only knew where else in between. Hawaii
and Alaska were left out because they were small states in
terms of political importance, and poles apart ideologically,
anyway. They would only confuse matters, or so the position
paper told him.

'Why can't I just stay here and work, Arnie?' Ryan asked
his arriving chief of staff.

'Because out there *is* work, Mr President.' Van Damm took
his seat to commence the latest class in Presidency 101.
'Because, as you put it, "It's a leadership function" – did I get
that right?' Arnie asked with a sardonic growl. 'And leading
means getting out with the troops, or, in this case, the citizens. Are we clear on that, Mr President?'

'Are you enjoying this?' Jack closed his eyes and ⟨...⟩ them under the glasses. He hated the goddamned g⟨...⟩ too.

'About as much as you are.' Which was an altogether ⟨...⟩ comment.

'Sorry.'

'Most people who come here genuinely like escaping from this museum and meeting real people. Of course, it makes people like Andrea nervous. They'd probably agree with keeping you here all the time. But it already feels like a prison, doesn't it?' Arnie asked.

'Only when I'm awake.'

'So get out. Meet people. Tell them what you think, tell them what you want. Hell, they might even listen. They might even tell you what *they* think, and maybe *you* will learn something from it. In any case, you can't *be* President and not do it.'

Jack lifted the position paper he'd just finished. 'Did you read this thing?'

Arnie nodded. 'Yep.'

'It's confusing garbage,' Ryan said, quite surprised.

'It's a political document. Since when is politics consistent or sensible?' He paused. 'The people I've worked with for the last twenty years got this sort of thing with their mother's milk – well, they were probably all bottle babies.'

'*What!*'

'Ask Cathy. It's one of those behavioral theories, that New Age stuff that's supposed to explain everything about everything to everybody everywhere. Politicians are all bottle babies. Mommy never nursed them, and they never bonded properly, felt rejected and all that, and so as compensation they go out and make speeches and tell people in different places the different things they want to hear so that they can get the love and devotion from strangers that their mothers denied them – not to mention the ones like Kealty, who're getting laid all the time. Properly nurtured infants, on the other hand, grow up to become – oh, doctors, I suppose, or maybe rabbis –'

'What the *hell*!' the President nearly shouted. His chief of staff just grinned.

'Had you going for a second, didn't I? You know,' van

went on, 'I figured out what we really missed when ⸱ this country up.'

⸱kay, I'll bite,' Jack said, eyes still closed, and finding the ⸱mor in the moment. Damn, but Arnie knew how to run ⸱ classroom.

'A court jester, make it a Cabinet post. You know, a dwarf – excuse me, a male person with an unusually large degree of vertical challenge – dressed in multicolored tights and the funny hat with bells on it. Give him a little stool in the corner – 'course, there isn't a corner here, but what the hell – and every fifteen minutes or so, he's supposed to jump up on your desk and shake his rattle in your face just to remind you that you have to take a leak every so often, just like the rest of us. Do you get it now, Jack?'

'No,' the President admitted.

'You dumbass! This job can be *fun*! Getting out and seeing your citizens is *fun*. Learning what they want is important, but there's also an exhilaration to it. They *want* to love you, Jack. They *want* to support you. They *want* to know what you think. They most of all *want* to know that you're one of them – and you know what? You're the first President in one hell of a long time who really *is*! So get the hell off the bench, tell the air scouts to fire up the Big Blue Bird, and play the damned game.' He didn't have to add that the schedule was already set sufficiently in stone that he couldn't back out.

'Not everybody will like what I say and believe, Arnie, and I'll be damned if I'm going to lie to people just to kiss ass or get votes or whatever.'

'You expect everybody to love you?' van Damm asked, sardonic again. 'Most Presidents will settle for fifty-one percent. Quite a few have had to settle for less. I tore your head off over your abortion statement – why? Because your statement was confused.'

'No, it wasn't, I –'

'You going to listen to your teacher or not?'

'Go ahead,' the President said.

'Start off, about forty percent of the people vote Democrat. About forty percent vote Republican. Of those eighty percent, most wouldn't change their votes if Adolf Hitler was running against Abe Lincoln – or against FDR, just to cover both sides.'

'But why –'

Exasperation: 'Why is the sky blue, Jack? It jus... Even if you can explain why, and I suppose there is ... some astronomer can explain, the sky *is* blue, and s... just accept the fact, okay? That leaves twenty percent o... people who swing back one way or another. Maybe they ... the true independents, like you. That twenty percent con trols the destiny of the country, and if you want things to happen your way, those are the people you have to reach. Now, here's the funny part. Those twenty percent don't especially care what you think.' This conclusion was delivered with a wry smile.

'Wait a minute –'

Arnie held up his hand. 'You keep interrupting teacher. The hard eighty percent that votes the party line doesn't care much about character. They vote party because they believe in the philosophy of the party – or because Mom and Dad always voted that way; the reason doesn't really matter. It happens. It's a fact. Deal with it. Now, back to the twenty percent that *does* matter. They care less about what you believe than they do in *you*. There is your advantage, Mr President. Politically speaking, you have as much place in this office as a three-year-old has in a gun shop, but you have character up the ass. That's what we play on.'

Ryan frowned at the 'play on' part, but this time kept his peace. He nodded for the chief of staff to go on.

'Just tell the people what you believe. Make it simple. Good ideas are expressed simply and efficiently. Make it consistent. That twenty percent wants to believe that *you* really do believe in what you say. Jack, do you respect a man who says what he believes, even if you disagree with it?'

'Of course, that's what –'

'A man is supposed to do,' Arnie said, completing the thought. 'So does the twenty percent. They will respect you and support you even though in some cases they disagree with you. Why? Because they will know that you are a man of your word. And they want the occupant of this office to be a man of character and integrity. Because if things go to shit, you can depend on somebody like that to at least try to do the right thing.'

t is packaging. And don't disparage packaging and
..., okay? There's nothing wrong about being intelli-
...bout how you get your ideas across. In the book you
...e about Halsey, *Fighting Sailor*, you chose your words
...efully to present your ideas, right?' The President nodded.
So it is with these ideas – hell, these ideas are even more
important, and so you have to package them with proportion-
ately greater skill, don't you?' The lesson plan was moving
along nicely, the chief of staff thought.

'Arnie, how many of those ideas will you agree with?'

'Not all of them. I think you're wrong on abortion – a
woman should have the right to choose. I bet you and I
disagree on affirmative action and a passel of other things, but
you know, Mr President, I've never doubted your integrity for
one single minute. I can't tell you what to believe, but you
know how to listen. I love this country, Jack. My family
escaped from Holland, crossed the English Channel in a boat
when I was three years old. I can still remember puking my
guts out.'

'You're Jewish?' Jack asked in surprise. He had no idea
what church, if any, Arnie attended.

'No, my father was in the Resistance and got himself fingered by a German plant. We skipped just in time, or he
would have been shot, and Mom and I would have ended up
in the same camp as Anne Frank. Didn't do the rest of the
family much good, though. His name was Willem, and after
the war ended, he decided that we'd come over here, and I
grew up hearing about the old country, and how this place
was different. It is different. I became what I am to protect the
system. What makes America different? The Constitution,
I guess. People change, governments change, ideologies
change, but the Constitution stays pretty much the same.
You and Pat Martin both swore an oath. So did I,' van Damm
went on. 'Except mine was made to me, and my mom and
my dad. I don't have to agree with you on all the issues, Jack.
I know you'll try to do the right thing. My job, then, is to
protect you so that you can. That means you have to listen,
and that you'll sometimes have to do things you don't like,
but this job you have, Mr President, has its own rules. You
have to follow them,' the chief of staff concluded quietly.

'How have I been doing, Arnie?' Ryan asked, absorb. largest lesson of the week.

'Not bad, but you have to do better. Kealty is still an ann ance rather than a real threat to us. Getting out and lookr presidential will further marginalize him. Now, somethin, else. As soon as you go out, go off campus, people are going to start asking you about reelection. So what will you say?'

Ryan shook his head emphatically. 'I do *not* want this job, Arnie. Let somebody else take over when – '

'In that case, you're screwed. Nobody will take you seriously. You will not get the people in Congress you want. You will be crippled and unable to accomplish the things you're thinking about. You will become politically ineffective. America cannot afford that, Mr President. Foreign governments – those are run by politicians, remember – will not take you seriously, and *that* has national security implications, both immediate and long-term. So what do you say when reporters ask you that question?'

The President felt like a student holding up his hand in third grade. 'I haven't decided yet?'

'Correct. You are carrying out your job of reconstituting the government, and that is a question which you will address in due course. I will quietly leak the fact that you're thinking about staying on, that you feel your first duty is to the country, and when reporters ask you about *that*, you will simply repeat your original position. That sends out a message to foreign governments that they will understand and take seriously, and the American people will also understand and respect it. As a practical matter, the presidential primaries for both parties will not select the marginal candidates who didn't get wiped out on the Hill. They'll vote for uncommitted delegations. We might even want you to speak on that issue. I'll talk that one over with Callie.' He didn't add that the media would just *love* that prospect. Covering *two* brokered, wide-open political conventions was a dream such as few of them had ever dared to consider. Arnie was keeping it as simple as he could. No matter what positions Ryan took, as soon as he took them, no less than forty percent of the people would object to it, and probably more. The funny thing about the twenty percent he kept harping on was that they covered the whole political spectrum – like f, less concerned with ideology than with character. e of them would object vociferously, and in that they ld be indistinguishable from whichever forty percent ouping shared that particular ideological stance, though at he end of the day they would vote the man. They always did, honest people that they were, placing country before prejudice, but joining in a process that most often honestly selected people who lacked the honor of their electors. Ryan didn't yet grasp the opportunity he held in his hands, and it was probably better that he didn't, for in thinking about it too much – perhaps at all – he would try to control the spin, which he'd never learn to do well. Even honorable men could make mistakes, and Ryan was no different from the rest. That was why people like Arnold van Damm existed, to teach and to guide from the inside and the outside of the system at the same time. He looked at his President, noting the confusion that came along with new thoughts. He was trying to make sense of it, and he'd probably succeed, because he was a good listener and a particularly adept processor of information. He wouldn't see it through to the natural conclusion, however. Only Arnie and maybe Callie Weston were able to look that far into the future. In the past weeks, van Damm had decided that Ryan had the makings of a real President. It would be his job, the chief of staff decided, to make sure that Jack stayed here.

'We cannot do that,' the Indian Prime Minister protested, with the admission: 'We only recently had a lesson from the American navy.'

'It was a harsh one,' Zhang agreed. 'But it did no permanent harm. I believe the damage to your ships will be made good in two more weeks.' That statement turned India's head around. She'd learned that fact herself only a few days earlier. The repairs were using up a sizable portion of the Indian navy's annual operating budget, which had been her principal concern. It wasn't every day that a foreign country, particularly one which had once been a shooting enemy, revealed its penetration of another's government.

'America is a façade, a giant with a sick heart and a damaged brain,' Daryaei said. 'You told us yourself, Prime Minister. President Ryan is a small man in a large job. If we make

the job larger and harder, then America will lose its abir
to interfere with us, for a long enough time that we ca
achieve our goals. The American government is paralyzed,
and will remain so for some weeks to come. All we need do
is to increase the degree of paralysis.'

'And how might one do that?' India asked.

'Through the simple means of stretching their commitments while at the same time disturbing their internal stability. On the one hand, mere demonstrations will suffice on
your part. On the other, that is my concern. It is better, I
think, that you have no knowledge of it.'

Had he been able to do so, Zhang would not even have
breathed at the moment, the better to control his feelings.
It wasn't every day that he met someone more ruthless than
himself, and, no, he didn't want to know what Daryaei had
in mind. Better for another country to commit an act of war.
'Do go on,' he said, reaching inside his jacket for a cigarette.

'Each of us represents a country with great abilities and
greater needs. China and India have large populations and
need both space and resources. I will soon have resources,
and the capital that comes with them, and also the ability
to control how both are distributed. The United Islamic
Republic will become a great power, as you are already great
powers. The West has dominated the East for too long.' Daryaei looked directly at Zhang. 'To our north is a rotting
corpse. Many millions of the Faithful are there and require
liberation. There are also resources and space which your
country needs. These I offer to you, if you will in turn offer
the lands of the Faithful to me.' Then he looked at the Indian
Prime Minister. 'To your south lies an empty continent with
the space and resources you need. For your cooperation, I
think the United Islamic Republic and the People's Republic
are willing to offer their protection. From each of you I ask
only quiet cooperation without direct risk.'

India remarked to herself that she'd heard that one before,
but her needs had not changed from before, either. China
immediately came up with a means of providing a distraction
that offered little in the way of danger. It had happened
before. Iran – what *was* this United Islamic Republic ... oh,
of course, Zhang thought. Of course. The UIR would take
all the real risks, though it would seem that those were

usually well calculated. He would do his own check of the correlation of forces on his return to Beijing.

'I ask no commitments at this point, obviously. You will need to assure yourselves that I am serious in my abilities and intentions. I do ask that you give full consideration to my proposed – informal – alliance.'

'Pakistan,' the Prime Minister said, foolishing tipping her hand, Zhang thought.

'Islamabad has been an American puppet for too long, and cannot be trusted,' Daryaei replied at once, having thought that one through already, though he hadn't really expected India to jump so readily. This woman hated America as much as he did. Well, the 'lesson' as she'd called it must have injured her pride even more deeply than his diplomats had told him. How typical for a woman to value her pride so highly. And how weak. Excellent. He looked over at Zhang.

'Our arrangements with Pakistan are commercial only, and as such are subject to modification,' China observed, equally delighted at India's weakness. It was no one's fault but her own. She'd committed forces to the field – well, the sea – in support of Japan's inefficient attack on America ... while China had done nothing and risked nothing, and emerged from the 'war' unhurt and uninvolved. Even Zhang's most cautious superiors had not objected to his play, failed though it was. And now, again, someone else would take the risks, and India would move in pacifist support, and China would have to do nothing but repeat an earlier policy that seemingly had nothing to do with this new UIR, but was rather a test of a new American President, and that sort of thing happened all the time anyway. Besides, Taiwan was still an annoyance. It was so curious. Iran, motivated by religion of all things. India, motivated by greed and anger. China, on the other hand, thought for the long term, dispassionately, seeking what really mattered, but with circumspection, as always. Iran's goal was self-evident, and if Daryaei was willing to risk war for it, then, why not watch in safety, and hope for his success? But he wouldn't commit his country now. Why appear too eager? India *was* eager, enough so to overlook the obvious: If Daryaei was successful, then Pakistan would make its peace with the new UIR, perhaps even join it, and then India would be isolated and vulnerable. Well, it was dangerous to be a vassal, and all the more so if you had aspirations to graduate to the next level – but without the wherewithal to make it happen. One had to be careful choosing allies. Gratitude among nations was a hothouse flower, easily wilted by exposure to the real world.

The Prime Minister nodded in acknowledgment of her victory over Pakistan, and said no more.

'In that case, my friends, I thank you for graciously agreeing to meet with me, and with your permission, I will take my leave.' The three stood. Handshakes were exchanged, and they headed to the door. Minutes after that, Daryaei's aircraft rotated off the bumpy fighter strip. The mullah looked at the coffeepot and decided against it. He wanted a few hours of sleep before morning prayers. But first –

'Your predictions were entirely correct.'

'The Russians called these things "objective conditions." They are and remain unbelievers, but their formulas for analysis of problems have a certain precision to them,' Badrayn explained. 'That is why I have learned to assemble information so carefully.'

'So I have seen. Your next task will be to sketch in some operations.' With that, Daryaei pushed back his seat and closed his eyes, wondering if he would dream again of dead lions.

Much as he wished for a return to clinical medicine, Pierre Alexandre didn't especially like it, at least this matter of treating people who would not survive. The former Army officer in him figured that defending Bataan had been like this. Doing all you could, firing off your best rounds, but knowing that relief would never come. At the moment, it was three AIDS patients, all homosexual men, all in their thirties, and all with less than a year to live. Alexandre was a fairly religious man, and he didn't approve of the gay lifestyle, but nobody deserved to die like this. And even if they did, he was a physician, not God sitting in judgment. Damn, he thought, walking off the elevator and speaking his patient notes into a mini-tape recorder.

It's part of a doctor's job to compartmentalize his life. The three patients on his unit would still be there tomorrow, and none of them would require emergency attention that night.

Putting their problems aside was not cruel. It was just business, and their lives, were they to have any hope at all, would depend on his ability to turn away from their stricken bodies and back to researching the microsized organisms that were attacking them. He handed the tape cassette to his secretary, who'd type up the notes.

'Dr Lorenz down in Atlanta returned your call returning his call returning your original call,' she told him as he passed. As soon as he sat down, he dialed the direct line from memory.

'Yes?'

'Gus? Alex here at Hopkins. Tag,' he chuckled, 'you're it.' He heard a good laugh at the other end of the line. Phone tag could be the biggest pain in the ass.

'How's the fishing, Colonel?'

'Would you believe I haven't had a chance yet? Ralph's working me pretty hard.'

'What did you want from me – you did call first, didn't you?' Lorenz wasn't sure anymore, another sign of a man working too hard.

'Yeah, I did, Gus. Ralph tells me you're starting a new look at the Ebola structure – from that mini-break in Zaire, right?'

'Well, I would be, except somebody stole my monkeys,' the director of CDC reported sourly. 'The replacement shipment is due in here in a day or two, so they tell me.'

'You have a break-in?' Alexandre asked. One of the troublesome developments for labs that had experimental animals was that animal-rights fanatics occasionally tried to bust in and 'liberate' the animals. Someday, if everyone wasn't careful, some screw-ball would walk out with a monkey under his arm and discover it had Lassa fever – or worse. How the hell were physicians supposed to study the goddamned bug without animals – and who'd ever said that a monkey was more important than a human being? The answer to that was simple: in America there were people who believed in damned near anything, and there was a constitutional right to be an ass. Because of that, CDC, Hopkins, and other research labs had armed guards, protecting monkey cages. And even *rat* cages, which really made Alex roll his eyes to the ceiling.

'No, they were highjacked in Africa. Somebody else is playing with them now. Anyway, so it kicks me back a week. What the hell. I've been looking at this little bastard for fifteen years.'

'How fresh is the sample?'

'It's off the Index Patient. Positive identification, Ebola Zaire, the Mayinga strain. We have another sample from the only other patient. That one disappeared –'

'What?' Alexandre asked in immediate alarm.

'Lost at sea in a plane crash. They were evidently flying her to Paris to see Rousseau. No further cases, Alex. We dodged the bullet this time for a change,' Lorenz assured his younger colleague.

Better, Alexandre thought, *to crunch in a plane crash than bleed out from that little fucker*. He still thought like a soldier, profanity and all. 'Okay.'

'So, why did you call?'

'Polynomials,' Lorenz heard.

'What do you mean?' the doctor asked in Atlanta.

'When you map this one out, let's think about doing a mathematical analysis of the structure.'

'I've been playing with that idea for a while. Right now, though, I want to examine the reproduction cycle and –'

'Exactly, Gus, the mathematical nature of the interaction. I was talking to a colleague up here – eye cutter, you believe? She said something interesting. If the amino acids have a quantifiable mathematical value, and they should, then *how* they interact with other codon strings may tell us something.' Alexandre paused and heard a match striking. Gus was smoking his pipe in the office again.

'Keep going.'

'Still reaching for this one, Gus. What if it's like you've been thinking, it's all an equation? The trick is cracking it, right? How do we do that? Okay, Ralph told me about your time-cycle study. I think you're onto something. If we have the virus RNA mapped, and we have the host DNA mapped, then –'

'Gotcha! The interactions will tell us something about the values of the elements in the polynomial –'

'And that will tell us a lot about how the little fuck replicates, and just maybe –'

'How to attack it.' A pause, and a loud puff came over the phone line. 'Alex, that's pretty good.'

'You're the best guy for the job, Gus, and you're setting up the experiment anyway.'

'Something's missing, though.'

'Always is.'

'Let me think about that one for a day or so and get back to you. Good one, Alex.'

'Thank you, sir.' Professor Alexandre replaced the phone and figured he'd done his duty of the day for medical science. It wasn't much, and there *was* an element missing from the suggestion.

23

EXPERIMENTS

It took several days to get everything in place. President Ryan had to meet with yet another class of new senators – some of the states were a little slow in getting things done, mainly because some of the governors established something akin to search committees to evaluate a list of candidates. That was a surprise to a lot of Washington insiders who'd expected the state executives to do things as they'd always been done to appoint replacements to the upper house just as soon as the bodies were cold – but it turned out that Ryan's speech *had* mattered a little bit. Eight governors had realized that this situation was unique, and had therefore acted in a different way, earning, on reflection, the praise of their local papers, if not the complete approval of the establishment press.

Jack's first political trip was an experimental one. He rose early, kissed his wife and kids on the way out the door, and boarded the helicopter on the South Lawn just before seven in the morning. Ten minutes later, he left the aircraft to trot up the stairs onto Air Force One, technically known to the Pentagon as a VC-25A, a 747 expensively modified to be the President's personal conveyance. He boarded just as the pilot, a very senior colonel, was making his airline-like preflight announcements. Looking aft, Ryan could see eighty or so reporters belting into their better-than-first-class leather seats – actually some *didn't* strap in, because Air Force One generally rode more smoothly than an ocean liner on calm seas – and when he turned to head forward, he heard, '*And this is a nonsmoking flight!*'

'Who said that?' the President asked.

'One of the TV pukes,' Andrea replied. 'He thinks it's his airplane.'

'In a way, it is,' Arnie pointed out. 'Remember that.'

'That's Tom Donner,' Callie Weston added. 'The NBC

anchor. His personal feces are not odorific, and he uses more hair spray than I do. But part of it's glued on.'

'This way, Mr President.' Andrea pointed forward. The President's cabin in Air Force One is in the extreme nose on the main deck, where there are regular, if very plush, seats, plus a pair of couches that fold out into beds for long trips. As the principal agent watched, her principal strapped in. Passengers could get away with breaking the rules – the USSS wasn't all that concerned with journalists – but not POTUS. When that was done, she waved to an Air Force crewman, who lifted a phone and told the pilot that he could go now. With that, the engines started up. Jack had mostly lost his fear of flying, but this was the part of the flight where he closed his eyes and thought (earlier in his life he'd whispered) a prayer for the collective safety of the people aboard – in the belief that praying merely for yourself might appear selfish to God. About the time that was finished, the takeoff roll began, rather more quickly than was normal on a 747. Lightly loaded, it felt like an airplane instead of a train pulling out of a station.

'Okay,' Arnie said, as the nose lifted off. The President studiously did not grip the armrests as he usually did. 'This is going to be an easy one. Indianapolis, Oklahoma City, and back home for dinner. The crowds will be friendly, and about as reactionary as you are,' he added with a twinkle. 'So you don't really have anything to worry about.'

Special Agent Price, sitting in the same compartment for the takeoff, hated it when anybody said that. Chief of Staff van Damm – CARPENTER to the Secret Service; Callie Weston was CALLIOPE – was one of the staffers who never quite appreciated the headaches the Service went through. He thought of danger as a political hazard, even after the 747 crash. Remarkable, she thought. A few feet aft, Agent Raman was in an aft-facing seat watching access forward, in case a reporter showed up with a gun instead of a pencil. There were six more agents aboard to keep an eye on everyone, even the uniformed crewmen, and a platoon of them standing by in each of the two destination cities, along with a huge collection of local cops. At Tinker Air Force Base in Oklahoma City, the fuel truck was already under USSS guard, lest someone contaminate the JP to go into the presidential aircraft; it would remain so until well *after* the 747 returned to Andrews. A C-5B Galaxy transport was already in Indianapolis, having ferried the presidential automobiles there. Moving the President around was rather like transporting the Ringling Brothers, Barnum & Bailey Circus, except people generally didn't worry about people trying to assassinate the man on the flying trapeze.

Ryan, Agent Price saw, was going over his speech. That was one of his few normal acts. They were almost always nervous about speeches – generally not so much stage fright as concern for the content spin. The thought made Price smile. Ryan wasn't worried about the content, but *was* worried about blowing the delivery. Well, he'd learn, and his good fortune was that Callie Weston, administrative pain in the ass that she was, wrote one hell of a speech.

'Breakfast?' a steward asked now that the aircraft was leveled off. The President shook his head.

'Not hungry, thanks.'

'Get him ham and eggs, toast, and decaf,' van Damm ordered.

'Never try to give a speech on an empty stomach,' Callie advised. 'Trust me.'

'And not too much real coffee. Caffeine can make you jumpy. When a President gives a speech,' Arnie explained for this morning's lesson, 'he's – Callie, help me out here?'

'Nothing dramatic for these two today. You're the smart neighbor coming over because the guy next door wants your advice on something he's been thinking about. Friendly. Reasonable. Quiet. "Gee, Fred, I really think you might want to do it this way,"' Weston explained with raised eyebrows.

'Kindly family doctor telling a guy to go easy on the greasy food and maybe play an extra round of golf – exercise is supposed to be fun, that sort of thing,' the chief of staff explained on. 'You do it all the time in real life.'

'Just do it this morning in front of four thousand people, right?' Ryan asked.

'And C-SPAN cameras, and it'll be on all the evening network news broadcasts –'

'CNN will be doing it live, too, 'cuz it's your first speech out in the country,' Callie added. No sense lying to the man.

Jesus. Jack looked back down at the text of his speech.

'You're right, Arnie. Better decaf.' He looked up suddenly. 'Any smokers aboard?'

It was the way he asked it that made the Air Force steward turn. 'Want one, sir?'

The answer was somewhat shameful, but – 'Yes.'

She handed him a Virginia Slim and lit it with a warm smile. It wasn't every day one got a chance to provide so personal a service to the Commander-in-Chief. Ryan took a puff and looked up.

'If you tell my wife, Sergeant –'

'Our secret, sir.' She disappeared aft to get breakfast, her day already made.

The fluid was surprisingly horrid in color, deep scarlet with a hint of brown. They'd monitored the process with small samples under an electron microscope. The monkey kidneys exposed to the infected blood were composed of discrete and highly specialized cells, and for whatever reason, Ebola loved those cells as a glutton loves his chocolate mousse. It had been both fascinating and horrifying to watch. The micron-sized virus strands touched the cells, penetrated them – and started to replicate in the warm, rich biosphere. It was like something from a science-fiction movie, but quite real. This virus, like all the others, was only equivocally alive. It could act only with help, and that help had to come from its host, which by providing the means for the virus to activate, also conspired at its own death. The Ebola strands contained only RNA, and for mitosis to take place, both RNA and DNA are required. The kidney cells had both, the virus strands sought them out, and when they were joined, the Ebola started to reproduce. To do that required energy, and that energy was supplied by the kidney cells, which were, of course, completely destroyed in the process. The multiplication process was a microcosm of the disease process in a human community. It started slowly, then accelerated geometrically – the faster it went, the faster it went: $2-4-16-256-65,536$ – until all of the nutrients were eaten up and only virus strands remained, then went dormant and awaited their next opportunity. People applied all manner of false images to disease. It would lie in wait for its chance; it would kill without mercy; it would seek out victims. All of that was anthropomorphic rubbish, Moudi and his colleague knew. It didn't think. It didn't do anything overly malevolent. All Ebola did was to eat and reproduce and go back to its dormant state. But as a computer is only a collection of electrical switches which can only distinguish between the numerals 1 and 0 – but does so more rapidly and efficiently than its human users – so Ebola was supremely well adapted to reproduce so rapidly that the human body's immune system, ordinarily a ruthlessly effective defense mechanism, was simply overwhelmed, as though by an army of carnivorous ants. In that lay Ebola's historic weakness. It was *too* efficient. It killed *too* fast. Its survival mechanism within the human host also tended to kill the host before it could pass the disease along. It was also super-adapted to a specific ecosystem. Ebola didn't survive long in the open, and only then in a jungle environment. For this reason, and since it could not survive in a human host without killing that host in ten days or less, it had also evolved slowly – without taking the next evolutionary step of becoming airborne.

Or so everyone thought. Perhaps 'hoped' would be a better word, Moudi reflected. An Ebola variant that could be spread by aerosol would be catastrophically deadly. It was possible they had exactly that. This was the Mayinga strain, as repeated microscopy had established, and *that* strain was suspected to be capable of aerosol transmission, and that was what they had to prove.

Deep-freezing, using liquid nitrogen as the refrigerant, for example, killed most normal human cells. When they froze, the expansion of the water, which accounted for most of the cellular mass, burst the cell walls, leaving nothing behind but wreckage. Ebola, on the other hand, was too primitive for that to happen. Too much heat could kill it. Ultraviolet light could kill it. Micro-changes in the chemical environment could kill it. But give it a cold, dark place to sleep, and it was content to slumber in peace.

They worked in a glove box. It was a highly controlled and lethally contaminated environment bordered with clear lexan strong enough to stop a pistol bullet. On two sides holes were cut into the sturdy plastic, and riveted at each workstation was a pair of heavy rubber gloves. Moudi withdrew 10cc's of the virus-rich liquid and transferred it to a small container, which he sealed. The sluggishness of the process was less from physical danger than from the awkwardness of the gloves. When the container was sealed, he transferred it from one gloved hand to another, then off to the director, who performed a similar switch, finally moving it into a small airlock. When that door was closed, as indicated by a light which read off a pressure sensor, the small compartment was flooded with disinfectant spray – dilute phenol – and allowed to sit for three minutes, until it was certain that the air and the transfer container were safe to release. Even then no one would touch it with ungloved hands, and despite the safety of the glove box, both physicians also wore full protective gear. The director removed the container, cradling it in both hands for the three-meter walk to the worktable.

For experimental purposes, the aerosol can was of the type used for insect spray, the sort one can place on a floor, activate, and leave to fog a whole room. It had been fully disassembled, cleaned out three times with live steam, and put back together – the plastic parts had been a problem, but that had been figured out a few months earlier. It was a crude device. The production versions would be far more elegant. The only danger here was from the liquid nitrogen, a watery-appearing fluid which, if spilled on the gloves, would freeze them immediately and soon thereafter cause them to fragment like black crystal glass. The director stood aside as Moudi poured the cryogenic liquid around the pressure vessel. Only a few cc's were required for the purpose of the experiment. Next, the Ebola-rich liquid was injected into the stainless-steel inner container, and the top screwed in place. When the cap was sealed, the new container was sprayed with disinfectant, then washed with sterile saline. The smaller transfer container went into a disposal bin for incineration.

'There,' the director said. 'We are ready.'

Inside the spray can, the Ebola was already deep-frozen, but not for long. The nitrogen would boil off relatively rapidly, and the sample would thaw. In that time, the rest of the experiment would be set up. And in that time, the two physicians would remove their protective clothing and have dinner.

The colonel driving the airplane touched down with consummate skill. It was his first time flying this President, and he had something to prove. The rollout was routine, with the reverse-thrusters slowing the jumbo to auto-speed before the nose came around to the left. Out the windows, Ryan could see hundreds – no, he realized, *thousands* – of people. *All there to see me!* he wondered. *Damn.* In their hands, dangling over the low perimeter fence were the red, white, and blue colors of the national flag, and when the aircraft finally stopped, those flags came up at one time, as though in a wave. The mobile stairs came to the door, which was opened by the steward – to call her a stewardess would have been incorrect – who'd given him a cigarette.

'Want another one?' she whispered.

Ryan grinned. 'Maybe later. And thanks, Sarge.'

'Break a leg, Mr President – but not on the stairs, okay?' She got a chuckle as reward.

'All ready for the Boss,' Price heard over her radio circuit from the leader of the advance team. With that, she nodded at President Ryan.

'Showtime, Mr President.'

Ryan took a deep breath and stood in the center of the door, looking out into the bright Midwestern sunlight.

The protocol was that he had to walk down first and alone. Barely had he stood in the opening when a cheer went up, and this from people who scarcely knew a thing about him. His coat buttoned, his hair combed down and sprayed into place despite his objections, Jack Ryan walked down the steps, feeling more like a fool than a President until he got to the bottom. There an Air Force chief master sergeant snapped a salute, which Ryan, so imprinted by his brief months in the Marine Corps, returned smartly – and another cheer went up. He looked around to see Secret Service and other Treasury agents deployed around, almost all of them looking outward. The first person to come close was the governor of the state.

'Welcome to Indiana, Mr President!' He seized Ryan's hand and shook it vigorously. 'We're honored to host your first official visit.'

They'd laid out everything for this one. A company of the

local National Guard was formed up. The band crashed out 'Ruffles and Flourishes,' immediately followed by 'Hail to the Chief,' and Ryan felt himself to be a singular fraud. With the governor to his left and half a step behind, Ryan followed the red – what else? – carpet. The assembled soldiers came to present arms, and their ancient regimental standard dipped, though not the Stars and Stripes, of course, which, an American athlete had once proclaimed, dips to no earthly king or potentate (he'd been an Irish-American unwilling so to honor the King of England at the 1908 Olympiad). Jack moved his right hand over his heart as he passed, a gesture remembered from his youth, and looked at the assembled guardsmen. He was their commander-in-chief now, the President told himself. He could give orders sending them off to the field of battle, and he had to look at their faces. There they were, clean-shaven and young and proud, as he would have been twenty-odd years earlier. They were here for him. And he always had to be there for them. *Yeah*, Jack told himself. *Have to remember that.*

'May I introduce you to some local citizens, sir?' the governor asked, pointing to the fence. Ryan nodded and followed.

'Heads up, pressin' flesh,' Andrea called over her radio microphone. For as many times as they'd seen it happen, the agents on presidential Detail detested this above all things. Price would be with POTUS at all times. Raman and three others hovered on both sides of him, their eyes scanning the crowd from behind dark sunglasses, looking for guns, for the wrong expression, for faces memorized from photographs, for anything out of the ordinary.

There were so many of them, Jack thought. None of them had voted for him, and until very recently few had even known his name. Yet they were here. Some, perhaps, state-government employees getting half a day off, but not the ones holding kids, not all of them, and the looks in their eyes stunned the President, who'd never in his life experienced anything even close to this. Hands extended frantically, and he shook all that he could, moving to his left down the line, trying to hear individual voices through the cacophony of screams.

'Welcome to Indiana!' – 'How are ya!' – 'MISTER PRESI-

DENT!' – 'We trust you!' – 'Good job so far!' – 'We're with ya!'

Ryan tried to answer back, achieving little more than a repeated thank-you, his mouth mainly open in surprise at the overpowering warmth of the moment, and all directed at him. It was enough to make him overlook the pain in his hand, but finally he had to step away from the fence and wave, to yet another roar of love for the new President.

Damn. If they only knew what a fraud he was, Jack thought, what would they do then? *What the hell am I doing here?* his mind demanded, as he headed for the open door of the presidential limousine.

There were ten of them, down in the basement of the building. All were men. Only one was a political prisoner, and his crime was apostasy. The rest were singularly undesirable people, four murderers, a rapist, two child molesters, and two thieves who were repeat offenders and, under the Koranic law of their nation, subject to removal of their right hands. They were in a single, climate-controlled room, each of them secured to the foot of the bed by leg cuffs. All were condemned to death, except the thieves who were only supposed to be mutilated, and knew it, and wondered why they were here with the rest. Why the others were still alive was a mystery to them, which none questioned but from which none took satisfaction, either. Their diet over the past few weeks had been particularly poor, enough to reduce their physical energy and their level of alertness. One of their number stuck a finger in his mouth to feel his sore and bleeding gums. The finger came out when the door opened.

It was someone in a blue plastic suit, which none of them had seen before. The person – a man, though they could barely make out the face through the plastic mask – set a cylindrical container down on the concrete floor, took off the blue plastic cap, and pressed down on a button. Then he hastily withdrew. Scarcely had the door closed when there came a hiss from the container, and a steamlike fog sprayed up into the room.

One of their number screamed, thinking that it was a poison gas, seizing the thin bedsheet and clasping it over his face. The one closest to the spray was slower-witted and merely watched, and when the cloud came over him, he looked around at it while the others waited for him to die. When he didn't, they were more curious than fearful. After a few minutes, the incident passed into their limited history. The lights were turned off, and they went to sleep.

'Three days to find out,' the director said, turning off the TV that fed from the cell. 'The spray system appears to work well, proper dispersion. They had a problem with the delay device. On the production version, it has to be good for – what? Five minutes, I think.'

Three days, Moudi thought. Seventy-two hours to see what evil they had wrought.

For all the money and hype, for all the exquisite planning, Ryan was sitting on a simple folding metal chair, the sort to make a person's rump sore. In front of him was a wooden rail covered with red, white, and blue bunting. Under the bunting was sheet steel supposed to stop a bullet. The podium was similarly armored – steel *and* Kevlar in this case; Kevlar is both stronger and lighter – and would protect nearly all of his body below the shoulders. The university field house – a very large gymnasium, though not the one used for the school's basketball team, already eliminated in the NCAA tournament – was packed 'to the rafters,' reporters would probably say, that being the stock phrase for a building with all its seats occupied. Most of the audience were probably students, but it was hard to tell. Ryan was the target of numerous bright lights, and the flood of brilliance denied him the ability to see most of the crowd. They'd arrived via the back door, walking through a smelly locker room because the President took the fast way in and out. The motorcade had come down a highway for most of the way, but in the regular city streets that had occupied maybe a quarter of the distance, there had been people on the sidewalks, waving to him while their governor extolled the virtues of the city and the Hoosier State. Jack had thought to ask the origin of 'Hoosier,' but decided not to.

The governor was talking again now, succeeding three others. A student, followed by the university president, followed by the mayor of the local town. The President actually tried listening to the speeches, but while on one hand they

462

all said mainly the same thing, on the other little of it was true. It was as though they were speaking of someone else, a theoretical President with generic virtues to deal with the misstated duties. Maybe it was just that the local speech-writers dealt with local issues only, Jack decided. So much the better for them.

'. . . my great honor to introduce the President of the United States.' The governor turned and gestured. Ryan rose, approached the podium, shook the governor's hand. As he set his speech folder on the top of the podium, he nodded embarrassed appreciation at the crowd he could barely see. In the first few rows, right on the hardwood of the basketball court, were local big shots. In other times and circumstances, they'd be major contributors. In this case, Ryan didn't know. Maybe from both parties, even. Then he remembered that major contributors donated money to *both* parties anyway, to hedge their bets by guaranteeing themselves access to power no matter who was there. They were prob-ably already trying to figure how to donate money to *his* campaign.

'Thank you, Governor, for that introduction.' Ryan turned to gesture to the people on the dais with him, naming them from the list on the first page of his speech folder, good friends whom he'd never see again after this first time, whose faces were illuminated by the simple fact that he spoke their names in the correct order.

'Ladies and gentlemen, I've never been to Indiana before. This is my first visit to the Hoosier State, but after experienc-ing your welcome, I hope it won't be the last –'

It was as though someone had held up the APPLAUSE sign on a TV show. He'd just spoken the truth, followed by some-thing that might or might not have been a lie, and while they had to know it, they didn't care a whit. And then Jack Ryan learned something important for the first time.

God, it's like a narcotic, Jack thought, understanding just then why people entered politics. No man could stand here like this, hearing the noise, seeing the faces, and not love the moment. It came through the stage fright, through the overwhelming sense of not belonging. Here he was, before four thousand people, fellow citizens each of them, equal to him before the law, but in their minds he was something else entirely. He *was* the United States of America. He was their President, but more than that, he was the embodiment of their hopes, their desires, the image of their own nation, and because of that they were willing to love someone they didn't know, to cheer his every word, to hope that for a brief moment they could believe that he'd looked directly into each individual pair of eyes so that the moment would be forever special, never to be forgotten. It was power such as he had never known to exist. This crowd was his to command. *This* was why men devoted their lives to seeking the presidency, to bathe in this moment like a warm ocean wave, a moment of utter perfection.

But why did they think he was so different? What made him special in their minds? Ryan wondered. It was only chance in his case, and in every other instance, it was they who'd done the choosing, they who had elevated the man to the podium, they who by their act had changed the ordinary into something else – and perhaps not even that. It was only perception. Ryan was the same man he'd been a month or a year before. He'd acquired little in the way of new knowledge and less in the way of wisdom. He was the same person with a different job, and while the trappings of the new post were all around him, the person within the protective ring of bodyguards, the person surrounded by a flood of love which he'd never sought, was merely the product of parents, a childhood, an education, and experiences, just as they all were. They thought him different and special and perhaps even great, but that was perception, not reality. The reality of the moment was sweaty hands on the armored podium, a speech written by someone else, and a man who knew that he was out of place, however pleasant the moment might be.

So, what do I do now? the President of the United States asked himself, his mind racing as the current wave of applause diminished. He'd never be what they thought he was. He was a good man, he thought, but not a great one, and the presidency was a job, a post, a government office that came with duties defined by James Madison, and, as with all things in life, a place of transition from one reality to another. The past was something you couldn't change. The future was something you tried to see. The present was where you were, and that's where you had to do your best –

and if you were lucky, maybe you'd be worthy of the moment. It wasn't enough to feel the love. He had to earn it, to make the looks on the assembled faces something other than a lie, for in giving power they also gave responsibility, and in giving love they demanded devotion in return. Chastened, Jack looked at the glass panel that reflected the text of his speech, took a deep breath, and started talking as he'd done as a history instructor in Annapolis.

'I come here today to speak to you about America . . .'

Below the President were five Secret Service agents standing in line, their sunglasses shielding their eyes so that those in the audience could not always tell where they were looking, and also because people without eyes are intimidating at a visceral level. Their hands were clasped in front, and radio earpieces kept them in contact with one another as they scanned the crowd. In the rear of the field house were others, this group scanning with binoculars, because they knew that the love in the building was not uniform, or even that there were some who sought to kill the things they loved. For that reason, the advance team had erected portable metal-detector arches at all the entrances. For that reason Belgian Malinois dogs had sniffed the building for explosives. For that reason they watched everything in the same way an infantryman in a combat zone was careful to examine every shadow.

'. . . and the strength of America lies not in Washington, but in Indiana, and New Mexico, and in every place Americans live and work, wherever it might be. We in Washington are not America. You are,' the President's voice boomed through the PA system – not a good system, the agents thought, but this event had been laid on a little fast. 'And we work for you.' The audience cheered again anyway.

The TV cameras all fed into vans outside the building, and those had uplink dishes to relay the sound and pictures to satellites. The reporters were mainly in the back today, taking notes despite the fact that they had the full text, along with a written promise that the President really would deliver this one. 'The President's speech today,' all would say this evening, but it wasn't really the President's speech at all. They knew who'd written it. Callie Weston had already talked to several of their number about it. They read the crowd, an easier task for them because they didn't have the klieg lights in their faces.

'. . . is not an opportunity, but a responsibility which we all share, because if America belongs to us all, so then the duty for running our country starts here, not in Washington.' More applause.

'Good speech,' Tom Donner observed to his commentator/analyst, John Plumber.

'Pretty good delivery, too. I talked to the superintendent of the Naval Academy. They say he was an excellent teacher once,' Plumber replied.

'Good audience for him, mainly kids. And he's not talking major policy issues.'

'Getting his feet wet,' John agreed. 'You have a team working the other segment for tonight, right?'

Donner checked his watch and nodded. 'Should be there now.'

'So, Dr Ryan, how do you like being First Lady?' Krystin Matthews asked, with a warm smile.

'I'm still figuring it out.' They were talking in Cathy's cubbyhole office overlooking central Baltimore. It had barely enough room for a desk and three chairs (a good one for the doctor, one for the patient, and the other for the spouse or mother of the patient), and with all the cameras and lights in the room, she felt trapped. 'You know, I miss cooking for my family.'

'You're a surgeon – and your husband expects you to cook, too?' the NBC co-anchor asked, in surprise bordering on outrage.

'I've always loved cooking. It's a good way for me to relax when I get home.' *Instead of watching TV*, Professor Caroline Ryan didn't add. She was wearing a new starched lab coat. She'd had to take fifteen minutes with her hair and makeup, and she had patients waiting. 'Besides, I'm pretty good at it.'

Ah, well, that was different. A cloying smile: 'What's the President's favorite meal?'

A smile returned. 'That's easy. Steak, baked potato, fresh corn on the cob, and my spinach salad – and I know, the physician in me tells him that it's a little heavy on the cholesterol. Jack's pretty good with a grill. In fact, he's a pretty handy man to have around the house. He doesn't even mind cutting the grass.'

'Let me take you back to the night your son was born, that awful night when the terrorists – '

'I haven't forgotten,' Cathy said in a quieter voice.

'Your husband has killed people. You're a doctor. How does that make you feel?'

'Jack and Robby – he's Admiral Jackson now – Robby and Sissy are our closest friends,' Cathy explained. 'Anyway, they did what they had to do, or we would not have survived that night. I don't like violence. I'm a surgeon. Last week I had a trauma case, a man lost his eye as a result of a fistfight in a bar a few blocks from here. But what Jack did is different from what *they* did. My husband fought to protect me and Sally, and Little Jack, who wasn't even born yet.'

'You like being a doctor?'

'I love my work. I wouldn't leave it for anything.'

'But usually a First Lady – '

'I know what you want to say. I'm not a political wife. I practice medicine. I'm a research scientist, and I work in the best eye institute in the world. I have patients waiting for me now. They need me – and you know, I need them, too. My job is who I am. I'm also a wife and a mother, and I like nearly everything about my life.'

'Except this?' Krystin asked, with a smile.

Cathy's blue eyes twinkled. 'I really don't have to answer that, do I?' And Matthews knew she had the tagline for the interview.

'What sort of man is your husband?'

'Well, I can't be totally objective, can I? I love him. He's risked his life for me and my children. Whenever I've needed him, he was there. And I do the same for him. That's what love and marriage mean. Jack is smart. He's honest. I guess he's something of a worrier. Sometimes he'll wake up in the middle of the night – at home, I mean – and spend half an hour looking out the windows at the water. I don't think he knows that I know that.'

'Does he still do that?'

'Not lately. He's pretty tired when he gets to bed. These are the worst hours he's ever worked.'

'His other government posts, at CIA, for example, there are reports that he –'

Cathy stopped that one with a raised hand. 'I do not have a security clearance. I don't know, and probably I don't want to know. It's the same with me. I am not allowed to discuss confidential patient information with Jack, or anyone else outside the faculty here.'

'We'd like to see you with patients and –' FLOTUS shook her head, stopping the question dead.

'No, this is a hospital, not a TV studio. It's not so much my privacy as that of my patients. To them, I am not the First Lady. To them, I am Dr Ryan. I'm not a celebrity. I'm a physician and a surgeon. To my students, I'm a professor and teacher.'

'And reportedly one of the best in the world at what you do,' Matthews added, just to see the reaction.

A smile resulted. 'Yes, I've won the Lasker prize, and the respect of my colleagues is a gift that's worth more than money – but you know, that isn't it, either. Sometimes – not very often – but sometimes after a major procedure, I'm the one who takes the bandages off in a darkened room, and we turn the lights up slowly, and I see it. I can see it on the patient's face. I fixed the eyes, and they work again, and the look you see on his or her face – well, nobody's in medicine for the money, at least not here at Hopkins. We're here to make sick people well, and for me to preserve and restore sight, and the look you see when that job is done is like having God tap you on the shoulder and say, "Nice job." That's why I'll never, *never* leave medicine,' Cathy Ryan said, almost lyrically, knowing that they'd use this on TV tonight, and hoping that maybe some bright young high-school kid would see her face and hear the words and decide to think about medicine. If she had to put up with this waste of her time, perhaps she could use it to serve her art.

It was a pretty good sequence, Krystin Matthews thought, but with only two minutes and thirty seconds of air time, they would not be able to use it. Better the part about how she hated being First Lady. Everybody was used to hearing doctors talk.

24

ON THE FLY

The return to the airplane was quick and efficient. The governor went his way. The people who'd lined the sidewalks were mainly back to their jobs, and those who turned and looked were shoppers who probably wondered what the sirens were all about – or if they knew, were annoyed with the noise. Ryan was able to lean back in the plush leather seats, deflated by the fatigue that comes after a stressful moment.

'So, how'd I do?' he asked, looking out the window as Indiana passed by at seventy miles per hour. He smiled inwardly at the thought of driving this fast in the outskirts of a city without getting a ticket.

'Very well, actually,' Callie Weston said first. 'You talked like a teacher.'

'I *was* a teacher once,' the President said. *And with luck, I may be again someday.*

'That's okay for a speech like this, but for others you'll need a little fire,' Arnie observed.

'One thing at a time,' Callie advised the chief of staff. 'You crawl before you walk.'

'Same speech in Oklahoma, right?' POTUS asked.

'A few changes, but no big deal. Just remember you're not in Indiana anymore. Sooner State, not Hoosier State. Same line about tornadoes, but football instead of basketball.'

'They also lost both senators, but they still have a congressman left, and he'll be on the dais with you,' van Damm advised.

'How'd he make it?' Jack asked idly.

'Probably getting laid that night,' was the curt answer. 'You'll announce a new contract for Tinker Air Force Base. It means about five hundred new jobs, consolidating a few operations at the new location. That'll make the local papers happy.'

*   *   *

Ben Goodley didn't know if he was the new National Security Advisor or not. If so, he was rather young for the job, but at least the President he served was well grounded in foreign affairs. That made him more a high-class secretary than an adviser. It was a function he didn't mind. He'd learned much in his brief time at Langley, and had advanced rapidly, becoming one of the youngest men ever to win the coveted NIO card because he knew how to organize information, and because he had the political savvy to grade the important stuff. He especially liked working directly for President Ryan. Goodley knew that he could play it straight with the Boss, and that Jack – he still thought of him by that name, though he could no longer use it – would always let him know what he was thinking. It would be another learning experience for Dr Goodley, and a priceless one for someone whose new life dream was someday becoming DCI on merit and not through politics.

On the wall opposite his desk was the sort of clock that shows the sun position for the entire world. He'd ordered it the very day he'd arrived – and to his surprise it had appeared literally overnight, instead of perking its way through five levels of procurement bureaucracy. He'd heard stories that the White House was one portion of the government that actually did work, and had not believed them – the Harvard graduate had been in government service about four years now, and figured he knew what worked and what didn't. The surprise was welcome, and the clock, he'd found from his work in the CIA Operations Center, was an instant reference, better than the array of regular clocks that some places had. Your eye instantly saw where noon was and could automatically grasp what time it was anywhere in the world. More to the point, you instantly knew if something was happening at an unusual hour, and that told you as much as the Signals Intelligence – SigInt – bulletin. Such as the one that had just come in over his personal fax machine that was connected to his STU-4 secure phone.

The National Security Agency was in the habit of posting periodic summaries of activity across the world. Its own watch center was staffed by senior military people, and while their outlook was more technical and less political than his own, they were not fools. Ben had gotten to know many of them by name in addition to reputation, and had also learned their individual strengths. The USAF colonel who had command of the NSA Watch Center on weekday afternoons didn't bother people with trivia. That was left to lower-level people and lower-level signals. When the colonel put his name on something, it was usually worth reading. And so it was just after noon, Washington time.

Goodley saw that the FLASH concerned Iraq. That was another thing about the colonel. He didn't go using CRITIC headers for the fun of it, as some did. Ben looked up to check the wall clock. After sundown, local time, a time of relaxation for some, and action for others. The action would be the sort to last all night, the better to get things accomplished without interference, so that the next day would be genuinely new, and genuinely different.

'Oh, boy,' Goodley breathed. He read down the page again, then turned his swivel chair and picked up the phone, touching the #3 speed-dial button.

'Director's office,' a fiftyish female voice answered.

'Goodley for Foley.'

'Please hold, Dr Goodley.' Then: 'Hi, Ben.'

'Hello, Director.' He felt it improper to first-name the DCI. He'd probably go back to work at Langley within the year, and not as a seventh-floor-rank official. 'You have what I have?' The page was still warm in his hand from the printer.

'Iraq?'

'Right.'

'You must have read it twice, Ben. I just told Bert Vasco to get his ass up here.' CIA's own Iraq desk was weak, both thought, while this State guy was very good indeed.

'Looks pretty hot to me.'

'Agreed,' Ed Foley replied, with an unseen nod. 'Jesus, but they're moving fast over there. Give me an hour, maybe ninety minutes.'

'I think the President needs to know,' Goodley said, with a voice that concealed the urgency he felt. Or so he thought.

'He needs to know more than we can tell him now. Ben?' the DCI added.

'Yes, Director?'

'Jack won't kill you for patience, and we can't do any more than watch it develop anyway. Remember, we can't overload him with information. He doesn't have the time to see it all anymore. What he sees has to be concise. That's your job,' Ed Foley explained. 'It'll take you a few weeks to figure it out. I'll help,' the DCI went on, reminding Goodley how junior he was.

'Okay. I'll be waiting.' The line clicked off.

Goodley had about a minute during which he reread the NSA bulletin, and then the phone rang again.

'Dr Goodley.'

'Doctor, this is the President's office,' one of the senior secretaries said. 'I have a Mr Golovko on the President's private line. Can you take the call?'

'Yes,' he replied, thinking, *Oh, shit.*

'Go ahead, please,' she said, clicking off the line.

'This is Ben Goodley.'

'This is Golovko. Who are you?'

'I am acting National Security Advisor to the President.' *And I know who you are.*

'Goodley?' Ben could hear the voice searching his memory. 'Ah, yes, you are national intelligence officer who just learned to shave. My congratulations on your promotion.'

The gamesmanship was impressive, though Goodley figured that there was a file on the Russian's desk with everything down to his shoe size. Even Golovko's memory couldn't be that good, and Goodley had been in the White House long enough that the word would have gotten out, and the RVS/KGB would have done its homework.

'Well, somebody has to answer the phones, Minister.' Gamesmanship could go two ways. Golovko wasn't really a minister, though he acted as such, and that was technically a secret. It was a weak reply, but it was something. 'What can I do for you?'

'You know the arrangement I have with Ivan Emmetovich?'

'Yes, sir, I do.'

'Very well, tell him that a new country is about to be born. It will be called the United Islamic Republic. It will include, for the moment, Iran and Iraq. I rather suspect that it will wish to grow further.'

'How reliable is that information, sir?' Better to be polite. It would make the Russian feel bigger.

'Young man, I would not make a report to your President unless I felt it to be reliable, but,' he added generously, 'I understand you must ask the question. The point of origin for the report does not concern you. The reliability of the source is sufficient for me to pass the information along with my own confidence. There will be more to follow. Do you have similar indications?'

The question froze Goodley's eyeballs in place, staring down at a blank spot on his desk. He had no guidance on this. Yes, he'd learned that President Ryan had discussed cooperation with Golovko, that he'd also discussed the matter with Ed Foley, and that both had decided to go forward with it. But nobody had told him the parameters for giving information back to Moscow, and he didn't have time to call Langley for instructions, else he would appear weak to the Russians, and the Russians didn't want America to appear weak at the moment, and he was the man on the spot, and he had to make a decision. That entire thought process required about a third of a second.

'Yes, Minister, we do. Your timing is excellent. Director Foley and I were just discussing the development.'

'Ah, yes, Dr Goodley, I see that your signals people are as efficient as ever. What a pity that your human sources do not match their performance.'

Ben didn't dare to respond at all to the observation, though its accuracy caused his stomach to contract. Goodley had more respect for Jack Ryan than he did for any man, and now he remembered the admiration Jack had often expressed for the man on the other end of the phone. Welcome to the bigs, kid. Don't hang any curveballs. He ought to have said that Foley had called *him*.

'Minister, I will be speaking to President Ryan within the hour, and I will pass your information along. Thank you for your timely call, sir.'

'Good day, Dr Goodley.'

United Islamic Republic, Ben read on his desk pad. There had once been a United Arab Republic, an unlikely alliance between Syria and Egypt doomed to failure in two respects. The separated countries had been fundamentally incompatible, and the alliance had been made only to destroy Israel, which had objected to the goal, and done so effectively. More to the point, a United *Islamic* Republic was a religious statement as much as a political one, because Iran was not an Arab nation – as Iraq was – but rather an Aryan one with different ethnic and linguistic roots. Islam was the world's only major religion to condemn in its scripture all forms of racism and proclaim the equality of all men before God, regardless of color – a fact often overlooked by the West. So, Islam was overtly designed to be a unifying force, and this new notional country would play on that fact with its very name. That said a lot, enough that Golovko didn't even need to explain it, and it also said that Golovko felt that he and Ryan were on the same wavelength. Goodley checked the wall clock again. It was nighttime in Moscow, too. Golovko was working late – well, not all *that* late for a senior official. Ben lifted the phone and hit #3 again. It took him less than a minute to summarize the call from Moscow.

'We can believe anything he says – on this issue, anyway. Sergey Nikolay'ch is a pro from way back. I imagine he twisted your tail just a little, right?' the DCI asked.

'Ruffled the fur some,' Goodley admitted.

'It's a carryover from old days. They do like their status games. Don't let it bother you, and don't shoot back. Better just to ignore it,' Foley explained. 'Okay, what's he worried about?'

'A lot of republics with "-stan" at the end,' Goodley blurted out, without thinking.

'Concur.' This came from another voice.

'Vasco?'

'Yeah, just walked in.' And then Goodley had to repeat what he'd told Ed Foley. Probably Mary Pat was there, too. Individually, both were good at what they did. In the same room, thinking together, they were a deadly weapon. It was something you had to see to understand, Ben knew.

'This looks to me like a big deal,' Goodley observed.

'Looks that way to me, too,' Vasco said over the speakerphone. 'Let us kick a few things around. Be back to you in fifteen or twenty.'

'Would you believe Avi ben Jakob is checking in with us?' Ed reported, after a background noise on the line. 'They must be having a really tough day.'

For the moment it was just irony that the Russians were

both the first to check in with America (and that they were doing so at all), and that they were the only ones calling straight into the White House, beating the Israelis on both scores. But the amusement wouldn't last, and all the players knew that. Israel was probably having the worst day of all. Russia was merely having a very bad one. And America was getting to share the experience.

It would have been uncivilized to deny them a chance at prayer. Cruel though they were, and criminals though they had been, they had to have their chance at prayer, albeit a brief one. Each was in the presence of a learned mullah, who, with firm but not unkind voice, told them of their fates, and cited scripture, and spoke to them of their chance to reconcile with Allah before meeting Him face to face. Every one did – whether they believed in what they did was another issue, and one left for Allah to judge, but the mullahs had done their duty – and then every one was led out into the prison yard.

It was a sort of assembly-line process, carefully timed so that the three clergymen gave each condemned criminal exactly three times the interval required to take each out in his turn, tie him to the post, shoot him, remove the body, and restart the process. It worked out to five minutes per execution and fifteen minutes for prayer.

The commanding general of the 41st Armored Division was typical, except that his religion was something more than vestigial. His hands were bound in his cell before his imam – the general preferred the Arabic term to the Farsi one – and he was led out by soldiers who a week before would have saluted and trembled at his passage. He'd reconciled himself to his fate, and he would not give the Persian bastards he'd fought in the border swamps the least bit of satisfaction, though inwardly he cursed to God the cowardly superiors who had skipped the country and left him behind. Perhaps he might have killed the President himself and taken over, he thought as his handcuffs were looped to the post. The general took a moment to look back at the wall to gauge how good was the marksmanship of the firing squad. He found strange humor in the fact that it might take him a few extra seconds to die, and he snorted in disgust.

Russian-trained and competent, he'd tried to be an honest soldier – nonpolitical, following his orders faithfully and without question, whatever they might be – and therefore had never been fully trusted by his country's political leadership, and this was his reward for it. A captain came up with a blindfold.

'A cigarette, if you please. You may keep *that* for when you sleep later tonight.'

The captain nodded without expression, his emotions already numbed by the ten killings done in the past hour. Shaking a cigarette from his pack, he put it into the man's lips and lit it with a match. That done, he said what he felt he must:

'*Salaam alaykum.*' Peace be unto you.

'I will have more than you, young man. Do your duty. Make sure your pistol is loaded, will you?' The general closed his eyes for a long, pleasurable puff. His doctor had told him only a few days before that it was bad for his health. Wasn't that a joke? He looked back on his career, marveling that he was still alive after what the Americans had done to his division in 1991. Well, he'd avoided death more than once, and that was a race a man could lengthen, but never win, not really. And so it was written. He managed another long puff. An American Winston. He recognized the taste. How did a mere captain ever get a pack of those? The soldiers brought their rifles up to 'aim.' There was no expression on their faces. Well, killing did that to men, he reflected. What was supposed to be cruel and horrible just became a job that –

The captain came over to the body that was slumped forward, suspended by the nylon rope that looped around the handcuffs. Again, he thought, drawing his 9mm Browning and aiming from a meter away. A final *crack* put an end to the groans. Then two soldiers cut the rope and dragged the body off. Another soldier replaced the rope on the post. A fourth used a gardener's rake to move the dirt around, not so much to conceal the blood as to mix dirt with it, because blood was slippery to walk on. The next one would be a politician, not a soldier. The soldiers, at least, died with dignity for the most part, as the last one had. Not the civilians. They whimpered and wept and cried out to Allah. And they always wanted the blindfold. It was something of a learning experience for the captain, who'd never done anything like this before.

It had taken a few days to get things organized, but they were all now in separate houses in separate parts of town – and once that had been accomplished, the generals and their entourages had started worrying about it. Separately quartered, they'd all thought, they could be picked up one by one and jailed preparatory to a return flight to Baghdad, but it wouldn't really have mattered very much. None of the families had more than two bodyguards, and what could they do, really, except to keep beggars away when they went outside? They met frequently – every general had a car assigned – mainly with the purpose of making further travel arrangements. They also bickered over whether they should continue to travel together to a new collective home or begin to go their separate ways. Some argued that it would be both more secure and more cost-effective to buy a large piece of land and build on it, for example. Others were making it clear that now that they were out of Iraq once and for all (two of them had illusions about going back in triumph to reclaim the government, but that was fantasy, as all but those two knew), they would be just as happy not to see some of their number ever again. The petty rivalries among them had long concealed genuine antipathy, which their new circumstances didn't so much exacerbate as liberate. The least of them had personal fortunes of over $40 million – one had nearly $300 million salted away in various Swiss banks – more than enough to live a comfortable life in any country in the world. Most chose Switzerland, always a haven to those with money and a desire to live quietly, though a few looked farther to the east. The Sultan of Brunei wanted some people to reorganize his army, and three of the Iraqi generals thought to apply for the job. The local Sudanese government had also begun informal discussions about using a few as advisers for ongoing military operations against animist minorities in the southern part of that country – the Iraqis had long experience dealing with Kurds.

But the generals had more to worry about than themselves alone. All had brought their families out. Many had brought mistresses, who now lived, to everyone's discomfort, in the homes of their patrons. These were as ignored now as they had been in Baghdad. That would change.

Sudan is mostly a desert country, known for its blistering dry heat. Once a British protectorate, its capital has a hospital catering to foreigners, with a largely English staff. Not the world's best facility, it was better than most in Saharan Africa, staffed mostly with young and somewhat idealistic physicians who'd arrived with romantic ideas about both Africa and their careers (the same thing had been going on for over a hundred years). They learned better, but they did their best and that, for the most part, was pretty good.

The two patients arrived scarcely an hour apart. The young girl came in first, accompanied by her worried mother. She was four years old, Dr Ian MacGregor learned, and had been a healthy child, except for a mild case of asthma, which, the mother correctly said, ought not to have been a problem in Khartoum, with its dry air. Where were they from? Iraq? The doctor neither knew nor cared about politics. He was twenty-eight, newly certified for internal medicine, a small man with prematurely receding sandy hair. What mattered was that he'd seen no bulletin concerning that country and a major infectious disease. He and his staff had been alerted about the Ebola blip in Zaire, but it had been only a blip.

The patient's temperature was 38.0, hardly an alarming fever for a child, all the more so in a country where the noon temperature was always at least that high. Blood pressure, heart rate, and respiration were unremarkable. She appeared listless. How long in Khartoum, did you say? Only a few days? Well, it could be merely jet lag. Some people were more sensitive to it than others, MacGregor explained. New surroundings, and so forth, could make a child out of sorts. Maybe a cold or the flu, nothing serious. Sudan has a hot climate, but really a fairly healthy one, you see, not like other parts of Africa. He slipped his hands into rubber gloves, not for any particular need but because his medical training at the University of Edinburgh had drilled it into him that you did it the same way every time, because the one time you forgot, you might end up like Dr Sinclair – oh, didn't you hear how he caught AIDS from a patient? One such story was generally enough. The patient was not in great distress. Eyes a little puffy. Throat slightly inflamed, but nothing serious. Probably a good night's sleep or two. Nothing to be prescribed. Aspirin for the fever and aches, and if the problem persists, please call me. She's a lovely child. I'm sure she'll be fine. Mother took child away. The doctor decided it was time for a cup of tea. Along the way to the doctor's lounge, he stripped off the latex gloves which had saved his life, and dropped them in the disposal bin.

The other came in thirty minutes later, male, thirty-three, looking rather like a thug, surly and suspicious toward the African staff, but solicitous to the Europeans. Obviously a man who knew Africa, MacGregor thought. Probably an Arab businessman. Do you travel a great deal? Recently? Oh, well, that could be it. You want to be careful drinking the local water, that could explain the stomach discomfort. And he, too, went home with a bottle of aspirin, plus an over-the-counter medication for his GI problems, and presently Mac-Gregor went off duty after one more routine day.

'Mr President? Ben Goodley coming through on the STU,' a sergeant told him. Then she showed him how the phones worked up front.

'Yeah, Ben?' Jack said.

'We have reports of a lot of Iraqi big shots getting put up against the wall. I'm faxing the report down to you. The Russians and the Israelis both confirm.' And on cue, another Air Force NCO appeared and handed Ryan three sheets of paper. The first one merely said TOP SECRET – PRESIDENT'S EYES ONLY, even though three or four communications types had seen it, and that was just in the airplane, now beginning its descent into Tinker.

'Got it now, let me read it.' He took his time, first scanning the report, then going back to the beginning for a slower read. 'Okay, who's going to be left?'

'Vasco says nobody worth mentioning. This is the entire Ba'ath Party leadership and all the remaining senior military commanders. That leaves nobody with status behind. Okay, the scary part comes from PALM BOWL, and –'

'Who's this Major Sabah?'

'I called on that myself, sir,' Goodley replied. 'He's a Kuwaiti spook. Our people say he's pretty swift. Vasco oncurs in his assessment. It's going down the track we were afraid of, and it's going real fast.'

'Saudi response?' Ryan was jolted by a minor bump as the VC-25A came through some clouds. It looked to be raining outside.

'None yet. They're still talking things over.'

'Okay, thanks for the heads-up, Ben. Keep me posted.'

'Will do, sir.'

Ryan put the phone back in its cradle and frowned.

'Trouble?' Arnie asked.

'Iraq, it's going fast. They're executing people at a brisk clip at the moment.' The President handed the pages over to his chief of staff.

There was always a huge sense of unreality to it. The NSA report, as amended and augmented by CIA and others, gave a list of men. Had he been in his office, Ryan would also have looked at photos of men he'd never met, and now never would, because while he was descending into Oklahoma to give a nonpolitical political speech, the lives of the men on that list were ending – more likely already had. It was rather like listening to a ballgame on the radio, except in this game real people were being shot. Reality was coming to an end for human beings seven thousand miles away, and Ryan was hearing about it from radio intercepts made even farther away and relayed to him, and it was real, but at the same time not real. There was just something about distance which did that – and his surroundings. *A hundred or so senior Iraqi officials are being shot – want a sandwich before you get off the airplane?* The dualism might have been amusing except for the foreign-policy implications. No, that wasn't true, either. There wasn't anything funny about it at all.

'What are you thinking?' van Damm asked.

'I ought to be back at the office,' Ryan replied. 'This is important, and I need to keep track of it.'

'Wrong!' Arnie said at once with a shake of the head and a pointing finger. 'You are not the National Security Advisor anymore. You have people to do that for you. You're the President, and you have a lot of things to do, and they're all important. The President never gets tied down on one issue and he never gets trapped in the Oval Office. The people out there don't want to see that. It means you're not in control.

It means events are controlling you. Ask Jimmy Carter about how great his second term was. Hell, this isn't all *that* important.'

'It could be,' Jack protested, as the aircraft touched down.

'What's important right now is your speech for the Sooner State.' He paused before going on. 'It isn't just charity that begins at home. It's political power, too. It starts right out there.' He pointed out the windows, as Oklahoma slowed to a halt outside.

Ryan looked, but what he saw was the *United Islamic Republic*.

It had once been hard to enter the Soviet Union. There had been a vast organization called the Chief Border Guards Directorate of the Committee for State Security which had patrolled the fences – in some cases minefields and genuine fortifications, as well – with the dual purpose of keeping people both in and out, but these had long since fallen into disrepair, and the main purpose of the border checkpoints today was for the new crop of regional border guards to accept the bribes that came from smugglers who now used large trucks to bring their wares into the nation that had once been ruled with an iron hand in Moscow, but was now a collection of semi-independent republics that were mostly on their own in economic, and because of that, political terms as well. It hadn't been planned that way. When he'd established the country's central-planned economy, Stalin had made a deliberate effort to spread out production sites, so that each segment of the vast empire would depend for vital commodities upon every other, but he'd overlooked the discordant fact that if the entire economy went to pot, then needing something you couldn't get from one source meant that you had to get it from another, and with the dissolution of the Soviet Union, smuggling, which had been well controlled under Communist rule, had become a genuine industry of its own. And with wares also came ideas, hard enough to stop, and impossible to tax.

The only thing lacking was a welcoming committee, but that wouldn't have done. The corruption of the border guards went both ways. They might well have told their superiors about things while sharing the requisite percentage of the loot from their informal tariff collection, and so the representative merely sat in the right seat of the truck while the driver handled business – out the back of the truck in this case, an offer to the guards of a selection of his cargo. They weren't the least bit greedy about it, instead taking little more than they could easily conceal in the back of their personal automobiles. (The only concession to the illegality of the entire business was that it took place at night.) With that, the proper stamps were affixed to the proper documents, and the truck pulled off, heading down the cross-border highway, which was probably the only decently surfaced road in the area. The remaining drive took a little over an hour, and then, entering the large town which had once serviced the caravan trade, the truck stopped briefly and the representative got out and walked to a private automobile to continue his journey, carrying only a small bag with a change of clothes or two.

The president of this semiautonomous republic claimed to be a Muslim, but he was mainly an opportunist, a former senior party official who as a matter of course had denied God regularly to ensure his political advancement and then, with the changing of the political wind, embraced Islam with public enthusiasm and private disinterest. His faith, if one could call it that, was entirely about his secular well-being. There were several passages in the Koran concerning such people, none of them flattering. He lived a comfortable life in a comfortable personal palace which had once quartered the party boss of this former Soviet republic. In that official residence, he drank liquor, fornicated, and ruled his republic with a hand that was by turns too firm and too gentle. Too firmly he controlled the regional economy (with his Communist training, he was hopelessly inept) and too gently he allowed Islam to flourish, so, he thought, to give his people the illusion of personal freedom (and in that he clearly misunderstood the nature of the Islamic Faith he professed to have, for Islamic law was written to apply to the secular as well as the spiritual). Like all presidents before him, he thought himself beloved of his people. It was, the representative knew, a common illusion of fools. In due course, the representative arrived at the modest private home of a friend of the local religious leader. This was a man of simple faith and quiet honor, beloved by all who knew him and disliked by no one, for his was a kindly voice in most things, and his occasional anger was founded on principles that even unbelievers could respect. In his middle fifties, he'd suffered at the hands of the previous regime, but never wavered in the strength of his beliefs. He was perfectly suited to the task at hand, and around him were his closest associates.

There were the usual greetings in God's Holy Name, followed by the serving of tea, and then it was time for business.

'It is a sad thing,' the representative began, 'to see the faithful living in such poverty.'

'It has always been so, but today we can practice our religion in freedom. My people are coming back to the Faith. Our mosques have been repaired, and every day they are more full. What are material possessions compared to the Faith?' the local leader responded, with the reasonable voice of a teacher.

'So true that is,' the representative agreed. 'And yet Allah wishes for His Faithful to prosper, does He not?' There was general agreement. Every man in the room was an Islamic scholar, and few prefer poverty to comfort.

'Most of all, my people need schools, proper schools,' was the reply. 'We need better medical facilities – I grow weary of consoling the parents of a dead child who needed not to have died. We need many things. I do not deny that.'

'All these things are easily provided – if one has money,' the representative pointed out.

'But this has always been a poor land. We have resources, yes, but they have never been properly exploited, and now we have lost the support of the central government – at the very moment when we have the freedom to control our own destiny, while that fool of a president we have gets drunk and abuses women in his palace. If only he were a just man, a faithful man, for then we might bring prosperity to this land,' he observed, more in sadness than in anger.

'That, and a little foreign capital,' one of the more economically literate of his retinue suggested modestly. Islam has never had a rule against commercial activity. Though it is remembered by the West for spreading by the sword, it had gone east on the ships of traders, much as Christianity had spread through the word and example of its own adherents.

'In Tehran, it is thought that the time has arrived for the faithful to act as the Prophet commands. We have made the error common to unbelievers, of thinking in terms of national greed rather than the needs of all people. My own teacher, Mahmoud Haji Daryaei, has preached of the need to return to the foundations of our Faith,' the representative said, sipping his tea. He spoke as a teacher himself, his voice quiet. Passion he saved for the public arena. In a closed room, sitting on the floor with men as learned as himself, he, too, spoke only with reason's voice. 'We have wealth – such wealth as only Allah could have awarded by His own plan. And now we have the moment as well. You men in this room, you kept the Faith, honored the Word in the face of persecution, while others of us grew rich. It is now our obligation to reward you, to welcome you back into the fold, to share our bounty with you. This is what my teacher proposes.'

'It is good to hear such words,' was the cautious reply. That the man was primarily a man of God did not make him naive. He guarded his thoughts with the greatest care – growing up under Communist rule had taught him that – but what he had to be thinking was obvious.

'It is our hope to unite all Islam under one roof, to bring the Faithful together as the Prophet Mohammed, blessings and peace be upon him, desired. We are different in place, in language, often in color, but in our Faith we are one. We *are* the elect of Allah.'

'And so?'

'And so, we wish your republic to join our own so that we may be as one. We will bring you schools and medical assistance for your people. We will help you take control of your own land, so that what we give you will be returned to all many-fold, and we shall be as the brothers Allah intends us to be.'

The casual Western observer might have remarked that these men all appeared unsophisticated, due to their less-than-splendid clothing, their simple mode of speech, or merely the fact that they sat on the floor. Such was not exactly the case, and what the visitor from Iran proposed was hardly less startling than an embassy from another planet might have been. There were differences between his nation and this one, between his people and theirs. Language and culture, for starters. They had fought wars over the centuries, there had been banditry and brigandage, this despite the most serious strictures in the Holy Koran about armed conflict between Islamic nations. There was, in fact, virtually no common ground between them at all – except for one. That one might have been called accidental, but the truly Faithful didn't believe in accidents. When Russia, first under the czars and then under Marxism-Leninism, had conquered their land (a lengthy process rather than an event), they'd stripped so much away. Culture, for one. History and heritage; everything but language, a sop to what the Soviets for generations had uneasily called 'the nationalities question.' They'd brought schooling aimed first at destroying everything and then at rebuilding it in a new and godless mode, until the only unifying force left to the people was their Faith, which they'd tried hard to suppress. And even that was good, they all thought now, because the Faith could never be suppressed, and such attempts only made the truly Faithful more determined. It might even – *had* to have been a plan from Allah Himself, to show the people that their one salvation could only be the Faith. Now they were coming back to it, to the leaders who had kept the flame alight, and now, all in the room reflected, as their visitor knew they must, Allah Himself had washed away their petty differences so that they could unify as their God wished. So much the better to do so with the promise of material prosperity, as Charity was one of the Pillars of Islam, and so long denied by people calling themselves faithful to the Holy Word. And now the Soviet Union was dead, and its successor state crippled, and the distant and unloved children of Moscow left largely on their own, all of them governed by an echo of what was gone. If it were not a sign from Allah that this opportunity should present itself, then what was it? they all asked themselves.

They only had to do one thing to bring it all about. And *he* was an unbeliever. And Allah would judge him – through their hands.

'And although I can't say that I liked the way you treated my Boston College Eagles last October,' Ryan said, with a smile, to the assembled NCAA football champions from the

University of Oklahoma at Norman, 'your tradition of excellence is part of the American soul.' Which hadn't been much of a pleasure for the University of Florida in the last Orange Bowl, in a 35-10 blowout.

And the people applauded again. Jack was so pleased by this that he almost forgot the fact that the speech was not really his. His smile, crooked teeth and all, lit up the arena, and he waved his right hand, this time not tentatively. One could tell the difference on the C-SPAN cameras.

'He's a fast learner,' Ed Kealty said. He was objective about such matters. His public face was one thing, but politicians are realists, at least in the tactical sense.

'He's very well coached, remember,' the former Vice President's chief of staff reminded his boss. 'They don't come any better than Arnie. Our initial play got their attention, Ed, and van Damm must have laid the word on Ryan pretty hard and pretty fast.'

He didn't have to add that their 'play' had gone nowhere fast after that. The newspapers had written their initial editorials, but then reflected a little and backed off – not editorially, since the media rarely admits to error, but the news stories coming from the White House press room, if not praising Ryan, hadn't used the usual assassination buzzwords: *unsure, confused, disorganized*, and the like. No White House with Arnie van Damm in it would ever be disorganized, and the whole Washington establishment knew it.

Ryan's major Cabinet appointments had shaken things up, but then the officials had all started doing the right things. Adler was another insider who'd worked his way to the top; as a junior official he'd briefed in too many foreign-affairs correspondents over the years for them to turn on him – and *he* never lost a chance to extol Ryan's expertise on foreign policy. George Winston, outsider and plutocrat though he was, had initiated a 'quiet' reexamination of his entire department, and Winston had on his Rolodex the number of every financial editor from Berlin to Tokyo, and was seeking out their views and counsel on his internal study. Most surprising of all was Tony Bretano in the Pentagon. A vociferous outsider for the last ten years, he'd promised the defense-reporting community that he'd clean out the temple or die in the attempt, that the Pentagon *was* wasteful now as they'd always proclaimed, but that he, with the President's approval, was going to do his damnedest to de-corrupt the acquisition process once and for all. It was a singularly uncharming collection of people, Washington outsiders all, but, damn it, they were charming the media in the best possible way, quietly, in the back rooms of power. Most disturbingly of all, the *Washington Post*, an internal spy had told Kealty earlier in the day, was preparing a multipart story about Ryan's history at CIA, and it would be a canonization piece by no less than Bob Holtzman. Holtzman was the quintessential media insider, and for reasons unknown, he liked Ryan personally – and he had one hell of a source inside somewhere. That was the Trojan horse. If the story ran, and if it were picked up around the nation – both likely, since it would increase the prestige both of Holtzman and the *Post* – then his media contacts would back away rapidly; the editorials would counsel him to withdraw his claim for the good of the nation and he'd have no leverage at all, and his political career would end in greater disgrace than he'd accepted only a short time before. Historians who might have overlooked his personal indiscretions would instead focus on his overreaching ambition, and instead of seeing it as an irregularity, would then fold it back into his entire career, questioning everything he'd ever done, seeing him in a different and unfavorable light at every step, saying that the good things he'd done were the irregularities. Kealty wasn't so much looking into his political grave as at eternal damnation.

'You left out Callie,' Ed grumped, still watching the speech, listening to the content and paying close attention to the delivery – academic, he thought, fitting for an audience mainly of students, who cheered this Ryan as though he were a football coach or someone of similar irrelevance.

'One of her speeches could make Pee-Wee Herman look presidential,' the chief of staff agreed. And that was the greatest danger of all. To win, Ryan just had to *appear* presidential, whether he really was or not – and he *wasn't*, of course, as Kealty kept reminding himself. How could he be?

'I never said he was stupid,' Kealty admitted. He had to be objective. This wasn't a game anymore. It was even more than life.

'It's gotta happen soon, Ed.'

'I know.' But he had to have something bigger to shoot, Kealty told himself. It was a curious metaphor for someone who'd advocated gun control all of his political life.

25

BLOOMS

The farm had come with a barn. It mainly served as a garage now. Ernie Brown had been in the construction business, and had earned a good deal of money, first in the late 1970s as a union plumber, then he'd established his own business in the 1980s to partake in the California building boom. Though a pair of divorces had depleted his funds, the selling of the business had been well timed, and he'd taken the money and run, and bought a sizable parcel of land in an area not yet chic enough to have its property values driven up by Hollywood types. What had resulted was almost a full 'section' – a square mile of privacy. Actually more than that, because the neighboring ranches were dormant at this time of year, the pastures frozen, and the cattle in pens comfortably eating silage. You could go several days without seeing so much as another car on the road, or so it seemed out in Big Sky Country. School buses, they told themselves, didn't count.

A five-ton flatbed truck also had been conveyed with the ranch – a diesel, conveniently enough – along with a buried two-thousand-gallon fuel tank right by the barn. The family which had sold off the ranch and barn and house to the newcomer from California hadn't known that they were giving over title to a bomb factory. The first order of business for Ernie and Pete was to get the old truck started up. That proved to be a forty-minute exercise, because it wasn't just a case of a dead battery, but Pete Holbrook was a competent mechanic, and in due course the truck's engine roared to unmuffled life and showed every sign of remaining with the living. The truck was not licensed, but that wasn't terribly unusual in this area of huge holdings, and their drive of forty miles north to the farm-supplies store was untroubled.

It could hardly have been a better portent of spring for the store. Planting season was coming (there were a lot of wheat armers around), and here was the first major customer for the virtual mountain of fertilizer just trucked in from the distributor's warehouse in Helena. The men bought four tons, not an unusual quantity, which a propane-powered forklift deposited on the flatbed of the truck, and they paid cash for it, then drove off with a handshake and a smile.

'This is going to be hard work,' Holbrook observed, halfway back.

'That's right, and we're going to do it all ourselves.' Brown turned. 'Or do you want to bring in somebody who might be an informer?'

'I hear you, Ernie,' Pete replied, as a state police car went the other way. The cop didn't even turn his head, chilling though the moment was for the two Mountain Men. 'How much more?'

Brown had done the calculations a dozen times. 'One more truckload. It's a shame this stuff is so bulky.' They'd make the second purchase tomorrow, at a store thirty miles southwest of the ranch. This evening would be busy enough, unloading all this crap inside the barn. A good workout. Why didn't the goddamn farm have a forklift? Holbrook wondered. At least when they refilled the fuel tank, the local oil company would do it. That was some consolation.

It was cold on the Chinese coast, and that made things easier for the satellites to see a series of thermal blooms at two naval bases. Actually, the 'Chinese navy' was the naval service of the People's Liberation Army, so gross a disregard for tradition that Western navies ignored the correct name in favor of custom. The imagery was recorded and cross-linked to the National Military Command Center in the Pentagon, where the senior watch officer turned to his intelligence specialist.

'Do the Chinese have an exercise laid on?'

'Not that we know of.' The photos showed that twelve ships, all of them alongside, had their engines running, instead of the normal procedure by which they drew electrical power from the dock. A closer look at the photo showed a half-dozen tugboats moving around the harbor, as well. The intel specialist for this watch was Army. He called a naval officer over.

'Sailing some ships,' was the obvious analysis.

'Not just doing an engineering exam or something?'

'They wouldn't need tugboats for that. When's the next pass?' the Navy commander asked, meaning a satellite pass, checking the time reference on the photo. It was thirty minutes old.

'Fifty minutes.'

'Then it ought to show three or maybe four ships standing out to sea at both bases. That'll make it certain. For right now, two chances out of three, they're laying on a major exercise.' He paused. 'Any political hoo-rah going on?'

The senior watch officer shook his head. 'Nothing.'

'Then it's a FleetEx. Maybe somebody decided to check out their readiness.' They would learn more with a press release from Beijing, but that was thirty minutes into a future they couldn't see, paid though they were to do so.

The director was a religious man, as was to be expected, what with the sensitivity of his post. Gifted physician that he had been, and scientist-virologist that he still was, he lived in a country where political reliability was measured by devotion to the Shi'a branch of Islam, and in this there was no doubt. His prayers were always on time, and he scheduled his laboratory work around them. He required the same of his people, for such was his devotion that he went beyond the teachings of Islam without even knowing it, bending such rules as stood in his way as though they were made of rubber, and at the same time telling himself that, no, he never violated the Prophet's Holy Word, or Allah's Will. How could he be doing that? He was helping to bring the world back to the Faith.

The prisoners, the experimental subjects, were all condemned men in one way or another. Even the thieves, lesser criminals, had four times violated the Holy Koran, and they had probably committed other crimes as well, perhaps – probably, he told himself – those worthy of death. Every day they were informed of the time for prayer, and though they knelt and bowed and mouthed the prayers, you could tell by watching them on the TV monitor that they were merely going through the ritual, not truly praying to Allah in the manner prescribed. That made them all apostates – and apostasy was a capital crime in their country – even though only one had been convicted of that crime.

That one was of the Baha'i religion, a minority almost stamped out, a belief structure that had evolved *after* Islam. Christians and Jews were at least People of the Book; however misguided their religions, at least they acknowledged the same God of the Universe, of whom Mohammed was the final messenger. The Baha'i had come later, *inventing* something both new and false that relegated them to the status of pagans, denying the True Faith, and earning the wrath of their government. It was fitting that this man was the first to show that the experiment was successful.

It was remarkable that the prisoners were so brain-dulled by their conditions that the onset of flu symptoms caused no special reaction at first. The medical corpsmen went in, as always in full protective gear, to take blood samples, and one additional benefit of the prisoners' condition was that they were far too cowed to make trouble. All of them had been in prison for some time, subject to a deficient diet which had its own effects on their energy levels, plus a discipline regime so harsh that they didn't dare resist. Even the condemned prisoners who knew they faced death had no wish to accelerate the process. All meekly submitted to having their blood drawn by exquisitely careful medics. The test tubes were carefully labeled in accordance with the numbers on the beds, and the medics withdrew.

In the lab, it was Patient Three's blood which went under the microscope first. The antibody test was prone to give some false positive readings, and this was too important to risk error. So slides were prepared and placed under the electron microscopes, first set at magnification 20,000 for area search. The fine adjustments for the instruments were handled by exquisitely machined gears, as the slide was moved left and right, up and down, until . . .

'Ah,' the director said. He centered the target in the viewing field and increased the magnification to 112,000 . . . and there it was, projected onto the computer monitor in black-and-white display. His culture knew much of shepherding, and the aphorism 'Shepherd's Crook' seemed to him a perfect description. Centered was the RNA strand, thin and curved at the bottom, with the protein loops at the top. These were the key to the action of the virus, or so everyone thought. Their precise function was not understood, and that also pleased the director's identity as a bio-war technician. 'Moudi,' he called.

'Yes, I see it,' the younger doctor said, with a slow nod, as he walked to that side of the room. Ebola Zaire Mayinga was in the apostate's blood. He'd just run the antibody test as well, and watched the tiny sample change color. This one was not a false positive.

'Airborne transmission is confirmed.'

'Agreed.' Moudi's face didn't change. He was not surprised.

'We will wait another day – no, two days for the second phase. And then we will know.' For now, he had a report to make.

The announcement in Beijing caught the American embassy by surprise. It was couched in routine terms. The Chinese navy would be holding a major exercise in the Taiwan Strait. There would be some live firings of surface-to-air and surface-to-surface missiles on dates yet unspecified (weather considerations had yet to be resolved, the release said). The People's Republic of China government was issuing Notice to Airmen and Notice to Mariner alerts, so that both airlines and shipping companies would be able to adjust their routings accordingly. Other than that, the release said nothing at all, and that was somewhat disturbing to the deputy chief of mission in Beijing. The DCM immediately conferred with his military attachés and the CIA chief of station, none of whom had any insights to offer, except that the release had nothing at all to say about the Republic of China government on Taiwan. On the one hand, that was good news – there was no complaint about the continued political independence of what Beijing deemed a rebel province. On the other hand, it was bad news – the release did *not* say that this was a routine exercise and not intended to disturb anyone. The notice was just that, with no explanation at all attached to it. The information was dispatched to the NMCC in the Pentagon, to the State Department, and to CIA headquarters at Langley.

Daryaei had to search his memory for the face that went with the name, and the face he remembered was the wrong e, really, for it was that of a boy from Qom, and the message came from a grown man half a world away. Raman . . . oh, yes, Aref Raman, what a bright lad he'd been. His father had been a dealer in automobiles, Mercedes cars, and had sold them in Tehran to the powerful, a man whose faith had wavered. But his son's had not. His son had not even blinked on learning of the death of his parents, killed by accident, really, at the hands of the Shah's army, for having been on the wrong street at the wrong time, caught up in a civil disturbance in which they'd had no part at all. Together, he and his teacher had prayed for them. Dead by the hands of those they trusted was the lesson from that event, but the lesson had not been a necessary one. Raman had already been a lad of deep faith, offended by the fact that his elder sister had taken up with an American officer, and so disgraced her family and his own name. She, too, had disappeared in the revolution, condemned by an Islamic court for adultery, which left only the son. They could have used him in many ways, but the chosen one had been Daryaei's own doing. Linked up with two elderly people, the new 'family' had fled the country with the Raman family wealth and gone first to Europe and then almost immediately thereafter to America. There they had done nothing more than live quietly; Daryaei imagined they were dead by now. The son, selected for the mission because of his early mastery of English, had continued his education and entered government service, performing his duties with all the excellence he'd displayed in the revolution's earliest phases, during which he'd killed two senior officers in the Shah's air force while they drank whiskey in a hotel bar.

Since then, he'd done as he'd been told. Nothing. Blend in. Disappear. Remember your mission, *but do nothing*. It was gratifying for the Ayatollah that he'd judged the boy well, for now he knew from the brief message that the mission was almost fully accomplished.

The word *assassin* is itself derived from *hashshash*, the Arabic word for the narcotic hashish, the tool once used by members of the Nizari subsect of Islam to give themselves a drug-induced vision of Paradise prior to setting out on missions of murder. In fact, they'd been heretics to Daryaei's way of thinking – and the use of drugs was an abomination.

They'd been weak-minded but effective servants of a serr
of master terrorists such as Hasan and Rashid ad-Din, and
for a time that stretched between two centuries, had served
the political balance of power in a region stretching from
Syria to Persia. But there was a brilliance in the concept
which had fascinated the cleric since learning of it as a boy.
To get one faithful agent inside the enemy's camp. It was
the task of years, and for that reason a task of faith. Where
the Nizaris had failed was that they *were* heretics, separate
from the True Faith, able to recruit a few extremists into
their cult, but not the multitude, and so they served a single
man and not Allah, and so they needed drugs to fortify themselves, as an unbeliever did with liquor. A brilliant idea
flawed. But a brilliant idea nonetheless. Daryaei had merely
perfected it, and so now he had a man close, something he'd
hoped for but not known. Better yet, he had a man close and
waiting for instructions, at the far end of an unknown message path that had never been used, all composed of people
who'd gone abroad no more recently than fifteen years ago,
an altogether better state of affairs than that which he'd set
in place in Iraq, for in America people who might be scrutin-
ized were either arrested or cleared, or if they were watched,
only for a little while, until the watchers became bored and
went on to other tasks. In some countries when that happened, the watchers became bored, picked up those whom
they watched, and frequently killed them.

So it was just timing before Raman completed his mission,
and after all these years, he still used his head, unaddled by
drugs and trained by the Great Satan himself. The news was
too sublime even to occasion a smile.

Then the phone rang. The private one. 'Yes?'

'I have good news,' the director said, 'from the Monkey
Farm.'

'You know, Arnie, you were right,' Jack said, in the breezeway to the West Wing. 'It was great to get the hell out of
here.'

The chief of staff noted the spring in his step, but didn't
get overly excited about it. Air Force One had brought the
President back in time for a quiet dinner with his family
instead of the usual rigors of three or four such speeches,

dless hours of schmoozing with major contributors, and ne usual four-hour night that resulted – and that, often enough, in the aircraft – followed by a quick shower and a working day artificially extended by the revelries in the hustings. It was remarkable, he thought, that any President was able to do any work at all. The real duties of the office were difficult enough, and those were almost always subordinated to what was little more than public relations, albeit a necessary function in a democracy, in which the people needed to see the President doing more than sitting at his desk and doing . . . his work. The presidency was a job which one could love without liking it, a phrase seemingly contradictory until you came here and saw it.

'You did just fine,' van Damm said. 'The stuff on TV was perfect, and the segment NBC ran with your wife was okay, too.'

'She didn't like it. She didn't think they used her best line,' Ryan reported lightly.

'Could have been a lot worse.' *They didn't ask her about abortion*, Arnie thought. To keep that from happening, he'd used up a few large markers with NBC, and made sure that Tom Donner had been treated at least as well as a senator, maybe even a Cabinet member, on the flight the previous day, including a rare taped segment in flight. The following week, Donner would be the first network anchor to have a one-on-one with the President in the upstairs sitting room, and for that there was no agreement on the scope of the questions, meaning that Ryan would have to be briefed for hours to make sure he didn't step on the presidential crank. But for now the chief of staff allowed his President to bask in the afterglow of what had been a pretty good day in the Midwest, whose real mission, aside from getting Ryan out of Washington and so get a feel for what the presidency really was, was to have him *look* like a President, and further marginalize that bastard Kealty.

The Secret Service people were as upbeat as their President, as they so often drew their mood from POTUS, returning his smiles and nods with spoken greetings of their own: 'Good morning, Mr President!' repeated by four of them as Ryan passed, finding his way to the Oval Office.

'Good morning, Ben,' Ryan said cheerily, heading to his

desk and falling into the comfortable swivel chair. 'Tell me how the world looks.'

'We may have a problem. The PRC navy's putting to sea,' the acting National Security Advisor said. The Secret Service had just assigned him a code name, CARDSHARP.

'And?' Ryan asked, annoyed that the morning might be spoiled.

'And it looks like a major fleet exercise, and they're saying there will be live-fire missile shoots. No reaction from Taipei yet.'

'They don't have elections or anything coming up, do they?' Jack asked.

Goodley shook his head. 'No, not for another year. The ROC has continued to spend money with the UN, and they're quietly lobbying a lot of countries in case they go through with a request for representation, but nothing remarkable about that, either. Taipei is playing its cards close to the vest, and not making any noise to offend the mainland. Their commercial relationship is stable. In short, we have no explanation for the exercise.'

'What do we have in the area?'

'One submarine in the Formosa Strait, keeping an eye on a Chinese SSN.'

'Carriers?'

'Nothing closer than the Indian Ocean. *Stennis* is back in Pearl for engine repairs, along with *Enterprise*, and they'll be there for a while. The cupboard is still pretty bare.' CARDSHARP reminded the President what he had himself said to *his* President only months before.

'What about their army?' the President asked next.

'Again, nothing new. We have higher-than-usual levels of activity, like the Russians said, but that's been going on for a while.'

Ryan leaned back in his chair and contemplated a cup of decaf. He'd found on his speechifying trip that his stomach really did feel better that way, and remarked on it to Cathy, who'd merely smiled and said *I told you so!* 'Okay, Ben, speculate.'

'I talked it over with some China people at State and the Agency,' Goodley replied. 'Maybe their military is making a political move, interior politics, I mean, increasing their eadiness state to let the other people on the Beijing Politburo know that they're still around and still matter. Aside from that, anything else is *pure* speculation, and I'm not supposed to do that here, boss, remember?'

'And "don't know" means *don't know*, doesn't it?' It was a rhetorical question, and one of Ryan's favored aphorisms.

'You taught me that on the other side of the river, Mr President,' Goodley agreed, but without the expected smile. 'You also taught me not to like things I can't explain.' The national intelligence officer paused. 'They know we'll know, and they know we'll be interested, and they know you're new here, and they know you don't need a hassle. So, why do it?' Goodley asked, also rhetorically.

'Yeah,' the President agreed quietly. 'Andrea?' he said. Price, as usual, was in the room, pretending not to pay attention.

'Yes, sir?'

'Where's the nearest smoker?' Ryan said it entirely without shame.

'Mr President, I don't –'

'The hell you don't. I want one.'

Price nodded and disappeared into the secretaries' room. She knew the signs as well as anyone. Switching from regular coffee to decaf, and now a smoke. In a way it was surprising that it had taken this long, and it told her more about the intelligence briefing than the words of Dr Benjamin Goodley did.

It had to be a woman smoker, the President saw a minute later. Another one of the thin ones. Price even brought a match and an ashtray along with her disapproving look. He wondered if they'd acted the same way with FDR and Eisenhower.

Ryan took his first drag, deep in thought. China had been the silent partner in the conflict – he still couldn't use the word *war*, not even in his own mind – with Japan. At least that was the supposition. It all made sense, and it all fitted together nicely, but there was no proof of the sort to flesh out a SNIE – a Special National Intelligence Estimate – much less present to the media, which often as not required the same degree of reliability as an especially conservative judge. *So...* Ryan lifted the phone. 'I want Director Murray.'

One of the nice things about the presidency was the t
of the telephone. 'Please hold for the President,' a simp**₁
phrase spoken by a White House secretary in the same voice
one might use for ordering out a pizza, never failed to cause
an instant, almost panicked, reaction on the other end of
whatever line she might use. It rarely took longer than ten
seconds to get the call through. This time it took six.

'Good morning, Mr President.'

'Morning, Dan. I need something. What's the name of that
Japanese police inspector who came over?'

'Jisaburo Tanaka,' Murray replied at once.

'Is he any good?' Jack said next.

'Solid. As good as anybody I have working here. What do
you want from him?'

'I presume they're talking a lot with that Yamata guy.'

'You may safely assume that a wild bear goes potty in the
woods, too, Mr President,' the acting Director of the FBI
managed to say without a laugh.

'I want to know about his conversations with China,
especially who his contact was.'

'That we can do. I'll try to get him right now. Call back
to you?'

'No, brief Ben Goodley in, and he'll coordinate with the
people down the hall,' Ryan said, using an old catch-phrase
between the two. 'Ben's here now in my old office.'

'Yes, sir. Let me do it now. It's heading up to midnight in
Tokyo.'

'Thanks, Dan. Bye.' Jack put the phone back. 'Let's start
figuring this one out.'

'You got it, boss,' Goodley promised.

'Anything else happening in the world? Iraq?'

'Same news as yesterday, lots of people executed. The Russians fed us this "United Islamic Republic" thing, and we
all think it likely, but no overt move yet. That's what I'd
planned to do today, and –'

'Okay, then, get to it.'

'Okay, what's the drill for this?' Tony Bretano asked.

Robby Jackson didn't especially like doing things on the
fly, but that was the job of the newly promoted J-3, Director
of Operations for the Joint Chiefs of Staff. In the previous

ek, he'd come to like the designate – Secretary of Defense. etano was one tough-minded little guy, but his snarl was mainly for show, and concealed a very thoughtful brain able to make quick decisions. And the man was an engineer – he knew what he didn't know, and was quick to ask questions.

'We have *Pasadena* – fast-attack sub – in the strait already doing routine surveillance. We break her off the current job of trailing the PRC SSN and have her move northwest. Next, we move two or three additional boats into the area, assign them operating areas, and let them keep an eye on things. We open a line of communications with Taipei and have them feed us what they see and know. They'll play ball. They always do. Ordinarily, we'd move a carrier a little closer, but this time, well, we don't have one very close, and absent a political threat to Taiwan, it would appear to be an over-reaction. We stage electronics-intelligence aircraft over the area out of Anderson Air Force Base in Guam. We're hampered by the lack of a nearby base.'

'So, essentially we gather intelligence information and do nothing substantive?' the SecDef asked.

'Gathering intelligence *is* substantive, sir, but, yes.'

Bretano smiled. 'I know. I built the satellites you'll be using. What will they tell us?'

'We'll probably get a lot of in-the-clear chatter that'll use up every Mandarin-speaker they have at Fort Meade and tell us not very much about their overall intentions. The operational stuff will be useful – it'll tell us a lot about their capabilities. If I know Admiral Mancuso – COMSUBPAC – he'll have one or two of his boats play a little fast and loose to see if the Chinese can acquire one and prosecute it, but nothing overt. That's one of our options if we don't like the way this exercise is going.'

'What do you mean?'

'I mean if you really want to put the fear of God in a naval officer, you let him know there's a submarine around – which is to say, Mr Secretary, one appears unexpectedly in the middle of your formation and immediately disappears again. It's a head game, and a nasty one. Our people are good at that, and Bart Mancuso knows how to use his boats. We couldn't have defeated the Japanese without him,' Jackson said positively.

'He's that good?' Mancuso was just a name to the ne
SecDef.

'None better. He's one of the people you listen to. So's
your CinCPac, Dave Seaton.'

'Admiral DeMarco told me –'

'Sir, may I speak freely?' the J-3 asked.

'Jackson, in here that's the only way.'

'Bruno DeMarco was made Vice Chief of Naval Operations
for a reason.'

Bretano got it at once. 'Oh, to give speeches and not do
anything that can hurt the Navy?' Robby's reply was a nod.
'Noted, Admiral Jackson.'

'Sir, I don't know much about industry, but there's something you need to learn about this building. There's two kinds
of officer in the Pentagon, operators and bureaucrats. Admiral
DeMarco has been here for more than half of his career.
Mancuso and Seaton are operators, and they try very hard to
stay out of this building.'

'So have you,' Bretano observed.

'I guess I just like the smell of salt air, Mr Secretary. I'm
not polishing my own apple here, sir. You'll decide if you
like me or not – what the hell, I'm out of the flying business
anyway, and that's what I signed up to do. But, damn it,
when Seaton and Mancuso talk, I hope you'll listen.'

'What's the matter with you, Robby?' the SecDef asked
with sudden concern. He knew a good employee when he
saw one.

Jackson shrugged. 'Arthritis. Runs in the family. Could be
worse, sir. It won't hurt my golf game, and flag officers don't
get to fly very much anyway.'

'You don't care about getting promoted, do you?' Bretano
was about to recommend another star for Jackson.

'Mr Secretary, I'm the son of a preacher man in Mississippi.
I got into Annapolis, flew fighters for twenty years, and I'm
still alive to talk about it.' All too many of his friends were
not, a fact Robby never forgot. 'I can retire whenever I want
and get a good job. I figure I'm ahead of the game whatever
happens. But America's been pretty good to me, and I owe
something back. What I owe, sir, is to tell the truth and do
my best and screw the consequences.'

'So you're not a bureaucrat, either.' Bretano wondered what

ckson's degree was in. He sure talked like a competent engineer. He even smiled like one.

'I'd rather play piano in a whorehouse, sir. It's more honest work.'

'We're going to get along, Robby. Put a plan together. Let's keep a close eye on the Chinese.'

'Actually, I'm just supposed to advise and –'

'Then coordinate with Seaton. I imagine he listens to you, too.'

The UN inspection teams had become so accustomed to frustration that they hardly knew how to deal with satisfaction. The various staffs at the various facilities had given over reams of paper, still photographs, and videotapes, and practically raced the inspectors through the installations, pointing out the important aspects of the workings, and often demonstrating the easiest method of deactivating the more offensive features. There was the minor problem that the difference between a chemical-weapons plant and a factory for insecticide was essentially nil. Nerve gas had been an accidental invention of research into killing bugs (most insecticides are nerve poisons), and what it came down to, really, were the chemical ingredients, called 'precursors.' Besides which, any country with oil resources and a petrochemical industry routinely produced all manner of specialized products, most of them toxic to humans anyway.

But the game had rules, and one of the rules was that honest people were assumed not to produce forbidden weapons, and overnight Iraq had become an honest member of the world community.

This fact was made clear at the meeting of the United Nations Security Council. The Iraqi ambassador spoke from his seat at the annular table, using charts to show what had already been opened to the inspection teams, and lamenting the fact that he'd been unable to speak the truth before. The other diplomats in the room understood. Many of them lied so much that they scarcely knew what the truth was. And so it was now that they saw truth and didn't recognize the lie behind it.

'In view of the full compliance of my country with all United Nations resolutions, we respectfully request that, in view of the needs of the citizens of my country, the embargo on foodstuffs be lifted as quickly as possible,' the ambassador concluded. Even his tone was reasonable now, the other diplomats noted with satisfaction.

'The chair recognizes the ambassador of the Islamic Republic of Iran,' said the Chinese ambassador, who currently had the rotating chairmanship for the Security Council.

'No country in this body has greater reason to dislike Iraq. The chemical-weapons plants inspected today manufactured weapons of mass destruction which were then used against the people of my country. At the same time, we feel it is incumbent upon us to recognize the new day that has dawned over our neighbor. The citizens of Iraq have suffered long because of the actions of their former ruler. That ruler is gone, and the new government shows every sign of reentering the community of nations. In view of that, the Islamic Republic of Iran will support an immediate suspension of the embargo. We will, moreover, initiate an emergency transfer of foodstuffs to bring relief to the Iraqi citizens. Iran proposes that the suspension should be conditional upon Iraq's continued good faith. To that end, we submit Draft Resolution 3659 . . .'

Scott Adler had flown up to New York to take the American seat at the Council. The American ambassador to the UN was an experienced diplomat, but for some situations the proximity of Washington was just too convenient, and this was one. For what little good it did, Adler thought. The Secretary of State had no cards to play at all. Often the cleverest ploy in diplomacy was to do exactly what your adversary requested. That had been the greatest fear in 1991, that Iraq could have simply withdrawn from Kuwait, leaving America and her allies with nothing to do, and preserving the Iraqi military to fight another day. It had been, fortunately, an option just a little too clever for Iraq to exercise. But someone had learned from that. When you demanded that someone should do something or else be denied something that he needed, and then that person did it – well, then you could no longer deny what he wanted, could you?

Adler had been fully briefed on the situation, for all the good it did him. It was rather like sitting at a poker game with three aces after the draw, only to learn that your

503

pponent had a straight flush. Good information didn't always help. The only thing that could delay the proceedings was the turgid pace of the United Nations, and even that had limitations when diplomats had an attack of enthusiasm. Adler could have asked for a postponement of the vote to ensure Iraqi compliance with the long-standing UN demands, but Iran had already handled that by submitting a resolution that specified the temporary and conditional nature of the embargo suspension. They'd also made it very clear that they were going to ship food anyway – in fact already had, via truck, on the theory that doing something illegal in public made it acceptable. The SecState looked over at his ambassador – they'd been friends for years – and caught the ironic wink. The British ambassador was looking down at a pad of penciled doodles. The Russian one was reading dispatches. Nobody was listening, really. They didn't have to. In two hours, the Iranian resolution would pass. Well, it could have been worse. At least he'd have a chance to speak face-to-face with the Chinese ambassador and ask about their naval maneuvers. He knew the answer he'd get, but he wouldn't know if it was the truth or not. Of course. *I'm the Secretary of State of the world's most powerful nation*, Adler thought, *but I'm just a spectator today.*

26

WEEDS

There were few things sadder than a sick child. Sohaila, her name was, Dr MacGregor remembered. A pretty name, for a pretty, elfin little girl. Her father carried her in his arms. He appeared to be a brutish man – that was MacGregor's first impression, and he'd learned to trust them – but if so, one transformed by concern for his child. His wife was in his wake, along with another Arabic-appearing man wearing a jacket, and behind *him* was an official-looking Sudanese, all of which the physician noted and ignored. They weren't sick. Sohaila was.

'Well, hello again, young lady,' he said, with a comforting smile. 'You are not feeling at all well, are you? We'll have to see about that, won't we? Come with me,' he said to the father.

Clearly these people were important to someone, and they would be treated accordingly. MacGregor led them to an examining room. The father set the little girl down on the table and backed away, letting his wife hold Sohaila's hand. The bodyguards – that's what they had to be – remained outside. The physician touched his hand to the child's forehead. She was burning up – 39 at least. Okay. He washed his hands thoroughly and donned gloves, again because this was Africa, and in Africa you took every precaution. His first considered action was to take her temperature via the ear: 39.4. Pulse was rapid but not worrisome for a child. A quick check with a stethoscope confirmed normal heart sounds and no particular problem with the lungs, though her breathing was rapid as well. So far she had a fever, something hardly uncommon with young children, especially those recently arrived into a new environment. He looked up.

'What seems to be the problem with your daughter?' The father answered this time.

...ne cannot eat, and her other end –'

'Vomiting and diarrhea?' MacGregor asked, checking her ...es out next. They seemed unremarkable as well.

'Yes, Doctor.'

'You've arrived here recently, I believe?' He looked up when the answer was hesitation. 'I need to know.'

'Correct. From Iraq, just a few days.'

'And your daughter has a mild case of asthma, nothing else, no other health problems, correct?'

'That is true, yes. She's had all her shots and such. She's never been ill like this.' The mother just nodded. The father clearly had taken over, probably to get the feeling of authority, to make things happen, the physician surmised. It was fine with him.

'Since arriving here, any unusual things to eat? You see,' MacGregor explained, 'travel can be very unsettling to some people, and children are unusually vulnerable. It could just be the local water.'

'I gave her the medicine, but it got worse,' the mother said.

'It is not the water,' the father said positively. 'The house has its own well. The water is good.'

As though on cue, Sohaila moaned and turned, vomiting off the examining table and onto the tile floor. It wasn't the right color. There were traces of red and black. Red for new blood, black for old. It wasn't jet lag or bad water. Perhaps an ulcer? Food poisoning? MacGregor blinked and instinctively checked to be sure his hands were gloved. The mother was looking for a paper towel to –

'Don't touch that,' he said mildly. He next took the child's blood pressure. It was low, confirming an internal bleed. 'Sohaila, I'm afraid you will be spending the night with us so that we can make you well again.'

It could have been many things, but the doctor had been in Africa long enough to know that you acted as though it were the worst. The young physician consoled himself with the belief that it couldn't be all *that* bad.

It wasn't quite like the old days – what was? – but Mancuso enjoyed the work. He'd had a good war – *he* thought of it as a war; his submarines had done exactly what they'd been designed to do. After losing *Asheville* and *Charlotte* – those

before the known commencement of hostilities – he'd
no more. His boats had delivered on every mission assign
savaging the enemy submarine force in a carefully planne
ambush, supporting a brilliant special operation, conducting
deep-strike missile launches, and, as always, gathering vital
tactical intelligence. His best play, COMSUBPAC judged, had
been in recalling the boomers from retirement. They were
too big and too unwieldy to be fast-attack boats, but God
damn if they hadn't done the job for him. Enough so that
they were all down the hill from his headquarters, tied alongside, their crews swaggering around town a bit, with brooms
still prominent on their sails. Okay, so he wasn't Charlie
Lockwood exactly, modesty told him. He'd done the job he'd
been paid to do. And now he had another.

'So what are they supposed to be up to?' he asked his
immediate boss, Admiral Dave Seaton.

'Nobody seems to know.' Seaton had come over to look
around. Like any good officer, he tried to get the hell out of
his office as much as possible, even if it only meant visiting
another. 'Maybe just a FleetEx, but with a new President,
maybe they want to flex their muscles and see what happens.'
People in uniform did not like such international examin-
ations, since they were usually the ones whose lives were
part of the grading procedure.

'I know this guy, boss,' Bart said soberly.

'Oh?'

'Not all that well, but you know about *Red October*.'

Seaton grinned. 'Bart, if you ever tell me that story, one
of us has to kill the other, and I'm bigger.' The story, one of
the most closely guarded secrets in the Navy's history, still
was not widely known, though the rumors – one would never
stop those – were many and diverse.

'You need to know, Admiral. You need to know what
National Command Authority has hanging between his legs.
I've been shipmates with the guy.'

That earned Mancuso a hard blink from CINCPAC. 'You're
kidding.'

'Ryan was aboard the boomer with me. Matter of fact, he
got aboard before I did.' Mancuso closed his eyes, delighted
that he could finally tell this sea story and get away with it.
Dave Seaton was a theater commander-in-chief, and he had

ght to know what sort of man was sending the orders
wn from Washington.

'I heard he was involved in the operation, even that he got
aboard, but I thought that was at Norfolk, when they parked
her at the Eight-Ten Dock. I mean, he's a spook, right, an
intel weenie . . .'

'Not hardly. He killed a guy – shot him, right in the missile
room – before I got aboard. He was on the helm when we
clobbered the Alfa. He was scared shitless, but he didn't cave.
This President we've got's been there and done that. Anyway,
if they want to test our President, my money's on him. Two
big brass ones, Dave, that's what he's got hangin'. He may
not look like it on TV, but I'll follow that son of a bitch
anywhere.' Mancuso surprised himself with the conclusion.
It was the first time he'd thought it all the way through.

'Good to know,' Seaton thought.

'So what's the mission?' SUBPAC asked.

'J-3 wants us to shadow.'

'You know Jackson better than I do. What are the parameters?'

'If this is a FleetEx and nothing else, we observe covertly.
If things change, we let them know we care. You've got point,
Bart. My cupboard's pretty damned bare.'

They had only to look out the windows to see that. *Enterprise* and *John Stennis* were both in drydock. CINCPAC did
not have a single carrier to deploy, and wouldn't for two
more months. They'd run *Johnnie Reb* on two shafts for the
retaking of the Marianas, but now she lay alongside her older
sister, with huge holes torched from the flight deck down to
the first platform level while new turbines and reduction
gears were fabricated. The aircraft carrier was the usual
means for the United States Navy to make a show of force.
Probably that was part of the Chinese plan, to see how
America would react when a substantive reaction was not
possible, or so it would appear to some.

'Will you cover for me with DeMarco?' Mancuso asked.

'What do you mean?'

'I mean that Bruno's from the old school. He thinks it's
bad to get detected. Personally, I think sometimes it can be
a good thing. If you want me to rattle John Chinaman's cage,
he has to hear the bars shake, doesn't he?'

'I'll write the orders accordingly. How you run it is business. For the moment, if some 'can skipper talks to XO about getting laid on the beach, I want it on tape for n collection.'

'Dave, that's an order a man can understand. I'll even get you the phone number, sir.'

'And not a damned thing we can do,' Cliff Rutledge concluded his assessment. 'Gee, Cliff,' Scott Adler responded. 'I kinda figured that one out for myself.' The idea was that subordinates gave you alternatives instead of taking them away – or in this case, telling you what you already knew.

They'd been fairly lucky to this point. Nothing much had gotten out to the media. Washington was still too shell-shocked, the junior people filling senior posts were not yet confident enough to leak information without authorization, and the senior posts President Ryan had filled were remarkably loyal to their Commander-in-Chief, an unexpected benefit of picking outsiders who didn't know from politics. But it couldn't last, especially with something as juicy as a new country about to be born from two enemies, both of whom had shed American blood.

'I suppose we could always just do nothing,' Rutledge observed lightly, wondering what the reaction would be. This alternative was distinct from not being able to do anything, a metaphysical subtlety not lost on official Washington.

'Taking that position only encourages developments adverse to our interests,' another senior staffer observed crossly.

'As opposed to proclaiming our impotence?' Rutledge replied. 'If we say we don't like it, and then we fail to stop it, that's worse than our taking no position at all.'

Adler reflected that you could always depend on a Harvard man for good grammar and finely split hairs and, in Rutledge's case, not much more than that. This career foreign service officer had gotten to the seventh floor by never putting a foot wrong, which was another way of saying that he'd never led a dance partner in his life. On the other hand, he was superbly connected – or had been. Cliff had the deadliest disease of a FSO, however. Everything was negotiable. Adler didn't think that way. You had to stand and fight for some

...s, because if you didn't, the other guy would decide
...ere the battlefield was, and then *he* had control. The
...ission of diplomats was to prevent war, a serious business,
...dler thought, which one accomplished by knowing where
to stand firm and where the limits on negotiation were. For
the Assistant Secretary of State for Policy, it was just an
unending dance. With someone else leading. Alas, Adler
didn't yet have the political capital to fire the man, or maybe
make him an ambassador to some harmless post. He himself
still had to be confirmed by the new Senate, for example.

'So just call it a regional issue?' another senior diplomat
asked. Adler's head turned slowly. Was Rutledge building a
consensus?

'No, it is not that,' the Secretary of State pronounced,
making his stand within his own conference room. 'It is a
vital security interest of the United States. We have pledged
our support to the Saudis.'

'Line in the sand?' Cliff asked. 'There's no reason to do
that yet. Look, let's be sensible about this, okay? Iran and
Iraq merge and form this new United Islamic Republic, fine.
Then what? It takes them years to get the new country organized. In that time, forces which we know to be under way
in Iran weaken the theocratic regime that's been giving us
such a royal pain in the butt. This is not a one-way deal, is
it? We can expect that from the influence the secular
elements in Iraqi society will necessarily have in Iran. If we
panic and get pushy, we make life easier for Daryaei and his
fanatics. But if we take it easy, then we lessen the imperative
for them to stoke up the rhetoric against us. Okay, we can't
stop this merger, can we?' Rutledge went on. 'So if we can't,
what do we do? We think of it as an opportunity to open a
dialogue with the new country.'

There was a certain logic to the proposal, Adler noted,
noting also the tentative nods around the conference table.
He knew the proper buzzwords. Opportunity. Dialogue.

'That'll really make the Saudis feel warm and fuzzy,' a
voice objected from the far end of the table. It was Bert Vasco,
the most junior man here. 'Mr Rutledge, I think you underestimate the situation. Iran managed the assassination –'

'We have no proof of that, do we?'

'And Al Capone was never convicted for Valentine's Day,

but I saw the movie.' Being called into the Oval Office enlivened the desk officer's rhetoric. Adler raised an amu eyebrow. 'Somebody is orchestrating this, starting with t shooting, continuing with the elimination first of the mili tary high command, and then second with the slaughter of the Ba'ath Party leadership. Next, we have this religious revival now under way. The picture I have of this is one of renewed national and religious identity. *That* will attenuate the moderating influences you referred to. The internal dissent in Iran will be knocked back a full year at least by these developments – and we don't know what *else* might be going on. Daryaei's a plotter, and a good one. He's patient, dedicated, and one ruthless son of a bitch –'

'Who's on his last legs,' one of Rutledge's allies in the room objected.

'Says who?' Vasco shot back. 'He's managed this one pretty sharp.'

'He's in his seventies.'

'He doesn't smoke or drink. Every tape we have of him in public, he looks vigorous enough. Underestimating this man is a mistake we've made before.'

'He's out of touch with his own people.'

'Maybe he doesn't know that. He's having a good year so far, and everybody likes a winner,' Vasco concluded.

'Bert, maybe you're just worried about losing your desk when they form the UIR,' someone joked. It was a low blow, aimed by a senior man at a junior, with chuckles around the table to remind him of that. The resulting silence told the Secretary of State that there *was* a consensus forming, and not the one he wanted. Time to take control again.

'Okay, moving on,' Adler said. 'The FBI will be back tomorrow to talk to us about the purloined letter. And guess what they'll be bringing?'

'Not the Box again,' someone groaned. Nobody noticed the way Rutledge's head turned.

'Just think of it as a routine test for our security clearances,' SecState told his principal subordinates. Polygraphs weren't exactly unknown for the senior people here.

'God damn it, Scott,' Cliff said, speaking for the others. 'Either we're trusted or we're not. I've already wasted hours with those people.'

ou know, they never found Nixon's letter of resignation, .er,' another said.

Maybe Henry kept it,' a third joked.

'Tomorrow. Starting at ten o'clock. Myself included,' Adler told them. He thought it a waste of time as well.

His skin was very fair, his eyes gray, and his hair had a reddish tinge, the result, he thought, of an Englishwoman somewhere in his ancestry, or such was the family joke. One advantage was his ability to pass for any Caucasian ethnicity. That he could still do so was the result of his caution. On his few 'public' operations, he'd tinted his hair, worn dark glasses, and let his beard grow – that was black – which resulted in jokes within his own community: 'Movie star,' they said. But many of the jokers were dead, and he was not. Perhaps the Israelis had photos of him – one never knew about them, but one did know that they rarely shared information with anyone, even their American patrons, which was foolish. And you couldn't worry about everything, even photographs in some Mossad file cabinet.

He came through Dulles International Airport after the flight from Frankfurt, with the requisite two bags of the serious businessman he was, with nothing more to declare than a liter of Scotch purchased in a German duty-free store. Purpose of his visit to America? Business and pleasure. Is it safe to move around Washington now? Terrible thing, saw the replay on the TV news, must be a thousand times, dreadful. It is? Really? Things are back to normal now? Good. His rental car was waiting. He drove to a nearby hotel, tired from the long flight. There he purchased a paper, ordered dinner in, and switched on the TV. That done, he plugged his portable computer into the room's phone – they all had data jacks now – and accessed the Net to tell Badrayn that he was safely in-country for his reconnaissance mission. A commercial encryption program transformed what was a meaningless code phrase into total gibberish.

'Welcome aboard. My name is Clark,' John told the first class. He was turned out much better than was his custom, wearing a properly tailored suit, button-down shirt, and a striped tie. For the moment, he had to impress in one way. Soon he'd do it in another. Getting the first group in had been easier than expected. The CIA, Hollywood notwithstanding, is an agency popular among American citizens, with at least ten applications for every opening, and it was just a matter of doing a computer search of the applications to find a group which fit the parameters of Clark's PLAN BLUE. Every one was a police officer with a college degree, at least four years of service, and an unblemished record which would be further checked by the FBI. For the moment, all were men, probably a mistake, John thought, but for the moment it wasn't important. Seven were white, two black, and one Asian. They were, mainly, from big-city police forces. All were at least bilingual.

'I am a field intelligence officer. Not an "agent," not a "spy," not an "operative." An *officer*,' he explained. 'I've been in the business for quite some time. I'm married and I have two children. If any of you have ideas about meeting a sleek blonde and shooting people, you can leave now. This business is mainly dull, especially if you're smart enough to do it right. You're all cops, and therefore you already know how important this job is. We deal with high-level crime, and the job is about getting information so that those major crimes can be stopped before people get killed. We do that by gathering information and passing it on to those who need it. Others look at satellite pictures or try to read the other guy's mail. We do the hard part. We get our information from *people*. Some are good people with good motives. Some are not such good people who want money, who want to get even, or who want to feel important. What these people are doesn't matter. You've all worked informants on the street, and they're not all Mother Teresa, are they? Same thing here. Your informants will often be better educated, more powerful people, but they won't be very different from the ones you've been working with. And just like your street informants, you have to be loyal to them, you have to protect them, and you'll have to wring their scrawny little necks from time to time. If you fuck up, those people die, and in some of the places you'll be working, their wives and children will die, too. If you think I'm kidding on that, you're wrong, people. You will work in countries where due process of law means whatever somebody wants it to mean. You've seen that on television just in the last few days, right?' he asked. Some of the Ba'ath officials shot in Baghdad had made world news telecasts, with the usual warnings about children and the sensitive, who invariably watched anyway. The heads nodded soberly.

'You will, for the most part, *not* be armed in the field. You will survive by your wits. You will sometimes be at risk of your life. I've lost friends in the field, some in places you know about, and some in places you don't. The world may be kinder and gentler now, but not everywhere. You're not going to be going to the nice places, guys,' John promised them. In the back of the room, Ding Chavez was struggling hard not to smile. *That little greasy guy is my partner and he's engaged to my little girl*. No sense, Domingo knew, in scaring them all away.

'What's good about the job? Well, what's good about being a cop? Answer: every bad guy you put away saves lives on the street. In this job, getting the right information to the right people saves lives, too. Lots,' Clark emphasized. 'When we do the job right, wars *don't* happen.

'Anyway, welcome aboard. I am your supervising teacher. You will find the training here stimulating and difficult. It starts at eight-thirty tomorrow morning.' With that John left the podium and walked to the back of the room. Chavez opened the door for him and they walked out into the fresh air.

'Gee, Mr C., where do I sign up?'

'God damn it, Ding, I had to say *something*.' It had been John's longest oration in some years.

'So, to get these rookies aboard, what did Foley have to do?'

'The RIFs have begun, m'boy. Hell, Ding, we had to get things started, didn't we?'

'I think you should have waited a few weeks. Foley isn't confirmed by the Senate yet. Better to wait,' Chavez thought. 'But I'm just a junior spook.'

'I keep forgetting how smart you've gotten.'

'So who the hell is Zhang Han San?' Ryan asked.

'Somewhere in his fifties, but young looking for his age, ten kilos overweight, five four or so, medium everything, so says our friend,' Dan Murray reported from his written notes. 'Quiet and thoughtful, and he stiffed Yamata.'

'Oh?' Mary Pat Foley said. 'How so?'

'Yamata was on Saipan when we got control of things. He placed a call to Beijing, looking to bug out to a safe place. Mr Zhang reacted as though it were a cold call. "What deal? We don't have any deal,"' the FBI Director mimicked. 'And after that, the calls didn't go through at all. Our Japanese friend regards that as a personal betrayal.'

'Sounds as though he's singing like a canary,' Ed Foley observed. 'Does that strike anybody as suspicious?'

'No,' Ryan said. 'In World War Two, what Japanese prisoners we took talked plenty.'

'The President's right,' Murray confirmed. 'I asked Tanaka about that myself. He says it's a cultural thing. Yamata wants to take his own life – the honorable way out in their cultural context – but they've got him on suicide watch – not even shoestrings. The resulting disgrace is so great for the guy that he has no particular reason to keep secrets. Hell of an interrogation technique. Anyway, Zhang is supposedly a diplomat – Yamata said he was titularly part of a trade delegation – but State's never heard of him. The Japanese have no records of the name on any diplomatic list. That makes him a spook, as far as I'm concerned, and so . . .' He looked over at the Foleys.

'I ran the name,' Mary Pat said. 'Zippo. But who's to say it's a real name?'

'Even if it were,' her husband added, 'we don't know that much about their intelligence people. If I had to guess' – and he did – 'he's political. Why? He cut a deal, a quiet one but a big one. Their military is still on an increased readiness and training regime because of that deal, which is why the Russians are still nervous. Whoever this guy is, best guess, he's a very serious player.' Which wasn't exactly an earthshaking revelation.

'Anything you can do to find out?' Murray inquired delicately.

Mrs Foley shook her head. 'No assets in place, at least nothing we can use for this. We have a good husband-wife team in Hong Kong, setting up a nice little network. We have a couple of assets in Shanghai. In Beijing we have some low-level agents in the defense ministry, but they're long-term prospects and using them on this issue wouldn't accomplish much more than to endanger them. Dan, the problem we have with China is that we don't really know how their government works. It has levels of complexity that we can only guess at. The Politburo members, we know who they are – we think. One of the biggies might be dead now, and we've been fishing for that tidbit for over a month. Even the Russians let us know when they buried people,' the DDO noted, as she sipped her wine. Ryan had come to like bringing his closest advisers in for drinks after the close of regular office hours. It hadn't quite occurred to him that he was extending their working day. He was also short-circuiting his own National Security Advisor, but as loyal and clever as Ben Goodley was, Jack Ryan still wanted to hear it directly when he could.

Ed took up the explanation. 'You see, sure, we think we know the political varsity over there, but we've never had a real handle on the second-string players. The dynamic is simple when you think about it, but it took us long enough to twig to it. We're talking elderly folks over there. They can't get around all that well. They need mobile eyes and ears, and over the years those gofers have accumulated a lot of power. Who's really calling the shots? We don't know for sure, and without ID'ing people, we can't find out.'

'I can dig it, guys.' Murray grunted, and reached for his beer. 'When I was working OC – organized crime – sometimes we ID'd Mafia *capi* by who held the car door open for whom. Hell of a way to do business.' It was the friendliest thing the Foleys remembered hearing from the FBI about CIA. 'Operational security really isn't all that hard if you think about it a little.'

'Makes a good case for PLAN BLUE,' Jack said next.

'Well, then you might be pleased to know the first group are in the pipeline even as we speak. John should have given them their welcoming speech a few hours ago,' the DCI announced.

Ryan had gone over Foley's reduction-in-force plan for CIA. Ed planned to swing a mean ax, ultimately reducing the Agency budget by $500 million over five years while increasing the field force. It was something to make people on the Hill happy, though with much of CIA's real budget in the black part of federal expenditures, few would ever know. Or maybe not, Jack thought. That was likely to leak.

Leaks. He'd hated them over his entire career. But now they were part of statecraft, weren't they? the President reflected. But what was he supposed to think? That leaks were *okay* now that he was the one doing it or allowing it? Damn. Laws and principles weren't supposed to work that way, were they? What exactly, what idea or ideal or principle or rock was he supposed to hold on to?

The bodyguard's name was Saleh. He was a physically robust individual, as his work demanded, and, as such, one who tried to deny illness or discomfort of any sort. A man of his station in life simply did not admit to difficulty. But when discomfort didn't go away as he'd expected and as the doctor had told him – Saleh knew that all men were vulnerable to stomach problems – and then he saw blood in the toilet . . . it was that, really. The body isn't supposed to issue blood except from a shaving cut or a bullet wound. Not in any case from moving one's bowels, and it was the sort of indicator certain to shake any man, all the more so a strong and otherwise confident one. Like many, he delayed somewhat, asking himself if it might be a temporary problem that would go away, that the discomfort would peak and abate, as flu symptoms always did. But these kept getting worse, and finally his fear got the better of him. Before dawn he left the villa, taking the car and driving to the hospital. Along the way he had to stop the car to vomit, deliberately not looking to see what he'd left on the street before heading on, his body weakening with every minute, until the walk from the car to the door seemed to take every bit of energy he had. In what passed here for an emergency room, he waited while people searched for his records. It was the smell of hospitals which frightened him, the same disinfectant odor which makes a dog stop dead and strain backward at the leash and whimper and pull away, because the smell is associated with pain, until finally a black nurse called his name, and then he rose, assembled his dignity and composure, and walked into the same examining room he'd visited before.

The second group of ten criminals was little different from the first, except that in this one there was not a condemned apostate. It was easy to dislike them, Moudi thought, looking

at the group with their sallow faces and slinking manner-
isms. It was their expressions most of all. They looked like
criminals, never quite meeting his eyes, glancing this way
and that, always, it seemed, searching for a way out, a trick,
an angle, something underhanded. The combination of fear
and lingering brutality on their faces. They were not just
men, and while that seemed to the doctor a puerile observation, it did mark them as different from himself and the
people he knew, and therefore as the bearers of lives which
were unimportant.

'We have some sick people here,' he told them. 'You have
been assigned to look after them. If you do this job well, you
will be trained as hospital aides for work at your prisons. If
not, you will be returned to your cells and your sentences.
If any of you misbehaves, your punishment will be immediate and severe.' They all nodded. They knew about severe
treatment. Iranian prisons were not noted for their amenities.
Nor, it would seem, for good food. They all had pale skin
and rheumy eyes. Well, what solicitude did such people
merit? the physician asked himself. Each of them was guilty
of known crimes, all of them serious, and what unknown
crimes lay in their pasts only the criminals and Allah knew.
What pity Moudi felt for them was residual, a result of his
medical training, which compelled him to view them as
human beings no matter what. That he could overcome. Robbers, thieves, pederasts all, they'd violated the law in a
country where law was a thing of God, and if it was stern,
it was also fair. If their treatment was harsh by Western
standards – Europeans and Americans had the strangest ideas
about human rights; what of the rights of the victims of
such people? – that was just too bad, Moudi told himself,
distancing himself from the people before him. Amnesty
International had long since stopped complaining about his
country's prisons. Perhaps they could devote their attention
to other things, like the treatment of the Faithful in other
lands. There was not a Sister Jean Baptiste among them, and
she was dead, and that was written, and what remained was
to see if their fates had been penned by the same hand in the
book of life and death. He nodded to the head guard, who
shouted at the new 'aides.' They even stood insolently,
Moudi saw. Well, they'd all see about that.

They'd all been pre-processed, stripped, showered, shaved, disinfected, and dressed in surgical greens with single-digit numbers on the back. They wore cloth slippers. The armed guards led them off to the air-lock doors, inside of which were the army medics, supplemented by a single armed guard, who kept his distance, a pistol in his gloved hands. Moudi returned to the security room to watch on the TV system. On the black-and-white monitors he watched them pad down the corridor, eyes shifting left and right in curiosity – and doubtless looking for a way out. All the eyes lingered on the guard, who was never less than four meters distant. Along the way, each of the new arrivals was handed a plastic bucket with various simple tools inside – the buckets also were numbered.

They'd all started somewhat at seeing the medics in their protective suits, but shuffled along anyway. It was at the entrance of the treatment room that they stopped. It must have been the smell, or perhaps the sight. Slow to pick up on the situation, one of their number had finally realized that whatever this was –

On the monitor, a medic gestured at the one who froze in the doorway. The man hesitated, then started speaking back. A moment later, he hurled his bucket down at the floor and started shaking his fist, while the others watched to see what would result. Then the security guard appeared out of the corner of the picture, his arm coming up and his pistol extended. At a range of two meters, he fired – so strange to see the shot but not hear it – straight into the criminal's face. The body fell to the tile floor, leaving a pattern of black spots on the gray wall. The nearest medic pointed to one of the prisoners, who immediately retrieved the fallen bucket and went into the room. There would be no more disciplinary trouble with this group. Moudi shifted his gaze to the next monitor.

This one was a color camera. It had to be. It could also be panned and zoomed. Moudi indicated the corner bed, Patient 1. The new arrival with 1 on his back and bucket just stood there at the foot of the bed at first, bucket in his hand, not knowing what he beheld. There was a sound pickup for this room, but it didn't work terribly well because it was a single nondirectional mike, and the security staff had long since turned it down to zero, because the sound was so piteous as to be debilitating to those who listened – moans, whimpers, cries from dying men who in their current state did not appear so sinister. The apostate, predictably, was the worst. He prayed and even tried to comfort those he could reach from his bed. He'd even attempted to lead a few in prayer, but they'd been the wrong prayers, and his roommates were not of the sort to speak to God under the best of circumstances.

Aide 1 continued to stand for a minute or so, looking down at Patient 1, a convicted murderer, his ankle chained to the bed. Moudi took control of the camera and zoomed it in further to see that the shackles had worn away the skin. There was a red stain on the mattress from it. The man – the *condemned patient*, Moudi corrected himself – was writhing slowly, and then Aide 1 remembered what he'd been told. He donned his plastic gloves, wet his sponge, and rubbed it across the patient's forehead. Moudi backed the camera off. One by one, the others did the same, and the army medics withdrew.

The treatment regime for the patients was not going to be a serious one. There was no point in it, since they'd already fulfilled their purpose in the project. That made life much easier on everyone. No IV lines to run, no needles to stick – and no 'sharps' to worry about. In contracting Ebola, they'd confirmed that the Mayinga strain was indeed airborne, and now all that was left was to prove that the virus had not attenuated itself in the reproductive process ... and that it could be passed on by the same aerosol process which had infected the first grouping of criminals. Most of the new arrivals, he saw, did what they'd been told to do – but badly, crassly, wiping off their charges with quick, ungentle strokes of the sponges. A few seemed genuinely compassionate. Perhaps Allah would notice their charity and show them mercy when the time came, less than ten days from now.

'Report cards,' Cathy said when Jack came into the bedroom.

'Good or bad?' her husband asked.

'See for yourself,' his wife suggested.

Uh-oh, the President thought, taking them from her hand. For all that, it wasn't so bad. The attached commentary sheets – every teacher did a short paragraph to supplement the letter grade – noted that the quality of the homework turned in had improved in the past few weeks ... so, the Secret Service agents *were* helping with that, Jack realized. At one level, it was amusing. At another – strangers were doing the father's job, and that thought made his stomach contract a little. The loyalty of the agents merely illustrated something that he was failing to do for his own kids.

'If Sally wants to get into Hopkins, she's going to have to pay more attention to her science courses,' Cathy observed.

'She's just a kid.' To her father she'd always be the little girl who –

'She's growing up, and guess what? She's interested in a young soccer player. Name of Kenny, and he's way cool,' SURGEON reported. 'Also needs a haircut. His is longer than mine.'

'Oh, shit,' SWORDSMAN replied.

'Surprised it took this long. I started dating when I was – '

'I don't want to hear about it – '

'I married *you*, didn't I?' Pause. 'Mr President . . .'

Jack turned. 'It has been a while.'

'Any way we can get to the Lincoln Bedroom?' Cathy asked. Jack looked over and saw a glass on her nightstand. She'd had a drink or two. Tomorrow wouldn't be a surgery day.

'He never slept there, babe. They call it that because – '

'The picture. I know. I asked. I like the bed,' she explained with a smile. Cathy set her patient notes down and took off her reading glasses. Then she held her arms up, almost like a toddler soliciting a pickup and a hug. 'You know, I've never made love to the most powerful man in the world before – at least not this week.'

'What about the timing?' Cathy had never used the pill.

'What *about* the timing?' she replied. And she'd always been as regular as a metronome.

'You don't want another – '

'Maybe I don't especially care.'

'You're forty,' POTUS objected.

'Well, thank you! That's well short of the record. What are you worried about?'

Jack thought about that for a moment. 'Nothing, I guess. Never did get that vasectomy, did I?'

'Nope, you never even talked to Pat about it like you said you would – and if you do it now,' FLOTUS went on with a positively wicked grin, 'it'll be in *all* the papers. Maybe even on live TV. Arnie might tell you that it'll set a good example for the Zero Population Growth people, and you'll cave on that. Except for the national security implications . . .'

'*What?*'

'President of the United States has his nuts cut, and they won't respect America anymore, will they?'

Jack almost started laughing, but stopped himself. The Detail people in the corridor might hear and –

'What got into you?'

'Maybe I'm finally getting comfortable with all this – or maybe I just want to get laid,' she added.

That's when the phone next to the bed rang. Cathy's face made a noiseless snarl as she reached for it. 'Hello? Yes, Dr Sabo. Mrs Emory? Okay . . . no, I don't think so . . . No, definitely not, I don't care if she's agitated or not, not till tomorrow. Get her something to help her sleep . . . whatever it takes. The bandages stay on till I say otherwise, and make sure that's on her chart, she's too good at whining. Yes. Night, Doctor.' She replaced the phone and grumbled. 'The lens replacement I did the other day. She doesn't like being blindfolded, but if we take the coverings off too soon –'

'Wait a minute, he called –'

'They have our number at Wilmer.'

'The direct residence?' That one even bypassed Signals, though it, like all White House lines, was bugged. Or probably was. Ryan hadn't asked, and probably didn't want to know.

'They had it for home, didn't they?' Cathy asked. 'Me surgeon, me treat patients, me professor, always on call when me have patients – especially the pain-in-the-ass ones.'

'Interruptions.' Jack lay down next to his wife. 'You don't really want another baby, do you?'

'What I want is to make love to my husband. I can't be picky about timing anymore, can I?'

'Has it been that bad?' He kissed her gently.

'Yes, but I'm not mad about it. You're trying very hard.

You remind me of my new residents – older, though.' touched his face and smiled. 'If something happens, it h pens. I like being a woman.'

'I rather like it myself.'

27

RESULTS

Some of them had degrees in psychology. It was a common and favored degree for law-enforcement officers. Some even had advanced degrees, and one member of the Detail had a doctorate, having done his dissertation on the sub-specialty of profiling criminals. All were at the least gifted amateurs in the science of reading minds; Andrea Price was one of these. SURGEON had a spring in her step as she walked out to her helicopter. SWORDSMAN walked her out to the ground-floor door and kissed her good-bye – the kiss was routine, the walk-out and the hand-holding were not, or hadn't been lately. Price shared a glance with two of her agents, and they read one another's minds, as cops can do, and they judged it to be good, except for Raman, who was as smart as the rest of them, but rather more straitlaced. He devoted more passion to sports than anything else, and Price imagined him in front of his TV every night. He probably knew even how to program his VCR. Well, there were many personality types in the Service.

'What's today look like?' POTUS asked, turning away when the Black Hawk lifted off.

'SURGEON is airborne,' Andrea heard in her earpiece. 'Everything's clear,' the overwatch people reported from their perches on the government buildings around the White House. They'd been scanning the perimeter for the last hour, as they did every day. There were the usual people out there, the 'regulars,' known by sight to the Detail members. These were people who seemed to turn up a lot. Some were just fascinated by the First Family, whichever family it might be. For them, the White House was America's real soap opera, *Dallas* writ large, and the trappings, the mechanics, really, of life in this most famous of dwellings drew them for some reason that Service psychologists struggled to understand, because for the armed agents on the Detail, 'regulars' were

dangerous by their very existence. And so the snipers on th⸺
Old Executive Office Building – OEOB – and Treasury knew
them all by sight through their powerful spotting glasses,
and knew them all by name, too, because Detail members
were out there, too, disguised as street rats or passersby. At
one time or another, the 'regulars' had all been trailed to
whatever homes they might have, and identified, and investigated, quietly. Those with irregularities were profiled for personality type – they all had a few kinks – and then they'd be
carefully scanned by the Detail members who worked outside for weapons – up to and including being bumped into
by a 'jogger' and expertly groped while being helped to their
feet during the embarrassed apology. But that danger was
past, for now.

'Didn't you check your schedule last night?' Price asked,
distracted from her duties into asking a dumb question.

'No, decided to catch some TV,' SWORDSMAN lied, not
knowing that they spotted the lie. He didn't even blush, Price
saw. For her part, she didn't allow her face to change. Even
POTUS was allowed to have a secret or two, or at least the
illusion of it.

'Okay, here's my copy.' She handed it over. Ryan scanned
the first page, which took him to lunch. 'SecTreas is on the
way in for breakfast right after CARDSHARP.'

'What do you guys call George?' Jack asked, entering the
West Wing.

'TRADER. He likes that,' Andrea reported.

'Just so you pronounce it right.' Which wasn't a bad line
for 7:50 AM, POTUS thought. But it was hard to tell. The
Detail liked nearly all of his jokes. Maybe they were just
being polite?

'Good morning, Mr President.' Goodley stood, as usual,
when Jack entered the Oval Office.

'Hi, Ben.' Ryan dropped the schedule down on his desk,
made a quick scan for important documents, and took his
seat. 'Go.'

'You stole my thunder talking with the crew last night.
We have gornischt on Mr Zhang. I could give you the long
version, but I imagine you've already heard it.' The President
nodded for him to go on.

'Okay, developments in the Taiwan Strait. The PRC has

teen surface ships at sea, two formations, one of six, one of nine. I have compositions if you want, but they're all destroyers and frigates. Deployed in regular squadron groupings, the Pentagon tells us. We have an EC-135 listening in. We have a submarine, *Pasadena*, camped between the two groups, with two more boats en route from central Pacific, timed to arrive in-area in thirty-six and fifty hours, respectively. CinCPac, Admiral Seaton, is up to speed and tasking out a full surveillance package. His parameters are on Secretary Bretano's desk now. I've discussed it over the phone. Sounds like Seaton knows his business.

'Political side, the ROC government is taking no official notice of the exercise. They put out a press release to that effect, *but* their military is in contact with ours – through CinCPac. We'll have people in their listening posts' – Goodley checked his watch – 'may be there already. State doesn't think this is a very big deal, but they're watching.'

'Overall picture?' Ryan asked.

'Could just be routine, but we wish their timing was a little better. They're not overtly pushing anything.'

'And until they do, we don't push back. Okay, we take no official notice of this exercise. Let's keep our deployments quiet. No press releases, no briefings to the media. If we get any questions, it's no big deal.'

Goodley nodded. 'That's the plan, Mr President.

'Next, Iraq, again, we have little in the way of direct information. Local TV is on a religious kick. It's all Shi'a. The Iranian clergymen we've been seeing are getting a lot of air time. The TV news coverage is almost entirely religion-based. The anchors are getting rhapsodic. The executions are done. We don't have a full body count, but it's over one hundred. That appears to be over. The Ba'ath leadership is gone for good. The littler fish are in the can. There was some stuff about how merciful the provisional government was to the "lesser criminals" – that's a quote. The "mercy" is religiously justified, and it seems that some of the "lesser criminals" have come back to Jesus – excuse me, back to Allah – in one big hurry. There's TV pictures of them sitting with an imam and discussing their misdeeds.

'Next indicator, we're seeing more organized activity within the Iranian military. Troops are training. We're get-

ting intercepts of tactical radio traffic. It's routine, but ther
a lot of it. They had an all-nighter at Foggy Bottom to g
over all this stuff. The Under Secretary for Political Affairs,
Rutledge, set it up. He evidently ran the I and R division
pretty ragged.' The State Department's Office of Intelligence
and Research was the smaller and much poorer cousin to the
intelligence community, but in it were a handful of very
astute analysts whose diplomatic perspective occasionally
gave insights the intelligence community missed.

'Conclusions?' Jack asked. 'From the all-nighter, I mean.'

'None.' *Of course*, Goodley could have added, but didn't.
'I'll be talking to them in an hour or so.'

'Pay attention to what I and R says. Pay particular attention
to – '

'Bert Vasco. Yes,' Goodley agreed. 'He's all right, but I'll
bet the seventh floor is giving him a pain in the ass. I talked to
him twenty minutes ago. He says, are you ready, forty-eight
hours. Nobody agrees with that. *Nobody*,' CARDSHARP
emphasized.

'But . . . ?' Ryan rocked back in his chair.

'But I won't bet against him, boss. I have nothing to support
his assessment. Our desk people at CIA don't agree. State
won't back him up – they didn't even give it to me; I got it
from Vasco directly, okay? But, you know, I am *not* going to
say he's wrong.' Goodley paused, realizing that he was not
sounding like every other NIO. 'We have to consider this
one, boss. Vasco has good instincts, and he's got balls, too.'

'We'll know quickly enough. Right or wrong, I agree that
he's the best guy over there. Make sure Adler talks to him,
and tell Scott I don't want him stomped, regardless of how
it turns out.'

Ben nodded emphatically as he made a note. 'Vasco gets
high-level protection. I like that, sir. It might even encourage
other people to make a gut call once in a while.'

'The Saudis?'

'Nothing from them. Almost like they're catatonic. I think
they're afraid to ask for any help until there's a reason for
it.'

'Call Ali within the hour,' the President ordered. 'I want
his opinion.'

'Yes, sir.'

And if he wants to talk to me, at any time, night or day, ll him he's my friend, and I always have time for him.'

'And that's the morning news, sir.' He rose and stopped. 'Who ever decided on CARDSHARP, by the way?'

'We did,' Price said from the far end of the room. Her left hand went up to her earpiece. 'It's in your file. You evidently played a good game of poker in your frat house.'

'I won't ask you what my girlfriends said about me,' the acting National Security Advisor said, on his way out the door.

'I didn't know that, Andrea.'

'He's even won some money at Atlantic City. Everybody underestimates him 'cause of his age. TRADER just pulled in.'

Ryan checked his agenda. Okay, this was about George's appearance before the Senate. The President took a minute to review his morning appointment list, while a Navy mess steward brought in a light breakfast tray.

'Mr President, the Secretary of the Treasury,' Agent Price announced at the side door to the corridor.

'Thank you, we can handle this alone,' Ryan said, rising from his desk as George Winston came in.

'Morning, sir,' SecTreas said, as the door closed quietly. He was dressed in one of his handmade suits, and was carrying a manila folder. Unlike his President, the Secretary of the Treasury was used to wearing a jacket most of the time. Ryan took his off and dropped it on the desk. Both sat on the twin couches, with the coffee table between them.

'Okay, how are things across the street?' Ryan asked, pouring himself some coffee, with the caffeine in this morning.

'If I ran my brokerage house like that, the SEC would have my hide on the barn door, my head over the fireplace, and my ass in Leavenworth. I'm going to – hell, I've already started bringing in some of my administrative folks down from New York. There are just too many people over there whose only job is looking at each other and telling them how important they all are. Nobody's *responsible* for anything. Damn it, at Columbus Group, we often make decisions by committee, but we make by-God *decisions* in time for them to matter. There are too many people, Mr Pres –'

'You can call me Jack, at least in here, George, I –' The door to the secretaries' room opened and the photographer

came in with his Nikon. He didn't say anything. He
did. He just snapped away, and the rubric was for ever
to pretend he simply wasn't there. It would have been a ⎕
of an assignment for a spy, Ryan thought.

'Fine. Jack, how far can I go?' TRADER asked.

'I already told you that. It's your department to run. Just
so you tell me about it first.'

'I'm telling you, then. I'm going to cut staff. I'm going to
set that department up like a business.' He stopped for a
second. 'And I'm going to rewrite the tax code. God, I didn't
know how screwed up it was until two days ago. I had some
in-house lawyers come in and – '

'It has to be revenue-neutral. We can't go dicking around
with the budget. None of us has the expertise yet, and until
the House of Representatives is reconstituted – ' the photographer left, having caught the President in a great pose,
both hands extended over the coffee tray.

'Playmate of the Month,' Winston said, with a hearty
laugh. He lifted a croissant and buttered it. 'We've run the
models. The effect on revenue will be neutral on the basis
of raw numbers, Jack, but there will probably be an overall
increase in usable funds.'

'Are you sure? Don't you need to study all the – '

'No, Jack. I don't need to study anything. I brought Mark
Gant in to be my executive assistant. He knows computer
modeling better than anybody I've ever met. He spent last
week chewing through the – didn't anybody ever tell you?
They never *stop* looking at the tax system over there. Study?
I pick up the phone, and inside half an hour I'll have a thou-
sand-page document on my desk telling me how things were
in 1952, what the tax code *then* did in every segment of the
economy – or what people think it did, as opposed to what
they thought *then* that it did, or as opposed to what the
studies in the 1960s said *they* thought that it did.' SecTreas
paused for a bite. 'Bottom line? Wall Street is far more complex, and uses simpler models, and those models *work*. Why?
Because they're simpler. And I'm going to tell the Senate
that in ninety minutes, with your permission.'

'You're sure you're right on this, George?' POTUS asked.
That was one of the problems, perhaps the largest of all. The
President couldn't check everything that was done in his

- even checking one percent would have been an heroic
- but he was responsible for it all. It was that knowledge
  had doomed so many Presidents to micro-managerial
  lure. 'Jack, I'm sure enough to bet my investors' money
  on it.'

Two pairs of eyes met over the table. Each man knew the
measure of the other. The President could have said that the
welfare of the nation was a matter of greater moment than
the few billions of dollars Winston had managed at the Columbus Group, but he didn't. Winston had built his investment house from nothing. Like Ryan, a man of humble
origins, he'd created a business in a ferociously competitive
environment on the basis of brains and integrity. Money
entrusted to him by his clients had to be *more* precious than
his own, and because it had always been so, he'd grown rich
and powerful, but never forgotten the how and why of it all.
The first important public-policy statement to be made by
Ryan's administration would ride on Winston's savvy and
honor. The President thought it over for a second, and then
he nodded.

'Then run with it, TRADER.' But then Winston had his
misgivings. It was instructive to the President that even so
powerful a figure as the Secretary of the Treasury lowered
his eyes for a second, and then said something quieter and
less positive than his confident assertion of five seconds
earlier.

'You know, politically this is going to –'

'What you're going to say to the Senate, George, is it good
for the country as a whole?'

'Yes, sir!' An emphatic nod of the head.

'Then don't wimp out on me.'

SecTreas wiped his mouth with the monogrammed nap-
kin, and looked down again. 'You know, after this is all over
and we go back to normal life, we really have to find a way
to work together. There aren't many people like us, Ryan.'

'Actually there are,' the President said, after a moment's
reflection. 'The problem is that they never come here to
work. You know who I learned that from? Cathy,' Jack told
him. 'She fucks up, somebody goes blind, but she can't run
away from making the call, can she? Imagine, you fuck up,
and somebody loses his sight forever – or dies. The guys who

work the emergency room are really on the ragged edge when Cathy and Sally went into Shock-Trauma. You make the call, and somebody is gone forever. Big deal, George, bigger than trading equities like we used to do. Same thing with cops. Same thing with soldiers. You have to make the call, right now, or something really bad happens. But those kinds of people don't come here to Washington, do they? And mainly that sort of guy goes to the place he – or she – has to be, where the real action is,' Ryan said, almost wistfully. 'The really good ones go where they're needed, and they always seem to know where that is.'

'But the really good ones don't like the bullshit. So they don't come here?' Winston asked, getting his own course in Government 101, and finding Ryan a teacher of note.

'Some do. Adler at State. Another guy over there I've discovered, name of Vasco. But those are the ones who buck the system. The system works against them. Those are the ones we have to identify and protect. Mostly little ones, but what they do isn't little. They keep the system running, and mainly they go unnoticed because they don't care much about being noticed. They care about getting it done, serving the people out there. You know what I'd really like to do?' Ryan asked, for the first time revealing something from the depths of his soul. He hadn't even had the guts to say this to Arnie.

'Yeah, set up a system that really works, a system that recognizes the good ones and gives them what they deserve. You know how hard that is in *any* organization? Hell, it was a struggle at my shop, and Treasury has more janitors than I had trading executives. I'm not even sure where to *start* a job like that,' Winston said. He would be one to grasp the scope of the dream, his President thought.

'Harder than you think, even. The guys who really do the work don't want to be bosses. They want to work. Cathy could be an administrator. They offered her the chair at the University of Virginia Medical School – and that would have been a big deal. But it would have cut her patient time in half, and she likes doing what she does. Someday Bernie Katz at Hopkins is going to retire, and they'll offer his chair to her, and she'll turn *that* down. Probably,' Jack thought. 'Unless I can talk her out of it.'

't be done, Jack.' TRADER shook his head. 'Hell of an
  though.'
    rover Cleveland reformed the Civil Service over a hun-
    ed years ago,' POTUS reminded his breakfast guest. 'I know
  we can't make it perfect, but we *can* make it better. You're
already trying – you just told me that. Think about it some.'

'I'll do that,' SecTreas promised, standing. 'But for now, I
have another revolution to foment. How many enemies can
we afford to make?'

'There's always enemies, George. Jesus had enemies.'

He liked the sobriquet 'Movie Star,' and having learned of it
fifteen years before, he had also learned to make it work for
him. The mission was reconnaissance, and the weapon was
charm. He had a choice of accents in his repertoire. Since he
had German travel documents, he affected the speech of a
person from Frankfurt to go along with German clothing,
complete to shoes and wallet, all purchased with money that
came from whatever sponsor Ali Badrayn had recently found.
The rental-car company had provided him with excellent
maps, all spread on the bucket seat next to his. That saved
him from memorizing all his routes, which was tiresome,
and wasteful of both his time and his photographic memory.

The first stop was St Mary's School, located a few miles
outside Annapolis. It was a religious school, Roman Catholic,
that ran from pre-kindergarten to twelfth grade, and had just
under six hundred students. That made it a borderline case
in terms of economics. The Star would get two or perhaps
three passes, made somewhat easier by the fact that the
school was on a point of land that had once been a sizable
farm which the Catholic Church had talked out of some
wealthy family or other. There was only one access road.
The school's land ended at the water, and there was a river
on the far side, past the athletic fields. The road had houses
on one side, a residential development perhaps thirty years
old. The school had eleven buildings, some closely bunched,
others more spread out. Movie Star knew the ages of the
targets, and from that it was easy enough to guess the buildings where they would spend much, if not all, of their time.
The tactical environment was not a favorable one, and
became less so when he spotted the protection. The school

had plenty of land – at least two hundred hectares – an[d] [•] [m]ade for a sizable defense perimeter, penetrating which [•] instant risks. He spotted a total of three large, dark vehic[e] Chevy Suburbans, which could not have been more obv[i]- ously the transport for the targets and their protectors. How many? He saw two people standing in the open, but the vehicles would have at least four guards each. The vehicles would be armored, and equipped with heavy weapons. One way in, and one way out. Almost a kilometer out to the main road. What about the water? Movie Star thought, driving to the end. Ah. There was a Coast Guard cutter there, a small one, but it would have a radio, and that made it large enough.

He stopped the car at the cul-de-sac, getting out to look at a house with a for-sale sign in the yard. He retrieved the morning paper from the car, ostentatiously checking the folded page against the number, then looking around some more. He had to be quick about it. The guards would be wary, and though they couldn't check everything – even the American Secret Service had limits on its time and resources – he couldn't afford to dawdle. His initial impressions were not at all favorable. Access was limited. So many students – picking out the right two would be difficult. The guards were many and dispersed. That was the bad part. Numbers mat- tered less than physical space. The most difficult defense to breach was a defense in depth, because depth meant both space *and* time. You could neutralize any number of people in a matter of seconds if you had the proper weapons and they were bunched up. But give them anything more than five seconds, and their training would kick in. The guards would be well-drilled. They'd have plans, some predictable, some not. That Coast Guard boat, for example, could dart into shore and take the targets clear. Or the guards could retreat with their charges to an isolated point and fight it out, and Movie Star had no illusions about their training and dedication. Give them as much as five minutes, and they'd win. They'd call in help from the local police force – which even had helicopters; he'd checked – and the attacking force would be cut off. No, this was not a favored site. He tossed the newspaper back into the car and drove off. On the way out, he looked on the street for a covert vehicle. There were

533

ans parked in driveways, none of them with darkened
c on the windows which might conceal a man with a
era. His peripheral vision confirmed his assessment. This
as not a good location. To take these targets, it would be
ar better to do it on the fly. On the road, more correctly.
But not much better. The protection for that would probably
be excellent. Kevlar panels. Lexan windows. Special tires.
And doubtless overhead protection in the form of helicopters.
That didn't even count the unmarked cars and ready access
to supplementary police reinforcement.

Okay, Movie Star thought, using in his mind an American-
ism that had universal application. Giant Steps Day Care
Center and Nursery School, Ritchie Highway above Joyce
Lane. Only one target there, but a better one, and probably,
Movie Star hoped, a more favorable tactical environment.

Winston had been in the business of selling himself and his
ideas for more than twenty years. Along with it had come a
certain theatrical sense. Better yet, the stage fright went in
both directions. Only one of the senators on the committee
had previous experience, and he was in the minority party –
the polarity of the Senate had changed with the 747 crash,
and done so in his ideological favor. As a result, the men and
women taking their seats behind the massive oak bench were
every bit as nervous as he was. While he took his seat and
set out his papers, a total of six people were piling up huge
bound volumes on the next table over. Winston ignored
them. The C-SPAN cameras did not.

It soon got better. While the Secretary-designate chatted
with Mark Gant, the latter's portable computer open and
operating in front of him, the table to their left groaned and
crashed, spilling the pile of books to the floor, to the collective gasp of everyone in the room. Winston turned, startled
and pleased. His gofers had done exactly what he'd told them,
piling the collected volumes of the United States Tax Code
right in the middle of the table instead of distributing the
load evenly.

'Oh, shit, George,' Gant whispered, struggling not to laugh.

'Maybe God really is on our side.' He jumped up to see
that nobody had been hurt. Nobody had. The first oaken cry
of protest had made the people stand back. Now security

guards darted in, only to see that nothing, really, ha[...]
pened. Winston leaned into the microphone.

'Mr Chairman, sorry about that, but it doesn't really [...]
anything. Can we proceed without further delay?'

The chairman gaveled the room to order, without taking
his eyes off the disaster. A minute later, George Winston was
sworn.

'Do you have an opening statement, Mr Winston?'

'Sir, I did.' SecTreas shook his head and stifled a laugh,
though not quite all the way. 'I guess I have to apologize to
the members of the committee for our little accident. I'd
meant that to be an illustration of one of my points, but . . .
well . . .' He rearranged his papers and sat more erect in his
chair.

'Mr Chairman, members of the committee, my name is
George Winston, and President Ryan has asked me to step
away from my business to serve my country in the capacity
of Secretary of the Treasury. Let me tell you a little bit about
myself . . .'

'What do we know about him?' Kealty asked.

'Plenty. He's smart. He's tough. He's pretty honest. And
he's richer 'n God.' *Even richer than you*, the aide didn't say.

'Ever investigated?'

'Never.' His chief of staff shook his head. 'Maybe he's
skated on thin ice, but – no, Ed, I can't even say that. The
book on Winston is that he plays by the rules. His investment
group is highly rated for performance and integrity. He had
a bad trader working for him eight years ago, and George
personally testified against him in court. He also made good
the guy's shenanigans out of his own pocket. His own *personal* pocket, that is. Forty million dollars' worth. The crook
served five years. He's a good choice for Ryan. He's no politician, but he's well respected on the Street.'

'Shit,' Kealty observed.

'Mr Chairman, there are a lot of things that need to be done.'
Winston set his opening statement aside and continued off
the cuff. Or so it seemed. He jerked his left hand to the pile
of books. 'That broken table over there. That's the US Tax
Code. It's a principle of common law that ignorance of the

...ot a defense before the bar of justice. But that doesn't sense anymore. The Treasury Department and the ...nal Revenue Service both promulgate and enforce the ... law of our country. Excuse me, those laws are passed by ...e Congress, as we all know, but mainly they happen because my department submits the proposed set of rules, and the Congress modifies and approves them, and then we enforce them. In many cases, the interpretation of the code you pass is left to people who work for me, and as we all know, the interpretation can be as important as the laws themselves. We have special tax courts to make further rulings – but what we end up with is that pile of printed paper over there, and I would submit to this committee that *nobody*, not even an experienced member of the bar, can possibly understand it all.

'We even have the absurd situation that when a citizen brings his tax records and return forms into an IRS office for assistance from the people who enforce the law, and those IRS employees make a mistake, then the *citizen* who comes to his government for help is responsible for the mistakes the *government* makes. Now, when I was in the trading business, if I gave my client a bad piece of advice, I had to take the responsibility for it.

'The purpose of taxes is to provide revenue for the country's government so that the government can serve the people. But along the way we've created an entire industry that takes billions of dollars from the public. Why? To explain a tax code that gets more complex every year, a code that the enforcement people themselves do not understand with a sufficient degree of confidence to undertake responsibility for getting it right. You already know, or you should' – they didn't – 'the amount of money we spend on *enforcing* that tax code, and that's not especially productive, either. We're supposed to be working for the people, not confusing them.

'And so, Mr Chairman, there are some things I hope to be able to accomplish during my term at Treasury, if the committee sees fit to confirm my nomination. First, I want the tax code completely rewritten into something a normal person can understand. I want that tax code to make sense. I want a code with no special breaks. I want the same rules

to apply equally to everybody. I am prepared to presen
proposal to do exactly that. I want to work with the comm,
tee to make that into law. I want to work with you ladie.
and gentlemen. I will *not* let any corporate or any other form
of lobbyist into my office to discuss this matter, and here
and now, I beseech you to do the same. Mr Chairman, when
we start talking to every Tom, Dick, and Harry who has a
little suggestion to take care of a special group with special
needs, we end up with that!' Winston pointed to the broken
table again. 'We're all Americans. We're supposed to work
together, and in the long run, tweaking the tax laws of our
country for every lobbyist with an office and a clientele ultimately takes *more* money from everybody. The laws of our
country are not supposed to be a jobs program for accountants
and lawyers in the private sector, and bureaucrats in the
public sector. The laws which you pass and which people
like me enforce are supposed to serve the needs of the citizens, not the needs of the government.

'Second, I want my department to run efficiently. *Efficiency* is not a word that government knows how to spell,
much less implement. That has to change. Well, I can't
change this whole city, but I *can* change the department with
which the President has entrusted me, and which, I hope,
you will let me have. I know how to run a business. The
Columbus Group serves literally millions of people, directly
and indirectly, and I've borne that burden with pride. I will,
in the next few months, submit a budget for a Department
of the Treasury that doesn't have so much as *one* excess
position.' It was a considerable exaggeration, but nonetheless
an impressive one. 'This room has heard such claims before,
and I will not blame you for taking my words with a ton of
salt, but I am a man accustomed to backing up my words
with results, and that's going to happen here, too

'President Ryan had to yell at me to get me to move into
Washington. I don't *like* it here, Mr Chairman,' Winston told
the committee. He had them now. 'I want to do my job and
leave. But the job is going to get done, if you let me. That
concludes my opening statement.'

The most experienced people in the room were the
reporters in the second row – the first row had Winston's
wife and family. They knew how things were done and how

...gs were said. A cabinet officer was supposed to wax rhap-
...ic about the honor of being allowed to serve, about the
...y of being entrusted with power, about the responsibility
...hat would bear heavily upon him or her.

I don't like it here! The reporters stopped writing their
notes and looked up, first at the dais, and then at one another.

Movie Star liked what he saw. Though the danger to him
was greater, the risk was balanced. Here there was a main
four-lane highway within a few meters of the objective, and
that led to an infinite network of side roads. Best of all, you
could see almost everything. Directly behind the objective
was a clump of woods, dense enough that it could not hold
a support vehicle. There had to be one, and where would it
be . . . ? Hmm, *there*, he thought. There was one house close
enough with an attached garage that actually faced the day-
care center and that one . . . yes. Two cars parked right in
front of that house – why weren't they parked inside? So
probably the Secret Service had made an arrangement with
the owners. It was ideal, fifty meters from the demi-school,
facing in the right direction. If something untoward happened, the alarm would be issued, and the support vehicle
would instantly be manned, the garage door opened, and out
it would race like a tank, except that it wasn't a tank.

The problem with security in a case such as this was that
you had to set your procedures in stone, and clever as the
Secret Service people undoubtedly were, their arrangements
had to fit parameters both known and predictable. He
checked his watch. How to confirm his suspicions? For starters, he needed a few minutes at rest. Directly across from
Giant Steps was a convenience store, and that he'd check,
because the enemy would have a person there, maybe more
than one. He pulled in, parked the car, and went in, spending
a minute or so blundering about.

'Can I help you?' a voice asked. Female, twenty-five – no
older than that, but trying to look young. One did that with
the cut of the hair and a little makeup, Movie Star knew.
He'd used female operatives himself, and that's what he'd
told them. Younger people always appear less threatening,
especially the females. With a smile of confusion and embarrassment, he walked to the counter.

'I'm looking for your maps,' he said.

'Right there under the counter.' The clerk pointed smile. She was Secret Service. The eyes were too brig the person to be in such a menial job.

'*Ach*,' he said in disgust, selecting a large book map th would show every residential street in the district – county, they called them in America. He lifted it and flipped pages, one eye trained across the street. The children were being led outside to the playground. Four adults with them. Two would have been the normal number. So, at least two – three, he realized, spotting a man in the shadows, hardly moving at all. Large man, 180 centimeters or so, wearing casual clothes. Yes, the playground faced the dwelling with the garage. The watchers *had* to be there. Two more, perhaps three, would be in the dwelling, always watching. This would not exactly be easy, but he *would* know where the opposition was. 'How much for the map?'

'Printed right there on the cover.'

'*Ach, ja*, excuse me.' He reached into his pocket. 'Five dollar, ninety-five,' he said to himself, fishing for the change.

'Plus tax.' She rang it up on the register. 'Are you new to the area?'

'Yes, I am. I am teacher.'

'Oh, what do you teach?'

'German,' he replied, taking his change, and counting it. 'I want to see what houses are like here. Thank you for the map. I have much to do.' A curt European nod punctuated the encounter, and he left without a further look across the street. Movie Star had a sudden chill. The clerk had definitely been a police type. She'd be watching him right now, probably taking down his license number, but if she did, and if the Secret Service ran the number, they'd find that his name was Dieter Kolb, a German citizen from Frankfurt, a teacher of English, currently out of the country, and unless they pressed, that cover would be sufficient. He pulled north on Ritchie Highway, turning right at the first opportunity. There was a community college on a hill nearby, and in America those all had parking lots.

It was just a matter of finding a good spot. This was it. The intervening woods would soon fill out with the coming of spring, blocking visual access to Giant Steps. The rear of

, whose garage probably held the Chevy Suburban vehicle had only a few windows facing in this direc- nd those were curtained. The same was true of the nool itself. Movie Star/Kolb lifted a pair of compact oculars and scanned. It wasn't easy with all the tree unks between him and the objective, but thorough as the American Secret Service was, its people weren't perfect. None were. More to the point, Giant Steps was not a favorable location for quartering so important a child, but that wasn't surprising. The Ryan family had sent all of its children here. The teachers were probably excellent, and Ryan and his physician wife probably knew them and were friendly with them, and the news stories he'd copied down from the Internet emphasized the fact that the Ryans wanted to keep their family life intact. Very human. And foolish.

He watched the children cavort on the playground. It seemed to be covered with wood chips. How natural it all was, the little ones cocooned in bulky winter clothes – the temperature was eleven or twelve, he estimated – and running about, some on the monkey bars, others on swings, still more playing in what dirt they could find. The manner of dress told him that these children were well looked-after, and they were, after all, children. Except for one. Which one he couldn't tell from this distance – they'd need photos for that, when the time came – but that one wasn't a child at all. That one was a political statement for someone to make. Who would make the statement, and exactly why the statement would be made didn't concern Movie Star. He'd remain in his perch for several hours, not thinking at all about what might result from his activities. Or might not. He didn't care. He'd write up his memorized notes, draw his detailed maps and diagrams, and forget about it. 'Kolb' was years past caring about it all. What had begun with religious fervor for the liberating Holy War of his people had, with the passage of time, become work for which he was paid. If, in the end, something happened which he found politically beneficial, so much the better, but somehow that had never taken place, despite all the hopes and dreams and fiery rhetoric, and what sustained him was the work and his skill at it. How strange, Movie Star thought, that it should have become so, but the passionate ones were mainly dead, victims of their own dedi-

cation. His face grimaced at the irony of it. The true be__
done in by their own passion, and those who sustaine__
hope of his people were those who . . . didn't care anym__
Was that true?

'Many people will object to the nature of your proposed tax plan. A really fair plan is progressive,' the senator went on. Predictably, he was one of the survivors, not one of the new arrivals. He had the mantra down. 'Doesn't this place rather a high burden on working Americans?'

'Senator, I understand what you're saying,' Winston replied after taking a sip from his water glass. 'But what do you mean when you say "working" Americans? I work. I built my business from the ground up and, believe me, that's work. The First Lady, Cathy Ryan, makes something like four hundred thousand dollars per year – much more than her husband, I might add. Does that mean she doesn't work? I think she does. She's a surgeon. I have a brother who's a physician, and I know the hours he works. True, those two people make more than the average American does, but the market-place has long since decided that the work they do is more valuable than what some other people do. If you're going blind, a union auto worker can't help you; neither can a lawyer. A physician can. That doesn't mean that the physician doesn't *work*, Senator. It means that the work requires higher qualifications and much longer training, and that as a result the work is more highly compensated. What about a baseball player? That's another category of skilled work, and nobody in this room objects to the salary paid Ken Griffey, Jr., for example. Why? Because he's superb at what he does, one of the – what? – four or five best in the entire world, and he is lavishly compensated for it. Again, that's the marketplace at work.

'In a broader sense, speaking in my capacity as a mere citizen instead of a Secretary-designate, I object strongly to the artificial and mainly false dichotomy that some people in the political arena place between blue-collar and white-collar workers. There is no way to earn an honest living in this country except by providing a product or a service to the public and, generally speaking, the harder and smarter you work, the more money you make. It's just that some people

eater abilities than others. If there is an idle-rich class
.....erica, I think the only place you find them is in the
.....ies. Who in this room, if you had the choice, would not
.....tantly trade places with Ken Griffey or Jack Nicklaus?
.....on't all of us dream about being *that* good at something? I
do,' Winston admitted. 'But I can't swing a bat that hard.

'Okay, what about a really talented software engineer? I
can't do that, either. What about an inventor? What about
an executive who transforms a company from a loser to a
profit-maker – remember what Samuel Gompers said? The
worst failure of a captain of industry is to fail to show a
profit. Why? Because a profitable company is one that does
its job well, and only those companies can compensate their
workers properly, and at the same time return money to their
shareholders – and those are the people who invest
their money in the *company* which generated *jobs* for its
workers.

'Senator, the thing we forget is why we're here and what
we're trying to do. The government doesn't provide productive jobs. That's not what we're supposed to do. General
Motors and Boeing and Microsoft are the ones who employ
workers to turn out products the people need. The job of
government is to protect the people, to enforce the law, and
to make sure people play by the rules, like the umpires on
a ball field. It's not supposed to be our job, I think, to punish
people for playing the game well.

'We collect taxes so that the government can perform its
functions. But we've gotten away from that. We should collect those taxes in such a way as to do minimum harm to
the economy as a whole. Taxes are by their very nature a
negative influence, and we can't get away from that, but
what we can do is at least structure the tax system in such a
way that it does minimum harm, and maybe even encourages
people to use their money in such a way as to encourage the
overall system to work.'

'I know where you're going. You're going to talk about
cutting capital-gains taxes, but that benefits only the few, at
the cost of – '

'Senator, excuse me for interrupting, but that simply is not
true, and you know it's not true,' Winston chided brusquely.
'Reducing the rate of tax on capital gains means the follow-

ing: it encourages people to invest their money – n...
back up a little.

'Let's say I make a thousand dollars. I pay taxes on...
money, pay my mortgage, pay for food, pay for the car,...
what I have left I invest in, oh, XYZ Computer Compan...
XYZ takes my money and hires somebody. That perso...
works at his job like I work at mine, and from what work
he does – he's making a product which the public likes and
buys, right? – the company generates a profit, which the
company shares with me. *That* money is taxed as regular
income. Then I sell the stock and buy into another company,
so that *it* can hire somebody else. The money realized from
selling the stock issue is capital gains. People don't put their
money under the mattress anymore,' he reminded them, 'and
we don't want them to. We want them to invest in America,
in their fellow citizens.

'Now, I've already paid tax on the money which I invested,
right? Okay, then I help give some fellow citizen a job. That
job makes something for the public. And for *helping* give a
worker a job, and for *helping* that worker make something
for the public, I get a modest return. That's good for that
worker I helped to hire, and good for the public. Then I move
on to do the same thing somewhere else. Why punish me
for that? Doesn't it make more sense to *encourage* people to
do that? And, remember, we've already taxed that investment money once anyway – in actual practice, more than
once.

'That isn't good for the country. It's bad enough that we
take so much, but the manner in which we take it is egregi-
ously counterproductive. Why are we here, Senator? We're
supposed to be *helping* things along, not hurting. And the
net result, remember, is a tax system so complicated that
we need to collect billions to administer it – and *that* money
is totally wasted. Toss in all the accountants and tax lawyers
who make their living off something the public can't understand,' SecTreas concluded.

'America isn't about envy. America isn't about class
rivalry. We don't *have* a class system in America. Nobody
tells an American citizen what they can do. Birth doesn't
count for much. Look at the committee members. Son of a
farmer, son of a teacher, son of a truck driver, son of a lawyer,

543

ator Nikolides, son of an immigrant. If America was defined society, then how the heck did you people re?' he demanded. His current questioner was a pro-onal politician, son of another, not to mention an arro-t son of a bitch, Winston thought, and didn't get classified. Everyone he'd just pointed to *kvelled* a little at being singled out for the cameras. 'Gentlemen, let's try and make it easier for people to do what we've all done. If we have to skew the system, then let's do it in such a way that it encourages our fellow citizens to help one another. If America has a struc-tural economic problem, it's that we don't generate as many opportunities as we should and can do. The system isn't perfect. Fine, let's try to fix it some. That's why we're all here.'

'But the system must demand that everyone pay their fair share,' the senator said, trying to take the floor back.

'What does "fair" mean? In the dictionary, it means that everyone has to do about the same. Ten percent of a million dollars is still ten times more than ten percent of a hundred thousand dollars, and *twenty* times more than ten percent of fifty thousand. But "fairness" in the tax code has come to mean that we take all the money we can from successful people and dole it back – and, oh, by the way, those rich people hire lawyers and lobbyists who talk to people in the political arena and get a million special exceptions written into the system so that they *don't* get totally fleeced – and they don't, and we all know that – and what do we end up with?' Winston waved his hand at the pile of books on the floor of the committee room. 'We end up with a jobs program for bureaucrats, and accountants, and lawyers, and lobbyists, and somewhere along the way the taxpaying citizens are just plain forgotten. We don't *care* that they can't make sense of the system that's supposed to serve them. It's not supposed to be that way.' Winston leaned into the microphone. 'I'll tell you what I think "fair" means. I think it means that we all bear the same burden in the same proportion. I think it means that the system not only allows but encourages us to participate in the economy. I think it means that we promul-gate simple and comprehensible laws so that people know where they stand. I think "fair" means that it's a level playing field, and everybody gets the same breaks, and that we don't

punish Ken Griffey for hitting home runs. We admi
We try to emulate him. We try to make more like him.
we keep out of his way.'

'Let 'em eat cake?' the chief of staff said.

'We can't say hot dogs, can we?' Kealty asked. Then r
smiled broadly. 'Finally.'

'Finally,' another aide agreed.

The results were *all* equivocal. The FBI polygrapher had been
working all morning, and every single set of tracings on the
fan-fold paper was iffy. It couldn't be helped. An all-night
session, they'd all told him, looking into something important which he wasn't cleared for. That made it the Iran/Iraq
situation, of course. He could watch CNN as well as anyone.
The men he'd put on the box were all tired and irritable, and
some had fluttered badly on telling him their proper names
and job descriptions, and the whole exercise had been useless.
Probably.

'Did I pass?' Rutledge asked, when he took off the pressur-
ized armband in the manner of someone who'd done this all
before.

'Well, I'm sure you've been told before –'

'It's not a pass-or-fail examination process,' the Under
Secretary of State said tiredly. 'Yeah, tell that to somebody
who lost his clearance because of a session on the box. I hate
the damned things, always have.'

It was right up – or down – there with being a dentist, the
FBI agent thought, and though he was one of the best around
at this particular black art, he'd learned nothing this day that
would help the investigation.

'The session you had last night –'

Rutledge cut him off cold. 'Can't discuss it, sorry.'

'No, I mean, this sort of thing normal here?'

'It will be for a while, probably. Look, you know what it's
about, probably.' The agent nodded, and the Under Secretary
did the same. 'Fine. Then you know it's a big deal, and we're
going to be burning a lot of midnight oil over it, especially
my people. So, lots of coffee and long hours and short tem-
pers.' He checked his watch. 'My working group gets together
in ten minutes. Anything else?'

'No, sir.'

nks for a fun ninety minutes,' Rutledge said, heading
e door. It was so easy. You just had to know how the
gs worked. They wanted relaxed and peaceful subjects
get proper results – the polygraph essentially measured
ension induced by awkward questions. So make everybody
tense. That was simple enough. And really the Iranians were
doing the work. All he had to do was stoke the fires a little.
That was good for a smile as he entered the executive
washroom.

There. Movie Star checked his watch and made a further
mental note . Two men walked out of the private dwelling.
One of them turned to say something as he closed the door.
They walked to the parking lot of Giant Steps, eyes scanning
around in a way that identified them as positively as uniforms and rifles. The Chevy Suburban emerged from the private garage. A good hiding place, but a little too obvious to
the skilled observer. Two children came out together, one
led by a woman, the other by a man . . . yes, the one who'd
been in the shadowed doorway when they'd gone out for
their afternoon playtime. Large man, formidable one. Two
women, one in front, one behind. All the heads turning and
scanning. They took the child to a plain car. The Suburban
halted in front of the driveway, and the other cars followed it
down the highway, with a police car, he saw, fifteen seconds
behind.
   It would be a difficult task, but not an impossible one, and
the mission had several different outcomes, all acceptable to
his patrons. Just as well that he didn't get sentimental about
children. He'd been involved in such missions before, and
you simply couldn't look at them as children at all. The one
who'd been led by the large hand of her bodyguard was what
he'd decided before, a political statement to be made by
someone else. Allah would not have approved. Movie Star
knew that. There was not a religion in the world that sanc-
tioned harm to a child, but religions were not instruments
of statecraft, regardless of what Badrayn's current superior
might believe. Religions were something for an ideal world,
and the world wasn't ideal. And so one might use unusual
means to serve religious goals, and that meant . . . something
he simply didn't think about. It was business, his business,

to see what could be done, rules or not, and Movie Star wasn't the least bit sanctimonious about it, which, he thought, was probably why he was still alive while others were not – and, if he read this properly, still others would not be.

28

. . . BUT A WHIMPER

Politicians rarely like surprises. Much as they enjoy dropping them on others – mainly other politicians, usually in public, and invariably delivered with all the care and planning of a jungle ambush – they reciprocally detest being on the receiving end. And that was just the political sort, in countries where politics was a fairly civilized business.

In Turkmenistan, things had not gotten that far yet. The Premier – he had a wide variety of titles to choose from, and he liked this one better than 'president' – enjoyed everything about his life and his office. As a chieftain of the semi-departed Communist Party, he would have lived under greater personal restrictions than were now the case, and would always be at the end of a telephone line to Moscow, like a brook fish at the end of a long leader. But not now. Moscow no longer had the reach, and he had become too large a fish. He was a vigorous man in his late fifties and, as he liked to joke, a man of the people. The 'people' in this case had been an attractive clerk of twenty years who, after an evening of fine dining and a little ethnic dancing (at which he excelled), had entertained him as only a young woman could, and now he was driving back to his official residence under a clear, starry sky, sitting in the right-front seat of his black Mercedes with the sated smile of a man who'd just proven that that's what he was, in the best possible way. Perhaps he'd wangle a promotion for the girl . . . in a few weeks. His was the exercise of, if not absolute power, then surely enough for any man, and with that came near-utter contentment. Popular with his people as an earthy, common-folk sort of leader, he knew how to act, how to sit with the people, how to grasp a hand or a shoulder, always in front of TV cameras to show that he was one of them. 'Cult of personality' was what the former regime had called it, and that's what it was, and that, he knew for sure, was what all politics had to be. His was a great responsibility, and he met that duty, and in return he was owed some things. One of them was this fine German automobile – smuggling that into the country had been an exercise in panache rather than corruption – and another was now returning to her bed with a smile and a sigh. And life was good. He didn't know he had less than sixty seconds of it left.

He didn't bother with a police escort. His people loved him. He was sure of that, too, and besides it was late. But there was a police car, he saw, at an intersection, its light turning and flashing, blocking the way, just beyond the cross street. A dismounted policeman raised his hand while talking into his radio, hardly even looking at them. The Premier wondered what the problem was. His driver/bodyguard slowed the Mercedes with an annoyed snort, stopping it right in the intersection and making sure his pistol was readily accessible. Barely had the official car stopped when both of them heard a noise to their right. The Premier turned that way, and scarcely had time for his eyes to go wide before the Zil-157 truck hit him at forty kilometers per hour. The high military-style bumper hit just at the bottom of the door glass, and the official car was thrown ten meters to the left, stopping when it hit the stone walls of an office building. Then it was time for the policeman to walk over, assisted by two others who had appeared from the shadows. The driver was dead from a broken neck. The policemen could see that from the angle of his head, and one of them reached through the shattered windshield to shake it around, just to make sure. But the Premier, to everyone's astonishment, was still moaning, despite his injuries. Due to all the drink, they thought, his body limp and limber. Well, that was easily fixed. The senior cop walked to the truck, flipped open the tool box, took a tire iron, returned, and smashed it against the side of his Premier's head just forward of the ear. That task completed, he tossed the tool back to the truck driver, and the premier of Turkmenistan was dead as the result of an auto accident. Well, then, their country would have to have elections, wouldn't it? That would be something of a first, and it would call for a leader whom the people knew and respected.

*   *   *

'Senator, it's been a long day,' Tony Bretano agreed. 'And it's been rather a long couple of weeks for me, learning the ropes and meeting the people, but, you know, management is management, and the Department of Defense has been without it for quite some time. I am especially concerned with the procurement system. It takes too long and costs too much. The problem isn't so much corruption as an attempt to impose a standard of fairness so exacting that – well, as a pedestrian example, if you bought food the way DOD is forced to buy weapons, you'd starve to death in the supermarket while trying to decide between Libby and DelMonte pears. TRW is an engineering company, and to my way of thinking, a very good one. There's no way I could run my company like this. My stockholders would lynch me. We can do better, and I intend to see that we do.'

'Mr Secretary-designate,' the senator asked, 'how much longer does this have to go on? We just won a war and –'

'Senator, America has the best medical care in the world, but people still die from cancer and heart disease. The best isn't always good enough, is it? But more than that, and more to the point, we can do better for less money. I am not going to come to you with a request for increased overall funding. Acquisition funding will have to be higher, yes. Training and readiness will be higher also. But the real money in defense goes out in personnel costs, and that is where we can make a difference. The whole department is overmanned in the wrong places. That wastes the taxpayers' money. I know. I pay a lot of taxes. We do not utilize our people effectively, and nothing, Senator, is more wasteful than that. I think I can promise you a net reduction of two or three percent. Maybe more if I can get a handle on the acquisition system. For the latter, I need statutory assistance. There's no reason why we have to wait eight to twelve years to field a new airplane. We study things to death. That was once meant to save money, and maybe once it was a good idea, but now we spend more money on studies than we do on real R and D. It's time to stop inventing the wheel every two years. Our citizens *work* for the money we spend, and we owe it to them to spend it intelligently.

'Most important of all, when America sends her sons and daughters into harm's way, they *must be* the best-trained, best-supported, best-equipped forces we can put into the field. The fact of the matter is that we can do that and save money also, by making the system work more efficiently.' The nice thing about this new crop of senators, Bretano reflected, was they didn't know what was impossible. He would never have gotten away with what he'd just said as recently as a year earlier. Efficiency was a concept foreign to most government agencies, not because there was anything wrong with the people, but because nobody had ever told them to do better. There was much to be said for working at the place that printed the money, but there was much to be said for eating eclairs, too, until your arteries clogged up. If the heart of America were its government, the nation would long since have fallen over dead. Fortunately, his country's heart was elsewhere, and surviving on healthier food.

'But why do we need so much defense in an age when –'

Bretano cut him off again. It was a habit he'd have to break, which he knew even as he did it – but this was too much. 'Senator, have you checked the building across the street lately?'

It was amusing to see the way the man's head jerked back, even though the aide to Bretano's left flinched almost as badly. That senator had a vote, both on the committee and on the floor of the Senate chamber, which was still open for business now that they'd gotten the smoke out of the building. But the point got across to most of the others, and the SecDef was willing to settle for that. In due course, the chairman gaveled the session to a close, and scheduled a vote for the following morning. The senators had already made their votes clear with their praise for Bretano's forthright and positive statement, pledging their desire to work with him in words almost as naive as his own, and with that another day ended on one place, with a new one soon to begin in another.

No sooner had the UN resolution passed, than the first ship had sailed for the brief steam to the Iraqi port of Bushire, there to be unloaded by the huge vacuum cleanerlike structures, and from that point on, things had gone quickly. For the first morning in many years, there would be bread enough on the breakfast tables of Iraq for everyone. Morning television proclaimed the fact for all – with the predictable live shots of neighborhood bakeries selling off their wares to happy, smiling crowds – and then concluding with word that the new revolutionary government was meeting today to discuss other matters of national importance. These signals were duly copied down at PALM BOWL and STORM TRACK and passed along, but the real news that day came from another source.

Golovko told himself that the Turkoman Premier might well have died in an accident. His personal proclivities were well known to the RVS, and vehicle accidents were hardly unknown in his country or any other – in fact, auto mishaps had been hugely disproportionate in the Soviet Union, especially those associated with drink. But Golovko had never been one to believe in coincidences of any sort, most particularly those which happened in ways and at times inconvenient to his country. It didn't help that he had ample assets in place to diagnose the problem. The Premier was dead. There would be elections. The likely winner was obvious because the departed politician had been wonderfully effective stifling political opposition. And now also, he saw, Iranian military units were forming up for road marches to their west. Two dead chiefs of state, in such a short time, within such a short radius, both in countries bordering Iran . . . no, even if it had been a coincidence, he would not have believed it. With that, Golovko changed hats – the Western aphorism – and lifted his phone.

USS *Pasadena* was positioned between the two PRC surface-action groups, currently operating about nine miles apart. The submarine had a full load of weapons, war shots all, but for all that, it was rather like being the only cop in Times Square at midnight on New Year's, trying to keep track of everything at the same time. Having a loaded gun didn't amount to very much. Every few minutes he deployed his ESM mast to get a feel for the electronic signals being radiated about, and his sonar department also fed data to the tracking party in the after portion of the attack center – as many men as could fit around the chart table were busily keeping tabs on the various contacts. The skipper ordered his boat to go deep, to three hundred feet, just below the layer, so that he could take a few minutes to examine the plot, which had become far too complex for him to keep it all in his head. With the boat steadied up on her new depth, he took the three steps aft to look.

It was a FleetEx, but the type of FleetEx wasn't quite ... ordinarily one group played the 'good guys' against the theoretical 'bad guys' in the other group, and you could tell what was what by the way the ships were arrayed. Instead of orienting toward each other, however, both groups were oriented to the east. This was called the 'threat axis,' meaning the direction from which the enemy was expected to strike. To the east lay the Republic of China, which comprised mainly the island of Taiwan. The senior chief operations specialist supervising the plot was marking up the acetate overlay, and the picture was about as clear as it needed to be.

'Conn, sonar,' came the next call.

'Conn, aye,' the captain acknowledged, taking the microphone.

'Two new contacts, sir, designate Sierra Twenty and Twenty-one. Both appear to be submerged contacts. Sierra Twenty, bearing three-two-five, direct path and faint ... stand by ... okay, looks like a Han-class SSN, good cut on the fifty-Hertz line, plant noise also. Twenty-one, also submerged contact, at three-three-zero, starting to look like a Xia, sir.'

'A boomer in a FleetEx?' the senior chief wondered.

'How good's the cut on Twenty-one?'

'Improving now, sir,' the sonar chief replied. The entire sonar crew was in their compartment, just forward of the attack center on the starboard side. 'Plant noise says Xia to me, Cap'n. The Han is maneuvering south, bearing now three-two-one, getting a blade rate ... call its speed eighteen knots.'

'Sir?' The operations chief made a quick, notional plot. The SSN and the boomer would be behind the northern surface group.

'Anything else, sonar?' the captain asked.

'Sir, getting a little complicated with all these tracks.'

'Tell me about it,' someone breathed at the tracking table, while making another change.

'Anything to the east?' the CO persisted.

'Sir, easterly we have six contacts, all classified as merchant traffic.'

'We got 'em all here, sir,' the operations chief confirmed. 'Nothing yet from the Taiwan navy.'

'That's gonna change,' the captain thought aloud.

General Bondarenko didn't believe in coincidences, either. More than that, the southern part of the country once known as the Union of Soviet Socialist Republics held little charm for him. His time in Afghanistan and a frantic night in Tajikistan had seen to that. In the abstract he would not have minded the total divorce of the Russian Republic from the Muslim proto-nations arrayed on his country's southern border, but the real world wasn't abstract.

'So, what do you think is going on?' the general-lieutenant asked.

'Are you briefed in on Iraq?'

'Yes, I am, Comrade Chairman.'

'Then you tell me, Gennady Iosefovich,' Golovko commanded.

Bondarenko leaned across the map table, and spoke while moving a finger about. 'I would say that what concerns you is the possibility that Iran is making a bid for superpower status. In uniting with Iraq, they increase their oil wealth by something like forty percent. Moreover, that would give them contiguous borders with Kuwait and the Saudi kingdom. The conquest of those nations would redouble their wealth – one may safely assume that the lesser nations would fall as well. The objective circumstances here are self-evident,' the general went on, speaking in the calm voice of a professional soldier analyzing disaster. 'Combined, Iran and Iraq outnumber the combined populations of the other states by a considerable margin – five to one, Comrade Chairman? More? I do not recall exactly, but certainly the manpower advantage is decisive, which would make outright conquest or at least great political influence likely. That alone would give this new United Islamic Republic enormous economic power, the ability to choke off the energy supply to Western Europe and Asia at will.

'Now, Turkmenistan. If this is, as you suspect, not a coincidence, then we see that Iran wishes to move north also, perhaps to absorb Azerbaijan' – his finger traced along the map – 'Uzbekistan, Tajikistan, at least part of Kazakhstan. That would triple their population, add a significant resource base to their United Islamic Republic, and next, one assumes, Afghanistan and Pakistan, and we have a new nation stretching from the Red Sea to the Hindu Kush – *nyet*, more to the point, from the Red Sea to China, and then our southern border is completely lined with nations hostile to us.' Then he looked up.

'This is much worse than I had been led to expect, Sergey Nikolay'ch,' he concluded soberly. 'We know the Chinese covet what we have in the east. This new state threatens *our* southern oil fields in the Transcaucasus – I cannot defend this border. My God, defending against Hitler was child's play compared to this.'

Golovko was on the other side of the map table. He'd called Bondarenko for a reason. The senior leadership of his country's military was composed of holdovers from the earlier era – but these were finally dying off, and Gennady Iosefovich was one of the new breed, battle-tested in the misbegotten Afghan War, old enough to know what battle was – perversely, this made him and his peers the superiors of those whom they would soon replace – and young enough that they didn't have the ideological baggage of the former generation, either. Not a pessimist, but an optimist ready to learn from the West, where he'd just spent over a month with the various NATO armies, learning everything he could – especially, it would seem, from the Americans. But Bondarenko was looking down at the map in alarm.

'How long?' the general asked. 'How long to establish this new state?'

Golovko shrugged. 'Who can say? Three years, perhaps two at the worst. At best, five.'

'Give me five years and the ability to rebuild our country's military power, and we can . . . probably . . . no.' Bondarenko shook his head. 'I can give you no guarantee. The government will not give me the money and resources I require. It can't. We do not have the money to spend.'

'And then?' The general looked up, straight into the RVS chairman's eyes.

'And then I would prefer to be the operations officer for

the other side. In the east we have mountains to defend, and that is good, but we have only two rail lines for logistical support, and that is *not* so good. In the center, what if they absorb all of Kazakhstan?' He tapped the map. 'Look how close that puts them to Moscow. And what about alliances? With Ukraine, perhaps? What about Turkey? What about Syria? All of the Middle East will have to come to terms with this new state . . . we lose, Comrade Chairman. We can threaten to use nuclear arms – but what real good does that do us? China can afford the loss of five hundred million, and still outnumber us. Their economy grows strong while ours continues to stagnate. They can afford to buy weapons from the West, or better yet to license the designs to manufacture their own. Our use of nuclear arms is dangerous, both tactically and strategically, and there is the political dimension which I will leave to you. Militarily, we will be outnumbered in all relevant categories. The enemy will have superiority in terms of arms, manpower, and geographic location. Their ability to cut off the oil supply to the rest of the world limits our hope of securing foreign help – assuming that any Western nation will have such a desire in the first place. What you have shown me is the potential destruction of our country.' That he delivered this assessment calmly was the most disturbing fact of all. Bondarenko was not an alarmist. He was merely stating objective fact.

'And to prevent it?'

'We cannot permit the loss of the southern republics, but at the same time, how do we hold them? Take control of Turkmenistan? Fight the guerrilla campaign that would surely result? Our army is in no shape to fight that sort of war – not even one of them, and it won't be just one, will it?' Bondarenko's predecessor had been fired over the failure of the Red Army – the term and the thought died hard – to deal effectively with the Chechens. What should have been a relatively simple effort at pacification had advertised to the world that the Russian army was scarcely a shadow of what it had been only a few years before.

The Soviet Union had operated on the principle of fear, they both knew. Fear of the KGB had kept the citizens in line, and fear of what the Red Army could and *would* do to any systematic rebellion had prevented large-scale political disturbances. But what happened when the fear went away? The Soviet failure to pacify Afghanistan, that despite the most brutal measures imaginable, had been a signal to the Muslim republics that their fear was misplaced. Now the Soviet Union was gone, and what remained was a mere shadow, and now that shadow could be erased by a brighter sun to the south. Golovko could see it on his visitor's face. Russia didn't have the power she needed. For all the bluster his country could still summon to awe the West – the West still remembered the Warsaw Pact, and the specter of the massive Red Army, ready to march to the Bay of Biscay – other parts of the world knew better. Western Europe and America still remembered the steel fist which they'd seen but never felt. Those who *had* felt it knew at once when the grip lessened. More to the point, they knew the significance of the relaxed grip.

'What will you need?'

'Time and money. Political support to rebuild our military. Help from the West.' The general was still staring at the map. It was, he reflected, like being the scion of a powerful capitalist family. The patriarch had died, and he was the heir to a vast fortune – only to discover that it was gone, leaving only debts. He'd come back from America upbeat, feeling that he'd seen the way, seen the future, found a way to secure his country and do it in the proper way, with a professional army composed of long-service experts, held together by esprit de corps, proud guardians and servants of a free nation, the way the Red Army had been on its march to Berlin. But that would take years to build. As it was . . . if Golovko and the RVS were right, then the best he could hope for was that his nation would rally as it had in 1941, trade space for time, as it had in 1941, and struggle back as it had in 1942–43. The general told himself that no one could see the future; that was a gift given to no man. And perhaps that was just as well, because the past, which all men knew, rarely repeated itself. Russia had been lucky against the fascists. One could not depend upon luck.

One could depend on a cunning and unpredictable adversary. Other people could look at a map the same as he, see the distances and obstacles, discern the correlation of forces, and know that the wild card lay on another sheet of printed paper, on the other side of the globe. The classical formula was first to cripple the strong, then crush the weak, and then, later, confront the strong again in one's own good time. Knowing that, Bondarenko could do nothing about it. He was the weak one. He had his own problems. His nation could not count on friends, only the enemies she had labored so long and so hard to create.

Saleh had never known such agony. He'd seen it, and had even inflicted it in his time as part of his country's security service – but not like this, not this bad. It was as though he were now paying for every such episode all at once. His body was racked with pain throughout its entire length. His strength was formidable, his muscles firm, his personal toughness manifest. But not now. Now every gram of his tissue hurt, and when he moved slightly to assuage the hurt, all he accomplished was to move it about to a fractionally different place. The pain was so great as to blot out even the fear which should have attended it.

But not for the doctor. Ian MacGregor was wearing full surgical garb, a mask over his face, and his hands gloved – only his concentration prevented them from shaking. He'd just drawn blood with the greatest care of his life, more than he'd ever exercised with AIDS patients, with two male orderlies clamping the patient's arm while he took the samples. He'd never seen a case of hemorrhagic fever. It had been for him nothing more than an entry in a textbook, or an article in the *Lancet*. Something intellectually interesting, and distantly frightening, as was cancer, as were other African diseases, but this was here and now.

'Saleh?' the physician asked.

'. . . yes.' A word, a gasp.

'You came here how? I must know if I am to help you.'

There was no mental hesitation, no consideration of secrets or security. He paused only to take a breath, to summon the energy to answer the question. 'From Baghdad. Airplane,' he added unnecessarily.

'Africa? Have you visited Africa recently?'

'Never before.' The head turned left and right not so much as a centimeter, the eyes screwed shut. The patient was trying to be brave, and largely succeeding. 'First time Africa.'

'Have you had sexual relations recently? Last week or so,' MacGregor clarified. It seemed so cruel a question. One could theoretically get such diseases through sexual contact – maybe a local prostitute? Perhaps there was another case of this at another local hospital and it was being hushed up . . . ?

It took a moment for the man to realize what the man was asking, then another shake. 'No, no women in long time.' MacGregor could see it on his face: *Never again, not for me . . .*

'Have you had any blood lately, been given blood, I mean?'

'No.'

'Have you been in contact with anyone who had traveled anywhere?'

'No, only Baghdad, only Baghdad, I am security guard for my general, with him all time, nothing else.'

'Thank you. We're going to give you something for the pain. We're going to give you some blood, too, and try to cool you down with ice. I'll be back in a little while.' The patient nodded, and the doctor left the room, carrying the blood-filled tubes in his gloved hands. 'Bloody hell,' MacGregor breathed.

While the nurses and orderlies did their job, MacGregor had his to do. One of the blood samples he split into two, packing both with the greatest care, one for Paris and the Pasteur Institute, and the other for the Centers for Disease Control and Prevention in Atlanta. They'd go out via air express. The rest went to his lead technician, a competent Sudanese, while the doctor drafted a fax. Possible hemorrhagic fever case, it would read, giving country, city, and hospital – but first . . . he lifted his phone and called his contact in the government health department.

'Here?' the government doctor asked. 'In Khartoum? Are you sure? Where is the patient from?'

'That is correct,' MacGregor replied. 'The patient says that he came here from Iraq.'

'Iraq? Why would this disease come from there? Have you tested for the proper antibodies?' the official demanded.

'The test is being set up right now,' the Scot told the African.

'How long?'

'An hour.'

'Before you make any notifications, let me come over to see,' the official directed.

To supervise, the man meant. MacGregor closed his eyes and tightened his grip on the phone. This putative physician was a government appointee, the son of a longtime minister, and the best that could be said for this professional colleague was that while seated in his plush office he didn't endanger any living patients. MacGregor had to struggle to keep his temper in check. It was the same all over Africa. It was as though the local government were desirous to protect their tourist industry – something Sudan singularly lacked, except for some anthropologists doing digs for primitive man down south, near the Ethiopian border. But it was the same everywhere on this lush continent. The government health departments denied everything, one reason why AIDS was so out of control in central Africa. They'd all denied and denied, and they would keep denying until what percentage of their populations were dead? Ten? Thirty? Fifty? But everyone was afraid to criticize African governments and their bureaucrats. It was so easy to be called a racist – and so, better to keep quiet . . . and let people die.

'Doctor,' MacGregor persisted, 'I am confident in my diagnosis, and I have a professional duty to –'

'It can wait until I come over,' was the casual reply. It was just the African way, MacGregor knew, and there was no sense in fighting it. This battle he could not win. The Sudanese health department could have his visa lifted in minutes, and then who would treat his patients?

'Very well, Doctor. Please come over directly,' he urged.

'I have a few things I must do, and then I will come over.' That could mean all day, or even longer, and both men knew it. 'The patient is isolated?'

'Full precautions are in place,' MacGregor assured him.

'You are a fine physician, Ian, and I know I can trust you to see to it that nothing serious will happen.' The line clicked off. He'd scarcely replaced the phone receiver when the instrument rang again.

'Yes?'

'Doctor, please come to Twenty-four,' a nurse's voice told him.

He was there in three minutes. It was Sohaila. An orderly

was carrying out the emesis tray. There was blood in it. She also had come here from Iraq, MacGregor knew. Oh, my God.

'None of you have anything to fear.'

The words were somewhat reassuring, though not as much as the members of the Revolutionary Council would have liked. The Iranian mullahs were probably telling the truth, but the colonels and generals around the table had fought against Iran as captains and majors, and one never forgets battlefield enemies.

'We need you to take control of your country's military,' the senior one went on. 'As a result of your cooperation, you will retain your positions. We require only that you swear your loyalty to your new government in God's name.' There would be more to it than that. They'd be watched closely. The officers all knew that. If they put a single foot wrong, they'd be shot for it. But they had nothing in the way of options, except perhaps to be taken out and shot this afternoon. Summary execution was not exactly unknown in either Iran or Iraq, an efficient way of dealing with dissidents, real or imagined, in both countries.

Facing such a thing was so different from one side to the other. On the side of the guns, one saw it as a quick, efficient, and final way of settling things in one's favor. From the other side, it had the abrupt injustice of a helicopter crash – just enough time for your spirit to scream *No!* before the racing earth blotted everything out, the disbelief and outrage of it. Except that in this case, they actually had a choice of sorts. Certain death now, or the chance of death later. The senior surviving officers of the Iraqi military shared furtive looks. They were *not* in control of their country's military. The military, the soldiers, were with the people, or with their company officers. The former was pleased to have a surplus of food to eat for the first time in almost a full decade. The latter was pleased as well to see a new day for their country. The break from the old regime was complete. It was just a bad memory now, and there was no return to it. The men in this room could reestablish control only through the good offices of the former enemies who stood at the end of the table with the serene smiles that went along with winning, that went along with holding the gift of life in their hands like pocket change, easily given and just as easily put away. They offered no choice, really.

The titular leader of the council nodded his submission, followed in seconds by all the others, and with the gesture, the identity of their country faded into history.

From that point on, it was just a matter of making some telephone calls.

The only surprise was that it didn't happen on television. For once, the listening posts at STORM TRACK and PALM BOWL were beaten by analysts elsewhere. The TV cameras were in place, as would later be seen, but first there was business to be done, and that was recorded on satellite.

The first Iranians across the border were in motorized units which speeded down the highways under radio silence, but it was daylight, and overhead came two KH-11 satellites which cross-linked their signals to communications birds, and from there down to the reception points. The nearest to Washington were at Fort Belvoir.

'Yes,' Ryan said, lifting the phone to his ear.

'It's Ben Goodley, Mr President. It's happening now. Iranian troops are crossing the border without any opposition we can see.'

'Announcement?'

'Nothing as yet. It looks like they want to be in control first.'

Jack checked the clock on the night table. 'Okay, we'll handle it at the morning brief.' There was no sense in ruining his sleep. He had people who would work through the night for him, Ryan told himself. He'd done it often enough himself.

'Yes, sir.'

Ryan replaced the phone, and was able to go back to sleep. It was one presidential skill he was learning to master. Maybe, he thought, as he faded out again, maybe he'd learn to play golf during a crisis . . . wouldn't that be . . .

Fittingly, it was one of the pederasts. He'd been looking after a fellow criminal – this one was a murderer – and doing a proper job of it, judging by the video-tapes, which had accelerated the process.

Moudi had been careful to tell the medical orderlies to supervise the new caregivers closely. The latter had taken the ordinary precautions, wearing their gloves, washing up carefully, keeping the room clean, mopping up all the fluids. This last task had become increasingly difficult with the advancing disease process in the first group of exposed subjects. Their collective moans came through the sound pickup with enough clarity for him to know what they were going through, especially with the absence of pain medications – a violation of the Muslim rules of mercy, which Moudi set aside. The second group of subjects were doing what they'd been told, but they'd not been issued masks, and that was for a reason.

The pederast was a young man, perhaps early twenties, and he'd been surprisingly attentive to his charge. Whether out of an appreciation for the murderer's pain or just to appear to be worthy of mercy himself, it didn't matter. Moudi zoomed the camera in. The man's skin was flushed and dry, his movements slow and achy. The doctor lifted the phone. A minute later, one of the army medics came into the picture. He spoke briefly with the pederast, then poked the thermometer into his ear before leaving the room and lifting a corridor phone.

'Subject Eight has a temperature of thirty-nine-point-two and reports fatigue and aches in his extremities. His eyes are red and puffy,' the medic reported brusquely. It was to be expected that the medics would not feel the same degree of empathy for any of the test subjects that they'd felt for Sister Jean Baptiste. Even though the latter had been an infidel, at least she'd been a woman of virtue. That was manifestly not true of the men in the room, and it made things easier for everyone.

'Thank you.'

So, it was true, Moudi told himself. The Mayinga strain was indeed airborne. Now it only remained to be seen if it had fully transmitted itself, that this new victim would die from it. When half of the second group showed symptoms, they would be moved across the hall to a treatment room of their own, and the first group – they were all fatally afflicted with the Ebola – would be medically terminated.

The director would be pleased, Moudi knew. The latest

step in the experiment had been as successful as those before. It was now increasingly certain that they had a weapon in their hands such as no man had ever wielded. Isn't that wonderful, the physician observed to himself.

The flight out was always easier on the disposition. Movie Star walked through the metal detector, stopped, had the magic wand waved over him, resulting in the usual embarrassment over his gold Cross pen, and then he walked to the first-class lounge, without even looking around for the policemen who, if they were about, would stop him here and now. But they weren't, and they didn't. His carry-on bag had a leather-bound clipboard in it, but he wouldn't take that out quite yet. The flight was called in due course, and he walked to the jetway, and quickly found his seat in the front of the 747. The flight was only half full, and that made things very convenient. No sooner had the aircraft lifted off than he took out his pad and started recording all the things he'd not wished to commit to paper just yet. As usual, his photographic memory helped, and he worked for three solid hours until, over mid-Atlantic, he succumbed to the need for sleep. He suspected, correctly, that he'd need it.

29

FULL COURT

It might be his last shot, Kealty knew, again using in his own mind a metaphor denoting firearms. The irony of it never registered. He had more important things to do. The previous evening he had been summoning his remaining press contacts – the reliable ones. Others had, if not exactly backed away, at least maintained a discreet distance in their uncertainty, but for most, it wasn't all that hard to get their attention, and his two-hour midnight meeting had been called on the basis of a few key words and phrases known to excite their professional sensibilities. After that all he had to do was set the rules. This was all on background, not for attribution, not to be quoted. The reporters agreed, of course.

'It's pretty disturbing. The FBI subjected the whole top floor of the State Department to lie-detector tests,' he told them. It was something they'd heard about but not yet confirmed. This would count as confirmation. 'But more disturbingly, look at the policies we're seeing now. Build up defense under this Bretano guy – a guy who's grown up within the military-industrial complex. He says he wants to eliminate all the safeguards within the procurement system, wants to slash congressional oversight. And George Winston, what does he want to do? Wreck the tax system, make it more regressive, do away with capital-gains entirely – and why? To lay the country's whole tax burden on the middle and working classes and give the big shots a free ride, that's why.

'I never figured Ryan for a professional, for a competent sort of man to occupy the presidency, but I have to tell you, this is not what I expected. He's a reactionary, a radical conservative – I'm not sure what you'd call him.'

'Are you sure about the thing at State?' the *New York Times* asked.

Kealty nodded. 'Positive, hundred percent. You mean you people haven't – come on, are you doing *your* job?' he asked tiredly. 'In the middle of a Mideast crisis, he has the FBI harassing the most senior people we have, trying to accuse them of stealing a letter that was never there.'

'And now,' Kealty's chief of staff added, seeming to speak out of turn, 'we have the *Washington Post* about to run a canonization piece on Ryan.'

'Wait a minute,' the *Post* reporter said, straightening his back, 'that's Bob Holtzman, not my doing. I *told* my AME that it wasn't a good idea.'

'Who's the leak?' Kealty asked.

'I don't have a clue. Bob never lets that out. You know that.'

'So what is Ryan doing at CIA? He wants to *triple* the Directorate of Operations – the spies. Just what the country needs, right? What is Ryan doing?' Kealty asked rhetorically. 'Beefing up defense. Rewriting the tax code to benefit the fat cats. And taking CIA back to the days of the Cold War. We're going back to the 1950s – *why?*' Kealty demanded. '*Why* is he doing all this? What is he thinking about? Am I the only one in this city asking questions? When are you people going to do your job? He's trying to bully Congress, and succeeding, and where is the media? Who's protecting the people out there?'

'What are you saying, Ed?' the *Times* asked.

The gesture of frustration was done with consummate skill. 'I'm standing in my own political grave here. I have nothing to gain by this, but I *can't* just stand by and do nothing. Even if Ryan has the entire power of our government behind him, I can't just let him and his cronies try to concentrate all of the power of our government in a few hands, increase their own ability to spy on us, load the tax system in such a way as to further enrich people who've never paid their fair share, reward the defense industry – what's next, trashing the civil rights laws? He's flying his wife to work every day, and you people haven't even remarked that that's never happened before. This is an imperial presidency like Lyndon Johnson never dreamed of, *without* a Congress to do anything about it. You know what we have here now?' Kealty gave them a moment. 'King Jack the First. Somebody's supposed to care about that. Why is it that you people don't?'

'What do you know about the Holtzman piece?' the *Boston Globe* wanted to know.

'Ryan has a lively history in CIA. He's killed people.'

'James fucking Bond,' Kealty's chief of staff said on cue. The *Post* reporter then had to defend his publication's honor:

'Holtzman doesn't say that. If you mean the time the terrorists came to –'

'No, not that. Holtzman's going to write about the Moscow thing. Ryan didn't even set that up. It was Judge Arthur Moore, when he was DCI. Ryan was the front man. It's bad enough anyway. It interfered with the inner workings of the old Soviet Union, and it never occurred to anyone that *maybe* that wasn't such a great idea – I mean, what the hell, right, screwing around with the government of a country with ten thousand warheads pointed at us – you know, people, that's called an act of war, like? And why? To rescue their head thug from a purge for stepping over the line *so that* we could crack a spy ring inside CIA. I bet he didn't tell Holtzman that, did he?'

'I haven't seen the story,' the *Post* reporter admitted. 'I've only heard a few things.' It was almost worthy of a smile. Kealty's sources inside the paper were better than those of the senior political reporter. 'Okay, you say Ryan has killed people like James Bond. Support that,' he said in a flat voice.

'Four years ago, remember the bombs in Colombia, took out some cartel members?' Kealty waited for the nod. 'That was a CIA operation. Ryan went to Colombia – and that was *another* act of war, people. That's two that I know about.'

It was amusing to Kealty that Ryan was so skillfully conniving at his own destruction. The PLAN BLUE move within CIA was already rippling through the Directorate of Intelligence, many of whose senior people faced either early retirement or the diminution of their bureaucratic empires, and many of those enjoyed walking the corridors of power. It was easy for them to think that they were vital to the security of their country, and thinking that, they had to do something, didn't they? More than that, Ryan had stepped on a lot of bureaucratic toes at Langley, and now it was payback time, all the better that he was a higher target than ever before, that the sources were, after all, merely talking to the former Vice President of the United States – maybe even the real

President, they could say – and not to the media, which was, after all, against the law, as opposed to a legitimate discussion of vital national policy.

'How sure of that are you?' the *Globe* asked.

'I have dates. Remember when Admiral James Greer died? He was Ryan's mentor. He probably set up the operation from his deathbed. Ryan didn't attend the funeral. He was in Colombia then. That's a fact, and you can check it,' Kealty insisted. 'Probably that's why James Cutter committed suicide –'

'I thought that was an accident,' the *Times* said. 'He was out jogging, and –'

'And he just happened to step in front of a transit bus? Look, I'm not saying that Cutter was murdered. I am saying that he was implicated in the illegal operation that Ryan was running, and he didn't want to face the music. That gave Jack Ryan the chance to cover his tracks. You know,' Kealty concluded, 'I've underestimated this Ryan fellow. He's as slick an operator as this town has seen since Allen Dulles, maybe Bill Donovan – but the time for that is past. We don't need a CIA with three times as many spies. We don't need to pile more dollars into defense. We don't need to redraft the tax code to protect the millionaires Ryan hangs out with. For sure we don't need a President who thinks the 1950s were just great. He's doing things to our country which we cannot allow to happen. I don't know' – another gesture of frustration – 'maybe I have to go it all alone on this. I'm – I know I risk ruining my reputation for all history, standing up like this . . . but, damn it, once I swore an oath to the Constitution of our country . . . first time,' he went on in a quiet, reflective voice, 'when I won my first House seat . . . then into the Senate . . . and then when Roger asked me to step up and be his Vice President. You know, you don't forget that sort of thing . . . an', an', an' maybe I'm not the right guy for this, okay? Yes, I've done some pretty awful things, betrayed my wife, lived in a bottle for so many years. The American people probably deserve somebody better than me to stand up and do what's right . . . but I'm all there is, and I can't – I *can't* break faith with the people who sent me to this town, no matter what it costs. Ryan is *not* the President of the United States. He knows that. Why else is he trying to change so many things so fast? Why is he trying to bully the senior people at State into lying? Why is he playing with abortion rights? Why is he playing with the tax code through this plutocrat Winston? He's trying to buy it. He's going to continue to bully Congress until the fat cats try to have him elected king or something. I mean, who represents the *people* right now?'

'I just don't see him that way, Ed,' the *Globe* responded, after a few seconds. 'His politics are pretty far to the right, but he comes across as sincere as hell.'

'What's the first rule of politics?' the *Times* asked with a chuckle. Then he continued: 'I tell you, if this stuff about Russia and Colombia is true . . . whoa! It is the '50s, fucking around with other governments that way. We're not supposed to do that anymore, sure as hell not at that level.'

'You never got this from us, and you can't reveal the source at Langley.' The chief of staff handed out tape cassettes. 'But there are enough verifiable facts here to back up everything we've told you.'

'It's going to take a couple of days,' the *San Francisco Examiner* said, fingering the cassette and looking at his colleagues. The race started now. Every reporter in the room would want to be the first to break the story. That process would start with them playing their tapes in their cars during the drive to their homes, and the one with the shortest drive had the advantage.

'Gentlemen, all I can say is, this is an important story, and you have to apply your best professional conduct to it. It's not for me,' Kealty said. 'I wish I could pick someone else to do this, someone with a better record – but I can't. Not for me. It's for the country, and that means you have to play it as straight as you can.'

'We will, Ed,' the *Times* promised. He checked his watch. Almost three in the morning. He'd work all day to make the ten PM deadline. In that time he'd have to verify, re-verify, and conference in with his assistant managing editor to make sure that he got the front page, above the fold. The West Coast papers had the advantage – three more hours because of time zones – but he knew how to beat them to the punch. The coffee cups went down on the table, and the journalists rose, tucking their personal minitape machines in their jacket pockets, and each holding his personal cassette in the left hand while the right fished for the car keys.

'Talk to me, Ben,' Jack commanded barely four hours later.

'Still nothing on the local TV, but we've caught microwave stuff transmitted for later broadcast.' Goodley paused as Ryan took his seat behind the desk. 'Quality is too poor to show you, but we have the audio tracks. Anyway, they spent all day consolidating power. Tomorrow, they go public. Probably the word's out on the street, and the official stuff will be for the rest of the world.'

'Smart,' the President observed.

'Agreed.' Goodley nodded. 'New wild card. The Premier of Turkmenistan bit the big one, supposedly an automobile accident. Golovko called me about – just after five, I think – to let us know. He ain't a real happy camper at the moment. He thinks that Iraq and Turko-land are part of the same play –'

'Do we have anything to support that?' Ryan asked, tying his necktie. It was a dumb question.

'You kidding, boss? We don't have crap, not even overheads in this case.'

Jack looked down at his desktop for a second. 'You know, for all the things people say about how powerful CIA is –'

'Hey, I work there, remember? Thank God for CNN. Yeah, I know. Good news, the Russians are telling us at least some of what they know.'

'Scared,' the President observed.

'Very,' the national intelligence officer agreed.

'Okay, we have Iran taking over Iraq. We have a dead leader in Turkmenistan. Analysis?' Jack asked.

'I won't contradict Golovko on this one. He doubtless does have agents in place, and it sounds like he's in the same situation we're in. He can watch and worry, but he doesn't have any real operational possibilities. Maybe it's a coincidence, but spooks aren't supposed to believe in such things. Damned sure Sergey doesn't. He thinks it's all one play. I think that's a definite possibility. I'll be talking to Vasco about that, too. What he says is shaping up is starting to look a little scary. We'll be hearing from the Saudis today.' And Israel could not be far behind, Ryan knew.

'China?' the President asked next. Maybe the other side of the world was a little better. It wasn't.

'Major exercise. Surface and sub-surface combatants, no air yet, but the overheads show the fighter bases are tooling up –'

'Wait a minute –'

'Yes, sir. If it's a planned exercise, why weren't they ready for it? I'll be talking to the Pentagon about that one at eight-thirty. The ambassador had a little talk with a foreign minis-try type. Feedback is, no big deal, the ministry didn't even know about it, routine training.'

'Bullshit.'

'Maybe. Taiwan is still low-keying it, but they'll be send-ing some ships out today – well, tonight over there. We have assets heading to the area. The Taiwanese are playing ball, full cooperation with our observers in their listening posts. Soon they will ask us what we will do if "A" or "B" happens. We need to think about that. The Pentagon says that the PRC doesn't have the assets to launch an invasion, same as back in '96. The ROC air force is stronger now than it was. So, I don't see that this is likely to lead anywhere. Maybe it really is just an exercise. Maybe they want to see how we – you, that is – will react.'

'What's Adler think?'

'He says to ignore it. I think he's right. Taiwan is playing low-key. I think we do the same. We move ships, especially subs, but we keep them out of sight. CINCPAC seems to have a handle on it. We let him run it for the time being?'

Ryan nodded. 'Through SecDef, yes. Europe?'

'Nice and quiet, ditto our hemisphere, ditto Africa. You know, if the Chinese are just being their usual obnoxious selves, then the only real problem is the Persian Gulf – and the truth of the matter is that we've been there and done that, sir. We've told the Saudis that we're not going to back off of them. That word will get to the other side in due course, and it ought to make the other side stop and think before making any plans to go farther. I don't like the UIR thing, but I think we can deal with it. Iran is fundamentally unstable; the people in that country want more freedom, and when they get a taste, that country will change. We can ride it out.'

Ryan smiled and poured himself a cup of decaf. 'You're getting very confident, Dr Goodley.'

'You pay me to think. I might as well tell you what's moving around between the ears, boss.'

'Okay, get on with your work and keep me posted. I have to figure a way to reconstitute the Supreme Court today.' Ryan sipped his coffee and waited for Arnie to come in. This job wasn't all that tough, was it? Not when you had a good team working for you.

'It's about seduction,' Clark said to the shiny new faces in the auditorium, catching Ding's grin in the back of the room and cringing. The training film they'd just watched had gone over the history of six important cases. There were only five prints of the film, and this one was already being rewound for the walk back to the vault. Two of the cases he'd worked himself. One of the agents had been executed in the basement of 2 Dzerzhinskiy Square after being burned by a KGB mole inside Langley. The other had a small farm in the birch country of northern New Hampshire, probably still wishing that he could go home – but Russia was still Russia, and the narrow view their culture took of high treason wasn't an invention of the previous regime. Such people were forever orphans . . . Clark turned the page and continued from his notes.

'You will seek out people with problems. You will sympathize with those problems. The people with whom you will work are not perfect. They will all have beefs. Some of them will come to you. You don't have to love them, but you do have to be loyal to them.

'What do I mean by seduction? Everyone in this room has done it once or twice, right? You listen more than you talk. You nod. You agree. Sure, you're smarter than your boss – I know about him, we have the same sort of jerk in our government. I had a boss like that once myself. It's hard to be an honest man in that kind of government, isn't it? You bet, honor really is important.

'When they say *that*, you know they want money. That's fine,' Clark told them. 'They never expect as much as they ask for. We have the budget to pay anything they want – but the important thing is getting them on the hook. Once they lose their virginity, people, they can't get it back.

'Your agents, the people you recruit, will get addicted to what they do. It's *fun* to be a spy. Even the most ideologically pure people you recruit will giggle from time to time because they know something nobody else knows.

'They will *all* have something wrong with them. The most idealistic ones are often the worst. They experience guilt. They drink. Some might go to their priest, even – I've had that happen to me. Some break the rules for the first time and figure no rules matter anymore. Those kind will start boffing every girl that crosses their path and taking all sorts of chances.

'Handling agents is an art. You are mother, father, priest, and teacher to them. You have to settle them down. You have to tell them to look after their families, and look after their own ass, especially the "good" ideological recruits. They're dependable for a lot of things, but one of them is to get too much into it. A lot of these agents self-destruct. They can turn into crusaders. Few of the crusaders,' Clark went on, 'died of old age.

'The agent who wants money is often the most reliable. They don't take too many chances. They want out eventually, so they can live the good life in Hollywood and get laid by a starlet or something. Nice thing about agents who work for money – they want to live to spend it. On the other hand, when you need something done in a hurry, when you need somebody to take a risk, you can use a money guy – just be ready to evac him the next day. Sooner or later he'll figure that he's done enough, and demand to be got out.

'What am I telling you? There are no hard and fast rules in this business. You have to use your heads. You have to know about people, how they are, how they act, how they think. You must have genuine empathy with your agents, whether you like them or not. Most you will not like,' he promised them. 'You saw the film. Every word was real. Three of those cases ended with a dead agent. One ended with a dead officer. Remember that.

'Okay, you now have a break. Mr Revell will have you in the next class.' Clark assembled his notes and walked to the back of the room while the trainees absorbed the lessons in silence.

'Gee, Mr C., does that mean seduction is okay?' Ding asked.

'Only when you get paid for it, Domingo.'

All of Group Two was sick now. It was as though they'd all punched in on some sort of time clock. Within ten hours, they'd all complained of fever and aches – flu symptoms. Some knew, Moudi saw, or certainly suspected what had happened to them. Some of them continued to help the sicker subjects to whom they were assigned. Others called for the army medics to complain, or just sat on the floor in the treatment room and did nothing but savor their own illness in fear that they would become what they saw. Again the conditions of their prior imprisonment and diet worked against them. The hungry and debilitated are more easily controlled than the healthy and well fed.

The original group was deteriorating at the expected rate. Their pain grew worse, to the point that their slow writhing lessened because it hurt more to move than to remain still. One seemed very close to death, and Moudi wondered if, as with Benedict Mkusa, this victim's heart was unusually vulnerable to the Ebola Mayinga strain – perhaps this sub-type of the disease had a previously unsuspected affinity for heart tissue? That would have been interesting to learn in the abstract, but he'd gone well beyond the abstract study of the disease.

'We gain nothing by continuing this phase, Moudi,' the director observed, standing beside the younger man and watching the TV monitors. 'Next step.'

'As you wish.' Dr Moudi lifted the phone and spoke for a minute or so.

It took fifteen minutes to get things moving, and then the medical orderlies entered the picture, taking all of the nine members of the second group out of that room, then across the corridor to a second large treatment room, where, on a different set of monitors, the physicians saw that each was assigned a bed and given a medication which, in but a few minutes, had them all asleep. The medics then returned to the original group. Half of them were asleep anyway, and all the others stuporous, unable to resist. The wakeful ones were killed first, with injections of Dilaudid, a powerful synthetic narcotic into whatever vein was the most convenient. The executions took but a few minutes and were, in the end, merciful. The bodies were loaded one by one onto gurneys for transport to the incinerator. Next the mattresses and bedclothes were bundled for burning, leaving only the metal frames of the beds. These, along with the rest of the room, were sprayed with caustic chemicals. The room would be sealed for several days, then sprayed again, and the collective attention of the facility's staff would transfer to Group Two, nine condemned criminals who had proven, or so it would seem, that Ebola Zaire Mayinga could be transmitted through the air.

The health department official took a whole day to arrive, doubtless delayed, Dr MacGregor suspected, by a pile of paperwork on his desk, a fine dinner, and a night with whatever woman spiced up his daily life. And probably the paperwork was still there on his desk, the Scot told himself.

At least he knew about the proper precautions. The government doctor barely entered the room at all – he had to come an additional, reluctant step so that the door could be closed behind him, but moved no farther than that, standing there, his head tilting and his eyes squinting, the better to observe the patient from two meters away. The lights in the room were turned down so as not to hurt Saleh's eyes. Despite that the discoloration of his skin was obvious. The two hanging units of type-O blood and the morphine drip told the rest, along with the chart, which the government official held in his gloved, trembling hands.

'The antibody tests?' he asked quietly, summoning his official dignity.

'Positive,' MacGregor told him.

The first documented Ebola outbreak – no one knew how far back the disease went, how many jungle villages it might have exterminated a hundred years earlier, for example – had gone through the nearest hospital's staff with frightening speed, to the point that the medical personnel had left the facility in panic. And that, perversely, had helped end the outbreak more rapidly than continued treatment might have done – the victims died, and nobody got close enough to them to catch what they had. African medics now knew what precautions to take. Everyone was masked and gloved, and disinfection procedures were ruthlessly enforced. As casual and careless as many African personnel often were, this was one lesson they'd taken to heart, and with that feeling of safety established, they, like medical personnel all over the world, did the best they could.

For this patient, that was very little use. The chart showed that, too.

'From *Iraq*?' the official asked.

Dr MacGregor nodded. 'That is what he told me.'

'I must check on that with the proper authorities.'

'Doctor, I have a report to make,' MacGregor insisted. 'This is a possible outbreak and –'

'No.' The official shook his head. 'Not until we know more. When we make a report, if we do, we must forward all of the necessary information for the alert to be useful.'

'But –'

'But this is *my* responsibility, and it is *my* duty to see that the responsibility is properly executed.' He pointed the chart to the patient. His hand wasn't shaking now that he had established his power over the case. 'Does he have a family? Who can tell us more about him?'

'I don't know.'

'Let me check that out,' the government doctor said. 'Have your people make copies of all records and send them to me at once.' With a stern order given, the health department representative felt as though he had done his duty to his profession and his country.

MacGregor nodded his submission. Moments like this made him hate Africa. His country had been here for more than a century. A fellow Scot named Gordon had come to the Sudan, fallen in love with it – was the man mad? MacGregor wondered – and died right in this city 120 years earlier. Then the Sudan had become a British protectorate. A regiment of infantry had been raised from this country, and that regiment had fought bravely and well under British officers. But then Sudan had been returned to the Sudanese – too quickly, without the time and money spent to create the institutional infrastructure to turn a tribal wasteland into a viable nation. The same story had been told in the same way all over the continent, and the people of Africa were still paying the price for that disservice. It was one more thing neither he nor any other European could speak aloud except with one another – and sometimes not even then – for fear of being called a racist. But if he were a racist, then *why* had he come here?

'You will have them in two hours.'

'Very well.' The official walked out the door. There the head nurse for the unit would take him to the disinfection area, and for that the official would follow orders like a child under the eye of a stern mother.

Pat Martin came in with a well-stuffed briefcase, from which he took fourteen folders, laddering them across the coffee table in alphabetical order. Actually they were labeled *A* to *N*, because President Ryan had specifically asked that he not know the names at first.

'You know, I'd feel a lot better if you hadn't given me all this power,' Martin said without looking up.

'Why's that?' Jack asked.

'I'm just a prosecutor, Mr President. A pretty good one, sure, and now I run the Criminal Division, and that's nice, too, but I'm only –'

'How do you think I feel?' Ryan demanded, then softened his voice. 'Nobody since Washington has been stuck with this job, and what makes you think *I* know what I'm supposed to be doing? Hell, I'm not even a lawyer to understand all this stuff without a crib sheet.'

Martin looked up with half a smile. 'Okay, I deserved that.'

But Ryan had set the criteria. Before him was a roster of the senior federal judiciary. Each of the fourteen folders gave the professional history of a judge in the United States Court of Appeals, ranging from one in Boston to another in Seattle. The President had ordered Martin and his people to select judges of no less than ten years' experience, with no less than fifty important written decisions (as distinguished from routine matters like which side won in a liability case), none of which had been overturned by the Supreme Court – or if one or two had been overturned, had been vindicated by a later reversal in Washington.

'This is a good bunch,' Martin said.

'Death penalty?'

'The Constitution specifically provides for that, remember.

Fifth Amendment,' Martin quoted from memory: ' "Nor shall any person be subject for the same offense to be twice put in jeopardy of life or limb; nor shall be compelled in any criminal case to be a witness against himself, nor be deprived of life, liberty, or property, without due process of law." So *with* due process, you can take a person's life, but you can only try him once for it. The Court established the criteria for that in a number of cases in the '70s and '80s – guilt trial followed by penalty trial, with the penalty phase dependent upon "special" circumstances. All of these judges have upheld that rule – with a few exceptions. *D* here struck down a Mississippi case on the basis of mental incompetence. That was a good call, even though the crime was pretty gruesome – the Supreme Court affirmed it without comment or hearing. Sir, the problem with the system is one that nobody can really fix. It's just the nature of law. A lot of legal principles are based on decisions from unusual cases. There's a dictum that hard cases make for bad law. Like that case in England, remember? Two little kids murder a younger kid. What the hell is a judge supposed to do when the defendants are eight years old, definitely guilty of a brutal murder, but only eight years old? What you do then is, you pray some other judge gets stuck with it. Somehow we all try to make cohesive legal doctrine out of that. It's not really possible, but we do it anyway.'

'I figure you picked tough ones, Pat. Did you pick fair ones?' the President asked.

'Remember what I said a minute ago? I don't want this sort of power? I didn't dare do otherwise. *E* here reversed a conviction one of my best people got on a technicality – an issue of admissibility – and when he did it, we were all pretty mad. The issue was entrapment, where the line is. The defendant was guilty as hell, no doubt of it. But Judge . . . *E* looked at the arguments and probably made the right call, and that ruling is part of FBI guidelines now.'

Jack looked at the folders. It would be a full week's reading. This, as Arnie had told him a few days before, would be his most important act as President. No Chief Executive since Washington had been faced with the necessity of appointing the entire Supreme Court, and even that had been in an age when the national consensus on law had been far firmer and deeper than what existed in America now. Back then 'cruel and unusual punishment' had meant the rack and burning at the stake – both of those things that *had* been used in pre-Revolutionary America – but in more recent rulings had been taken to mean the absence of cable television and denial of sex-change operations, or just overcrowding in the prisons. *So fine*, Ryan thought, *the prisons are too crowded, and then why not release dangerous criminals on society for fear of being cruel to convicted felons?*

Now he had the power to change that. All he had to do was select judges who took as harsh a view on crime as he did, an outlook he'd learned from listening to his father's occasional rant about a particularly vile crime, or an especially bat-brained judge who hadn't ever viewed a crime scene, and therefore never really known what the issues were. And for Ryan there was the personal element. He'd been the subject of attempted murder, as had his wife and children. He *knew* what it was all about, the outrage at facing the fact that there were people who could take a life as easily as buying candy at a drug store, who preyed on others as though they were game animals, and whose actions cried out for retribution. He could remember looking into Sean Miller's eyes more than once and seeing *nothing*, nothing in there at all. No humanity, no empathy, no feelings – not even hatred, so outside the human community he'd taken himself that there was no returning . . .

And yet.

Ryan closed his eyes, remembering the moment, a loaded Browning pistol in his grip, his blood boiling in his veins but his hands like ice, the exquisite moment at which he could have ended the life of the man who had so wanted to end his own – and Cathy's, and Sally's, and Little Jack, yet unborn. Looking in his eyes, and finally seeing the fear at last, breaking through the shell of inhumanity . . . but how many times had he thanked a merciful God that he'd neglected to cock the hammer on his pistol? He would have done it. He'd wanted to do it more than anything in his life, and he *could* remember pulling the trigger, only to be surprised when it hadn't moved – and then the moment had passed away. Jack could remember killing. The terrorist in London. The one in the boat at the base of his cliff. The cook on the submarine.

Surely he'd killed others – that horrible night in Colombia which had given him nightmares for years after. But Sean Miller was different. It hadn't been necessity for Miller. For him it had been justice of a sort, and he'd been there, and he'd been the Law, and, God, how he'd wanted to take that worthless life! But he hadn't. The Law that had ended the life of that terrorist and his colleagues had been well considered, cold and detached . . . as it had to be – and for *that* reason he had to select the best possible people to repopulate the Court, because the decisions they would make were not about one enraged man trying at the same time to protect and avenge his family. They would say what the law was for everyone, and that wasn't about personal desires. This thing people called civilization was about something more than one man's passion. It had to be. And it was his duty to make sure that it was, by picking the right people.

'Yeah,' Martin said, reading the President's face. 'Big deal, isn't it?'

'Wait a minute.' Jack rose and walked out the door to the secretaries' room. 'Which one of you smokes?' he asked there.

'It's me,' said Ellen Sumter. She was of Jack's age, and probably trying to quit, as all smokers of that age at least claimed. Without another question, she handed her President a Virginia Slim – the same as the crewwoman on his airplane, Jack realized – and a butane lighter. The President nodded his thanks and walked back into his office, lighting it. Before he could close the door, Mrs Sumter raced to follow him with an ashtray taken from her desk drawer.

Sitting down, Ryan took a long drag, eyes on the carpet, which was of the Great Seal of the President of the United States, covered though it was with furniture.

'How the hell,' Jack asked quietly, 'did anybody ever decide that one man could have this much power? I mean, what I'm doing here –'

'Yes, sir. Kind of like being James Madison, isn't it? You pick the people who decide what the Constitution really means. They're all in their late forties or fifties, and so they'll be there for a while,' Martin told him. 'Cheer up. At least it's not a game for you. At least you're doing it the right way. You're not picking women because they're women, or blacks because they're black. I gave you a good mix, color, bathrooms, and everything, but all the names have been redacted out – and you won't be able to tell who's who unless you follow cases, which you probably don't. I give you my word, sir, they're all good ones. I spent a lot of time assembling the list for you. Your guidelines helped, and they were good guidelines. For what it's worth, they're all people who think the way you do. People who like power scare me,' the attorney said. 'Good ones reflect a lot on what they're doing before they do it. Picking real judges who've made some hard calls – well, read their decisions. You'll see how hard they worked at what they did.'

Another puff. He tapped the folders. 'I don't know the law well enough to understand all the points in there. I don't know crap about the law, except you're not supposed to break it.'

Martin grinned at that one: 'Not a bad place to start when you think about it.' He didn't have to go any further. Not every occupant of this office had thought of things quite that way. Both men knew it, but it wasn't the sort of thing one said to the sitting President.

'I know the things I don't like. I know the things I'd like to see changed, but, God damn it' – Ryan looked up, eyes wide now – 'do I have the *right* to make that sort of call?'

'Yes, Mr President, you do, because the Senate has to look over your shoulder, remember? Maybe they'll disagree on one or two. All these judges have been checked out by the FBI. They're all honest. They're all smart. None of them ever wanted or expected to make it to the Supreme Court except through a certiori grant. If you can't come up with nine you like, we'll search some more – better then if you have somebody else do it. The head of the Civil Rights Division is also a pretty good man – he's off to my left some, but he's another thinker.'

Civil rights, Jack thought. Did he have to make government policy on *that*, too? How was he supposed to know what might be the right way to treat people who might or might not be a little different from everybody else? Sooner or later you lost the ability to be objective, and then your beliefs took over – and were you then making policy based on personal prejudice? How were you supposed to know what was right? Jesus.

Ryan took a last puff and stubbed the cigarette out, rewarded as always by a dizzying buzz from the renewed vice. 'Well, I guess I have a lot of reading to do.'

'I'd offer you some help, but probably better that you try to do it yourself. That way, nobody pollutes the process – more than I've already done, that is. You want to keep that in mind. I might not be the best guy for this, but you asked me, and that's the best I have.'

'I suppose that's all any of us can do, eh?' Ryan observed, staring at the pile of folders.

The chief of the Civil Rights Division of the United States Department of Justice was a political appointee dating back to President Fowler. Formerly a corporate lawyer and lobbyist – it paid far better than the academic post he'd held before his first political appointment – he'd been politically active since before his admission to law school, and as with so many occupants of official offices he had become, if not his post, then his vision of it. He had a constituency, even though he'd never been elected to anything, and even though his government service had been intermittent, a series of increasingly high posts made possible by his proximity to the power that rested in this city, the power lunches, the parties, the office visits made while representing people he might or might not really care about, because a lawyer had an obligation to serve the interests of his clients – and the clients chose him, not the reverse. One often needed the fees of the few to serve the needs of the many – which was, in fact, his own philosophy of government. Thus he'd unknowingly come to live Ben Jonson's dictum about 'speaking to mere contraries, yet all be law.' But he'd never lost his passion for civil rights, and he'd never lobbied for anything contrary to that core belief – of course, nobody since the 1960s had lobbied *against* civil rights *per se*, but he told himself that was important. A white man with stock originating well before the Revolutionary War, he spoke at all the right forums, and from that he'd earned the admiration of people whose political views were the same as his. From that admiration came power, and it was hard to say which aspect of his life influenced the other more. Because of his early work in the Justice Department he'd won the attention of political figures. Because he'd done that work with skill, he'd also earned the attention of a powerful Washington law firm. Leaving the government to enter that firm, he'd used his political contacts to practice his profession more effectively, and from that effectiveness he'd generated additional credibility in the political world, one hand constantly washing the other until he couldn't really discern which hand was which. Along the way the cases he argued had become his identity in a process so gradual and seemingly so logical that he hardly knew what had taken place. He was what he'd argued for over the years.

And that was the problem right now. He knew and admired Patrick Martin as a lesser legal talent who'd advanced at Justice by working exclusively in the courts – never even a proper United States Attorney (those were political appointments, mainly selected by senators for their home states), but rather one of the apolitical professional worker bees who did the real casework while their appointed boss worked on speeches, caseload management, and political ambition. And the fact of the matter was that Martin was a gifted legal tactician, forty-one and one in his formal trials, better yet as a legal administrator guiding young prosecutors. But he didn't know much about politics, the Civil Rights chief thought, and for that reason he was the wrong man to advise President Ryan.

He had the list. One of his people had helped Martin put it together, and his people were loyal, because they knew that the real path to advancement in this city was to move in and out as their chief had done, and their chief could by lifting a phone get them that job at a big firm, and so one of them handed his chief the list, with the names *not* redacted out.

The chief of the Civil Rights Division had only to read off the fourteen names. He didn't need to call up the paperwork on their cases. He knew them all. This one, at the Fourth Circuit in Richmond, had reversed a lower-court ruling and written a lengthy opinion questioning the constitutionality of affirmative action – too good a discourse, it had persuaded the Supreme Court in a sharply divided 5–4 decision. The case had been a narrow one, and the affirmation of it in Washington had been similarly narrow, but the chief didn't like *any* chips in that particular wall of stone.

That one in New York had affirmed the government's position in another area, but in doing so had limited the applicability of the principle – and *that* case hadn't gone further, and was law for a large part of the country.

These were the wrong people. Their view of judicial power was too circumscribed. They deferred too much to Congress and the state legislatures. Pat Martin's view of law was different from his own. Martin didn't see that judges were *supposed* to right what was wrong – the two had often debated the issue over lunch in conversations spirited but always good-natured. Martin was a pleasant man, and a sufficiently good debater that he was hard to move off any position, whether he was wrong or not, and while that made him a fine prosecutor he just didn't have the temperament, he just didn't *see* the way things were supposed to be, and he'd picked judges the same way, and the Senate might be dumb enough to consent to the selections, and that *couldn't happen*. For this sort of power, you had to pick people who knew how to exercise it in the proper way.

He really had no choice. He bundled the list into an envelope and tucked it into the pocket of his jacket and made a phone call for lunch with one of his many contacts.

30

PRESS

They did it for the morning news, so pervasive had become the influence of television. This was how reality was defined, changed, and announced. A new day had surely dawned. The viewer was left in little doubt. There was a new flag hanging behind the announcer, a green field, the color of Islam, with two small gold stars. He started off with an invocation from the Koran, and then went into political matters. There was a new country. It was called the United Islamic Republic. It would be comprised of the former nations of Iran and Iraq. The new nation would be guided by the Islamic principles of peace and brotherhood. There would be an elected parliament called a majlis. Elections, he promised, would be held by the end of the year. In the interim there would be a revolutionary council comprised of political figures from both countries, in proportion to population – which gave Iran the whip hand, the announcer didn't say; he didn't have to.

There was no reason, he went on, for any other country to fear the UIR. The new nation proclaimed its goodwill for all Muslim nations, and all nations who had friendly relations with the former divided segments of the new land. That this statement was contradictory in numerous ways was not explored. The other Gulf nations, all of them Islamic, had *not* actually enjoyed friendly relations with either of the partners. The elimination of the former Iraqi weapons facilities would continue apace so that there would be no question of hostility to the international community. Political prisoners would be freed at once –

'And now they can make room for the new ones,' Major Sabah observed at PALM BOWL. 'So, it's happened.' He didn't have to phone anyone. The TV feed was being viewed all over the Gulf, and in every room with a functioning television the only happy face was the one on the screen – that is, until the scene changed to show spontaneous demonstrations at the various mosques, where people made their morning prayers, and walked outside to display their joy.

'Hello, Ali,' Jack said. He'd stayed up reading the folders Martin had left, knowing that the call would come, suffering, again, from a headache that he seemed to acquire just from walking into the Oval Office. It was surprising that the Saudis had been so long in authorizing the call from their Prince/Minister-Without-Portfolio. Maybe they'd just hoped to wish it away, a characteristic not exactly unique to that part of the world. 'Yes, I'm watching the TV now.' At the bottom of the display, like the captioning for the hearing-impaired, was a dialogue box being typed by intelligence specialists at the National Security Agency. The rhetoric was a little flowery, but the content was clear to everyone in the room. Adler, Vasco, and Goodley had come in as soon as the feed arrived, liberating Ryan from his reading, if not his headache.

'This is very unsettling, if not especially surprising,' the Prince said over the encrypted line.

'There was no stopping it. I know how it looks to you, Your Highness,' the President said tiredly. He could have indulged in coffee, but he did want to get *some* sleep tonight.

'We are going to place our military at a higher state of readiness.'

'Is there anything you want us to do?' Ryan asked.

'For the moment, just to know that your support has not changed.'

'It hasn't. I've told you before. Our security commitment to the Kingdom remains the same. If you want us to do something to demonstrate that, we're ready to take whatever steps seem reasonable and appropriate. Do you –'

'No, Mr President, we have no formal requests at this time.' That statement was delivered in a tone that made Jack's eyes flicker off the speakerphone and to his visitors.

'In that case, might I suggest that you have some of your people discuss options with some of mine?'

'It must be kept quiet. My government has no wish to inflame the situation.'

'We'll do what we can. You can start talking to Admiral Jackson – he's J-3 in the –'

'Yes, Mr President, I met him in the East Room. I will have our working-level people contact him later today.'

'Okay. If you need me, Ali, I'm always at the end of the phone.'

'Thank you, Jack. I hope you will sleep well.' *You'll need it. We all will.* And the line went dead. Ryan killed the button on the phone to make sure.

'Opinions?'

'Ali wants us to do something, but the King hasn't decided yet,' Adler said.

'They'll try to establish contacts with the UIR.' Vasco took up the conversation. 'Their first instinct will be to get a dialogue going, try to do a little business. The Saudis will take the lead. Figure Kuwait and the rest of the lesser states will let them handle the contacts, but we'll be hearing from them soon, probably through channels.'

'We have a good ambassador in Kuwait?' the President asked.

'Will Bach,' Adler said, with an emphatic nod. 'Career FSO. Good man. Not real imaginative, but a good plugger, knows the language and culture, lots of friends in their royal family. Good commercial guy. He's been pretty effective as a middle-man between our businesspeople and their government.'

'Good deputy chief of mission to back him up,' Vasco went on, 'and the attachés there are tops, all spooks, good ones.'

'Okay, Bert.' Ryan took off his reading glasses and rubbed his eyes. 'Tell me what happens next.'

'The whole south side of the Gulf is scared shitless. This is their nightmare come true.'

Ryan nodded and shifted his gaze. 'Ben, I want CIA's assessment of the UIR's intentions, and I want you to call Robby and see what kind of options we have. Get Tony Bretano into the loop. He wanted to be SecDef, and I want him to start thinking about the non-admin part of the job.'

'Langley doesn't have much of a clue,' Adler pointed out. 'Not their fault, but that's how it is.' And so their assessment would present a range of potential options, from theater nuclear war – Iran might have nukes, after all – to the Second Coming, and three or four options in between, each with its theoretical justification. That way, as usual, the President had the chance to choose the wrong one, and it wouldn't be anyone's fault but his own.

'Yeah, I know. Scott, let's see if we can establish some contacts with the UIR, too.'

'Extend the olive branch?'

'You got it,' the President agreed. 'Everyone figure they need time to consolidate before they do anything radical?'

There were nods with the President's assessment, but not from everyone.

'Mr President?' Vasco said.

'Yeah, Bert – by the way, good call. You weren't exactly right on timing, but damned if you weren't right enough.'

'Thanks. Mr President, on the consolidation issue, that's about people, right?'

'Sure.' Ryan and the rest nodded. Consolidating a government meant little more than that the people got used to the new system of rule and accepted it.

'Sir, if you look at the number of people in Iraq who have to get used to this new government, compare that number to the population of the Gulf states. It's a big jump in terms of distance and territory, but not in terms of population,' Vasco said, reminding them that although Saudi Arabia was larger than all of America east of the Mississippi, it had fewer people than the Philadelphia metropolitan area.

'They're not going to do anything right away,' Adler objected.

'They might. Depends on what you mean by "right away," Mr Secretary.'

'Iran has too many internal problems,' Goodley started to say.

Vasco had come to like presidential access and attention, and decided to seize the floor. 'Don't underestimate the religious dimension,' he warned. 'That is a unifying factor which could erase or at least suppress their internal problems. Their flag says it. The name of the country says it. People all over the world like a winner. Daryaei sure looks like a winner now, doesn't he? One other thing.'

'What's that, Bert?' Adler asked.

'You notice the flag? The two stars are pretty small,' Vasco said pensively.

'So?' This was Goodley. Ryan looked back at the TV

and the announcer. The flag was still there behind him and –

'So, there's plenty of room for more.'

It was a moment such as he had dreamed of, but the culmination of such a dream is always better than its contemplation, because now the cheers were real, striking his ears from the outside, not the inside. Mahmoud Haji Daryaei had flown in before dawn, and with the rising of the sun he'd walked into the central mosque, removing his shoes, washing his hands and forearms, because a man was supposed to be clean before his God. Humbly, he'd listened to the incantation from the minaret, calling the faithful to prayer, and this day people didn't roll back over and try to capture a few more hours of sleep. Today they flocked to the mosque from blocks around in a gesture of devotion that moved their visitor to his core. Daryaei took no special place, but he appreciated the singularity of the moment, and tears streamed down his dark, deeply lined cheeks at the overwhelming emotion of the moment. He had fulfilled the first of his tasks. He had fulfilled the wishes of the Prophet Mohammed. He had restored a measure of unity to the Faith, the first step in his holy quest. In the reverent hush following the conclusion of morning prayers, he rose and walked out into the street, and there he was recognized. To the despairing panic of his security guards, he walked along the street, returning the greetings of people at first stupefied and then ecstatic to see the former enemy of their country walking among them as a guest.

There were no cameras to record this. It was not a moment to be polluted by publicity, and though there was danger, he accepted it. What he was doing would tell him much. It would tell him of the power of his Faith, and the renewed faith of these people, and it would tell him whether or not he had Allah's blessing on his quest, for Daryaei truly was a humble man, doing what he had to do, not for himself, but for his God. Why else, he often asked himself, would he have chosen a life of danger and denial? Soon the sidewalk traffic turned into a crowd, and from a crowd to a mob. People he'd never met appointed themselves to be his guardians, forcing a path for him through the bodies and the cheers as his aged legs made their way while his now-serene dark eyes swept left and right, wondering if danger would come, but finding only joy that reflected his own. He gazed and gestured to the crowd as a grandfather might greet his progeny, not smiling, but composed, accepting their love and respect, and with his benign eyes promising greater things, because great deeds had to be followed by greater ones, and the moment was right.

'So, what sort of man is he?' Movie Star asked. His flight to Frankfurt had been followed by one to Athens, and from there to Beirut, and from there to Tehran. He knew Daryaei only by reputation.

'He knows power,' Badrayn answered, listening to the demonstrations outside. There was something about peace, he imagined. The war between Iraq and Iran had lasted close to a decade. Children had been sent off to die. Rockets had blasted the cities of both countries. The human cost would never be fully assessed, and though the war had ended years before, now it was truly ended – a thing of the heart rather than of law, perhaps. Or maybe a thing of God's law, which was different from that of man. The resulting euphoria was something he'd once felt himself. But now he knew better. Feelings like that were weapons of statecraft, things to be used. Outside were people who a short time before had chafed at what they had and what they did not have, who questioned the wisdom of their leader, who bridled – as much as one could in so tightly controlled a society as this one was – at the freedoms they lacked. That was gone now, and it would remain gone for – how long? That was the question, and that was why such moments had to be properly used. And Daryaei knew all of those things.

'So,' Badrayn said, turning off the outside noise of the faithful, 'what have you learned?'

'The most interesting things I learned from watching television. President Ryan is doing well, but he has difficulties. The government is not yet fully functional. The lower house of their parliament has not yet been replaced – the elections for that will begin to take place next month. Ryan is popular. The Americans love to poll one another,' he explained. 'They call people on the telephone and ask questions – only a few thousand, often not that many, and from this they report to one another what everyone thinks.'

'The result?' Badrayn asked.

'A large majority seems to approve what he is doing – but he isn't really doing anything except to continue. He hasn't even chosen a Vice President yet.'

Badrayn knew that, but not the reason. 'Why?' he asked.

Movie Star grinned. 'I asked that question myself. The full parliament must approve such a thing, and the full parliament has not yet been reestablished. It will not be so for some time. Moreover, there is the problem with the former Vice President, that Kealty fellow, who claims that *he* is the President – and this Ryan has not imprisoned him. Their legal system doesn't deal with treason effectively.'

'And if we were able to kill Ryan ... ?'

Movie Star shook his head. 'Very difficult. I took an afternoon to walk around Washington. Security at the palace is very strict. It is not open to public tours. The street in front of the building is closed. I sat on a bench for an hour, reading, and watched for signs around the place. Riflemen on all the buildings. I suppose we would have a chance on one of his official trips, but that would require extensive planning for which we lack the necessary time. And so, that leaves us with –'

'His children,' Badrayn observed.

Jesus, I hardly see them anymore, Jack thought. He'd just gotten off the elevator, accompanied by Jeff Raman, and checked his watch. Just after midnight. Damn. He'd managed to sit through a hurried dinner with them and Cathy before hustling back downstairs for his reading and meetings, and now ... everyone was asleep.

The upstairs corridor was a lonely place, too wide for the intimacy of a real home. Three agents were in view, 'standing post,' as they called it, and the warrant officer with 'the Football' full of its nuclear codes. It was quiet because of the time of night, and the overall impression was rather like that of an upscale funeral home, not a house with a family in it. No clutter, no toys lying on the rug, no empty glasses in front of a TV. Too neat, too tidy, too cold. Always somebody around. Raman traded looks with the other agents, whose nods meant 'Okay, everything clear.' *Nobody with guns around*, Ryan thought. *Super.*

The bedrooms were too far apart up here. He turned left, heading for Katie's room first. Opening the door, he saw his youngest, recently graduated from crib to bed, lying on her side, a fuzzy brown teddy bear next to her. She still wore sleepers with feet on them. Jack could remember when Sally had worn the same, and how cute children looked that way, like little packages. But Sally now looked forward to the day she'd buy things from Victoria's Secret, and Little Jack – he had taken to objecting to that label of late – now insisted on boxer shorts because that was the new 'in' thing for boys of his age group, and they had to be pulled down low, because the 'in' thing was to risk having them fall off. Well, he still had a toddler. Jack approached the bed, and stood there for a minute, just looking at Katie and quietly enjoying the status of fatherhood. He looked around, and again the room was unnaturally neat. Everything was picked up. Not a loose item on the floor. Her clothing for the coming day was neatly laid out on a wooden valet. Even the white socks were folded next to the diminutive sneakers with cartoon animals on them. Was this a way for a child to live? It seemed like a Shirley Temple movie from when his mom and dad were kids – some upper-class thing that he'd always wondered about: *Did people really live that way?*

Not real people, just royalty, and the family of the man sentenced to the presidency. Jack smiled, shook his head, and left the room. Agent Raman closed the door for him, not even letting POTUS do that. Somewhere else in the building, Ryan was sure, an electronic status board showed that the door had been opened and closed, probably sensors told that someone had entered the room, and probably someone had asked over the radio link the Service people used to be told that SWORDSMAN was tucking SANDBOX in.

He stuck his head in Sally's room. His elder daughter was similarly asleep, doubtless dreaming of some boy or other in her class – Kenny or something, wasn't it? Somebody who was way cool. Little Jack's bedroom floor was actually polluted by the presence of a comic book, but his white shirt was pressed and hanging on another valet, and someone had shined his shoes.

Another day shot to hell, the President thought. He turned to his bodyguard. 'Night, Jeff.'

'Good night, sir,' Agent Raman said outside the door to the master bedroom. Ryan nodded his farewell to the man, and Raman waited for the door to shut. Then he looked left and right at the other Detail agents. His right hand brushed against the service pistol under his jacket, and his eyes smiled in a private way, knowing what might so easily have been. Word had not come back. Well, his contact was doubtless being careful, as well he should. Aref Raman had the duty tonight as supervisor for the Detail. He walked up the corridor, nodding to the agents on post, asked one innocuous question, then headed down the elevator to the State Floor, and outside to get some air, stretch, and look at the perimeter guard posts, where, also, everything was quiet. There were some protesters in Lafayette Park across the street, this time of night huddled together, many of them smoking – exactly what he didn't know but had suspicions. Maybe hashish? he wondered with a cryptic smile. Wouldn't that be funny. Beyond that there were only the traffic sounds, a distant siren to the east, and people standing at their posts, trying to stay alert by talking about basketball, or hockey, or spring training for baseball, eyes sweeping outward, looking for dangers in the shadows of the city. The wrong place to look, Raman thought, turning back to head for the command post.

'Is it possible to kidnap them?'

'The two older ones, no, too inconvenient, too difficult, but the youngest, that is possible. It could be both dangerous and costly,' Movie Star warned.

Badrayn nodded. That meant picking especially reliable people. Daryaei had such people. That was obvious from what had taken place in Iraq. He looked over the diagrams in silence for a few minutes while his guest stood to look out the window. The demonstration was still under way. Now they were shouting 'Death to America!' The crowds and the cheerleaders who organized them had long experience with that particular mantra. Then his intelligence man came back.

'What exactly,' Movie Star asked, 'is the mission, Ali?'

'The strategic mission would be to prevent America from

interfering with us.' Badrayn looked up. *Us* now meant whatever Daryaei wanted it to mean.

All nine of them, Moudi saw. He ran the antibody tests himself. He actually did each three times, and the tests were all positive. Every one of them was infected. For the sake of security, they were given drugs and told that they'd be all right – as they would until it was determined that the disease had been transmitted in its full virulence, not attenuated by reproduction in the previous set of hosts. Mainly they were dosed with morphine, the better to keep them quiet and stuporous. So first Benedict Mkusa, then Sister Jean Baptiste, then ten criminals, and now nine more. Twenty-two victims, if one also counted Sister Maria Magdalena. He wondered if Jean Baptiste was still praying for him in Paradise and shook his head.

Sohaila, Dr MacGregor thought, looking over his notes. She was ill, but she had stabilized. Her temperature had abated a whole degree. She was occasionally alert. He'd thought jet lag at first, until there had been blood in her vomit and stool, but that had stopped . . . Food poisoning? That had seemed the likely diagnosis. She'd probably eaten the same things as the rest of her family, but it could have been one bad piece of meat, or maybe she'd done what every child did, and swallowed the wrong thing. It happened literally every week in every doctor's office in the world, and was particularly common among the Western community in Khartoum. But she was from Iraq, too, just as Patient Saleh was. He'd rerun the antibody tests on the latter, and there was no doubt. The bodyguard fellow was gravely ill, and unless his immune system rallied itself –

Children, MacGregor remembered, somewhat startled by the connection, have powerful immune systems, rather more so than adults had. Though every parent knew that every child could come down with a disease and high fever in a matter of hours, the reason was simply that children, as they grew, were exposed to all manner of ailments for the first time. Each organism attacked the child, and in each child the immune system fought back, generating antibodies which would forever defeat that particular enemy (measles, mumps, and all the rest) whenever it again appeared – and rapidly defeating it the first time in nearly all cases, which was why a child could spike a high fever one day and be out playing the next, another characteristic of childhood that first terrified and then vexed parents. The so-called childhood diseases were those *defeated* in childhood. An adult exposed to them for the first time was in far greater distress – mumps could render a healthy man impotent; chicken pox, a childhood annoyance, could *kill* adults; measles had killed off whole peoples. Why? Because for all its apparent frailty, the human child was one of the toughest organisms known to exist. Vaccines for the childhood diseases had been developed not to save the many, but the few who for whatever reason – probably genetic, but that was still being investigated – were unusually vulnerable. Even polio, a devastating neuromuscular disease, had done permanent harm to only a fraction of its victims – but they were mostly children, and adults protected children with a ferocity usually associated with the animal kingdom – and properly so, MacGregor thought, because the human psyche was programmed to be solicitous to children – which was why so much scientific effort had been devoted to childhood disease over the years . . . Where was this line of thought taking him? the doctor wondered. So often his brain went off on its own, as though wandering in a library of thoughts, searching for the right reference, the right connection . . .

Saleh had come from Iraq.

Sohaila had also come from Iraq.

Saleh had Ebola.

Sohaila showed symptoms of flu, or food poisoning, or –

But Ebola initially presented itself as flu . . .

'My God,' MacGregor breathed. He rose from his desk and his notes and walked to her room. Along the way he got a syringe and some vacuum tubes. There was the usual whining from the child about a needle, but MacGregor had a good touch, and it was all over before she was able to start crying, which problem he left to her mother, who'd slept overnight in the room.

Why didn't I run this test before? the young doctor raged at himself. *Damn.*

*   *   *

'They are not officially here,' the foreign ministry official told the health department official. 'What exactly is the problem?'

'He seems to have Ebola virus.' That got the other man's attention. His eyes blinked hard, and he leaned forward across his desk.

'Are you certain?'

'Quite,' the Sudanese physician confirmed with a nod. 'I've seen the test data. The doctor on the case is Ian MacGregor, one of our British visitors. He's actually a fine practitioner.'

'Has anyone been told?'

'No.' The doctor shook his head emphatically. 'There is no cause to panic. The patient is fully isolated. The hospital staff know their business. We are supposed to make the proper notifications to the World Health Organization, informing them of the case and –'

'You are certain there is no risk of an epidemic?'

'None. As I said, full isolation procedures are in place. Ebola is a dangerous disease, but we know how to deal with it,' the physician answered confidently.

'Then why must you notify the WHO?'

'In these cases, they dispatch a team to oversee the situation, to advise on procedures, and to look for the focal source of the infection so that –'

'This Saleh chap, he didn't catch the disease here, did he?'

'Certainly not. If we had that problem here, I would know of it straightaway,' he assured his host.

'So, there is no danger of spreading the disease, and he brought it in with him, so there is no question that there is a public-health danger to our country?'

'Correct.'

'I see.' The official turned to look out the window. The presence of the former Iraqi officers in Sudan was still a secret, and it was in his country's interest to make sure it stayed that way. Keeping secrets meant keeping secrets from everyone. He turned back. 'You will *not* notify the World Health Organization. If the presence of this Iraqi in our country became widely known, it would be a diplomatic embarrassment for us.'

'That might be a problem. Dr MacGregor is young and idealistic and –'

'You tell him. If he objects, I will have someone else speak to him,' the official said, with a raised eyebrow. Such warnings, properly delivered, rarely failed to get someone's attention.

'As you wish.'

'Will this Saleh fellow survive?'

'Probably not. The mortality rate is roughly eight of ten, and his symptoms are advancing rapidly.'

'Any idea how he contracted the disease?'

'None. He denies ever having been in Africa before, but such people do not always speak the truth. I can speak with him further.'

'That would be useful.'

President Eyes Conservatives for the Supreme Court, the headline ran. The White House staff never sleeps, though this privilege is occasionally granted to POTUS. Copies of various papers arrived while the rest of the city slept, and staff workers would take one of the copies and scan it for items of particular interest to the government. Those stories would be clipped, pasted together, and photocopied for the *Early Bird*, an informal publication which allowed the powerful to find out what was happening – or at least what the press thought was happening, which was sometimes true, sometimes false, and mainly in between.

'We got a major leak,' one of them said, using an X-Acto knife to cut out the story from the *Washington Post*.

'Look like it. Looks like it gets around, too,' her counterpart on the *Times* agreed.

An internal Justice Department document lists the judges being reviewed by the Ryan administration for possible nomination to fill the nine vacant seats on the Supreme Court.

Each of the jurists listed is a senior appeals court judge. The list is a highly conservative roster. Not a single judicial appointee from presidents Fowler or Durling is to be found on it.

Ordinarily such nominees are first submitted to a committee of the American Bar Association, but in this case the list was prepared internally by senior career officials at the Justice Department, overseen by Patrick J. Martin, a career prosecutor and chief of the Criminal Division.

'The press doesn't like this.'

'Think that's bad? Check this editorial out. Boy, they really responded fast to this one.'

They'd never worked so hard on anything. The mission had turned into sixteen-hour days, not much beer in the evenings, hasty pre-cooked meals, and only a radio for entertainment. That had to be played loud at the moment. They had lead boiling. The rig was the same as that used by plumbers, a propane tank with a burner on top, like an inverted rocket being static-tested, and atop that was a metal pot filled with lead kept in a liquid state by the roaring flame. A ladle came with the pot and this was dipped, then poured into bullet molds. The latter were .58 caliber, 505-grain, made for muzzle-loading rifles, rather like what the original mountain men had carried west back in the 1820s. These had been ordered from catalogs. There were ten of the molds, with four cavities per mold.

So far, Ernie Brown thought, things were going well, especially on the security side. Fertilizer was not a controlled substance. Neither was diesel fuel. Neither was lead, and every purchase had been made at more than one place, so that no single acquisition was so large as to cause comment.

It was still time-consuming menial labor, but as Pete had remarked, Jim Bridger hadn't come west by helicopter. No, he'd traveled the distance on horseback, doubtless with a packhorse or two, making maybe fifteen or twenty miles per day, then trapping his beaver one at a time, doing everything the hard way, the individual way, occasionally bumping into another of his kind and trading for jugged liquor or tobacco. So what they did was in the tradition of their kind. That was important.

The timing worked out nicely. Pete was doing the ladle work now, and from the time he poured into the first mold-set until he poured the last, the first set hardened enough that, when dipped in water and opened – the two-piece tool was like a pair of pliers – the mini-ball-type projectiles were fully formed and solid. These were tossed into an empty oil drum, and the molds replaced in their holders. Ernie collected the spilled lead and dumped it back in the pot so that none would be wasted.

The only hard part was getting the cement truck, but a search of local papers had found an auction sale for a contractor going out of business, and for a mere $21,000 they'd acquired a three-year-old vehicle with a Mack truck body, only 70,567.1 miles on the odometer, and in pretty good running shape. They'd driven that down at night, of course, and it was now parked in the barn, sitting twenty feet away, its headlights watching them like a pair of eyes.

The work was menial and repetitive, but even that helped. Hanging on the barn wall was a map of downtown Washington, and as Ernie stirred the lead, he turned to look at it, his brain churning over the flat paper image and his own mental picture. He knew all the distances, and distance was the prime factor. The Secret Service thought it was pretty smart. They'd closed off Pennsylvania Avenue for the very purpose of keeping bombs away from the President's house. Well, hell, weren't they smart. They'd overlooked only one little thing.

'But I *have* to,' MacGregor said. 'We're *required* to.'

'You will not,' the health department official told him. 'It is not necessary. The Index Patient brought the disease with him. You have initiated proper containment procedures. The staff are doing their job – you trained them well, Ian,' he added to assuage the heat of the moment. 'It would be inconvenient for my country for this word to go out. I discussed it with the foreign ministry, and word will *not* go out. Is that clear?'

'But –'

'If you pursue this, we will have to ask you to leave the country.'

MacGregor flushed. He had a pale, northern complexion, and his face too easily showed his emotional state. This bastard could and would make another telephone call, and he would have a policeman – so they called them here, though they were decidedly not the civilized, friendly sort he'd known in Edinburgh – come to his house to tell him to pack his things for the ride to the airport. It had happened before to a Londoner who'd lectured a government official a little too harshly about AIDS dangers. And if he left, he'd be leaving patients behind, and that was his vulnerability, as the official knew, and as MacGregor knew that he knew. Young and dedicated, he looked after his patients as a doctor should, and leaving them to another's care wasn't something he could do easily, not here, not when there were just too few really competent physicians for the patient load.

'How is Patient Saleh?'

'I doubt he will survive.'

'That is unfortunate, but it cannot be helped. Do we have any idea how this man was exposed to the disease?'

The younger man flushed again. 'No, and that's the point!'

'I will speak to him myself.'

Bloody hard thing to do from three meters away, Mac-Gregor thought. But he had other things to think about.

Sohaila had tested positive for antibodies also. But the little girl was getting better. Her temperature was down another half a degree. She'd stopped her GI bleeding. MacGregor had rerun a number of tests, and baselined others. Patient Sohaila's liver function was nearly normal. He was certain she'd survive. Somehow she'd been exposed to Ebola, and somehow she'd defeated it – but without knowing the former, he could only guess at the reason for the latter. Part of him wondered if Sohaila and Saleh had been exposed in the same way – no, not exactly. As formidable as a child's immune defenses were, they were not all *that* much more powerful than a healthy adult's, and Saleh showed no underlying health problems. But the adult was surely dying while the child was going to live. Why?

What other factors had entered into the two cases? There was no Ebola outbreak in Iraq – there had never been such a thing, and in a populous country like that – didn't Iraq have a bio-war program? Could they have had an outbreak and hushed it up? But, no, the government of that country was in turmoil. So said the SkyNews service he had at his apartment, and in such circumstances secrets like this could not be kept. There would be panic.

MacGregor was a doctor, not a detective. The physicians who could do both worked for the World Health Organization, at the Pasteur Institute in Paris, and at CDC in America. Not so much brighter than he as more experienced and differently trained.

Sohaila. He had to manage her case, keep checking her

blood. Could she still infect others? MacGregor had to check the literature on that. All he knew for sure was that one immune system was losing and another was winning. If he were to figure anything out, he had to stay on the case. Maybe later he could get the word out, but he had to stay here to accomplish anything.

Besides, before telling anyone, he had gotten the blood samples out to Pasteur and CDC. This strutting bureaucrat didn't know that, and the phone calls, if they came, would come to this hospital and to MacGregor. He *could* get some word out. He could tell them what the political problem was. He could ask some questions, and relay others. He had to submit.

'As you wish, Doctor,' he told the official. 'You will, of course, follow the necessary procedures.'

31

RIPPLES AND WAVES

The payoff was this morning, and again President Ryan suffered through the ordeal of makeup and hair spray.

'We should at least have a proper barber chair,' Jack observed while Mrs Abbot did her duty. He'd just learned the day before, that the presidential barber came to the Oval Office and did *his* job at the President's swivel chair. That must be a real treat for the Secret Service, he thought, having a man with scissors and a straight razor an inch from his carotid artery. 'Okay, Arnie, what do I do with Mr Donner?'

'Number one, he asks any question he wants. That means you have to think about the answers.'

'I do try, Arnie,' Ryan observed with a frown.

'Emphasize the fact that you're a citizen and not a politician. It might not matter to Donner, but it will matter to the people who watch the interview tonight,' van Damm advised. 'Expect a hit on the court thing.'

'Who leaked that?' Ryan demanded crossly.

'We'll never know, and trying to find out only makes you look like Nixon.'

'Why is it that no matter what I do, somebody – damn,' Ryan sighed as Mary Abbot finished with his hair. 'I told George Winston that, didn't I?'

'You're learning. If you help some little old lady to cross the street, some feminist will say that it was condescending. If you don't help her, the AARP will say you're insensitive to the needs of the elderly. Throw in every other interest group there is. They all have agendas, Jack, and those agendas are a lot more important to them than you are. The idea is to offend as few people as possible. That's different from offending nobody. Trying to do that offends everybody,' the chief of staff explained.

Ryan's eyes went wide. 'I got it! I'll say something to piss everybody off – and then they'll all love me.'

Arnie wasn't buying: 'And every joke you tell will piss somebody off. Why? Humor is always cruel to someone, and some people just don't have a sense of humor to begin with.'

'In other words, there's people out there who *want* to get mad at something, and I'm the highest-profile target.'

'You're learning,' the chief of staff observed with a grim nod. He was worried about this one.

'We have Maritime Pre-Positioning Ships at Diego Garcia,' Jackson said, touching the proper point on the map.

'How much is there?' Bretano asked.

'We just reconfigured the TOE –'

'What's that?' SecDef asked.

'Table of Organization and Equipment.' General Michael Moore was the Army's chief of staff. He'd commanded a brigade of the First Armored Division in the Persian Gulf War. 'The load-out is enough for a little better than a brigade, a full-sized heavy Army brigade, along with all the consumables they need for a month's combat operations. Added to that, we have some units set in Saudi Arabia. The equipment is almost all new, M1A2 main battle tanks, Bradleys, MLRS. The new artillery tracks will be shipped out in three months. The Saudis,' he added, 'have been helping on the funding side. Some of the equipment is technically theirs, supposedly reserve equipment for their army, but we maintain it, and all we have to do is fly our people over to roll it out of the warehouses.'

'Who would go first, if they ask for help?'

'Depends,' Jackson answered. 'Probably the first out would be an ACR – Armored Cavalry Regiment. In a real emergency, we'd airlift the personnel from the 10th ACR in the Negev Desert. That can be done in as little as a single day. For exercises, the 3rd ACR out of Texas or the 2nd out of Louisiana.'

'An ACR, Mr Secretary, is a well-balanced brigade-sized formation. Lots of teeth, but not much tail. It can take care of itself, and people will think twice before taking it on,' Mickey Moore explained, adding, 'Before they can deploy for a lengthy stay, however, they need a combat-support battalion – supply and repair troops.'

'We still have a carrier in the Indian Ocean – she's at Diego now with the rest of the battle group to give the crews some shore leave,' Jackson went on. Which just about covered that atoll with sailors, but it was something. At least they could have a beer or two, and stretch their legs and play softball. 'We have an F-16 wing – well, most of one – in the Negev as well, as part of our commitment to Israeli security. That and the 10th Cav are pretty good. Their continuing mission is to train up the IDF, and it keeps them busy.'

'Soldiers love to train, Mr Secretary. They'd rather do that than anything,' General Moore added.

'I need to get out and see some of this stuff,' Bretano observed. 'Soon as I get the budget thing worked out – the start of it, anyway. It sounds thin, gentlemen.'

'It is, sir,' Jackson agreed. 'Not enough to fight a war, but probably enough to deter one, if it comes to that.'

'Will there be another war in the Persian Gulf?' Tom Donner asked.

'I see no reason to expect it,' the President replied. The hard part was controlling his voice. The answer was wary, but his words had to sound positive and reassuring. It was yet another form of lying, though telling the truth might change the equation. That was the nature of 'spin,' a game so false and artificial that it became a kind of international reality. Saying what wasn't true in order to serve the truth. Churchill had said it once: in time of war, truth was so precious as to need a bodyguard of lies. But in peacetime?

'But our relations with Iran and Iraq have not been friendly for some time.'

'The past is the past, Tom. Nobody can change it, but we can learn from it. There is no good reason for animosity between America and the countries in that region. Why should we be enemies?' the President asked rhetorically.

'So will we be talking to the United Islamic Republic?' Donner asked.

'We are always willing to talk to people, especially in the interest of fostering friendly relations. The Persian Gulf is a region of great importance to the entire world. It is in everyone's interest for that region to remain peaceful and stable. There's been enough war. Iran and Iraq fought for – what? – eight years, at enormous human cost to both countries. Then all the conflicts between Israel and her neighbors. Enough is enough. Now we have a new nation being born. This new country has much work to do. Its citizens have needs, and fortunately they also have the resources to address those needs. We wish them well. If we can help them, we will. America has always been willing to extend the hand of friendship.'

There was a brief break, which probably denoted a commercial. The interview would run this evening at nine o'clock. Then Donner turned to his senior colleague, John Plumber, who took the next segment.

'So, how do you like being President?'

Ryan tilted his head and smiled. 'I keep telling myself that I wasn't elected, I was sentenced. Honestly? The hours are long, the work is hard, much harder than I ever appreciated, but I've been pretty lucky. Arnie van Damm is a genius at organization. The staff here at the White House is just outstanding. I've gotten tens of thousands of letters of support from the people outside the Beltway, and I'd like to take this opportunity to thank them, and to let them know that it really helps.'

'Mr Ryan' – Jack supposed that his Ph.D. didn't count anymore – 'what things are you going to try and change?' Plumber asked.

'John, that depends on what you mean by "change." My foremost task is to keep the government operating. So, not "change," but "restore," is what I'm trying to do. We still don't really have a Congress yet – not until the House of Representatives is reestablished – and so I cannot submit a budget. I've tried to pick good people to take over the major Cabinet departments. Their job is to run those departments efficiently.'

'Your Secretary of the Treasury, George Winston, has been criticized for his rather abrupt desire to change the federal tax code,' Plumber said.

'All I can say is that I support Secretary Winston fully. The tax code *is* unconscionably complicated, and that is fundamentally unfair. What he wants to do will be revenue-neutral. Actually, that may be overly pessimistic. The net effect will be to enhance government revenues because of administrative savings in other areas.'

'But there has been a lot of adverse comment about the regressive nature –'

Ryan held up his hand. 'Wait a minute. John, one of the problems in this town is that the language used by people has been warped. Charging everyone the same is not *regressive*. That word means a backward step, charging the poor more than the rich. We will *not* be doing that. When you use that word in the incorrect way, you're misleading people.'

'But that's the way people have described the tax system for years.' Plumber hadn't had his grammar challenged in years.

'That doesn't make it right,' Jack pointed out. 'In any case, as I keep saying, I am not a politician, John. I only know how to talk straight. Charging everyone the same tax rate fulfills the dictionary's definition of "fair." Come on, John, you know how the game is played. You and Tom make a lot of money – far more than I do – and every year your lawyer and accountant go over everything. You probably have investments that are designed to reduce your tax payments, right? How did those loopholes happen? Easy, lobbyists talked Congress into changing the law a little. Why? Because rich people paid them to do so. So what happens? The supposedly "progressive" system is manipulated in such a way that the increased rates for the rich don't actually apply, because their lawyers and accountants tell them how to beat the system, and they *do* beat the system, for a fee. So, the increased rates they pay are a lie, aren't they? Politicians know all this when they pass the laws.

'You see where all this takes us? Nowhere, John. It takes us nowhere. It's a great big game, that's all. Just a game that wastes time, misleads the public, and makes a lot of money for people who work the system – and where does the money come from? The citizens, the people who pay for everything that happens. So George Winston wants to change the system – and we agreed on that – and what happens? The people who play the game and work the system use the same misleading words to make it look as though we're doing something unfair. These insiders are the most dangerous and pernicious special-interest group there is.'

'And you don't like that.' John smiled.

'Every job I've ever had, stock broker, history teacher, everything else, I've had to tell the truth as best I could. I'm not going to stop that now. Maybe some things do need changing, and I'll tell you what one of them is:

'Every parent in America sooner or later tells every child that politics is a dirty business, a rough business, a nasty business. Your dad told you. My dad told me – and we accept that as though it makes sense, as though it's normal and right and proper. But it's *not*, John. For years we've accepted the fact that politics – wait, let's define terms, shall we? The political system is the way we govern the country, pass the laws we all have to follow, levy taxes. These are important things, aren't they? But at the same time we accept people into that system whom we would not willingly invite into our homes, whom we would not trust to baby-sit our children. Does this strike you as just a little odd, John?

'We allow people into the political system who routinely distort facts, who twist laws in order to suit patrons who give them campaign money. Some of whom just plain lie. And we accept this. You people in the media do. You would not accept that sort of behavior in your own profession, would you? Or in medicine, or in science, or in business, or in law enforcement.

'There's something wrong here,' the President went on, leaning forward and talking passionately for the first time. 'This is our *country* we're talking about, and the standards of behavior we demand of our representatives shouldn't be lower – they should be higher. We should demand intelligence and integrity. That's why I've been giving speeches around the country. John, I'm a registered independent. I don't *have* a party affiliation. I don't have an agenda except for wanting to make things work for everyone. I swore an oath to do that, and I take my oaths seriously. Well, I've learned that this upsets people, and I'm sorry about that, but I will *not* compromise my beliefs to accommodate every special group with an army of paid lobbyists. I'm here to serve everybody, not just to serve the people who make the most noise and offer the most money.'

Plumber didn't show his pleasure at the outburst. 'Okay, Mr President, for starters, then, what about civil rights?'

'The Constitution is color-blind as far as I am concerned.

Discrimination against people because of how they look, how they sound, what church they go to, or the country their ancestors came from is against the laws of our country. Those laws will be enforced. We are all supposed to be equal in the eyes of the law, whether we obey them or break them. In the latter case, those people will have the Department of Justice to worry about.'

'Isn't that idealistic?'

'What's wrong with idealism?' Ryan asked in return. 'At the same time, what about a little common sense once in a while? Instead of a lot of people chiseling for advantages for themselves or whatever small group they represent, why can't we all work together? Aren't we all Americans before we're anything else? Why can't we all try a little harder to work together and find reasonable solutions to problems? This country wasn't set up to have every group at the throat of every other group.'

'Some would say that's the way we fight things out to make sure that everyone gets a fair share,' Plumber observed.

'And along the way, we corrupt the political system.'

They had to stop for the crew to change tapes on their cameras. Jack looked longingly at the door to the secretaries' office, wishing for a smoke. He rubbed his hands together, trying to look relaxed, but though he'd been given the chance to say things he'd wanted to say for years, the opportunity to do so only made him more tense.

'The cameras are off,' Tom Donner said, settling back in his seat a little. 'Do you really think you can bring *any* of this off?'

'If I don't try, what does that make me?' Jack sighed. 'The government's a mess. We all know that. If nobody tries to fix it, then it'll just get worse.'

Donner almost felt sympathy for his subject at that point. This Ryan guy's sincerity was manifest, as though his heart were beating right there on the sleeve of his jacket. But he just didn't get it. It wasn't that Ryan was a bad guy. He was just out of his depth, just as everyone else said. Kealty was right, and because he was right, Donner had his job to do.

'Ready,' the producer said.

'The Supreme Court,' Donner said, taking up the questioning from his colleague. 'It's been reported that you are now looking over a list of prospective justices for submission to the Senate.'

'Yes, I am,' Ryan replied.

'What can you tell us about them?'

'I instructed the Justice Department to send me a list of experienced appeals-court judges. That's been done. I'm looking over the list now.'

'What exactly are you looking for?' Donner asked next.

'I'm looking for good judges. The Supreme Court is our nation's primary custodian of the Constitution. We need people who understand that responsibility, and who will interpret the laws fairly.'

'Strict-constructionists?'

'Tom, the Constitution says that the Congress makes the law, the Executive Branch enforces the law, and the courts explain the law. That's called checks and balances.'

'But historically the Supreme Court has been an important force for change in our country,' Donner said.

'And not all of those changes have been good ones.' *Dred Scott* started the Civil War. *Plessy v. Ferguson* was a disgrace that set our country back seventy years. Please, you need to remember that as far as the law is concerned, I'm a layman –'

'That's why the American Bar Association routinely goes over judicial appointments. Will you submit your list to the ABA?'

'No.' Ryan shook his head. 'First, all of these judges have already passed that hurdle in order to get where they are. Second, the ABA is also an interest group, isn't it? Fine, they have a right to look out for the interests of their members, but the Supreme Court is the body of government which decides the law for everybody, and the ABA is the organization of people who use the law to make a living. Isn't it a conflict of interest for the group which makes use of the law to select the people who define the law? It would be in any other field, wouldn't it?'

'Not everyone will see it that way.'

'Yes, and the ABA has a big office here in Washington, and it's full of lobbyists,' the President agreed. 'Tom, my job isn't to serve the interest groups. My job is to preserve, protect, and defend the Constitution to the best of my ability. To help me do that, I'm trying to find people who think the same way I do, that the oath means what it says, without any game-playing under the table.'

Donner turned. 'John?'

'You spent many years at the Central Intelligence Agency,' Plumber said.

'Yes, I did,' Jack agreed.

'Doing what?' Plumber asked.

'Mainly I worked in the Directorate of Intelligence, going over information that came in through various means, trying to figure out what it meant, and then passing it on to others. Eventually I headed the Intelligence Directorate, then under President Fowler I became Deputy Director. Then, as you know, I became National Security Advisor to President Durling,' Jack answered, trying to steer the talk forward rather than backward.

'Along the way, did you ever go out into the field?' Plumber asked.

'Well, I advised the arms-control negotiations team, and I went off to a lot of conferences,' the President replied.

'Mr Ryan, there are reports that you did more than that, that you participated in operations that resulted in the deaths of, well, the deaths of Soviet citizens.'

Jack hesitated for a moment, long enough that he knew the impression he'd be giving to the viewers for this 'special.' 'John, it's been a principle of our government for many years that we never comment on intelligence operations. I will not change that principle.'

'The American people have a right and a need to know what sort of man sits in this office,' Plumber insisted.

'This administration will never discuss intelligence operations. As far as what sort of person I am, that's the purpose of this interview. Our country has to keep some secrets. So do you, John,' Ryan said with a level gaze into the commentator's eyes. 'If you reveal sources, you're out of business. If America does the same thing, people get hurt.'

'But –'

'The subject is closed, John. Our intelligence services operate under congressional oversight. I've always supported that law, and I will continue to uphold it, and that's it on this subject.'

Both reporters blinked pretty hard at that, and surely, Ryan thought, that part of the tape wouldn't make it onto the network tonight.

Badrayn needed to select thirty people, and while the number wasn't especially difficult – nor was the required dedication – brains were. He had the contacts. If there was a surplus of anything in the Middle East, it was terrorists, men like himself, if somewhat younger, who had dedicated their lives to the Cause, only to have it wither before their eyes. And that only made their anger and dedication worse – and better, depending on one's point of view. On reflection, he needed only twenty smart ones. The rest just had to be dedicated, with one or two intelligent overseers. They all had to follow orders. They all had to be willing to die, or at least to take the chance. Well, that wasn't much of a problem, either. Hezbollah still had a supply of people willing to strap explosives to their bodies, and there were others.

It was part of the region's tradition – probably not one that Mohammed would have approved entirely, but Badrayn wasn't particularly religious, and terrorist operations were his business. Historically, Arabs had not been the world's most efficient soldiers. Nomadic tribesmen for most of their history, their military tradition was one of raiding, later quantified as guerrilla tactics, rather than set-piece battle, which was, in fact, an invention of the Greeks, passed along to the Romans and thence to all Western nations. Historically, a single person would step forward to become a sacrifice – in Viking tradition the person was called a 'berzerker,' and in Japan they'd been part of the special attack corps also known as kamikaze – on the field of battle, to swing his sword gloriously, and take as many of his foes off to be his servants in Paradise as possible. This was especially true in a *jihad*, or 'holy war,' whose objective was to serve the interests of the Faith. It ultimately proved that Islam, like any religion, could be corrupted by its adherents. For the moment, it meant that Badrayn had a supply of people who would do what he told them to do, his instructions relayed from Daryaei, who would also tell them that this was, indeed, a *jihad* service in which lay their individual keys to a glorious afterlife.

He had his list. He made three telephone calls. The calls were relayed through several cutout chains, and in Lebanon and elsewhere, people made travel plans.

'So, how'd we do, coach?' Jack asked with a smile.

'The ice got pretty thin, but I guess you didn't get wet,' Arnie van Damm said with visible relief. 'You hit the interest groups pretty hard.'

'Isn't it *okay* to trash the special interests? Hell, everybody else does!'

'It depends on which groups and which interests, Mr President. They all have spokespersons, too, and some of them can come across like Mother Teresa after a nice-pill – right before they slash your throat with a machete.' The chief of staff paused. 'Still, you handled yourself pretty well. You didn't say anything they could turn against you too badly. We'll see how they cut it up for tonight, and then what Donner and Plumber say at the end. The last couple of minutes count the most.'

The tubes arrived in Atlanta in a very secure container called a 'hatbox' because of its shape. It was in its way a highly sophisticated device, designed to hold the most dangerous of materials in total safety, multiple-sealed, and spec'd to survive violent impacts. It was covered with biohazard warning labels and was treated with great respect by the handlers, including the FedEx deliveryman who'd handed it over this morning at 9:14.

The hatbox was taken to a secure lab, where the outside was checked for damage, sprayed with a powerful chemical disinfectant, and then opened under strict containment procedures. The accompanying documents explained why this was necessary. The two blood tubes were suspected to contain viruses which caused hemorrhagic fever. That could mean any of several such diseases from Africa – the indicated continent of origin – all of which were things to be avoided. A technician working in a glove box made the transfer after examining the containers for leaks. There were none he could see, and more disinfectant spray made sure of that. The blood would be tested for antibodies and compared with other samples. The documentation went off to the office of Dr Lorenz in the Special Pathogens Branch.

'Gus, Alex,' Dr Lorenz heard on the phone.

'Still not getting any fishing in?'

'Maybe this weekend. There's a guy in neurosurgery with a boat, and we have the house pretty well set up, finally.' Dr Alexandre was looking out the window of his office at east Baltimore. One could see the harbor, which led to the Chesapeake Bay, and there *were* supposed to be rockfish out there.

'What's happening?' Gus asked, as his secretary came in with a folder.

'Just checking in on the outbreak in Zaire. Anything new?'

'Zip, thank God. We're out of the critical time. This one burned out in a hurry. We were very –' Lorenz stopped when he opened the folder and scanned the cover sheet. 'Wait a minute. Khartoum?' he muttered to himself.

Alexandre waited patiently. Lorenz was a slow, careful reader. An elderly man, rather like Ralph Forster, he took his time with things, which was one of the reasons he was a brilliant experimental scientist. Lorenz rarely took a false step. He thought too much before moving his feet.

'We just had two samples come in from Khartoum. Cover sheet is from a Dr MacGregor, the English Hospital in Khartoum, two patients, adult male and four-year-old female, possible hemorrhagic fever. The samples are in the lab now.'

'Khartoum? Sudan?'

'That's what it says,' Gus confirmed.

'Long way from the Congo, man.'

'Airplanes, Alex, airplanes,' Lorenz observed. If there was one thing that frightened epidemiologists, it was international air travel. The cover sheet didn't say much, but it did give phone and fax numbers. 'Okay, well, we have to run the tests and see.'

'What about the samples from before?'

'Finished the mapping yesterday. Ebola Zaire, Mayinga sub-type, identical with the samples from 1976, down to the last amino acid.'

'The airborne one,' Alexandre muttered, 'the one that got George Westphal.'

'That was never established, Alex,' Lorenz reminded him.

'George was careful, Gus. You know that. You trained him.' Pierre Alexandre rubbed his eyes. Headaches. He needed a new desk light. 'Let me know what those samples tell you, okay?'

'Sure. I wouldn't worry too much. Sudan is a crummy environment for this little bastard. Hot, dry, lots of sunlight. The virus wouldn't last two minutes in the open. Anyway, let me talk to my lab chief. I'll see if I can micrograph it myself later today – no, more likely tomorrow morning. I have a staff meeting in an hour.'

'Yeah, and I need some lunch. Talk to you tomorrow, Gus.' Alexandre – he still thought of himself more as 'Colonel' than 'Professor' – replaced the phone and walked out, heading off to the cafeteria. He was pleased to find Cathy Ryan in the food line again, along with her bodyguard.

'Hey, Prof.'

'How's the bug business?' she asked, with a smile.

'Same-o, same-o. I need a consult, Doctor,' he said, selecting a sandwich off the counter.

'I don't do viruses.' But she did enough work with AIDS patients whose eye troubles were secondary to their main problem. 'What's the problem?'

'Headaches,' he said on the way to the cashier.

'Oh?' Cathy turned and took his glasses right off his face. She held them up to the light. 'You might try cleaning them once in a while. You're about two diopters of minus, pretty strong astigmatism. How long since you had the prescription checked?' She handed them back with a final look at the encrusted dirt around the lenses, already knowing the answer to her question.

'Oh, three –'

'Years. You should know better. Have your secretary call mine and I'll have you checked out. Join us?'

They selected a table by the window, with Roy Altman in tow, scanning the room, and catching looks from the other detail members doing the same. All clear.

'You know, you might be a good candidate for our new laser technique. We can re-shape your cornea and bring you right down to 20–20,' she told him. She'd helped ramrod that program, too.

'Is it safe?' Professor Alexandre asked dubiously.

'The only unsafe procedures I perform are in the kitchen,' Professor Ryan replied with a raised eyebrow.

'Yes, ma'am.' Alex grinned.

'What's new on your side of the house?'

It was all in the editing. Well, mostly in the editing, Tom Donner thought, typing on his office computer. From that he would slide in his own commentary, explaining and clarifying what Ryan had really meant with his seemingly sincere ... seemingly? The word had leaped into his mind of its own accord, startling the reporter. Donner had been in the business for quite a few years, and before his promotion to network anchor, he'd been in Washington. He'd covered them all and knew them all. On his well-stuffed Rolodex was a card with every important name and number in town. Like any good reporter, he was *connected*. He could lift a phone and get through to anyone, because in Washington the rules for dealing with the media were elegantly simple: either you were a source or a target. If you didn't play ball with the media, they would quickly find an enemy of yours who did. In other contexts, the technical term was 'blackmail.'

Donner's instincts told him that he'd never met anyone like President Ryan before, at least not in public life ... or was that true? The I'm-one-of-you, Everyman stance went at least as far back as Julius Caesar. It was always a ploy, a sham to make voters think that the guy really was like them. But he never was, really. Normal people didn't get this far in any field. Ryan had advanced in CIA by playing office politics just like everyone else – he must have. He'd made enemies and allies, as everyone did, and maneuvered his way up. And the leaks he'd gotten about Ryan's tenure at CIA. . . could he use them? Not in the special. Maybe in the news show, which would contain a teaser anyway to make people watch it instead of their usual evening TV fare.

Donner knew he had to be careful on this. You didn't go after a sitting President for the fun of it – well, that wasn't true, was it? Going after a President *was* the best sort of fun, but there were rules about how you did it. Your information had to be pretty solid. That meant multiple sources, and they had to be good sources. Donner would have to take them to a senior official of his news organization, and people would hem and haw, and then they'd go over the copy for his story, and then they'd let him run it.

Everyman. But Everyman didn't work for CIA and go into the field to be a spy, did he? Damned sure Ryan was the first spy who'd ever made it to the Oval Office . . . was that good?

There were so many blanks in his life. The thing in London. He'd killed there. The terrorists who'd attacked his home – he'd killed at least one of them there, too. This incredible story about stealing a Soviet submarine, during which, his source said, he'd killed a Russian sailor. The other things. Was this the sort of person the American people wanted in the White House?

And yet he tried to come across as . . . Everyman. Common sense. This is what the law says. I take my oaths seriously.

It's a lie, Donner thought. *It has to be a lie.*

You're one clever son of a bitch, Ryan, the anchorman thought.

And if it was that he was clever, and if it *was* a lie, then what? Changing the tax system. Changes in the Supreme Court. Changes in the name of efficiency, Secretary Bretano's activities at Defense . . . damn.

The next leap of imagination was that CIA and Ryan had had a role in the crash at the Capitol – no, that was too crazy. Ryan was an opportunist. They all were, the people Donner had covered for all of his professional life, all the way back to his first job at the network affiliate in Des Moines, where his work had landed a county commissioner in jail, and so gotten Donner noticed by the network executives at 30 Rock. Political figures. Donner reported on all manner of news from avalanches to warfare, but it was politicians whom he had studied as a profession and a hobby.

They were all the same, really. Right place, right time, and they already had the agenda. If he'd learned anything at all, he'd learned that. Donner looked out his window and lifted his phone with one hand while flipping the Rolodex with the other.

'Ed, this is Tom. Just how good are those sources, and how quickly can I meet them?' He couldn't hear the smile on the other end of the line.

*   *   *

Sohaila was sitting up now. Such situations provided a relief that never failed to awe the young doctor. Medicine was the most demanding of the professions, MacGregor believed. Every day, to a greater or lesser degree, he diced with Death. He didn't think of himself as a soldier, or a warrior knight on a blooded charger, at least not in conscious terms, because Death was an enemy who never showed himself – but he was always there, even so. Every patient he treated had that enemy inside, or hovering about somewhere, and his job as a physician was to discover his hiding place, seek him out, and destroy him, and you saw the victory in the face of the patient, and you savored every one.

Sohaila was still unwell, but that would pass. She was on liquids now, and she was keeping them down. Still weak, she would grow no weaker. Her temperature was down. All her vital signs were either stabilized or heading back to normal. This was a victory. Death wouldn't claim this child. In the normal course of events, she would grow and play and learn and marry and have children of her own.

But it was a victory for which MacGregor could not really take credit, at least not all of it. His care for the child had been merely supportive, not curative. Had it helped? Probably, he told himself. You couldn't know where the line was between what would have happened on its own and what had made a real difference. Medicine would be far easier if its practitioners possessed that degree of sight, but they didn't yet and probably never would. Had he not treated her – well, in this climate, just the heat might have done it, or certainly the dehydration, or maybe some opportunistic secondary infection. People so often expired not from their primary ailment, but from something else that took hold from the general weakening of the body. And so, yes, he *would* claim this victory, better yet that it was the life of a charming and attractive little girl who would in just a short time learn to smile again. MacGregor took her pulse, savoring the touch of the patient as he always did, and the remote contact with a heart that would still be beating a week from now, and as he watched, she fell off to sleep. He gently replaced the hand on the bed and turned.

'Your daughter will recover fully,' he told the parents, confirming their hopes and crushing their fears with five quiet words and a warm smile.

The mother gasped as though punched, her mouth open, tears exploding from her eyes as she covered her face with her hands. The father took the news in what he deemed a more manly way, his face impassive – but not his eyes, which relaxed and looked up to the ceiling in relief. Then he seized the doctor's hand, and his dark eyes came back down to bore in on MacGregor's.

'I will not forget,' the general told him.

Then it was time to see Saleh, something he'd consciously delayed. MacGregor left the room and walked down the corridor. Outside he changed into a different set of clothing. Inside he saw a defeat. The man was under restraints. The disease had entered his brain. Dementia was yet another symptom of Ebola, and a merciful one. Saleh's eyes were vacant and stared at the water marks on the ceiling. The nurse in attendance handed him the chart, the news on which was uniformly bad. MacGregor scanned it, grimaced, and wrote an order to increase the morphine drip. Supportive care in this case hadn't mattered a damn. One victory, one loss, and if he'd had the choice of which to save and which to lose, this was how he'd have written the story, for Saleh was grown and had had a life of sorts. That life had but five days to run, and MacGregor could do nothing now to save it, only a few things to make its final passage less gruesome for the patient – and the staff. After five minutes he left the room, stripped off his protective garb, and walked to his office, his face locked in a frown of thought.

Where had it come from? Why would one survive and one die? What didn't he know that he needed to know? The physician poured himself a cup of tea and tried to think past the victory and the defeat in order to find the information that had decided both issues. Same disease, same time. Two very different outcomes. Why?

32

RERUNS

'I can't give this to you, and I can't let you copy any of it, but I can let you look at it.' He handed the photo over. He had light cotton gloves on, and he'd already given a pair to Donner. 'Fingerprints,' he explained quietly.

'Is this what I think it is?' It was a black-and-white photograph, eight-by-ten glossy, but there was no classification stamp on it, at least not on the front. Donner didn't turn it over.

'You really don't want to know, do you?' It was a question and a warning.

'I guess not.' Donner nodded, getting the message. He didn't know how the Espionage Act – 18 USC §793E – interacted with his First Amendment rights, but if he didn't know that the photo was classified, then he didn't have to find out.

'That's a Soviet nuclear missile submarine, and that's Jack Ryan on the gangway. You'll notice he's wearing a Navy uniform. This was a CIA operation, run in cooperation with the Navy, and that's what we got out of it.' The man handed over a magnifying glass to make sure that the identifications were positive. 'We conned the Soviets into thinking she'd exploded and sunk about halfway between Florida and Bermuda. They probably still think that.'

'Where is it now?' Donner asked.

'They sank her a year later, off Puerto Rico,' the CIA official explained.

'Why there?'

'Deepest Atlantic water close to American territory, about five miles down, so nobody will ever find her, and nobody can even look without us knowing.'

'This was back – I remember!' Donner said. 'The Russians had a big exercise going and we raised hell about it, and they actually lost a submarine, didn't –'

'Two.' Another photo came out of the folder. 'See the

damage to the submarine's bow? *Red October* rammed and sank another Russian sub off the Carolinas. It's still there. The Navy didn't recover that one, but they sent down robots and stripped a lot of useful things off the hulk. It was covered as salvage activity on the first one, that sank from a reactor accident. The Russians never found out what happened to the second Alfa.'

'And this never leaked?' It was pretty amazing to a man who'd spent years extracting facts from the government, like a dentist with an unwilling patient.

'Ryan knows how to hush things up.' Another photo. 'That's a body bag. The person inside was a Russian crewman. Ryan killed him – shot him with a pistol. That's how he got his first Intelligence Star. I guess he figured we couldn't risk having him tell – well, isn't too hard to figure, is it?'

'Murder?'

'No.' The CIA man wasn't willing to go that far. 'The official story is that it was a real shoot-out, that other people got hurt also. That's how the documents read in the file, but . . .'

'Yeah. You have to wonder, don't you?' Donner nodded, staring down at the photos. 'Could this possibly be faked?'

'Possibly, yes,' he admitted. 'But it's not. The other people in the photo: Admiral Dan Foster, he was Chief of Naval Operations back then. This one is Commander Bartolomeo Mancuso. Back then he commanded USS *Dallas*. He was transferred to *Red October* to facilitate the defection. He's still on active duty, by the way, an admiral now. He commands all the submarines in the Pacific. And that one is Captain Marko Aleksandrovich Ramius of the Soviet navy. He was the captain of *Red October*. They're all still alive. Ramius lives in Jacksonville, Florida, now. He works at the Navy's base at Mayport under the name Mark Ramsey. Consulting contract,' he explained. 'The usual thing. Got a big stipend from the government, too, but God knows he earned it.'

Donner noted the details, and he recognized one of the extraneous faces. Sure as hell this wasn't faked. There were rules for that, too. If somebody lied to a reporter, it wasn't all that hard to make sure the right people found out who had broken the law – worse yet, that person became a target, and the media was in its way a crueler prosecutor than anyone in the Justice Department could ever hope to be. The court system, after all, required due process of law.

'Okay,' the journalist said. The first set of photos went back in their folder. Another folder appeared, and from it a photograph.

'Recognize this guy?'

'He was – wait a minute. Gera-something. He was –'

'Nikolay Gerasimov. He was chairman of the old KGB.'

'Killed in a plane crash back in –'

Another photo went down. The subject was older, grayer, and looking far more prosperous. 'This picture was taken in Winchester, Virginia, two years ago. Ryan went to Moscow, covered as a technical adviser to the START talks. He got Gerasimov to defect. Nobody's exactly sure how. His wife and daughter got out, too. That op was run directly out of Judge Moore's office. Ryan worked that way a lot. He was never really part of the system. Ryan knows – well, look, in fairness to the guy, he's one hell of a spook, okay? He supposedly worked directly for Jim Greer as part of the DI, not the DO. A cover within a cover. Ryan's never made an operational mistake that I know of, and that's some record. Not too many others can claim that, but one reason for it is he's one ruthless son of a bitch. Effective, yes, but ruthless. He cut through all the bureaucracy whenever he wanted. He does it his way every time, and if you get in his way – well, there's one dead Russian we buried off the *Red October*, and a whole Alfa crew off the Carolinas, to keep that op a secret. This one, I'm not sure. Nothing in the file, but the file has a lot of blanks. How the wife and daughter got out, it's not in the file. All I have for that are rumors, and they're pretty thin.'

'Damn, I wish I'd had this a few hours ago.'

'Rolled you, did he?' This question came from Ed Kealty over a speaker phone.

'I know the problem,' the CIA official said. 'Ryan is slick. I mean, *slick*. He's skated through CIA like Dorothy Hamill at Innsbruck, done it for years. Congress loves him. Why? He comes across as the most straightforward guy this side of Honest Abe. Except he's killed people.' The man's name was Paul Webb, and he was a senior official in the Directorate of Intelligence, but not senior enough to prevent his whole unit from ending up on the RIF list. He should have been DDI now, Webb thought, and he would have been except for the way Ryan had gotten James Greer's ear and never let go of it. And so his career had ended as an entry-level supergrade at CIA, and now *that* was being taken away from him. He had his retirement. Nobody could take that away – well, if it became known that he'd smuggled these files out of Langley, he'd be in very deep trouble . . . or maybe not. What really happened to whistle-blowers, after all? The media protected them pretty well, and he had his time in service, and . . . he didn't *like* being part of a reduction-in-force exercise. In another age, though he didn't admit it even to himself, his anger might have prompted him to make contact with – no, not that. Not to an enemy. But the media wasn't an enemy, was it? He told himself that it was not, despite an entire career of thinking otherwise.

'You've been rolled, Tom,' Kealty said again over the phone line. 'Welcome to the club. *I* don't even know all the stuff he can pull off. Paul, tell him about Colombia.'

'There's no file on that one that I can find,' Webb admitted. 'Wherever it is – well, there are special files, the ones with date-stamps on them. Like 2050 at the earliest. Nobody sees those.'

'How does *that* happen?' Donner demanded. 'I've heard that before, but I've never been able to confirm –'

'How they keep those off the books? It's a deal that has to go through Congress, an unwritten part of the oversight process. The Agency goes there with a little problem, asks for special treatment, and if Congress agrees, off the file goes into the special vault – hell, for all I know, the whole thing's been shredded and turned into compost, but I can give you a few verifiable facts,' Webb concluded with an elegant dangle.

'I'm listening,' Donner replied. And so was his tape recorder.

'How do you suppose the Colombians broke up the Medellín cartel?' Webb asked, drawing Donner in further. It wasn't all that hard. These people thought they knew about intrigue, Webb thought with a benign smile.

'Well, they had some sort of internal faction fight, a couple of bombs went off and –'

'They were CIA bombs. Somehow – I'm not sure exactly how, we initiated the faction fight. This I do know: Ryan was down there. His mentor at Langley was James Greer – they were like father and son. But when James died, Ryan wasn't there for the funeral, and he wasn't at home, and he wasn't away on CIA business – he'd just come *back* from a NATO conference in Belgium. But then he just dropped off the map, like he's done any number of times. Soon thereafter the President's National Security Advisor, Jim Cutter, is *accidentally* run down by a DC transit bus on the GW, right? He didn't look? He just ran in front of a bus. That's what the FBI said, but the guy running that was Dan Murray, and what job does he have now? FBI Director, right? It just so happens he and Ryan go back more than ten years. Murray was the "special" guy for both Emil Jacobs *and* Bill Shaw. When the Bureau needed something done quietly, they called in Murray. Before that he was legal attaché in London – that's a spook post, lots of contacts with the intelligence communities over there; Murray's the black side of FBI, big time and well connected. And *he* picked Pat Martin to advise Ryan on Supreme Court appointments. Is the picture becoming clear?'

'Wait a minute. I *know* Dan Murray. He's a tough son of a bitch, but he's an honest cop –'

'He was in Colombia with Ryan, which is to say, he was off the map at exactly the same time. Okay, remember, I do *not* have the file on this operation, okay? I can't prove any of this. Look at the sequence of events. Director Jacobs and all the others were killed, and right after that we have bombs going off in Colombia, and a lot of the cartel boys go to talk it over with God – but a lot of innocent people got killed, too. That's the problem with bombs. Remember how Bob Fowler made an issue of that? So what happens then? Ryan disappears. Murray does, too. I figure they went down to turn the operation off before it got totally out of hand – and then Cutter dies at a very convenient moment. Cutter didn't have the balls for wet work, he probably knew that, and people probably were afraid he'd crack because he just didn't have the nerve. But Ryan sure as hell did – and still does. Murray

– well, you kill the FBI Director, and you piss off a very serious organization, and I can't say I disapprove. Those Medellín bastards stepped way over the line, and they did it in an election year, and Ryan was in the right place to play a little catch-up ball, and so somebody issued him a hunting license, and maybe things got a little out of hand – it happens – and so he goes down there to shut it down. Successfully,' Webb emphasized. 'In fact, the whole operation was a success. The cartel came apart –'

'Another one took its place,' Donner objected. Webb nodded with an insider's smile.

'True, and they haven't killed any American officials, have they? Somebody explained to them what the rules are. Again, I will not say that what Ryan did was wrong, except for one little thing.'

'What's that?' Donner asked, disappointing Webb, though he was fully caught up in the story now.

'When you deploy military forces into a foreign country, and kill people, it's called an act of war. But, again, Ryan skated. The boy's got some beautiful moves. Jim Greer trained him well. You could drop Ryan in a septic tank and he'll come out smelling like Old Spice.'

'So, what's your beef with him?'

'You finally asked,' Webb observed. 'Jack Ryan is probably the best intelligence operator we've had in thirty years, the best since Allen Dulles, maybe the best since Bill Donovan. *Red October* was a brilliant coup. Getting the chairman of KGB out was even better. The thing in Colombia, well, they twisted the tiger's tail, and they forgot that the tiger has great big claws. Okay,' Webb allowed. 'Ryan's a king spook – but he needs somebody to tell him what the law is, Tom.'

'A guy like this would never get elected,' Kealty observed, straining himself to say as little as possible. Three miles away his own chief of staff almost pulled the phone away from him, they were so close to getting the message across. Fortunately, Webb carried on.

'He's done a great job at the Agency. He was even a good adviser for Roger Durling, but that's not the same as being President. Yeah, he rolled you, Mr Donner. Maybe he rolled Durling – probably not, but who can say? But this guy is rebuilding the whole fucking government, and he's building

624

it in *his* image, in case you didn't notice. Every appointment he's made, they're all people he's worked with, some for a long time – or they were selected for him by close associates. Murray running the FBI. Do you want Dan Murray in charge of America's most powerful law enforcement agency? You want these two people picking the Supreme Court? Where will he take us?' Webb paused, and sighed. 'I hate doing this. He's one of us at Langley, but he isn't supposed to be President, okay? I have an obligation to my country, and my country isn't Jack Ryan.' Webb collected the photos and tucked them back in the folders. 'I gotta get back. If anyone finds out what I've done, well, look what happened to Jim Cutter . . .'

'Thank you,' Donner said. Then he had some decisions to make. His watch said three-fifteen, and he had to make them fast. Driving that decision would be a well-understood fact. There was something in creation even more furious than a woman scorned. It was a reporter who'd discovered that he'd been rolled.

All nine were dying. It would take from five to eight days, but they were all doomed, and they all knew it. Their faces stared at the overhead cameras, and they had no illusions now. Their executions would be even crueller than the courts had decided for them. Or so they thought. This group promised to be more dangerous than the first – they just knew more of what was going on – and as a result they were more fully restrained. As Moudi watched, the army medics went in to draw blood samples from the subjects, which would be necessary to confirm and then to quantify the degree of their infection. On their own, the medics had come up with a way to keep the 'patients' from struggling during the process – a jerked arm at the wrong moment could make one of the medical corpsmen stab the needle into the wrong body, and so while one man did the sample, the other held a knife across the subject's throat. Doomed though the criminals believed themselves to be, they *were* criminals, and cowards, and therefore unwilling to hasten their deaths. It wasn't good medical technique, but then nobody in the building was practicing good medicine. Moudi watched the process for a few minutes and left the monitoring room.

They'd been overly pessimistic on many things, and one of them was the quantity of virus that would be needed. In the culturing tank, the Ebola had consumed the monkey kidneys and blood with a gusto whose results chilled even the director. Though it happened fundamentally at the molecular level, overall it was like seeing ants going after dead fruit, seeming to come from nowhere and then covering it, turning it black with their bodies. So it was with the Ebola virus; even though it was too small to see, there were literally trillions of them eating and displacing the tissue offered them as food. What had been one color was now another, and you didn't have to be a physician to know that the contents of the chamber were hateful beyond words. It chilled his blood merely to look at the dreadful 'soup.' There were liters of it now, and they were growing more, using human blood taken from the Tehran central blood bank.

The director was examining a sample under the electron microscope, comparing it with another. As Moudi approached, he could see the date-stamp labels on each. One was from Jean Baptiste. The other was newly arrived from a 'patient' in the second group of nine.

'They're identical, Moudi,' he said, turning when the younger man approached.

This was not as much to be expected as one might think. One of the problems with viruses was that, since they were scarcely alive at all, they were actually ill suited for proper reproduction. The RNA strand lacked an 'editing function' to ensure that each generation would fully follow in the footsteps of its predecessor. It was a serious adaptive weakness of Ebola, and many other similar organisms. Sooner or later each Ebola outbreak petered out, and this was one of the reasons. The virus itself, maladapted to the human host, became less virulent. And *that* was what made it the ideal biological weapon. It would kill. It would spread. Then it would die before doing too much of the latter. How much it did of the former was a function of the initial distribution. It was both horribly lethal and also self-limiting.

'So, we have at least three generations of stability,' Moudi observed.

'And by extrapolation, probably seven to nine.' The project director, whatever his perversion of medical science, was a conservative on technical issues. Moudi would have said nine to eleven. Better that the director was right, he admitted to himself, turning away.

On a table at the far wall were twenty cans. Similar to the ones used to infect the first collection of criminals, but slightly modified, they were labeled as economy-size cans of a popular European shaving cream. (The company was actually American-owned, which amused everyone associated with the project.) They'd been exactly what they said, and been bought singly in twelve different cities in five different countries, as the lot numbers inked on their curving bottoms showed. Here in the Monkey House they'd been emptied and carefully disassembled for modification. Each would contain a half liter of the thinned-out 'soup,' plus a neutral-gas propellant (nitrogen, which would not involve any chemical reaction with the 'soup' and would not support combustion) and a small quantity of coolant. Another part of the team had already tested the delivery system. There would be no degradation of the Ebola at all for more than nine hours. After that, with the loss of the coolant, the virus particles would start to die in a linear function. At 9 + 8 hours, less than ten percent of the particles would be dead – but those, Moudi told himself, were the weak ones anyway, and probably the particles that would be unlikely to cause illness. At 9 + 16 hours, fifteen percent would be dead. Thereafter, experiments had revealed, every eight hours – for some reason the numbers seemed to track with thirds of days – an additional five percent would die. And so . . .

It was simple enough. The travelers would all fly out of Tehran. Flight time to London, seven hours. Flight time to Paris, thirty minutes less. Flight time to Frankfurt, less still. Much of that factor was the time of day, Moudi had learned. In the three cities there would be easy connecting flights. Baggage would not be checked because the travelers would be moving on to another country, and therefore customs inspection wasn't necessary, and therefore no one would notice the cans of unusually cold shaving cream. About the time the coolant ran out, the travelers would be in their first-class seats, climbing to cruising altitude to their cities of final destination, and there again international air travel worked out nicely. There were direct flights from Europe to

New York, to Washington, to Boston, to Philadelphia, to Chicago, to San Francisco, to Los Angeles, to Atlanta, to Dallas, to Orlando, and regular connecting flights to Las Vegas, and Atlantic City – in fact to all of America's convention cities. The travelers would all fly first class, the quicker to claim their luggage and get through customs. They would have good hotel reservations, and return tickets that took them out from different airports. From time-zero to delivery no more than twenty-four hours would pass, and therefore eighty percent of the Ebola released would be active. After that, it was all random, in Allah's hands – *no!* Moudi shook his head. He was not the director. He would not apply this act to the will of his God. Whatever it might be, however necessary it was to his country – and a new one at that – he would not defile his religious beliefs by saying or even thinking *that.*

Simple enough? It had been simple once, but then – it was a legacy of sorts. Sister Jean Baptiste, her body long since incinerated ... instead of leaving children behind as a woman's body ought, disease was its only physical legacy, and that was an act of such malignance that surely Allah must be offended. But she'd left something else, too, a real legacy. Moudi had once hated all Westerners as unbelievers. In school he'd learned of the Crusades, and how those supposed soldiers of the prophet Jesus had slaughtered Muslims, as Hitler had later slaughtered Jews, and from that he'd taken the lesson that all Westerners and all Christians were something less than the people of his own Faith, and it was easy to hate such people, easy to write them off as irrelevancies in a world of virtue and belief. But that one woman. What was the West and what was Christianity? The criminals of the eleventh century, or a virtuous woman of the twentieth who denied every human wish she might have had – and for what? To serve the sick, to teach her faith. Always humble, always respectful. She'd never broken her vows of poverty, chastity, and obedience – Moudi was sure of that – and though those vows and those beliefs might have been false, they hadn't been *that* false. He'd learned from her the same thing that the Prophet had learned. There was but one God. There was but one Book. She had served both with a pure heart, however misguided her religious beliefs might have been.

Not just Sister Jean Baptiste, he reminded himself. *Sister Maria Magdalena, too*. And she had been murdered – and why? Loyalty to her faith, loyalty to her vows, loyalty to her friend, not one of which the Holy Koran found the least bit objectionable.

It would have been so much easier for him had he only worked with black Africans. Their religious beliefs were things the Koran abhorred, since many of them were still pagans in deed if not in word, ignorant of the One God, and he could easily have looked down on them, and not worried at all about Christians – but he had met Jean Baptiste and Maria Magdalena. Why? Why had that happened?

Unfortunately for him it was too late to ask such questions. What was past was past. Moudi walked to the far corner of the room and got himself some coffee. He'd been awake for more than a day, and with fatigue came doubts, and he hoped the drink would chase them away until sleep could come, and with it rest, and with that, perhaps, peace.

'You have to be kidding!' Arnie snarled into the phone.

Tom Donner's voice was as apologetic as it could be. 'Maybe it was the metal detectors on the way out. The tape – I mean, it's damaged. You can still see it and hear it just fine, but there's a little noise on the audio track. Not broadcast quality. The whole hour's worth is shot. We can't use it.'

'So?' van Damm demanded.

'So, we have a problem, Arnie. The segment is supposed to run at nine.'

'So, what do you want me to do about it?'

'Is Ryan up to redoing it live? We'll get better share that way,' the anchorman offered.

The President's chief of staff almost said something else. If this had been sweeps week – during which the networks did their best to inflate their audiences in order to get additional commercial fees – he might have accused Donner of having done this deliberately. No, that was a line even *he* couldn't cross. Dealing with the press on this level was rather like being Clyde Beatty in center ring, armed with a bottomless chair and a blank-loaded revolver, holding great jungle cats at bay for the audience, having the upper hand at all times, but knowing that the cats needed to get lucky only once. Instead he just offered silence, forcing Donner to make the next move.

'Look, Arnie, it'll be the same agenda. How often do we give the President a chance to rehearse his lines? And he did fine this morning. John thinks so, too.'

'You can't retape?' van Damm asked.

'Arnie, I go on the air in forty minutes, and I'm wrapped till seven-thirty. That gives me thirty minutes to scoot down to the White House, set up and shoot, and get the tape back here, all before nine? You want to lend me one of his helicopters?' He paused. 'This way – tell you what. I will say on the air that we goofed on the tape, and that the Boss graciously agreed to go live with us. If that isn't a network blow job, I don't know what is.'

Arnold van Damm's alarm lights were all flashing red. The good news was that Jack had handled himself pretty well. Not perfect, but pretty well, especially on the sincerity. Even the controversial stuff, he'd come across as believing what he'd said. Ryan took coaching well, and he learned fast. He hadn't looked as relaxed as he should, but that was okay. Ryan *wasn't* a politician – he'd said that two or three times – and therefore looking a little tense was all right. Focus groups in seven different cities all said that they liked Jack because he acted like one of them. Ryan didn't know that Arnie and the political staff were doing that. *That* little program was as secret as a CIA operation, but Arnie justified it to himself as a reality check on how the President could best project his agenda and his image in order to govern effectively – and no President had ever known all the things done in his name. So, yes, Ryan *did* come across as presidential – not in the normal way, but in *his own* way, and that, the focus groups all agreed, was good, too. And going live, yes, that would *really* look good, and it *would* get a lot more people to flip the channel to NBC, and Arnie wanted the people to get to know Ryan better.

'Okay, Tom, a tentative yes. But I *do* have to ask him.'

'Fast, please,' Donner replied. 'If he cancels out, then we have to jerk around the whole network schedule for tonight, and that could mean *my* ass, okay?'

'Back to you in five,' van Damm promised. He killed the

button on the phone and hustled out of the room, leaving the receiver on his desk pad.

'On the way to see the Boss,' he told the Secret Service agents in the east-west corridor. His stride told them to jump out of his way even before they saw his eyes.

'Yes?' Ryan said. It wasn't often his door opened without warning.

'We have to redo the interview,' Arnie said somewhat breathlessly.

Jack shook his head in surprise. 'Why? Didn't I have my fly zipped?'

'Mary always checks that. The tape got screwed up, and there isn't time to reshoot. So Donner asked me to ask you if you would do it live at nine o'clock. Same questions and everything – no, no,' Arnie said, thinking fast. 'What about we get your wife down here, too?'

'Cathy won't like that. Why?' the President asked.

'Really, all she has to do is sit there and smile. It will look good for the people out there. Jack, she has to act like the First Lady occasionally. This should be an easy one. Maybe we can even bring the kids in toward the end –'

'No. My kids stay out of the public eye, period. Cathy and I have talked about that.'

'But –'

'No, Arnie, no now, no tomorrow, no in the future, no.' Ryan's voice was as final as a death sentence.

The chief of staff figured he couldn't talk Ryan into everything. This would take a little time, but he'd come around eventually. You couldn't be one of the people without letting them meet your kids, but now wasn't the time to press on that one. 'Will you ask Cathy?'

Ryan sighed and nodded. 'Okay.'

'Right, okay, I'll tell Donner that she might be on, but we're not sure yet because of her medical obligations. It'll give him something to think about. It will also take some of the heat off you. That's the First Lady's main job, remember.'

'You want to tell her that, Arnie? Remember, she's a surgeon, good with knives.'

Van Damm laughed. 'I'll tell you what she is. She's a hell of a lady, and she's tougher than either one of us. Ask nicely,' he advised.

'Yeah.' Right before dinner, Jack thought.

'Okay, he'll do it. But we want to ask his wife to join us, too.'

'Why?'

'Why not?' Arnie asked. 'Not sure yet. She isn't back from work,' he added, and that was a line that made the reporters smile.

'Okay, Arnie, thanks, I owe you one.' Donner turned off the speakerphone.

'You realize that you just lied to the President of the United States,' John Plumber observed pensively. Plumber was an older pro than Donner. He wasn't of the Edward R. Murrow generation – quite. Pushing seventy now, he'd been a teenager in World War II, but had gone to Korea as a young reporter, and been foreign correspondent in London, Paris, Bonn, and finally Moscow. Plumber had been ejected from Moscow, and his somewhat left political stance had nonetheless never turned into sympathy with the Soviet Union. But more than that, though he was not of Murrow's generation, he had grown up listening to the immortal CBS correspondent, and he could still close his eyes and hear the gravelly voice which had somehow carried a measure of authority usually associated with the clergy. Maybe it was because Ed had started on the radio, when one's voice was the currency of the profession. He'd certainly known language better than most of his own time, and infinitely better than the semiliterate reporters and newswriters of the current generation. Plumber was something of a scholar in his own right, a devoted student of Elizabethan literature, and he tried to draft his copy and his spontaneous comments with an elegance in keeping with that of the teacher he'd only watched and heard, but never actually met. More than anything else, people had listened to Ed Murrow because of his honor, John Plumber reminded himself. He'd been as tough as any of the later generation of 'investigative journalists' that the schools turned out now, but you always knew that Ed Murrow was fair. And you knew that he didn't break the rules. Plumber was of the generation that believed that his profession was supposed to have rules, one of which was you *never* told a lie. You could bend, warp, and twist the truth in

632

order to get information out of someone – that was different – but you *never* told someone something that was deliberately and definitely false. That troubled John Plumber. Ed would never have done that. Not a chance.

'John, he rolled us.'

'You think.'

'The information I got – well, *what* do you think?' It had been a frantic two hours, with the entire network research staff running down bits of such minor trivia that even two or three of the pieces, put together, didn't amount to much of anything. But they'd *all* checked out, and that was something else entirely.

'I'm not sure, Tom.' Plumber rubbed his eyes. 'Is Ryan a little out of his depth? Yes, he is. But is he trying pretty hard? Definitely. Is he honest? I think so. Well, as honest as any of them ever can be,' he amended himself.

'Then we'll give him the chance to prove it, won't we?'

Plumber didn't say anything. Visions of ratings, and maybe even an Emmy were dancing in the eyes of his junior colleague like sugar plums on Christmas Eve. In any case, Donner was the anchor, and Plumber was the commentator, and Tom had the ear of the front office in New York, which had once been peopled by men of his own generation, but was now entirely populated by people of Donner's, businessmen more than journalists, who saw ratings as the Holy Grail on their quarterly earnings statements. Well, Ryan liked businessmen, didn't he?

'I suppose.'

The helicopter landed on the South Lawn pad. The crew chief jerked the door open and jumped out, next helping the First Lady out with a smile. Her portion of the Detail followed, walking up the gentle slope to the south entrance, then to the elevator, where Roy Altman pushed the button for her, since the First Lady wasn't allowed to do that, either.

'SURGEON is in the elevator, heading for the residence,' Agent Raman reported from the ground floor.

'Roger,' Andrea Price acknowledged upstairs. She'd already had some people from the Technical Security Unit check all the metal detectors the NBC crew had passed on the way out. The TSU chief commented that occasionally they got a little fluky, and the large-format Beta tapes the networks used could easily be damaged – but he didn't think so. Maybe a line surge, she'd asked. No chance, he'd replied, reminding her archly that even the *air* in the White House was checked continuously by his people. Andrea debated discussing that with the chief of staff, but it would have been no use. Damn the reporters anyway. They were the biggest pain in the ass on the campus.

'Hi, Andrea,' Cathy said, breezing past her.

'Hello, Dr Ryan. Dinner is just coming up now.'

'Thank you,' Surgeon replied on her way into the bedroom. She stopped on entering, seeing that a dress and jewelry were on her valet. Frowning, she kicked off her shoes and got casual clothes for dinner, wondering, as always, if there were cameras hidden somewhere to record the event.

The White House cook, George Butler, was by far her superior. He'd even improved on her spinach salad, adding a pinch of rosemary to the dressing she'd perfected over the years. Cathy kibitzed with him at least once a week, and in turn he showed her how to use the institutional-class appliances. She sometimes wondered how good a cook she might have become had she not opted for medicine. The executive chef hadn't told her that she had a gift for it, being fearful of patronizing her – Surgeon *was* a surgeon, after all. Along the way he'd learned the family preferences, and cooking for a toddler, he'd discovered, was a treat, especially when she occasionally came down with her towering bodyguard to search for snacks. Don Russell and she had milk and cookies at least twice a week. Sandbox had become the darling of the staff.

'Mommy!' Katie Ryan said when Cathy came through the door.

'Hi, honey.' Sandbox got the first hug and kiss. POTUS got the second. The older kids resisted, as always. 'Jack, why are my clothes out?'

'We're going to be on TV tonight,' Swordsman replied warily.

'Why?'

'The tape from this morning got all farbled up, and they want to do it live at nine, and if you're willing, I want you to be there, too.'

634

'To answer what?'

'About what you'd expect as far as I'm concerned.'

'So, what do I do, walk in with a tray of cookies?'

'George makes the *best* cookies!' SANDBOX added to the conversation. The other kids laughed. It broke the tension somewhat.

'You don't *have* to if you don't want, but Arnie thinks it's a good idea.'

'Great,' Cathy observed. Her head tilted as she looked at her husband. Sometimes she wondered where the puppet strings were, the ones Arnie used to jerk her husband around.

Bondarenko was working late – or early, depending on one's point of view. He'd been at his desk for twenty hours, and since his promotion to general officer he'd learned that life was far better as a colonel. As a colonel he'd gotten out to jog, and even managed to sleep with his wife most of the time. Now – well, he'd always aspired to higher rank. He'd always had ambition, else why would a Signal Corps officer have gone into the Afghan mountains with the Spetznaz? Recognized for his talent, his colonelcy had almost been his undoing, as he'd worked as a close aide for another colonel who'd turned out to be a spy – that fact still boggled him. Misha Filitov a spy for the West? It had shaken his faith in many things, most of all his faith in his country – but then the country had died. The Soviet Union which had raised him and uniformed him and trained him had died one cold December night, to be replaced with something smaller and more ... comfortable to serve. It was easier to love Mother Russia than a huge polyglot empire. Now it was as though the adopted children had all moved away, and the true children remained, and that made for a happier family.

But a poorer one. Why hadn't he seen it before? His country's military had been the world's largest and most impressive, or so he had once thought, with its huge masses of men and arms, and its proud history of destroying the German invaders in history's most brutal war. But that military had died in Afghanistan, or if not quite that, then lost its soul and its confidence, as America's had done in Vietnam. But America had recovered, a process his country had yet to begin.

All that money wasted. Wasted on the departed provinces, those ungrateful wretches whom the Union had supported for generations, now gone, taking so much wealth with them, and in some cases turning away to join with others, then, he feared, to turn back as enemies. Just like unfaithful adopted children.

Golovko was right. If that danger was to be stopped, it had to be stopped early. But how? Dealing with a few bandit Chechens had proved difficult enough.

He was operations chief now. In five more years, he'd be commanding general. Bondarenko had no illusions about that. He was the best officer of his age group, and his perform-ance in the field had won him high-level attention, ever the determining factor in the ultimate advancement. He could get that job just in time to fight Russia's last losing battle. Or maybe not. In five years, given funding and a free hand to reshape doctrine and training, he might just convert the Russian army into a force such as it had never been. He would shamelessly use the American model, as the Americans had shamelessly used Soviet tactical doctrine in the Persian Gulf War. But for that to happen he needed a few years of relative peace. If his forces were to be trapped into fighting brushfires all along its southern periphery, he would not have the needed time or funding to save the army.

So what was he supposed to do? He was the operations chief. He was supposed to know. It was his job to know. Except he didn't. Turkmenistan was first. If he didn't stop it there, he never would. On the left side of his desk was a roster of available divisions and brigades, with their supposed states of readiness. On the right side was a map. The two made a poor match.

'You have such nice hair,' Mary Abbot said.

'I didn't do surgery today,' Cathy explained. 'The cap always ruins it.'

'You've had the same hairstyle for how long?'

'Since we got married.'

'Never changed it?' *That* surprised Mrs Abbot. Cathy just shook her head. She thought that she looked rather like the actress Susannah York – or at least she'd liked the look from a movie she'd seen while in college. And the same was true of Jack, wasn't it? He'd never changed *his* haircut, except when he didn't have the time to get a trim, something else the White House staff took care of, every two weeks. They were far better at managing Jack's life than she'd ever been. They probably just did things and scheduled things instead of asking first, as she had always done. A much more efficient system, Cathy told herself.

She was more nervous than she let on, worse than the first day of medical school, worse than her first surgical procedure, when she'd had to close her eyes and scream inwardly at her hands to keep them from shaking. But at least they'd listened then, and they listened now, too. Okay, she thought, that was the key. This was a surgical procedure, and she was a surgeon, and a surgeon was always in control.

'I think that does it,' Mrs Abbot said.

'Thank you. Do you like working with Jack?'

An insider's smile. 'He *hates* makeup. But most men do,' she allowed.

'I have a secret for you – so do I.'

'I didn't do much,' Mary observed at once. 'Your skin doesn't need much.'

The woman-to-woman observation made Dr Ryan smile. 'Thank you.'

'Can I make a suggestion?'

'Sure.'

'Let your hair grow another inch, maybe two. It would complement the shape of your face better.'

'That's what Elaine says – she's my hairdresser in Baltimore. I tried it once. The surgical caps make it all scrunchy.'

'We can make bigger caps for you. We try to take care of our First Ladies.'

'Oh!' *And why didn't I think of that!* Cathy asked herself. It had to be cheaper than taking the helicopter to work ... 'Thank you!'

'This way.' Mrs Abbot led FLOTUS to the Oval Office.

Surprisingly, Cathy had been in the room only twice before, and only once to see Jack there. It suddenly struck her as odd. Her bedroom wasn't fifty yards away from her husband's place of work, after all. The desk struck her as grossly old-fashioned, but the office itself was huge and airy compared to hers at Hopkins, even now with the TV lights and cameras set up. Over the mantel opposite the desk was what the Secret Service called the world's most photographed plant. The furniture was too formal to be comfortable, and the rug with the President's Seal embroidered on it was downright tacky, she thought. But it wasn't a normal office for a normal person.

'Hi, honey.' Jack kissed her and handled introductions. 'This is Tom Donner and John Plumber.'

'Hello.' Cathy smiled. 'I used to listen to you while fixing dinner.'

'Not anymore?' Plumber asked with a smile.

'No TV in the dining room upstairs, and they won't let me fix dinner.'

'Doesn't your husband help?' Donner asked.

'Jack in the kitchen? Well, he's okay on a grill, but the kitchen is my territory.' She sat down, looking at their eyes. It wasn't easy. The TV lights were already on. She made the extra effort. Plumber she liked. Donner was hiding something. The realization made her blink, and her face changed over to her doctor's look. She had the sudden desire to say something to Jack, but there wasn't –

'One minute,' the producer said. Andrea Price, as always, was in the room, standing by the door to the secretaries' space, and the door behind Cathy was open to the corridor. Jeff Raman was there. He was another odd duck, Cathy thought, but the problem with the White House was that everyone treated you like you were Julius Caesar or something. It was so hard just being friendly with people. It seemed that there was always something in the way. Fundamentally, neither Jack nor Cathy was used to having servants. Employees, yes, but not servants. She was popular with her nurses and technicians at Hopkins because she treated them all like the professionals they were, and she was trying to do the same thing here, but for some reason it didn't work quite the same way, and that was bothersome in a distant way.

'Fifteen seconds.'

'Are we having fun yet?' Jack whispered.

Why couldn't you just have stayed at Merrill Lynch? Cathy almost said aloud. He would have been a senior VP by now – but, no. He would never have been happy. Jack was as driven to do his work as she was to fix people's eyes. In that they were the same.

'Good evening,' Donner said to the camera behind the Ryans. 'We're here in the Oval Office to speak with President Jack Ryan and the First Lady. As I said on *NBC Nightly News*, a technical glitch damaged the taping we did earlier today. The President has graciously allowed us to come back and talk live.' His head turned. 'And for that, sir, we thank you.'

'Glad to see you again, Tom,' the President said, comfortably. He was getting better at concealing his thoughts.

'Also joining us is Mrs Ryan –'

'Please,' Cathy said, with a smile of her own. 'It's Dr Ryan. I worked pretty hard for that.'

'Yes, ma'am,' Donner said with a charm that made Cathy think about a bad trauma case rolling off on Monument Street at lunchtime. 'You're both doctors, aren't you?'

'Yes, Mr Donner, Jack in history, and me in ophthalmology.'

'And you're a distinguished eye surgeon with the Lasker Public Service Award,' he observed, applying his anchorman's charm.

'Well, I've been working in medical research for over fifteen years. At Johns Hopkins we're all clinicians and researchers, too. I work with a wonderful group of people, and, really, the Lasker Prize is more a tribute to them than it is to me. Back fifteen years ago, Professor Bernard Katz encouraged me to look into how we could use lasers to correct various eye problems. I found it interesting, and I've been working in that area ever since, in addition to my normal surgical practice.'

'Do you really make more money than your husband?' Donner asked with a grin for the cameras.

'Lots,' she confirmed with a chuckle.

'I always said that Cathy was the brains of the outfit,' Jack went on, patting his wife's hand. 'She's too modest to say that she's just about the best in the world at what she does.'

'So, how do you like being First Lady?'

'Do I have to answer?' A charming smile. Then she turned serious. 'The way we got here – well, it's not something anyone would wish for, but I guess it's like what I do at the hospital. Sometimes a trauma case comes in, and that person didn't choose to be injured, and we try our best to fix what's wrong. Jack's never turned away from a problem or a challenge in his life.'

Then it was time for business. 'Mr President, how do you like *your* job?'

'Well, the hours are pretty long. As much time as I have spent in government service, I don't think I ever really understood how difficult this job is. I am blessed with a very fine staff, and our government has thousands of dedicated workers doing the public's business. That helps a lot.'

'As you see it, sir, what is *your* job?' John Plumber asked.

'The oath says to preserve, protect, and defend the Constitution of the United States,' Ryan replied. 'We're working to restore the government. We now have the Senate fully in place, and as the several states get on with their elections, we'll soon have a new House of Representatives. I've got most of the Cabinet posts filled – for HHS and Education, we still have the sitting Deputy Secretaries doing a fine job.'

'We spoke this morning about events in the Persian Gulf. What are the problems there as you see them?' It was Plumber again. Ryan was handling himself well, much more relaxed, and Plumber noted the look in his wife's eyes. She *was* smart.

'The United States wants nothing more than peace and stability in that region. We have every wish to establish friendly relations with the new United Islamic Republic. There's been enough strife there and elsewhere in the world. I'd like to think that we've turned the corner on that. We've made peace – a real peace, not just the absence of war – with the Russians, after generations of turmoil. I want us to build on that. Maybe the world's never been fully at peace, but that is no reason why we can't do it. John, we've come a very long way in the past twenty years. There's a lot more for us to do, but we have a lot of good work to build on.'

'We'll be back after this break,' Donner told the cameras. He could see that Ryan was pretty pleased with himself. Excellent.

A staffer came in from the back door with water glasses.

Everyone had a sip while they waited for the two commercials to run. 'You really hate all this, don't you?' he asked Cathy.

'As long as I can do my work, I can live with almost anything, but I do worry about the kids. After this is over, they have to go back to being normal children, and we didn't raise them for all this hoopla.' Then everyone was quiet for the rest of the commercial time.

'We're back in the Oval Office with the President and First Lady. Mr President,' Donner asked, 'what about the changes you are making?'

'Mainly my job isn't to "change," Tom, it's to "restore." Along the way we will try to do a few things. I've tried to select my new Cabinet members with an eye toward making the government function more efficiently. As you know, I've been in government service for quite a while, and along the way I've seen numerous examples of inefficiency. The citizens out there pay a lot of money in taxes, and we owe it to them to see that the money is spent wisely – and efficiently. So I've told my Cabinet officers to examine all of the executive departments with an eye to doing the same work for less cost.'

'A lot of presidents have said that.'

'This one means it,' Ryan said seriously.

'But your first major policy act has been to attack the tax system,' Donner observed.

'Not "attack," Tom. "Change." George Winston has my full support. The tax code we have now is totally unfair – and I mean unfair in many ways. People can't understand it, for one. That means that they have to hire people to explain the tax system to them, and it's hard to see how it makes sense for people to pay good money for people to explain how the law takes more of their money away – especially when the government writes the laws. Why make laws that the people can't understand? Why make laws that are so complicated?' Ryan asked.

'But along the way, your administration's goal is to make the tax system *regressive*, not *progressive*.'

'We've been over that,' the President replied, and Donner knew he had him then. It was one of Ryan's more obvious weaknesses that he didn't like repeating himself. He really was *not* a politician. They loved to repeat themselves. 'Charging everyone the same amount is just as fair as anything can be. Doing so in a way that everyone can understand will actually *save* money for people. Our proposed tax changes will be revenue-neutral. Nobody's getting any special breaks.'

'But the tax rates for the rich will fall dramatically.'

'That's true, but we'll also eliminate all the breaks that their lobbyists have written into the system. They'll actually end up paying the same, or more probably, a little more than they already do. Secretary Winston has studied that very carefully, and I concur in his judgment.'

'Sir, it's hard to see how a thirty percent rate reduction will make them pay more. That's fourth-grade arithmetic.'

'Ask your accountant.' Ryan smiled. 'Or for that matter, look at your own tax returns, if you can figure them out. You know, Tom, I used to be an accountant – I passed the exam before I went into the Marine Corps – and *I* can't even figure the darned things out. The government does not serve the public interest by doing things that the people can't understand. There's been too much of that. I'm going to try to dial it back a bit.'

Bingo. To Donner's left, John Plumber grimaced. The director with his selection of camera feeds made sure that one didn't go out. Instead he picked Donner's winning anchorman smile.

'I'm glad you feel that way, Mr President, because there are many things that the American people would like to know about government operations. Nearly all of your government service has been in the Central Intelligence Agency.'

'That's true but, Tom, as I told you this morning, no President has ever spoken about intelligence operations. There's a good reason for that.' Ryan was still cool, not knowing what door had just opened.

'But, Mr President, you have personally been involved in numerous intelligence operations which had important effects on bringing that end to the Cold War. For example, the defection of the Soviet missile submarine *Red October*. You played a personal part in that, didn't you?'

The director, cued ahead of time to the question, had selected the camera zeroed in on Ryan's face just in time to see his eyes go as wide as doorknobs. He really wasn't all that good at controlling his emotions. 'Tom, I –'

'The viewers should know that you played a decisive role in one of the greatest intelligence coups of all time. We got our hands on an intact Soviet ballistic-missile submarine, didn't we?'

'I won't comment on that story.' By this time his makeup couldn't hide the pale look. Cathy turned to look at her husband, having felt his hand in hers turn to ice.

'And then less than two years later, you personally arranged the defection of the head of the Russian KGB.'

Jack managed to control his face, finally, but his voice was wooden. 'Tom, this has to stop. You're making unfounded speculations.'

'Mr President, that individual, Nikolay Gerasimov, formerly of the KGB, now lives with his family in Virginia. The captain of the submarine lives in Florida. It's not a "story" ' – he smiled – 'and you know it. Sir, I don't understand your reticence. You played a major role in bringing that peace to the world that you talked about a few minutes ago.'

'Tom, let me make this clear. I will not ever discuss intelligence operations in any public forum. Period.'

'But the American people have a right to know what sort of man sits in this office.' The same thing had been said eleven hours before by John Plumber, who winced inwardly to hear himself quoted in this way, but who could not turn on his own colleague in public.

'Tom, I have served my country to the best of my ability for a number of years, but just as you cannot reveal your news sources, so our intelligence agencies cannot reveal many of the things they do, for fear of getting real people killed.'

'But, Mr President, you have done that. You have killed people.'

'Yes, I have, and more than one President has been a soldier or –'

'Wait a minute,' Cathy interrupted, and now her eyes were flaring. 'I want to say something. Jack joined CIA after our family was attacked by terrorists. If he hadn't done those things back then, none of us would be alive. I was pregnant with our son then, and they tried to kill me and our daughter in my car in Annapolis and –'

'Excuse me, Mrs Ryan, but we have to take a break now.'

'This has to stop, Tom. This has to stop right now,' Ryan said forcefully. 'When people talk about field operations in the open, real people can get killed. Do you understand that?' The camera lights were off, but the tapes were still rolling.

'Mr President, the people have a right to know, and it's my job to report the facts. Have I lied about anything?'

'I can't even comment on that, and you know it,' Ryan said, having almost snarled an accurate answer. *Temper, Jack, temper* he reminded himself. *A President can't have a temper, damned sure not on live TV.* Damn, Marko would never cooperate with the – or would he? He was Lithuanian, and maybe he might like the idea of becoming a national hero, though Jack figured he might just talk him out of such a thing. But Gerasimov was something else. Ryan had disgraced the man, threatened him with death – at the hands of his own countrymen, but that didn't matter to a man like him – and stripped him of all his power. Gerasimov now enjoyed a life far more comfortable than anything he might have enjoyed in the Soviet Union, which he had sought to maintain and rule, but he wasn't the sort of man to enjoy comfort so much as power. Gerasimov had aspired to the sort of position Ryan now enjoyed himself, and would have felt very comfortable in this office or another like it. But those who aspired to power were most often those who misused it, which distinguished him from Jack in one more way. Not that it mattered at the moment. Gerasimov would talk. Sure as hell. And they knew where he was.

So what do I do now?

'We're back in the Oval Office with President and Mrs Ryan,' Donner intoned for anyone who might have forgotten.

'Mr President, you are an expert in national security and foreign affairs,' Plumber said before his colleague could speak. 'But our country faces more problems than that. You now have to reestablish the Supreme Court. How do you propose to do that?'

'I asked the Justice Department to send me a list of experienced judges from federal appeals courts. I'm going over that list now, and I hope to make my nominations to the Senate in the next two weeks.'

'Normally the American Bar Association assists the government in screening such judges, but evidently that's not being done in this case. May I ask why, sir?'

'Tom, all of the judges on the list have been through that process already, and since then all have sat on the appeals bench for a minimum of ten years.'

'The list was assembled by prosecutors?' Donner asked.

'By experienced professionals in the Justice Department. The head of the search group is Patrick Martin, who just took over the Criminal Division. He was assisted by other Justice Department officials, like the head of the Civil Rights Division, for example.'

'But they're all prosecutors, or people whose job it is to prosecute cases. Who suggested Mr Martin to you?'

'It's true that I don't personally know the Department of Justice all that well. Acting FBI Director Murray recommended Mr Martin to me. He did a good job supervising the investigation of the airplane crash into the Capitol building, and I asked him to assemble the list for me.'

'And you and Mr Murray have been friends for a long time.'

'Yes, we have.' Ryan nodded.

'On another of those intelligence operations, Mr Murray accompanied you, didn't he?'

'Excuse me?' Jack asked.

'The CIA operation in Colombia, when you played a role in breaking up the Medellín cartel.'

'Tom, I'm going to say this one last time: I will not discuss intelligence operations, real ones or made-up ones, at all – ever. Are we clear on that?'

'Mr President, that operation resulted in the death of Admiral James Cutter. Sir,' Donner went on, a sincerely pained expression on his face, 'a lot of stories are coming out now about your tenure at CIA. These stories are going to break, and we really want you to have the chance to set the record straight as rapidly as possible. You were not elected to this office, and you have never been examined in the way that political candidates usually are. The American people want to know the man who sits in this office, sir.'

'Tom, the world of intelligence is a secret world. It has to be. Our government has to do many things. Not all of those things can be discussed openly. Everyone has secrets. Every viewer out there has them. You have them. In the case of the government, keeping those secrets is vitally important to the well-being of our country, and also, by the way, to the safety of the lives of the people who do our country's business. Once upon a time the media respected that rule, especially in times of war, but also in other times. I wish you still did.'

'But at what point, Mr President, does secrecy work against our national interests?'

'That's why we have a law that mandates Congress's right to oversee intelligence operations. If it were just the Executive Branch making these decisions, yes, you would have just cause to worry. But it isn't that way. Congress also examines what we do. I have myself reported to Congress on many of these things.'

'Was there a secret operation to Colombia? Did you participate in it? Did Daniel Murray accompany you there after the death of then-FBI Director Emil Jacobs?'

'I have nothing to say on that or on any of the other stories you brought up.'

And there was another commercial break.

'Why are you doing this?' To everyone's surprise, the question came from Cathy.

'Mrs Ryan –'

'Dr Ryan,' she said at once.

'Excuse me. Dr Ryan, these allegations must be laid to rest.'

'We've been through this before. Once people tried to break our marriage up – and that was all lies, too, and –'

'Cathy,' Jack said quietly. Her head turned toward his.

'I know about that one, Jack, remember?' she whispered.

'No, you don't. Not really.'

'That's the problem,' Tom Donner pointed out. 'These stories will be followed up. The people want to know. The people have a right to know.'

Had the world been just, Ryan thought, he would have stood, tossed the microphone to Donner, and asked him to leave his house, but that wasn't possible, and so here he was, supposedly powerful, trapped by circumstance like a criminal in an interrogation room. Then the camera lights came back on.

'Mr President, I know this is a difficult subject for you.'

'Tom, okay, I will say this. As part of my service with CIA, I occasionally had to serve my country in ways that cannot be revealed for a very long time, but at no time have I ever violated the law, and every such activity was fully reported to the appropriate members of the Congress. Let me tell you why I joined CIA.

'I didn't want to. I was a teacher. I taught history at the Naval Academy. I love teaching, and I had time to write a couple of history books, and I like that, too. But then a group of terrorists came after me and my family. There were two very serious attempts to kill us – all of us. You know that. It was all over the media when it happened. I decided then that my place was in the Agency. Why? To protect others against the same sort of dangers. I never liked it all that much, but it was the job I decided I had to do. Now I'm here, and you know what? I don't much like this job, either. I don't like the pressure. I don't like the responsibility. No one person should have this much power. But I *am* here, and I swore an oath to do my best, and I'm doing that.'

'But, Mr President, you are the first person to sit in this office who's never been a political figure. Your views on many things have never been shaped by public opinion, and what is disturbing to a lot of people is that you seem to be leaning on others who have never achieved high office, either. The danger, as some people see it, is that we have a small group of people who lack political experience but who are shaping policy for our country for some time to come. How do you answer that concern?'

'I haven't even *heard* that concern anywhere, Tom.'

'Sir, you've also been criticized for spending too much time in this office and not enough out among the people. Could that be a problem?' Now that he'd sunk the hook, Donner could afford to appear plaintive.

'Unfortunately I do have a lot of work to do, and this is where I have to do that work. For the team I've put together, where do I start?' Jack asked. Next to him, Cathy was seething. Now her hand felt cold in his. 'Secretary of State, Scott Adler, a career foreign service officer, son of a Holocaust survivor. I've known Scott for years. He's the best man I know to run State. Treasury, George Winston, a self-made man. He was instrumental in saving our financial system during the conflict with Japan; he has the respect of the financial community, and he's a real thinker. Defense, Anthony Bretano, is a highly successful engineer and businessman who's already making needed reforms at the Pentagon. FBI, Dan Murray, a career cop, and a good one. You know what I'm doing with my choices, Tom? I'm picking pros, people who know the work because they've done it, not political types who just talk about it. If you think that's wrong, well, I'm sorry about that, but I've worked my way up inside the government, and I have more faith in the professionals I've come to know than I do in the political appointees I've seen along the way. And, oh, by the way, how is that different from a politician who selects the people he knows – or, worse, people who contributed to his campaign organization?'

'Some would say that the difference is that ordinarily people selected to high office have much broader experience.'

'I would not say that, and I have worked under such people for years. The appointments I've made are all people whose abilities I know. Moreover, a President is supposed to have the right, with the assent of the people's elected representatives, to pick people he can work with.'

'But with so much to do, how do you expect to succeed without experienced political guidance? This is a political town.'

'Maybe that's the problem,' Ryan shot back. 'Maybe the political process that we've all studied over the years gets in the way more than it helps. Tom, I didn't ask for this job, okay? The idea, when Roger asked me to be Vice President, was that I serve out the remaining term and leave government service for good. I wanted to go back to teaching. But then that dreadful event happened, and here I am. I am not a politician. I never wanted to be one, and as far as I'm concerned, I'm not a politician now. Am I the best man for this job? Probably not. I am, however, the President of the United States, and I have a job to do, and I'm going to do it to the best of my ability. That's all I can do.'

'And that's the last word. Thank you, Mr President.'

Jack barely waited for the camera lights to go off a final time before unclipping the microphone from his tie and standing. The two reporters didn't say a word. Cathy glared at them.

'Why did you do that?'

'Excuse me?' Donner replied.

'Why do people like you always attack people like us? What have we done to deserve it? My husband is the most honorable man I know.'

'All we do is ask questions.'

'Don't give me that! The way you ask them and the questions you choose, you give the answers before anyone has a chance to say anything.'

Neither reporter responded to that. The Ryans left without another word. Then Arnie came in.

'Okay,' he observed, 'who set this up?'

'They gutted him like a fish,' Holbrook thought aloud. They were due for some time off, and it was always a good thing to know your enemy.

'This guy's scary,' Ernie Brown thought, considering things a little more deeply.

'At least, politicians you can depend on to be crooks. This guy, Jesus, he's going to try to – we're talking a police state here, Pete.'

It was actually a frightening thought for the Mountain Man. He'd always thought that politicians were the worst thing in creation, but suddenly he realized that they were not. Politicians played the power game because they liked it, liked the idea of power and jerking people around because it made them feel big. Ryan was worse. He thought it was *right*.

'God damn,' he breathed. 'The court he wants to appoint . . .'

'They made him look like a fool, Ernie.'

'No, they didn't. Don't you get it? They were playing *their* game.'

33

REBOUNDS

The editorials were established by front-page stories in every major paper. In the more enterprising of them, there were even photographs of Marko Ramius's house – it turned out that he was away at the moment – and that of the Gerasimov family – he was home, but a security guard managed to persuade people to leave, after getting his own photo shot a few hundred times.

Donner came into work very early, and was actually the most surprised by all of that. Plumber walked into his office five minutes later, holding up the front page of the *New York Times*.

'So who rolled whom, Tom?'

'What do you –'

'That's a little weak,' Plumber observed acidly. 'I suppose after you walked out of the meeting, Kealty's people had another little kaffeeklatsch. But you've trapped everybody, haven't you? If it ever gets out that your tape wasn't –'

'It won't,' Donner said. 'And all this coverage does is make our interview look better.'

'Better to whom?' Plumber demanded on his way out the door. It was early in the day for him, too, and his first irrelevant thought of the day was that Ed Murrow would never have used hair spray.

Dr Gus Lorenz finished his morning staff meeting early. Spring was coming early to Atlanta. The trees and bushes were budding, and soon the air would be filled with the fragrances of all the flowering plants for which the southern city was so famous – and a lot of pollen, Gus thought, which would get his sinuses all stuffed, but it was a fair trade for living in a vibrant and yet gracious southern city. With the meeting done, he donned his white lab coat and headed off to his own special fiefdom in the Centers for Disease Control and Prevention. CDC ('and P' had never been added to the acronym) was one of the government's crown jewels, an elite agency that was one of the world's important centers of medical research – many would say the most important. For that reason the center in Atlanta attracted the best of the profession. Some stayed. Some left to teach at the nation's medical schools, but all were forever marked as CDC people, as others might boast of having served their time in the Marine Corps, and for much the same reason. They were the first people their country sent to trouble spots. They were the first to fight diseases, instead of armed enemies, and that cachet engendered an *esprit de corps* which more often than not retained the best of them despite the capped government salaries.

'Morning, Melissa,' Lorenz said to his chief lab assistant – she had a master's and was finishing up her doctorate in molecular biology at nearby Emory University, after which she'd get a sizable promotion.

'Good morning, Doctor. Our friend is back,' she added.

'Oh?' The specimen was all set up on the microscope. Lorenz took his seat, careful as always to take his time. He checked the paperwork to identify the proper sample against the record he'd had on his desk: 98–3–063A. Yes, the numbers matched. Then it was just a matter of zooming in on the sample ... and there it was, the Shepherd's Crook.

'You're right. Got the other one set up?'

'Yes, Doctor.' The computer screen split into two vertical halves, and next to the first was a specimen from 1976. They weren't quite identical. The curve at the bottom of the RNA chain was seemingly never the same way twice, as snowflakes had almost infinite patterns, but that didn't matter. What mattered was the protein loops at the top, and those were –

'Mayinga strain.' He spoke the words matter-of-factly.

'I agree,' Melissa said from just behind him. She leaned across to type on the keyboard, calling up -063B. 'These were a lot harder to isolate, but –'

'Yes, identical again. This one's from the child?'

'A little girl, yes.' Both voices were detached. One can only bear so much exposure to sadness before the mind's defense mechanism kicks in, and the samples become samples, disembodied from the people who donated them.

'Okay, I have some calling to do.'

The two groups were kept separate for obvious reasons, and in fact neither knew of the existence of the other. Badrayn spoke to one group of twenty. The Movie Star spoke to the second group, composed of nine. For both groups there were similarities of preparation. Iran was a nation-state, with the resources of a nation-state. Its foreign ministry had a passport office, and its treasury had a department of printing and engraving. Both allowed the printing of passports from any number of countries and the duplication of entry-exit stamps. In fact such documents could be prepared in any number of places, mostly illegally, but this source made for somewhat higher quality without the risk of revealing the place of origin.

The more important of the two missions was, perversely, the safer in terms of actual physical danger – well, depending on how one looked at it. Badrayn could see the looks on their faces. The very idea of what they were doing was the sort of thing to make a person's skin crawl, though in the case of these people, it was merely one more example of the vagaries of human nature. The job, he told them, was simple. Get in. Deliver. Get out. He emphasized that they were completely safe, as long as they followed the procedures on which they would be fully briefed. There would be no contacts on the other side. They needed none, and doing without them just made things safer. Each had a choice of cover stories, and such were the parameters of the mission that having more than one of the group select the same one didn't matter. What did matter was that the stories could be plausibly presented, and so each traveler would pick a field of business activity in which he had some knowledge. Nearly all had a university degree, and those who didn't could talk about trading or machine tools or some field better known to them than any customs official asking questions out of mere boredom.

The Movie Star's group was far more comfortable with their task. He supposed it was some flaw in the character of his culture that this was so. This group was younger and less experienced, and part of it was that the young simply know less of life, and therefore less of death. They were motivated by passion, by a tradition of sacrifice, and by their own hatreds and demons, all of which clouded their judgment in a way that pleased the masters, who always felt free to expend the hatreds and the passions, along with the people who bore them. This briefing was more detailed. Photographs were displayed, along with maps and diagrams, and the group drew closer, the better to see the details. None of them remarked on the character of the target. Life and death was so simple a question to those who didn't know the ultimate answers – or who thought they did, even if they did not – and that was better for all, really. With an answer to the Great Question fixed in their minds, the lesser ones would not even occur to them. The Movie Star had no such illusions. He asked the questions within his own mind, but never answered them. For him the Great Question had become something else. For him it was all a political act, not a matter of religion, and one didn't measure one's destiny by politics. At least not willingly. He looked at their faces, knowing that they were doing exactly that, but without realizing it. They were the best sort of people for the task, really. They thought they knew everything, but in reality they knew very little, only the physical tasks.

The Movie Star felt rather like a murderer, but it was something he'd done before, at secondhand, anyway. Doing it firsthand was dangerous, and this promised to be the most dangerous such mission in years.

How remarkable that they didn't know better. Each of them inwardly styled himself the stone in Allah's own sling, without reflecting that such stones are by their very nature thrown away. Or maybe not. Perhaps they would be lucky, and for that eventuality he gave them the best data he'd managed to generate, and that data was pretty good. The best time would be afternoon, just before people got out from work, the better to use crowded highways to confuse their pursuers. He himself would go into the field again, he told them, to facilitate their ultimate escape – he didn't tell them, *if it came to that.*

'Okay, Arnie, what's going on?' Ryan asked. It was just as well that Cathy didn't have any procedures scheduled for today. She had seethed all night and was not in a proper mental state to do her normal work. He wasn't feeling much better, but there was neither justice nor much point in snapping at his chief of staff.

'Well, for damned sure there's a leak at CIA, or maybe in the Hill, somebody who knows about some of the things you did.'

'Colombia, the only people who know are Fellows and Trent. And they also know that Murray wasn't there – not exactly, anyway. The rest of that operation is locked up tight.'

'What actually happened?' And need-to-know applied to Arnie now. The President gestured and spoke as one explaining something to a parent:

'There were two operations, SHOWBOAT and RECIPROCITY. One of them involved putting troops into Colombia, the idea was to bird-dog drug flights. Those flights were then splashed –'

'What?'

'Shot down, by the Air Force – well, some were intercepted, the crews arrested and processed quietly. Some other things happened, and then Emil Jacobs got killed, and RECIPROCITY got laid on. We started dropping bombs on places. Things got a little out of hand. Some civilians got killed, and it all started coming apart.'

'How much did you know?' van Damm asked.

'I didn't know jack shit until late in the game. Jim Greer was dying then, and I was handling his work, but that was mostly NATO stuff. I was cut out of it until after the bombs started falling – I was in Belgium when that happened. I saw it on TV, would you believe? Cutter was actually running the operation. He suckered Judge Moore and Bob Ritter into starting it, and then he tried to close it down. That's when things got crazy. Cutter tried to cut off the soldiers – the idea was that they'd just disappear. I found out. I got into Ritter's personal records vault. So I went down into Colombia with the rescue crew, and we got most of them out. It wasn't much fun,' Ryan reported. 'There was some shooting involved, and I worked one of the guns on the chopper. A crewman, a sergeant named Buck Zimmer, got killed on the last extraction, and I've been looking after his family ever since. Liz Elliot got a hold of that and tried to use it against me a while later.'

'There's more to it,' Arnie said quietly.

'Oh, yeah. I had to report the operations to the Select Committee, but I didn't want to rip the government apart. So I talked it over with Trent and Fellows, and I came in to see the President. We talked for a while, and then I stepped out of the room, and Sam and Al talked with him for a while. I'm not exactly sure what they agreed on, but –'

'But he threw the election. He dumped his campaign manager and his campaign was for crap the whole way. Christ, Jack, what did you do?' Arnie demanded. His face was pale now, but for political reasons. And all along van Damm had figured that he'd run a brilliant and successful campaign for Bob Fowler, unseating a popular sitting President. And so, a fix had been in? And he'd never found out?

Ryan closed his eyes. He'd just forced himself to relive a dreadful night. 'I terminated an operation that was technically legal, but teetering right on the edge. I closed it down quietly. The Colombians never found out. I thought I prevented another Watergate, domestically – and a god-awful international incident. Sam and Al signed off on it, the records are sealed until long after we're all dead. Whoever leaked that must have picked up on a couple of rumors and made a few good guesses. What did *I* do? I think I obeyed the law as best I could – no, Arnie, I did *not* break the law. I followed the rules. It wasn't easy, but I did.' The eyes opened. 'So, Arnie, how will that play in Peoria?'

'Why couldn't you have just reported to Congress and –'

'Think back,' the President said. 'It wasn't just the one thing, okay? That's when Eastern Europe was coming unglued, the Soviet Union was still there but teetering, some really big things were happening, and if our government had come apart, right then, with everything else happening, hell, it could have been a mess like nobody's ever seen. America couldn't – we would not have been able to help settle Europe down if we'd been pissing around with a domestic scandal. And I was the guy who had to make the call and take the action, *right now*, or those soldiers would have been killed. Think about the box I was in, will you?

'Arnie, I couldn't go to anybody for guidance on that one,

okay? Admiral Greer was dead. Moore and Ritter were compromised. The President was up to his eyeballs in it; at the time I thought *he* was running the show through Cutter – he wasn't; he got finessed into it by that incompetent political bastard. I didn't know where to go, so I went to the FBI for help. I couldn't trust *anybody* but Dan Murray and Bill Shaw, and one of our people at Langley on the operational side. Bill – did you know he was a JD? – worked me through the law part of it, and Murray helped with the recovery operation. They had an investigation started on Cutter. It was a code-word op, I think they called it ODYSSEY, and they were about to go to a US magistrate for criminal conspiracy, but Cutter killed himself. There was an FBI agent fifty yards behind him when he jumped in front of the bus. You've met him, Pat O'Day. Nobody *ever* broke the law except for Cutter. The operations themselves were within the Constitution – at least that's what Shaw said.'

'But politically . . .'

'Yeah, even I'm not that ignorant. So here I am, Arnie. I didn't break the law. I served my country's interests as best I could under the circumstances, and look what good it's done me.'

'Damn. How is it that Bob Fowler never was told?'

'That was Sam and Al. They thought it would have poisoned Fowler's presidency. Besides, I don't really *know* what the two of them said to the President, do I? I never wanted to know, I never found out, and all I have is speculation – pretty good speculation,' Ryan admitted, 'but that's all.'

'Jack, it's not often I don't know what to say.'

'Say it anyway,' the President ordered.

'It's going to get out. The media has enough now to put some pieces together, and that will force Congress to launch an investigation. What about the other stuff?'

'It's all true,' Ryan said. 'Yeah, we got our hands on *Red October*, yeah, I got Gerasimov out myself. My idea, my operation, nearly got my ass killed, but there you go. If we hadn't, then Gerasimov was poised to launch his own coup to topple Andrey Narmonov – and then there might still be a Warsaw Pact, and the bad old days might never have gone away. So we compromised the bastard, and he didn't have any choices but to get on the airplane. He's still pissed despite all we did to get him set up over here, but I understand his wife and daughter like America just fine.'

'Did you kill anybody?' Arnie asked.

'In Moscow, no. In the sub – he was trying to self-destruct the submarine. He killed one of the ship's officers and shot up two others pretty bad, but I punched his ticket myself – and I had nightmares about it for years.'

In another reality, van Damm thought, his President would be a hero. But reality and public politics had little in common. He noted that Ryan hadn't recounted his story about Bob Fowler and the aborted nuclear launch. The chief of staff had been around for that one, and he knew that three days later, J. Robert Fowler had come nearly apart at the realization at how he'd been saved from mass murder on a Hitlerian scale. There was a line in Hugo's *Les Misérables* that had struck the older man when he'd first read the book in high school: 'What evil good can be.' Here was another case. Ryan had served his country bravely and well more than once, but not one of the things he'd done would survive public scrutiny. Intelligence, love of country, and courage merely added up to a series of events which anyone could twist out of recognition into scandal. And Ed Kealty knew how to do just that.

'How do we spin-control all this?' the President asked. 'What else do I need to know?'

'The files on *Red October* and Gerasimov are at Langley. The Colombian thing, well, you know what you need to know. I'm not sure even I have the legal right to unseal the records. On the other hand, you want to destabilize Russia? This will do it.'

Red October, Golovko thought, then he looked up at the high ceiling of his office. 'Ivan Emmetovich, you clever bastard. *Zvo tvoyu maht!*'

The curse was spoken in quiet admiration. From the first moment he'd met Ryan, he'd underestimated him, and even with all the contacts, direct and indirect, that had followed, he had to admit, he'd never stopped doing it. So *that* was how he'd compromised Gerasimov! And in so doing, he'd saved Russia, perhaps – but a country was supposed to be saved from within, not without. Some secrets were supposed to be kept forever, because they protected everyone equally. This was such a secret. It would embarrass both countries now. For the Russians, it was the loss of a valuable national asset through high treason – worse still, something their intelligence organs had not discovered, which was quite incredible on reflection, but the cover stories had been good ones, and the loss of two hunter submarines in the same operation had made the affair something that the Soviet navy had every desire to forget – and so they hadn't looked far beyond the cover story.

Sergey Nikolay'ch knew the second part better than the first. Ryan had forestalled a coup d'état. Golovko supposed that Ryan might as easily have told him what was happening and left it to the Soviet Union's internal organs – but, no. Intelligence services turned everything to their advantage, and Ryan would have been mad not to have done so here. Gerasimov must have sung like a canary – he knew the Western aphorism – and given up everything he'd known; Ames, for one, had been identified that way, he was sure, and Ames had been a virtual diamond mine for KGB.

And you always told yourself that Ivan Emmetovich was a gifted amateur, Golovko thought.

But even his professional admiration was tempered. Russia might soon need help. How could she go for that help to someone who, it would now be known, had tampered with his country's internal politics like a puppeteer? That realization was worth another oath, not spoken in admiration of anything.

Public waterways are free for the passage of all, and so the Navy couldn't do anything more than prevent the charter boat from getting too close to the Eight-Ten Dock. Soon it was joined by another, then more still, until a total of eleven cameras were pointing at the covered graving dock, now empty with the demise of most of America's missile submarines, and also empty of another which had briefly lived there, not American, or so the story went.

It was possible to access the Navy's personnel records via computer, and some were doing that right now, checking for former crewmen of USS *Dallas*. An early-morning call to

ComSubPac concerning his tenure as commanding officer of *Dallas* got no farther than his public affairs officer, who was well-schooled in no-commenting sensitive inquiries. Today he'd get more than his fair share. So would others.

'This is Ron Jones.'

'This is Tom Donner at NBC News.'

'That's nice,' Jonesy said diffidently. 'I watch CNN myself.'

'Well, maybe you want to watch our show tonight. I'd like to talk to you about –'

'I read the *Times* this morning. It's delivered up here. No comment,' he added.

'But –'

'But, yes, I used to be a submariner, and they call us the Silent Service. Besides, that was a long time ago. I run my own business now. Married, kids, the whole nine yards, y'know?'

'You were lead sonar man aboard USS *Dallas* when –'

'Mr Donner, I signed a secrecy agreement when I left the Navy. I don't talk about the things we did, okay?' It was his first encounter with a reporter, and it was living up to everything he'd ever been told to expect.

'Then all you have to do is tell us that it never happened.'

'That what never happened?' Jones asked.

'The defection of a Russian sub named *Red October*.'

'You know the craziest thing I ever heard as a sonar man?'

'What's that?'

'Elvis.' He hung up. Then he called Pearl Harbor.

With daylight, the TV trucks rolled through Winchester, Virginia, rather like the Civil War armies that had exchanged possession of the town over forty times.

He didn't actually own the house. It could not even be said that CIA did. The land title was in the name of a paper corporation, in turn owned by a foundation whose directors were obscure, but since real-property ownership in America is a matter of public record, and since all corporations and foundations were also, that data would be run down in less than two days, despite the tag on the files which told the clerks in the county courthouse to be creatively incompetent in finding the documents.

The reporters who showed up had still photos and taped file footage of Nikolay Gerasimov, and long lenses were set up on tripods to aim at the windows, a quarter mile away, past a few grazing horses which made for a nice touch on the story: CIA TREATS RUSSIAN SPYMASTER LIKE VISITING KING.

The two security guards at the house were going ape, calling Langley for instructions, but the CIA's public affairs office – itself rather an odd institution – didn't have a clue on this one, other than falling back on the stance that this *was* private property (whether or not that was legally correct under the circumstances was something CIA's lawyers were checking out) and that, therefore, the reporters couldn't trespass.

It had been years since he'd had much to laugh about. Sure, there had been the occasional light moment, but this was something so special that he'd never even considered its possibility. He'd always thought himself an expert on America. Gerasimov had run numerous spy operations against the 'Main Enemy,' as the United States had once been called in the nonexistent country he'd once served, but he admitted to himself that you had to come here and live here for a few years to understand how incomprehensible America was, how nothing made sense, how literally anything could happen, and the madder it was, the more likely it seemed. No imagination was sufficient to predict what would happen in a day, much less a year. And here was the proof of it.

Poor Ryan, he thought, standing by the window and sipping his coffee. In his country – for him it would always be the Soviet Union – this would never have happened. A few uniformed guards and a hard look would have driven people off, or if the look alone didn't, then there were other options. But not in America, where the media had all the freedom of a wolf in the Siberian pines – he nearly laughed at *that* thought, too. In America, wolves were a protected species. Didn't these fools know that wolves killed people?

'Perhaps they will go away,' Maria said, appearing at his side.

'I think not.'

'Then we must stay inside until they do,' his wife said, terrified at the development.

He shook his head. 'No, Maria.'

'But what if they send us back?'

'They won't. They can't. One doesn't do that with defectors. It's a rule,' he explained. 'We never sent Philby, or Burgess, or MacLean back – drunks and degenerates. Oh, no, we protected them, bought them their liquor, and let them diddle with their perversions, because that's the rule.' He finished his coffee and walked back to the kitchen to put the cup and saucer in the dishwasher. He looked at it with a grimace. His apartment in Moscow and his dacha in the Lenin Hills – probably renamed since his departure – hadn't had an appliance like that one. He'd had servants to do such things. No more. In America convenience was a substitute for power, and comfort the substitute for status.

Servants. It could all have been his. The status, the servants, the power. The Soviet Union could still have been a great nation, respected and admired across the world. He would have become General Secretary of the Communist Party of the Soviet Union. He could then have initiated the needed reforms to clear out the corruption and get the country moving again. He would probably have made a full rapprochement with the West, and made a peace, but a peace of equals it would have been, not a total collapse. He'd never been an ideologue, after all, though poor old Alexandrov had thought him so, since Gerasimov had always been a Party man – well, what else could you be in a one-party state? Especially if you knew that destiny had selected you for power.

But, no. Destiny had betrayed him, in the person of John Patrick Ryan, on a cold, snowy Moscow night, sitting, he recalled, in a streetcar barn, sitting in a resting tram. And so now he had comfort and security. His daughter would soon be married to what the Americans called 'old money,' what other countries called the nobility, and what he called worthless drones – the very reason the Communist Party had won its revolution. His wife was content with her appliances and her small circle of friends. And his own anger had never died. Ryan had robbed him of his destiny, of the sheer joy of power and responsibility, of being the arbiter of his nation's path – and then Ryan had taken to himself that same destiny, and the fool didn't know how to make use of it. The real disgrace was to have been done in by such a person. Well, there was one thing to be done, wasn't there? Gerasimov walked into the mud room that led out the back, selected a leather jacket, and walked outside. He thought for a moment. Yes, he'd light a cigarette, and just walk up the driveway to where they were, four hundred meters away. Along the way he would consider how to couch his remarks, and his gratitude to President Ryan. He'd never stopped studying America, and his observations on how the media thought would now stand him in good stead, he thought.

'Did I wake you up, Skipper?' Jones asked. It was about four in the morning at Pearl Harbor.

'Not hardly. You know, my PAO is a woman, and she's pregnant. I hope all this crap doesn't put her into early labor.' Rear Admiral (Vice Admiral selectee, now) Mancuso was at his desk, and his phone, on his instructions, wasn't ringing without a good reason. An old shipmate was such a reason.

'I got a call from NBC, asking about a little job we did in the Atlantic.'

'What did you say?'

'What do you think, Skipper? Zip.' In addition to the honor of the situation, there was also the fact that Jones did most of his work with the Navy. 'But –'

'Yeah, but somebody is gonna talk. Somebody always does.'

'They know too much already. The *Today Show* is doing a live shot from Norfolk, the Eight-Ten Dock. You can guess what they're saying.'

Mancuso thought about flipping his office TV on, but it was still too early for the NBC morning news show – no. He did flip it on and selected CNN. They were doing sports now, and the top of the hour was coming.

'Next they might ask about another job we did, the one involving a swimmer.'

'Open line, Dr Jones,' ComSubPac warned.

'I didn't say where, Skipper. It's just something you'll want to think about.'

'Yeah,' Mancuso agreed.

'Maybe you can tell me one thing.'

'What's that, Ron?'

'What's the big deal? I mean, sure, I won't talk and neither will you, but somebody will, sure as hell. Too good a sea story not to tell. But what's the big deal, Bart? Didn't we do the right thing?'

'I think so,' the admiral replied. 'But I guess people just like a story.'

'You know, I hope Ryan runs. I'll vote for him. Pretty cool stuff, bagging the head of the KGB and –'

'Ron!'

'Skipper, I'm just repeating what they're saying on TV, right? I have no personal knowledge of that at all.' *Damn*, Jonesy thought, *what a sea story this one is. And it's all true.*

At the other end of the line the 'Breaking News' graphic came up on Mancuso's TV screen.

'Yes, I am Nikolay Gerasimov,' the face said on screens all over the world. There were at least twenty reporters clustered on the other side of the stone fence, and the hard part was hearing one of the shouted questions.

'Is it true that you were –'

'Are you –'

'Were you –'

'Is it true that –'

'Silence, please.' He held up his hand. It took fifteen seconds or so. 'Yes, I was at one time the chairman of KGB. Your President Ryan induced me to defect, and I have lived in America ever since, along with my family.'

'*How* did he get you to defect?' a reporter shouted.

'You must understand that the intelligence business is, as you say, rough. Mr Ryan plays the game well. At the time there was ongoing power struggle. CIA opposed my faction in favor of Andrey Il'ych Narmonov. So, he came to Moscow under cover of advisor to START talks. He claimed that he wanted to give me information to make the meeting happen, yes?' Gerasimov had decided that downgrading his English skills would make him seem more credible to the cameras and microphones. 'Actually, you can say he trap me with accusation that I was going to create, how you say, treason? Not true, but effective, and so I decide to come to America with my family. I come by airplane. My family come by submarine.'

'What? Submarine?'

'Yes, was submarine *Dallas*.' He paused and smiled rather grimly. 'Why are you so hard on President Ryan? He serve his country well. A master spy,' Gerasimov said admiringly.

'Well, there goes that story.' Bob Holtzman muted his television and turned to his managing editor.

'Sorry, Bob.' The editor handed the copy back. It was to have run in three days. Holtzman had done a masterful job of assembling his information, and then taken the time to integrate it all into a cohesive and flattering picture of the man whose office was only five blocks from his own. It was about spin, that most favored of Washington words. Somebody had changed the spin, and that was that. Once the initial story went out, it was impossible even for an experienced journalist like Holtzman to change it, especially if his own paper didn't support him.

'Bob,' the editor said with a measure of embarrassment, 'your take on this is different than mine. What if this guy's a cowboy? I mean, okay, getting the submarine was one thing, Cold War and all that, but tampering with internal Soviet politics – isn't that close to an act of war?'

'That's not what it was really about. He was trying to get an agent out, code name CARDINAL. Gerasimov and Aleksandrov were using that spy case to topple Narmonov and kill off the reforms he was trying to initiate.'

'Well, Ryan can say that all day if he wants. That's not how it's going to come across. "Master spy"? Just what we need to run the country, hmph?'

'Ryan isn't like that, God damn it!' Holtzman swore. 'He's a straight shooter right out of –'

'Yeah, he shoots straight, all right. He's killed at least three people. *Killed*, Bob! How the hell did Roger Durling ever get it into his head that this was the right guy to be Vice President. I mean, Ed Kealty isn't much of a prize, but at least –'

'At least he knows how to manipulate us, Ben. He suckered

that airhead on TV, and then he suckered the rest of us into following the story his way.'

'Well . . .' Ben Saddler ran out of things to say at that point. 'It's factual, isn't it?'

'That isn't the same as "true," Ben, and you know it.'

'This is going to have to be looked into. Ryan looks like a guy who's played fast and loose with everything he's touched. Next, I want this Colombian story run down. Now, can you do it? Your contacts at the Agency are pretty good, but I have to tell you, I worry about your objectivity on this.'

'You don't have a choice, Ben. If you want to keep up, it's my story – course you can always just reword what the *Times* says,' Holtzman added, making his editor flush. Life could be tough in the media, too.

'Your story, Bob. Just make sure you deliver. Somebody broke the law, and Ryan's the one who covered everything up and came out smelling like a rose. I want that story.' Saddler stood. 'I have an editorial to write.'

Daryaei could scarcely believe it. The timing could scarcely have been better. He was days away from his next goal, and his target was about to descend into the abyss entirely without his help. With his help, of course, the fall would be farther still.

'Is that what it appears to be?'

'It would seem so,' Badrayn replied. 'I can do some quick research and be back to you in the morning.'

'Is it truly possible?' the Ayatollah persisted.

'Remember what I told you about lions and hyenas? For America it is a national sport. It is no trick. They don't do such tricks. However, let me make sure. I have my methods.'

'Tomorrow morning, then.'

34

WWW.TERROR.ORG

He had much work to do along those lines anyway. Back in his office, Badrayn activated his desktop computer. This had a high-speed modem and a dedicated fiber-optic telephone line that ran to an Iranian – UIR, now – embassy in Pakistan, and from there another line to London, where he could link into the World Wide Web without fear of a trace. What had once been a fairly simple exercise for police agencies – that's what counterespionage and counterterrorism was, after all – was now virtually impossible. Literally millions of people could access all the information mankind had ever developed, and more quickly than one could walk to one's car for a trip to the local library. Badrayn started by hitting press areas, major newspapers from the *Times* in Los Angeles to the *Times* in London, with Washington and New York in between. The major papers all presented much the same basic story – quicker on the Web than in the printed editions, in fact – though the initial editorial comment differed somewhat from one to another. The stories were vague on dates, and he had to remind himself that the mere repetition of the content didn't guarantee accuracy, but it *felt* real. He knew Ryan had been an intelligence officer, knew that the British, the Russians, *and* the Israelis respected him. Surely stories such as these would explain that respect. They also made him slightly uneasy, a fact which would have surprised his master. Ryan was potentially a more formidable adversary than Daryaei appreciated. He knew how to take decisive action in difficult circumstances, and such people were not to be underestimated.

It was just that Ryan was out of his element now, and that was plain from the news coverage. As he changed from one home page to another, a brand-new editorial came up. It called for a congressional inquiry into Ryan's activities at CIA. A statement from the Colombian government asked in clipped diplomatic terms for an explanation of the allegations – and *that* would start another firestorm. How would Ryan respond to the charges and the demands? An open question, Badrayn judged. He was an unknown quantity. That was disturbing. He printed up the more important articles and editorials for later use, and then went on with his real business.

There was a dedicated home page for conventions and trade shows in America. Probably for the use of travel agents, he thought. Well, that wasn't far off. Then it was just a matter of selecting them by city. That told him the identity of the convention centers, typically large barnlike buildings. Each of those had a home page as well, to boast of their capabilities. Many showed diagrams and travel directions. All gave phone and fax numbers. These he collected as well until he had twenty-four, a few extra, just in case. One could not send one of his travelers to a ladies' underwear show, for example – although . . . he chuckled to himself. Fashion and fabric shows – these would be for the winter season, though summer had not yet come even to Iran. Automobile shows. These, he saw, traced across America as the various car and truck manufacturers showed their wares like a traveling circus . . . so much the better.

Circus, he thought, and punched up another home page – but, no, it was just a few weeks too early in the year for that. Too bad. Too bad indeed! Badrayn groused. Didn't the big circuses travel in private trains? Damn. But that was just bad timing, and bad timing could not be helped. The auto show would have to do.

And all the others.

Group Two's members were all fatally ill now, and it was time to end their suffering. It wasn't so much mercy as efficiency. There was no point at all in risking the lives of the medical corpsmen by treating people condemned to death by law and science both, and so like the first group they were dispatched by large injections of Dilaudid, as Moudi watched the TV. The relief for the medics was visible, even through the cumbersome plastic suits. In just a few minutes all of the test subjects were dead. The same procedures as before would be exercised, and the doctor congratulated himself that they'd worked so well, and no extraneous personnel had been infected. That was mainly because of their ruthlessness. Other places – proper hospitals – would not be so lucky, he knew, already mourning the loss of fellow practitioners.

It was a strange truism of life that second thoughts came only when it was too late for them. He could no more stop what was to come than he could stop the turning of the earth.

The medics started loading the infected bodies on the gurneys, and he turned away. He didn't need to see it again. Moudi walked into the lab.

Another set of technicians was now loading the 'soup' into containers known as flasks. They had a thousand times more than was needed for the operations, but the nature of the exercise was such that it was actually easier to make too much than it was to make just enough and, the director had explained offhandedly, one never knew when more might be needed. The flasks were all made of stainless steel, actually a specialized alloy that didn't lose its strength in extreme cold. Each was three-quarters filled and sealed. Then it would be sprayed with a caustic chemical to make certain the outside was clean. Next it would be placed on a cart and rolled to the cold-storage locker in the building's basement, there to be immersed in liquid nitrogen. The Ebola virus particles could stay there for decades, too cold to die, completely inert, waiting for their next exposure to warmth and humidity, and a chance to reproduce and kill. One of the flasks stayed in the lab, sitting in a smaller cryogenic container, about the size of an oil drum but somewhat taller, with an LED display showing the interior temperature.

It was something of a relief that his part in the drama would soon be over. Moudi stood by the door, watching the lesser personnel do their jobs, and probably they felt the same. Soon the twenty spray containers would be filled and removed from the building, and every square centimeter of the building would be rigorously cleaned, making everything safe again. The director would spend all of his time in his office, and Moudi – well, he couldn't reappear at the WHO, could he? He was dead, after all, killed in the airplane crash just off the Libyan coast. Someone would have to generate a new identity and passport for him before he could travel again, assuming that he ever could. Or perhaps as a security measure – no, even the director wasn't that ruthless, was he?

'Hello, I'm calling for Dr Ian MacGregor.'

'Who's calling, please?'

'This is Dr Lorenz at CDC Atlanta.'

'Wait, please.'

Gus had to wait for two minutes, by his watch, long enough to light his pipe and open a window. The younger staffers occasionally chided him about the habit, but he didn't inhale, and it was good for thinking . . .

'This is Dr MacGregor,' a young voice said.

'This is Gus Lorenz in Atlanta.'

'Oh! How do you do, Professor?'

'How are your patients doing?' Lorenz asked from seven time zones away. He liked the sound of MacGregor, clearly working a little late. The good ones did a lot of that.

'The male patient isn't doing well at all, I'm afraid. The child, however, is recovering nicely.'

'Indeed? Well, we examined the specimens you sent. Both contained the Ebola virus, Mayinga sub-strain.'

'You're quite certain?' the younger man asked.

'No doubt about it, Doctor. I ran the tests myself.'

'I was afraid of that. I sent another set to Paris, but they haven't got back to me yet.'

'I need to know a few things.' On his end of the line, Lorenz had a pad out. 'Tell me more about your patients.'

'There's a problem with that, Professor Lorenz,' MacGregor had to say. He didn't know if the line might be bugged, but in a country like Sudan, it was not something he could discount. On the other hand, he had to say something, and so he started picking his way through the facts he could disclose.

'I saw you on TV last night.' Dr Alexandre had decided to see Cathy Ryan at lunch again for that very reason. He'd taken a liking to her. Who would have expected an eye cutter and laser jockey (for Alex, these were more mechanical specialties than the true medicine he practiced – even that profession had its rivalries, and he felt that way about almost all surgical specialties) to take an interest in genetics? Besides, she probably needed a friendly voice.

'That's nice,' Caroline Ryan replied, looking down at her chicken salad as he took his seat. The bodyguard, Alexandre saw, merely looked unhappily tense.

'You did okay.'

'Think so?' She looked up, saying evenly: 'I wanted to rip his face off.'

'Well, that didn't quite come across. You were pretty supportive of your husband. You came across smart.'

'What is it with reporters? I mean, why –'

Alex smiled. 'Doctor, when a dog urinates on a fire hydrant, he's not committing vandalism. He's just being a dog.' Roy Altman nearly choked on his drink.

'Neither one of us ever wanted this, you know?' she said, still unhappy enough to miss the jibe.

Professor Alexandre held his hands up in mock surrender. 'Been there, done that, ma'am. Hey, I never wanted to join the Army. They drafted me right out of med school. It turned out all right, making colonel and all. I found an interesting field to keep the brain busy, and it pays the bills, y'know?'

'*I* don't get paid for this abuse!' Cathy objected, albeit with a smile.

'And your husband doesn't get paid enough,' Alex added.

'He never has. Sometimes I wonder why he doesn't just do the job for free, turn the checks back in, just to make the point that he's worth more than they pay him.'

'You think he would have made a good doc?'

Her eyes brightened. 'I've told him that. Jack would have been a surgeon, I think – no, maybe something else, like what you're in. He's always liked poking around and figuring things out.'

'And saying what he thinks.'

That almost started a laugh. 'Always!'

'Well, guess what? He comes across as a good guy. I've never met him, but I liked what I saw. Sure as hell he's no politician, and maybe that's not a bad thing once in a while. You want to lighten up a little, Doctor? What's the worst thing that can happen? He leaves the job, goes back to whatever he wants to do – teaching, I guess from what he said – and you're still a doc with a Lasker on the wall.'

'The worst thing that can happen –'

'You have Mr Altman here to take care of that, don't you?' Alexandre looked him over. 'I imagine you're big enough to stand in the way of the bullet.' The Secret Service agent didn't reply, but his look at Alex told the tale. Yes, he'd stop one for his principal. 'You guys can't talk about this sort of thing, can you?'

'Yes, sir, we can, if you ask.' Altman had wanted to say this all day. He'd seen the TV special, too, and as had often happened before, there was light talk in the Detail this morning about popping a cap on the reporter in question. The Secret Service had a fantasy life, too. 'Dr Ryan, we like your family a lot, and I'm not just saying that to be polite, okay? We don't always like our principals. But we like all of you.'

'Hey, Cathy.' It was Dean James, passing by with a smile and a wave.

'Hi, Dave.' Then she noted a few waves from faculty friends. So, she wasn't as alone as she thought.

'Okay, Cathy, are you married to James Bond or what?' In a different context the question might have set her off, but Alexandre's Creole eyes were twinkling at her.

'I know a little. I got briefed in on some of it when President Durling asked Jack to be Vice President, but I can't –'

He held up his hand. 'I know. I still have a security clearance because I still drive up to Fort Detrick once in a while.'

'It isn't like the movies. You don't do stuff like that and have a drink, kiss the girl, and drive away. He used to have nightmares and I – well, I'd hug him in his sleep and usually that calmed him down, then when he wakes up, he pretends it never happened at all. I know some of it, not all. When we were in Moscow last year, a Russian comes up and says that he had a gun to Jack's head once' – Altman's head turned at that one – 'but he said it like a joke or something, then he said the gun wasn't loaded. Then we had dinner together, like we were pals or something, and I met his wife – pediatrician, would you believe it? She's a doc and her husband is the head Russian spy and –'

'It does sound a little far-fetched,' Dr Alexandre agreed with a judiciously raised eyebrow, and then a real laugh happened on the other side of the table.

'It's all so crazy,' she concluded.

'You want crazy? We have two Ebola cases reported in Sudan.' Now that her mood had changed, he could talk about his problems.

'Funny place for that virus to turn up. Did they come in from Zaire?'

'Gus Lorenz is checking that out. I'm waiting for him to get back to me,' Professor Alexandre reported. 'It can't be a local outbreak.'

'Why's that?' Altman asked.

'Worst possible environment,' Cathy explained, finally picking at her lunch. 'Hot, dry, lots of direct sun. The UV from the sunlight kills it.'

'Like a flamethrower,' Alex agreed. 'And no jungle for a host animal to live in.'

'Only two cases?' Cathy asked with a mouthful of salad. At least, Alexandre thought, he'd gotten her to eat. Yep, he still had a good bedside manner, even in a cafeteria.

He nodded. 'Adult male and a little girl, that's all I know right now. Gus is supposed to run the tests today, probably already has.'

'Damn, that's a nasty little bug. And you still don't know the host.'

'Twenty years of looking,' Alex confirmed. 'Never found one sick animal – well, the host wouldn't be sick, but you know what I mean.'

'Like a criminal case, eh?' Altman asked. 'Poking around for physical evidence?'

'Pretty much,' Alex agreed. 'Just we're trying to search a whole country, and we've never figured exactly what we're looking for.'

Don Russell watched as the cots went out. After lunch – today it was ham-and-cheese sandwiches on wheat bread, glass of milk, and an apple – the kids all went down for their afternoon nap. An altogether good idea, all the adults thought. Mrs Daggett was a superb organizer, and the kids all knew the routine. The beds came out of the storage room, and the kids knew their spaces. SANDBOX was getting along well with young Megan O'Day. Both usually dressed in Oshkosh B'gosh outfits decorated with flowers or bunnies – at least a third of the kids had them; it was a popular label. The only hard part was parading the children into the bathrooms so that no 'accidents' happened during the naps – some happened anyway, but that was kids for you. It took fifteen minutes, less than before because two of his agents helped. Then the kids were all down in their cots, with their blankets and bears, and the lights went down. Mrs Daggett and her helpers found chairs to sit in and books to read.

'SANDBOX is sleeping,' Russell said, stepping outside for some fresh air.

'Sounds like a winner,' the mobile team thought, sitting in the den of the house across the street. Their Chevy Suburban was parked in the family garage. There were three agents there, two of whom were always on watch, seated close to the window which faced Giant Steps. Probably playing cards, ever a good way to pass dead time. Every fifteen minutes – not quite regularly in case someone was watching – Russell or another of the crew would walk around the grounds. TV cameras kept track of traffic on Ritchie Highway. One of the inside people was always positioned to cover the doors in and out of the center. At the moment it was Marcella Hilton; young and pretty, she always had her purse with her. A special purse of a type made for female cops, it had a side pocket she could just reach into for her SigSauer 9mm automatic, and two spare magazines. She was letting her hair grow to something approaching hippie length (he'd had to tell her what a hippie was) to accentuate her 'disguise.'

He still didn't like it. The place was too easy to approach, too close to the highway with its heavy volume of traffic, and there was a parking lot within plain sight, a perfect spot for notional bad guys to do surveillance. At least reporters had been shooed away. On that one SURGEON had been ruthlessly direct. After an initial spate of stories about Katie Ryan and her friends, the foot had come down hard. Now visiting journalists who called were told, firmly but politely, to stay away. Those who came anyway had to talk to Russell, whose grandfatherly demeanor was saved for the children at Giant Steps. With adults he was simply intimidating, usually donning his Secret Service sunglasses, the better to appear like Schwarzenegger, who was shorter than he by a good three inches.

But his sub-detail had been cut down to six. Three directly on site, and three across the street. The latter trio had shoulder weapons, Uzi submachine guns and a scoped M-16. In another location, six would have been plenty, but not this one, he judged. Unfortunately, any more than that would have made this day-care center appear to be an armed camp, and President Ryan was having trouble enough.

'What's the word, Gus?' Alexandre asked, back in his office before starting afternoon rounds. One of his AIDS patients had taken a bad turn, and Alex was trying to figure what to do about it.

'ID is confirmed. Ebola Mayinga, same as the two Zairean cases. The male patient isn't going to make it, but the child is reportedly recovering nicely.'

'Oh? Good. What's the difference in the cases?'

'Not sure, Alex,' Lorenz replied. 'I don't have much patient information, just first names, Saleh for the male and Sohaila for the child, ages and such.'

'Arabic names, right?' But Sudan was an Islamic country. 'I think so.'

'It would help to know what's different about the cases.'

'I made that point. The attending physician is an Ian Mac-Gregor, sounds pretty good, University of Edinburgh, I think he said. Anyway, he doesn't know any differences between them. Neither has any idea how they were exposed. They appeared at the hospital at roughly the same time, in roughly the same shape. Initial presentation was as flu and/or jet lag, he said –'

'Travel from where, then?' Alexandre interrupted.

'I asked. He said he couldn't say.'

'How come?'

'I asked that, too. He said he couldn't say that, either, but that it had no apparent connection with the cases.' Lorenz's tone indicated what he thought of that. Both men knew it had to be local politics, a real problem in Africa, especially with AIDS.

'Nothing more in Zaire?'

'Nothing,' Gus confirmed. 'That one's over. It's a head-scratcher, Alex. Same disease turned up in two different places, two thousand miles apart, two cases each, two dead, one dying, one apparently recovering. MacGregor has initiated proper containment procedures at his hospital, and it sounds as though he knows his business.' You could almost hear the shrug over the phone.

What the Secret Service guy had said over lunch was right on target, Alexandre thought. It was more detective work than medicine, and this one didn't make a hell of a lot of sense, like some sort of serial-murder case with no clues. Entertaining in book form, maybe, but not in reality.

'Okay, what *do* we know?'

'We know that Mayinga strain is alive and kicking. Visual inspection is identical. We're running some analysis on the proteins and sequences, but my gut says it's a one-to-one match.'

'God damn, what's the host, Gus? If we could only find that!'

'Thank you for that observation, Doctor.' Gus was annoyed – enraged – in the same way and for the same reason. But it was an old story for both of them. Well, the older man thought, it had taken a few *thousand* years to figure malaria out. They'd been playing with Ebola for only twenty-five or so. The bug had been around, probably, for at least that long, appearing and disappearing, just like a fictional serial killer. But Ebola didn't have a brain, didn't have a strategy, didn't even move of its own accord. It was super-adapted to something very limited and exceedingly narrow. But they didn't know what. 'It's enough to drive a man to drink, isn't it?'

'I imagine a stiff shot of bourbon will kill it, too, Gus. I have patients to see.'

'How do you like regular clinical rounds, Alex?' Lorenz missed them, too.

'Good to be a real doc again. I just wish my patients had a little more hope. But that's the job, ain't it?'

'I'll fax you data on the structural analysis on the samples if you want. The good news is that it seems pretty well contained,' Lorenz repeated.

'I'd appreciate it. See ya, Gus.' Alexandre hung up. *Pretty well contained? That's what we thought before...* But then his thoughts shifted, as they had to. *White male patient, thirty-four, gay, resistant TB that came out of left field. How do we stabilize him?* He lifted the chart and walked out of his office.

* * *

'So I'm the wrong guy to help with the court selections?' Pat Martin asked.

'Don't feel too bad,' Arnie answered. 'We're *all* the wrong guy for everything.'

'Except you,' the President noted with a smile.

'We all make errors of judgment,' van Damm admitted. 'I could have left with Bob Fowler, but Roger said he needed me to keep this shop running, and –'

'Yeah.' Ryan nodded. 'That's how I got here, too. So, Mr Martin?'

'No laws were broken by any of this.' He'd spent the last three hours going over the CIA files and Jack's dictated summary of the Colombian operations. Now one of his secretaries, Ellen Sumter, knew about some rather restricted things – but she was a *presidential* secretary, and besides, Jack had gotten a smoke out of it. 'At least not by you. Ritter and Moore could be brought up on failure to fully report their covert activities to the Congress, but their defense would be that the sitting President told them to do it that way, and the Special and Hazardous Operations guidelines appended to the oversight statute give them an arguable defense. I suppose I could get them indicted, but I wouldn't want to prosecute the case myself,' he went on. 'They were trying to work on the drug problem, and most jurors wouldn't want to hurt them for doing so, especially since the Medellín cartel came apart partly as a result. The real problem on that one is the international-relations angle. Colombia's going to be pissed, sir, and with very good reason. There are issues of international law and treaties which applied to the activity, but I'm not good enough in that field to render an opinion. From the domestic point of view, it's the Constitution, the supreme law of the land. The President is Commander-in-Chief. The President decides what is or is not in the country's security interest as part of his executive powers. The President can, therefore, take whatever action he deems appropriate to protect those interests – that's what *executive* power means. The brake on that, aside from statutory violations that mainly apply *inside* the country, is found in the checks and balances exercised by the Congress. They can deny funds to prevent something, but that's about all. Even the War Powers Resolution is written in such a way as to let you act first before they try and stop you. You see, the Constitution is flexible on the really important issues. It's designed for reasonable people to work things out in a reasonable way. The elected representatives are supposed to know what the people want, and act accordingly, again, within reasonable limits.'

The people who wrote the Constitution, Ryan wondered to himself, *were they politicians or something else?*

'And the rest?' the chief of staff asked.

'The CIA operations? Not even close to any sort of violation, but again the problem is one of politics. Speaking for myself – I used to run espionage investigations, remember – Mr President, what beautiful jobs they were. But the media is going to have a ball,' he warned.

Arnie thought that was a pretty good start. His third President didn't have to worry about going to jail. The political stuff came *after* that, which was, for him, a first of sorts.

'Closed hearings or open?' van Damm asked.

'That's political. The main issue there is the international side. Best to kick that one around with State. By the way, you've got me right against the edge here, ethically speaking. Had I discovered a possible violation against you in any of these three cases, I'd be unable to discuss them with you. As it is, my cover is to say that you, Mr President, asked me for an opinion on the possible criminal violations of others, to which inquiry I must, as a federal official, respond as part of my official duties.'

'You know, it would be nice if everybody around me didn't talk like a lawyer all the time,' Ryan observed crossly. 'I have real problems to deal with. A new country in the Middle East that doesn't like us, the Chinese making trouble at sea for reasons I don't understand, and I still don't have a Congress.'

'This *is* a real problem,' Arnie told him. Again.

'I can read.' Ryan gestured to the pile of clippings on his desk. He'd just discovered that the media graced him with early drafts of adverse editorials scheduled to run the next day. How nice of them. 'I used to think CIA was Alice in Wonderland. That's not even Triple-A ball. Okay, the Supreme Court. I've read over about half of the list.

They're all good people. I'll have my selections this time next week.'

'ABA is going to raise hell,' Arnie said.

'Let 'em. I can't show weakness. I've learned that much last night. What's Kealty going to do?' the President asked next.

'The only thing he can do, weaken you politically, threaten you with scandal, and force you to resign.' Arnie held his hand up again. 'I'm not saying it makes sense.'

'Damned little in this town does, Arnie. That's why I'm trying.'

One crucial element in the consolidation of the new country was, of course, its military. The former Republican Guards divisions would keep their identity. There had to be a few adjustments in the officer corps. The executions of previous weeks hadn't totally expunged undesirable elements, but in the interest of amity, the new eliminations were made into simple retirements – the departure briefings were forcefully direct: *Step out of line and disappear*. It was not a warning to be disregarded. The departing officers invariably nodded their submission, grateful to be allowed to live.

These units had mainly survived the Persian Gulf War – at least a majority of their personnel had, and the shock of their treatment at American hands had been assuaged by their later campaigns to crush rebellious civilian elements, replacing part of their swagger and much of their bravado. Their equipment had been replaced from stocks and other means, and that would soon be augmented as well.

The convoys moved out of Iran, down the Abadan highway, through border check-points already dismantled. They moved under cover of darkness, and with a minimum of radio traffic, but that didn't matter to satellites.

'Three divisions, heavies at that,' was the instant analysis at I-TAC, the Army's Intelligence and Threat Analysis Center, a windowless building located in the Washington Navy Yard. The same conclusion was rapidly reached at DIA and CIA. A new Order of Battle assessment for the new country was already under way, and though it was not yet complete, the first back-of-the-envelope calculations showed that the UIR had more than double the military power of all the other Gulf states combined. It would probably be worse when all the factors were fully evaluated.

'Headed where, exactly, I wonder,' the senior watch officer said aloud as the tapes were rewound.

'Bottom end of Iraq has always been Shi'a, sir,' a warrant officer area specialist reminded the colonel.

'And that's the closest part to our friends.'

'Roge-o.'

Mahmoud Haji Daryaei had much to think about, and he usually tried to do it outside, not inside, a mosque. In this case it was one of the oldest in the former country of Iraq, within sight of the world's oldest city, Ur. A man of his God and his Faith, Daryaei was also a man of history and political reality who told himself that all came together in a unified whole that defined the shape of the world, and that all had to be considered. It was easy in moments of weakness or enthusiasm (the two were the same in his mind) to tell himself that certain things were written by Allah's own immortal hand, but circumspection was also a virtue taught by the Koran, and he found he was able to achieve that most easily by walking outside a holy place, usually in a garden, such as this mosque had.

Civilization had started here. Pagan civilization, to be sure, but all things began somewhere, and it was not the fault of those who had first built this city five thousand years before that God had not yet fully revealed Himself. The faithful who had built this mosque and its garden had also rectified the oversight.

The mosque was in disrepair. He bent down to pick up a piece of tile that had fallen off the wall. It was blue, the color of the ancient city, a color somewhere between that of sky and sea, made by local artisans to the same shade and texture for more than fifty centuries, adopted in turn for temples to pagan statues, palaces of kings, and now a mosque. One could pluck a new one off a building or dig ten meters into the earth to find one over three thousand years old, and the two would be indistinguishable. In that there was such continuity here as at no other place in the world. A kind of peace came from it, especially in the chill of a cloudless midnight, when he alone was walking here, and even his bodyguards were out of sight, knowing their leader's mood.

A waning moon was overhead, and that gave emphasis to the numberless stars which kept him company. To the west was ancient Ur, once a great city as things had been reckoned, and surely even today it would be a noteworthy sight, with its towering brick walls and its towering ziggurat to whatever false god the people here had worshiped. Caravans would travel in and out of the fortified gates, bringing everything from grain to slaves. The surrounding land would be green with planted fields instead of mere sand, and the air alive with the chatter of merchants and tradesmen. The tale of Eden itself had probably begun not far from here, somewhere in the parallel valleys of the Tigris and Euphrates that emptied into the Persian Gulf. Yes, if humanity were all one vast tree, then the oldest roots were right here, virtually in the center of the country he had just created.

The ancients would have had the same sense of centrality, he was sure. Here are *we*, they would have thought, and out there were . . . *they*, the universal appellation for those who were not part of one's own community. *They* were dangerous. At first *they* would have been nomadic travelers for whom the idea of a city was incomprehensible. How could one stay in one place and live? Didn't the grass for the goats and sheep run out? On the other hand, what a fine place to raid, they would have thought. That was why the city had sprouted defensive walls, further emphasizing the primacy of place and the dichotomy of *we* and *they*, the civilized and the uncivilized.

And so it was today, Daryaei knew, Faithful and Infidel. Even within the first category there were differences. He stood in the center of a country which was also the center of the Faith, at least in geographic terms, for Islam had spread west and east. The true center of his religion lay in the direction in which he always prayed, southwest, in Mecca, home of the Ka'aba stone, where the Prophet had taught.

Civilization had begun in Ur, and spread, slowly and fitfully, and in the waves of time, the city had risen and fallen because, he thought, of its false gods, its lack of the single unifying idea which civilization needed.

The continuity of this place told him much about the

people. One could almost hear their voices, and they were no different, really, from himself. They'd looked up on quiet nights into the same sky and wondered at the beauty of the same stars. They'd heard the silence, the best of them, just as he did, and used it as a sounding board for their most private thoughts, to consider the Great Questions and find their answers as best they could. But they'd been flawed answers, and that was why the walls had fallen, along with all the civilizations here – but one.

And so, his task was to restore, Daryaei told the stars. As his religion was the final revelation, so his culture would grow from here, down-river from the original Eden. Yes, he'd build his city here. Mecca would remain a holy city, blessed and pure, not commercialized, not polluted. There was room here for the administrative buildings. A fresh beginning would take place on the site of the oldest beginning, and a great new nation would grow.

But first . . .

Daryaei looked at his hand, old and gnarled, scarred by torture and persecution, but still the hand of a man and the servant of his mind, an imperfect tool, as he himself was an imperfect tool for his God, but a faithful tool even so, able to smite, able to heal. Both would be necessary. He knew the entire Koran by heart – memorization of the entire book was encouraged by his religion – and more than that he was a theologian who could quote a verse to any purpose, some of them contradictory, he admitted to himself, but it was the Will of Allah that mattered more than His words. His words often applied to a specific context. To kill for murder was evil, and the Koranic law on that was harsh indeed. To kill in defense of the Faith was not. Sometimes the difference between the two was clouded, and for that one had the Will of Allah as a guide. Allah wished the Faithful to be under one spiritual roof, and while many had attempted to accomplish that by reason and example, men were weak and some had to be shown more forcefully than others – and perhaps the differences between Sunni and Shi'a *could* be resolved in peace and love, with his hand extended in friendship and both sides giving respectful consideration to the views of the other – Daryaei was willing to go that far in his quest – but first the proper conditions had to be established. Beyond the horizon of Islam were others, and while God's Mercy applied to them as well, after a fashion, it did not apply while they sought to injure the Faith. For those people, his hand was for smiting. There was no avoiding it.

Because they *did* injure the Faith, polluting it with their money and strange ideas, taking the oil away, taking the children away to educate them in corrupt ways. They sought to limit the Faith even as they did business with those who called themselves Faithful. They would resist his efforts to unify Islam. They'd call it economics or politics or something else, but really they knew that a unified Islam would threaten their apostasy and temporal power. They were the worst kind of enemies in that they called themselves friends, and disguised their intentions well enough to be mistaken for such. For Islam to unify, they had to be broken.

There really was no choice for him. He'd come here to be alone and to think, to ask God quietly if there might be another way. But the blue piece of tile had told him of all that had been, the time that had passed, the civilizations that had left nothing behind but imperfect memories and ruined buildings. He had the idea and the faith that they had all lacked. It was merely a question of applying those ideas, guided by the same Will that had placed the stars in the sky. His God had brought flood and plague and misfortune as tools of the Faith. Mohammed had himself fought wars. And so, reluctantly, he told himself, would he.

35

OPERATIONAL CONCEPT

When military forces move, other forces watch with interest, though what they do about it depends on the instructions of their leaders. The move of Iranian forces into Iraq was entirely administrative. The tanks and other tracked vehicles came by low-hauler trailers, while the trucks rolled on their own wheels. There were the usual problems. A few units took wrong turns, to the embarrassment of their officers and the rage of superiors, but soon enough each of the three divisions had found a new home, in every case co-located with a formerly Iraqi division of the same type. The traumatically enforced downsizing of the Iraqi army had made for almost enough room for the new occupants of the bases, and scarcely had they arrived but the staffs were integrated in corps units, and joint exercises began to acquaint one grouping with the other. Here, too, there were the usual difficulties of language and culture, but both sides used much the same weapons and doctrine; and the staff officers, the same all over the world, worked to hammer out a common ground. This, too, was watched from satellite.

'How much?'

'Call it three corps formations,' the briefing officer told Admiral Jackson. 'One of two armored divisions, and two of an armored and a heavy mechanized. They're a little light in artillery, but they have all the rolling stock they need. We spotted a bunch of command-and-control vehicles running around in the desert, probably doing unit-movement simulations for a CPX.' That was a Command-Post Exercise, a war game for professionals.

'Anything else?' Robby asked.

'The gunnery ranges at this base here, west of Abu Sukayr, are being bulldozed and cleaned up, and the air base just north at Nejef has a few new tenants, MiGs and Sukhois, but on IR their engines are cold.'

'Assessment?' This came from Tony Bretano.

'Sir, you can call it anything,' the colonel replied. 'New country integrating their military, there's going to be a lot of getting-to-know-you stuff. We're surprised by the integrated corps formations. It's going to pose administrative difficulties, but it might be a good move from the political-psychological side. This way, they're acting like they really are one country.'

'Nothing threatening at all?' the SecDef asked.

'Nothing overtly threatening, not at this time.'

'How quick could that corps move to the Saudi border?' Jackson asked, to make sure his boss got the real picture.

'Once they're fully fueled and trained up? Call it forty-eight to seventy-two hours. We could do it in less than half the time, but we're trained better.'

'Force composition?'

'Total for the three corps, we're talking six heavy divisions, just over fifteen hundred main battle tanks, over twenty-five hundred infantry fighting vehicles, upwards of six hundred tubes – still haven't got a handle on their red team, Admiral. That's artillery, Mr Secretary,' the colonel explained. 'Logistically they're on the old Soviet model.'

'What's that mean?'

'Their loggies are organic to the divisions. We do that also, but we maintain separate formations to keep our maneuver forces running.'

'Reservists for the most part,' Jackson told the Secretary. 'The Soviet model allows for a more integrated maneuver force, but only for the short term. They can't sustain operations as long as we can, in terms of time or distance.'

'The admiral is correct, sir,' the briefing officer went on. 'In 1990, when the Iraqis jumped into Kuwait, they went about as far as their logistical tail allowed. They had to stop to replenish.'

'That's part of it. Tell him the other part,' Jackson ordered.

'After a pause of from twelve to twenty-four hours, they *were* ready to move again. The reason they didn't was political.'

'I always wondered about that. Could they have taken the Saudi oil fields?'

'Easy,' the colonel said. 'He must have thought a lot about

that in later months,' the officer added without sympathy.

'So, we have a threat here?' Bretano was asking simple questions and listening to the answers. Jackson liked that. He knew what he didn't know, and wasn't embarrassed about learning things.

'Yes, sir. These three corps represent a potential striking force about equal in power to what Hussein used. There would be other units involved, but they're just occupying forces. That's the fist right here,' the colonel said, tapping the map with his pointer.

'But it's still in their pocket. How long to change that?'

'A few months at minimum to do it right, Mr Secretary. It depends most of all on their overall political intentions. All of these units are individually trained up to snuff by local standards. Integrating their corps staffs and organizations is the real task ahead for them.'

'Explain,' Bretano ordered.

'Sir, I guess you could call it a management team. Everybody has to get to know everybody else so that they can communicate properly, start thinking the same way.'

'Maybe it's easier to think of it as a football team, sir.' Robby took it further. 'You don't just take eleven guys and put them in a huddle together and expect them to perform properly. You have to have everybody reading out of the same playbook, and everybody has to know what everybody else is able to do.'

SecDef nodded. 'So it's not the hardware we're worried about. It's the people.'

'That's right, sir,' the colonel said. 'I can teach you to drive a tank in a few minutes, but it'll be a while before I want you driving around in my brigade.'

'That's why you people must love having a new Secretary come in every few years,' Bretano observed with a wry smile.

'Mostly they learn pretty fast.'

'So, what do we tell the President?'

The Chinese and Taiwanese navies were keeping their respective distances, as though an invisible line were drawn north-south down the Formosa Strait. The latter kept pacing the former, interposing itself between its island home, but informal rules were established and so far none was being violated.

This was good for the CO of USS *Pasadena*, whose sonar and tracking parties were trying to keep tabs on both sides, all the while hoping that a shooting war wouldn't start with them in the middle. Getting killed by mistake seemed such a tawdry end.

'Torpedo in the water, bearing two-seven-four!' was the next call from the sonar compartment. Heads turned and ears perked up at once.

'Stay cool,' the captain ordered quietly. 'Sonar, Conn, I need more than that!' That statement was not quiet.

'Same bearing as contact Sierra Four-Two, a Luda II-class 'can, sir, probably launched from there.'

'Four-Two is bearing two-seven-four, range thirty thousand yards,' a petty officer in the tracking party interjected at once.

'Sounds like one of their new homers, sir, six blades, turning at high speed, bearing is changing north to south, definite side aspect on the fish.'

'Very well,' the captain said, allowing himself to stay as calm as he pretended to be.

'Could be targeted on Sierra-Fifteen, sir.' That contact was an old Ming-class submarine, a Chinese copy of the old Russian Romeo-class, a clunker whose design dated from the 1950s which had snorted less than an hour before to recharge batteries. 'He's at two-six-one, range about the same.' That came from the officer in charge of the tracking party. The senior chief at his left nodded agreement.

The captain closed his eyes and allowed himself a breath. He'd heard the stories about the Good Old Days of the Cold War, when people like Bart Mancuso had gone Up North into the Barents Sea and, occasionally, found themselves right in the middle of a live-fire ShootEx of the Soviet navy – perhaps mistaken for practice targets, even. A fine opportunity to figure out how good Soviet weapons really were, they joked now, sitting in their offices. Now he knew what they'd really felt at the time. Fortunately, his private head was a mere twenty feet away, if it came to that . . .

'Transient, transient, mechanical transient bearing two-six-one, sounds like a noisemaker, probably released by contact Sierra-Fifteen. The torpedo bearing is now two-six-seven, estimated speed four-four knots, bearing continues to change north to south,' sonar reported next. 'Hold it – *another* torpedo in the water bearing two-five-five!'

'No contact on that bearing, could be a helo launch,' the senior chief said.

He'd have to discuss one of those sea stories with Mancuso when he got back to Pearl, the captain thought.

'Same acoustical signature, sir, another homing fish, drifting north, could also be targeted on Sierra-Fifteen.'

'Bracketed the poor bastard.' This came from the XO.

'It's dark topside, isn't it?' the captain thought suddenly. Sometimes it was easy to lose track.

'Sure is, sir.' From the XO again.

'Have we seen them do night helo ops this week?'

'No, sir. Intel says they don't like to fly off their 'cans at night.'

'That just changed, didn't it? Let's see. Raise the ESM mast.'

'Raise the ESM, aye.' A sailor pulled the proper handle and the reed-thin electronics-sensor antenna hissed up on hydraulic power. *Pasadena* was running at periscope depth, her long sonar 'tail' streamed out behind her as the submarine stayed roughly on what they hoped was the borderline between the two enemy fleets. It was the safest place to be until such time as real shooting started.

'Looking for –'

'Got it, sir, a Ku-band emitter at bearing two-five-four, aircraft type, frequency and pulse-repetition rate like that new French one. Wow, *lots* of radars turning, sir, take a while to classify them.'

'French Dauphin helos on some of their frigates, sir,' the XO observed.

'Doing night ops,' the captain emphasized. That was unexpected. Helicopters were expensive, and landing on tin cans at night was always dicey. The Chinese navy was training up to do something.

Things could be slippery in Washington. The nation's capital invariably panics at the report of a single snowflake despite the realization that a blizzard might do little more than fill the potholes in the street, if only people would plow the snow that way. But there was more to it than that. As soldiers once followed flags onto a battlefield, so senior Washington officials follow leaders or ideologies, but near the top it got slippery. A lower- or middle-level bureaucrat might just sit at his post and ignore his sitting department Secretary's identity, but the higher one went, the closer one came to something akin to decision or policy making. In such positions, one actually had to do things, or tell others to do things, from time to time, other than what someone else had already written down. One regularly went in and out of top-floor offices and became identified with whoever might be there, ultimately all the way to the President's office in the West Wing, and though access to the top meant power of a sort, and prestige, and an autographed photo on the office wall to tell *your* visitors how important you were, if something happened to the *other* person in the photo, then the photo and its signature might become a liability rather than an asset. The ultimate risk lay in changing from an insider, always welcome, to an outsider, if not quite *always* shunned, then forced to earn one's way back inside, a prospect not attractive to those who had spent so much time getting there in the first place.

The most obvious defense, of course, was to be *networked*, to have a circle of friends and associates which didn't have to be deep so much as broad, and include people in all parts of the political spectrum. You had to be known by a sufficiently wide number of fellow insiders so that no matter what happened at the very top there was always a safe platform just below, a safety net of sorts. The net was close enough to the top that the people in it had the upward access without the risk of falling off. With care, those at the top positions enjoyed its protection, too, always able to slide in and out of appropriate postings, to and from other offices not too far away – usually less than a mile – to await the next opportunity, and so even though *out*, to remain in the Network, to retain the access, and also rent out that access to those who needed it. In that sense, nothing had changed since the pharaonic court in the ancient Nile city of Thebes, where knowing a nobleman who had access to Pharaoh gave one a power which translated into both money and the pure joy of being important enough to bow and scrape for profit.

But in Washington as in Thebes, being too close to the wrong leader's court meant you ran the risk of becoming tarnished, especially when the Pharaoh didn't play ball (actually jackals and hounds in the Middle Kingdom) with the system.

And President Ryan didn't. It was as though a foreigner had usurped the throne, not necessarily a bad man, but a *different* man who didn't assemble people from the Establishment. They'd waited patiently for him to come to them, as all Presidents did, to seek their wisdom and counsel, to give access and get it in return, as courtiers had for centuries. They handled things for a busy chief, doling out justice, seeing to it that things were done in the same old way, which had to be the right way, since all of their number agreed with it while serving and being served by it.

But the old system hadn't so much been destroyed as ignored, and that befuddled the thousands of members of the Great Network. They held their cocktail parties and discussed the new President over Perrier and pâté, smiling tolerantly at his new ideas and waiting for him to see the light. But it had been quite a while now since that awful night, and it hadn't happened yet. Networked people still working inside as appointees of the Fowler-Durling administration came to the parties and reported that they didn't understand what was going on. Senior lobbyists tried to make appointments through the office of the President, only to be told that the President was extremely tied up, and didn't have time.

Didn't have time?

Didn't have time for *them?*

It was as though Pharaoh had told all the nobles and courtiers to go home and tend their estates up and down the river kingdom, and *that* was no fun – to live in the provinces . . . with the . . . common folk?

Worse, the new Senate, or a large part of it, was following the President's example. Worst of all, many, if not most, were curt with them. A new senator from Indiana was reported to have a kitchen timer on his desk and to twist it to a mere five minutes for lobbyists, and to none at all for people talking to him about the *absurd* ideas for rewriting the tax code. Worst of all, he even lacked the courtesy to have his executive secretary deflect appointment requests. He'd actually *told* the chief of a powerful Washington law firm – a man who'd only wanted to educate the newcomer from Peoria – that he would *not* listen to such people, ever. Told the man himself. In another context it would have been an amusing story. Such people occasionally came to Washington with such purity of purpose as to justify a white horse, but in due course they would learn that horses were out of date – and in most cases, they were merely doing it for show anyway.

But not this time. The story had spread. First reported in the local DC papers with whimsy, it had been picked up in Indianapolis as something genuinely new and decidedly 'Hoosier,' and then respread through a couple of the news syndicates. This new senator had talked forcefully with his new colleagues, and won a few converts. Not all that many, but enough to be worrisome. Enough to give him a chairmanship of a powerful subcommittee, what was too bully a pulpit for one such as he, especially since he had a flair for the dramatic and an effective, if not exactly nice, turn of phrase that reporters couldn't avoid quoting. Even reporters in the Great Network enjoyed reporting genuinely new things – which was what 'news' meant, something everyone mainly forgot.

At the parties, people joked that it was a fad, like hula hoops, amusing to watch and soon to fade, but every so often one of them would worry. The tolerant smile would freeze on his or her face in mid-joke, and they'd wonder if something genuinely new might be happening.

No, nothing genuinely new ever happened here. Everybody knew that. The system had rules, and the rules had to be obeyed.

Even so, a few of them worried at their dinner parties in Georgetown. They had expensive houses to pay off, children to educate, and status to maintain. All had come from somewhere else, and none wanted to go back there.

It was just so outrageous. How did the newcomers expect to find out what they needed to, without lobbyists from the Network to guide and educate them – and didn't *they* represent the people, too? Weren't they paid to do exactly that? Didn't *they* tell the elected representatives – worse, these new ones weren't elected, they were all appointed, many of them by governors who, in their wish to get reelected themselves, had bowed to President Ryan's impassioned but utterly unrealistic televised speech. As though some new religion had broken out.

At the parties in Chevy Chase, many of them worried that the new laws these new senators would pass would be ... laws, just like the ones produced by the system, at least in their power if not in their wisdom. These new people could actually pass new laws without being 'helped.' That was so genuinely new an idea as to be ... frightening. But only if you really believed it.

And then there were the House races, just about to start around the country, the special elections required to repopulate the People's House, as everyone liked to call it, which was Disneyland for lobbyists, so many meetings all in one convenient complex of buildings, 435 lawmakers and their staffs within a mere twenty acres. Polling data that had been reported mainly in local papers was now being picked up by the national media in shocked disbelief. There were people running who had never run for anything before; businessmen, community leaders who had never worked the system, lawyers, ministers, even some physicians. Some of them might win as they spewed forth neo-populist-type speeches about supporting the President and 'restoring America' – a phrase that had gained wide currency. But America had never died, the Network people told themselves. *They* were still here, weren't they?

It was all Ryan's doing. He'd never been one of them. He'd actually said more than once that he didn't like being President!

Didn't like it?

How could any man – 'person' to the Network Establishment in the new age of enlightenment – not *like* having the ability to do so much, to pass out so many favors, to be courted and flattered like a king of old?

Didn't like it?

Then he didn't belong, did he?

They knew how to handle that. Someone had already started it. Leaks. Not just from inside. Those were little people with lesser agendas. There was more. There was the big picture, and for that, access still counted, because the

Network had many voices, and there were still ears to listen. There would be no plan and no conspiracy *per se*. It would all happen naturally, or as naturally as anything happened here. In fact, it had already begun.

For Badrayn, again, it was time on his computer. The task, he learned, was time-critical. Such things often were, but the reason was new in this case. The travel time itself had to be minimized, rather than arranged in such a way as to meet a specific deadline or rendezvous. The limiting factor here was the fact that Iran was still something of an outlaw country with surprisingly little in the way of air travel options.

Flights with convenient times were astoundingly limited:

KLM 534 to Amsterdam left just after one AM, and arrived in Holland at 6:10 AM after an intermediary stop;

Lufthansa's nonstop 601 left at 2:55, and got to Frankfurt at 5:50;

Austrian Airlines 774, leaving at 3:40 AM, arrived in Vienna nonstop at 6:00 AM;

Air France 165 left at 5:25 AM, arrived at Charles de Gaulle at nine AM;

British Airways 102 left at six AM, stopping en route, arriving at Heathrow at 12:45 PM;

Aeroflot 516 left at three AM for Moscow, arrived there at 7:10.

Only one nonstop to Rome, no direct flights to Athens, not even a nonstop to Beirut! He could have his people connect through Dubai – remarkably, Emirates Airlines *did* fly out of Tehran into its own international hub, as did Kuwait's flag carrier, but they, he thought, were not a very good idea.

Just a handful of flights to use, all of them easily observed by foreign intelligence services – if they were competent, as he had to assume they were, either they'd have their own people aboard the flights or the cabin staff would be briefed on what to look for and how to report it while the aircraft was still in the air. So, it wasn't just time, was it?

The people he'd selected were good ones; educated for the most part, they knew how to dress respectably, how to carry on a conversation, or at least to deflect one politely – on international flights the easiest thing was to feign the need for sleep, which most often wasn't feigned anyway. But only one mistake, and the consequences could be serious. He'd told them that, and all had listened.

Badrayn had never been given a mission like this one, and the intellectual challenge was noteworthy. Just a handful of really useable flights out, and the one to Moscow wasn't all that attractive. The gateway cities of London, Frankfurt, Paris, Vienna, and Amsterdam would have to do – and one flight each per day. The good news was that all five of them offered a wide choice of connections via American and other flag carriers. So one group would take 601 to Frankfurt, and there, some would disperse through Brussels (Sabena to New York-JFK) and Paris (Air France to Washington-Dulles; Delta to Atlanta; American Airlines to Orlando; United to Chicago) via conveniently timed connecting flights, while others took Lufthansa to Los Angeles. The British Airways team had the most options of all. One would take Concorde Flight 3 into New York. The only trick was getting them through the first series of flights. After that, the whole massive system of international air travel would handle the dispersal.

Still, twenty people, twenty possible mistakes. Operational security was always a worry. He'd spent half his life trying to outfox the Israelis, and while his continued life was some testimony to his success – or lack of total failure, which was somewhat more honest – the hoops he'd had to leap through had nearly driven him mad more than once. Well. At least he had the flights figured out. Tomorrow he would brief them in. He checked his watch. Tomorrow wasn't all that far away.

Not every insider agreed. Every group had its cynics and rebels, some good, some bad, some not even outcasts. Then there was also anger. The Network members, when thwarted by other members in one of their endeavors often took a philosophical view of the matter – one could always get even later, and still stay friends – but not always. This was especially true of the media members who both were and were not part of it all. They were, in the sense that they did have their own personal relationships and friendships with the government in and out people; they could go to them for information and insights, and stories about their enemies. They were not, in that the insiders never really trusted them, because the media could be used and fooled – most often cajoled, which was easier for one side of the political spectrum than the other. But trust? Not exactly. Or more exactly, not at all.

Some of them even had principles.

'Arnie, we need to talk.'

'I think we do,' van Damm agreed, recognizing the voice that had come in on *his* direct line.

'Tonight?'

'Sure. Where?'

'My place?'

The chief of staff gave it a few seconds of consideration. 'Why not?'

The delegation came just in time for evening prayers. The greetings were cordial and modest on both sides, and then all three of them entered the mosque and performed their daily ritual. Ordinarily, all would have felt purified by their devotions as they walked back out to the garden. But not this time. Only long practice in the concealment of emotions prevented overt displays of tension, but even that told much to all three, and especially to the one.

'Thank you for receiving us,' Prince Ali bin Sheik said first of all. He didn't add that it had taken long enough.

'I am pleased to welcome you in peace,' Daryaei replied. 'It is well that we should pray together.' He led them to a table prepared by his security people, where coffee was served, the strong, bitter brew favored in the Middle East. 'The blessings of God on this meeting, my friends. How may I be of service?'

'We are here to discuss recent developments,' the Royal Prince observed after a sip. His eyes locked in on Daryaei. His Kuwaiti colleague, Mohammed Adman Sabah, his country's foreign minister, remained quiet for the moment.

'What do you wish to know?' Daryaei asked.

'Your intentions,' Ali replied bluntly.

The spiritual head of the United Islamic Republic sighed. 'There is much work to be done. All the years of war and suffering, all the lives lost to so many causes, the destruction to so much. Even this mosque' – he gestured to the obvious need for repairs – 'is a symbol of it all, don't you think?'

'There has been much cause for sorrow,' Ali agreed.

'My intentions? To restore. These unhappy people have been through so much. Such sacrifices – and for what? The secular ambitions of a godless man. The injustice of it all cried out to Allah, and Allah answered the cries. And now, perhaps, we can be one prosperous and godly people.' The *again* hung unspoken on the end of the statement.

'That is the task of years,' the Kuwaiti observed.

'Certainly it is,' Daryaei agreed. 'But now with the embargo lifted, we have sufficient resources to see to the task, and the will to see it done. There will be a new beginning here.'

'In peace,' Ali added.

'Certainly in peace,' Daryaei agreed seriously.

'May we be of assistance? One of the Pillars of our Faith is charity, after all,' Foreign Minister Sabah observed.

A gracious nod. 'Your kindness is noted with gratitude, Mohammed Adman. It is well that we should be guided by our Faith rather than worldly influences that have so sadly swept over this region in recent years, but for the moment, as you can see, the task is so vast that we can scarcely begin to determine what things need to be done, and in what order. Perhaps at a later time we might discuss that again.'

It wasn't quite a flat rejection of aid, but close. The UIR wasn't interested in doing business, just as Prince Ali had feared.

'At the next meeting of OPEC,' Ali offered, 'we can discuss the rearrangement of production quotas so that you can share more fairly in the revenue we collect from our clients.'

'That would indeed be useful,' Daryaei agreed. 'We do not ask for all that much. A minor adjustment,' he allowed.

'Then on that we are agreed?' Sabah asked.

'Certainly. That is a technical issue which we can delegate to our respective functionaries.'

Both visitors nodded, noting to themselves that the allocation of oil production quotas was *the* most rancorous of issues. If every country produced too much, then the world price would fall, and all would suffer. On the other hand, if production were overly restricted, the price would rise, damaging the economies of their client states, which would then reduce demand and revenues with it. The proper balance – hard to strike, like all economic issues – was the yearly subject of high-level diplomatic missions, each with its own economic model, no two ever the same, and considerable discord within the mainly Muslim association. This was going far too easily.

'Is there a message you wish to convey to our governments?' Sabah asked next.

'We desire only peace, peace so that we can accomplish our tasks of restoring our societies into one, as Allah intends it to be. There is nothing for you to fear from us.'

'So what do you think?' Another training rotation was completed. Present at the final review of operations were some very senior Israeli officers, at least one of whom was a senior spook. Colonel Sean Magruder was a cavalryman, but in a real sense every senior officer was an intelligence consumer, and willing to shop at any source.

'I think the Saudis are very nervous, along with all their neighbors.'

'And you?' Magruder asked. He'd unconsciously adopted the informal and direct mode of address common in the country, especially its military.

Avi ben Jakob, still titularly a military officer – he was wearing a uniform now – was deputy chief of the Mossad. He wondered how far he could go, but with his job title, that was really for him to decide.

'We are not pleased at all by the development.'

'Historically,' Colonel Magruder observed, 'Israel has had a working relationship with Iran, even after the Shah fell. That goes all the way back to the Persian Empire. I believe your festival of Purim results from that period. Israeli air force pilots flew missions for the Iranians during the Iran-Iraq war and –'

'We had a large number of Jews then in Iran, and that was intended to get them out,' Jakob said quickly.

'And the arms-for-hostages mess that Reagan got into went through here, probably your agency,' Magruder added, just to show that he, too, was a player in the game.

'You are well informed.'

'That's my job, part of it anyway. Sir, I am not making value judgments here. Getting your people out of Iran back then was, as we say at home, business, and all countries have to do business. I'm just asking what you think of the UIR.'

'We think Daryaei is the most dangerous man in the world.'

Magruder thought of the eyes-only brief he'd had earlier in the day about the Iranian troop movements into Iraq. 'I agree.'

He'd come to like the Israelis. That hadn't always been true. For years, the United States Army had cordially disliked the Jewish state, along with the other branches of the service, mainly because of the corporate arrogance adopted by the small nation's senior military officers. But the IDF had learned humility in Lebanon, and learned to respect American arms as observers in the Persian Gulf War – after literally months of telling American officers that they needed advice on how to fight first the air war and then the ground war, they'd quickly taken to asking, politely, to look over some of the American plans because there *might* be some few *minor* things worthy of a *little* study.

The descent of the Buffalo Cav into the Negev had changed things some more. America's tragedy in Vietnam had broken another type of arrogance, and from that had grown a new type of professionalism. Under Marion Diggs, first CO of the reborn 10th United States Cavalry, quite a few harsh lessons had been handed out, and while Magruder was continuing that tradition, the Israeli troopers were learning, just as Americans had done at Fort Irwin. After the initial screams and near fistfights, common sense had broken out. Even Benny Eitan, commander of the Israeli 7th Armored Brigade, had rallied from the first set of drubbings to finish his training rotation with a pair of break-evens, and come away thanking his American hosts for the lessons – and promising to kick their asses when he returned the next year. In the central computer in the local Star Wars building, a complex mathematical model said that the performance of the Israeli army had improved by fully forty percent in just a few years, and now that they again had something to be arrogant about, the Israeli officers were showing disarming humility and an almost ruthless desire to learn – ever signs of truly professional soldiers.

And now one of their head spooks wasn't talking about

how his forces could handle anything the Islamic world might throw at his country. That was worth a contact report to Washington, Magruder thought.

The business jet once 'lost' in the Mediterranean could no longer leave the country. Even using it to ferry the Iraqi generals to Sudan had been a mistake, but a necessary one, and perhaps the odd covert mission was all right as well, but for the most part it had become Daryaei's personal transport, and a useful one, for his time was short, and his new country large. Within two hours of seeing his Sunni visitors off, he was back in Tehran.

'So?'

Badrayn laid out his papers on the desk, showing cities and routes and times. It was mere mechanics. Daryaei looked the plans over with a cursory eye, and while they seemed overly complex, that was not a major concern for him. He'd seen maps before. He looked up for the explanation that had to come with the paperwork.

'The primary issue is time,' Badrayn said. 'We want to have each traveler to his destination no more than thirty hours after departure. This one, for example, leaves Tehran at six AM, and arrives in New York at two AM Tehran time, elapsed time twenty hours. The trade show he will attend – it is at the Jacob Javits Center in New York – will be open past ten in the evening. This one departs at 2:55 AM, and ultimately arrives in Los Angeles twenty-three hours later early afternoon, local time. His trade show will be open all day. That is the most lengthy in terms of distance and time, and his "package" will still be more than eighty-five percent effective.'

'And security?'

'They are all fully briefed. I have selected intelligent, educated people. All they need do is be pleasant en route. After that, a little caution. Twenty at once, yes, that is troublesome, but those were your orders.'

'And the other group?'

'They will go out two days later via similar arrangements,' Badrayn reported. 'That mission is far more dangerous.'

'I am aware of that. Are the people faithful?'

'They are that.' Badrayn nodded, knowing that the question

698

really asked if they were fools. 'The political risks concern me.'

'Why?' The observation didn't surprise Daryaei, but he wanted the reason.

'The obvious question of discovering who sent them, though their travel documents will be properly prepared, and the usual security measures put in place. No, I mean the American political context. An unhappy event to a politician can often create sympathy for him, and from that sympathy can come political support.'

'Indeed! It does not make him appear weak?' That was rather much to swallow.

'In our context, yes, but not necessarily in theirs.'

Daryaei considered that and compared it with other analyses he'd ordered and reviewed. 'I have met Ryan. He *is* weak. He does *not* deal effectively with his political difficulties. He still has no true government behind him. Between the first mission and the second, we will break him – or at least we will distract him long enough to achieve our next goal. After that is accomplished, America becomes irrelevant.'

'Better the first mission only,' Badrayn advised.

'We must shake their people. If what you say of their government is true, we will do such harm as they have never known. We will shake their leader, we will shake his confidence, we will shake the confidence of the people in him.'

He had to respond to that carefully. This was a Holy Man with a Holy Mission. He was not fully amenable to reason. And yet there was one other factor which he didn't know about. There had to be. Daryaei was more given to wishes than considered action – no, that wasn't true, was it? He united the two while giving another impression entirely. What the cleric did appreciate was that the American government was still vulnerable, since its lower house of parliament had not yet been replaced, a process just beginning.

'Best of all merely to kill Ryan, if we could. An attack on children will inflame them. Americans are very sentimental about little ones.'

'The second mission goes on only after the first is known to be successful?' Daryaei demanded.

'Yes, that is true.'

'Then that is sufficient,' he said, looking back down at the travel arrangements, and leaving Badrayn to his own thoughts.

There is *a third element*. There had to be.

'He says his intentions are peaceful.'

'So did Hitler, Ali,' the President reminded his friend. He checked his watch. It was after midnight in Saudi Arabia. Ali had flown back and conferred with his government before calling Washington, as one would expect. 'You know about the troop movement.'

'Yes, your people briefed our military earlier today. It will be some time before they are ready to make any threat. Such things take time. Remember, I was once in uniform.'

'True, that's what they told me, too.' Ryan paused. 'Okay, what does the Kingdom propose?'

'We will observe closely. Our military is training. We have your pledge of support. We are concerned, but not overly so.'

'We could schedule some joint exercises,' Jack offered.

'That might only inflame matters,' the Prince replied. The absence of total conviction in his voice was not accidental. He'd probably fielded the idea in council himself and gotten a negative reply.

'Well, I guess you've had a long day. Tell me, how did Daryaei look? I haven't seen the guy since you introduced him to me.'

'His health appears good. He looks tired, but he's had a busy time.'

'I can relate to that. Ali?'

'Yes, Jack?'

The President stopped then, reminding himself that he was unschooled in diplomatic exchange. 'How concerned should I be about all this?'

'What do your people tell you?' the Prince replied.

'About the same as you do, but not all of them. We need to keep this line open, my friend.'

'I understand, Mr President. Good-bye for now.'

It was an unsatisfactory conclusion to an unsatisfactory call. Ryan replaced the phone and looked around at his empty office. Ali wasn't saying what he wanted to say because the position of his government was different from what he thought it should be. The same had happened to Jack often enough, and the same rules applied. Ali had to be loyal to that government – hell, it was mainly his own family – but he had allowed himself one slip, and the Prince was too clever to do that sort of thing by mistake. It probably would have been easier before, when Ryan had not been President and both could talk without the worry of making policy with every word. Now Jack *was* America to those beyond the borders, and governmental officials could talk to him only that way, instead of remembering that he was also a thinking man who needed to explore options before making decisions. Maybe if it hadn't been over the phone, Jack thought. Maybe face-to-face would have been better. But even Presidents were limited by time and space.

36

TRAVELERS

KLM – Royal Dutch Airlines – Flight 534 – left the gate on time at 1:10 AM The aircraft was full – at this hour, full of weary people who stumbled to their seats, strapped in, and accepted pillows and blankets. The more experienced travelers among them waited for the sound of the wheels being retracted, then pushed their seats as far back as they could go, and closed their eyes in the hope of a smooth ride and something akin to real sleep.

Five of Badrayn's men were aboard, two in first class, three in business. They all had baggage in the cargo hold, and a carry-on tucked under the seat in front. All had a minor case of nerves, and all would have had a drink to ameliorate it – religious prohibition or not – but the aircraft had landed in an Islamic airport and would not serve alcohol until it had left United Islamic Republic airspace. To a man, they considered their situation and bowed to circumstance. They'd been well briefed and properly prepared. They'd come through the airport like ordinary travelers, and submitted their carry-ons to X-ray inspection by security personnel who were every bit as careful as their Western counterparts – actually more so, since the flights were relatively few, and the local paranoia relatively greater. In every case, the X-ray display had shown a shaving kit, along with papers, books and other sundries.

They were all educated men, many of them having attended the American University of Beirut, some to obtain degrees, the others simply to learn about the enemy. They were dressed neatly, all with ties, loose now in their collars, and their coats hung in the mini-closets throughout the aircraft. Within forty minutes, they, along with the rest of the passengers, were fitfully asleep.

'So what's your take on all this?' van Damm asked.

Holtzman swirled his drink, watching the ice cubes circle

around. 'Under different circumstances I might call it a conspiracy, but it's not. For a guy who says he's just trying to put things back together, Jack sure is doing a lot of new and crazy things.'

'"Crazy" is a little strong, Bob.'

'Not for them, it isn't. Everybody's saying "he isn't one of us," and they're reacting strongly to his initiatives. Even you have to admit that his tax ideas are a little way off the usual playing field, but that's the excuse for what's happening – one of the excuses, anyway. The game's the same one it always was. A couple of leaks, and the manner of their presentation, that's what determines how it's played.'

Arnie had to nod. It was like highway littering. If someone dumped all the trash in the proper barrel, then things were neat, and the task was done in a few seconds. If that same someone tossed it all out the window of a moving car, then you had to spend hours picking it all up. The other side was now dumping the trash haphazardly, and the President was having to use his limited time doing wasteful and unproductive things instead of the real work of driving down the road. The simile was ugly, but apt. Politics was so often less about doing constructive work than about spreading garbage around for others to clean up.

'Who leaked?'

The reporter shrugged. 'I can only guess. Somebody in the Agency, probably somebody who's being RIF'd. You have to admit that building up the spy side of the house looks kind of Neanderthal. How far are they cutting the Intelligence Directorate?'

'More than enough to compensate for the new field people. The idea is to save money overall, better information, more efficient overall performance, that sort of thing. I don't,' he added, 'tell the President how to do intelligence stuff. On that, he really is an expert.'

'I know that. I had my story almost ready to run. I was about to call you for an interview with him when the bubble broke.'

'Oh? And –'

'What was my angle? He's the most contradictory son of a bitch in this town. In some ways he's brilliant – but in others? Babe-in-the-woods is charitable.'

'Go on.'

'I like the guy,' Holtzman admitted. 'For damned sure, he's honest – not relatively honest, really honest. I was going to tell it pretty much the way it was. You want to know what has *me* pissed?' He paused for a sip of the bourbon, hesitated again before proceeding, and then spoke with unconcealed anger. 'Somebody at the *Post* leaked my story, probably to Ed Kealty. Then Kealty probably arranged a leak to Donner and Plumber.'

'And they used your story to hang him?'

'Pretty much,' Holtzman admitted.

Van Damm nearly laughed. He held it back for as long as he could, but it was too delicious to resist: 'Welcome to Washington, Bob.'

'You know, some of us really do take our professional ethics seriously,' the reporter shot back, rather lamely. 'It was a good story. I researched the hell out of it. I got my own source in CIA – well, I have several, but I got a new one for this, somebody who really knew the stuff. I took what he gave me, and I back-checked the hell out of it, verified everything I could, wrote the piece stating what I knew and what I thought – careful to explain the difference at all times,' he assured his host. 'And you know? Ryan comes out looking pretty good. Yeah, sure, sometimes he short-circuits the system, but the guy's never broken the rules far as I can tell. If we ever have a major crisis, that's the guy I want in the Oval Office. But some son of a *bitch* took *my* story, *my* information from *my* sources, and played with it, I don't like that, Arnie. *I* have a public trust, too, and so does my paper, and somebody *fucked* with that.' He set his drink down. 'Hey, I know what you think about me and my –'

'No, you don't,' van Damm interrupted.

'But you've always –'

'I'm the chief of staff, Bob. I *have* to be loyal to my boss, and so I have to play the game from my side, but if you think I don't respect the press, you're not as smart as you're supposed to be. We're not always friends. Sometimes we're enemies, but we need you as much as you need us. For Christ's sake, if I didn't respect you, why the hell are you drinking my booze?'

It was either an elegant roll or a truthful statement, Holtzman thought, and Arnie was too skillful a player for him to tell the difference right off. But the smart thing to do was finish the drink, which he did. A pity that his host preferred cheap booze to go along with his L.L. Bean shirts. Arnie didn't know how to dress, either. Or maybe that was a considered part of his mystique. The political game was so intricate as to be a cross between classical metaphysics and experimental science. You could never know it all, and finding out one part as often as not denied you the ability to find out another, equally important part. But that was why it was the best game in town.

'Okay, Arnie, I'll accept that.'

'Good of you.' Van Damm smiled, and refilled the glass. 'So why did you call me?'

'It's almost embarrassing.' Another pause. 'I will not participate in the public hanging of an innocent man.'

'You've done that before,' Arnie objected.

'Maybe so, but they were all politicians, and they all had it coming in one way or another. I don't know what – okay, how about I'm not into child abuse? Ryan deserves a fair chance.'

'And you're pissed about losing your story and the Pulitzer that –'

'I have two of them already,' Holtzman reminded him. Otherwise, he would have been taken off the story by his managing editor, but internal politics at the *Washington Post* were as vicious as those elsewhere in the city.

'So?'

'So, I need to know about Colombia. I need to know about Jimmy Cutter and how he died.'

'Jesus, Bob, you don't know what our ambassador went through down there today.'

'Great language for invective, Spanish.' A reporter's smile. 'The story can't be told, Bob. It just can't.'

'The story *will* be told. It's just a question of who tells it, and that will determine *how* it's told. Arnie, I know enough now to write something, okay?'

As so often happened in Washington at times like this, everyone was trapped by circumstance. Holtzman had a story to write. Doing it the right way would, perhaps, resurrect his original story, put him in the running for another Pulitzer

– it was still important to him, previous denials notwithstanding, and Arnie knew it – and tell whoever had leaked his story to Ed Kealty that he or she had better leave the *Post* before Holtzman nailed that name down and wrecked his or her career with a few well-placed whispers and more than a few dead-end assignments. Arnie was trapped by his duty to protect his President, and the only way to do it was to violate the law and his President's trust. There had to be an easier way, the chief of staff thought, to earn a living. He could have made Holtzman wait for his decision, but that would have been mere theatrics, and both men were past that.

'No notes, no tape recorder.'

'Off the record. "Senior official," not even "senior administration official,"' Bob agreed.

'And I can tell you who to confirm it with.'

'They know it all?'

'Even more than I do,' van Damm told him. 'Hell, I just found out about the important part.'

A raised eyebrow. 'That's nice, and the same rules will apply to them. Who really knows about this?'

'Even the President doesn't know it all. I'm not sure if anybody knows it all.'

Holtzman took another sip. It would be his last. Like a doctor in an operating room, he didn't believe in mixing alcohol and work.

Flight 534 touched down at Istanbul at 2:55 AM local time, after a flight of 1,270 miles and three hours, fifteen minutes. The passengers were groggily awake, having been roused by the cabin staff thirty minutes earlier and told to put their seat-backs to the upright position in a series of languages. The landing was smooth, and a few of them raised the plastic shades on the windows to see that they were indeed on the ground at one more anonymous piece of real-estate with white runway lights and blue taxiway lights, just like those all over the world. Those getting out stood at the proper time to stumble off into the Turkish night. The rest pushed their seats back for another snooze during the forty-five-minute layover, before the aircraft left yet another gate at 3:40 AM for the second half of the trip.

Lufthansa 601 was a European-made Airbus 310 twin-jet, roughly the same as the KLM Boeing in size and capacity. This one, too, had five travelers aboard, and left its gate at 2:55 for the nonstop flight to Frankfurt. The departure was routine in all details.

'That's some story, Arnie.'

'Oh, yeah. I didn't know the important parts until this week.'

'How sure are you of this?' Holtzman asked.

'The pieces all fit.' He shrugged again. 'I can't say I liked hearing it. I think we would have won the election anyway, but, Jesus, the guy threw it. He *tanked* on a presidential election, but you know,' van Damm said wistfully, 'that might have been the most courageous and generous political act of the century. I didn't think he had it in him.'

'Does Fowler know?'

'I haven't told him. Maybe I should.'

'Wait a minute. Remember how Liz Elliot planted a story on me about Ryan and how –'

'Yes, that all folds into this. Jack went down personally to get those soldiers out. The guy next to him in the chopper was killed, and he's looked after the family ever since. Liz paid for it. She came apart the night the bomb went off in Denver.'

'And Jack really did . . . you know that's one story that never came out all the way. Fowler lost it and almost launched a missile at Iran – it was Ryan, wasn't it? He's the one who stopped it.' Holtzman looked down at his drink and decided on another sip. 'How?'

'He got onto the Hot Line,' Arnie replied. 'He cut the President off and talked directly with Narmonov, and persuaded him to back things off some. Fowler flipped out and told the Secret Service to go arrest him, but by the time they got to the Pentagon, things *were* calmed down. It worked, thank God.'

It took Holtzman a minute or so to absorb that, but again, the story fit with the fragments he knew. Fowler had resigned two days later, a broken man, but an honorable one who knew that his moral right to govern his country had died with his order to launch a nuclear weapon at an innocent city. And Ryan had also been shaken by the event, badly enough to leave government service at once, until Roger Durling had brought him back in.

'Ryan's broken every rule there is. Almost as if he likes it.' But that wasn't fair, was it?

'If he hadn't, we might not be here.' The chief of staff poured himself another. Holtzman waved him off. 'You see what I mean about the story, Bob? If you tell it all, the country gets hurt.'

'But then why did Fowler recommend Ryan to Roger Durling?' the reporter asked. 'He couldn't stand the guy and –'

'Whatever his faults, and he has them, Bob Fowler is an honest politician, that's why. No, he doesn't like Ryan personally, maybe it's chemistry, I don't know, but Ryan saved him and he told Roger – what was it? "Good man in a storm." That's it,' Arnie remembered.

'Shame he doesn't know politics.'

'He learns pretty fast. Might surprise you.'

'He's going to gut the government if he gets the chance. I can't – I mean, I *do* like the guy personally, but his policies . . .'

'Every time I think I have him figured out, he swerves on me, and then I have to remind myself that he doesn't have an agenda,' van Damm said. 'He just does the job. I give him papers to read, and he acts on them. He listens to what people tell him – asks good questions, and always listens to the answers – but he makes his own decisions, as though he knows what's right and what's wrong – but the hell of it is, mostly he does. Bob, he's rolled *me*! But that's not it, either. Sometimes I'm not sure what it is with him, you know?'

'A total outsider,' Holtzman observed quietly. 'But –'

The chief of staff nodded. 'Yeah, *but*. *But* he's being analyzed as though he's an insider with a hidden agenda, and they're playing the insider games as if they apply to him, but they don't.'

'So the key to the guy is there's nothing to figure out . . . son of a bitch,' Bob concluded. 'He hates the job, doesn't he?'

'Most of the time. You should have been there when he spoke in the Midwest. He got it then. All those people loving him, and he loved them back, and it showed – and it scared the shit out of him. Nothing to figure out? Exactly. Like they say in golf, the hardest thing to do is to hit a straight ball, right? Everybody's looking for curves. There aren't any.'

Holtzman snorted. 'So, what's the angle if there isn't an angle?'

'Bob, I just try to control the media, remember? Damned if I know how you report this, except to state the facts – you know, like you're *supposed* to do.'

That was a lot for the journalist to take. He'd been in Washington for all of his professional life. 'And every politician is *supposed* to be like Ryan. But they're not.'

'This one is,' Arnie shot back.

'How am I supposed to tell my readers that? Who'll believe it?'

'Ain't that the problem?' he breathed. 'I've been in politics all my life, and I thought I knew it all. Hell, I *do* know it all. I'm one of the best operators ever was, everybody knows that, and all of a sudden this yahoo comes into the Oval Office and says the emperor's naked, and he's right, and nobody knows what to do about it except to say that he isn't. The system isn't ready for this. The system is only ready for itself.'

'And the system will destroy anybody who says different.' Holtzman snorted with the thought: If Hans Christian Andersen had written 'The Emperor's Clothes' about Washington, then the kid who'd spoken the truth out loud would have been killed on the spot by the assembled crowd of insiders.

'It'll try,' Arnie agreed.

'And what are we supposed to do about it?'

'You're the one who said that you don't want to officiate at the hanging of an innocent man, remember?'

'Where's that leave us?'

'Maybe to talk about the unruly mob,' Arnie suggested, 'or the emperor's corrupt court.

Next to go was Austrian Airlines 774. It was down to a routine now, and the arrangements were well within the technical parameters. The cans of shaving cream had been filled a bare forty minutes before departure. The proximity of the Monkey House to the airport helped, as did the time of day, and having people race the last few hundred meters to the gate was not unusual anywhere in the world, particularly for flights like this one. The 'soup' was sprayed into the bottom of the can, by a plastic valve that was invisible to X-ray examination. The nitrogen went in the top to a separate insulated container located in the center of the cans. The process was clean and safe – for extra but really unnecessary safety, the cans were sprayed and wiped; that was just to make the travelers happy. The cans were quite cold, of course, though not dangerously so. As the liquid nitrogen boiled off, it would vent through a pressure valve into the ambient atmosphere, where it merely joined the air. Though nitrogen is an important element in explosives, by itself it is totally inert, clear, and odorless. Nor would it react chemically with the contents of the cans, and so the pressure-relief valve retained a precise quantity of the warming gas to act as a safe propellant for the 'soup' when the time came.

The filling was done by the medical corpsmen in their protective suits – they refused to work without them, and ordering them otherwise would only have made them nervous and sloppy, and so the director indulged their fears. Two groups of five remained, to be done. The cans could really all have been prepared at the same time, Moudi knew, but no unnecessary chances were being taken, a thought that made him stop cold. No unnecessary chances? Sure.

Daryaei didn't sleep that night, which was unusual for him. Though with increasing years he found that he needed less of it, getting off to sleep had never been difficult for him. On a really quiet night, if the winds were right, he could hear the airliners bring their engines to the roar of takeoff power – a distant sound, rather like a waterfall, he sometimes thought, or perhaps an earthquake. Some fundamental sound of nature, distant and foreboding. And now he found himself listening for it, and with his imagination, wondering if he heard it or not.

Had he gone too fast? He was an old man in a country where so many died young. He remembered the diseases of his youth, and later he'd learned their scientific causes, mainly poor water and sanitation, for Iran had been a backward country for most of his lifetime, despite its long history of civilization and power. Then it had been resurrected by

oil and the immense riches that had come with it. Mohammad Reza Pahlavi, Shahanshah – *King of kings!* the phrase
proclaimed – had begun to raise the country, but made the
mistake of moving too fast and making too many enemies.
In Iran's dark age, as in every other such time, secular power
had devolved to the Islamic clergy, and in liberating the
nation's peasantry, he'd trod on too many toes, making
enemies of people whose power was spiritual and to whom
the common folk looked for order in lives made chaotic by
change. Even so, the Shah had almost succeeded, but not
quite, and *not quite* was as damning a curse as the world
produced for those who would be great.

What did such men think? Just as he himself was old, so
the Shah had grown old and sick with cancer, and watched
the work of a lifetime evaporate in a matter of weeks, his
associates executed in a brief orgy of settled scores, bitter at
his betrayal by his American friends. Had he thought that
he'd gone too far – or not far enough? Daryaei didn't know,
and now he would have liked to know, as he listened for the
distant sounds of waterfalls in the still of a Persian night.

To move too fast was a grievous error, which the young
learned and the old knew, but not to move enough, fast
enough, far enough, strongly enough, that was what really
denied goals to those who would be great. How bitter it must
be to lie in bed, without the sleep one needed to think clearly,
and wonder and curse oneself for chances missed and chances
lost.

Perhaps he knew what the Shah had thought, Daryaei
admitted to himself. His own country was drifting again.
Even insulated as he was, he knew the signs. It showed up
as subtle differences in dress, especially the dress of women.
Not much, not quite enough for his true believers to per-
secute them, for even the true believers had softened their
devotion, and there were gray areas into which people could
venture to see what might happen. Yes, the people still
believed in Islam, and yes, they still believed in him, but,
really, the Holy Koran wasn't *that* strict, and their nation
was rich, and to grow richer it needed to do business. How
could it be a champion of the Faith unless it grew richer,
after all? The best and brightest of Iran's young went abroad
to be educated, for his country did not possess the schools

that the infidel West had – and, for the most part, they came back, educated in skills which his country needed. But they also came back with other things, invisible, doubts and questions, and memories of a freewheeling life in a different society where the pleasures of the flesh were available to the weak, and all men were weak. What if all Khomeini and he had accomplished was to delay what the Shah had started? The people who had come back to Islam in reaction to Pahlavi were now drifting back to the promise of freedom he'd offered them. Didn't they *know*? Didn't they *see*? They could have all the trappings of power and all the blessings of what people called civilization and still remain faithful, still have the spiritual anchor – without which all was nothing.

But to have all that, his country needed to be more than it was, and so he could not afford to be *not quite*. Daryaei had to deliver the things that would show he'd been right all along, that uncompromising faith *was* the true root of power.

The assassination of the Iraqi leader, the misfortune that had befallen America – these things had to be a sign, didn't they? He'd studied them carefully. Now Iraq and Iran were one, and *that* had been the quest of decades – and at virtually the same instant, America had been crippled. It wasn't just Badrayn who was telling him things. He had his own America experts who knew the workings of that country's government. He knew Ryan from a single important meeting, had seen his eyes, heard the bold but hollow words, and so he knew the measure of the man who might be his principal adversary. He knew that Ryan had not, and by the laws of his country *could* not, have a replacement selected for himself, and so there was only this moment, and he had to act in it, or else assume for himself the curse of *not quite*.

No, he would not be remembered as another Mohammad Pahlavi. If he did not covet the trappings of power, he lusted for the fact of it. Before his death he would lead all Islam. In a month he would have the oil of the Persian Gulf and the keys to Mecca, secular *and* spiritual power. From that his influence would expand in all directions. In but a few years his country would be a superpower in every way, and he would leave to his successors a legacy such as the world hadn't seen since Alexander, but with the added security that it was founded in the words of God. To achieve that end, to unite Islam, to fulfill the Will of Allah and the words of the Prophet Mohammed, he would do what was needed, and if that meant moving fast, then he would move fast. Overall, the process was a simple one, three simple steps, the third and most difficult of which was already established and nothing could stop, even if Badrayn's plans all failed completely.

Was he moving too fast? Daryaei asked himself for the last time. No, he was moving decisively, with surprise, with calculation, with boldness. That was what history would say.

'Flying at night is a big deal?' Jack asked.

'Sure is, for them it is,' Robby replied. He liked briefing the President this way, late evening in the Oval Office, with a drink. 'They've always been more parsimonious with equipment than they are with people. Helicopters – French ones in this case, same model the Coast Guard has a bunch of – cost money, and we haven't seen much in the way of night operations. The operation they're running is heavy on ASW. So maybe they're thinking about dealing with all those Dutch subs the Republic of China bought last year. We're also seeing a lot of combined operations with their air force.'

'Conclusion?'

'They're training up for something.' The Pentagon's Director of Operations closed his briefing book. 'Sir, we –'

'Robby,' Ryan said, looking over the new reading glasses Cathy had just gotten him, 'if you don't start calling me "Jack" when we're alone, I'm going to break you back to ensign by executive order.'

'We're not alone,' Admiral Jackson objected, nodding toward Agent Price.

'Andrea doesn't count – oh, shit, I mean –' Ryan blushed.

'He's right, Admiral, I don't count,' she said, with a barely contained laugh. 'Mr President, I've been waiting *weeks* for you to say that.'

Jack looked down at the table and shook his head. 'This is no way for a man to live. Now my best friend calls me "sir," and I'm being impolite to a lady.'

'*Jack*, you are my commander-in-chief,' Robby pointed out, with a relaxed grin at his friend's discomfort. 'And I'm just a poor sailor man.'

First things first, the President thought: 'Agent Price?'

'Yes, Mr President?'

'Pour yourself a drink and sit down.'

'Sir, I'm on duty, and regulations –'

'Then make it a light one, but that's an order from your President. Do it!'

She actually hesitated, but then decided that POTUS was trying to make some sort of point. Price poured a large thimbleful of whiskey into the Old Fashioned glass and added a lot of ice and Evian to it. Then she sat next to the J-3. His wife, Sissy, was upstairs in the House with the Ryan family.

'As a practical matter, people, the President needs to relax, and it's easier for me to do that if I don't make ladies stand up, and my friend can call me by my name once in a while. Are we agreed on that?'

'Aye aye,' Robby said, still smiling but seeing the logic and desperation of the moment. 'Yes, Jack, we are all relaxed now, and we *will* enjoy it.' He looked over at Price. 'You're here to shoot me if I misbehave, right?'

'Right in the head,' she confirmed.

'I prefer missiles myself. Safer,' he added.

'You did okay with a shotgun one night, or so the Boss has told me. By the way, thanks.'

'Huh?'

'For keeping him alive. We actually like taking care of the Boss, even if he gets too familiar with the hired help.'

Jack freshened his drink while they relaxed on the other sofa. Remarkable, he thought. For the first time, there was a genuinely relaxed atmosphere in the office, to the point that two people could joke about him, right in front of him, as though he were a human being instead of POTUS.

'I like this a lot better.' The President looked up. 'Robby, this gal has been around more crap than we have, listened in on all sorts of things. She has a master's degree, she's smart, but I'm supposed to treat her like she's a knuckle-dragger.'

'Well, hell, I'm just a fighter jock with a bad knee.'

'And I still don't know what the hell I'm supposed to be. Andrea?'

'Yes, Mr President?' Getting her to call him by his name was an impossible goal, Jack knew.

'China, what do you think?'

'I think I'm no expert, but since you ask, I don't know.'

'You're expert enough,' Robby observed with a grunt. 'All the king's horses and all the king's men don't know much, either. The additional subs are arriving,' he told the President. 'Mancuso wants them on the north-south line between the two navies. I've concurred on that, and the Secretary's signed off on it.'

'How's Bretano doing?'

'He knows what he doesn't know, Jack. He listens to us on operational stuff, asks good questions, and listens some more. He wants to start getting out into the field next week, poke around and see the kids at work to educate himself. His managerial skills are downright awesome, but he's swinging a big ax – he's going to, that is. I've seen his draft plan for downsizing the bureaucracy. Whoa,' Admiral Jackson concluded, with an eye-roll.

'You have problems with that?' Jack asked.

'No way. It's about fifty years overdue. Ms Price, I'm an operator,' he explained. 'I like greasy flight suits and the smell of jet fuel and pulling g's. But us guys at the sharp end always have the desk-sitters after us like a bunch of little dogs at our ankles all the time. Bretano loves engineers and people who do things, but along the way he's learned to hate bureaucrats and cost accountants. My kind of guy.'

'Back to China,' Ryan said.

'Okay, we still have the electronics-intelligence flights working out of Kadena. We're getting routine training stuff. We do not know what intentions the ChiComs have. CIA isn't giving us much. Signal intelligence is unremarkable. State says that their government says, "What's the big deal?" And that's it. The Taiwanese navy is big enough to handle the threat, if there is one, unless they get coldcocked. That's not going to happen. They're bright-eyed and bushy-tailed, doing their own training ops. A lot of sound and fury, signifying nothing I can make out.'

'The Gulf?'

'Well, we're hearing from our people in Israel that they're taking a very close look, but I gather they're not getting much in the way of hard intel. Whatever sources they had were probably with the generals who bugged out to Sudan

– aides and such, probably. I got a fax in from Sean Magruder –'

'Who's that?' Ryan asked.

'He's an Army colonel, boss-man of the 10th Cav in the Negev. I met him last year; he's a guy we listen to. "Most dangerous man in the world," is what our good pal Avi ben Jakob says of Daryaei. Magruder thought that was insightful enough to pass it along.'

'And?'

'And we need to keep an eye on it. It's probably a ways off, but Daryaei has imperial ambitions. The Saudis are playing it wrong. We should have people on the way over now, maybe not many, but some, to show the other side that we're in the game.'

'I talked to Ali about that. His government wants to cool it.'

'Wrong signal,' Jackson observed.

'Agreed.' POTUS nodded. 'We'll work on that.'

'What's the state of the Saudi military?' Price asked.

'Not as good as it ought to be. After the Persian Gulf War, it got fashionable to join their National Guard, and they bought equipment like it was a bunch of Mercedes cars from a wholesaler. For a while they had themselves a fine old time playing soldier, but then they found out that you have to maintain the stuff. They hired people to do that for them. Kinda like squires and knights back in the old days. Ain't the same,' Jackson said. 'And now they're not training. Oh, sure, they run around in their tanks, and they do their gunnery – the M1 is a fun tank to shoot, and they do a lot of that – but they're not training in units. Knights and squires. Their tradition is guys on horses going after other guys on horses – one-on-one, like in the movies. War ain't like that. War is a great big team working together. Their culture and history are against that model, and they haven't had the chance to learn. Bottom line, they're not as good as they think they are. If the UIR gets its military act together someday and comes south, the Saudis are outgunned and damned sure outmanned.'

'How do we fix that?' Ryan asked.

'For starters, get some of our people over there, and some of their people over here, out to the National Training Center for a crash course in reality. I've talked it over with Mary Diggs at the NTC –'

'Mary?'

'General Marion Diggs. "Mary" goes back to the Point. It's a uniform thing,' Robby told Price. 'I'd like to fly a Saudi heavy battalion over here and have the OpFor pound them into the sand for a few weeks to get the message across. That's how our people learned. That's how the Israelis learned. And that's how the Saudis are going to have to learn, damned sight easier that way than in a shooting war. Diggs is for it, big time. Give us two or three years, maybe less if we set up a proper training establishment in Saudi, and we can snap their army into shape – except for politics,' he added.

POTUS nodded. 'Yeah, it'll make the Israelis nervous, and the Saudis have always worried about having too strong a military, for domestic reasons.'

'You could tell them the story about the three little pigs. It might not fly with their culture, but the big bad wolf just moved in next door to them, and they'd better start paying attention before he starts a-huffin' and a-puffin'.'

'I hear you, Robby. I'll have Adler and Vasco think that one over.' Ryan checked his watch. Another fifteen-hour day. One more drink would have been nice, but as it was, he'd be lucky to get six hours of sleep, and he didn't want to wake up with a larger headache than necessary. He set his drink down and waved for the other two to follow, down the ramp and out the door.

'SWORDSMAN heading to the residence,' Andrea spoke into her radio mike. A minute later, they were in the elevator and going up.

'Try not to let the booze show,' Jack remarked to his principal agent.

'What *are* we going to do with you?' she asked the ceiling, as the doors opened.

Jack walked out first, leaving the other two behind as he took his jacket off. He hated wearing a jacket all the time.

'Well, now you know,' Robby said to the Secret Service agent. She turned to look in his eyes.

'Yeah.' Actually she'd known for quite a while, but she kept learning more and more about SWORDSMAN.

'Take good care of him, Price. When he escapes from this place, I want my friend back.'

The vagaries of winds made the Lufthansa flight first to arrive at the international terminal in Frankfurt, Germany. For the travelers it was like an inverted funnel. The jetway was the narrow part, and on entering the concourse they all spread out, checking the video monitors for their gates. The layovers ranged from one to three hours, and their luggage would be automatically transferred from one aircraft to another – for all the complaints about airport luggage-handlers, 99.9 percent is a passing grade in most human endeavors; and the Germans were notoriously efficient. Customs control points didn't worry them, because none of them were spending any more time in Europe than was necessary. They studiously avoided eye contact, even when three of them entered a coffee shop, and all three, on reflection, decided on decaf. Two walked into the men's rooms for the usual reason, and then looked into the mirrors to check their faces. They'd all shaved just before leaving, but one of them, especially heavily-bearded, saw that his jaw was already shadowed. Perhaps he should shave? Not a good idea, he thought, smiling at the mirror. Then he lifted his carry-on bag and walked off to the first-class lounge to wait for the flight to Dallas-Fort Worth.

'Long day?' Jack asked, after everyone had gone home, and just the usual squad of guards patrolled outside.

'Yeah. Grand rounds tomorrow with Bernie. Some procedures the next day, though.' Cathy changed into her night-gown, as tired as her husband was.

'Anything new?'

'Not in my shop. Had lunch with Pierre Alexandre. He's a new associate professor working under Ralph Forster, ex-Army, pretty smart.'

'Infectious diseases?' Jack vaguely remembered meeting the guy at some function or other. 'AIDS and stuff?'

'Yeah.'

'Nasty,' Ryan observed, getting into bed.

'They just dodged a bullet. There was a mini-outbreak of Ebola in Zaire,' Cathy said, getting in the other side. 'Two deaths. Then two more cases turned up in Sudan, but it doesn't look like it's going anywhere.'

'Is that as bad as people say?' Jack turned the light off.

'Eighty percent mortality – pretty bad.' She adjusted the covers and moved toward him. 'But enough of that stuff. Sissy says she's got a concert scheduled for two weeks from now at Kennedy Center. Beethoven's Fifth, with Fritz Bayerlein conducting, would you believe? Think we can get tickets?' He could sense his wife's smile in the dark.

'I think I know the theater owner. I'll see what I can do.' A kiss. A day ended.

'See you in the morning, Jeff.' Price went to the right for her car. Raman went to the left for his.

A mind could be dulled by this job, Aref Raman told himself. The sheer mechanics of it, the hours, the watching and waiting and doing nothing – but always being ready.

Hmph. Why should he complain about that? It was the story of his adult life. He drove north, waited for the security gate to open and headed northwest. The empty streets made it go quickly. By the time he got to his home, the bled-off stress of working the Detail in the White House had him nodding, but there were still mechanics.

Unlocking the door, he next turned off the security system, picked up the mail that had come through the slot in the door and scanned it. One bill, and the rest was junk mail offering him the chance of a lifetime to buy things he didn't need. He hung up his coat, removed the pistol and holster from his belt, and walked into the kitchen. The light was blinking on the answering machine. There was one message.

'Mr Sloan,' the digital recorder said to him in a voice that was familiar, though he'd only heard it once before, 'this is Mr Alahad. Your rug just came in, and is ready for delivery.'

37

DISCHARGES

America was sleeping when they boarded their flights in Amsterdam, and London, and Vienna, and Paris. This time no two were on the same aircraft, and the schedules were staggered so that the same customs inspector would not have the chance to open two shaving kits and find the same brand of cream and then wonder about it, however unlikely that might be. The real risk had been in placing so many men on the same flights out of Tehran, but they'd been properly briefed on how to act. While the ever-watchful German police, for example, might have taken note of a gaggle of Middle Eastern men huddling together after arriving on the same flight, airports have always been anonymous places full of semi-confused wandering people, often tired and usually disoriented, and one lonely, aimless traveler looked much like another.

The first to board a transatlantic flight walked onto a Singapore Airlines 747 at Amsterdam's Schiphol International Airport. Coded as SQ26, the airliner pulled away at eight-thirty AM and got into the air on time, then angled northwest for a great-circle course that would take it over the southern tip of Greenland. The flight would last just under eight hours. The traveler was in a first-class window seat, which he tilted all the way back. It was not even three in the morning in his next destination city, and he preferred sleep to a movie, along with most of the other people in the nose of the aircraft. He had his itinerary memorized, and if his memory failed, with the confusion of long-distance travel, he still had his tickets to remind him of what to do next. For the moment, sleep was enough, and he turned his head on the pillow, soothed by the swish of passing air outside the double windows.

Around him, in the air, were other flights, with other travelers heading for Boston, Philadelphia, Washington-Dulles,

Atlanta, Orlando, Dallas-Fort Worth, Chicago, San Francisco, Miami, and Los Angeles, the ten principal gateway cities into America. Each of them had a trade show or convention of some sort underway now. Ten other cities, Baltimore, Pittsburgh, St Louis, Nashville, Atlantic City, Las Vegas, Seattle, Phoenix, Houston, and New Orleans, also had events, and each was but a brief flight – in two cases, a drive – from the nearest port of entry.

The traveler on SQ26 thought about that as he faded off. The shaving kit was tucked in his carry-on bag under the seat in front of him, carefully insulated and wrapped, and he made certain that his feet didn't touch, much less kick, the bag.

It was approaching noon outside Tehran. The Movie Star watched as his group conducted weapons practice. It was a formality really, designed more for morale than anything else. They all knew how to shoot, having learned and practiced in the Bekaa Valley, and though they weren't using the same weapons they'd have in America, it didn't really matter. A gun was a gun, and targets were targets, and they knew about both. They couldn't simulate everything, of course, but all of them knew how to drive, and they spent hours every day going over the diagram and the models. They would go in during the late afternoon, when parents came in to pick up their children for the daily trip home, when the bodyguards would be tired and bored from a day of watching the children doing childish things. Movie Star had gotten descriptions of several of the 'regular' cars, and some were common types which could be rented. The opposition was as trained and experienced as they had to be, but they were not supermen. Some were even women, and for all his exposure to the West, the Movie Star could not take women seriously as adversaries, guns or no guns. But their biggest tactical advantage was that his team was willing to use deadly force with profligate abandon. With over twenty toddlers about, plus the school staff, and probably a few parents in the way as well, the opposition would be greatly hampered. So, no, the initial part of the mission was the easiest. The hard part would be getting away – if things got that far. He had to tell his team that they would get away, and that there was a plan. But really it didn't matter, and in their hearts all of them knew it.

They were all willing to become sacrifices in the unannounced *jihad*, else they would never have joined Hezbollah in the first place. They were also willing to see their victims as sacrifices. But that was just a convenient label. Religion was really nothing more than a façade for what they did and who they were. A true scholar of their religion would have blanched at their purpose, but Islam had many adherents, and among them were many who chose to read the scriptures in unconventional ways, and they too, had their following. What Allah might have thought of their actions was not something they considered very deeply, and the Movie Star didn't trouble himself to think about it at all. For him, it was business, a political statement, a professional challenge, one more task to occupy his days. Perhaps, too, it was a step toward a larger goal, the achievement of which would mean a life of comfort, and perhaps even some personal power and stability – but in his heart he didn't really believe that, either. At first, yes, he'd thought that Israel might be overthrown, the Jews expunged from the face of the earth, but those careless beliefs of his youth had long since faded. For him, it was all mere process now, and this was one more task. The substance of the task didn't really matter all that much, did it? he asked himself, watching the team's grimly enthusiastic faces, as the men hit the targets. Oh, it seemed to matter to them. But he knew better.

The day began at five-thirty AM for Inspector Patrick O'Day. A clock-radio roused him from his bed, then off to the bathroom for the usual start-up functions, a look in the mirror, and off to the kitchen to get the coffee going. It was the quiet of the day. Most people (the sensible ones) weren't up yet. No traffic on the streets. Even the birds still slumbering on their perches. Outside to get the papers, he could feel the silence and wonder why the world wasn't always this way. Through the trees to the east was the glow of a coming dawn, though the stronger of the stars still burned overhead. Not a single light showing in the rest of the houses in the development. Damn. Was he the only one who had to work such punishing hours?

Back inside, he took ten minutes to scan the morning *Post* and *Sun*. He kept track of the news, especially crime cases. As a roving inspector working directly out of the office of the Director, he never knew from one day to the next when he might be sent off on a case, which often meant calling in a sitter, to the point that he sometimes thought about getting a full-time nanny. He could afford it – the insurance settlement for his wife's death in the plane crash had actually given him a measure of financial independence, though its circumstances seemed altogether blasphemous, but they had offered it and he, on advice of counsel, had taken it. But a nanny? No. It would be a woman, and Megan would think of her as Mommy, and, no, he couldn't have that. Instead, he did the hours and denied himself so that he could be both parents, and no grizzly bear had ever been more protective of a cub. Maybe Megan didn't know the difference. Maybe kids thrived under the care of a mother and bonded firmly to her but could as easily bond to a father. When asked about her mommy by other kids, she explained that Mommy had gone to heaven early – and this is my daddy! Whatever the psychological circumstances, the closeness of the two which seemed so natural to Megan – she'd scarcely had the chance to know anything else – was something that occasionally brought tears to her father's eyes. The love of a child is ever unconditional, all the more so when there is but one object for it. Inspector O'Day was sometimes grateful for the fact that he hadn't worked a kidnapping in years. Were he to do so today . . . he took a sip of coffee and admitted to himself that he might just find himself searching for an excuse not to bring the subject in. There were always ways. He'd worked on six of those cases as a young agent – kidnapping for money was a very rare crime today; the word had gotten out that it was a losing game, that the full power of the FBI descended on such cases like the wrath of God – and only now did he understand how hateful such crimes were. You had to be a parent, you had to know the feel of tiny arms around your neck to understand the magnitude of such a violation – but then your blood turned to ice, and you didn't so much turn off your emotions as block them out for as long as you had to before letting them free again. He remembered his first squad supervisor, Dominic DiNapoli – 'the toughest wop this side of the Gambino family' was the office joke – crying like a baby himself as he carried the living victim of such a crime to see her parents. Only now did he understand how it was just one more sign of Dom's toughness. Yeah. And *that* subject would *never* get out of Atlanta Federal Penitentiary.

Then it was time to get Megan up. She was curled up in her full-body sleeper, the blue one with Casper the Friendly Ghost on it. She was outgrowing it, he saw. Her little toes were pushing at the plastic feet. They did grow so fast. He tickled her nose, and her eyes opened.

'Daddy!' She sat up, then stood to give him a kiss, and Pat wondered how kids woke up with a smile. No adult ever did. And the day began in earnest with another trip to the bathroom. He noted with pleasure that her training pants were dry. Megan was catching on to sleeping through the night – it had been a struggle for a while – though it seemed a very strange thing to be proud about, he thought. He started to shave, a daily event that utterly fascinated his daughter. Done, he bent down so that she could feel his face and pronounce it, 'Okay!'

Breakfast this morning was oatmeal with sliced banana and a glass of apple juice, and watching the Disney Channel on the kitchen TV while Daddy returned to his paper. Megan took her bowl and glass to the dishwasher all by herself, a very serious task which she was learning to master. The hard part was getting the bowl into the holder properly. Megan was still working on that. It was harder than doing her own shoes, which had Velcro closures. Mrs Daggett had told him that Megan was an unusually bright child, one more thing to beam with pride about, followed by the sadness, always, of remembering his wife. Pat told himself that he could see Deborah's face in hers, but the honest part of the agent occasionally wondered how much of that was a wish and how much fact. At least she seemed to have her mother's brains. Maybe the bright expression was what he saw?

The ride in the truck was routine. The sun was up now, and the traffic still light. Megan was in her safety seat, as usual looking at the other cars with wonderment.

The arrival was routine also. There was the agent working in the 7-Eleven, of course, plus the advance team at Giant Steps. Well, nobody would ever kidnap *his* little girl. At the working level, rivalry between the Bureau and the Service largely disappeared, except for the occasional inside joke or two. He was glad they were there, and they didn't mind having *this* armed man come in. He walked Megan in, and she immediately ran off to hug Mrs Daggett and put her blanky in her cubby in the back, and her day of learning and play began.

'Hey, Pat,' the agent at the door greeted him.

''Morning, Norm.' Both men enjoyed an early-morning yawn.

'Your schedule's as screwed up as mine,' Special Agent Jeffers replied. He was one of the agents who rotated on and off the SANDBOX detail, this morning working as part of the advance team.

'How's the wife?'

'Six more weeks, and then we have to think about shopping for a place like this. Is she as good as she seems?'

'Mrs Daggett? Ask the President,' O'Day joked. 'They've sent all their kids here.'

'I guess it can't be too bad,' the Secret Service man agreed. 'What's the story on the Kealty case?'

'Somebody at State is lying. That's what the OPR guys think.' He shrugged. 'Not sure which. The polygraph data was worthless. Your guys picking up on anything?'

'You know, it's funny. He sends his detail off a lot. He's actually said to them that he doesn't want to put them in a position where they'd have to –'

'Gotcha.' Pat nodded. 'And they have to play along?'

'No choice. He's meeting with people, but we don't always know who, and we're not allowed to find out what he's doing against SWORDSMAN.' A wry shake of the head. 'Don't you love it?'

'I like Ryan.' His eyes scanned the area, looking for trouble. It was automatic, just like breathing.

'We love the guy,' Norm agreed. 'We think he's going to make it. Kealty's full of crap. Hey, I worked his detail back when he was VP, okay? I fuckin' stood post outside the door while he was inside boffin' some cookie or other. Part of the job,' he concluded sourly. The two federal agents shared a look. This was an inside story, to be repeated only within the federal law-enforcement community, and while the Secret

Service was paid to protect their principals and keep all the secrets, that didn't mean they liked it.

'I think you're right. So things here okay?'

'Russell wants three more people, but I don't think he's going to get it. Hell, we have three good agents inside, and three doing overwatch next door' – he wasn't revealing anything; O'Day had figured that one out – 'and –'

'Yeah, across the street. Russell looks like he knows his stuff.'

'Grandpa's the best,' Norm offered. 'Hell, he's trained half the people in the Service, and you oughta see him shoot. Both hands.'

O'Day smiled. 'People keep telling me that. One day I'll have to invite him over for a friendly match.'

A grin. 'Andrea told me. She, uh, pulled your Bureau file –'

'What?'

'Hey, Pat, it's business. We check everybody out. We have a principal in here every day, y'dig?' Norm Jeffers went on. 'Besides, she wanted to see your firearms card. I hear you're pretty decent, but I'm telling you, man, you want to play with Russell, bring money, y'hear?'

'That's what makes a horse race, Mr Jeffers.' O'Day loved such challenges, and he'd yet to lose one.

'Bet your white ass, Mr O'Day.' His hand went up. He checked his earpiece, then his watch. 'They just started moving. SANDBOX is on the way. Our kid and your kid are real buddies.'

'She seems like a great little girl.'

'They're all good kids. A couple of rough spots, but that's kids. SHADOW is going to be a handful when she starts dating for real.'

'I don't want to hear it!'

Jeffers had a good laugh. 'Yeah, I'm hoping ours'll be a boy. My dad – he's a city police captain in Atlanta – he says that daughters are God's punishment on ya for being a man. You live in fear that they'll meet somebody like you were at seventeen.'

'Enough! Let me go to work and deal with some criminals.' He slapped Jeffers on the shoulder.

'She'll be here when you get back, Pat.'

O'Day passed on the usual coffee refill across Ritchie Highway, instead heading south to Route 50. He had to admit that the Service guys knew their stuff. But there was at least one aspect of presidential security that the Bureau was handling. He'd have to talk to the OPR guys this morning – informally, of course.

One died, one went home, and at roughly the same time. It was MacGregor's first Ebola death. He'd seen enough others, heart-attack failures-to-resuscitate, strokes, cancer, or just old age. More often than not, doctors weren't there, and the job fell on nurses. But he was there for this one. At the end, it wasn't so much peace as exhaustion. Saleh's body had fought as best it could, and his strength had merely extended the struggle and the pain, like a soldier in a hopeless battle. But his strength had given out, finally, and the body collapsed, and waited for death to come. The alarm chirp on the cardiac monitor went off, and there was nothing to do but flip it off. There would be no reviving this patient. IV leads were removed, and the sharps carefully placed in the red-plastic container. Literally everything that had touched the patient would be burned. It wasn't all that remarkable. AIDS and some hepatitis victims were similarly treated as objects of deadly contamination. Just with Ebola, burning the bodies was preferable – and besides, the government had insisted. So, one battle lost.

MacGregor was relieved, somewhat to his shame, as he stripped off the protective suit for the last time, washed thoroughly, then went to see Sohaila. She was still weak, but ready to leave to complete her recovery. The most recent tests showed her blood full of antibodies. Somehow her system had met the enemy and passed the test. There was no active virus in her. She could be hugged. In another country she would have been kept in for further tests, and would have donated a good deal of blood for extensive laboratory studies, but again the local government had said that such things would not take place, that she was to be released from the hospital the first minute that it was safe to do so. MacGregor had hedged on that, but now he was certain that there would be no more complications. The doctor himself lifted her and placed her in the wheelchair.

'When you feel better, will you come back to see me?' he

asked, with a warm smile. She nodded. A bright child. Her English was good. A pretty child, with a charming smile despite her fatigue, glad to be going home.

'Doctor?' It was her father. He must have had a military background, so straight of back was he. What he was trying to say was evident on his face, before he could even think the words.

'I did very little. Your daughter is young and strong, and that is what saved her.'

'Even so, I will not forget this debt.' A firm handshake, and MacGregor remembered Kipling's line about East and West. Whatever this man was – the doctor had his suspicions – there was a commonality among all men.

'She will be weak for another fortnight or so. Let her eat whatever she wants, and best to let her sleep as long as possible.'

'It will be as you say,' Sohaila's father promised.

'You have my number, here and at home, if you have any questions at all.'

'And if you have any difficulties, with the government, for example, please let me know.' The measure of the man's gratitude came across. For what it was worth, MacGregor had a protector of sorts. It couldn't hurt, he decided, walking them to the door. Then it was back to his office.

'So,' the official said after listening to the report, 'everything is stabilized.'

'That is correct.'

'The staff have been checked?'

'Yes, and we will rerun the tests tomorrow to be sure. Both patient rooms will be fully disinfected today. All contaminated items are being burned right now.'

'The body?'

'Also bagged and to be burned, as you directed.'

'Excellent. Dr MacGregor, you have done well, and I thank you for that. Now we can forget that this unhappy incident ever happened.'

'But *how* did the Ebola get here?' MacGregor demanded – plaintively, which was as far as he could go.

The official didn't know, and so he spoke confidently: 'That does not concern you, and it does not concern me. It will not be repeated. Of that I am certain.'

'As you say.' After a few more words, MacGregor hung the phone up and stared at the wall. One more fax to CDC, he decided. The government couldn't object to that. He had to tell them that the outbreak, such as it was, was closed out. And that was a relief, too. Better to go back to the normal practice of medicine, and diseases he could defeat.

It turned out that Kuwait had been more forthcoming than Saudi on forwarding the substance of the meeting, perhaps because the Kuwaiti government really was a family business, and their establishment happened to be on a very dangerous street corner. Adler handed the transcript over. The President scanned it quickly.

'It reads like, "Get lost."'

'You got it,' the Secretary of State agreed.

'Either Foreign Minister Sabah edited all the polite stuff out, or what he heard scared him. I'm betting on number two,' Bert Vasco decided.

'Ben?' Jack asked.

Dr Goodley shook his head. 'We may have a problem here.'

'"May?"' Vasco asked. 'This goes beyond "may."'

'Okay, Bert, you're our champ prognosticator for the Persian Gulf,' the President observed. 'How about another forecast?'

'The culture over there is one of bargaining. There are elaborate verbal rituals for important meetings. "Hi, how are you?" can take an hour. If we're to believe that such things did not take place, there's a message in their absence. You said it, Mr President: *Get lost*.' Though it was interesting, Vasco thought, that they'd begun by praying together. Perhaps that was a signal that had meant something to the Saudis but not the Kuwaitis? Even he didn't know every aspect of the local culture.

'Then why are the Saudis low-keying this?'

'You told me that Prince Ali gave you another impression?'

Ryan nodded. 'That's right. Go on.'

'The Kingdom is a little schizophrenic. They like us, and they trust us as strategic partners, but they also dislike us and distrust us as a culture. It's not even that simple, and it goes round and round, but they're afraid that too much exposure to the West will adversely affect their society.

They're highly conservative on what we call social issues, like when our Army was over there in '91, and they requested that Army chaplains remove the religious insignia from their uniforms, and seeing women drive cars and carry guns drove them a little nuts. So, on one hand, they depend on us as guarantor of their security – Prince Ali keeps asking you about that, right? – but on the other hand they worry that in protecting them we might mess up their country. It keeps coming back to religion. They'd probably prefer to make a deal with Daryaei than to have to invite us back to guard their border, and so the majority of their government is going to run down that track in the knowledge that we *will* come in if asked. Kuwait's going to be a different story. If we ask to be allowed to stage an exercise, they'll say "yes" in a heartbeat, even if the Saudis ask them not to. Good news, Daryaei knows that, and he can't move all that fast. If he starts moving troops south –'

'The Agency will give us warning,' Goodley said confidently. 'We know what to look for, and they're not sophisticated enough to hide it.'

'If we run troops into Kuwait now, it will be perceived as an aggressive act,' Adler warned. 'Better we should meet with Daryaei first and sound him out.'

'Just so we give him the right signal,' Vasco put in.

'Oh, we won't make that mistake, and I think he knows that the status of the Gulf countries is a top-drawer item with us. No mixed signals this time.' Ambassador April Glaspie had been accused of giving such a signal to Saddam Hussein in the summer of 1990 – but she'd denied Hussein's account, and the latter wasn't all that reliable a source of information. Maybe it had been a linguistic nuance. Most likely of all, he'd heard exactly what he'd wanted to hear and not what had actually been said, a habit frequently shared by heads of state and children.

'How fast can you set it up?' the President asked.

'Pretty fast,' the Secretary of State replied.

'Do it,' Ryan ordered. 'All possible speed. Ben?'

'Yes, sir.'

'I talked with Robby Jackson already. Coordinate with him for a plan to get a modest security force rapid-deployed over there. Enough to show that we're interested, not enough to provoke them. Let's also call Kuwait and tell them that we're here if they need us, and that we *can* deploy to their country if they so request. Who's on-deck for this?'

'Twenty-fourth Mech, Fort Stewart, Georgia. I checked,' Goodley said, rather proud of himself. 'Their second brigade is on rotating alert-status now. Also a brigade of the 82nd at Fort Bragg. With the equipment warehoused in Kuwait, we can do the match-up and be rolling in as little as forty-eight hours. I'd also advise increasing the readiness state of the Maritime Pre-Positioning Ships at Diego Garcia. That we can do quietly.'

'Nice job, Ben. Call the SecDef and tell him I want it done – quietly.'

'Yes, Mr President.'

'I'll tell Daryaei that we offer a friendly hand to the United Islamic Republic,' Adler said. 'Also that we're committed to peace and stability in that region, and that means territorial integrity. I wonder what he'll say . . . ?'

Eyes turned to Bert Vasco, who was learning to curse his newly acquired status as resident genius. 'He might just have wanted to rattle their cage. I don't think he wants to rattle ours.'

'That's your first hedge,' Ryan observed.

'Not enough information,' Vasco replied. 'I don't see that he wants a conflict with us. That happened once, and everybody watched. Yes, he doesn't like us. Yes, he doesn't like the Saudis or any of the other states. But, no, he doesn't want to take us on. Maybe he *could* knock them all off. That's a military call, and I'm just an FSO. But not with us in the game, and he knows it. So, political pressure on Kuwait and the Kingdom, sure. Beyond that, however, I don't see enough to be worried about.'

'Yet,' the President added.

'Yes, sir, *yet*,' Vasco agreed.

'Am I leaning on you too hard, Bert?'

'It's okay, Mr President. At least you listen to me. It wouldn't hurt for us to generate a Special National Intelligence Estimate of the UIR's full capabilities and intentions. I need broader access to what the intel community's generating.'

Jack turned. 'Ben, the SNIE is ordered. Bert's on the team

with full access, by my order. You know, guys, giving orders can be fun,' the President added, with a smile to break up the tension that the meeting had generated. 'This is a potential problem, but not a ball-buster yet, correct?' There were nods. 'Okay. Thank you, gentlemen. Let's keep an eye on this one.'

Singapore Airlines Flight 26 landed five minutes later, coming to the terminal at 10:25 AM The first-class passengers, having enjoyed wider, softer seats, now enjoyed quicker access to the entry rigmarole which America inflicts on her visitors. The traveler recovered his two-suiter from the carousel, and with his carry-on slung on his other shoulder, picked a line to stand in, in his hand held his entry card, which declared nothing of interest to the United States government. The truth would not have been pleasing to them in any case.

'Hello,' the inspector said, taking the card and scanning it. The passport came next. It seemed an old one, its pages liberally covered with exit and entry stamps. He found a blank page and prepared to make a new mark. 'Purpose of your visit to America?'

'Business,' the traveler replied. 'I am here for the auto show at Javits Center.'

'Uh-huh.' The inspector had scarcely heard the answer. The stamp was placed and the visitor pointed to another line. There his bags were X-rayed instead of opened. 'Anything to declare?'

'No.' Simple answers were best. Another inspector looked at the TV display of the bag and saw nothing interesting. The traveler was waved through, and he collected his bags from the conveyor and walked out to where the taxis were.

Amazing, he thought, finding a place in another line, and getting into a cab in less than five minutes. His first concern, being caught at the customs checkpoint, was behind him. For his next, the taxi he was in could not have been preselected for him. He'd fumbled with his bags and let a woman go ahead of him in order to keep that from happening. Now he slumped back in his seat and made a show of looking around, while in reality looking to see if there was a car following the cab into town. The pre-lunchtime traffic was so dense that it hardly seemed possible, all the more so that he was in one of thousands of yellow vehicles, darting in and out of traffic like cattle in a stampede. About the only bad news was that his hotel was sufficiently far from the convention center that he'd need another cab. Well, that couldn't be helped, and he needed to check in first anyway.

Another thirty minutes and he was in the hotel, in the elevator, going up to the sixth floor, a helpful bellman holding his two-suiter while the traveler retained his carry-on. He tipped the bellman two dollars – he'd been briefed on what to tip; better to give a modest one than to be remembered as one who'd tipped too much or not at all – which was taken with gratitude, but not too much. With his entry tasks complete, the traveler unpacked his suits and shirts, also removing extraneous items from his carry-on. The shaving kit he left in, using what the hotel provided to re-shave his bristly face after a cleansing shower. Despite the tension, he was amazed at how good he felt. He'd been on the go for – what? Twenty-two hours? Something like that. But he'd gotten a lot of sleep, and air travel didn't make him anxious, as it did for so many. He ordered lunch from the room-service menu, then dressed, and slinging his carry-on over his shoulder, walked downstairs and got a cab for the Javits Center. The auto show, he thought. He'd always liked cars.

Behind him in space and time, most of the nineteen others were still in the air. Some were just landing – Boston first, then more in New York, and one at Dulles – to make their own way through customs, testing their knowledge and their luck against the Great Satan, or whatever rubbish Daryaei termed their collective enemy. Satan, after all, had great powers and was worthy of respect. Satan could look in a man's eyes and see his thoughts, almost as Allah could. No, these Americans were functionaries, only dangerous to them if given warning.

'You have to know how to read people,' Clark told them. It was a good class. Unlike people in a conventional school, they all wanted to learn. It almost took him back to his own days here at the Farm, at the height of the Cold War, when everyone had wanted to be James Bond and actually believed a little in it despite everything the instructors had said. Most of his classmates had been recent college grads, well educated from books but not yet from life. Most had learned pretty well. Some hadn't, and the flunking grade out in the field could be more than a red mark on a blue book, but mainly it had been less dramatic than what they showed in the movies. Just the realization that it was time for a career change. Clark had higher hopes for this bunch. Maybe they hadn't arrived with degrees in history from Dartmouth or Brown, but they had studied something, somewhere, then learned more on the streets of some big cities. Maybe they even knew that *everything* they learned would be important to them someday.

'Will they lie to us – our agents, I mean?'

'You're from Pittsburgh, Mr Stone, right?'

'Yes, sir.'

'You worked confidential informants on the street. They ever lie to you?'

'Sometimes,' Stone admitted.

'There's your answer. They will lie about their importance, the danger they're in, damned near anything, depending on how they feel today. You have to know them and know their moods. Stone, did you know when your informants were telling sea stories?'

'Most of the time.'

'How did you tell?' Clark asked.

'Whenever they know a little too much, whenever it doesn't fit –'

'You know,' their instructor observed with a grin, 'you people are so smart that sometimes I wonder what I'm doing here. It's about knowing people. In your careers at the Agency, you will always be running into folks who think they can tell it all from overheads – the satellite knows all and tells all. Not exactly,' Clark went on. 'Satellites can be fooled, and it's easier than people like to admit. People have their weaknesses, too, ego foremost among them, and there is never a substitute for looking them in the eyes. But the nice thing about working agents in the field is, even their lies will reveal some of the truth to you. Case in point, Moscow, Kutuzovkiy Prospyekt, 1983. This agent we brought out, and he'll be here next week for you to meet. He was having a hard time with his boss and –'

Chavez appeared at the back door and held up a phone-message form. Clark hurried through the rest of the lesson and handed the class over to his assistant.

'What is it, Ding?' John asked.

'Mary Pat wants us up in DC in a hurry, something about an SNIE.'

'The United Islamic Republic, I bet.'

'Hardly worth taking the message down, Mr C.,' Chavez observed. 'They want us up in time for dinner. Want me to drive?'

There were four Maritime Pre-Positioning Ships at Diego Garcia. They were relatively new ships, built for their purpose, which was to be floating parking garages for military vehicles. A third of those were tanks, mobile artillery, and armored personnel carriers, and the rest were the less dramatic 'trains,' vehicles pre-loaded with everything from ammunition to rations to water. The ships were painted Navy gray, but with colored bands around their funnels to designate them as part of the National Defense Reserve Fleet, crewed by merchant sailors whose job was to maintain them. That wasn't overly difficult. Every few months they'd light off the huge diesel engines and sail around for a few hours, just to be absolutely sure everything worked. This evening they got a new message to increase their alert status.

One by one, the engine-room crews went below and fired up the engines. Fuel quantities were verified against written records, and various benchmark tests made to ensure that the ship was ready to sail – which was why they were maintained so lovingly. Testing the engines was not abnormal. Testing all at the same time was, and the collection of monster engines made for a thermal bloom that was obvious to infrared detectors overhead, especially at night.

That came to the attention of Sergey Golovko within thirty minutes of its detection, and like intelligence chiefs all over the world, he assembled a team of specialists to discuss it.

'Where is the American carrier battle group?' he asked first of all. America loved to throw them around the oceans of the world.

'They left the atoll yesterday, heading east.'

'Away from the Persian Gulf?'

'Correct. They have exercises scheduled with Australia.

It's called SOUTHERN CUP. We have no information to suggest that the exercise is being canceled.'

'Then why exercise their troopships?'

The analyst gestured. 'It could be an exercise, but the turmoil in the Persian Gulf suggests otherwise.'

'Nothing in Washington?' Golovko asked.

'Our friend Ryan continues to navigate the political rapids,' the chief of the American political section reported. 'Badly.'

'Will he survive?'

'Our ambassador believes so, and the *rezident* concurs, but neither thinks he is firmly in command. It's a classic muddle. America has always prided herself on the smooth transition of government power, but their laws did not anticipate such events as we have seen. He cannot move decisively against his political enemy –'

'What Kealty's doing is state treason,' Golovko observed, the penalty for which in Russia had always been severe. Even the phrase was enough to lower the temperature of a room.

'Not according to their law, but my legal experts tell me that the issue is sufficiently confused that there will be no clear winner, and in such a case Ryan remains in command because of his position – he got there first.'

Golovko nodded, but his expression was decidedly unhappy. *Red October* and the Gerasimov business should never have become public knowledge. He and his government had known the latter, but only suspected the former. On the submarine business, American security had been superb – so *that* was the card Ryan had played to make Kolya defect. It had to be. It all made sense from the distance of time, and a fine play it had been. Except for one thing: it had become public knowledge in Russia as well, and he was now forbidden to contact Ryan directly until the diplomatic fallout had been determined. America was doing something. He did not yet know what that was, and instead of calling to ask, and perhaps even getting a truthful answer, he'd have to wait for his field officers to discern it on their own. The problem lay in the harm that had been done to the American government, and in Ryan's own habit, learned at CIA, of working with a small number of people instead of playing the entire bureaucracy like a symphony orchestra. Instinct told him that Ryan would be cooperative, he'd trust former enemies to act in collective self-interest, but one thing the traitor Kealty had accomplished – who else could have told the American press those stories! – was to create a political impasse. Politics!

Politics had once been the center of Golovko's life. A party member since the age of eighteen, he'd studied his Lenin and Marx with all the fervor of a theology student, and though the fervor had changed over time to something else, those logical but foolish theories *had* shaped his adult life, until they'd evaporated, leaving him, at least, a profession at which he excelled. He'd been able to rationalize his previous antipathy to America in historical terms, two great powers, two great alliances, two differing philosophies acting in perverse unison to create the last great world conflict. National pride still wished that his nation had won, but the *Rodina* hadn't, and that was that. The important part was that the Cold War was over, and with it the deadly confrontation between America and his country. Now they could actually recognize their common interests, and at times act in cooperation. It had actually happened already. Ivan Emmetovich Ryan had come to him for help in the American conflict with Japan, and together the two countries had accomplished a vital goal – something still secret. Why the hell, Golovko thought, couldn't the traitor Kealty have revealed *that* secret instead of the others? But, no, now his country was embarrassed, and while the newly freed media had as great a field day with this story as the Americans were having – or even more – he was unable to make a simple phone call.

Those ships were turning their engines for a reason. Ryan was doing something or thinking about doing something, and instead of merely asking, he had to be a spy again, working against another spy instead of working with an ally. Well, he had no choice.

'Form a special study group for the Persian Gulf. Everything we have, bring it together as quickly as possible. America will have to react somehow to the developing situation. First, we must determine what is happening. Second, what America probably knows. Third, what America will do. That general, G. I. Bondarenko, get him involved. He just spent time with their military.'

'Immediately, Comrade Chairman,' his principal deputy

replied for the rest of the meeting. At least *that* hadn't changed!

Conditions, he thought, were excellent. Not too hot, not too cold. The Javits Center was right on the river, and that made for relatively high local humidity, and that was good also. He'd be inside, and so there was no concern about ultraviolet radiation harming the contents of his container. For the rest, the theory of what he was doing was not his concern; he'd been briefed on it and would do exactly what he'd been told. Whether or not it worked, well, that was in Allah's hands, wasn't it? The traveler got out of his cab and walked in.

He'd never been in so capacious a building, and there was a little disorientation after he got his visitor's badge and program book, which showed a map of the interior. With that came an index that allowed him to see the location of various exhibits, and with a muted smile he decided that he had hours to accomplish his goal, and would spend the time looking at cars, just like everybody else.

There were lots of them, sparkling like jewels, some on turntables for those too lazy to walk around them, many with scantily clad women gesturing at them as though one might have sexual relations with them – the cars, that is, though some of the women might be possibilities, he thought, watching their faces with concealed amusement. He'd known intellectually that America made millions of cars, and in almost that many shapes and colors. It seemed hugely wasteful – what was a car, after all, except for a method of moving from one place to another, and in the course of use they got damaged and dirty, and the show here was a lie in that it showed them as they would be for less time than it took to drive one home – even in America, as he'd seen in the drive here from his hotel –

But it was a pleasant experience even so. He would have thought of it as shopping, but this was not the souk which he connected with the process, not an alley full of small shops operated by merchants for whom bargaining was as important as the air. No, America was different. Here they prostituted women to sell things for a predetermined price. It wasn't that he was personally against such use of women; the traveler was not married and had the usual carnal desires, but to proclaim it in this way attacked the puritanical modesty of his culture, and so while he never once looked away from the women standing by the cars, he was glad that none of them was from his part of the world.

All the makes and models. Cadillac had a huge display in the General Motors section. Ford had another area of its own for all of its trademark products. He wandered through the Chrysler section, and then off to the foreign makers. The Japanese section, he saw, was being avoided, doubtless as a result of the American conflict with that country – though above many of the displays were signs proclaiming *MADE IN AMERICA BY AMERICANS!* in three-meter letters to those few who seemed to care. Toyota, Nissan, and the rest would have a bad year, even the sporty Cressida, regardless of where they might be assembled. You could tell that by the lack of people in the area, and with that realization, his interest in Asian cars died. No, he decided, not around here.

European cars were profiting from Japan's misfortune, he saw. Mercedes especially was drawing a huge crowd, especially a new model of their most expensive sports car, painted a glossy midnight black that reflected the overhead lighting like a piece of the clear desert sky. Along the way, the traveler picked up a brochure at every booth from a friendly manufacturer's representative. These he tucked into his carry-on bag so as to make himself look like every other visitor. He found a food booth and got something to eat – it was a hot dog, and he didn't worry if it had pork in it or not; America wasn't an Islamic country, after all, and he didn't have to worry about such things. He spent a good deal of time looking at all-terrain vehicles, first wondering if they'd survive the primitive roads of Lebanon and Iran, and deciding that they probably would. One was based on a military type he'd seen before, and if he'd had a choice, it would have been that one, wide and powerful. He got the entire publicity package for that one, then leaned against a post so that he might read it. Sports cars were for the effete. This was something of substance. What a pity he'd never own one. He checked his watch. Early evening. More visitors were crowding in as work let out and people took the evening to indulge their fantasies. Perfect.

Along the way he'd noted the air conditioning. It would

have been better to set his canister in the system itself, but he'd been briefed on that, too. The Legionnaire's disease outbreak years before in Philadelphia had taught Americans about the need for keeping such systems clean; they often used chlorine to treat the condensate water which humidified the recirculating air, and chlorine would kill the virus as surely as a bullet killed a man. Looking up from the color-printed brochure, he noted the huge circular vents. Cool air descended from them, and washed invisibly along the floor. On being heated by the bodies in the room, the warm air would rise back into the returns and go through the system for cooling – and some degree of disinfection. So he had to pick a spot where the air flow would be his ally, not his enemy, and he considered that, standing there like an interested car shopper. He started wandering more, walking under some of the vents, feeling the gentle, cooling breeze with his skin, evaluating one and another and looking for a good spot to leave his canister. The latter was equally important. The spray period would last for about fifteen seconds. There would be a hissing sound – probably lost in the noise of the crowded building – and a brief fog. The cloud would turn invisible in just a few more seconds; the particulate matter was so small and, being as dense as the surrounding air, would become part of the ambient atmosphere and spread around randomly for at least thirty minutes, perhaps more, depending on the efficiency of the environmental systems in the center. He wanted to expose as many people as possible, consistent with those parameters, and with that renewed thought in his mind, he started wandering again.

It helped that, vast as the auto show was, it did not fill the Javits Center. Every exhibit was constructed of prefabricated parts like those in a business office, and behind many of those were large swatches of cloth, like vertical banners, whose only purpose was to break up the line of sight to empty portions of the building. They were easily accessible, the traveler saw. Nothing was fenced off. You simply ducked around an exhibit. He saw some people holding mini-meetings there, and some circulating maintenance personnel, but little else. The maintenance personnel were a potential problem, though. It wouldn't do to have his canister picked up before it discharged. But such people would be on regular routines, wouldn't they? It was just a matter of discerning the patterns of their movement. Of course. So, he thought, where is the best spot? The show would be open for several more hours. He wanted to pick a perfect place and time, but he'd been briefed not to worry too greatly about that. He took that advice to heart. Better to be covert. That was his primary mission.

The main entrance is ... there. People entered and left through the same side of the building. Emergency exits were everywhere, all of them properly marked, but with alarm buzzers on them. At the entrance was a bank of air-conditioning vents to form a thermal barrier of sorts, and the returns were mainly in the center of the exhibit hall. So the air flow was designed to move inward from the periphery ... and everyone had to come in and out the same way ... how to make that work for him ... ? A bank of rest rooms was on that side, with regular traffic back and forth – too dangerous; someone might see the can and pick it up and put it in a trash can. He walked to the other side, fumbling with his program as he did so, bumping into people, and finding himself again at the edge of the General Motors section. Beyond that were Mercedes and BMW, all on the way to the returns, and there were lots of people in all three areas – plus the downward bloom of the air would wash across part of the entrance/exit. The green banners blocked view of the wall, but there was space under them, open area ... partially shielded from view. This was it. He walked away, checking his watch and then the program for the show's hours. The program he tucked into the carry-on bag while his other hand unzipped the shaving kit. He circulated around one more time, looking for another likely place, and while he found one, it wasn't as good as the first. Then he made a final check to see if someone might be following him. No, nobody knew he was here, and he wouldn't announce his presence or his mission with a burst from an AK-47 or the crash of a tossed grenade. There was more than one way to be a terrorist, and he regretted not having discovered this one sooner. How much he might have enjoyed setting a canister like this one into a theater in Jerusalem ... but, no, the time for that would come later, perhaps, once the main enemy of his culture was crippled. He looked at the faces now, these

Americans who so hated him and his people. Shuffling around, like cattle, purposeless. And then it was time.

The traveler ducked behind an exhibit, extracted the can and set it on its side on the concrete floor. It was weighted to roll to the proper position, and, lying on its side, it would be harder to see. With that done, he pressed the simple mechanical timer and walked away, back into the exhibition area, turning left to leave the building. He was in a taxi in five minutes, on the way back to his hotel. Before he got there, the timer-spring released the valve, and for fifteen seconds the canister emptied its contents into the air. The noise was lost in the cacophony of the crowd. The vapor cloud dispersed before it could be seen.

In Atlanta, it was the Spring Boat Show. About half of the people there might have serious thoughts of buying a boat, this year or some other. The rest were just dreaming. Let them dream, this traveler thought on the way out.

In Orlando, it was recreational vehicles. That was particularly easy. A traveler looked under a Winnebago, as though to check the chassis, slid his canister there, and left.

In Chicago's McCormick Center, it was housewares, a vast hall full of every manner of furniture and appliance, and the women who wished to have them.

In Houston, it was one of America's greatest horse shows. Many of them were Arabians, he was surprised to note, and the traveler whispered a prayer that the disease didn't hurt those noble creatures, so beloved of Allah.

In Phoenix, it was golf equipment, a game that the traveler didn't know a thing about, though he had several kilos of free literature which he might read on the flight back to the Eastern Hemisphere. He'd found an empty golf bag with a hard-plastic lining that would conceal the canister, set the timer, and dropped it in.

In San Francisco, it was computers, the most crowded show of all that day, with over twenty thousand people in the

Moscone Convention Center, so many that this traveler feared he might not get outside to the garden area before the can released its contents. But he did, walking upwind to his hotel, four blocks away, his job complete.

The rug shop was just closing down when Aref Raman walked in. Mr Alahad locked the front door and switched off the lights.

'My instructions?'

'You will do nothing without direct orders, but it is important to know if you are able to complete your mission.'

'Is that not plain?' Raman asked in irritation. 'Why do you think –'

'I have my instructions,' Alahad said gently.

'I am able. I am ready,' the assassin assured his cutout. The decision had been made years before, but it was good to say it out loud to another, here, now.

'You will be told at the proper time. It will be soon.'

'The political situation . . .'

'We are aware of that, and we are confident of your devotion. Be at peace, Aref. Great things are happening. I know not what they are, merely that they are under way, and at the proper time, your act will be the capstone of the Holy Jihad. Mahmoud Haji sends his greetings and his prayers.'

'Thank you.' Raman inclined his head at word of the distant but powerful blessing. It had been a very long time since he'd heard the man's voice over anything but a television, and then he'd been forced to turn away, lest others see his reaction to it.

'It has been hard for you,' Alahad said.

'It has.' Raman nodded.

'It will soon be over, my young friend. Come to the back with me. Do you have time?'

'I do.'

'It is time for prayer.'

38

GRACE PERIOD

'I'm not an area specialist,' Clark objected. He'd been to Iran before.

Ed Foley would have none of that: 'You've been on the ground there, and I think you're the one who always talks about how there's no substitute for dirty hands and a good nose.'

'He was just laying more of that on the kiddies at the Farm this afternoon,' Ding reported with a sly look. 'Well, today it was about reading people by lookin' in their eyes, but it's the same thing. Good eye, good nose, good senses.' *He* hadn't been to Iran, and they wouldn't send Mr C. alone, would they?

'You're in, John,' Mary Pat Foley said, and since she was the DDO, that was that. 'Secretary Adler may be flying over real soon. I want you and Ding to go over as SPOs. Keep him alive, and sniff around, nothing covert or anything. I want your read on what the street feels like. That's all, just a quick recon.' It was the sort of thing usually done by watching footage on CNN, but Mary Pat wanted an experienced officer to take the local pulse, and it was her call.

If there were a curse in being a good training officer, it was that the people you trained often got promoted, and remembered their lessons – and worse, who'd taught them. Clark could recall both of the Foleys in his classes at the Farm. From the start, she'd been the cowboy – well, cow*girl* – of the pair, with brilliant instincts, fantastically good Russian skills, and the sort of gift for reading people more often found in a professor of psychiatry ... but somewhat wanting in caution, trusting a little too much on the baby blues and dumb blonde act to keep her safe. Ed lacked her passion but had the ability to formulate The Big Picture, to take a long view that made sense most of the time. Neither was quite perfect. Together they were a piece of work, and John took pride in having taught them his way. Most of the time.

'Okay. We have anything in the way of assets over there?'

'Nothing useful. Adler wants to eyeball Daryaei and tell him what the rules are. You'll be quartered in the French embassy. The trip is secret. VC-20 to Paris, French transport from there. In and out in a hurry,' Mary Pat told them. 'But I want you to spend an hour or two walking around, just to get a feel for things, price of bread, how people dress, you know the drill.'

'And we'll have diplomatic passports, so nobody can hassle us,' John added wryly. 'Yeah, heard that one before. So did everyone else in the embassy back in 1979, remember?'

'Adler's Secretary of State,' Ed reminded him.

'I think they know that.' *They know he's Jewish, too,* he didn't add.

The flight into Barstow, California, was how the exercise always started. Buses and trucks rolled up to the airplanes, and the troops came down the stairs for the short drive up the only road into the NTC. General Diggs and Colonel Hamm watched from their parked helicopter as the soldiers formed up. This group was from the North Carolina National Guard, a reinforced brigade. It wasn't often that the Guard came to Fort Irwin, and this one was supposed to be pretty special. Because the state was blessed with very senior senators and congressmen – well, until recently – over the years, the men from Carolina had gotten the very best in modern equipment, and been designated a round-out brigade for one of the Regular Army's armored divisions. Sure enough, they strutted like real soldiers, and their officers had been prepping for a year in anticipation of this training rotation. They'd even managed to get their hands on additional fuel with which they'd trained a few extra weeks. Now the officers formed their men up in regular lines before putting them on the transport, and from a distance of a quarter mile, Diggs and Hamm could see their officers talking to their men over the noise of the arriving aircraft.

'They look proud, boss,' Hamm observed.

They heard a distant shout, as a company of tankers told their captain they were ready to kick some ass. A news crew was even out there to immortalize the event for local TV.

'They *are* proud,' the general said. 'Soldiers should be proud, Colonel.'

'Only one thing missing, sir.'

'What's that, Al?'

'*Baaaaaaaaaa*,' Colonel Hamm said around his cigar. 'Lambs to the slaughter.' The two officers shared a look. The first mission of the OpFor was to take away that pride. The Blackhorse Cav had never lost so much as a single simulated engagement to anything other than a regular formation – and that rarely enough. Hamm didn't plan to start this month. Two battalions of Abrams tanks, one more of Bradleys, another of artillery, a cavalry company, and a combat-support battalion against his three squadrons of Opposing Force. It hardly seemed fair. For the visitors.

They were almost done. The most annoying work of all was mixing the AmFo, which turned out to be a pretty good upper-body workout for the Mountain Men. The proper proportions of the fertilizer (which was mainly an ammonia-based chemical compound) and the diesel fuel came from a book. It struck both men as amusing that plants should like to eat a deadly explosive. The propellant used in artillery rounds was also ammonia-based, and once upon a time, in post-World War I Germany, a chemical plant making fertilizer had exploded and wiped out the neighboring village. The addition of diesel fuel was partly to provide an additional element of chemical energy, but mainly to act as a wetting agent, the better for the internal shock wave to propagate within the explosive mass and hasten the detonation. They used a large tub for the mixing, and an oar, like a canoe's, to stir the mass into the proper consistency (that came from a book also). The result was a large glob of mud-like slurry which formed into blocks of a sort. These they lifted by hand.

It was dirty and smelly and a little dangerous inside the drum of the cement truck.

They took turns doing the filling. The access hatch, which was designed to admit semi-liquid cement, was just over three feet in diameter. Holbrook had rigged an electric fan to blow fresh air into the drum, because the fumes from the fresh AmFo mix were unpleasant and possibly dangerous –

it gave them headaches, which was warning enough. It was the work of over a week, but now the drum was as filled as they needed it to be, about three-quarters, when the last block was nested in with all the rest. Every layer had been somewhat uneven, and the void spaces were filled with a mix that was more liquid and had been handed in by bucket, so that the circular body of the drum was as full as two men working alone could make it. If one could have seen through the steel, it would have looked like a pie chart, the unfilled part a V-shape, facing upwards.

'I think that does it, Pete,' Ernie Brown said. 'We have about another hundred pounds or so, but – '

'No place for it to go,' Holbrook agreed, climbing out. He clambered down the ladder and the two walked outside, sat in lawn chairs and got some fresh air. 'Damn, I'm glad *that*'s done!'

'You bet.' Brown rubbed his face and took a deep breath. His head hurt so badly that he wondered if his face might come off. They'd stay out here for a long while, until they got all those goddamned fumes out of their lungs.

'This has got to be bad for us,' Pete said.

'Sure as hell gonna be bad for somebody. Good idea on the bullets,' he added. There were two oil drums full of them inside, probably too many, but that was okay.

'What's a brownie without some walnuts?' Holbrook asked.

'You bastard!' Brown laughed so hard he nearly came out of the chair. 'Oh, Jesus, my head hurts!'

Approval for French cooperation on the meeting came from the Quai d'Orsay with remarkable speed. France had diplomatic interests with every country bordering on the Gulf that connected to all manner of commercial relationships, from tanks to pharmaceuticals. French troops had deployed in the Persian Gulf War to find themselves fighting against French products, but that sort of thing wasn't all that unusual. It made for lots of markets. Approval of the mission was phoned to the American Ambassador at nine in the morning, who telexed Foggy Bottom in less than five minutes, where it was relayed to Secretary Adler while he was still in his bed. Action officers made other notifications, first of all to the 89th Military Airlift Wing at Andrews Air Force Base.

Getting the Secretary of State out of town quietly was never the easiest of tasks. People tended to notice empty offices of that magnitude, and so an easy cover story was laid on. Adler was going to consult with European allies on several issues. The French were far better able to control their media, a task which was more than anything else a matter of timing.

'Yeah?' Clark said, lifting the phone at the Marriott closest to Langley.

'It's on for today,' the voice said.

A blink. A shake of the head. 'Super. Okay, I'm packed.' Then he rolled back over for some more sleep. At least there didn't have to be a mission brief for this one. Keep an eye on Adler, take a walk, and come home. There wasn't any real worry about security. If the Iranians – UIR-ians was a phrase he hadn't come to terms with yet – wanted to do something, two men with pistols wouldn't be able to do much about it except hand their weapons over unused, and either locals or Iranian security would keep the hostile peons away. He was going to be there for show, because it was something you did, for some reason or other.

'We goin'?' Chavez asked from the other bed.

'Yep.'

'*Bueno.*'

Daryaei checked his desk clock, subtracting eight, nine, ten, and eleven hours, and wondering if anything had gone wrong. Second thoughts were the bane of people in his position. You made your decisions and took the action, and only then did you really worry, despite all the planning and thought that might have gone into what you did. There was no royal road to success. You had to take risks, a fact never appreciated by those who merely *thought* about being a chief of state.

No, nothing had gone wrong. He'd received the French Ambassador, a very pleasant unbeliever who spoke the local language so beautifully that Daryaei wondered what it might be like to have him read some of his country's poetry. And a courtly man, ever polite and deferential, he'd posed his secondhand request like a man arranging a marriage of family alliance, his hopeful smile also conveying the wishes of his government. The Americans would not have made the request if they'd had any pre-warning of Badrayn's people and their mission. No, in a case like that, the meeting would have been on neutral ground – Switzerland was always a possibility – for informal but direct contact. In this case, they would send their own Foreign Minister into what they had to consider to be enemy country – and a Jew at that! *Friendly contact, friendly exchange of views, friendly offers of friendly relations*, the Frenchman had said, pitching the meeting, doubtless hoping that if it went well, then France would be remembered as the country that fostered a new friendship – well, maybe a 'working relationship' – and if the meeting went badly, then all that would be remembered was that France had *tried* to be an honest broker. Had Daryaei known about ballet, he would have used it as a visual image for the exchange.

Damn the French, anyway, he thought. *Had their warrior chief Martel not stopped 'Abd-ar-Rahman in 732 at Poitiers, then the whole world might be. . .* but even Allah couldn't change history. Rahman had lost that battle because his men had grown greedy, fallen away from the purity of the Faith. Exposed to the riches of the West, they'd stopped fighting and started looting, and given Martel's forces the chance to reform and counterattack. Yes, that was the lesson to be remembered. There was always time for looting. You had to win the battle first. First destroy the enemy's forces, and *then* take that which you wanted to take.

He walked from his office into the next room. There on the wall was a map of his new country and its neighbors, and a comfortable seat from which to view it. There came the usual error from looking at maps. Distances were truncated. Everything seemed so close, all the more so after all the lost time of his life. Close enough to reach. Close enough to grasp. Nothing could go wrong now. Not with everything so close.

Leaving was easier than arriving. Like most Western countries, America was more concerned with what people might bring in than with what they might take out – and properly so, the first traveler thought, as his passport was processed at JFK. It was 7:05 AM, and Air France Flight 1, a supersonic

Concorde, was waiting to take him part of the way home. He had a huge collection of auto brochures, and a story he'd spent some time concocting should anyone ask about them, but his cover wasn't challenged, or even examined. He was leaving, and that was okay. The passport was duly stamped. The customs agent didn't even ask why he had come one day and left the next. Business travelers were business travelers. Besides, it was early in the morning, and nothing important happened before ten.

The Air France first-class lounge served coffee, but the traveler didn't want any. He was almost done. Only now did his body want to tremble. It was amazing how easily it had gone. Badrayn's mission brief had told them how easy it would be, but he hadn't quite believed it, used, as he was, to dealing with Israeli security with their numberless soldiers and guns. After all the tension he'd felt, like being wrapped tightly with rope, it was all diminishing now. He'd slept poorly in his hotel the previous night, and now he'd get on the aircraft and sleep all the way across. On getting back to Tehran, he'd look at Badrayn and laugh and ask for another such mission. On passing the buffet, he saw a bottle of champagne, and poured himself a glass. It made him sneeze, and it was contrary to his religion, but it was the Western way to celebrate, and indeed he had something to celebrate. Twenty minutes later, his flight was called, and he walked off to the jetway with the others. His only concern now was jet lag. The flight would leave at eight sharp, then arrive in Paris at 5:45 PM! From breakfast to dinner without the intervening midday meal. Well, such was the miracle of modern travel.

They drove separately to Andrews, Adler in his official car, Clark and Chavez in the latter's personal auto, and while the Secretary of State was waved through the gate, the CIA officers had to show ID, which at least earned them a salute from the armed airman.

'You really don't like the place, do you?' the junior officer asked.

'Well, Domingo, back when you were taking the training wheels off your bike, I was in Tehran with a cover so thin you could read an insurance policy through it, yelling "Death to America!" with the gomers and watching our people being paraded around blindfolded by a bunch of crazy kids with guns. For a while there, I thought they were going to be lined up against a wall and hosed. I knew the station chief. Hell, I recognized him. They had him in the bag, too, gave him a rough time.' Just standing there, he remembered, only fifty yards away, not able to do a damned thing . . .

'What were you doing?'

'First time, it was a quick recon for the Agency. Second time, it was to be part of the rescue mission that went tits-up at Desert One. We all thought it was bad luck at the time, but that operation really scared me. Probably better it failed,' John concluded. 'At least we got them all out alive in the end.'

'So, bad memories, you don't like the place?'

Clark shrugged. 'Not really. Never figured them out. The Saudis I understand – I like 'em a lot. Once you get through the crust, they make friends for life. Some of the rules are a little funny to us, but that's okay. Kinda like old movies, sense of honor and all that, hospitality,' he went on. 'Anyway, lots of good experiences there. Not on the other side of the Gulf. Just as soon leave that place alone.' Ding parked his car. Both men retrieved their bags as a sergeant came up to them.

'Going to Paris, Sarge,' Clark said, holding up his ID again.

'You gentlemen want to come with me?' She waved them towards the VIP terminal. The low, one-story building had been cleared of other distinguished visitors. Scott Adler was on one of the couches, going over some papers.

'Mr Secretary?'

Adler looked up. 'Let me guess, this one is Clark, and this one is Chavez.'

'You might even have a future in the intelligence business.' John smiled. Handshakes were exchanged.

'Good morning, sir,' Chavez said.

'Foley says, with you, my life is in good hands,' SecState offered, closing his briefing book.

'He exaggerates.' Clark walked a few feet to get a Danish. Was it nerves? John asked himself. Ed and Mary Pat were right. This should be a routine operation, in and out, Hi, how are you, eat shit and die, so long. And he'd been in tighter spots than Tehran in 1979–80 – not many, but some. He frowned at the pastry. Something had brought the old feeling back, the creepy-crawly sensation on his skin, like something was blowing on the hairs there, the one that told him to turn around and look real hard at things.

'He also tells me you're on the SNIE team, and I should listen to you,' Adler went on. At least he seemed relaxed, Clark saw.

'The Foleys and I go back some,' John explained.

'You've been there before?'

'Yes, Mr Secretary.' Clark followed with two minutes of explanation that earned a thoughtful nod from the senior official.

'Me, too. I was one of the people the Canadians snuck out. Just showed up a week before. I was out apartment-hunting when they seized the embassy. Missed all the fun,' SecState concluded. 'Thank God.'

'So you know the country some?'

Adler shook his head. 'Not really. A few words of the language. I was there to learn up on the place, but it didn't work out, and I branched off into other areas. I want to hear more about your experiences, though.'

'I'll do what I can, sir,' John told him. Then a young captain came in to say that the flight was ready. A sergeant got Adler's things.

The CIA officers lifted their own bags. In addition to two changes of clothes, they had their sidearms – John preferred his Smith & Wesson; Ding liked the Beretta .40 – and compact cameras. You never knew when you might see something useful.

Bob Holtzman had a lot to think about, as he sat alone in his office. It was a classic newsman's place of work, the walls glass, which allowed him a modicum of acoustic privacy while also letting him see out into the city room and the reporters there to see in. All he really needed was a cigarette, but you couldn't smoke in the *Post* building anymore, which would have amused the hell out of Ben Hecht.

Somebody'd got to Tom Donner and John Plumber. It had to be Kealty. Holtzman's views on Kealty were an exact mirror image of his feelings toward Ryan. Kealty's political ideas, he thought, were pretty good, progressive and sensible.

It was just the man who was useless. In another age, his womanizing would have been overlooked, and in fact, Kealty's political career had straddled those ages, the old and the new. Washington was full of women drawn to power like bees to honey – or like flies to something else – and they got used. Mainly they went away sadder and wiser; in the age of abortion on demand, more permanent consequences were a thing of the past. Politicians were so charming by nature that most of the cookies – that euphemism went *way* back – even went away with a smile, hardly realizing how they'd been used. But some got hurt, and Kealty had hurt several. One woman had even committed suicide. Bob's wife, Libby Holtzman, had worked that story, only to see it lost in the shuffle during the brief conflict with Japan, and in the interim the media had decided in some collective way that the story was history, and Kealty had been rehabilitated in everyone's memory. Even women's groups had looked at his personal behavior, then compared it with his political views, and decided that the balance fell one way and not another. It all offended Holtzman in a distant way. People had to have *some* principles, didn't they?

But this was Washington.

Kealty had *got* to Donner and Plumber, and must have done so between the taped morning interview and the live evening broadcast. And that meant . . .

'Oh, shit,' Holtzman breathed, when the lightbulb flashed on in his head.

That was a story! Better yet, it was a story his managing editor would love. Donner had said on live TV that the morning tape had been damaged. *It had to be a lie.* A reporter who lied directly to the public. There weren't all that many rules in the business of journalism, and most of them were amorphous things that could be bent or skirted. But not that one. The print and TV media didn't get along all that well. They competed for the same audience, and the lesser of the two was winning. *Lesser?* Holtzman asked himself. Of course. TV was flashy, that was all, and maybe a picture was worth a thousand words, but not when the frames were selected with an eye more towards entertainment than information. TV was the girl you looked at. The print media was the one who had your kids.

But how to prove it?

What could be sweeter? He could destroy that peacock, with his perfect suits and his hair spray. He could cast a pall over all television news, and wouldn't *that* boost circulation! He could couch it all as a religious ceremony on the altar of Journalistic Integrity. Wrecking careers was part of his business. He'd never broken a fellow reporter before, but there was an anticipatory delight in drumming this one out of the corps.

But what about Plumber? Holtzman knew and respected him. Plumber had come to TV at a different time, when the industry had been trying to gain respectability, and hired journalistic craftsmen on the basis of their professional reputations rather than their movie-star looks. Plumber had to know. And he probably didn't like it.

Ryan couldn't *not* see the Colombian Ambassador. The latter, he saw, was a career diplomat from the aristocracy, immaculately dressed for a meeting with the American chief of state. The handshake was strong and cordial. The usual pleasantries were exchanged in front of the official photographer, and then it was time to talk business.

'Mr President,' he began formally, 'my government has instructed me to inquire about some unusual allegations in your news media.'

Jack nodded soberly. 'What do you wish to know?'

'It has been reported that some years ago the United States government may have invaded my country. We find this assertion disturbing, not to mention a violation of international law and various treaty relationships between our two democracies.'

'I understand your feelings on the matter. In your position I would feel much the same way. Let me say now that my administration will not countenance such action under any circumstances. On that, sir, you have my personal word, and I trust you will convey it to your government.' Ryan decided to pour the man some coffee. He'd learned that such small personal gestures were vastly powerful in diplomatic exchanges, for reasons he didn't quite understand, but was quite willing to accept when they worked for him. It worked this time, too, and broke the tension of the moment.

'Thank you,' the ambassador said, lifting his cup.

'I believe it's even Colombian coffee,' the President offered.

'Regrettably, not our most famous export product,' Pedro Ochoa admitted.

'I don't blame you for that,' Jack told his visitor.

'Oh?'

'Mr Ambassador, I am fully aware that your country has paid a bitter price for America's bad habits. While I was at CIA, yes, I did look over all manner of information concerning the drug trade and the effects it's had in your part of the world. I had no part at all in initiating any improper activity in your country, but, yes, I did look over a lot of data. I know about the policemen who've been killed – my own father was a police officer, as you know – and the judges, and the journalists. I know that Colombia has worked harder and longer than any other country in your region to bring about a true democratic government, and I will say one more thing, sir. I am ashamed at some of the things that have been said in this city about your country. The drug problem does not begin in Colombia, or Ecuador, or Peru. The drug problem starts here, and you are as much a victim as we are – actually more so. It's American money that's poisoning your country. It is not you who hurts us. It is we who hurt you.'

Ochoa had expected many things from this meeting, but not this. He set his cup down, and his peripheral vision suddenly reported that they were alone in the room. The bodyguards had withdrawn. There wasn't even an aide to take notes. This was unusual. More than that, Ryan had just admitted that the stories were true – partly true, anyway.

'Mr President,' he said, in English learned at home and polished at Princeton, 'we have not often heard such words from your country.'

'You're hearing them now, sir.' Two very level pairs of eyes crossed the table. 'I will not criticize your country unless you deserve it, and on the basis of what I know, such criticism is not deserved. Diminishing the drug trade, most of all, means attacking the demand side, and that will be a priority of this administration. We are now drafting legislation to punish those who *use* drugs, not merely those who sell them. When the Congress is properly reestablished, I will press hard for passage of that legislation. I also wish to establish an informal working group, composed of members of my government and yours, to discuss how we may better assist you in your part of the problem – but always with full respect for your national integrity. America has not always been a good neighbor to you. I can't change the past, but I can try to change the future. Tell me, might your President accept an invitation so that we could discuss this issue face-to-face?' *I want to make up for all this lunacy.*

'I think it likely that he would view such an invitation favorably, with due consideration for time and other duties, of course.' Which meant, *damned right he will!*

'Yes, sir, I am myself learning just how demanding such a job can be. Perhaps,' Jack added with a smile, 'he might give *me* some advice.'

'Less than you think.' Ambassador Ochoa was wondering how he'd explain this meeting to his government. Clearly, the basis of a deal was on the table. Ryan was offering what could only be seen in South America as an elaborate apology for something that would never be admitted, and whose full revelation could only damage everyone involved. And yet this was not being done for political reasons, was it?

Was it?

'Your proposed legislation, Mr President, what will you seek to accomplish?'

'We're studying that now. For the most part, I believe, people use drugs because it's fun – escape from reality, whatever you might want to call it – it comes down to personal amusement of one sort or another. Our data suggests that at least half of the drugs sold in the country are for recreational users rather than true addicts. I think we should make the use of drugs un-fun, by which I mean some form of punishment for any level of possession or intoxication. Obviously, we do not have the prison space for all the drug users in America, but we do have lots of streets that need sweeping. For recreational users, thirty days – for the first offense – of sweeping streets and collecting garbage' in an economically disadvantaged area, wearing distinctive clothing, of course, will take much of the fun out of it. You are Catholic, I believe?'

'Yes, I am, as you are.'

Ryan grinned. 'Then you know about shame. We learned

it in school, didn't we? It's a starting place, that's all it is for the moment. The administrative issues need to be looked at. Justice is also examining some constitutional questions, but those appear to be less troublesome than I expected. I want this to be law by the end of the year. I've got three kids, and the drug problem here frightens the hell out of me at the personal level. This isn't a perfect response to the problem. The truly addicted people need professional help of one sort or another, and we're now looking at a variety of state and local programs for things that really work – but, hell, if we can kill off recreational use, that's at least half of the trade, and where I come from, half is a good start.'

'We will watch this process with great interest,' Ambassador Ochoa promised. Cutting the income of the drug traffickers by that much would reduce their ability to buy protection, and help his government do what it had so earnestly tried to do, for the monetary power of the drug trade was a political cancer in the body of his country.

'I regret the circumstances that brought this meeting about, but I am glad that we've had a chance to discuss the issues. Thank you, Mr Ambassador, for being so forthright. I want you to know that I am always open to any exchange of views. Most of all, I want you and your government to know that I have great respect for the rule of law, and that respect does not stop at our borders. Whatever may have happened in the past, I propose a new beginning, and I will back up my words with action.'

Both men stood, and Ryan took his hand again, and led him outside. There followed a few minutes on the edge of the Rose Garden in front of some TV cameras. The White House Press Office would release a statement about a friendly meeting between the two men. The photos would run on the news to show that it might not be a lie.

'It promises to be a good spring,' Ochoa said, noting the clear sky and warming breezes.

'But summers here can be very unpleasant. Tell me, what's it like in Bogotá?'

'We are high up. It's never terribly hot, but the sun can be punishing. This is a fine garden. My wife loves flowers. She's becoming famous,' the Ambassador said. 'She's developed her own new type of rose. Somehow she cross-bred yellow and pink and produced something that's almost golden in color.'

'What does she call it?' Ryan's entire knowledge of roses was that you had to be careful about the branches, or stalks, or whatever you called the thorny part. But the cameras were rolling.

'In English, it would be "Dawn Display." All the good names for roses, it seems, have already been taken,' Ochoa noted, with a friendly smile.

'Perhaps we might have some for the garden here?'

'Maria would be greatly honored, Mr President.'

'Then we have more than one agreement, *señor*.' Another handshake.

Ochoa knew the game, too. For the cameras his Latin face broke into the friendliest of diplomatic smiles, but the handshake also had genuine warmth in it. 'Dawn Display – for a truly new day between us, Mr President.'

'My word on it.' And they took their leave. Ryan walked back into the West Wing. Arnie was waiting inside the door. It was widely known but little acknowledged that the Oval Office *was* wired like a pinball machine – or more properly, a recording studio.

'You're learning. You're really learning,' the chief of staff observed.

'That one was easy, Arnie. We've been fucking those people over for too long. All I had to do was tell the truth. I want that legislation fast-tracked. When will the draft be ready?'

'Couple of weeks. It's going to raise some hell,' van Damm warned.

'I don't care,' the President replied. 'How about we try something that might work instead of spending money for show all the time? We've tried shooting the airplanes down. We've tried murder. We've tried interdiction. We've tried going after pushers. We've exhausted all the other possibilities, and they don't work because there's too much money involved for people not to give it a go. How about we go after the source of the problem for a change? That's where the problem starts, and that's where the money comes from.'

'I'm just telling you it's going to be hard.'

'What useful thing isn't?' Ryan asked, heading back to his

office. Instead of the direct door off the corridor, he went through the secretaries' room. 'Ellen?' he said, gesturing to the Oval Office.

'Am I corrupting you?' Mrs Sumter asked, bringing her cigarettes, to the semi-concealed smiles of the other ladies in the room.

'Cathy might see it that way, but we don't have to tell her, do we?' In the sanctity of his office, the President of the United States lit up a skinny woman's cigarette, celebrating with one addiction an attack on another – and, oh, by the way, having neutralized a potential diplomatic earthquake.

The last of the travelers left America, strangely enough, from Minneapolis–St Paul International Airport, via Northwest and KLM flights. Badrayn would sweat it out for hours more. In the interest of security, none of them had so much as a telephone number to call to announce success, warn of failure, or to give to whomever might have arrested them, tying them to the UIR with something more than their own words. Instead, Badrayn had people at all of the return airports with flight schedules. When the travelers got off their flights in Europe and were visually recognized, then calls would be made circuitously, from public phones, using pre-paid and anonymous calling cards.

The successful return of the travelers to Tehran would start the next operation. Sitting in an office there, Badrayn had nothing more to do than look at the clock and worry. He was logged onto the Net via his computer, and had been scanning the news wires, and finding nothing of note. Nothing would be certain until all the travelers got back and made their individual reports. Not even then, really. It would take three or four days, maybe five, before the e-mail lines to CDC would be screaming. Then he'd know.

39

FACE TIME

The flight across the pond was pleasant. The VC-20B was more a mini-airliner than a business jet, and the Air Force crewmen, who looked to Clark as though they might be old enough to take driving lessons, kept things smooth. The aircraft began its descent into the enveloping darkness of the European night, finally landing at a military airfield west of Paris.

There was no arrival ceremony *per se*, but Adler was an official of ministerial rank, and he had to be met, even on a covert mission. In this case, a high-level official – a civil servant – walked up to the aircraft as soon as the engines wound down. Adler recognized him as the stairs descended.

'Claude!'

'Scott. Congratulations on your promotion, my old friend!' In deference to American tastes, kisses were not exchanged.

Clark and Chavez scanned the area for danger, but all they saw were French troops, or maybe police – they couldn't tell at this distance – standing in a circle, with weapons in evidence. Europeans had a penchant for showing people machine guns, even on city streets. It probably had a salutary effect on street muggings, John thought, but it seemed a little excessive. In any case, they'd expected no special dangers in France, and indeed there were none. Adler and his friend got in an official vehicle. Clark and Chavez got in the chase car. The flight crew would head off for mandated crew rest, which was USAF-talk for having a few with their French colleagues.

'We go to the lounge for a few minutes before your aircraft is ready,' a French air force colonel explained. 'Perhaps you wish to freshen up?'

'*Merci, mon commandant*,' Ding replied. Yeah, he thought, the Frenchies do know how to make you feel safe.

'Thank you for helping to arrange this,' Adler said to his friend. They'd been FSOs together, once in Moscow and once more in Pretoria. Both had specialized in sensitive assignments.

'It is nothing, Scott.' Which it wasn't, but diplomats talk like diplomats even when they don't have to. Claude had once helped him get through a divorce in a uniquely French way, all the while speaking as though conducting treaty negotiations. It was almost a joke between the two. 'Our ambassador reports that he will be receptive to the right sort of approach.'

'And what might that be?' SecState asked his colleague. They got out at what appeared to be the base officers club, and a minute later found themselves in a private dining room, with a carafe of fine Beaujolais on the table. 'What's your take on this, Claude? What does Daryaei want?'

The shrug was as much a part of the French character as the wine, which Claude poured. They toasted, and the wine was superb even by the standards of the French diplomatic service. Then came business.

'We're not sure. We wonder about the death of the Turkoman Premier.'

'You don't wonder about the death of –'

'I do not believe anyone has doubts about that, Scott, but that is a long-standing business, is it not?'

'Not exactly.' Another sip. 'Claude, you're still the best authority on wine I know. What's he thinking about?'

'Probably many things. His domestic troubles – you Americans don't appreciate them as well as you should. His people are restless, less so now that he's conquered Iraq, but the problem is still there. We feel that he must consolidate before he does anything else. We also feel that the process may turn out to be unsuccessful. We are hopeful, Scott. We are hopeful that the extreme aspects of the regime will moderate over time, perhaps not very much time. It must. It is no longer the eighth century, even in that part of the world.'

Adler took a few seconds to consider that, then nodded thoughtfully. 'Hope you're right. The guy's always scared me.'

'All men are mortal. He is seventy-two, and he works a hard schedule. In any case, we have to check on him, do we not? If he moves, then we will move, together, as we have done in the past. The Saudis and we have talked on this matter also. They are concerned, but not overly so. Our assessment is the same. We counsel you to keep an open mind.'

Claude might be correct, Adler thought. Daryaei *was* old, and consolidating the rule over a newly acquired country wasn't exactly a trivial undertaking. More than that, the easiest way to bring a hostile country down, if you have the patience for it, was to be nice to the bastards. A little trade, a few journalists, some CNN, and a couple of G-rated movies, such things could do wonders. If you have the patience. If you had the time. There were plenty of Iranian kids in American universities. That could be the most effective means for America to change the UIR. Problem was, Daryaei had to know that, too. And so here he was, Scott Adler, Secretary of State, a post he'd never expected to approach, much less have, and he was supposed to know what to do next. But he'd read enough diplomatic history to know better.

'I'll listen to what he has to say, and we're not looking to make any new enemies, Claude. I think you know that.'

'*D'accord*.' He topped off Adler's glass. 'Unfortunately, you will find none of this in Tehran.'

'And two is my limit when I'm working.'

'Your flight crew is excellent,' Claude assured him. 'They fly our own ministers.'

'When has your hospitality ever been lacking?'

For Clark and Chavez it was Perrier, cheaper to buy here, they both imagined, though the lemons probably were not.

'So how are things in Washington?' a French counterpart asked, just killing time, or so it seemed.

'Pretty strange. You know, it's amazing how quiet the country is. Maybe having a lot of the government turned off helps,' John said, trying to dodge.

'And this talk of your President and his adventures?'

'Sounds like a lot of movie stuff to me,' Ding said, with the open face of honesty.

'Stealing a Russian sub? All by himself? Damn.' Clark grinned. 'I wonder who made *that* up?'

'But the Russian spy chief,' their host objected. 'It is he, and he's been on the television.'

'Yeah, well, I bet we paid him a ton of money to come across, too.'

'Probably wants to do a book and make some more.' Chavez laughed. 'Sumbitch'll get it, too. Hey, *mon ami*, we're just worker bees, okay?'

It didn't fly any better than a lead glider. Clark looked into their interrogator's eyes and they just clicked. The man was DGSE, and he knew Agency when he saw it.

'Then be careful of the nectar you will find where you are going, my young friend. It is, perhaps, too sweet.' It was like the start of a card game. The deck was out, and he was shuffling. Probably just one hand, and maybe a friendly one, but the hand had to be played.

'What do you mean?'

'The man you go to meet, he is dangerous. He has the look of one who sees what we do not.'

'You've worked the country?' John asked.

'I have traveled through the country, yes.'

'And?' This was Chavez.

'And I have never understood them.'

'Yeah,' Clark agreed. 'I know what you're saying.'

'An interesting man, your President,' the Frenchman said again, and it was pure curiosity, actually an endearing thing to see in the eyes of an intelligence officer.

John looked right in those eyes and decided to thank the man for his warning, one pro to another. 'Yeah, he is. He's one of us,' Clark assured him.

'And those entertaining stories?'

'I cannot say.' Delivered with a smile. *Of course they're true. You think reporters have the wit to make such things up?*

Both men were thinking the same thing, and both men knew it, though neither could speak it aloud: *A shame we cannot get together some evening for a dinner and some stories.* But it just wasn't done.

'On the way back, I will offer you a drink.'

'On the way back, I will have it.'

Ding just listened and watched. The old bastard still had it, and there were still lessons to learn from how he did it. 'Nice to have a friend,' he said five minutes later on the way to the French aircraft.

'Better than a friend, a pro. You listen to people like him, Domingo.'

Nobody had ever said that governance was easy, even for those who invoked the word of God for nearly everything. The disappointment, even for Daryaei, who'd been governing Iran for nearly twenty years in one capacity or another, was in all the petty administrative rubbish that reached his desk and took from his time. He'd never grasped that it was almost entirely his fault. His rule was fair by his own reckoning, but harsh by most others. Most violations of the rules mandated death for the miscreant, and even small administrative errors on the part of bureaucrats could entail the end of a career – that degree of mercy depended on the magnitude of the error, of course. A bureaucrat who said no to everything, noting that the law was clear on an issue, whether it was or not, rarely got into trouble. One who broadened the scope of the government's power over the most minor of day-to-day activities was merely adding to the scope of Daryaei's rule. Such decisions came easily and caused little in the way of difficulty to the arbiter in question.

But real life wasn't that simple. Practical questions of commerce, for example, just the way in which the country did business in everything from the sale of melons to the honking of auto horns around a mosque required a certain degree of judgment, because the Holy Koran hadn't anticipated every situation, and neither had the civil law been based upon it. But to liberalize anything was a major undertaking, because any liberalization of any rule might be seen as a theological error – this in a country where apostasy was a capital crime. And so the lowest-level bureaucrats, when stuck with the necessity of saying yes to a request, from time to time, tended to hem and haw and kick things upstairs, which gave a higher-level official the chance to say no, which came just as easily to them after a career of doing so, but with somewhat greater authority, somewhat greater responsibility, and far more to lose in the event that someone higher still disagreed with the rare and erroneous yes decision. All that meant was that such calls kept perking up the pyramid. In between Daryaei and the bureaucracy was a council of religious leaders (he'd been a member under Khomeini), and a titular parliament, and experienced officials, but, disappointingly to the new UIR's religious leader, the principle held, and he found himself dealing with such weighty issues as the business hours for markets, the price of petrol, and the educational syllabus of grade-school females. The sour expression he'd adopted for such trivial issues merely made his lesser colleagues all the more obsequious in their presentation of the pros and cons, which added an additional measure of gravity to the absurd, while they sought favor for being strict (opposing whatever change was on the table) or for being practical (supporting it). Earning Daryaei's favor was the biggest political game in town, and he inevitably found himself as tied down as an insect in amber by small issues, while he needed all his time to deal with the big ones. The amazing part is that he never understood why people couldn't take *some* initiative, even as he destroyed people on occasion for taking any.

So it was that he landed in Baghdad this evening to meet with local religious leaders. The issue of the day was which mosque in need of repair would get repaired first. It was known that Mahmoud Haji had one personal favorite for his own prayers, another for its architectural beauty, and yet a third for its great historical significance, while the people of the city loved yet another – and wouldn't it be a better idea, politically, to deal with the maintenance needs of that one first, the better to ensure the political stability of the region? After that came a problem with the right of women to drive cars (the previous Iraqi regime had been overly liberal on that!), which was objectionable, but was it not difficult to take away a right already possessed, and what of women who lacked a man (widows, for example) to drive them, and also lacked the money with which to hire one? Should the government look after their needs? Some – physicians for one example, teachers for another – were important to the local society. On the other hand, since Iran and Iraq were now one, the law had to be the same, and so did one grant a right to Iranian women or deny it to the Iraqi? For these weighty issues and a few others, he had to take an evening flight to Baghdad.

Daryaei, sitting in his private jet, looked over the agenda for the meeting and wanted to scream, but he was too patient a man for that – or so he told himself. He had something important to prepare for, after all. In the morning he'd be meeting with the Jew American foreign minister. His expression, as he looked through the papers, frightened even the flight crew, though Mahmoud Haji didn't notice that, and even if he had, would not have understood why.

Why couldn't people take some *initiative!*

The jet was a Dassault Falcon 900B, about nine years old, similar in basic type and function to the USAF VC-20B twin-jet. The two-man flight crew was a pair of French air force officers, both rather senior for this 'charter,' and there was also a pair of cabin attendants, both female and as charming as they could be. At least one, Clark figured, was a DGSE spook. Maybe both. He liked the French, especially their intelligence services. As troublesome an ally as France occasionally was, when the French did business in the black world, they damned well did business as well as any and better than most. Fortunately, in the case at hand, aircraft are noisy and hard to bug. Perhaps that explained why one attendant or the other would come back every fifteen minutes or so to ask if they needed anything.

'Anything special we need to know?' John asked, when the latest offer was declined with a smile.

'Not really,' Adler replied. 'We want to get a feel for the guy, what he's up to. My friend Claude, back at Paris, says that things are not as bad as they look, and his reasoning seems pretty sound. Mainly I'm delivering the usual message.'

'Behave yourself,' Chavez said, with a smile.

The Secretary of State smiled. 'Somewhat more diplomatically, but yes. What's your background, Mr Chavez?'

Clark liked that one: 'You don't want to know where we got him from.'

'I just finished my master's thesis,' the young spook said proudly. 'Get hooded in June.'

'Where?'

'George Mason University. Professor Alpher.'

That perked Adler's interest. 'Really? She used to work for me. What's the thesis on?'

'It's called "A Study in Conventional Wisdom: Erroneous

Diplomatic Maneuvers in Turn-of-the-Century Europe."'

'The Germans and the Brits?'

Ding nodded. 'Mainly, especially the naval races.'

'Your conclusion?'

'People couldn't recognize the differences between tactical and strategic goals. The guys supposed to be thinking "future" were thinking "right now," instead. Because they confused politics with statecraft, they ended up in a war that brought down the entire European order, and replaced it with nothing more than scar tissue.' It was remarkable, Clark thought, listening to the brief discourse, that Ding's voice changed when discussing his school work.

'And you're an SPO?' SecState asked, with a certain degree of incredulity.

A very Latino grin reappeared. 'Used to be. Sorry if I don't drag my knuckles on the ground like I'm supposed to, sir.'

'So why did Ed Foley lay you two on me?'

'My fault,' Clark said. 'They want us to take a little stroll around and get a smell for things.'

'Your fault?' Scott asked.

'I was their training officer, once upon a time,' John explained, and that changed the complexion of the conversation entirely.

'You're the guys who got Koga out! You're the guys who –'

'Yeah, we were there,' Chavez confirmed. SecState was probably cleared for all that. 'Lots of fun.'

The Secretary of State told himself that he should be offended that he had two field spooks with him – and the younger one's remark about being a knuckle-dragger wasn't that far off. But a master's from George Mason . . .

'You're also the guys who sent that report that Brett Hanson pooh-poohed, the one about Goto. That was good work. In fact, it was excellent work.' He'd wondered what these two were doing on the SNIE team for the UIR situation. Now he knew.

'But nobody listened,' Chavez pointed out. It may have been a deciding factor in the war with Japan, and a very hairy time for them in that country. But it had also given him some real insight into how diplomacy and statecraft hadn't changed very much since 1905. It was an ill wind that blew no one good.

'I'll listen,' Adler promised. 'Let me know what your little stroll turns up, okay?'

'Sure will. I guess you have need-to-know on this,' John observed, with a raised eyebrow.

Adler turned and waved to one of the attendants, the pretty brunette one whom Clark had tagged as a certain spook. She was just as charming as hell, and drop-dead pretty, but seemed a little too clumsy in the galley to be a full-time flight attendant.

'Yes, Monsieur Minister?'

'How long until we land?'

'Four hours.'

'Okay, then, could we have a deck of cards and a bottle of wine?'

'Certainly.' She hustled the twelve feet to get them.

'Not supposed to drink on duty, sir,' Chavez said.

'You're off-duty until we land,' Adler told them. 'And I like to play cards before I go into one of these sessions. Good for the nerves. You gentlemen up to a friendly game?'

'Well, Mr Secretary, if you insist,' John replied. Now they'd all get a read on the mission. 'A little five-card stud, maybe?'

Everybody knew where the line was. No official communiqués had been exchanged, at least not between Beijing and Taipei, but it was known and understood even so, because people in uniform tend to be practical and observant. The PRC aircraft never flew closer than ten nautical miles (fifteen kilometers) to a certain north-south line, and the ROC aircraft, recognizing that fact, kept the same distance from the same invisible bit of longitude. On either side of the line, people could do anything they wanted, appear as aggressive as they wished, expend all the ordnance they could afford, and that was agreed to without so much as a single tactical radio message. It was all in the interest of stability. Playing with loaded guns was always dangerous, as much so for nation-states as for children, though the latter were more easily disciplined – the former were too big for that.

America now had four submarines in the Formosa Strait. These were spotted on – under – the invisible line, which was the safest place to be. A further collection of three ships was now at the north end of the passage, a cruiser, USS *Port*

Royal, along with destroyers *The Sullivans* and *Chandler*. All were SAM ships, equipped with a total of 250 SM2-MR missiles. Ordinarily, they were tasked to guard a carrier from air attack, but 'their' carrier was in Pearl Harbor having her engines replaced. *Port Royal* and *The Sullivans* – named for a family of sailors wiped out on the same ship in 1942 – were both Aegis ships with powerful SPY radars, which were now surveilling air activity while the submarines were handling the rest. *Chandler* had a special ELINT team aboard to keep track of voice radio transmissions. Like a cop on the beat, they were not so much there to interfere with anyone's exercises as to let people know that The Law was around, in a friendly sort of way, and as long as they were, things would not get out of hand. At least that was the idea. And if anyone objected to the presence of the American ships, their country would note that the seas were free for the innocent passage of all, and they weren't in anyone's way, were they? That they were actually part of someone *else's* plan was not immediately apparent to anyone. What happened next confused nearly everyone.

It was dawn in the air, if not yet on the surface, when a flight of four PRC fighters came off the mainland, heading east, followed five minutes later by four more. These were duly tracked by the American ships at the extreme range of their billboard radars. Routine track numbers were assigned, and the computer system followed their progress to the satisfaction of the officers and men in the CIC of *Port Royal*. Until they didn't turn. Then a lieutenant lifted a phone and pushed a button.

'Yes?' a groggy voice answered.

'Captain, Combat, we have a flight of PRC aircraft, probably fighters, about to cross the line, bearing two-one-zero, altitude fifteen thousand, course zero-niner-zero, speed five hundred. There's a flight of four more a few minutes behind.'

'On the way.' The captain, partially dressed, arrived in the combat information center two minutes later, not in time to see the PRC fighters break the rules, but in time to hear a petty officer report something:

'New track, four or more fighters coming west.'

For the purposes of convenience, the computer had been told to assign 'enemy' designator-graphics to the mainland fighters and 'friendly' symbols to the Taiwanese. (There were also a few American aircraft around from time to time, but these were electronic-intelligence gatherers and well out of harm's way.) At this point, there were two immediately converging flights of four each, about thirty miles apart, but with a closure speed of over a thousand miles per hour. The radar was also tracking six commercial airliners, all on the east side of the line, minding their own business as they skirted the agreed-upon 'exercise' areas.

'Raid Six is turning,' a sailor reported next. This was the first outbound flight off the mainland, and as the captain watched, the velocity vector turned southward, while the outbound flight off Taiwan bored in on them.

'Illuminators coming on,' the chief at the ESM console said. 'The ROCs are lighting up Raid Six. Their radars seem to be in tracking mode.'

'Maybe that's why they turned,' the captain thought.

'Maybe they got lost?' the CIC officer wondered.

'Still dark out. Maybe they just went too far.' They didn't know what sort of navigation gear the ChiCom fighters might have had, and driving a single-seat aircraft over the sea at night was not a precise business.

'More airborne radars coming on, easterly direction, probably Raid Seven,' the ESM chief said. This was the second flight off the mainland.

'Any electronic activity from Raid Six?' the CIC officer asked.

'Negative, sir.' These fighters continued their turn and were now heading west, back for the line, with the ROC F-16s in pursuit. It was at this point that things changed.

'Raid Seven is turning, course now zero-nine-seven.'

'That puts them on the -16s . . . and they're illuminating . . . ,' the lieutenant observed, with the first hint of worry in his voice. 'Raid Seven is lighting up the F-16's, radars in tracking mode.'

The Republic of China F-16s then turned also. They'd been getting a lot of work. The newer, American-made fighters and their elite pilots comprised only about a third of their fighter force, and were drawing the duty of covering and responding to the flight exercises of their mainland cousins. Leaving Raid Six to return, they necessarily got more interested in the trailing flight, still heading east. The closure rate was still a thousand miles per hour, and both sides had their missile-targeting radars up and running, aimed at each other. That was internationally recognized as an unfriendly act, and one to be avoided for the simple reason that it was the aerial equivalent of aiming a rifle at someone's head.

'Uh-oh,' the petty officer on the ESM board said. 'Sir, Raid Seven, their radars just shifted to tracking mode.' Instead of just searching for targets, the airborne systems were now operating in the manner used to guide air-to-air missiles. What had been merely unfriendly a few seconds ago now became overtly hostile.

The F-16s broke into two pairs – elements – and began maneuvering freely. The outbound PRC fighters did the same. The original flight of four, Raid Six, was now across the line, heading west on what appeared to be a direct line to their airfield.

'Oh, I think I know what's going on here, sir, look how –'

A very small pip appeared on the screen, leaving one of the ROC F-16s –

'Oh, shit,' a sailor said. 'We have a missile in the air –'

'Make that two,' his chief said.

Aloft, a pair of American-made AIM-120 missiles were now taking separate paths to separate targets.

'They thought it was an attack. Oh, Christ,' the captain said, turning to his communications. 'Get me CinCPac right now!'

It didn't take long. One of the mainland fighters turned into a puff on the screen. Warned, the other jinked hard and dodged its missile at the last second.

Then it turned back. The southern PRC fighter element maneuvered also, and Raid Six turned radically to the north, its illumination radars now on. Ten seconds later, six more missiles were airborne and tracking targets.

'We got a battle on our hands!' the chief of the watch said. The captain lifted the phone:

'Bridge, combat, general quarters, general quarters!' Then he grabbed the TBS microphone, getting the captains of his two companion ships, both ten miles away, east and west of his cruiser as the alarm gong started sounding on USS *Port Royal*.

'I have it,' *The Sullivans* reported. That destroyer was outboard.

'Me, too,' *Chandler* chimed in. That one was closer to the island nation, but getting the radar picture from the Aegis ships via data link.

'That's a kill!' Another ChiCom fighter took its hit and headed down to the still-dark surface. Five seconds later, an F-16 died. More crewmen arrived in CIC, taking their battle stations.

'Captain, Raid Six was just trying to simulate –'

'Yeah, I see that now, but we have a train wreck on our hands.'

And then, predictably, a missile went wild. These were so small as to be hard for the Aegis radar to track, but a technician boosted power, throwing six million watts of RF energy into the 'exercise' area, and the picture became more clear.

'Oh, shit!' a chief said, pointing to the main tactical display. 'Captain, look there!'

It was instantly obvious. Someone had loosed what was probably an infra-red-seeking missile, and the hottest target in town was an Air China Airbus 310, with two huge General Electric CF6 turbofans – the same basic engines as those which powered all three of the American warships – which looked like the sun to its single red eye.

'Chief Albertson, get him on guard!' the skipper shouted.

'Air China Six-Six-Six, this is a US Navy warship, you have a missile inbound on you from the northwest, I say again, maneuver immediately, you have a missile tracking you from the northwest!'

'What, what?' But the plane started moving, turning left and descending. Not that it mattered.

The plotted velocity vector of the missile never wavered from the target. There was a hope that it would burn out and fall short, but the missile was going at mach 3, and the Air China flight was already slowed down, commencing its approach to its home field. When the pilot put his nose down, he just made things easier for the missile.

'It's a big airplane,' the captain said.

'Only two engines, sir,' the weapons officer pointed out.

'That's a hit,' a radarman said.

'Get her down, pal, get her down. Oh, fuck,' the captain breathed, wanting to turn away. On the display, the 310's blip tripled in size and flashed the emergency code.

'He's calling Mayday, sir,' a radioman said. 'Air China flight triple-six is calling Mayday . . . engine and wing damage . . . possible fire aboard.'

'Only about fifty miles out,' a chief said. 'He's vectoring for a direct approach into Taipei.'

'Captain, all stations report manned and ready. Condition One is set throughout the ship,' the IC man of the watch told the skipper.

'Very well.' His eyes were locked on the center of the three radar displays. The fighter engagement, he saw, had ended as quickly as it had started, with three fighters splashed, another possibly damaged, and both sides withdrawing to lick their wounds and figure out what the hell had happened. On the Taiwanese side, another flight of fighters was up and forming just off their coast.

'Captain!' It was the ESM console. 'Looks like every radar on every ship just lit off. Sources all over the place, classifying them now.'

But that didn't matter, the captain knew. What mattered now was that Airbus 310 was slowing and descending, according to his display.

'CinCPac Operations, sir.' The radio chief pointed.

'This is Port Royal,' the captain said, lifting the phone-type receiver for the satellite radio link. 'We just had a little air battle here – and a missile went wild and it appears that it hit an airliner inbound from Hong Kong to Taipei. The aircraft is still in the air, but looks to be in trouble. We have two ChiCom MiGs and one ROC F-16 splashed, maybe one more -16 damaged.'

'Who started it?' the watch officer asked.

'We think the ROC pilots fired the first missile. It could have been a screwup.' He explained on for a few seconds. 'I'll upload our radar take as quick as I can.'

'Very well. Thank you, Captain. I'll pass that along to the boss. Please keep us informed.'

'Will do.' The skipper killed the radio link and turned to the IC man of the watch. 'Let's get a tape of the battle set up for uplinking to Pearl.'

'Aye, sir.'

Air China 666 was still heading toward the coast, but the radar track showed the aircraft snaking and yawing around its straight-line course into Taipei. The ELINT team on *Chandler* was now listening in on the radio circuits. English is the language of international aviation, and the pilot in command of the wounded airliner was speaking quickly and clearly, calling ahead for emergency procedures, while he and his co-pilot struggled with their wounded airliner. Only they, really, knew the magnitude of the problem. Everyone else was just a spectator, rooting and praying that he'd keep it together for another fifteen minutes.

This one went up the line fast. The communications nexus was Admiral David Seaton's office on the hilltop overlooking Pearl Harbor. The senior communications watch officer changed buttons on his phone to call the theater commander-in-chief, who immediately told him to shoot a CRITIC-level flash message to Washington. Seaton next ordered an alert message to the seven American warships in the area – mainly the submarines – to perk their ears up. After that, a message went off to the Americans who were 'observing' the exercise in various Republic of China military command posts – these would take time to get delivered. There was still no American embassy in Taipei, and therefore no attachés or CIA personnel to hustle down to the airport to see if the airliner made it in safely or not. At that point, there was nothing to do but wait, in anticipation of the questions that would start arriving from Washington, and which as yet he was in no real position to answer.

'Yes?' Ryan said, lifting the phone.

'Dr Goodley for you, sir.'

'Okay, put him on.' Pause. 'Ben, what is it?'

'Trouble off Taiwan, Mr President; could be a bad one.' The National Security Advisor explained on, telling what he knew. It didn't take long.

It was, on the whole, an impressive exercise in communications. The Airbus was still in the air, and the President of the United States knew that there was a problem – and nothing else.

774

'Okay, keep me posted.' Ryan looked down at the desk he was about to leave. 'Oh, shit.' It was such a pleasure, the power of the presidency. Now he had virtually instant knowledge of something he could do nothing about. Were there Americans on the aircraft? What did it all mean? What was happening?

It could have been worse. Daryaei got back on the aircraft after having been in Baghdad for less than four hours, having dealt with the problems even more tersely than usual, and taking some satisfaction from the fear he'd struck into a few hearts for having bothered him with such trivial matters. His sour stomach contributed to an even more sour expression as he boarded and found his seat, and waved to the attendant to tell the flight crew to get moving – the sort of wrist-snapping gesture that looked like *off with their heads* to so many. Thirty seconds later, the stairs were up and the engines turning.

'Where did you learn this game?' Adler asked.

'In the Navy, Mr Secretary,' Clark answered, collecting the pot. He was ten dollars up now, and it wasn't the money. It was the principle of the thing. He'd just bluffed the Secretary of State out of two bucks. Miller Time.

'I thought sailors were crummy gamblers.'

'That's what some people say.' Clark smiled, as he piled the quarters up.

'Watch his hands,' Chavez advised.

'I *am* watching his hands.' The attendant came aft and poured out the rest of the wine. Not even two full glasses for the men, just enough to pass the time. 'Excuse me, how much longer?'

'Less than an hour, Monsieur Minister.'

'Thank you.' Adler smiled at her as she moved back forward.

'King bets, Mr Secretary,' Clark told him.

Chavez checked his hole card. Pair of fives. Nice start. He tossed a quarter into the center of the table after Adler's.

The European-made Airbus 310 had lost its right-side engine to the missile, but that wasn't all. The heat-seeker had come in from the right rear and impacted on the side of the big GE turbofan, with fragments from the explosion ripping into the outboard wing panels. Some of these sliced into a fuel cell – fortunately almost empty – which trailed some burning fuel, panicking those who could look out their windows and see. But that wasn't the frightening part. Fire behind the aircraft couldn't hurt anyone, and the vented fuel tank didn't explode, as it might have done had it been hit as little as ten minutes earlier. The really bad news was the damage to the aircraft's control surfaces.

Forward, the two-man flight crew was as experienced as that of any international airline. The Airbus could fly quite well, thank you, on one engine, and the left-side engine was undamaged, and now turning at full power while the co-pilot shut down the right side of the aircraft and punched the manual controls on the elaborate fire-suppression systems. In seconds, the fire-warning alarms went silent and the co-pilot started breathing again.

'Elevator damage,' the pilot reported next, working the controls and finding that the Airbus wasn't responding as it should.

But the problem wasn't with the flight crew, either. The Airbus actually flew via computer software, a huge executive program that took inputs directly from the airframe as well as from the control movements of the pilots, analyzed them, and then told the control surfaces what to do next. Battle damage was not something the software engineers had anticipated in the design of the aircraft. The program noted the traumatic loss of the engine and decided it was an engine explosion, which it had been taught to think about. The onboard computers evaluated the damage to the aircraft, what control surfaces worked and how well, and adjusted itself to the situation.

'Twenty miles,' the co-pilot reported, as the Airbus settled in on its direct-penetration vector. The pilot adjusted his throttle, and the computers – the aircraft actually had seven of them – decided this was all right, and lowered engine power. The aircraft, having burned off most of its fuel, was light. They had all the engine power they needed. The altitude was low enough that depressurization was not an issue. They could steer. They just might make this, they decided.

A 'helpful' fighter aircraft pulled alongside to look over their damage and tried to call them on the guard frequency, only to be told to keep out of the way, in very irate Mandarin.

The fighter could see skin peeling off the Airbus, and tried to report that, only to be rebuffed. His F-5E backed off to observe, talking to his base all the while.

'Ten miles.' Speed was below two hundred knots now, and they tried to lower flaps and slats, but the ones on the right side didn't deploy properly, and the computers, sensing this, didn't deploy them on the left side, either. The landing would have to be overly fast. Both pilots frowned, cursed, and got on with it.

'Gear,' the pilot ordered. The co-pilot flipped the levers, and the wheels went down – and locked in place, which was worth a sigh of relief to both drivers. They couldn't tell that both tires on the right side were damaged.

They had the field in view now, and both could see the flashing lights of emergency equipment as they crossed the perimeter fencing, and the Airbus settled. Normal approach speed was about 135 knots. They were coming in at 195. The pilot knew he'd need every available foot of space, and touched down within two hundred meters of the near edge.

The Airbus hit hard, and started rolling, but not for long. The damaged right-side tires lasted about three seconds before they both lost pressure, and one second after that, the metal strut started digging a furrow in the concrete. Both men and computers tried to maintain a straight-line course for the aircraft, but it didn't work. The 310 yawed to the right. The left-side gear snapped with a cannon-shot report, and the twin-jet bellied out. For a second, it appeared that it might pinwheel onto the grass, but then a wingtip caught, and the plane started turning over. The fuselage broke into three uneven sections. There was a gout of flame when the left wing separated – mercifully, the forward bit of fuselage shot clear, as did the after section, but the middle section stopped almost cold in the middle of the burning jet fuel, and all the efforts of the racing firefighters couldn't change that. It would later be determined that the 127 people killed quickly asphyxiated. Another 104 escaped with varying degrees of injury, including the flight crew. The TV footage would be uplinked within the hour, and a full-blown international incident was now world news.

Clark felt a slight chill as his aircraft touched down. Looking out the window, he imagined a certain familiarity, but admitted it was probably imaginary, and besides, all international airports looked pretty much alike in the dark. Forward, the French aviators followed directions, taxiing to the air force terminal for security, instructed to follow another business-type jet which had landed a minute ahead of them.

'Well, we're here,' Ding said, with a yawn. He had two watches on, one for local time and one for Washington, and from them he tried to decide what time his body thought it was. Then he looked outside with all the curiosity of a tourist, and suffered the usual disappointment. It might as easily have been Denver from what he could see.

'Excuse me,' the brunette attendant said. 'They've instructed us to remain in the aircraft while another is serviced first.'

'What's a few more minutes?' Secretary Adler thought, as tired as the rest of them.

Chavez looked out the window. 'There, he must have gotten in ahead of us.'

'Kill the cabin lights, will you?' Clark asked. Then he pointed at his partner.

'Why –' Clark cut the SecState off with a gesture. The attendant did as she was told. Ding took his cue and pulled the camera out of his bag.

'What gives?' Adler asked more quietly, as the lights went off.

'There's a G right in front of us,' John replied, taking his own look. 'Not many of them around, and he's going to a secure terminal. Let's see if we can tell who it is, okay?'

Spooks had to be spooks, Adler knew. He didn't object. Diplomats gathered information, too, and knowing who had access to such expensive official transport could tell them something about who really rated in the UIR government. In a few seconds, just as their own wheels were chocked, a parade of cars rolled up to the Gulfstream fifty meters away from them on the Iranian – UIR-ian – air force ramp.

'Somebody important,' Ding said.

'How you loaded?'

'ASA 1200, Mr C.,' Chavez replied, selecting the telephoto setting. The whole aircraft fit into the frame. He couldn't zoom any closer. He started shooting as the steps came down.

'Oh,' Adler said first. 'Well, that shouldn't be much of a surprise.'

'Daryaei, isn't it?' Clark asked.

'That's our friend,' SecState confirmed.

Hearing this, Chavez got off ten rapid frames, showing the man getting off, to be greeted by some colleagues, who embraced him like a long-lost uncle, then guided him into the car. The vehicles pulled off. Chavez fired off one more, then put the camera back in his bag. They waited another five minutes before they were allowed to de-plane.

'Do I want to know what time it is?' Adler asked, heading for the door.

'Probably not,' Clark decided. 'I guess we'll get a few hours of rack time before the meeting.'

At the bottom of the steps was the French ambassador, with one obvious security guard, and ten more locals. They would travel to the French embassy in two cars, with two Iranian vehicles leading and two more trailing the semi-official procession. Adler went with the ambassador in the first one. Clark and Chavez bundled into the second. They had a driver and another man in the front seat. Both would have to be spooks.

'Welcome to Tehran, my friends,' the guy riding shotgun said.

'*Merci*,' Ding replied, with a yawn.

'Sorry to get you up so early,' Clark added. This one would probably be the station chief. The people he and Ding had sat with at Paris would have called ahead to let him know that they were probably not State Department security types.

The Frenchman confirmed it. 'Not your first time, I am told.'

'How long have you been here?' John asked.

'Two years. The car is safe,' he added, meaning that it probably wasn't bugged.

'We have a message for you from Washington,' the ambassador told Adler in the leading car. Then he relayed what he knew about the Airbus incident at Taipei. 'You will be busy when you return home, I'm afraid.'

'Oh, Christ!' the Secretary observed. 'Just what we need. Any reaction yet?'

'Nothing I know of. But that will change within hours. You are scheduled to see the Ayatollah Daryaei at ten-thirty, so you have time for some sleep. Your flight back to Paris will leave just after lunch. We will give you all the assistance you request.'

'Thank you, Mr Ambassador.' Adler was too tired to say much else.

'Any idea what happened?' Chavez asked in the trail car.

'We have only what your government has told us to pass along. Evidently there was a brief clash over the Strait of Taiwan, and a missile hit an unintended target.'

'Casualties?' Clark said next.

'Unknown at this time,' the local DGSE station chief said.

'Kinda hard to hit an airliner without killing somebody.' Ding closed his eyes in anticipation of a soft bed at the embassy.

The same news was given to Daryaei at exactly the same time. He surprised his fellow cleric by taking it without a visible reaction. Mahmoud Haji had long since decided that people who didn't know anything couldn't interfere with much.

French hospitality was not disgraced even by its transplantation to a place which could hardly have been more different from the City of Light. Inside the compound, three uniformed soldiers collected the Americans' bags, while another man in some sort of livery conducted them to their quarters. The beds were turned down, and there was ice water on the nightstands. Chavez checked his watches again, groaned, and collapsed into the bed. For Clark, sleep came harder. The last time he'd looked at an embassy compound in this city ... *what was it!* he asked himself. What was bothering him so much about this?

Admiral Jackson did the brief, complete with videotape.

'This is the upload from *Port Royal*. We have a similar

tape from *The Sullivans*, no real differences, so we'll just use the one,' he told those in the Sit Room. He had a wooden pointer and started moving it around the large-screen TV display.

'This is a flight of four fighters, probably Jianjiji Hongzhaji-7s – we call it the B-7 for the obvious reason. Two engines and two seats, performance and capabilities like an old F-4 Phantom. The flight departs the mainland, and comes out a little too far. There's a no-man's-land right about here that neither side had violated until today. Here's another flight, probably the same aircraft and –'

'You're not sure?' Ben Goodley asked.

'We've ID'd the aircraft from their avionics, their radar emissions. A radar can't directly identify an airplane by type,' Robby explained. 'You have to deduce types by what they do, or from the electronic signatures of their equipment, okay? Anyway, the lead group is coming east, and crosses the invisible line here.' The pointer moved. 'Here's a flight of four Taiwanese F-16s with all the bells and whistles. They see the lead PRC group come too far and vector in on them. Then the lead group turns back west. Soon thereafter, right about . . . now, the trailing group lights off their radars, but instead of tracking their own lead group, they're hitting the F-16s.'

'What are you saying, Rob?' the President asked.

'What this looks like, the lead group was simulating a dawn attack on the mainland, and the trail group was supposed to defend against the simulated attack. On the surface, it looks like a fairly standard training exercise. The trail group, however, lit up the wrong people, and when they shifted radar modes to the attack setting, one of the Taiwanese pilots must have thought he was under attack and so he pickled off a missile. Then his wingman did the same. Zap! Right here, a B-7 eats a Slammer, but this one evades it – damned lucky for him – and he gets off a missile of his own. Then everybody starts shooting. This F-16 jinks around one but walks right into another – see here, the pilot ejects, and we think he survived. But this element launches four missiles, and one of those acquires this airliner. Must have just barely made it all the way. We've checked the range, and it's actually two miles over what we thought the missile could do. By the time it caught up and hit, the fighters have all turned back, the PRC guys because they were probably bingo-fuel, and the ROC guys because they were Winchester – out of missiles. All in all, it was a fairly sloppy engagement on both sides.'

'You're saying it was a goof?' This came from Tony Bretano.

'It certainly looks that way, except for one thing –'

'Why carry live missiles on an exercise?' Ryan said.

'Close, Mr President. The ROC pilots, sure, they're carrying white ones because they see the whole PRC exercise as a threat –'

'White ones?' It was Bretano again.

'Excuse me, Mr Secretary. White missiles are war shots. Exercise missiles are usually painted blue. The PRC guys, though, why carry heat-seekers? In situations like this, we usually don't, because you can't turn them off – once they go they're entirely on their own, fire-and-forget, we call it. One other thing. All the birds fired at the F-16s were radar-homers. This one, the one that went for the airliner, seems to be the *only* heat-seeker that was launched. I don't much like the smell of that.'

'Deliberate act?' Jack asked quietly.

'That is a possibility, Mr President. The whole show looks just like a screwup, classic case. A couple fighter jocks get really hyped on something, you have an instant furball, some people get killed, and we'll never be able to prove otherwise, but if you look at this two-plane element, I think they were aiming for the airliner all along – unless they took it for a ROC fighter, and I don't buy that –'

'Why?'

'It was heading the wrong way all the time,' Admiral Jackson answered.

'Buck fever,' Secretary Bretano offered.

'Why not engage people heading right for you instead of somebody heading away? Mr Secretary, I'm a fighter pilot. I don't buy it. If I'm in an unexpected combat situation, first thing I do is identify the threats to me and shoot 'em right in the lips.'

'How many deaths?' Jack asked bleakly.

Ben Goodley handled that one: 'News reports say over a

hundred. There are survivors, but we don't have any kind of count yet. And we should expect that there were some Americans aboard. A lot of business goes on between Hong Kong and Taiwan.'

'Options?'

'Before we do anything, Mr President, we need to know if any of our people are involved. We only have one carrier anywhere close, the *Eisenhower* battle group on the way to Australia for SOUTHERN CUP. But it's a good bet that this won't exactly help things out between Beijing and Taipei.'

'We'll need some kind of press release,' Arnie told the President.

'We need to know if we lost any citizens first,' Ryan said. 'If we did . . . well, what do we do, demand an explanation?'

'They'll say it was a mistake,' Jackson repeated. 'They might even blame the Taiwanese for shooting first and starting it, then disclaim all responsibility.'

'But you don't buy it, Robby?'

'No, Jack – excuse me, no, Mr President, I don't think so. I want to go over the tapes with a few people, to back-check me some. Maybe I'm wrong . . . but I don't think so. Fighter pilots are fighter pilots. The only reason to shoot the guy who's running away instead of the guy who's closing in is because you want to.'

'Move the *Ike* group north?' Bretano wondered.

'Get me contingency plans to do just that,' the President said.

'That leaves the Indian Ocean uncovered, sir,' Jackson pointed out. '*Carl Vinson* is most of the way home to Norfolk now. *John Stennis* and *Enterprise* are still in the yard at Pearl, and we do not have a deployable carrier in the Pacific. We're out of carriers on that whole half of the world, and we'll need a month at best to move another one in from LantFleet.'

Ryan turned to Ed Foley. 'What are the chances this could blow all the way up?'

'Taiwan's going to be pretty unhappy about this. We have shots fired and people dead. National-flag airline clobbered. Countries tend to be protective of those,' the DCI observed. 'It's possible.'

'Intentions?' Goodley asked the DCI.

'If Admiral Jackson is correct – I'm not ready to buy into

that yet, by the way,' Ed Foley added for Robby's benefit. He got an understanding nod. 'Then we have something going on, but what it is, I don't know. Better for everybody if this was an accident. I can't say I like the idea of pulling the carrier out of the Indian Ocean with the developing situation in the Persian Gulf.'

'What's the worst thing that can happen between the PRC and Taiwan?' Bretano asked, annoyed that he had to ask the question at all. He was still too new in his job to be as effective as his President needed.

'Mr Secretary, the People's Republic has nuclear-tipped missiles, enough to turn Formosa into a cinder, but we have reason to believe that the Republic of China has them too and –'

'Roughly twenty,' Foley interrupted. 'And those F-16s can one-way a couple all the way to Beijing if they want. They can't destroy the People's Republic, but twenty thermo-nuclear weapons will knock their economy back at least ten years, maybe twenty. The PRC does not want that to happen. They're not crazy, Admiral. Keep it conventional, okay?'

'Very well, sir. The PRC does *not* have the ability to invade Taiwan. They lack the necessary amphibious assets to move large numbers of troops for a forced-entry assault. So what happens if things blow up anyway? Most likely scenario is a nasty air and sea battle, but one that leads to no resolution, since neither side can finish off the other. That also means a shooting war astride one of the world's most important trade routes, with all sorts of adverse diplomatic consequences for all the players. I can't see the purpose in doing this intentionally. Just too destructive to be deliberate policy ... I think.' He shrugged. It didn't make sense, but neither did a deliberate attack on a harmless airliner – and he'd just told his audience that *had* probably been deliberate.

'And we have large trade relationships with both,' the President noted. 'We want to prevent that, don't we? I'm afraid it's looking like we have to move that carrier, Robby. Let's get some options put together, and let's *try* to figure out what the hell the PRC might be up to.'

Clark woke up first, feeling quite miserable. But that wasn't allowed under the circumstances. Ten minutes later, he was shaved, dressed, and heading out the door, leaving Chavez in bed. Ding didn't speak the language anyway.

'Morning walk?' It was the guy who'd brought them in from the airport.

'I could use a stretch,' John admitted. 'And you are?'

'Marcel Lefevre.'

'Station chief?' John asked bluntly.

'Actually, I am the commercial attaché,' the Frenchman replied – meaning, *yes*. 'You mind if I come along?'

'Not at all,' Clark replied, surprising his companion as they headed for the door. 'Just wanted to take a walk. Any markets around here?'

'Yes, I will show you.'

Ten minutes later, they were in a street of commerce. Two Iranian shadows were fifty feet behind them, and obvious about it, though they did nothing more than to observe.

The sounds brought it all back. Clark's Farsi was not all that impressive, especially since it was over fifteen years since he'd practiced it, but though his speech might not have been terribly good, his hearing clicked back in, soon catching the chatter and bargaining as the two Westerners passed stalls on both sides of the street.

'How are food prices?'

'Fairly high,' Lefevre answered. 'Especially with all the supplies they shipped to Iraq. A few grumbles about that.'

There was something lacking, John saw, after a few minutes of contemplation. Passing half a block of food stalls, they were now in another area – gold, always a popular trade item in this part of the world. People were buying and selling. But there wasn't the enthusiasm he remembered from before. He looked at the stalls as he passed, trying to figure what it was.

'Something for your wife?' Lefevre asked.

Clark tried an unconvincing smile. 'Oh, you never know. Anniversary coming up soon.' He stopped to look at a necklace.

'Where are you from?' the dealer asked.

'America,' John replied, also in English. The man had picked out his nationality at once, probably from his clothes, and taken the chance to speak in that language.

'We do not see many Americans here.'

'Too bad. In my younger days I traveled here quite a lot.'
It was actually rather a nice necklace, and on checking the price tag and doing the mental calculation, the cost was reasonable as hell. And he *did* have an anniversary approaching.

'Perhaps someday that will change,' the goldsmith said.

'There are many differences between my country and yours,' John observed sadly. Yes, he *could* afford it, and as usual he had plenty of cash with him. One nice thing about American currency was that it was damned near universally accepted.

'Things change,' the man said next.

'Things have changed,' John agreed. He looked at a slightly more expensive necklace. It wasn't any problem handling them. One thing about Islamic countries, they had a way of discouraging thieves. 'There's so little smiling here, and this is a market street.'

'You have two men following you.'

'Really? Well, I'm not breaking any laws, am I?' Clark asked with some obvious concern.

'No, you are not.' But the man was nervous.

'This one,' John said, handing it to the goldsmith.

'How will you pay?'

'American dollars, is that okay?'

'Yes, and the price is nine hundred of your dollars.'

It required all of his control not to show surprise. Even in a New York wholesale shop, this necklace would have been triple that, and while he wasn't quite prepared to spend that much, haggling was part of the fun of shopping in this part of the world. He'd figured that he could talk the guy down to maybe fifteen hundred, still a considerable bargain. Had he heard the man properly?

'Nine hundred?'

An emphatic finger pointed right at his heart. 'Eight hundred, not a dollar less – you wish to ruin me?' he added loudly.

'You bargain hard.' Clark adopted a defensive posture for the benefit of the watchers, who were coming closer.

'You are an unbeliever! You expect charity? This is a fine necklace, and I hope you will give it to your honorable wife and not a lesser, debauched woman!'

Clark figured he'd put the man in enough danger. He pulled out his wallet and counted off the bills, handing them over.

'You pay me too much, I am not a thief!' The goldsmith handed one back.

Seven hundred dollars for this?

'Excuse me, I meant no insult,' John said, pocketing the necklace, which the man not quite tossed to him without a case.

'We are not all barbarians,' the dealer said quietly, abruptly turning his back a split-second later. Clark and Lefevre walked to the end of the street and headed to the right. They moved quickly, forcing their tail to follow.

'What the hell?' the CIA officer observed. He hadn't expected anything like that to happen.

'Yes. The enthusiasm for the regime has abated somewhat. What you saw is representative. That was nicely done, Monsieur Clark. How long in the Agency?'

'Long enough that I don't like being surprised that much. I believe your word is *merde*.'

'So, is it for your wife?'

John nodded. 'Yeah. Will he get into any trouble?'

'Unlikely,' Lefevre said. 'He may have lost money on the exchange, Clark. An interesting gesture, was it not?'

'Let's get back. I have a Cabinet secretary to wake up.' They were back in fifteen minutes. John went right to his room.

'What's the weather like outside, Mr C.?' Clark reached into his pocket and tossed something across the room. Chavez caught it. 'Heavy.'

'What do you suppose it costs, Domingo?'

'Looks like twenty-one carat, feels like it too ... coupla grand, easy.'

'Would you believe seven hundred?'

'You related to the guy, John?' Chavez asked with a laugh. The laugh stopped. 'I thought they didn't like us here?'

'Things change,' John said quietly, quoting the goldsmith.

'How bad was it?' Cathy asked.

'One hundred four survivors, it says, some pretty beat up, ninety confirmed dead, about thirty still unaccounted for, meaning they're dead, too, just haven't identified the body parts yet,' Jack said, reading the dispatch just brought to the bedroom door by Agent Raman. 'Sixteen Americans in the survivor category. Five dead. Nine unknown and presumed dead. Christ, there were forty PRC citizens aboard.' He shook his head.

'How come – if they don't get along –'

'Why do they do so much business? They do, and that's a fact, honey. They spit and snarl at each other like alley cats, but they need each other, too.'

'What will we do?' his wife asked.

'I don't know yet. We're saving the press release for tomorrow morning, when we have more information. How the hell am I supposed to sleep on a night like this?' the President of the United States asked. 'We have fourteen dead Americans halfway around the world from here. I was supposed to protect them, wasn't I? I'm not supposed to let people kill our citizens.'

'People die every day, Jack,' the First Lady pointed out.

'Not from air-to-air missiles.' Ryan put the dispatch on his night table and switched off the light, wondering when sleep would come, wondering how the meeting would go in Tehran.

It started with handshakes. A foreign ministry official met them outside the building. The French ambassador handled introductions, and everyone swiftly moved inside, the better to avoid the coverage of a TV camera, though none appeared to be in evidence on the street. Clark and Chavez played their parts, standing close to their principal, but not too close, looking around nervously, as they were supposed to do.

Secretary Adler followed the official, with everyone else in trail. The French ambassador stopped in the anteroom with the others, as Adler and his guide went all the way into the rather modest official office of the UIR's spiritual leader.

'I welcome you in peace,' Daryaei said, rising from his chair to greet his guest. He spoke through an interpreter. It was a normal ploy for such meetings. It made for greater precision in communications – and also if something went badly wrong, it could be said that the interpreter had made the mistake, which gave both sides a convenient way out. 'Allah's blessing on this meeting.'

'Thank you for receiving me on such short notice,' Adler said, taking his seat.

'You have come far. Your journey was a good one?' Daryaei inquired pleasantly. The entire ritual would be pleasant, or at least the beginning of it.

'It was uneventful,' Adler allowed. He struggled not to yawn or show fatigue. Three cups of strong European coffee helped, though they made his stomach a little jumpy. Diplomats in serious meetings were supposed to act like surgeons in an operating room, and he had long practice in showing none of his emotions, jumpy stomach or not.

'I regret that we cannot show you more of our city. There is so much history and beauty here.' Both men waited for the words to be translated. The translator was thirtyish, male, intense, and, Adler saw . . . afraid of Daryaei? he wondered. He was probably a ministry official, dressed in a suit that needed a little pressing, but the Ayatollah was in robes, emphasizing his national and clerical identity. Mahmoud Haji was grave, but not hostile in demeanor – and, strangely, he seemed totally lacking in curiosity.

'Perhaps the next time I visit.'

A friendly nod. 'Yes.' This was said in English, which reminded Adler that the man understood his visitor's language. Nothing all that unusual in form, SecState noted.

'It has been a long time since there were direct contacts between your country and mine, certainly at this level.'

'This is true, but we welcome such contacts. How may I be of service to you, Secretary Adler?'

'If you do not object, I would like to discuss stability in this region.'

'Stability?' Daryaei asked innocently. 'What do you mean?'

'The establishment of the United Islamic Republic has created the largest country in the region. This is a matter of concern to some.'

'I would say that we have improved stability. Was not the Iraqi regime the destabilizing influence? Did not Iraq start two aggressive wars? We certainly did no such thing.'

'This is true,' Adler agreed.

'Islam is a religion of peace and brotherhood,' Daryaei went on, speaking as the teacher he'd been for years. *Probably a*

789

tough one, Adler thought to himself, *with steel under the gentle voice.*

'That is also true, but in the world of men the rules of religion are not always followed by those who call themselves religious,' the American pointed out.

'Other countries do not accept the rule of God as we do. Only in the recognition of that rule can men hope to find peace and justice. That means more than saying the words. One must also live the words.'

And thank you for the Sunday school lesson, Adler thought, with a respectful nod. *Then why the hell do you support Hezbollah?*

'My country wishes no more than peace in this region – throughout the world, for that matter.'

'As is indeed the wish of Allah, as revealed to us through the Prophet.'

He was sticking to the script, Adler saw. Once upon a time, President Jimmy Carter had dispatched an emissary to visit this man's boss, Khomeini, at his exile home in France. The Shah had been in deep political trouble then, and the opposition had been sounded out, just to hedge America's bets. The emissary had come home after the meeting to tell his President that Khomeini was a 'saint.' Carter had accepted the report at face value, and brought about the removal of Mohammad Reza Pahlavi, allowing the 'saint' to supplant him.

Oops.

The next administration had dealt with the same man and gotten nothing more for it than a scandal and world ridicule.

Ouch.

Those were mistakes Adler was determined not to repeat.

'It is also one of my country's principles that international borders are to be honored. Respect for territorial integrity is the sine qua non of regional and global stability.'

'Secretary Adler, all men are brothers, this is the will of Allah. Brothers may quarrel from time to time, but to make war is hateful to God. In any case, I find the substance of your remarks somewhat unsettling. You seem to suggest that we have unfriendly intentions to our neighbors. Why do you say such a thing?'

'Excuse me, I think you misunderstand. I make no such

suggestions. I have come merely to discuss mutual concerns.'

'Your country and its associates and allies depend on this region for their economic health. We will not do harm to that. You need our oil. We need the things that oil money can buy. Ours is a trading culture. You know that. Our culture is also Islamic, and it is a source of great pain to me that the West seems never to appreciate the substance of our Faith. We are not barbarians, despite what your Jewish friends may say. We have, in fact, no religious quarrel with the Jews. Their patriarch, Abraham, came from this region. They were the first to proclaim the true God, and truly there should be peace between us.'

'It pleases me to hear those words. How may we bring this peace about?' Adler asked, wondering when the last time had been that someone had tried to drop a whole olive *tree* on his head.

'With time, and with talk. Perhaps it is better that we should have direct contacts. They, too, are people of trade in addition to being people of faith.'

Adler wondered what he meant by that. Direct contacts with Israel. Was it an offer, or a sop to toss at the American government?

'And your Islamic neighbors?'

'We share the Faith. We share oil. We share a culture. We are already one in so many ways.'

Outside, Clark, Chavez, and the ambassador sat quietly. The office personnel studiously ignored them, after having provided the usual refreshments. The security people stood about, not looking at the visitors, but not looking away from them, either. For Chavez it was a chance to meet a new people. He noted that the setting was old-fashioned, and oddly shabby, as though the building hadn't changed much since the departure of the previous government – a long time ago, he reminded himself – and it wasn't so much that things were run down as that they weren't modern. There was a real tension here, though. That he could feel in the air. An American office staff would have looked at him with curiosity. The six people in this room did not. Why?

Clark had expected that. Being ignored didn't surprise him. He and Ding were here as security troops, and they were just furniture, unworthy of notice. The people here would be trusted aides and underlings, faithful to their boss because they had to be. They had a measure of power because of him. These visitors would either ratify that power in the international sense or threaten it, and while that was important to their individual well-being, they could no more affect it than they could affect the weather, and so they just tuned their visitors out, except for the security pukes, who were trained to view everyone as a threat even though protocol disallowed them from the physical intimidation which they would have preferred to show.

For the ambassador it was one more exercise in diplomacy, conversations in carefully chosen words selected to show little on the one hand, and to uncover much on the other. He could guess at what was being said by both sides. He could even guess at the real meaning of the words. It was their truth that interested him. What *did* Daryaei have planned? The ambassador and his country hoped for peace in the region, and so he and his colleagues had prepped Adler to feel open to that possibility, while at the same time not knowing how this would really go. An interesting man, Daryaei. A man of God who had surely murdered the Iraqi President. A man of peace and justice who ruled his country with an iron hand. A man of mercy who clearly had his own personal staff terrified of him. You had only to look around the room to see that. A modern, Middle Eastern Richelieu? There was a novel thought, the Frenchman joked to himself, behind an impassive face. He'd have to run that idea past his ministry later today. And in with him right now was a brand-new American minister. He allowed for the fact that Adler had a fine reputation as a career diplomat, but was he good enough for *this* task?

'Why do we discuss this? Why should I have territorial ambitions?' Daryaei asked, almost pleasantly, but telegraphing his irritation. 'My people desire only peace. There has been too much strife here. For all my life I have studied and taught the Faith, and now, finally, in the closing days of my life, there *is* peace.'

'We have no more wish for this region than that, except perhaps to reestablish our friendship with your country.'

'On that we should talk further. I thank your country for not hindering the removal of trade sanctions against the former country of Iraq. Perhaps that is a beginning. At the same time, we would prefer that America did not interfere in the internal affairs of our neighbors.'

'We are committed to the integrity of Israel,' Adler pointed out.

'Israel is not, strictly speaking, a neighbor,' Daryaei replied. 'But if Israel can live in peace, then we can also live in peace.'

The guy was good, Adler thought. He wasn't revealing very much, just denying everything. He made no policy statements aside from the usual protestations of peaceful intent. Every chief of state did that, though not many invoked the name of God so much. Peace. Peace. Peace.

Except that Adler didn't believe him for an instant on the subject of Israel. If he'd had peaceful intentions, he would have told Jerusalem first, the better to get them on his side for dealing with Washington. Israel had been the unnamed middleman for the arms-for-hostages disaster, and they'd been suckered, too.

'I hope that is a foundation upon which we can build.'

'If your country treats my country with respect, then we can talk. Then we can discuss an improvement in relations.'

'I will tell my President that.'

'Your country, too, has endured much sorrow of late. I wish him the strength to heal your nation's wounds.'

'Thank you.' Both men stood. Handshakes were exchanged again, and Daryaei conducted Adler to the door.

Clark noted the way the office staff jumped to their feet. Daryaei conveyed Adler to the outer door, took his hand one more time, and let the man leave with his escorts. Two minutes later, they were in their official cars and on the way directly to the airport.

'I wonder how that went?' John asked nobody in particular. Everyone else wondered the same thing, but not another word was spoken. Thirty minutes later, aided by their official escort, the cars were back at Mehrabad International, and pulling up to the air force part of the facility, where their French jet was waiting.

There had to be a departure ceremony, too. The French

ambassador talked with Adler for several minutes, all the while holding his hand in an extended farewell shake. With ample UIR-ian security, there was nothing for Clark and Chavez to do but look around, as they were supposed to do. In plain view were six fighter aircraft, with maintenance people working on them. The mechanics walked in and out of a large hangar that had doubtless been built under the Shah. Ding looked inside, and nobody made a fuss about it. Another airplane was in there, seemingly half disassembled. An engine was sitting on a cart, with another team of people tinkering with it.

'Chicken coops, you believe it?' Chavez asked.

'What's that?' Clark said, looking the other way.

'Check it out, Mr C.'

John turned. Stacked against the far wall of the hangar were rows of wire cages, about the size of those used for moving poultry. Hundreds of them. Funny thing for an air force base, he thought.

On the other side of the airport, the Movie Star watched the last of his team board a flight to Vienna. He happened to gaze across the expansive vista to see the private jets on the far side, with some people and cars close to one of them. He wondered briefly what that was about. Probably some government function. So was what he had planned, of course, but one that would never be acknowledged. The Austrian Airlines flight pulled away from the gate on time, and would head off just behind the business jet, or whatever it was. Then he walked to another gate to board his own flight.

40

OPENINGS

Most Americans woke up to learn what their President already knew. Eleven American citizens were dead, with three more unaccounted for, in an airliner disaster on the opposite side of the world. A local TV crew had made it to the airport just in time, having learned of the emergency from a helpful source at the terminal. Their video showed little more than a distant fireball erupting into the sky, followed by some closer shots that were so typical that they, too, might have come from anywhere. Ten fire trucks surrounded the burning wreckage, blasting it with foam and water, both too late to save anyone. Ambulances scurried about. Some people, obvious survivors, wandered in the haze of shock and disorientation. Others, their faces blackened, staggered into the arms of rescue personnel. There were wives without husbands, parents without children, and the sort of chaos that always appeared dramatic but which passed on nothing in the way of explanation, even as it cried out for action of some kind.

The Republic of China's government issued a blistering statement about air piracy, then requested an emergency meeting of the UN Security Council. Beijing issued its own statement minutes later, stating that its aircraft, on a peaceful training exercise, had been attacked entirely without provocation, then returned fire in self-defense. Beijing totally disavowed any involvement in the damage to the airliner, and blamed the entire episode on their rebellious province.

'So, what else have we turned up?' Ryan asked Admiral Jackson at seven-thirty.

'We went over both tapes for about two hours. I brought in a few fighter pilots I've worked with, and a pair of Air Force guys, and we kicked it around some. Number one, the ChiComs –'

'Not supposed to call them that, Robby,' the President observed.

'Old habit, sorry. The *gentlemen* of the PRC – hey, they knew we had ships there. The electronic signature of an Aegis ship is like Mount St Helens with an attitude, okay? And the capabilities of the ships ain't exactly a secret. They've been in service for almost twenty years. So they knew we were watching, and they knew we'd see everything. Let's keep that one in mind.'

'Keep going,' Jack told his friend.

'Number two, we have a spook team on the *Chandler*, listening in on radio chatter. We have translated the voice transmissions of the Chinese fighter pilots. Quoting now – this is thirty seconds into the engagement – "I have him, I have him, taking the shot." Okay, the time stamp on that is exactly the same as the heat-seeker launch on the airliner.

'Number three, every driver I talked to said the same as I did – why shoot at an airliner on the edge of your missile range when you have fighters in your face? Jack, this one smells – real bad, man.

'Unfortunately, we can't prove the voice transmission came from the fighter that launched on the Airbus, but it is my opinion, and that of my pals across the river, that this was a deliberate act. They tried to splash that airliner on purpose,' the Pentagon's director of operations concluded. 'We're lucky anybody got off at all.'

'Admiral,' Arnie van Damm asked, 'could you take that into a court of law?'

'Sir, I'm not a lawyer. I'm an airplane driver. I don't have to prove things for a living, but I'm telling you, it's a hundred-to-one against that we're wrong on this.'

'I can't say this in front of the cameras, though,' Ryan said, checking his watch. He'd have to do makeup in a few minutes. 'If they did it on purpose –'

'No "if," Jack, okay?'

'Damn it, Robby, I heard you the first time!' Ryan snapped. He paused and took a breath. 'I can't accuse a sovereign country of an act of war without absolute proof. Next, okay, fine, they *did* do it on purpose, and they did it with the knowledge that we'd know they did. What's that *mean!*'

Jack's national security team had had a long night. Goodley took the lead. 'Hard to say, Mr President.'

'Are they making a move on Taiwan?' the President asked.

'They *can't*,' Jackson said, shaking off his Commander-in-Chief's tantrum. 'They do not have the physical ability to invade. There is no sign of unusual activity in their ground forces in this area, just the stuff they've been doing in the northwest that has the Russians so annoyed. So from a military point of view the answer is no.'

'Airborne invasion?' Ed Foley asked. Robby shook his head.

'They don't have the airlift capacity, and even if they tried, the ROC has enough air-defense assets to turn it into early duck season. They could stage an air-sea battle like I told you last night, but it'll cost them ships and planes – *for what purpose?*' the J-3 asked.

'So did they splash an airliner to test *us?*' POTUS wondered. 'That doesn't make sense, either.'

'If you say "me" instead of "us," that's a possibility,' the DCI said quietly.

'Come on, Director,' Goodley objected. 'There were two hundred people on that plane, and they must have thought they'd kill them all.'

'Let's not be too naive, Ben,' Foley observed tolerantly. 'They don't share our sentimentality for human life over there, do they?'

'No, but –'

Ryan interrupted: 'Okay, hold it. We think this was a deliberate act, but we don't have positive proof, and we have no idea what its purpose might have been – and if we don't, I can't call it a deliberate act, right?' There were nods. 'Fine, now in fifteen minutes I have to go down to the Press Room and deliver this statement and then the reporters will ask me questions, and the only answers I can give them will be lies.'

'That about sums it up, Mr President,' van Damm confirmed.

'Well, isn't that just *great*,' Jack snarled. 'And Beijing will know, or at least suspect, that I'm lying.'

'Possible, but not certain on that,' Ed Foley observed.

'I'm not good at lying,' Ryan told them.

'Learn how,' the chief of staff advised. 'Quickly.'

*　　*　　*

There was no talking on the flight from Tehran to Paris. Adler took a comfortable seat in the back, got out a legal pad, and wrote the whole way, using his trained memory to reconstruct the conversation, then added a series of personal observations on everything from Daryaei's physical appearance to the clutter on his desk. After that, he examined the notes for an hour, and started making analytical comments. In the process, he wore down half a dozen pencils. The layover in Paris lasted less than an hour, enough for Adler to spend a little time with Claude again and for his escorts to have a quick drink. Then it was off again in their Air Force VC-20B.

'How'd it go?' John asked.

Adler had to remind himself that Clark was on the SNIE team, and not just a gun-toting SPO.

'First, what did you find out on your walk?'

The senior CIA officer reached in his pocket and handed the Secretary of State a gold necklace.

'Does this mean we're engaged?' Adler asked, with a surprised chuckle.

Clark gestured to his partner. 'No, sir. He's engaged.'

Now that they were aloft, the cabin crewman who ran the communications panel turned on his equipment. The fax machine started chirping at once.

'. . . we have confirmed eleven American deaths, with three more US citizens missing. Four of the American survivors are injured and are being treated in local hospitals. That concludes my opening statement,' the President told them.

'Mister President!' thirty voices called at once.

'One at a time, please.' Jack pointed to a woman in the front row.

'Beijing claims that Taiwan shot first. Can we confirm that?'

'We are examining some information, but it takes a while to figure these things out, and until such time as we have definitive information, I do not think it proper to draw any conclusions at this time.'

'But both sides traded shots, didn't they?' she asked as a follow-up.

'That would seem to be the case, yes.'

'So then do we know whose missile hit the Airbus?'

'As I said, we are still examining the data.' *Keep it short, Jack*, he told himself. And that wasn't quite a lie, was it? 'Yes?' He pointed to another reporter.

'Mr President, with so many American citizens lost, what action will you be taking to ensure this does not happen again?' At least this one he could answer truthfully.

'We are examining options right now. Beyond that, I have nothing to say, except that we call on both Chinas to step back and think about their actions. The loss of innocent life is in the interest of no country. Military exercises there have been ongoing for some time now, and the resulting tension is not helpful to regional stability.'

'So you're asking both countries to suspend their exercises?'

'We're going to ask them to consider that, yes.'

'Mr President,' said John Plumber, 'this is your first foreign policy crisis and . . .'

Ryan looked down at the elderly reporter and wanted to observe that his first *domestic* crisis had been of *his* making, but you couldn't afford to make enemies of the press, and you could only make friends with them if they liked you – an altogether unlikely possibility, he'd come to understand.

'Mr Plumber, before you do anything, you have to find out the facts. We're working on that just as hard as we can. I had my national security team in this morning – '

'But not Secretary Adler,' Plumber pointed out. Good reporter that he was, he'd checked the official cars on West Executive Drive. 'Why wasn't he here?'

'He'll be in later today,' Ryan dodged.

'Where is he now?' Plumber persisted.

Ryan just shook his head. 'Can we limit this to just one topic? It's a little early in the morning for so many questions, and as you pointed out, I *do* have a situation to deal with, Mr Plumber.'

'And he is your principal foreign policy adviser, sir. Where is he now?'

'Next question,' the President said tersely. He got about what he deserved from Barry of CNN:

'Mr President, a moment ago you said *both* Chinas.

Sir, does this signal a change in our China policy, and if so –'

It was just after eight in the evening in Beijing, and things were good. He could see it on TV. How strange to watch a political figure so singularly lacking in charm and adroitness, especially an American. Zhang Han San lit a cigarette and congratulated himself. He'd done it again. There had been a danger in staging the 'exercise,' most particularly the recent air sorties – but then the Republic's aviators had so kindly obliged by shooting first, just as he'd hoped they would, and now there was a crisis which he could control precisely, and end it at any time, merely by recalling his own forces to their bases. He'd force America to react not so much by action as by inaction – and then someone else would take the lead in provoking its new President. He had no idea what Daryaei had in mind. An assassination attempt, perhaps? Something else? All he had to do was watch, as he was doing now, and reap the harvest when the opportunity arose, which it surely would. America couldn't stay lucky forever. Not with this young fool in the White House.

'Barry, one country calls itself the People's Republic of China, and the other calls itself the Republic of China. I have to call them something, don't I?' Ryan asked testily. *Oh, shit, have I done it* again?
   'Yes, Mr President, but –'
   'But we probably have fourteen American citizens dead, and this is not a time to worry about semantics.' *There, take that.*
   'What are we going to do?' a female voice demanded.
   'First, we're going to try to find out what took place. *Then* we can start thinking about reactions.'
   'But *why* don't we know yet?'
   'Because as much as we would like to know everything that takes place in the world every minute, it's simply impossible.'
   'Is that why your administration is radically increasing the size of the CIA?'
   'As I have said before, we do not discuss intelligence matters, ever.'

'Mr President, there are published reports that –'

'There are published reports that UFOs land here on a regular basis,' Ryan shot back. 'Do you believe *that*, too?'

The room actually went quiet for a moment. It wasn't every day that you saw a President lose his temper. They loved it.

'Ladies and gentlemen, I regret the fact that I cannot answer all your questions to your satisfaction. In fact, I am asking some of the same questions myself, but correct answers take time. If I have to wait for the information, so do you,' he said, trying to get the news conference back on track.

'Mr President, a man who looks very much like the former Chairman of the Soviet KGB has appeared on live television and –' The reporter stopped, as he saw Ryan's face glow red under the makeup. He expected another blowup, but it didn't happen. The President's knuckles went ivory-white on the lectern, and he took a breath.

'Please go on with your question, Sam.'

'And that gentleman said that he is who he is. Now, sir, the cat is well out of the bag, and I think my question is a legitimate one.'

'I haven't heard a question yet, Sam.'

'Is he who he says he is?'

'You don't need me to tell you that.'

'Mr President, this event, this . . . operation has great international significance. At some point, intelligence operations, sensitive though they may well be, have a serious effect on our foreign relations. At that point, the American people want to know what such things are all about.'

'Sam, I will say this one last time: I will never, not ever, discuss intelligence matters. I am here this morning to inform our citizens of a tragic and so far unexplained incident in which over a hundred people, including fourteen American citizens, have lost their lives. This government will do its utmost to determine what took place, and then to decide upon a proper course of action.'

'Very well, Mr President. Do we have a one-China policy, or a two-China policy?'

'We have made no changes.'

'Might a change result from this incident?'

'I will not speculate on something so important as that. And now, with your permission, I have to get back to work.'

'Thank you, Mr President!' Jack heard on his way out the door. Just around the corner was a well-hidden gun cabinet. POTUS slammed it with his hand hard enough to rattle a few of the Uzis inside.

'God damn it!' he swore on the fifty-yard walk back to his office.

'Mr President?' Ryan spun around. It was Robby, holding his briefcase. It seemed so out of place for an aviator to be toting one of those.

'I owe you an apology,' Jack said, before Robby could get another word out. 'Sorry I blew up.'

Admiral Jackson popped his friend on the arm. 'Next time we play golf, it's a buck a hole, and if you're going to get mad, do it at me, not them, okay? I've seen your temper before, man. Dial it back. A commander can only get pissed in front of the troops for show – leadership technique, we call it – not for real. Yelling at staff is something else. I'm staff,' Robby said. 'Yell at me.'

'Yeah, I know. Keep me posted and –'

'Jack?'

'Yeah, Rob?'

'You're doing fine, just keep it cool.'

'I'm not supposed to let people kill Americans, Robby. That's not what I'm here for.' His hands balled into fists again.

'Shit happens, Mr President. If you think you can stop it all, you're just kidding yourself. And I don't have to tell you that. You're not God, Jack, but you are a pretty good guy doing a pretty good job. We'll have more information for you as soon as we can put it together.'

'When things settle down, how about another golf lesson?'

'I am yours to command.' The two friends shook hands. It wasn't enough for either of them at this moment, but it had to do. Jackson headed for the door, and Ryan turned back toward his office. 'Mrs Sumter!' he called on the way in. Maybe a smoke would help.

'So what gives, Mr Secretary?' Chavez asked. The three-page fax off the secure satellite link told them everything the President had. He'd let them read it, too.

'I don't know,' Adler admitted. 'Chavez, that thesis paper you told me about?'

'What about it, sir?'

'You should have waited to write it. Now you know what it's like up here. Like playing dodge ball as a kid, except it ain't a rubber ball we're trying to dodge, is it?' The Secretary of State tucked his notes into his briefcase and waved to the Air Force sergeant who was supposed to look after them. He wasn't as cute as the French attendant had been.

'Yes, sir?'

'Did Claude leave us anything?'

'A couple of bottles from the Loire Valley,' the NCO replied, with a smile.

'You want to uncork one and get some glasses out?'

'Cards?' John Clark asked.

'No, I think I'm going to have a glass or two, and then I'm going to get a little sleep. Looks like I have another trip laid on,' SecState told them.

'Beijing.' No surprise, John thought.

'It won't be Philadelphia,' Scott said, as the bottle and glasses arrived. Thirty minutes later, all three men pushed their seat backs down all the way. The sergeant closed the window shades for them.

This time Clark got some sleep, but Chavez did not. There was truth in what Adler had remarked to him. His thesis had savagely attacked turn-of-the-century statesmen for their inability to see beyond immediate problems. Now Ding did know a little better. It was hard to tell the difference between an immediate tactical problem and a truly strategic one when you were dodging the bullets on a minute-to-minute basis, and history books couldn't fully convey the temper, the *feel* of the times on which they supposedly reported. Not all of it. They also gave the wrong impression of people. Secretary Adler, now snoring in his leather reclining seat, was a career diplomat, Chavez reminded himself, and he'd earned the trust and respect of the President – a man he himself deeply respected. He wasn't stupid. He wasn't venal. But he was merely a man, and men made mistakes . . . and great men made big ones. Someday some historian would write about this trip they'd just taken, but would that historian really know what it had been like – and, not knowing, how could he really comment on what had taken place?

What's going on? Ding asked himself. Iran gets real frisky and knocks over Iraq and starts a new country, and just as America is trying to deal with that, something else happens. An event minor in the great scheme of things, perhaps – but you never knew that until it was all over, did you? How could you tell? That was always the problem. Statesmen over the centuries had made mistakes because when you were stuck in the middle of things, you couldn't step outside and take a more detached look. That's what they were paid to do, but it *was* pretty hard, wasn't it? He had just finished his master's thesis, and he'd get hooded later this year, and officially proclaimed an expert in international relations. But that was a lie, Ding thought, settling back into his own seat. A flippant observation he'd once made on another long flight came back to him. All too often international relations was simply one country fucking another. Domingo Chavez, soon-to-be master's in international relations, smiled at the thought, but it wasn't very funny, really. Not when people got killed. Especially not when he and Mr C. were front-line worker-bees. Something happening in the Middle East. Something else happening with China ... four thousand miles away, wasn't it? Could those two things be related? What if they were? But how could you tell? Historians assumed that people *could* tell if only they'd been smart enough. But historians didn't have to do the work ...

'Not his best performance,' Plumber said, sipping his iced tea.

'Twelve hours, not even that much, to get a handle on something halfway 'round the world, John,' Holtzman suggested.

It was a typical Washington restaurant, pseudo-French with cute little tassels on a menu listing overpriced dishes of mediocre quality – but, then, both men were on expense accounts.

'He's supposed to handle himself better,' Plumber observed.

'You're complaining that he can't lie effectively?'

'That's one of the things a President is supposed to do –'

'And when we catch him at it . . .' Holtzman didn't have to go on.

'Who ever said it was supposed to be an easy job, Bob?'

'Sometimes I wonder if we're really supposed to make the job harder.' But Plumber didn't bite.

'Where do you suppose Adler is?' the NBC correspondent wondered aloud.

'That was a good question this morning,' the *Post* reporter granted, lifting his glass. 'I have somebody looking into that.'

'So do we. All Ryan had to do was say he was preparing to meet with the PRC ambassador. That would have covered things nicely.'

'But it would have been a lie.'

'It would have been the *right* lie. Bob, that's the game. The government tries to do things in secret, and we try to find out. Ryan likes this secrecy stuff a little too much.'

'But when we burn him for it, whose agenda are we following?'

'What do you mean?'

'Come on, John. Ed Kealty leaked all that stuff to you. I don't have to be a rocket scientist to figure that one out. Everybody knows it.' Bob picked at his salad.

'It's all true, isn't it?'

'Yes, it is,' Holtzman admitted. 'And there's a lot more.'

'Really? Well, I know you had a story working.' He didn't add that he was sorry to have scooped the younger man, mainly because he wasn't.

'Even more than I can write about.'

'Really?' That got John Plumber's attention. Holtzman was one of the younger generation in relation to the TV correspondent, and one of the older generation for the newest class of reporters – which regarded Plumber as a fuddy-duddy even as they attended his seminars at Columbia University's journalism program.

'Really,' Bob assured him.

'Like?'

'Like things that I can't write about,' Holtzman repeated. 'Not for a long time, anyway. John, I've been on part of this story for years. I know the CIA officer who got Gerasimov's wife and daughter out. We have a little deal. In a couple years he tells me how it was done. The submarine story is true and – '

'I know. I've seen a photograph of Ryan on the boat. Why he doesn't let that one leak is beyond me.'

'He doesn't break the rules. Nobody ever explained to him that it's okay to do that – '

'He needs more time with Arnie – '

'As opposed to Ed.'

'Kealty knows how the game is played.'

'Yes, he does, John, maybe a little too well. You know, there's one thing I've never quite been able to figure out,' Bob Holtzman remarked.

'What's that?'

'The game we're in, are we supposed to be spectators, referees, or players?'

'Bob, our job is to report the truth to our readers – well, viewers for me.'

'Whose facts, John?' Holtzman asked.

'A flustered and angry President Jack Ryan . . .' Jack picked up the remote and muted the CNN reporter who'd zapped him with the China question. 'Angry, yes, flustered, n – '

'Also yes,' van Damm said. 'You bungled the thing on China, and where Adler is – where is he, by the way?'

The President checked his watch. 'He should be getting into Andrews in about ninety minutes. Probably over Canada now, I guess. He comes straight here, and then probably off again to China. What the *hell* are they up to?'

'You got me,' the chief of staff admitted. 'But that's why you have a national security team.'

'I know as much as they do, and I don't know shit,' Jack breathed, leaning back in his chair. 'We've *got* to increase our human-intelligence capability. The President can't be stuck here all the time not knowing what's going on. I can't make decisions without information, and all we have now are guesses – except for what Robby told us. That's a hard data-point, but it doesn't make sense, because it doesn't fit in with anything else.'

'You have to learn to wait, Mr President. Even if the press doesn't, you do, and you have to learn to focus on what you can do when you can do it. Now,' Arnie went on, 'we have the first set of House elections coming up next week. We have you scheduled to go out and make speeches. If you want the right kind of people in Congress, then that's what you have to go out and do. I have Callie preparing a couple of speeches for you.'

'What's the focus?'

'Tax policy, management improvement, integrity, all your favorites. We'll have the drafts to you tomorrow morning. Time to spend some more time out among the people. Let them love you some, and you can love them back some more.' The chief of staff earned himself a wry look. 'I've told you before, you can't be trapped in here, and the radios on the airplane work just fine.'

'A change of scenery would be nice,' POTUS admitted.

'You know what would really be good now?'

'What's that?'

Arnie grinned. 'A natural disaster, gives you the chance to fly out and look presidential, meet people, console them and promise federal disaster relief and –'

'God damn it!' It was so loud the secretaries heard it through the three-inch door.

Arnie sighed. 'You gotta learn to take a joke, Jack. Put that temper of yours in a box and lock it the hell up. I just set you off for fun, and I'm on *your* side, remember?' Arnie headed back to his office, and the President was alone again.

Yet another lesson in Presidency 101. Jack wondered when they would stop. Sooner or later he'd have to *act* presidential, wouldn't he? But he hadn't quite made it yet. Arnie hadn't said that, exactly, and neither had Robby, but they didn't have to. He still didn't belong. He was doing his best, but his best wasn't good enough – yet, his mind added. Yet? Maybe never. *One thing at a time*, he thought. What every father said to every son, except they never warned you that one at a time was a luxury some people couldn't afford. Fourteen dead Americans on a runway on an island eight thousand miles away, killed on purpose probably, for a purpose he could scarcely guess at, and he was supposed to set that fact aside and get on with other things, like a trip back out to meet the people he was supposed to preserve, protect, and defend, even as he tried to figure out how he'd failed to do so for fourteen of them. What was it you needed in order to do this job? Turn off dead citizens and fix on other things? You had to be a sociopath to accomplish that, didn't you? Well, no. Others had to – doctors, soldiers, cops. And now him. *And* control his temper, salve his frustration, and focus on something else for the rest of the day.

Movie Star looked down at the sea, six kilometers below, he estimated. To the north he could see an iceberg on the blue-gray surface, glistening in the bright sunlight. Wasn't that remarkable? As often as he'd flown, he'd never seen one of those before. For someone from his part of the world, the sea was strange enough, like a desert, impossible to live on, though a different way. Strange how it looked like the desert in all but color, the surface crinkling in almost-regular parallel lines just like dunes, but uninvitingly. Despite his looks – about which he was quite vain; he liked the smiles he got from flight attendants, for example – almost nothing was inviting to him. The world hated him and his kind, and even those who made use of his services preferred to keep him at arm's length, like a vicious but occasionally useful dog. He grimaced, looking down. Dogs were not favored animals in his culture. And so here he was, back on another airplane, alone, with his people on other aircraft in groups of three, heading to a place where they would be decidedly not welcome, sent from a place where they were scarcely more so.

Success would bring him – what? Intelligence officers would seek to identify and track him, but the Israelis had been doing that for years, and he was still alive. What was he doing this *for*? Movie Star asked himself. It was a little late for that. If he canceled the mission, then he wouldn't be welcome anywhere at all. He was supposed to be fighting for Allah, wasn't he? *Jihad*. A holy war. It was a religious term for a military-religious act, one meant to protect the Faith, but he didn't really believe that anymore, and it was vaguely frightening to have no country, no home, and then . . . no faith? Did he even have *that* anymore? He asked himself, then admitted that if he had to ask – he didn't. He and his kind, at least the ones who survived, became automatons, skilled robots – computers in the modern age. Machines that did things at the bidding of others, to be thrown away when convenient, and below him the surface of the sea or the desert never changed. Yet he had no choice.

Perhaps the people who were sending him on the mission would win, and he would have some sort of reward. He kept telling himself that, after all, even though there was nothing in his living experience to support the belief – and if he'd lost his faith in God, then why was it that he could remain faithful to a profession that even his employers regarded with distaste?

Children. He'd never married, never fathered one to his knowledge. The women he'd had, perhaps – but, no, they were debauched women, and his religious training had taught him to despise them even as he made use of their bodies, and if they produced offspring, then the children, too, would be cursed. How was it that a man could chase an idea for all his life and then realize that here he was, looking down at the most inhospitable of scenes – a place where neither he nor any man could live – and be more at home here than anyplace else? And so he would assist in the deaths of children. Unbelievers, political expressions, things. But they were not. They were innocent of any guilt at that age, their bodies not yet formed, their minds not yet taught the nature of good and evil.

Movie Star told himself that such thoughts had come to him before, that doubts were normal to men on difficult tasks, and that each previous time he'd set them aside and gotten on with it. If the world had changed, then perhaps –

But the only changes that had taken place were contrary to his lifelong quest, and was it that having killed for nothing, he had to keep killing in the hope of achieving *something*? Where did that path lead? If there were a God and there were a Faith, and there were a Law, then –

Well, he had to believe in something. He checked his watch. Four more hours. He had a mission. He had to believe in that.

They came by car instead of helicopter. Helicopters were too visible, and maybe this way nobody would notice. To make things more covert still, the cars came to the East Wing entrance. Adler, Clark, and Chavez walked into the White House the same way Jack had on his first night, hustled along by the Secret Service, and they managed to arrive unseen by the press. The Oval Office was a little crowded. Goodley and the Foleys were there, as well, along with Arnie, of course.

'How's the jet lag, Scott?' Jack asked first, meeting him at the door.

'If it's Tuesday, it must be Washington,' the Secretary of State replied.

'It isn't Tuesday,' Goodley observed, not getting it.

'Then I guess the jet lag is pretty bad.' Adler took his seat and brought out his notes. A Navy mess steward came in with coffee, the fuel of Washington. The arrivals from the UIR all had a cup.

'Tell us about Daryaei,' Ryan commanded.

'He looks healthy. A little tired,' Adler allowed. 'His desk is fairly clean. He spoke quietly, but he's never been one to raise his voice in public, to the best of my knowledge. Interestingly, he was getting into town about the same time we were.'

'Oh?' Ed Foley said, looking up from some of his own notes.

'Yeah, he came in on a business jet, a Gulfstream,' Clark reported. 'Ding got a few pictures.'

'So, he's hopping around some? I guess that makes sense,' POTUS observed. Strangely, Ryan could identify with Daryaei's problems. They weren't all that different from his own, though the Iranian's methods could hardly have been more different.

'His staff's afraid of him,' Chavez added impulsively. 'Like something from an old World War II Nazi movie. The staff in his outer office was pretty wired. If somebody had yelled "boo," they would have hit the ceiling.'

'I'd agree with that,' Adler said, not vexed at the interruption. 'His demeanor with me was very old-world, quiet, platitudes, that sort of thing. The fact of the matter is that he said nothing of real significance – maybe good, maybe bad. He's willing to have continued contacts with us. He says he desires peace for everybody. He even hinted at a certain degree of goodwill for Israel. For a lot of the meeting, he lectured me on how peaceful he and his religion are. He emphasized the value of oil and the resulting commercial relationships for all parties involved. He denied having any territorial ambitions. No surprises in any of it.'

'Okay,' the President said. 'What about body language?'

'He appears very confident, very secure. He likes where he is now.'

'As well he might.' It was Ed Foley again.

Adler nodded. 'Agreed. If I had to describe him in one word, it would be "serene."'

'When I met him a few years ago,' Jack remembered, 'he was aggressive, hostile, looking for enemies, that sort of thing.'

'None of that earlier today.' SecState stopped and asked himself if it was still the same day. Probably, he decided. 'Like I said, serene, but then on the way back, Mr Clark here brought something up.'

'What's that?' Goodley asked.

'It set off the metal detector.' John pulled the necklace out again, and handed it to the President.

'Get some shopping done?'

'Well, everybody wanted me to do a walkabout,' he reminded his audience. 'What better place than a market?' Clark went on to report the incident with the goldsmith, while POTUS examined the necklace.

'If he sells these things for seven hundred bucks, maybe we should all get his address. Isolated incident, John?'

'The French station chief was walking with me. He said that this guy was pretty representative.'

'So?' van Damm asked.

'So maybe Daryaei doesn't have much to be all that serene about,' Scott Adler suggested.

'People like that don't always know what the peasants are thinking,' the chief of staff thought.

'That's what brought the Shah down,' Ed Foley told him. 'And Daryaei is one of the people who made that happen. I don't think it likely that he's forgotten that particular lesson . . . and we know that he's still cracking down on people who step out of line.' The DCI turned to look at his field officer. 'Good one, John.'

'Lefevre – the French spook – told me twice that we don't have a very good feel for the mood in the street over there. Maybe he was shining me on,' Clark continued, 'but I don't think so.'

'We know there's dissent. There always is,' Ben Goodley said.

'But we don't know how much.' It was Adler again. 'On the whole, I think we have a man here who wants to project serenity for a reason. He's had a couple of good months. He's knocked over a major enemy. He has some internal problems whose magnitude we need to evaluate. He's hopping back and forth to Iraq – we saw that. He's tired-looking. Tense staff. I'd say he has a full plate right now. Okay, he told me how he wants peace. I almost buy it. I think he needs time to consolidate. Clark here tells me that food prices are high. That's an inherently rich country, and Daryaei can best quiet things down by playing on his political success and turning that into economic success as quickly as possible. Putting food on the table won't hurt. For the moment, he needs to look in instead of looking out.

'So I think it's possible that we have a window of opportunity here,' SecState concluded.

'Extend the open hand of friendship?' Arnie asked.

'I think we keep the contacts quiet and informal for the time being. I can pick somebody to handle the meetings. And then we see what develops.'

The President nodded. 'Good one, Scott. Now I guess we'd better get you up to speed on China.'

'When do I leave?' SecState inquired, with a pained expression.

'You'll have a bigger airplane this time,' his President promised him.

41

HYENAS

Movie Star felt the main landing gear thump down at Dulles International Airport. The physical sensation didn't exactly end his doubts, but it did announce that it was time to put them aside. He lived in a practical world. The entry routine was – routine, again.

'Back so soon?' the immigration officer asked, flipping to the last entry in the passport.

'*Ja, doch.*' Movie Star replied in his German identity. 'Perhaps I get apartment here soon.'

'The prices in Washington are kinda steep,' the man reported, stamping the booklet yet again. 'Have a pleasant stay, sir.'

'Thank you.'

It wasn't that he had anything to fear. He was carrying nothing illegal, except what was in his head, and he knew that American intelligence had virtually never caused substantive harm to a terrorist group, but this trip was different, even if only he knew it, as he walked alone in the mob of the terminal. As before, no one would meet him. They had a rendezvous to which he would be the last to arrive. He was more valuable than the other members of the team. Again he rented a car, and again he drove toward Washington, checking his mirror, taking the wrong exit deliberately and watching to see if anyone followed as he reversed direction to get back on the proper road. Again as before, the coast was clear. If there were anyone on him, the coverage was so sophisticated that he had no chance at all to survive. He knew how that worked: multiple cars, even a helicopter or two, but such an investment of time and resources only happened if the opposition knew nearly everything – it took time to organize – and that could only mean deep penetration of his group by the American CIA. The Israelis were capable of such a thing, or so everyone in the terrorist movement feared, but over the years a brutally Darwinian process had ended the lives of all the careless men; the Israeli Mossad had never once blanched at the sight of Islamic blood, and had he been discovered by that agency, he would long since have been dead. Or that's what he told himself, still watching his rear-view mirror because that was how he stayed alive.

On the other hand, it amused him greatly that this mission would not have been possible without the Israelis. Islamic terrorist groups existed in America, but they had all the hall-marks of amateurs. They were overtly religious. They held meetings in known places. They talked among themselves. They could be seen, spotted, and positively identified as being *different* from the other fish in their adopted sea. And then they wondered how they were caught. *Fools*, Movie Star thought. But they served their purpose. In being visible, they attracted attention, and the American FBI had only so many assets. However formidable the world's intelligence services, they were also human institutions, and humans universally pounded on the nails that stuck up.

Israel had taught him that, after a fashion. Before the fall of the Shah, his own intelligence service, the Savak, had received training from the Israeli Mossad, and not all Savak members had been executed with the arrival of the new Islamic regime. The tradecraft they'd learned had also been taught to those like Movie Star, and the truth of the matter was that it was very easy to understand. The more important the mission, the more caution was required. If you wanted to avoid being spotted, then you had to disappear into your surroundings. In a secular country, do not be obviously devout. In a Christian and Jewish country, do not be Muslim. In a nation that had learned to distrust people from the Middle East, be from somewhere else – or better yet, on occasion, be truthful after a fashion. Yes, I come from *there*, but I am a Christian, or a Baha'i, or a Kurd, or an Armenian, and *they* persecuted my family cruelly, and so I came to America, the land of opportunity, to experience true freedom. And if you followed those simple rules, the opportunity was quite real, for America made it so easy. This country wel-comed foreigners with an openness that reminded Movie Star of his own culture's stern law of hospitality.

Here he was in the camp of his enemy, and his doubts

faded, as the exhilaration of it increased his heart rate and brought a smile to his face. He *was* the best at what he did. The Israelis, having trained him at second hand, had never gotten close to him, and if they couldn't, then neither could the Americans. You just had to be careful.

In each team of three there was one man like him, not quite as experienced as he was, but close enough. Able to rent a car and drive safely. To know to be polite and friendly with all he met. If a policeman were to stop him, he knew to be contrite and apologetic, to ask what he'd done wrong, and then ask for directions, because people remembered hostility more clearly than amity. To profess to be a physician or engineer or something else respectable. It was easy if you were careful.

Movie Star reached his first destination, a middle-level hotel on the outskirts of Annapolis, and checked in under his cover name, Dieter Kolb. The Americans were so foolish. Even their police thought that all Muslims were Arabs, never remembering that Iran was an Aryan country – the very same ethnic identity which Hitler had claimed for his nation. He went to his room, and checked his watch. If everything went according to plan, they would meet in two hours. To be sure, he placed a call to the 1–800 numbers for the proper airlines – and inquired about arriving flights. They'd all arrived on time. There might have been a problem with customs, or bad traffic, but the plan had allowed for that. It was a cautious one.

They were already on the road for their next stop, which was Atlantic City, New Jersey, where there was a huge convention center. The various new-model and 'concept' cars were wrapped in covers to protect their finish, most of them on conventional auto trailers, but a few in covered trailers like those used by racing teams. One of the manufacturer's representatives was going over handwritten comments his company had solicited from people who'd stopped by to look at their products. The man rubbed his eyes. Damned headache, sniffles. He hoped he wasn't coming down with something. Achy, too. That's what you got for standing around all day right under the air-conditioning vent.

* * *

The official telegram was hardly unexpected. The American Secretary of State requested an official consultation with his government to discuss matters of mutual interest. Zhang knew there was no avoiding this, and all the better to receive him in a friendly way, protesting innocence – and inquiring delicately if the American President had merely misspoken himself or had changed long-standing US policy at his press conference. That side issue alone would tie up Adler for some hours, he imagined. The American would probably offer to be an intermediary between Beijing and Taipei, to shuttle back and forth between the two cities, hoping to calm things down. That would be very useful.

For the moment, the exercises were continuing, albeit with somewhat greater respect for the neutral space between the two sets of forces. The heat was still on, but at the 'simmer' setting. The People's Republic, the ambassador had already explained in Washington, had done nothing wrong, had *not* fired the first shot, and had no desire to initiate hostilities. The problem was with the breakaway province, and if only America would accede to the obvious solution to the problem – there is *one* China – then the matter would be settled, and quickly.

But America had long held to a policy that made sense to none of the countries involved, wanting to be friendly with Beijing *and* Taipei, treating the latter as the lesser nation it was, but unwilling to take that to its logical conclusion. Instead, America said that, yes, there was only one China, but that the one China did not have the right to enforce its rule on the 'other' China, which, according to official American policy, didn't actually exist. Such was American consistency. It would be such a pleasure to point this out to Secretary Adler.

'"The People's Republic is pleased to welcome Secretary Adler in the interests of peace and regional stability." Well, isn't that nice of them,' Ryan said, still in his office at nine in the evening, and wondering what TV his kids were watching without him. He handed the message back to Adler.

'You're really sure they did it?' SecState asked Admiral Jackson.

'If I go over it any more, the tape will wear out.'

'You know, sometimes people just screw up.'

'Sir, this is not one of those times,' Robby said, wondering if he'd have to run the videotape *again*. 'And they've been exercising their fleet for quite a while now.'

'Oh?' Ryan asked.

'To the point that they must be wearing things out by now. They're not as good on maintenance as we are. Besides that, they're using up a lot of fuel. This is the most at-sea time we've ever seen them do. Why are they stringing things out? This shoot-down looks to me like a great excuse to call it a day and head back to port and say they've made their point.'

'National pride,' Adler suggested. 'Face saving.'

'Well, since then they've curtailed operations somewhat. Not approaching the line I showed you. The Taiwanese are really at full alert now. Hell, maybe that's it,' the J-3 opined. 'You don't attack a pissed-off enemy. You let him relax some first.'

'Rob, you said that a real attack isn't possible,' Ryan said.

'Jack, in the absence of knowledge of their intentions, I have to go by capabilities. They *can* stage a major engagement in the strait, and they will probably come off winners if they do. Maybe that will put sufficient political pressure on Taiwan to force some sort of major concession. They killed people,' Jackson reminded the other two. 'Sure, the value they place on human life isn't the same as ours, but when you kill people you cross another invisible line – and they know how *we* feel about that.'

'Move the carrier up,' Adler said.

'Why, Scott?'

'Mr President, it gives me a face card to lay on the table. It shows that we're taking this seriously. As Admiral Jackson just told us, we *do* take the loss of life seriously, and they will just have to accept the fact that we don't want and might not *allow* this to go any further.'

'What if they press anyway – what if there's another "accident" that might involve us?'

'Mr President, that's operations, and that's my business. We'd park *Ike* on the east side of the island. They can't get to her by accident then. They'd have to come through three defense belts to do so, the ROC one over the strait, then Taiwan itself, and then the wall the battle-group commander puts up. I could also spot an Aegis at the bottom end of the strait to give us full radar coverage of the entire passage. If, that is, you order us to move *Ike*. The advantage for Taiwan, well, four squadrons of fighters, plus air-borne radar coverage. That should make them feel more secure.'

'Which will allow me to play a better game if I shuttle back and forth,' the Secretary concluded.

'But that still leaves the IO uncovered. It's been a long time since we did that.' Robby kept coming back to that, the other two noticed.

'Nothing else there?' Jack asked. He realized that he should have found out before.

'A cruiser, *Anzio*, two destroyers, plus two frigates guarding an under way-replenishment group based at Diego Garcia. We never leave Diego uncovered by warships, not with the Pre-Positioning Ships there. We have a 688-class sub in the area, too. It's enough to matter, but not enough to project power. Mr Adler, you understand what a carrier means.'

SecState nodded. 'People take them seriously. That's why I think we need it off China.'

'He makes a good case, Rob. Where is *Ike* now?'

'Between Australia and Sumatra, should be approaching the Sunda Strait. Exercise SOUTHERN CUP is supposed to simulate an Indian attack on their northwest coast. If we move her now, she can be to Formosa in four days plus a couple hours.'

'Get her moving that way, Rob, all possible speed.'

'Aye aye, sir,' Jackson acknowledged, his doubts still visible on his face. He gestured to the phone and, getting a nod, he called the National Military Command Center. 'This is Admiral Jackson with orders from National Command Authority. Execute GREYHOUND BLUE. Acknowledge that, Colonel.' Robby listened and nodded. 'Very well, thank you.' Then he turned to his President. 'Okay, *Ike* will turn north in about ten minutes and make a speed run to Taiwan.'

'That fast?' Adler allowed himself to be impressed.

'The miracle of modern communications, and we already had alert orders to Admiral Dubro. This won't be a covert move. The battle group will head through several narrows, and people will notice,' he warned.

'Press release won't hurt,' Adler said. 'We've done it before.'

'Well, there's your card to play in Beijing and Taipei,' Ryan said, having exercised yet another executive order, but distantly concerned that Robby was unhappy about it. The really difficult matter was fuel. A fleet-replenishment group would have to move as well, to refill the bunkers of *Eisenhower*'s non-nuclear escort ships.

'Will you let on that we know about the shoot-down?'

Adler shook his head. 'No, definitely not. It will be more unsettling to them if they think we don't know.'

'Oh?' This came from a somewhat surprised President.

'Then I can decide *when* we "find out," boss, and when that happens, I have another card to play – that way I can make it a big card.' He turned. 'Admiral, don't overestimate the intelligence of your enemy. Diplomats like me aren't all that savvy on the technical aspects of what you do. That applies to people in foreign countries, too. A lot of our capabilities are unknown to them.'

'They have spooks to keep them informed,' Jackson objected.

'You think they always listen? Do we?'

The J-3 blinked at that lesson and filed it away for future use.

It happened in a large shopping mall, an American invention that seemed designed for covert operations, with its many entrances, bustling people, and near-perfect anonymity. The first rendezvous wasn't really a meeting at all. Nothing more than eye contact was made, and that not at a distance closer than ten meters, as the groups strolled past one another. Instead, each of the sub-groups performed a count, confirmed identity visually, and then each checked to be sure that there was no surveillance on the others. With that done, they all returned to their hotel accommodations. The real rendezvous would take place tomorrow.

Movie Star was pleased. The sheer audacity of this was very exciting indeed. This wasn't the relatively simple task of getting one bomb-clad fool – *heroic martyr*, he corrected himself – into Israel, and the beauty of it was that had one of his teams been spotted, the enemy couldn't possibly risk ignoring them. You *could* force the opposition into showing its hand, and so much the better to do it at a point in time when none of your people had done anything more than enter the country with false travel documents.

Doubts be damned, the leader of the operation told himself. There was the sheer beauty of being ready to do something right in the lion's own den, and *that* was what kept him in the business of terrorism. In the lion's own den? He smiled at the cars as he walked across the parking lot. The lion's own *cubs*.

'So what are you doing?' Cathy asked in the dark.

'Scott leaves for China tomorrow morning,' Jack answered, lying next to his wife. People said that the President of the United States was the world's most powerful man, but at the end of every day the exercise of that power surely seemed to exhaust him. Even his time at Langley, with an auto commute each way every day, hadn't worn him out as this job did.

'To say what?'

'Try to get them calmed down, defuse the situation.'

'You're really sure that they deliberately –'

'Yes. Robby is positive, about as much as you are with a diagnosis,' her husband confirmed, staring up at the ceiling.

'And we're going to negotiate with them?' SURGEON asked.

'Have to.'

'But –'

'Honey, sometimes – hell, most of the time a nation-state commits murder, they get away with it. I'm supposed to think about "the big picture," "the larger issues," and all that stuff.'

'That's awful,' Cathy told him.

'Yes, it sure is. This game you have to play by its own rules. If you mess up, more people suffer. You can't talk to a nation-state the way you talk to a criminal. There are thousands of Americans over there, businessmen and like that. If I get too far out of line, then things might happen to some of them, and then things escalate and get worse,' POTUS explained to her.

'What's worse than killing people?' his physician-wife asked.

Jack didn't have an answer. He'd come to accept the fact that he didn't have all the answers for press conferences, or for all the people out there, or even for his own staff sometimes. Now he didn't even have a single answer for his wife's simple and logical question. Most powerful man in the world? Sure. With that thought, another day ended at 1600 Pennsylvania Avenue.

Even important people got careless, an eventuality made easier by a little creativity on the part of more careful folk. The National Reconnaissance Office was working hard to keep track of two places. Every pass of the reconsats over the Middle East and now the Formosa Strait resulted in copious numbers of download pictures, literally thousands of images which photo-interpretation specialists had to examine one by one in their new building close to Dulles Airport. It was just one more task that couldn't be done by computer. The readiness state of the UIR military had become the number-one priority item for the American government, as part of the Special National Intelligence Estimate now in preparation on White House orders. That meant the entire attention of the team fell that way, and for the other things, more people were called in to work overtime. These looked continuously at the photos downloaded from over China. If the PRC was going to make a real military move, then it would show in many ways. People's Liberation Army troops would be out training and maintaining their equipment, or loading their tanks onto trains and the parking areas would look different. Aircraft would have weapons hanging from their wings. These were things a satellite photo would reveal. More care was taken to spot ships at sea – that was far harder, since they were not in fixed locations. America still had three photographic satellites aloft, each making two passes per day over the areas of interest, and they were spaced so that there was little 'sad time.' That made the technicians feel pretty good about things. They had a continuous feed of data with which to firm up their estimates and so do their duty for their President and their country.

But they couldn't watch everything everywhere, and one place they didn't watch was Bombay, western headquarters of the Indian navy. The orbits of the American KH-11 satellites were well defined, as were their schedules. Just after the newest satellite swept over the area, with the other new one on the far side of the world, came a four-hour window, which would end with the overhead passage of the oldest and least reliable of the trio. Happily, it also coincided with a high tide.

Two carriers, their repairs recently completed, and their escorts, slipped their mooring lines and stood out to sea. They would be conducting training exercises in the Arabian Sea, in case anyone noticed and asked about it.

Damn. The Cobra representative woke up, feeling a little feverish. It took him a few seconds to orient himself. Different motel, different city, different room lights. He fumbled for the proper switch, then put on his glasses, squinting in the uncomfortable light, and spotted his bag. Yeah. Shaving kit. He took that into the bathroom, pulled the paper cover off the glass, and half filled it with water. Then he worked the childproof top on the aspirin bottle, tipped two tablets into his hand and washed them down. He ought not to have had all those beers after dinner, the sales rep told himself, but he'd made a fairly decent deal with a couple of club pros, and beer was always a good lubricant for the golf business. He'd feel better in the morning. A former touring professional who hadn't been quite good enough to make it big, he was now a very successful manufacturer's representative. What the hell, he thought, heading back to his bed. He still had a minus handicap, the pace was easier, and he was making a pretty good living – plus being able to play a new course practically every week, the better to demonstrate his wares. He hoped the aspirin would work. He had an eight-thirty tee time.

STORM TRACK and PALM BOWL were connected by a fiber-optic communications cable, the better to share information. Another training exercise was under way in the former Iraq and this one wasn't a CPX. The three heavy corps of integrated Iraqi and Iranian units were in the field. Direction-finding radios placed them well away from the Saudi and Kuwaiti borders, and so no special danger was attached to their activities, but the ELINT troops were listening closely to get a feel for the skill level of the commanders who were moving tanks and infantry fighting vehicles across the broad, dry plains southeast of Baghdad.

'Here's good news, Major,' the American lieutenant said, handing over a telex. The UIR SNIE had generated something positive for a change.

Two hundred miles northwest of Kuwait, at a spot five miles south of the 'berm' – actually a man-made dune – that marked the border between the Kingdom and the UIR, a deuce-and-a-half truck stopped. The crew got out, attached the extension to the launch ramp and fired up their Predator drone. But 'drone' was an obsolete term. This mini-aircraft was an Unmanned Aerial Vehicle, or UAV, a blue-gray-colored, propeller-driven spy. It took about twenty minutes to attach the wings, run diagnostics on the electronics, and spin up the engine, and then it was launched, the annoying buzz of its engine fading rapidly as it climbed to its operating altitude and headed north.

The product of three decades of research, Predator was fairly stealthy, difficult to detect on radar due to its small size, the inclusion of radar-absorbing material in its design, and the fact that its operating speed was so slow that modern computer-controlled radars, if they caught it at all, classified it as a bird and erased it from the operator's scope. The paint covering the airframe was the same IR-suppressive product the Navy had taken to using. It was both ugly and prone to provide a sticky home to anything that touched it – the technicians had to brush sand off their baby all the time – but that was balanced by the fact that the color blended in with the sky exceedingly well. Armed only with a TV camera, this one soared up to ten thousand feet, and cruised north under the control of another team at STORM TRACK, the better to keep an eye on the UIR exercises. It was a technical violation of the new country's sovereignty, but two pounds of explosive in the UAV would ensure that if it hit the ground in the wrong place, no one would be able to tell what it was. A directional antenna beamed the 'take' from the camera to receivers in the Kingdom.

The fiber-optic data link crossloaded the same signal to PALM BOWL, and when a USAF enlisted woman switched on the room's monitor, they were looking down at a nearly featureless landscape while the Predator was guided to its destination by its operators.

'It'll be good to see if they know what they're doing,' the lieutenant observed to Major Sabah.

'Better if we see that they don't,' the Kuwaiti officer replied thoughtfully. Other members of his extended family were increasingly concerned. Enough so, the major thought, that their country's military was quietly ramping up to a very high state of readiness. Like the Saudis, the Kuwaiti citizens who'd flocked enthusiastically to man the best equipment that their small but wealthy country could obtain felt that maintenance of their tanks was a task for lesser men, but, unlike their Saudi cousins, they had experience with being on the bottom side of conquest. Many of them had lost family members, and a long memory was characteristic of this part of the world. For that reason, they trained with a will. They weren't yet near the level of the Americans who taught them or the Israelis who held them in distant contempt, Major Sabah knew. His countrymen had first of all learned how to shoot. They'd burned out at least one gun tube per tank in the pure joy of learning that skill, and they had been firing real rounds, not just practice – war shots fly straighter and farther – as they combined a diverting hobby with a national survival skill. Able now to hit their targets, their current task was to learn to maneuver and fight on the move. Again, they couldn't do it well, not yet, but they were learning. The developing crisis put emphasis on their training, and even now his countrymen were leaving their banking, oil, and trading offices to mount their vehicles. An American advisory team would take them into the field again, give them a battle problem, and watch their performance. While it pained the major that his countrymen, many of them relatives, were not yet ready, it was a source of pride to him that they were making a real effort. Bright as he was, however, it never occurred to him how close his military was to the Israeli model: citizen soldiers learning to fight after the harsh lesson of not having known.

'SWORDSMAN is awake,' Andrea Price heard in her earpiece. They were in the kitchen, the Detail commander with her sub-detail chiefs, standing and sipping coffee around one of the stainless-steel countertops used for preparing food. 'Roy?'

'Another routine day,' Special Agent Altman said. 'She's got three procedures scheduled for the morning, then a lecture to some Spanish docs in the afternoon – University of Barcelona, ten of them, eight males, two females. We checked the names with the Spanish police. They're all clean. No special threats reported against SURGEON. Looks like a normal day at the office.'

'Mike?' she asked Special Agent Michael Brennan, principal agent to Little Jack.

'Well, SHORTSTOP has a first-period biology test today and baseball practice after school. Pretty good with a glove, but his batting needs help,' the agent added. 'Otherwise, same-o same-o.'

'Wendy?' Special Agent Gwendolyn Merritt was principal agent for Sally Ryan.

'Chemistry exam for SHADOW in third period today. She's getting very interested in Kenny. Nice kid, needs a haircut and a new tie. She's thinking about going out for the girls' lacrosse team.' A few faces winced at that revelation. How do you protect someone being chased by teenagers with sticks?

'What's the family background on Master Kenny again?' Price asked. Even she couldn't remember everything.

'Father and mother both lawyers, tax stuff mainly.'

'SHADOW needs better taste,' Brennan observed to general amusement around the counter. He was the joker on the crew. 'There is a potential threat there, Wendy.'

'Huh? What?'

'If POTUS gets the new tax laws passed, they're in the shitter.'

Andrea Price made another check mark on her morning list. 'Don?'

'Today's routine is the same as usual, Introductory Crayon. I'm still not happy with the setup, Andrea. I want some more people, one more inside, and two more for over-watch on the south side,' Don Russell announced. 'We're too exposed. We just don't have enough defensive depth there. The outer perimeter is essentially the only one, and I am not comfortable with that.'

'SURGEON doesn't want us to overpower the place. You have yourself and two agents inside, three for immediate backup, and one surveillance agent across the road,' Price reminded him.

'Andrea, I want three more. We're too exposed there,' Russell repeated. His voice was reasonable and professional as ever. 'The family has to listen to us on professional questions.'

'How about I come over tomorrow afternoon to look things over again?' Price asked. 'If I agree, then I go to the Boss.'

'Fine.' Special Agent Russell nodded.

'Any more problems with Mrs Walker?'

'Sheila tried to get a petition drive started with the other Giant Steps parents – get SANDBOX out of there, that sort of thing. It turns out that Mrs Daggett gets a lot of repeat business, and more than half the parents know the Ryans and like 'em. So, that crapped out in a hurry. You know what the only real problem is?'

'What's that, Don?'

He smiled. 'At that age – sometimes I turn around and the kids move and when I turn back I can't tell which one SAND-BOX is. You know there's only two kinds of hair-cuts for little girls, and half the mothers there think Oshkosh is the only brand of kid's clothes.'

'Don, it's a woman thing,' Wendy Merritt observed. 'If the First Toddler wears it, it *has* to be fashionable.'

'Probably the same thing with the hair,' Andrea added. 'By the way, I forgot to tell you, Pat O'Day wants a little match with you,' she told the Detail's most senior member.

'The Bureau guy?' Russell's eyes lit up. 'Where? When? Tell him to bring money, Andrea.' It occurred to Russell that he was due to have some playtime of his own. He hadn't lost a pistol match in seven years – his last bout with the flu.

'We all set?' Price asked her senior agents.

'How's the Boss doing?' Altman asked.

'They're keeping him pretty busy. Cutting into his sleep time.'

'Want me to talk to SURGEON about it? She keeps a good eye on him,' Roy told her.

'Well –'

'I know how. Gee, Dr Ryan, is the Boss doing okay? He looked a little tired this morning . . .' Altman suggested.

The four agents exchanged looks. President-management

826

was their most delicate duty. This President listened to his wife almost as though he were a normal husband. So why not make SURGEON into an ally? All four nodded at once.

'Go with it,' Price told him.

'Son of a bitch,' Colonel Hamm said inside his command track.

'Surprised you, did they?' General Diggs inquired delicately.

'They have a ringer in there?' the CO of the Blackhorse Cav wanted to know.

'No, but they sprung one on me, Al. They didn't let anybody know they had IVIS training. Well, that is, I found out last night.'

'Nice guy, sir.'

'Surprises work both ways, Colonel,' Diggs reminded him.

'How the *hell* did they get the funding for that?'

'Their fairy god-senators, I suppose.'

Visiting units didn't bring their own equipment to Fort Irwin, for the obvious reason that it was too expensive to transport it all back and forth. Instead they mated up with vehicle sets permanent to the base, and those were top-of-the-line. Included in all of them was IVIS, the Inter-Vehicle Information System, a battlefield data link that projected data onto a computer screen inside the tanks and Bradleys. It was something the 11th Cav had been issued for only its own vehicles (their real ones, not the simulated enemy sets) six months earlier. Seemingly a simple system for trading data – it even ordered spare parts automatically when something broke – it presented the crew with a comprehensive overview of the battlefield, and converted hard-won reconnaissance information into general knowledge in a matter of seconds. No longer was data on a developing engagement limited to a harried and distracted unit commander. Now sergeants knew everything the Colonel did, and information was still the most valuable commodity known to man. The visiting tankers from the Carolina Guard were fully trained up on its use. So were the troopers of the Blackhorse, but their pseudo-Soviet OpFor vehicles didn't have it.

'Colonel, now we really know how good the system is. It beat you.'

The simulated engagement had been a bloody one. Hamm and his operations officer had contrived a devilish ambush, only to have the Weekend Warriors detect it, avoid it, and enter into a battle of maneuver which had caught the OpFor leaning the wrong way. A daring counterstroke by one of his squadron commanders had almost saved the day, and killed off half of the Blue Force, but it hadn't been enough. The first night engagement had gone to the good guys, and the Guardsmen were whooping it up as if after an ACC basketball game.

'I'll know better next time,' Hamm promised.

'Humility is good for the soul,' Marion Diggs said, enjoying the sunrise.

'Death is bad for the body, sir,' the colonel reminded him.

'*Baaaaaaaaa*,' Diggs said, grinning on the way to his personal Hummer. Even Al Hamm needed the occasional lesson.

They took their time. Movie Star handled the car rentals. He had duplicate IDs, enough to rent four vehicles, three four-door private cars and a U-Haul van. The former had been selected to match vehicles owned by parents who had children at the nursery school. The latter was for their escape – an eventuality which he now thought likely and not merely possible. His men were smarter than he'd appreciated. Driving past the objective in their rented cars, they didn't turn their heads to stare, but allowed their peripheral vision to take in the scene. They already had exact knowledge from the model they'd built, based on data from their leader's photographs. Driving past the site gave them a better full-size, three-dimensional view, and added more substance to their mental image, and to their growing confidence. With that task done, they drove west, turned off Route 50 and proceeded to a lonely farmhouse in southern Anne Arundel County.

The house was owned by a man thought by his neighbors to be a Syrian-born Jew who'd lived in the area for eleven years, but who was a sleeper agent. Over the past few years, he'd made discreet purchases of arms and ammunition, all of them legal, and all made before restrictive laws on some of the weapons had been passed – he could have evaded them anyway. In his coat pocket were airline tickets under a different name and passport. This was the final rendezvous point. They would bring the child here. Then six of them would leave the country at once, all on separate flights, and the remaining three would enter the homeowner's personal car and drive to yet another predetermined location to await developments. America was a vast country, with many roads. Cellular telephones were difficult to track. They'd give a devil of a time to their pursuers, Movie Star thought. He knew how he'd do things, if it got that far. The team with the child would have one phone. He would have two, one to make brief calls to the American government, and another to call his friends. They would demand much for the life of the child, enough to throw this country into chaos. Perhaps the child might even be set free alive. He wasn't sure about that, but he supposed it was possible.

42

PREDATOR/PREY

CIA has its own photo shop, of course. The film shot out the aircraft window by Field Officer Domingo Chavez was tagged by the technician in a manner little different from that used by commercial shops, and then processed on standard equipment. There the routine treatment stopped. The grainy ASA-1200 film produced a poor-quality image, and one couldn't give *that* to the people on the seventh floor. The employees in the photo shop knew about the RIF order, and the best way to avoid being laid off, in this or any other business, was to be indispensable. So the developed roll of film went into a computer-enhancement system. It took only three minutes per frame to convert the images into something that might have been shot by an expert with a Hasselblad under studio conditions. Less than an hour after the film's arrival, the tech produced a set of eight-by-ten glossies that positively identified the airplane passenger as the Ayatollah Mahmoud Haji Daryaei, and provided a shot of his aircraft, so clear and dramatic that the manufacturer might have used it on a sales brochure. The film was put in an envelope and sent off to secure storage. The photos themselves were stored in digital form on tape, their precise identity – date, time of day, location, photographer, and subject – also coded into a computer register for extensive cross-referencing. It was standard procedure. The technician had long since stopped caring about what he developed, though he still did see the occasional frame showing someone on the news in a position that never made the TV screen . . . but not this guy. From what he'd heard about Daryaei, the man probably didn't have much interest in boys or girls, and the dour expression on his face seemed to confirm it. What the hell, he did have nice taste in airplanes, a G-IV, it looked like. Odd, wasn't that a Swiss registration code on the tail, though . . . ?

When the photos went upstairs, one complete set was also

set aside for a different kind of analysis. A physician would examine them closely. Some diseases left visible signs, and the Agency always kept an eye on the health of foreign leaders.

'. . . Secretary Adler will be leaving for Beijing this morning,' Ryan told *them*. Arnie had told *him* that, as unpleasant as these news appearances were, being seen on TV doing presidential things was good for him politically – and *that*, Arnie always went on, meant being more effective in the job. The President also remembered hearing from his mom how important it was to go to the dentist twice a year, too, and just as the antiseptic smells of that place were certain to frighten a child, so he had come to loathe the damp of this room. The walls leaked, some of the windows were cracked, and this part of the West Wing of the White House was about as neat and well kept as a high-school locker room, something the citizens couldn't tell from watching TV. Though the area was only a few yards from his own office, nobody really cared much about tidying things up. Reporters were such slobs, the staff claimed, that it wouldn't have mattered much anyway. What the hell, the reporters didn't seem to worry about it.

'Mr President, have we learned anything more about the airliner incident?'

'It's been announced that the body count is complete. The flight-data recorders have been recovered and – '

'Will we have access to the black-box information?'

Why did they call it the *black* box when it was *orange*? Jack had always wondered about that, but knew he'd never get a sensible answer. 'We've asked for that access, and the Republic of China government has promised its full cooperation. They don't have to do that. The aircraft is registered in that country, and the aircraft is made in Europe. But they are being helpful. We acknowledge that with thanks. I should add that none of the Americans who survived the crash itself are in any medical danger – some of the injuries are severe, but not life-threatening.'

'Who shot it down?' another reporter asked.

'We're still examining the data, and – '

'Mr President, the Navy has two Aegis-class ships in that

immediate area. You must have a good idea of what happened.' This guy had done his homework.

'I really can't comment further on that. Secretary Adler will discuss the incident with the parties concerned. We want, first of all, to make sure that no further loss of life takes place.'

'Mr President, a follow-up: you *must* know more than you're saying. Fourteen Americans were killed in this incident. The American people have a right to know why.'

The hell of it was, the man was right. The hell of it also was that Ryan had to evade: 'We really do not know what happened yet. I cannot make a definitive statement until we do.' Which was philosophically true, anyway. He knew who'd taken the shot. He didn't know why. Adler had made a good point yesterday on keeping that knowledge close.

'Mr Adler returned from somewhere yesterday. Why is that a secret?' It was Plumber again, chasing down his question from the previous day.

I'm going to kill Arnie for exposing me this way all the time. 'John, the Secretary was engaged in some important consultations. That's all I have to say on the issue.'

'He was in the Middle East, wasn't he?'

'Next question?'

'Sir, the Pentagon has announced that the carrier *Eisenhower* is moving into the South China Sea. Did you order that?'

'Yes, I did. We feel that the situation warrants our close attention. We have vital interests in that region. I point out that we are not taking sides in this dispute, but we are going to look after our own interests.'

'Will moving the carrier cool things down or heat them up?'

'Obviously, we're not trying to make things worse. We're trying to make them better. It's in the interests of both parties to take a step back and think about what they are doing. Lives have been lost,' the President reminded them. 'Some of those were American lives. That gives us a direct interest in the matter. The reason we have a government and a military is to look after American interests and to protect the lives of our citizens. The naval forces heading for the region will observe what is happening and conduct routine training operations. That is all.'

Zhang Han San checked his watch again and remarked to himself that it was becoming a fine way to end his working day – the sight of the American President doing exactly what he wanted him to do. Now China had fulfilled her obligations to that Daryaei barbarian. The Indian Ocean was devoid of a major American naval presence for the first time in twenty years. The American foreign minister would leave Washington in another two hours or so. Another eighteen hours to fly to Beijing, and then the platitudes could be exchanged. He'd see what concessions he could wring out of America and the Taiwanese puppet state. Maybe a few good ones, he thought, with the trouble America was sure to face elsewhere . . .

Adler was in his office. His bags were packed and in his official car, which would take him to the White House to catch a helicopter to Andrews after a presidential handshake and a brief departure statement which would be as bland as oatmeal. The more dramatic departure would look good on TV, make his mission appear to be a matter of importance, and cause additional wrinkling to his clothes – but the Air Force crew had an ironing board on the plane.

'What do we know?' Under Secretary Rutledge asked of the Secretary's senior staff.

'The missile was shot by a PRC aircraft. That's pretty positive from the Navy's radar tapes. No idea why, though Admiral Jackson is very positive in saying that it was not an accident.'

'How was it in Tehran?' another assistant secretary inquired.

'Equivocal. I'll get that written up on the flight and fax it back here.' Adler, too, was pressed for time and hadn't had enough to think through his meeting with Daryaei.

'We need that if we're going to be much use on the SNIE,' Rutledge pointed out. He really wanted *that* document. With it, Ed Kealty could prove that Ryan was up to his old tricks, playing secret agent man, and even suborning Scott Adler into doing the same. It was out there somewhere, the key to destroying Ryan's political legitimacy. He was dodging and counterpunching well, doubtless due to Arnie van Damm's coaching, but his gaffe yesterday on China policy had sent rumbles throughout the building. Like many people at State, he wished that Taiwan would just go away, and enable America to get on with the business of conducting normal relations with the world's newest superpower.

'One thing at a time, Cliff.'

The meeting returned to the China issue. By mutual consent, it was decided that the UIR problem was on the back burner for the next few days.

'Any change in China policy from the White House?' Rutledge asked.

Adler shook his head. 'No, the President was just trying to talk his way through things – and, yeah, I know, he shouldn't have called the Republic of China China, but maybe it rattled their cage just a little in Beijing, and I'm not all that displeased about it. They do need to learn about not killing Americans. We have crossed a line here, people. One of the things I have to do is let them know that we take that line seriously.'

'Accidents happen,' someone observed.

'The Navy says it wasn't an accident.'

'Come on, Mr Secretary,' Rutledge groaned. 'Why the hell would they do that on purpose?'

'It's our job to find out. Admiral Jackson made a good case for his position. If you're a cop on the street and you have an armed robber in front of you, why shoot the little old lady down the block?'

'Accident, obviously,' Rutledge persisted.

'Cliff, there are accidents, and there are accidents. This one killed Americans, and in case anybody in this room forgot, we are supposed to take that seriously.'

They weren't used to that sort of reprimand. What was *with* Adler, anyway? The job of the State Department was to maintain the peace, to forestall conflict that killed people in the thousands. Accidents were accidents. They were unfortunate, but they happened, like cancer and heart attacks. State was supposed to deal with the Big Picture.

*   *   *

'Thank you, Mr President.' Ryan left the podium, having again survived the slings and arrows of the media. He checked his watch. Damn. He'd missed seeing the kids off to school – again – and hadn't kissed Cathy good-bye, either. Where in the Constitution, he wondered, was it written down that the President wasn't a human being?

On reaching his office, he scanned the printed sheet of his daily schedule. Adler was due over in an hour for the send-off to China. Winston at ten o'clock to go over the details of his administrative changes across the street at Treasury. Arnie and Callie at eleven to go through his speeches for next week. Lunch with Tony Bretano. A meeting after lunch with – who? The Anaheim Mighty Ducks? Ryan shook his head. Oh. They'd won the Stanley Cup, and this would be a photo opportunity for them and for him. He had to talk to Arnie about that political crap. Hmph. Ought to have Ed Foley over for that, Jack smiled to himself. He was a hockey fanatic . . .

'You're running late,' Don Russell said, as Pat O'Day dropped Megan off.

The FBI inspector continued past him, saw to Megan's coat and blanky, then returned. 'The power went off last night and reset my clock-radio for me,' he explained.

'Big day planned?'

Pat shook his head. 'Desk day. I have to finish up a few things – you know the drill.' Both did. It was essentially editing and indexing reports, a secretarial function which on sensitive cases was often done by sworn, gun-toting agents.

'I hear you want to have a little contest,' Russell said.

'They say you're pretty good.'

'Oh, fair, I guess,' the Secret Service agent allowed.

'Yeah, I try to keep the shots inside the lines, too.'

'Like the SigSauer?'

The FBI agent shook his head. 'Smith 1076 stainless.'

'The ten-millimeter.'

'It makes a bigger hole,' O'Day pointed out.

'Nine's always been enough for me,' Russell reported. Then both men laughed.

'You hustle pool, too?' the FBI agent asked.

'Not since high school, Pat. Shall we set the amount of the wager?'

'It has to be serious,' O'Day thought.

'Case of Samuel Adams?' Russell suggested.

'An honorable bet, sir,' the inspector agreed.

'How about at Beltsville?' That was the site of the Secret Service Academy. 'The outside range. Indoors is always too artificial.'

'Standard combat match?'

'I haven't shot bull's-eye in years. I don't ever expect one of my principals to be attacked by a black dot.'

'Tomorrow?' It seemed a good Saturday diversion.

'That's probably a little quick. I can check. I'll know this afternoon.'

'Don, you have a deal. And may the best man win.' They shook hands.

'The best man will, Pat. He always does.' Both men knew who it would be, though one of them would have to be wrong. Both also knew that the other would be a good guy to have at your back, and that the beer would taste pretty good either way when the issue was decided.

The weapons weren't fully automatic. A good machinist could have changed that, but the sleeper agent wasn't one of those. Movie Star and his people didn't mind all that much. They were trained marksmen and knew that full-auto was only good for three rounds unless you had the arms of a gorilla – after that, the gun jumped up and you were just drilling holes in the sky instead of the target, who just might fire back at you. There was neither time nor space for another round of shooting, but they were familiar with the weapon type, the Chinese knock-off of the Soviet AK-47, itself a development of a German weapon from the 1940s. It fired a short-case 7.62mm cartridge. The magazines held thirty rounds each. The team members used duct tape to double them up, inserting and ejecting the magazines to be sure that everything fit properly. With that task completed, they resumed their examination of the objective. Each of them knew his place and his task. Each also knew the dangers involved, but they didn't dwell on that. Nor, Movie Star saw, did they dwell on the nature of the mission. They were so dehumanized by their years of activity within the terrorist community that, though this was the first real mission, for

836

most of them, all they really thought about was proving themselves. How they did it, exactly, was less important.

'They're going to bring up a lot of things,' Adler said.

'Think so?' Jack asked.

'You bet. Most-favored nation, copyright disputes, you name it, it'll all come up.'

The President grimaced. It seemed obscene to place the copyright protection for Barbra Streisand CDs alongside the deliberate killing of so many people, but –

'Yeah, Jack. They just don't think about stuff the same way we do.'

'Reading my mind?'

'I'm a diplomat, remember? You think I just listen to what people say out loud? Hell, we'd never get any negotiations done that way. It's like playing a long low-stakes card game, boring and tense all at the same time.'

'I've been thinking about the lives lost . . .'

'I have, too,' SecState replied with a nod. 'You can't dwell on it – it's a sign of weakness in their context – but I won't forget it, either.' That got a rise out of his Commander-in-Chief.

'Why is it, Scott, that we always have to respect their cultural context? Why is it that they never seem to respect ours?' POTUS wanted to know.

'It's always been that way at State.'

'That doesn't answer the question,' Jack pointed out.

'If we lean too hard on that, Mr President, it's like being a hostage. Then the other side always knows that they can hang a couple of lives over us and use it to pressure us. It gives them an advantage.'

'Only if we allow it. The Chinese need us as much as we need them – more, with the trade surplus. Taking lives is playing rough. We can play rough, too. I've always wondered why we don't.'

SecState adjusted his glasses. 'Sir, I do not disagree with that, but it has to be thought through very carefully, and we do not have the time to do that now. You're talking a doctrinal change in American policy. You don't shoot from the hip on something that big.'

'When you get back, let's get together over a weekend with

a few others and see if there are any options. I don't like what we've been doing on this issue in a moral sense, and I don't like it because it makes us a little too predictable.'

'How so?'

'Playing by a given set of rules is all well and good, as long as everybody plays by the same rules, but playing by a known set of rules when the other guy *doesn't* just makes us an easy mark,' Ryan speculated. 'On the other hand, if somebody else breaks the rules and then we break them, too, maybe in a different way, but break them even so, it gives him something to think about. You want to be predictable to your friends, yes, but what your enemy needs to predict is that messing with you gets him hurt. How hurt he gets, that part we make unpredictable.'

'Not without merit, Mr President. Sounds like a nice subject for a weekend up at Camp David.' Both men stopped talking when the helicopter came down on the pad. 'There's my driver. Got your statement?'

'Yeah, and about as dramatic as a weather report on a sunny day.'

'That's how the game is played, Jack,' Adler pointed out. He reflected that Ryan was hearing a lot of that song. No wonder he was bridling at it.

'I've never run across a game where they never change the rules. Baseball went to a designated hitter to liven things up,' POTUS remarked casually.

Designated hitter, SecState wondered on his way out the door. *Great choice of words . . .*

Fifteen minutes later, Ryan watched the helicopter lift off. He'd done the handshake for the cameras, made his brief statement for the cameras, looked serious but upbeat for the cameras. Maybe C-SPAN had covered it live, but nobody else would. Were it to be a slow news day – Friday in Washington often was – it might get a minute and a half on one or two of the evening news shows. More likely not. Friday was their day to summarize the week's events, recognize some person or other for doing something or other, and toss in a fluff story.

'Mr President!' Jack turned to see TRADER, his Secretary of the Treasury, walking over a few minutes early.

'Hi, George.'

'That tunnel between here and my building?'

'What about it?'

'I took a look at it this morning. It's a real mess. You have any beefs about cleaning it up?' Winston asked.

'George, that's a Secret Service function, and *you* own them, remember?'

'Yeah, I know, but it does come to your house, and so I thought I ought to ask. Okay, I'll get it taken care of. Might be nice for when it rains.'

'How's the tax plan coming?' Ryan asked, on his way to the door. An agent yanked it open and held it for him. Such things still made Jack uncomfortable. A man had to do *some* things for himself.

'We'll have the computer models done next week. I really want the case tight on this one, revenue-neutral, easier on the little guy, fair on the big guy, and I have my people jumping through hoops on the administrative savings. Jesus, Jack, was I wrong about that!'

'What do you mean?' They turned the corner for the Oval Office.

'I thought I was the only guy pissing money away to work the tax code. Everybody does. It's a huge industry. It'll put a lot of people out of work –'

'I'm supposed to be happy about that?'

'They'll all find honest work, except for the lawyers, maybe. And we'll save the taxpayers a few billion dollars by giving them a tax form they can figure out from fourth-grade math. Mr President, the government doesn't insist that people buy buggy whips, does it?'

Ryan told his secretary to call Arnie in. He'd want a little political guidance on the ramifications of George's plan.

'Yes, Admiral?'

'You asked for a report on the *Eisenhower* group,' Jackson said, walking to the large wall map and consulting a slip of paper. 'They're right here, making good speed.' Then Robby's pager started vibrating in his pocket. He pulled it out and checked the number. His eyebrows went up. 'Sir, do you mind . . . ?'

'Go ahead,' Secretary Bretano said. Jackson took the phone on the other side of the room, dialing five digits. 'J-3 here

... oh? Where are they? Then let's find out, shall we, Commander? Correct.' He put the phone back. 'That was the NMCC. The NRO reports that the Indian navy's missing – their two carriers, that is.'

'What does that mean, Admiral?'

Robby walked back to the map and walked his hand across the blue part west of the Indian subcontinent. 'Thirty-six hours since the last time we checked. Figure three hours to clear the port and form up . . . twenty knots times thirty-three is six hundred sixty nautical miles, that's seven hundred sixty statute miles . . . about halfway between their home port and the Horn of Africa.' He turned. 'Mr Secretary, they have two carriers, nine escorts, and an UnRep group missing from their piers. The fleet oilers mean they might be planning to stay out for a while. We had no intelligence information to warn us about this.' *As usual*, he didn't add.

'So where exactly are they?'

'That's the point. We don't know. We have some P-3 Orion aircraft based at Diego Garcia. They're going to launch a couple to go looking. We can task some satellite assets to the job also. We need to tell State about this. Maybe the embassy can find out something.'

'Fair enough. I'll tell the President in a few minutes. Anything to worry about?'

'Could be they're just putting out after completing repairs – we rattled their cage pretty hard a while back, as you know.'

'But now the only two aircraft carriers in the Indian Ocean are somebody else's?'

'Yes, sir.' *And our nearest one is heading the wrong way.* But at least SecDef was catching on some.

Adler was in a former Air Force One, an old but solid version of the venerable 707-320B. His official party comprised eight people, with five Air Force stewards to look after them. For the moment, he looked at his watch, computed the travel time – they had to stop for fuel at Elmendorf Air Force Base in Alaska – and decided he'd catch up on his sleep during the last leg. What a shame, he thought, that the government didn't award frequent-flyer miles. He'd be traveling free for the rest of his life. For now, he took out his Tehran notes and started examining them again. He closed his eyes, trying to recall additional details as he relived the experience from his arrival at Mehrabad to the departure, visualizing every single episode. Every few minutes, he opened his eyes, flipped to the page in his notes, and made a few marginal comments. With luck, he'd be able to have them typed up and sent by secure fax to Washington for the SNIE team.

'Ding, maybe you have another career ahead of you,' Mary Pat observed, as she examined the photo through a magnifying glass. Her voice went on in some disappointment. 'He looks healthy.'

'You suppose being a son of a bitch is good for longevity?' Clark asked.

'Worked for you, Mr C.,' Chavez joked.

'I may have to put up with this for the next thirty years.'

'But such handsome grandsons you will have, *jefe*. And bilingual.'

'Back to business, shall we?' Mrs Foley suggested, Friday afternoon or not.

It's never fun to be ill on an airplane. He wondered what he'd eaten, or maybe he'd picked up something in San Francisco at the computer show, all those damned people around. The executive was an experienced traveler, and his personal 'first-aid kit' never left his side. In with his razor and such he found some Tylenol. He washed two down with a glass of wine and decided that he'd just try to sleep it off. With luck, he'd feel better by the time his flight made it into Newark. Sure as hell, he didn't want to drive home feeling like this. He eased the seat all the way back, clicked off the light, and closed his eyes.

It was time. The rental cars pulled away from the farmhouse. Each driver knew the route to and from the objective. There were no maps or other written material in their vehicles aside from photos of their prey. If any of them had uneasy feelings about kidnapping a small child, none showed it. Instead, their weapons were loaded and set on safe, and in every case sat on the floor, covered with a blanket or cloth. All wore suits and ties so that if a police car pulled alongside, a look would reveal only three well-groomed men, probably businessmen in nice private cars. The team thought that last part amusing. The Movie Star was a stickler for proper appearance, probably, they all thought, because of his vanity.

Price watched the arrival of the Mighty Ducks with no small amusement. She'd seen it all before. The most powerful of men walked into this place and were turned into children by it. What to her and her colleagues was just part of the scenery, the paintings and so forth, was to others the trappings of ultimate power. And in a way, she admitted to herself, they were right and she was wrong. Anything can become routine after sufficient repetition, whereas the new visitor, seeing everything for the first time, may have seen more clearly. The processing helped make it that way, as they came through the metal detectors under the watchful eyes of members of the USSS Uniformed Division. They'd get a quick walk-around while the President finished his meeting with the SecDef, which was reportedly running very late. The hockey players, bearing gifts for the President – the usual sticks, pucks, and a jersey-sweater with his name on it (actually they had them for the whole family) – shuffled through the passage from the East Entrance, their eyes sweeping left and right over the decorations on the white-painted walls of what for Andrea was a place of work and for them something else, powerful and special. An interesting dualism, she thought, walking over to Jeff Raman.

'I'm heading over to check out arrangements for SANDBOX.'

'I heard Don was getting a little antsy. Anything I need to know?'

She shook her head. 'POTUS isn't planning anything special. Callie Weston will be over later. They changed her slot. Otherwise, everything's routine.'

'Fair enough,' Raman acknowledged.

'This is Price,' she said into her microphone. 'Show me in transit to SANDBOX.'

'Roger that,' the command post replied.

The Detail chief headed out the way the Mighty Ducks had come in, and turned left for her personal vehicle, a Ford Crown Victoria. The vehicle looked ordinary, but wasn't. Under the hood was the biggest standard engine Ford made. There were two cellular phones and a pair of secure radios.

The tires had steel disks inside so that were one to be flattened, the car could still drive. Like all members of the Detail, she'd been trained in the Service's special evasive-driving course at Beltsville – it was something they all loved. And in her purse was her SigSauer 9mm automatic, along with two spare clips, plus her lipstick and credit cards.

Price was a fairly ordinary-looking woman. Not as pretty as Helen D'Agustino . . . she sighed at the memory. Andrea and Daga had been close. The latter had helped her through a divorce and gotten her some dates. Good friend, good agent, dead with all the rest that night on the Hill. Daga – nobody in the Service had called her Helen – had been blessed with Mediterranean features that stopped just short of voluptuous, and that had made for a fine disguise. She just hadn't looked at all like a cop. Presidential aide, secretary, or mistress, maybe . . . but Andrea was more ordinary, and so she donned the sunglasses that agents on the Detail adopted. She was no-nonsense, maybe a little strident? They'd said that about her once, back when it had been a novelty for women to join up and carry guns. The system was over that now. Now she was one of the boys, to the point that she laughed at the jokes and told some of her own. Her instant assumption of command on that night with SWORDSMAN, getting his family to safety – she owed Ryan, Andrea knew. He'd made the call because he liked the way she did things. She would never have made Detail chief so rapidly but for his instant decision. Yes, she had the savvy. Yes, she knew the personnel very well. Yes, she genuinely loved the work. But she was young for the responsibility – and female. POTUS didn't seem to care, however. He hadn't picked her because she was female and it might therefore look good to the voting public. He'd done it because she'd gotten the job done during a tough time. That made it right, and that made SWORDSMAN special. He even asked her questions about things. That was unique.

She didn't have a husband. She didn't have kids, probably never would. Andrea Price wasn't one of those who sought to escape her womanhood in pursuit of a career. She wanted it all, but she hadn't quite managed that. Her career was important – she could think of nothing more vital to her country than what she did – and the good news was that it was so all-encompassing that she rarely had the time to dwell on what was missing . . . a good man to share her bed, and a small voice to call her Mommy. But on drives alone, she did think about it, like now, heading up New York Avenue.

'Not all that liberated at all, are we?' she asked the windshield. But the Service didn't pay her to be liberated. It paid her to look after the First Family. Her personal life was supposed to run on her personal time, though the Service didn't issue her any of that, either.

Inspector O'Day was already on Route 50. Friday was best of all. He'd done his duty for the week. His tie and suit jacket were on the seat next to him, and he was back in his leather bomber jacket and his lucky John Deere ballcap, without which he'd never consider playing golf or going out to hunt. This weekend he had a ton of things to do around the house. Megan would help with many of them. Somehow she knew. Pat didn't fully understand it. Maybe it was instinct. Maybe she just responded to her father's devotion. However it came about, the two were inseparable. At home, she left his side only to sleep, and only then after a major hug and kiss, her little arms tight around his neck. O'Day chuckled to himself. 'Tough guy.'

Russell supposed it was the grandfather in him. All these little munchkins. They were playing outside now, every one in his or her parka, about half with the hoods up, because little kids liked that for some reason. Serious playtime here. SANDBOX was in the sandbox, along with the O'Day kid who so closely resembled her, and a little boy – the Walker kid, the rather nice young son of that pain in the ass with the Volvo wagon. Agent Hilton was out, too, supervising. Strangely, they could relax more out here. The playground was on the north side of the Giant Steps building, under the direct view of the support team just across the street. The third member of the team was inside on the phone. She ordinarily worked the back room, where the TV monitors were. The kids knew her as Miss Anne.

Too thin, Russell told himself, even as he watched the toddlers having the purest sort of fun. In the extreme case, somebody could drive by on Ritchie Highway and hose the place. Trying to talk the Ryans out of sending Katie here was a wasted effort, and, sure, they wanted their youngest to be a normal kid. But . . .

But it was all insane, wasn't it? Russell's entire professional life had revolved around the knowledge that there were people who hated the President and everyone around him. Some were truly crazy. Some were something else. He'd studied the psychology of it. He had to, since learning about them helped to predict what to look for, but that wasn't the same as understanding it. These were *kids*. Even the fucking Mafia, he knew, didn't mess with children. He sometimes envied the FBI for its statutory authority to track down kidnappers. To rescue a child and apprehend the criminal in that sort of case must be a sweet moment indeed, though part of him wondered how hard it was to bring in alive that kind of subject instead of just sending him off to have his Miranda rights read to him by God Himself. That random thought evoked a smile. Or maybe what really happened was better yet. Kidnappers had a *very bad time* in prison. Even hardened robbers couldn't stomach the abusers of children, and so that variety of hood learned a whole new form of recreation in the federal corrections system: survival.

'Russell, Command Post,' his earpiece said.

'Russell.'

'Price is heading out here like you requested,' Special Agent Norm Jeffers said from the house across the street. 'Forty minutes, she says.'

'Right. Thanks.'

'I see the Walker lad is continuing his engineering studies,' the voice continued.

'Yeah, maybe he'll do bridges next,' Don agreed. The youngster had the second level building on his sand castle, to the rapt admiration of Katie Ryan and Megan O'Day.

'Mr President,' the team captain said, 'I hope you'll like this.'

Ryan had a good laugh and donned the team jersey for the cameras. The team bunched around him for the shot.

'My CIA Director is a big hockey fan,' Jack said.

'Really?' Bob Albertsen asked. He was a very physical defenseman, the terror of his conference for his board checking, but as docile as a kitten in this setting.

'Yeah, he has a kid who's pretty good, played in the kids' leagues in Russia.'

'Then maybe he learned something. Where's he go to school?'

'I'm not sure what colleges they're thinking about. I think they said Eddie wants to study engineering.' It was so damned pleasant, Jack thought, to talk about normal things like a normal person to other normal people once in a while.

'Tell them to send the kid to Rensselaer. It's a good tech school up by Albany.'

'Why there?'

'Those damned nerds win the college championship every other year. I went to Minnesota, and they cleaned our clock twice in a row. Send me his name and I'll see he gets some stuff. His dad, too, if that's okay, Mr President.'

'I'll do that,' the President promised. Six feet away, Agent Raman heard the exchange and nodded.

O'Day arrived just as the kids were trooping back in the side door for bathroom call. This, he knew, was a major undertaking. He pulled his diesel pickup in just after four. He watched the Secret Service agents switch positions. Russell appeared at the front door, his regular post for when the children were inside.

'We got us a match for tomorrow?'

Russell shook his head. 'Too quick. Two weeks from tomorrow, two in the afternoon. It'll give you a chance to practice.'

'And you won't?' O'Day asked, passing inside. He watched Megan enter the girls' bathroom without seeing her daddy in the room. Well, then. He squatted down outside the door to surprise her when she came out.

Movie Star, too, was at his surveillance position in the school parking lot to the northeast. The trees were starting to fill in, he realized. He could see, but his view was somewhat obstructed. Things appeared normal even so, and from this point on, it was in Allah's hands, he told himself, surprised that he used the term for a decidedly ungodly act. As he watched, Car 1 turned right just north of the day-care center.

It would proceed down the street, reverse directions, and head back.

Car 2 was a white Lincoln Town Car, the twin of one belonging to a family with a child here. That family comprised two physicians, though none of the terrorists knew that. Immediately behind it was a red Chrysler whose twin belonged to the again-pregnant wife of an accountant. As Movie Star watched, both pulled into parking spaces opposite each other, as close to the highway as the parking lot allowed.

Price would be here soon. Russell took note of the cars' arrival, thinking over his arguments for the Detail chief. The afternoon sun reflected off the windshields, preventing him from seeing anything more inside than the outline of the drivers. Both cars were early, but it was a Friday . . .

. . . the tag numbers . . . ?

. . . his eyes narrowed slightly as he shook his head, asking himself why he hadn't –

Someone else had. Jeffers lifted his binoculars, scanning the arriving cars as part of his surveillance duties. He didn't even know he had a photographic memory. Remembering things was as natural to him as breathing. He thought everyone could do it.

'Wait, wait, something's wrong here. They're not – ' He lifted the radio mike. 'Russell, those are not our cars!' It was almost in time.

In one smooth motion, two drivers opened their car doors and swung their legs out, lifting their weapons off the front seats as they did so. In the back of both cars, two pairs of men came up, also armed.

Russell's right hand moved back and down, reaching for his automatic while his left lifted the collar-mounted radio microphone: *'Gun!'*

Inside the building, Inspector O'Day heard something but wasn't sure what, and he was facing the wrong way to see how Agent Marcella Hilton turned away from a child who was asking her a question and shoved her hand into her gun purse.

It was the simplest of code words. An instant later, he heard the same word repeated over his earpiece as Norm Jeffers shouted it from the command post. The black agent's hand pushed another button, activating a radio link to Washington. '*SANDSTORM SANDSTORM SANDSTORM*!'

Like most career cops, Special Agent Don Russell had never fired his side arm in anger, but years of training made his every action as automatic as gravity. The first thing he'd seen was the elevated front sight of an AK-47-class automatic rifle. With that, as though a switch had been thrown, he changed from a watchful cop into a guidance system for a firearm. His SigSauer was out now. His left hand was racing to meet his right on the grip of the weapon, as the rest of his body dropped to one knee to lower his profile and give him better control. The man with the rifle would get the first shot off, but it would miss high, Russell's mind reported. Three such rounds did, passing over his head into the door frame as the area exploded with staccato noise. While that was happening, his tritium-coated front sight matched up with the face behind the weapon. Russell depressed the trigger, and from fifteen yards, he fired a round straight into the shooter's left eye.

Inside, O'Day's own instincts were just lighting off when Megan emerged from the bathroom, struggling with the suspender clips on her Oshkosh coveralls. Just then, the agent the kids knew as Miss Anne bolted out of the back room, her pistol in both hands and pointed up.

'Jesus,' the FBI inspector had time to say, when Miss Anne bounded right through him like an NFL fullback, knocking him down at his daughter's feet and banging his head against the wall in the process.

Across the street, two agents ran out the front door of the residence, both holding Uzi submachine guns while Jeffers worked the communications inside. He'd already gotten the emergency code word to headquarters. Next he activated the direct drop lines to Barracks J of the Maryland State Police on Rowe Boulevard in Annapolis. There was noise and confusion, but the agents were expertly drilled. Jeffers's function was to make sure that the word got out, then to back up the other two members of his team, already crossing the lawn of the house –

– they never had a chance. From fifty yards away, the shooters from Car 1 dropped both of them with aimed fire. Jeffers watched them go down while he got the word to the state police. He didn't have time for shock. As soon as his information was acknowledged, he lifted his M-16 rifle, flipped off the safety, and moved for the door.

Russell shifted fire. Another shooter made the mistake of standing to get a better shot. He never made it. Two quick rounds exploded his head like a melon, saw the agent, who was not thinking, not feeling, not doing anything but servicing targets as quickly as he could identify them. The enemy rounds were still going over his head. Then he heard a scream. His mind reported that it was Marcella Hilton, and he felt something heavy fall on his back and knock him to the ground. Dear God, it had to be Marcella. Her body – something – was on his legs, and as he rolled to get clear of the obstruction, four men came into view, advancing toward him, now with a clear line of sight to where he was. He fired one round that scored, drilling one of them right through the heart. The man's eyes went wide with the shock of the impact, until a second round took him in the face. It was like he'd always dreamed it would be. The gun was doing all the work. His peripheral vision showed movement to his left – the support group – but no, it was a car, driving across the playground right at them – not the Suburban, something else. He scarcely could tell as his pistol centered on another shooter, but that man went down, shot three times by Anne Pemberton in the doorway behind him. The remaining two – only two, he had a chance – then Annie got one in the chest, then fell forward, and Russell knew he was alone, all alone now, only him between SANDBOX and these mother-fuckers.

Don Russell rolled to his right to avoid fire on the ground to his left, shooting as his body turned, getting off two rounds that went wild. Then his Sig locked open on an empty magazine. He had another ready, and instantly he ejected the empty and slapped in a full one, but that took time and he felt a round enter his lower back, the impact like a kick that shook his body, as his right thumb dropped the slide lever and another bullet struck him in the left shoulder, ripping all the way down his torso to exit out his right leg. One more round, but he couldn't get the gun high enough, something wasn't working right, and he hit somebody straight through the kneecap an instant before a series of shots lowered his face to the ground.

O'Day was just trying to get up when two men came through the door, both armed with AKs. He looked around the room, now full of stunned, silent kids. The silence seemed to hang for a long moment, then turn to the shrill screams of toddlers. One of the men had blood all over his leg, and was gritting his teeth in pain and rage.

Outside, the three men from Car 1 surveyed the carnage. Four men were dead, they saw, as they jumped out of the car, but they'd done for the covering group and –

– the first one out the right-rear door fell facedown. The other two turned around to see a black man in a white shirt with a gray rifle.

'Eat shit and die.' His memory would fail him on this occasion. Norman Jeffers would never remember saying that as he shifted to the next target and squeezed off a three-round burst into his head. The third man of the team which had killed his two friends dropped behind the front of his car, but the car was stuck in the middle of the playground with open air to the left and right. 'Come on, stick it up and say hi, Charlie,' the agent breathed –

– and sure enough he did, swinging his weapon around to shoot back at the remaining bodyguard, but not fast enough. His eyes as open and unblinking as an owl's, Jeffers watched the blood cloud fly back as the target disappeared.

'Norm!' It was Paula Michaels, the afternoon surveillance agent from the 7-Eleven across the street, her pistol out and in both hands.

Jeffers dropped to one knee behind the car whose occupants he'd just killed. She joined him, and with the sudden negation of activity, both agents started breathing heavily, their hearts racing, their heads pounding.

'Get a count?' she asked.

'At least one made it inside –'

'Two, I saw two, one hit in the leg. Oh, Jesus, Don, Anne, Marcella –'

'Save it. We got kids in there, Paula. Fuck!'

So, Movie Star thought, it wasn't going to work out after all. Damn it, he swore silently. He'd *told* them there were *three* people in the house to the north. Why hadn't they waited to kill the third? They could have had the child away from here by now! Well. He shook his head clear. He'd never fully expected the mission to succeed. He'd warned Badrayn of that – and picked his people accordingly. Now all he had to do was watch to make sure – what? Would they kill the child? That was something they'd discussed. But they might not fulfill their duty before they died.

Price had been five miles out when the emergency call had come over her radio. In less than two seconds, she'd had the pedal to the floor, and the car accelerating through traffic, the flashing light in place, and siren screaming. Turning north onto Ritchie Highway, she could see cars blocking the road. Immediately, she maneuvered left onto the median, the car side-slipping as it clawed its way across the inward-sloping surface. She arrived a few seconds ahead of the first olive-and-black Maryland State Police radio car.

'Price, is that you?'

'Say who?' she replied.

'Norm Jeffers. I think we have two subjects inside. We have five agents down. Michaels is with me now. I'm sending her around the back.'

'There in a second.'

'Watch your ass, Andrea,' Jeffers warned.

O'Day shook his head. His ears were still ringing and his head sore from the hit on the wall. His daughter was ncxt to him, shielded by his body from the two – terrorists – who were now sweeping their weapons left and right around the room while the children screamed. Mrs Daggett moved slowly, standing between them and 'her' kids, instinctively holding her hands in the open. Around them, all the kids were cowering. There were cries for Mommy – none for Daddy, oddly enough, O'Day realized. And a lot of wet pants.

'Mr President?' Raman said, pressing his earpiece in tight. *What the hell was this?*

At St Mary's, the call of 'SANDSTORM' over the radio links had hit the SHADOW/SHORTSTOP details with a thunderbolt. Agents standing outside the classrooms of the Ryan kids slammed in, weapons drawn, to drag their protectees out to the corridor. Questions were asked, but none answered, as the Detail fell into the pre-set plan for such an event. Both kids entered the same Chevy Suburban, which drove not out to the road but off to a service building across the athletic field. One way in, one way out of this place, and an ambush team might be right out there, disguised as Christ knew what. In Washington, a Marine helicopter spooled up to fly to the school and extract the Ryan children. The second Suburban took position on the field, one hundred fifty yards from where the kids were. The class that had been doing gym outside was chased off, and agents stood behind their kevlar-armored vehicle, heavy weapons out, looking for targets.

'Doc!'
    Cathy Ryan looked up from her desk. Roy had never called her that before. He'd never had his pistol out in her presence, either, knowing that she was not fond of firearms. Her reaction was probably instinctive. Cathy's face went as white as her lab coat.
    'Is it Jack or –'
    'It's Katie. That's all I know, Doc. Please come with me right now.'
    'No! Not again, not again!' Altman wrapped his arm around SURGEON to guide her out into the corridor. Four more agents were there, weapons out and faces grim. Hospital security people kept out of the way, though uniformed Baltimore City Police made up an outer perimeter, all of them trying to remember to look outward toward a possible threat, not inward toward a mother whose child was in peril.

*   *   *

Ryan stretched out his arm, placed his hand against the wall of his office, looked down, and bit his lip for a second before speaking: 'Tell me what you know, Jeff.'

'Two subjects are in the building. Don Russell is dead, so are four other agents, sir, but we have it contained, okay? Let us do the work,' Agent Raman said, touching the extended arm to steady the President.

'Why my kids, Jeff? I'm the one – here. If people get mad, it's supposed to be at me. Why do people like this go after children, tell me that . . .'

'It's a hateful act, Mr President, hateful to God and man,' Raman said, as three more agents came into the Oval Office. What was he doing now? the assassin asked himself. What in hell was he doing? Why had he said *that*?

They were talking in a language he didn't understand. O'Day stayed down, sitting on the floor with his little girl, holding her in his lap with both arms and trying to look as harmless as she did. Dear God, all the years he'd trained for things like this – but never to be inside, never to be *in* the crime scene while the crime happened. Outside, you knew what to do. He knew exactly what was happening. If any Service people were left – probably some, yes, there had to be. Somebody had fired three or four bursts with an M-16 – O'Day knew the distinctive chatter of that weapon. No more bad guys had entered. His mind added those facts up. Okay, there were good guys outside. First they'd establish a perimeter to make sure nobody got in or out. Next they'd call in – who? The Service probably had its own SWAT team, but also close by would be the FBI Hostage Rescue Team, with its own choppers to get them here. Almost on cue, he heard a helicopter overhead.

'This is Trooper Three, we're orbiting the area now,' a voice said over the radio. 'Who's in charge down there?'

'This is Special Agent Price, United States Secret Service. How long you with us, Trooper?' she asked over a state police radio.

'We have gas for ninety minutes, and then another chopper will relieve us. Looking down now, Agent Price,' the pilot reported. 'I have one individual to the west, looks like a female behind a dead tree, looking into the scene. She one of yours?'

'Michaels, Price,' Andrea said over her personal radio system. 'Wave to the chopper.'

'Just waved at us,' Trooper Three reported at once.

'Okay, that's one of mine, covering the back.'

'All right. We have no movement around the building, and no other people within a hundred yards. We will continue to orbit and observe until you say otherwise.'

'Thank you. Out.'

The Marine VH-60 landed on the athletic field. Sally and Little Jack were fairly thrown aboard, and Colonel Goodman lifted off at once, heading east toward the water, which, the Coast Guard had told him moments before, was free of unknown craft. He rocketed the Black Hawk to altitude, going north over the water. To his left he could see the shape of a French-made police helicopter orbiting a few miles north of Annapolis. It didn't require much insight to explain it, and behind calm eyes he wished for a couple of squads of recon Marines to deliver to the site. He'd once heard that criminals who hurt children faced a rough go in prison, but that wasn't half of what Marines would do if they got the chance. His reverie ended there. He didn't even look back to see how the other two kids were doing. He had an aircraft to fly. That was his function. He had to trust others to do theirs.

They were looking out the windows now. They were being careful about it. While the wounded one stood leaning against the wall – looked like a kneecap, O'Day saw; good – the other one allowed his eye to peer around the edge. It wasn't too hard to guess what he saw. Sirens announced the arrival of police cars. Okay, they probably had the perimeter forming now. Mrs Daggett and her three women helpers had the kids in a single bunch on the corner, while the two subjects traded words. Good, that was smart. They weren't doing all that well, O'Day thought. One of them was always sweeping the room with eyes and muzzle, but they hadn't –

Just then one of them reached into his shirt pocket and pulled out a photo. He said something else in whatever tongue they spoke. Then he closed the shades. Damn. That would prevent scoped rifles from seeing inside. They were smart enough to know that people might just shoot. Few of the kids here were tall enough to look out and –

The one with the photo held it up again and walked toward the kids. He pointed.

'That one.'

Strangely, it was only now, it seemed, that they saw O'Day in the room. The knee-shot one blinked his eyes and aimed the AK right at him. The inspector took his arms from around his daughter's chest and held them up.

'Enough people been hurt, pal,' he said. It didn't require all that much effort to make his voice shake. He'd made a mistake, too, holding his Megan that way. *That fuck might shoot through her to get to me*, he realized, a sudden wave of nausea rippling through his stomach at the thought. Slowly, carefully, he lifted her and moved her off his lap, and onto the floor to his left.

'No!' It was Marlene Daggett's voice.

'Bring her to me!' the man insisted.

Do it, do it, O'Day thought. *Save your resistance for when it counts. It doesn't change anything right now.* But she couldn't hear his thoughts.

'Bring her!' the shooter repeated.

'*No!*'

The man shot Daggett in the chest from a range of three feet.

'What was that?' Price snapped. Ambulances were coming up Ritchie Highway now, their whooping sirens different from the monotonal screams of the police cars. Down to her left, state troopers were trying to get the road clear, shunting traffic away from the area while their hands rubbed on their holsters, wishing they were there to help. Their angry gestures conveyed their mental state to the puzzled drivers.

Closer to Giant Steps, those immediately outside heard a renewed wave of screams, little kids in terror, for what reason they could only guess.

The leather jacket rode up when you were sitting down like this. If anyone had been behind him, he'd see the holster in the small of his back, the inspector knew. He'd never seen a murder before. He'd investigated his share of them, but to see one . . . a lady who worked with kids. The shock on his face was as real as any man's, watching life vanish . . . innocent life, his mind added. So he really had no choice.

When he next looked at Marlene Daggett, he wished that he might tell her that her murderers would not be leaving this building alive.

It was miraculous that none of the kids were wounded as yet. All the shooting had gone high, and he realized that had Miss Anne not knocked him down, he might be dead beside his daughter now. There were holes in the wall, and the bullets that had made them would have transited the space he'd been in a second or two before. He looked down a second, to see his hands shaking. His hands knew what they had to do. They knew their task and they didn't understand why they weren't doing it, why the mind which commanded them hadn't yet given them the release. But his hands had to be patient. This was a job of the mind.

The subject lifted Katie Ryan by her arm, wrenching it, making her cry out as he twisted it. O'Day thought about his first supervisor, working that first kidnapping case, Dom DiNapoli, that big, tough guinea who'd wept bringing the child back to her family: 'Never forget, they're *all* our kids.'

They might just as easily have selected Megan, they were so close – and that thought *did* cross from mind to mind as the one with SANDBOX looked at the photo again, and over toward Pat O'Day.

'Who are you?' the voice demanded, while his partner moaned with increasing pain.

'What d'ya mean?' the inspector asked in nervous reply. *Look dumb and scared.*

'Whose child is that?' He pointed at Megan.

'She's mine, okay? I don't know who that one belongs to,' the FBI agent lied.

'She is the one we want, she is President's child, yes?'

'How the hell should I know? My wife usually picks Megan up, not me. Do what you gotta do and get the fuck outa here, okay?'

'You inside,' a female voice boomed from outside. 'This is the United States Secret Service. We want you to come out. You will not be hurt if you do. You have no place to go.

Come out where we can see you, and you will not be hurt.'

'That's good advice, man,' Pat told him. 'Nobody's gonna get out of here, you know?'

'You know who this girl is? She is daughter of your President Ryan! They will not dare shoot me!' the subject proclaimed. His English was pretty good, O'Day noted, nodding.

'What about all the other kids, man? That's the only one you want, that's the only other one that matters – hey, why not, you know, like, let some out, eh?'

The man was partly right. The Service guys wouldn't shoot at one target for fear that someone else might be in here, as one surely was, his rifle leveled at Pat's chest. And they were smart enough that they were never less than five feet apart. Shooting them would take two separate moves.

What really scared O'Day was the casual, reflexive way he'd killed Marlene Daggett. They just plain didn't care. You couldn't predict that sort of criminal. You could talk to them, try to calm them down, distract them, but beyond that, there was only one way to deal with them.

'We give them children, they give us car, yes?'

'Hey, that works for me, okay? I think that's just fine. I just want to get my daughter home tonight, y'know?'

'Yes, you take good care of your little one. Sit there.'

'No problem.' He relaxed his hands, bringing them closer to his chest, right at the top of the zipper on his jacket. Undo that and the leather would hang better, concealing his gun.

'Attention,' the voice called again. 'We want to talk.'

Cathy Ryan joined her children in the helicopter. The agents' faces were grim enough. Sally and Jack were coming out of the initial shock and sobbing now, looking to their mother for solace as the Black Hawk leaped into the sky again, heading southwest for Washington with another in trail. The pilot, she saw, was not taking the usual route, but was instead going directly west, away from where Katie was. That was when SURGEON collapsed into the arms of her kids.

'O'Day is in there,' Jeffers told her.

'You sure, Norm?'

'That's his truck. I saw him going in right before this went down.'

'Shit,' Price swore. 'That's probably the shot we heard.'

'Yah.' Jeffers nodded grimly.

The President was in the Situation Room, the best spot to keep track of things. Perhaps he might have been elsewhere, but he couldn't face his office, and he wasn't President enough to pretend that –

'Jack?' It was Robby Jackson. He came over as his President stood, but they'd been friends much longer than that, and the two shared an embrace. 'Been here before, man. It worked out then, too, remember?'

'We have tag numbers off the cars in the parking lot. Three are rentals. We're running them now,' Raman said, a phone to his ear. 'Should be able to get some kind of ID.'

How dumb might they be? O'Day asked himself. They'd have to be pretty fucking stupid to think they had any chance at all of getting out of here . . . and if they didn't have that hope, then they had nothing to lose . . . not a damned thing . . . and they didn't seem to care about killing. It had happened before, in Israel, Pat remembered. He didn't recall the name or the date, but a couple of terrorists had had a bunch of kids and hosed them before the commandos were able to . . .

He'd taught tactics for every possible situation, or so he'd thought, and would have said as recently as twenty minutes before – but to have your only child next to you . . .

They're all our kids, Dom's voice told him again.

The unhurt killer had Katie Ryan by the upper arm. She was only whimpering now, exhausted from her earlier screams, almost hanging from his hand as the subject stood there to the left of the wounded one. His right hand held the AK. If he'd had a pistol, he could have held that weapon to her head, but the AK was too lengthy for that. Ever so slowly, Inspector O'Day moved his hand down, opening the zipper on his jacket.

They started talking back and forth again. The wounded one was in considerable discomfort. At first, the adrenaline rush had blocked it out, but now things were settling down somewhat, and with the release of tension also went the pain-blocking mechanism that protected the body in periods of great stress. He was saying something, but Pat couldn't tell what it was. The other one snarled a reply, gesturing to the door, speaking with passion and frustration. The scary part would come when they came to a decision. They might just shoot the kids. Those outside would probably rush the building if they heard more than a shot or two. They might be fast enough to save some of the kids, but . . .

He started thinking of them as Hurt and Unhurt. They were pumped up but confused, excited but undecided, wanting to live but coming to the realization that they would not . . .

'Hey, uh, guys,' Pat said, holding his arms up and moving them to distract them from the open zipper. 'Can I say something?'

'What?' Hurt demanded, as Unhurt watched.

'All these kids you have here, it's like too many to cover, right?' he asked, with an emphatic nod to get the idea across. 'How about I take my little girl out and some of the others, okay? Make things easier for you, maybe?'

That generated some more jabbering. The idea actually seemed attractive to Unhurt, or so it appeared to O'Day.

'Attention, this is the Secret Service!' the voice called yet again. It sounded like Price, the FBI agent thought. Unhurt was looking toward the door, and his body language was leaning him that way, and to get there he had to pass in front of Hurt.

'Hey, come on, okay, let some of us go, will ya?' O'Day pleaded. 'Maybe I can tell them to give you a car or something.'

Unhurt waved his rifle in the inspector's direction. 'Stand!' he commanded.

'Okay, okay, be cool, all right?' O'Day stood slowly, keeping his hands well away from his body. Would they see his holster if he turned around? The Service people had spotted it the first time he'd come in, and if he fucked this one up, then Megan . . . there was no turning back. There just wasn't.

'You tell them, you tell them they give us car or I kill this one and all the rest!'

'Let me take my daughter with me, okay?'

'No!' Hurt said.

Unhurt said something in his native tongue, looking down at Hurt, his weapon still pointed at the floor while Hurt's was aimed at O'Day's chest.

'Hey, whatcha got to lose?'

It was almost as though Unhurt said the same thing to his wounded friend, and with that he gave Katie Ryan a yank on the arm. She cried out loudly again as he walked across the room, pushing her ahead of him, blocking Hurt's field of view as he did so. It had taken twenty minutes to achieve. Now he had one second to see if it would work.

The drill was the same for O'Day as it had been for Don Russell. His right hand raced back, whipped inside the jacket, and pulled the pistol out, as he dropped to one knee. The moment Unhurt's body cleared the target, the Smith 1076 loosed two perfect rounds, both of the stainless-steel cases flying in the air, as Hurt became Dead. Unhurt's eyes went wide in surprise, as the children's screams erupted again.

'*DROP IT*,' O'Day bellowed at him.

Unhurt's first reaction was to yank again at Katie Ryan's arm, and at the same time the gun started to move up, as though it were a pistol, but the AK was far too heavy to be used that way. O'Day wanted him alive, but there wasn't the time for chances. His right index finger pushed back on the trigger, then pushed again. The body fell straight down, behind it a red shadow on the white walls of Giant Steps.

Inspector Patrick O'Day jumped across the room, kicking one, then the other rifle free of their dead owners' hands. He gave each body a careful look, and for all the years of practice and instruction he'd given and taken, it still came as a surprise that it all had worked. Only then did his heart start beating again, or so it seemed, as a vacuum filled his chest. His body slumped down for a moment. Then he tensed his muscles and knelt beside the body of Katie Ryan, SANDBOX to the Secret Service, and a *thing* to the people he'd just killed.

'You okay, honey?' he asked. She didn't answer. She was holding her arm and sobbing, but there was no blood on her. 'Come on,' he said gently, wrapping his arms around a daughter who now would forever be partly his. Next he picked up his Megan and walked to the door.

'There's shooting in the building!' a voice said on the desk-mounted speaker. Ryan just froze. The rest of the people in the Sit Room cringed.

860

'Sounded like a pistol. Do they have pistols?' another voice asked on the same radio circuit.

'Holy shit, look there!'

'Who's that?'

'Coming out!' a voice called. 'Coming out!'

'*HOLD FIRE*!' Price called over the loudspeaker. Guns didn't move away from the door, but hands relaxed a fraction.

'Jesus!' Jeffers said, standing and racing to join him in the doorway.

'Both subjects dead, Mrs Daggett, too,' O'Day said. 'All clear, Norm. All clear.'

'Let me –'

'No!' Katie Ryan screamed.

He had to get out of the way. Pat looked down to see the blood-soaked clothing of three agents of his rival agency. There were at least ten rounds by Don Russell's body, and an empty magazine. Beyond were four dead criminals. Two, he saw, walking to the perimeter, head shots. He stopped by his pickup. His knees were a little weak now, and he set the kids down, sitting himself on the bumper. A female agent came up. Pat took the Smith from his belt and handed it over without really looking.

'You hurt?' It was Andrea Price.

He shook his head; it took him a moment to speak again. 'I might start shaking in a minute.' The agent looked at his two little girls. A state trooper scooped Katie Ryan up, but Megan refused to leave his side. That was when he hugged his daughter to his chest, and the tears began for both of them.

'SANDBOX is safe!' he heard Price say. 'SANDBOX is safe and unhurt!'

Price looked around. Backup Service agents hadn't arrived yet, and most of the law-enforcement personnel on the scene were troopers of the Maryland State Police in their starched khaki shirts. Ten of them formed a ring around SANDBOX, guarding her like a pride of lions.

Jeffers rejoined them. O'Day had never fully appreciated the way time changed in such moments as this. When he looked up, the children were being let out the side door. Paramedics were flooding the area, going to the children first. 'Here,' the black agent said, handing over a handkerchief.

'Thanks, Norm.' O'Day wiped his eyes, blew his nose, and stood. 'Sorry about that, guys.'

'It's okay, Pat you did –'

'Better if I'd've taken the last one alive, but couldn't . . . couldn't take the chance.' He was able to stand now, as he held Megan by the hand. 'Oh, damn,' he added.

'I think we should get you out of here,' Andrea observed. 'We can do the interviews in a better place than this.'

'Thirsty,' O'Day said next. He shook his head again. 'Never expected this, Andrea. Kids around. Not supposed to be this way, is it?' Why was he babbling? the inspector asked himself.

'Come on, Pat. You did just fine.'

'Wait a minute.' The FBI inspector rubbed his face with two large hands, took a deep breath, and looked around the crime scene. Christ, what a mess. Three dead just this side of the playground. That would be Jeffers, he thought, with his M-16. Not bad. But there was one other thing he had to do. By each of the rented cars was a body, each a head shot. Another one, one round in the chest, and one in the head, it looked like. The fourth, he wasn't sure who'd gotten him. Probably one of the girls. Ballistics tests would determine which one, he knew. O'Day walked back toward the front door, to the body of Special Agent Donald Russell. There he turned, looking back at the parking lot. He'd seen his share of crime scenes. He knew the signs, knew how to figure things out. No warning, not a damned bit, maybe a second, no more than that, and he'd stood his ground against six armed subjects and gotten three of them. Inspector Patrick O'Day knelt beside the body. He removed the Sig pistol from Russell's hand, gave it to Price, then took the hand in his own for what seemed a long time.

'See y'around, champ,' O'Day whispered, letting go after a few seconds. It was time to leave.

43

RETREAT

The nearest convenient place to land a Marine helicopter was the Naval Academy, and the hard part was finding available Secret Service personnel to ride with SANDBOX. Andrea Price, senior agent on the crime scene as well as Detail chief, had to stay at Giant Steps, so USSS personnel racing to Annapolis were diverted, met the state troopers at the Academy, and took custody of Katie. And so it happened that the first team of federal officers to arrive at the scene were FBI agents from the small Annapolis office, a satellite of the Baltimore Field Division. What orders they needed they took from Price, but for the moment their duties were straightforward, and quite a few more were on the way.

O'Day walked across the street to the house which had been Norm Jeffers' local command post, whose owner, a grandmother, overcame her shock to make coffee. A tape recorder was set up, and the FBI inspector ran through an uninterrupted narrative, really just a long ramble which was actually the best way to get fresh information. Later, they would walk him back through it, probing for additional facts. From where he was sitting, O'Day could see out the window. Ambulance crews were standing by to remove the bodies, but first, photographers had to record the event for posterity.

They couldn't know that Movie Star was still looking down, along with what was now a crowd of several hundred, students and teachers from the community college plus others who'd guessed the nature of the event and wanted to watch. Movie Star had already seen enough, however, and he made his way to his car, picking his way across the parking lot, and then drove north on Ritchie Highway.

'Hey, I gave him a chance. I told him to drop his weapon,' O'Day said. 'I yelled so loud I'm surprised you didn't hear it outside, Price. But the gun started moving, and I wasn't in a mood to take chances, you know?' His hands were steady now. The immediate shock period was over. Others would come later.

'Any idea who they were?' Price asked, after he'd gone through it the first time.

'They were talking in some language, but I don't know what one. Wasn't German or Russian – aside from that, I don't know. Foreign languages sound like foreign languages. I couldn't recognize any words or phrases. Their English was pretty good, accented, but again, not sure what the accent was. Physical appearance, Mediterranean. Maybe from the Middle East. Maybe from some other place. Absolutely ruthless. He shot Mrs Daggett down, not a blink, no emotion – no, that's wrong. He was pissed, very pumped up. No hesitation at all. *Boom*, she's down. Nothing I could have done,' the inspector went on. 'The other one had his gun on me, and it happened so fast, I didn't really see that happening so fast.'

'Pat.' Andrea took his hand. 'You did great.'

The helicopter landed on the White House pad, just south of the ground-floor entrance. Again a ring of agents with weapons was in evidence, as Ryan ran to the aircraft while the rotor was still turning, and nobody tried to stop him. A Marine crewman in a green flight suit pulled the door open and stepped out, which allowed the agents on the helicopter to carry SANDBOX off and hand her off to her father.

Jack cradled her like the baby she no longer was but always would be in his mind, and walked up the slope to the house, where the rest of his family was waiting under cover. News cameras recorded the event, though no reporter got within fifty yards of POTUS. The Secret Service members of the Detail were in a mood to kill; for the first time in the memory of the White House press corps, they looked overly dangerous.

'Mommy!' Katie twisted in her father's arms, reaching for her mother, who took her away from Jack at once. Sally and Little Jack closed in on the pair, leaving their father standing alone. That didn't last for long.

'How you doing?' Arnie van Damm asked quietly.

'Better now, I guess.' His face was still ashen, his body limp but still able to stand. 'Do we know any more?'

'Look, first thing, how about we get all of you out of here? Up to Camp David. You can calm down there. Security is airtight. It's a good place to relax.'

Ryan thought about that. The family hadn't been up there yet, and he'd only been there twice, most recently on a dreadful January day several years before. 'Arnie, we don't have clothes or –'

'We can take care of that,' the chief of staff assured him.

The President nodded. 'Get it set up. Fast,' he added. While Cathy took the kids upstairs, Jack headed back out and over to the West Wing. Two minutes later, he was back in the Situation Room. The mood was better there. The initial shock and fear were gone, replaced with a quiet determination.

'Okay,' Ryan said quietly. 'What do we know?'

'Is that you, Mr President?' It was Dan Murray on the table-mounted speakerphone.

'Talk to me, Dan,' SWORDSMAN commanded.

'We had a guy inside, one of mine. You know him. Pat O'Day, one of my roving inspectors. His daughter – Megan, I think – goes there, too. He got the drop on the subjects and blew 'em both away. The Secret Service people killed the rest – the total count is nine, two by Pat and the rest by Andrea's people. There are five Service agents dead, plus Mrs Daggett. No children were wounded, thank God. Price is interviewing Pat right now. I have about ten agents on the scene to assist with the investigation, with a lot of Service people on the way there, too.'

'Who runs the investigation?' POTUS asked.

'Two statutes on this one. An attack on you or any member of your family is under the purview of the Secret Service. Terrorism is our bailiwick. I'd give the Service lead on this one, and we'll provide all possible assistance,' Murray promised. 'No pissin' contest on this one, my word on it. I've already called Justice. Martin will assign us a senior attorney to coordinate the criminal investigation. Jack?' the FBI Director added.

'What, Dan?'

'Get your family put back together. We know how to do this. I know you're the President, but for the next day or two, just be a guy, okay?'

'Good advice, Jack,' Admiral Jackson observed.

'Jeff?' Ryan said to Agent Raman. All his friends were saying the same thing. They were probably right.

'Yes, sir?'

'Let's get us the hell out of town.'

'Yes, Mr President.' Raman left the room.

'Robby, how about you and Sissy fly up, too. I'll have a helo waiting for you here.'

'Anything you say, pal.'

'Okay, Dan,' Ryan told the speakerphone. 'We're going to Camp David. Keep me informed.'

'Will do,' the FBI Director promised.

They heard it on the radio. Brown and Holbrook were heading north on US Route 287 to join Interstate 90-East. The cement truck drove like a pig, even with its multirange gearbox, top-heavy, slow to accelerate, and almost as slow to brake. Maybe the interstate would be better driving, they hoped. But it did have a decent radio.

'Damn,' Brown said, adjusting the dial.

'Kids.' Holbrook shook his head. 'We have to make sure no kids are around, Ernie.'

'I think we can handle that, Pete, assuming we can horse this rig all the way there.'

'What do you figure?'

A grunt. 'Five days.'

Daryaei took it well, Badrayn saw, especially with the news that all of them were dead.

'Forgive me for saying so, but I did warn you that –'

'I know. I remember,' Mahmoud Haji acknowledged. 'The success of this mission was never really necessary, so long as the security arrangements were properly looked after.' With that, the cleric looked closely at his guest.

'They all had false travel documents. None had a criminal file anywhere in the world, so far as I know. None had anything to connect him with your country. Had one been taken alive, there was a chance, and I warned you about that, but it appears that none were.'

The Ayatollah nodded, and spoke their epitaph: 'Yes, they were faithful.'

Faithful to what? Badrayn asked himself. Overtly religious political leaders weren't exactly uncommon in this part of the world, but it was tiresome to hear. Now, supposedly, all nine of them were in Paradise. He wondered if Daryaei actually believed that. He probably did; he was probably so sure that he believed that he could speak with God's own voice, or at least had told himself so often that he thought he did. One could do that to himself, Ali knew, just keep repeating any idea enough, and however it had first entered one's mind – for political advantage, personal revenge, greed, any of the baser motivations – after enough repetitions it became an article of faith, as pure in purpose as the words of the Prophet himself. Daryaei was seventy-two, Badrayn reminded himself, a long life of self-denial, focused on something outside himself, continuing on a journey that had begun in his youth with shining purpose toward a holy goal. He was a long way from the beginning now, and very close to the end. Now the goal could be seen so clearly that the purpose itself could be forgotten, couldn't it? That was the trap for all such men. At least he knew better, Badrayn told himself. For him it was just business, devoid of illusions and devoid of hypocrisy.

'And the rest?' Daryaei asked, after a prayer for their souls.

'We will know by Monday, perhaps, certainly by Wednesday,' Ali replied.

'And security for that?'

'Perfect.' Badrayn was totally confident. All of the travelers had returned safely, and reported in every case that their missions had been properly carried out. Whatever physical evidence they'd left behind – just the spray cans – would have been collected as trash and carted away. The plague would appear, and there would never be any evidence of how it might have gotten there. And so what had apparently failed today was not a failure at all. This Ryan fellow, relieved though he might be at the rescue of his child, was now a weakened man, as America was a weakened country, and Daryaei had a plan. A good one, Badrayn thought, and for his help in implementing it, his life would change forever now. His days as an international terrorist were a thing of the past. He might have some position in the expanding UIR government – security or intelligence, probably, with a comfortable office and a sizable stipend, able finally to settle down in peace and safety. Daryaei had his dream, and might even achieve it. For Badrayn, the dream was closer still, and he need now not do a thing more to make it a reality. Nine men had died to make it so. That was their misfortune. Were they truly in Paradise for their sacrificial act? Perhaps Allah truly was that merciful, enough to forgive any act done in His Name, mistakenly or not. Perhaps.

It didn't really matter, did it?

They tried to make the departure look normal. The kids had changed clothes. Bags were packed and would go out on a later flight. Security looked tighter than usual, but not grossly so. That was mistaken. Atop the Treasury Building to the east and the Old Executive Office Building to the west, the Secret Service people who usually crouched were now standing, showing their full profiles as they scanned the area with their binoculars. Beside each was a man with a rifle. Eight agents were on the south perimeter fence, examining the people who were passing by or had come just to be there after hearing the horrid news, for whatever purpose. Most had probably come because they cared to some degree or another, maybe even to offer a prayer for the Ryans' safety. For those who had some other purpose, the agents watched, and this time, as with all the others, saw nothing unusual.

Jack strapped in, as did the rest of his family. The engines over their heads started whining, and the rotor turning. Inside with them were Agent Raman and another guard, plus the Marine crew chief. The VH-3 helicopter vibrated, then lifted off, climbing rapidly into the westerly wind, first heading toward the OEOB, then south, then northwest, its curving flight path designed to confuse someone who might be out there with a surface-to-air missile. Light conditions were good enough that such a person would probably be spotted – it takes a few seconds to make a successful launch – and anyway the helicopter was equipped with the newest variant of the Black Hole IR-suppression system, which made Marine One a hard kill. The pilot – it was Colonel Hank Goodman again – knew all this, took the proper protective measures, and did his best to forget about it as he did so.

It was quiet in the back. President Ryan had his thoughts. His wife had hers. The kids looked out the windows, for helicopter flying is one of the greatest thrill rides known to man. Even little Katie twisted in her seat belt to look down, her dreadful afternoon suppressed by the wonder of the moment. Jack turned, and seeing that, he decided that the short attention span of children was as much a blessing as a curse. His own hands were shaking a little now. Fear or rage, he couldn't tell. Cathy just looked bereft, her face slack in the golden light of sunset. Their talk tonight would not be a pleasant one.

Behind them, a Secret Service car had collected Cecilia Jackson from their Fort Myers home. Admiral Jackson and his wife boarded a backup VH-60, along with some carry-on bags, and more substantial luggage for the Ryan family. There were no cameras to record this. The President and First Family were gone, and the cameras with them, while pundits put together their thoughts for the evening news broadcasts, trying to find a deeper significance in the events of the day, coming to conclusions well in advance of the federal officers who only now were allowing the ambulance crews to remove the fifteen bodies from the crime scene. The flashing police lights looked dramatic as TV crews set up to do live broadcasts, one of them from the very spot where Movie Star had observed the burned operation.

He had prepared for this eventuality, of course. He drove north on Ritchie Highway – the traffic wasn't bad at all, considering the police still had the road blocked at Giant Steps – and at Baltimore-Washington International he even had time to turn in his rental car and catch the British Airways 767 for Heathrow. Not first-class this time, he realized. The aircraft was all business class. He didn't smile. He had hoped the kidnapping might actually succeed, though from the beginning he had planned also for its failure. For Movie Star the mission hadn't failed at all. He was still alive, and escaping yet again. Here he was, lifting off, soon to be in another country, and there to disappear completely, even while the American police were trying to establish if there might have been another member of the criminal conspiracy. He decided to have a few glasses of wine, the better to help him sleep after a very stressful day. The thought that it was against his religion, made him smile. What aspect of his life wasn't?

Sunset comes quickly. By the time they started circling at Camp David, the ground was an undulating shadow punctuated by the stationary lights of private homes and the moving lights of automobiles. The helicopter descended slowly, flared out fifty feet above the ground, then settled vertically for a whisper-soft landing. There were few lights beyond the square landing pad's perimeter. When the crew chief opened the door, Raman and the other agent stepped down first. The President undid his lap belt and walked forward. He stopped just behind the flight crew, tapping the pilot on the shoulder.

'Thanks, Colonel.'

'You have a lot of friends, Mr President. We're here when you need us,' Goodman told his Commander-in-Chief.

Jack nodded, went down the steps, and beyond the lights he saw the spectral outlines of Marine riflemen in camouflaged utilities.

'Welcome to Camp David, sir.' It was a Marine captain.

Jack turned to help his wife down. Sally led Katie down. Little Jack came out last. It hit Ryan that his son was almost as tall as his mother now. He might have to call his son something else.

Cathy looked around nervously. The captain saw it.

'Ma'am, there's sixty Marines out there,' he assured her. He didn't have to add what they were there for. He didn't have to tell the President how alert they were.

'Where?' Little Jack asked, looking and seeing nothing.

'Try this.' The captain handed over his PVS-7 night-vision goggles. SHORTSTOP held them to his eyes.

'*Cool!*' His arm reached out, pointing to those he could see. Then he lowered the goggles, and the Marines turned invisible again.

'They're great for spotting deer, and there's a bear that wanders on and off the grounds every so often. We call him Yogi.' Captain Larry Overton, USMC, congratulated himself for calming them down, and led them toward the HMMWVs that would transport them to quarters. Yogi, he'd explain later, had a radio collar on so that he wouldn't surprise anybody, least of all a Marine with a loaded rifle.

The quarters at Camp David appeared rustic, and truly were not anywhere near as plush as those in the White House, but could accurately be described as the sort of hide-

away a millionaire might set up for himself outside Aspen –
in fact, Presidential Quarters are officially known as Aspen
Cottage. Maintained by Naval Surface Detachment, Thur-
mont (Maryland), and guarded by a short company of hand-
picked Marines, the compound was as remote and secure a
location as anything within a hundred miles of Washington
could possibly be. There were Marines at the presidential
cabin to let them in, and inside were sailors to guide each
to a private bedroom. Outside were twelve additional cot-
tages, and the closer you were to Aspen, of course, the more
important you were.

'What's for dinner?' Jack Junior asked.

'Just about anything you want,' a Navy chief steward
replied.

Jack turned to Cathy. She nodded. This would be a what-
ever-you-want night. The President took off his jacket and
tie. A steward darted up to collect them. 'The food is great
here, Mr President,' he promised.

'That's a fact, sir,' the chief confirmed. 'We have a deal
with some local folks. Fresh everything, right off the farm.
Can I get you something to drink?' he asked hopefully.

'That sounds like a great plan, chief. Cathy?'

'White wine?' she asked, the stress bleeding off her, finally.

'We have a pretty good selection, ma'am. For domestic,
how about a Chateau Ste. Michelle reserve chardonnay? It's
a 1991 vintage, and about as good as a chardonnay gets.'

'You're a Navy chief?' POTUS asked.

'Yes, sir. I used to take care of admirals, but I got promoted,
and if I may say so, sir, I do know my wines.'

Ryan held up two fingers. The chief nodded and went out
the door.

'This is insane,' Cathy said after he left.

'Don't knock it.' While they waited for drinks, the two big
kids agreed on a pizza. Katie wanted a burger and fries. They
heard the buzz of another helicopter coming into the pad.
Cathy was right, her husband thought. This is insane.

The door reopened, and the chief returned with two bottles
and a silver bucket. Another steward followed with glasses.

'Chief, I just meant two glasses.'

'Yes, Mr President, but we have two more guests arriving,
Admiral and Mrs Jackson. Mrs Jackson likes a good white

also, sir.' He popped the cork and poured a splash for SUR-GEON. She nodded.

'Doesn't it have a wonderful nose?' He filled her glass and one other, handing that to the President. Then he withdrew.

'They always told me the Navy had guys like that, but I never believed it.'

'Oh, Jack.' Cathy turned. The kids were watching TV, all three sitting on the floor, even Sally, who was trying to become an elegant lady. They were retreating into the familiar, while their parents did what parents always did, came to terms with a new reality, in order to buffer their children from the world.

Jack saw the lights of a HMMWV go past to the left. Robby and Sissy would have their own cabin, he imagined. They'd change before coming over. He turned back and wrapped his arms around his wife from behind. 'It's okay, babe.'

Cathy shook her head. 'It'll never be okay, Jack. It'll never be okay again. Roy told me, as long as we live, we'll have bodyguards with us. Everywhere we go, we'll need protection. Forever,' she said, sipping her wine, not so much angry as resigned, not so much dazed as comprehending something she'd never dreamed. The trappings of power were seductive sometimes. A helicopter to work. People to take care of your clothes, look after the kids, whatever food you wanted as close as the phone, escorts everywhere, fast track into everything.

But the price of it? No big deal. Just every so often somebody might try to murder one of your children. There was no running away from it. It was as though she'd been given a diagnosis of cancer, of the breast, the ovaries, something else. Horrible as it was, you had to do what you had to do. Crying didn't help, though she'd do a lot of that, SURGEON was sure. Screaming at Jack wouldn't help – and she wasn't a screamer anyway, and it wasn't Jack's fault, was it? She just had to roll with the punch, like patients at Hopkins did when you told them they had to go see the Oncology Department – *oh, please, don't worry. They're the best, the very best, and times have changed, and they really know what they're doing now*. Her colleagues in the Department of Oncology were the best. And they had a nice new building now. But who really wanted to go there?

And so she and Jack had a nice house of sorts, with a wonderful staff, some of whom were even wine experts, she thought, taking another sip from her glass. *But who really wants to go there?*

So many agents were assigned to the case that they didn't know what to do yet. They didn't have enough rough information to generate leads, but that was changing fast. Most of the dead terrorists had been photographed – two of them, shot from behind by Norm Jeffers's M-16 rifle, didn't have faces to photograph – and all of the bodies fingerprinted. Blood samples would be taken for DNA records in case that later became useful – a possibility, since identity *could* be confirmed by a genetic match with close relatives. For now they went with the photos. These were transmitted to the Mossad first of all. The terrorists had probably been Islamic, everyone thought, and the Israelis had the best data on them. CIA handled the initial notice, followed by the FBI. Full cooperation was promised at once, personally, by Avi ben Jakob.

All of the bodies were taken to Annapolis for postmortem examination. This was required by law, even in cases where the cause of death was as obvious as an earthquake. The pre-death condition of each body would be established, plus a full blood-toxicology check to see if any were on drugs.

The clothing of each was removed for full examination at the FBI laboratory in Washington. The brand names were established first of all to determine country of origin. That and general condition, would determine time of purchase, which could be important. More than that, the technicians now working overtime on a Friday evening would use ordinary Scotch tape to collect loose fibres, and especially pollen particles, which could determine many things, because some plants grew only in limited regions of the world. Such results could take weeks, but with a case such as this, there was no limit on resources. The FBI had a lengthy roster of scientific experts to consult.

Tag numbers for the cars had been transmitted even before O'Day had done his shooting, and already agents were at the car-rental agencies, checking the computerized records.

At Giant Steps, the adult survivors were being interviewed.

They mainly confirmed O'Day's reportage. Some of the details were askew, but that was not unexpected. None of the young women recognized the language the terrorists had spoken. The children were subjected to far gentler interrogations, in every case sitting on a parent's lap. Two of the parents were from the Middle East, and it was thought that perhaps the children knew something of foreign languages, but that proved to be a false hope.

The weapons had all been collected, and their serial numbers checked with a computerized database. The date of manufacture was easily established, and the makers' records checked to see which distributor had purchased them, and from there which store had sold them. That trail proved cold indeed. The weapons were old ones, a fact belied by their new condition, which was established by visual inspection of the barrel and bolt mechanisms. They hardly had any wear at all. That tidbit of information went up the line even before they had a purchaser's name.

'Damn, I wish Bill was here,' Murray said aloud, for the first time in his career feeling inadequate to a task. His division chiefs were arrayed around his conference table. From the first it was certain that this investigation would be a joint venture between the Criminal and Foreign Counter-Intelligence divisions, aided, as always, by Laboratory. Things were moving so rapidly that there wasn't yet a Secret Service official to join them. 'Thoughts?'

'Dan, whoever bought these guns has been in-country a long time,' FCI said.

'Sleeper.' Murray nodded agreement.

'Pat didn't recognize their language. He would probably have recognized a European one. Has to be the Middle East,' Criminal said. This wasn't exactly Nobel-class work, but even the FBI had to follow form in what it did. 'Well, Western Europe, anyway. I suppose we have to consider the Balkan countries.' There was reluctant agreement around the table.

'How old are those guns again?' the Director asked.

'Eleven years. Long before the ban was passed,' Criminal answered for FCI. 'They may have been totally unused until today, virgins, Dan.'

'Somebody's set up a network that we didn't know about.

Somebody real patient. Whoever the purchaser turns out to be, I think we'll find that it's a nicely faked ID, and he's already flown the coop. It's a classic intelligence job, Dan,' FCI went on, saying what everybody was thinking. 'We're talking pros here.'

'That's a little speculative,' the Director objected.

'When's the last time I was wrong, Danny?' the assistant director asked.

'Not lately. Keep going.'

'Maybe the Lab guys can develop some good forensic stuff' – he nodded to the assistant director for the Laboratory Division – 'but even then, what we're going to end up with won't be good enough to take into a court, unless we get real lucky and bag either the purchaser, or the other people who had to be involved in this mission.'

'Flight records and passports,' Criminal said. 'Two weeks back for starters. Look for repeaters. Somebody reconned the objective. Must have been since Ryan became President. That's a start.' Sure, he didn't go on, only about ten million records to check. But that was what cops did.

'Christ, I hope you're wrong on the sleeper,' Murray said, after a further moment's reflection.

'So do I, Dan,' FCI replied. 'But I'm not. We'll need time to ID his house, assembly point, whatever, interview his neighbors, check the real-estate records to come up with a cover name and try to proceed from there. He's probably already gone, but that's not the scary part, is it? Eleven years at least he's been here. He was bankrolled. He was trained. He kept the faith all the way to today to help with that mission. All that time, and he still believed enough to help kill kids.'

'He won't be the only one,' Murray concluded bleakly.

'I don't think so.'

'Will you come with me, please?'

'I've seen you before, but –'

'Jeff Raman, sir.'

The admiral took his hand. 'Robby Jackson.'

The agent smiled. 'I know that, sir.'

It was a pleasant walk, though it would have been more so without the obvious presence of armed men. The mountain air was cool and clear, lots of stars blinking overhead.

'How's he doing?' Robby asked the agent.

'Tough day. A lot of good people dead.'

'And some bad ones, too.' Jackson would always be a fighter pilot, for whom inflicted death was part of the job description. They turned into the Presidential Quarters.

Both Robby and Sissy were struck by the scene. Not parents themselves – Cecilia's medical problem had not allowed it, despite the best of efforts – they didn't fully understand how it was with kids. The most horrific events, if followed by a parent's hug and other signs of security, were usually set aside. The world, especially for Katie, had resumed its proper shape. But there would be nightmares, too, and those would last for weeks, maybe longer, until the memories faded. Embraces were exchanged, and then also as usual, man paired with man and woman with woman. Robby got himself a glass of wine and followed Jack outside.

'How you doing, Jack?' By unspoken agreement, here and now Ryan wasn't the President.

'The shock comes and goes,' he admitted. 'It's all come back from before. The bastards can't just come after me – oh, no, they have to go for the soft targets. *Those cowardly fucks!*' Jack cursed as it came back again.

Jackson sipped at his glass. There wasn't a whole hell of a lot to be said right now, but that would change.

'It's my first time here,' Robby said, just to say something.

'My first time – would you believe we buried a guy up here?' Jack remarked, remembering. 'He was a Russian colonel, an agent we had in their Defense Ministry. Hell of a soldier, hero of the Soviet Union, three or four times, I think, we buried him in his uniform with all the decorations. I read off the citations myself. That's when we got Gerasimov out.'

'The KGB head. So, that's true, eh?'

'Yep.' Ryan nodded. 'And you know about Colombia, and you know about the submarine. How the hell did those newsies find out, though?'

Robby almost laughed aloud, but settled for a chuckle. 'Holy God, and I thought my career was eventful.'

'You volunteered for yours,' Jack observed crossly.

'So did you, my friend.'

'Think so?' Ryan went back inside for a refill. He returned with the night-vision goggles and switched them on, scanning the surroundings. 'I didn't volunteer for having my family guarded by a company of Marines. There's three of them down there, flak jackets, helmets, and rifles – and why? Because there's people in the world who want to kill us. Why? Because –'

'I'll tell you why. Because you're better than they are, Jack. You stand for things, and they're good things. Because you've got balls, and you don't run away from shit. I don't want to hear this, Jack,' Robby told his friend. 'Don't give me this "oh, my God" stuff, okay? I know who you are. I'm a fighter pilot because I chose to be one. You're where you are because you chose, too. Nobody ever said it was supposed to be easy, okay?'

'But –'

'But, my ass, Mr President. There's people out there who don't like you? Okay, fine. You just figure out how to find them, and then you can ask those Marines out there to go take care of business. You know what they'll say. You may be hated by some, but you're respected and loved by a lot more, and I'm telling you now, there's not one person in our country's uniform who isn't willing to dust *anybody* who fucks with you and your family. It's not just what you are, it's who you are, okay?'

Who am I? SWORDSMAN asked himself. At that moment, one of his weaknesses asserted itself.

'Come on.' Ryan walked over to the west. He'd just seen a sudden flare of light, and thirty seconds later, at the corner of another cabin, he found a Navy cook smoking a cigarette. President or not, he wasn't going to be overly proud tonight. 'Hello.'

'Jesus!' the sailor blurted, snapping to attention and dropping his smoke into the grass. 'I mean, hello, Mr President.'

'Wrong the first time, right the second time. Got a smoke?' POTUS asked, entirely without shame, Robby Jackson noted.

'You bet, sir.' The cook fished one out and lit it.

'Sailor, if the First Lady sees you do that again, she'll have the Marines shoot you,' Jackson warned.

'Admiral Jackson!' Those words made the kid brace again. 'I think the Marines work for me. How's dinner coming?'

'Sir, the pizza is being cut right now. Baked it myself, sir. They oughta like it,' he promised.

'Settle down. Thanks for the cigarette.'

'Anytime, sir.' Ryan shook his hand and wandered off with his friend.

'I needed that,' Jack admitted, somewhat shamefully, taking a long drag.

'If I had a place like this, I'd use it a lot. Almost like being at sea,' Jackson went on. 'Sometimes you go outside, stand on one of the galleries off the flight deck, and just sort of enjoy the sea and the stars. The simple pleasures.'

'It's hard to turn it off, isn't it? Even when you went communing with the sea and the stars, you didn't turn it off, not really.'

'No,' the admiral admitted. 'It makes thinking a little easier, makes the atmosphere a little less intense, but you're right. It doesn't really go away.' And it didn't now, either.

'Tony said India's navy's gone missing on us.'

'Both carriers at sea, with escorts and oilers. We're looking for them.'

'What if there's a connection?' Ryan asked.

'With what?'

'The Chinese make trouble in one place, the Indian navy goes to sea again, and *this* happens to me – am I being paranoid?' SWORDSMAN asked.

'Probably. Could be the Indians put out when they finished their repairs, and maybe to show us that we didn't teach them all that big a lesson. The China thing, well, it's happened before, and it's not going anywhere, especially after Mike Dubro gets there. I know Mike. He'll have fighters up and poking around. The attempt on Katie? Too early to say, and it's not my field. You have Murray and the rest for that. In any case, they failed, didn't they? Your family's in there, watching TV, and it'll be a long time before somebody tries anything else.'

It was becoming an all-nighter all over the world. In Tel Aviv, where it was now after four in the morning, Avi ben Jakob had called in his top terrorism experts. Together they went over the photos transmitted from Washington and were comparing them with their own surveillance photographs that had been taken over the years in Lebanon and elsewhere. The problem was that many of their photos showed young men with beards – the simplest method of disguise known to man – and the photos were not of high quality. By the same token, the American-transmitted images were not exactly graduation pictures, either.

'Anything useful?' the director of Mossad asked.

Eyes turned to one of the Mossad's experts, a fortyish woman named Sarah Peled. Behind her back, they called her the witch. She had some special gift for ID'ing people from photographs, and was right just over half the time in cases where other trained intelligence officers threw up their hands in frustration.

'This one.' She slid two photos across the table. 'This is a definite match.'

Ben Jakob looked at the two side by side – and saw nothing to confirm her opinion. He'd asked her many times what keyed her in on such things. Sarah always said it was the eyes, and so Avi took another look, comparing the eyes of one with the eyes of the other photo. All he saw were eyes. He turned the Israeli photo over. The printed data on the back said that he was a suspected Hezbollah member, name unknown, age about twenty in their photo, which was dated six years earlier.

'Any others, Sarah?' he asked.

'No, none at all.'

'How confident are you on this one?' one of the counter-intelligence people asked, looking at the photos himself now and, like Avi, seeing nothing.

'One hundred percent, Benny. I said "definite," didn't I?' Sarah was often testy, especially with unbelieving men at four in the morning.

'How far do we go on this?' another staff member asked.

'Ryan is a friend of our country, and President of the United States. We go as far as we can. I want inquiries to go out. All contacts, Lebanon, Syria, Iraq and Iran, everywhere.'

'Swine.' Bondarenko ran a hand through his hair. His tie was long since gone. His watch told him it was Saturday, but he didn't know what that day was anymore.

'Yes,' Golovko agreed.

'A black operation – a "wet" one, you used to call it?' the general asked.

'Wet and incompetent,' the RVS chairman said crossly. 'But Ivan Emmetovich was lucky, Comrade General. This time.'

'Perhaps,' Gennady Iosefovich allowed.

'You disagree?'

'The terrorists underestimated their opponents. You will recall that I recently spent time with the American army. Their training is like nothing else in the world, and the training of their presidential guard must be equally as expert. Why is it that people so often underestimate the Americans?' he wondered.

That was a good question, Sergey Nikolay'ch recognized, nodding for the chief of operations to go on.

'America often suffers from a lack of political direction. That is not the same as incompetence. You know what they are like? A vicious dog held on a short leash – and because he cannot break the leash, people delude themselves that they need not fear him, but within the arc of that leash he is invincible, and a leash, Comrade Chairman, is a temporary thing. You know this Ryan fellow.'

'I know him well,' Golovko agreed.

'And? The stories in their press, are they true?'

'All of them.'

'I tell you what I think, Sergey Nikolay'ch. If you regard him as a formidable adversary, and he has that vicious dog on the leash, I would not go far out of my way to offend him. An attack on a child? *His* child?' The general shook his head.

That was it, Golovko realized. They were both tired, but here was a moment of clarity. He'd spent too much time reading over the political reports from Washington, from his own embassy, and directly from the American media. They all said that Ivan Emmetovich . . . was that the key? From the beginning he'd called Ryan that, thinking to honor the man with the Russian version of his name and the Russian patronymic. And an honor it was in Golovko's context . . .

'You are thinking what I am thinking, *da*?' the general asked, seeing the man's face and gesturing for him to speak.

'Someone has made a calculation . . .'

'And it is not an accurate one. I think we need to find out

who has done so. I think a systematic attack on American interests, an attempt to weaken America, Comrade Chairman, is really an attack against our interests. Why is China doing what she is doing, eh? Why did they force America to change her naval dispositions? And now this? American forces are being stretched, and at the same time a strike at the very heart of the American leader. This is no coincidence. Now we can stand aside and do nothing more than observe, or –'

'There is nothing we can do, and with the revelations in the American press –'

'Comrade Chairman,' Bondarenko interrupted. 'For seventy years, our country has confused political theory with objective fact, and that was almost our undoing as a nation. There are objective conditions here,' he went on, using a phrase beloved of the Soviet military – a reaction, perhaps, to their three generations of political oversight. 'I see the patterns of a clever operation, a coordinated operation, but one which has a fatal flaw, and that flaw is a misestimation of the American President. Do you disagree?'

Golovko gave that a few seconds of thought, noting also that Bondarenko might just be seeing something real – but did the Americans? It was so much harder to see something from the inside than the outside. A coordinated operation? Back to Ryan, he told himself.

'No. I made that mistake myself. Ryan appears much less than what he is. The signs are all there, but people don't see them.'

'When I was in America, that General Diggs told me the story of the time terrorists attacked Ryan's house. He took up arms and defeated them, courageously and decisively. From what you say, it appears he is also highly effective as an intelligence officer. His only flaw, if one may call it that, is that he is not politically adept, and politicians invariably take that for weakness. Perhaps it is,' Bondarenko allowed. 'But if this is a hostile operation against America, then his political weaknesses are far less important than his other gifts.'

'And?'

'Help the man,' the general urged. 'Better that we should be on the winning side, and if we do not help, then we might be on the other. Nobody will attack America directly. We are not so fortunate, Comrade Chairman.' He was almost right.

44

INCUBATION

Ryan awoke at dawn, wondering why. The quiet. Almost like his home on the Bay. He strained to listen for traffic or other sounds, but there were none. Moving out of the bed was difficult. Cathy had decided to have Katie in with them, and there she was in her pink sleeper, looking angelic as toddlers did, still babies at that age whatever others might say. He had to smile, then made his way to the bathroom. Casual clothes had been set out in the dressing room, and he put them on, with a pair of sneaks and a sweater, to head outside.

The air was brisk, with traces of frost on the boxwoods, and the sky clear. Not bad. Robby was right. This wasn't a bad place to come to. It put a distance between himself and other things, and he needed that right now.

'Morning, sir.' It was Captain Overton.

'Not bad duty, is it?'

The young officer nodded. 'We do the security. The Navy does the petunias. It's a fair division of labor, Mr President. Even the Secret Service guys can sleep in here, sir.'

Ryan looked around and saw why. There were two armed Marines immediately around the cabin, and three more within fifty yards. And those were just the ones he could see.

'Get you anything, Mr President?'

'Coffee'll do for a start.'

'Follow me, sir.'

'Attention on deck!' a sailor shouted a few seconds later, when Ryan went into the cook shed – or whatever they called it here.

'As you were,' the President told them. 'I thought this was the Presidential Retreat, not boot camp.' He picked a seat at the table the staff used. Coffee appeared as if by magic. Then more magic happened.

'Good morning, Mr President.'

'Hi, Andrea. When did you get in?'

'Around two, helicopter,' she explained.

'Get any sleep?'

'About four hours.'

Ryan took a sip. Navy coffee was still Navy coffee. 'And?'

'The investigation is under way. The team's put together. Everybody's got a seat at the table.' She handed over a folder, which Ryan would get to read before his morning paper. Anne Arundel County and Maryland State Police, Secret Service, FBI, ATF, and all the intelligence agencies were working the case. They were running IDs on the terrorists, but the two whose documents had so far been checked turned out to be non-persons. Their papers were false, probably of European origin. Big surprise. Any competent European criminal, much less a terrorist organization, could procure phony passports. He looked up.

'What about the agents we lost?'

A sigh, a shrug. 'They all have families.'

'Let's get it set up so that I can meet with them . . . should it be all at once or one at a time?'

'Your choice, sir,' Price told him.

'No, it has to be what's best for them. They're your people, Andrea. You work that out for me, okay? I owe them my daughter's life, and I have to do what's right for them,' POTUS said soberly, remembering why he was in this quiet and peaceful place. 'And I presume that they will be properly looked after. Get me the details on that, insurance, pensions, and stuff, okay? I want to look that over.'

'Yes, sir.'

'Do we know anything important yet?'

'No, not really. The terrorists who've been posted, their dental work definitely isn't American, that's it for now.'

Ryan flipped through the papers he had. One preliminary conclusion leaped off the page at him: 'Eleven years?'

'Yes, sir.'

'So this is a major operation for somebody – a country.'

'That's a real possibility.'

'Who else would have the resources?' he asked, and Price reminded herself that he'd been an intelligence officer for a long time.

Agent Raman came in and took his seat. He'd heard that observation, and he and Price traded a look and a nod.

The wall phone rang. Captain Overton walked over to get it. 'Yes?' He listened for a few minutes, then turned. 'Mr President, this is Mrs Foley at CIA.'

The President went to take the call. 'Yeah, Mary Pat.'

'Sir, we had a call a few minutes ago from Moscow. Our friend Golovko asks if he can be of any assistance. I recommend a "yes" on that.'

'Agreed. Anything else?'

'Avi ben Jakob wants to talk to you later today. Ears-only,' the DDO told him.

'About an hour, let me get woke up first.'

'Yes, sir . . . Jack?'

'Yeah, MP?'

'Thank God about Katie,' she said, mother to father, then going on as mother alone: 'If we can get a line on this, we will.'

'I know you're our best,' Mrs Foley heard. 'We're doing okay right now.'

'Good. Ed and I will be in all day.' She hung up.

'How's he sound?' Clark asked.

'He'll make it, John.'

Chavez rubbed his hand over the night's growth of beard. The three of them plus quite a few others had spent the night reviewing everything CIA had on terrorist groups. 'We have to do something about this, guys. This is an act of war.' His voice was devoid of accent now, as it tended to be when he got serious enough to call on his education instead of his L.A. origins.

'We don't know much. Hell,' the DDO said, 'we don't know anything yet.'

'Shame he couldn't have taken one alive.' This observation, to the surprise of the two others, came from Clark.

'He probably didn't have much of a chance to snap the cuffs on the guy,' Ding replied.

'True.' Clark lifted the set of crime-scene photos that had been couriered over from the FBI just after midnight. He'd worked the Middle East, and it had been hoped that he might have recognized a face, but he hadn't. Mainly he'd learned that whichever FBI puke had been inside, the gent could shoot as well as he ever had. Lucky man, to have been there, to have had that chance, and to take it.

'Somebody's taking one hell of a big chance,' John said.

'That's a fact,' Mary Pat agreed automatically, but then they all wondered about it.

The question was not how big the chance was, but rather how big the chance was perceived to be by whoever had tossed the dice. The nine terrorists had all been throwaways, as surely marked for death as the Hezbollah fanatics who'd gone strolling down Israeli streets in clothing made by DuPont – that was the CIA joke about it, though in fact the plastic explosives had probably come from the Skoda Works in the former Czechoslovakia. 'Not-so-smart bombs' was the other in-house sobriquet. Had they really believed that they could pull it off? The problem with some of the fanatics was that they didn't weigh things very well . . . maybe they hadn't even cared.

That was also the problem of those who sent them. This mission had been different, after all. Ordinarily, terrorists boasted widely of what they did, however odious the act, and at CIA and elsewhere they'd waited for fifteen hours for the press release. But it never came, and if it hadn't by now, then it never would. If they didn't make the release, then they didn't want anyone to know. But that was an illusion. Terrorists always proclaimed their acts, but they didn't always appreciate that police agencies could figure things out anyway.

Nation-states knew better, or were supposed to. Okay, fine, the dealers hadn't had anything that could identify their point of origin – or so some might think. But Mary Pat was under no such illusions. The FBI was better than good, good enough that the Secret Service was letting the Bureau handle all of the forensics. And so it was likely that whoever had initiated the mission might actually expect that the story would eventually unravel. Knowing that – probably – they'd gone ahead with it anyway. If this line of speculation were true, then –

'Part of something else?' Clark asked. 'Not a stand-alone. Something else, too.'

'Maybe,' Mary Pat observed.

'If it is, it's big,' Chavez went on for them. 'Maybe that's why the Russians called in to us.'

'So big ... so big that even if we figure it out, it won't matter when we do.'

'That's pretty big, Mary Pat,' Clark said quietly. 'What could it be ... ?'

'Something permanent, something we can't change after it's done,' Domingo offered. His time at George Mason University hadn't been wasted.

Mrs Foley wished her husband were in on this, but Ed was meeting with Murray right now.

Saturdays in the spring are often days of dull but hopeful routine, but in just over two hundred homes little was done. Gardens were not planted. Cars were not washed. Garage sales were not attended. Paint cans went unopened. That wasn't counting government employees or news personnel working the big story of the week. Mainly the people suffering from the flu were men. Thirty of them were in hotel rooms. Several even tried to work, attending their trade shows in the new cities. Wiping their faces, blowing their noses, and wishing the aspirin or Tylenol would kick in. Of the last group, most went back to the hotel rooms to relax – no sense in getting the customers sick, was there? In not a single case did anyone seek medical attention. There was the usual winter/spring flu bug circulating around, and everybody got it sooner or later. They weren't that sick, after all, were they?

News coverage of the incident at Giant Steps was entirely predictable, starting with camera shots taken from about fifty yards away, and the same words repeated by all of the correspondents, followed by the same words delivered by 'experts' in terrorism and/or other fields. One of the networks took the viewer all the way back to Abraham Lincoln for no other reason than that it was otherwise a very slow news day. All of the coverage pointed to the Middle East, though the investigating agencies had declined any comment at all on the event so far, except to cite an FBI agent's heroic interference and the spirited battle put up by the Secret Service bodyguards of little Katie Ryan. Words like 'heroic,' 'dedicated,' and 'determined' were bandied about with great frequency, leading to the 'dramatic conclusion.'

Something very simple had gone wrong, Badrayn was certain, though he wouldn't know for sure until his colleague got back to Tehran from London, via Brussels and Vienna, on several different sets of travel documents.

'The President and his family are at the Presidential Retreat at Camp David,' the reporter concluded, 'to recover from the shock of this dreadful event just north of peaceful Annapolis, Maryland. This is . . .'

'Retreat?' Daryaei asked.

'It means many things in English, first among them is to run away,' Badrayn answered, mainly because he was sure that's what his employer would like to hear.

'If he thinks he can run away from me, he is mistaken,' the cleric observed in dark amusement, the spirit of the moment getting the better of his discretion.

Badrayn didn't react to the revelation. It was easy at the instant of his realization, since he was looking at the TV and not at his host, but things then became more clear. There was not all that much risk at all, was there? Mahmoud Haji had a way to kill this man, perhaps whenever he wished to do so, and it was all being orchestrated. Could he really do it? But, of course, he already had.

IVIS made life hard on the OpFor. Not all that hard. Colonel Hamm and the Blackhorse had won this one, but what only a year before would have been a wipeout of cosmic proportions – Fort Irwin *was* in California, and some linguistic peculiarities were inevitable – had been a narrow victory. War was about information. It was always the lesson of the National Training Center: Find the enemy. Don't let the enemy find you. Reconnaissance. Reconnaissance. Reconnaissance. The IVIS system, operated by halfway competent people, shot the information out to everyone so fast that the soldiers were leaning in the right direction even before the orders came down. That had nearly negated a maneuver on the OpFor's part, which would have been worthy of Erwin Rommel on his best day, and as he watched the fast-play of the exercise on the big screen in the Star Wars Room, Hamm saw just how close it had been. If one of those Blue Force tank companies had moved just five minutes faster, he would have lost this one, too. The NTC would surely lose its effectiveness if the Good Guys won regularly.

'That was a beautiful move, Hamm,' the colonel of the Carolina Guard admitted, reaching in his pocket for a cigar and handing it over. 'But we'll whip your ass tomorrow.'

Ordinarily, he would have smiled and said, *Sure you will*. But the cracker son of a bitch just might pull it off, and that would take a lot of the fun out of Hamm's life. The colonel of the 11th Armored Cavalry Regiment would now have to come up with ways of spoofing IVIS. It was something he'd thought about, and had been the subject of a few discussions over beers with his operations officer, but so far they had only agreed that it was no small feat, probably involving dummy vehicles . . . like Rommel had used. He'd have to get funding for those. He walked outside to smoke his cigar. It had been honorably won. He found the Guard colonel there, too.

'For Guardsmen, you're pretty damned good,' Hamm had to admit. He'd never said such a thing to a Guard formation before. He rarely said it to anyone at all. Except for one deployment error, the Blue Force plan had been a thing of beauty.

'Thank you for saying that, Colonel. IVIS came as a rude surprise, didn't it?'

'You might say that.'

'My people love it. A lot come in on their own time to play on the simulators. Hell, I'm surprised you took us on this one.'

'Your reserve was too close in,' Hamm told him. 'You thought you knew what to exploit. Instead, I caught you out of position to meet my counterattack.' It wasn't a revelation. The senior observer/controller had made that lesson clear to the momentarily contrite tank commander.

'I'll try to remember that. Catch the news?'

'Yeah, that sucks,' Hamm thought aloud.

'Little kids. I wonder if they award medals to the Secret Service?'

'They have something, I imagine. I can think of worse things to die for.' And that's what it was all about. Those five agents had died doing their jobs, running to the sound of the guns. They must have made some mistakes, but sometimes you didn't have a choice in the matter. All soldiers knew that.

'God rest their brave souls.' The man sounded like Robert Edward Lee. It triggered something in Hamm.

'What's the story on you guys? You, Colonel Eddington, you're not supposed – what the hell do you do in real life?' The guy was over fifty, very marginal for an officer in command of a brigade, even in the Guard.

'I'm professor of military history at the University of North Carolina. What's the story? This brigade was supposed to be the round-out for 24th Mech back in 1991, and we came here for workups and got our ass handed to us. Never got to deploy. I was a battalion XO then, Hamm. We wanted to go. Our regimental standards go back to the Revolution. It hurt our pride. We've been waiting to come back here near on ten years, boy, and this IVIS box gives us a fair chance.' He was a tall, thin man, and when he turned, he was looking down at the regular officer. 'We are going to make use of that chance, son. I know the theory. I been readin' and studyin' on it for over thirty years, and my men ain't'a'gonna roll over and die for you, you he'ah?' When aroused, Nicholas Eddington tended to adopt an accent.

''Specially not for Yankees?'

'Damn right!' Then it was time for a laugh. Nick Eddington was a teacher, with a flair for the impromptu dramatic. The voice softened. 'I know, if we didn't have IVIS, you'd murder us –'

'Ain't technology wonderful?'

'It almost makes us your equal, and your men are the best. Everybody knows that,' Eddington conceded. It was a worthy peace gesture.

'With the hours we keep, kinda hard to get a beer at the club when you need one. Can I offer you one at my home, sir?'

'Lead on, Colonel Hamm.'

'What's your area of specialty?' BLACKHORSE SIX asked on the way to his car.

'My dissertation was on the operational art of Nathan Bedford Forrest.'

'Oh? I've always admired Buford, myself.'

'He only had a couple of days, but they were all good days. He might have won the war for Lincoln at Gettysburg.'

'The Spencer carbines gave his troopers the technical edge,' Hamm announced. 'People overlook that factor.'

'Choosing the best ground didn't hurt, and the Spencers helped, but what he did best was to remember his mission,' Eddingon replied.

'As opposed to Stuart. Jeb definitely had a bad day. I suppose he was due for one.' Hamm opened the car door for his colleague. It would be a few hours before they had to prepare for the next exercise, and Hamm was a serious student of history, especially of the cavalry. This would be an interesting breakfast: beer, eggs, and the Civil War.

They bumped into each other in the parking lot of the 7-Eleven, which was doing a great business in coffee and donuts at the moment.

'Hi, John,' Holtzman said, looking at the crime scene from across the street.

'Bob,' Plumber acknowledged with a nod. The area was alive with cameras, TV and still, recording the scene for history.

'You're up early for a Saturday – TV guy, too,' the *Post* reporter noted with a friendly smile. 'What do you make of it?'

'This really is a terrible thing.' Plumber was himself a grandfather many times over.

'Was it Ma'alot, the one in Israel, back – what? 1975, something like that?' They all seemed to blend together, these terrorist incidents.

Holtzman wasn't sure, either. 'I think so. I have somebody checking it back at the office.'

'Terrorists make for good stories, but, dear God, we'd be better off without them.'

The crime scene was almost pristine. The bodies were gone. The autopsies were complete by now, they both imagined. But everything else was intact, or nearly so. The cars were there, and as the reporters watched, ballistics experts were running strings to simulate shots at mannequins brought in from a local department store, trying to re-create every detail of the event. The black guy in the Secret Service wind-breaker was Norman Jeffers, one of the heroes of the day, now demonstrating how he'd come down from the house across the street. Inside was Inspector Patrick O'Day. Some agents were simulating the movements of the terrorists. One man lay on the ground by the front door, aiming a red plastic 'play gun' around. In criminal investigations, the dress rehearsals always came after the play.

'His name was Don Russell?' Plumber asked.

'One of the oldest guys in the Service,' Holtzman confirmed.

'Damn.' Plumber shook his head. 'Horatius at the bridge, like something from a movie. "Heroic" isn't a word we use often, is it?'

'No, that isn't something we're supposed to believe in any more, is it? We know better. Everybody's got an angle, right?' Holtzman finished off his coffee and dumped the cup in the trash bin. 'Imagine, giving up your life to protect other people's kids.'

Some reports talked about it in Western terms. 'Gunfight at the Kiddy Corral' some local TV reporter had tried out, winning the low-taste award for last night, and earning his station a few hundred negative calls, confirming to the station manager that his outlet had a solid nighttime viewership. None had been more irate about that than Plumber, Bob Holtzman noted. He still thought it was supposed to mean something, this news business they both shared.

'Any word on Ryan?' Plumber asked.

'Just a press release. Callie Weston wrote it, and Arnie delivered it. I can't blame him for taking the family away. He deserves a break from somebody, John.'

'Bob, I seem to remember when –'

'Yeah, I know. I got snookered. Elizabeth Elliot fed me a story on Ryan back when he was Deputy at CIA.' He turned to look at his older colleague. 'It was all a lie. I apologized to him personally. You know what it was really all about?'

'No,' Plumber admitted.

'The Colombian mission. He was there, all right. Along the way, some people got killed. One of them was an Air

Force sergeant. Ryan looks after the family. He's putting them all through college, all on his own.'

'You never printed that,' the TV reporter objected.

'No, I didn't. The family – well, they're not public figures, are they? By the time I found out, it was old news. I just didn't think it was newsworthy.' That last word was one of the keys to their profession. It was news personnel who decided what got before the public eye and what did not, and in choosing what got out and what didn't, it was they who controlled the news, and decided what, exactly, the public had a right to know. And in so choosing, they could make or break everyone, because not every story started off big enough to notice, especially the political ones.

'Maybe you were wrong.'

Holtzman shrugged. 'Maybe I was, but I didn't expect Ryan to become President any more than he did. He did an honorable thing – hell, a lot more than honorable. John, there are things about the Colombian story that can't ever see the light of day. I think I know it all now, but I can't write it. It would hurt the country and it wouldn't help anybody at all.'

'What did Ryan do, Bob?'

'He prevented an international incident. He saw that the guilty got punished one way or another –'

'Jim Cutter?' Plumber asked, still wondering what Ryan was capable of.

'No, that really was a suicide. Inspector O'Day, the FBI guy who was right there across the street?'

'What about him?'

'He was following Cutter, watched him jump in front of the bus.'

'You're sure of this?'

'As sure as I've ever been. Ryan doesn't know that I'm into all this. I have a couple of good sources, and everything matches up with the known facts. Either it's all the truth or it's the cleverest lie I've ever run into. You know what we have in the White House, John?'

'What's that?'

'An honest man. Not "relatively honest," not "hasn't been caught yet." Honest. I don't think he's ever done a crooked thing in his life.'

'He's still a babe in the woods,' Plumber replied. It was

893

almost bluster, if not disbelief, because his conscience was starting to make noise.

'Maybe he is. But who ever said we were wolves? No, that's not right. We're supposed to chase after the crooks, but we've been doing it so long and so well that we forgot that there are some people in government who aren't.' He looked over at his colleague again. 'And so then we play one off against another to get our stories – and along the way we got corrupted, too. What do we do about that, John?'

'I know what you're asking. The answer is no.'

'In an age of relative values, nice to find an absolute, Mr Plumber. Even if it is the wrong one,' Holtzman added, getting the reaction he'd hoped for.

'Bob, you're good. Very good, in fact, but you can't roll me, okay?' The commentator managed a smile, though. It was an expert attempt, and he had to admire that. Holtzman was a throwback to the days Plumber remembered so fondly.

'What if I can prove I'm right?'

'They why didn't you write the story?' Plumber demanded. No real reporter could turn away from this one.

'I didn't print it. I never said I didn't write it,' Bob corrected his friend.

'Your editor would fire you for –'

'So? Aren't there things you never did, even after you had everything you needed?'

Plumber dodged that one: 'You talked about proof.'

'Thirty minutes away. But this story can't ever get out.'

'How can I trust you on that?'

'How can I trust you, John? What do we put first? Getting the story out, right? What about the country, what about the people? Where does professional responsibility end and public responsibility begin? I didn't run this one because a family lost a father. He left a pregnant wife behind. The government couldn't acknowledge what happened, and so Jack Ryan stepped in himself to make things right. He did it with his own money. He never expected people to find out. So what was I supposed to do? Expose the family? For what, John? To break a story that hurts the country – no, that hurts one family that doesn't need any more hurt. It could jeopardize the kids' educations. There's plenty of news we can cover without that. But I'm telling you this, John:

You've hurt an innocent man, and your friend with the big smile *lied* to the public to do it. We're supposed to care about that.'

'So why don't you write *that!*'

Holtzman made him wait a few seconds for the answer. 'I'm willing to give you the chance to set things right. That's why. You were there, too. But I have to have your word, John. I'll take yours.'

There was more to it than that. There had to be. For Plumber, it was a matter of two professional insults. First, that he'd been steamrolled by his younger associate at NBC, one of the new generation who thought journalism was how you looked in front of a camera. Second, that he'd also been rolled by Ed Kealty – used . . . to hurt an innocent man? If nothing else, he had to find out. He had to, otherwise he'd be spending a lot of time looking in mirrors.

The TV commentator took Holtzman's mini-tape recorder from his hand and punched the record button.

'This is John Plumber, it's Saturday, seven-fifty in the morning, and we're standing across the street from the Giant Steps Day Care Center. Robert Holtzman and I are about to leave this location to go somewhere. I have given my word that what we are about to investigate will remain absolutely confidential between us. This tape recording is a permanent record of that promise on my part. John Plumber,' he concluded, 'NBC News.' He clicked it off, then clicked it back on again. 'However, if Bob has misrepresented himself to me, all bets are off.'

'That's fair,' Holtzman agreed, removing the tape cassette from the recorder and pocketing it. The promise had no legal standing at all. Even if it had been a contractual agreement, the First Amendment would probably negate it, but it was a man's word, and both of the reporters knew that something had to hold up, even in the modern age. On the way to Bob's car, Plumber grabbed his field producer.

'We'll be back in an hour or so.'

The Predator was circling at just under ten thousand feet. For purposes of convenience, the three UIR army corps were identified as I, II, and III by the intelligence officers at STORM TRACK and PALM BOWL. The UAV was circling I Corps now, a reconstituted Iraqi Republican Guard armored division and a similar division from the former Iranian army, 'The Immortals,' it was called, harkening back to the personal guard of Xerxes. The deployment was conventional. The regimental formations were in the classic two-up/one-back disposition, a triangle of sorts, with the third forming the divisional reserve. The two divisions were abreast. Their frontage was surprisingly narrow, however, with each division covering a mere thirty kilometers of linear space, and only a five-kilometer gap between the two.

They were training hard. Every few kilometers were targets, plywood cutouts of tanks. When they came into view, they were shot at. The Predator couldn't tell how good the gunnery was, though most of the targets were knocked over by the time the first echelon of fighting vehicles passed. The vehicles were mainly of Russian/Soviet origin. The heavy ones were T-72 and T-80 main battle tanks made at the huge Chelyabinsk works. The infantry vehicles were BMPs. The tactics were Soviet, too. That was evident from the way they moved. Sub-units were kept under tight control. The huge formations moved with geometric precision, like harvesting machines in a Kansas wheatfield, sweeping across the terrain in regular lines.

'Geez, I've seen the movie,' the chief master sergeant observed at the Kuwaiti ELINT station.

'Yes?' Major Sabah asked.

'The Russians – well, the Soviets, used to make movies of this, sir.'

'How would you compare the two?' And *that*, the NCO intelligence-specialist thought, was a pretty good question.

'Not much different, Major.' He pointed to the lower half of the screen. 'See here? The company commander has everything on line, proper distance and interval. Before, the Predator was over the division reconnaissance screen, and that was right out of the book, too. Have you read up on Soviet tactics, Major Sabah?'

'Only as the Iraqis implemented them,' the Kuwaiti officer admitted.

'Well, it's pretty close. You hit hard and fast, just go right through your enemy, don't give him a chance to react. You keep your own people under control. It's all mathematics to them.'

'And the level of their training?'

'Not bad, sir.'

'Elliot had surveillance on Ryan, right over there,' Holtzman pointed as he brought the car into the 7-Eleven.

'She was having him followed?'

'Liz hated his guts. I never – well, okay, I did figure it out. It was personal. She really had it in for Ryan, something that happened before Bob Fowler got elected. Enough that she leaked a story that was supposed to hurt his family. Nice, eh?'

Plumber wasn't all that impressed. 'That's Washington.'

'True, but what about using official government assets for a personal vendetta? That may be real Washington, too, but it's against the law.' He switched off the car and motioned for Plumber to get out.

Inside they found a diminutive owner, female, and a bunch of Amerasian kids stocking the shelves on this Saturday morning.

'Hello,' Carol Zimmer said. She recognized Holtzman from previous visits to buy bread and milk – and to eyeball the establishment. She had no idea he was a reporter. But she did recognize John Plumber. She pointed. 'You on TV!'

'Yes, I am,' the commentator admitted with a smile.

The eldest son – his name tag said Laurence – came up with a less friendly look on his face. 'Can I help you with something, sir?' His voice was unaccented, his eyes bright and suspicious.

'I'd like to talk to you, if I might,' Plumber asked politely.

'About what, sir?'

'You know the President, don't you?'

'Coffee machine's that way, sir. You can see where the doughnuts are.' The young man turned his back. His height must have come from his father, Plumber saw, and he had education.

'Wait a minute!' Plumber said.

Laurence turned back. 'Why? We have a business to run here. Excuse me.'

'Larry, be nice to man.'

'Mom, I told you what he did, remember?' When Laurence

897

looked back at the reporters, his eyes told the tale. They wounded Plumber in a way he hadn't known in years.

'Excuse me. Please,' the commentator said. 'I just want to talk to you. There aren't any cameras with me.'

'Are you in medical school now, Laurence?' Holtzman asked.

'How did you know that? Who the hell are you?'

'Laurence!' his mother objected.

'Wait a minute, please.' Plumber held his hands up. 'I just want to talk. No cameras, no recorders. Everything is off the record.'

'Oh, sure. You give us your word on that?'

'Laurence!'

'Mom, let me handle this!' the student snapped, then instantly apologized. 'Sorry, Mom, but you don't know what this is about.'

'I'm just trying to figure out –'

'I saw what you did, Mr Plumber. Didn't anybody tell you? When you spit on the President, you spit on my father, too! Now, why don't you buy what you need and take a hike.' The back turned again.

'I didn't know,' John protested. 'If I've done something wrong, then why don't you tell me about it? I promise, you have my word, I will not do anything to hurt you or your family. But if I've done something wrong, please tell me.'

'Why you hurt Mr Ryan?' Carol Zimmer asked. 'He good man. He look after us. He –'

'Mom, please. These people don't care about that!' Laurence had to come back and handle this. His mom was just too naive.

'Laurence, my name is Bob Holtzman. I'm with the *Washington Post*. I've known about your family for several years now. I never ran the story because I didn't want to invade your privacy. I know what President Ryan is doing for you. I want John to hear it from you. It will *not* become public information. If I wanted that to happen, I would have done it myself.'

'Why should I trust you?' Laurence Zimmer demanded. 'You're reporters.' That remark broke through Plumber's demeanor hard and sharp enough to cause physical pain. Had his profession sunk so low as that?

'You're studying to be a doctor?' Plumber asked, starting at square one.

'Second year at Georgetown. I have a brother who's a senior at MIT, and a sister who just started at UVA.'

'It's expensive. Too expensive for what you make off this business. I know. I had to educate my kids.'

'We all work here. I work weekends.'

'You're studying to be a physician. That's an honorable profession,' Plumber said. 'And when you make mistakes, you try to learn from them. So do I, Laurence.'

'You sure talk the talk, Mr Plumber, but lots of people do that.'

'The President helps, doesn't he?'

'If I tell you something off the record, does that mean you can't report it at all?'

'No, actually "off the record" doesn't quite mean that. But if I tell you, right here and right now, that I will never use it in any way – and there are other people around to back you up – and then I break my word, you can wreck my career. People in my business are allowed to get away with a lot, maybe even too much,' Plumber conceded, 'but we can't lie.' And that was the point, wasn't it?

Laurence looked over to his mother. Her poor English did not denote a poor mind. She nodded to him.

'He was with my dad when he got killed,' the youth reported. 'He promised Pop that he would look after us. He does, and yeah, he pays for school and stuff, him and his friends at CIA.'

'They had some trouble here with some rowdies,' Holtzman added. 'A guy I know at Langley came over here and –'

'He shouldna done that!' Laurence objected. 'Mr Clar – well, he didn't have to.'

'How come you didn't go to Johns Hopkins?' Holtzman asked.

'They accepted me,' Laurence told them, hostility still in his voice. 'This way I can commute easier, and help out here with the store. Dr Ryan – Mrs Ryan, I mean – she didn't know at first, but when she found out, well, 'nother sister starts at the university this fall. Pre-med, like me.'

'But why . . . ?' Plumber's voice trailed off.

'Cuz maybe that's the kind of guy he is, and you fucked him over.'

'Laurence!'

Plumber didn't speak for fifteen seconds or so. He turned to the lady behind the counter. 'Mrs Zimmer, thank you for your time. None of this will ever be repeated. I promise.' He turned. 'Good luck with your studies, Laurence. Thank you for telling me that. I will not be bothering you any-more.'

The two reporters walked back outside, straight to Holtz-man's Lexus.

Why should I trust you! You're reporters. The artless words of a student, perhaps, but deeply wounding even so. Because those words had been earned, Plumber told himself.

'What else?' he asked.

'As far as I know they don't even know the circumstances of Buck Zimmer's death, just that he died on duty. Evidently, Carol was pregnant with their youngest when he died. Liz Elliot tried to get a story out that Ryan was fooling around and the baby was his. I got suckered.'

A long breath. 'Yeah. Me, too.'

'So, what are you going to do about it, John?'

He looked up. 'I want to confirm a few things.'

'The one at MIT is named Peter. Computer science. The one going to Charlottesville, I think her name is Alisha. I don't know the name of the one graduating high school, but I could look that up. I have dates for the purchase of this business. It's a sub-chapter-S corporation. It all tallies with the Colombian mission. Ryan does Christmas for them every year. Cathy, too. I don't know how they'll work that now. Pretty well, probably.' Holtzman chuckled. 'He's good at keeping secrets.'

'And the CIA guy who –'

'I know him. No names. He found out that some punks were annoying Carol. He had a little chat with them. The police have records. I've seen them,' Holtzman told him. 'He's an interesting guy. He's the one who got Gerasimov's wife and daughter out. Carol thinks he's a great big teddy bear. He's also the guy who rescued Koga. Serious player.'

'Give me a day. One day,' Plumber said.

'Fair enough.' The drive back to Ritchie Highway passed without another word.

'Dr Ryan?' both heads turned. It was Captain Overton, sticking his head in the door.

'What is it?' Cathy asked, looking up from a journal article.

'Ma'am, there's something happening that the kids might like to see, with your permission. All of you, if you want.'

Two minutes later they were all in the back of a Hummer, heading into the woods, close to the perimeter fence. The vehicle stopped two hundred yards away. The captain and a corporal led them the rest of the way, to within fifty feet.

'Shh,' the corporal said to SANDBOX. He held binoculars to her eyes.

'Neat!' Jack Junior thought.

'Will she be scared of us?' Sally asked.

'No, nobody hunts them here, and they're used to the vehicles,' Overton told them. 'That's Elvira, she's the second-oldest doe here.'

She'd given birth only minutes before. Elvira was getting up now, licking the new-born fawn whose eyes were confused by a new world it had no reason to expect.

'Bambi!' Katie Ryan observed, being an expert on the Disney film. It only took minutes, and then the fawn wobbled to its – they couldn't tell the gender yet – feet.

'Okay. Katie?'

'Yes?' she asked, not looking away.

'*You* get to give her her name,' Captain Overton told the toddler. It was a tradition here.

'Miss Marlene,' SANDBOX said without hesitation.

45

CONFIRMATION

As the saying went, miles and miles of miles and miles. The road was about as boring as any civil engineer could make, but it hadn't been anyone's fault. So was the land. Brown and Holbrook now knew why the Mountain Men had become Mountain Men. At least there was scenery there. They could have driven faster, but it took time to learn the handling characteristics of this beast, and so they rarely got above fifty. That earned them the poisonous looks of every other driver on I-90, especially the cowboy-hatted K-Whopper owner-operators who thought the unlimited speed limit in eastern Montana was just great, plus the occasional lawyer – they *had* to be lawyers – in German muscle cars who blazed by their truck as though it were a cattle-feeder.

They also found it was hard work. Both men were pretty tired from all the preparation. All the weeks of effort to set up the truck, mix the explosives, cast the bullets, and then embed them. It had all made for little sleep, and there was nothing like driving a western interstate highway to put a man to sleep. Their first overnight was at a motel in Sheridan, just over the line into Wyoming. Getting that far, their first day driving the damned thing, had almost been their undoing, especially negotiating the split of I-90 and I-94 in Billings. They'd known that the cement truck would corner about as well as a hog on ice, but actually experiencing it had exceeded their worst fears. They ended up sleeping past eight that morning.

The motel was actually a truck stop of sorts that catered both to private cars and to interstate freight carriers. The dining room served a hearty breakfast, wolfed down by a lot of rugged-looking independent men, and a few similarly minded women. Breakfast conversation was predictable.

'Gotta be rag-head sunzabitches,' opined a big-bellied trucker with tattoos on his beefy forearms.

'Think so?' Ernie Brown asked from down the counter, hoping to get a feel for how these kindred souls felt about things.

'Who *else* would go after younguns? Sunzabitches.' The driver returned to his blueberry pancakes.

'If the TV has it right, those two cops got it done,' a milk hauler announced. 'Five head shots. Whoa!'

'What about the one guy who went down hard, standing up like that against six riflemen! With a *pistol*. Dropped three of them, maybe four. There died a real American lawman.' He looked up from his pancakes again. This one had a load of cattle. 'He's earned his place in Valhalla, and that's for *damn* sure.'

'Hey, they were feds, man,' Holbrook said, chewing on his toast. 'They ain't heroes. What about –'

'You can stick that one, good buddy,' the milk hauler warned. 'I don't wanna hear it. There was twenty, thirty children in that place.'

Another driver chimed in. 'And that black kid, rollin' on in with his -16. Damn, like when I was in the Cav for the Second of Happy Valley. I wouldn't mind buying that boy a beer, maybe shake his hand.'

'You were AirCav?' the cattle hauler asked, turning away from his breakfast.

'Charlie, First of the Seventh.' He turned to show the over-sized patch of the First Air Cavalry Division on his leather jacket.

'Gary Owen, bro'! Delta, Second/Seventh.' He stood up from the counter and walked over to take the man's hand. 'Where you outa?'

'Seattle. That's mine out there with the machine parts. Heading for St Louis. Gary Owen. Jesus, nice to hear that one again.'

'Every time I drive through here . . .'

'You bet. We got brothers buried out yonder at Little Big Horn. Always say a little prayer for 'em when I come through.'

'Shit.' The two men shook hands again. 'Mike Fallon.'

'Tim Yeager.'

The two Mountain Men had not just come into the room for breakfast. These were their kind of people. Supposed to be, anyway. Rugged individualists. Federal cops as heroes? What the hell was that all about?

'Boy, we find out who bankrolled this job, I hope that Ryan fella knows what to do 'bout it,' machine parts said.

'Ex-Marine,' cattle replied. 'He ain't one of them. He's one of us. Finally.'

'You may be right. Somebody's gotta pay for this one, and I hope we get the right people to do the collectin'.'

'Damn right,' the milk hauler agreed from his spot on the counter.

'Well.' Ernie Brown stood. 'Time for us to boogie on down the road.'

The others nearby took a cursory look, and that was all, as the truckers returned to their informal opinion poll.

'If you don't feel better by tomorrow, you're going to the doctor, and that's final!' she said.

'Oh, I'll be all right.' But that protestation came out as a groan. He wondered if this was Hong Kong flu or something else. Not that he knew the difference. Few people did, and in a real sense that included docs – and he did know that. What would they tell him? Rest, liquids, aspirin, which he was already doing. He felt as though he'd been placed in a bag and beaten with baseball bats, and all the traveling didn't help. Nobody liked traveling. Everyone liked *being* somewhere else, but getting there was always a pain in the . . . everywhere, he grumped. He allowed himself to fade back off to sleep, hoping his wife wouldn't worry too much. He'd feel better by tomorrow. These things always went away. He had a comfortable bed, and a TV controller. As long as he didn't move around it didn't hurt . . . much. It couldn't get any worse. Then it would get better. It always did.

When people got to a certain point, their work never really stopped. They could go away, but then the work came to them, found them wherever they might be, and the only issue, really, was how expensive it was to bring the work to them. That was a problem for both Jack Ryan and Robby Jackson.

For Jack it was the speeches Callie Weston had prepared for him – he'd be flying tomorrow, to Tennessee, then to

Kansas, then to Colorado, then to California, and finally back to Washington, arriving at three in the morning on what was going to be the biggest special-election day in American history. Just over a third of the House seats vacated by that Sato guy would be selected, with the remainder to be done over the following two weeks. Then he'd have a full Congress to work with, and maybe, just maybe, he could get some real work done. Pure politics loomed in his immediate future. This coming week he'd be going over the detailed plans to streamline two of the government's most powerful bureaucracies, Defense and Treasury. The rest were in the works, too.

Since he was here with the President, Admiral Jackson was also getting everything developed by the office of J-2, the Pentagon's chief of intelligence, so that he could conduct the daily around-the-world brief. It took him an hour just to go over the materials.

'What's happening, Rob?' Jack asked, and instead of a friendly inquiry into how a guy's week was going, the President was asking the state of the entire planet. The J-3's eyebrows jerked up.

'Where do you want me to start?'

'Pick a spot,' the President suggested.

'Okay, Mike Dubro and the *Ike* group are still heading north to China, making good time. Good weather and calm seas, they're averaging twenty-five knots. That advances their ETA by a few hours. Exercises continue on the Formosa Strait, but both sides are hugging their coasts now. Looks like maybe the shoot-downs got everybody to calm down a bit. Secretary Adler is supposed to be in there right now, talking to them about things.

'Middle East. We're watching the UIR military run exercises, too. Six heavy divisions, plus attachments and tactical air. Our people on the scene have Predators up and watching pretty closely –'

'Who authorized that?' the President asked.

'I did,' Jackson replied.

'Invading another country's airspace?'

'J-2 and I are running this. You want us to know what they're up to and what their capabilities are, don't you?'

'Yes, I need that.'

'Good, you tell me what to do, and let me worry about how, all right? It's a stealthy platform. It self-destructs if it goes out of control or the guys directing it don't like something, and it gives us very good real-time data we can't get from satellites, or even from J-STARS, and we don't have one of those over there at the moment. Any other questions, Mr President?'

'Touché, Admiral. What's the take look like?'

'They're looking better than our initial intelligence assessment led us to expect. Nobody's panicking yet, but this is starting to get our attention.'

'What about Turkestan?' Ryan asked.

'They're evidently trying to get elections going, but that's old information, and that's all we know on the political side. The overall situation there is quiet at the moment. Satellites show increased cross-border traffic – mainly trade, the overhead-intelligence guys think, nothing more than that.'

'Anybody looking at Iranian – damn, UIR – troop dispositions on the border?'

'I don't know. I can check.' Jackson made a note. 'Next, we've spotted the Indian navy.'

'How?'

'They're not making a secret of anything. I had 'em send a pair of Orions off from Diego Garcia. They spotted our friends from three hundred miles out, electronic emissions. They are about four hundred miles offshore from their base. And, by the way, that places them directly between Diego and the entrance to the Persian Gulf. Our defense attaché will drop in tomorrow to ask what they're up to. They probably won't tell him very much.'

'If they don't, I think maybe Ambassador Williams will have to make a call of his own.'

'Good idea. And that's the summary of today's news, unless you want the trivia.' Robby tucked his documents away. 'What do your speeches look like?'

'The theme is common sense,' the President reported.

'In Washington?'

Adler was not overly pleased. On arriving in Beijing, he'd learned that the timing wasn't good. His aircraft had gotten in on what had turned out to be a Saturday evening – the date line again, he realized – then he learned that the important ministers were out of town, studiously downplaying the significance of the air battle over the strait, and giving him a chance to recover from jet lag so that he would be up to a serious meeting. Or so they'd said.

'What a pleasure to have you here,' the Foreign Minister said, taking the American's hand and guiding him into his private office. Another man was waiting in there. 'Do you know Zhang Han San?'

'No, how do you do, Minister?' Adler asked, taking his hand as well. *So, this was what he looked like.*

People took their seats. Adler was alone. In addition to the two PRC ministers, there was an interpreter, a woman in her early thirties.

'Your flight was a pleasant one?' the Foreign Minister inquired.

'Coming to your country is always pleasant, but I do wish the flight were faster,' Adler admitted.

'The effects of travel on the body are often difficult, and the body does affect the mind. I trust you have had some time to recover. It is important,' the Foreign Minister went on, 'that high-level discussions, especially in times of unpleasantness, are not clouded by extraneous complications.'

'I am well rested,' Adler assured them. He'd gotten plenty of sleep. It was just that he wasn't sure what time it was in whatever location his body thought itself to be. 'And the interests of peace and stability compel us to make the occasional sacrifice.'

'That is so true.'

'Minister, the unfortunate events of the last week have troubled my country,' SecState told his hosts.

'Why do those bandits seek to provoke us?' the Foreign Minister asked. 'Our forces are conducting exercises, that is all. And they shot down two of our aircraft. The crewmen are all dead. They have families. This is very sad, but I hope you have noted that the People's Republic has not retaliated.'

'We have noted this with gratitude.'

'The bandits shot first. You also know that.'

'We are unclear on that issue. One of the reasons for my coming here is to ascertain the facts,' Adler replied.

'Ah.'

Had he surprised them? SecState wondered. It was like a card game, though the difference was that you never really knew the value of the cards in your own hand. A flush still beat a straight, but the hole card was always down, even for its owner. In this case, he had lied, but while the other side might suspect the lie, they didn't know for sure, and that affected the game. If they thought he knew, they would say one thing. If they thought he didn't know, they'd say another. In this case, they thought he knew, but they weren't sure. He'd just told them otherwise, which could be a lie or the truth. Advantage, America. Adler had thought about this all the way over.

'You have said publicly that the first shot was taken by the other side. Are you sure of this?'

'Completely,' the Foreign Minister assured him.

'Excuse me, but what if the shot were taken by one of your lost pilots? How would we ever know?'

'Our pilots were under strict orders not to fire except in self-defense.'

'That is both a reasonable and prudent guide for your personnel. But in the heat of battle – or if not battle, a somewhat tense situation, mistakes do happen. We have the problem ourselves. I find aviators to be impulsive, especially the young, proud ones.'

'Is not the same true of the other side as well?' the Foreign Minister asked.

'Certainly,' Adler admitted. 'That is the problem, isn't it? Which is why,' he went on, 'it is the business of people like ourselves to ensure that such situations do not arise.'

'But they always provoke us. They hope to garner your favor, and we find it troubling that this may have succeeded.'

'Excuse me?'

'Your President Ryan spoke of *two* Chinas. There is only one China, Secretary Adler. I'd thought that issue settled a long time ago.'

'That was a semantic error on the President's part, a linguistic nuance,' Adler replied, dismissing the observation. 'The President has many qualities, but he has yet to learn the niceties of diplomatic exchange, and then a foolish reporter seized on the issue. Nothing more than that. There have been no changes in policies toward this region.' But Adler had deliberately *not* said 'our policies,' and 'have been' instead of 'are.' There were times when he thought that he might have made a fortune for himself by drafting insurance policies.

'Such linguistic errors can be seen as things other than errors,' the Foreign Minister replied.

'Have I not made our position clear on this issue? You will recall that he was responding to a most unfortunate incident in which American lives were lost, and in searching for words to use, he selected words which have one meaning in our language, and another in yours.' This was going a lot easier than he'd expected.

'Chinese lives were lost as well.'

Zhang, Adler saw, was doing a lot of listening but wasn't uttering a single word. In the Western context, that made him an aide, a technical assistant, there to assist his minister on an issue of law or interpretation. He wasn't so sure that rule applied in this case. More likely, the reverse applied. If Zhang were what the American thought him to be, and if Zhang were smart enough to suspect that the American would be thinking along those lines – then why the hell was he here?

'Yes, and various others, to little purpose and great sorrow. I hope you will understand that our President takes such things seriously.'

'Indeed, and I am remiss in not saying sooner that we view with horror the attack on his daughter. I trust you will convey to President Ryan our heartfelt sympathy at this inhuman act, and our pleasure that no harm has come to his child.'

'I thank you on his behalf, and I will pass your good wishes along.' Twice in a row now the Foreign Minister had temporized. He had an opening. He reminded himself that his interlocutors thought themselves smarter and shrewder than everybody else. 'My President is a sentimental man,' the Secretary admitted. 'It is an American trait. Moreover, he feels strongly about his duty to protect all of our citizens.'

'Then you need to speak to the rebels on Taiwan. We believe that it is they who destroyed the airliner.'

'But why do such a thing?' Adler asked, ignoring the really surprising part. Was it a slip? Talk to Taiwan. The PRC was asking him to do that?

'To foment this incident, obviously. To play upon your President's personal feelings. To cloud the real issues between the People's Republic and our wayward province.'

'Do you really think so?'

'Yes, we do,' the Foreign Minister assured him. 'We do not wish to have hostilities. Such things are so wasteful of people and resources, and we have greater concerns for our country. The Taiwan issue will be decided in due course. So long as America does not interfere,' he added.

'As I have already told you, Minister, we have made no policy changes. All we wish is the restoration of peace and stability,' Adler said, the obvious import being the indeterminate maintenance of the status quo, which was decidedly *not* part of the People's Republic game plan.

'Then we are agreed.'

'You will not object to our naval deployments?'

The Foreign Minister sighed. 'The sea is free for the innocent passage of all. It is not our place to give orders to the United States of America, as it is not your place to give orders to the People's Republic. The movement of your forces gives the impression that you will influence local events, and we will make pro forma comments on this. But in the interests of peace,' he went on in a voice that was both patient and weary, 'we will not object too strongly, especially if it encourages the rebels to cease their foolish provocations.'

'It would be useful to know if your naval exercises will end soon. That would be a very favorable gesture.'

'The spring maneuvers will continue. They do not threaten anyone, as your increased naval presence will determine quite clearly. We do not ask you to take our word. Let our deeds speak for us. It would be well also if our rebellious cousins reduce their own activities. Perhaps you might speak to them on this?' Twice now? He hadn't misspoken before, then.

'If you request it, yes, I would be pleased to add my voice and that of my country to the quest for peace.'

'We value the good offices of the United States, and we trust you to be an honest broker for this occasion, in view of the fact that, regrettably, American lives were lost in this tragic incident.'

Secretary Adler yawned. 'Oh, excuse me.'

'Travel is a curse, is it not?' These words came from Zhang, speaking for the first time.

'It truly can be,' Adler agreed. 'Please allow me to consult my government. I think our response to your request will be favorable.'

'Excellent,' the Foreign Minister observed. 'We seek to make no precedent here. I hope you understand this, but in view of the singular circumstances here, we welcome your assistance.'

'I shall have a reply for you in the morning,' Adler promised, rising. 'Forgive me for extending your day.'

'Such is duty, for all of us.'

Scott Adler took his leave, wondering what exactly this bombshell was that had landed on him. He wasn't sure who'd won the card game, and realized that he wasn't even sure what game it had been. It certainly hadn't gone as expected. It seemed like he'd won, and won easily. The other side had been more accommodating than he would have been in their place.

Some called it checkbook journalism, but it wasn't new, and it wasn't expensive at the working level. Any experienced reporter had people he could call, people who, for a modest fee, would check things. It wasn't in any way illegal, to ask a favor of a friend, at least not grossly so. The information was rarely sensitive – and in this case was public record. It was just that the offices weren't always open on Sunday.

A mid-level bureaucrat in the office of Maryland's Secretary of State drove into his office in Baltimore, used his cardpass to get to his parking place, then walked in and unlocked the right number of doors until he got to a musty file room. Finding the right cabinet, he pulled open a drawer and found a file. He left a marker in the drawer and carried the file to the nearest copying machine. Copies of all the documents were made in less than a minute, and then he replaced everything. With that task done, he walked back to his car and drove home. He did this often enough that he had a personal fax machine at home, and within ten minutes, the documents had been sent off, then taken to the kitchen and dumped in the trash. For this he would receive five hundred dollars. He got extra for working weekends.

John Plumber was reading the documents even before the transmission was complete. Sure enough, a Ryan, John P., had established a sub-S corporation at the time Holtzman had told him. Control of that corporation had conveyed to Zimmer, Carol (none), four days later (a weekend had stood in the way), and that corporation now owned a 7-Eleven in southern Maryland. The corporate officers included Zimmer, Laurence; Zimmer, Alisha; and one other child, and the stockholders all shared the same surname. He recognized Ryan's signature on the transfer documents. The legal work had been done by a firm in Washington – a big one, he knew that name, too. There had been some tricky, but entirely legal, maneuvering to make the transaction tax-free for the Zimmer family. There was no further paperwork on that subject. Nothing else was needed, really.

He had other documents as well. Plumber knew the registrar at MIT, and had learned the previous evening, also via fax, that the tuition and housing expenses for Peter Zimmer were paid by a private foundation, the checks issued and signed by a partner in the same law firm that had set up the sub-S corp for the Zimmer family. He even had a transcript for the graduating senior. Sure enough, he was in computer science, and would be staying in Cambridge for his graduate work in the MIT Media Lab. Aside from mediocre marks in his freshman literature courses – even MIT wanted people to be literate, but evidently Peter Zimmer didn't care for poetry – the kid was straight A.

'So, it's true.' Plumber settled back in his swivel chair and examined his conscience. ' "Why should I trust you? You're reporters," ' he repeated to himself.

The problem with his profession was one that its members almost never talked about, just as a wealthy man will not often bemoan low taxes. Back in the 1960s, a man named Sullivan had sued the *New York Times* over defamation of character, and had demonstrated that the newspaper had not been entirely correct in its commentary. But the paper had argued, and the court had agreed, that in the absence of true malice, the mistake was not really culpable, and that the public's interest in learning the goings-on in their nation superseded protection of an individual. It left the door open for suits, technically, and people did still bring action against the media, and sometimes they even won. About as often as Slippery Rock University knocked off Penn State.

That court ruling was necessary, Plumber thought. The First Amendment guaranteed freedom of the press, and the reason for it was that the press was America's first and, in many ways, only guardian of freedom. People lied all the time. Especially people in government, but others, too, and it was the job of the media to get the facts – the *truth* – out to the people, so that they could make their own choices.

But there was a trap built into the hunting license the Supreme Court had issued. The media could destroy people. There was recourse against almost any improper action in American society, but reporters had such protections as those once enjoyed by kings, and, as a practical matter, his profession was above the law. As a practical matter, also, it worked hard to stay that way. To admit error was not only a legal faux pas, for which money might have to be paid. It would also weaken the faith of the public in their profession. And so they never admitted error when they didn't have to, and when they did, the retractions were almost never given the prominence of the initial, incorrect, assertions – the minimum necessary effort defined by lawyers who knew exactly the height of the castle walls they defended. There were occasional exceptions, but everyone knew that exceptions they were.

Plumber had seen his profession change. There was too much arrogance, and too little realization of the fact that the public they served no longer trusted them – and *that* wounded Plumber. He deemed himself worthy of that trust. He deemed himself a professional descendant of Ed Murrow, whose voice *every* American had learned to trust. And that was how it was supposed to be. But it wasn't, because the profession could not be policed from without, and it would never be trusted again until it was policed from within. Reporters called down every other profession – medicine, law, politics – for failing to meet a level of professional responsibility which they would allow no one to enforce on themselves, and which they themselves would too rarely enforce on their own. *Do as I say, not as I do* was something you couldn't say to a six-year-old, but it had become a ready cant for grown-ups. And if it got any worse, then what?

Plumber considered his situation. He could retire whenever he wanted. Columbia University had more than once invited him in to be an adjunct professor of journalism ... and ethics, because his was a trusted voice, a reasoned voice, an honest voice. An old voice, he added to himself. Maybe the last voice?

But it all came down, really, to one man's conscience, to ideas inculcated by parents long dead, and teachers whose names he had forgotten. He had to be loyal to something. If he were to be loyal to his profession, then he had to be loyal to its foundation. To tell the truth and let the chips fall. He lifted his phone.

'Holtzman,' the reporter answered, because it was the business line in his Georgetown home.

'Plumber. I've done some checking. It appears you were right.'

'Okay, now what, John?'

'I have to do this myself. I'll give you the exclusive on print coverage.'

'That's generous, John. Thank you,' Bob acknowledged.

'I still don't like Ryan very much as a President,' Plumber added, rather defensively, the other thought. That made sense. He couldn't appear to be doing this to curry favor.

'You know that's not what this is about. That's why I talked to you about it. When?' Bob Holtzman asked.

'Tomorrow night, live.'

'How about we sit down and work out a few things? This will be a biggie for the *Post*. Want to share the byline?'

'I might just be looking for another job by tomorrow night,' Plumber observed, with a rueful chuckle. 'Okay, we'll do that.'

'So, what's that mean?' Jack asked.

'They do not mind anything we're doing. It's almost like they want the carrier there. They have requested that I shuttle back and forth to Taipei –'

'Directly?' The President was astonished. Such direct

flights would give the appearance of legitimacy to the Republic of China government. An American Secretary of State would be shuttling back and forth, and a ministerial official did so only between capitals of sovereign countries. Lesser disputes were left to 'special envoys,' who might carry the same power, but nothing approaching the same status.

'Yeah, that kinda surprised me, too,' Adler replied over the encrypted channel. 'Next, the dogs that didn't bark: a cursory objection to your "two Chinas" gaffe at the press conference, and trade never raised its ugly head. They're being real docile for people who killed a hundred-plus airline passengers.'

'Their naval exercises?'

'They will continue, and they practically invited us to observe how routine they are.'

Admiral Jackson was listening on the speakerphone. 'Mr Secretary? This is Robby Jackson.'

'Yes, Admiral?'

'They staged a crisis, we move a carrier, and now they say they want us around, am I getting this right?'

'That's correct. They do not know that we know, at least I don't think they do – but you know, I'm not sure that matters at the moment.'

'Something's wrong,' the J-3 said immediately. 'Big-time wrong.'

'Admiral, I think you might be correct on that one, too.'

'Next move?' Ryan asked.

'I guess I go to Taipei in the morning. I can't evade this one, can I?'

'Agreed. Keep me informed, Scott.'

'Yes, Mr President.' The line went dead.

'Jack – no, Mr President, I just had a big red flashing light go off.'

Ryan grimaced. 'I have to go be political tomorrow, too. I fly out at, uh' – he checked his schedule – 'leave the House at six-fifty, to speak in Nashville at eight-thirty. We need an assessment on this in one big hurry. Shit. Adler's over there, I'm on the road, and Ben Goodley isn't experienced enough for this. I want you there, Rob. If there's operational ramifications to this, that's your bailiwick. The Foleys. Arnie on the political side. We need a good China hand from State . . .'

* * *

915

Adler was settling into his bed in the embassy VIP quarters. He went over his notes, trying to figure the angle. People made mistakes at every level. The wide belief that senior officials were canny players was not nearly as true as people thought. They made mistakes. They made slips. They loved to be clever.

'Travel is a curse,' Zhang had said. His only words. Why then, and why those? It was so obvious that Adler didn't get it then.

'Bedford Forrest, eh?' Diggs said, spreading relish on his hot dog.

'Best cavalry commander we've ever had,' Eddington said.

'You'll pardon me, Professor, if I show diminished enthusiasm for the gentleman,' the general observed. 'The son of a bitch *did* found the Ku Klux Klan.'

'I never said the man was politically astute, sir, and I do not defend his personal character, but if we've ever had a better man with a cavalry command, I have not learned his name,' Eddington replied.

'He's got us there,' Hamm had to admit.

'Stuart was overrated, sometimes petulant, and very lucky. Nathan had the *Fingerspitzengefühl*, knew how to make decisions on the fly, and damned if he made many bad ones. I'm afraid we just have to overlook his other failings.'

History discussions among senior Army officers could last for hours, as this one had, and were as learned as those in any university's seminar room. Diggs had come over for a chat with Colonel Hamm, then found himself embroiled in the millionth refighting of the Civil War. Millionth? Diggs wondered. No, a *lot* more than that.

'What about Grierson?' Diggs asked.

'His deep raid was a thing of beauty, but he didn't actually conceive it, remember. Actually, I think his best work was as commander of the 10th.'

'Now you're talking, Dr Eddington.'

'See how the boss's eyes just lit up. You –'

'That's right! You had that regiment until a little while ago. Ready and Forward!' the colonel of the Carolina Guard added.

'You even know our regimental motto?' Maybe this guy

was a serious historian after all, even if he did admire that racist murderer, Diggs thought.

'Grierson built that regiment from the ground up, mainly illiterate troopers. He had to grow his own NCOs, and they drew every shit job in the Southwest, but they're the ones who defeated the Apaches – and only one damned movie ever made about 'em. I've been thinking about a book on the subject after I retire. He was our first real desert fighter, and he figured things out in a hurry. He knew about deep strike, he knew how to pick his fights, and once he got hold, he didn't let go. I was glad to see that regimental standard come back.'

'Colonel Eddington, I take back what I was thinking.' Diggs lifted his beer can in salute. 'That's what the cav is all about.'

46

OUTBREAK

It would have been better to come back Monday morning, but it would have meant getting the kids up too early. As it was, Jack Junior and Sally had to study for tests, and for the moment, Katie needed new arrangements of her own. Camp David had been so different it was very much like returning from a vacation, and coming back was something of a shock. As soon as the Executive Mansion appeared in the windows of the descending helicopter, faces and moods changed. Security was vastly increased. The body count around the perimeter was noticeably different, and that, too, was a reminder of how undesirable this place and the life it contained were for them. Ryan stepped off first, saluted the Marine at the bottom of the stairs then looked up at the south face of the White House. It was like a slap in the face. Welcome back to reality. After seeing his family safely inside, President Ryan headed west for his office.

'Okay, what's happening?' he asked van Damm, who hadn't had much of a weekend himself – but then, nobody was trying to kill him or his family, either.

'The investigation hasn't turned up much of anything yet. Murray says to be patient, things are happening. Best advice, Jack, just keep going with it,' the chief of staff advised. 'You have a full day tomorrow. The country's mood is for you. There's always an outpouring of sympathy in times like –'

'Arnie, I'm not going out after votes for myself, remember? It's nice that people think better of me after some terrorists attack my daughter, but, you know, I really don't want to look at things in those terms,' Jack observed, his anger returning after two days of relief. 'If I ever had thoughts about staying in this job, last week cured me.'

'Well, yes, but –'

'"But," hell! Arnie, when it's all said and done, what will

I take away from this place? A place in the history books? By the time that's written, I'll be dead, and I won't be around to care what historians say, will I? I have a friend in the history business who says that all history is really nothing more than the application of ideology to the past – and I won't be around to read it anyway. The only thing I want to take away from here is my life and the lives of my family. That's all. If somebody else wants the pomp and circumstance of this fucking prison, then let 'em have it. I've learned better. Fine,' POTUS said bitterly, his mood totally back in his office now. 'I'll do the job, make the speeches, and try to get some useful work done, but it ain't worth it all, Arnie. For goddamned sure it isn't worth having nine terrorists try to kill your daughter. There's only one thing you leave behind on this planet. That's your kids. Everything else, hell, other people just make it up to suit themselves anyway, just like the news.'

'It's been a rough couple of days, and –'

'What about the agents who died? What about their families? I had a nice two-day vacation. They sure as hell didn't. I've gotten used enough to this job that I hardly thought about them at all. Over a hundred people worked hard to make sure I forgot about it. And I let them do it! It's important that I don't dwell on such things, right? What am I supposed to concentrate on? "Duty, Honor, Country"? Anybody who can do that and turn his humanity off doesn't belong here, and that's what this job is turning me into.'

'You finished, or do I have to get a box of Kleenex for you?' For one brief moment the President looked ready to punch van Damm. Arnie plunged on. 'Those agents died because they chose jobs they thought were important. Soldiers do the same thing. What's with you, anyway, Ryan? How the hell do you think a country happens? You think it's just nice thoughts? You weren't always that stupid. You were a Marine once. You did other stuff for CIA. You had balls then. You have a job. You didn't get drafted, remember? You volunteered for this, whether you admit it or not. You knew it was possible this would happen. And so now you're here. You want to run away, fine – run away. But don't tell me it isn't worth it. Don't tell me it doesn't matter. If people *died* to protect your family, don't you fucking *dare* tell me it doesn't matter!' Van Damm stormed out of the office, without even bothering to close the door behind him.

Ryan didn't know what to do right then. He sat down behind his desk. There were the usual piles of paper, neatly arrayed by a staff that never slept. Here was China. Here was the Middle East. Here was India. Here was advance information on the leading economic indicators. Here were political projections for the 161 House seats to be decided in two days. Here was a report on the terrorist incident. Here was a list of the names of the dead agents, and under each was a list of wives and husbands, parents and children, and in the case of Don Russell, grandchildren. He knew all the faces, but Jack had to admit that he hadn't remembered all the names. They'd died to protect his child, and he didn't even know all the names. Worst of all, he'd allowed himself to be carted away, to indulge himself in yet more artificial comfort – and forget. But here it all was, on his desk, waiting for him, and it wouldn't go away. And he couldn't run away, either. He stood and walked out the door, heading left for the chief of staff's corner office, passing Secret Service agents who'd heard the exchange, probably traded looks, certainly developed their own thoughts, and now concealed them.

'Arnie?'

'Yes, Mr President?'

'I'm sorry.'

'Okay, honey,' he groaned. He'd go to see the doctor tomorrow morning. It hadn't gotten better at all. If anything, it had gotten worse. The headaches were punishing, and that despite two extra-strength Tylenol every four hours. If only he could sleep it off, but that was proving hard. Only exhaustion allowed him an hour here and an hour there. Just getting up to use the bathroom required a few minutes of concentrated effort, enough that his wife offered to help, but, no, a man didn't need an escort for that. On the other hand, she was right. He did need to see a doctor. Would have been smarter to do it yesterday, he thought. Then he might have felt better now.

It had been easy for Plumber, at least on the procedural side. The tape-storage vault was the size of a respectable public library, and finding things was easy. There, on the fifth shelf were three boxed Beta-format cassettes. Plumber took them down, removed the tapes from the boxes, and replaced them with blanks. The three tapes he placed in his briefcase. He was home twenty minutes later. There, for his own convenience, he had a commercial-type Betamax, and he ran the tapes of the first interview, just to make sure, just to confirm the fact that the tapes were undamaged. And they were. These would have to be sent to a secure place.

Next, John Plumber drafted his three-minute commentary piece for the next day's evening news broadcast. It would be a mildly critical piece on the Ryan presidency. He spent an hour on it, since, unlike the current crop of TV reporters, he liked to achieve a certain elegance in his language, a task which came easily to him, as his grammar was correct. This he printed up and read over because he both edited and detected errors more easily on paper than on a computer monitor. Satisfied, he copied the piece over to disk, which would later be used at the studio to generate copy for the TelePrompTer. Next, he composed another commentary piece of the same overall length (it turned out to be four words shorter), and that he printed also. Plumber spent rather more time with this one. If it were to be his professional swan song, then it had to be done properly, and this reporter, who had drafted quite a few obituaries for others, both admired and not, wanted his own to be just right. Satisfied with the final copy, he printed that up as well, tucking the pages into his briefcase, with the cassettes. This one he would not copy to disk.

'I guess they're finished,' the chief master sergeant said.

The take from the Predator showed the tank columns heading back to their laagers, hatches open on the turrets, crewmen visible, mainly smoking. The exercise had gone well for the newly constituted UIR army, and even now they were conducting their road movement in good order.

Major Sabah spent so much time looking over this man's shoulder that they really should have spoken on a more informal basis, he thought. It was all routine. Too routine. He'd expected – hoped – that his country's new neighbor would require much more time to integrate its military forces, but the commonality of weapons and doctrine had worked in their favor. Radio messages copied down here and at Storm Track suggested that the exercise was concluded. The TV coverage from the UAV confirmed it, however, and confirmation was important.

'That's funny . . .' the sergeant observed, to his own surprise.

'What is that?' Sabah asked.

'Excuse me, sir.' The NCO stood and walked over to a corner cabinet, from which he extracted a map, and brought it back to his workstation. 'There's no road there. Look, sir.' He unfolded the map, matched the coordinates with those on the screen – the Predator had its own Global Positioning Satellite navigation system and automatically told its operators where it was – and tapped the right section on the paper. 'See?'

The Kuwaiti officer looked back and forth from map to screen. On the latter, there *was* a road, now. But that was easily explained. A column of a hundred tanks would convert almost any surface into a hard-packed highway of sorts, and that had happened here.

But there hadn't been a road there before. The tanks had made it over the last few hours.

'That's a change, Major. The Iraqi army was always road-bound before.'

Sabah nodded. It was so obvious that he hadn't seen it. Though native to the desert, and supposedly schooled in traveling there, the Iraqi army in 1991 had connived at its own destruction by sticking close to roads, because its officers always seemed to get lost when moving cross-country. Not as mad as it sounded – the desert was essentially as featureless as the sea – it had made their movements predictable, never a good thing in a war, and given advancing allied forces free rein to approach from unexpected directions.

That had just changed.

'You suppose they have GPS, too?' the chief master sergeant asked.

'We couldn't expect them to stay stupid forever, could we?'

*   *   *

President Ryan kissed his wife on the way to the elevator. The kids weren't up yet. One sort of work lay ahead. Another sort lay behind. Today there wasn't time for both, though some efforts would be made. Ben Goodley was waiting on the helicopter.

'Here's the notes from Adler on his Tehran trip.' The National Security Advisor passed them over. 'Also the write-up from Beijing. The working group is getting together at ten to go over that situation. The SNIE team will be meeting at Langley later today, too.'

'Thanks.' Jack strapped into his seat and started reading. Arnie and Callie came aboard and took their seats forward of his.

'Any ideas, Mr President?' Goodley asked.

'Ben, you're supposed to tell me, remember?'

'How about I tell you that it doesn't make much sense?'

'I already know that part. You guard the phones and faxes today. Scott should be in Taipei now. Whatever comes from him, fast-track it to me.'

'Yes, sir.'

The helicopter lurched aloft. Ryan hardly noticed that. His mind was on the job, crummy though it was. Price and Raman were with him. There would be more agents on the 747, and more still waiting even now in Nashville. The presidency of John Patrick Ryan went on, whether he liked it or not.

This country might be small, might be unimportant, might be a pariah in the international community – not because of anything it had done, except perhaps to prosper, but because of its larger and less prosperous neighbor to the west – but it did have an *elected* government, and that was supposed to count for something in the community of nations, especially those with popularly elected governments themselves. The People's Republic had come to exist by force of arms – well, most countries did, SecState reminded himself – and had immediately thereafter slaughtered millions of its own citizens (nobody knew how many; nobody was terribly interested in finding out), launched into a revolutionary development program ('the Great Leap Forward'), which had turned out more disastrously than was the norm even for

Marxist nations; and launched yet another internal 'reform' effort ('the Cultural Revolution') which had come *after* something called the 'Hundred Flowers' campaign, whose real purpose had been to smoke out potential dissidents for later elimination at the hands of students whose revolutionary enthusiasm had indeed been revolutionary toward Chinese culture – they'd come close to destroying it entirely, in favor of *The Little Red Book*. Then had come more reform, the supposed changeover from Marxism to something else, another student revolution – this one against the existing political system – arrogantly cut down with tanks and machine guns on global television. Despite all that, the rest of the world was entirely willing to let the People's Republic crush their cousins on Taiwan.

This was called *realpolitik*, Scott Adler thought. Something similar had resulted in an event called the Holocaust, an event his father had survived, with a number tattooed on his forearm to prove it. Even his own country officially had a one-China policy, though the unspoken codicil was that the PRC would not attack the ROC – and if it did, then America might just react. Or might not.

Adler was a career diplomat, a graduate of Cornell and the Fletcher School of Law and Diplomacy at Tufts University. He loved his country. He was often an instrument of his country's policy, and now found himself to be his country's very voice of international affairs. But what he often had to say was not terribly just, and at moments like this, he wondered if he might himself be doing the same things that had been done sixty years earlier by other Fletcher grads, well-educated and well-meaning, who, after it was all over, wondered how the hell they'd been so blind as not to have seen it coming.

'We have fragments – and actually some rather large pieces from the missile that were lodged in the wing. It is definitely of PRC origin,' the ROC Defense Minister said. 'We will allow your technical people to look them over and make your own tests to confirm matters.'

'Thank you. I will discuss that with my government.'

'So.' This was the Foreign Minister. 'They allow a direct flight from Beijing to Taipei. They do not object privately to the dispatch of an aircraft carrier. They disclaim any responsibility for the Airbus incident. I confess I see no rationale for this behavior.'

'I am gratified that they express interest only in the restoration of regional stability.'

'How good of them,' Defense said. 'After they deliberately upset it.'

'This has caused us great economic harm. Again, foreign investors get nervous, and with the flight of their capital, we face some minor embarrassments. Was that their plan, do you suppose?'

'Minister, if that were the case, why did they ask me to fly here directly?'

'Some manner of subterfuge, obviously,' the Foreign Minister answered, before Defense could say anything.

'But if so, what for?' Adler wanted to know. Hell, *they* were Chinese. Maybe they could figure it out.

'We are secure here. We know that, even if foreign investors do not. Even so, the situation is not an entirely happy one. It is rather like living in a castle with a moat. Across the moat is a lion. The lion would kill and eat us if he had the chance. He cannot leap the moat, and he knows that, but he keeps trying to do so, even with that knowledge. I hope you can understand our concern.'

'I do, sir,' SecState assured him. 'If the PRC reduces the level of its activity, will you do the same?' Even if they couldn't figure out what the PRC was up to, perhaps they could de-stress the situation anyway.

'In principle, yes. Exactly how, is a technical question for my colleague here. You will not find us unreasonable.'

And the entire trip had been staged for that simple statement. Now Adler had to fly back to Beijing to deliver it. Matchmaker, matchmaker . . .

Hopkins had its own day-care center, staffed by permanent people and always some students from the university doing lab work for their child-care major. Katie walked in, looked around and was pleased by the multicolored environment. Behind her were four agents, all male, because there weren't any unassigned women. One carried a FAG bag. Nearby was a trio of plainclothes officers of the Baltimore City Police, who exchanged credentials with the USSS to confirm identity, and so another day started for SURGEON and SANDBOX. Katie had enjoyed the helicopter ride. Today she'd make some new friends, but tonight, her mother knew, she'd ask where Miss Marlene was. How did one explain death to a not-yet-three-year-old?

The crowd applauded with something more than the usual warmth. Ryan could feel it. Here he was, not yet three days after an attempt on the life of his youngest daughter, doing his job for them, showing strength and courage and all that other bullshit, POTUS thought. He'd led off with a prayer for the fallen agents, and Nashville was the Bible Belt, where such things were taken seriously. The rest of the speech had actually been pretty good, the President thought, covered things he really believed in. Common sense. Honesty. Duty. It was just that hearing his own voice speaking words written by somebody else made it seem hollow, and it was hard to keep his mind from wandering so early in the morning.

'Thank you, and God bless America,' he concluded. The crowd stood and cheered. The band struck up. Ryan turned away from the armored podium to shake hands again with the local officials, and made his way off the stage, waving as he did so. Arnie was waiting behind the curtain.

'For a phony, you still do pretty good.' Ryan didn't have time to respond to that before Andrea came up.

'FLASH-traffic waiting for you on the bird, sir. From Mr Adler.'

'Okay, let's roll. Stay close,' he told his principal agent on the way out the back.

'Always,' Price assured him.

'Mr President!' a reporter shouted. There were a bunch of them. He was the loudest this morning. He was one of the NBC team. Ryan turned and stopped. 'Will you press Congress for a new gun-control law?'

'What for?'

'The attack on your daughter was –'

Ryan held his hand up. 'Okay. As I understand it, the weapons used were of a type already illegal. I don't see how a new law would accomplish much, unfortunately.'

'But gun-control advocates say –'

'I know what they say. And now they're using an attack

on my little girl, and the deaths of five superb Americans, to advance a political agenda of their own. What do you think of that?' the President asked, turning away.

'What's the problem?'

He described his symptoms. His family physician was an old friend. They even played golf together. It wasn't hard. At the end of every year, the Cobra representative had plenty of demonstrator clubs in nearly mint condition. Most were donated to youth programs or sold to country clubs as rental sticks. But some he could give to his friends, not to mention some Greg Norman autographs.

'Well, you have a temperature, one hundred and three, and that's a little high. Your BP's one hundred over sixty-five, and that's a little low for you. Your color's rotten –'

'I know, I feel sick.'

'You are sick, but I wouldn't worry about it. Probably a flu bug you picked up in some bar, and all the air travel doesn't help much, either – and I've been telling you for years about cutting back on the booze. What happened is you picked something up, and other factors worsened it. Started Friday, right?'

'Thursday night, maybe Friday morning.'

'Played a round anyway?'

'Ended up with a snowman for my trouble,' he admitted, meaning a score of 80.

'I'd settle for that myself, healthy and stone-sober.' The doctor had a handicap of twenty. 'You're over fifty and you can't wallow with the pigs at night and expect to soar with the eagles in the morning. Complete rest. A lot of liquids – non-alcoholic. Stay on the Tylenol.'

'No prescription?'

The doc shook his head. 'Antibiotics don't work on viral infections. Your immune system has to handle those, and it will if you let it. But while you're here, I want to draw some blood. You're overdue for a cholesterol check. I'll send my nurse in. You have somebody here to drive you home?'

'Yeah. I didn't want to drive myself.'

'Good. Give it a few days. Cobra can do without you, and the golf courses will still be there when you feel better.'

'Thanks.' He felt better already. You always did when the doc told you that you weren't going to die.

'Here you go.' Goodley handed the paper over. Few office buildings, even secure government ones, had the communications facilities that were shoehorned into the upper-level lounge area of the VC-25, whose call sign was Air Force One. 'Not bad news at all,' Ben added.

SWORDSMAN skimmed it once, then sat down to read it more slowly. 'Okay, fine, he thinks he can defuse the situation,' Ryan noted. 'But he still doesn't know what the goddamned situation is.'

'Better than nothing.'

'Does the working group have this?'

'Yes, Mr President.'

'Maybe they can make some sense out of it. Andrea?'

'Yes, Mr President?'

'Tell the driver it's time to get moving.' He looked around. 'Where's Arnie?'

'I'm calling you on a cellular,' Plumber said.

'Fine,' van Damm replied. 'I'm on one, too, as a matter of fact.' The instruments on the aircraft were also secure, with STU-4 capability. He didn't say that. He just needed a retort. John Plumber was no longer on his Christmas card list. Unfortunately, his direct line was still on Plumber's Rolodex. What a shame he couldn't change it. And he'd have to tell his secretary *not* to put this guy through anymore, at least not when he was traveling.

'I know what you're thinking.'

'Good, John. Then I don't have to say what I think.'

'Catch the broadcast tonight. I'll be on at the end.'

'Why?'

'See for yourself, Arnie. So long.'

The chief of staff thumbed the kill switch on the phone and wondered what Plumber meant. He'd once trusted the man. Hell, he'd once trusted the man's colleague. He could have told the President about the call, but decided not to. He'd just delivered a pretty good speech, distractions and all, doing well in spite of himself, because the poor son of a bitch really did believe in more than he knew. It wouldn't be smart to drop something else on him. They'd tape the speech on the flight into California, and if it were fit to view, then he'd show it to POTUS.

'I didn't know there was a flu bug around,' he said, putting his shirt back on. It took time. The auto executive was sore all over.

'There always is. Just it doesn't always make the news,' the physician replied, looking over the vital signs his nurse had just written down. 'And you got it.'

'So?'

'So, take it easy. Don't go to the office. No sense infecting your whole company. Ride it out. You should be fine by the end of the week.'

The SNIE team met at Langley. A ton of new information had come across from the Persian Gulf region, and they were sorting through it in a conference room on the sixth floor. Chavez's photo of Mahmoud Haji Daryaei had been blown up by the inhouse photo lab and was now hanging on the wall. Maybe somebody would throw darts at it, Ding thought.

'Track toads,' the former infantryman snorted, watching the Predator video.

'Kinda big to take on with a rifle, Sundance,' Clark observed. 'Those things always scared the hell out of me.'

'LAWS rocket'll do 'em fine, Mr C.'

'What's the range on a LAWS, Domingo?'

'Four, five hundred meters.'

'Those guns shoot two or three kilometers,' John pointed out. 'Think about it.'

'I'm not up on the hardware,' Bert Vasco said. He waved at the screen. 'What's this mean?'

The answer came from one of CIA's military analysts. 'It means the UIR military is in much better shape than we'd expected.'

An Army major brought over from the Defense Intelligence Agency didn't dispute that. 'I'm fairly impressed. It was a pretty vanilla exercise, nothing really complicated on the maneuver side, but they kept themselves organized for all of it. Nobody got lost –'

'You suppose they're using GPS now?' the CIA analyst asked.

'Anybody who subscribes to *Yachting* magazine can buy the things. The price is down to four hundred bucks, last time I looked,' the officer told his civilian counterpart. 'It means they can navigate their mobile forces a lot better. More than that, it means their artillery will become a whole lot more effective. If you know where your guns are, where your forward observer is, and where the target is in relation to him, then your first round is going to be pretty much on the money.'

'Fourfold increase in performance?'

'Easy,' the major replied. 'That elderly gent on the wall has a big stick to wave at his neighbors. I imagine he'll let them know about it, too.'

'Bert?' Clark asked.

Vasco squirmed in his seat. 'I'm starting to worry. This is going faster than I expected. If Daryaei didn't have other things to worry about, I'd be more worried.'

'Like?' Chavez asked.

'Like he has a country to consolidate, and he has to know that if he starts rattling sabers, we'll react.' The FSO paused. 'Sure as hell, he wants to let his neighbors know who the big boy on the block is. How close is he to being able to do something?'

'Militarily?' the civilian analyst asked. He gestured to the guy from DIA.

'If we were not in the picture, now. But we are in the picture.'

'I ask now that you will join me in a moment of silence,' Ryan told the audience in Topeka. It was eleven here. That made it noon back home. Next stop Colorado Springs, then Sacramento, then, blessedly, home.

'You have to ask yourself what kind of man we have here,' Kealty said in front of cameras of his own. 'Five men and women dead, and he doesn't see the need for a law to control these guns. It's just beyond my comprehension how anyone can be as coldly heartless as that. Well, if he doesn't care about those brave agents, I do. How many Americans will have to die before he sees the need for this? Will he have to actually lose a family member? I'm sorry, I just can't believe that remark,' the politician went on for the minicam.

'We can all remember when people ran for reelection to Congress, and one of the things they told us was, "Vote for me, because for every dollar that taxes take from this district, a dollar-twenty comes back." Do you remember those claims?' the President asked.

'What they didn't say was – well, it was actually a lot of things. Number one, who ever said that you depend on the government for money? We don't vote for Santa Claus, do we? It's the other way around. The government can't exist unless *you* give *it* money.

'Number two, are they telling you, "Vote for me, 'cause I really stick it to those rotten people in North Dakota"? Aren't they Americans, too?

'Number three, the real reason this happens is that the government deficit means *every* district gets more in federal payments than it lost in federal taxes – excuse me, I mean *direct* federal taxes. The ones you can see.

'So they were bragging to you that they were spending more money than they had. If your next-door neighbor told you he was kiting checks drafted on your personal bank, you think maybe you might call the police about it?

'We all know that the government *does* take more than it gives back. They've just learned to hide it. The federal budget deficit means that every time you borrow money, it costs more than it should – why? Because the government borrows so much money that it drives up interest rates.

'And so, ladies and gentlemen, every house payment, every car payment, every credit-card bill is also a *tax*. And maybe they give you a tax break on interest payments. Isn't that nice?' POTUS asked. 'Your government gives you a tax break on money you ought not to have to pay in the first place, and then it tells you that you get back more than you pay out.' Ryan paused.

'Does anybody out there really believe that? Does anybody really believe it when people say that the United States can't *afford* – *not* to spend more money than it has? Are these the words of Adam Smith or Lucy Ricardo? I have a degree in economics, and *I Love Lucy* wasn't on the course.

'Ladies and gentlemen. I am not a politician, and I am not here to speak on behalf of any of your local candidates for the vacant seats in the People's House. I am here to ask you to think. You, too, have a duty. The government belongs to you. You don't belong to it. When you go out to vote tomorrow, please take the time to think about what the candidates say and what they stand for. Ask yourself, "Does this make sense?" and then make the best choice you can – and if you don't like any of them, go to the polls anyway, go into the voting booth, and then go home without giving your vote to anyone, but at least show up. You owe that to your country.'

The heating and air-conditioning van pulled up the driveway, and a pair of men got out and walked up to the porch. One of them knocked.

'Yes?' the lady of the house asked in puzzlement.

'FBI, Mrs Sminton.' He showed his credentials. 'Could we come in, please?'

'Why?' the sixty-two-year-old widow asked.

'We'd like you to help us with something, if you might.' It had taken longer than expected. The guns used in the SANDBOX case had been traced to a manufacturer, from the manufacturer to a wholesaler, from the wholesaler to a dealer, and from the dealer to a name, and from a name to an address. With the address, the Bureau and Secret Service had gone to a United States District Court judge for a search-and-seizure warrant.

'Please come in.'

'Thank you. Mrs Sminton, do you know the gentleman who lives next door?'

'Mr Azir, you mean?'

'That's right.'

'Not very well. Sometimes I wave.'

'Do you know if he's home now?'

'His car's not there,' she replied, after looking. The agents already knew that. He owned a blue Oldsmobile wagon with Maryland tags. Every cop in two hundred miles was looking for it.

'Do you know when the last time was you saw him?'

'Friday, I guess. There were some other cars there, and a truck.'

'Okay.' The agent reached in his coveralls pocket and pulled out a radio. 'Move in, move in. Bird is probably – say again, *probably* – out of the coop.'

Before the widow's astonished eyes, a helicopter appeared directly over the house three hundred yards away. Zip lines dropped from both sides, and armed agents slid down them. At the same time, four vehicles converged from both directions on the country road, all of them driving off the road, onto the wide lawn straight toward the dwelling. Ordinarily, things would have gone slower, with some period of discreet surveillance, but the word was out on this one. Front and back doors were kicked in – and thirty seconds later, a siren went off. Mr Azir, it seemed, had a burglar alarm. Then the radio crackled.

'Clear, building is clear. This is Betz. Search complete, building is clear. Bring in the lab troops.' With that, two vans appeared. These proceeded up the driveway, and one of the first things the passengers did was to take samples of the gravel there, plus grass, to match with scrapings from the rented cars left at Giant Steps.

'Mrs Sminton, could we sit down, please? There are a couple questions we'd like to ask you about Mr Azir.'

'So?' Murray asked, arriving in the FBI Command Center.

'No joy,' the agent at the console said.

'Damn.' It wasn't said with passion. He'd never really expected it. But he expected some important information anyway. The Lab had collected all manner of physical evidence. Gravel samples could match the driveway. Grass and dirt found on the inside of fenders and bumpers could link the vehicles to the Azir house. Carpet fibers – maroon wool – on the shoes of the dead terrorists could put them inside the house. Even now, a team of ten agents was beginning the process of discovering exactly who 'Mordecai Azir' was. Smart money was that he was about as Jewish as Adolf Eichmann. Nobody was covering that wager.

'Commander Center, this is Betz.' Billy Betz was assistant special agent in charge of the Baltimore Field Division, and a former HRT shooter, hence his dramatic descent from the helicopter, leading his men . . . and a woman.

'Billy, this is Dan Murray. What do you have?'

'Would you believe it? A half-empty crate of seven-six-two ball ammo, and the lot numbers match, Director. Living room has a dark red wool rug. This is our place. Some clothes missing from the master-bedroom closet. I'd say nobody's been here for a couple of days. Location is secure. No booby traps. The lab troops are starting their routine.' And all eighty minutes from the time the Baltimore SAC had walked into the Garmatz Federal Courthouse. Not fast enough, but fast.

The forensics experts were a mix of Bureau, Service, and the Bureau of Alcohol, Tobacco, and Firearms, a troubled agency whose technical staff was nonetheless excellent. They'd all be shaking the house for hours. Everyone wore gloves. Every surface would be dusted for fingerprints to match with those of the dead terrorists.

'Some weeks ago you saw me take an oath to preserve, protect, and defend the Constitution of the United States. That's the second time I did that. The first time was as a brand-new Marine second lieutenant, when I graduated from Boston College. Right after that, I read the Constitution, to make sure I knew what it was that I was supposed to be defending.

'Ladies and gentlemen, we often hear politicians saying how they want government to empower you, so that you can do things.

'That's not the way it is,' Ryan told them forcefully. 'Thomas Jefferson wrote that governments derive their just powers from the *consent* of the governed. That's you. The Constitution is something you should all read. The Constitution of the United States was not written to tell you what to do. The Constitution establishes the relationship among the three branches of government. It tells the government what it may do, and it also tells the government what it may *not* do. The government may *not* restrict your speech. The government may *not* tell you how to pray. The government may *not* do a lot of things. Government is a lot better at taking things away than it is at giving, but most of all, the government does not empower you. You empower the government. Ours is a government of the people. You are *not* people who belong to the government.

'Tomorrow you will not be electing masters, you will be choosing employees, servants of your will, guardians of your rights. We do not tell you what to do. You tell us what to do.

'It is not my job to take your money and give it back. It is my job to take what money I must have to protect and serve you – and to do that job as efficiently as possible. Government service may be an important duty, and a great responsibility, but it is not supposed to be a blessing for those who serve. It is your government servants who are supposed to sacrifice for you, not you who sacrifice for them.

'Last Friday, three good men and two good women lost their lives in the service of our country. They were there to protect my daughter, Katie. But there were other children there, too, and in protecting one child, you protect all children. People like that do not ask for much more than your respect. They deserve that. They deserve it because they do things that we cannot easily do for ourselves. That's why we hire them. They sign on because they know that service is important, because they care about us, because they *are* us. You and I know that not all government employees are like that. That's not their fault. That's *your* fault. If you do not demand the best, you will not get the best. If you do not give the right measure of power to the right kind of people, then the wrong people will take more power than they need and they will use it the way they want, not the way you want.

'Ladies and gentlemen, that's why your duty tomorrow to elect the right people to serve you is so important. Many of you operate your own businesses and you hire people to work for you. Most of you own your own homes, and sometimes you hire plumbers, electricians, carpenters to do work for you. You try to hire the right people for the work because you pay for that work, and you want it done right. When your child is sick, you try to pick the best physician – and you pay attention to what that doctor does and how well he or she does it. Why? Because there is nothing more important to you than the life of your child.

'America is also your child. America is a country forever

young. America needs the right people to look after her. It is *your* job to pick the right people, regardless of party, or race, or gender, or anything other than talent and integrity. I can't and I won't tell you which candidate merits your vote. God gave you a free will. The Constitution is there to protect your right to exercise that will. If you fail to exercise your will intelligently, then you have betrayed yourselves, and neither I nor anyone else can fix that for you.

'Thank you for coming to see me on my first visit to Colorado Springs. Tomorrow is your day. Please use it to hire the right people.'

'In a series of speeches clearly designed to reach conservative voters, President Ryan is stumping the country on the eve of the House elections, but even as federal officials investigate the vicious terrorist attack on his own daughter, the President flatly *rejected* the idea of improved gun-control laws. We have this report from NBC correspondent Hank Roberts, traveling with the presidential party today.' Tom Donner continued looking into the camera until the red light went off.

'I thought he said some pretty good things today,' Plumber observed while the tape ran.

'Invoking *I Love Lucy* must have come from Callie Weston on a serious PMS day,' Donner observed, flipping through his copy. 'Funny, she used to do great speeches for Bob Fowler.'

'Did you *read* the speech?'

'John, come on, we don't have to read what he says. We *know* what he's going to say.'

'Ten seconds,' the director called over their earpieces.

'Nice copy for later, by the way, John.' The face broke into the smile at 'three.'

'A huge federal task force is now investigating Friday's attack on the President's daughter. We have this report from Karen Stabler in Washington.'

'I thought you'd like it, Tom,' Plumber replied, when the light went dark again. So much the better, he thought. His conscience was clear now.

The VC-25 lifted off on time, and headed north to avoid some adverse weather over northern New Mexico. Arnie van

Damm was topside in the communications area. There were enough important-looking boxes to run half the world here, or so it seemed, and hidden in the skin of the aircraft was a satellite dish whose expensive aiming system could track almost anything. At the chief of staff's direction, it was now getting the NBC feed off a Hughes bird.

'We have this closing comment from special correspondent John Plumber.' Donner turned graciously. 'John.'

'Thank you, Tom. The profession of journalism is one I entered many years ago, because I was inspired in my youth. I remember my crystal radio set – those of you old enough might recall how you had to ground them to a pipe,' he explained, with a smile. 'I remember listening to Ed Murrow in London during the blitz, to Eric Sevareid from the jungles of Burma, to all the founding fathers – giants, really – of our profession. I grew up with pictures in my mind painted by the words of men whom all America could trust to tell the truth to the best of their ability. I decided that finding the truth and communicating it to people was as noble a calling as any to which a man – or woman – could aspire.

'We're not always perfect in this profession. No one is,' Plumber went on.

To his right, Donner was looking at the TelePrompTer in puzzlement. This *wasn't* what was rolling in front of the camera lens, and he realized that, though Plumber had printed pages in front of him, he was giving a *memorized* speech. Imagine that. Just like the old days, apparently.

'I would like to say that I am proud to be in this profession. And I was, once.

'I was on the microphone when Neil Armstrong stepped down on the moon, and on sadder occasions, like the funeral of Jack Kennedy. But to be a professional does not mean merely being there. It means that you have to profess something, to believe in something, to stand for something.

'Some weeks ago, we interviewed President Ryan twice in one day. The first interview in the morning was taped, and the second one was done live. The questions were a little different. There's a reason for that. Between the first interview and the second, we were called over to see someone. I will not say who that was right now. I will later. That person gave us information. It was sensitive information aimed at hurting the President, and it looked like a good story at the time. It wasn't, but we didn't know that then. At the time, it seemed as though we had asked the wrong questions. We wanted to ask better ones.

'And so we lied. We lied to the President's chief of staff, Arnold van Damm. We told him that the tape had been damaged somehow. In doing that, we also lied to the President. But worst of all, we lied to you. I have the tapes in my possession. They are not damaged in any way.

'No law was broken. The First Amendment allows us to do almost anything we want, and that's all right, because you people out there are the final judge of what we do and who we are. But one thing we may not do is to break faith with you.

'I have no brief for President Ryan. Speaking personally, I disagree with him on many policy issues. If he should run for reelection, I will probably vote for someone else. But I was part of that lie, and I cannot live with it. Whatever his faults, John Patrick Ryan is an honorable man, and I am not supposed to allow my personal animus for or against anyone or anything to affect my work.

'In this case, I did. I was wrong. I owe an apology to the President, and I owe an apology to you. This might well be the end of my career as a broadcast journalist. If so, I want to leave it as I entered it, telling the truth as best I can.

'Good night, from NBC News.' Plumber took a very deep breath as he stared at the camera.

'What the hell was *that* all about?'

Plumber stood before he answered. 'If you have to ask that question, Tom –'

The phone on his desk rang – actually, it had a blinking light. Plumber decided not to answer it, and instead walked to his dressing room. Tom Donner would have to figure it out all by himself.

Two thousand miles away, over Rocky Mountain National Park, Arnold van Damm stopped the machine, ejected the tape, and carried it down the circular stairs to the President's compartment in the nose. He saw Ryan going over his next and final speech of the day.

'Jack, I think you will want to see this,' the chief of staff told him, with a broad grin.

There has to be a first one of everything. This time it happened in Chicago. She'd seen her physician on Saturday afternoon and been told the same as everyone else. Flu. Aspirin. Liquids. Bed rest. But looking in the mirror, she saw some discoloration on her fair skin, and that frightened her even more than the other symptoms she'd had to that point. She called her doctor, but she got only an answering machine, and those blotches could not wait, and so she got in her car and drove to the University of Chicago Medical Center, one of America's finest. She waited in the emergency room for about forty minutes, and when her name was called, she stood and walked toward the desk, but she didn't make it, instead falling to the tile floor in sight of the administrative people. That caused some instant reactions, and a minute later, two orderlies had her on a gurney and were wheeling her back to the treatment area, her paperwork carried behind by one of the admissions people.

The first physician to see her was a young resident most of the way through his first year of post-graduate study in internal medicine, doing his ER rotation and liking it.

'What's the problem?' he asked, as the nursing staff went to work, checking pulse, blood pressure, and respiration.

'Here,' the woman from admissions said, handing over the paper forms. The physician scanned them.

'Flu symptoms, looks like, but what's this?'

'Heart rate is one twenty, BP is – wait a minute.' The nurse ran it again. 'Blood pressure is ninety over fifty?' She looked much too normal for that.

The doctor was unbuttoning the woman's blouse. And there it was. The clarity of the moment made passages from his textbooks leap into his mind. The young resident held up his hands.

'Everybody, stop what you're doing. We may have a major problem here. I want everybody regloved, everybody masked, right now.'

'Temp is one-oh-four-point-four,' another nurse said, stepping back from the patient.

'This isn't flu. We have a major internal bleed, and those

are petechiae.' The resident got a mask and changed gloves as he spoke. 'Get Dr Quinn over here.'

A nurse trotted out, while the resident looked again at the admission papers. Might be vomiting blood, darkened stool. Depressed blood pressure, high fever, and subcutaneous bleeding. But this was Chicago, his mind protested. He got a needle.

'Everybody stay clear, okay, nobody get close to my hands and arms,' he said, slipping the needle into the vein, then drawing four 5cc tubes.

'What gives?' Dr Joe Quinn asked. The resident recited the symptoms, and posed his own question as he moved the blood tubes onto a table.

'What do you think, Joe?'

'If we were somewhere else . . .'

'Yeah. Hemorrhagic fever, if that's possible.'

'Anybody ask her where she's been?' Quinn asked.

'No, Doctor,' the admissions clerk replied.

'Cold packs,' the head nurse said, handing over an armload of them. These went under the armpits, under the neck, and elsewhere to bleed off the body's potentially lethal heat.

'Dilantin?' Quinn wondered.

'She's not convulsing yet. Hell.' The chief resident took out his surgical scissors and cut off the patient's bra. There were more petechiae forming on her torso. 'We have a very sick lady here. Nurse, call Dr Klein in infectious disease. He'll be at home now. Tell him we need him here at once. We have to get her temp down, wake her up, and find out where the hell she's been.'

47

INDEX CASE

Mark Klein was a full professor at the medical school, and therefore a man accustomed to regular working hours. Getting called in at almost nine in the evening wasn't the usual thing for him, but he was a physician, and when called, he went. It was a twenty minute drive on this Monday night to his reserved parking space. He walked through the security staff with a nod, changed into scrubs, came into the emergency room from the back, and asked the charge nurse where Quinn was.

'Isolation Two, Doctor.'

He was there in twenty seconds, and stopped cold when he saw the warning signs posted on the door. Okay, he thought, donning a mask and gloves, then walking in.

'Hi, Joe.'

'I don't want to make this call without you, Professor,' Quinn said quietly, handing the chart over.

Klein scanned it, then his brain stopped cold, and he started from the beginning, looking up to compare the patient with the data. Female Caucasian, yes, age forty-one, about right, divorced, that was her business, apartment about two miles away, fine, temperature on admission 104.4, pretty damn high, BP, that was awfully low. Petechiae?

'Let me take a look here,' Klein said. The patient was coming around. The head was moving a little, and she was making some noise. 'What's her temp now?'

'One-oh-two-two, coming down nicely,' the admitting resident replied, as Klein pulled the green sheet back. The patient was nude now, and the marks could hardly have been more plain on her otherwise very fair skin. Klein looked at the other doctors.

'Where's she been?'

'We don't know,' Quinn admitted. 'We looked through her

purse. It seems she's an executive with Sears, office over in the tower.'

'Have you examined her?'

'Yes, Doctor,' Quinn and the younger resident said together.

'Animal bites?' Klein asked.

'None. No evidence of needles, nothing unusual at all. She's clean.'

'I'm calling it possible hemorrhagic fever, method of transmission unknown for now. I want her upstairs, total isolation, full precautions. I want this room scrubbed – everything she touched.'

'I thought these viruses only passed –'

'Nobody knows, Doctor, and things I can't explain scare me. I've been to Africa. I've seen Lassa and Q fever. Haven't seen Ebola. But what she has looks a hell of a lot like one of those,' Klein said, speaking those awful names for the first time.

'But how –'

'When you don't know, it means you don't know,' Professor Klein said to the resident. 'For infectious diseases, if you do not know the means of transmission, you assume the worst. The worst case is aerosol, and that's how this patient will be handled. Let's get her moved up to my unit. Everybody who's been in contact with her, I want you to scrub down. Like AIDS or hepatitis. Full precautions,' he emphasized again. 'Where's the blood you drew?'

'Right there.' The admitting physician pointed to a red plastic container.

'What's next?' Quinn asked.

'We get a sample off to Atlanta, but I think I'm going to take a look myself.' Klein had a superb laboratory in which he worked every day, mainly on AIDS, which was his passion.

'Can I come with?' Quinn asked. 'I go off duty in a few minutes anyway.' Monday was usually a quiet day for emergency rooms. Their hectic time was generally weekends.

'Sure.'

'I knew Holtzman would come through for me,' Arnie said. He was having a drink to celebrate, as the 747 began its descent into Sacramento.

'What?' the President asked.

'Bob's a tough son of a bitch, but he's an honest son of a bitch. That also means that he will honestly burn you at the stake if he thinks you have it coming. Always remember that,' the chief of staff advised.

'Donner and Plumber lied,' Jack said aloud. 'Damn.'

'Everybody lies, Jack. Even you. It's a question of context. Some lies are designed to protect the truth. Some lies are designed to conceal it. Some are designed to deny it. And some lies happen because nobody gives a damn.'

'And what happened here?'

'A combination, Mr President. Ed Kealty wanted 'em to ambush you for him, and he suckered them. But I got that treacherous bastard for you. I'll bet that tomorrow there will be a front-page article in the *Post* exposing Kcalty as the guy who suborned two very senior reporters, and the press will turn on him like a pack of wolves.' The reporters riding in the back of the plane were already buzzing about it. Arnie had seen to it that the NBC news tape had run on the cabin video system.

'Because he's the one who made them look bad . . .'

'You got it, boss,' van Damm confirmed, tossing off the remainder of his drink. He couldn't add that it might not have happened without the attack on Katie Ryan. Even reporters felt sympathy on occasion, which might have been decisive in Plumber's change of heart on the matter. But he was the one who'd made the carefully measured leaks to Bob Holtzman. He decided that he'd have a Secret Service agent find him a good cigar once they got on the ground. He felt like having one right now.

Adler's body clock was totally confused now. He found that catching catnaps helped, and it also helped that the message he was delivering was a simple and favorable one. The car stopped. A minor official opened the door for him and bowed curtly. Adler stifled a yawn as he walked into the ministry building.

'So good to see you again,' the PRC Foreign Minister said, through his interpreter. Zhang Han San was there again, too, and made his own greeting.

'Your gracious agreement to allow direct flights certainly

makes the process easier for me. Thank you for that,' Sec-State replied, taking his seat.

'Just so you understand that these are exceptional circumstances,' the Foreign Minister observed.

'Of course.'

'What news do you bring us from our wayward cousins?'

'They are entirely willing to match your reductions in activity, with an eye toward reducing tension.'

'And their insulting accusations?'

'Minister, that issue never arose. I believe that they are as interested as you in returning to peaceful circumstances.'

'How good of them,' Zhang commented. 'They initiate hostilities, shoot down two of our aircraft, damage one of their own airliners, kill over a hundred people, whether by deliberate act or by incompetence, and then they say that they will match *us* in reducing provocative acts. I hope your government appreciates the forbearance we are showing here.'

'Mr Minister, peace serves everyone's best interests, does it not? America appreciates the actions of both parties in these informal proceedings. The People's Republic has indeed been gracious in more than one way, and the government in Taiwan is willing to match your actions. What more is required than that?'

'Very little,' the Foreign Minister replied. 'Merely compensation for the deaths of our four aviators. Each of them left a family behind.'

'Their fighters did shoot first,' Zhang pointed out.

'That may be true, but the question of the airliner is still undetermined.'

'Certainly, *we* had nothing to do that that.' This came from the Foreign Minister.

There were few things more boring than negotiations between countries, but there was actually a reason for that. Sudden or surprise moves could force a country into making impromptu decisions. Unexpected pressure caused anger, and anger had no place in high-level discussions and decisions. Therefore, important talks were almost never decisive, but were, rather, evolutionary in nature, which gave each side time to think through its position, and that of the other side, carefully, so to arrive at a final communiqué with which both sides could be relatively content. Thus the demand for compensation was a violation of the rules. More properly done, this would have been said at the first session, and Adler would have taken it to Taipei and probably presented it as his own suggestion after the Republic of China government had agreed to cooperate in the reduction of tension. But they had already done that, and now the PRC wanted him to take back the request for compensation instead of a formula for local détente. That was an insult to the Taiwanese government, and also a measured insult to the American government for having been used as a stalking horse for another country.

This was all the more true since Adler and the ROC knew who'd killed the airliner, and who had therefore shown contempt for human life – for which the PRC now demanded compensation! And now Adler wondered again how much of what he knew of the incident was known to the PRC. If they knew a lot, then this was definitely a game whose rules had yet to be decoded.

'I think it would be more useful if both sides were to cover their individual losses and needs,' Secretary Adler suggested.

'I regret that we cannot accept that. It is a matter of principle, you see. He who commits the improper act must make amends.'

'But what if – I do not have any evidence to suggest this, but what if it is determined that the PRC inadvertently damaged the airliner? In such a case your request for compensation might appear unjust.'

'That is not possible. We have interviewed our surviving pilots and their reports are unequivocal.' Again it was Zhang.

'What precisely do you request?' Adler asked.

'Two hundred thousand dollars for each of the four aviators lost. The money will go to their families, of course,' Zhang promised.

'I can present this request to –'

'Excuse me. It is not a request. It is a requirement,' the Foreign Minister told Adler.

'I see. I can present your position to them, but I must urge you not to make this a condition of your promise to reduce tension.'

'That *is* our position.' The Foreign Minister's eyes were quite serene.

'. . . and God bless America,' Ryan concluded. The crowd stood and cheered. The band struck up – there had to be a band everywhere he went, Jack supposed – and he made his way off the dais behind a wall of nervous Secret Service agents. Well, the President thought, no gunfire out of the blinding lights this time, either. He stifled another yawn. He'd been on the move for over twelve hours. Four speeches didn't seem to be all that much physical work, but Ryan was learning just how exhausting public speaking could be. You had the shakes every time before getting up there, and though you got over it in a few minutes, the accumulated stress did take its toll. The dinner hadn't helped much. The food had been bland, so carefully chosen to offend no one that it wasn't worth anyone's attention. But it had given him heartburn anyway.

'Okay,' Arnie told him, as the presidential party assembled to head out the back door. 'For a guy who was ready to chuck it yesterday, you did awfully well.'

'Mr President!' a reporter called.

'Talk to him,' Arnie whispered.

'Yes?' Jack said, walking over, to the displeasure of his security force.

'Do you know about what John Plumber said this evening on NBC?' The reporter was ABC, and unlikely to pass on the chance to slam a competing network.

'Yes, I've heard about it,' the President replied soberly.

'Do you have any comment?'

'Obviously, I do not like learning about all this, but as far as Mr Plumber is concerned, that's as gracious an act of moral courage as I've seen in quite a while. He's okay in my book.'

'Do you know who it was who –'

'Please, let Mr Plumber handle that. It's his story, and he knows how to tell it. Now if you will excuse me, I have a plane to catch.'

'Thank you, Mr President,' the ABC reporter said to Ryan's back.

'Just right,' Arnie said, with a smile. 'We've had a long day, but it's been a good day.'

Ryan let out a long breath. 'You say so.'

'Oh, my God,' Professor Klein whispered. There it was on the display monitor. The Shepherd's Crook, right out of a medical text. How the hell had it come to Chicago?

'That's Ebola,' Dr Quinn said, adding, 'That's not possible.'

'How thorough was your physical examination?' the senior man asked again.

'Could have been better, but – no bite marks, no needle marks. Mark, it's *Chicago*. I had *frost* on my windshield the other day.'

Professor Klein pressed his hands together, and pushed his gloved fingers up against his nose. Then he stopped the gesture when he realized that he was still wearing a surgical mask. 'Keys in her purse?'

'Yes, sir.'

'First, we have cops around the ER. Get one, tell him we need a police escort to go to her apartment and allow us to look around. Tell him this woman's life is in danger. Maybe she's got a pet, a tropical plant, something. We have the name of her physician. Get him up, get him in here. We need to find out what he knows about her.'

'Treatment?'

'We cool her down, we keep her hydrated, we medicate for pain, but there isn't anything that really works on this. Rousseau in Paris has tried interferon and a few other things, but no luck so far.' He frowned at the display again. 'How'd she get it? How the hell did she contract this little bastard?'

'CDC?'

'You get the cop up here. I'll get a fax off to Gus Lorenz.' Klein checked his watch. Damn.

The Predator drones were back in Saudi, having never been discovered. It was felt that having them circle over a stationary position, like a divisional encampment, was a little too dangerous, however, and now the overhead work was being done by satellites, whose photos downloaded to the National Reconnaissance Office.

'Check this out,' one of the night crew said to the guy at the next workstation. 'What are these?'

The tanks of the UIR 'Immortals' division were grouped

in what was essentially a large parking lot, all evenly spaced in long, regular lines so that they could be counted – a stolen tank with a full basic load of shells was a dangerous thing to have on the loose, and all armies took security of the tank laagers seriously. It also made things more convenient for the maintenance personnel to have them all together. Now they were all back, and men were swarming over the tanks and other fighting vehicles, doing the normal maintenance that followed a major exercise. In front of every tank in the first row were two dark lines, each about a meter across, and ten meters long. The man on the screen was ex-Air Force, and more expert on airplanes than land-combat vehicles.

His neighbor only needed one look. 'Tracks.'

'What?'

'They're rotating the tires, like. Tracks wear out, and you put new ones on. The old ones go into the shop to be worked on, replacing pads and stuff,' the former soldier explained. 'It's no big deal.'

Closer examination showed how it was done. The new tracks were laid in front of the old ones. The old ones were then disconnected, and attached to the new, and the tank, its motor running, simply drove forward, the sprocket wheel pulling the new track in place over the road wheels. It required several men and was hot, heavy work, but it could be done by a well-trained tank crew in about an hour under ideal conditions, which, the ex-soldier explained, these were. Essentially, the tank drove onto the new tracks.

'I never knew how they did that.'

'Beats having to jack the sumbitch off the ground.'

'What's a track good for?'

'On one of these, cross-country in a desert? Oh, call it a thousand miles, maybe a little less.'

Sure enough, the two couches in Air Force One's forward cabin folded out to make beds. After dismissing his staff, Ryan hung up his clothes and lay down. Clean sheets and everything, and he was weary enough that he didn't mind being on an airplane. Flight time to Washington was four and a half hours, and then he'd be able to sleep some more in his own bed. Unlike normal red-eye travelers, he might even be able to do some useful work the next day.

In the big cabin, aft, the reporters were doing the same, having decided to leave the issue of Plumber's astounding revelation to the next day. They had no choice in the matter; a story of this magnitude was handled at least at the assistant managing editor level. Many of the print journalists were dreaming about the editorials that would appear in the papers. The TV reporters were trying not to cringe at what this would mean to their credibility.

In between were the President's staff members. They were all smiles, or nearly so.

'Well, I finally saw his temper,' Arnie told Callie Weston. 'Big-time.'

'And I bet he saw yours, too.'

'And mine won.' Arnie sipped at his drink. 'You know, the way things are going, I think we have a pretty good President here.'

'He hates it.' Weston had one of her own.

Arnie van Damm didn't care: 'Fabulous speeches, Callie.'

'There's such an engaging way about how he delivers them,' she thought. 'Every time, he starts off tight, embarrassed, and then the teacher in him takes over, and he really gets into it. He doesn't even know it, either.'

'Honesty. It really does come out, doesn't it?' Arnie paused. 'There's going to be a memorial service for the dead agents.'

'I'm already thinking about it,' Weston assured him. 'What are you going to do about Kealty?'

'I'm thinking about *that*. We're going to sink that bastard once and for all.'

Badrayn was back on his computer, checking the proper Internet sites. Still nothing. In another day he might start worrying, though it wasn't really his problem if nothing happened, was it? Everything he'd done had gone perfectly.

Patient Zero opened her eyes, which got everyone's attention. Her temperature was down to 101.6, entirely due to the cold packs that now surrounded her body like a fish in the market. The combination of pain and exhaustion was plain on her face. In that way, she looked like a patient with advanced AIDS, a disease with which the physician was all too familiar.

'Hello, I'm Dr Klein,' the professor told her from behind his mask. 'You had us a little worried there for a minute, but things are under control now.'

'Hurts,' she said.

'I know, and we're going to help you with that, but I need to ask you a few questions. Can you help me with a few things?' Klein asked.

'Okay.'

'Have you been doing any traveling lately?'

'What do you mean?' Every word she spoke drew down on her energy reserves.

'Have you been out of the country?'

'No. Flew to Kansas City . . . ten days ago, that's all. Day trip,' she added.

'Okay.' It wasn't. 'Have you had any contact with someone who's been out of the country?'

'No.' She tried to shake her head. It moved maybe a quarter inch.

'Forgive me, but I have to ask this. Do you have any ongoing sexual relationships at the moment?'

That question shook her. 'AIDS?' she gasped, thinking that was the worst thing she might have.

Klein shook his head emphatically. 'No, definitely not. Please don't worry about that.'

'Divorced,' the patient said. 'Just a few months. No new . . . men in my life yet.'

'Well, as pretty as you are, that'll have to change soon,' Klein observed, trying to get a smile out of her. 'What do you do at Sears?'

'Housewares, buyer. Just had . . . big show . . . McCormick Center . . . lots of paperwork, orders and things.'

This was going nowhere. Klein tried a few more questions. They led nowhere. He turned and pointed to the nurse.

'Okay, we're going to do something about the pain now,' the professor told her. He stepped away so as not to crowd the nurse when she started the morphine on the IV tree. 'This will start working in a few seconds, okay? I'll be back soon.'

Quinn was waiting out in the hall with a uniformed police officer, a checkerboard band around his cap.

'Doc, what's the story?' the cop asked.

'The patient has something very serious, possibly very contagious. I need to look over her apartment.'

'That's not really legal, you know. You're supposed to go to a judge and get – '

'Officer, there's no time for that. We have her keys. We could just break in, but I want you there so that you can say we didn't do anything wrong.' And besides, if she had a burglar alarm, it wouldn't do for them to be arrested. 'There's no time to waste. This woman is very sick.'

'Okay, my car is outside.' The cop pointed and the doctors followed.

'Get the fax off to Atlanta?' Quinn asked. Klein shook his head.

'Let's look at her place first.' He decided not to wear a coat. It was cold outside, and the temperature would be very inhospitable to the virus in the unlikely event that it had somehow gotten on his scrubs. Reason told him that there was no real danger here. He'd never encountered Ebola clinically, but he knew as much about it as any man could. It was regrettably normal for people to show up with diseases whose presence they could not explain. Most of the time, careful investigation would reveal how it had been contracted, but not always. Even with AIDS, there was the handful of unexplained cases. But only a handful, and you didn't start with one of those as your Index Case. Professor Klein shivered when he got outside. The temperature was in the low thirties, with a north wind blowing down off Lake Michigan. But that wasn't the reason for his shaking.

Price opened the door to the nose cabin. The lights were off except for a few faint indirect ones. The President was lying on his back and snoring loudly enough to be heard over the whining drone of the engines. She had to resist the temptation to tiptoe in and cover him with a blanket. Instead, she smiled and closed the door.

'Maybe there is such a thing as justice, Jeff,' she observed to Agent Raman.

'The newsie thing, you mean?'

'Yeah.'

'Don't bet on it,' the other agent said.

They looked around. Finally everyone was asleep, even the

chief of staff. Topside, the flight crew was doing their job, along with the other USAF personnel, and it really was like a red-eye flight back to the East Coast, as Air Force One passed over central Illinois. The two agents moved back to their seating area. Three members of the Detail were playing cards, quietly. Others were reading or dozing.

An Air Force sergeant came down the circular steps, holding a folder.

'FLASH-traffic for the Boss,' she announced.

'Is it that important? We get into Andrews in about ninety minutes.'

'I just take 'em off the fax machine,' the sergeant pointed out.

'Okay.' Price took the message and headed aft. To where Ben Goodley was. It was his job to be around to tell the President what he needed to know about the important happenings in the world – or, in this case, to evaluate the importance of a message. Price shook the man's shoulder. The national intelligence officer opened one eye.

'Yeah?'

'Do we wake the Boss for this?'

The intelligence specialist scanned it and shook his head. 'It can wait. Adler knows what he's doing, and there's a working group at State for this.' He turned back into his seat without another word.

'Don't touch anything,' Klein told the policeman. 'Best for you to stand right by the door, but if you want to follow us around, don't touch a thing. Wait.' The physician reached into the plastic trash bag he'd brought along, and pulled out a surgical mask in a sterile container. 'Put this on, okay?'

'Anything you say, Doc.'

Klein handed over the house key. The police officer opened the door. It turned out that there was an alarm system. The control panel was just inside the door, but not turned on. The two physicians put on their own masks and donned latex gloves. First, they turned on all the lights.

'What are we looking for?' Quinn asked.

Klein was already looking. No cat or dog had come to note their arrival. He saw no bird cages – part of him had hoped for a pet monkey, but somehow he knew that wasn't in the cards. Ebola didn't seem to like monkeys very much, anyway. It killed them with all the alacrity it applied to human victims. Plants, then, he thought. Wouldn't it be odd if Ebola's host was something other than an animal? That would be a first of sorts.

There were plants, but nothing exotic. They stood in the center of the living room, not touching anything with their gloved hands or even with their green-trousered legs, as they turned around slowly, looking.

'I don't see anything,' Quinn reported.

'Neither do I. Kitchen.'

There were some more plants there, two that looked like herbs in small pots. Klein didn't recognize their type and decided to lift them.

'Wait. Here,' Quinn said, opening a drawer and finding freezer bags. The plants went into those bags, which the younger physician sealed carefully. Klein opened the refrigerator. Nothing unusual there. The same was true of the freezer. He'd thought it possible that some exotic food product ... but, no. Everything the patient ate was typically American.

The bedroom was a bedroom and nothing more. No plants there, they saw.

'Some article of clothing? Leather?' Quinn asked. 'Anthrax can –'

'Ebola can't. It's too delicate. We know the organism we're dealing with. It can't survive in this environment. It just *can't*,' the professor insisted. They didn't know much about the little bastard, but one of the things they did at CDC was to establish the environmental parameters, how long the virus could survive in a whole series of conditions. Chicago at this time of year was as inhospitable to that sort of virus as a blast furnace. Orlando, some place in the South, maybe. But Chicago? 'We got nothing,' he concluded in frustration.

'Maybe the plants?'

'You know how hard it is to get a plant through customs?'

'I've never tried.'

'I have, tried to bring some wild orchids back from Venezuela once ...' He looked around some more. 'There's nothing here, Joe.'

'Is her prognosis as bad as –'

'Yeah.' A pair of gloved hands rubbed against the scrub pants. Inside the latex rubber, his hands were sweating now. 'If we can't determine where it came from ... if we can't explain it ...' He looked at his younger, taller colleague. 'I have to get back. I want to take another look at that structure.'

'Hello,' Gus Lorenz said. He checked his clock. What the hell?

'Gus?' the voice asked.

'Yes, who's this?'

'Mark Klein in Chicago.'

'Something wrong?' Lorenz asked groggily. The reply opened his eyes all the way.

'I think – no, Gus, I *know* I have an Ebola case up here.'

'How can you be sure?'

'I have the crook. I micrographed it myself. It's the Shepherd's Crook, and no mistake, Gus. I wish it were.'

'Where's he been?'

'It's a she, and she hasn't been anywhere special.' Klein summarized what he knew in less than a minute. 'There is no immediately apparent explanation for this.'

Lorenz could have objected that this was not possible, but the medical community is an intimate one at its higher levels; he knew Mark Klein was a full professor at one of the world's finest medical schools. 'Just one case?'

'They all start with one, Gus,' Klein reminded his friend. A thousand miles away, Lorenz swung his legs off the bed and onto the floor.

'Okay. I need a specimen.'

'I have a courier on the way to O'Hare now. He'll catch the first flight down. I can e-mail you the micrographs right now.'

'Give me about forty minutes to get in.'

'Gus?'

'Yes?'

'Is there anything on the treatment side that I don't know? We have a very sick patient here,' Klein said, hoping that for once maybe he wasn't fully up to speed on something in his field.

''Fraid not, Mark. Nothing new that I know about.'

'Damn. Okay, we'll do what we can here. Call me when you get there. I'm in my office.'

Lorenz went into the bathroom and ran some water to splash in his face, proving to himself that this wasn't a dream. No, he thought. Nightmare.

This presidential perk was one even the press respected. Ryan walked down the steps first, saluted the USAF sergeant at the bottom, and walked the fifty yards to the helicopter. Inside, he promptly buckled his belt and went back to sleep. Fifteen minutes later he was roused from his seat again, walked down another set of stairs, saluted a Marine this time, and headed into the White House. Ten minutes after that, he was in a sleeping place that didn't move.

'Good trip?' Cathy asked, one eye partly open.

'Long one,' her husband reported, falling back to sleep.

The first flight from Chicago to Atlanta left the gate at 6:15 AM, Central Time. Before then, Lorenz was in his office, on his computer terminal, dialed into the Internet and on the phone at the same time.

'I'm downloading the image now.'

As the older man watched, the micrograph grew from top to bottom, one line at a time, faster than a fax would come out of a machine, and far more detailed.

'Tell me I'm wrong, Gus,' Klein said, no hope in his voice at all.

'I think you know better, Mark.' He paused as the image finished forming. 'That's our friend.'

'Where's he been lately?'

'Well, we had a couple of cases in Zaire, and two more reported in Sudan. That's it, as far as I know. Your patient, has she been –'

'No. There aren't any risk factors that I have been able to identify so far. Given the incubation period, she must almost certainly have contracted it here in Chicago. And that's not possible, is it?'

'Sex?' Lorenz asked. He could almost hear the shake of the head over the phone.

'I asked. She says she's not getting any of that. Any reports anyplace else?'

'None, none anywhere. Mark, are you sure of what you've told me?' As insulting as the question was, it had to be asked.

'I wish I weren't. The micrograph I sent is the third one, I wanted good isolation for it. Her blood is full of it, Gus. Wait a minute.' He heard a muffled conversation. 'She just came around again. Says she had a tooth extracted a week or so ago. We have the name of her dentist. We'll run that one down. That's all we have here.'

'All right, let me get set up for your sample. It's only one case. Let's not get too excited.'

Raman got home shortly before dawn. It was just as well that the streets were almost entirely devoid of traffic at this time of day. He was in no condition for safe driving. Arriving home, he followed the usual routine. On his answering machine was another wrong number, the voice of Mr Alahad.

The pain was so severe that it woke him up from the sleep of exhaustion. Just walking the twenty feet around the bed and into the bathroom seemed like a marathon's effort, but he managed to stagger that far. The cramping was terrible, which amazed him, because he hadn't eaten all that much in the past couple of days despite his wife's insistence on chicken soup and toast, but with all the urgency he could suffer, he dropped his shorts and sat down just in time. Simultaneously, his upper GI seemed to explode as well, and the former golf pro doubled over, vomiting on the tiles. There was an instant's embarrassment at having done so unmanly a thing. Then he saw what was there at his feet.

'Honey?' he called weakly. 'Help . . .'

48

HEMORRHAGE

Six hours of sleep, maybe a little more, was better than nothing. This morning, Cathy got up first, and the father of the First Family came into the breakfast room unshaven, following the smell of coffee.

'When you feel this rotten, you should at least have a hangover to blame it on,' the President announced. His morning papers were in the usual place. A Post-it note was affixed to the front page of the Washington Post, just over an article bylined to Bob Holtzman and John Plumber. Now, there was something to start off his day, Jack told himself.

'That's really sleazy,' Sally Ryan said. She'd already heard TV coverage of the controversy. 'What finks.' She would have said 'dicks,' a newly favored term among the young ladies at St Mary's School, but Dad wasn't ready to acknowledge the fact that his Sally was talking like a grown-up.

'Uh-huh,' her father replied. The story gave far more detail than was possible in a couple of minutes of air time. And it named Ed Kealty, who had, it seemed – unsurprisingly, but still against the law – a CIA source who had leaked information which, the story explained, had not been entirely truthful and, even worse, had been a deliberate political attack on the President, using the media as an attack dog. Jack snorted. As though that were new. The Post's emphasis was on the gross violation of journalistic integrity. Plumber's recantation of his actions was very sincere, it said. The article said that senior executives at NBC's news division had declined comment, pending their own inquiry. It also said that the Post had custody of the tapes, which were entirely undamaged.

The Washington Times, he saw, was just as irate but not in quite the same way. There would be a colossal internecine battle in the Washington press corps over this, something, the *Times* editorial observed, that the politicians would clearly watch with amusement.

Well, Ryan told himself, *that ought to keep them off my back for a while.*

Next, he opened the manila folder with the secret-tape borders on it. This document, he saw, was pretty old.

'Bastards,' POTUS whispered.

'They really did it to themselves this time,' Cathy said, reading her own paper.

'No,' SWORDSMAN replied. 'China.'

It wasn't an epidemic yet, because nobody knew about it. Doctors were already reacting in surprise to telephone calls. Excited, if not frantic, calls to answering services had already awakened over twenty of them across the country. Bloody vomit and diarrhea were reported in every case, but only one to a customer, and there were various medical problems that could explain that. Bleeding ulcers, for example, and many of the calls came from businesspeople for whom stress came with the tie and white shirt. Most were told to drive to the nearest hospital's emergency room, and in nearly all cases the doctor got dressed to meet his or her patient there, or to have a trusted associate do so. Some were instructed to be at the office first thing, usually between eight and nine in the morning, to be the first patient of the day and thus not interfere with the daily schedule.

Gus Lorenz hadn't felt like being in his office alone, and had called in a few senior staff members to join him at his computer. They noted that his pipe was lit when they came in. One of them might have objected – it was contrary to federal regulations – but she stopped short, looking at the image on the screen.

'Where's this one from?' the epidemiologist asked.

'Chicago.'

'*Our* Chicago?'

Pierre Alexandre arrived at his office on the eleventh floor of the Ross Building just before eight. His morning routine began with checking his fax machine. Attending physicians with AIDS cases regularly sent him patient information that way. It allowed him to monitor a large number of patients, both to advise treatment options and to increase his own knowledge base. There was only one fax this morning, and it was relatively good news. Merck had just fielded a new drug which the FDA was fast-tracking into clinical trials, and a friend of his at Penn State was reporting some interesting results. That's when his phone rang.

'Dr Alexandre.'

'This is the ER, sir. Could you come down here? I got a patient here, Caucasian male, thirty-seven. High fever, internal bleeding. I don't know what this is – I mean,' the resident said, 'I mean, I know what it looks like, but –'

'Give me five minutes.'

'Yes, sir,' she acknowledged.

The internist/virologist/molecular biologist donned his starched lab coat, buttoned it, and headed down toward the emergency room, which was in a separate building on the sprawling Hopkins campus. Even in the military, he'd dressed the same way. The Doctor Look, he called it. Stethoscope in the right-side pocket. Name embroidered onto the left side. A calm expression on his face as he walked into the largely idle ER. Nighttime was the busy period here. There she was, cute as a button . . . putting on a surgical mask, he saw. What could be all that wrong this early on a spring day?

'Good morning, Doctor,' he said, in his most charming Creole accent. 'What seems to be the problem?' She handed him the chart and started talking while he read.

'His wife brought him in. High fever, some disorientation, BP is low, probable internal bleed, bloody vomit and stool. And there are some marks on his face,' she reported. 'And I'm not sure enough to say.'

'Okay, let's take a look.' She sounded like a promising young doc, Alexandre thought pleasantly. She knew what she didn't know, and she'd called for consultation . . . but why not one of the internal-medicine guys? the former colonel asked himself, taking another look at her face. He put on mask and gloves and walked past the isolation curtain.

'Good morning, I'm Dr Alexandre,' he said to the patient. The man's eyes were listless, but it was the marks on his cheeks that made Alexandre's breath stop. It was George

Westphal's face, come back from more than a decade in Alex's past.

'How did he get here?'

'His personal physician told his wife to drive him in. He has privileges at Hopkins.'

'What's he do? News photographer? Diplomat? Something to do with traveling?'

The resident shook her head. 'He sells Winnebagos, RVs and like that, dealership over on Pulaski Highway.'

Alexandre looked around the area. There were a medical student and two nurses, in addition to the resident who was running the case. All gloved, all masked. Good. She was smart, and now Alex knew why she was scared.

'Blood?'

'Already taken, Doctor. Doing the cross-match now, and specimens for analysis in your lab.'

The professor nodded. 'Good. Admit him right now. My unit. I need a container for the tubes. Be careful with all the sharps.' A nurse went off to get the things.

'Professor, this looks like – I mean, it can't be, but –'

'It can't be,' he agreed. 'But it does look that way. Those are petechiae, right out of the book. So we'll treat it like it is for the moment, okay?' The nurse returned with the proper containers. Alexandre took the extra blood specimens. 'As soon as you send him upstairs, everybody strip, everybody scrub. There's not that much danger involved, as long as you take the proper precautions. Is his wife around?'

'Yes, Doctor, out in the waiting room.'

'Have somebody bring her up to my office. I have to ask her some things. Questions?' There were none. 'Then let's get moving.'

Dr Alexandre visually checked the plastic container for the blood and tucked it into the left-side pocket of his lab coat, after determining that it was properly sealed. The calm Doctor's Look was gone, as he walked to the elevator. Looking at the burnished steel of the automatic doors, he told himself that, no, this wasn't possible. Maybe something else. But what? Leukemia had some of the same symptoms, and as dreaded as that diagnosis was, it was preferable to what it looked like to him. The doors opened, and he headed off to his lab.

'Morning, Janet,' he said, walking into the hot lab.

'Alex,' replied Janet Clemenger, a Ph.D. molecular biologist.

He took the plastic box from his pocket. 'I need this done in a hurry. Like, immediately.'

'What is it?' She wasn't often told to stop everything she was doing, especially at the start of a working day.

'Looks like hemorrhagic fever. Treat it as level . . . four.'

Her eyes went a little wide. 'Here?' People were asking the same question all over America, but none of them knew it yet.

'They should be bringing the patient up now. I have to talk to his wife.'

She took the container and set it gently on the worktable. 'The usual antibody tests?'

'Yes, and please be careful with it, Janet.'

'Always,' she assured him. Like Alexandre, she worked a lot of AIDS experiments.

Alexandre next went to his office to call Dave James.

'How certain are you?' the dean asked two minutes later.

'Dave, it's just a heads-up for now, but – I've seen it before. Just like it was with George Westphal. I have Jan Clemenger working on it right now. Until further notice, I think we have to take this one seriously. If the lab results are what I expect, I get on the phone to Gus and we declare a for-real alert.'

'Well, Ralph gets back from London day after tomorrow. It's your department for the moment, Alex. Keep me posted.'

'Roger,' the former soldier said. Then it was time to speak to the patient's wife.

In the emergency room, orderlies were scrubbing the floor where the bed had been, overseen by the ER charge nurse. Overhead they could hear the distinctively powerful sound of a Sikorsky helicopter. The First Lady was coming to work.

The courier arrived at CDC, carrying his 'hatbox,' and handed it over to one of Lorenz's lab technicians. From there everything was fast-tracked. The antibody tests were already set up on the lab benches, and under exquisitely precise handling precautions, a drop of blood was dipped into a small glass tube. The liquid in the tube changed color almost instantly.

'It's Ebola, Doctor,' the technician reported. In another room a sample was being set up for the scanning electron microscope. Lorenz walked there, his legs feeling tired for so early in the morning. The instrument was already switched on. It was just a matter of getting things aimed properly before the images appeared on the TV display.

'Take your pick, Gus.' This was a senior physician, not a lab tech. As the magnification was adjusted, the picture was instantly clear. This blood sample was alive with the tiny strands. And soon it would be alive with nothing else. 'Where's this one from?'

'Chicago,' Lorenz answered.

'Welcome to the New World,' he told the screen as he worked the fine control to isolate one particular strand for full magnification. 'You little son of a bitch.'

Next came a closer examination to see if they could sub-type it. That would take a while.

'And so he has not traveled out of the country?' Alex was running down his list of stock questions.

'No, no he hasn't,' she assured him. 'Just to the big RV show. He goes to that every year.'

'Ma'am, I have to ask a number of questions, and some of them may seem offensive. Please understand that I have to do this in order to help your husband.' She nodded. Alexandre had a quiet way of getting past that problem. 'Do you have any reason to suspect that your husband has been seeing other women?'

'No.'

'Sorry, I had to ask that. Do you have any exotic pets?'

'Just two Chesapeake Bay retrievers,' she replied, surprised at the question.

'Monkeys? Anything from out of the country?'

'No, nothing like that.'

This isn't going anywhere. Alex couldn't think of another relevant question. They were supposed to say *yes* to the travel one. 'Do you know anybody, family member, friend, whatever, who does a lot of traveling?'

'No – can I see him?'

'Yes, you can, but first we have to get him settled into his room and get some treatment going.'

'Is he going to – I mean, he's never been sick at all, he runs and doesn't smoke and doesn't drink much and we've always been careful.' And then she started losing control.

'I won't lie to you. Your husband appears to be a very sick man, but your family doctor sent you to the best hospital in the world. I just started here. I spent more than twenty years in the Army, all of that in the area of infectious diseases. So you are in the right place, and I am the right doc.' You had to say things like that, empty words though they might be. The one thing you could never, ever, do was take hope away. The phone rang.

'Dr Alexandre.'

'Alex, it's Janet. Antibody test is positive for Ebola. I ran it twice,' she told him. 'I have the spare tube packaged to go to CDC, and the microscopy will be ready to go in about fifteen minutes.'

'Very well. I'll be over for that.' He hung up. 'Here,' he told the patient's wife. 'Let me get you out to the waiting room and introduce you to the nurses. We have some very good ones on my unit.'

This was not the fun part, even though infectious diseases was not a particularly fun field. In trying to give her hope, he'd probably given her too much. Now she'd listen to him, thinking that he spoke with God's voice, but right now God didn't have any answers, and next he had to explain to her that the nurses would be taking some of her blood for examination, too.

'What gives, Scott?' Ryan asked across thirteen time zones.

'Well, they sure as hell tossed a wrench into it. Jack?'

'Yes?'

'This guy Zhang, I've met him twice now. He doesn't talk a hell of a lot, but he's a bigger fish than we thought. I think he's the one keeping an eye on the Foreign Minister. He's a player, Mr President. Tell the Foleys to open a file on the guy and put a big flag on it.'

'Will Taipei spring for compensation?' SWORDSMAN asked.

'Would you?'

'My instinct would be to tell them where they could shove it, but I'm not supposed to lose my temper, remember?'

'They will listen to the demand, and then they will ask

963

me where the United States of America stands. What do I tell them?'

'For the moment, we stand for renewed peace and stability.'

'I can make that last an hour, maybe two hours. Then what?' SecState persisted.

'You know that area better than I do. What's the game, Scott?'

'I don't know. I thought I did, but I don't. First, I kinda hoped it was an accident. Then I thought they might be rattling their cage – Taiwan's, I mean. No, it's not that. They're pushing too hard and in the wrong way for that. Third option, they're doing all this to test you. If so, they're playing very rough – too rough. They don't know you well enough yet, Jack. It's too big a pot for the first hand of the night. Bottom line, I do not know what they're thinking. Without that, I can't tell you how to play it out.'

'We know they were behind Japan – Zhang personally was behind that Yamata bastard and –'

'Yes, I know. And they must know that we know, and that's one more reason not to piss us off. There are a lot of chips on the table, Jack,' Adler emphasized again. 'And I do not see a reason for this.'

'Tell Taiwan we're behind them?'

'Okay, if you do that, and it gets out, and the PRC ups the ante, we have thousands – hell, close to a hundred thousand citizens over here, and they're hostages. I won't go into the trade considerations, but that's a big chip in political-economic terms.'

'But if we don't back Taiwan up, then they'll think they're on their own and cornered –'

'Yes, sir, and the same thing happens from the other direction. My best suggestion is to ride with it. I deliver the demand, Taipei says no, then I suggest that they suggest the issue is held in abeyance until the issue of the airliner is determined. For that, we call in the U.N. We, that is, the United States, call the question before the Security Council. That strings it out. Sooner or later, their friggin' navy's gotta run out of fuel. We have a carrier group in the neighborhood, and so nothing *can* happen, really.'

Ryan frowned. 'I won't say I like it, but run with it. It'll last a day or two anyway. My instinct is to back up Taiwan and tell the PRC to suck wind.'

'The world isn't that simple, and you know it,' Adler's voice told him.

'Ain't it the truth. Run with what you said, Scott, and keep me posted.'

'Yes, sir.'

Alex checked his watch. Next to the electron microscope was Dr Clemenger's notebook. At 10:16, she lifted it, made a time notation, and described how both she and her fellow associate professor confirmed the presence of the Ebola virus. On the other side of the lab, a technician was running a test on blood drawn from the wife of Patient Zero. It was positive for Ebola antibodies. She had it, too, though she didn't know it yet.

'They have any children?' Janet asked, when the news arrived.

'Two, both away in school.'

'Alex, unless you know something I don't . . . I hope their insurance is paid up.' Clemenger didn't quite have the status of an M.D. here, but at moments like this she didn't mind. Physicians got to know the patients a lot better than the pure scientists did.

'What else can you tell me?'

'I need to map the genes out a little, but look here.' She tapped the screen. 'See the way the protein loops are grouped, and this structure down here?' Janet was the lab's top expert on how viruses were formed.

'Mayinga?' *Christ, that's what got George. . .* And nobody knew how George had gotten it, and he didn't know now how this patient . . .

'Too early to be sure. You know what I have to do to run that down, but . . .'

'It fits. No known risk factors for him, maybe not for her, either. Jesus, Janet, if this is airborne.'

'I know, Alex. You call Atlanta or me?'

'I'll do it.'

'I'll start picking the little bastard apart,' she promised.

It seemed a long walk from the lab back to his office. His secretary was in now, and noticed his mood.

* * *

'Dr Lorenz is in a meeting now,' another secretary said. That usually put people off. Not this time:

'Break in, if you would, please. Tell him it's Pierre Alexandre at Johns Hopkins, and it's important.'

'Yes, Doctor. Please hold.' She pressed one button and then another, ringing the line in the conference room down the hall. 'Dr Lorenz, please, it's urgent.'

'Yes, Marjorie?'

'I have Dr Alexandre holding on three. He says it's important, sir.'

'Thank you.' Gus switched lines. 'Talk fast, Alex, we have a developing situation here,' he said in an unusually businesslike voice.

'I know. Ebola's made it to this side of the world,' Alexandre announced.

'Have you been talking to Mark, too?'

'Mark? Mark who?' the professor asked.

'Wait, wait, back up, Alex. Why did you call here?'

'We have two patients on my unit, and they've both got it, Gus.'

'In Baltimore?'

'Yes, now what – where else, Gus?'

'Mark Klein in Chicago has one, female, forty-one. I've already micrographed the blood sample.' In two widely separated cities, two world-class experts did exactly the same thing. One pair of eyes looked at a wall in a small office. The other pair looked down a conference table at ten other physicians and scientists. The expressions were exactly the same. 'Has either one been to Chicago or Kansas City?'

'Negative,' the former colonel said. 'When did Klein's case show up?'

'Last night, ten or so. Yours?'

'Just before eight. Husband has all the symptoms. Wife doesn't, but her blood's positive . . . oh, shit, Gus . . .'

'I have to call Detrick next.'

'You do that. Keep an eye on the fax machine, Gus,' Professor Alexandre advised. 'And hope it's all a fucking mistake.' But it wasn't, and both knew it now.

'Stay close to the phone. I may want your input.'

'You bet.' Alex thought about that as he hung up. He had a call to make, too.

'Dave, Alex.'

'Well?' the dean asked.

'Husband and wife both positive. Wife is not yet symptomatic. Husband is showing all the classic signs.'

'So what's the story, Alex?' the dean asked guardedly.

'Dave, the story is I caught Gus at a staff meeting. They were discussing an Ebola case in Chicago. Mark Klein called it in around midnight, I gather. No commonalties between that one and our Index Case here. I, uh, think we have a potential epidemic on our hands. We need to alert our emergency people. There might be some very dangerous stuff coming in.'

'Epidemic? But –'

'That's my call to make, Dave. CDC is talking to the Army. I know what exactly they're going to say up at Detrick. Six months ago it would have been me making that call, too.' Alexandre's other line started ringing. His secretary got it in the outer office. A moment later, her head appeared in the doorway.

'Doctor, that's ER, they say they need you stat.' Alex relayed that message to the dean.

'I'll meet you there, Alex,' Dave James told him.

'At the next call on your machine, you will be free to complete your mission,' Mr Alahad said. 'The timing is yours to decide.' He didn't have to add that it would be better for him if Raman erased all his messages. To do so would have appeared venal to one who was willing to sacrifice himself. 'We will not meet again in this lifetime.'

'I must go to my workplace.' Raman hesitated. So the order had really come, after a fashion. The two men embraced, and the younger one took his leave.

'Cathy?' She looked up to see Bernie Katz's head sticking in her office door.

'Yeah, Bernie?'

'Dave has called a department head meeting in his office at two. I'm leaving for New York to do that conference at Columbia, and Hal's operating this afternoon. Sit in for me?'

'Sure, I'm clear.'

'Thanks, Cath.' His head vanished again. Surgeon went back to her patient records.

Actually the dean had told his secretary to call the meeting on his way out the door. David James was in the emergency room. Behind the mask he looked like any other physician.

This patient had nothing at all to do with the other two. Watching from ten feet away in a corner of the ER already set aside for the situation, they watched him vomit into a plastic container. There was ample evidence of blood.

It was the same young resident working this one, too. 'No traveling to speak of. Says he was in New York for some stuff. Theater, auto show, regular tourist stuff. What about the first one?'

'Positive for Ebola virus,' Alex told her. That snapped her head around like an owl's.

'Here?'

'Here. Don't be too surprised, Doctor. You called me, remember?' He turned to Dean James and raised an eyebrow.

'All department heads in my office at two. I can't go any faster, Alex. A third of them are operating or seeing patients right now.'

'Ross for this one?' the resident asked. She had a patient to deal with.

'Quick as you can.' Alexandre took the dean by the arm and walked him outside. There, dressed in greens, he lit a cigar, to the surprise of the security guards, who enforced a smoking ban out there.

'What the hell's going on?'

'You know, there is something to be said for these things.' Alex took a few puffs. 'I can tell you what they're going to say up at Detrick, sure as hell.'

'Go on.'

'Two separate index cases, Dave, a thousand miles apart in distance, and eight hours apart in time. No connection of any kind. No commonalties at all. Think it through,' Pierre Alexandre said, taking another worried puff.

'Not enough data to support it,' James objected.

'I hope I'm wrong. They're going to be scrambling down in Atlanta. Good people down there. The best. But they don't look at this sort of the thing the way I do. I wore that green suit a long time. Well' – another puff – 'we're going to see what the best possible supportive care can do. We're better than anyplace in Africa. So's Chicago. So are all the other places that are going to phone in, I suppose.'

'Others?' As fine a physician as he was, James still wasn't getting it.

'The first attempt at biological warfare was undertaken by Alexander the Great. He launched bodies of plague victims into a besieged city with catapults. I don't know if it worked or not. He took the city anyway, slaughtered all the citizens, and moved on.'

He got it now, Alex could see. The dean was as pale as the new patient inside.

'Jeff?' Raman was in the local command post going over the coming schedule for POTUS. He had a mission to complete now, and it was time to start doing some planning. Andrea walked over to him. 'We have a trip to Pittsburgh on Friday. You want to hop up there with the advance team? There are a couple local problems that have cropped up at the hotel.'

'Okay. When do I leave?' Agent Raman asked.

'Flight leaves in ninety minutes.' She handed him a ticket. 'You get back tomorrow night.'

How much the better, Raman thought, if he might even survive. Were he to structure all the security at one of these events, that might actually be possible. The idea of martyr-dom didn't turn his head all that much, but if survival were possible, then he would opt for that.

'Fair enough,' the assassin replied. He didn't have to worry about packing. The agents on the Detail always had a bag in the car.

It took three satellite passes before NRO was willing to make its estimate of the situation. All six of the UIR heavy div-isions which had participated in the war game were now in a full-maintenance stand-down. Some might say that such a thing was normal. A unit went into a heavy-maintenance cycle after a major training exercise, but six divisions – three heavy corps – at once was a bit much. The data was immedi-ately forwarded to the Saudi and Kuwaiti governments. In the meantime, the Pentagon called the White House.

'Yes, Mr Secretary,' Ryan said.

'The SNIE isn't ready yet for the UIR, but we have received . . . well, some disturbing information. I'll let Admiral Jackson present it.'

The President listened, and didn't need much in the way of analysis, though he wished the Special National Intelligence Estimates were on his desk to give him a better feel for the UIR's political intentions. 'Recommendations?' he asked, when Robby was done.

'I think it's a good time to get the boats at Diego moving. It never hurts to exercise them. We can move them to within two steaming days of the Gulf without anybody noticing. Next, I recommend that we issue warning orders to XVIII Airborne Corps. That's the 82nd, 101st, and 24th Mechanized.'

'Will it make noise?' Jack asked.

'No, sir. It's treated as a practice alert. We do those all the time. All it really does is to get staff officers thinking.'

'Make it so. Keep it quiet.'

'This would be a good time to do a joint training exercise with friendly nations in the region,' J-3 suggested.

'I'll see about that. Anything else?'

'No, Mr President,' Bretano replied. 'We'll keep you informed.'

By noon, the fax count at CDC Atlanta was over thirty, from ten different states. These were forwarded to Fort Detrick, Maryland, home of the United States Army Medical Research Institute of Infectious Diseases – USAMRIID – the military counterpart to the Centers for Disease Control and Prevention in Atlanta. As chilling as the data was, it was just a little too chilling for snap judgment. A major staff meeting was called for just after lunch, while the commissioned officers and civilians tried to get their data organized. More senior officers from Walter Reed got in their staff cars for the ride up Interstate-70.

'Dr Ryan?'

'Yes?' Cathy looked up.

'The meeting in Dr James's office has been moved up,' her secretary said. 'They want you over there right now.'

'I guess I better head over, then.' She stood and headed for the door. Roy Altman was standing there.

'Anything I need to know about?' SURGEON's principal agent asked.

'Something's up. I don't know what it is.'

'Where is the dean's office?' He'd never been there before. All of the staff meetings she'd attended recently were in Maumenee.

'That way.' She pointed. 'Other side of Monument Street in the admin building.'

'SURGEON is moving, going north to Monument.' The agents just appeared out of nowhere, it seemed. It might have seemed funny except for recent events. 'If you don't mind, I'll stand in the room. I'll keep out of the way,' Altman assured her.

Cathy nodded. There was no fighting it. He'd hate the dean's office for all the big windows there, she was sure. It was a ten-minute walk over, almost all of it undercover. She headed outdoors to cross the street, wanting a little fresh air. Entering the building, she saw a lot of her friends, either department chairmen or senior staffers standing in as she was doing. The director-level people were always traveling, one reason why she wasn't sure if she ever wanted to be that senior herself. Pierre Alexandre stormed in, wearing greens, carrying a folder, and looking positively grim as he almost bumped into her. A Secret Service agent prevented that.

'Glad you're here, Cathy,' he said on the way past. 'Them, too.'

'Nice to be appreciated,' Altman observed to a colleague, as the dean appeared at the door.

'Come in.'

One look at the conference room convinced Altman to lower the shades with his own hands. The windows faced a street of anonymous brick houses. A few of the doctors looked on with annoyance, but they knew who he was and didn't object.

'Calling the meeting to order,' Dave James said, before everyone was seated. 'Alex has something important to tell us.'

There was no preamble: 'We have five Ebola cases in Ross right now. They all came in today.'

Heads turned sharply. Cathy blinked at her seat at the end of the table.

'Students from someplace?' the surgery director asked. 'Zaire?'

'One auto dealer and his wife, a boat salesman from Annapolis, three more people. Answering your question, no. No international travel at all. Four of the five are fully symptomatic. The auto dealer's wife shows antibodies, but no symptoms as yet. That's the good news. Our case wasn't the first. CDC has cases reported in Chicago, Philadelphia, New York, Boston, and Dallas. That's as of an hour ago. Total reported cases is twenty, and that number doubled between ten and eleven. Probably still going up.'

'Jesus Christ,' the director of medicine whispered.

'You all know what I did before I got here. Right now I imagine they're having a staff meeting at Fort Detrick. The conclusion from that meeting will be that this is not an accidental outbreak. Somebody has initiated a biological-warfare campaign against our country.'

Nobody objected to Alexandre's analysis, Cathy saw. She knew why. The other physicians in the room were so bright that sometimes she wondered if she belonged on the same faculty with them – she had never considered that most of them might harbor the same thoughts. All of them were world experts in their fields, at least four the very best there was. But all of them also spent time as she did, having lunch with a colleague in a different field to exchange information, because, like her, they were all truly fanatical about learning. They all wanted to know everything, and even though they knew that such a thing was impossible, even within one professional field, that didn't stop them from trying. In this case, the suddenly rigid faces concealed the same analytical process.

Ebola was an infectious disease, and such diseases started from a single place. There was always a first victim, called Patient Zero or the Index Case, and it spread from there. No disease just exploded in this way. CDC and USAMRIID, which had to make that conclusion official, would have the duty to assemble, organize, and present information in what was almost a legalistic structure to prove their case. For their medical institution, it was simpler, all the more so because

Alex had commanded one of the divisions at Fort Detrick. Moreover, since there was a plan for everything, Johns Hopkins was one of the institutions tapped to receive cases in the event something like this took place.

'Alex,' the director of urology said, 'the literature says that Ebola is only spread by large particles of liquid. How could it explode so fast, even at the local level?'

'There's a sub-strain called Mayinga. It's named for a nurse who picked it up and died. The method of her infection was never determined. A colleague of mine, George Westphal, died of the same thing in 1990. We never determined the means of transmission in his case, either. There is thought that this sub-strain may spread by aerosol. It's never been proven one way or the other,' Alex explained. 'Besides, there are ways to fortify a virus, as you know. You admit some cancer genes into the structure.'

'And there's no treatment, nothing experimental even?' Urology asked.

'Rousseau is doing some interesting work at Pasteur, but so far he hasn't produced any positive results.'

A physical reaction rippled down the conference table from one physician to another. They were among the best in the world, and they knew it. They also knew now that it didn't matter against this enemy.

'How about a vaccine?' Medicine asked. 'That shouldn't be too hard.'

'USAMRIID has been playing with that for about ten years. The first issue is that there seems to be a specificity problem. What works for one sub-strain may not always work with another. Also, the quality-control issue is a killer. Studies I've seen predict a two-percent infection rate from the vaccine itself. Merck thinks they can do better, but trials take time to run.'

'Ouch,' Surgery commented with a wince. Giving one person out of fifty a disease with an eighty-percent mortality rate – twenty thousand people infected per million doses, of whom roughly sixteen thousand might die from it. Applied to the population of the United States, it could mean three *million* deaths from an attempt to safeguard the population. 'Hobson's choice.'

'But it's too early to determine the extent of the notional

epidemic, and we do not have hard data on the ability of the disease to spread in existing environmental conditions,' Urology thought. 'So we really aren't sure what measures need to be taken yet.'

'Correct.' At least it was easy to explain things to these people.

'My people will see it first,' Emergency said. 'I have to get them warned. We can't risk losing our people unnecessarily.'

'Who tells Jack?' Cathy wondered aloud. 'He's got to know, and he's got to know fast.'

'Well, that's the job of USAMRIID and the Surgeon General.'

'They're not ready to make the call yet. You just said that,' Cathy replied. 'You're sure about this?'

'Yes.'

Surgeon turned to Roy Altman: 'Get my helicopter up here stat.'

49

REACTION TIME

Colonel Goodman was surprised by the call. He was having a late lunch after a check-flight for a spare VH-60 just out of the maintenance shop for engine replacement. The one he used for SURGEON was on the ramp. The three-man crew walked out to it and spooled up the engines, not knowing why the schedule for the day had changed. Ten minutes after the call, he was airborne and heading northeast. Twenty minutes after that, he was circling the landing pad. Well, there was SURGEON, with SANDBOX by her side, and the Secret Service squad . . . and one other he didn't know, wearing a white coat. The colonel checked the wind and began his descent.

The faculty meeting had gone on until five minutes before. Decisions had to be made. Two complete medical floors would be cleared and tooled up for possible Ebola arrivals. The director of emergency medicine was even now assembling his staff for a lecture. Two of Alexandre's people were on the phone to Atlanta, getting updates on the total number of known cases, and announcing that Hopkins had activated its emergency plan for this contingency. It meant that Alex hadn't been able to go to his office and change clothes. Cathy was wearing her lab coat, too, but in her case it was over a normal dress. He'd been wearing greens – his third set of the day – for the meeting, and still was. Cathy told him not to worry about it. They had to wait for the rotor to stop before the Secret Service allowed their protectees to board the aircraft. Alex noted the presence of a backup chopper, circling a mile away, and a third circling closer in. It looked like a police bird, probably for security, he imagined.

Everyone was bundled aboard. Katie – he'd never met her before – got the jump seat behind the pilots, supposedly the safest place on the aircraft. Alexandre hadn't ridden in a Black Hawk in years. The four-point safety belt still worked, though. Cathy snapped hers right in place. Little Katie had to be helped, but she loved her helmet, painted pink, with a bunny on it, doubtless some Marine's idea. Seconds later the rotor started turning.

'This is going a little fast,' Alex said over the intercom.

'You really think we should wait?' Cathy replied, keying her microphone.

'No.' And it wouldn't do to say that he wasn't dressed for seeing the President. The aircraft lifted off, climbed about three hundred feet, and turned south.

'Colonel?' Cathy said to the pilot in the right-front seat.

'Yes, ma'am.'

'Make it fast,' she ordered.

Goodman had never heard Surgeon talk like a surgeon before. It was a voice of command that any Marine would recognize. He dropped the nose and brought the Black Hawk to 160 knots.

'You in a hurry, Colonel?' the backup chopper called.

'The lady is. Bravo routing, direct approach.' Next he called to BWI Airport to tell the controllers to hold arrivals and departures until he'd passed overhead. It wouldn't take long. Nobody on the ground really noticed, but two USAir 737s had to go around once, to the annoyance of their passengers. Watching from the jump seat, Sandbox thought it was pretty neat.

'Mr President?'

'Yes, Andrea?' Ryan looked up.

'Your wife is inbound from Baltimore. She needs to see you about something. I don't know what. About fifteen minutes,' Price told him.

'Nothing's wrong?' Jack asked.

'No, no, everybody's fine, sir. Sandbox is with her,' the agent assured him.

'Okay.' Ryan went back to the most recent update of the investigation.

'Well, it's officially a clean shoot, Pat.' Murray wanted to tell his inspector that himself. There hadn't been much doubt of that, of course.

'Wish I could have taken the last one alive,' O'Day remarked with a grimace.

'You can stow that one. There was no chance, not with kids around. I think we'll probably arrange a little decoration for you.'

'We have anything on that Azir guy yet?'

'His driver's license photo and a lot of written records, but aside from that, we'd have a hard time proving he ever existed.' It was a classic set of circumstances. Sometime Friday afternoon, 'Mordecai Azir' had driven his car to Baltimore-Washington International Airport and caught a flight to New York-Kennedy. They knew that much from the USAir desk clerk who'd issued him the ticket in that name. Then he'd disappeared, like a cloud of smoke on a windy day. He doubtless had had a virgin set of travel documents. Maybe he'd used them in New York for an international flight. If he'd really been smart, he would have caught a cab to Newark or LaGuardia first, and taken an overseas flight from the former, or maybe a flight to Canada from the latter. Even now agents from the New York office were interviewing people at every airline counter. But nearly every airline in the world came into Kennedy, and the clerks there saw thousands per day. Maybe they would establish what flight he'd taken. If so, he'd be on the moon before they managed that feat.

'Trained spook,' Pat O'Day observed. 'It's really not all that hard, is it?'

What came back to Murray were the words of his FCI chief. If you could do it once, you could do it more than once. There was every reason to believe that there was a complete espionage – worse, a terrorist – network in his country, sitting tight and waiting for orders ... to do what? And to avoid detection, all its members really had to do was *nothing*. Samuel Johnson had once remarked that everybody could manage that feat.

The helicopter flared and landed, rather to the surprise of the newspeople who always kept an eye out. Anything unexpected at the White House was newsworthy. They recognized Cathy Ryan. Her white doctor's coat was unusual, however, and on seeing another person dressed in the same way but wearing greens, the immediate impression was of a medical emergency involving the President. This was actually correct, though a spokesman came over to say that, no, the President was fine, working at his desk; no, he didn't know why Dr Ryan had come home early.

I'm not dressed for this, Alex thought. The looks of the agents on the way to the West Wing confirmed that, and now a few of *them* wondered if SWORDSMAN might be ill, resulting in a few radio calls that were immediately rebuffed. Cathy led him down the corridor, then tried the wrong door until an agent pointed and opened the one into the Oval Office. They noted that she didn't bother with anger or embarrassment at the mistake. They'd never seen SURGEON so focused.

'Jack, this is Pierre Alexandre,' she said without a greeting.

Ryan stood. He didn't have any major appointments for another two hours, and had shed his suit coat. 'Hello, Doctor,' he said, extending his hand and taking in the manner of his visitor's dress. Then he realized that Cathy had her work coat on as well. 'What's going on, Cathy?' he asked his wife.

'Alex?' Nobody had even sat down yet. Two Secret Service agents had followed the physicians in, and the tension in the room was like an alarm bell for them, though they didn't know what was going on, either. Roy Altman was in another room, talking to Price.

'Mr President, do you know what the Ebola virus is?'

'Africa,' Jack said. 'Some jungle disease, right? Deadly as hell. I saw a movie –'

'Pretty close,' Alexandre confirmed. 'It's a negative-strand RNA virus. We don't know where it lives – I mean, we know the place but not the host. That's the animal it lives in,' he explained. 'And it's a killer, sir. The crude mortality rate is eighty percent.'

'Okay,' POTUS said, still standing. 'Go on.'

'It's here now.'

'Where?'

'At last count we had five cases at Hopkins. More than twenty countrywide – that number is about three hours old now. Can I use the phone?'

* * *

Gus Lorenz was alone in his office when the phone rang. 'It's Dr Alexandre again.'

'Yes, Alex?'

'Gus, what's the count now?'

'Sixty-seven,' the speakerphone replied. Alex was leaning over it.

'Where?'

'Mainly big cities. The reports are coming in mostly from major medical centers. Boston, New Haven, New York, Philadelphia, Baltimore, one in Richmond, seven right here in Atlanta, three in Orlando . . .' They could hear a door open and a paper being handled. 'Eighty-nine, Alex. They're still coming in.'

'Has USAMRIID put the alert out yet?'

'I expect that within the hour. They are having a meeting to determine –'

'Gus, I am in the White House right now. The President is here with me. I want you to tell him what you think,' Alexandre commanded, speaking like an Army colonel again.

'What – how did you – Alex, it's not sure yet.'

'Either you say it or I will. Better that you do.'

'Mr President?' It was Ellen Sumter at the side door. 'I have a General Pickett on the phone for you, sir. He says it's most urgent.'

'Tell him to stand by.'

'John's good, but he's a little conservative,' Alex observed. 'Gus, talk to us!'

'Sir, Mr President, this appears to be something other than a natural event. It looks very much like a deliberate act.'

'Biological warfare?' Ryan asked.

'Yes, Mr President. Our data isn't yet complete enough for a real conclusion, but naturally occurring epidemics don't start this way, not all over the place.'

'Mrs Sumter, can you put the general on this line?'

'Yes, sir.'

'Mr President?' a new voice asked.

'General, I have a Dr Lorenz on the line, and next to me is Dr Alexandre from up the road at Hopkins.'

'Hi, Alex.'

'Hi, John,' Alexandre responded.

'Then you know.'

'How confident are you in this estimate?' SWORDSMAN asked.

'We have at least ten focal centers. A disease doesn't get around like that by itself. The data is still coming in, sir. All these cases appearing in twenty-four hours, it's no accident, and it's no natural process. You have Alex there to explain things further. He used to work for me. He's pretty good,' Pickett told his commander-in-chief.

'Dr Lorenz, you concur in this?'

'Yes, Mr President.'

'Jesus.' Jack looked at his wife. 'What's next?'

'Sir, we have some options,' Pickett replied. 'I need to get down to see you.'

Ryan turned: 'Andrea!'

'Yes, sir?'

'Get a chopper up to Fort Detrick, right now!'

'Yes, Mr President.'

'I'll be waiting, General. Dr Lorenz, thank you. Anything else I need to know now?'

'Dr Alexandre can handle that.'

'Very well, I will put Mrs Sumter on the phone to give you the direct lines to this office.' Jack walked to the door. 'Get on and give them what they need. Then get Arnie and Ben in here.'

'Yes, Mr President.'

Jack walked back to sit on the edge of his desk. He was silent for a moment. In a way, he was now grateful for the failed attack on his daughter. That had hit him with a dreadful immediacy. This one as yet had not, and though intellectually he knew that the ramifications were far worse, he didn't need the emotional impact for the time being.

'What do I need to know?'

'Most of the important stuff we can't tell you yet. The issues are technical,' Alex explained. 'How easily the disease spreads, all we have now is anecdotal and unreliable. That's the key issue. If it spreads easily by aerosol –'

'What's that?' POTUS asked.

'Spray, little droplets, like a cough or a sneeze. If it spreads that way, we're in very deep trouble.'

'It's not supposed to,' Cathy objected. 'Jack, this bug is

980

very delicate. It doesn't last in the open for more than – what, Alex, a few seconds?'

'That's the theory, but some strains are more robust than others. Even if it can survive just a few minutes in the open – that's pretty damned bad. If this is a strain we call Mayinga, well, we just don't know how robust it is. But it goes farther than that. Once a person gets it, then they take it home. A house is a pretty benign environment for pathogens. We have heating and air-conditioning to make it that way, and family members are in close contact. They hug. They kiss. They make love. And once somebody has it in their system, they're always pumping the things out.'

'Things?'

'Virus particles, Mr President. The size of these things is measured in microns. They're far smaller than dust particles, smaller than anything you can see.'

'You used to work at Detrick?'

'Yes, sir, I was a colonel, head of pathogens. I retired, and Hopkins hired me.'

'So you have an idea what General Pickett's plans are, the options, I mean?'

'Yes, sir. That stuff is reevaluated at least once a year. I've sat in on the committee that draws the plans up.'

'Sit down, Doctor. I want to hear this.'

The Maritime Pre-Position Ships had just gotten back from an exercise, and what little maintenance had been required was already done. On receiving orders from CIN-CLANTFLT, they initiated engine-start procedures, which mainly meant warming up the fuel and lubricating oils. To the north, the cruiser *Anzio*, plus destroyers *Kidd* and *O'Bannon*, got orders of their own and turned west for a projected rendezvous point. The senior officer present was the skipper of the Aegis cruiser, who wondered how the hell he was supposed to get those fat merchants into the Persian Gulf without air cover, if it came to that. The United States Navy didn't go anywhere without air cover, and the nearest carrier was *Ike*, 3,000 miles away, with Malaya in the way. On the other hand, it wasn't all that bad to be a mere captain in command of a task force without an admiral to look over his shoulder.

The first of the MPS ships to sortie from the large anchorage was USNS *Bob Hope*, a newly built military-type roll-on/roll-off transport displacing close to 80,000 tons, and carrying 952 vehicles. Her civilian crew had a little tradition for their movements. Oversized speakers blared 'Thanks for the Memories' at the naval base as she passed by, just after midnight, followed by four of her sisters. Aboard, they had the full vehicle complement for a reinforced heavy brigade. Passing the reef-marked entrance, the handles were pushed down on the enunciators, demanding twenty-six knots of the big Colt-Pielstick diesels.

They waited for Goodley and van Damm to come in, and then it took ten minutes to bring them up to speed on what was going on. By this time, the enormity of it was sinking into the President's consciousness, and he had to struggle with emotions now in addition to intellect. He noted that Cathy, though she had to be as horrified as he was, was taking everything calmly, at least outwardly so. Well, it was her field, wasn't it?

'I didn't think Ebola could survive outside a jungle,' Goodley said.

'It can't, at least not long-term, or it would have traveled around the world by now.'

'It kills too fast for that,' SURGEON objected.

'Cathy, we've had jet travel for over thirty years now. This little bastard is delicate. That works for us.'

'How do we find out who did it?' This came from Arnie.

'We interview all the victims, find out where they've been, and try to narrow the focal centers down to one point if we can. That's an investigative function. Epidemiologists are pretty good at that . . . but this one's a little big,' Alexandre added.

'Could the FBI help, Doctor?' van Damm asked.

'Can't hurt.'

'I'll get Murray over here,' the chief of staff told the President.

'You can't treat it?' POTUS asked.

'No, what happens is the epidemic burns itself out over several generational cycles. What I mean by that – okay, one person gets it. The virus reproduces in them, and then they pass it on to somebody else. Every victim becomes an imperfect host. As the disease reproduces and kills the victim, the victim passes it on to the next one. *But*, and here's the good news, Ebola doesn't reproduce efficiently. As it goes through these generational cycles, it becomes less virulent. Most of the survivors in an outbreak happen toward the end, because the virus progressively mutates itself into a less dangerous form. The organism is so primitive that it doesn't do everything well.'

'How many cycles before that happens, Alex?' Cathy asked.

He shrugged. 'It's empirical. We know the process, but we can't quantify it.'

'Lots of unknowns.' She grimaced.

'Mr President?'

'Yes, Doctor?'

'The movie you saw?'

'What about it?'

'The budget for that movie is quite a bit more than all the funding for research in virology. Keep that in mind. I guess it isn't sexy enough.' Arnie started to say something. Alex cut him off with a raised hand. 'I'm not on the government payroll anymore, sir. I don't have any empire to build. My research is privately funded. I'm just stating a fact. What the hell, I guess we can't fund everything.'

'If we can't treat it, how do we stop it?' Ryan asked, getting things back on track. His head turned. A shadow crossed the South Lawn, and the roar of a helicopter came through the bulletproof windows.

'Ahh,' Badrayn observed with a smile. The Internet was designed to give access to information, not to conceal it, and from a friend of a friend of a friend who was a medical student at Emory University in Atlanta, he had the password to crack into that medical center's electronic mail. Another keyword eliminated all of the clutter, and there it was. It was 1400 hours on America's east coast, and Emory reported to CDC that it now had six cases of suspected hemorrhagic fever. Better yet, CDC had already replied, and that told him a lot more. Badrayn printed up both letters, and made a telephone call. Now he really had good news to deliver.

*　　*　　*

Raman felt the DC-9 thump down in Pittsburgh after a brief flight that had allowed him to sit alone and think through several options. His colleague – brother – in Baghdad had been a little too sacrificial in his attitude, a little too dramatic, and the detail around the Iraqi leader had been pretty large, actually larger than the one on which he himself served. How to do it? The trick was to create as much confusion as possible. Perhaps when Ryan walked into the crowd to press the flesh. Take the shot, kill one or two of the other agents, then race into the crowd. If he could make it past the first line or two of spectators, all he had to do was hold up his Secret Service ID, better than a gun for getting through things – everyone would think that he was chasing the subject. The key to escaping from an assassination – the USSS had taught him this – was in the first thirty seconds. Survive that, and you have a better-than-even chance of surviving it all. And he would be the one setting all the security arrangements for the Friday trip. How, then, could he get the President to a spot in which he would have that option? Take POTUS. Take Price. Take one other. Then melt into the crowd. Probably better to fire from the hip. Best if the citizens didn't see the gun in his hand until after the shots. Yes, that might work, he thought, taking off the lap belt and standing. There would be a local Treasury agent at the end of the jetway. They'd go right to the hotel whose large dining room would host President Ryan's speech. Raman would have all day and part of tomorrow to think it through, under the very eyes of fellow agents. How challenging.

Major General John Pickett, it turned out, was a graduate of Yale Medical School, added to which were a pair of doctorates – molecular biology from Harvard, and public health from UCLA. He was a pale, spare man who looked small in his uniform – he hadn't had time to change and was wearing camouflage BDUs – making his parachutist's wings look very out of place. Two colonels came with him, followed by Director Murray of the FBI, who'd raced over from the Hoover Building. The three officers came to attention as they walked in, but now the Oval Office was too small, and the President led them across the hall into the Roosevelt Room. On the way a Secret Service agent handed the general a fax that was still warm from the machine in the secretaries' room.

'Case count is now one hundred thirty-seven, according to Atlanta,' Pickett said. 'Fifteen cities, fifteen states, coast-to-coast.'

'Hi, John,' Alexandre said, taking his hand. 'I've seen three of them myself.'

'Alex, glad to see you, buddy.' He looked up. 'I guess Alex has briefed everybody in on the baseline stuff?'

'Correct,' Ryan said.

'Do you have any immediate questions, Mr President?'

'You're certain that this is a deliberate act?'

'Bombs do not go off by accident.' Pickett unfolded a map. A number of cities were marked with red dots. One of his attending colonels placed three more down: San Francisco, Los Angeles, and Las Vegas.

'Convention cities. Just how I would have done it,' Alexandre breathed. 'Looks like Bio-War 95, John.'

'Close. That's a wargame we played with the Defense Nuclear Agency. We used anthrax for that one. Alex here was one of our best for planning offensive bio,' Pickett told his audience. 'He was Red Team commander for this.'

'Isn't that against the law?' Cathy said, her face outraged at the revelation.

'Offense and defense are two sides of the same coin, Dr Ryan,' Pickett replied, defending his former subordinate. 'We have to think like the bad guys do if we're going to stop them.'

'Operational concept?' the President asked. He understood that better than his wife did.

'Biological warfare at the strategic level means starting a chain reaction within your target population. You try to infect as many people as possible – and that's not very many; we're not talking nuclear weapons here. The idea is for the people, the victims, to spread it for you. That's the elegance of bio-warfare. Your victims actually do most of the killing. Any epidemic starts low and ramps up, slowly at first, like a tangential curve, and then it rockets up geometrically. So, if you're using bio in the offensive role, you try to jump-start it by infecting as large a number of people as you can, and you opt for people who travel. Las Vegas is the tip-off. It's a convention city, and sure enough they just had a big one.

The conventioneers get infected, get on the airplanes to fly home, and they spread it for you.'

'Any chance of discovering how they did it?' Murray asked. He showed his ID so that the general would know who he was.

'Probably a waste of time. The other nice thing about bio weapons is – well, in this case the incubation period is a minimum of three days. Whatever distribution system was used has been picked up, bagged, and trucked off to a landfill. No physical evidence, no proof of who did it to us.'

'Save that for later, General. What do we do? I see a lot of states with no infection –'

'That's just for now, Mr President. There's a three- to ten-day lead time on Ebola. We don't know how far it's gotten already. The only way we can find out is by waiting.'

'But we have to initiate CURTAIN CALL, John,' Alexandre said. 'And we have to do it fast.'

Mahmoud Haji was reading. He had an office adjoining his bedroom, and actually preferred working here because of the familiar surroundings. He did not enjoy being disturbed here, however, and so his security people were surprised at his response to the telephone call. Twenty minutes later, they let the visitor in, without an escort.

'Has it begun?'

'It has begun.' Badrayn handed over the CDC printout. 'We will know more tomorrow.'

'You have served well,' Daryaei told him, dismissing him. When the door was closed, he made a telephone call.

Alahad didn't know how circuitous the link to him was, merely that it was an overseas call. He suspected London, but he didn't know and wouldn't ask. The inquiry was entirely routine, except for the time of day – it was evening in England, after business hours. The variety of the rug and the price were the key parts, telling him what he needed to know, in a code long since memorized and never written down. In knowing little, he could reveal little. That part of the tradecraft he did fully understand. His own part came next. Placing the Back in a Few Minutes sign in his window, he walked out, locked the door, and went around the corner, proceeding two blocks to a pay phone. There he made a call to pass on his last order to Aref Raman.

The meetings had started in the Oval Office, were transferred to the Roosevelt Room, and were now all the way down the hall in the Cabinet Room, where more than one image of George Washington could watch the proceedings. The Cabinet secretaries arrived almost together, and their arrival couldn't be a secret. Too many official cars, too many guards, too many faces known to the reporters.

Pat Martin came, representing Justice. Bretano was SecDef, with Admiral Jackson sitting on the wall behind him. (Everyone brought a deputy of some sort, mainly to take notes.) Winston was SecTreas, having walked from across the street. Commerce and Interior were survivors from the Durling presidency, actually having been appointed by Bob Fowler. Most of the rest were of undersecretary rank, holding on from presidential apathy in some cases, and in others because they appeared to know what they were doing. But none of them knew what he was doing now. Ed Foley arrived, summoned by the President despite CIA's previous loss of Cabinet rank. Also present were Arnie van Damm, Ben Goodley, Director Murray, the First Lady, three Army officers, and Dr Alexandre.

'We will be in order,' the President said. 'Ladies and gentlemen, thank you for coming. There's no time for a preamble here. We face a national emergency. The decisions we make here today will have serious effects on our country. In the corner is Major General John Pickett. He's a physician and scientist, and I will now turn the meeting over to him. General, do your brief.'

'Thank you, Mr President. Ladies and gentlemen, I am commanding general at Fort Detrick. Earlier today, we started getting some very disturbing reports . . .'

Ryan tuned the general out. He'd heard it all twice now. Instead he read over the file Pickett had handed him. The folder was bordered in the usual red-and-white-striped tape. The sticker in the center read TOP SECRET – AFFLICTION, rather an appropriate code name for the special-access compartment this one was in, SWORDSMAN thought. Then he opened the folder and started reading OpPlan CURTAIN CALL.

987

There were four variants of the plan, Jack saw. He turned to Option Four. That was called SOLITARY, and that name, too, was appropriate. Reading through the executive summary chilled him, and Jack found himself turning to look over at George, hanging there on the wall, and wanting to ask, *Now what the hell do I do?* But George wouldn't have understood. He didn't know from airliners and viruses and nuclear weapons, did he?

'How bad is it now?' HHS asked.

'Just over two hundred cases have been reported to CDC as of fifteen minutes ago. I emphasize that these have all appeared in less than twenty-four hours,' General Pickett told the Secretary.

'Who did it?' Agriculture asked.

'Set that aside,' the President said. 'We will address that issue later. What we have to decide now is the best chance we have to contain the epidemic.'

'I just can't believe that we can't treat –'

'Believe it,' Cathy Ryan said. 'You know how many viral diseases we know how to cure?'

'Well, no,' HUD admitted.

'None.' It constantly amazed her how ignorant some people could be on medical issues.

'Therefore containment is the only option,' General Pickett went on.

'How do you contain a whole country?' It was Cliff Rutledge, Assistant Secretary of State for Policy, sitting in for Scott Adler.

'That's the problem we face,' President Ryan said. 'Thank you, General. I'll take it from here. The only way to contain the epidemic is to shut down all places of assembly – theaters, shopping malls, sports stadia, business offices, everything – and also to shut off all interstate travel. To the best of our information, at least thirty states are so far untouched by this disease. We would do well to keep it that way. We can accomplish that by preventing all interstate travel until such time as we have a handle on the severity of the disease organism we are facing, and then we can come up with less severe countermeasures.'

'Mr President, that's unconstitutional,' Pat Martin said at once.

'Explain,' Ryan ordered.

'Travel is a constitutionally protected right. Even inside states, any restriction of travel is a constitutional violation under the Lemuel Penn case – he was a black Army officer who was murdered by the Klan in the sixties. That's a Supreme Court precedent,' the head of the Criminal Division reported.

'I understand that I – excuse me, just about everybody in the room – was sworn to uphold the Constitution. But if upholding it means killing off a few million citizens, what have we accomplished?' POTUS asked.

'We can't *do* that!' HUD insisted.

'General, what happens if we don't?' Martin asked, surprising Ryan.

'There is no precise answer. There cannot be, because we do not know the ease of transmission for this virus yet. If it is an aerosol, and there is reason to suspect that it is – well, we've got a hundred computer models we can use. Problem is deciding which one. Worst case? Twenty million deaths. At that point, what happens is that society breaks down. Doctors and nurses flee the hospitals, people lock themselves in their homes, and the epidemic burns out pretty much like the Black Death did in the fourteenth century. Human interactions cease, and because of that the disease stops spreading.'

'Twenty million? How bad was the Black Death?' Martin asked, his face somewhat ashen.

'Records are sketchy. There was no real census system back then. Best data is England,' Pickett replied. 'It depopulated that country by half. The plague lasted about four years. Europe took about one hundred fifty years to return to the 1347 population level.'

'*Shit*,' breathed Interior.

'Is it really that dangerous, General?' Martin persisted.

'Potentially yes. The problem, sir, is that if you take no action at all, and then you find out that it is that virulent, then it's just too late.'

'I see.' Martin turned. 'Mr President, I do not see that we have much of a choice here.'

'You just said it was against the law, damn it!' HUD shouted.

'Mr Secretary, the Constitution is not a suicide pact, and although I think I know how the Supreme Court would rule on this, there has never been a case in point, and it could be argued, and the process would have to deal with it.'

'What changed your mind, Pat?' Ryan asked.

'Twenty million reasons, Mr President.'

'If we flout our own laws, then what are we?' Cliff Rutledge asked.

'Alive,' Martin answered quietly. 'Maybe.'

'I am willing to listen to arguments for fifteen minutes,' Ryan said. 'Then we have to come to a decision.'

It was lively.

'If we violate our own Constitution,' Rutledge said, 'then nobody in the world can trust us!' HUD and HHS agreed.

'What about the practical considerations?' Agriculture objected. 'People have to eat.'

'What kind of country are we going to turn over to our children if we –'

'What do we turn over to them if they're dead?' George Winston snapped back at HUD.

'Things like this don't happen today!'

'Mr Secretary, would you like to come up to my hospital and see, sir?' Alexandre asked from his seat in the corner.

'Thank you,' Ryan said, checking his watch. 'I am calling the issue on the table.'

Defense, Treasury, Justice, and Commerce voted aye. All the rest voted no. Ryan looked at them for a long few seconds.

'The ayes have it,' the President said coldly. 'Thank you for your support. Director Murray, the FBI will render all assistance required by CDC and USAMRIID to ascertain the focal centers of this epidemic. That has absolute and unconditional priority over any other matter.'

'Yes, Mr President.'

'Mr Foley, every intelligence asset we have goes into this. You will also work in conjunction with the medical experts. This came from somewhere, and whoever did it has committed an act of war, using weapons of mass destruction against our country. We need to find out who that was, Ed. All the intelligence agencies will report directly to you. You have statutory authority to coordinate all intelligence activities.

Tell the other agencies that you have my order to exercise it.'

'We'll do our best, sir.'

'Secretary Bretano, I am declaring a state of national emergency. All Reserve and National Guard formations are to be activated immediately and placed under federal command. You have this contingency plan in the Pentagon.' Ryan held the CURTAIN CALL folder up. 'You will execute Option Four, SOLITARY, at the earliest possible moment.'

'I will do that, sir.'

Ryan looked down the table at the Secretary of Transportation. 'Mr Secretary, the air-traffic-control system belongs to you. When you get back to your office, you will order all aircraft in flight to proceed to their destinations and stop there. All aircraft on the ground will remain there, commencing at six o'clock this evening.'

'No.' SecTrans stood. 'Mr President, I will not do that. I believe it to be an illegal act, and I will not break the law.'

'Very well, sir. I will accept your resignation effective immediately. You're the deputy?' Ryan said to the woman sitting behind him.

'Yes, Mr President, I am.'

'Will you execute my order?'

She looked around the room without really knowing what to do. She'd heard it all, but she was a career civil servant, unaccustomed to making a hard call without political coverage.

'I don't like it, either,' Ryan said. The room was invaded by the roar of jet engines, an aircraft taking off from Washington National. 'What if that airplane's carrying death somewhere? Do we just let it happen?' he asked so quietly she could barely hear.

'I will carry out your order, sir.'

'You know, Murray,' the former – he wasn't sure yet – SecTrans said, 'you could arrest the man right now. He's breaking the law.'

'Not today, sir,' Murray replied, staring at his President. 'Somebody's going to have to decide what the law is first.'

'If anyone else in the room feels the need to leave federal service over this issue, I will accept your resignations without prejudice – but *please* think what you are doing. If I'm wrong on this, fine, I'm wrong, and I'll pay the price for that. But if the doctors are right and we do nothing, we've got more blood on our hands than Hitler ever did. I need your help and your support.' Ryan stood and walked out of the room as the others struggled to their feet. He moved fast. He had to. He entered the Oval Office, turned right to the presidential sitting room, and barely made it to the bathroom in time. Seconds later, Cathy found him there, flushing down a bowlful of vomit. 'Am I doing the right thing?' he asked, still on his knees.

'You've got my vote, Jack,' SURGEON told him.

'You look great,' van Damm observed, catching POTUS in rather an undignified posture.

'Why didn't you say anything, Arnie?'

'Because you didn't need me to, Mr President,' the chief of staff replied.

General Pickett and the other physicians were waiting when he came back into the office. 'Sir, we just had a fax from CDC. There are two cases at Fort Stewart. That's the 24th Mech's home base.'

50

SPECIAL REPORT

It started with National Guard armories. Virtually every city and town in America had one, and in each was a duty sergeant, or perhaps an officer, sitting at a desk to answer the phone. When the phone rang, a voice from the Pentagon spoke a code word that designated an activation order. The duty person in the armory would then alert the unit commander, and more calls were made, branching out like the limbs of a tree, with every recipient detailed to call several others. It usually took an hour or so for everyone to get the word – or nearly everyone, as some were inevitably out of town, traveling for either work or vacation. Senior Guard commanders usually worked directly for the governors of the several states, as the National Guard is a hybrid institution, partly a state militia and partly United States Army (or Air Force, in the case of the Air National Guard, which gave many of the state governors access to state-of-the-art fighter aircraft). These senior Guard officers, surprised by the activation orders, reported the situation to their governors, asking for guidance which the state executives were as yet in no position to give, since mainly they didn't know what was going on yet, either. But at the company and battalion level, officers and men (and women) hurried home from their civilian jobs, citizen soldiers that they were, donned their woodland-pattern BDU fatigues, buffed their boots, and drove to the local armory to form up with their squads and platoons. Once there they were startled to see that they were supposed to draw weapons and, more disturbingly, their MOPP gear. MOPP, for Mission-Oriented Protective Posture, was the chemical-warfare equipment in which they had all trained at one time or another, and which every person in uniform cordially detested. There were the usual jokes and good humor, stories of work, tales of spouses and children, while the officers and senior non-coms met in conference rooms to find out what the hell was going on. They emerged from those brief meetings angry, confused, and for the better informed of them, frightened. Outside the armories, vehicles were fired up. Inside, TV sets were switched on.

In Atlanta, the special agent in charge of the FBI's Atlanta Field Division drove with sirens screaming to CDC, followed by ten more agents. In Washington, a number of CIA and other intelligence officers drove more sedately to the Hoover Building to set up a joint task force. In both cases, the job was to figure out how the epidemic had started and from that to try to determine its point of origin. These people were not all civilians. The Defense Intelligence Agency and National Security Agency were mainly uniformed organizations, and among that grouping grim-faced officers let everyone know that something new in American history had taken place. If this truly were a deliberate attack against the United States of America, then a nation-state had made use of what was delicately termed a 'weapon of mass destruction.' Then they explained to their civilian counterparts what had been US policy for two generations for responding to such an eventuality.

It was all happening too fast, of course, since emergencies are by definition things for which one cannot plan terribly well. That extended to the President himself, who walked into the White House press room, accompanied by General Pickett of USAMRIID. Only thirty minutes earlier the White House had told the major networks that the President had an announcement to make, and that on this occasion, the government would exercise its option to demand airtime instead of requesting it – since the 1920s, the government had adopted the position that it owned the airwaves – thus supplanting all the talk shows and other programming which preceded the evening news. Lead-in commentary told viewers that nobody knew what this was about, but that there had been an emergency Cabinet meeting only minutes before.

'My fellow Americans,' President Ryan began, his face in most American homes, and his voice in every car on the road. Those who had become accustomed to their new President took note of the pale face (Mrs Abbot hadn't had time to do his makeup) and grim voice. The message was grimmer still.

The cement truck had a radio, of course. It even had a tape and CD player, since, work-vehicle or not, it had been designed for the use of an American citizen. They were in Indiana now, having crossed both the Mississippi River and Illinois earlier in the day on their trek to their nation's capital. Holbrook, who had no use for the words of any President, hit the scan button, only to find that the same voice was on all the stations. That was sufficiently unusual that he stayed with one of them. Brown, driving the truck, saw that cars and trucks were pulling over – not many at first, but more and more as the speech progressed, their drivers, like himself, leaning down to listen to the radio.

'Accordingly, by executive order of the President, your government is taking the following actions:

'One, until further notice, all schools and colleges in the country will be closed.

'Two, all businesses except for those providing essential services – the media, health care, food, law-enforcement, and fire protection – will also be closed until further notice.

'Three, all places of public assembly, theaters, restaurants, bars and the like, will be closed.

'Fourth, all interstate travel is suspended until further notice. This means all commercial air travel, interstate trains and buses, and private-passenger automobiles. Trucks carrying foodstuffs will be allowed to travel under military escort. The same is true of essential supplies, pharmaceuticals and the like.

'Fifth, I have activated the National Guard in all the fifty states and placed it under federal control to maintain public order. A state of martial law is now in force throughout the country.

'We urge our citizens – no, let me speak more informally. Ladies and gentlemen, all that is required for us to weather this crisis is a little common sense. We do not yet know how dangerous this disease is. The measures I have ordered today are precautionary in nature. They seem, and indeed they are, extreme measures. The reason for that, as I have told you, is that this virus is potentially the most deadly organism on the planet, but we do not yet know how dangerous it is. We *do* know that a few simple measures can limit its spread, no matter how deadly it is, and in the interest of public safety, I have ordered those measures. This action is being taken on the best scientific advice available. To protect yourselves, remember how the disease is spread. I have General John Pickett, a senior Army physician and an expert in the field of infectious diseases, to provide medical advice to all of us. General?' Ryan stepped away from the microphone.

'What the fuck!' Holbrook shouted. 'He can't do that!'

'Think so?' Brown followed an eighteen-wheeler onto the shoulder. They were a hundred miles from the Indiana-Ohio border. About two hours driving this pig, he thought. No way he'd get there before the local Guard closed the road.

'I think we better find a motel, Pete.'

'So what do I do?' the FBI agent asked in Chicago.

'Strip. Hang your clothes on the door.' There was no time and little spare room for the niceties, and he was, after all, a physician. His guest didn't blush. Dr Klein decided on full surgical garb, long-sleeve greens instead of the more popular sort. There were not enough of the plastic space suits to go around, and his staff would use all of those. They had to. They got closer. They handled liquids. They touched the patients. His medical center now had nine symptomatic patients who tested positive. Six of those were married, and of the spouses, four tested positive for Ebola antibodies. The test gave an occasional false-positive reading; even so it was not the least bit pleasant to tell someone – well, he did that often enough with AIDS patients. They were testing children now. That really hurt.

The protective outfit he gave the agent was made of the usual cotton, but the hospital had taken a number of sets and sprayed them with disinfectant, especially the masks. The agent also was given a pair of laboratory glasses, the broad plastic ones known to chemistry students.

'Okay,' Klein told the agent. 'Don't get close. No closer

than six feet, and you should be completely safe. If she vomits or coughs, if she has a convulsion, stay clear. Dealing with that sort of thing is our job, not yours. Even if she dies right in front of you, don't touch anything.'

'I understand. You going to lock the office up?' She pointed to the gun hanging with her clothes.

'Yes, I will. And when you're done, give me your notes. I'll run them through the copying machine.'

'How come?'

'It uses a very bright light to make copies. The ultraviolet will almost certainly kill any virus particle that might find its way to the paper,' Professor Klein explained. Even now in Atlanta, rapid experiments were under way to determine just how robust the Ebola particles were. That would help define the level of precaution that was necessary in hospitals first of all, and perhaps also provide useful guidance for the general population.

'Uh, Doc, why not just let me make the copies?'

'Oh.' Klein shook his head. 'Yes, I suppose that will work, too, won't it?'

'Mr President.' It was Barry of CNN. 'These steps you're taking, sir, are they legal?'

'Barry, I do not have the answer to that,' Ryan said, his face tired and drawn. 'Whether they're legal or not, I am convinced that they are necessary.' As he spoke, a White House staffer was passing out surgical masks for the assembled reporters. That was Arnie's idea. They'd been procured from the nearby George Washington University Hospital.

'But, Mr President, you can't break the law. What if you're wrong?'

'Barry, there's a fundamental difference between what I do in my job and what you do in yours. If you make a mistake, you can make a retraction. We just saw that, only yesterday, with one of your colleagues, didn't we? But, Barry, if I make a mistake in a situation like this, how do I retract a death? How do I retract thousands of deaths? I don't have that luxury, Barry,' the President said. 'If it turns out that what I am doing is wrong, then you can have at me all you want. That's part of my job, too, and I'm getting used to that. Maybe I'm a coward. Maybe I'm just afraid of letting people die for no good reason when I have the power to prevent it.'

'But you don't really know, do you?'

'No,' Jack admitted, 'none of us really knows. This is one of those times when you have to go with your best guess. I wish I could sound more confident, but I can't, and I won't lie about it.'

'Who did it, Mr President?' another reporter asked.

'We don't know, and for the moment I will not speculate as to the origin of this epidemic.' And that was a lie, Ryan knew even as he was saying it, speaking the lie right after stating that he wouldn't lie, because the situation demanded that, too. What a crazy fucking world it was.

It was the worst interview of her life. The woman, she saw, called the Index Case, was attractive, or had been so a day or two previously. Now skin that had so recently qualified as a peaches-and-cream complexion was sallow and mottled with red-purple blotches. Worst of all, she knew. She had to know, the agent thought, hiding behind her mask, holding her felt-tip pen in the rubber gloves (nothing sharp that might penetrate the thin latex), taking her notes, and learning not very much. She had to know that this sort of medical care was not the usual thing, that the medics were afraid to touch her, and that now a special agent of the Federal Bureau of Investigation would not even approach her bed.

'Aside from the trip to Kansas City?'

'Nothing really,' the voice replied, as though from the bottom of a grave. 'Working at my desk, getting ready for the fall orders. Went to the housewares show at McCormick Center two days.'

There were some more questions, none of which turned up any immediately useful information. The woman in the agent wanted to reach out, touch her hand, provide some measure of comfort and sympathy – but no. The agent had just learned the previous week that she was pregnant with her first child. She had custody of two lives now, not just her own, and it was all she could do to keep her hand from shaking.

'Thank you. We'll be back to you,' the agent said, rising from her metal chair and moving to the door. Opening it, she pulled her shoulders in so as not to touch the door frame, and proceeded to the next room down the hall for the next interview. Klein was in the corridor, discussing something with another staffer – doc or nurse, the agent couldn't tell.

'How'd it go?' the professor asked.

'What are her chances?' the agent asked.

'Essentially zero,' Mark Klein replied. For diseases like this one, Patient Zero was just that.

'Compensation? They ask *us* for compensation!' the Defense Minister demanded before the Foreign Minister could speak.

'Minister, I merely convey the words of others,' Adler reminded his hosts.

'We have had two officers from your Air Force examine the missile fragments. Their judgment confirms our own. It is a Pen-Lung-13, their new heat-seeker with the long range, a development of a Russian weapon. It's definite now, in addition to the radar evidence developed from your ships,' Defense added. 'The shooting of the airliner was a deliberate act. You know that. So do we. So, tell me, Mr Adler, where does America stand in this dispute?'

'We wish nothing more than the restoration of peace,' SecState replied, confirming his own predictions. 'I would also point out that the PRC, in allowing my direct flights between their capital and yours, are showing a measure of goodwill.'

'Quite so,' the Foreign Minister replied. 'Or so it might seem to the casual observer, but tell me, Mr Adler, what do they really want?'

So much, the American Secretary of State told himself, for settling the situation down. These two were as smart as he was, and even more angry. Then that changed.

A secretary knocked, then entered, annoying his boss until they exchanged a few words in Mandarin. A telex was passed over and read. Then another was given directly to the American.

'It seems that there is a serious problem in your country, Mr Secretary.'

The press conference was cut off. Ryan left the room, returned to the Oval Office and sat on the couch with his wife.

'How did it go?'

'Didn't you watch?' Jack asked.

'We were talking over some things,' Cathy explained. Then Arnie came in.

'Not bad, boss,' the chief of staff opined. 'You will have to meet with people from the Senate this evening. I just worked that out with the leadership on both sides. This will make the elections today a little interesting and –'

'Arnie, until further notice we will not discuss politics in this building. Politics is about ideology and theory. We have to deal with cold facts now,' SWORDSMAN said.

'You can't get away from it, Jack. Politics *is* real, and if this is the deliberate attack the general here says it is, then it's war, and war *is* a political act. You're leading the government. You have to lead the Congress, and that is a political act. You're not a philosopher king. You're the President of a democratic country,' van Damm reminded him.

'All right.' Ryan sighed his surrender to the moment. 'What else?'

'Bretano called. The plan is being implemented right now. In a few minutes, the air-traffic system tells all the airliners to stop flying. There's probably a lot of chaos in the airports right now.'

'I bet.' Jack closed his eyes, and rubbed them.

'Sir, you don't have much choice in the matter,' General Pickett told the President.

'How do I get back to Hopkins?' Alexandre asked. 'I have a department to run and patients to treat.'

'I told Bretano that people will be allowed to leave Washington,' van Damm informed the others in the room. 'The same will be true of all big cities with borders nearby. New York, Philadelphia and like that. We have to let people go home, right?'

Pickett nodded. 'Yes, they're safer there. It's unrealistic to assume that the plan will be properly implemented until midnight or so.'

Then Cathy spoke: 'Alex, I guess you'll come with me. I have to fly up, too.'

'What?' Ryan's eyes opened.

'Jack, I'm a doctor, remember?'

'You're an *eye* doctor, Cathy. People can wait to get new glasses,' Jack insisted.

'At the staff meeting today, we agreed that everybody has to pitch in. We can't just leave it to the nurses and the kids – the residents – to treat these patients. I'm a clinician. We all have to take our turn on this, honey,' Surgeon told her husband.

'No! No, Cathy, it's too dangerous.' Jack turned to face her. 'I won't let you.'

'Jack, all those times you went away, the things you never told me about, the dangerous things, you were doing your job,' she said reasonably. 'I'm a doctor. I have a job, too.'

'It's not all that dangerous, Mr President,' Alexandre put in. 'You just have to follow the procedures. I work with AIDS patients every day and –'

'No, God damn it!'

'Because I'm a girl?' Caroline Ryan asked gently. 'It worries me some, too, Jack, but I'm a professor at a medical school. I teach students how to be doctors. I teach them what their professional responsibilities are. One of those responsibilities is to be there for your patients. You can't run away from your duties. I can't, either, Jack.'

'I'd like to see the procedures you've set up, Alex,' Pickett said.

'Glad to have you, John.'

Jack continued to look in his wife's face. He knew she was strong, and he'd always known that she sometimes treated patients with contagious diseases – AIDS produced some serious eye complications. He'd just never thought much about it. Now he had to: 'What if –'

'It won't. I have to be careful. I think you did it to me again.' She kissed him in front of the others. 'My husband has the most remarkable timing,' she told the audience.

It was too much for Ryan. His hands started to shake a little and his eyes teared up. He blinked them away. 'Please, Cathy . . .'

'Would you have listened to me on the way to that submarine, Jack?' She kissed him again and stood.

There was resistance, but not all that much. Four governors told their adjutant generals – the usual title for a state's senior National Guard officer – not to obey the presidential order, and three of those wavered until the Secretary of Defense called to make the order clear and personal, threatening them with immediate relief, arrest, and court-martial. Some talked about organizing protests, but that took time, and the green vehicles were already starting to move, their orders modified in many cases, like the Philadelphia Cavalry, one of the Army's most ancient and revered units, whose members had escorted George Washington to his inauguration more than two centuries earlier, and whose current troopers now headed for the bridges on the Delaware River. Local TV and radio told people that commuters would be allowed to go home without inhibitions until nine that night, and until midnight with identification check. If it was easy, people would be allowed to get home. That happened in most cases, but not all, and motels filled up all across America.

Children, told that schools would be closed for at least a week, greeted the news with enthusiasm, puzzled at the concern and even outright fear their parents displayed.

Pharmacies which sold things like surgical masks ran out of them in a matter of minutes, their clerks mainly not knowing why until someone switched on a radio.

In Pittsburgh, strangely, the Secret Service agents going over security arrangements for President Ryan's coming visit were late getting the word. While most on the advance team hustled into the bar to watch the President on TV, Raman broke away to make a phone call. He called his home, waited for the four rings until his answering machine kicked in, then punched the code to access the messages. It was a false one, as before, announcing the arrival of a rug he hadn't ordered and a price he would not have to pay. Raman experienced a slight chill. He was now free to complete his mission at his discretion. That meant soon, as it was expected that he would die in the effort. This he was willing to do, though he thought he might have a chance now, as he walked to the bar. The other three agents stood right by the TV. When someone objected to their blockage of his view, a set of credentials were held up.

'Holy shit!' the senior man from the Pittsburgh office said for the rest. 'Now what do we do?'

*   *   *

It was tricky with international flights. The word was only now getting to the embassies in Washington. They communicated the nature of the emergency to their governments, but for the European ones, senior officials were at home, many getting into bed when the calls came. These had to get into their offices, have their own meetings, and decide what to do, but the long duration of over-water flights mainly gave time for that. Soon it was decided that all passengers on flights from America would be quarantined – how long, they didn't know yet. Urgent calls to the American Federal Aviation Administration made arrangements to allow flights to America to sit on the ground, be refueled, and then depart for their points of origin. These aircraft were identified as uncontaminated, their passengers allowed to proceed home, though there would be bureaucratic mistakes along the way.

That the financial markets would be closed was made apparent by an Ebola case which arrived in Northwestern University Medical Center. He was a commodities trader who customarily worked on the raucous floor of the Chicago Board of Trade, and the news was quick to get out. All the exchanges would be closed, and the next worry for the business and financial community was the effect this would have on their activities. But mainly people watched the TV coverage. Every network found its medical expert and gave him or her free rein to explain the problem, usually in too much detail. Cable channels ran science specials on Ebola outbreaks in Zaire, showing just how far flu symptoms might lead. What resulted was a quiet, private sort of panic throughout the nation, people in their homes, inspecting their pantries to see how much food they had, watching TV and worrying as they also struggled to ignore. When neighbors talked, it was at a distance.

The case count reached five hundred just before eight o'clock in Atlanta. It had been a long day for Gus Lorenz, gyrating as he did between his laboratory and his office. There was danger for him and his staff. Fatigue made for errors and accidents. Normally a sedate establishment, one of the world's finest research laboratories, the people there were accustomed to working in a calm, orderly way. Now it was frantic. Blood samples couriered to them had to be tagged and tested, and the results faxed to the hospital of origin. Lorenz struggled throughout the day to reorganize his people and their functions, so as to keep staff on duty around the clock, but also not to overly fatigue anyone. He had to apply that to himself as well, and when he returned to his office to catch a nap, he found someone waiting inside.

'FBI,' the man said, holding up his ID folder. It was actually the local SAC, a very senior agent who'd been running his own office over a cellular phone. He was a tall, quiet man, slow to excite. In crisis situations, he told his force of agents, you think first. There was always time to screw things up, and there had to be time to get them right, too.

'What can I do for you?' Lorenz asked, taking his seat.

'Sir, I need you to brief me in. The Bureau is working with a few other agencies to see how this all started. We're interviewing every victim to try and determine where they got sick, and we figure you're the expert to ask about the overall situation. Where did all this start?'

The military didn't know where it had started, but it was rapidly becoming apparent where it had gotten to. Fort Stewart, Georgia, had only been the first. Nearly every Army base was near some big city or other. Fort Stewart was within easy driving distance of Savannah and Atlanta. Fort Hood was close to Dallas–Fort Worth. Fort Campbell an hour from Nashville, where Vanderbilt had already reported cases. The personnel lived mainly in barracks, where they shared common showers and toilet facilities, and at these bases the senior medical officers were quite literally terrified. Naval personnel lived the most closely of all. Their ships were enclosed environments. Those ships at sea were instantly ordered to remain there while the shoreside situation was evaluated. It was soon determined that every major base was at risk, and though some units – mainly infantry and military police – deployed to augment the National Guard, medics kept an eye on every soldier and Marine. Soon they started finding men and women with flu symptoms. These were instantly isolated, put in protective MOPP gear and flown by helicopter to the nearest hospital that was receiving suspected Ebola cases. By midnight it would be clear that, until further notice, the US military was a contaminated instrument. Urgent calls into the National Military Command Center reported which units had found cases, and on that information whole battalions were separated from others and kept that way, the personnel eating combat rations because their mess halls were closed, and thinking about an enemy they couldn't see.

'Jesus, John,' Chavez said in the latter's office.

Clark nodded silently. His wife, Sandy, was an instructor in nursing in a teaching hospital, and her life, he knew, might be at risk. She worked a medical floor. If an infected patient arrived, he would come to her unit, and Sandy would take the lead to show her students how to treat such patients safely.

Safely? he asked himself. Sure. The thought brought back dark memories and the sort of fear he hadn't known in many years. This attack on his country – Clark hadn't been told yet, but he never had learned to believe in coincidences – didn't put him at risk, but it put his wife at risk.

'Who do you suppose did it?' It was a dumb question, and it generated a dumber reply.

'Somebody who doesn't like us a whole hell of a lot,' John answered crossly.

'Sorry.' Chavez looked out the window and thought for a few seconds. 'It's one hell of a gamble, John.'

'If we find out it is . . . and operational security on something like this is a motherfucker.'

'Roge-o, Mr C. The people we've been looking at?'

'That's a possibility. Others, too, I suppose.' He checked his watch. Director Foley should be back from Washington by now, and they should head up to his office. It took only a couple of minutes.

'Hi, John,' the DCI said, looking up from his desk. Mary Pat was there, too.

'Not an accident, is it?' Clark asked.

'No, it's not. We're setting up a joint task force. The FBI is talking to people inside the country. If we get leads, it'll be our job to work outside the borders. You two will stand by to handle that. I'm trying to figure a way now to get people overseas.'

'The SNIE?' Ding asked.

'Everything else is on the back burner now. Jack even gave me authority to order NSA and DIA around.' Though the DCI by law had the power to do just that, in fact the other large agencies had always been their own independent empires. Until now.

'How are the kids, guys?' Clark asked.

'Home,' Mary Pat replied. Queen spook or not, she was still a mother with a mother's concerns. 'They say they feel fine.'

'Weapons of mass destruction,' Chavez said next. He didn't have to say anything more.

'Yeah.' The DCI nodded. Somebody either had overlooked or didn't care about the fact that United States policy for years had been explicit on that issue. A nuke was a germ was a gas shell, and the reply to a germ or a gas shell was a nuke, because America had those, and didn't have the others. Foley's desk phone rang. 'Yes?' He listened for a few seconds. 'Fine, could you send a team here for that? Good, thank you.'

'What was that?'

'USAMRIID at Fort Detrick. Okay, they'll be here in an hour. We can send people overseas, but they have to have their blood tested first. The European countries are – well, you can imagine. Shit, you can't take a fucking *dog* into England without leaving him in a kennel for six months to make sure he doesn't have rabies. You'll probably have to be tested on the other side of the pond, too. Flight crew also,' the DCI added.

'We're not packed,' Clark said.

'Buy what you need over there, John, okay?' Mary Pat paused. 'Sorry.'

'Do we have any leads to run down?'

'Not yet, but that will change. You can't do something like this without leaving *some* footprints.'

'Something's strange here,' Chavez observed, looking down the long, narrow top-floor office. 'John, remember what I said the other day?'

'No,' Clark said. 'What do you mean?'

'Some things you can't retaliate about, some things you can't reverse. Hey, if this was a terrorist op –'

'Too big,' Mary Pat objected. 'Too sophisticated.'

'Fine, ma'am, even if it was, hell, we could turn the Bekaa Valley into a parking lot, and send the Marines in to paint the lines after it cools down. That ain't no secret. Same thing's true of a nation-state, isn't it? We ditched the ballistic missiles, but we still have nuclear bombs. We can burn any country down to bedrock, and President Ryan would do it – least I wouldn't bet the house against it. I've seen the guy in action, and he ain't no pantywaist.'

'So?' the DCI asked. He didn't say that it wasn't that simple. Before Ryan or anyone else initiated a nuclear-release order, the evidence would have to be of the sort to pass scrutiny with the Supreme Court, and he *didn't* think Ryan was the sort to do such a thing under most circumstances.

'So whoever ran this op is thinking one of two things. Either it won't matter if we find out, or we can't respond that way, or . . .' There was a third one, wasn't there? It was almost there, but not quite.

'Or they take the President out – but then why try for his little girl first?' Mary Pat asked. 'That just increases security around him, makes the job harder instead of easier. We have things happening all over. The Chinese thing. The UIR. The Indian navy sneaked out to sea. All the political crap here, and now this Ebola. There's no picture. All these things are unconnected.'

'Except they're all making *our* life hard, aren't they?' The room got quiet for a few seconds.

'The boy's got a point,' Clark told the other two.

'It always starts in Africa,' Lorenz said, filling his pipe. 'That's where it lives. There was an outbreak in Zaire a few months ago.'

'Didn't make the news,' the FBI agent said.

'Only two victims, a young boy and a nurse – nursing nun, I think, but she was lost in a plane crash. Then there was a mini-break in Sudan, again two victims, an adult male and a little girl. The man died. The child survived. That was weeks ago, too. We have blood samples from the Index Case. We've been experimenting with that one for a while now.'

'How do you do that?'

'You culture the virus in tissue. Monkey kidneys, as a matter of fact – oh, yeah,' he remembered.

'What's that?'

'I put in an order for some African greens. That's the monkey we use. You euthanatize them and extract the kidneys. Somebody got there first, and I had to wait for another order.'

'Do you know who it was?'

Lorenz shook his head. 'No, never found out. Put me back a week, ten days, that's all.'

'Who else would want the monkeys?' the SAC asked.

'Pharmaceutical houses, medical labs, like that.'

'Who would I talk to about that?'

'You serious?'

'Yes, sir.'

Lorenz shrugged and pulled the card off his Rolodex. 'Here.'

The breakfast meeting had taken a little time to arrange. Ambassador David L. Williams left his car, then was escorted into the Prime Minister's official residence. He was grateful for the time of day. India could be a furnace, and at his age the heat became increasingly oppressive, especially since he had to dress like an Ambassador, instead of a governor of Pennsylvania, where it was okay to look working class. In this country, working class meant even more informal clothing, and that made the upper crust even haughtier with their beloved symbols of status. World's largest democracy they liked to call this place, the retired politician thought. Sure.

The PM was already seated at the table. She rose when he entered the room, took his hand and conveyed him to his seat. The china was gold-trimmed, and a liveried servant came in to serve coffee. Breakfast started with melon.

'Thank you for receiving me,' Williams said.

'You are always welcome in my house,' the PM replied graciously. About as much as a snake, the Ambassador knew. The hi-how-are-you chitchat lasted for ten minutes. Spouses were fine. Children were fine. Grandchildren were fine. Yes, it was warming up with the approach of summer. 'So what business do we have to discuss?'

'I understand that your navy has sailed.'

'Yes, it has, I believe. After the unpleasantness your forces inflicted on us, they had to make repairs. I suppose they are making sure all their machines work,' the PM replied.

'Just exercises?' Williams asked. 'My government merely asks the question, madam.'

'Mr Ambassador, I remind you that we are a sovereign nation. Our armed forces operate under our law, and you keep reminding us that the sea is free for the innocent passage of all. Are you now telling me that your country wishes to deny us that right?'

'Not at all, Prime Minister. We merely find it curious that you are evidently staging so large an exercise.' He didn't add, *with your limited resources.*

'Mr Ambassador, no one likes to be bullied. Only a few months ago you falsely accused us of harboring aggressive intentions to a neighbor. You threatened our country. You actually staged an attack on our navy and damaged our ships. What have we done to merit such unfriendly acts?' she asked, leaning back in her chair.

Unfriendly acts was not a phrase used lightly, the Ambassador noted, and was not accidentally spoken here.

'Madam, there has been no such act. I would suggest that if there were misperceptions, perhaps they were mutual, and to prevent further such errors, I come here to ask a simple question. America makes no threats. We simply inquire as to the intentions of your naval forces.'

'And I have answered. We are conducting exercises.' A moment before, Williams noted, she had *supposed* that something was going on. Now she seemed more certain of it. 'Nothing more.'

'Then my question is answered,' Williams commented with a benign smile. Jesus, but she thought she was clever. Williams had grown up in one of America's most complex political environments, the Pennsylvania Democratic party, and had fought his way to the top of it. He'd met people like her before, just less sanctimonious. Lying was such a habit for political figures that they thought they could always get away with it. 'Thank you, Prime Minister.'

The engagement was a wipeout, the first such in this training rotation. Pretty bad timing, Hamm thought, watching the vehicle returning up the dirt roads. They'd headed into it just after the President's announcement. They were Guardsmen, and they were far from home, and they were worried about their families. That had distracted them badly, since they hadn't had time to let things settle down a little, to call home and make sure things were okay with Mom and Dad, or honey and the kids. And they'd paid for it, but professional soldier that he was, Hamm knew it wasn't fair to mark this one down against the Carolina brigade. This sort of thing wouldn't happen in the field. Realistic as the NTC was, it was still play. Nobody died here except by accident, while at home the real thing might well be taking place. That wasn't how it was supposed to be with soldiers, was it?

Clark and Chavez had their blood drawn by an Army medic who also ran the screening test. They watched it with morbid fascination, especially since the medic wore thick gloves and a mask.

'You're both clean,' he told them, with a sigh of his own.

'Thanks, Sarge,' Chavez said. It was very real now. His dark Latino eyes were showing something other than relief. Like John, Domingo was putting on his mission face.

With that, they bundled into an official car for the drive to Andrews. The streets in the Washington metropolitan area were unusually empty. It made for a swift passage that didn't assuage the sense of foreboding they both felt. Crossing one of the bridges, they stopped and had to wait for three other vehicles to pass a checkpoint. There was a National Guard Hummer in the middle of the eastbound lanes, and when Clark pulled up, he showed his CIA picture-pass.

'Agency,' he told the MP.

'Pass,' the Spec-4 replied.

'So, where we going, Mr C.?'

'Africa, via the Azores.'

51

INVESTIGATIONS

The meeting with the Senate leadership went predictably. Issuing them surgical masks had set the tone of the evening for them – again, van Damm's idea. General Pickett had been to Hopkins to review procedures there, then flown back to give the main part of the briefing. The fifteen senators assembled in the East Room listened gravely, only their eyes showing above the masks.

'I'm not comfortable with your actions, Mr President,' one of them said. Jack couldn't tell which one.

'You think *I* am?' he replied. 'If anybody has a better idea, let's hear it. I have to go with the best medical advice. If this thing is as deadly as the general says, then any mistake could kill people in the thousands – even millions. If we err, we have to err on the side of caution.'

'But what about civil liberties?' another one demanded.

'Does any of those come before life?' Jack asked. 'People, if anyone wants to give me a better option, I will listen – we have one of our experts here to help evaluate it. *But* I will *not* listen to objections that are not based on scientific fact. The Constitution and the law cannot anticipate every eventuality. In cases like this, we're supposed to use our heads –'

'We're supposed to be guided by principle!' It was the civil liberties Senator again.

'Fine, then let's talk about it. If there's a balance between what I have done and whatever else will keep the country moving – *and safe!* – let's find it. I *want* options! *Give me something I can use!*' There followed a silence and a lot of crossed looks. Even that was hard. The senators were spaced out in their seating.

'Why did you have to move so fast?'

'People may be dying, you jackass!' another senator snarled at his good friend and distinguished colleague. He had to be one of the new crop, Jack thought. Someone who didn't know the mantras yet.

'But what if you're wrong?' a voice asked.

'Then you can hold your impeachment trial after the House indicts me,' Jack replied. 'Then somebody else can make these decisions, and God help him. Senators, my wife is in Hopkins right now, and she's going to take her turn treating these people. I don't like *that*, either. I would like to have your support. It's lonely standing up by myself like this, but whether you support your President or not, I have to do the best I can. I'll say it one more time: if anybody here has a better idea, let's hear it.'

But nobody did, and it wasn't their fault. As little time as he'd had to come to terms with the situation, they'd had less.

The Air Force had managed tropical uniforms for them out of the Andrews Post Exchange – a medium-sized department store – since their Washington clothes were a little too heavy for a tropical environment. It made for good cover, too. Clark wore the silver eagles of a colonel, and Chavez was a major, complete with silver pilot's wings and ribbons donated by the flight crew of their VC-20B. There were, in fact, two sets of pilots. The backup crew was sleeping in the two most-forward passenger seats.

'Not bad for a retired E-6,' Ding noted, though the uniform didn't fit all that well.

'Not bad for a retired E-7, either, and that's "sir," to you, Major Chavez.'

'Three bags full, sir.' It was their only light moment. The military version of the Gulfstream business jet had a ton of communications gear, and a sergeant to run it. The documents coming over the equipment threatened to exhaust the on-board supply of paper as they passed over Cape Verde, inbound to Kinshasa.

'Second stop is Kenya, sir.' The communications sergeant was really an intelligence specialist. She read all the inbound traffic. 'You have to see a man about some monkeys.'

Clark took the page – he was the colonel, after all – and read it, while Chavez figured out how the ribbons went on the blue uniform shirt. He decided he didn't have to be too careful. It wasn't as though the Air Force were really a military service – at least according to the Army in which he'd once served, where it was an article of faith.

'Check this out,' John said, handing the page over.

'That's a lead, Mr C.,' Ding observed at once. They traded a look. This was a pure intelligence mission, one of the few on which they'd been dispatched. They were tasked to gather vitally important information for their country, and nothing else. For now. Though they didn't say so, neither would have objected to doing something more. Though both were field officers of the CIA's Directorate of Operations, both were also former combat soldiers (in Clark's case, a former SEAL) who more often than not dropped into the DO's paramilitary side, where they did things that the pure spooks regarded as a little too exciting. But often satisfying, Chavez told himself. Very satisfying. He was learning to control his temper – in fact, that part of his genetic heritage, as he called it now, had always been under tight control – but it didn't stop him from thinking about finding whoever it was who had attacked his country, and then dealing with him as soldiers did.

'You know him better than I do, John. What's he going to do?'

'Jack?' Clark shrugged. 'That depends on what we get for him, Domingo. That's our job, remember?'

'Yes, sir,' the younger man said seriously.

The President did not sleep well that night, though he told himself, and was told by others that sleep was a prerequisite to making good decisions – and *that*, everyone emphasized, was his only real function. It was what the citizens expected him to do above all other things. He'd only had about six hours the previous day after an exhausting schedule of travel and speeches, but even so, sleep came hard. His staff and the staffs of many other federal agencies slept less, because, as sweeping as the executive orders were, they had to be implemented in a practical world, and that meant interpretation of the orders in the context of a living nation. A final complication was the fact that there was a problem with the two Chinas, who were thirteen hours ahead of Washington; another potential problem with India, ten hours ahead; and the Persian Gulf, eight hours ahead; in addition to the major crisis in America, which stretched across seven time zones all by itself, if one counted Hawaii – or even more if you added lingering possessions in the Pacific. Lying in bed on the residence floor of the White House, Ryan's mind danced around the globe, finally wondering what part of the world *wasn't* an area of some kind of concern. Around three he gave up the effort and rose, put on casual clothes and headed to the West Wing for the Signals Office, with members of the Detail in tow.

'What's happening?' he asked the senior officer present. It was Major Charles Canon, USMC, who'd been the one to inform him of the Iraqi assassination . . . which had seemed to start everything, he remembered. People started to jump to their feet. Jack waved them back into their seats. 'As you were.'

'Busy night, sir. Sure you want to be up for all this?' the major asked.

'I don't feel much like sleeping, Major,' Ryan replied. The three Service agents behind him made faces behind SWORDS-MAN's back. They knew better even if POTUS didn't.

'Okay, Mr President, we're linked in now with CDC and USAMRIID communications lines, so we're copying all their data. On the map there we have all the cases plotted.' Canon pointed. Someone had installed a new, large map of the United States mounted on a corkboard. Red pushpins obviously designated Ebola cases. There was a supply of black ones, too, whose import was all too obvious, though none were on the board yet. The pins were mainly clustered in eighteen cities now, with seemingly random singles and pairs spread all over the map. There were still a number of states untouched. Idaho, Alabama, both the Dakotas, even, strangely, Minnesota with its Mayo Clinic, were among the states so far protected by Ryan's executive order – or chance, and how did one tell the difference? There were several computer printouts – the printers were all running now. Ryan picked one up. The victim-patients were listed alphabetically by name, by state, by city, and by occupation. Roughly fifteen percent of them were in the 'maintenance custodial' category, and that was the largest statistical grouping other than 'sales marketing.' This data came from the FBI and CDC, which were working together to study patterns of infection. Another printout showed suspected sites of infection, and that confirmed General Pickett's statement that trade shows had been selected as primary targets.

In all his time at CIA, Ryan had studied all manner of theoretical attacks against his country. Somehow this sort had never made it to his desk. Biological warfare was beyond the pale. He'd spent thousands of hours thinking about nuclear attack. What we had, what they had, what targets, what casualties, the hundreds of possible targeting options selected for political, military, or economic factors, and for each option there was a range of possible outcomes depending on weather, time of year, time of day, and other variables until the result could be addressed only by computers, and even then the likely results were only expressions of probability calculations. He'd hated every moment of that, and rejoiced at the end of the Cold War and its constant, implied threat of megadeaths. He'd even lived through a crisis that might have led that far. The nightmares from that, he remembered . . .

The President had never taken a course in government per se, just the usual political science courses at Boston College in pursuit of his first degree in economics. Mainly he remembered the words of an aristocratic planter, written almost thirty years before his ascension to become the country's third President: '. . . Life, Liberty, and the Pursuit of Happiness. That to secure these Rights, Governments are instituted among men, deriving their just Powers from the consent of the governed.' That was the mission statement right there. The Constitution he'd sworn to Preserve, Protect, and Defend was itself designed to preserve, protect, and defend the lives and rights of the people out there, and he wasn't supposed to be here going over lists of names and places and occupations of people, at least eighty percent of whom were going to die. They were entitled to their lives. They were entitled to their liberty. They were entitled to the pursuit – by which Jefferson had meant the *vocation of*, not the chase after – of happiness. Well, somebody was taking lives. Ryan had ordered the suspension of their liberty. Sure as hell not many were happy right now . . .

'Here's actually a little bit of good news, Mr President.'

Canon handed over the previous day's election results. It startled Ryan. He'd allowed himself to forget about that. Someone had compiled a list of the winners by profession, and less than half of them were lawyers. Twenty-seven were physicians. Twenty-three were engineers. Nineteen were farmers. Eighteen were teachers. Fourteen were businessmen of one sort or another. Well, that was something, wasn't it? Now he had about a third of a House of Representatives. How to get them to Washington, he wondered. They could not be impeded from that. The Constitution was explicit on that issue. While Pat Martin might argue that the suspension of interstate travel had never been argued before the high court, the Constitution mandated that members of the Congress could not be stopped from coming to a session except on cause of treason . . . ? Something like that. Jack couldn't remember exactly, but he knew that congressional immunity was a big deal.

Then a telex machine started chattering. An Army Spec-5 walked over to it.

'FLASH-traffic from State, from Ambassador Williams in India,' he announced.

'Let's see.' Ryan walked over, too. It wasn't good news. Neither was the next one from Taipei.

The physicians were working four-hour shifts. For every young resident there was a senior staff member. They were largely doing nurses' work, and though they mainly were doing it well, they also knew that it wouldn't matter all that much.

It was Cathy's first time in a space suit. She'd operated on thirty or so AIDS patients for eye complications of their disease, but that hadn't been terribly difficult. You used regular gloves, and the only real worry was the number of hands allowed in the surgical field, and for ophthalmic surgery that wasn't nearly the problem it was for thoracic. You went a little slower, were a little more careful in your movements, but that was it, really. Not now. Now she was in a big, thick plastic bag, wearing a helmet whose clear faceplate often fogged from her breath, looking at patients who were going to die despite the attention of professor-rank physicians.

But they had to try anyway. She was looking down at the local Index Case, the Winnebago dealer whose wife was in the next room. There were two IVs running, one of fluids and electrolytes and morphine, the other of whole blood, both held rigidly in place so as not to damage the steel-vein interface. The only thing they could do was to support. It had once been thought that interferon might help, but that hadn't worked. Antibiotics didn't touch viral diseases, a fact which was not widely appreciated. There was nothing else, though a hundred people were now examining options in their labs. No one had ever taken the time with Ebola. CDC, the Army, and a few other labs across the world had done some work, but there hadn't been the effort devoted to other diseases that raged through 'civilized' countries. In America and Europe research priority went to diseases that killed many, or which attracted a lot of political attention, because the allocation of government research money was a political act, and for private funding it tracked with what rich or prominent person had been unlucky. Myasthenia gravis had killed Aristotle Onassis, and the resultant funding, while not fast enough to help the shipping magnate, had made significant progress almost overnight – largely luck, Dr Ryan knew, but true even so, and a blessing to other victims. The same principle extended to oncology, where the funding for breast cancer, which attacked roughly one woman in ten, far outstripped research in prostate cancer, which afflicted roughly half of the male population. A huge amount went into childhood cancers, which were statistically quite rare – only twelve cases a year per hundred thousand kids – but what was more valuable than a child? Nobody objected to that; certainly she did not. It came down to minuscule funding for Ebola and other tropical diseases because they didn't have a high profile in the countries which spent the money. That would change now, but not soon enough for the patients filling up the hospital.

The patient started gagging and turned to his right. Cathy grabbed the plastic trash can – emesis trays were too small and tended to spill – and held it for him. Bile and blood, she saw. Black blood. Dead blood. Blood full of the little crystalline 'bricks' of Ebola virus. When he was done, she gave him a water container, the sort with a straw that gave a little bit of water from a squeeze. Just enough to wet his mouth.

'Thanks,' the patient groaned. His skin was pale except in the places where it was blotched from subcutaneous bleeding. Petechiae. Must be Latin, Cathy thought. A dead language's word to designate the sign of approaching death. He looked at her, and he knew. He had to know. The pain was fighting up against the border of the current morphine dosage, reaching his consciousness in waves, like the battering of a tide against a seawall.

'How am I doing?' he asked.

'Well, you're pretty sick,' Cathy told him. 'But you're fighting back very well. If you can hang in there long enough, your immune system can beat this thing down, but you have to hang tough for us.' And that wasn't quite a lie.

'I don't know you. You a nurse?'

'No, I'm actually a professor.' She smiled at him through the plastic shield.

'Be careful,' he told her. 'You really don't want this. Trust me.' He even managed to smile back in the way that severely afflicted patients did. It nearly tore Cathy's heart from her chest.

'We're being careful. Sorry about the suit.' She so needed to touch the man, to show that she really did care, and you couldn't do that through rubber and plastic, damn it!

'Hurts real bad, Doc.'

'Lie back. Sleep as much as you can. Let me adjust the morphine for you.' She walked to the other side of the bed to increase the drip, waiting a few minutes before his eyes closed. Then she walked back to the bucket and sprayed it with a harsh chemical disinfectant. The container was already soaked in it, to the point that the chemical had impregnated the plastic, and anything alive that fell into it would quickly be extinguished. Spraying the thirty or so cc's that he'd brought up was probably unnecessary, but there was no such thing as too many precautions now. A nurse came in and handed over the printout with the newest blood work. The patient's liver function was nearly off the scale, automatically highlighted by asterisks as though she wouldn't have noticed. Ebola had a nasty affinity for that organ. Other chemical indicators confirmed the start of systemic necrosis. The internal organs had started to die, the tissues to rot, eaten by the tiny virus strands. It was theoretically possible that his immune system could still summon its energy and launch a counterattack, but that was only theory, one chance in several hundred. *Some* patients *did* fight this off. It was in the literature which she and her colleagues had studied over the last twelve hours, and in that case, they were already speculating, if they could isolate the antibodies, they might have something they could use therapeutically.

If – maybe – might – could – possibly.

That wasn't medicine as she knew it. Certainly it wasn't the clean, antiseptic medicine she practiced at Wilmer, fixing eyes, restoring and perfecting sight. She thought again about her decision to enter ophthalmology. One of her professors had pressed her hard to look at oncology. She had the brains, she had the curiosity, she had the gift for connecting things, he'd told her. But looking down at this sleeping, dying patient, she knew that, no, she didn't have the heart to do this every day. Not to lose so many. So did that make her a failure? Cathy Ryan asked herself. With this patient, she had to admit, yes, it did.

'Damn,' Chavez said. 'It's like Colombia.'

'Or Vietnam,' Clark agreed on being greeted with the tropical heat. There was an embassy official, and a representative of the Zaire government. The latter wore a uniform and saluted the arriving 'officers,' which courtesy John returned.

'This way, if you please, Colonel.' The helicopter, it turned out, was French, and the service was excellent. America had dropped a lot of money into this country. It was payback time now.

Clark looked down. Triple-canopy jungle. He'd seen that before, in more than one country. In his youth, he'd been underneath, looking for enemies, and with enemies looking for him – little men in black pajamas or khaki uniforms, carrying AK-47s, people who wanted to take his life. Now he appreciated the fact that there was something down there even smaller, that was not carrying any weapon, and was targeted not merely on him, but at the heart of his country. It seemed so damned unreal. John Clark was a creature of his country. He'd been wounded in combat operations and other, more personal events, and every time was restored quickly to full health. There had been that one time, when he'd rescued an A-6 pilot up some river in North Vietnam whose name he couldn't remember anymore. He'd gotten cut, and the polluted river had infected him, and *that* had been fairly unpleasant, but drugs and time had fixed it. He'd come away from all the experiences with a deeply held belief that his country produced doctors who could fix just about anything – not old age, and not cancer, yet, but they were working on it, and in due course they'd win their battles as he'd won most of his. That was an illusion. He had to admit that now. As he and his country had lost their struggle in a jungle like this one, a thousand feet below the racing helicopter, so now the jungle was reaching out, somehow. No. He shook that off. The jungle wasn't reaching out. People had done that.

The four Ro/Ro ships formed up six hundred miles north-northwest of Diego Garcia. They were in a box formation, spaced a thousand yards abeam and a thousand yards fore and aft. The destroyer *O'Bannon* took position five thousand yards dead ahead. *Kidd* was ten thousand yards northeast of the ASW ship, with *Anzio* twenty miles in advance of the rest. The replenishment group with its two frigates was westbound and would join up around sunset.

It was a good opportunity for an exercise. Six P-3C Orion aircraft were based at Diego Garcia – the number had once been larger – and one of them was patrolling ahead of the mini-convoy, dropping sonobuoys, a complex undertaking for so rapidly moving a formation, and listening for possible submarines. Another Orion was well in advance, tracking the Indian navy's two-carrier battle group from their radar emissions while staying well out of detection range. The lead Orion was not armed with anything but anti-sub weapons at the moment, and its mission was routine surveillance.

'Yes, Mr President,' the J-3 said. *Why aren't you asleep, Jack?* he couldn't say.

'Robby, did you see this thing from Ambassador Williams?'
'It got my attention,' Admiral Jackson confirmed.

David Williams had taken his time drafting the communiqué. That had annoyed people at State, and caused two requests for his report which he had ignored. The former governor was drawing on all of his political savvy to consider the words the Prime Minister had chosen, her tone, her body language – the look in her eyes most of all. There was no substitute for that. Dave Williams had learned that lesson more than once. One thing he hadn't learned was diplomatic verbiage. His report was straight-from-the-shoulder, and his conclusion was that India was up to something. He further noted that the Ebola crisis in America had not come up. Not a word of sympathy. That, he wrote, was probably a mistake in one sense, and a very deliberate act in another. India should have cared about it, or should have expressed concern even if she didn't. Instead it had been ignored. If asked, the Prime Minister would have said that she hadn't yet been informed, but that would be a lie, Williams added. In the age of CNN, things like that never went unnoticed. Instead, she had harped on being bullied by America, reminded him of the 'attack' on her navy not once but twice, and then extended the remark into calling it an 'unfriendly act,' a phrase used in diplomacy right before a hand descended toward the holster. He concluded that India's naval exercise was not a mistake in either timing or location. The message he'd received was: *In your face!*

'So, what do you think, Rob?'

'I think Ambassador Williams is one shrewd son of a bitch, sir. The only thing he didn't say is something he didn't know: we don't have a carrier there. Now, the Indians haven't been tracking us in any way, but it's public knowledge that *Ike* is heading toward China, and if their intel officers are halfway competent, they definitely *do* know. Then, *shazam*, they put out to sea. And now, we get this from the Ambassador. Sir –'

'Stow that, Robby,' Ryan told him. 'You've said that enough for one day.'

'Fine. Jack, we have every reason to believe that China and India were working together before. So what happens now? China stages an incident. It gets nastier. We move a carrier. The Indians put to sea. Their fleet is on a direct line between Diego Garcia and the Persian Gulf. The Persian Gulf heats up.'

'And we have a plague,' Ryan added. He leaned forward on the cheap desk in Signals. He couldn't sleep, but that didn't mean he was fully awake, either. 'Coincidences?'

'Maybe. Maybe the Indian Prime Minister is pissed at us because we rattled their cage a while back. Maybe she just wants to show us that we can't push her around. Maybe it's petty bullshit, Mr President. But maybe it ain't.'

'Options?'

'We have a surface-action group in the Eastern Med, two Aegis cruisers, a Burke-class 'can, and three figs. The Med's quiet. I suggest that we consider moving that group through Suez to back up the *Anzio* group. I further suggest that we consider moving a carrier from WestLant to the Med. That will take a while, Jack. It's six thousand miles; even with a speed of advance of twenty-five knots that's almost nine days just to get a carrier close. We have more than a third of the world without a carrier handy, and the part that isn't covered is starting to make me nervous. If we have to do something, Jack, I'm not sure we can.'

'Hello, Sister,' Clark said, taking her hand gently. He hadn't seen a nun in quite a few years.

'Welcome, Colonel Clark. Major.' She nodded to Chavez.

'Afternoon, ma'am.'

'What brings you to our hospital?' Sister Mary Charles's English was excellent, almost as though she taught it, with a Belgian accent that sounded just like French to the two Americans.

'Sister, we're here to ask about the death of one of your colleagues, Sister Jean Baptiste,' Clark told her.

'I see.' She waved to the chairs. 'Please sit down.'

'Thank you, Sister,' Clark said politely.

'You are Catholic?' she asked. It was important to her.

'Yes, ma'am, we both are.' Chavez nodded agreement with the 'colonel.'

'Your education?'

'Actually all Catholic schools for me,' Clark said, indulging her. 'Grade school was the School Sisters of Notre Dame, and Jesuits after that.'

'Ah.' She smiled, pleased at the news. 'I have heard of the sickness that has broken out in your country. This is very sad. And so you are here to ask about poor Benedict Mkusa, Sister Jean, and Sister Maria Magdalena. But I fear we cannot be of much help to you.'

'Why is that, Sister?'

'Benedict died and his body was cremated on government order,' Sister Mary Charles explained. 'Jean was taken ill, yes, but she left for Paris on a medical evacuation flight, you see, to visit the Pasteur Institute. The airplane crashed into the sea, however, and all were lost.'

'All?' Clark asked.

'Sister Maria Magdalena flew off also, and Dr Moudi, of course.'

'Who was he?' John inquired next.

'He was part of the World Health Organization mission to this area. Some of his colleagues are in the next building.' She pointed.

'Moudi, you said, ma'am?' Chavez asked, taking his notes.

'Yes.' She spelled it for him. 'Mohammed Moudi. A good doctor,' she added. 'It was very sad to lose them all.'

'Mohammed Moudi, you said. Any idea where he was from?' It was Chavez again.

'Iran – no, that's just changed, hasn't it? He was educated in Europe, a fine young physician, and very respectful of us.'

'I see.' Clark adjusted himself in his seat. 'Could we talk with his colleagues?'

'I think the President's gone much too far,' the doctor said on TV. He had to be interviewed in a local affiliate since he was unable to drive from Connecticut to New York this morning.

'Why is that, Bob?' the host asked. He'd come in from his home in New Jersey to the New York studio off Central Park West, just before the bridges and tunnels had been closed, and was sleeping in his office now. Understandably, he wasn't very happy about it.

'Ebola is a nasty one. There's no doubt of that,' said the network's medical correspondent. He was a physician who didn't practice, though he spoke the language quite well. He mainly presented medical news, in the morning concentrating on the benefits of jogging and good diet. 'But it's never been here, and the reason is that the virus can't survive here.

However, these people contracted it – and for the moment I will leave speculation on that aside – it *can't* spread very far. I'm afraid the President's actions are precipitous.'

'And unconstitutional,' the legal correspondent added. 'There's no doubt of that. The President has panicked, and that's not good for the country in medical or legal terms.'

'Thanks a bunch, fellas,' Ryan said, muting the set.

'We have to work on this,' Arnie said.

'How?'

'You fight bad information with good information.'

'Super, Arnie, except that proving I did the right thing means people have to die.'

'We have a panic to prevent, Mr President.'

So far that hadn't happened, which was remarkable. Timing had helped. The news had mainly hit people in the evening. For the most part, they'd gone home, they had enough food in the pantry to see them through a few days, and the news had shocked enough that there had not been a nationwide raid on supermarkets. Those things would change today, however. In a few hours people would be protesting. The news media would cover that, and some sort of public opinion would form. Arnie was right. He had to do something about it. But what?

'How, Arnie?'

'Jack, I thought you'd never ask.'

The next stop was the airport. There it was confirmed that, yes, a privately owned, Swiss-registered G-IV business jet had indeed lifted off with a flight plan taking it to Paris via Libya, for refueling. The chief controller had a Xerox copy of the airport records and the aircraft's manifest ready for the visiting Americans. It was a remarkably comprehensive document, since it had to allow for customs control as well. Even the names for the flight crew were on it.

'Well?' Chavez asked.

Clark looked at the officials. 'Thank you for your valuable assistance.' Then he and Ding headed for the car that would take them to their aircraft.

'Well?' Ding repeated.

'Cool it, partner.' The five-minute ride passed in silence.

Clark looked out the window. Thunderheads were building. He hated flying in the things.

'No way. We wait a few minutes.' The backup pilot was a lieutenant colonel. 'We have rules.'

Clark tapped the eagles on his epaulets and leaned right into his face. 'Me colonel. Me say go, air scout. Right the *fuck* now!'

'Look, Mr Clark, I know who you are and –'

'Sir,' Chavez said, 'I'm only an artificial major, but this mission's more important than your rules. Steer around the worst parts, will ya? We have barf bags if we need 'em.' The pilot glared at them, but moved back into the front office. Chavez turned. 'Temper, John.'

Clark handed over the paper. 'Check the names for the flight crew. They ain't Swiss, and the registration of the aircraft is.'

Chavez looked for that. HX-NJA was the registration code. And the names for the flight crew weren't Germanic, Gallic, or Italian.

'Sergeant?' Clark called as the engines started up.

'Yes, sir!' The NCO had seen this man tear the driver a new asshole.

'Fax this to Langley, please. You have the right number to use. Quick as you can, ma'am,' he added, since she was a lady, and not just a sergeant. The NCO didn't get it, but didn't mind, either.

'Cinch those belts in tight,' the pilot called over the intercom as the VC-20B started to taxi.

It took three tries because of electrical interference from the storm, but the facsimile transmission went through the satellite, downlinked to Fort Belvoir, Virginia, and reappeared in Mercury, the Agency's communications nexus. The senior watch officer had his deputy run it to the seventh floor. By that time, Clark was on the phone to him.

'Getting some interference,' the watch officer said. Digital satellite radio and all, a thunderstorm was still a thunderstorm.

'It's a little bumpy at the moment. Run the registration number and the names on that manifest. Everything you can get on them.'

'Say again.'

Clark did. It got through this time.

'Will do. Somebody's got a file on this. Anything else?'

'Back to you later. Out,' he heard.

'So?' Ding asked, reefing his belt in tighter as the G took a ten-foot drop.

'Those names are in Farsi, Ding – oh, shit.' Another major bump. He looked out the window. It was like a huge arena, a cylindrical formation of clouds with lightning all over the place. It wasn't often he looked down at that. 'The bastard's doing this on purpose.'

But he wasn't. The lieutenant colonel on the controls was scared. Air Force regulations not to mention common sense prohibited what he was doing. The weather radar in the nose showed red twenty degrees left and right of his projected course to Nairobi. Left looked better. He turned thirty degrees, banking the executive jet like a fighter, searching for a smooth spot as he continued the climb-out. What he found wasn't smooth, but it was better. Ten minutes later the VC-20B broke into sunlight.

One of the spare pilots turned in her front row seat: 'Satisfied, Colonel?' she asked.

Clark unbuckled his belt in defiance of the sign and went to the lavatory to splash water in his face. Then he knelt down on the floor next to her and showed her the paper that had just been transmitted. 'Can you tell me anything about this?' She only needed one look.

'Oh, yeah,' the captain said. 'We got a notice on that.'

'What?'

'This is essentially the same aircraft. When one breaks, the manufacturer tells everybody about it – I mean, we'd ask anyway, but it's almost automatic. He came out of here, flew north to Libya, landed to refuel, right? Took off right away, practically – medical flight, I think, wasn't it?'

'Correct. Go on.'

'He called emergency, said he lost power on one engine, then the other, and went in. Three radars tracked it. Libya, Malta, and a Navy ship, destroyer, I think.'

'Anything funny about it, Captain?'

She shrugged. 'This is a good airplane. I don't think the

military's ever broke one. You just saw how good. A couple of those bumps were two and a half, maybe three gees, and the engines – Jerry, have we ever lost an engine in flight on a -20?'

'Twice, I think. First one there was a defect on the fuel pump – Rolls-Royce sent out a fix on all of those. The other one, it was in November, a few years back. They ate a goose.'

'That'll do it every time,' she told Clark. 'Goose weighs maybe fifteen, twenty pounds. We try to keep clear of them.'

'This guy lost both engines, though?'

'They haven't figured out why yet. Maybe bad fuel. That happens, but the engines are isolated units, sir. Separate everything, pumps, electronics, you name it –'

'Except fuel,' Jerry said. 'That all comes out of one truck.'

'What else? What happens when you lose an engine?'

'If you're not careful you can lose control. You get a full shutdown, the aircraft yaws into the dead engine. That changes airflow over the control surfaces. We lost a Lear, a VC-21, that way once. If it catches you in a transition maneuver when it happens, well, then it can get a little bit exciting. But we train for that, and the flight crew on this one, that was in the report. They were both experienced drivers, and they go in the box – the training simulator – pretty regular. You have to, or they take your insurance away. Anyway, the radar didn't show them maneuvering. So, no, that shouldn't have done it to them. The best guess was bad fuel, but the Libyans said the fuel was okay.'

'Unless the crew just totally screwed up,' Jerry added. 'But even that's hard. I mean, they make these things so you really have to try to break 'em, y'know? I got two thousand hours.'

'Two and a half for me,' the captain said. 'It's safer 'n driving a car in DC, sir. We all love these things.'

Clark nodded and went forward.

'Enjoying the ride?' the pilot in command said over his shoulder. His voice wasn't exactly friendly, and he didn't exactly have to worry about insubordination. Not with an 'officer' wearing his own ribbons.

'I don't like leaning on people, Colonel. This is very important shit. That's all I can say.'

'My wife's a nurse in the base hospital.' He didn't have to say more. He was worried about her.

'So's mine, down in Williamsburg.' The pilot turned on learning that, and nodded at his passenger.

'No real harm done. Three hours to Nairobi, Colonel.'

'Well, how do *I* get back?' Raman asked over the phone.

'You don't for now,' Andrea told him. 'Sit tight. Maybe you can help the FBI with the investigation they have running.'

'Well, that's just great!'

'Deal with it, Jeff. I don't have time for this,' she told her subordinate crossly.

'Sure.' He hung up.

That was odd, Andrea thought. Jeff was always one of the cool ones. But who was cool at the moment?

'Ever been here before, John?' Chavez asked as their aircraft descended to meet its shadow on the runway.

'Passed through once. Didn't see much more than the terminal.' Clark slipped off his belt and stretched. Sunset was descending here, too, and with it *not* the end of a very long day for the two intelligence officers. 'Most of what I know comes from books by a guy named Ruark, hunting and stuff.'

'You don't hunt – not animals, anyway,' Ding added.

'Used to. I still like reading about it. Nice to hunt things that don't shoot back.' John turned with part of a smile.

'Not as exciting. Safer, maybe,' the junior agent allowed. How dangerous could a lion really be? he wondered.

The rollout took them to the military terminal. Kenya had a small air force, though what it did was a mystery to the visiting CIA/Air Force 'officers,' and seemed likely to remain so. The aircraft was met, again, by an embassy official, this one the Defense attaché, a black Army officer with the rank of colonel, and a Combat Infantryman's Badge that marked him as a veteran of the Persian Gulf War.

'Colonel Clark, Major Chavez.' Then his voice stopped. 'Chavez, do I know you?'

'Ninja!' Ding grinned. 'You were brigade staff then, First of the Seventh.'

'Cold Steel! You're one of the guys who got lost. I guess they found you. Relax, gentlemen, I know where you're from, but our hosts do not,' the officer warned.

'Where's the CIB from, Colonel?' the former staff sergeant asked on the walk over to where the cars were.

'I had a battalion of the Big Red One in Iraq. We kicked a few and took a few.' Then his mood changed. 'So how are things at home?'

'Scary,' Ding replied.

'Something to remember, bio-war is mainly a psychological weapon, like the threat of gas was against us back in '91.'

'Maybe so,' Clark responded. 'It sure as hell's got my attention, Colonel.'

'Got mine, too,' the Defense attaché admitted. 'I got family in Atlanta. CNN says there's cases there.'

'Read fast.' John handed over the last data sent to them on the airplane. 'This ought to be better than what's on TV.' Not that *better* was the right word, he thought.

The colonel rated a driver, it seemed. He took the front seat in the embassy car and flipped through the pages.

'No official greeting this time?' Chavez asked.

'Not here. We'll have a cop where we're going. I asked my friends in the ministry to low-profile this one. I have some pretty good contacts around town.'

'Good call,' Clark said as the car started moving. Getting there only took ten minutes.

The animal dealer had his place of business on the outskirts of the city, conveniently located to the airport and the main highway west into the bush, but not too close to much else. The CIA officers soon discovered why.

'Christ,' Chavez observed, getting out of the car.

'Yeah, they're noisy, aren't they? I was here earlier today. He's getting a shipment of greens ready for Atlanta.' He opened a briefcase and handed something over. 'Here, you'll need this.'

'Right.' Clark slid the envelope into his clipboard.

'Hello!' the dealer said, coming out of his office. He was a big man and, judging by his gut, knew his way around a case of beer. With him was a uniformed police officer, evidently a senior one. The attaché went to speak with him, and move him aside. The cop didn't seem to object. This infantry colonel, Clark saw, knew how the game was played.

'Howdy,' John said, taking his hand. 'I'm Colonel Clark. This is Major Chavez.'

'You are American Air Force?'

'That's right, sir,' Ding replied.

'I love airplanes. What do you fly?'

'All sorts of things,' Clark answered. The local businessman was already half in the bag. 'We have a few questions, if you don't mind.'

'About monkeys? Why are you interested in monkeys? The chief constable didn't explain.'

'Is it all that important?' John asked, handing over an envelope. The dealer pocketed it without opening it to count. He'd felt how thick it was.

'Truly it is not, but I do love to watch airplanes. So what can I tell you?' he asked next, his voice friendly and open.

'You sell monkeys,' John said.

'Yes, I deal in them. For zoos, for private collectors, and for medical laboratories. Come, I will show you.' He led them toward a three-sided building made of corrugated iron, it looked like. Two trucks were there, and five workers were loading cages onto them, their hands in thick leather gloves.

'We just had an order from your CDC in Atlanta,' the dealer explained, 'for a hundred greens. They are pretty animals, but very unpleasant. The local farmers hate them.'

'Why?' Ding asked, looking at the cages. They were made of steel wire, with handles at the top. From a distance they appeared to be of the size used to transport chickens to market . . . viewed closer, they were a little large for that, but . . .

'They ravage crops. They are a pest, like rats, but more clever, and people from America think they are gods or something, the way they complain on how they are used in medical experiments.' The dealer laughed. 'As though we would run out of them. There are millions. We raid a place, take thirty, and a month later we can come back and take thirty more. The farmers beg us to come and trap them.'

'You had a shipment ready for Atlanta earlier this year, but you sold them to someone else, didn't you?' Clark asked. He looked over to his partner, who didn't approach the building. Rather, he separated from Clark and the dealer, and walked on a line away from it. He seemed to be staring at the empty cages. Maybe the smell bothered him. It was pretty thick.

'They did not pay me on time, and another customer came along, and he had his money all ready,' the dealer pointed out. 'This is a business, Colonel Clark.'

John grinned. 'Hey, I'm not here from the Better Business Bureau. I just want to know who you sold them to.'

'A buyer,' the dealer said. 'What else do I need to know?'

'Where was he from?' Clark persisted.

'I do not know. He paid me in dollars, but he was probably not an American. He was a quiet fellow,' the dealer remembered, 'not very friendly. Yes, I know I was late getting the new shipment to Atlanta, but they were late in paying me,' he reminded his guest. 'You, fortunately, were not.'

'They went out by air?'

'Yes, it was an old 707. It was full. They were not just my monkeys. They had gotten them elsewhere, too. You see, the green is so common. It lives all over Africa. Your animal worshippers need not worry about extinction for the green. The gorilla, now, I admit that is something else.' Besides, they mainly lived in Uganda and Rwanda, and more was the pity. People paid real money for them.

'Do you have records? The name of the buyer, the manifest, the registration of the airplane?'

'Customs records, you mean.' He shook his head. 'Sadly, I do not. Perhaps they were lost.'

'You have an arrangement with the airport officials,' John said with a smile that he didn't feel.

'I have many friends in the government, yes.' Another smile, the sly sort that confirmed his arrangement. Well, it wasn't as though there was no such thing as official corruption in America, was it? Clark thought.

'And you don't know where they went, then?'

'No, there I cannot help you. If I could, I would gladly do so,' the dealer replied, patting his pocket. Where the envelope was. 'I regret to say that my records are incomplete for some of my transactions.'

Clark wondered if he could press the man further on this issue. He suspected not. He'd never worked Kenya, though he had worked Angola, briefly, in the 1970s, and Africa was a very informal continent, and cash was the lubricant. He looked over to where the Defense attaché was talking to the chief constable – the title was a holdover from British rule, which he'd read about in one of Ruark's books, and so were the shorts and kneesocks. He was probably confirming that, no, the dealer wasn't a criminal, just creative in his relationships with local authorities who, for a modest fee, looked the other way when asked. And monkeys were hardly a vital national commodity, assuming the dealer was truthful about the numbers of the things. And he probably was. It sounded true. The farmers would probably be just as happy to be rid of the damned things just to make the noise stop. It sounded like a riot in the biggest bar in town on a Friday night. And they were nasty little bastards, reaching and snapping at the gloved hands transferring the cages. What the hell, they were having a bad day. And on getting to CDC Atlanta, it wouldn't get much better, would it? Were they smart enough to know? Damned sure Clark knew. You didn't ship this many to pet stores. But he didn't have enough solicitude to waste on monkeys at the moment.

'Thank you for your help. Perhaps someone will be back to speak with you.'

'I regret that I could not tell you more.' He was sincere enough about it. For five thousand dollars in cash, he thought he should do more. Not that he'd return any, of course.

The two men walked back toward the car. Chavez joined up, looking pensive, but not saying anything. As they approached, the cop and the attaché shook hands. Then it was time for the Americans to leave. As the car pulled off, John looked back to see the dealer take the envelope from his pocket and extract a few bills to hand over to the friendly chief constable. That made sense, too.

'What did you learn?' the real colonel asked.

'No records,' John replied.

'It's the way they do business here. There's an export fee for those things, but the cops and the customs people usually have an –'

'Arrangement,' John interrupted with a frown.

'That's the word. Hey, my father came from Mississippi. They used to say down there that one term as county sheriff fixed a guy up for life, y'know?'

'Cages,' Ding said suddenly.

'Huh?' Clark asked.

'Didn't you see, John, the cages! We seen 'em before, just like those – in Tehran, in the air force hangar.' He'd kept his distance in order to duplicate what he'd seen at Mehrabad. The relative size and proportions were the same. 'Chicken coops or cages or whatever in a hangar with fighter planes, remember?'

'Shit!'

'One more indicator, Mr C. Them coincidences are piling up, 'mano. Where we goin' next?'

'Khartoum.'

'I saw the movie.'

News coverage continued, but little else. Every network affiliate became more important as the 'name' correspondents were trapped in their base offices of New York, Washington, Chicago, and Los Angeles, and the news devoted a great deal of time to visuals of National Guardsmen on the major interstate highways, blocking the roads physically with Hummers or medium trucks. No one really tried to run the blockades there. Food and medical supply trucks were allowed through, after each was inspected, and in a day or two, the drivers would be tested for Ebola antibodies, and given picture passes to make their way more efficiently. The truckers were playing ball.

It was different for other vehicles and other roads. Though most interstate highway traffic went on the major highways, there was not a state in the Union that didn't have an extensive network of side roads that interconnected with those of neighboring states, and all of these had to be blocked, too. That took time to accomplish, and there were interviews of people who'd gotten across and thought it something of a joke, followed by learned commentary that this proved that the President's order was impossible to implement completely, in addition to being wrong, stupid, and unconstitutional.

'It just isn't possible,' one transportation expert said on the morning news.

But that hadn't accounted for the fact that National Guardsmen lived in the country they guarded, and could read maps. They were also offended by the implied statement that they were fools. By noon on Wednesday there was a vehicle on every country road, crewed by men with rifles and wearing the chemical-protective suits that made them look like men (and women, though that was almost impossible to tell) from Mars.

On the side roads, if not the main ones, there were clashes. Some were mere words – my family is right over there, give a guy a break, okay? Sometimes the rule was enforced with a little common sense, after an identification check and a radio call. In other cases, the enforcement was literal, and here and there words were exchanged, some of them heated, and some of those escalated, and in two cases shots were fired, and in one of them a man was killed. Reported rapidly up the line, it was national news in two hours, and again commentators wondered at the wisdom of the President's order. One of them laid the death on the front steps of the White House.

For the most part, even those most determined to make their way to their cross-border destinations saw the uniformed men with guns and decided that it wasn't worth the risk.

The same applied to international borders. The Canadian military and police closed all border-crossing points. American citizens in Canada were asked to report to the nearest hospital for testing, and there they were detained, in a civilized way. Something similar happened in Europe, though there the treatment differed from one country to another. For the first time, it was the Mexican army which closed America's southern border, in cooperation with US authorities, this time against traffic mainly moving south.

Some local traffic was moving. Supermarkets and convenience stores allowed people in, mainly in small numbers, to purchase necessities. Pharmacies sold out of surgical masks. Many called local hardware and paint dealers to get protective masks made for other uses, and TV coverage helped there by telling people that such masks, sprayed with common household disinfectants, offered better protection against a virus than the Army's chemical gear. But inevitably, some people overdid the spraying, and that resulted in allergic reactions, respiratory difficulties, and a few deaths.

Physicians all across the country were frantically busy. It was rapidly known that the initial presentation of Ebola was similar to flu symptoms, and any doctor could relate that people could *think* themselves into those. Telling the truly sick from the hypochondriac was rapidly becoming the most demanding of medical skills.

Despite it all, however, people dealt with it, watched their televisions, looked at one another, and wondered how much substance there was to the scare.

*   *   *

That was the job of CDC and USAMRIID, aided by the FBI. There were now five hundred confirmed cases, each of which had been tied directly or indirectly to eighteen trade shows. That gave them time references. It also identified four other trade shows from which no illnesses had as yet developed. All twenty-two had been visited by agents, all of whom learned that in every case the rubbish from the shows had long since been hauled off. There was some thought that the trash might be picked through, but USAMRIID waved the Bureau off, and said that identifying the distribution system would mean comparing the contents of thousands of tons of material, a task that simply was not possible, and might even be dangerous. The important discovery was the time window. That information was made public at once. Americans who had traveled out of the country prior to the start dates of the trade shows that were known to have been focal centers were not dangerous. That fact was made known to national health services worldwide, most of which tacked on from two days to a full week. From them, the information became global knowledge within a few hours. There was no stopping it, and there was no purpose in keeping the secret, even if it were possible to do so.

'Well, that means we're all safe,' General Diggs told his staff at the morning conference. Fort Irwin was one of the most isolated encampments in America. There was only one way in and out, and that road was now blocked by a Bradley.

That wasn't true of other military bases; the problem was global. A senior Army officer from the Pentagon had flown to Germany to hold a conference with V Corps headquarters, and two days later collapsed, in the process infecting a doctor and two nurses. The news had shaken NATO allies, who instantly quarantined American encampments that dated back to the 1940s. The news was also instantly on global TV. What was worse in the Pentagon was that nearly every base had a case, real or suspected. The effect on unit morale was horrific, and that information, also, was impossible to conceal. Transatlantic phone lines burned with worry headed in both directions.

*   *   *

Things were frantic in Washington, too. The joint task force included members of all the intelligence services, plus FBI and the federal law-enforcement establishment. The President had given them a lot of power to use, and they intended to use it. The manifest of the lost Gulfstream business jet had started things moving in a new and unexpected direction, but that was the way of investigations.

In Savannah, Georgia, an FBI agent knocked on the door of the president of Gulfstream and handed him a surgical mask. The factory was shut down, as were most American businesses, but that executive order would be bent today. The president called his chief safety officer and told him to head in, along with the firm's senior test pilot. Six FBI agents sat down with them for a lengthy chat. That soon evolved into a conference call. The most important immediate result was the discovery that the lost aircraft's flight recorder hadn't been recovered. *That* resulted in a call to the CO of USS *Radford*, who confirmed that his ship, now in drydock, had tracked the lost aircraft and then had searched for the sonar pings of the black box, but to no avail. The naval officer could not explain that. Gulfstream's chief test pilot explained that if the aircraft hit hard enough, the instrument could break despite its robust design. But it hadn't been going all *that* fast, the *Radford*'s skipper remembered, and no debris had been found, either. As a result of that, the FAA and NTSB were called in and told to produce records instantly.

In Washington – the working group was in the FBI Building – looks were exchanged over the masks everyone was wearing. The FAA part of the team had run down the identity of the flight crew and their qualifications. It turned out that they were both former Iranian air force pilots, trained in America in the late 1970s. From that came photos and fingerprints. Another pair of pilots, flying the same sort of aircraft for the same Swiss corporation, had similar training, and the FBI's legal attaché in Bern made an immediate call to his Swiss colleagues to request assistance in interviewing them.

'Okay,' Dan Murray summarized. 'We got a sick Belgian nun and a friend with an Iranian doctor. They fly off in a Swiss-registered airplane that disappears without a trace. The airplane belongs to a little trading company – the leg-alt will run that down for us pretty fast, but we know the flight crew was Iranian.'

'It does seem to be heading in a certain direction, Dan,' Ed Foley said. Just then an agent came in with a fax for the CIA Director. 'Check this out.' He slid it across the table. It wasn't a long message.

'People think they're so fuckin' smart,' Murray told the people around the table. He passed the new dispatch around.

'Don't underestimate 'em,' Ed Foley warned. 'We don't have anything hard yet. The President can't take any action at all on anything until we do.' And maybe not even then, his mind went on, as gutted as the military is right now. There was also the thing Chavez had said before flying off. Damn, but that kid was getting smart. Foley wondered whether to bring that up. There were more pressing matters for now, he decided. He could discuss it with Murray privately.

Chavez didn't feel smart as he dozed in his leather seat. It was another three-hour hop to Khartoum, and he was having dreams, fitful ones. He'd done his share of flying as a CIA officer, but even on a plush executive jet with all the bells and whistles, you got tired of it in a hurry. The diminished air pressure meant diminished oxygen, and that made you tired. The air was dry, and that dehydrated you. The noise of the engines made it like sleeping out in the boonies with insects swarming around all the time, always ready to suck your blood, and you could never make the little bastards go away.

Whoever was doing whatever was happening wasn't all that smart. Okay, an airplane had disappeared with five people aboard, but that wasn't necessarily a dead end, was it? HX-NJA, he remembered from the customs document. Hmph. They'd probably kept records because they were shipping out people, rather than monkeys. HX for Switzerland. Why HX? he wondered. 'H' for Helvetia, maybe? Wasn't that an old name for Switzerland? Didn't some languages still call it that? He seemed to remember that some did. German, maybe. NJA to identify the individual aircraft. They used letters instead of numbers because it made for more permutations. Even this one had such a code, with an 'N' prefix because American aircraft used that letter code. NJA, he thought with his eyes closed. NJA. Ninja. That generated a smile. The sobriquet for his old outfit, 1st Battalion of the 17th Infantry Regiment. 'We own the night!' Yeah, those were the days, humping the hills at Fort Ord and Hunter-Liggett. But the 7th Infantry Division (Light) had been de-established, its standards furled and cased for retirement, or maybe later use ... Ninja. That seemed important. Why?

His eyes opened. Chavez stood, stretched, and went forward. There he woke the pilot with whom Clark had had that little tiff. 'Colonel?'

'What is it?' Only one eye opened.

'What's one of these things cost?'

'More 'n either one of us can afford.' The eye closed back down.

'Seriously.'

'Upwards of twenty million dollars, depending on the version and the avionics package. If somebody makes a better business jet, I don't know what it is.'

'Thanks.' Chavez returned to his seat. There was no sense in trying to fade back out. He felt the nose lower and heard the engines reduce their annoying sound. They were starting their descent into Khartoum. The local CIA station chief would be meeting – excuse me, he thought to himself. Commercial attaché. Or was it political officer? Whatever. He knew that this city wouldn't be as friendly as the last two.

The helicopter landed at Fort McHenry, close to the statue of Orpheus that someone had decided was appropriate to honor the name of Francis Scott Key, Ryan noted irrelevantly. About as irrelevant as Arnie's idea for a fucking photo opportunity. He had to show he was concerned. Jack wondered about that. Did people think that at times like this the President threw a party? Hadn't Poe written a story like that? 'The Mask of the Red Death'? Something like that. But that plague had gotten into the party, hadn't it? The President rubbed his face. *Sleep. Have to sleep. Thinking crazy shit.* It was like flashbulbs. Your mind got tired and random thoughts blinked into your mind for no apparent reason, and then you had to fight them back, and get your mind going on the important stuff.

The usual Chevy Suburbans were there, but not the presidential limo. Ryan would ride in the obviously armored vehicle. There were cops around, too, looking grim. Well, everybody else did, too. Why not them?

He, too, was wearing a mask, and there were three TV cameras to record the fact. Maybe it was going out live. He didn't know, and scarcely looked at the cameras on the short walk to the cars. They started moving almost at once, up Fort Avenue, then north onto Key Highway. It was ten fast minutes over vacated city streets, heading toward Johns Hopkins, where the President and First Lady would show how concerned they were for other cameras. A leadership function, Arnie had told him, picking a phrase he was sure to recognize as something he had to respect whether he liked it or not. And the hell of it was, Arnie was right. He was the President, and he couldn't isolate himself from the people – whether he could do anything substantive to help them or not, they had to see him being concerned. It was something that did and didn't make sense, all at the same time.

The motorcade pulled into the Wolfe Street entrance. There were soldiers there, Guardsmen of the 175th Infantry Regiment, the Maryland Line. The local commander had decided that all hospitals had to be guarded, and Ryan supposed that was one of the things that did make sense. The Detail was nervous to have men around with loaded rifles, but they were soldiers, and that was that – disarming them might have made the news, after all. They all saluted, masked as they were in their MOPP gear, rifles slung over their shoulders. Nobody had threatened the hospital. Perhaps they were the reason why, or maybe it was just that people were scared. Enough that one cop had remarked to a Service agent that street crime had dropped to almost nil. Even the drug dealers were nowhere to be seen.

There were not very many people to be seen anywhere at this hour, but all of them were masked, and even the lobby was heavy with the chemical smell that was now the national scent. How much of that was a necessary physical measure, and how much psychological? Jack wondered. But, then, that's what his trip was.

'Hi, Dave,' the President said to the dean. He was wearing greens instead of his suit, masked like everyone else, and gloved, too. They didn't shake hands.

'Mr President, thank you for coming.' There were cameras in the lobby – they'd followed him in from outside. Before any of the reporters could shout a request for a statement, Jack pointed, and the dean led the party off. Ryan supposed it would look businesslike. Secret Service agents hustled to get ahead as they walked from the elevator bank to the medical floor. The doors slid open to reveal a busy corridor. Here there was bustle and people.

'What's the score, Dave?'

'We have thirty-four patients admitted here. Total for the area is one hundred forty – well, was the last time I checked. We have all the space we need for now, and all the staff, too. We've released about half of our patients, the ones we could sign out safely. All elective procedures are canceled for now, but there is the usual activity. I mean, babies are being born. People get sick from the normal diseases. Some outpatient treatments have to be continued, epidemic or not.'

'Where's Cathy?' Ryan asked, as the next elevator arrived with a single camera whose tape would be pooled with all the networks. The hospital didn't want or need to be crowded with extraneous people, and while media management people had made a little noise, their field personnel weren't all that eager, either. Maybe it was the antiseptic smell. Maybe it affected people the same way it affected dogs taken to the vet. It was the smell of danger for everyone.

'This way. Let's get you suited up.' The floor had a doctors' lounge, and one for nurses. Both were being used. The one at the far end was 'hot,' used for disrobing and decontamination. The near one was supposed to be safe, used for suiting up. There wasn't time or space for all the niceties. The Secret Service agents went in first and saw a woman in bra and panties, picking a plastic suit that was her size. She didn't blush. It was her fourth shift on the unit, and she was beyond that.

'Hang your clothes over there.' She pointed. 'Oh!' she added, recognizing the President.

'Thank you,' Ryan said, taking his shoes off and taking a clothes hanger from Andrea. Price examined the woman briefly. Clearly she wasn't carrying a weapon. 'How is it?' Jack asked.

She was the charge nurse for the floor. She didn't turn to answer. 'Pretty bad.' She paused for a second and then decided she had to turn. 'We appreciate the fact that your wife is up here with us.'

'I tried to talk her out of it,' he admitted to her. He didn't feel the least bit guilty about it, either, and wondered if he should or not.

'So'd my husband.' She came over. 'Here, the helmet goes on like this.' Ryan experienced a brief moment of panic. It was a most unnatural act to put a plastic bag over one's head. The nurse read his face. 'Me, too. You get used to it.'

Across the room, Dean James was already in his. He also came over to check the President's protective gear.

'Can you hear me?'

'Yeah.' Jack was sweating now, despite the portable air-conditioning pack that hooked on his belt.

The dean turned to the Secret Service personnel. 'From here on, I'm the boss,' he told them. 'I won't let him get into any danger, but we don't have enough suits for you people. If you stay in the corridors, you'll be safe. Don't touch anything. Not the walls, not the floors, nothing. Somebody goes past you with a cart, get out of the way. If you can't get out of the way, walk to the end of the corridor. If you see any kind of plastic container, stay clear of it. Do you understand?'

'Yes, sir.' For once, Andrea Price was cowed, POTUS saw. As was he. The psychological impact of this was horrific. Dr James tapped the President on the shoulder.

'Follow me. I know it's scary, but you are safe in this thing. We all had to get used to it, too, didn't we, Tisha?'

The nurse turned, now fully in hers. 'Yes, Doctor.'

You could hear your breathing. There was the whir of the A/C pack, but everything else was muted. Ryan felt a frightening sense of confinement as he walked behind the dean.

'Cathy's in here.' He opened the door. Ryan entered.

It was a child, a boy, aged eight or so, Jack saw. Two blue-clad figures were ministering to him. From behind he couldn't tell which one was his wife. Dr James held his hand up, forbidding Ryan from taking another step. One of the two was trying to restart an IV, and there couldn't be any distractions. The child was moaning, writhing on the bed. Ryan couldn't see much of him, but he saw enough for his stomach to turn.

'Hold still now. This will make you feel better.' It was Cathy's voice; evidently she was doing the stick. The other two hands were holding the arm in place. '. . . there. Tape,' she added, lifting her hands.

'Good stick, Doctor.'

'Thank you.' Cathy went to the electronic box that controlled the morphine and pushed in the right numbers, checking to be sure that the machine started functioning properly. With that done, she turned. 'Oh.'

'Hi, honey.'

'Jack, you don't belong here,' Surgeon told him firmly.

'Who does?'

'Okay, I have a line on this Dr MacGregor,' the station chief told them, driving his red Chevy. His name was Frank Clayton, a graduate of Grambling, whom Clark had seen through the Farm some years earlier.

'Then let's go see him, Frank.' Clark checked his watch, did the calculations, and decided that it was two hours after midnight. He grunted. Yeah, that was about right. First stop was the embassy, where they changed clothes. American military uniforms weren't all that welcome here. In fact, the station chief warned, few things American were. Chavez noted that a car followed them in from the airport.

'Don't sweat it. We'll lose him at the embassy. You know, sometimes I wonder if it wasn't a good deal when my folks got kidnapped out of Africa. Don't tell anybody I said that, okay? South Alabama is like heaven on earth compared to this shithole.'

He parked the car in the embassy's back lot and took them inside. A minute later one of his people walked out, started the Chevy, and headed right back out. The tail car went with him.

'Shirts,' the CIA resident officer said, handing them over. 'I suppose you can leave the pants on.'

'Have you talked to MacGregor?' Clark asked.

'On the phone a few hours ago. We're going to drive over to where he lives, and he's going to get into the car. I have a nice quiet parking spot picked out for our chat,' Clayton told them.

'Any danger to him?'

'I doubt it. The locals are pretty sloppy. If we have anybody tailing us, I know what to do about it.'

'Then let's move, buddy,' John said. 'We're burning moonlight.'

MacGregor's quarters weren't all that bad, located in a district favored by Europeans, and, the station chief related, fairly secure. He lifted his cellular phone and dialed the doctor's beeper number – there was a local paging service. Less than a minute later his door opened, and a figure walked to the car, got in the back, and closed the door a second before it moved off.

'This is rather unusual for me.' He was younger than Chavez, John was surprised to note, and eager in rather a shy way. 'Who exactly are you chaps?'

'CIA,' Clark told him.

'Indeed!'

'Indeed, Doctor,' Clayton said from the front seat. His eyes checked the mirrors. They were clear. Just to make sure, he took the next left, then a right, and then another left. Good.

'Are you allowed to tell people that?' MacGregor asked as the car pulled back onto what passed locally as the main drag. 'Do you have to kill me now?'

'Doc, save that for the movies, okay?' Chavez suggested. 'Real life ain't like that, and if we told you we were from the State Department, you wouldn't believe us anyway, right?'

'You don't look like diplomats,' MacGregor decided.

Clark turned in the front seat. 'Sir, thank you for agreeing to meet with us.'

'The only reason I did so – well, the local government forced me to disregard normal procedures for my two cases. There's a reason for those procedures, you know.'

'Okay, first of all, could you please tell me all you can about them?' John asked, switching on the tape recorder.

'You look tired, Cathy.' Not that it was all that easy to tell through the plastic mask. Even her body language was disguised.

SURGEON looked over to the wall clock behind the nursing

station. She was technically off duty now. She would never learn that Arnie van Damm had called the hospital to make sure the timing went right for this. It would have enraged her, and she was mad enough at the whole world already.

'The kids started arriving this afternoon. Second-generation cases. That one in there must have got it from his father. His name is Timothy. He's in the third grade. His dad's on the next floor up.'

'Rest of the family?'

'His mom tested positive. They're admitting her now. He has a big sister. She's clean so far. We have her sitting over in the outpatient building. They set up a holding area there for people who've been exposed but don't test out. Come on. I'll show you around the floor.' A minute later they were in Room 1, temporary home of the Index Case.

Ryan thought he must be imagining the smell. There was a dark stain on the bedclothes which two people – nurses, doctors, he couldn't tell – were struggling to change. The man was semiconscious, and fighting the restraints that held his arms to the bed bars. That had the two medics concerned, but they had to change the sheets first. Those went into a plastic bag.

'They'll get burned,' Cathy said, pressing her helmet against her husband's. 'We've really dialed up the safety precautions.'

'How bad?'

She pointed back to the door and followed Jack into the corridor. Once there, with the door closed behind them, she poked an angry finger into his chest. 'Jack, you never, *ever* discuss a patient's prognosis in front of them, unless you know it's good. *Never!*' She paused, and went on without an apology for the outburst: 'He's three days into frank symptoms.'

'Any chance?'

Her head shook inside the helmet. They walked back up the corridor, stopping in some more rooms where the story was dismally the same.

'Cathy?' It was the dean's voice. 'You're off duty. Move,' he commanded.

'Where's Alexandre?' Jack asked on the way to the former physicians' lounge.

'He's got the floor upstairs. Dave has taken this one himself. We hoped Ralph Forster would get back and help out, but there aren't any flights.' Then she saw the cameras. 'What the hell are *they* doing here?'

'Come on.' Ryan led his wife into the changing room. The clothing he'd worn to the hospital was bagged somewhere. He put on scrubs, in front of three women and a man who didn't seem all that interested in ogling any of the females. Leaving the room, he headed for the elevator.

'Stop!' a female voice called. 'There's a case coming up from ER! Use the stairs.' And obediently, the Secret Service Detail did just that. Ryan led his wife down to the main floor, and from there out front, still wearing masks.

'How are you holding up?'

Before she could answer, a voice screamed, '*Mr President!*' Two Guardsmen got in the way of the reporter and cameraman, but Ryan waved them off. The pair approached under armed scrutiny, uniformed and plainclothes.

'Yes, what is it?' Ryan asked, pulling his mask down. The reporter held the microphone at full arm's length. It would have been comical under other circumstances. Everybody was spooked.

'What are you doing here, sir?'

'Well, I guess it's part of my job to see what's going on, and also I wanted to see how Cathy is doing.'

'We know the First Lady is working upstairs. Are you trying to make a statement to the nation –'

'I'm a *doctor*!' Cathy snapped. 'We're all taking turns up there. It's my job.'

'Is it bad?'

Ryan spoke before she could explode at them. 'Look, I know you have to ask that question, but you know the answer. These people are extremely ill, and the docs here, and everyplace else, are doing their best. It's hard on Cathy and her colleagues. It's really hard on the patients and their families.'

'Dr Ryan, is Ebola really as deadly as everyone has been saying?'

She nodded. 'It's pretty awful, yes. But we're giving these people the best we got.'

'Some have suggested that since the hope for the patients is so bleak, and since their pain is so extreme –'

'What are you saying? Kill them?'

'Well, if they're really suffering as much as everyone reports –'

'I'm not that kind of doctor,' she replied, her face flushed. 'We're going to save some of these people. From those we save, maybe we can learn to save more, and you don't learn *anything* by giving up. That's why real doctors don't kill patients! What is the matter with you? Those are *people* in there, and my job is fighting for their lives – and don't you dare tell me how to do it!' She stopped when her husband's arm squeezed her shoulder. 'Sorry. It's a little tough in there.'

'Could you excuse us for a few minutes?' Ryan asked. 'We haven't talked since yesterday. You know, we are husband and wife, just like real people.'

'Yes, sir.' They pulled back, but the camera stayed on them.

'Come here, babe.' Jack embraced her for the first time in more than a day.

'We're going to lose them all, Jack. Every one, starting tomorrow or the next day,' she whispered. Then she started crying.

'Yeah.' He lowered his head on hers. 'You know, you're allowed to be human, too, Doctor.'

'How do they think we learned anything? Oh, we can't fix it, so let 'em all die with dignity. Give up. That's not what they taught me here.'

'I know.'

She sniffed and wiped her eyes on his shirt. 'Okay, back under control now. I'm off duty for eight hours.'

'Where are you sleeping?'

A deep breath. A shudder. 'Maumenee. They have some cots set up. Bernie's up in New York, helping out at Columbia. They have a couple hundred cases there.'

'You're pretty tough, Doctor.' He smiled down at his wife.

'Jack, if you find out who did this to us . . .'

'Working on it,' POTUS said.

'Know any of these people?' The station chief handed over some photos he'd shot himself. He handed over a flashlight, too.

'That's Saleh! Who was he, exactly? He didn't say and I never found out.'

'These are all Iraqis. When the government came down, they flew here. I have a bunch of photos. You're sure of this one?'

'Quite sure, I treated him for over a week. The poor chap died.' MacGregor went through some more. 'And that looks like Sohaila. She survived, thank God. Lovely child – and that's her father.'

'What the hell?' Chavez asked. 'Nobody told us that.'

'We were at the Farm then, weren't we?'

'Back to being a training officer, John?' Frank Clayton grinned. 'Well, I got the word, and so I went out to shoot the pictures. They came in first class, by God, a big ol' G. Here, see?'

Clark looked at it and grunted – it was almost a twin to the one they were using for their round-the-world jaunt. 'Nice shots.'

'Thank you, sir.'

'Let me see that.' Chavez took the photo. He held the light right up against it. '*Ninja*,' he whispered. 'Fucking *ninja* . . .'

'What?'

'John, read those letters off the tail,' Ding said quietly.

'HX-NJA. . . my God.'

'Clayton,' Chavez said, 'is that cellular phone secure?'

The station chief turned it on and punched in three digits. 'It is now. Where do you want to call?'

'Langley.'

'Mr President, can we talk to you now?'

Jack nodded. 'Yeah, sure, come on.' He needed to walk some, and waved for them to follow. 'Maybe I should apologize for Cathy. She's not like that. She's a good doc,' Swordsman said tiredly. 'They're all pretty stressed out up there. The first thing they teach 'em here, I think it goes *primum non nocere*, "First of all, do no harm." It's a pretty good rule. Anyway, my wife's had a couple of hard days in there. But so have all of us.'

'It is possible that this was a deliberate act, sir?'

'We're not sure, and I can't talk about that until I have good information one way or the other.'

'You've had a busy time, Mr President.' The reporter was local, not part of the Washington scene. He didn't know how to talk to a President, or so others might think. Regardless, this one was going out live on NBC, though even the reporter didn't know that.

'Yeah, I guess I have.'

'Sir, can you give us any hope?'

Ryan turned at that. 'For the people who're sick, well, the hope comes from the docs and the nurses. They're fine people. You can see that here. They're fighters, warriors. I'm very proud of my wife and what she does. I'm proud of her now. I asked her not to do this. I suppose that's selfish of me, but I said it anyway. Some people tried to kill her once before, you know. I don't mind danger to me, but my wife and kids, no, it's not supposed to happen to them. Not supposed to happen to any of these people. But it did, and now we have to do our best to treat the sick ones and make sure people don't get sick unnecessarily. I know my executive order has upset a lot of people, but I can't live with not doing something that might save lives. I wish there were an easier way, but if there is, nobody's told me about it yet. You see, it's not enough to say, "No, I don't like that." Anybody can do that. We need more right now. Look, I'm pretty tired,' he said, looking away from the camera. 'Can we call it a day for now?'

'Yes, sir. Thank you, Mr President.'

'Sure.' Ryan turned away, walking south, just wandering really, toward the big parking garages. He saw a man smoking a cigarette there, a black man about forty, in defiance of the signs that prohibited the vice within sight of this shrine of medical learning. POTUS walked up to him, heedless of the three agents and two soldiers behind him.

'Got a spare?'

'Sure.' The man didn't even look up as he sat on the edge of the brick planter, looking down at the concrete. His left hand held out the pack and a butane lighter at arm's length. By unspoken consent they didn't sit close together.

'Thanks.' Ryan sat down about four feet away from the man, reaching to hand the items back.

'You, too, man?'

'What do you mean?'

'My wife's in there, got the sickness. She work with a family, nanny, like. They're all sick. Now she is, too.'

'My wife's a doc, she's up there with 'em.'

'Ain't gonna matter, man. Ain't gonna matter at all.'

'I know.' Ryan took a long pull and let it out.

'Won't even let me in, say it too dangerous. Takin' *my* blood, say I gotta stay close, won't let me smoke, won't let me see her. Sweet Jesus, man, how come?'

'If it was you who was sick, and you knew that you might give it to your wife, what would you do?'

He nodded with angry resignation. 'I know. The doctor said that. He's right. I know. But that don't *make* it right.' He paused. 'Helps to talk.'

'Yeah, I guess it does.'

'The fuckers did this, like they say on TV, somebody did this. Fuckers gotta pay, man.'

Ryan didn't know what to say then. Somebody else did. It was Andrea Price:

'Mr President? I have the DCI for you.'

That turned the man's head. He looked at Ryan in the yellow-orange lighting. 'You're him.'

'Yes, sir,' Jack answered quietly.

'You say your wife is workin' up there?'

A nod. A sigh. 'Yeah, she's been working here for fifteen years. I came in to see her, and see how it is, how it's going. I'm sorry . . .'

'What'd'ya mean?'

'They won't let you in, but they let me in.'

He grimaced. 'Guess you gotta see, eh? Tough what happened with your little girl last week. She okay?'

'Yeah, she's fine. At that age, well, you know how it is.'

'Good. Hey, thanks for talking with me.'

'Thanks for the smoke,' the President said, standing and walking to Agent Price. He took the phone. 'Ed, it's Jack.'

'Mr President, we need you back. We have something you need to see,' Ed Foley told him. He wondered how he would explain that the evidence was hanging on the wall of a conference room in CIA Headquarters.

'Give me an hour, Ed.'

'Yes, sir. We're getting it organized now.'

Jack hit the END switch on the phone and handed it back. 'Let's move.'

53

SNIE

Before flying home, everyone had to be decontaminated. Hopkins had set up a large room with separation of the sexes this time. The water was hot, and stank of chemicals, but the smell gave Ryan a needed sense of safety. Then he donned a new set of greens. He'd worn them before, when he'd attended the births of his children. Happy connotations. No longer, he thought, as he headed for the Suburban for the drive back to Fort McHenry and the helicopter hop back to the White House. At least the shower had enlivened him. It might even last a few hours, POTUS thought, as the VH-3 lifted off and turned southwest. If he were lucky.

It was the most lackluster performance in the history of the National Training Center. The troopers of the 11th Cav and the tankers of the Carolina Guard had blundered about for five hours, barely executing the plans that both had set up. The replay in the Star Wars Room showed cases where tanks had been less than a thousand meters apart and in plain sight, yet hadn't exchanged fire. Nothing had worked on either side, and the simulated engagement had not so much ended as stopped by apathetic consent. Just before midnight, the units formed up for the drive back to their respective laagers, and the senior commanders went to General Diggs's home on the hill.

'Hi, Nick,' Colonel Hamm said.

'Hi, Al,' Colonel Eddington replied, in about the same tone of voice.

'And what the hell was that all about?' Diggs demanded.

'The men are coming a little unglued, sir,' the Guardsman replied first. 'We're all worried about our people back home. We're safe here. They're in danger there. I can't blame them for being distracted, General. They're human.'

'Best thing I can say is that our immediate families seem

to be safe here, General,' Hamm agreed with his older comrade in arms. 'But we all got family back in the world.'

'Okay, gentlemen, we've all had a chance to cry in our beer. I don't like this shit, either, y'hear? But *your* job is to lead your people, and that means *lead*, God damn it! In case you two warrior chiefs haven't noticed yet, the whole fuckin' United States Army is tied up in this epidemic – *except us!* You two colonels want to think about that? Maybe get your people thinking about it? Nobody ever told me soldiering was an easy job, and damned sure command isn't, but it is the job we do, and if you gentlemen can't get it done, well, there are others who can.'

'Sir, that isn't going to work. Ain't nobody to relieve us with,' Hamm pointed out wryly.

'Colonel –'

'The man's right, Diggs,' Eddington said. 'Some things are too much. There's an enemy out there we can't fight. Our people'll come around once they have a chance to get used to it, maybe get some good news for a change. Come on, General, you know better. You know history. Those are people out there – yes, soldiers, but people first. They're shook. So am I, Diggs.'

'I also know that there are no bad regiments, only bad colonels,' Diggs retorted, with one of Napoleon's best aphorisms, but he saw that neither man rose to the bait. Jesus, this really was bad.

'How was it?' van Damm asked.

'Horrible,' Ryan replied. 'I saw six or seven people who're going to die. One of 'em's a kid. Cathy says there'll be more of them showing up.'

'How's she doing?'

'Pretty stressed, but okay. She really let a reporter have it.'

'I know, it was on TV,' the chief of staff informed him.

'Already?'

'You were on live.' Arnie managed a smile. 'You looked great. Concerned. Sincere as hell. You said nice things about your wife. You even apologized for what she said – really good, boss, especially since she looked wonderful. Dedicated. Intense. Just like a doctor is supposed to be.'

'Arnie, this isn't theater.' Ryan was too tired to be angry.

The reviving effects of the shower, disappointingly, had already worn off.

'No, it's leadership. Someday you're going to learn that – shit, maybe not. Just keep goin' like you're goin',' Arnie advised. 'You do it without even knowing it, Jack. Don't think about it at all.'

NBC shared their tape with the whole world. As competitive as the news business was, a consciousness of public responsibility *did* pervade the profession, and the tape of the President's brief conversation went out an hour later on television sets across the globe.

She'd been right from the first instant, the Prime Minister told herself. He was far out of his depth. He couldn't even stand up straight. His words rambled. He let his wife speak for him – and she was frantic, emotional, weak. America's time as a major power was ending, because the country lacked firm leadership. She didn't *know* who had caused this plague to happen, but it was easy to guess. It had to be the UIR. Why else had he called them together in western China? With her fleet at sea guarding the approaches to the Persian Gulf, she was doing her part. She was sure she would be rewarded for it in due course.

'Your President is distracted,' Zhang said. 'Understandably so.'

'Such a great misfortune. You have our deepest sympathy,' the Foreign Minister added. The three, plus the translator, had also just seen the tape.

Adler had been slow in getting the news of the epidemic, but he was up to speed now. He had to set it all aside, however. 'Shall we proceed?'

'Does our distant province agree to our compensation demand?' the Foreign Minister asked.

'Unfortunately not. They take the position that the entire incident results from your extended maneuvers. Viewed abstractly, that point of view is not entirely without merit,' the Secretary of State told them in diplo-speak.

'But the situation is not abstract. We are conducting peaceful exercises. One of their pilots saw fit to attack our aircraft, and in the process another of their foolish aviators destroyed an airliner. Who is to say if it was an accident or not?'

'Not an accident?' Adler asked. 'What possible purpose could there be for such a thing?'

'Who can say with these bandits?' the Foreign Minister asked in return, stirring the pot a little more.

Ed and Mary Pat Foley came in together. Ed was carrying a large rolled poster or something, Jack saw as he sat in the Cabinet Room, still wearing greens with HOPKINS stenciled on them. Next came Murray, with Inspector O'Day in his wake. Ryan stood to go to him.

'I owe you, sorry I didn't get to see you sooner.' He took the man's hand.

'That was pretty easy compared to this,' Pat said. 'And my little girl was there, too. But, yeah, glad I was there. I won't have any nightmares about that shoot.' He turned. 'Oh, hi, Andrea.'

Price smiled for the first time that day. 'How's your daughter, Pat?'

'Home with the sitter. They're both okay,' he assured her.

'Mr President?' It was Goodley. 'This is pretty hot.'

'Okay, then shall we get to work? Who starts?'

'I do,' the DCI said. He slid a sheet of paper across the table. 'Here.'

Ryan took it and scanned it. It was some sort of official form, and the words were all in French. 'What's this?'

'It's the immigration and customs clearance form for an airplane. Check the ID box, top-left corner.'

'HX-NJA. Okay, so?' SWORDSMAN asked. His chief of staff sat at his side, keeping his peace. He felt the tension that the executives had brought into the room.

The blowup of Chavez's photo at Mehrabad Airport was actually larger than a poster, and had been printed up mainly as a joke. Mary Pat unrolled it, and laid it flat on the table. Two briefcases were used to keep it from rolling back up. 'Check the tail,' the DDO advised.

'HX-NJA. I don't have time for Agatha Christie, people,' the President warned them.

'Mr President.' This was Dan Murray. 'Let me walk you through this, but I'll say up front, that photo is something I could take into court and get a conviction with.

'The customs form identifies a business jet, a Gulfstream G-IV belonging to this Swiss-based corporation.' A piece of paper went down on the conference table. 'Flown by this flight crew.' Two photos and fingerprint cards. 'It left Zaire with three passengers. Two were nuns, Sister Jean Baptiste and Sister Maria Magdalena. They were both nurses at a Catholic hospital down there. Sister Jean treated Benedict Mkusa, a little boy who contracted Ebola and died of it. Somehow, Sister Jean caught it, too, and the third passenger, Dr Mohammed Moudi – we don't have a photo of him yet; we're working on it – decided to fly the sick one to Paris for treatment. Sister Maria tagged along, too. Dr Moudi is an Iranian national working with the WHO. He told the boss-nun that she might have a chance there and said that he could whistle up a private jet to get her there. With me so far?'

'And this is the jet.'

'Correct, Mr President. This is the jet. Except for one thing. This jet supposedly crashed into the sea after taking off after a refueling stop in Libya. We have a ton of paperwork about that. Except for one thing.' He tapped the poster again. 'That photo was taken by Domingo Chavez –'

'You know him,' Mary Pat put in.

'Go on. When did Ding shoot the frame?'

'Clark and Chavez accompanied Secretary Adler to Tehran, just last week.'

'The aircraft was reported lost some time before that. It was even tracked by one of our destroyers when it squawked emergency. No trace was ever found, however,' Murray went on. 'Ed?'

'When Iraq came apart, Iran allowed the senior military leadership to skip. They all had golden parachutes. Our friend Daryaei let them jump out of the airplane. He *even* provided transport, all right? This started the day after the jet disappeared,' Foley told them. 'They were flown to Khartoum, in the Sudan. Our station chief there is Frank Clayton, and he drove to the airport and shot these pictures to confirm our intelligence information.' The DCI slid them across.

'Looks like the same airplane, but what if somebody just played with the numbers – letters, whatever?' Ryan asked.

'Next indicator,' Murray said. 'There were two Ebola cases in Khartoum.'

'Clark and Chavez talked to the attending physician a few hours ago,' Mary Pat added.

'Both the patients flew on this airplane. We have photos of them getting off. So,' the FBI Director said, 'now, we have an airplane with a sick person aboard. The airplane disappears – *but* it turns up less than twenty-four hours later somewhere else, and two of the passengers come down with the same illness that the nun had. The passengers came from Iraq, via Iran, to the Sudan.'

'Who owns the airplane?' Arnie asked.

'It's a corporation. We should have further details in a few hours from the Swiss. But the flight crew is Iranian. We have info on them because they learned how to fly over here,' Murray explained. 'And, finally, we have our friend Daryaei here on the same airplane. Looks like it's been taken out of international service. Maybe Daryaei is using it to hop around his new country now. So, Mr President, we have the disease, the airplane, and the owner, all tied up. Tomorrow we'll work with Gulfstream to see if the aircraft has any unique characteristics that we can identify in addition to the registration code. We'll have the Swiss pull info on the ownership and the flight logs for the rest of their fleet.

'We now know who did this, sir,' Murray concluded. 'This chain of evidence is hard to beat.'

'There are more details to flesh out,' Mary Pat said. 'Background on this Dr Moudi. Tracking down some monkey shipments – they use monkeys to study the disease. How they staged the faked airplane crash – you believe it? The bastards even made an insurance claim.'

'We're going to suspend this meeting for a moment. Andrea?'

'Yes, Mr President.'

'Get Secretary Bretano and Admiral Jackson in here.'

'Yes, sir.' She left the room.

Ed Foley waited for the door to close behind her. 'Uh, Mr President?'

'Yeah, Ed?'

'There is one other thing. I haven't even told Dan this yet. We now know that the UIR – really, our friend Mahmoud

Haji Daryaei – is behind this. Chavez brought something up before we sent him and John off. The other side could well expect us to trace this back to them. Operational security for something like this is almost impossible to achieve.'

'So?'

'So, two things, Jack. First, whatever they're planning, they may think it's irreversible, and therefore it doesn't matter whether we figure this out or not. Second, let's remember how they knocked off Iraq. They got somebody all the way inside.'

Those were two very big thoughts. Ryan started pondering the first one. Dan Murray's head turned to his roving inspector and they traded looks on the second.

'Christ, Ed,' the FBI Director said a moment later.

'Think it through, Dan,' the DCI said. 'We have a President. We have a Senate. We have a third of the House. We do not have a Vice President yet. The presidential succession is still dicey, no really powerful figures, and the top level of the government is still gutted. Toss in this epidemic, which has the whole country tied up in knots. To almost anybody outside, we look weak and vulnerable.'

Ryan looked up as Andrea came back in. 'Wait a minute. They made a play for Katie. Why do that if they want me out of the way?'

'What's this?' Price asked.

'The other side has demonstrated a frightening capability. One,' Foley said, 'they got all the way into the Iraqi President's security detail and blew him away. Two, the operation last week was run by a sleeper agent who's been here more than a decade, and in that time did nothing at all, but when he woke up, he cared enough to assist in an attempt on a child.'

Murray had to agree with that: 'That's occurred to us, too. The Intelligence Division is thinking about it right now.'

'Wait a minute,' Andrea objected. 'I know every person on the Detail. For God's sake, we lost five of them defending SANDBOX!'

'Agent Price,' Mary Pat Foley said. 'You know how many times CIA's been burned by people we knew all about – people I knew. Hell, I lost three agents to one of those fucking moles. I *knew* them, and I *knew* the guy who shopped 'em.

Don't tell me about paranoia. We are up against a very capable enemy here. And it only takes one.'

Murray whistled as the argument took its full form. His mind had been racing for the past few hours in one direction. Now it had to race in another.

'Mrs Foley, I –'

'Andrea,' Inspector O'Day said, 'this isn't personal. Take a step back and think about it. If you had the resources of a nation-state, if you were patient, and if you had people who were really motivated, how would you do it?'

'How did they do Iraq?' Ed Foley took up the argument. 'Would you have thought that was possible?'

The President looked around the room. *Fabulous, now they're telling me not to trust the Secret Service.*

'It all makes sense if you think like the other guy,' Mary Pat told them. 'It's part of their tradition, remember?'

'Okay, but what do we do about it?' Andrea asked, her face openly stunned at the possibility.

'Pat, you have a new assignment,' Murray told his subordinate. 'With the President's permission, that is.'

'Granted,' POTUS breathed.

'Rules?' O'Day wanted to know.

'None, none at all,' Price told him.

It was approaching noon over the United Islamic Republic. Maintenance was going well on the six heavy divisions based in the south-central part of the country. Nearly all the tracks on the mechanized fighting vehicles had been replaced. A healthy spirit of competition had developed between the former Iraqi divisions and those moved down from Iran. With their vehicles restored to full fighting order, the troopers drew ammunition to bring all of the T-80 tanks and BMP infantry carriers to full basic loads.

The battalion commanders looked over the results of their training exercise with satisfaction. Their newly acquired GPS locators had been like magic, and now the Iraqis understood one of the reasons why the Americans had treated them so harshly in 1991. With GPS one didn't need roads at all. The Arabic culture had long termed the desert a sea, and now they could navigate on it like sailors, moving from point to point with a confidence they had never known before.

Corps and divisional staff officers knew why this was so important. They had just been issued new maps, and with them a new mission. They also learned that their three-corps mechanized force had a name, the Army of God. By tomorrow, sub-unit commanders would be briefed in on that, and many other things.

It took an hour for them to get in. Admiral Jackson had been sleeping in his office, but Secretary Bretano had gone home after a marathon session of reviewing deployments within the country. The White House dress code had been relaxed, they saw. The President, also red-eyed, was wearing doctor clothes.

Dan Murray and Ed Foley repeated their brief.

Jackson took it well: 'All right. Now we know what we're up against.'

Bretano did not: 'This is an overt act of war.'

'But we're not the objective,' the DCI told him. 'It's Saudi Arabia, and all the other Gulf states. It's the only thing that makes sense. He figures that if he takes over those states, we *can't* nuke him – it would turn off the oil for the whole world.' The DCI almost had it right, but not quite.

'And he has India and China in his pocket,' Robby Jackson went on. 'They're just running interference, but it's good interference. *Ike*'s in the wrong place. The Indians have their carriers blocking the Straits of Hormuz. We can't get the MPS ships in without air cover. Zap, he moved those three corps down. The Saudis'll fight, but they're outmanned. It's over in a week, maybe less. Not a bad operational concept,' the J-3 concluded.

'The bio-attack's pretty clever, too. I think they got more than they bargained for. Almost every base and unit we have is out of business at the moment,' SecDef observed, catching up fast on the operational side.

'Mr President, when I was a boy in Mississippi, I remember the Klukkers used to say, when you see a mad dog, don't kill the poor thing – toss it in somebody's backyard. You know, some sheet-head actually did that to us once, 'cause my pap was real big on getting people registered to vote.'

'What did you do, Rob?'

'Pap blew it away with his Fox double,' Admiral Jackson

replied. 'And continued the mission. We have to move fast if we're going to move. Problem is, what with?'

'How long before the MPS ships get to Saudi?'

'Just under three days, but there's somebody in the way. CinCLant's cut orders for that surface group to scoot down the Suez, and they can be at the strait in time, but we gotta get those tank-carriers past the Indians first. Those four boats are escorted by one cruiser, two 'cans, and two frigates, and if we lose them, nearest equipment resupply's in Savannah, sir.'

'What do we have in storage in Saudi?' Ben Goodley asked.

'Enough for a heavy brigade. Same in Kuwait. The third brigade-set is afloat and standing in harm's way.'

'Kuwait's first in line,' the President said. 'What can we get there?'

'If we're balls-to-the-wall, we can fly the 10th ACR out of Israel to mate up with the POMCUS site south of Kuwait City. That we can do in twenty-four hours. The Kuwaitis'll handle transport. They have a quiet understanding with Israel on that. We helped broker it,' Robby said. 'The plan's called Buffalo Forward.'

'Anybody think that's a bad idea?' Jack asked.

'One armored cavalry regiment – I don't think it's enough to deter them, sir,' Goodley said.

'The man's right,' the J-3 agreed.

Ryan looked around the table. Knowing was one thing. Being able to act was something else. He *could* order a strategic nuclear attack on Iran. He had B-2A stealth bombers at Whiteman Air Force Base, and with the information he'd been given in the past two hours, getting CinC-Strike to validate the order under the two-man rule would not be a problem. The 'Spirits,' as the B-2s were called, could be there in less than eighteen hours, and turn that nation into a smoking, poisoned ruin.

But he couldn't do that. Even if he had to, he probably couldn't. Though American Presidents had long been faced with the necessity of telling the world that, yes, we *will* launch our missiles and bombers if we have to, it was a duty Ryan never expected to carry out. Even this attack on his country, the use of weapons of mass destruction – to America the equivalent of nuclear arms – had been the decision of one man, and carried out by a relative handful. Could he flatten whole cities in response, kill the innocent as Daryaei had done, because the other guy had done it first? And live with himself afterward? There had to be something better, some other option. Killing Daryaei was one.

'Ed?'

'Yes, Mr President?'

'Where are Clark and Chavez right now?'

'Khartoum, still, awaiting instructions.'

'Think they can get into Tehran again?'

'Won't be easy, sir.' He turned to his wife.

'The Russians have helped us in the past. I can ask. What would their mission be?'

'Find out if they can get in first. We'll figure out the mission in a little while. Robby?'

'Yes, Mr President?'

'The 10th Regiment moves to Kuwait at once.'

Jackson took a deep and skeptical breath. 'Aye aye, sir.'

There was the intermediary step of getting the approval of the Kuwaiti government. The Ambassador handled that. It did not prove to be hard. Major Sabah had kept his government informed of developments in their new neighbor to the north, and the satellite photos of the retracking of the UIR tanks turned the trick. With their own military fully activated, the Kuwait government telexed a formal request for America to commence an extended training exercise in the western part of their nation. This moved fast. The rulers of the small nation had fresh memories of earlier mistakes. Their only proviso was that the movement be made secretly, and America did not object. Within four hours, the plush, brand-new airliners of the national airline started lifting off, headed southwest over Saudi Arabia, and later turned north, up the Gulf of Aqaba.

The order was issued by Training and Doctrine Command, which administratively owned the 10th ACR, since it was technically a training establishment. Most other state-side units belonged to Forces Command, FORCE COM. The emergency-deployment order went by CRITIC-priority to Colonel Sean Magruder. He had roughly five thousand personnel to move, and that would require twenty jumbo flights. The roundabout routing made for a distance of 1,300 miles and three hours in each direction, with an hour's turnaround time at both ends. But it had all been thought through, and the diminution of international air travel had made more aircraft available than the plan had anticipated for BUFFALO FORWARD. Even the Israelis cooperated. The pilots of the Kuwaiti jumbos had the singular experience of seeing F-15 fighters with blue Star of David markings flying escort as they came into the big Israeli air base in the Negev.

The first group out comprised senior officers and a security group to supplement the Kuwaiti guard force at the POMCUS site. The site was a group of warehouses containing the complete equipment set of a heavy brigade, which was exactly what the armored cavalry regiment was. The equipment was lovingly maintained by contractors, who were well paid by their Kuwaiti hosts.

The second aircraft had A-Troop, 1st of the 10th. Buses took them through the late-afternoon sun to their vehicles, which in every case started up at once, fully loaded with fuel and ammunition. A troop of the 1st 'Guidon' Squadron rolled out under the watchful eyes of their squadron CO, Lieutenant Colonel Duke Masterman. He had family in the Philadelphia area, and he could add two and two together. Something very bad was happening in his country, and out of a clear sky BUFFALO FORWARD had been activated. That was fine with him, he decided, and his troopers.

Magruder and his staff also watched. He'd even insisted that the command group bring the regimental standard. This was the Cav.

'Foleyeva, is it that bad?' Golovko asked, meaning the epidemic. They were speaking in Russian. Though his English was nearly perfect, the CIA official spoke his native language with a poetic elegance learned from her grandfather.

'We don't know, Sergey Nikolay'ch, and I have been looking at other things.'

'Ivan Emmetovich is bearing up?'

'What do you think? I know you saw the TV interview a few hours ago.'

'An interesting man, your President. So easy to underestimate. I did that once myself.'

'And Daryaei?'

'Formidable, but an uncultured barbarian.' Mary Pat could almost hear the man spit.

'Quite.'

'Tell Ivan Emmetovich to think the scenario through, Foleyeva,' Golovko suggested. 'Yes, we will cooperate,' he added, answering a question not yet asked. 'Fully.'

'*Spasiba*. I will be back to you.' Mary Pat looked over at her husband. 'You have to love the guy.'

'I wish he was on our side,' the DCI observed.

'He is, Ed.'

The dog had stopped barking, they noted in STORM TRACK. The three corps they were trying to observe had stopped using their radios around noon. Zero. As sophisticated as their computer-aided ELINT equipment was, nothing was still nothing. It was an obvious sign, and just as often overlooked. The direct lines to Washington burned constantly now. More Saudi officers were coming in, demonstrating the increased alert state of their own military, which was quietly deploying to the field around King Khalid Military City. That was some comfort to the intelligence people in the listening post, but not much. They were far closer to the mouth of the lion. Being spooks, they thought like spooks, and by consensus they decided that the events in America had somehow started here. Elsewhere, such thoughts engendered a feeling of helplessness; here they had a different effect. The rage was real, and they had a mission to fulfill, exposed position or not.

'Okay,' Jackson said on the conference line, 'who *can* we deploy?'

The answer was a brief silence. The Army was half the size it had been less than a decade before. There were two heavy divisions in Europe, V Corps, but they were quarantined by the Germans. The same was true of the two armored divisions at Fort Hood, Texas, and the 1st Infantry Division (Mechanized) at Fort Riley, Kansas. Parts of the 82nd at Fort Bragg and the 101st at Fort Campbell *were* deployed to support National Guard units, but the units that had been kept back at their bases had soldiers who'd tested positive for

Ebola. The same was true of the two stateside Marine divisions, based at Lejeune in North Carolina and Pendleton in California.

'Look,' FORCE COM said. 'We got the 11th ACR and a Guard brigade training up at the NTC. That base is totally clean, we can move them out as quick as you can whistle up the airplanes. The rest? Before we can move them, we have to sort everybody out. I don't dare move them before we've tested every soldier for this damned bug, and the kits ain't out everywhere yet.'

'He's right,' another voice said. Every head on the conference line nodded. The pharmaceutical companies were racing to produce them. Millions of test kits were needed, but only a few tens of thousands were available, and those were being used for targeted people, the ones who showed symptoms, relatives or close associates of known cases, truckers delivering food and medical supplies, and most of all, the medical personnel themselves, who were the most exposed to the virus. Worse still, one 'clear' reading wasn't enough. Some people would have to be tested daily for three days or more, because although the test was reliable, the immune systems of potential victims were not. The antibodies could start showing up an hour after a negative test reading. Doctors and hospitals throughout the country were screaming for the kits, and in this case the Army was sucking hind tit.

The UIR is going to throw a war, J-3 thought, *and nobody's going to come.* Robby wondered if some hippie from the sixties might find that amusing.

'How long on that?'

'End of the week, at best,' FORCE COM replied. 'I have an officer on it.'

'I got the 366th Wing at Mountain Home. They're all clean,' Air Combat Command reported. 'We have the F-16 wing in Israel. My European units are being held hostage, though, all of them.'

'Airplanes are nice, Paul,' FORCE COM said. 'So are ships, but we need soldiers over there in one big fucking hurry.'

'Cut warning orders to Fort Irwin,' Jackson said. 'I'll have the SecDef authorize their release within the hour.'

'Done.'

* * *

'Moscow?' Chavez asked. 'Jesu Cristo, we are getting around.'

'Ours is not to reason why.'

'Yeah, I know the second part, Mr C. If we're going to the right place, I'll take that chance.'

'Your carriage awaits, gents,' Clayton said. 'The blue suits are turning the airplane over for you.'

'Yeah, that reminds me.' Clark pulled the uniform shirt out of the closet. In a minute, he was a colonel again. Five minutes after that, they were off for the airport, soon to leave the Sudan to the ministrations of Frank Clayton and memories of 'Chinese' Gordon.

There was an aspect of schadenfreude about it. O'Day assembled a team of FBI agents to go over the personnel packets of every Secret Service agent who got close to the President, both the plainclothes and Uniformed Division officers. There were quite a few. Ordinarily some would have been tossed for obvious no-hit indicators – a name like O'Connor, for example – but this case was too important for that, and every file had to be examined in full before it could be set aside. This job he left to others. Another team was examining something not widely known. There was a computerized record of every telephone call made in the Washington, DC, metropolitan area. Legal in a strict sense, the program, had it extended farther afield, would have excited Big Brother-ish outrage from even the most extreme law-enforcement hawk, but the President lived in Washington, and America had lost Presidents there. It was almost too much to hope for. By definition, a conspirator in the Secret Service would be an expert on security measures. Their target, if there was one, would be one of the boys. He might stand out in professional excellence – you had to, in order to make the Detail – but nothing else. He'd fit in. He'd have a good service reputation. He'd tell jokes, bet on ballgames, have a beer at the local hangout – he'd be just like all the others who would willingly guard the life of the President as courageously as Don Russell had done, O'Day knew, and part of him hated the rest of him for having to treat them like suspects in a criminal investigation. It wasn't supposed to be this way. But then, what was?

* * *

Diggs called both colonels to his office to give them the news: 'We have warning orders to deploy overseas.'

'Who?' Eddington asked.

'Both of your units,' the general answered.

'Where to, sir?' Hamm asked next.

'Saudi. We've both been there and done that before, Al, and here's your chance, Colonel Eddington.'

'Why?' the Guardsman asked.

'They haven't said yet. I have background information coming into the fax machine now. All they told me over the phone was that the UIR is getting frisky. The 10th is mating up with their POMCUS gear right now –'

'BUFFALO FORWARD?' Hamm asked. 'No warning?'

'Correct, Al.'

'Is this related to the epidemic?' Eddington asked.

Diggs shook his head. 'Nobody's told me anything about that.'

It had to be done in Federal District Court in Baltimore. Edward J. Kealty filed a suit naming John Patrick Ryan as defendant. The substance of the complaint was that the former wanted to cross a state line, and the latter wouldn't let him. The filing asked for summary judgment, the vacating of the executive order of the President (strangely, the complaint named Ryan as President of the United States) immediately. Kealty figured that he'd win this one. The Constitution was on his side, and he'd chosen the judge with care.

The Special National Intelligence Estimate was now complete, and irrelevant. The intentions of the United Islamic Republic were totally clear. The trick now was to do something about them, but that was not, strictly speaking, an intelligence function.

54

FRIENDS AND NEIGHBORS

They didn't see it coming, and it did get their attention. By dawn the next day, all three ground squadrons of the 10th Cavalry were fully deployed, while the fourth squadron, composed of attack helicopters, needed one more day to get up to speed. Kuwaiti regular officers – their standing army was still relatively small, with the ranks fleshed out by enthusiastic reservists – greeted their American counterparts with waving swords and embraces in front of the cameras, and serious, quiet conversation in the command tents. For his part, Colonel Magruder arranged for one of his squadrons to assemble in parade formation with standards flying. It was good for everyone's morale, and the fifty-two tanks massed together looked like the fist of an angry god. The UIR intelligence service expected something to happen, but not this, and not this fast.

'What is this?' Daryaei demanded, allowing his deadly rage to show for once. Ordinarily, it was enough that people knew it was hidden there, somewhere.

'It's a sham.' After the initial shock, his chief of intelligence had taken the time to get a feel for the reality of the situation. 'That is a *regiment*. Each of the six divisions in the Army of God has three – in two cases, four – brigades. And so, we are twenty to their one. Did you expect that the Americans would not respond at all? That is unrealistic. But here we see they have responded. With one regiment, moved in from Israel, and sent in the wrong place. With this they intend to frighten us.'

'Go on.' The dark eyes softened slightly, merely simmering rather than dangerously hostile.

'America cannot deploy its divisions from Europe. They are contaminated. The same is true of their heavy divisions in America. So we will face the Saudis first of all. It will be a great battle, which we shall win. The rump states will surrender to us, or be crushed – and then Kuwait will stand alone, at the top of the Gulf, with its own forces and this American regiment, and then we shall see about that. They probably expect us to invade Kuwait first. We will not repeat that error, will we?'

'And if they reinforce the Saudis?'

'Again, they have the equipment for but one brigade in the Kingdom. The second is afloat. You talked to India about that, did you not?' It was so normal that he might have predicted it, the chief UIR spook thought behind outwardly cowed eyes. They always got nervous just before things started, as though expecting everyone to follow the script they'd written. The enemy was the enemy. He didn't always cooperate. 'And I doubt they have the troops to move. Aircraft, perhaps, but there is no carrier within ten thousand kilometers, and aircraft, though they are an annoyance, can neither take nor hold ground.'

'Thank you for making that clear.' The old man's mood softened.

'At last we meet, Comrade Colonel,' Golovko said to the CIA officer.

Clark had always wondered if he'd see the inside of KGB headquarters. He'd never quite expected to be offered drinks there in the Chairman's office. Early in the morning or not, he took a slug of the Starka-brand vodka. 'Your hospitality is not what I was trained to expect, Comrade Chairman.'

'We don't do that here anymore. Lefortovo Prison is more convenient.' He paused, set down his glass, and switched back to tea. A drink with the man was mandatory, but it was early in the day. 'I must ask. Was it you who brought Madam Gerasimov and the girl out?'

Clark nodded. There was nothing to be gained from lying to the man. 'Yes, that was me.'

'You are welcome to all three of them, Ivan ... your father's name?'

'Timothy. I am Ivan Timofeyevich, Sergey Nikolay'ch.'

'Ah.' Golovko had a good laugh. 'As hard as the Cold War was, my friend, it is good now, at the end of it, to see old enemies. Fifty years from now, when all of us are dead, historians will compare CIA records with ours, and they will decide who won the intelligence war. Have you any idea what they will decide?'

'You forget, I was a foot soldier, not a commander, for most of it.'

'Our Major Scherenko was impressed with you and your young partner here. Your rescue of Koga was impressive. And now we will work together again. Have you been briefed in?'

For Chavez, who'd come to manhood watching Rambo movies, and whose early Army training had taught him to expect going head-to-head with the Soviets at any time, it was an experience which he wanted to ascribe to jet lag, though both CIA officers had noted how empty the corridors were for their passage. There was no sense letting them see faces they might remember in some other time and some other place.

'No, mainly we've been gathering information.'

Golovko hit a button on his desk. 'Is Bondarenko here?' A few seconds later, the door opened, revealing a senior Russian general officer.

Both Americans stood. Clark read the medals and gave the man a hard look. Bondarenko did the same. The handshakes exchanged were wary, curious, and strangely warm. They were of an age, raised in one, growing into another.

'Gennady Iosefovich is chief of operations. Ivan Timofeyevich is a CIA spy,' the Chairman explained. 'As is his quiet young partner. Tell me, Clark, the plague, it comes from Iran?'

'Yes, that is certain.'

'Then he is a barbarian, but a clever one. General?'

'Last night you moved your cavalry regiment from Israel to Kuwait,' Bondarenko said. 'They are fine troops, but the correlation of forces is adverse in the extreme. Your country cannot deploy large numbers of troops for at least two weeks. He will not give you two weeks. We estimate that the heavy divisions southeast of Baghdad will be ready to move in three days, four at the most. One day for the approach march to the border area, and then? Then we will see what their plan is.'

'Any thoughts?'

'We have no more intelligence on this than you do,' Golovko said. 'Regrettably, most of our assets in the area have been shot, and the generals we befriended in the previous Iraqi regime have left the country.'

'The high command of the army is Iranian, many were trained in Britain or America under the Shah as junior officers, and they survived the purges,' Bondarenko said. 'We have dossiers on many of them, and these are being transmitted to the Pentagon.'

'That's very cordial of you.'

'You bet,' Ding observed. 'If they dust us off, next they come north.'

'Alliances, young man, do not occur for reasons of love, but from mutual interests,' Golovko agreed.

'If you cannot deal with this maniac today, then we will have to deal with him in three years,' Bondarenko said seriously. 'Better today, I think, for all of us.'

'We have offered our support to Foleyeva. She has accepted. When you learn your mission, let us know, and we will see what we can do.'

Some would last longer than others. Some would last less. The first recorded death happened in Texas, a golf-equipment representative who expired due to heart complications three days after being admitted, one day after his wife entered the hospital with her own symptoms. Doctors interviewing her determined that she'd probably contracted the disease by cleaning up after her husband had vomited in the bathroom, not from any intimate contact, because he'd felt too ill even to kiss her after returning from Phoenix. Though seemingly an insignificant conclusion from obvious data, it was faxed to Atlanta, as the CDC had requested all possible information, however minor it might seem. It certainly seemed minor to the medical team in Dallas. The first death for them was both a relief and a horror. A relief because the man's condition toward the end was both hopeless and agonizing; a horror, because there would be others just as vile, only longer in coming.

The same thing happened six hours later in Baltimore. The Winnebago dealer had a preexisting GI complaint, peptic ulcer disease, which, though controlled by an over-the-counter medication, gave Ebola an easy target. His stomach lining disintegrated, and the patient rapidly bled out while unconscious with his massive dose of pain-killers. This, too, came as something of a surprise to the attending physician and nurse. Soon thereafter more deaths started occurring nationwide. The media reported them, and the country's horror deepened. In the first series of cases, the husband died first, with the wife soon to follow. In many similar cases, children would be next.

It was more real for everyone now. For most, the crisis had seemed a distant event. Businesses and schools were closed, and travel was restricted, but the rest of it was a TV event, as things tended to be in Western countries. It was something you saw on a phosphor screen, a moving image augmented by sound, something both real and not. But now the word *death* was being used with some frequency. Photos of the victims appeared on the screens, in some cases home videos, and the moving pictures of people now dead, their private pasts revealed in moments of pleasure and relaxation, followed by the somber words of reporters who were themselves becoming as familiar as family members – it all entered the public consciousness with an immediacy that was as new and different as it was horrid. It was no longer the sort of nightmare from which one awoke. It was one which went on and on, seeming to grow, like the child's dream in which a black cloud entered a room, growing and growing, approaching despite all attempts at evasion, and you knew that if it touched you, you were lost.

Grumbles about the federally imposed travel restrictions died the same day as the golfer in Texas and the recreational vehicle dealer in Maryland. Interpersonal contact, which had first been cut way back, then started to grow again, was restricted to the family-member level. People lived on telephones now. Long-distance lines were jammed with calls to ascertain the well-being of relatives and friends, to the point that AT&T, MCI, and the rest ran commercial messages requesting that such calls be kept short, and special-access lines were set aside for government and medical use. There was a true national panic now, though it was a quiet, personal one. There were no public demonstrations. Traffic on the streets was virtually nil in the major cities. People even stopped heading for supermarkets, and instead stayed at home, living out of cans or freezers for the time being.

Reporters, still moving around with their mobile cameras, reported on all that, and in doing so, they both increased the degree of tension, and contributed to its solution.

'It's working,' General Pickett said over the phone to his former subordinate in Baltimore.

'Where are you, John?' Alexandre asked.

'Dallas. It's working, Colonel. I need you to do something.'

'What's that?'

'Stop playing practitioner. You have residents to do that. I have a working group at Walter Reed. Get the hell over there. You're too big an asset on the theoretical side to waste in a Racal suit doing sticks, Alex.'

'John, this is my department now, and I have to lead my troops.' It was a lesson well remembered from his time in green suits.

'Fine, your people know you care, Colonel. Now you can put the damned rifle down and start thinking like a god-damned *commander*. This battle's not going to be won in hospitals, is it?' Pickett asked more reasonably. 'I have transport waiting for you. There should be a Hummer downstairs to bring you into Reed. Want me to reactivate you and make it an order?'

And he could do that, Alexandre knew. 'Give me half an hour.' The associate professor hung up the phone and looked down the corridor. Another body bag was being carried out of a room by some orderlies in plastic suits. There was a pride in being here. Even though he was losing patients and would lose more, he was here, being a doctor, doing his best, showing his staff that, yes, he was one of them, ministering to the sick, taking his chances in accordance with the oath he'd sworn at the age of twenty-six. When this was over, the entire team would look back on this with a feeling of solidarity. As horrible as it had been, they'd done the job –

'Damn,' he swore. John Pickett was right. The battle was being fought here, but it wouldn't be won here. He told his chief assistant that he was heading down to the next floor, which was being run by Dean James.

There was an interesting case there. Female, thirty-nine, admitted two days earlier. Her common-law significant other was dying, and she was distraught, and her blood showed

Ebola antibodies, and she'd presented the classic flu symptoms, but the disease hadn't gone further. It had, in fact, seemed to stop.

'What gives with this one?' Cathy Ryan was speculating with Dean James.

'Don't knock it, Cath,' he responded tiredly.

'I'm not, Dave, but I want to know why. I interviewed her myself. She slept in the same bed with him two days before she brought him in –'

'Did they have sex?' Alex asked, entering the conversation.

'No, Alex, they didn't. I asked that. He didn't feel well enough. I think this one's going to survive.' And that was a first for Baltimore.

'We keep her in for at least a week, Cathy.'

'I *know* that, Dave, but this is the first one,' SURGEON pointed out. 'Something's different here. What is it? We have to know!'

'Chart?' Cathy handed it over to Alexandre.

He scanned it. Temperature down to 100.2, blood work . . . not normal, but . . . 'What does she say, Cathy?' Alexandre asked, flipping back through some pages.

'How she says she feels, you mean? Panicked, frightened to death. Massive headaches, abdominal cramps – I think a lot of that is pure stress. Can't blame her, can we?'

'These values are all improving. Liver function blipped hard, but that stopped last night, and it's coming back . . .'

'That's what got my attention. She's fighting it off, Alex,' Dr Ryan said. 'First one, I think we're going to win with her. But *why*? What's different? What can we learn from this? What can we apply to other patients?'

That turned the trick for Dr Alexandre. John Pickett was right. He had to get to Reed.

'Dave, they want me in Washington right now.'

'Go,' the dean replied at once. 'We're covered here. If you can help make sense of this, get yourself down there.'

'Cathy, the most likely answer to your question is the simple one. Your ability to fight this thing off is inversely proportional to the number of particles that get into your system. Everybody thinks that just one strand can kill you. That's not true. Nothing's that dangerous. Ebola kills first of all by overpowering the immune system; *then* it goes to

1074

work on the organs. If she only got a small number of the little bastards, then her immune system fought the battle and won. Talk to her some more, Cathy. Every detail of her contact with her husband-whatever in the last week. I'll call you in a couple of hours. How are you guys doing?'

'Alex, if there's some hope in this,' Dr James replied, 'then I think we can hack it.'

Alexandre went back upstairs for decontamination. First his suit was thoroughly sprayed. Then he disrobed and changed into greens and a mask, took the 'clean' elevator down to the lobby, and out the door.

'You Colonel Alexandre?' a sergeant asked.

'Yes.'

The NCO saluted. 'Follow me, sir. We got a Hummer and a driver for you. You want a jacket, sir? Kinda cool out.'

'Thanks.' He donned the rubberized chemical-warfare parka. They were so miserable to wear that it would surely keep him warm all the way down. A female Spec-4 was at the wheel. Alexandre got into the uncomfortable seat, buckled the belt, and turned to her. 'Go!' Only then did he rethink what he'd told Ryan and James upstairs. His head shook as though to repel an insect. Pickett *was* right. Maybe.

'Mr President, please, let us reexamine the data first. I even called Dr Alexandre down from Hopkins to work with the group I set up at Reed. It's much too soon for any conclusions. Please, let us do our work.'

'Okay, General,' Ryan said angrily. 'I'll be here. Damn,' he swore after hanging up.

'We have other things to do, sir,' Goodley pointed out.

'Yeah.'

It was still dark when it started in the Pacific Time Zone. At least getting the aircraft was easy. Jumbos from most of the major airlines were heading for Barstow, California, their flight crews screened for Ebola antibodies and passed by Army doctors with test kits which were just now coming on line. There were also modifications to the aircraft ventilation systems. At the National Training Center, soldiers were boarding buses. That was normal for the Blue Force, but not for the OpFor, whose families watched the uniformed soldiers leave their homes for the deployment. Little was known except that they were leaving. The destination was a secret for now; the soldiers would learn it only after lifting off for the sixteen-hour flights. Over ten thousand men and women meant forty flights, leaving at a rate of only four per hour from the rudimentary facilities in the high desert of California. If asked, the local public affairs officers would tell whoever called that the units at Fort Irwin were moving out to assist with the national quarantine. In Washington, a few reporters learned something else.

'Thomas Donner?' the woman in the mask asked.

'That's right,' the reporter answered crossly, pulled away from his breakfast table, dressed in jeans and a flannel shirt.

'FBI. Would you come with me, sir? We have to talk to you about some things.'

'Am I under arrest?' the TV personality demanded.

'Only if you want to be, Mr Donner,' the agent told him. 'But I need you to come with me, right now. You won't need anything special, except your wallet and ID and stuff,' she added, handing over a surgical mask in a plastic container.

'Fine. Give me a minute.' The door closed, allowing Donner to kiss his wife, get a jacket, and change shoes. He emerged, put the mask on, and followed the agent to her car. 'So what is this all about?'

'I'm just the limo service,' she said, ending the morning's conversation. If he was too dumb to remember that he was a member of the press pool pre-selected for Pentagon operations, it wasn't her lookout.

'The biggest mistake the Iraqis made in 1990 was logistics,' Admiral Jackson explained, moving his pointer on the map. 'Everybody thinks it's about guns and bombs. It isn't. It's about fuel and information. If you have enough fuel to keep moving, and you know what the other guy's doing, chances are you'll win.' The slide changed on the screen next to the map. The pointer moved there next. 'Here.'

The satellite photos were clear. Every tank and BMP laager was accompanied by something else. A large collection of fuel bowsers. Artillery limbers were attached to their trucks. Blowups showed fuel drums attached to the rear decks of the

T-80 tanks. Each contained fifty-five gallons of diesel. These greatly increased the tank's vulnerability to damage, but could be dropped off by flipping a switch inside the turret.

'No doubt about it. They're getting ready to move, probably within the week. We have the 10th Cavalry in place in Kuwait. We have the 11th and the First Brigade of the North Carolina National Guard moving now. That's all we can do for the moment. It won't be till Friday at the earliest that we can cut any more units loose from the quarantine.'

'And that's public information,' Ed Foley added.

'Essentially, we're deploying one division, a very heavy one, but only one,' Jackson concluded. 'The Kuwait military is fully in the field. The Saudis are spinning up, too.'

'And the third brigade depends on getting the MPS ships past the Indian navy,' Secretary Bretano pointed out.

'We can't do that,' Admiral DeMarco informed them. 'We don't have the combat power to fight our way through.'

Jackson didn't reply to that. He couldn't. The acting Chief of Naval Operations was his senior, despite what he thought of him.

'Look, Brucie,' Mickey Moore said, turning to look right at him, 'my boys need those vehicles, or the Carolina Guard is gonna be facing an advancing enemy mechanized force with side arms. You blue-suits been telling us for years how ballsy those Aegis cruisers are. Put up or shut up, okay? By this time tomorrow, I'll have fifteen thousand soldiers at risk.'

'Admiral Jackson,' the President said. 'You're Operations.'

'Mr President, without air cover –'

'Can we do it or can't we?' Ryan demanded.

'No,' DeMarco replied. 'I won't see ships wasted that way. Not without air cover.'

'Robby, I want your best judgment on this,' Secretary Bretano said.

'Okay.' Jackson took a breath. 'They have a total of about forty Harriers. Nice airplanes, but not really high-performance. The escorting force has a total of maybe thirty surface-to-surface missiles. We don't have to worry about a gunfight. *Anzio* currently carries seventy-five SAMs, fifteen Tomahawks, and eight Harpoons. *Kidd* has seventy SAMs, and eight Harpoons. *O'Bannon* isn't a SAM ship. She just has point-defense weapons, but she has Harpoons, too. The two frigates that just joined up have about twenty SAMs each. Theoretically, they can fight through.'

'It's too dangerous, Jackson! You don't send a surface force against a carrier group by itself, *ever!*'

'What if we shoot first?' Ryan asked. *That* caused heads to turn.

'Mr President.' It was DeMarco again. 'We don't do that. We're not even sure that they are hostile.'

'The ambassador thinks they are,' Bretano told them.

'Admiral DeMarco, that equipment has to be delivered,' the President said, his own face coloring up.

'The Air Force is deploying to Saudi now. Two extra days and we can deal with it, but until then –'

'Admiral, call your relief.' Secretary Bretano looked down at his briefing folder. 'Your services are not needed here anymore. We don't have two days to bicker.'

That was actually a violation of protocol. The Joint Chiefs were presidential appointments, and while they were titularly military advisers to the Secretary of Defense *and* the President, supposedly only the latter could ask one to resign. Admiral DeMarco looked to Ryan's place in the center of the conference table.

'Mr President, I have to give you my best feel for this.'

'Admiral, we have fifteen thousand men standing in harm's way. You can't tell us that the Navy will not support them. You are relieved of duty effective now,' the President said. 'Good day.' The other uniformed Chiefs glanced at one another. This hadn't happened before. 'How long before contact with the Indians?' Ryan asked, moving on.

'About twenty-four hours, sir.'

'Any way we can provide additional support?'

'There's a submarine there also, loaded with torpedoes and missiles. She's about fifty miles in advance of *Anzio*,' Jackson said, as a stunned admiral and his aide left the room. 'We can speed her up. That risks detection, but the Indians aren't all that swift on ASW. She would be an offensive weapon, sir. Submarines can't defend passively. They sink ships.'

'I think the Indian Prime Minister and I need to have a little chat,' POTUS observed. 'After we get through them, then what?'

'Well, then we have to transit the strait and make it up to the unloading ports.'

'That I can help you with,' the Air Force chief of staff promised. 'We'll have the F-16s in-country and in range for that part of the passage. The 366th Wing won't be ready yet, but the boys from Israel will be.'

'We're going to need that cover, General,' Jackson emphasized.

'Well, God damn, the Navy's asking for help from us Air Scouts,' the Air Force said lightly, then turned serious. 'We'll kill every rag-head son of a bitch who gets in the air, Robby. Those forty-eight-16-Charlies are locked and cocked. As soon as you're within a hundred miles of the Strait, you have a friend overhead.'

'Is it enough?' the President asked.

'Strictly speaking, no. The other side has four hundred top-of-the-line airplanes. When the 366th gets fully set up – in three days, minimum – we'll have eighty fighters for air-to-air, but the Saudis aren't bad. We have AWACS in place. Your tanks will fight under a neutral sky at worst, Mickey.' The general checked his watch. 'They should be getting off right about now.'

The first flight of four F-15C fighter-interceptors rotated aloft together. Twenty minutes later, they formed up with their KC-135R tankers. There were six of them from their own wing, and others would join from the Montana and North and South Dakota Air National Guard, their home states as yet untouched by the epidemic. For most of the way to the Arabian Peninsula, they'd hold position ten miles from the lead commercial aircraft coming out of California. The flight path took them north to the Pole, then over the hump and south toward Russia, continuing over Eastern Europe. West of Cyprus, they would be joined by an Israeli escort, which would convey them as far as Jordan. From there on, the American Eagle fighters would be augmented by Saudi F-15s. They might make the first few arrivals covertly, the planning officers thought in their own commercial transports, but if the other side woke up, then there would be an air battle. The pilots in the lead Eagle flight really didn't mind that very much. There was no extraneous chatter on the radios as they saw dawn to their right. It would be a flight of two dawns. The next one would be to their left.

'Okay, ladies and gentlemen,' the public affairs officer told the fifteen assembled journalists. 'Here's the scoop. You have been called up for a military deployment. Sergeant Astor is now handing out consent forms. You will please sign them and hand them back.'

'What's this?' one of them asked.

'You maybe want to try reading it?' the Marine colonel suggested from behind his mask.

'Blood test,' one muttered. 'I guess so. But what about the rest?'

'Ma'am, those of you who sign the form will find out more. Those who do not will be driven home.' Curiosity won in every case. They all signed.

'Thank you.' The colonel examined all the forms. 'Now if you will go through the door to your left, some Navy corpsmen are waiting for you.'

He was pleading his own case. Though a member of the bar for thirty years, Ed Kealty had been in a court of law only as a spectator, though on many occasions he'd stood on the steps of a courthouse to make a speech or announcement. It was always dramatic, and so was this.

'May it please the court,' the former Vice President began, 'I stand here to request summary judgment. My right to cross a state line has been violated by the executive order of the President. This is contrary to explicit constitutional guarantees, and also to Supreme Court precedent, to wit, the Lemuel Penn case, in which the Court ruled unanimously . . .'

Pat Martin sat beside the Solicitor General, who would speak for the government. There was a camera from *Court TV* to send the case up and down via satellite into homes across the nation. It was a strange scene. The judge, the court reporter, the bailiff, all the attorneys, the ten reporters, and four spectators were all wearing surgical masks and rubber gloves. All had just seen Ed Kealty make the greatest political miscalculation of his career, though none had grasped it yet. Martin had come in anticipation of that very fact.

'Freedom of travel is central to all of the freedoms established and protected by the Constitution. The President has neither constitutional nor statutory authority to deny this freedom to the citizens, most particularly not by the application of armed force, which has already resulted in the death of a citizen, and the wounding of several others. This is a simple point of law,' Kealty was saying, half an hour later, 'and on behalf of myself and our fellow citizens, I beg the court to set this illegal order aside.' With that, Edward J. Kealty took his place.

'Your Honor,' the Solicitor General said, walking to the podium with the TV microphone, 'as the complainant tells us, this is a most important case, but not one of great legal complexity at its foundation.

'The government cites Mr Justice Holmes in the celebrated free speech case where he told us that the suspension of freedoms *is* permissible when the danger to the country as a whole is both real and present. The Constitution, Your Honor, is not a suicide pact. The crisis which the country faces today is deadly, as press reports have told us, and it is of a nature that the drafters could not have anticipated. In the late eighteenth century, I remind learned counsel, the nature of infectious disease was not yet known. But quarantining of ships at the time was both common and accepted. We have Jefferson's embargo of foreign trade as a precedent, but most of all, Your Honor, we have common sense. We cannot sacrifice our citizens on the altar of legal theory . . .'

Martin listened, rubbing his nose under the mask. It smelled as though a barrel of Lysol had been spilled in the room.

It might have been comical, but was not, when each of the fifteen reporters reacted the same way to the blood test. A blink. A sigh of relief. Each one stood and walked to the far side of the room, taking the opportunity to remove his or her mask. When the tests were complete, they were led into another briefing room.

'Okay, we have a bus outside to take you to Andrews. You will receive further information after you take off,' the PAO colonel told them.

'Wait a minute!' Tom Donner objected.

'Sir, that was on your consent form, remember?'

*   *   *

'You were right, John,' Alexandre said. Epidemiology was the medical profession's version of accounting, and as that dull profession was vital to running a business, so the study of diseases and how they spread was actually the mother of modern medicine, when in the 1830s a French physician had determined that people who became ill died or recovered at the same rate whether they were treated or not. That awkward discovery had forced the medical community to study itself, to look for things that worked and things that did not, and along the way changed medicine from a trade into a scientific art.

The devil was always in the details. In this case, it might not be a devil at all, Alex realized.

There were now 3,451 Ebola cases in the country. That included those who had started dying, those who showed frank symptoms, and those who showed antibodies. The number by itself wasn't large. Lower than AIDS deaths, lower by more than two orders of magnitude than cancer and heart disease. The statistical study, aided by FBI interviews and feedback from local physicians all over the country, had established 223 primary cases, all of them infected at trade shows, and all of whom had infected others who had in turn infected more. Though the incoming cases were still on the upslope, the rate was lower than that predicted by preexisting computer models ... and at Hopkins they'd had the first case of someone who showed antibodies, but no symptoms ...

'There should have been more primary cases, Alex,' Pickett said. 'We started seeing that last night. The first one who died, he flew from Phoenix to Dallas. The FBI got the flight records, and University of Texas tested everybody aboard, finished this morning. Only one shows antibodies, and he isn't really symptomatic.'

'Risk factors?'

'Gingivitis. Bleeding gums,' General Pickett reported.

'It's trying to be an aerosol ... but ...'

'That's what I think, Alex. The secondary cases appear to be mostly intimate contact. Hugs, kisses, taking personal care of a loved one. If we're right, this will peak in three days, and then it'll stop. Along the way we'll start seeing survivors.'

'We have one of those at Hopkins. She's got the antibodies, but it didn't get beyond the initial presentation.'

'We need to get Gus working on environmental degradation. He should be already.'

'Agreed. You call him. I'm doing some follow-ups down here.'

The judge was an old friend of Kealty. Martin wasn't exactly sure how he'd fiddled with the docket in this particular district, but that didn't matter now. The two presentations had taken about thirty minutes each. It was, as Kealty had said and the Solicitor General had agreed, a fundamentally simple point of law, though the practical applications of it led into all manner of complexity. It was also a matter of great urgency, as a result of which the judge reappeared from chambers after a mere hour's contemplation. He would read his decision from his notes, and type up a full opinion later in the day.

'The Court,' he began, 'is cognizant of the grave danger facing the country, and must sympathize with President Ryan's sincerely felt duty to safeguard the lives of Americans in addition to their freedoms.

'However, the Court must acknowledge the fact that the Constitution is, and remains, the supreme law of the land. To violate that legal bulwark is a step that potentially sets a precedent with consequences so grave as to reach beyond the current crisis, and though the President is certainly acting under the best motives, this Court must vacate the executive order, trusting our citizens to act intelligently and prudently in the pursuit of their own safety. So ordered.'

'Your Honor.' The Solicitor General stood. 'The government will and must, appeal your ruling immediately to the Fourth Circuit in Richmond. We request a stay until the paperwork can be processed, later today.'

'Request is denied. Court is adjourned.' The judge stood and left the bench without a further word. The room, of course, erupted.

'What does this mean?' the Court TV correspondent – himself a lawyer, who knew what it probably meant – said to Ed Kealty, his microphone extended, as reporters tended to do at the moment.

'It means that so-called President Ryan cannot break the law. I think I have shown here that the rule of law still exists in our country,' the politician replied. He was not being overtly smug.

'What does the government say?' the reporter asked the Solicitor General.

'Not very much. We will have papers filed with the Fourth US Circuit Court of Appeals before Judge Venable has his opinion drafted. The order of the court is not officially binding until it is written up, signed, and properly filed. We'll have our appeal drafted first. The Fourth Circuit will stay the order –'

'And if it doesn't?'

Martin took that on. 'In that case, sir, the executive order will remain in place in the interest of public safety until the case can be argued in a more structured setting. But there is every reason to believe that the Fourth Circuit will stay the order. Judges are people of reality in addition to being people of the written word. There is one other thing, however.'

'Yes?' the reporter asked. Kealty was watching from ten feet away.

'The court has settled another important constitutional issue here. In referring to President Ryan by both his name and the title of his office, the court has settled the succession question raised by former Vice President Kealty. Further, the court said that that order was vacated. Had Mr Ryan not been the President, the order would have been invalid and never legally binding, and the court could have stated that as well. Instead, the Court acted improperly on point, I believe, but properly in a procedural sense. Thank you. The Solicitor General and I have to get some paperwork done.'

It wasn't often you shut reporters up. Shutting political figures up was harder still.

'Now, wait a minute!' Kealty shouted.

'You never were a very good lawyer, Ed,' Martin said on his way past.

'I think he's right,' Lorenz said. 'Jesus, I sure hope he is.'

CDC laboratories had been frantically at work since the beginning, studying how the virus survived in the open. Environmental chambers were set up with differing values of temperature and humidity, and different light-intensity levels, and the data, incomprehensibly, kept telling them the same thing. The disease that had to be spreading by aerosol – wasn't, or at most it was barely doing so. Its survival in the open, even under benign conditions, was measured in minutes.

'I wish I understood the warfare side of this a little better,' Lorenz went on after a moment's thought.

'Two-two-three primary cases. That's all. If there were more, we'd know by now. Eighteen confirmed sites, four additional trade shows that generated no hits. Why eighteen and not the other four?' Alex wondered. 'What if they did hit all twenty-two, but four didn't work?'

'On the basis of our experimental data, that's a real possibility, Alex.' Lorenz was pulling on his pipe. 'Our models now predict a total of eight thousand cases. We're going to get survivors, and the numbers on that will alter the model somewhat. This quarantine stuff has scared the shit out of people. You know, I don't think the travel ban really matters directly, but it scared people enough that they're not interacting enough to –'

'Doctor, that's the third good piece of news today,' Alexandre breathed. The first had been the woman at Hopkins. The second was Pickett's analytical data. Now the third was Gus's lab work and the logical conclusion it led to. 'John always said that bio-war was more psychological than real.'

'John's a smart doc, Alex. So are you, my friend.'

'Three days and we'll know.'

'Agreed. Rattle some beads, Alex.'

'You can reach me through Reed for the time being.'

'I'm sleeping in the office, too.'

'See ya.' Alexandre punched off the speakerphone. Around him were six Army physicians, three from Walter Reed, three from USAMRIID. 'Comments?' he asked them.

'Crazy situation,' a major observed with an exhausted smile. 'It's a psychological weapon, all right. Scares the hell out of everybody. But that works for us, too. And somebody goofed on the other side. I wonder how . . . ?'

Alex thought about that for a moment. Then he lifted the phone and dialed Johns Hopkins. 'This is Dr Alexandre,' he told the desk nurse on the medical floor. 'I need to talk to

Dr Ryan, it's very important . . . okay, I'll hold.' It took a few minutes. 'Cathy? Alex here. I need to talk to your husband, and it's better if you're there, too . . . It's damned important,' he told her a moment later.

55

COMMENCEMENT

Two hundred files meant two hundred birth certificates, two hundred driver's licenses, houses or apartments, sets of credit cards, and all manner of other permutations to be checked out. It was inevitable that once such an investigation started, Special Agent Aref Raman would garner special attention from the three hundred FBI agents assigned to the case. But in fact every Secret Service employee who had regular access to the White House was on the immediate checklist. All across the country (the USSS draws personnel from as wide a field as any other government agency), agents did start with birth certificates and move on, also checking high-school yearbooks for graduation pictures to be compared with ID photos of all the agents. Three agents on the Detail turned out to be immigrants, some of whose exact personal details could not be easily checked. One was French-born, having come to America in his mother's arms. Another hailed from Mexico, having actually come illegally with her parents; she'd later legitimatized her status and distinguished herself as a genius with the Technical Security Division – and a ferociously patriotic member of the team. That left 'Jeff' Raman as an agent with some missing documentation, which was reasonably explained by his parents' reported refugee status.

In many ways, it was too easy. It was on his record that he'd been born in Iran and had come to America when his parents had fled the country with the fall of the Shah's regime. Every indicator since showed that he had fully adapted to his new country, even adopting a fanaticism for basketball that was a minor legend in the Service. He almost never lost a wager on a game, and it was a standing joke that professional gamblers consulted him on the line for an important game. He was always one to enjoy a beer with his colleagues. He'd developed an outstanding service reputation as a field agent. He was unmarried. That was not terribly unusual for a federal law enforcement officer. The Secret Service was especially tough on spouses who had to share their loved ones (mainly husbands) with a job far more unforgiving than the most demanding mistress – which made divorce more common than marriage. He'd been seen around with female company, but didn't talk about that much. Insofar as he had a private life, it was a quiet one. It was certain that he'd had no contacts at all with other Iranian-born citizens or aliens, that he was not the least bit religious, that he'd never once brought up Islam in a conversation, except to say, as he'd told the President once, that religion had caused his family so much grief that it was a subject he was just as happy to leave alone.

Inspector O'Day, back at work because Director Murray trusted him with the sensitive cases, was not the least bit impressed with this or any other story. He supervised the investigation. He assumed that the adversary, if he existed, would be an expert, and therefore the most plausible and consistent identity was to him only a potential cover to be examined. Better yet, there were no rules on this one. Agent Price had made that determination herself. He picked the local investigating team himself from Headquarters Division and the Washington Field Office. The best of them he assigned to Aref Raman, now, conveniently, in Pittsburgh.

His apartment in northwest DC was modest, but comfortable. It had a burglar alarm, but that was not a problem. The agents selected for the illegal breaking-and-entering included a technical wizard who, after defeating the locks in two minutes, recognized the control panel and punched in the maker's emergency code – he had them all memorized – to deactivate the system. This procedure had once been called a 'black bag job,' a term which had fallen by the wayside, though the function itself had not quite done so. Now the term 'special operation' was used, which could mean anything one wanted it to.

The first two agents in the door called three more into the apartment after the break-in had been effected. They photographed the apartment first of all, looking for possible telltales: seemingly innocent or random objects which, if disturbed in any way, warned the occupant that someone had been inside. These could be devilishly hard things to detect and defeat, but all five of the agents were part of the FBI's Foreign Counterintelligence Division, both trained against and trained by professional spooks. 'Shaking' the apartment would take hours of exquisitely tedious effort. They knew that at least five other teams were doing the same thing to other potential subjects.

The P-3C was hovering at the edge of the radar coverage for the Indian ships, keeping low and bumping through the roiled air over the warm surface of the Arabian Sea. They had tracks on thirty emitters from nineteen sources. The powerful, low-frequency search radars were the ones they worried about most, though the threat-receivers were getting traces of SAM radars as well. Supposedly, the Indians were running exercises, their fleet back at sea after a long stand-down for maintenance. The problem was that such workup exercises were quite indistinguishable from battle readiness. The data being analyzed by the on-board ELINT crew was downlinked to *Anzio* and the rest of the escorts for Task Group COMEDY, as the sailors had taken to calling the four *Bob Hopes* and their escorts.

The group commander was sitting in his cruiser's combat information center. The three large billboard displays (actually rear-projection televisions linked to the Aegis radar-computer system) showed the location of the Indian battle group with a fair degree of precision. He even knew which of the blips were probably the carriers. His task was a complex one. COMEDY was now fully formed. Under way–replenishment ships *Platte* and *Supply* were now attached to the group, along with their escorts *Hawes* and *Carr*, and over the next few hours all of the escorts would take turns alongside to top off their fuel bunkers – for a Navy captain, having too much fuel was like having too much money: impossible. After that, the UNREP ships would be ordered to take position outboard of the leading tank carriers, and the frigates outboard of the trailers. *O'Bannon* would move forward to continue her ASW search – the Indians had two nuclear submarines, and nobody seemed to know where they were at the moment. *Kidd* and *Anzio*, both SAM ships, would back into the formation, providing close air defense.

Ordinarily the Aegis cruiser would stand farther out, but not now.

The reason for that came not from his mission orders, but from TV. Every naval vessel in the group had its own satellite-TV receiver; in the modern Navy, the sailors wanted and got their own cable system, and while the crew spent most of their time watching the various movie channels – *Playboy* was always a favorite, sailors being sailors – the group commander was overdosing on CNN, because while his mission orders didn't always give him all the background information he needed for his missions, very often commercial TV did. The crews were tense. The news of events at home could not have been concealed from them in any case, and the images of sick and dying people, blocked interstates, and empty city streets had initially shaken them badly, causing officers and chiefs to sit down with the men on the mess decks to talk things through. Then had come these orders. Things were happening in the Persian Gulf, things were happening at home, and all of a sudden the MPS ships, with their brigade set of combat vehicles, were heading for the Saudi port of Dhahran . . . and the Indian navy was in the way. The crew was quiet now, Captain Greg Kemper of USS *Anzio* saw. His chiefs reported that the 'troops' were not laughing and cutting up in the mess rooms, and the constant simulations on the Aegis combat system in the past few days had conveyed their own message. COMEDY was sailing in harm's way.

Each of the escorting ships had a helicopter. These coordinated with the crack ASW team on *O'Bannon*, namesake of the Navy's golden ship of World War II, a Fletcher-class destroyer which had fought in every major Pacific engagement without a casualty or a scratch; the new one had a gold A on her superstructure, the mark of a submarine-killer of note – at least in simulation. *Kidd*'s heritage was less lucky. Named for Admiral Isaac Kidd, who had died aboard USS *Arizona* on the morning of December 7, 1941, she was a member of the 'dead-admiral class' of four missile destroyers originally built for the Iranian navy under the Shah, forced on a reluctant President Carter, and then perversely all named for admirals who'd died in losing battles. *Anzio*, in one of the Navy's stranger traditions, was named for a land battle, part of the Italian campaign in 1944, in which a daring invasion had developed into a desperate struggle. Ships of war were actually made for that sort of business, but it was the business of their commanders to see that the desperate part applied to the other guy.

In a real war, that would have been easy. *Anzio* had fifteen Tomahawk missiles aboard, each with a thousand-pound warhead, and nearly in range of the Indian battle group. In an ideal world he'd loose them at just over two hundred miles, based on targeting information from the Orions – his helicopters could do that, too, but the P-3Cs were far more survivable.

'Captain!' It was a petty officer on the ESM board. 'We're getting airborne radars. The Orion has some company approaching, looks like two Harriers, distance unknown, constant bearing, signal strength increasing.'

'Thank you. It's a free sky until somebody says different,' Kemper reminded everybody.

Maybe it was an exercise, but the Indian battle group hadn't moved forty miles in the past day, instead traveling back and forth, east and west, crossing and recrossing its own course track. Exercises were supposed to be more free-form than that. What the situation told the captain of USS *Anzio* was that they'd staked out this piece of ocean as their own. And the Indians just happened to be between where COMEDY was and where it wanted to be.

Nothing was very secret about it, either. Everyone pretended that normal peace-time conditions were in effect. *Anzio* had her SPY-1 radar operating, pumping out millions of watts. The Indians were using theirs as well. It was almost like a game of chicken.

'Captain, we have bogies, we have unknown multiple air contacts bearing zero-seven-zero, range two-one-five miles. No squawk ident, they are not commercial. Designate Raid-One.' The symbols came up on the center screen.

'No emitters on that bearing,' ESM reported.

'Very well.' The captain crossed his legs in his command chair. In the movies this was where Gary Cooper lit up a smoke.

'Raid-One appears to be four aircraft in formation, speed four-five-zero knots, course two-four-five.' Which made them inbounds, though not quite directly at COMEDY.

'Projected CPA?' the captain asked.

'They will pass within twenty miles on their current course, sir,' a sailor responded crisply.

'Very well. Okay, people, listen up. I want this place cool and businesslike. You all know the job. When there's reason to be excited, I will be the one to tell you,' he told the CIC crew. 'Weapons tight.' Meaning that peacetime rules still applied, and nothing was actually ready to fire – a situation that could be remedied by turning a few keys.

'*Anzio*, this is Gonzo-Four, over,' a voice called on the air-to-surface radio.

'Gonzo-Four, *Anzio*, over.'

'*Anzio*,' the aviator reported, 'we got two Harriers playing tag with us. One just zipped by at about fifty yards. He's got white ones on the rails.' Real missiles hanging under the wings, not pretend ones.

'Doing anything?' the air-control officer asked.

'Negative, just like he's playing a little.'

'Tell him to continue the mission,' the captain said. 'And pretend he doesn't care.'

'Aye, sir.' The message was relayed.

This sort of thing wasn't all that unusual. Fighter pilots were fighter pilots, the captain knew. They never grew up past the stage of buzzing by girls on their bikes. He directed his attention to Raid-One. Course and speed were unchanged. This wasn't a hostile act. The Indians were letting him know that they knew who was in their neighborhood. That was evident from the appearance of fighters in two places at the same time. It was definitely a game of chicken now.

What to do now? he wondered. *Play tough? Play dumb? Play apathetic?* People so often overlooked the psychological aspect of military operations. Raid-One was now 150 miles out, rapidly approaching the range of his SM-2 MR SAMs.

'What d'ya think, Weps?' he asked his weapons officer.

'I think they're just trying to piss us off.'

'Agreed.' The captain flipped a mental coin. 'Well, they're harassing the Orion. Let 'em know we see 'em,' he ordered.

Two seconds later, the SPY search radar jacked up its power to four million watts, sent all of it down one degree of bearing at the inbound fighters, and increased the 'dwell' on the targets, which meant they were being hit almost continuously. It was enough to peg the threat-detection gear they had to have aboard. Inside of twenty miles, it could even start damaging such equipment, depending on how delicate it was. That was called a 'zorch,' and the captain still had another two million watts of power up his sleeve. The joke was that if you really pissed off an Aegis, you might start producing two-headed kids.

'*Kidd* just went to battle stations, sir,' the officer of the deck reported.

'Good training time, isn't it?' Range to Raid-One was just over one hundred miles now. 'Weps, light 'em up.'

With that command, the ship's four SPG-51 target-illumination radars turned, sending pencil beams of X-band energy at the inbound fighters. These radars told the missiles how to find their targets. The Indian threat gear would pick that up, too. The fighters didn't change course or speed.

'Okay, that means we're not playing rough today. If they were of a mind to do something, they'd be maneuvering now,' the captain told his crew. 'You know, like turning the corner when you see a cop.' Or they had ice water in their veins, which didn't seem likely.

'Going to eyeball the formation?' Weps asked.

'That's what I'd do. Take some pictures, see what's here,' Kemper thought.

'A lot of things happening at once, sir.'

'Yep,' the captain agreed, watching the display. He lifted the growler phone.

'Bridge,' the OOD answered.

'Tell your lookouts I want to know what they are. Photos, if possible. How's visibility topside?'

'Surface haze, not bad aloft, sir. I've got men on the Big Eyes now.'

'Very well.'

'They'll go past us to the north, turn left, and come down our port side,' the captain predicted.

'Sir, Gonzo-Four reports a very close pass a few seconds ago,' air control said.

'Tell him to stay cool.'

'Aye, Cap'n.' The situation developed quickly after that. The fighters circled COMEDY twice, never closer than five nautical miles. The Indian Harriers spent another fifteen minutes around the patrolling Orion, then had to return back to their carrier to refuel, and another day at sea continued with no shots fired and no overtly hostile acts, unless you counted the fighter play, and that was pretty routine. When all was settled down, the captain of USS *Anzio* turned to his communications officer.

'I need to talk to CINCLANT. Oh, Weps?' Kemper added.

'Yes, sir?'

'I want every combat system on this ship fully checked out.'

'Sir, we just ran a full check twelve hours –'

'Right now, Weps,' he emphasized quietly.

'And that's good news?' Cathy asked.

'Doctor, that's real simple,' Alexandre said in reply. 'You watched some people die this morning. You will watch more die tomorrow, and that stinks. But thousands is better than millions, isn't it? I think this epidemic is going to burn out.' He didn't add that it was somewhat easier for him. Cathy was an eye cutter. She wasn't used to dealing with death. He was infectious diseases, and he was used to it. Easier? Was that the word? 'We'll know in a couple of days from statistical analysis of the cases.'

The President nodded silently. Van Damm spoke for him: 'What's the count going to be?'

'Less than ten thousand, according to the computer models at Reed and Detrick. Sir, I am not being cavalier about this. I'm saying that ten thousand is better than ten million.'

'One death is a tragedy, and a million is a statistic,' Ryan said finally.

'Yes, sir. I know that one.' The good news didn't make Alexandre all that happy. But how else to tell people that a disaster was better than a catastrophe?

'Iosef Vissarionovich Stalin,' SWORDSMAN told them. 'He did have a way with words.'

'You know who did it,' Alex observed.

'What makes you say that?' Jack asked.

'You didn't react normally to what I told you, Mr President.'

'Doctor, I haven't done much of anything normally over

1094

the past few months. What does this mean about the no-travel order?'

'It means we leave it in place for at least another week. Our prediction is not carved in stone. The incubation period for the disease is somewhat variable. You don't send the fire trucks home as soon as the last flame disappears. You sit there and watch for another possible flare-up. That will happen here, too. What's worked to this point is that people are frightened to death. Because of that, personal interactions are minimized, and *that*'s how you stop one of these things. We keep 'em that way. The new cases will be very circumscribed. We attack those like we did with smallpox. Identify the cases, test everyone with whom they've had contact, isolate the ones with antibodies, and see how they do. It's *working*, okay? Whoever did this miscalculated. The disease isn't anywhere near as contagious as they thought – or maybe the whole thing was just a psychological exercise. That's what bio-war is. The great plagues of the past really happened because people didn't know how diseases spread. They didn't know about microbes and fleas and contaminated water. We do. Everybody does, you learn it in health class in school. Hell, that's why we haven't had any medics infected. We've had lots of practice dealing with AIDS and hepatitis. The same precautions that work with those also work with this.'

'How do we keep it from happening again?' van Damm asked.

'I told you that already. Funding. Basic research on the genetic side, and more focused work on the diseases we know about. There's no particular reason why we can't develop safe vaccines for Ebola and a lot of others.'

'AIDS?' Ryan asked.

'That's a toughie. That virus is an agile little bastard. No attempt for a vaccine has even come close yet. No, on that side, basic genetic research to determine how the biologic mechanism works, and from that to get the immune system to recognize it and kill it – some sort of vaccine; that's what a vaccine is. But how to make it work, well, we haven't figured that one yet. We'd better. In twenty years, we might have to write Africa off. Hey,' the Creole said, 'I got kin over there, y'know?

'That's one way to keep it from happening again. You, Mr

President, are already working on the other way. Who was it?'

He didn't have to tell anybody how secret it was: 'Iran. The Ayatollah Mahmoud Haji Daryaei and his merry men.'

Alexandre reverted to officer in the United States Army: 'Sir, you can kill all of them you want, as far as I'm concerned.'

It was interesting to see Mehrabad International Airport in daylight. Clark had never experienced Iran as a friendly country. Supposedly, before the fall of the Shah, the people had been friendly enough, but he hadn't made the trip soon enough for that. He'd come in covertly in 1979 and again in 1980, first to develop information for, and then to participate in, the attempt to rescue the hostages. There were no words to describe what it was like to be in a country in a revolutionary condition. His time on the ground in the Soviet Union had been far more comfortable. Enemy or not, Russia had always been a civilized country with lots of rules and citizens who broke them. But Iran had ignited like a dry forest in a lightning storm. 'Death to America' had been a chant on everyone's lips, and *that*, he remembered, was about as scary as things got when you were in the middle of the mob singing *that* song. One little mistake, just contacting an agent who'd been turned, would have been his death, rather a frightening thought to a man with young children, spook or no spook. Locally they shot some criminals, but spies they mostly hanged. It seemed a gratuitously cruel way to take a man's life.

Some things had changed in the intervening years. Some had not. There was still a suspicion of foreigners here at the customs post. The clerk was backed up by armed men, and their job was to prevent the entry of people like him. For the new UIR, as for the previous country, every new face was a potential spy.

'Klerk,' he said, handing over his passport, 'Ivan Sergeyevich.' What the hell, the Russian cover identity had worked before, and he already had it memorized. Better yet, his Russian was letter-perfect. He'd passed as a Soviet citizen before a uniformed official more than once.

'Chekov, Yevgeniy Pavlovich,' Chavez told the next clerk over.

They were, again, news correspondents. Rules prohibited CIA officers from covering themselves as *American* reporters, but that didn't apply to the foreign media.

'The purpose of your visit?' the first clerk asked.

'To learn about your new country,' Ivan Sergeyevich replied. 'It must be very exciting for everyone.' For their work in Japan, they'd brought camera gear, and a useful little gadget that looked like, and indeed was, a bright light. Not this time.

'He and I are together,' Yevgeniy Pavlovich told his clerk.

The passports were brand-new, though one could not have told it from casual inspection. It was one of the few things Clark and Chavez didn't have to worry about. RVS tradecraft was every bit as good as the former KGB's had been. They made some of the best fake documents in the world. The pages were covered with stamps, many overlapping, and were creased and dog-eared from years of apparent use. An inspector grabbed their bags and opened them. He found clothing, clearly much used, two books, which he flipped through to see if they were pornographic, two cameras of medium quality, their black enamel well-chipped but the lenses new. Each had a carry-on bag with note pads and mini-tape recorders. The inspectors took their time, even after the clerks had done their work, finally passing their country's visitors through with a palpable reluctance.

'*Spasiba*,' John said pleasantly, getting his bags and moving off. Over the years, he'd learned not to conceal his relief completely. Normal travelers were intimidated. He had to be, too, lest he stand apart from them. The two CIA officers went outside to catch a cab, standing together in line silently as the rank of taxis ate up the new arrivals. When they were two back, Chavez dropped his travel bag, and the contents spilled out. He and Clark let two people jump ahead of them in line while he repacked the bag. That almost certainly guaranteed a random cab, unless they were all being driven by spooks.

The trick was to look normal in all respects. Not too stupid. Never too smart. To get disoriented and ask for directions, but not too often. To stay in cheap hotels. And in their particular case, to pray that none of the people who'd seen them during their brief visit to this city crossed their path. The mission was supposed to be a simple one. That was usually the idea. You rarely sent intelligence officers out on complex missions – they'd have the good sense to refuse. The simple ones were hairy enough once you got out there.

'It's called Task Group COMEDY,' Robby told him. 'They got their doorbell rung this morning.' The J-3 explained on for a few minutes.

'Playing rough?' the President asked.

'Evidently, they gave the P-3 a real air show. I've done that myself a few times, back in my young-and-foolish days. They want us to know they're there, and they're not intimidated. The group commander is Greg Kemper. I don't know him, but his rep's pretty good. CINCLANT likes him. He's asking for a ROE change.'

'Not yet. Later today.'

'Okay. I would not expect a night attack, but remember dawn there is midnight here, sir.'

'Arnie, what's the book on the PM?'

'She and Ambassador Williams don't exchange Christmas presents,' the chief of staff replied. 'You met her in the East Room a while back.'

'Warning her off risks having her call Daryaei,' Ben Goodley reminded them all. 'If you confront her, she'll weasel on you.'

'And? Robby?'

'If we get past the Indians, but she warns Daryaei? They can try to block the strait. The Med force will turn the corner in a few hours and join up fifty miles off the entrance. We'll have air cover. It could be exciting, but they should make it. Mines are the scary part. The strait there is pretty deep for them. Closer into Dhahran is another story. The longer the UIR's in the dark, the better, but they may already know what COMEDY is made up of.'

'Or maybe not,' van Damm thought. 'If she thinks she can handle it herself, she might just try to show him what kind of balls she has.'

* * *

The transfer was called Operation CUSTER. All forty aircraft were aloft now, each carrying roughly 250 soldiers in a sky train six thousand miles long. The lead aircraft were now six hours out from Dhahran, leaving Russian airspace and overflying Ukraine.

The F-15 pilots had traded waves with a handful of Russian fighters which had come up to say hello. They were tired now. Their rumps were like painful lead from all the time in the same seat – the airliner pilots behind them could get up and move around; they even had toilets, quite a luxury for a fighter pilot who had an appliance called a relief tube. Arms tightened up. Muscles were sore from staying in the same position. It was to the point that tanking from their KC-135s was becoming difficult, and gradually they came to the opinion that an air-to-air engagement an hour out from their destination might not be much fun at all. Most drank coffee, tried to shift hands on the stick, and stretched as much as they could.

The soldiers were mainly sleeping, still ignorant of the nature of their mission. The airlines had stocked their aircraft normally, and the troops indulged what would be their last chance to have a drink for some time to come. Those who had deployed to Saudi in 1990 and 1991 told their war stories, chief among which was the memory that the Kingdom wasn't a place you went to for the nightlife.

Neither was Indiana, Brown and Holbrook had found, at least not now. They had at least been smart enough to get into a motel before the general panic, and here they were trapped. This motel, like the ones they'd used in Wyoming and Nebraska, catered to truckers. It had a large restaurant, the old-fashioned sort with a counter and booths, and now with masked waitresses and customers who didn't group closely together to socialize. Instead, they ate their meals and went back to their rooms, or to sleep in their trucks. There was a daily dance of sorts. The trucks had to be moved, lest staying in the exact same spot damage the tires. Everyone listened to the radio for hourly news broadcasts. The rooms, the restaurant, and even some of the trucks had televisions for further information and distraction. There was boredom, the tense sort familiar to soldiers but not known to the two Mountain Men.

'Goddamned government,' a furniture hauler said. He had family two states away.

'I guess they showed us who was boss, eh?' Ernie Brown said, for general consumption.

Later, data would show that not a single interstate trucker had caught the virus. Their existence was too solitary for that. But their working lives depended on movement, both because they earned their living that way and because they had chosen to do so. Sitting still was not in their nature. Being told to sit still was even less so.

'What the hell,' another driver added. He couldn't think of anything else to say. 'Goddamned glad I got outa Chicago when I did. That news is scary.'

'You suppose this all makes sense?' someone asked.

'Since when does the government make sense?' Holbrook griped.

'I hear that,' a voice chimed in, and finally the Mountain Men felt at home somewhere. Then, by unspoken consent, it was time for them to leave.

'How the hell much longer will we be stuck here, Pete?' Ernie Brown wanted to know.

'You're askin' me?'

'A whole lot of nothing,' concluded the lead agent. Aref Raman was a little neat for a single man living alone, but not grossly so. One of the FBI agents had noted with surprise that even the man's socks were neatly folded, along with everything else in the bureau drawers. Then one of the group remembered a study of NFL football players. A psychologist had determined after months of study that offensive linemen, whose job was to protect the quarterback, had neat lockers, while defensive linemen, whose job it was to pound the opposing quarterbacks into the turf, were slobs in every respect. It was good for a laugh, and an explanation. Nothing else was found. There was a photo of his parents, both dead. He subscribed to two news magazines, had the full cable options for his two televisions, had no booze in the house, and ate healthy. He had a particular affinity for kosher hot dogs, judging by the freezer. There were no hidden drawers or compartments – they would have found them – and nothing the least bit suspicious. That was both good news and bad.

The phone rang. Nobody answered it, because they weren't there, and they had beepers and cellular phones for their own communications needs.

'Hello, this is 536–3040,' the recording of Raman's voice said, after the second ring. 'Nobody's here to answer the phone right now, but if you leave a message, somebody will get back to you.' Followed by a beep, and in this case, a click.

'Wrong number,' one of the agents said.

'Pull the messages,' the lead agent ordered the technical genius on the team.

Raman owned a digital recording system, and again there was a punch code programmed in by the manufacturer. The agent hit the six digits and another took notes. There were three clicks and a wrong number. Somebody calling for Mr Sloan, whoever that was.

'Rug? Mr Alahad?'

'Sounds like the name of a rug dealer,' another one said. But when they looked around, there was no such rug in the apartment, just the usual cheap wall-to-wall carpet you found in apartments of this type.

'Wrong number.'

'Run the names anyway.' It was more habit than anything else. You checked everything. It was like working FCI. You just never knew.

Just then the phone rang again, and all five of the agents turned to stare at the answering machine, as though it were a real witness with a real voice.

Shit, Raman thought, he'd forgotten to erase the messages from before. There was nothing new. His control officer hadn't called again. It would have been a surprise if he had. With that determined, Raman, sitting in a Pittsburgh hotel room, punched the erase-all code. One nice thing about the new digitals was that, once erased, they were gone forever. That wasn't necessarily true of the ones using tape cassettes.

The FBI agents took note of that, sharing looks.

'Hey, we all do that.' There was general agreement. And everybody got wrong numbers, too. And this was a brother officer. But they'd run the numbers anyway.

*   *   *

Surgeon, to the relief of her detail, was sleeping upstairs in the residence. Roy Altman and the rest assigned to guard her had been going crazy with her on the fever ward – their term for it – at Johns Hopkins, as much from the physical danger as for the fact that she had run herself right into the ground. The kids, being kids, had spent the time like most other American children, watching TV and playing under the eyes of their agents, who now worried about seeing the onset of flu symptoms, blessedly absent from the entire campus. SWORDSMAN was in the Situation Room.

'What's the time there?'

'Ten hours ahead, sir.'

'Make the call,' POTUS ordered.

The first 747, in United livery, crossed into Saudi airspace a few minutes earlier than expected, due to favorable arctic winds. A more circuitous routing at this point would not have helped very much. Sudan had airports and radars, too, as did Egypt and Jordan, and it was assumed that the UIR had informants somewhere in those countries. The Saudi Air Force, augmented by the F-16Cs which had sneaked in from Israel the previous day as part of BUFFALO FORWARD, stood combat air patrol along the Saudi-UIR border. Two E-3B AWACS were up and turning their rotodomes. The sun was rising now in that part of the world – at least one could see first light from their cruising altitude, though the surface, six miles below, was still black.

'Good morning, Prime Minister. This is Jack Ryan,' the President said.

'A pleasure to hear your voice. It is late in Washington, is it not?' she asked.

'We both work irregular hours. I imagine your day is just beginning.'

'So it is,' the voice answered. Ryan had a conventional receiver to his ear. The conversation was on speakerphone as well, and feeding into a digital tape recorder. The CIA had even supplied a voice-stress analyzer. 'Mr President, the troubles in your country, have they improved?'

'We have some hope, but, no, not quite yet.'

'Is there any way in which we might be of assistance?'

Neither voice showed the least emotion beyond the false amity of people suspicious of each other, and trying to hide it.

'Well, yes, actually, there is.'

'Please, then, how may we be of help?'

'Prime Minister, we have some ships heading through the Arabian Sea at the moment,' Ryan told her.

'Is that so?' Total neutrality in the voice.

'Yes, ma'am, it is, and you know it is, and I want your personal assurance that your navy, which is also at sea, will not interfere with their passage.'

'But why do you ask this? Why should we interfere – for that matter, what is the purpose of your ship movement?'

'Your word on the matter will suffice, Prime Minister,' Ryan told her. His right hand gripped a number 2 lead pencil.

'But, Mr President, I fail to understand the purpose of this call.'

'The purpose of this call is to seek your personal assurance that the Indian navy will not interfere with the peaceful passage of United States Navy ships through the Arabian Sea.'

He was so weak, she thought, repeating himself that way.

'Mr President, I find your call unsettling. America has never spoken to us about such a matter before. You say you move warships close to my country, but not the purpose for the move. The movement of such vessels without an explanation is not the act of a friend.' What if she could make him back down?

What did I tell you? the note from Ben Goodley read.

'Very well, Prime Minister, for the third time, will you give me your assurance that there will be no interference in this activity?'

'But why are you invading our waters?' she asked again.

'Very well.' Ryan paused, and then his voice changed. 'Prime Minister, the purpose of the movement does not directly concern your country, but I assure you, those ships will sail on to their destination. Since their mission is one of importance to us, we will not, I repeat not, brook interference of any kind, and I must warn you that should any unidentified ship or aircraft approach our formation, there might be adverse consequences. No, please excuse me, there *will* be such consequences. To avoid that, I give you notice of the passage, and I request your personal assurance to the United States of America that there will be no attack on our ships.'

'And now you threaten me? Mr President, I understand the stress which has come to you of late, but, please, you may not treat sovereign countries in this way.'

'Prime Minister, then I will speak very clearly. An overt act of war has been committed against the United States of America. Any interference with, or attack on, any part of our military will be deemed a further act of war, and whatever country commits such an act will face the most serious possible consequences.'

'But who has done this to you?'

'Prime Minister, that is not your concern unless you wish it to be. I think in the interests of both your country and mine, it would be well if your navy returned to port forthwith.'

'And you blame us, you order us?'

'I began with a request, Prime Minister. You saw fit to evade my request three times. I regard that as an unfriendly act. And so I have a new question: Is it your desire to be at war with the United States of America?'

'Mr President –'

'Because if those ships don't move, Prime Minister, you will be.' The pencil snapped in Ryan's hand. 'I think you may have associated yourself with the wrong friends, Prime Minister. I hope I am incorrect, but if my impression is correct, then your country could well pay dearly for that misjudgment. We have experienced a direct attack on our citizens. It is a particularly cruel and barbaric attack, utilizing weapons of mass destruction.' He enunciated these words very clearly. 'This is not yet known to our citizens. That will soon change,' he told her. 'When it does, Prime Minister, those guilty of launching that attack will face our justice. We will not send notes of protest. We will not call a special meeting of the UN Security Council in New York. We will make war, Prime Minister. We will make war with all the power and rage this country and her citizens can muster.

Do you now understand what I am saying? Ordinary men, women, and now even children have been murdered within our borders by a foreign power. There has even been an attack upon my own child, Prime Minister. Does your country wish to be associated with those acts? If so, Prime Minister, if you wish to be part of that, then the war commences now.'

56

DEPLOYMENT

'Jesus, Jack, you had me convinced,' Jackson breathed.

'Our friend in the clergy won't be as easy,' the President said. He rubbed his two sweaty hands together. 'And we still don't know if she'll keep her word. Okay, Task Group COMEDY is at DEFCON 1. If they think it's hostile, kill it. But for Christ's sake, make sure that commander knows how to use his head.'

The Situation Room was quiet now, and President Ryan felt very alone, despite the people assembled around him. Secretary Bretano and the Joint Chiefs were there. Rutledge was there for State. Secretary Winston, because Ryan trusted his judgment. Goodley, because he was fully briefed in on all the intelligence information; plus his chief of staff and the usual bodyguards. They all showed their support, but it really didn't help all that much. He alone had talked to India, because despite all the help and staff and advice, Jack Ryan was now the United States of America, and the country was going to war.

The media pool learned that over the Atlantic Ocean. America expected an attack at any time from the United Islamic Republic into the other Gulf states. They would be there to cover the story. They also learned about the forces being deployed.

'That's all?' one of the more knowledgeable of them asked.

'That's it for the moment,' the public affairs officer confirmed. 'We hope that the show of force will be sufficient to deter the attack, but if not, it's going to be exciting.'

'Exciting ain't the word.'

Then the PAO told them why it was happening, and the windowless KC-135 that was taking them to Saudi Arabia became very quiet indeed.

*   *   *

Kuwait essentially had two heavy brigades, complemented by a motorized reconnaissance brigade equipped with anti-tank weapons and designed to be a screening force on the border. The two heavy brigades, equipped and trained on the American model, were held back from the border in the usual way so as to be able to move to counter an incursion rather than having to meet the initial attack – possibly in the wrong place. The 10th US Cavalry stood between and slightly behind those two. Overall command was somewhat equivocal. Colonel Magruder was the most senior officer in time of service, and the most experienced tactician, but there were Kuwaitis more senior in rank – all three brigades were commanded by brigadier generals – and it *was* their country. On the other hand, the country was small enough to require only one primary command post, and Magruder was there, both to command his regiment and to advise the Kuwaiti commanders. The latter were both proud and nervous. They were understandably pleased by the strides their small country had made since 1990. No longer the comic-opera force which had disintegrated on the Iraqi invasion – though some sub-units had fought bravely – they had what looked on paper and to the eye like a very capable mechanized force. They were nervous because they were heavily outnumbered, and their mainly reservist soldiers had a long way to go before they met the American training standards to which they aspired. But the one thing they knew was gunnery. Shooting tanks is as enjoyable a pastime as it is a vital one; the empty slots in their formations were explained by the fact that twenty tanks were in the shop for replacement of their main gun tubes. That was being done by civilian contractors while the tank crews paced and waited.

The 10th Cav's helicopters were flying around the country's border, their Longbow radars looking deep into the UIR for movement, and so far seeing nothing of particular note. The Kuwaiti air force was standing a four-plane combat air patrol, with the rest of the force on high alert. Outmanned though they were, this would not be a repeat of 1990. The busiest people were the engineers, who were digging holes for all the tanks so that they could fight hull-down, with only their turrets showing. These were covered with netting to make them invisible from the air.

'And so, Colonel?' the senior Kuwaiti commander asked.

'Nothing wrong with your deployments, General,' Magruder replied, scanning the map again. He didn't show everything he felt. Two or three weeks of intensive training would have been a blessing. He'd run one very simple exercise, one of his squadrons against the Kuwaiti 1st Brigade, and even then he'd gone very easy on them. It wasn't the time to break their confidence. They had enthusiasm, and their gunnery was about seventy percent of American standards, but they had a lot to learn about maneuver warfare. Well, it took time to raise an army, and more time to train field officers, and they were doing their best.

'Your Highness, I need to thank you for your cooperation to this point,' Ryan said over the phone. The wall clock in the Sit Room said 2:10.

'Jack, with luck they will see this and not move,' Prince Ali bin Sheik replied.

'I wish I could agree with that. It is time for me to tell you something you do not yet know, Ali. Our ambassador will present you with full information later in the day. For the moment, you need to know what your neighbors have been up to. It isn't just about the oil, Your Highness.' He went on for five minutes.

'Are you certain of this?'

'The evidence we have will be in your hands in four hours,' Ryan promised. 'We haven't even told our soldiers yet.'

'Might they use these weapons against us?' The natural question. Biological warfare made everyone's skin crawl.

'We don't think so, Ali. Environmental conditions militate against it.' That had been checked, too. The weather forecast for the next week was hot, dry, and clear.

'Those who would use such weapons, Mr President, this is an act of utter barbarism.'

'That's why we do not expect them to back down. They can't –'

'Not "they," Mr President. One man. One godless man. When will you speak to your people about this?'

'Soon,' Ryan replied.

'Please, Jack, this is not our religion, this is not our faith. Please tell your people that.'

'I know that, Your Highness. It isn't about God. It's about power. It always is. I'm afraid I have other things to do.'

'As do I. I must see the King.'

'Please give him my respects. We stand together, Ali, just like before.' With that the line went dead.

'Next, where exactly is Adler right now?'

'Shuttling back to Taiwan,' Rutledge answered. Those negotiations were still going on, though their purpose was now rather clear.

'Okay, he has secure comm links on the plane. You brief him in,' he told the Under Secretary. 'Anything else I need to do right now?'

'Sleep,' Admiral Jackson told him. 'Let us do the all-nighter, Jack.'

'That's a plan.' Ryan rose. He wobbled a bit from the stress and lack of sleep. 'Wake me up if you need me.'

We won't, nobody said.

'Well,' Captain Kemper said, reading the CRITIC message from CINCLANT. 'That makes things a lot simpler.' Range to the Indian battle group was now two hundred miles, about eight hours of steaming – still the term they used, though all the combatant ships were now powered by jet-turbine engines. Kemper lifted the phone and flipped a switch to speak on the ship's 1-MC address system. 'Now hear this. This is the captain speaking.

'Task Group COMEDY is now at DefCon 1. That means if anybody gets close, we shoot him. The mission is to deliver our tank-carriers to Saudi Arabia. Our country is flying in the soldiers to drive them in anticipation of an attack on our allies in the region by the new United Islamic Republic.

'In sixteen hours, we will link up with a surface action making a speed-run down from the Med. We will then enter the Persian Gulf to make our delivery. The group will have friendly air cover in the form of Air Force F-16C fighters, but it is to be expected that the UIR – our old Iranian friends – will not be happy with our arrival.

'USS *Anzio* is going to war, people. That is all for now.' He flipped the switch back. 'Okay, let's start running simulations. I want to see everything those bastards might try on us. We will have an updated intelligence estimate here in two hours. For now, let's see what we can do about aircraft and missile attacks.'

'What about the Indians?' Weps asked.

'We'll be keeping an eye on them, too.' The main tactical display showed a P-3C Orion passing COMEDY to relieve the aircraft now on station. The battle group was heading east, again recrossing its wake, as it had been doing for some time now.

A KH-11 satellite was just sweeping down, northwest-to-southeast, over the Persian Gulf. Its cameras, having already looked at the three heavy corps of the Army of God, were now photographing the entire Iranian coast, looking for the launch sites of Chinese-made Silkworm missiles. The take from the electronic cameras was cross-linked to a communications satellite over the Indian Ocean, and from there to the Washington area, where technicians still wearing chemically impregnated surgical masks started looking for the airplane-shaped surface-to-surface missiles. The fixed launch sites were well known, but the weapon also could be fired off the back of a large truck, and there were plenty of coastal roads to survey.

The first group of four airliners touched down without incident outside Dhahran. There was no arrival ceremony. It was already hot. Spring had come early to the region after the surprisingly cold and wet winter season, and that meant noon temperatures close to 100 degrees, as opposed to the 120 of high summer, but night temperatures down in the forties. It was humid this close to the coast as well.

When the first airliner stopped, the truck-mounted stairs were driven up, and Brigadier General Marion Diggs was the first off. He would be the ground commander for this operation. The virus epidemic still raging in America had also compromised MacDill Air Force Base in Florida, home of Central Command, which had responsibility for this area. The briefing papers he'd seen to this point said that the commander of the 366th Air Combat Wing was also a one-star, but junior to him. It had been a long time since so vital an operation had been turned over to someone as junior as himself, Marion Diggs thought on the way down the steps.

At the bottom was a Saudi three-star. The two men exchanged salutes and entered a car for the ride to the local command post, and an intelligence update. Behind Diggs was the command group of the 11th ACR, and on the other three aircraft, a security group and most of the Second Squadron of the Black Horse. Buses waited to take them to the POMCUS site. It was all rather like the REFORGER exercises of the Cold War, which had anticipated a NATO-Warsaw Pact clash requiring American soldiers to get off the airplanes, board their vehicles, and march off to the front. That had never happened except in simulation, but now, again, it was happening, and this time it was for real. Two hours later, 2nd of the Blackhorse was rolling into the open.

'What do you mean?' Daryaei asked.

'There appears to be a major troop movement under way,' his intelligence chief told him. 'Radar sites in western Iraq have detected commercial aircraft entering Saudi Arabia from Israeli airspace. We also show fighters escorting them and patrolling the border.'

'What else?'

'Nothing at the moment, but it would seem likely that America is moving another force into the Kingdom. I am not sure what it could be – certainly, it cannot be very large. Their German-based divisions are under quarantine, and all their home-quartered divisions are in the same condition. Most of their army is actually deployed for internal security.'

'We should attack them anyway,' his air force adviser urged.

'I think that would be a mistake,' Intelligence said. 'It would be an invasion of Saudi airspace, alerting those goatherds too soon. The Americans can at most move one brigade-sized force. There is a second based at Diego Garcia – the equipment, that is – but we have no information to suggest that it has moved, and even if it does, we expect that our Indian friends can stop it.'

'We trust pagans?' Air Force asked with contempt. That was how Muslims viewed the official religion of the Subcontinent.

'We can trust their antipathy to America. And we can ask

them if their fleet has spotted anything. In any case, the Americans can deploy another brigade-sized force. That is all.'

'Kill it anyway!'

'That throws away operational security,' Intelligence pointed out.

'If they don't know we are coming by now, then they are fools,' Air Force objected.

'The Americans have no reason to suspect that we have taken hostile actions against them. To attack their aircraft, if that's what they are, will alert *them* unnecessarily, not just the Saudis. They are probably concerned about our troop movements in Iraq. So they fly in some small reinforcements. We can deal with them when the time comes,' Intelligence told them.

'I will call India,' Daryaei said, temporizing.

'Navigation radars only . . . make that two air-search, probably from the carriers,' the petty officer said. 'Their course track is zero-niner-zero, speed about sixteen.'

The tactical officer on the Orion, called a tacco, looked down at his chart. The Indian battle group was at the extreme eastern edge of the racetrack pattern they'd been following for the last several days. In less than twenty minutes, they should reverse course to head west. If they turned, things would become exciting. COMEDY was now 120 miles away from the other formation, and his aircraft was feeding constant information to *Anzio* and *Kidd*. Under the wings of the four-engine Lockheed turboprop were four Harpoon missiles. White ones, war shots. The aircraft was now under the tactical command of Captain Kemper on *Anzio*, and on his order they could launch those missiles, two each at the Indian carriers, because they were the long gun of the opposing navy. A few minutes behind would be a swarm of Tomahawks and more Harpoons headed the same way.

'Are they EMCON'D?' the officer wondered.

'With nav sets emitting?' the sailor replied. 'COMEDY must have 'em on their ESM gear by now. Damned sure our guys are lighting up the sky, sir.' COMEDY had essentially two choices. Adopt EMCON – for emissions control – turning off their radars to make the other side expend time and fuel searching for them, or simply light everything off, creating an electronic bubble which the other side could easily see, but the penetration of which would be dangerous. *Anzio* had gone with the second option.

'Any airplane chatter?' the tacco asked another crewman.

'Negative, sir, none at all.'

'Hmph.' As low as the Orion was flying, its presence was probably not known to the Indians, despite their use of air-search gear. He was sorely tempted to pop up and illuminate himself with his own search radar. What were they up to? Might a few ships have broken away from the group, heading west, say, to launch an off-axis missile attack? He couldn't know what they were saying or thinking. All he had were computer-generated course tracks based on radar signals. The computer knew exactly where the aircraft was at all times off the Global Positioning Satellite system. From that the bearing to the radar sources enabled calculation of their location and . . .

'Course change?'

'Negative, system shows them still leading zero-niner-zero at sixteen knots. They are passing out of the box now, sir. This is farther east than we've seen them in three days. They are now thirty miles east of COMEDY's course to the Strait.'

'I wonder if they changed their minds about this . . .'

'Yes, our fleet is at sea,' the Prime Minister told him.

'Have you seen the American ships?'

The leader of the Indian government was all alone in her office. Her Foreign Minister had been in earlier, and was on his way back at this moment. This phone call had been anticipated, but not hoped for.

The situation had changed. President Ryan, weak though she still thought him to be – who else but a weak man would have threatened a sovereign country so? – had nonetheless frightened her. What if the plague in America had been initiated by Daryaei? She had no evidence that it had, and she would never seek such information out. Her country could never be associated with such an act. Ryan had asked – what was it, four times? five? – for her word that the Indian navy would not hinder the American fleet movement. But only one time had he said *weapons of mass destruction*. That was the deadliest code phrase in international exchange. All the more so, her Foreign Minister had told her, because America only possessed one kind of such weapons, and for that reason, America regarded biological weapons and chemical weapons *to be* nuclear weapons. That led to another calculation. Aircraft fought aircraft. Ships fought ships. Tanks fought tanks. One answered an attack with the same weapon used by one's enemy. *Full power and rage*, she remembered also. Ryan had overtly suggested that he would take action based on the nature of the supposed attack by the UIR. Nor, finally, did she discount the lunatic attack on his little daughter. She remembered that from the East Room, the reception after the funeral, how Ryan doted on his children. Weak man though he had to be, he was an *angry* weak man, armed with weapons more dangerous than any others.

Daryaei had been foolish to provoke America in that way. Better just to have launched his attack on Saudi and win with conventional arms on the field of battle, and that would have been that. But, no, he had to try to cripple America at home, to provoke them in a way that was the purest form of lunacy – and now she and her government *and her country* could be implicated, the PM realized.

She hadn't bargained for any of that. Deploying her fleet was chance enough – and the Chinese, what had they done? Launched an exercise, perhaps damaged that air liner – five thousand kilometers away! What risks were *they* taking? Why, none at all. Daryaei expected much of her country, and with his attack on the very citizens of America, it was too much.

'No,' she told him, choosing her words carefully. 'Our fleet units have seen American patrol aircraft, but no ships at all. We have heard, as you perhaps have, that an American ship group is transiting Suez, but only warships and nothing more.'

'You are sure of this?' Daryaei asked.

'My friend, neither our ships nor our naval aircraft have spotted any American ships in the Arabian Sea at all.' The one overflight had been by land-based MiG-23s of the Indian air force. She hadn't lied to her supposed ally. Quite. 'The sea is large,' she added. 'But the Americans are not that clever, are they?'

'Your friendship will not be forgotten,' Daryaei promised her.

The Prime Minister replaced the phone, wondering if she'd done the right thing. Well. If the American ships got to the Gulf, she could always say that they hadn't been spotted. That was the truth, wasn't it? Mistakes happened, didn't they?

'Heads up. I got four aircraft lifting off from Gasr Amu,' a captain said aboard the AWACS. The newly-constituted UIR air force had been working up, too, but mainly over what was the central part of the new country, and hard to spot even from the airborne radar platform.

Whoever had timed this wasn't doing all that badly. The fourth quartet of inbound airliners had just crossed into Saudi airspace, less than two hundred miles from the UIR fighters doing their climb-out. It had been quiet on the air front to this point. Two fighters had been tracked over the last few hours, but those appeared to be check-hops from the mission profiles, probably aircraft that had been fixed for some major or minor defect, then taken up to see if the new widgets worked properly. But this was a flight of four which had taken off in two closely spaced elements. That made them fighters on a mission.

The current air cover for Operation CUSTER in this sector was a flight of four American F-16s, orbiting within twenty miles of the border.

'Kingston Lead, this is Sky-Eye Six, over.'

'Sky, Lead.'

'We have four bandits, zero-three-five your position, angels ten and climbing, course two-niner-zero.' The four American fighters moved west to interpose themselves between the UIR fighters and the inbound airliners.

Aboard the AWACS, a Saudi officer listened in to the radio chatter between the ground radar station controlling the flight of four and the fighters. The UIR fighters, now identified as French-made F-1s, continued to close the border, then turn ten miles short of it, finally tracing only one mile inside. The F-16s did much the same, and the pilots saw each other, and examined one another's aircraft from four thousand yards apart, through the protective visors of their helmets. The air-to-air missiles were clearly visible under the wings of all the aircraft.

'Y' all want to come over and say hello?' the USAF major leading the F-16s said over guard. There was no response. The next installment of Operation Custer proceeded unhindered to Dhahran.

O'Day was in early. His sitter, with no classes to worry about, rather enjoyed the thought of all the money that would come in from this, and the most important bit of news for everyone was that not a single case of the new illness had happened within ten miles of his home. Despite the inconvenience, he had slept at home every night – even though on one occasion that had been a mere four hours. He couldn't be a daddy if he didn't kiss his little girl at least once a day, even in her sleep. At least the ride into work was easy. He'd gotten a Bureau car. It was faster than his pickup, complete with a flashing light that allowed him to zip through all the checkpoints on the way.

On his desk were the case summaries from the background checks of all the Secret Service personnel. The work in nearly every case had been stultifyingly duplicative. Full background checks had been done on every USSS employee, or else they could not have held the security clearances that were an automatic part of their jobs. Birth certificates, high-school photos, and everything else matched up perfectly. But ten files showed loose ends, and all of those would be run down later in the day. O'Day went over all of them. He kept coming back to one.

Raman was of Iranian birth. But America was a nation of immigrants. The FBI had originally been constructed of Irish-Americans, preferably those educated at Jesuit institutions – Boston College and Holy Cross were the favorites, according to the legend – because J. Edgar Hoover was supposed to have believed that no Irish-American with a Jesuit education could conceivably betray his country. Doubtless, there had been some words about that at the time, and even today, anti-Catholicism was the last of the respectable prejudices. But it was well-known that immigrants so often made the most loyal of citizens, some ferociously so. The military and other security agencies often profited from that. Well,

Pat thought, it was easily settled. Just check out the rug thing and let it be. He wondered who Mr Sloan was. A guy who wanted a rug, probably.

There was a quiet to the streets of Tehran. Clark didn't remember them that way from 1979–80. His more recent trip had been different, more like the rest of the region, bustling but not dangerous. Being journalists, they acted like journalists. Clark reentered market areas, talking politely to people about business conditions, the availability of food, what they thought of the unification with Iraq, what their hopes for the future were, and what he got was pure vanilla. Platitudes. The political comments were especially bland, singularly lacking in the passion he remembered from the hostage crisis, when every heart and mind had been turned against the entire outside world – especially America. Death to America. Well, they'd given substance to that wish, John thought. Or someone had. He didn't sense that animus anymore among the people, remembering the strangely cordial jeweler. Probably they just wanted to live, just like everyone else. The apathy reminded him of Soviet citizens in the 1980s. They'd just wanted to get along, just wanted to live a little better, just wanted their society to respond to their needs. There was no revolutionary rage left in them. So why, then, had Daryaei taken his action? How would the people respond to that? The obvious answer was that he'd lost touch, as Great Men so often did. He'd have his coterie of true believers, and a larger number of people willing to ride the bus and enjoy the comfortable seating while everyone else walked and kept out of the way, but that was it. It was fertile ground to recruit agents, to identify those who'd had enough and were willing to talk. What a shame that there was no time to run a proper intelligence operation here. He checked his watch. Time to head back to the hotel. Their first day had been both a waste and part of their cover. Their Russian colleagues would arrive tomorrow.

The first order of business was to check out the names Sloan and Alahad. That started with a check of the telephone book. Sure enough, there was a Mohammed Alahad. He had an ad in the Yellow Pages. Persian and Oriental Rugs. For some reason, people didn't connect 'Persia' with 'Iran,' a saving grace for a lot of rug merchants. The shop was on Wisconsin Avenue, about a mile from Raman's apartment, which was not in the least way remarkable. Similarly, there was a Mr Joseph Sloan in the criss-cross, whose telephone number was 536–4040, as opposed to Raman's 536–3040. A one-digit goof, which easily explained the wrong number on the Secret Service agent's answering machine.

The next step was pure form. The computer records of telephone calls were run by command. The massive numbers of them took almost a minute to run, even with knowledge of the probable dates . . . and there it came up on the agent's screen, a call to 202–536-3040 from 202–459-6777. But that wasn't Alahad's store number, was it? A further check showed -6777 as a pay phone two blocks from the shop. Odd. If he were that close to his shop, why drop a dime – actually a quarter now – to make the call?

Why not make another check? The agent was his squad's techno-genius, with a mustache and a marginal haircut. He'd been something less than a raving success working bank robberies, but had found foreign counterintelligence to his liking. It was like the engineering classes of his college days. You just kept picking at things. He'd also found that the foreign spies he chased thought the same way he did. Toss in his technical prowess . . . hmph, in the past month there had *not* been a call from the rug shop to 536–4040. He went back another month. No. How about the other direction? No, 536–4040 had *never* called 457–1100. Now, if he'd ordered a rug, and those things took time – must have, if the dealer had called to let the guy know it had finally come in . . . why hadn't there been a call about it in either direction?

The agent leaned over to the next desk. 'Sylvia, want to take a look at this?'

'What is it, Donny?'

The Blackhorse was fully on the ground now. Most of them were in their vehicles or attending their aircraft. The 11th Armored Cavalry Regiment comprised 123 M1A2 Abrams main-battle tanks, 127 M3A4 Bradley scout vehicles, 16 M109A6 Paladin 155mm mobile guns, and 8 M270 Multiple-Launch Rocket System tracks, plus a total of 83 helicopters,

26 of which were AH-54D Apache attack choppers. Those were the shooting platforms. They were supported by hundreds of soft vehicles – mostly trucks to carry fuel, food, and ammunition – plus twenty extras locally called Water Buffaloes, a vital need in this part of the world.

The first order of business was to get everyone away from the POMCUS site. The tracked vehicles were driven onto low-boy trailers for the ride north to Abu Hadriyah, a small town with an airport and the designated assembly point for the 11th Cav. As every vehicle rolled out of its warehouse, it stopped on a pre-selected spot painted red. There the GPS navigation systems were checked against a known reference point. Two of the IVIS boxes were down. One of them announced the fact all by itself, sending a coded radio message to the regiment's support troop, demanding that it be replaced and repaired. The other was completely dead, and the crew had to figure it out for themselves. The large red square helped.

The trailer trucks were driven by Pakistanis, a few hundred of the thousands imported into the Saudi Kingdom to do menial labor. For the Abrams and Bradley crews, it would prove to be exciting, while they worked inside their tracks to make sure that everything was working. With the routine tasks done, drivers, loaders, and commanders stuck their heads out of their hatches, hoping to enjoy the view. What they saw was different from Fort Irwin but not terribly exciting. To the east was an oil pipeline. To the west was a lot of nothing. The crews watched anyway – the view was better than they'd experienced on the flight – except for the gunners, many of whom fought motion-sickness, a common problem for people in that position. It was almost as bad for those who could see. The local truckers, it seemed, were paid by the mile and not the hour. They drove like maniacs.

The Guardsmen were beginning to arrive now. They had nothing to do at the moment except set up the tents provided for them, drink lots of water, and exercise.

Supervisor Special Agent Hazel Loomis commanded this squad of ten agents. 'Sissy' Loomis had been in FCI from the beginning of her career, virtually all of it in Washington. Approaching forty now, she still had the cheerleader look that had served her so well earlier in her time as a street agent. She also had a number of successful cases under her belt.

'This looks a little odd,' Donny Selig told her, laying out his notes on her desk.

It didn't require much by way of explanation. Phone contacts between intelligence agents never included the words, 'I have the microfilm.' The most innocuous of messages were pre-selected to convey the proper information. Which was why they were called 'code words.' And it wasn't that the tradecraft was bad. It was just that if you knew what to look for, it looked like tradecraft. Loomis looked the data over, then looked up.

'Got addresses?'

'You bet, Sis,' Selig told her.

'Then let's go see Mr Sloan.' The one bad part about promotion was that being a supervisor denied her the chance to hit the bricks. Not for this one, Loomis told herself.

At least the F-15E Strike Eagle had a crew of two, allowing the pilot and weapons-systems operator to engage in conversation for the endless flight. The same was true of the six B-1B bomber crews; the Lancer even had enough area that people could lie down and sleep – not to mention a sit-down toilet. This meant that, unlike the fighter crews, they didn't have to shower immediately upon reaching Al Kharj, their final destination, south of Riyadh. The 366th Air Combat Wing had three designated 'checkered flag' locations throughout the world. These were bases in anticipated trouble spots, with support equipment, fuel, and ordnance facilities maintained by small caretaker crews, who would be augmented by the 366th's own personnel, mainly flying in by chartered airliners. That included additional flight crews, so that, theoretically, the crew which had flown in from Mountain Home Air Force Base in Idaho could indulge in crew rest, while another relief crew could, theoretically, fly the aircraft off to battle. Fortunately for all concerned, this wasn't necessary. Thoroughly exhausted airmen (and, now, -women) brought their birds in for landing, taxied off to their shelters, and dismounted, handing their charges over to maintenance personnel. The bomb-bay fuel tanks were removed first of all, and replaced with the appliances made to hold weapons, while the crews went off for long showers and briefings from intelligence officers. Over a period of five hours, the entire 366th combat strength was in Saudi, less one F-16C, which had developed avionics trouble and diverted to Bentwaters Royal Air Force Base in England.

'Yes?' The elderly woman wasn't wearing a surgical mask. Sissy Loomis handed her one. It was the new form of greeting in America.

'Good morning, Mrs Sloan. FBI,' the agent said, holding up her ID.

'Yes?' She wasn't intimidated, but she was surprised.

'Mrs Sloan, we're conducting an investigation, and we'd like to ask you a few questions. We just need to clear something up. Could you help us, please?'

'I suppose.' Mrs Joseph Sloan was over sixty, dressed neatly, and looked pleasant enough, if somewhat surprised by all this. Inside the apartment the TV was on, tuned to a local station by the sound of it. The weather forecast was running.

'May we come in? This is Agent Don Selig,' she said, nodding her head to the techno-weenie. As usual, her friendly smile won the day; Mrs Sloan didn't even put the mask on.

'Surely.' The lady of the house backed away from the door.

It took only a single glance to tell Sissy Loomis that something was not quite right here. For one thing, there was no Persian rug to be seen in the living room – in her experience people didn't just buy one of the things. For another, this apartment was just too neat.

'Excuse me, is your husband in?' The response was immediate, and pained.

'My husband passed away last September,' she told the agent.

'Oh, I am sorry, Mrs Sloan. We didn't know.' And with that a fairly routine follow-up changed into something very different indeed.

'He was older than me. Joe was seventy-eight,' she said, pointing to a picture on the coffee table of two people a long time ago, one about thirty and one in her late teens.

'Does the name Alahad mean anything to you, Mrs Sloan?' Loomis asked after sitting down.

'No. Should it?'

'He deals in Persian and Oriental rugs.'

'Oh, we don't have any of those. I'm allergic to wool, you see.'

57

NIGHT PASSAGE

'Jack?' Ryan's eyes clicked open to see that there was bright sunlight coming through the windows. His watch said it was just after eight in the morning.

'What the hell? Why didn't anybody –'

'You even slept through the alarm,' Cathy told him. 'Andrea said that Arnie said to let you sleep till about now. I guess I needed it, too,' SURGEON added. She'd been in bed for over ten hours before waking at seven. 'Dave told me to take the day off,' she added.

Jack jolted up and moved at once into the bathroom. When he came back, Cathy, in her housecoat, handed over his briefing papers. The President stood in the center of the room, reading them. Reason told him that if anything serious had happened he would have been awakened – he had slept through the clock-radio alarm before, but he'd never failed to be aroused by a phone. The papers told him that all was, if not exactly well, then relatively stable. Ten minutes after that, he was dressed. He took the time to say hello to his kids, and kiss his wife. Then he headed out.

'SWORDSMAN is moving,' Andrea said into her radio mike. 'Sit Room?' she asked POTUS.

'Yeah. Whose idea was it to –'

'Mr President, that was the chief of staff, but he was right, sir.'

Ryan looked at her as she punched the elevator button for the ground floor. 'I guess I'm outvoted, then.'

The national-security team had clearly been up all night on his behalf. Ryan had coffee waiting at his place. They'd been living on it.

'Okay, what's happening over there?'

'COMEDY is now one hundred thirty miles beyond the Indians – would you believe they resumed their patrol station *behind* us?' Admiral Jackson told his Commander-in-Chief.

'Playing both sides of the street,' Ben Goodley concluded.
'It's a good way to get hit by traffic in both directions,'
Arnie put in.

'Go on.'

'Operation CUSTER is just about done. The 366th is also
in Saudi, less one broke fighter that diverted to England. The
11th Cav is rolling out of its storage site to an assembly area.
So far,' the J-3 said, 'so good. The other side sortied some
fighters to the border, but we and the Saudis had a blocking
force, and nothing happened aside from some mean looks.'

'Anybody think they're going to back down?' Ryan asked.

'No.' This came from Ed Foley. 'They can't, not now.'

The rendezvous took place fifty miles off Cape Rass al Hadd,
the far southeast corner of the Arabian Peninsula. Cruisers
Normandy and *Yorktown*, destroyer *John Paul Jones*, and
frigates *Underwood, Doyle,* and *Nicholas* took a trailing position so that *Platte* and *Supply* could take them alongside
after their high-speed run down from Alexandria, to top off
their bunkers. Helicopters ferried the captains to *Anzio*,
whose captain was senior, for an hour's worth of discussion
of the mission. Their destination was Dhahran. To get there
they had to drive northwest into the Strait of Hormuz. Getting there would take just over six hours, 2200 hours local
time. The strait was twenty miles across and speckled with
islands, plus it was one of the most heavily traveled waterways in the world – even now, despite the growing crisis.
Supertankers, one of which displaced more water than all of
the warships in the now-designated TF-61.1 combined, were
merely the best-known vessels transiting the area. There
were also massive container ships wearing the flags of ten
nations, and even a multilevel sheep carrier which looked
like a big-city parking garage, which was bringing in live
mutton from Australia. The smell of it was famous on all
the oceans of the world. The strait was covered by radar to
establish traffic control – the possibility of a ramming incident between two supertankers didn't bear thinking about –
which meant that TF-61.1 would be unlikely to sneak in
entirely unnoticed. But they could do a few things. At the
narrowest point, the Navy ships would hold to the south,
dodging between islands belonging to Oman, and hopefully

somewhat obscured by the clutter. Next they'd move south of Abu Musa, past the crowd of oil platforms, again using them for radar cover, and then make a straight run for Dhahran, past the mini-states of Qatar and Bahrain. Opposition, the intelligence officers said, included ships of American, British, Chinese, Russian, and French origin, all of them armed with one sort of missile or another. The most important ships in the group, of course, were totally unarmed. Maintaining their box formation, *Anzio* would lead them, 2,000 yards in front. *Normandy* and *Yorktown* would take position 2,000 yards to starboard, with *Jones* in trail. The two under way-replenishment ships, with *O'Bannon* and all the frigates in close escort, would form a second, decoy group. Helicopters would be aloft, both to patrol and, with their radar transponders on, to simulate much larger targets. The various COs agreed on the plan and waited for their helicopters to return them to their commands. It was the first time in ages that an American naval formation had stood in harm's way without a carrier in close support. Their bunkers full of fuel, the group formed up as planned, pointed their bows northwest, and bent on twenty-six knots. At 1800 local time, a flight of four F-16 fighters blazed overhead, both to give the Aegis ships a chance to practice fire-control against live targets and also to verify the IFF codes to be used for the night's mission.

Mohammed Alahad, they saw, was just as ordinary as hell. He'd come to America more than fifteen years earlier. He was said to be widowed and childless. He ran a decent and profitable business on one of Washington's nicer shopping streets. He was, in fact, in there right now. Though the CLOSED sign was on the door, they supposed he had nothing better to do but sit in his shop and go over his bills.

One of Loomis's squad went up to the shop and knocked on the door. Alahad came to open it, and a brief conversation ensued, with the expected gestures, and they could figure what was being said. *I'm sorry, but all businesses are closed because of the President's order – Yeah, sure, but I don't have anything to do, and neither do you, right? – Yes, but it is an order – Hey, who's gonna know, what'd'ya say?* Finally the agent went in, wearing a surgical mask. He stayed there for ten minutes before coming back out, walking around the corner, and making a radio call from his car.

'It's a rug shop,' the agent told Loomis over the encrypted radio channel. 'If we want to toss the place, we'll have to wait.' There was already a tap on the phone line, but so far there had not been a single call in or out.

The other half of her squad was in Alahad's apartment. There they found a photo of a woman and a child, probably his son, wearing something like a uniform – about fourteen, the agent thought, photographing them with a Polaroid. But again, everything was pure vanilla. It was exactly the way a businessman would live in the Washington area, or an intelligence officer. You just couldn't tell. They had the beginning of a case, but not enough evidence to take to a judge, certainly not enough for a search warrant. Their probable-cause quotient was a little on the thin side. But this was a national-security investigation involving the personal safety of the President, and headquarters *had* told them that there were no rules. They'd already committed two technical violations of the law in invading two apartments without a warrant, and two more in tapping a couple of phone lines. With all that work accomplished, Loomis and Selig made their way into an apartment building across the street. From the manager, they learned that there was a vacant apartment facing Alahad's storefront. They got the keys to that without any difficulty and set up their surveillance of the front, while two more agents watched the back door. Sissy Loomis then used her cellular phone to call headquarters. Maybe it wasn't enough to take to a judge or a US attorney, but it was enough to talk to another agent about.

One other potential subject wasn't completely clear yet, O'Day noted. There was Raman, and a black agent whose wife was a Muslim and who was evidently trying to convert her husband – but the agent had discussed it with his comrades, and there was a notation in his file that this agent's marriage, like others in the Service, was on shaky ground.

The phone rang.

'Inspector O'Day.'

'Pat? It's Sissy.'

'How's Raman looking?' He'd worked three cases with her, all involving Russian spies. The cheerleader had the jaw of a pit bull once she got onto something.

'The message on his phone, the wrong number?'

'Yeah?'

'Our rug merchant was calling a dead person whose wife is allergic to wool,' Loomis told him.

Click.

'Keep going, Sis.' She read off her notes and the information garnered by the people who'd entered the dealer's apartment.

'This one feels real, Pat. The tradecraft is just too good. Right out of the book. It looks so normal that you don't think about it. But why the pay phone, except that he's worried somebody might have a tap on his phone? Why call a dead man by mistake? And why did the wrong number go to somebody on the Detail?'

'Well, Raman's out of town.'

'Keep him there,' Loomis advised. They didn't have a case. They were still struggling for probable cause. If they arrested Alahad, he'd have the sense to ask for a lawyer – and what did they have? He'd made a phone call. He wouldn't have to defend the call. He just had to say nothing. His lawyer would say it was all some kind of mistake – Alahad might even have a plausible explanation already prepared; he'd keep that one in his pocket, of course – ask for evidence, and the FBI would have nothing to show.

'That tips our hand, too, doesn't it?'

'Better safe than sorry, Pat.'

'I have to take this to Dan. When are you tossing the shop?'

'Tonight.'

The troopers of the Blackhorse were thoroughly exhausted. Fit and desert-trained soldiers that they were, they'd spent two-thirds of a day in airplanes with dry air, sitting in cramped seats, their personal weapons in the overhead bins – that always got a curious reaction from the stewardesses – and then arrived eleven time zones away in blazing heat. But they did what they had to do.

First came gunnery. The Saudis had established a large shooting range for their own use, with pop-up steel targets as close as three hundred meters and as far as five thousand.

Gunners bore-sighted their weapons, then tried them out, using real ammunition instead of practice, then learned that the war shots were far more accurate, the projectiles flying 'right through the dot,' meaning the circular reticle in the center of their sighting systems. Once off the transport trailers, drivers exercised their mounts to make sure that everything worked properly, but the tanks and Bradleys were in the nearly mint condition promised on the flight over. Radio checks were made so that everyone could talk to everyone else. Then they verified the all-important IVIS data links. The more mundane tasks came last of all. The Saudi-deployed M1A2s did not yet have the newest modification to the vehicle series, pallet-loaded ammunition racks. Instead there was a large steel-wire bustle for personal things, especially water. One by one, the crews cycled their vehicles through the course. The Bradley crews even got to fire a single TOW missile each. Then they entered the reloading area, taking on new ammunition to replace what had been expended on the range.

It was all quiet and businesslike. The Blackhorse, because they trained other soldiers so regularly in the fine art of mechanized death, were utterly desensitized to the routine tasks of soldiering. They had to remind themselves that this was not *their* desert – deserts all look pretty much alike; this one, however, didn't have creosote bushes and coyotes. It did have camels and merchants. The Saudis honored their hospitality laws by providing food and soft drinks in abundance to the troopers, while their senior officers conferred over maps with the region's bitter coffee.

Marion Diggs was not a big man. A cavalryman all of his life, he'd always enjoyed the ability to direct sixty tons of steel with his fingertips, to reach out and touch someone else's vehicle at three miles' distance. Now he was a senior commander, effectively commanding a division, but with a third of it two hundred miles to the north, and another third aboard some ships which would be running a gauntlet later this evening.

'So what are we really up against, how ready are they?' the general asked.

Satellite photos went down, and the senior American intelligence officer, based at KKMC, went through his mission brief. It took thirty terse minutes, during which Diggs stood. He was very tired of sitting.

'STORM TRACK reports minimal radio traffic,' the briefing officer, a colonel, reported. 'We need to remember that they're pretty exposed where they are, by the way.'

'I have a company moving to cover it,' a Saudi officer reported. 'They should be in position by morning.'

'What's Buffalo doing?' Diggs asked. Another map went down. The Kuwaiti dispositions looked all right to his eye. At least they were not forward-deployed. Just the screening force on the berm, he saw, with the three heavy brigades in position to counter a penetration. He knew Magruder. In fact, he knew all three of the ground-squadron commanders. If the UIR hit there first, outnumbered or not, the Blue Force would give the Red one hell of a bloody nose.

'Enemy intentions?' he inquired next.

'Unknown, sir. There are elements to this we do not understand yet. Washington has told us to expect an attack, but not why.'

'What the hell?'

'Tonight or tomorrow morning for that, best I can tell you, sir,' the intel officer replied. 'Oh, we have newsies assigned to us. They flew in a few hours ago. They're in a hotel in Riyadh.'

'Marvelous.'

'In the absence of knowledge of what they plan to do . . .'

'The objective is plain, is it not?' the senior Saudi commander observed. 'Our Shi'ite neighbors have all the desert they need.' He tapped the map. 'There is our economic center of gravity.'

'General?' another voice asked. Diggs turned to his left. 'Colonel Eddington?'

'Center of gravity is political, not military. We might want to keep that in mind, gentlemen,' the colonel from Carolina pointed out. 'If they want to go for the coastal oil fields, we'll have a lot of strategic warning.'

'They do have us outnumbered, Nick. That does give them a certain degree of strategic flexibility. Sir, I see a lot of fuel trucks in these photos,' the American general noted.

'They stopped at the Kuwait border the last time because they were out of fuel,' the Saudi commander reminded them.

The Saudi army – actually called their National Guard – comprised five heavy brigades, almost all of it American equipment. Three were deployed south of Kuwait, with one at Ras al Khafji, site of the only invasion of the Kingdom, but right on the water, and nobody expected an attack from the sea. It was not unusual for soldiers to prepare to fight the last war, the American remembered.

For his part, Eddington remembered a quote from Napoleon. When shown a defense plan that had troops evenly spaced on the French border, he'd asked the officer if the idea was to prevent smuggling. That defensive concept had been given the patina of legitimacy by NATO's doctrine of forward defense on the inner German border, but it had never been tested, and if there were ever a place to trade space for time, it was the Saudi desert. Eddington kept his mouth shut on that one. He was junior to Diggs, and the Saudis seemed quite possessive about their territory, as most people were. He and Diggs shared a look. As the 10th Cav was the theater reserve for the Kuwaitis, so the 11th would perform the same function for the Saudis. That might change when his Guardsmen mounted their tracks at Dhahran, but for the moment this deployment would have to do.

One big problem with the situation was the command relationship in place. Diggs was a one-star – one hell of a good one, Eddington knew, but just a brigadier. Had CENTCOM been able to fly over, he would have had the rank status to make firmer suggestions to the Saudis. Evidently, Colonel Magruder of the Buffalo Cav had done something like that, but Diggs's position was just a little ticklish.

'Well, we'll have a couple of days, anyway.' The American general turned. 'Get additional recon assets in place. If those six divisions fart, I want to know what they had for dinner.'

'We'll have Predators going up at sunset,' the intel colonel promised.

Eddington walked outside to light a cigar. He needn't have troubled himself, he realized after a few puffs. The Saudis all smoked.

'Well, Nick?' Diggs asked, joining him.

'Beer'd be nice.'

'Just empty calories,' the general observed.

'Four-to-one odds, and they have the initiative. That's if

my people get their gear in time. This could get right interesting, Diggs.' Another puff. 'Their deployments suck.' A phrase acquired from his students, his senior thought. 'By the way, what are we calling this?'

'BUFORD, Operation BUFORD. Pick a moniker for your brigade, Nick?'

'How's WOLFPACK grab you? It's the wrong school, but TARHEEL just doesn't sound right. This damned thing's going pretty fast, General.'

'One lesson the other side *must* have learned from the last one: don't give us time to build our forces up.'

'True. Well, I have to see after my people.'

'Use my chopper,' Diggs told him. 'I'll be here a while.'

'Yes, sir.' Eddington turned, saluted, and started walking off. Then he turned. 'Diggs?'

'Yes?'

'Maybe we're not as well-trained as Hamm and his boys, but we'll get it done, y'hear?' He saluted again, tossed his cigar, and walked off to the Black Hawk.

Nothing moves as quietly as a ship. An automobile moving at this speed, a fraction below thirty miles per hour, made noise one could hear for hundreds of yards on a silent night, but for a ship it was the high-frequency *swish* of steel hull cutting through what were at the moment calm seas, and that didn't carry very far at all. Those aboard could feel the vibrations of the engine, or hear the deep sucking breath of the turbine engines, but that was all, and those sounds scarcely carried a hundred yards across the water at night. Just the swish, and behind every ship was a foaming wake, a ghostly shade of green in the water from tiny organisms upset by the pressure wave of their passage, and phosphorescing as some sort of biological protest to the disturbance. To those on the ships, it seemed hellishly bright. On every bridge, the lights were turned down, so that night vision wouldn't be compromised. Navigation lights were turned off, a rules-of-the-road violation in these confined waters. Lookouts used conventional binoculars and light-amplification gear to scan forward. The formation was just now turning the corner, in the narrowest part of the passage.

In every combat information center, people hovered over

scopes and charts, talking in whispers lest they somehow be heard. Those who smoked wished they could in the anti-septic spaces, and those who'd quit now wondered why. Something about a health hazard, they remembered as they contemplated surface-to-surface missiles mounted in emplacements about fifteen thousand yards away, each of them with a ton of explosives right behind the seeker-head.

'Coming left, new course two-eight-five,' the officer of the deck reported on *Anzio*.

On the main plot, there were over forty 'targets,' as radar contacts were called, each with a vector showing approximate course and speed. The number of inbounds and outbounds was about the same. Some of them were huge, the radar returns of supertankers being about that of a medium-sized island.

'Well, we've made it this far,' Weps said to Captain Kemper. 'Maybe they're asleep.'

'Maybe there really is a Great Pumpkin, Charlie Brown.'

Only navigation radars were turning now. The Iranian/UIR-ians had to have ESM gear over there, but if they were standing a patrol in the Strait of Hormuz, they hadn't spotted it yet. There were unexplained targets. Fishing boats? Smugglers? Somebody in a pleasure craft? There was no telling. Probably the enemy was a little reticent about sending their vessels too far over the centerline of the strait. The Arabs were as territorial as everyone else, Kemper imagined.

The ships were all at battle stations. All combat systems were fully powered up, but on standby. If somebody turned toward them, they would first try to get a visual. If somebody lit them up with a targeting radar, then the ship on the clearest bearing would step up her alert level somewhat and make a few sweeps with the SPY radars to see if there might be an inbound track. But that would be tough. Those missiles all had independent seeker-heads, and the strait was crowded, and a missile just might acquire something unintended. The other side couldn't be all that trigger-happy. They might even end up slaughtering a few thousand sheep, Kemper thought with a smile. As tense as this part of the mission was, the task for the other side wasn't all *that* easy.

'Course change on track four-four, coming left,' a quarter-master said.

That one was a surface contact just inside UIR-ian waters, seven miles away and passing aft. Kemper leaned forward. A computer command showed the contact's course-track for the last twenty minutes. It had been moving along at mere steerage speed, about five knots. It was now doing ten, and had turned ... toward the trailing decoy group. That data was linked to USS *O'Bannon*, whose captain was the senior officer for the group. The range between the two ships was 16,000 yards and closing.

Things got more interesting. *Normandy*'s helicopter closed on the track from behind, keeping low. The pilots saw a green-white bloom as the unknown craft increased power, stirring the water and disturbing more of the organisms which somehow survived all the pollution here. A sudden burst of power meant ...

'That's a gunboat,' the pilot reported over the data link. 'He just goosed it. Target has just increased power.'

Kemper grimaced. He had a choice now. Do nothing, and maybe nothing would happen. Do nothing, and maybe give the gun/missile boat the first shot at *O'Bannon* and her group. Do something, and risk alerting the other side. But if the enemy craft shot first, the enemy would know something anyway, right? Maybe. Maybe not. It was a complex set of data for five seconds. He waited five more.

'Target is a missile boat, I see two launchers, target steadying down on course.'

'He's got a direct line to *O'Bannon*, sir,' Weps reported.

'Radio chatter, I have radio chatter on UHF, bearing zero-one-five.'

'Take the shot,' Kemper said instantly.

'Shoot!' Weps said over the voice channel to the helo.

'Roger, engaging!'

'Combat, lookout, sir, I have a flash like a missile launch on the port quarter – make that two, sir,' a speaker announced.

'Give it a sweep –'

'Two more launches, sir.'

Shit, Kemper thought. The helo carried only two Penguin antiship missiles. The enemy had gotten the first two off. And he couldn't do anything now. The decoy group was fulfilling its function. It was getting shot at.

'Two vampires inbound – target destroyed,' the pilot added, announcing the destruction of the missile boat – confirmed a moment later by the topside lookout. 'Say again, two vampires inbound *O'Bannon*.'

'Silkworms are big targets,' Weps said.

They watched the mini-battle imperfectly. The navigation-radar display showed *O'Bannon* changing course to port. That would be to unmask her point-defense missile system, located far aft. It would also provide a huge radar target to the inbound missiles. The destroyer did not fire off her decoys for fear that spoofing the inbounds would only divert them to the replenishment ships she was guarding. An automatic decision? Kemper wondered. A considered one? Ballsy either way. The destroyer's illumination radar came on. That meant she was firing her missiles, but the navigation radar couldn't tell. Then at least one of the frigates joined in.

'All kinda flashes aft,' the topside lookout said next. '*Wow*, that was a big one! There goes another!' Then five seconds of silence.

'*O'Bannon* to group, we're okay,' a voice reported.

For now, Kemper thought.

The Predators were up, three of them, one each for the three corps encamped southwest of Baghdad, motoring through the air at only twice the speed of a tank. None of them got as far as planned. Thirty miles short of their objectives, their look-down thermal cameras showed the glowing shapes of armored vehicles. The Army of God was moving. The feed to STORM TRACK was instantly cross-loaded to KKMC, and from there all over the world.

'Another couple of days would have been nice,' Ben Goodley thought aloud.

'How ready are our people?' Ryan turned to the J-3.

'The 10th's ready to rock. The 11th needs at least a day. The other brigade doesn't even have its equipment yet,' Jackson replied.

'How long before contact?' the President asked next.

'At least twelve hours, maybe eighteen. Depends on where they're going, exactly.'

Jack nodded. 'Arnie, has Callie been briefed in on all this?'

'No, not at all.'
'Then let's get that done. I have a speech to make.'

Alahad must have gotten bored running a business with no customers, Loomis thought. He left early, walked to where his car was parked, and drove off. Tailing him on such empty streets would probably be fairly easy. A few minutes later, the subject was observed to park his car and enter his apartment building. Then she and Selig walked out of the unit they'd been in, crossed the street, and walked around the back. There were two locks on the door, which caused the junior agent to take ten minutes to defeat them, much to his own annoyance. Then came the alarm system, but that was more easily accomplished. It was an old one with a socket key and a very simple disarming code. Inside they found a few more photos, one, probably, of his son. They checked the Rolodex first, and there was the card for J. Sloan, with the number 536–4040, but no address.

'Tell me what you think,' Loomis said.

'I think it's a new card, not dog-eared or anything like that, and I think there's a dot over the first numeral *four*. Tells him which number to change, Sis.'

'This guy's a player, Donny.'

'I think you're right, and that makes Aref Raman one, too.'

But how to prove it?

The cover might or might not have been blown. There was no knowing. Kemper assessed the situation as best he could. Maybe the missile boat had gotten off a broadcast and received permission to fire . . . Maybe the young commander had decided to shoot on his own . . . probably not. Dictatorial countries didn't give much autonomy to their military commanders. If you were the dictator and you started doing that, it was a sure way to find your back to a wall sooner or later. The score to this point was USN 1 and UIR 0. Both groups were continuing, going southwest now into a widening gulf, still doing twenty-six knots, still surrounded by merchant traffic, and the electronic environment was alive with ship-to-ship chatter wondering what the hell had just happened north of Abu Masa.

Omani patrol boats were out now, and *they* were talking back and forth with somebody, perhaps the UIR, asking what was going on.

In confusion, Kemper decided, there was profit. It was dark out, and identifying ships in darkness was never an easy business.

'When's nautical twilight?'

'Five hours, sir,' the quartermaster of the watch replied.

'That's a hundred fifty miles to the good. We continue as before. Let them sort things out if they can.' Getting as far as Bahrain without detection would be miracle enough.

They laid it all out on Inspector O'Day's desk. 'It all' amounted to three pages of notes and a couple of Polaroid photographs. The most important-looking tidbit was a printout of the phone records, duplicating Selig's scribbling. That was also the only legal piece of evidence they had.

'Not exactly the thickest pile of proof I've ever seen,' Pat noted.

'Hey, Pat, you said to move fast,' Loomis reminded him. 'They're both dirty. I can't prove it to a jury, but that's enough to start a major investigation, assuming we have the luxury of time, which I don't think we do.'

'Correct. Come on,' he said, rising. 'We have to see the Director.'

It wasn't as though Murray weren't busy enough. The FBI wasn't exactly running the epidemiological investigation of all the Ebola cases, but the Bureau's agents were doing a lot of legwork. There was the ongoing, and practically new, case on the attack on Giant Steps, which was both criminal and FCI – and an inter-agency case to boot. And now this, the third 'put everything else aside' situation in less than ten days. The inspector waved his way past the secretaries and walked into the Director's office without a knock.

'It's a good thing I wasn't taking a leak,' Murray observed.

'I didn't think you'd have time for that. I don't,' Pat told him. 'There's probably a mole in the Service after all, Dan.'

'Oh?'

'Oh, yeah, and oh, shit. I'll let Loomis and Selig walk you through it.'

'Can I take this to Andrea Price without getting shot?' the Director asked.

'I think so.'

58

THE LIGHT OF DAY

It wasn't something to celebrate, but for the second day in a row, new Ebola cases had dropped. Of the new cases identified, moreover, about a third were people who tested positive for the antibodies but were asymptomatic. CDC and USAM-RIID rechecked the data twice before reporting it to the White House, also cautioning that it was too preliminary to be released to the public. The travel ban, it seemed, and the spinoff effects it was having on interpersonal contacts, was working – but the President couldn't say it was working, because then it would stop working.

The Giant Steps case was also ongoing, mainly a task of the FBI laboratory division. There, electronic microscopes were being used for something other than the identification of Ebola strands, and were narrowing in on pollen and other tiny particles. This was complicated by the fact that the Giant Steps attack had been made in the spring, when the air was full of pollens.

Mordecai Azir, it was now firmly established, was a quintessential unperson who had sprung into existence seemingly for a single purpose and, fulfilling it, had disappeared. But he had left behind photographs, and there were ways of dealing with that, Ryan learned. He wondered if there might be some good news to end the day. There wouldn't be.

'Hi, Dan.' He was back in his office. The Situation Room was just one more reminder that his next major order was to send people into combat.

'Mr President,' the FBI Director said, entering with Inspector O'Day and Andrea Price.

'Why do you look so happy?'

And then they told him.

It was a brave man who awoke the Ayatollah Mahmoud Haji Daryaei before dawn, and since those around him feared his wrath, it took two hours for them to summon the courage to do so. Not that it would help matters. At four in the morning in Tehran, the phone by the side of his bed rang. Ten minutes after that, he was in the sitting room of his private apartment, his dark, sunken eyes waiting to punish those responsible.

'We have a report that American ships have entered the Gulf,' the intelligence chief told him.

'When and where?' the Ayatollah asked quietly.

'It was after midnight at the narrows. One of our missile-patrol boats spotted what it reported to be an American destroyer. It was ordered in to attack by the local naval commander, but we've heard nothing more from the boat.'

'That is all?' *You awakened me for* this?

'There was some radio traffic in the area, ships talking back and forth. They talked about several explosions. We have reason to believe that our missile boat was attacked and destroyed by someone, probably an aircraft – but an aircraft from where?'

'We want your permission to commence air operations to sweep the Gulf after dawn. We have never done this without your word,' the air force chief pointed out.

'Permission is *given*,' Daryaei told them. Well, he *was* awake now, the cleric told himself. 'What else?'

'The Army of God is making its approach march to the border area. The operation is proceeding as scheduled.' Surely this news would please him, the intelligence chief thought.

Mahmoud Haji nodded. He'd hoped for a decent night's sleep, in anticipation of being up long hours for the next few days, but it was his nature that, once awakened, he could not return to sleep. He looked at his desk clock – he didn't wear a watch – and decided that the day would have to begin.

'Will we surprise them?'

'Somewhat, certainly,' Intelligence responded. 'The army is under strict orders to maintain radio silence. The American listening posts are very sensitive, but they cannot hear nothing. When they reach Al Busayyah, we must expect detection, but then we will be ready to jump off, and it will be at night.'

Daryaei shook his head. 'Wait, what did our patrol boat tell us?'

'He reported an American destroyer or frigate, possibly

with other ships, but that was all. We will have aircraft up to look in two hours.'

'Their transport ships?'

'We don't know,' Intelligence admitted. He'd hoped that they were past that.

'*Find out!*'

The two men took their leave with that order. Daryaei rang his servant for tea. He had another thought just then. All would be settled, or at least solved, when the Raman boy fulfilled his mission. The report was that he was in place, and had received his order. Why, then, hadn't he fulfilled it! the Ayatollah asked himself, with a building anger. He looked at the clock again. It was too early to make a call.

Kemper had given his crew something akin to a stand-down. The automation of the Aegis ships made that possible, and so, starting two hours after the incident with the gunboat – missile boat, he corrected himself – crewmen were allowed to rotate off their battle stations, to relieve themselves, to get something to eat, and in many cases to pump a little iron. That had lasted an hour, with each officer and man having had fifteen minutes. They were all back now. It was two hours to nautical twilight. They were just under a hundred miles from Qatar, now heading west-northwest, after having dodged behind every island and oil platform that might confuse an enemy radar post. COMEDY had been through the tough part. The Gulf was far wider here. There was sea room to maneuver in and to make full use of his powerful sensors. The radar picture in *Anzio*'s CIC showed a flight of four F-16s twenty miles north of his formation, their IFF codes clear on the display – his people had to be careful about that. It would have been better if there could be an AWACS aloft, but, he had just learned an hour before, all of those were deployed up north. Today, there would be a fight. It would not be the sort of thing Aegis had been designed for, or quite what he'd been trained for, but that was the Navy for you.

The decoy group he ordered south. Their job was done for now. With the sun up, there would be no disguising what COMEDY was and where they were going, he thought.

* * *

'How sure of this are you?' POTUS asked. 'Christ, I've been alone with the guy a hundred times!'

'We know,' Price assured him. 'We know. Sir, it's hard to believe. I've known Jeff on and off –'

'He's the basketball guy. He told me who was going to win the NCAA finals. He was right. His *point spread* was right on.'

'Yes, sir.' Andrea had to agree with that, too. 'Unfortunately, these items are a little hard to explain.'

'Are you going to arrest him?'

'We can't.' Murray took that one. 'It's one of those situations where you know, or think you know, but can't prove anything. Pat here had an idea, though.'

'Then let's hear it,' Ryan ordered. His headache was back. No, that wasn't right. The intervening, brief period without a headache had ended. Bad enough that he'd been told of the vague possibility that the Secret Service was compromised, but now they thought they had proof – no, worse, he corrected himself, not good enough for proof, just more fucking suspicion! – that one of the people trusted to be around him and his family was a potential assassin. Would this never end? But he listened anyway.

'Actually, it's pretty simple,' O'Day concluded.

'No!' Price said immediately. 'What if –'

'We can control that. There won't be any real danger,' the inspector assured everyone.

'Hold it,' SWORDSMAN said. 'You say you can smoke the guy out?'

'Yes, sir.'

'And I actually get to *do* something instead of just sitting here like a goddamned king?'

'Yes, sir,' Pat repeated.

'Where do I sign up?' Ryan asked rhetorically. 'Let's do it.'

'Mr President –'

'Andrea, you'll be here, right?'

'Well, yes, but –'

'Then it's approved,' POTUS told her. 'He doesn't get *near* my family. I mean that. If he even looks at the elevator, you take him down yourself, Andrea, got that?'

'I understand, Mr President. West Wing only.'

With that, they walked downstairs to the Situation Room,

where Arnie and the rest of the national-security team were watching a map display on a large-screen TV.

'Okay, let's light up the sky,' Kemper told the CIC crew. On command, *Anzio* and the other four Aegis ships flipped their SPY radars from standby to full radiated power. There was no percentage in hiding anymore. They were right under a commercial air route designated W-15, and any airline pilot could look down and see the small box of ships. When one did, he'd probably talk about it. The element of surprise had its practical limits.

In a second, the three big screens showed numerous air tracks. This had to be the busiest hunk of airspace outside O'Hare, Kemper thought. The IFF scan showed a flight of four F-16 fighters deployed northwest of his formation. There were six airliners aloft, and the day had scarcely started. Missile specialists ran practice tracks just to exercise the computers, but really the Aegis system was designed to be one of those supposedly all-powerful things that could sit still one second and raise hell the next. They'd come to the right place to do that.

The first Iranian fighters to head into the sky that day were two aged F-14 Tomcats from Shiraz. The Shah had purchased about eighty of the fighters from Grumman in the 1970s. Ten could still fly, with parts cannibalized from all the others or procured on the world's lively black market in combat-aircraft components. These flew southeast, overland to Bandar Abbas, then they increased speed and darted south to Abu Musa, passing just north of it, with the pilots driving and the backseaters scanning the surface with binoculars. The sun was plainly visible at twenty thousand feet, but on the surface there was still the semidarkness of nautical twilight.

One doesn't see ships from aloft, a fact often lost on both sailors and airmen. In most cases, ships are too small, and the surface of the sea too vast. What one sees, whether from a satellite photo or the unaided human eye, is the wake, a disturbance in the water much like an arrow with an over-sized head – the bow and stern waves generated by the ship's passage through the water – and the foaming a straight line caused by the propellers is the arrow's shaft. The eye is drawn to such shapes as naturally as to the body of a woman, and at the apex of the V-shape, there one finds the ship. Or, in this case, many ships. They spotted the decoy group first, from forty miles away. The main body of COMEDY was identified a minute later.

The problem for the ships was positive identification. Kemper couldn't risk killing an airliner, as USS *Vincennes* had once done. The four F-16s had already turned toward them when the radio call went out. He didn't have anyone aboard who spoke the language well enough to catch what they'd just said.

'Tally-ho,' the F-16 flight leader called. 'Looks like F-14s.' And he knew the Navy didn't have any of those around.

'*Anzio* to STARFIGHTER, weapons free, splash 'em.'

'Roger that.'

'Flight, Lead, go Slammer.' They were too busy looking down instead of looking around. Recon flight, Starfighter Lead figured. Tough. He selected AIM-120 and fired, a fraction before the other three aircraft in his formation did the same. 'Fox-One, Fox-One!' And the Battle of Qatar was under way.

The UIR Tomcats were just a little too busy for their own good. Their radar-warning receivers were reporting all manner of emitters at the moment, and the air-to-air radar on the Vipers was just one of many. The leader of the two was trying to get a count of the warships below and talking on his radio at the same time, when a pair of AMRAAM missiles exploded twenty meters in front of his aging fighter. The second pilot at least looked up in time to see death coming.

'*Anzio*, Starfighter, splash two, no 'chutes, say again, splash two.'

'Roger that.'

'What a nice way to start the day,' commented a USAF major who'd just spent sixteen months playing against the Israeli air force in the Negev. 'Returning to station. Out.'

'I'm not sure that's a good idea,' van Damm said. The radar picture from *John Paul Jones* had been uplinked from the new ship via satellite to Washington. They were seeing things less than half a second after they really happened.

'Those ships cannot be stopped, sir,' Robby Jackson told the chief of staff. 'We can't take chances.'

'But they can say we shot first and –'

'Wrong, sir. Their missile boat shot first five hours ago,' the J-3 reminded him.

'But they won't say that.'

'Save it, Arnie,' Ryan said. 'My order, remember. The rules of engagement are in place. What now, Robby?'

'Depends on whether the Iranians got the word out. That first kill was easy. The first one usually is,' Jackson said, remembering the ones he'd made in his career, nothing at all like what he'd trained for at Top Gun, but there were no fair-play rules in real combat, were there?

The narrowest part of the passage was just over a hundred miles between Qatar and the Iranian town of Basatin. There was an air base there, and satellite coverage said there were fighters sitting on the ramp.

'Hi, Jeff.'

'What's happening, Andrea?' Raman asked, adding, 'Glad you remembered that you left me up here.'

'It's pretty busy with all this fever stuff. We need you back here. Got a car?'

'I think I can steal one from the local office.' In fact, he had an official car already.

'Okay,' she told him, 'come on down. I don't suppose we really need the advance work up there. Your ID will get you through the roadblocks on I-70. Quick as you can. Things are happening here.'

'Give me four hours.'

'You have a change of clothes?'

'Yeah, why?'

'You're going to need it. We've set up decontamination procedures here. Everybody has to scrub down before getting into the West Wing. You'll see when you get here,' the chief of the Detail told him.

'Fine with me.'

* * *

Alahad wasn't doing anything. Bugs planted in his house had determined that he was watching TV, flipping channels from one cable station to another in search of a movie he hadn't seen before, and before going to bed he'd listened to *CNN Headline News*. After that, nothing. The lights were all out, and even the thermal-viewing cameras couldn't see through the curtained windows of his bedroom. The agents doing surveillance drank their coffee from plastic cups and looked on, at nothing, while discussing their worries about the epidemic, just like everyone else in America. The media continued to devote virtually all of its airtime to the story. There was little else. Sports had stopped. Weather continued, but few were outside to notice. Everything else rotated around the Ebola crisis. There were science segments explaining what the virus was and how it spread – actually, how it *might* be spreading, as there was still diverse opinion on that – and the agents with the headphones had listened to the latest installment over Alahad's own TV. It was all nature's revenge, one environmental advocate was preaching. Man had gone into the jungle, cut down trees, killed animals, upset the ecosystem, and now the ecosystem was getting even. Or something like that.

There was legal analysis of the court case Edward Kealty had brought, but there simply was no enthusiasm for lifting the travel ban. Stories showed airplanes at airports, buses in terminals, trains at stations, and a lot of empty roads. Stories showed people in hotels, and how they were coping. Stories showed how to reuse surgical masks, and told people that this simple safety measure worked almost flawlessly; most people seemed to believe that. But to counter that, most of the stories showed hospitals and, now, body bags. Reports on how the bodies of the dead were being burned ran without showing the flames; that was by mutual consent. The raw data was distasteful enough without the image of its reality. Reporters and medical consultants were starting to comment on the lack of data on the number of cases – which was alarming to many – but hinting that the space in hospitals to deal with the Ebola cases had not expanded – which was comforting to some. The extreme doom-and-gloom-sayers were still distributing their cant, but others said quietly that the data didn't support that view, that the situation might be stabilizing, though in every case they added that it was much too soon to tell.

They were starting to say that people were coping, that some states were totally clean, that many regions within those states that had cases were similarly healthy. And, finally, some people were coming forward to say with some authority that the epidemic had definitely not been a natural event. There was no public opinion on the issue that the media could really measure. People didn't interact enough, share thoughts enough to make informed judgments, but with the beginnings of confidence that the world was *not* going to end came the big question: How had this begun?

Secretary of State Adler was back in his airplane, flying west to the People's Republic. While aloft, and in the Beijing embassy, he had access to the latest news. It had caused rage and, perversely, some degree of satisfaction. It was Zhang who was leading his government in this direction. That was fairly certain, now that they knew India had been involved – again – this time duped by Iran and China. The real question was whether or not the Prime Minister would let her partners know that she'd reneged on her part of the deal. Probably not, Adler thought. She'd outmaneuvered herself again. She seemed able to do that standing still.

But the rage kept coming back. His country had been attacked, and by someone he'd met only a few days before. Diplomacy had failed. He had failed to stop a conflict – and wasn't that his job? Worse than that, he and his country had been duped. China had maneuvered *him* and a vital naval force out of position. The PRC was now stringing out a crisis they'd made themselves, for the purpose of hurting American interests, and probably for the ultimate purpose of reshaping the world into their own design. They were being clever about it. China had not directly done anything to anyone, except a few air passengers, but had let others take the lead, and the risks that went with them. However this turned out, they would still have their trade, they would still have the respect due a superpower, and influence over American policy, and they planned to maintain all of those things until such time as they made the changes they desired. They'd killed Americans on the Airbus. Through their maneuvers they were helping to kill others, to do real and permanent harm to his country, and doing so entirely without risk, SecState thought quietly, gazing out the window as his aircraft made landfall.

But they didn't know that he knew these things, did they?

The next attack would be a little more serious. The UIR had a large supply of C-802 missiles, so intelligence said. Made by China Precision Machine Import and Export Corporation, these were similar in type and capabilities to the French Exocet, with a range of about seventy miles. However, again the problem was targeting. There were just too many ships in the Gulf. To get the right destination for their missiles, the Iranians would have to get close enough for the look-down radars on their fighters to brush the edge of COMEDY's missile envelope.

Well, Kemper decided, he'd have to see about that. *John Paul Jones* increased speed to thirty-two knots and moved north. The new destroyer was stealthy – on a radar set she looked rather like a medium-sized fishing boat – and to accentuate it she turned off all her radars. COMEDY had shown them one look. Now they would show them another. He also radioed Riyadh and screamed for AWACS support. The three cruisers, *Anzio*, *Normandy*, and *Yorktown*, maintained position close to the cargo ships, and it was now pretty clear to the civilian crews on the *Bob Hopes* that the warships were not there merely for missile defense. Any inbound vampire would have to go through a cruiser to get to them. But there was nothing to be done about that. The civilian seamen were all at their duty stations. Firefighting gear was deployed throughout the cargo decks. Their diesels were pounding out all the continuous power that the manuals allowed.

Aloft, the dawn patrol of F-16s was replaced by another. Weapons were free, and word was getting out now to the civilian traffic that the air over the Persian Gulf was not a good place to be. It would make everyone's task a lot easier. It was no secret that they were there. Iranian radar had to have them, but there was no helping that at the moment.

*   *   *

'It appears that there are two naval forces in the Gulf,' Intelligence told him.

'We are not sure of their composition, but it is possible that they are military transport ships.'

'And?'

'And two of our fighters have been shot down approaching them,' Air Force went on.

'The American ships – some of them are warships of a very modern type. The report from our aircraft said that there are others as well, looking like merchant ships. It is likely that these are tank transports from Diego Garcia –'

'The ones the Indians were supposed to stop!'

'That is probably correct.'

What a fool I was to trust that woman! 'Sink them!' he ordered, thinking that his wish could become a fact.

Raman liked to drive fast. The nearly clear interstate, the dark night, and the powerful Service car allowed him to indulge that pastime, as he tore down Interstate 70 toward Maryland. The number of trucks on the road surprised him. He hadn't known that there were so many vehicles dedicated to moving food and medical supplies. His rotating red light told them to keep out of his way, and also allowed his passage at speeds approaching a hundred miles per hour without interference from the Pennsylvania State Police.

It also gave him time to think. It would have been better for everyone if he'd known beforehand about all the things that were happening. Certainly it would have been better for him. The attack on SANDBOX had not pleased him. She was a child, too young, too innocent to be an enemy – he *knew* her by face and name and sound – and the shock of it had disturbed him, briefly . He didn't quite understand why it had been ordered . . . unless to draw the protective circle even more tightly around POTUS, and so make his own mission easier. But that hadn't been necessary, not really. America was not Iraq, which Mahmoud Haji probably didn't fully understand.

The disease attack, that was something else. The manner of its spread was a matter of God's Will. It was distasteful, but that was life. He remembered the burning of the theater in Tehran. People had died there, too, ordinary people whose mistake had been to watch a movie instead of attending to their devotions. The world was hard, and the only thing that made its burden easier to bear was faith in something larger than oneself. Raman had that faith. The world didn't change its shape by accident. Great events had to be cruel ones, for the most part. The Faith had spread with the help of the sword, despite the Prophet's own admonition that the sword could not make one faithful . . . a dichotomy he did not fully understand, but that, too, was the nature of the world. One man could hardly comprehend it all. For so many things, one had to depend on the guidance of those wiser than oneself, to tell one what had to be done, what was acceptable to Allah, what served His purpose.

That he had not been told things that would have been useful – well, he had to admit, that was a reasonable security measure . . . if one accepted the fact that one was not supposed to survive. The realization did not bring a chill along with it. He had accepted that possibility a long time before, and if his distant brother could have fulfilled his mission in Baghdad, then he could fulfill his own in Washington. But he would try to survive if the chance offered itself. There wasn't anything wrong with that, was there?

Clearly, they were still figuring this operation out, Kemper told himself. In 1990–91 there had been the luxury of time to decide things, to allocate assets, to set up communications links and all the rest. But not this time. When he'd called for the AWACS, some Air Force puke had replied, 'What, you don't have one? Why didn't you ask?' The commanding officer of USS *Anzio* and Task Force 61.1 hadn't vented his temper at the man. It probably wasn't his fault anyway, and the good news was that they had one now. The timing was good enough, too. Four fighter aircraft, type unknown, were just rotating off the ground at Basatin, ninety miles away.

'COMEDY, this is Sky-Two, we show four inbounds.' The data link came up on one of the Aegis screens. His own radar couldn't see that far, because it was well under the horizon. The AWACS showed four blips in two pairs.

'Sky, COMEDY, they're yours. Splash 'em.'

'Roger – stand by, four more coming up.'

* * *

'Here's where it gets interesting,' Jackson told them in the Sit Room. 'Kemper has a missile trap set up outboard of the main formation. If anybody gets past the -16s, we'll see if it works.'

A third group of four lifted off a minute later. The twelve fighter aircraft climbed to ten thousand feet, then turned south at high speed.

The flight of F-16s couldn't risk straying too far from COMEDY, but moved to meet the threat in the center of the Gulf under direction from the AWACS. Both sides switched on their targeting radars, the UIR force controlled by ground-based sets, and the USAF teams guided by the E-3B circling a hundred miles behind them. It wasn't elegant. The -16s, with their longer-ranging missiles, shot first, and turned away as the southbound Iranian interceptors loosed their own and tried to evade. Then the first group of four dived down for the water. Jamming pods went on, aided by powerful shore-based interference, which the Americans hadn't expected. Three UIR fighters, still heading in, fell to the missile volley, while the Americans outran the return volley, then turned back to reengage. The American flight split into two-plane elements, racing east, then turned again to conduct an anvil attack. But the speeds involved were high, and one Iranian flight was now within fifty miles of COMEDY. That was when they appeared on *Anzio*'s radar.

'Cap'n,' the chief on the ESM board said into his microphone, 'I am getting acquisition radar signals, bearing three-five-five. These are detection values, sir. They may have us.'

'Very well.' Kemper reached to turn his key. On *Yorktown* and *Normandy* the same thing happened. The former was an older version of the cruiser. In her case, four white painted SM-2 MR came out of the fore and aft magazines onto the launch rails. For *Anzio* and *Normandy* nothing changed visually. Their missiles were in vertical launch cells. The SPY radars were now pumping out six *million* watts of RF energy, and dwelling almost continuously on the inbound fighter-bombers, which were just out of range of the cruisers.

But not out of range for *John Paul Jones*, ten miles to the north of the main body. In the space of three seconds, her main radar went active, and then the first of eight missiles erupted from her launch cells, rocketing skyward on columns of smoke and flame, then changing direction in skidding turns to level out and burn north.

The fighters hadn't seen *Jones*. Her stealthy profile had not shown as a real target on their scopes, and neither had they noticed the fact that a fourth SPY radar was now tracking them. The series of white smoke trails came as an unpleasant surprise when the pilots looked up from their own radar scopes. But two of them triggered off their C-802s just in time.

Four seconds out from their targets, the SM-2 missiles received terminal guidance signals from the SPG-62 illumination radars. It was too sudden, too unexpected for them to jink clear. All four fighters were blotted out on massive clouds of yellow and black, but they'd managed to launch six antiship missiles.

'Vampire, vampire! I show inbound missile seekers, bearing three-five-zero.'

'Okay, here we go.' Kemper turned the key another notch, to the 'special-auto' setting. Aegis would now go fully automatic. Topside, the CIWS gatling guns turned to starboard. Everywhere aboard the four warships, sailors listened and tried not to cringe. The merchant crews they guarded simply didn't know to be scared yet.

Aloft, the F-16s closed on the still-intact flight of four. These were also antiship-missile carriers, but they'd looked in the wrong place, probably for the decoy group. The first group had seen a close gaggle of ships. The second hadn't yet, and never would. They'd just turned into the signals of the Aegis radars to their west when the sky filled with down-bound smoke trails. The four scattered. Two exploded in midair. Another was damaged and tried to limp back northwest before he lost power and went in, while a fourth, missed entirely, reefed into a left turn, punched burner, and jettisoned his exterior weapons load. The four Air Force F-16s had splashed six enemy fighters in under four minutes.

Jones got one of the sea-skimmers on the way by, but none of them had locked into her radar return, and the resulting high-speed crossing targets were too difficult to engage. Three of four computer-launched attempts all failed. That left five. The destroyer's combat systems recycled and looked for additional targets.

They'd seen *Jones*'s smoke and wondered what it was, but the first real warning that something was badly wrong came when the near trio of cruisers started launching.

In *Anzio*'s CIC, Kemper decided, as *O'Bannon* had, not to launch his decoy rockets. Three of the inbounds seemed aimed at the after part of the formation, with only two at the lead. His cruiser and *Normandy* concentrated on those. You could feel the launches. The hull shivered when the first two went out. The radar display was changing every second now, showing inbound and outbound tracks. The 'vampires' were eight miles away now. At ten miles per minute, that meant less than fifty seconds to engage and destroy. It would seem like a week.

The system was programmed to adopt a fire-control mode appropriate to the moment. It was now doing shoot-shoot-look. Fire one missile, fire another, and then look to see if the target had survived the first two, and merit a third try. His target was exploded by the first SM-2 and the second SAM self-destructed. *Normandy*'s first missile missed, but the second nicked the C-802, tumbling it into the sea with an explosion they felt through the hull a second later.

Yorktown had an advantage and a disadvantage. Her older system allowed launches directly at the inbound missiles instead of forcing the missiles to turn in flight before they could engage. But she could not launch as fast. She had three targets and fifty seconds to destroy them. The first -802 splashed five miles out, killed by a double hit. The second was now at its terminal height of three meters, ten feet over the flat surface. The next outgoing SM-2 missed high, exploding harmless behind it. The following missile missed as well. The next ripple from the forward launchers obliterated that one three miles out, filling the air with fragments that confused the guidance of the next pair, causing both to explode in the shredded remains of a dead target. Both of the cruiser's launchers swiveled fore and aft and vertical to receive the next set of four SAMs. The last -802 passed through the spray and fragments, heading straight into the cruiser. *Yorktown* got off two more launches, but one faulty missile failed to guide at all, and the other missed. Then the CIWS systems located on the forward and after superstructure turned slightly, as the vampire entered their targeting envelope. Both opened up at eight hundred yards, missing, missing yet again, but then exploding the missile less than two hundred yards off the starboard beam. The five-hundred-pound warhead showered the cruiser with fragments, and parts of the missile body kept coming, striking the ship's foreright SPY radar panel and ripping into the superstructure, killing six sailors and wounding twenty more.

'Wow,' Secretary Bretano said. All the theoretical stuff he'd learned in the past weeks was suddenly real.

'Not bad. They've launched fourteen aircraft at us, and they're getting two or three back, that's all,' Robby said. 'That'll give them something to think about for the next time.'

'What about *Yorktown*?' the President asked.

'We have to wait and see.'

Their hotel was only half a mile from the Russian embassy, and like good parsimonious journalists, they decided to walk, and left a few minutes before eight. Clark and Chavez had gone a scarce hundred yards when they saw that something was wrong. People were moving listlessly for so early on the start of a working day. Had the war with the Saudis been announced? John took a turn onto another market street, and there he found people listening to portable radios in their stalls instead of moving their wares onto the shelves.

'Excuse me,' John said in Russian-accented Farsi. 'Is something the matter?'

'We are at war with America,' a fruit vendor said.

'Oh, when did this happen?'

'The radio says they have attacked our airplanes,' the fruit seller said next. 'Who are you?' he asked.

John pulled out his passport. 'We are Russian journalists. Can I ask what you think of this?'

'Haven't we fought enough?' the man asked.

'Told you. They're blaming us,' Arnie said, reading over the intercept report off Tehran radio. 'What will that do to the politics in the region?'

'The sides are pretty much drawn up,' Ed Foley said. 'You're either on one side or the other. The UIR is the other. Simpler than the last time.'

The President checked his watch. It was just past midnight. 'When do I go on the air?'

'Noon.'

Raman had to stop at the Maryland-Pennsylvania line. A good twenty or so trucks were waiting for clearance from the Maryland State Police, with the National Guard in close attendance, and they lined up two by two, completely blocking the road at this point. Ten angry minutes later, he showed his ID. The cop waved him through without a word. Raman turned his light back on and sped off. He turned on the radio, caught an all-news AM station, but missed the top-of-the-hour news summary and had to suffer through all the rest, largely the same thing he'd been hearing all week, until twelve-thirty, when the network news service announced a reported air battle in the Persian Gulf. Neither the White House nor the Pentagon had commented on the alleged incident. Iran claimed to have sunk two American ships and shot down four fighters.

Patriot and zealot that he was, Raman couldn't believe it. The problem with America, and the reason for his mission of sacrifice, was that this poorly organized, idolatrous, and misguided nation was lethally competent in the use of force. Even President Ryan, he had seen, discounted as he was by politicians, had a quiet strength to him. He didn't shout, didn't bluster, didn't act like most 'great' men. He wondered how many people appreciated just how dangerous SWORDS-MAN was, for that very reason. Well, that was why he had to kill him, and if that had to come at the cost of his own life, so be it.

TF61.1 turned south behind the Qatar Peninsula without further incident. *Yorktown's* forward superstructure was badly damaged, the electrical fire having done as much damage as the missile fragments, but with her stern turned to the enemy, that didn't matter. Kemper maneuvered his escorting ships yet again, placing all four behind the tank carriers, but another attack was not forthcoming. The result of the first had stung the enemy too badly. Eight F-15s, four each of the Saudi Air Force and the 366th, orbited overhead. A mixture of Saudi and other escort ships turned up. Mainly mine-hunters, they pinged the bottom in front of COMEDY, looking for danger and finding none. Six huge container ships had been moved off the Dhahran quay to make room for *Bob Hope* and her sisters, and now three tugs each appeared to move them alongside. The four Aegis ships maintained station even sitting still, dropping their anchors fore and aft, mooring five hundred yards off their charges to maintain air defense coverage through the unloading process. The decoy force, having suffered not a single scratch, pulled into Bahrain to await developments.

From the wheelhouse of USS *Anzio*, Captain Gregory Kemper watched as the first brown buses pulled up to the tank-carriers. Through his binoculars, he could see men in 'chocolate-chip' fatigues trot to the edge, and watched the stern ramps come down to meet them.

'We have no comment at this time,' van Damm told the latest reporter to call in. 'The President will be making a statement later today. That's all I can say right now.'
'But –'
'That's all we have to say right now.' The chief of staff killed the line.

Price had assembled all of the Detail agents in the West Wing, and gone through the game plan for what was coming. The same would be repeated for the people in the White House proper, and the reaction there would be pretty much the same, she was certain: shock, disbelief, and anger bordering on rage.

'Let's all get that out of our systems, shall we? We know what we're going to be doing about it. This is a criminal case, and we'll treat it like a criminal case. Nobody loses control. Nobody gives anything away. Questions?' There were none.

Daryaei checked his clock again. Yes, finally, it was time. He placed a telephone call over a secure line to the UIR embassy in Paris. There, the ambassador placed a call to someone else. That person made a call to London. In all cases, the words exchanged were innocuous. The message was not.

Past Cumberland, Hagerstown, Frederick, Raman turned south on I-270 for the last hour's worth into Washington. He was tired, but his hands tingled. He'd see a dawn this morning. Perhaps his last. If so, he hoped it would be a pretty one.

The noise made the agents jump. Both checked their watches. First of all, the number calling in came up on an LED display. It was overseas, code 44, which made it from the UK.

'Yes?' It was the voice of the subject, Mohammed Alahad.

'Sorry to disturb you so early. I call about the three-meter Isfahan, the red one. Has it arrived yet? My customer is very anxious.' The voice was accented, but not in quite the right way.

'Not yet,' the groggy voice replied. 'I have asked my supplier about it.'

'Very well, but as I said, my customer is quite anxious.'

'I will see what I can do. Good-bye.' And the line went dead.

Don Selig lifted his cellular phone, dialed headquarters, and gave them the UK number for a quick check.

'Lights just came on,' Agent Scott said. 'Looks like it woke our boy up. Heads up,' she said into her portable radio. 'Subject is up and moving.'

'Got the lights, Sylvia,' another agent assured her.

Five minutes later, he emerged from the front door of the garden-style apartment building. Tracking him was not the least bit easy, but the agents had taken the trouble to locate the four closest public phones and had people close to all of them. It turned out that he picked one at a combination gas station/convenience store. The computer monitor would tell them what number he called, but through a long-lens camera he was observed to drop in a quarter. The agent on the camera saw him hit 3–6–3 in rapid succession. It was clear a few seconds later, when another tapped phone rang, and was answered by a digital answering machine.

'Mr Sloan, this is Mr Alahad. Your rug is in. I don't understand why you do not call me, sir.' Click.

'Bingo!' another agent called over the radio net. 'That's it. He called Raman's number. Mr Sloan, we have your rug.'

Yet another voice came on. 'This is O'Day. Take him down right now!'

It wasn't really all *that* hard. Alahad went into the store to buy a quart of milk, and from there he walked directly back home. He had to use a key to enter his apartment house, and was surprised to find a man and a woman inside.

'FBI,' the man said.

'You're under arrest, Mr Alahad,' the woman said, producing handcuffs. No guns were in evidence, but he didn't resist – they rarely did – and if he had, there were two more agents just outside now.

'But why?' he asked.

'Conspiracy to murder the President of the United States,' Sylvia Scott said, pushing him against the wall.

'That's not so!'

'Mr Alahad, you made a mistake. Joseph Sloan died last year. How do you sell a rug to a dead man?' she asked. The man jerked back as though from an electric shock, the agents saw. The clever ones always did when they found out that they had not been so clever at all. They never expected to be caught. The next trick was in exploiting the moment. That would start in a few minutes, when they told him what the penalty was for violating 18 USC §1751.

The inside of USNS *Bob Hope* looked like the parking garage from hell, with vehicles jammed in so closely that a rat would have had a difficult time passing between them. To board a tank, an arriving crew had to walk on the decks of the vehicles, crouching lest they smash their skulls into the overhead, and they found themselves wondering about the sanity of those who'd periodically had to check the vehicles, turning over the engines and working the guns back and forth so that rubber and plastic seals wouldn't dry out.

Assigning crews to tracks and trucks had been an administrative task of no small proportions, but the ship was loaded in such a way as to allow the most important items off first. The Guardsmen arrived as units, with computerized printouts giving them the number and location of their assigned vehicles, and ship crewmen pointing them to the quickest way out. Less than an hour after the ship tied up, the first M1A2 main-battle tank rolled off the ramp onto the quay to board the same tank transporter used shortly before by a tank of the 11th Cav, and with the same drivers. Unloading would take more than a day, and most of another would be needed to get WOLFPACK Brigade organized.

The dawn proved to be a pretty one, Aref Raman saw with satisfaction as he pulled into West Executive Drive. It would be a clear day for his mission. The uniformed guard at the gate waved hello as the security barrier went down. Another car came in behind him, and that one went through as well. It parked two spaces from his spot, and Raman recognized the driver as that FBI guy, O'Day, who'd been so lucky at the day-care center. There was no sense in hating the man. He'd been defending his own child, after all.

'How are you doing?' the FBI inspector asked cordially.

'Just got in from Pittsburgh,' Raman replied, hefting his suitcase out of the trunk.

'What the hell were you doing up there?'

'Advance work – but that speech won't be happening, I guess. What are you in for?' Raman was grateful for the distraction. It allowed him to get his mind into the game, as it were.

'The Director and I have something to brief the Boss about. Gotta shower first, though.'

'Shower?'

'Disinfec – oh, you haven't been here. A White House staff member is sick with this virus thing. *Everybody* has to shower and disinfect on the way in now. Come on,' O'Day said, carrying a briefcase. Both men went through the West Entrance. Both buzzed the metal detectors, but since both were sworn federal officers, nothing was made of the fact that both were carrying side arms. The inspector pointed to the left.

'This is a treat, showing you something in the place,' he joked to Raman.

'Been in a lot lately?' The Secret Service agent saw that two offices had been converted into something. One marked

MEN and the other WOMEN. Andrea Price came out of one just then, her hair wet, and, he noted as she passed him, smelling of chemicals.

'Hey, Jeff, how was the drive? Pat, how's the hero?' she inquired.

'Hey, no big deal, Price. Just two rag-heads,' O'Day said with a grin. He opened the MEN door and went in, and set his briefcase down.

It had clearly been a rush job, Raman saw. Some minor functionary had had the office, but all the furniture was gone and the floor covered with plastic. A hanging rack was there for clothing. O'Day stripped down and headed into the canvas-enclosed shower.

'These damn chemicals at least wake you up,' the FBI inspector reported as the water started. He emerged two minutes later and started toweling off vigorously. 'Your turn, Raman.'

'Great,' the Service agent griped, removing his clothing and showing some of the lingering body modesty of his parent society. O'Day didn't look at him and didn't look away. Didn't do anything except dry off, until Raman was behind the canvas. The agent's service pistol, a SigSauer, had been set atop the clothing rack. O'Day opened his briefcase first. Then he pulled Raman's automatic, ejected the magazine, and quietly worked the action to remove the chambered round.

'How are the roads?' O'Day called.

'Clear, made great time – damn, this water stinks!'

'Ain't that the truth!' Raman kept two spare magazines for his pistol. O'Day saw. He put all three in the lid-pocket before unwrapping the four he'd prepared. One he slid into the butt of the Sig. He worked the action one more time to load a round, then replaced it with a new, full magazine, and two more for the agent's belt holder. Finished, he hefted the gun. Weight and balance were exactly the same as before. Everything went back in place as O'Day returned to dressing. He needn't have rushed. Raman evidently needed a shower. Maybe he was purifying himself, the inspector thought coldly.

'Here.' O'Day tossed over a towel as he put his shirt on.

'Glad I brought a change.' Raman pulled new underwear and socks from his two-suiter.

'I guess it's a rule you have to be all spiffy when you work in with the President, eh?' The FBI agent bent down to tie his shoes. He looked up. 'Morning, Director.'

'I don't know why I bothered at home,' Murray grumped. 'Got the paperwork, Pat?'

'Yes, sir. This is something to show him.'

'Damned right it is.' And Murray doffed his jacket and tie. 'White House locker room,' he noted. 'Morning, Raman.'

Both agents completed dressing, made sure their personal weapons were tucked in the right place, then stepped outside.

'Murray and I are going right in,' Pat told the other in the corridor. They didn't have to wait long for Murray, and then Price showed up again, just as the FBI Director reemerged. O'Day rubbed his nose to tell her all was done. She nodded back.

'Jeff, want to take these gentlemen into the office? I have to head to the command post. The Boss is waiting.'

'Sure, Andrea. This way,' Raman said, leading O'Day. Behind them, Price waited and did not head toward the command post.

In the next level up, Raman saw TV equipment being prepared for installation in the Oval Office. Arnie van Damm buzzed out the corridor entrance, trailed by Callie Weston. President Ryan was at his desk in the usual shirtsleeves, going through a folder. CIA Director Ed Foley was in there, too.

'Enjoy the shower, Dan?' the DCI asked.

'Oh, yeah, I'm losing the rest of my hair, Ed.'

'Hi, Jeff,' the President said, looking up.

'Good morning, Mr President,' Raman said, taking his usual place against the wall.

'Okay, Dan, what do you guys have for me?' Ryan asked.

'We've broken an Iranian espionage ring. We think it's associated with the attempt on your daughter.' While Murray talked, O'Day opened his briefcase and pulled out a folder.

'The Brits turned the connection,' Foley started to say. 'And the contact here is a guy named Alahad – would you believe the bastard has a business about a mile from here?'

'We have him under surveillance right now,' Murray put in. 'We're running his phone records.'

They were all looking down at the papers on the President's desk and didn't see Raman's face freeze in place. His mind started racing, as though a drug had been injected into his bloodstream. If they were doing that right now ... There might still be a chance, a slim one, but if not, here was the President, the directors of FBI and CIA, and he could deliver them all to Allah, and if that weren't sacrifice enough ... Raman unbuttoned his jacket with his left hand. He eased off the spot on the wall he was leaning against and closed his eyes for a quick prayer. Then, in a rapid, smooth movement, his right hand went to his automatic.

Raman was surprised to see the President's eyes move and stare right at him. Well, that wasn't so bad, was it? Ryan should know that his death was coming, and the only shame was he'd never quite understand why.

Ryan flinched as the pistol came out. The reaction was automatic, despite the briefing on what to expect, and the sign from O'Day that it was okay. He dodged anyway, wondering if he could really trust anyone, and saw that Jeff Raman's hands tracked him and pulled back on the trigger like an automaton, no emotion in his eyes at all –

The sound made everyone jump, albeit for different reasons.

Pop.

That was all. Raman's mouth dropped open in disbelief. The weapon was loaded. He could feel the added weight of the live rounds in it, and –

'Put it down,' O'Day said calmly, his Smith out and aimed now. An instant later, Murray had his service weapon out.

'We have Alahad in custody already,' the Director explained.

Raman had another weapon, a telescoping billy club called an Asp, but the President was fifteen feet away and ...

'I can put one right through your kneecap if you want,' O'Day said coldly.

'You fuckin' traitor!' Andrea said, entering the room with her pistol out, too. 'You fuckin' assassin! *On the floor now!*'

'Easy, Price. He's not going anywhere,' Pat told her.

But it was Ryan who nearly lost control: 'My little girl,

my *baby*, you helped plan to murder *her*?' He started around the desk, but Foley stopped him. 'No, not this time, Ed!'

'Stop!' the DCI told him. 'We have him, Jack. We've got him.'

'One way or another, you get on the floor,' Pat said, ignoring the others and aiming at Raman's knee. 'Drop the weapon and get down.'

He was trembling now, fear, rage, all manner of emotions assaulted him, everything but the one he'd expected. He racked the Sig's action and pulled the trigger again. It wasn't even aimed, it was just an act of denial.

'I couldn't use blanks. They don't weigh the same,' O'Day explained. 'They're real rounds. I just tapped the bullets out and dumped the powder. The primer makes a cute little pop, doesn't it?'

It was as though he'd forgotten to breathe for a minute or so. Raman's body collapsed in on itself. He dropped the pistol to the rug with the Seal of the President on it and fell to his knees. Price came over and pushed him the rest of the way. Murray, for the first time in years, snapped the cuffs on.

'You want to hear about your rights?' the FBI Director asked.

59

RULES OF ENGAGEMENT

Diggs had not received proper mission orders yet and what was even more disturbing, his Operation BUFORD did not really have much of a plan yet, either. The Army trained its commanders to act swiftly and decisively, but as with doctors in hospitals, emergency situations were not as welcome as planned procedures. The general was in continuous contact with the commanders of his two Cavalry regiments, the senior Air Force commander, the one-star who'd brought the 366th over, the Saudis, the Kuwaitis, and various intelligence assets, just trying to get a feel for what the enemy was actually doing, and from that to determine what the enemy might be planning – from which he would try to formulate some sort of plan of his own aside from mere ad-hoc reaction.

The orders and rules of engagement arrived on his fax machine around 11:00 Washington time, 16:00 Zulu time, and 19:00 Lima, or local time. Here was the explanation he'd lacked. He relayed it at once to his principal subordinates, and assembled his staff to brief them. The troops, he told the assembled officers, would learn from their Commander-in-Chief. Their officers would have to be with their people when *that* word came down.

Things were busy enough. According to the satellites, the Army of God – as the intelligence people had determined the name to be – was within one hundred miles of the Kuwaiti border, approaching from the west in good order, and following the roads as expected. That made the Saudi deployment look pretty good, since three of their five brigades were covering the approaches to the oil fields.

They still weren't ready. The 366th Wing was in the Kingdom, but it wasn't enough to have the airplanes on the right airfields. A thousand minor details had to be sorted out, and that job wasn't even half done yet. The F-16s from Israel were pretty well spun up, all forty-eight of their single-engine fighters running, and even some kills recorded in the initial skirmishes, but the rest needed another day. Similarly, the 10th Cav was fully ready, but the 11th was not; it was still assembling and moving to its initial deployment area. His third brigade had just started drawing equipment. An army wasn't a collection of weapons. It was a team composed of people with an idea of what they were supposed to be doing. But picking the time and place for war was usually the job of an aggressor, which was a role his country hadn't practiced very much.

He looked at the three-page fax again. It seemed quite literally explosive in his hands. His planning staff read their copies and were eerily quiet until the 11th's S-3, the regimental operations officer, said it for all of them:

'We're gonna get some.'

Three Russians had recently arrived. Clark and Chavez had to remind themselves that this wasn't some sort of alcohol-induced dream. The two CIA officers were being supported by Russians under mission orders from Langley by way of Moscow. Actually, they had two missions. The Russians had drawn the hard one, and had brought the necessary equipment in the diplomatic pouch for the two Americans to have a try at the easier one. A dispatch had also come from Washington, via Moscow, that all of them read.

'Too fast, John,' Ding breathed. Then his mission face came on. 'But what the hell.'

The press room was still underpopulated. So many of the regulars were elsewhere, some caught out of town and blocked by the travel ban, others just missing, and nobody quite sure why.

'The President will be making a major speech in one hour,' van Damm told them. 'Unfortunately, there will be no time to give you advance copies of the speech. Please inform your networks that this is a matter of the highest importance.'

'Arnie!' a reporter called, but the chief of staff had already turned his back.

The reporters in Saudi knew more than both their friends back in Washington, and they were moving out to join their assigned units. For Tom Donner, it was B-Troop, 1st of the 11th. He was fully outfitted in a desert battle-dress uniform, or BDU, and found the twenty-nine-year-old troop commander standing by his tank.

'Howdy,' the captain said, halfway looking up from his map.

'Where do you want me?' Donner asked.

The captain laughed. 'Never ask a soldier where he wants a reporter, sir.'

'With you, then?'

'I ride this,' the officer responded, nodding at the tank. 'I'll put you in one of the Brads.'

'I need a camera crew.'

'They're already here,' the captain told him, pointing. 'Over that way. Anything else?'

'Yeah, would you like to know what this is all about?' Donner asked. The journalists had been virtual prisoners in a Riyadh hotel, not even allowed to call home to tell their families where they were – all they'd known was that the reporters had been called up, and their parent corporations had signed agreements not to reveal the purpose of their absences for such deployments. In Donner's case, the network said that he was 'on assignment,' a difficult thing to explain with the travel ban. But they had been told the overall situation – there'd been no avoiding it – which put them one up on a lot of soldiers.

'We hear that in an hour or so, or that's what the colonel told us.' But the young officer was interested now.

'This is something you need to know now. Honest.'

'Mr Donner, I know what you pulled on the President and –'

'If you want to shoot me, do it later. Listen to me, Captain. This is important.'

'Say your say, sir.'

There seemed something perverse in being made up at a time like this. It was, as always, Mary Abbot doing the job, wearing her mask, and this time gloves as well, while both Tele-PrompTers ran their copy. Ryan hadn't had the time or really the inclination to rehearse. Important as the speech was, he only wished to do it once.

* * *

'They can't do cross-country,' the Saudi general insisted. 'They haven't trained for it, and they're still road-bound.'

'There is information to suggest otherwise, sir,' Diggs said.

'We are ready for them.'

'You're never ready enough, General. Nobody is.'

It was tense but otherwise normal at PALM BOWL. Downloaded satellite photos told them that the UIR forces were still moving, and if they continued, then they would be met by two Kuwaiti brigades fighting on their own turf, and an American regiment in reserve, and the Saudis ready to provide rapid support. They didn't know how the battle would turn out – the overall numbers weren't favorable – but it wouldn't be like the last time, Major Sabah told himself. It seemed so foolish to him that the allied forces could not strike first. They *knew* what was coming.

'Getting some radio chatter,' a technician reported. Outside, the sun was just starting to set. The satellite photos the intelligence officers looked at were four hours old. More would not be available for another two.

STORM TRACK was close to the Saudi-UIR border, too far for a mortar round, but not safe from real tube artillery. A company of fourteen Saudi tanks was now arrayed between the listening post and the berm. There also, for the first time in days, they were starting to copy radio transmissions. The signals were scrambled, more like the command sets than the regular tactical radios, which were far too numerous for easy encryption systems. Unable to read them immediately – that was the job of the computers back at KKMC – they did start trying to locate their points of origin. In twenty minutes, they had thirty point-sources. Twenty represented brigade headquarters. Six for the division command posts. Three for the corps commanders, and one for the army command. They seemed to be testing their commo net, the ELINT people decided. They'd have to wait for the computers to unscramble what was being said. The direction-finders had them arrayed on the road to Al Busayyah, still doing their approach march to Kuwait. The radio traffic wasn't all that remarkable. Maybe, most thought, the Army of God needed more practice in march discipline . . . though they hadn't done all that badly in their exercise . . .

With sunset the Predators were launched again, motoring north. They headed to the radio sources first of all. Their cameras turned on ten miles inside the UIR, and the first thing one of them saw was a battery of 203mm towed guns, off their trucks, their limbers spread out, and the tubes pointed south.

'Colonel!' a sergeant called urgently.

Outside, the Saudi tankers had selected hillocks to hide behind and were putting a few crewmen out to act as spotters. The first few had just started to settle into their observation points when the northern horizon flashed orange.

Diggs was still discussing deployment patterns when the first message came in:

'Sir, STORM TRACK reports they're taking artillery fire.'

'Good morning, my fellow Americans,' Ryan said to the cameras. His image was being carried worldwide. His voice would be heard even by those without TV sets at hand. In Saudi Arabia, his words went out on AM, FM, and shortwave bands so that every soldier, sailor, and airman would hear what he was about to say. 'We have been through much in the past two weeks.

'The first order of business is to tell you of progress we have made with the epidemic which has been inflicted upon our country.

'It was not easy for me to order the imposition of a ban on interstate travel. There are few freedoms more precious than the right to come and go as one pleases, but based on the best medical advice, I felt it necessary to take that action. I can report to you now that it has had the desired effect. New disease cases have been trending down for four days now. Partly that's because of what your government did, but it's more because you have taken the proper measures to protect yourselves. We will give more detailed information later in the day, but for the moment I can tell you that the Ebola epidemic is going to end, probably in the next week. Many of the new cases are people who will definitely survive. America's medical professionals have performed super-

1167

human work to help the afflicted, and to help us understand what has happened, and how best to combat it. This task is not yet complete, but our country will weather this storm, as we have weathered many others.

'A moment ago, I said that the epidemic has been inflicted upon us.

'The arrival of this disease into our country was not an accident. We have been struck with a new and barbaric form of attack. It's called biological warfare. That is something outlawed by international treaty. Biological warfare is designed to terrify and to cripple a nation, rather than to kill it. We've all felt the disgust and horror at what's been happening in our country, the way in which the disease attacks people at random. My own wife, Cathy, has worked around the clock with Ebola victims at her hospital in Baltimore. As you know, I was only there a few days ago to see for myself. I saw the victims, talked with the doctors and nurses, and outside the hospital I sat with a man whose wife was ill.

'I could not tell him then, but I can tell you now, that from the beginning we suspected that this epidemic was a man-made act, and over the last few days, our law-enforcement and intelligence agencies have formulated the proof we needed before I could tell you what you are about to hear.' On TV screens across the world appeared the faces of a young African boy, and a white-clad Belgian nun.

'This disease started some months ago in the country of Zaire,' the President went on. He had to walk everyone through it, slowly and carefully, and Ryan found it hard to keep his voice even.

The Saudi tankers remounted their vehicles at once, fired up the turbine engines, and moved to new locations lest their original points had been spotted. But the fire, they saw, was aimed at STORM TRACK. That made sense, their commander thought. The listening post was a prime intelligence-gathering point. Their job was to protect it, which they could do against tanks and troops, but not against artillery fire. The Saudi captain was a handsome, almost rakish young man of twenty-five. He was also devoutly religious, and therefore mindful of the fact that the Americans were guests of his country, and thus worthy of his protection. He got on his radio to call back to his battalion headquarters, and requested armored personnel carriers – helicopters would have been suicidal – to evacuate the intelligence specialists.

'And so, we have the disease traveling from Africa to Iran. How do we know this?' the President asked. 'We know it because the disease traveled back to Africa on this aircraft. Please note the registration code, HX-NJA. This is the same aircraft supposedly lost with Sister Jean Baptiste aboard . . .'

We need another day, damn it! Diggs thought. And the enemy forces were nearly two hundred miles west of where everyone planned to meet them.

'Who's closest?' he asked.

'Fourth Brigade's area,' the senior Saudi replied. But that brigade was spread over a front of over a hundred miles. There were some helicopter-reconnaissance assets there, but the attack choppers were also in the wrong place, fifty miles south of Wadi al Batin. The other side wasn't cooperating very well, was it?

Daryaei was shocked to see his photograph on TV. Worse, at least ten percent of the people in his country were seeing this. The American CNN was not available in the UIR, but the British Sky News service was, and nobody had thought to –

'This is the man behind the biological attack upon our country,' Ryan said, with the sort of calm that seemed robotic. 'He is the reason several thousand of our citizens have died. Now, I will tell you why he did this, why there was an attack on my daughter, Katie, and why there was an attempt on my own life, right in the Oval Office a few hours ago. I imagine Mr Daryaei is watching this broadcast, too, right now. Mahmoud Haji,' he said, right into the camera's eye, 'your man Aref Raman is now in federal custody. Do you really think America is as foolish as that?'

Like everyone else in the Blackhorse, Tom Donner was listening – in his case with a pair of headphones off the Bradley's radio. There weren't quite enough to go around, and the crewmen had to share. He watched their faces. They, too, were as blank and expressionless as Ryan's voice had been, until his last sentence of contempt.

'Fuck,' one spec-4 said. He was an 11-Delta, a Cavalry scout, and backup gunner for this track.

'My God,' Donner managed to say.

Ryan went on: 'UIR forces are now poised to invade our ally, the Kingdom of Saudi Arabia. Over the past two days, we have moved forces there to stand with our friends.

'There is something very important I must say now. The attack on my daughter, the attempt on my own life, and the barbaric attack on our country was undertaken by people who call themselves Muslims. We must all understand that religion has nothing at all to do with these inhuman acts. Islam is a *religion*. America is a country in which religious liberty is the *first* freedom expressed in our Bill of Rights, even before speech and all the others. Islam is not the enemy of our country or any other. Just as my family was once attacked by people calling themselves Catholics, so these people have twisted and defiled their own religious faith in the name of worldly power, and then hidden behind it like the cowards they are. What God thinks of that, I cannot say. I know that Islam, like Christianity and Judaism, teaches us about a God of love and mercy – and justice.

'Well, there will be justice. If the UIR forces arrayed on the Saudi border move to invade, we will meet them. Our armed forces are in the field even as I speak to you, and now I will speak directly to them:

'Now you know why you have been taken away from your homes and families. Now you know why you must take up arms in the defense of your country. Now you know the nature of your enemy, and the nature of his acts.

'But America does not have a tradition of deliberate attack on the innocent. You will act in accordance with our laws at all times. I must now send you into battle. I wish this were not necessary. I have myself served as a Marine, and I know what it is like to be in a foreign place. But you stand there for your country, and here at home your country stands up for you. You will be in our prayers.

'To our allies in Kuwait, the Kingdom of Saudi Arabia, Qatar, Oman, and all the Gulf states: America stands again

with you to stop aggression and restore the peace. Good luck.'
Ryan's voice changed then, for the first time allowing his
emotions to show. 'And good hunting.'

The crewmen in B-Troop's command track looked at one
another for several seconds before anyone spoke. They even
managed to forget the presence of the reporter. The youngest
of them, a PFC, looked down at shaking hands and had his
say.

'Fuckers gonna pay. Motherfuckers gonna pay for this,
guys.'

Four armored personnel carriers were racing across the desert
at about forty miles per hour. They avoided the beaten-dirt
road to STORM TRACK for fear that it would be targeted with
artillery fire; that proved to be a sensible precaution. Their
first view of their objective was a cloud of smoke and dust
drifting away from the antenna farm as fire continued to
pour into the site. One of the three buildings appeared to be
standing, but on fire, and the Saudi lieutenant leading the
scout platoon wondered if anyone could possibly be alive
there. To the north he saw a different sort of flash – five
miles away, the horizontal tongue of flame from a tank's
main gun illuminated the bumps and knolls of a landscape
that was not at all as level as it appeared in daylight. A
minute after that, the fire on STORM TRACK diminished
somewhat, shifting to where the tanks were evidently
engaging enemy vehicles invading his country. He thanked
Allah that his immediate job had just gotten a little easier
while his radio operator called ahead on the track's tactical
radio.

The four APCs picked their way through the fallen
antennas on the way into the wrecked compound. Then their
rear doors opened and the soldiers raced out to look around.
Thirty men and women worked here. They found nine
unhurt people, plus five wounded. The scout platoon took
about five minutes searching the wreckage, but no more living people were discovered, and there wasn't time to be fastidious about the dead. The tracks moved out, back toward
the battalion CP, where helicopters waited to ferry the
Americans out.

* * *

It amazed the Saudi tank commander that surprise had been achieved. He knew that most of his country's forces were two hundred miles to the east. But the enemy was *here* and coming south. They weren't going into Kuwait or after the oil fields at all. That became plain when the first UIR tanks appeared in his thermal viewer, cresting a low spot in the berm, out of gun range because he'd been ordered not to move too close. The young officer really didn't know what to do. Ordinarily, his military worked under fairly tight control, and so he radioed back for instructions. But his battalion commander was busy now, his own command of fifty-four tanks and other vehicles spread over a front of thirty kilometers, all of which was being hit with indirect artillery fire, and much of which was reporting enemy tanks crossing the border, with infantry carriers in support.

The officer decided he had to do something, so he ordered his tanks forward to meet the attack. At three thousand meters, his men opened fire, and the first fourteen shots resulted in eight hits, not bad under the circumstances for part-time soldiers, he thought as he decided to stand and fight right there, and defend his soil against the invader. His fourteen tanks were spread over a line three kilometers long. It was a defensible deployment, but a stationary one, and in the center of his own line he was too fixed on what lay before him. The second volley got another six kills at the long range, but then one of his tanks took a direct hit from an artillery round, which destroyed its engine and started a fire that made its crew bail out, only to be shredded by more of the artillery fire before they could run five meters. He was looking that way and saw them die, four hundred meters away, and he knew that there was a hole in his line now, and he was supposed to do something about that.

His gunner, like the others, was looking for and trying to engage enemy tanks, the T-80s with their domed turrets, when the first flight of antitank missiles zoomed away from the BMP infantry carriers that lay behind them. Those started getting hits, and though they could not penetrate the frontal armor on his tanks, tracks were knocked off, more engines set afire, and fire-control systems damaged. When half his command was burning, it was time to pull back. Four started moving again, turning and darting two kilometers south. The captain remained with the other three, and got another tank kill before he started to move. The air was filled with missiles now, and one of them hit the rear of his turret, igniting the ammo-storage box. The vertical flame sucked the air from the open hatch, asphyxiating his crew even as it burned him alive. Leaderless, the company fought on for thirty minutes, falling back again until the three surviving tanks ran south at fifty kilometers per hour, trying to find the battalion command post.

That was no longer there. It had been located by its radio transmissions and pounded by a full brigade of UIR artillery in its unprepared position just as the survivors from STORM TRACK arrived with the scout troop. In the first hour of the Second Persian Gulf War, a thirty-mile rent had been made in the Saudi lines, and there was a direct path to Riyadh. For that, the Army of God had lost half a brigade, a stiff price, but one which they were willing to pay.

The initial picture wasn't clear. It rarely was. That was the advantage the attacker almost always had, Diggs knew, and the job of the commander was to make order from chaos and use the former to inflict the latter on his enemy. With the destruction of STORM TRACK, his Predator capability was temporarily gone and would have to be reestablished. The 366th had deployed without J-STARS airborne radar capable of tracking the movement of ground troops. Aloft were two E-3B AWACS aircraft, each with four fighters in close attendance. Twenty UIR fighters came up and started going after them. That would be exciting for the Air Force.

But Diggs had his own problems. With the loss of STORM TRACK and its Predator drones, he was largely blind and his first remedial action was to order the 10th Cav's air squadron to probe west. Eddington's words had come back hard to him. The Saudi center of gravity might not be an economic target after all.

'Our troops are inside the Kingdom,' Intelligence told him. 'They are meeting opposition, but are breaking through. The American spy post has been destroyed.'

The news didn't make Daryaei any happier. 'How did they know – how did they know?'

The intelligence chief was afraid to ask how *they* knew *what*. So he dodged the issue: 'It does not matter. We will be in Riyadh in two days, and then nothing matters.'

'What do we know about the sickness in America? Why are not more people ill? How can they have troops to send?'

'This I do not know,' Intelligence admitted.

'What *do* you know?'

'It appears that the Americans have one regiment in Kuwait, and another in the Kingdom, with a third taking equipment from the ships – the ones the Indians failed to stop – in Dhahran.'

'So attack them!' Mahmoud Haji almost shouted. The arrogance of that American, calling him by name in a way that his own people might have seen and heard . . . and believed?

'Our air force is attacking in the north. That is the place of decision. Any diversion from that is a waste of time,' he replied reasonably.

'Missiles, then!'

'I will see.'

The brigadier commanding the Saudi 4th Brigade had been told to expect nothing more than a diversionary attack in his area and to stand ready to launch a counterattack into the UIR right upon the commencement of their massed attack into Kuwait. Like many generals throughout history, he had made the mistake of believing his intelligence a little too much. He had three mechanized battalions, each covering a thirty-mile sector, with a five- to ten-mile gap between them. In an offensive role, it would have been a flexible deployment for harassing the enemy's flank, but the early loss of his middle battalion had split his command in two, leaving him no easy way to command the separated parts. He next compounded the error by moving forward instead of backward. A courageous decision, it overlooked the fact that he had one hundred miles of depth behind him to King Khalid Military City, space in which he could have reorganized for a weighted counterstroke instead of a fragmented impromptu one.

The UIR attack was made on the model perfected by the Soviet army in the 1970s. The initial break-in phase had been composed on a heavy brigade surging forward behind massed artillery fire. The elimination of STORM TRACK had been intended from the beginning. It and PALM BOWL – they even knew the code names – were largely the eyes of their enemy's command structure. Satellites they could do nothing about, but ground-based intelligence-gathering posts were fair game. As expected, the Americans had deployed some assets, but not many, it appeared, and half of those would be day-flying aircraft. As with the Soviets, who had written the book to drive to the Bay of Biscay, the UIR would accept the cost, balancing lives against time to reach their political objective before the full weight of their potential enemies could come to bear. If the Saudis believed that Daryaei wanted their oil more than anything else, so be it, for in Riyadh was the royal family and the government. In doing so, the UIR risked its left flank, but Kuwait-based forces would have to negotiate the terrain of the Wadi al Batin, and then cross two hundred miles of desert just to get to where the Army of God had already been.

The key was speed, and the key to achieving speed was the rapid elimination of the Saudi 4th. The artillery still massed north of the berm tracked in on the urgent radio transmissions, and commenced a relentless area fire aimed at disrupting communications and cohesion in the units that they fully expected would be used to counter the initial invasion. It was a tactic almost certain to work, so long as they were willing to pay the price. One brigade each had been allocated to the three border battalions.

The 4th Brigade commander also had artillery of his own, but this, he decided, was best used on the center breakthrough, to punish the units with a clear road into the heart of his nation. The support mainly went there, to harass people just passing through rather than the brigades, which were just now making contact with his remaining mechanized forces. With their destruction, he would triple the width of the gap in the Saudi lines.

Diggs was in the main command post with all of this news coming in, and he realized what was happening to him, after a fashion. He'd done it to the Iraqis in 1991. He'd done it to the Israelis for a couple of years as CO of the Buffalo Cav. And he'd commanded the National Training Center for a time as well. Now he saw what it was like on the other side. Things were happening too fast for the Saudis. They were reacting rather than thinking, seeing the crisis in its magnitude but not its shape, semi-paralyzed by the speed of events which, had they been on the other side, would have seemed merely exciting and nothing more.

'Have the 4th pull back about thirty klicks,' he said quietly. 'You have plenty of room to maneuver in.'

'We will stop them right there!' the Saudi commander replied, too automatically.

'General, that is a mistake. You are risking that brigade when you don't have to. You can recover lost ground. You cannot recover lost time and lost men.'

But he wasn't listening, and Diggs didn't have enough stars on his collar to speak more insistently. *One more day*, he thought, *one more goddamned day*.

The helicopters took their time. M-Troop, 4th of the 10th, was made of six OH-58 Kiowa scout choppers and four AH-64 Apache attack birds, all carrying more extra fuel tanks than weapons. They had warning that enemy fighters were aloft, which prohibited flying very high. Their sensors were sniffing the air for the radar emissions of SAM radars – there had to be some around – while the pilots picked their way from hilltop to hilltop, scanning forward with low-light viewing systems and Longbow radars. Passing into UIR territory, they spotted the occasional scout vehicle, perhaps a company spread over twenty klicks within sight of the Kuwaiti border, they estimated, but that was all. The next fifty miles revealed much of the same, though the vehicles were heavier. Arriving on the outskirts of Al Busayyah, which the Army of God had been approaching according to satellite-intelligence information, all they really found were tracks in the sand and a few groups of support vehicles, mainly fuel trucks. Destroying them wasn't their mission. Their task was to locate the enemy's main body and determine its axis of advance.

That took another hour of ducking and side-slipping and darting, the helicopters leap-frogging. There were SAM vehicles around here, Russian- and French-made short-range ones that helicopters knew to avoid. One Kiowa-Apache team got close enough to see a column of tanks moving through a gap in the berm in brigade strength, and that was 150 miles from the point they'd left. With that information, the helicopters withdrew, without taking a shot at anything. The next time, they might well come in strength, and there was no sense in warning people about the gap in their air defenses before it could be properly exploited.

The 4th Brigade's easternmost battalion stood its ground, and mainly died there. By this time, UIR attack helicopters had joined in, and while the Saudis shot well, the inability to maneuver doomed them. It cost the Army of God another brigade to accomplish this mission, but at the end of it, the gap in Saudi lines was seventy miles wide.

It was different in the west. This battalion, commanded now by a major with the death of his colonel, broke contact and headed southwest with half its strength, then tried to turn east, to get ahead of the advancing attack. Lacking the strength to stand, he stung and moved, in the process accounting for twenty tanks and a number of other vehicles, before running out of fuel, thirty kilometers north of KKMC. The 4th Brigade's support vehicles had gotten lost somewhere. The major radioed for help and wondered if any might arrive.

It came as more of a surprise than it should have. A Defense Support System Program satellite over the Indian Ocean spotted the launch bloom. That word went to Sunnyvale, California, and from there to Dhahran. It had all happened before, but not with missiles launched from Iran. The ships were scarcely half unloaded. The war was only four hours old when the first Scud left its truck-bed launcher, heading south out of the Zagros Mountains.

'Now what?' Ryan asked.

'Now you see why the cruisers are still there,' Jackson replied.

Raid warning was scarcely needed. The three cruisers, plus *Jones*, had their radars sweeping the sky, and they all acquired the inbound ballistic track over a hundred miles out. National Guardsmen waiting their turn to fetch their tracked vehicles watched the fireballs of surface-to-air missiles lance into the sky, leaping after things that only radars could see. The initial launch of three exploded separately in the darkness, and that was that. But the soldiers were now even more motivated to collect their tanks as the triple boom came down from one hundred thousand feet.

On *Anzio*, Captain Kemper watched the track disappear from the display. This was one other thing Aegis should be good at, though sitting still under fire wasn't exactly his idea of fun.

The other event of the evening was a spirited air battle over the border. The AWACS aircraft had watched what turned out to be twenty-four fighters coming in directly for them in an attempt to deny the allies air coverage. That proved a costly exercise. No attack on the E-3B aircraft was actually accomplished. Instead, the UIR air force continued to demonstrate its ability to lose aircraft to no purpose. But would that matter? The senior American controller on one AWACS remembered an old NATO joke. One Soviet tank general ran into another in Paris and asked, 'By the way, who won the air war?' The point of it was that wars were ultimately won or lost on the ground. So it would be here.

60

BUFORD

It wasn't until six hours after the first artillery barrage that
enemy intentions were clear. It took the reports of the helicopter reconnaissance to give an initial picture, but what
finally turned the trick was satellite photography that was
impossible to discount. The historical precedents flooded
into Marion Diggs's mind. When the French high command
had got wind of the German Schlieffen Plan prior to World
War I, their reaction had been, 'So much the better for us!'
That assault had barely ground to a halt outside Paris. In
1940, the same high command had greeted initial news of
another German attack with smiles – and *that* attack had
ended at the Spanish border. The problem was that people
tended to wed their ideas more faithfully than their spouses,
and the tendency was universal. It was well after midnight,
therefore, when the Saudis realized that the main force of
their army was in the wrong place, and that their western
covering force had been steamrollered by an enemy who was
either too smart or too dumb to do what they'd expected
him to do. To counter that, they had to fight a battle of
maneuver, which they were unprepared for. The UIR sure as
hell was driving first to KKMC. There would be a battle for
that point on the map, after which the enemy would have
the option of turning east towards the Persian Gulf – and the
oil – thus trapping allied forces; or continuing south to
Riyadh to deliver a political knockout and win the war. All
in all, Diggs thought, it wasn't a terribly bad plan. If they
could execute it. Their problem was the same as the Saudis',
though. They had a plan. They thought it was pretty good,
and they, too, thought that *their* enemy would connive at
his own destruction. Sooner or later, everyone did, and the
key to being on the winning side was knowing what you
could do and what you couldn't. This enemy didn't know

the *couldn't* part yet. There was no sense in teaching them that too soon.

In the Situation Room, Ryan was on the phone with his friend in Riyadh.

'I have the picture, Ali,' the President assured him.

'This is serious.'

'The sun will be up soon, and you have space to trade for time. It's worked before, Your Highness.'

'And what will your forces do?'

'They can't exactly drive home from there, can they?'

'You are that confident?'

'You know what those bastards did to us, Your Highness.'

'Why, yes, but –'

'So do our troops, my friend.' And then Ryan had a request.

'This war has started badly for allied forces,' Tom Donner was saying live on *NBC Nightly News*. 'That's what we're hearing, anyway. The combined armies of Iraq and Iran have smashed through Saudi lines west of Kuwait and are driving south. I'm here with the troopers of the 11th Armored Cavalry Regiment, the Blackhorse. This is Sergeant Bryan Hutchinson of Syracuse, New York. Sergeant, what do you think of this?'

'I guess we're just going to have to see, sir. What I can tell you, B-Troop is ready for anything they got. I wonder if they're ready for us, sir. You come along and watch.' And that was all he had to say on the subject.

'As you see, despite the bad news from the battlefield, these soldiers are ready – even eager – for contact.'

The senior Saudi commander hung up the phone, having just talked with his sovereign. Then he turned to Diggs. 'What do you recommend?'

'For starters, I think we should move the 5th and 2nd Brigades southwest.'

'That leaves Riyadh uncovered.'

'No, sir, actually it doesn't.'

'We should counterattack at once!'

'General, we don't have to yet,' Diggs told him, staring down at the map. The 10th sure was in an interesting position . . . He looked up. 'Sir, have you ever heard the story about the old bull and the young bull?' Diggs proceeded to tell one of his favorite jokes, and one which, after a few seconds, had the senior Saudi officers nodding.

'You see, even the American television says that we are succeeding,' the intelligence chief told his boss.

The general commanding the UIR air force was less sanguine. In the past day, he'd lost thirty fighters, for perhaps two Saudi aircraft in return. His plan to bore in and kill the AWACS aircraft which so tilted the odds in the air had failed, and cost him a gaggle of his best-trained pilots in the process. The good news, for him, was that his enemies lacked the aircraft needed to invade his country and do serious damage. Now more ground forces were moving down from Iran to advance on Kuwait from the north, and with luck all he would have to do would be to cover the advance ground forces, which his people knew how to do, especially in daylight. They'd learn about that course in a few hours.

A total of fifteen Scud-type ballistic missiles had been launched at Dhahran. Hitting the COMEDY ships had been a long shot at best, and all of the inbounds had either been intercepted or, in most cases, had fallen harmlessly into the sea during a night of noise and fireworks. The last of the load – mainly trucks at this stage – were rolling off now, and Greg Kemper set his binoculars down, as he watched the line of brown-painted trucks fade into the dawn haze. Where they were heading, he didn't know. He did know that about five thousand very pissed-off National Guardsmen from North Carolina were ready to do something.

Eddington was already south of KKMC with his brigade staff. His WOLFPACK force would probably not get there in time to fight a battle. Instead, he had headed them to Al Artawiyah, one of those places which sometimes became important in history because roads led there. He wasn't sure if that would happen here, though he remembered that Gettysburg had been a place where Bobby Lee hoped to get some shoes for his men. While his staff did their work, the colonel lit a cigar and walked outside, to see two companies of men arriving with their vehicles. He decided to head over that way while the MPs got them scattered into hasty-defense locations. Fighters screamed overhead. American F-15Es, by the look of them. Okay, he thought, the enemy'd had a pretty good twelve hours. Let 'em think that.

'Colonel!' a staff sergeant Bradley commander saluted from his hatch. Eddington climbed up as soon as the vehicle stopped. 'Good morning, sir.'

'How is everybody?'

'We're just ready as hell, sir. Where are they?' the sergeant asked, taking off his dust-covered goggles.

Eddington pointed. 'About a hundred miles that way, coming this way. Tell me about how the troops feel, Sergeant.'

'How many can we kill before they make us stop, sir?'

'If it's a tank, kill it. If it's a BMP, kill it. If it's a truck, kill it. If it's south of the berm, and it's holding a weapon, kill it. *But* the rules are serious about killing unresisting people. We don't break those rules. That's important.'

'Fair 'nuff, Colonel.'

'Don't take any unnecessary chances with prisoners, either.'

'No, sir,' the track commander promised. 'I won't.'

Geometry put the Blackhorse first, advancing west from their assembly area toward KKMC. Colonel Hamm had his command advancing on line, 1st, 2nd, and 3rd Squadrons lined up south to north, each covering a twenty-mile frontage. The 4th (Aviation) Squadron he kept in his pocket, with just a few helo scouts probing forward while the ground-support elements of their battalion moved to set up an advanced base at a point which his leading troops had not yet reached. Hamm was in his M4 command track – called, naturally enough, the Star Wars (some called it 'God') Track – sitting athwartships, which made for motion-sickness, and starting to get that 'take' from his advanced units.

The IVIS system was starting to go on-line now in a real tactical environment. The Inter-Vehicle Information System was a data-link network the Army had been playing with for about five years. It had never been tested in combat, and it pleased Al Hamm that he would be the first to prove its worth. His command screens in the M4 got everything. Each single vehicle was both a source and a recipient of information. It began by telling everybody where all friendly units were, which, with GPS location equipment, was accurate to the meter, and that was supposed to prevent blue-on-blue 'friendly fire' losses. At the touch of a key, Hamm knew the location of every fighting vehicle he had, plotted on a map which showed all relevant terrain features. In time he would have a similarly accurate picture of enemy dispositions, and with the knowledge of everyone's location came the option to pick his spots. The Saudi 2nd and 5th Brigades were to his northwest, coming down from the Kuwaiti border area. He had about one hundred miles to move cross-country before he had to worry about making contact, and the four hours of approach march would serve to establish control of his units and make sure that everything was working. He had few doubts of that, but it was a drill he had to perform, because mistakes on the battlefield, however small, were expensive ones.

Remnants of the Saudi 4th Brigade tried to assemble north of KKMC. They amounted to perhaps two companies of tanks and infantry carriers, most having fought hit-and-run actions during the long desert night. Some had survived from pure luck, others through the brutally Darwinian process that was mobile warfare. The senior surviving officer was a major whose billet had been intelligence, and who had commandeered a tank from an angry NCO. His men had neglected practice on their IVIS gear, preferring gunnery and racing about instead of more structured battle drills. Well, they'd paid for that, the major knew. His first order of business was finding and calling in the scattered fuel trucks his brigade had kept to the rear, so that the surviving twenty-nine tanks and fifteen other tracks could fill up their tanks. Some ammunition trucks were also found, which allowed about half of his heavy vehicles to replenish their storage racks. With that done, he sent the support vehicles to the rear and selected a wadi – a dry riverbed – north and west of KKMC as his next defense position. It took another half hour for him to establish reliable contact with his high command and to call for support.

His force was not coherent. The tanks and tracks came from five different battalions. Some crews knew others only casually or not at all, and he was short of officers to command what force he had. With that knowledge came the realization that his job was to command rather than to fight himself. He reluctantly returned the tank to the sergeant who 'owned' it, and chose instead an infantry carrier with more radios and fewer distractions. It wasn't a warlike decision, not for a person whose cultural tradition was leading a mob of warriors on horseback with a sword waving in the air, but he'd learned a few hard lessons in the darkness south of the berm, which put him one up on a lot of men who'd died from not learning fast enough.

The day's fighting began after a pause from both movement and killing that would afterward seem as stylized as the halftime of a football game. The reason the Saudi 4th's survivors had garnered the time and space to reorganize and replenish was that the Army of God had to do the same. Trailing elements refueled from the bowsers, which had followed the combat units. Then they leapfrogged forward, allowing the fuel trucks to succor the erstwhile advance units. That process took four hours. The brigade and divisional commanders were pleased to this point. They were only ten kilometers behind the plan – plans are always too optimistic – in distance, and an hour in time. The refueling took place almost on schedule as well. They'd smashed the initial opposition, taking more losses than hoped, but crushing their foe in any case. Men were tired, but soldiers were supposed to be tired, too, everyone thought, and the time for refueling allowed most to nap enough to freshen them. With the coming of dawn, the Army of God started its diesel engines and renewed its drive south.

The first battles this day would be aloft. The allied air forces started taking off in numbers just after four from bases in the southern portion of the Kingdom. The first rank of aircraft were F-15 Eagles, which joined up with three circling E-3B AWACS aircraft lined up east and west of Riyadh. The UIR fighters rose as well, still in the control of ground radar stations inside the former country of Iraq. It began as a sort of dance between two chorus lines. Both sides wanted to know where the other side's SAMs were, information on which had been gathered during the dark hours. Both sides, it was gradually determined, would have a missile belt to hide behind, but in both cases the initial battles would be fought in an electronic no-man's-land. The first move was by a flight of four from the 390th Fighter Squadron, the Wild Boars. Alerted by their control aircraft that a UIR flight had turned east, the Eagles angled west, went to burner, and darted across the empty space, reversing course back toward the sea as they did so. The Americans expected to win, and they did. The UIR fighters – actually, Iranian F-4s left over from the time of the Shah – were caught looking the wrong way. Warned by their ground controllers, they turned back, but their problem was deeper than the tactical situation. They'd expected an engagement pattern in which one side would fire missiles, and the other would evade, then turn back to fire its own in a style of encounter as rigid as a medieval joust. Nobody had told them that this was not how their American enemies were trained.

The Eagles fired first, loosing one AMRAAM each. It was a fire-and-forget missile, which allowed them to retreat after shooting. But they didn't, and instead bored in behind them, following both their doctrine and inclinations after ten hours of contemplating what their President had said on the radio. It was all personal now, and the first team of Eagle drivers kept closing while their missiles tracked in on the first group of targets. Three of the four targets were destroyed, adversely surprised by the missile American pilots called the Slammer. The fourth evaded, blessed his luck, and turned back to fire off his own weapon, only to see on his radar that there was a fighter fifteen kilometers distant, with a closure rate of nearly two thousand knots. That made him flinch and turn south, a mistake. The Eagle pilot, his wingman half a mile behind, chopped power to slow down and got in a tail-chase position. He wanted an eyeball-kill, and he got it, closing on the enemy's 'six,' and selecting guns. The other guy was a little slow to catch on this morning. In fifteen more seconds, the F-4 expanded to fill the gunsight . . .

'Fox-Three, Fox-Three for a kill!'

A second flight of Eagles was in the combat area now,

going after their own targets. The UIR ground controllers were startled by the speed of the result, and ordered their fighters to point at the oncoming Americans and fire off their radar-guided long-range missiles – but even then, the Americans did not run away to evade as expected. Instead, their tactic was to roll ninety degrees to the ground, and maintain an even distance to the launching aircraft. That denied the fighter radars a Doppler, or range-rate change, to their targets, broke radar lock, and sent the missiles into random, unguided courses. Then the Eagles turned in, selected their own missiles, and shot from under ten miles while the UIR fighters were trying to reacquire and fire another volley, again boring in behind them. Warned that more missiles were in the air, the enemy fighters tried to turn and run, but they were too far inside the Slammer envelope, and all four of them were blotted out as well.

'Hey, dude, this is Bronco,' a voice taunted over the UIR guard channel. 'Send us some more. We're hungry. We're wanna shoot 'em *all* down and fuck their ol' ladies!' He switched channels to Sky-One. 'Razorback Lead, more business, over?'

'Not in your sector, stand by.'

'Roger that.' The lieutenant colonel commanding the 390th rolled sideways again, looking down to see the massed tanks moving out from their assembly points, and for the first time in his life he wished that he was air-to-mud instead of air-to-air. Colonel Winters came from New York. There were sick people there, he knew, and here he was at war against those who had caused it, but he'd killed only two aircraft, and just three people so far. 'Razorback, Lead, form up on me.' Then he checked his fuel state. He'd have to tank soon.

Next in were the Strike Eagles of the 391st, escorted by HARM-equipped F-16s. The smaller, single-seat fighters cruised in with their threat-receivers on, sniffing for mobile SAM launchers. There turned out to be a goodly collection of low-altitude missile vehicles, French Crotales and old Russian SA-6 Gainfuls, just behind the lead echelons. The Viper drivers jinked down to draw their attention, then fired off their anti-radar missiles to cover the inbound F-15Es. Those were looking for enemy artillery first of all.

* * *

The Predators were working on that. Three had crashed with the loss of their ground-control at STORM TRACK, creating a gap in intelligence coverage that had taken hours to rectify. There were only ten left in theater. Four of those were up and flying at eight thousand feet, loitering almost invisibly over the advancing divisions. The UIR forces relied mostly on towed tubes. These were now setting up for the next major attack, lined up behind two mechanized brigades about to make the next leap toward KKMC. One Predator found the six-battery group. The data went to a collection team, then up to the AWACS, and back down to the sixteen Strike Eagles of the 391st.

The Saudi formation waited tensely. Their forty-four fighting vehicles were spread over eight kilometers, as wide as the major commanding them dared, having to balance dispersal against firepower in what he hoped would be at least a delaying action, and maybe a stand. An approaching scream in the sky told him and his men to button up, as eight-inch shells started landing in front of his position. The initial bombardment lasted three minutes, the rounds advancing toward where his vehicles were . . .

'Tigers in hot!' the strike commander called. The enemy had evidently expected his first attack to go after the leading tanks. That's where the SAMs were, and the Vipers were trying to deal with them. The three flights of four separated, then split into elements of two, coming down to four thousand feet, smoking in at five hundred knots. The gun batteries were lined up nice and neat, in even lines, the cannons spaced about a hundred meters apart, along with their trucks, just like their manual must have said, LTC Steve Berman thought. His weapons-system operator selected cluster munitions and started sprinkling them with bomblets.

'Lookin' good.' They had dropped two canisters of BLU-97 combined-effects munitions, a total of over four hundred softball-sized mini-bombs. The first battery was wiped out when the pattern covered their position. Secondary explosions erupted from the ammo trucks. 'Next.' The pilot reefed his fighter into a tight right turn. His wizzo called him back around toward the next battery, then he spotted –

'Triple-A at ten.' That proved to be a ZSU-23 mobile anti-aircraft vehicle, whose four guns started sending tracers at their Strike Eagle. 'Selecting Mav.'

This death dance lasted just a few seconds. The Eagle evaded fire and got off a Maverick air-to-ground missile, which streaked down to obliterate the gun-track, and then the pilot went after the next battery of howitzers.

It was like Red Flag, the pilot thought in a blink. He'd been here in 1991 as a captain and killed targets, but mainly wasted his time in Scud-hunts. The experience of real combat had never measured up to battle practice in the Nellis Air Force Base weapons range. It did now. The mission was only planned in a general sense. He was looking for targets in real time with look-down radar and mark-one eyeball, and unlike his playtime at Nellis, these guys were shooting back with real bullets. Well, he was dropping real bombs, too. More ground fire started up as he lined his aircraft on the next collection of targets.

It seemed, of all things, like a cough in the middle of a conversation. There was a final crash of twenty or thirty rounds on the desert a hundred meters in front of his position. Thirty seconds later, ten more fell. Thirty seconds after that, only three. On the horizon, well behind the first row of tanks just appearing, there were dust clouds. Some seconds later, they felt something through their boots, and after that a distant rumble. It became clear in a few seconds. Green-painted fighters appeared, heading due south. They were friendly, he saw from their shape. Then another appeared, trailing smoke, staggering in the sky, then tipping over, and two objects jolted out of it, turning into parachutes that drifted to the ground a kilometer behind his position, as the fighter smashed down separately, making an immense fireball. The major dispatched a vehicle to pick them up, then returned his attention to tanks still out of range – and he had no artillery to call in on them as yet.

Well, shit, the colonel thought, it was like Red Flag after all, except this night wouldn't be spent telling lies in the O club and sneaking off to Vegas for a show and some time in a casino. His third pass had run him into fire, and the Eagle was too sick to make it all the way home. He wasn't even on the ground yet when he saw a vehicle coming toward him, and he wondered whose it was. A moment later, it looked like an American-made Hummer, fifty meters away when he hit the ground, jolting hard on the packed sand. He popped the release on his chute and pulled his pistol out, but sure enough the vehicle was friendly, with two Saudi soldiers in it. One came over to him while the other took the Hummer to where the wizzo was standing, half a mile away.

'Come, come!' the Saudi private said. A minute later, the Hummer was back with the wizzo, who was holding his knee and grimacing.

'Twisted it bad, boss. Landed on a fuckin' rock,' he explained, getting in one of the backseats.

Everything he'd heard about Saudi drivers was true, the colonel learned in a few seconds. It was like being inside a Burt Reynolds movie, as the Hummer bounded its way back to the safety of the wadi, but it was good to see the shapes of friendly vehicles there. The Hummer took him to what had to be the command post. There were still some shells falling forward of their position, but their aim had worsened, now dropping the shells five hundred meters short.

'Who are you?' Lieutenant Colonel Steve Berman asked.

'Major Abdullah.' The man even saluted. Berman holstered his pistol and looked around.

'I guess you're the guys we came to support. We took out their artillery pretty good, but some bastard got lucky with his Shilka. Can you get us a chopper?'

'I will try. Are you injured?'

'My wizzo had a bum knee. We could use something to drink, though.'

Major Abdullah handed over his canteen. 'We have an attack coming in.'

'Mind if I watch?' Berman asked.

One hundred miles to the south, Eddington's brigade was still forming. He had one battalion pretty much intact. This he moved twenty miles forward, left and right of the road to KKMC, to screen the rest of his forces as they came up the road from Dhahran. Unhappily, his artillery was the last group to have been off-loaded, and they weren't due for at least another four hours. But that couldn't be helped. As units arrived, he first of all got them to assembly areas where they could top off their fuel tanks. What with getting people off the road, directed to their intermediate destinations, and gassed up, it took about an hour per company to get things organized. His second battalion was just about ready to move. This one he would send west of the road, which would allow the first one to move laterally to the east, and double his advanced security force. It was so hard to explain to people that fighting battles was more about traffic control than killing people. That, and gathering information. A combat action was like the last act of a massive ballet – most of the time it was just getting the dancers to the right parts of the stage. The two acts – knowing where to send them and then getting them there – were interactive, and Eddington still didn't have a very clear picture. His brigade intelligence group was just setting up and starting to get hard information from Riyadh. Forward, his lead battalion had a reconnaissance screen of HMMWVs and Bradleys ten miles in advance of the main force, all of them hunkered down, their vehicles hidden as best they could be, and the troops on their bellies, scanning forward with binoculars, so far reporting nothing but the occasional wisp of dust well beyond the visible horizon and the rumbles of noise that carried amazingly far. Well, Eddington decided, so much the better. He had time to prepare, and time was the most valuable commodity a soldier could hope for.

'Lobo-Six, this is Wolfpack-Six, over.'

'Lobo-Six copies.'

'This is Wolfpack-Six-Actual. Whitefang is moving out now. They should be on your left in an hour. You may commence your lateral movement when they arrive on line. Over.'

'Lobo-Six-Actual copies, Colonel. Still nothing to see up here. We're in pretty good shape, sir.'

'Very well. Keep me informed. Out.' Eddington handed the radio phone back.

'Colonel!' It was the major who ran his intelligence section. 'We have some information for you.'

'Finally!'

*   *   *

1190

The artillery fire continued, with a few rounds dropping right in the wadi. It was Colonel Berman's first experience with that, and he found that he didn't like it very much. It also explained why the tanks and tracks were spread out so much, which had struck him as very odd at first. One round went off a hundred meters to the left of the tank behind which he and Major Abdullah were sheltering, thankfully to the far side. They both quite distinctly heard the *pings* of fragments hitting the brown-painted armor.

'This is not fun,' Berman observed, shaking his head to clear the noise of the shellburst.

'Thank you for dealing with the rest of their guns. It was quite frightening,' Abdullah said, looking through his binoculars. The advancing UIR T-80s were just over three thousand meters away, having not yet spotted his hull-down M1A2s.

'How long have you been in contact?'

'It started just after sunset yesterday. We are all that is left of the 4th Brigade.' And that didn't help Berman's confidence at all. Above their heads, the tank's turret made a slight adjustment to the left. There was a short phrase over the major's radio, and he replied with a single word – shouted, however. A second after that, the tank to the left of them jerked backward a foot or so, and a blast of fire erupted from the main gun. It made the artillery round seem like a firecracker in comparison. Against all logic, Berman raised his head. In the distance he saw a column of smoke, and tumbling atop it was a tank turret.

'Jesus!'

'You have a radio I can use?'

'Sky-One, this is Tiger Lead,' an AWACS officer heard on a side channel. 'I am on the ground with a Saudi tank group north of KKMC.' He gave the position next. 'We are in heavy contact here. Got any help you can send us? Over.'

'Tiger, can you authenticate?'

'No, God damn it, my fuckin' codes went down with my -15. This is Colonel Steve Berman out of Mountain Home, and I am one very pissed-off aviator right now, Sky. Forty minutes ago, we beat the snot out of some Iraqi artillery, and now we got tanks coming out the ass. You gonna believe me or not, over.'

'Sounds American to me,' a more senior officer thought.

'And if you look close, their tanks are round on top and pointing south and ours are flat on the top and pointing north, over.' That bit of information was followed by the crash of an explosion. 'This ground-pounder shit ain't no fun at all,' he told them.

'Me too,' the first controller decided. 'Tiger, stand by. Devil-Lead, this is Sky-One, we have some business for you . . .'

It wasn't supposed to be this way at all, but it was happening even so. There were supposed to be frag – for fragmentary – orders detailing 'packages' of tactical aircraft to hunting patches, but there weren't enough aircraft for that, and no time to select their patches, either. Sky-One had a flight of four F-16s waiting for some air-to-mud action, and this seemed as good a time as any.

The advancing tanks stopped to trade fire at first, but that was a losing game against the fire-control systems on the American-made Abrams tanks, and these Saudi crews had gotten a post-graduate course in gunnery earlier in the day. The enemy backed off and maneuvered left and right, blowing smoke from their rear decks to obscure the battlefield. More vehicles were left behind, contributing their own black columns to the morning sky as their ammunition racks cooled off. The initial part of the engagement had lasted five minutes and had cost the UIR twenty vehicles that Berman could see, with no losses for the friendlies. Maybe this wasn't so bad after all.

The Vipers came in from the west, hardly visible about four miles downrange, dropping their Mark-82 dumb bombs in the middle of the enemy formation.

'Brilliant!' the English-educated Major Abdullah said. They couldn't tell how many vehicles had died as a result, but now his men knew they were not alone in their engagement. That made a difference.

If anything, the streets of Tehran had become grimmer still. What struck Clark and Chavez (Klerk and Chekov, currently) was the absence of conversation. People moved along without speaking to one another. There was also a sudden shortage of men, as reserves were being called up to trek into their armories, draw weapons, and prepare to move into the war which their new country had halfheartedly announced after President Ryan's pre-emption.

The Russians had given them the location of Daryaei's home, and their job really was only to look at it – which was easily said, but rather a different task on the streets of the capital city of the country with which you were at war. Especially if you had been in that city shortly before, and seen by members of its security force. The complications were piling up.

The man lived modestly, they saw from two and a half blocks away. It was a three-story building on a middle-class street that displayed no trappings of power at all, except for the obvious presence of guards on the front steps, and a few cars spotted at the corners. Looking closer from two hundred meters away, they could also see that people avoided walking on that side of the street. Popular man, the Ayatollah.

'So, who else lives there?' Klerk asked the Russian *rezident*. He was covered as the embassy's second secretary, and performed many diplomatic functions to maintain his legend.

'Mainly his bodyguards, we believe.' They were sitting in a cafe, drinking coffee and studiously not looking directly at the building of their interest. 'To either side, we think the buildings have been vacated. He has his security concerns, this man of God. The people here are increasingly uneasy under his rule – even the enthusiasm of the Iraqi conquest fades now. You can see the mood as well as I, Klerk. These people have been under control for almost a generation. They grow tired of it. And it was clever of your President to announce hostilities before our friend did. The shock value was very effective, I think. I like your President,' he added. 'So does Sergey Nikolay'ch.'

'This building is close enough, Ivan Sergeyevich,' Chavez said quietly, calling the kaffeeklatsch back to order. 'Two hundred meters, direct line of sight.'

'What about collateral damage?' Clark wondered. It

required some circumlocutions to make that come out in Russian.

'You Americans are so sentimental about such things,' the *rezident* observed. It amused him.

'Comrade Klerk has always had a soft heart,' Chekov confirmed.

At Holloman Air Force Base in New Mexico, a total of eight pilots arrived at the base hospital to have their blood checked. The Ebola testing kits were finally coming out in numbers. The first major military deliveries went to the Air Force, which could deploy more power more quickly than the other branches of the service. There had been a few cases in nearby Albuquerque, all being treated at the University of New Mexico Medical Center and two on this very base, a sergeant and his wife, the former dead and the latter dying – the news of it was all over the base, further enraging warriors who already possessed a surfeit of passion. The aviators all checked out clean, and the relief they felt was not ordinary. Now, they knew, they could go out and do something. The ground crews came in next. These also tested negative. All went off to the flight line. Half of the pilots strapped into F-117 Nighthawks. The other half, with the ground crews, boarded KC-10 tanker/transport aircraft for the long flight to Saudi.

Word was coming in over the Air Force's own communications network. The 366th and the F-16s from the Israeli base were doing pretty well, but everyone wanted a piece of this one, and the men and women from Holloman would lead the second wave into the battle zone.

'Is he quite mad?' the diplomat asked an Iranian colleague. It was the RVS officers who had the dangerous – or at least most sensitive – part of the intelligence mission.

'You may not speak of our leader in that way,' the foreign ministry official replied as they walked down the street.

'Very well, does your learned holy man fully understand what happens when one employs weapons of mass destruction?' the intelligence officer asked delicately. Of course he did not, they both knew. No nation-state had done such a thing in over fifty years.

'He may have miscalculated,' the Iranian allowed.

'Indeed.' The Russian let it go at that for the moment. He'd been working this mid-level diplomat for over a year. 'The world now knows that you have this capability. So clever of him to have flown on the very aircraft that made it possible. He is quite mad. You know that. Your country will be a pariah –'

'Not if we can –'

'No, not if you can. But what if you cannot?' the Russian asked. 'Then the entire world will turn against you.'

'This is true?' the cleric asked.

'It is quite true,' the man from Moscow assured him. 'President Ryan is a man of honor. He was our enemy for most of his life, and a dangerous enemy, but now, with peace between us, he turns into a friend. He is well respected by both the Israelis and the Saudis. The Prince Ali bin Sheik and he are very close. That is well known.' This meeting was in Ashkhabad, capital of Turkmenistan, disagreeably close to the Iranian border, especially with the former Premier dead in a traffic accident – probably a creative one, Moscow knew – and elections pending. 'Ask yourself this: Why did President Ryan say those things about Islam? An attack on his country, an attack on his child, an attack on himself – but does he attack your religion, my friend? No, he does not. Who but an honorable man would say such things?'

The man on the other side of the table nodded. 'This is possible. What do you ask of me?'

'A simple question. You are a man of God. Can you condone those acts committed by the UIR?'

Indignation: 'The taking of innocent life is hateful to Allah. Everyone knows that.'

The Russian nodded. 'Then you must decide for yourself which is more important to you, political power, or your faith.'

But it wasn't quite that simple: 'What do you offer us? I have people who will soon look to me for their welfare. You may not use the Faith as a weapon against the Faithful.'

'Increased autonomy, free trade of your goods to the rest of the world, direct flights to foreign lands. We and the

Americans will help you to arrange lines of credit with the Islamic states of the Gulf. They do not forget acts of friendship,' he assured the next Premier of Turkmenistan.

'How can a man faithful to God do such things?'

'My friend' – he wasn't really, but that was what one said – 'how many men start to do something noble and then become corrupted? And then what do they stand for? Perhaps it is a lesson for you to remember. Power is a deadly thing, most deadly of all to those who hold it in their earthly hands. For yourself, you must decide. What sort of leader do you wish to be, and with what other leaders will you associate your country?' Golovko leaned back and sipped at his tea. How wrong his country had been not to understand religion – and yet, how right was the result. This man had clung to his Islamic faith as an anchor against the previous regime, finding in it a continuity of belief and values which the political reality of his youth had lacked. Now that his character, known to all in the land, was carrying him to political power, would he remain what he had been, or would he become something else? He had to recognize that danger now. He hadn't thought it all the way through, Golovko saw. Political figures so rarely did. This one had to do so, and right now, and the chairman of the RVS watched him search his soul – something the Marxist doctrine of his youth had told him did not exist. It turned out to be better that it did.

'Our religion, our Faith, it is a thing of God, not of murder. The Prophet teaches Holy War, yes, but it does not teach us to become our enemies. Unless Mahmoud Haji proves these things are false, I will not stand with him, for all his promises of money. I would like to meet this Ryan, when the time comes.'

By 13:00 Lima time, the picture was firming up nicely. The numbers were still pretty unattractive, Diggs thought, with five concentrated divisions on the move facing four brigade-sized forces, which were still dispersed. But there were things that could be done about that.

The small Saudi blocking force north of KKMC had held for three spectacular hours, but was now being enveloped and had to move, despite the wishes of the Saudi general staff. Diggs didn't even know the kid's name, but hoped to meet him later. With a couple years of proper training, he might really turn into something.

At his 'suggestion,' King Khalid Military City was being evacuated. The one part about that which hurt was turning off the intelligence assets there. Especially the Predator teams which now had to recall their birds for their withdrawal to WOLFPACK's line north of Al Artawiyah. Now that they'd all had time to think about it, the battle was like a huge training exercise at the NTC – three corps instead of battalions to face, but the principle was the same, wasn't it?

The lingering concern was an Iranian heavy division now known to be crossing the swamps west of Basra. The enemy's operational concept did leave one blank spot. In bypassing Kuwait, they had not had a covering force in place, perhaps because they thought it unnecessary, more likely because they didn't want to tip their hand, figuring to patch the hole as they were doing now. Well, every plan had a flaw.

So did the plan he'd put together for Operation BUFORD, probably. But he didn't see it, despite two hours of looking.

'Are we agreed, gentlemen?' he had to ask. Every Saudi officer in the room was still senior to him, but they'd come to see the logic of his proposal. They were going to fuck 'em all, not just a few. The assembled generals nodded. They didn't even complain any more about leaving KKMC to the enemy. They could always rebuild it. 'Then Operation BUFORD commences at sundown.'

They fell back by echelon. A few Saudi mobile guns had appeared and they now fired smoke to obscure the battlefield. As soon as they landed, half of Major Abdullah's vehicles backed off their positions and hurried south. The flanking units were already moving, fending off encirclement attempts which the enemy had adopted, probing expensively for the extreme ends of the Saudi line.

Berman's helicopter had never arrived, and the afternoon of noisy and confusing action – you couldn't see crap down here! he had come to learn – had been instructive. Calling in four more air strikes and seeing the effects on the ground was something he would keep in mind, if the Saudis clawed their way out of the trap the other side was casting about them.

'Come with me, Colonel,' Abdullah said, turning to run for his command track, ending the First Battle of KKMC.

61

GRIERSON'S RIDE

The view on the map was just awful. It was easy for anyone to see, a lot of long red arrows and short blue ones. The maps on the morning TV shows were not all that different from those in the Situation Room, and commentary – especially 'expert' commentary – talked about how American and Saudi forces were badly outnumbered and poorly deployed, with their backs to the sea. But then there was the direct satellite feed.

'We've heard stories of fierce air battles to the northwest,' Donner told the camera from 'somewhere in Saudi Arabia.' 'But the troopers of the Blackhorse Regiment have yet to see action. I can't say where I am right now – the fact of the matter is that I just don't know. B-Troop is stopped for refueling now, pouring hundred of gallons into those big M1 Abrams tanks. It's a real fuel-hog, the troopers tell me. But their mood remains the same. These are angry men – *and* women – back in the headquarters troop,' he added. 'I don't know what we will find at the western horizon. I can say that these soldiers are straining at the leash despite all the bad news that has come down from the Saudi high command. The enemy is somewhere out there, driving south in great strength, and soon after sundown, we expect to make contact. This is Tom Donner in the field with the B-Troop, 1st of the Blackhorse,' the report concluded.

'His poise isn't bad,' Ryan noted. 'When does that go on the air?'

Fortunately for all concerned, the television uplinks were over military channels, which were encrypted and controlled. It wasn't time for the UIR to learn exactly who was where. The negative commentary of the 'defeat' of the Saudi army *was*, however, going out. That news, leaked in Washington, and studiously not commented on by the Pentagon, was being accepted as gospel. Jack was still worried, however amusing it might have been in the abstract that the media was doing disinformation without even being asked.

'This evening. Maybe sooner,' General Mickey Moore replied. 'Sunset over there is in three hours.'

'Can we do it?' POTUS asked.

'Yes, sir.'

WOLFPACK, First Brigade, North Carolina National Guard, was fully formed now. Eddington took to a UH-60 Black Hawk helicopter for a flyover of his forward units. LOBO, his 1st Battalion Task Force, had its left edge on the road from Al Artawiyah to KKMC. WHITEFANG, the 2nd, was arrayed to the west side of the highway. COYOTE, the 3rd, was in reserve, his maneuver force, leaning to the west, because that's where he thought the possibilities were. His artillery battalion he split into two segments, able to cover the left or right extremes, and both able to cover the center. He lacked air assets and had been unable to get anything more than three Black Hawks for medevac. He also had an intelligence group, a combat-support battalion, medical personnel, MPs, and all the other things organic to a unit of brigade size. Forward of his two frontline battalions was a reconnaissance element whose mission was, first, to report, and second, to take out the enemy's eyes when they appeared. He'd thought of asking the 11th ACR for some of their helicopter assets, but he knew what Hamm had planned for those, and it was a waste of breath to ask. He *would* get the take from their reconnaissance efforts, and that would have to do.

Looking down, he saw that the forward line of M1A2s and Bradleys had all found comfortable spots, mainly behind berms and mini-dunes, where possible just behind high ground, so that at most the top of a turret was visible and mainly not even that. Just the track commander's head and a pair of binoculars would suffice in most cases. The tanks were spaced no less than three hundred meters apart, and mostly more than that. It made them an unattractively diluted target for artillery or air attack. He'd been told not to worry about the latter, but he worried anyway, as much as circumstance allowed. His subordinate commanders knew their jobs as well as reservists could, and the truth of the matter was that the mission was right out of the textbooks written by Guderian and practiced by Rommel and every mounted commander ever since.

The withdrawal started with a ten-mile dash at thirty-five miles per hour, enough to outrun artillery fire, and to look like the rout that Berman initially thought it to be – until he remembered that *he* made a practice of leaving enemy fire behind at least fifteen times as fast as these mechanized vehicles were doing. They were riding with top hatches open, and Berman stood to look behind, past the brown-black fountains of exploding artillery shells. He'd never known what a defensive stand was like. Mainly lonely, he thought. He'd expected bunched vehicles and men, forgetting what he himself did to such things when he spotted them from the air. He saw what had to be fifty columns of smoke, all vehicles blown apart by the Saudi National Guard. Maybe they didn't take training seriously enough – he had heard such things – but this team had stood their ground against a force at least five times as large, and held them for three hours.

Not without cost. He turned forward and counted only fifteen tanks, plus eight infantry tracks. Perhaps there were more he couldn't see in the clouds of dust, he hoped. He looked up, into what he hoped was a friendly sky.

It was. The score since dawn was forty UIR fighters down, all of them air-to-air, against six American and Saudi losses, all of them ground-to-air. The opposing air force had been unable to overcome the advantage of the allied airborne radar coverage, and the best thing that could be said for their effort was that they had distracted efforts to attack the ground forces, which would otherwise have been totally unimpeded. The ragtag collection of American-, French-, and Russian-made fighter aircraft looked impressive on paper and on the ramp, but less so in the air. But the allied air forces were far less capable at night. Only the small collection of F-15E Strike Eagles was really all-weather capable (night is considered a weather condition). There were about twenty of those, UIR intelligence estimated, and couldn't do all that much harm. The advancing divisions halted right before KKMC, again to refuel and rearm. One more such jump, their commanders thought, and they'd be to Riyadh before the

Americans were organized enough to take the field. They still had the initiative, and were halfway to their objective.

PALM BOWL kept track of all that, feeding what radio intercepts it was garnering from the southwest, but now facing a new threat to the north from an Iranian armored division. Perhaps the UIR had expected that, with the Kingdom out of the way or at least heavily engaged, the Kuwaitis would be intimidated into inaction. If so, it was wishful thinking. Borders could be crossed in two directions, and Kuwait's government made the correct assumption that doing nothing would only make things worse for them, not better. It turned out to be another case of one more day needed to patch things up, but this time it was the other side which needed the extra time.

The Air Cavalry Squadron, 4th of the 10th, lifted off twenty minutes after sunset, heading north. There were some light motorized units on border guard duty, soon, they thought, to be relieved by the unit now crossing the Tigris-Euphrates delta. It comprised two battalions of troops in trucks and light armored vehicles. They'd chatted quite a bit on their radios, the commanders moving units back and forth, but strangely unprepared to be invaded by a nation not a tenth the size of their own. For the next hour, all twenty-six of the Buffalo Cav's Apaches would hunt them with cannon and rocket fire, burning a path for Kuwait's own light mechanized brigade, whose reconnaissance vehicles fanned out, searching for and finding the lead elements of Iranian armor. Five kilometers back was a battalion of heavy armor guided by the reconnaissance information, and the first major surprise of the night for the UIR was the sundering of nightfall by twenty tank guns, followed two seconds later by fifteen kills. The next lesson applied was that of confidence. Their first contact with the enemy a successful one, the lead Kuwaiti elements pressed the attack with gusto. It was all coming together for them. The night-vision systems worked. The guns worked. They had an enemy with his back to unsuitable ground and noplace to go.

Listening at PALM BOWL, Major Sabah heard the radio calls, again experiencing things at second hand. It turned out that only one brigade of the Iranian 4th Armored Division, mainly a reserve formation, had gotten across, and had driven blithely and unwarned into an advancing armor force. It was, Sabah thought, just about as fair as what had happened to his country on the morning of 1 August 1990. By sunset plus three hours, the only usable access route into southern Iraq was completely blocked, and with it, easy reinforcement of the Army of God. Throughout the night, precision-guided bombs would drop bridges to make certain of that. It was a small battle for his small nation, but a winning one to set the stage for her nation's allies.

The Buffalo Cav was already moving its ground elements due west, while the Air Cav squadron returned to refuel and rearm, leaving a buoyant Kuwaiti army holding the allied rear and spoiling for another battle.

The UIR I Corps had been in reserve until this point. One division was the former Iranian 1st Armored, 'The Immortals,' accompanied by another armored division comprised mainly of surviving Republican Guards officers, and a new class of enlisted men untouched by the 1991 war. II Corps had made the breakthrough at the border and held the lead for the advance to KKMC, though in the course of combat action losing more than a third of its strength. That task accomplished, it moved left, east, clearing the path for I Corps, as yet untouched except by a few air attacks, and III Corps, similarly untouched. II Corps would now guard the flank of the advancing force against counterstrikes fully expected from the seaward side. All units, following their doctrine, sent out reconnaissance forces as darkness fell.

The lead units, advancing by bounds, skirted around King Khalid Military City, surprised to find no opposition. Emboldened, the commander of the reconnaissance battalion sent units directly into the city, then found it virtually empty of people, most of whom had driven out during the previous day. It seemed logical when he thought about it. The Army of God was advancing, and though it had taken a few heavy blows, nothing the Saudis had could stop it. Satisfied, he pressed south, a little more cautiously now. There had to be some opposition ahead.

*   *   *

Eddington's MP detachment had done its job conveying people south and out of the way. He'd seen a few faces, downcast mainly, until they'd gotten a look at what was waiting between KKMC and Al Artawiyah. WOLFPACK couldn't hide everything. Saudi MP units brought up the rear, passing through the recon screen at 21:00 local time. They'd said that there was nothing behind them. They were wrong.

With his soft vehicles in the lead and his fighting tracks guarding the rear with their turrets turned aft, Major Abdullah had thought about making one more stand, but didn't have the combat power to hold much of anything against what he knew had to be behind him. His men were exhausted by twenty-four hours of continuous combat operations, and the worst off were his tank drivers. Their position in the front of their vehicles was so comfortable as to cause them to fall asleep, only to be awakened by the shouts of their tank commanders, or the lurch of heading off the road into a ditch. His additional concern was that he'd expected to make contact with friendly units – battlefields, he'd learned in the past day, were anything but friendly places.

They appeared as white blobs at first on the thermal-imaging scopes, the vehicles straggling down the highway. Eddington, in his command post, knew that there might be some Saudi stragglers downbound, and had warned his recon screen to expect it, but it wasn't until the evening's Predators took to the sky that he was sure. Through the thermal viewers, the distinctive flat top of the M1A2 tanks was clearly visible. This information he relayed to HOOTOWL, his recon detachment, which lessened their tension as the shapeless thermal blobs on their ground-based viewing systems gradually turned into friendlier profiles. Even then, there was the chance that friendly vehicles had been captured and converted to enemy use.

Troopers cracked chemical-light wands and dropped them on the road. These were spotted and the advancing trucks stopped practically on top of them, even rolling slowly as they were, without lights. A handful of Saudi liaison officers assigned to WOLFPACK verified their identity and waved them south. Major Abdullah, arriving at the screening position ten minutes later, jumped out of his command track, along with

Colonel Berman. The American Guardsmen handed over food and water, first of all, quickly followed by GI coffee out of their MRE packs, the sort with triple the normal amount of caffeine.

'They're a ways back, but they're coming,' Berman said. 'My friend here – well, he's had a busy day.'

The Saudi major was at the point of collapse, the physical and mental exertions like nothing he'd ever known. He staggered over to the HOOTOWL command post and, over a map, relayed what he knew as coherently as he could.

'We must stop them,' he concluded.

'Major, why don't you head on down about ten miles, and you'll see the biggest fuckin' roadblock ever was. Nice job, son,' the lawyer from Charlotte told the young man. The major walked off toward his track. 'Was it that tough?' he asked Berman when the Saudi was out of earshot.

'I know they killed fifty tanks, and that's just the ones I could see,' Berman said, sipping coffee from a metal cup. 'A lot more coming, though.'

'Really?' the lawyer/lieutenant colonel said. 'That suits us just fine. No friendlies back of you?'

Berman shook his head. 'No chance.'

'You head on down the road now, Berman. Ten miles, and then you watch the show, y'hear?'

They looked like Americans, Berman saw, in their desert BDUs, their faces painted under the German-shaped Fritz helmets. There were red-shielded lights to point at the maps. It was dark out here, about as dark as a clear sky could get, just the stars enabling him to tell the difference between land and sky. A sliver of moon would appear later, but that wouldn't be much. The screen commander had a command HMMWV with lots of radios. Beyond, he could see a single Bradley, a few troops, and little else. But they stood like Americans and they spoke like Americans.

'HOOT-SIX, this is Two-Niner.'

'Two-Niner, Six, go,' the commander took the radio.

'We have some movement, five miles north of our position. Two vehicles nosing around right on the horizon.'

'Roger, Two-Niner. Keep us informed. Out.' He turned to Berman. 'Get going, Colonel. We have work to do here.'

* * *

There was a flanking screen. That would be the enemy II Corps, Colonel Hamm thought. His forward line of Kiowa scout helicopters was now watching it. The Kiowas – the military version of the Bell 206, the copter most often used in America for reporting on traffic congestion – specialized in hiding, most often behind hills and ridges, with just the top-mounted electronic periscope peering about the terrain while the pilot held his aircraft in hover, seeing but not seen, while the TV systems recorded the event, relaying their 'take' back. Hamm had six of them up now, advance scouts for his 4th Squadron, ten miles in front of his ground elements, now lying still thirty miles southeast of KKMC.

While he watched his display in the Star Wars Track, technicians converted the information from the Kiowa scouts into data that could be displayed graphically and distributed to the fighting vehicles in his command. Next came data from the Predator drones. They were up, covering the roads and desert south of the captured city, with one drone over it. The streets, he saw, were full of fuel and supply trucks. It was a convenient place to hide them.

Most important, electronic sensors were now at work. The UIR forces were moving too fast to rely on radio silence. Commanders had to talk back and forth. Those sources were moving, but they were moving predictably now, talking almost all the time, as commanders told sub-units where to go and what to do, got information and reported it up the chain. He had two brigade CPs positively identified, and probably a divisional one, too.

Hamm changed display to get the larger picture. Two divisions were moving south from KKMC now. That would be the enemy I Corps, spread on a ten-mile frontage, two divisions moving abreast in columns of brigades, a tank brigade in front, mobile artillery right behind it. II Corps was moving to their left, spread thin to provide flank guard. III Corps appeared to be in reserve. The deployment was conventional and predictable. First contact with WOLFPACK would be in about an hour, and he would hold back until then, allowing I Corps to pass north to south, right to left along his front.

There hadn't been time to prepare the battlefield properly. The Guard troops lacked a full engineer detachment and the antitank mines they might have strewn to dirty up the terrain. There hadn't been time to prepare proper obstacles and traps. They'd scarcely been in place for ten hours, and the full brigade less than that. All they really had was a fire plan. WOLFPACK could shoot short wherever it wanted, but all deep fire had to be west of the road.

'Pretty good picture here, sir,' his S-2 intelligence officer said.

'Send it out.' And with that, every fighting vehicle in the Blackhorse had the same digital picture of the enemy that he had. Then Hamm lifted his radio.

'WOLFPACK-SIX, this is BLACKHORSE-SIX.'

'This is WOLFPACK-SIX-ACTUAL. Thanks for the data feed, Colonel,' Eddington replied over the digital radio. Both units also knew where all the friendlies were. 'I'd say initial contact in about an hour.'

'Ready to rock, Nick?' Hamm asked.

'Al, it's all I can do to hold my boys back. We are locked and cocked,' the Guard commander assured him. 'We have visual on their advance screen now.'

'You know the drill, Nick. Good luck.'

'Blackhorse,' Eddington said in parting.

Hamm changed settings on his radio, calling BUFORD-SIX.

'I have the picture, Al,' Marion Diggs assured him, a hundred miles back and not liking *that* fact one bit. He was sending men into battle by remote control, and that came hard to a new general officer.

'Okay, sir, we are fully in place. All they have to do is walk in the door.'

'Roger, BLACKHORSE. Standing by here. Out.'

The most important work was now being done by the Predators. The UAV operators, sited with Hamm's intelligence section, circled their mini-aircraft higher to minimize the chance they might be spotted or heard. Cameras pointed down, counting and checking locations. The Immortals were on the enemy left, and the former Iraqi Guards Division on the right, west of the road. They were moving along steadily, battalions on line and tightly packed for maximum power and shock effect if they encountered opposition, ten miles behind their own reconnaissance screen. Behind the lead brigade was the divisional artillery. This force was divided in two, and as they watched in the intel track, one half halted, spread out, and set up to provide covering fire, while the other half took up and moved forward. Again, that was right out of the book. They would be in place for about ninety minutes. The Predators flew over the line of guns, marking their position from GPS signals. That data went down to the MLRS batteries. Two more Predators were sent along. These were dedicated to getting exact locations on enemy command vehicles.

'Well, I'm not sure when this will go out,' Donner told the camera. 'I'm here inside Bravo-Three-Two, number-two scout track in 3rd Platoon of B-Troop. We just got information on where the enemy is. He's about twenty miles west of us right now. There are at least two divisions moving south on the road from King Khalid Military City. I know now that a brigade of the North Carolina National Guard is in a blocking position. They deployed with the 11th Cavalry Regiment because they were at the National Training Center for routine training.

'The mood here – well, how can I explain this? The troopers of the Blackhorse Regiment, they're almost like doctors, strange as that may sound. These men are angry at what's happened to their country, and I've talked to them about it, but right now, like doctors waiting for the ambulance to come into the emergency room. It's quiet in the track. We just heard that we'll be moving west in a few minutes to the jump-off point.

'I want to add a personal note. Not long ago, as you all know, I violated a rule of my profession. I did something wrong. I was misled, but the fault was mine. I learned earlier today that the President himself requested that I should come here – maybe to get me killed?' Donner ad-libbed in an obvious joke. 'No, not that. This is the sort of situation that people in the news business live for. I am here where history may soon take place, surrounded by other Americans who have an important job to do, and however this turns out, this is where a reporter belongs. President Ryan, thank you for the chance.

'This is Tom Donner, southeast of KKMC, with B-Troop, 1st Squadron of the Blackhorse.' He lowered the mike. 'Got that?'

'Yes, sir,' the Army spec-5 told him. The soldier said something into his own microphone. 'Okay, that went up to the satellite, sir.'

'Good one, Tom,' the track commander said, lighting up a cigarette. 'Come here. I'll show you how this IVIS thing works and –' He stopped, holding his helmet with his hand to hear what was coming over the radio. 'Start 'er up, Stanley,' he told the driver. 'It's showtime.'

He let them come in. The man commanding the WOLFPACK's reconnaissance screen was a criminal-defense attorney by profession who'd actually graduated from West Point but later decided on a civilian career. He'd never quite lost the bug, as he thought of it, though he didn't quite know why. Age forty-five now, he'd been in uniformed service of one sort or another for almost thirty years of drills and exhausting exercise and mind-numbing routine which took away from his time and his family. Now, in the front line of his recon force, he knew why.

The lead scout vehicles were two miles to his front. He estimated two platoons that he could see, a total of ten vehicles spread across three miles, moving three or four at a time in the darkness. Maybe they had low-light gear. He wasn't sure of that, but had to assume that they did. On his thermal systems he could make them out as BRDM-2 scout cars, four-wheeled, equipped with a heavy machine gun or antitank missiles. He saw both versions, but he was especially looking for the one with four radio antennas. That would be the platoon or company commander's vehicle . . .

'Antenna track direct front,' a Bradley commander called from four hundred meters to the colonel's right. 'Range two-kay meters, moving in now.'

The lawyer-officer lifted his head above the abbreviated ridge and scanned the field with his thermal viewer. Now was as good a time as any.

'HOOTOWL, this is SIX, party in ten, I say again, party in ten seconds. Four-Three, stand by.'

'Four-Three is standing by, SIX.' That Bradley would take the first shot in 2nd of KKMC. The gunner selected high-explosive incendiary tracer. A BRDM wasn't tough enough to need the armor-piercing rounds he had in the dual-feed magazine of his

Bushmaster cannon. He centered the target in his pipper, and the on-board computer adjusted for the range.

'Eat shit and *die*,' the gunner said into the interphones.

'HOOTOWL, SIX, commence firing, commence firing.'

'Fire!' the track commander told the gunner. The spec-4 on the 25mm gun depressed the triggers for a three-round burst. All three tracers made a line across the desert, and all three hit. The command BRDM erupted into a fireball as the vehicle's gas tank – strangely for a Russian-made vehicle, it was not diesel-powered – exploded. 'Target!' the commander said instantly, confirming that the gunner had destroyed it. 'Traverse left, target *burdum*.'

'Identified!' the gunner said when he was locked on.

'Fire!' A second later: 'Target! Cease fire, traverse right! Target *burdum*, two o'clock, range fifteen hundred!' The Bradley's gun turret rotated the other way as the enemy vehicles started to react.

'Identified!'

'Fire!' And the third one was dead, ten seconds after the first.

Within a minute, all the BRDMs the screen commander had seen were burning. The brilliant white light made him cringe to see. Then other flashes appeared left and right of his position. Then: 'Move out, run 'em down!'

Across ten miles of desert, twenty Bradleys darted from behind their hiding places, going forward, not backward, their turrets traversing and their gunners hunting for enemy scout vehicles. A short, vicious, running gunfight began, lasting ten minutes and three klicks, with the BRDMs trying to pull back but unable to shoot back effectively. Two Sagger antitank missiles were launched, but both fell short and exploded in the sand when their launch vehicles were killed by Bushmaster fire. Their heavy machine guns weren't powerful enough to punch through the Bradley's frontal armor. The enemy screen, comprising a total of thirty vehicles, was exterminated by the end of it, and HOOTOWL owned this part of the battlefield.

'WOLFPACK, this is HOOT-SIX-ACTUAL, I think we got 'em all. Their lead screen is toast. No casualties,' he added. God damn, he thought, those Bradleys can shoot.

*   *   *

'Some radio chatter got out, sir,' the ELINT trooper next to Eddington reported. 'Getting some more now.'

'He's calling for artillery fire,' a Saudi intelligence officer said quickly.

'HOOT, you may expect some fire shortly,' Eddington warned.

'Roger, understand. HOOT is moving forward.'

It was safer than staying in place or falling back. On command, the Bradleys and Hummers darted two klicks to the north, looking for the enemy supplementary reconnaissance screen – there had to be some – which would move up now, probably cautiously, on direction of their brigade or divisional commanders. This, the Guard lieutenant colonel knew, would be the reconnaissance battle, the undercard for the main event, with the lightweights duking it out before the heavyweights closed. But there was a difference. He could continue to shape the battlefield for WOLFPACK. He expected to find another company of reconnaissance vehicles, closely followed by a heavy advanced guard of tanks and BMPs. The Bradley had TOW missiles to do the tanks, and the Bushmaster had been designed for the express purpose of killing the infantry carrier they called the *bimp*. Moreover, though the enemy now knew where the Blue Force recon screen was – had been – he would expect it to fall back, not advance.

That was plain two minutes later, when a planned-fire barrage dropped a klick behind the moving Bradleys. The other side was playing it by the book, the old Soviet book. And it wasn't a bad book, but the Americans had read it, too. HOOTOWL pressed on rapidly for another klick and stopped, finding a convenient line of low ridges, with blobs on the horizon again. The lawyer/colonel lifted his radio to report that.

'BUFORD, this is WOLFPACK, we are in contact, sir,' Eddington relayed to Diggs from his CP. 'We just clobbered their recon element. Our screening forces now have visual on the advance guard. My intentions are to engage briefly and pull them back and right, southeast. We have enemy artillery fire dropping between the screen and the main body. Over.'

'Roger, WOLFPACK.' On his command screen, Diggs saw

the advancing Bradleys, moving in a fairly even line, but well spread. Then they started spotting movement. The things they saw started appearing as unknown-enemy symbols on the IVIS command system.

It was immensely frustrating to the general in command. He had more knowledge of a developing battle than had ever been possible in the history of warfare. He had the ability now to tell platoons what to do, where to go, whom to shoot – *but he couldn't allow himself to do that.* He'd approved the intentions of Eddington, Hamm, and Magruder, coordinating their plans in space and time, and now as their commander he had to let them do it their way, interfering only if something went wrong or some new and unexpected situation offered itself. The commander of American forces in the Kingdom, he was now a spectator. The black general shook his head in wonderment. He'd known it would be like this. He hadn't known how hard it would hit him.

It was almost time. Hamm had his squadrons advancing abreast, covering only ten kilometers each, but separated by intervals of ten more. In every case, the squadron commanders had opted to have their scout troops in the lead, and their tank companies in reserve. Each troop had nine tanks and thirteen Brads, plus two mortar-carrying M113 tracks. In front of them, now seven kilometers away, were the brigades of UIR II Corps, bloodied by the breakthrough battles north of KKMC, weakened, but probably alert. There was nothing like violent death to get someone's attention. His helicopters and video feed from the Predators had well defined their positions. He knew where they were. They didn't know about him yet – probably, he had to admit. Certainly they were trying as hard as he would have done to make sure. His final order was for his helicopters to make one more sweep of the intervening terrain for an enemy outpost line. Everything else was pretty well locked into place, and fifty miles back, his Apaches started lifting off, along with their Kiowa scouts, for their part in the main event.

The F-15E Strike Eagles were all up north. Two of their number had been lost earlier in the day, including that of the squadron commander. Now, protected by HARM-equipped

F-16s, they were pounding the bridges and causeways across the twin-rivers estuary with smart bombs. They could see tanks on the ground, burning ones west of the swamps and intact ones bunched up to the east. In an exciting hour, every route across was destroyed by repeated hits.

The F-15Cs were over the KKMC area, as always under AWACS control. One group of four stayed high, outside the envelope of the mobile SAMs with the advancing land force. Their job was to watch for UIR fighters who might get in the way of things. The rest were hunting for helicopters belonging to the armored divisions. It didn't carry the prestige of a fighter kill – but a kill was a kill, and was something they could do with near-total impunity. Better still, generals traveled in helicopters, and most of all, those would be part of the UIR reconnaissance effort, and that, the plan said, couldn't be allowed.

Below them, word must have gotten out in a hurry. Only three choppers had been killed during the daylight hours, but with the coming of darkness a number had lifted off, half of them splashed in the first ten minutes. It was so different from the last time. The hunting was pretty easy. The enemy, on the offense, had to offer battle – couldn't hide in shelters, couldn't disperse. That suited the Eagle drivers. One driver, south of KKMC, was vectored by his AWACS, located a chopper on his look-down radar, selected AIM-120, and triggered the missile off in seconds. He watched the missile all the way in, spotting the fireball that jerked left and splattered widely on the ground. Part of him thought it a needless waste of a perfectly good Slammer. But a kill was a kill. That would be the last chopper kill of the evening. The pilots heard from their E-3B Sentry control aircraft that friendly choppers were now entering the battle area, and weapons went tight on the Eagles.

Less than half of his Bradley gunners had ever fired TOW missiles for real, though all had done so hundreds of times in simulation. HOOTOWL waited for the advance guard to get just within the margins. It was tricky. The supplementary recon screen was closer still. The Bradleys engaged them first, and this gunfight was a little more two-sided. Two BRDMs were actually behind the American scout line. Both turned at once. One nearly drove over a HMMWV, hosing it with its machine gun before a Bradley blew it apart. The armored vehicle raced to the site, finding one wounded survivor from the three-man crew on the Hummer. The infantrymen tended to him while the driver got up on a berm and the gunner elevated his TOW launcher.

The leading group of tanks was shooting now, seeking out the flashes of the Bradley guns, activating their own night-vision systems, and again there was a brief, vicious battle over the barren, unlit ground. One Bradley was hit and exploded, killing all aboard. The rest got off one or two missiles each, collecting twenty tanks in reply before their commander called them back, and just escaping the artillery barrage called in by the enemy tank commander on their positions. HOOTOWL left behind that one Bradley, and two Hummers, and the first American ground casualties of the Second Persian Gulf War. These were reported up the line.

It was right after lunch in Washington. The President had eaten lightly, and the word came into the Situation Room just after he'd finished, still able to look down at the gold-trimmed plate, the crust of bread from his sandwich, and the chips he'd not eaten. The news of the deaths hit him hard, harder, somehow, than the casualties on USS *Yorktown* or the six missing aviators – *missing* didn't necessarily mean *dead*, did it? he allowed himself to think. These men certainly were. National Guardsmen, he'd learned. Citizen soldiers most often used to help people after floods or hurricanes . . .

'Mr President, would you have gone over there for this mission?' General Moore asked, even before Robby Jackson could speak. 'If you were twenty-something again, a Marine lieutenant, and they told you to go, you'd go, right?'

'I suppose – no, no, I'd go. I'd have to.'

'So did they, sir,' Mickey Moore told him.

'That's the job, Jack,' Robby said quietly. 'That's what they pay us for.'

'Yeah.' And he had to admit that it was what they paid him for, too.

*   *   *

The four F-117 Nighthawks landed at Al Kharj, rolling out and taxiing to shelters. The transports carrying the spare pilots and ground crews were right behind. Intelligence officers down from Riyadh met the latter group, taking the spare pilots aside for their first mission briefing in a war which was just now getting started in a big way.

The major general in charge of the Immortals Division was in his command vehicle, trying to make sense of things. It had been a quite satisfactory war to this point. II Corps had done its job, blasting open the hole, allowing the main force to shoot through, and until an hour before, the picture had been both clear and pleasing. Yes, there were Saudi forces heading southwest for him, but they were the best part of a day away. By then, he'd be on the outskirts of their capital, and there were other plans for them as well. At dawn, II Corps would jump east from its covering position on his left, feinting toward the oil fields. That should give the Saudis second thoughts. Certainly it would give him another day in which, with luck, he'd get some, maybe all of the Saudi government. Maybe even the royal family – or, if they fled, as they might well do, then the Kingdom would be leaderless, and then his country would have won the war.

It had been costly to this point. II Corps had paid the price of half its combat power to deliver the Army of God this far, but victory had never been cheaply bought. Nor would it be the case here. His forward screen had disappeared right off the radio net. One call of contact with unknown forces, a request for artillery support, then nothing. He knew that a Saudi force was somewhere ahead of him. He knew it was the remains of the 4th Brigade, which II Corps had almost but not quite immolated. He knew it had fought hard north of KKMC and then pulled back ... it had probably been ordered to hold so that the city could be evacuated ... it was probably still strong enough to chew up his reconnaissance force. He didn't know where the American cavalry regiment was ... probably to his east. He knew that there might be another American brigade somewhere, probably also to his east. He wished for helicopters, but he'd just lost one to American fighters, along with his chief intelligence officer. So much for the air support he'd been promised. The only friendly fighter he'd seen all day had been a smoking hole in the ground just east of KKMC. But though Americans could annoy him, they couldn't stop him, and if he got to Riyadh on time, then he could send troops to cover most of the Saudi airfields and preempt that threat. So the key to the operation, as his Corps and Army command had told him, was to press on with all possible speed. With that decision made, he ordered his lead brigade to advance as scheduled, with his advance guard playing the reconnaissance role. They'd just reported contact and a battle, losses taken and inflicted on an enemy as yet unidentified, but who had withdrawn after a brief firefight. Probably that Saudi force, he decided, doing its best to sting and run, and he'd run it down after sunrise. He gave the orders, informed his staff of his intentions, and left the command post to drive forward, wanting to see things at the front, as a good general should, while the staff radioed orders to subordinate commanders.

There were some screening elements, the Kiowas reported. Not many. They'd probably been badly shot up on the drive south, Colonel Hamm thought. He directed one of his squadrons to maneuver left to avoid, and told his air commander to detail an Apache to deal with that one in a few minutes. One of the others could be bypassed easily. The third was directly in the path of 3rd Squadron, and that was just too bad. The position of the BRDMs was marked on the IVIS screens, along with most of UIR's battered II Corps.

So were the Immortals. Eddington saw that the advance guard, with the leading elements of the main force close behind, was just entering gun range of his tanks, advancing at about twenty kilometers per hour. He called Hamm.

'Five minutes from *now*. Good luck, Al.'

'You, too, Nick,' Eddington heard.

It was called synchronicity. Thirty miles apart, several groups of Paladin mobile guns elevated their tubes and pointed them to spots picked by Predator drones and ELINT intercepts. The cannoneers of the new age punched the proper coordinates into their computers so that the widely separated weapons could fire to the same point. Eyes were on clocks now, watching the digital numbers change, one second at a time, marching toward 22:30:00 Lima time, 19:30:00 Zulu, 14:30:00 Washington.

It was much the same in the Multiple-Launch Rocket System tracks. There the troops made sure their compartments were sealed, locked their suspension to stabilize the vehicles during the launch cycle, and then closed down windshield shutters. The exhaust from their rockets could be lethal.

South of KKMC, the Carolina Guard tankers watched the advancing white blobs. Gunners thumbed their laser rangefinders. The lead screening elements were now 2,500 meters distant, and the follow-on line of the main body a thousand behind them, mixed tanks and BMPs.

Southeast of KKMC, the Blackhorse was advancing at fifteen kph now, toward a line of targets on a ridge four thousand meters west.

It wasn't perfect. B-Troop, 1st of the 11th, stumbled right into an unsuspected BRDM position and opened fire on its own, starting fireballs into the air, turning eyes, and alerting people a few seconds too soon, but in the end that didn't matter, as the digital numbers kept changing at the same pace, either fast or slow, depending on the perceptions of the onlookers.

Eddington timed it to the second. Unable to smoke throughout the evening, for fear of making a glow that would show up on somebody's night viewer, he opened his Zippo and flicked it as 59 changed to 00. A little bit of light wouldn't matter . . . now.

The artillery went first, already ordered to time its fire to the second. The most spectacular were the MLRS rockets, twelve from each launcher, rippling out less than two seconds apart, their flaming motors illuminating the exhaust smoke as they streaked into a sky no longer dark. By 22:30:30, nearly two hundred of the M77 free-flight rockets were in the air. By that time, the mobile guns were being reloaded, their lanyards pulled, the guns discharged, and now their breeches open for the next set of rounds.

The night was clear, and the light show could not be missed by anyone within a hundred miles. Fighter pilots aloft to the northeast saw the rockets fly, and looked closely at their course. They didn't want to be in the same sky with the things.

Iraqi officers in the advancing Guards Armored Division saw them first, coming up from the south, and next they saw that all were angling west of the north-south road from KKMC to Al Artawiyah. Many of them had seen the same sight as lieutenants and captains, and knew exactly what they meant. Steel rain was coming. Some were paralyzed by the sight. Others shouted orders for men to get cover, close their hatches, and ride it out.

That wasn't possible for the divisional artillerymen. Most of their guns were towed, and most of the gunners were in the open, ammunition trucks standing by for the fire mission that had to be coming. They saw the rocket motors burn out, noted their direction, and there was little to be done but wait. Men dived to the ground, usually scattering first, holding their helmets in place and praying that the damned things were heading somewhere else.

The rockets tipped over on apogee, heading back to the ground. At several thousand feet, a timer blew open the noses, and each projectile released 644 submunitions, each weighing half a pound, which made for 7,728 for each of the launchers employed. All were targeted at the Guards Division's artillery. That was their longest-reaching weapon, and Eddington wanted it out of play immediately. As was the practice in the US Army, MLRS was the unit commander's personal shotgun. A few of the Iraqi gunners looked up. They couldn't see or hear them coming, but come they did.

From a distance, it looked like sparklers on the ground, or maybe firecrackers at Chinese New Year, dancing and exploding in celebration. It was noisy death for those on the ground, as a total of over seventy *thousand* of the munitions exploded over an area of about two hundred acres. Trucks caught fire and exploded in flame. Propellant charges lit off in secondary explosions, but most of all the artillerymen were slaughtered, over eighty percent of them killed or wounded by the first volley. There would be two more. Back of WOLFPACK's center, the launch vehicles scuttled back to their resupply trucks. Just before getting there, the expended 'six-pack' launch cells were ejected and new ones hoisted into place with rigging equipment. It took about five minutes to accomplish the reload.

It was faster for the 155mm guns. These, too, were gunning for their enemy counterparts, and their rounds were every bit as accurate as the rockets. It was the most mechanistic of military activities. The gun did the killing and the people served the gun. They couldn't see their work, and in this case didn't even have a forward-observer to tell them how they were doing, but they'd learned that with GPS doing the aiming, it didn't matter – and if things went as planned, they would later see the results of their deadly work.

Perversely, those with direct views of the advancing enemy fired last, the tankers waiting for the word, delivered as company commanders fired first for their units.

For all its lethality, the fire-control system for the Abrams tank is one of the simplest mechanisms ever placed in the hands of soldiers, and even easier to use than the million-dollar crew-training simulators. The gunners each had assigned sectors, and the initial rounds fired by the company commanders had been HEAT – high explosive antitank – rounds, which made a distinctive visual signature. Tanks were assigned areas left or right of those first kills. The thermal-imaging viewing systems keyed on heat, infrared radiation. Their targets were warmer than the desert landscape at night and announced their presence as clearly as lightbulbs. Each gunner was told what area to pick from, and each selected an advancing T-80. Centering the target in the sight, the laser buttons were depressed. The beam went out to the target and reflected back. The return signal told the ballistic computer the target's distance, speed, and direction of movement. Other sensors told it the outside temperature, the temperature of the ammunition, atmospheric density, wind direction and speed, the condition of the gun (hot ones droop), and how many shells had been fired through the tube to this point in its career. The computer digested this and other information, processed it, and when finished, flashed a white rectangle in the gunsight to tell the gunner the system was on target. Then it was just a matter of his closing his index fingers on the yoke's twin triggers. The tank lurched, the breech surged back, the muzzle flash blinded the sight momentarily, and the 'sabot' rounds streaked downrange at more than a mile a second. The projectiles were like overly thick arrows, less than the length of a man's arm, and two inches in diameter, with stubby fins on the tail that burned from air friction in their brief flight, and trailing tracers for the tank commander to watch the 'silver bullets' all the way in.

The targets were Russian-made T-80s, old tanks with old design histories. They were much smaller than their American adversaries, mainly due to their inadequate engine power, and their diminished size had made for a number of design compromises. There was a fuel tank in the front, the line for which went along the turret ring. Gun rounds were fitted in slots that nested in the rear fuel tank, so that their ammunition was surrounded by diesel fuel. Finally, to save on turret space, the loader had been replaced by an automated loading system, which in addition to being slower than a man, also required that a live round be in the open in the turret at all times. It might not have made all that much of a difference in any case, but it did make for spectacular kills.

The second T-80 to die took a 'silver bullet' at the base of the turret. The incoming round obliterated the fuel line first of all, and in the process of crashing through the armor created a lethal shower of fragments moving at over a thousand meters per second in the cramped confines, caroming off the inner surface and chopping the crewmen to bits; at the same time the ready round ignited on its tray and other rounds exploded in their racks. The crew was already dead when the ammunition exploded, also setting off the fuel and creating an explosion which blew the heavy turret fifty feet straight up in what the Army called a 'catastrophic kill.' Fifteen others died the same way in the space of three seconds. The Immortals Division's advance guard evaporated in ten more, and the only resistance they were able to offer was that the pyres of their vehicles obscured the battlefield.

Fire shifted at once to the main body, three battalions advancing on line, now just over three thousand meters away, a total of just over a hundred fifty advancing toward a battalion of fifty-four.

The commanders of the Iranian tanks were mainly still out of their turrets, the better to see, despite their having seen the rockets lifting off several miles downrange. They next saw a linear ripple of white and orange three kilometers in the distance, followed by explosions to their direct front. The quicker of the officers and conscripted tank commanders ordered their gunners to get rounds off at the muzzle flashes, and no less than ten did shoot, but they hadn't had time to gauge the range, and all their rounds fell short. The Iranian crews were drilled in what to do, and they hadn't as yet had time for fear to replace shock. Some started reload cycles, while others worked their range finders to get off properly aimed rounds, but then the horizon turned orange again, and what followed scarcely gave them the time to take note of the change of color in the sky.

The next volley of fifty-four main-gun rounds found forty-four marks, ten of the T-80s being double-targeted. This was less than twenty seconds into the engagement.

'Find one still moving,' one E-6 tank commander said to his gunner. The battlefield was lighting up now, and the fireballs interfered with the thermal viewers. There. The gunner got his laser range – 3,650m – the box came up, and he fired. The sights blanked, then came back, and he could see the tracer of his round arcing flat across the desert, all the way in –

'Target!' the commander said. 'Shift fire.'

'Identified – got one!'

'Fire!' the commander ordered.

'On the way!' the gunner fired his third round of the half-minute, and three seconds later, another T-80 turret became a ballistic object.

Just that fast, the tank phase of the battle was over.

The Bradleys were engaging the advancing BMPs, their Bushmaster cannons reaching out. It was slower for them, the range more difficult for their lighter guns, but the result was just as final.

The commander of the Immortals was just approaching the trail elements of the lead brigade when *he* saw the rockets fly. Telling his driver to pull over, he stood and turned in his command vehicle and saw the secondary explosions of his divisional artillery array, when, turning back forward, he saw the second volley of Eddington's tanks. Forty percent of his combat power had disappeared in less than a minute.

Even before the shock hit him, he knew that he'd walked into an ambush – but of what?

The MLRS rockets which had robbed the Immortals of their artillery had come from the east, not the south. It was Hamm's gift to the National Guardsmen, who were unable to go after the Iranian guns themselves with the existing fire plan. Blackhorse's MLRS had done that, then shifted fire to make way for the regiment's Apache attack helicopters, which were striking deep, actually beyond the II Corps units now being engaged by the three ground squadrons.

The division of labor on this battlefield had been determined in principle the previous day, and developments had not changed anyone's thoughts. Artillery would initially target artillery. Tanks would target tanks. The helicopters were out to kill commanders. The Immortals Division CP had stopped twenty minutes earlier. Ten minutes before the first rocket launch, Apache-Kiowa teams looped around from the north, approaching from the rear and heading for the places from which the radio signals were emitting. First would come the division-level targets, followed by the brigades.

The Immortals' staff was just coming to terms with the incoming signals. Some officers requested confirmation or clarification, information needed before they could react properly to the situation. That was the problem with command posts. They were the institutional brains of the units they commanded, and the people who made up the decision process had to be together to function.

From six kilometers away, the collection of vehicles was obvious. Four SAM-shooters were oriented south, and there was a ring of AAA guns, too. Those went first. The Apaches of P-(Attack)-Troop stopped in place, picking a spot with nothing dangerous around, and hovering at about a hundred feet. Front-seated gunners, all of them young warrant officers, used optical equipment to zoom in, selected the first group of targets, and selected Hellfire laser-guided missiles. The first launch was made by surprise, but an Iranian soldier saw the flash, and shouted to a gun crew, which slewed its guns around and started shooting before the missiles were all the way on. What followed was a madhouse. The targeted

Apache dodged left, accelerating sideways at fifty knots to throw them off, but also ruining the aim of the startled gunner, who had to shoot again, as the first missile went wide. The other AH-64s were not hampered, and of their six launches, five hit. In another minute, the antiair problem was neutralized, and the attack choppers closed. They could see people running now, out and away from the command tracks. Some soldiers in the command security group started firing their rifles into the sky, and there was more structured activity from machine-gunners, but surprise was on the other side. The gunners fired 2.75-inch rockets to blanket the area, Hellfires to eliminate the few remaining armored vehicles, and then shifted to their 30mm cannon. In display of their rage, they closed in now, like the oversized insects they appeared to be, buzzing and slipping from side to side while the gunners looked for people the heavier weapons had missed. There was noplace to hide on the flat terrain, and the human bodies glowed on the dark, colder surface, and the gunners hunted them down in groups, in pairs, and finally one by one, sweeping across the site like harvesters. In their pre-mission discussion on the flight line, it had been decided that, unlike in 1991, helicopters would not accept surrender in this war, and the 30mm projectiles had explosive tips. P-Troop – they called themselves the Predators – lingered for ten minutes before they were satisfied that every single vehicle was destroyed and every moving body dead before they twisted in the sky, dipped their noses, and headed back east for their rearm points.

The premature attack on II Corps's reconnaissance element had started one part of this battle a little too early, and alerted a reasonably intact tank company sooner than intended, but the enemy tanks were still white blobs on a black background, and less than four thousand meters away.

'Battlestars engage,' B-Troop's commander ordered, firing off his first round, soon to be followed by eight more. Six hit, even at this extreme range, and the attack by the Blackhorse on II Corps began even before the first MLRS volley. The next volley was delivered on the move, and five more tanks exploded, their return rounds falling short. It was a little harder to hit this way. Though the gun was stabilized, hitting a bump could throw the aim off, and misses were expected, if not exactly welcomed.

B-Troop's tanks were spaced fully half a kilometer apart, and each had a hunting zone exactly that wide, and the farther they went, the more targets appeared. The Bradley scout vehicles hung back a hundred yards or so, and their gunners looked for infantry who might wield antitank weapons. II Corps's two divisions were spread across twenty miles of linear space and about eight miles of depth, so said the IVIS gear. In ten minutes, B-Troop chopped its way through a battalion diminished by the Saudis and now erased by the Americans. The bonus came ten minutes later, when they spotted a battery of artillery setting up. The Bradleys got those, sweeping the area with their 25mm cannon and adding to the fireballs that gave the lie to the sunset only four hours old.

'Damn.' Eddington merely spoke the word, without any emphasis at all. He had been called forward by his battalion commanders and was now standing up in his HMMWV.

'You believe less than five minutes?' LOBO-SIX asked. He'd heard the amazement himself over his battalion net: 'Is that all?' more than one sergeant had asked aloud. It was crummy radio discipline, but everyone was thinking the same thing.

But there was more to do than admire the work. Eddington lifted his radio handset and called for his brigade S-2.

'What's Predator tell us?'

'We have two more brigades still southbound, but they slowed some, sir. They're roughly nine klicks north of your line on the near one, and twelve on the far one.'

'Put me through to BUFORD,' WOLFPACK-SIX ordered.

The general was still in the same place, with death before and behind. Scarcely ten minutes had passed. Three tanks and twelve BMPs had run backward, stopping at a depression and holding position while they waited for instructions. There were men coming back now, too, some wounded, most not. He could not scream at them. If anything, the shock of the moment was harder on him than it was on them.

He'd already tried contacting his divisional command post,

but gotten only static in return, and for all his experience in uniform, his time in command, the schools he'd attended, and the exercises he'd won and lost – nothing had prepared him for this.

But he still had more than half a division to command. Two of his brigades were still fully intact, and he hadn't come here to lose. He ordered his driver to turn and head back. To the surviving elements of the lead brigade went orders to hold until further word. He had to maneuver. He'd run into a nightmare, but it couldn't be everywhere.

'What do you propose, Eddington?'

'General Diggs, I want to move my people north. We just ate up two tank brigades easier'n a plate full of grits. The enemy's artillery is largely destroyed, sir, and I have a clear field in front of me.'

'Okay, take your time and watch your flanks. I'll notify BLACKHORSE.'

'Roger that, sir. We'll be moving in twenty.'

They'd thought about this possibility, of course. There was even a sketch plan on the maps. LOBO would shift and extend right. WHITEFANG would go straight north, straddling the road, and the so far unengaged Battalion Task Force COYOTE would take the left, echeloned to be able to sweep in from the rough terrain to the west. From their new positions, the brigade would grind north to phase-lines spaced ten kilometers apart. They'd have to move slowly because of the darkness, the unfamiliar ground, and the fact that it was only half a plan, but the activation code word was NATHAN, and the first phase-line was MANASSAS. Eddington hoped Diggs wouldn't mind.

'This is WOLFPACK-SIX to all sixes. Code word is NATHAN. I repeat, we are activating Plan NATHAN in two-zero minutes. Acknowledge,' he ordered.

All three battalion commanders chimed in seconds later.

Diggs had kept him in the loop, and the picture, such as it was, was up on the command screen in the M4 God Track. Colonel Magruder wasn't all that surprised at the initial results, except maybe that the Guardsmen had done so well. Rather more surprising was the progress the 10th had made.

Advancing at a steady thirty kilometers per hour, he was well into the former Iraq, and ready to turn south. This he did at 0200L. His helicopter squadron left behind to cover the Kuwaitis, he felt a little naked at the moment, but it was still dark and would be for another four hours. By then he'd be back in Saudi. BUFFALO-SIX judged that he had the best cavalry mission of all. Here he was, deep into enemy territory, and deeper still in his rear. Just like what Colonel John Grierson had done to Johnny Reb, and what he and the Buffalo Soldiers had done to the Apaches. He ordered his units to spread wide. Reconnaissance said there wasn't much out here to get in the way, that the enemy's main strength was deep in the Kingdom. Well, he didn't think it would get much deeper, and all he had to do was slam the door behind.

Donner was standing up in the top hatch of the scout track, behind the turret, with his Army cameraman next to him. It was like nothing he'd ever seen. He'd gotten the assault on the gun battery on tape, though he didn't think the tape would be all that usable, what with all the bouncing and bumping. All around him was destruction. Behind to the southeast were at least a hundred burned-out tanks, trucks, and other things he didn't recognize, and it had all happened in less than an hour. He lurched forward, striking his face on the hatch rim when the Bradley stopped.

'Get security out!' the track commander shouted. 'We're gonna be here for a bit.'

The Bradleys were arrayed in a circle, about a mile north of the wrecked UIR guns. There was nothing moving around them, which the gunner made sure of by traversing his turret around. The rear hatch opened, and two men jumped out, first looking and then running, rifles in hand.

'Come here,' the sergeant said, holding his hand out. Donner took it and climbed to the vehicle's roof. 'Want a smoke?'

Donner shook his head. 'Gave it up.'

'Yeah? Well, those folks'll stop smoking in a day or two,' he said, gesturing to the mess a mile back. The sergeant thought that was a pretty good one. He lifted binoculars to his eyes and looked around, confirming what the gunsights said.

'What do you think of this?' the reporter asked, tapping his cameraman.

'I think this is what they pay me for, and it all works.'

'What are we stopped for?'

'We'll get some fuel in half an hour, and we need to replenish ammo.' He put the glasses down.

'We need fuel? We haven't been moving that much.'

'Well, the colonel thinks tomorrow might be kinda busy, too.' He turned. 'What do *you* think, Tom?'

62

READY AND FORWARD!

What people call 'the initiative,' whether in war or any other field of human activity, is never anything more or less than a psychological advantage. It combines one side's feeling that they are winning with the other side's feeling that something has gone wrong – that they must now prepare for and respond to the actions of their enemy instead of preparing their own offensive action. Couched in terms of 'momentum' or 'ascendancy,' it really always comes down to who is doing what to whom, and a sudden change in that equation will have a stronger effect than that of a gradual buildup to the same set of circumstances. The expected, when replaced by the unexpected, lingers for a time, lingers in the mind, since it is easier, for a while, to deny rather than to adapt, and that just makes things harder for those who are being done *to*. For the doers, there are other tasks.

For the American forces in contact, there came a brief, unwelcome, but necessary pause. It should have been easiest of all for Colonel Nick Eddington of WOLFPACK, but it wasn't. His force of National Guard troops had done little more than stay in place for their first battle, which had allowed the enemy to come into their kill box, an ambush fifteen miles wide by fifteen deep. Except for the brigade's reconnaissance screen, the men from Carolina had hardly moved at all. But now that had to change, and Eddington was reminded of the fact that though he was after a fashion a ballet master, the things performing the maneuvering were tanks, ponderous and clumsy, moving in the dark across unfamiliar ground.

Technology helped. He had radios to tell his people when and where to go, and the IVIS system to tell them how. Task Force LOBO started by backing off the reverse-slope positions that had served them so well only forty minutes earlier, turning south and heading through pre-selected navigational way points to destinations less than ten kilometers south of their initial fighting positions. In the process, the augmented battalion diluted itself, spread itself more thinly than it had been, a feat made possible because the battalion staff was able to program the move electronically and transmit their intentions to sub-unit commanders, who, assigned areas of responsibility, were able to subdivide them almost automatically, until every single vehicle knew its destination to the meter. The initial delay of twenty minutes from notification that Plan NATHAN was about to be activated allowed that selection process to begin. The lateral shift required an hour, with the vehicles moving across what appeared to be vacant land at the speed of commuters in a particularly congested rush hour. Even so, it worked, and an hour from the time the movement was started, it had been completed. WOLF-PACK, now covering well over twenty miles of lateral space, wheeled, turned north, and started moving out at ten kilometers per hour, with recon teams darting forward faster still to take position five klicks in advance of the main body. That was well short of what the book said the interval should be. Eddington had to be mindful of the fact that he was maneuvering a large force of part-time soldiers whose dependence on their electronic technology was a little too great for his total comfort. He'd keep his force of three fighting battalions under tight control until contact was established and the overall picture was clear.

It surprised Tom Donner that the support vehicles, nearly all of them robust-looking trucks, were able to follow the fighting units as quickly as they did. Somehow he hadn't understood how important this was, accustomed as he was to hitting one particular gas station once or twice a week. Here the service personnel had to be as mobile as their customers, and that, he realized, was a major task. The fuel trucks set up. The Bradleys and battle tanks came to them two at a time, then went back to their perimeter posts, where ammunition was dropped off other trucks for the track crewmen to load up. Every Bradley, he learned, had a Sears socket wrench, in nearly every case bought out of the gunner's salary, to facilitate reloading of the Bushmaster magazine. It worked better than the tool designed for the purpose. That was probably worth a little story, he thought with a distant smile.

The troop commander, now in his command HMMWV instead of his M1A2, raced about from track to track to ascertain the condition of each vehicle and crew. He saved Three-Two for the last.

'Mr Donner, you doing okay, sir?'

The reporter sipped at coffee brewed up by the Bradley's driver, and nodded. 'Is it always like this?' he asked the young officer.

'First time for me, sir. Pretty much like training, though.'

'What do you *think* about all this?' the journalist asked. 'I mean, back there, you and your people, well, *killed* a lot of the enemy.'

The captain thought about that briefly. 'Sir, you ever cover tornadoes and hurricanes and stuff?'

'Yes.'

'And people get their lives all messed up, and you ask them what it's like, right?'

'That's my job.'

'Same with us. These guys made war on us. We're making war back. If they don't like it, well, maybe next time they'll think more about it. Sir, I got an uncle in Texas – uncle and an aunt, actually. Used to be a golf pro, he taught me how to play, then went to work for Cobra – the club company, okay? Right before we left Fort Irwin, my mom called and told me they both died of that Ebola shit, sir. You *really* want to know what we think of this?' asked an officer who'd killed five tanks this night. 'Saddle up, Mr Donner. The Blackhorse will be rolling in ten. You can expect contact right before dawn, sir.' There was a dull flash on the horizon, followed a minute or so later by the rumble of distant thunder. 'I guess the Apaches are starting early.'

Fifteen miles to the northwest, II Corps's command post had just been destroyed.

The plan was evolving. First Squadron would pivot and drive north through remaining II Corps units. Third Squadron would come south through lighter opposition, massing the regiment for the first attack into the enemy III Corps's left flank. Ten miles away, Hamm was moving his artillery to facilitate the destruction of the remains of II Corps, whose commanders his helicopter squadron had just eliminated.

Eddington reminded himself again that he had to keep it simple. Despite all his years of study and the name he'd assigned to his counterstroke, he *wasn't* Nathan Bedford Forrest, and this battlefield *wasn't* small enough for him to ad-lib his maneuvers, as that racist genius had done so often in the War of the Northern Aggression.

HOOTOWL was spread especially thin now, with the brigade's front almost doubled in the last ninety minutes, and that was slowing them down. Probably not a bad thing, the colonel thought. He had to be patient. The enemy force couldn't maneuver too far east for fear of running into the left of Blackhorse – assuming they knew it was there, he thought – and the ground to the west was too choppy to allow easy movement. They'd tried the middle and gotten pounded for it. So the logical move for the enemy I Corps was to try a limited envelopment maneuver, probably weighted to the east. Incoming pictures from the Predator drones started to confirm that.

The commander of the Immortals no longer had a proper command post to use, and so he absorbed what was left of the command post from the vanished 1st Brigade, having also learned that he had to keep moving at all times. The first order of business for him had been to reestablish contact with I Corps command, which had proved somewhat difficult, as that CP had been on the move when he'd walked into the American – it had to be American – ambush along the road to Al Artawiyah. Now I Corps was setting up again, and probably talking a lot to Army command. He broke in, got the three-star, a fellow Iranian, and told what he could as rapidly as possible.

'There cannot be more than a single brigade,' his immediate superior assured him. 'What will you do?'

'I shall mass my remaining forces and strike from both flanks before dawn,' the divisional commander replied. It wasn't as though he had much choice in the matter, and both senior officers knew it. I Corps couldn't retreat, because the government which had ordered it to march would not countenance that. Staying still meant waiting for the Saudi forces storming down from the Kuwaiti border. The task, then, was to regain the initiative by overpowering the American blocking force by maneuver and shock effect. That was what tanks were designed to do, and he had more than four hundred still under his command.

'Approved. I will dispatch you my corps artillery. Guards Armored on your right will do the same. Accomplish your breakthrough,' his fellow Iranian told him. 'Then we will drive to Riyadh by dusk.'

Very well, the Immortals commander thought. He ordered his 2nd Brigade to slow its advance, allowing 3rd to catch up, concentrate, and maneuver east. To his west, the Iraqis would be doing much the same in mirror image. Second would advance to contact, fix the enemy flank, and 3rd would sweep around, taking them in the rear. The center he would leave empty.

'They've stopped. The lead brigade has stopped. They're eight klicks north,' the brigade S-2 said. 'HOOT should have visual on them in a few minutes to confirm.' That explained what one of the enemy forces to his front was doing. The western group was somewhat farther back, not stopped, but moving slowly forward, evidently waiting for orders or some change in their dispositions. His opponent and his people were taking time to think.

Eddington couldn't allow that.

The only real problem with MLRS was that it had a minimum range far less convenient than the maximum. For the second mission that night, the rocket vehicles, which hadn't really moved at all, locked their suspensions in place and elevated their launcher boxes, again aimed by electronic information only. Again the night was disturbed by the streaks of rocket trails, though this time on much lower trajectories. Tube artillery did the same, with both forces dividing their attention between the advance brigades left and right of the highway.

The purpose was more psychological than real. The mini-bomblets of the MLRS rockets would not *kill* a tank. A lucky fall atop a rear deck might disable a diesel engine, and the sides of the BMP infantry carriers could sometimes be penetrated by a nearby detonation, but these were chance events.

The real effect was to make the enemy button up, to limit their ability to see, and with the falling steel rain, limit their ability to think. Officers who'd leaped from their command tanks to confer had to run back, some of them killed or wounded by the sudden barrage. Sitting safely in stationary vehicles, they heard the *ping* sound of fragments bounding off their armor, and peered out their vision systems to see if the artillery barrage presaged a proper attack. The less numerous 155mm artillery rounds were a greater danger, all the more so since the American gun rounds were not bursting in the air, but were 'common' shells that hit the ground first. The laws of probability guaranteed that some of the vehicles would be hit – and some were, erupting into fireballs as the rest of 2nd Brigade was forced to hold in place, ordered to do so while 3rd moved up to their left. Unable to move and, with the loss of their own divisional artillery, unable to respond in kind, they could do nothing but cringe and stay alert, look out of their vehicles, and watch the shells and bomblets fall.

B-Troop, 1st of the 11th, moved out on schedule, spreading out and travelling due north, with the Bradley scouts in the lead and the 'Battlestar' tanks half a klick behind, ready to respond to a report of contact. It provided a strange revelation to Donner. An intelligent man, and even an outdoorsman of sorts who enjoyed backpacking with his family on the Appalachian Trail, he spent as much time as he could looking out of the Bradley, and didn't have a clue as to what was really going on. He finally overcame his embarrassment and got on the interphones to ask the track commander how *he* knew, and was called forward, where he crammed himself as a third man in a space designed for two – more like one and a half, the reporter thought.

'We're here,' the staff sergeant told him, touching his finger to the IVIS screen. 'We're going that way. 'Cording to this, there's nobody around to bother us, but we're looking out for that. The enemy' – he changed the display somewhat – 'is here, and we're along this line.'

'How far?'

'About twelve klicks and we should start to see 'em.'

'How good is this information?' Donner asked.

'It got us this far, Tom,' the track commander pointed out.

The pattern of movement was annoying, and reminded the reporter of stop-and-go traffic on a Friday afternoon. The armored vehicles would dart – never faster than twenty miles per hour – from one terrain feature to another, scan ahead, then move some more. The sergeant explained that they'd move in a steadier manner on better ground, but that this part of the Saudi desert was marked by hillocks and ridges and dips that people might hide behind. The Brads were in a platoon, but actually seemed to move in pairs. Every M3 had a 'wingman,' a term borrowed from the Air Force.

'What if there's somebody out there?'

'Then he'll probably try to shoot at us,' the staff sergeant explained. All this time, the gunner was traversing his turret left and right, searching for the glow of a warm body on the chilled ground. They could actually see better at night, Donner learned, which was why Americans had adopted the darkness as their preferred hunting time. 'Stanley, come left and stop behind that bump,' he ordered the driver. 'If I was a grunt, I'd like that place over to the right. We'll cover Chuck as he comes around it.' The turret rotated and sighted in on a larger bump, while the Bradley's wingman drove past. 'Okay, Stanley, move out.'

The Army of God command section had proved devilishly hard to pin down, but now Hamm had two helo-scout troops detailed to that single mission, and his electronic-intelligence section had just set up again, co-located with 2nd Squadron's headquarters troop. They'd taken to calling their target the enchilada. Locate it, and disorganize the entire enemy force. Saudi intelligence officers attached to the ELINT tracks were listening to signals. The UIR forces had encrypted radios for the senior commanders, but those were good only for talking to other people with the same equipment, and with the gradual degradation of the enemy radio network, sooner or later the enchilada would have to start talking in the clear. One Corps and two divisional command posts had been hit, two of those almost totally destroyed and the other badly disrupted. Moreover, they knew roughly where III Corps was, and Army would have to start talking to that formation, since it was the only one so far not engaged except by a few air strikes. They didn't have to read the messages, nice though that would have been. They knew the frequency ranges for the high-command circuit, and a few minutes of traffic would enable them to localize it enough for M- and N-helicopter-scout troops to dart in and start ruining their whole morning.

It sounded like static, but digitally encrypted radios usually did. The ELINT officer, a first lieutenant, loved eavesdropping, but missed his jamming gear, which had been overlooked in the POMCUS equipment sets, probably, he thought, because that was supposed to be an Air Force mission. There was an art to this. His troopers, all military-intelligence specialists, had to tell the difference between real atmospheric static and manmade static as they swept the frequencies.

'Bingo!' One said, 'Bearing three-zero-five, hissin' like a snake.' It was too loud to be atmospheric noise, random though it might have sounded.

'How good?' the officer asked.

'Ninety percent, ell-tee.' A second vehicle, slaved electronically to the first, was a klick away, providing a baseline for triangulation ... 'There.' The location came up on the computer screen. The lieutenant lifted a radio for the 4th Squadron command post.

'ANGEL-SIX, this is PEEPER, we may have a posit for the enchilada ...'

M-Troop's four Apaches and six Kiowas were but twenty klicks away from the position, conducting a visual search. A minute later, they turned south.

'What is happening!' Mahmoud Haji demanded. He hated using this phone-radio lash-up, and just getting in contact with his own army commander had proved difficult enough.

'We have encountered opposition south of King Khalid Military City. We are dealing with it.'

'Ask him the nature of the opposition,' Intelligence advised his leader.

'Perhaps your guest could tell *me* that,' the general on the other side of the conversation suggested. 'We're still working to find out.'

'The Americans cannot have more than two brigades in theater!' the man insisted. 'One more brigade-equivalent in Kuwait, but that is all!'

'Is that so? Well, I have lost more than a division in strength in the last three hours, and I still don't know what I'm facing here. Two Corps has been badly mauled. One Corps has run into something and is continuing the attack now. Three Corps is so far untouched. I can continue the attack to Riyadh, but I need more information on what I'm facing.' The commanding general, a man of sixty years, was not a fool, and he still felt that he could win. He still had about four divisions' worth of combat power. It was just a matter of directing it properly. He actually felt lucky that air attacks from American and Saudi forces had been so light. He'd learned a few other lessons fast. The disappearance of three command sections had made him cautious, at least for his own safety. He was now a full kilometer from the radio transmitters attached to his armored command vehicle, a BMP-1KSh, his handset at the end of a lengthy spool of commo wire. He himself was surrounded by a squad of soldiers, who did their best not to listen to the excitement in their commander's voice.

'Damn, look at all those SAM tracks,' a Kiowa observer said over the radio, from eight klicks north. His pilot made the call while the observer did a count.

'MARAUDER-LEAD, this is MASCOT-THREE. I think we have the enchilada.'

'THREE, LEAD, go,' was the terse reply.

'Six *bimps*, ten trucks, five SAM tracks, two radar tracks, and three ZSU-23s in a wadi. Recommend approach from the west, say again, approach from the west.' It was far too much defensive firepower to be much of anything other than the Army of God's mobile command section. The SAM launchers were all French Crotales, and those little fuckers were scary, MASCOT-THREE knew. But they should have picked a different spot. This was one of those situations where you were better in the open, or even on high ground, so that your SAM radars could see better.

'THREE, LEAD, can you illuminate?'

'Affirmative. Tell us when. Radar tracks first.'

The Apache leader, a captain, was hugging the ground to the west, creeping forward at thirty knots now, coming up on what he thought was a ridgeline that would tip over into the wadi. Slowly, slowly, letting his own mast sensor do the looking. The pilot flew the airplane like a kid learning to parallel-park, while the gunner manned the sensors.

'Hold it right there, sir,' the gunner advised from his front seat.

'THREE, LEAD, start the music,' the pilot called.

The Kiowa lit up its laser-illuminator, an invisible infrared beam that aimed first at the far radar track. It was actually a wheeled vehicle, but nobody was being particular. On notification that the target was lit up, the Apache tilted its nose up and loosed first one Hellfire, then another five seconds later.

The general heard the shouted warning from a thousand meters away. Only one of the radar vehicles was actually transmitting, and that intermittently as an electronic-security measure. It was radiating now, and caught the inbound missile. One of the launcher trucks rotated its four-tube mount and fired, but the Crotale lost lock when the Hellfire angled down and went harmlessly ballistic. The radar vehicle blew apart a moment later, and the second one six seconds after that. The commanding general of the Army of God stopped talking then, and ignored the incoming conversation from Tehran. There was quite literally nothing for him to do but crouch down, which his bodyguards made him do.

All four Apaches of the troop were hovering in a semicircle now, waiting for their troop commander to ripple off his Hellfires. This he did, about five seconds apart, letting the Kiowa guide them in, switching from target to target. Next came the SAM-launcher vehicles, followed by the Russian-made gun tracks. Then there was nothing left to protect the BMP command tracks.

It was utterly heartless, the general saw. Men tried shooting back, but at first there was nothing to shoot at. Some people looked. Others pointed. Only a few ran. Most stayed and tried to fight. The missiles seemed to come from the west. He could see the yellow-white glow of rocket motors racing through the darkness like fireflies, but he couldn't see anything shooting them, and one after another the air defense vehicles were destroyed, then the BMPs, then the trucks. It took less than two minutes, and only then did the helicopters begin to appear. The security detachment for his mobile command post was a company of picked infantrymen. They fought back with heavy machine-gun fire and shoulder-launched rockets, but the ghostly shapes of the helicopters were too far away. The man-portable missiles couldn't seem to find them. His men tried, but then the tracers lanced out, reaching for them like beams of light into an area now bright with vehicle fires. A squad here, a section there, a pair there. The men tried to run, but the helicopters closed in, firing from only a few hundred meters away, herding them in a cruel, remorseless game. The radio handset was dead in his hand, but he still held it, watching.

'Lead, Two, I got a bunch to the east,' a pilot told the Apache commander.

'Get 'em,' the flight leader ordered, and one of the attack choppers ducked south around the remains of the command post.

Nothing to do. No place to flee. Three of his men shouldered their weapons and fired. Others tried to run, but there was no running and no hiding. Whoever flew those aircraft were killing everything they saw. Americans. Had to be. Angry at what they'd been told. Might even be true, the general thought, and if –

'How d'ya say *tough shit* in rag-head?' the gunner asked, taking his time to make sure he got every one.

'I think they got the message,' the pilot said, turning the chopper around and scanning for additional targets.

'Angel-Six, Angel-Six, this is Marauder-Six-Actual. This sure looked like a CP, and it's toast now,' the troop commander called. 'We are RTB for bullets and gas. Out.'

'Well, get him back!' Daryaei shouted at the communications officer on the line. The intelligence chief in the room didn't say anything, suspecting that they'd never talk to the army commander again in this lifetime. The worst part was not knowing why. His intelligence assessment on arriving

American units had been correct. He was sure of that. How could so few do so much harm . . . ?

'They had a pair of brigades – regiments, whatever – there, didn't they?' Ryan asked, getting the latest upload from the battlefield onto his projection TV in the Sit Room.

'Yep.' General Moore nodded. He noted with some pleasure that even Admiral Jackson was pretty quiet. 'Not anymore, Mr President. Jesus, those Guardsmen are doing just fine.'

'Sir,' Ed Foley said, 'just how far do you want to take this?'

'Do we have any doubts at all that it was Daryaei personally who made all these decisions?' It was, Ryan thought, a dumb question. Why else had he told the citizens that? But he had to ask the question, and the others in the Sit Room knew why.

'None,' the DCI replied.

'Then we take it all the way, Ed. Will the Russians play?'

'Yes, sir, I think they will.'

Jack thought of the plague now dying out in America. Thousands of the innocent had already died, with more yet to follow. He thought of the soldiers, sailors, and airmen at risk under his distant command. He found himself thinking, even, of the UIR troops who'd followed the wrong banner and wrong ideas because they hadn't had the chance to select their country or its leader, and were now paying the price for that mistake of birthplace. If they were not completely innocent, then neither were they completely guilty, because for the most part soldiers merely did what they were told. He also found himself remembering the look in his wife's eyes when Katie had arrived by helicopter on the South Lawn. There were times when he was allowed to be a man, just like other men, except for the power he held in his hands.

'Find out,' the President said coldly.

It was a sunny morning in Beijing, and Adler knew more than the other people in the discussion. It hadn't been much of a detailed dispatch, just the high points, which he'd shown to the Defense attaché, and the Army colonel had told him to trust every word. But the information wasn't widely known. The TV reports had to come out over military communications nets, and because of the time of day in most of

America, those hadn't reported much beyond the commencement of combat action. If the PRC was in cahoots with the UIR, they might yet believe that their distant friends held the upper hand. It was worth a try, SecState thought, sure that POTUS would back him up.

'Mr Secretary, welcome again,' the Foreign Minister said graciously. And again, Zhang was there, silent and enigmatic as he tried always to be.

'Thank you.' Adler took his regular seat. It wasn't as comfortable as the one in Taipei.

'These new developments – can it be true?' his official host asked.

'That is the public position of my President and my country,' the Secretary of State replied. Thus it *had* to be true.

'Do you have sufficient forces to protect your interests in that region?'

'Minister, I am not a military expert, and I cannot comment on that,' Adler replied. That was entirely true, but a man in a position of strength would probably have said something else.

'It would be a great misfortune if you cannot,' Zhang observed.

It might have been fun to inquire about the PRC's position on the matter, but the answer would have been neutral and meaningless. Nor would they have said anything about the presence of the *Eisenhower* battle group, now flying patrols over the 'international waters' of the Formosa Strait. The trick was to make them say anything at all.

'The world situation occasionally requires reexamination of one's position on many things, and one must sometimes think carefully about one's friendships,' Adler tried. It lay on the table for half a minute.

'We have been friends since your President Nixon first courageously came here,' the Foreign Minister said after reflection. 'And we remain so, despite the occasional misunderstanding.'

'That is good to hear, Minister. We have a saying about friendship in time of need.' Okay, think about that one. Maybe the news reports are true. Maybe your friend Daryaei will succeed. The bait dangled for another fifteen seconds.

'Really, our only area of permanent discord is America's position on what your President inadvertently called the "two Chinas." If only this could be regularized . . . ,' the Minister mused.

'Well, as I told you, the President was trying to express himself to reporters in a confusing situation.'

'And we are to disregard it?'

'America continues to feel that a peaceful solution to this provincial dispute serves the interests of all parties.' That was status quo ante, a position established by a strong, confident America whom China would not challenge openly.

'Peace is always preferable to conflict,' Zhang said. 'But how long must we show such great forbearance? These recent events have only served to illustrate the central problem.'

A very small push, Adler noted: 'I understand your frustration, but we all know that patience is the most valuable of virtues.'

'At some point, patience becomes indulgence.' The Foreign Minister reached for his tea. 'A helpful word from America would be most gratefully received.'

'You ask that we alter our policy somewhat?' SecState wondered if Zhang would speak again after altering the course of the conversation ever so slightly.

'Merely that you see the logic of the situation. It would make the friendship of our two nations far more substantial, and it is, after all, a minor issue to countries such as ours.'

'I see,' Adler replied. And he did. It was certain now. He congratulated himself for making them tip their hand. The next call on this would have to be made in Washington, assuming they had the time there for something other than a shooting war.

The 10th ACR crossed back into Saudi territory at 0330L. The Buffalo Cav was now spread in a line thirty miles across. In another hour, they would be astride the UIR army's supply line, having gotten here without any notice. The force was moving faster now, almost thirty miles in an hour. His lead elements had found a few patrol and internal-security units in UIR territory, mainly single vehicles which had been dispatched immediately upon sighting. There would be more now, as soon as they hit the next road. It would be MP units at first – whatever the enemy called them – used for traffic control. There had to be a lot of fuel rolling down the road to KKMC, and that was the first mission of the Buffalo Soldiers.

Second Brigade of the Immortals had been under fire for nearly an hour, when orders came to go forward, and the armored vehicles of the former Iranian armored division moved with a will. The two-star in command was in back of the flanking 3rd Brigade now, listening rather than talking, wondering about and thankful for the absence of American air power. Corps artillery had arrived and set up without firing to reveal its presence. They might not last long, but he wanted the benefit of their presence. The opposing force could hardly be as much as a full brigade on this side of the highway, and he had double that – and even if he did face a complete brigade, then his Iraqi comrades on the far side would loop around to support him, as he would for them if he found a clear field. Over the radio, on the move in order to prevent being attacked by artillery or helicopters, he exhorted his commanders to press the attack, as he followed on in an open-topped command vehicle. Now, if his enemy would just sit still in the positions they'd held successfully for the first attack, he would see about things . . .

Lobo passed phase-line Manassas twenty minutes late, to the quiet anger of Colonel Eddington, who thought that he'd allowed ample time for the maneuver. But that damned criminal lawyer – a redundancy, he'd joked more than once – commanding Hootowl was well forward again, covering the right while his battalion XO took the left, calling fire but not taking any shots of his own.

'Wolfpack-Six, this is Hoot-Six, over.'

'Six-Actual, Hoot,' Eddington replied.

'They're coming on, sir, two brigades on line, packed in pretty close, advancing over phase-line Highpoint right now.'

'How close are you, Colonel?'

'Three thousand. I am pulling my people back now.' They had designated safe-travel lanes for that. Hoot hoped that everybody remembered where they were. The redeployment would take them east, to screen the right edge of the flanking battalion task force.

'Okay, clear the field, counselor.'

'Roger that, Professor Eddington. HOOTOWL is flying,' the misplaced lawyer replied. 'Out.' In a minute he told his driver to see how fast he could go in the dark. It was something the NASCAR fan was just as pleased as hell to demonstrate.

The same report arrived four minutes later from the left. His one brigade was facing four. It was time to narrow those odds some. His artillery battalion shifted fire. His tank and Bradley commanders started sweeping the horizon for movement, and the three mechanized battalions started rolling forward to meet their enemy on the move. Company and platoon commanders checked their lines for proper interval. The battalion commander was in his own command tank on the left side of the line. The S-3 operations officer backed up the right. As usual, the Bradleys were slightly back on the fifty-four Abrams tanks, their mission to sweep the field for infantry and support vehicles.

The falling artillery was common shell, and now VT proximity, to make life very hard on tanks with open hatches and people dumb enough to be in the open. Nobody thought of armored knights. The battlefield was too dispersed for that. It was more like a naval battle fought on a sandy, rocky sea which was every bit as hostile to human life as the conventional kind, and about to become more so. Eddington stayed with WHITEFANG, which was essentially an advancing reserve force, as it became clear that the enemy was advancing on both flanks, and leaving the center with a screening force, if anything.

'Contact,' a platoon leader called on his company net. 'I have enemy armored vehicles at five thousand meters.' He checked his IVIS display to confirm, again, that there were no friendlies out there. Good. HOOTOWL was clear. There was only a Red Force to his front.

The moon was up now, less than a quarter of a waning moon, but it lit up the land enough for the lead Immortals to see movement on their visible horizon. The men of 2nd Brigade, furious at the pounding they'd taken in their wait to advance, were loaded up. Some of them had laser range-finders, which showed targets at nearly double their effective range. That word, too, went up the line, and back down came orders to increase speed, the quicker to close the distance and get out of the indirect fire that had to stop soon. Gunners centered on targets that were still too far away, in anticipation of that changing in two minutes or less. They felt their mounts speed up, heard the words of their tank commanders to stand by. There were enough targets to count now, and the opposing numbers were not impressive. They had the advantage. They must have, the Immortals all thought.

But why were the Americans advancing toward them?

'Commence firing at four thousand meters,' the company commander told his crews. The Abrams tanks were spread nearly five hundred meters apart in two staggered lines, covering a lot of ground for one mounted battalion. The TCs mainly kept their heads up and out of the vehicles for the approach phase, then ducked down to activate their own fire-control systems.

'I'm on one,' one gunner told his TC. 'T-80, identified, range forty-two-fifty.'

'Setting?' the tank commander asked, just to make sure.

'Set on Sabot. Loader, all silver bullets till I say different.'

'I hear you, gunner. Just don't miss any.'

'Forty-one,' the gunner breathed. He waited for another fifteen seconds and became the first in his company to fire, and to kill. The sixty-two-ton tank staggered with the shot, then kept moving.

'Target, cease fire, target tank at eleven,' the TC said over the interphones.

The loader stomped his boot down on the pedal, opened the ammo doors, and yanked out another 'silver bullet' round, then turned in a graceful move, first to guide, then to slam the mainly plastic round into the breech.

'Up!' he called.

'Identified!' the gunner told the TC.

'Fire!'

'On the way!' A pause. The tracer flew true. 'Right through the dot!'

Commander: 'Target! Cease fire! Traverse right, target tank at one.'

Loader: 'Up!'
Gunner: 'Identified!'
Commander: 'Fire!'

'On the waaaaay!' the gunner said, squeezing off his third shot in eleven seconds.

It wasn't like reality, the battalion commander saw, really too busy watching to take his own shots. It was like an advancing wave. First the lead rank of T-80s blew up, just a handful of misses that were corrected five seconds later, as the second rank of enemy vehicles started to go. They started to return fire. The flashes looked like the Hoffman simulation charges he'd so recently seen at the NTC, and turned out to be just as harmless. Enemy rounds were marked with their own tracers, and all of their first volley fell short. Some of the T-80s got off a second shot. None got off a third.

'Jesus, sir, give me a target!' his gunner called.

'Pick one.'

'*Bimp*,' the gunner said, mainly to himself. He fired off a high-explosive round, and got a kill at just over four thousand meters, but as before, the battle was over in less than a minute. The American line advanced. Some of the BMPs launched missiles, but now they were being engaged by tanks and Bradleys. Vehicles exploded, filling the sky with fire and smoke. Now individual men were visible, mainly running, some turning to fire or trying to deploy. The tank gunners, with nothing large left to shoot, switched to the coaxial machine guns. The Bradleys pulled up level with the tanks, and they did the serious hunting.

The lead line of tanks passed through the smoking wreckage of the Immortals division less than four minutes after the first volley. Turrets traversed left and right, looking for targets. Tank commanders had their heads back up, hands on their top-mounted heavy machine guns. Where fire originated, it was returned, and at first there was a race to see who could kill the most, because there is an excitement, a *rush* to battle unknown to those who have never felt it, the feeling of godlike power, the ability to make a life-and-death decision and then enforce it at the touch of a finger. More than that, these Guardsmen knew why they were here, knew what they had been sent to avenge. In some, that rage lasted for some minutes, as the vehicles rolled forward, grinding along at less than ten miles per hour, like farm tractors or harvesting combines, collecting life and converting it to death, looking like something from the dawn of time, utterly inhuman, utterly heartless.

But then it began to stop. It stopped being duty. It stopped being revenge. It stopped being the fun they'd expected it to be. It became murder, and one by one, the men on the weapons realized what they themselves were supposed to be and what they might become if they didn't turn away from this. It wasn't like being an aviator, hundreds of meters away, shooting at shapes that moved comically in their aiming systems and were never really human beings at all. These men were closer. They could see the faces and the wounds now, and the harmless backs of people running away. Even those fools who still shot back attracted pity from the gunners who dispatched them, but soon the futility of it was clear to everyone, and soldiers who'd arrived in the desert with rage grew sick at what the rage had become. The guns gradually fell silent, by common consent rather than order, as resistance stopped, and with it the need to kill. Battalion Task Force LOBO rolled completely through the smoking ruin of two heavy brigades, searching for targets worthy of professional attention, rather than personal, from which they had to turn away.

There was nothing left to be done. The general stood and walked away from his command vehicle, beckoning for the crew to do the same. On his order, they put their weapons down and stood on high ground to wait. They didn't have to wait long. The sun was rising. The first glow of orange was to the east, announcing a new day far different from the old.

The first convoy rolled right in front of them, thirty fuel trucks, driving at a good clip, and the drivers must have taken the south-moving vehicles for those of their own army. The Bradley gunners of I-Troop, 3rd of the 10th, took care of that with a series of shots that ignited the first five trucks. The rest of them halted, two of them turning over and exploding on their own when their drivers rolled them into ditches in their haste to escape. The Bradley crews mainly let the people get clear, plinked the trucks with high-explosive rounds, and kept moving south past the bewildered drivers, who just stood there and watched them pass.

It was a Bradley that found him. The vehicle pulled to within fifty meters before stopping. The general who, twelve hours before, had commanded a virtually intact armored division didn't move or resist. He stood quite still, as four infantrymen appeared from the back of the M2A4, advancing with rifles out, while their track covered his detail with even more authority.

'On the ground!' the corporal called.

'I will tell my men. I speak English. They do not,' the general said, then kept his word. His soldiers went facedown. He continued to stand, perhaps hoping that he could die.

'Get those hands up, partner.' This corporal was a police officer in civilian life. The officer – he didn't know what kind yet, but the uniform was too spiffy for a grunt – complied. The corporal next handed his rifle off and drew a pistol, walked in, and held it to the man's head while he searched him expertly. 'Okay, you can get down now. If you play smart, nobody gets hurt. Please tell your men that. We will kill them if we have to, but we ain't going to murder anybody, okay?'

'I will tell them.'

With the coming of daylight, Eddington got back into the helicopter he'd borrowed, and flew to survey the battlefield. It was soon plain that his brigade had crushed two complete divisions. He ordered his screen forward to scout ahead for the pursuit phase that had to come next, then called Diggs for instructions on what he was supposed to do with prisoners. Before anyone figured that out, a chopper arrived from Riyadh with a television crew.

Even before the pictures got out, the rumors did, as they always do in countries lacking a free press. A telephone call arrived in the home of a Russian embassy official. It came just before seven, and awakened him, but he was out of his house in minutes and driving his car through quiet streets to the rendezvous point with a man who, he thought, was finally crossing the line to become an agent of the RVS.

The Russian spent ten extra minutes checking his back, but anyone following him this morning would have to be invisible, and he imagined that a lot of the Ayatollah's security forces had been called up.

'Yes?' he said on meeting the man. There wasn't much time for formalities.

'You are right. Our army was – defeated last night. They called me in at three for an opinion of American intentions, and I heard it all. We cannot even talk with our units. The army commander simply vanished. The Foreign Ministry is in a panic.'

'As well it might be,' the diplomat thought. 'I should tell you that the Turkoman leader has –'

'We know. He called Daryaei last night to ask if the plague story was true.'

'And what did your leader say?'

'He said that it was an infidel lie – what do you expect?' The official paused. 'He was not entirely persuasive. Whatever you said to the man, he is neutralized. India has betrayed us – I learned about that, too. China does not yet know.'

'If you expect *them* to stand with you, you have violated your religion's laws on the consumption of alcohol. Of course, my government stands with America as well. You are quite alone,' the Russian told him. 'I need some information.'

'What information?'

'The location of the germ factory. I need that today.'

'The experimental farm north of the airport.'

That easy? the Russian thought. 'How can you be sure?'

'The equipment was bought from the Germans and the French. I was in the commercial section then. If you wish to confirm, it should be easy. How many farms have guards in uniform?' the man asked helplessly.

The Russian nodded. 'I will see about that. There are other problems. Your country will soon be fully – by which I mean *completely* – at war with America. My country may be able to offer her good offices to negotiate a settlement of some kind. If you whisper the right word into the right ear, our ambassador is at your disposal, and then you will have done the world a service.'

'That is simple. By noon we will be looking for a way out of this.'

'There *is* no way out for your government. None,' the RVS officer emphasized.

63

THE RYAN DOCTRINE

Wars usually begin at exact moments in time, but most often end neither cleanly nor precisely. Daylight found the 11th Armored Cavalry Regiment in command of yet another battlefield, having completed the destruction of one of UIR II Corps's divisions. The other division was now facing the Saudi 2nd Brigade, which was attacking from the rising sun while the American unit halted again to refuel and rearm in preparation for the continued attack on III Corps, still not decisively engaged.

But that was already changing. Those two divisions now had the full and undivided attention of all tactical aircraft in theater. First their air defense assets were targeted. Every radar which switched on drew the attention of HARM – High-speed Anti-Radiation Missile – equipped F-16s, and in two hours the skies were friendly to American and Saudi pilots. UIR fighters made an effort to strike down from their home bases to defend their beleaguered ground forces, but none made it past the radar-fighter screen set up well beyond the location of the forces they had been dispatched to support. They lost over sixty aircraft in the futile attempt. It was easier for them to lash out at the Kuwaiti brigades which had so impudently invaded their vastly larger and more powerful neighbor. The small air force of that country was on its own for most of the day, and the battle had little strategic relevance. The routes across the swamps were cut and would take days to repair. The resulting air battle was more a display of mutual anger than anything else, and here, too, the Kuwaiti forces held the day, not spectacularly so, but giving three kills for every one they absorbed. For a small country learning the martial arts, it was a battle that men would talk of for years, the magnitude of their deeds growing with every recounting. Yet all the deaths on this day would be useless, lives wasted in mere punctuation of a decision already reached.

Over III Corps, with the SAMs taken out, attention turned to more structured murder. There were over six hundred tanks on the ground, another eight hundred infantry carriers, more than two hundred pieces of towed and self-propelled artillery, several thousand trucks, and thirty thousand men, all of them well inside a foreign nation and trying to escape. The F-15E Strike Eagles circled at about 15,000 feet, almost loitering on low power settings, while the weapons-systems operators selected targets one by one for laser-guided bombs. The air was clear, the sun was bright, and the battlefield was flat. It was far easier than any exercise in the Nellis bombing range. Lower down in different hunting patches, F-16s joined in with Maverick and conventional bombs. Before noon, III Corps's three-star commander, correctly thinking himself the senior ground officer, ordered a general retreat, gathered up the support trucks laagered in KKMC, and tried to get his units out in something resembling order. Bombs falling on him from above, the Saudi 5th Brigade approaching from the east, and an American force closing on his rear, he turned northwest, hoping to cross back into friendly territory at the same point he had entered. On the ground, his vehicles used smoke to obscure themselves as best they could, which somewhat frustrated the allied aviators, who did not, however, come down low to press their attacks, since the UIR forces might have shot back with some effect. That gave the commander hope that he might make it back with something like two-thirds of his strength. Fuel was not a concern. The combined fuel trucks for the entire Army of God were with his corps now.

Diggs stopped off first to see Eddington's brigade. He'd seen the sights and smelled the smells before. Tanks could burn for a surprisingly long time, as much as two days, from all the fuel and ammunition they carried, and the stink of diesel oil and chemical propellants served to mask the revolting stench of burning human flesh. Armed enemies were always things to be killed, but dead ones soon enough became objects of pity, especially slaughtered as they had been. But only a few, in relative terms, had died by the guns of the men from

Carolina. Many more had surrendered. Those had to be gathered, disarmed, counted, and set to work, mainly in disposing of the bodies of their fallen comrades. It was a fact as old as warfare, and the lesson for the defeated was always the same: *This is why you don't want to mess with us again.*

'Now what?' Eddington asked, a cigar in his teeth. The victors suffered through many mood swings on the battlefield. Arriving in confusion and haste, facing the unknown with concealed fear, entering battle with determination – and, in their case, with such wrath as they had never felt – winning with exhilaration, and then feeling horror at the carnage and pity for the vanquished. The cycle changed anew. Most of the mechanized units had reorganized over the last few hours, and were ready to move again, while their own MPs and arriving Saudi units took possession of the prisoners gathered by the line units.

'Just sit tight,' Diggs replied, to Eddington's disappointment and relief. 'The remains are running hard. You'd never catch them, and we don't have orders to invade.'

'They just came at us in the same old way,' the Guard colonel said, remembering Wellington. 'And we stopped them in the same old way. What a terrible business.'

'Bobby Lee, remember, Chancellorsville?'

'Oh, yeah. He was right, too. Those couple of hours, Diggs, getting things set up, maneuvering my battalions, getting the information, acting on it.' He shook his head. 'I never knew anything could feel like that . . . but now . . .'

'"It is good that war is so terrible, else we should grow too fond of it." Funny thing is, you forget sometimes. Those poor bastards,' the general said, watching fifty men being herded off to trucks for the ride back to the rear. 'Clean up, Colonel. Get your units put back together. There may be orders to move, but I don't think so.'

'Three Corps?'

'Ain't goin' far, Nick. We're "keepin' up the skeer" and we're running them right into the 10th.'

'So you know Bedford Forrest after all.' It was one of the Confederate officer's most important aphorisms. *Keep up the skeer*: never give a fleeing enemy the chance to rest; harry him, punish him, force him into additional errors, run him into the ground. Even if it really didn't matter anymore.

'My doctoral dissertation was on Hitler as a political manipulator. I didn't much like him, either.' Diggs smiled and saluted. 'You and your people did just fine, Nick. Glad to have you on this trip.'

'Wouldn't have missed it, sir.'

The vehicle had diplomatic tags, but the driver and passenger knew that such things had not always been respected in Tehran. Things changed in a country at war, and you could often spot previously clandestine facilities by the fact that they got more guards in time of trouble instead of remaining the same. The latter would have been far smarter, but everyone did it. The car halted. The driver lifted binoculars. The passenger lifted a camera. Sure enough, the experimental farm had armed men around the research building, and that wasn't the normal sort of thing, was it? It was just that easy. The car turned in the road and headed back to the embassy.

They were getting only stragglers. The Blackhorse was in full pursuit now, and this tail chase was proving to be a long one. American vehicles were better and generally faster than those they were pursuing, but it was easier to run than to chase. Pursuers had to be a little careful about possible ambushes, and the lust to kill more of the enemy was muted by the concern at dying in a war already won. Enemy disorder had allowed the 11th to pull in tight, and the right-flank units were now in radio contact with the advancing Saudis, who were just now finishing off the last few battalions of II Corps and thinking about engaging III in a final decisive battle.

'Target tank,' one TC said. 'Ten o'clock, forty-one hundred.'

'Identified,' the gunner said as the Abrams halted to make the shot easier.

'Hold fire,' the TC said suddenly. 'They're bailing out. Give 'em a few seconds.'

'Right.' The gunner could see it, too. The T-80's main gun was pointed away, in any case. They waited for the crew to make a hundred meters or so.

'Okay, take it.'

'On the way.' The breech recoiled, the tank jolted, and the

round flew. Three seconds later, one more tank turret blew straight up. 'Jack-in-the-box.'

'Target. Cease fire. Driver, move out,' the TC ordered. That made the twelfth kill for their tank. The crew wondered what the unit record would be, while the TC made a position notation for the three-man enemy crew on his IVIS box, which automatically told the regimental security detail where to pick them up. The advancing cavalrymen gave them a wide berth. Unlikely though it was, one of them might shoot or do something stupid, and they had neither the time nor the inclination to waste ammunition. One more battle to fight, unless the other side got some brains and just called it a day.

'Comments?' POTUS asked.

'Sir, it sets a precedent,' Cliff Rutledge replied.

'That's the idea,' Ryan said. They were getting the battle-field video first, unedited. It included the usual horrors, body parts of those ripped to shreds by high explosives, whole bodies of those whose deaths had come from some mysterious cause, a hand reaching out of a personnel carrier whose interior still smoked, some poor bastard who'd almost gotten out, but not quite. There had to be something about carrying a mini-cam that just drew people to that sort of thing. The dead were dead, and the dead were all victims in one way or another – more than one way, Ryan thought. These soldiers of two previously separate countries and one overlapping culture had died at the hands of armed Americans, but they'd been sent to death by a man whose orders they'd had to follow, who had miscalculated, and who had been willing to use their lives as tokens, gambling chips, quarters in a big slot machine whose arm he'd yanked to see what would result. It wasn't supposed to be that way. Power carried responsibility. Jack knew that he would hand-write a letter to the family of every dead American, just as George Bush had done in 1991. The letters would serve two purposes. They would, perhaps, be some measure of comfort to the families of the lost. They would, certainly, remind the man who had ordered them to the field that the dead had once been living. He wondered what their faces had been like. Probably no different from the Guardsmen who'd formed that honor guard at Indianapolis, the day of his first public appearance. They looked the same, but each human life was individual, the most valuable possession of its owner, and Ryan had played a part in stripping it away, and though he knew it had been necessary, it was also necessary for him, now and for as long as he sat in this building, to remember that they were more than just faces. And that, he told himself, is the difference. I know about my responsibility. *He* doesn't know about *his*. *He* still lived with the illusion that people were responsible to him, and not the reverse.

'It's political dynamite, Mr President,' van Damm said.

'So?'

'There is a legal problem,' Pat Martin told them. 'It violates the executive order that President Ford put in place.'

'I know about that one,' Ryan responded. 'But who decides the executive orders?'

'The Chief Executive, sir,' Martin answered.

'Draft me a new one.'

'What is that smell?' Back at the Indiana motel, the truck drivers were out for the morning dance of moving the trucks around to protect the tires. They were sick of this place by now, and heartily wished the travel ban would be lifted soon. One driver had just exercised his Mack, and parked it back next to the cement truck. Spring was turning warm, and the metal bodies of the trucks turned the interiors into ovens. In the case of the cement truck, it was having an effect its owners hadn't thought about. 'You got a fuel leak?' he asked Holbrook, then bent down to look. 'No, your tank's okay.'

'Maybe somebody had a little spill over at the pumps,' the Mountain Man suggested.

'Don't think so. They just hosed it down a while ago. We better find this. I seen a KW burn once 'cuz some mechanic fucked up. Killed the driver, that was on I-40 back in '85. Hell of a mess.' He continued to walk around. 'You got a leak somewhere, ol' buddy. Let's check your fuel pump,' he said next, turning the locks on the hood panels.

'Hey, uh, wait a minute – I mean –'

'Don't sweat it, pard, I know how to fix the things. I save a good five grand a year doing my own work.' The hood went up, and the trucker looked inside, reached to shake a few hoses, then felt the fuel-line connectors. 'Okay, they're all right.' Next he looked at the line to the injectors. One nut was a little loose, but that was just the lock, and he twisted that back in place. There wasn't anything unusual. He bent down again to look underneath. 'Nothin' drippin'. Damn,' he concluded, standing back up. Next he checked the wind. Maybe the smell was coming from ... no. He could smell breakfast cooking in the restaurant, his next stop of the day. The smell was coming from right here ... something else, too, not just diesel, now that he thought about it.

'What's the problem, Coots?' another driver asked, walking over.

'Smell that?' And both men stood there, sniffing the air like woodchucks.

'Somebody got a bad tank?'

'Not that I can see.' The first one looked at Holbrook. 'Look, I don't want to be unneighborly, but I'm an owner-operator, and I get nervous about my rig, y'know? Would you mind moving your truck over there? And I'd have somebody give the engine a look, okay?'

'Hey, sure, no problem, don't mind a bit.' Holbrook remounted his truck, started it, and drove it slowly off, turning to park in a fairly vacant part of the lot. The other two watched him do it.

'The goddamned smell went away, didn't it, Coots?'

'That is a sick truck.'

'Fuck 'im. About time for the news. Come on.' The other driver waved.

'Whoa!' they heard on entering the restaurant. The TV was tuned to CNN. The scene looked like something from the special-effects department of a major studio. Nothing like that ever was real. But this was.

'Colonel, what happened last night?'

'Well, Barry, the enemy came in on us twice. The first time,' Eddington explained, holding a cigar in his extended hand, 'we sat on that ridge back there. The second time, we were advancing, and so were they, and we met right about here ...' The camera turned to show two tanks heading up the road, past where the colonel was giving his lecture.

'I bet those fuckers are fun to drive,' Coots said.

'I bet they're fun to shoot.' The scene changed again. The

reporter's familiar, handsome face was covered with dust, with the bags of exhaustion under his eyes.

'This is Tom Donner, with the press team assigned to the 11th Armored Cavalry Regiment. How can I describe the night we had? I've been riding with this Bradley crew, and our vehicle and the rest of B-Troop have gone through – I don't know how many of the enemy in the past twelve hours. It was *War of the Worlds* in Saudi Arabia last night, and we were the Martians.

'The UIR forces – the ones we faced were a mix of Iraqis and Iranians – fought back, or tried to, but nothing they did . . .'

'Shit, wish they'd've sent my unit,' a highway patrolman said, taking his usual seat for his beginning-of-watch coffee. He'd gotten to know some of the drivers.

'Smoky, you have those in the Ohio Guard?' Coots asked.

'Yeah, my unit's armored cavalry. Those boys from Carolina had a big night. Jesus.' The cop shook his head, and in the mirror noticed a man walking in from the parking lot.

'Enemy forces are in full flight now. You've just had a report from the National Guard force that defeated two complete armored divisions –'

'That many! Wow,' the cop observed, sipping his coffee.

' – the Blackhorse has annihilated another. It was like watching a movie. It was like watching a football game between the NFL and the Pop Warner League.'

'Welcome to the bigs, you bastards,' Coots told the TV screen.

'Hey, is that your cement truck?' the cop asked, turning.

'Yes, sir,' Holbrook answered, stopping on the way to join his friend for breakfast.

'Make sure it don't blow the hell up on you,' Coots said, not turning his head.

'What the hell is a cement truck from Montana doing here?' the cop asked lightly. 'Huh?' he added to Coots.

'He's got some kinda fuel problem. We asked him to move the rig. Thanks, by the way,' he added. 'Don't mean to be unneighborly, buddy.'

'It's all right. I'll have it checked for sure.'

'Why all the way from Montana?' the cop inquired again.

'Well, uh, we bought it there, and bringing it east for our business, y'know?'

'Hmmm.' Attention returned to the TV.

'Yes, they were coming south, and we drove right into them!' a Kuwaiti officer was telling another reporter now. He patted the gun tube of his tank with the affection he might have shown a prize stallion, a little man who'd grown about a foot in the last day or so, along with his country.

'Any word on when we can get back to work, Smoky?' Coots asked the cop.

The highway patrolman shook his head. 'You know as much as I do. When I leave here, I go up to the line to play roadblock some more.'

'Yeah, all that good ticket money you're losin', Smoky Bear!' a driver commented with a chuckle.

'I didn't notice the tags. Why the hell drive a cement truck in from Montana?' Coots wondered. Those guys just didn't fit in.

'Maybe he got it cheap,' the cop thought, finishing his coffee. 'I don't have anything on the sheet about a hot one. Damn, I wonder if anyone ever stole one of those?'

'Not that I heard of – zap!' Coots said. The current shot was of smart bombs. 'At least it can't hurt much.'

'Y'all have a good one,' the cop said on the way out. He entered his Chevy patrol car and headed back to the highway, then decided to give the cement truck a look. Might as well run the tag, he thought. Maybe it *was* hot. Then he smelled it, too, and to the cop it wasn't the diesel . . . ammonia . . . ? It was a smell he'd always associated with ice cream, having once worked a summer in a plant which made it . . . and also with the smell of propellant in his National Guard cavalry unit. His curiosity aroused, he drove back to the cafe. 'Excuse me, gentlemen, is that your truck parked over on the edge?'

'Yeah, why?' Brown asked. 'We do something wrong?'

It was his hands that betrayed him. The cop saw them twitch. Something was definitely not right. 'Would you gentlemen come with me, please?'

'Wait a minute, what's the beef here?'

'No beef. I just want to know what that smell is. Fair enough?'

1258

'We're going to have it looked at.'

'You're going to have it looked at right now, gentlemen.' He gestured. 'If you would, please?'

The cop followed them out, got back into his car, and drove behind them as they walked to the truck. They were talking back and forth. Something just wasn't right. His fellow highway cops were not terribly busy at the moment, and on instinct he called another car for backup, and told his headquarters to run the truck tag. That done, he got out and looked up at the truck again.

'You want to turn it over?'

'Okay, sure.' Brown got in and cranked the engine, which was noisy enough.

'What is going on here?' the cop asked Holbrook. 'Could I see some identification, please?'

'Hey, I don't understand what the beef is.'

'No beef, sir, but I do want to see your ID.'

Pete Holbrook pulled out his wallet as another police car arrived. Brown saw it, too, looked down to see Holbrook's wallet in his hand, and the cop's hand on the butt of his pistol. It was just the way cops stood, but Brown didn't think of that. Neither Mountain Man had a gun handy. They had them in their room, but hadn't thought to carry them to breakfast. The policeman took Pete's driver's license, then walked back to his car, lifting the microphone –

'The tag is clean, not in the computer as hot,' the lady at the station informed him.

'Thank you.' He tossed the mike back inside and walked back to Peter Holbrook, twirling the license in his hand –

Brown saw a cop with his friend, another cop, they'd just talked on the radio –

The highway patrolman looked up in surprise as the truck jerked forward. He yelled and pointed for the man to stop. The second car moved to block him, and then the cement truck did stop. That did it. Something was just not right.

'Out!' he shouted, his pistol in his hands now. The second officer took control of Holbrook, not having a clue what this was all about. Brown stepped down, and felt his collar grabbed and himself thrust against the body of the truck. 'What is the matter with you?' the cop demanded. It would take hours to find out, and then a very interesting time at the truck stop.

There was nothing for him to do but scream, and that, uncharacteristically, he did. The video was undeniable. There was an instant respectability to global TV, and he couldn't stop it from going out. The affluent in his country had their own satellite dishes, and so did many others, including little neighborhood groups. What would he do now? Order them turned off?

'Why aren't they attacking?' Daryaei demanded.

'The Army commander and all corps commanders are off the air. We have some contact with two of our divisions only. One brigade reported it is heading north with enemy forces in pursuit.'

'And?'

'And our forces have been defeated,' Intelligence said.

'*But how?*'

'Does that matter?'

They came on north. Buffalo came on south. UIR III Corps didn't know what lay ahead. The discovery took place in midafternoon. Masterman's 1st Squadron had so far eliminated a hundred or so fuel and other trucks, more than the other two battalions. The only question now was how much resistance the enemy would display. From air coverage, he knew exactly where the advancing force was, in what strength and concentration, and in what direction. It was much easier than the last time he'd seen action.

A-Troop was screening in advance, with B and C three klicks back, and the tank company in reserve. As fearful a pounding as their UIR forces were taking, he decided not to use his own artillery yet. No sense warning them that tanks were close by. With contact less than ten minutes away, he shifted A-Troop to the right. Unlike the first – and only previous – battle in his career, Duke Masterman wouldn't really see this one. Instead, he listened to it on the radio.

A-Troop engaged at extreme range with both gun tubes and TOW missiles, and crumpled the first ragged line of vehicles. The troop commander estimated at least battalion strength as he engaged them from their left-front, approaching obliquely in the planned opening maneuver. This UIR division was Iraqi in origin and recoiled the other way, without realizing that it was being herded right into two more cavalry troops.

'This is GUIDON-SIX. Punch left, say again punch left,' Masterman ordered from his command track. B and C turned to the east, sprinted about three kilometers, then wheeled back. At about the same time, Masterman let his artillery fire into the enemy's second echelon. There was no surprise to lose now, and it was time to hurt the enemy in every possible way. In another few minutes, it was clear that he was engaging at least a brigade with the 1st Squadron of the Buffalo, but the numbers didn't matter any more now than they had during the night.

For one last time, there was a mechanistic horror. The gun flashes were less brilliant in the light of day, and tanks drove through the dust of their own shots as they advanced. As planned, the enemy force recoiled again from the devastating effects of B- and C-Troop, turning back, hoping to find a gap between the first attacking force and the second. What they found were fourteen M1A2s of the squadron's tank company, spaced two hundred meters apart like a breakwater. As before, first the tanks were destroyed, then the mechanized infantry carriers, as GUIDON rolled into the enemy formation. Then it stopped. Vehicles not yet engaged stopped moving. Crews hopped out and ran away from them. It was the same, Masterman heard, all the way west on the line. Surprised, running, their exit blocked, the soldiers lucky enough to see what was rolling toward them in time decided that resistance was surely fatal, and the Third (and last) Battle of KKMC stopped thirty minutes after it had begun.

It wasn't quite that easy for the invaders. Advancing Saudi forces, finally in heavy contact, fought a deliberate battle, grinding their way through another brigade, this one Iranian and therefore getting more attention than an Arab unit might have, but by sunset, all six of the UIR divisions that had entered their country were destroyed. Sub-units with some lingering fight in them were ordered to surrender by senior officers, before enemies on three sides could enforce a more final decision.

The biggest administrative headache, as before, were the

prisoners, all the worse with the additional confusion of nightfall. That problem would last for at least a day, commanders reported. Fortunately, in most cases the UIR soldiers had water and rations of their own. They were moved away from their equipment and placed under guard, but this far from home, there was little danger of their striking across the desert on foot.

Clark and Chavez left the Russian embassy an hour after nightfall. In the back of their car was a large suitcase whose contents would not appear overly dangerous to anyone, and was in fact largely in keeping with their journalistic cover. The mission, they decided, was slightly crazy, but while that troubled the senior member of the team somewhat, it had Ding rather juiced. The premise of it seemed incredible, however, and that had to be verified. The drive to the alley behind the coffee shop was uneventful. The security perimeter around Daryaei's home stopped short of their destination. The coffee shop was closed, what with the blackout conditions imposed on a city half at war and half at peace – streetlights were off, and windows draped, but cars were allowed to drive about with lights, and domestic electricity was evidently on. That worked to their benefit. The door lock was easily defeated in the unlit alley. Chavez eased the door open and looked inside. Clark followed, lugging the case, and both men went inside, closing the door behind them. They were already on the second floor when they heard noises. A family lived here. It turned out to be a husband and wife in their fifties, proprietors of the eating place, watching television. Had the mission been properly planned, he knew, they would have established that sooner. Oh, well.

'Hello,' Clark said quietly. 'Please do not make any noise.'

'What –'

'We will not hurt you,' John said as Ding looked around for – yes, electric cords would do just fine. 'Please lie down on the floor.'

'Who –'

'We will let you go when we leave,' Clark went on in literate Farsi. 'But if you resist, we must hurt you.'

They were too terrified to resist the two men who had appeared like thieves in their home. Clark used the light cords to tie their arms, then their ankles. Chavez laid them on their sides, first getting the woman some water before he gagged her.

'Make sure they can breathe,' Clark said, in English this time. He checked all the knots, pleased that he remembered his basic seamanship skills from thirty years before. Satisfied, they went upstairs.

The truly crazy part was the communications lash-up. Chavez opened the case and started taking things out. The roof of the building was flat, and had a clear line of sight to another such building three blocks away. For that reason, they had to keep low. First of all, Ding set up the mini-dish. The tripod for it was heavy, with spiked feet to secure it to the roof. Next he had to turn it, to get the buzzing chirp of the carrier signal from the proper satellite. That done, he twisted the clamp to lock the dish in place. Then came the camera. This, too, had a tripod. Chavez set that up, screwed the camera in place, and aimed it, switching it on and pointing it at the center of the three buildings that held their interest. Then the cable from the camera went into the transmitter/power-supply box, which they left in the opened suitcase.

'It's running, John.'

The odd part was that they had an up-link, but not a down-link. They could download signals from the satellite, but there wasn't a separate audio channel for them to use. For that they needed additional equipment, which they didn't have.

'There it is,' Robby Jackson reported from the National Military Command Center.

'That's the one,' Mary Pat Foley confirmed, looking at the same picture. She dialed a phone number to the American embassy in Moscow, from there to the Russian Foreign Ministry, from there to the Russian embassy in Tehran, and from there by the digital phone in John's hand. 'Do you hear me, Ivan?' she asked in Russian. 'It's Foleyeva.' It took a very long second for the reply to come through.

'Ah, Maria, how good to hear your voice.' *Thank God for the phone company*, John thought to himself, letting out a long breath. *Even the one here.*

'I have your picture here on my desk,' she said next.
'I was so much younger then.'

'He's in place and everything's cool,' the DDO said.

'Okay.' Jackson lifted another phone. 'It's a go. I repeat, it's a go. Acknowledge.'

'Operation BOOTH is go,' Diggs confirmed from Riyadh.

The Iranian air defense system was about as tense as it could be. Though no attack at all had been launched into their territory, the radar operators were keeping a close eye on things. They watched several aircraft patrolling the Saudi and Qatari coasts, mainly running parallel, not even pushing toward the center of the waterway.

BANDIT-TWO-FIVE-ONE and BANDIT-TWO-FIVE-TWO completed refueling from their tankers within seconds of each other. It wasn't often that Stealth fighters operated in unison. They were, in fact, designed to operate entirely alone. But not this time. Both separated from the KC-10s and turned north for a flight of about one hour, albeit with a thousand feet of vertical separation. The tanker crews remained on station, and used the time to refuel the standing fighter patrol on the Saudi coast, exactly routine for night operations. Fifty miles away, an AWACS tracked everything – or almost. The E-3B couldn't detect an F-117, either.

'We keep meeting like this,' the President said to the makeup woman, with forced good humor.

'You look very tired,' Mary Abbot told him.

'I am pretty tired,' Ryan admitted.

'Your hands are shaking.'

'Lack of sleep.' This was a lie.

Callie Weston was typing alterations to the speech directly into the electronic memory of the TelePrompTer. Even the TV technicians were not allowed to see the content of this one, and in a way she was surprised, that she herself was. She finished, scanning the whole thing for typos, which, she'd learned over the years, could be very disconcerting to Presidents on live TV.

* * *

Some of them were smoking, Clark saw, the guards outside. Poor discipline, but maybe it did serve to keep people awake.

'John, you ever think that this job is maybe just a little too exciting?'

'Gotta take a leak?' It was the usual reaction, even for them.

'Yeah.'

'Me, too.' It was something that never made the James Bond movies. 'Hmph. I didn't know that.' Clark pressed the earpiece in, hearing a normal voice, as opposed to one of a known announcer, say that the President would be on in two minutes. Maybe some network director, he thought. With that, the last two items came out of the suitcase.

'My fellow Americans, I am here to give you an updated report on the situation in the Middle East,' the President said without preamble.

'Approximately four hours ago, organized resistance ceased among the forces of the United Islamic Republic which invaded the Kingdom of Saudi Arabia. Saudi, Kuwaiti, and American forces, working together, have destroyed six divisions in a battle which raged through a night and a day.

'I can now tell you that our country dispatched the 10th and 11th Cavalry regiments, plus the First Brigade of the North Carolina National Guard, and the 366th Wing from Mountain Home Air Force Base in Idaho. A massive battle was fought south of King Khalid Military City. You have already seen some of the details on TV. The final UIR units attempted to flee the battlefield to the north, but they were cut off, and after a brief engagement, they began to surrender. Ground combat in the area has, *for the moment*, concluded.

'I say "for the moment," because this war is unlike any most of us have known in the past fifty years. An attack was made directly upon our citizens, on our soil. It was an attack deliberately made upon civilians. It was an attack made using a weapon of mass destruction. The violations of international law are too numerous to list,' the President went on, 'but it would be wrong to say that this attack was made by the people of the United Islamic Republic upon America.

'*Peoples* do not make war. The decision to start a war is

most often made by one man. They used to be kings, or princes, or barbarian chiefs, but throughout history it's usually one man who decides, and never is the decision to start a war of aggression the result of a democratic process.

'We Americans have no quarrel with the people of the former Iran and Iraq. Their religion may be different from ours, but we are a country which protects freedom of religion. Their languages may be different, but America has welcomed people of many languages. If America has proven anything to the world, it is that all men are the same, and given the same freedom and the same opportunity, they will all prosper to the limit only of their own abilities.

'In the last twenty-four hours, we killed at least ten thousand soldiers of the UIR. Probably many more. We do not know now and probably never will know the total number of *enemy* deaths, and we need to remind ourselves that they did not choose their fates. Those fates were chosen for them by others, and ultimately by one person.' Ryan clasped his hands together theatrically. It seemed a very awkward gesture to all who watched.

'There it goes,' Chavez said, his face to the camera's small eyepiece screen, which was now showing the download from the orbiting satellite. 'Start the music.'

Clark thumbed the laser transmitter, careful to see that it was on the invisible infrared setting. A check through his eyepiece put the dot on the building's cornice – or parapet, he couldn't remember the difference. Whatever, there was a guard standing there, his foot on the structure.

Diggs in Riyadh: 'Final check.'

'BANDIT-TWO-FIVE-ONE,' he heard in reply –

'TWO-FIVE-TWO.'

'Throughout history, kings and princes have made war at their whim, sending people off to die. To the kings, they were just peasants, and the wars were just grabs for power and riches, a kind of entertainment, and if people died, nobody much cared, and when it was all over, for the most part the kings were still kings, whether they won or lost, because they were above it all. All the way into this century, it was assumed that a chief of state had a *right* to make war. At Nuremberg, after the Second World War, we changed that rule by trying and executing some of those responsible. But getting to that point, arresting the criminals, as it were, cost the lives of twenty million Russians, six million Jews, so many lives lost that historians don't even know . . .' Ryan looked up to see Andrea Price wave to him. She didn't smile. It was not a smiling matter. But she gave the signal anyway.

The ground-based laser was only insurance. They could have gone in without it, but picking out exactly the right house in the city would have been difficult, and they wanted to limit collateral damage. This way, also, the aircraft could drop their weapons from higher altitude. Simple ballistics would guarantee a drop to within a hundred yards, and the improved optics systems on the guidance packages cut that figure to one. Exactly on time, both BANDIT aircraft ('Bandit' was the semi-official call sign for the pilots of the Black Jets) opened their bomb-bay doors. Each aircraft carried a single five-hundred-pound weapon, the smallest that could take a PAVEWAY guidance package. These hung from a trapeze while the seeker heads looked for a modulated laser signal. Both acquired the laser dot, and so informed the pilots, who executed the release. Then they both did something neither had ever done before on a Stealth mission.

'BANDIT-TWO-FIVE-ONE, bomb away!'
'TWO-FIVE-TWO, bomb gone!'

'Every idea in the history of man, good or bad, has started in a single human mind, and wars begin because one mind thinks it profitable to kill and steal. This time, it's happened to us in a particularly cruel way. This time, we can be exactly sure who did it – and more.'

Worldwide, in every country with a satellite dish and TV cable, in over a billion homes, the picture changed from the Oval Office of the White House to a three-story building on a city street. Most viewers thought it some mad error, something from a movie, a bad connection –

*   *   *

A handful knew different, even before the President went on. Daryaei, too, was watching the President's speech, as much from pure curiosity as political advantage. What sort of man was this Ryan, really? he'd wondered so long. Too late, he found out.

'This is where he lives, Mahmoud Haji Daryaei, the man who attacked our country with disease, the man who attacked my child, the man who tried to attack me, the man who sent his army on a mission of conquest that turned into a mission of death. He is a man who has defiled his religion and the laws of men and nations, and now, Mr Daryaei, here is the reply of the United States of America.'

The President's voice stopped, and a second or two later, so did translations all over the world, replaced only by silence, as eyes watched an ordinary black-and-white picture of a quite ordinary building – and yet everyone knew that something extraordinary was about to happen. Those looking very closely saw a light go on in a window, and the front door open, but no one would ever know the identity of the person who might have been attempting to leave, because both weapons fell true, struck the roof of the building, and went off a hundredth of a second later.

The noise was awful. The passing pressure wave was worse. Both men watched, ignoring the danger. The echoes were punctuated by the tinkle of glass from half a mile around.

'You okay?' Ding asked.

'Yeah. Time to boogie, partner.'

'Fuckin' A, Mr C.'

They got down to the bedroom level as quickly as possible. Chavez cut most of the way through the cords with a pocket knife. He figured it would take them about five minutes to work themselves free. The alleys allowed them to drive from the area, and keep out of the way of emergency vehicles, which screamed their way to the remains of the three buildings. Half an hour later, they were back in the safety of the Russian embassy. Vodka was offered. Vodka was drunk. Chavez had never experienced so bad a case of the shakes. Clark had. The vodka helped.

* * *

'To the people of the United Islamic Republic, the United States of America says this:

'First, we know the exact location of the germ-warfare factory. We have asked for and received the help of the Russian Federation. They are neutrals in our dispute, but they have knowledge of this type of weapon. A team of technical experts is now on its way to Tehran. They will land, and you will take them immediately to the facility to supervise its neutralization. They will be accompanied by journalists for an independent verification of the facts. If this does not happen, then twelve hours from now we will destroy the site with a low-yield nuclear bomb to be delivered by a Stealth aircraft. Do not make the mistake of thinking that I am unwilling to give that order. The United States of America will not tolerate the existence of that facility and its inhuman weapons. The twelve-hour period starts now.

'Second, your prisoners will be treated in full accordance with international convention, and also the stern and admirable laws of hospitality which are part of your Islamic faith. Your prisoners will be returned as soon as you deliver to the United States the living bodies of every single person who had a role in preparing and delivering those weapons to our country, and those behind the attack on my daughter. On that there will be no compromise.

'Third, we will give your country a week to comply with this requirement. If you do not, then America will declare and wage unlimited war. You have seen what we can do, what we have done. I assure you that, if we have to, we can do more still. The choice is yours to make. Choose wisely.

'Finally, and I say this to all nations who may wish us ill, the United States of America will not tolerate attacks on our country, our possessions, or our citizens. From this day forward, whoever executes or orders such an attack, no matter who you are, no matter where you might hide, no matter how long it may take, we will come for you. I have sworn an oath before God to execute my duties as President. That I will do. To those who wish to be our friends, you will find no more faithful friend than we. To those who would be our enemies, remember that we can be faithful at that, too.

'My fellow Americans, it has been a hard time for us, for some of our allies, and for our enemies as well. We have defeated aggression. We have punished the person most guilty for the cruel deaths in our land, and we will have a reckoning also with those who followed his orders, but for the rest, let us now recall the words of President Abraham Lincoln:

' "With malice toward none; with charity for all; with firmness in the right, as God gives us to see the right, let us strive on to finish the work we are in: to bind up the nation's wounds . . . to do all which may achieve and cherish a just and lasting peace among ourselves, and with all nations."

'Thank you, and good day.'

EPILOGUE

PRESS ROOM

'. . . and finally, I am submitting to the Senate the name of Dr Pierre Alexandre to fill the post of Surgeon General. Dr Alexandre, after a distinguished career in the United States Army Medical Corps, then joined the Johns Hopkins University School of Medicine as an associate professor in the area of infectious disease. He was very helpful to me during the Ebola outbreak. Dr Alexandre is a brilliant clinician and researcher who will initiate and oversee several new programs, including basic research in rare infectious diseases, and will also head up a new federal oversight commission to coordinate AIDS research. This will not be bureaucratic,' the President said, 'there's enough of that. The idea here is to set up a new system by which physicians and other research scientists can more easily exchange research data. It is my hope that the Senate will see quickly to confirmation of his appointment.

'That concludes my opening statement.' Jack pointed. 'Yes, Helen?'

'Mr President, your opening remarks on China –'

'I thought I made that clear. We have had private discussions with the Republic of China and concluded that the restoration of full diplomatic relations is in the best interests of both our countries. It is not the policy of the United States to discourage countries with freely elected governments. The Republic of China is such a country, and merits our full respect and recognition.'

'But what will mainland China think of this?'

'What they think is their affair. We are both sovereign nations. So is Taiwan, and it's time we stopped pretending otherwise.'

'Does this have anything to do with the shoot-down of the airliner?'

'That matter is still under investigation. Next?' Ryan pointed.

'Mr President, the new Iranian provisional government is reportedly seeking to establish full diplomatic relations with our country. Will we entertain that request?'

'Yes, we certainly will,' Jack replied. 'If there's a better way to turn an enemy into a friend than by open discussion and trade, I don't know what it is. They have been very cooperative, and we still have an embassy building there, but I suppose we'll have to change the lock on the front door.' There was general laughter. 'Yes, Tom. Nice tan, by the way. Welcome home.'

'Mr President, thank you. Regarding the destruction of the germ-warfare lab outside Tehran, the only journalists who ever got in there were those two Russians that their embassy drafted for the purpose. How can we be sure –'

'Tom, the Russian experts who supervised the neutralization of the facility were indeed experts. We have video of their procedures from the reporters, and both I and my consultants on this matter are fully satisfied. Ed?'

'Mr President, the prisoner exchange is now concluded. How will we respond to Iranian and Iraqi requests for credit?'

'Secretaries Adler and Winston will be flying to London next week to discuss this with representatives of both governments.'

'Sir, a follow-up, will this mean preferential prices for imported oil, and if so, for how long?'

'Ed, those are subjects for negotiation, but I suppose they will offer us something in return for the credit approval they desire. The exact details will have to be worked out, and we have two very good men to handle that for us.'

'What about good women?' a female reporter asked.

'We have a lot of those around, Denise, including yourself. In case you haven't heard, Special Agent Andrea Price' – POTUS gestured toward the door at his right – 'has accepted a proposal of marriage. It will be a mixed marriage, however, as her fiancé, Inspector Patrick O'Day, is a special agent in the FBI. I wish them the very best, even if it means I may need a new bodyguard. Yes, Barry,' he said, pointing to the senior CNN reporter.

'So the big question that nobody has asked yet today, Mr President –'

Ryan held up his hand. 'There is so much – so many things

yet to be done just to get the government fully functional again after all we've been through –'

'Sir, we're not going to let you off the hook.'

A smile. A sigh. A nod. A surrender. 'The answer to your question, Barry, is, yes, I will.'

'Thank you, Mr President.'

It is now the moment when by common consent we pause to become conscious of our national life and to rejoice in it, to recall what our country has done for each of us, and to ask ourselves what we can do for our country in return.

OLIVER WENDELL HOLMES, JR.

The Hunt for Red October
Tom Clancy

THE RUNAWAY
INTERNATIONAL #1 BESTSELLER

The novel that launched Tom Clancy's phenomenal career and introduced Jack Ryan – the unforgettable story of a spellbinding battle of nerves, above and below the waves, unrivalled in its authenticity and breathtaking suspense.

Silently, beneath the chill Atlantic waters, Russia's ultra-secret missile submarine, the *Red October*, is heading west. The Americans want her. The Russians want her back. With all-out war only seconds away, the superpowers race across the ocean on the most desperate mission of a lifetime. The most incredible chase in history is on . . .

'Absolutely terrific: entertaining, suspenseful and masterfully written . . . superlative.'   *Washington Times*

'Offers an extraordinarily detailed glimpse into the secret world of nuclear submarines, and the potentially deadly cat-and-mouse games played by superpowers beneath the oceans.'   *Sunday Times*

'A snakily plotted, fast-moving blockbuster . . . terrifying tension to the last page.'   *Mail on Sunday*

'Gripping narrative . . . navy buffs and thriller adepts have been mesmerised by the story of Soviet submarine captain Marko Ramius, who seeks to defect to the US, bringing a billion-dollar present with him.'   *Time Magazine*

ISBN 0 00 617276 8

Red Storm Rising
Tom Clancy

The superpowers hurtle towards global conflict, in this chillingly authentic vision of modern warfare from the world's #1 thriller writer.

The Muslim terrorists who destroyed the Soviet Union's largest petro-chemical plant thought they were striking a blow for freedom. What they had done, unknowingly, was fire the first shots in World War III.

Desperately short of oil, the Kremlin hawks see only one way of solving their problem: seize supplies in the Persian Gulf. To do that, they must first neutralize NATO's forces and eliminate their response – and so they develop Red Storm, a dazzling master plan of diplomatic subterfuge and intense re-armament. The battle lines are drawn and Armageddon beckons. . .

'Packed with more nerve-shattering tension than anything in print today . . . gripping, audacious, brilliant storytelling at its very best.' *Washington Times*

'Has the fascination of being on a high-speed train which is about to crash. The description of a submarine patrol racing for the safety of the icepack is as vivid as I ever hope to read.' *Today*

'Frighteningly realistic, chillingly so . . . I dare you to read one chapter and put it down.' *Newsday*

'The supreme exponent of the technothriller.' *Sunday Times*

ISBN 0 00 617362 4

Patriot Games
Tom Clancy

Tom Clancy's acclaimed hero Jack Ryan is hunted by Irish terrorists in this phenomenally successful international #1 bestseller – which became a major Hollywood film.

When Jack Ryan foils an Ulster Liberation Army terrorist attack on the Prince of Wales and his family, his courageous actions not only win him the admiration of an entire nation, they also arouse the enmity and hatred of that nation's most dangerous men.

Now a ULA target himself, Ryan plunges into the murky world of counter-intelligence, where he uncovers a connection between the ULA and an international underground network that places him at the forefront of the deadly battle against international terrorism, and pitches him into the most desperate struggle of his life . . .

'Tom Clancy has done it again! Compelling and spine-tingling, superb . . . highly imaginative, believable and horrifying. He sustains a high pitch of excitement . . . a splendid read.' *Wall Street Journal*

'Fasten your seat belts: Clancy stuffs his story with authentic detail and cranks up the suspense toward unbearable.' *Chicago Tribune*

'Tom Clancy has picked up the fiction mantle where Frederick Forsyth left off . . . the fast action thriller that Clancy fans have come to expect.' *Sunday Times*

ISBN 0 00 617455 8

The Cardinal of the Kremlin
Tom Clancy

'Clancy is the best there is . . . He is a master.'
San Francisco Chronicle

The superpower arms negotiations appear to be making progress. But a US spy-satellite reveals that the Soviets are building a massive laser-defence system controlled from an other-worldly array of pillars and domes near the border of war-torn Afghanistan.

The Americans need more information. The man to give it is Colonel Mikhail Filitov, codename Cardinal, America's highest-placed agent in the Kremlin. But Filitov's cover is about to be betrayed to the KGB and CIA adviser Jack Ryan must rescue Filitov and bring him to safety . . .

Tom Clancy's international bestseller looks to the skies and one of the most remarkable technological competitions of our time – the race to develop 'Star Wars'.

'Has the authentic feel of espionage. A marvellous portrait of Moscow . . . as good as anything in *Gorky Park*. Tom Clancy has written a great spy novel.'
Bob Woodward, *Washington Post*

ISBN 0 00 617454 X

Clear and Present Danger
Tom Clancy

America's secret war against South American drug cartels spirals out of control, in Tom Clancy's highly acclaimed #1 bestseller – which became a major Hollywood film.

Colombian drug lords, tired of being harassed by US law enforcement agents, have assassinated the American Ambassador and the visiting head of the FBI. Their message is clear: leave us alone.

But they have pushed too far. The decision is made to send undercover teams into Colombia. Back in the USA, men armed with the most sophisticated tools their country can devise prepare to take the fight to the enemy. But does anyone know who the real enemy is?

Jack Ryan and CIA field officer John Clark must find the answer. They expect danger from without – yet the greatest danger of all may come from within . . .

'Clancy's most politically sophisticated and philosophically complex thriller.' *Time*

'A jump ahead of the headlines . . . moves with the speed of light.' *New York Times*

'A rousing performance . . . a crackling good yarn.' *Washington Post*

'The excitement is tremendous.' *Sunday Telegraph*

ISBN 0 00 617730 1

The Sum of All Fears
Tom Clancy

THE *SUNDAY TIMES* NO. 1 BESTSELLER

As those in power around the globe face up to the challenges of a new world order, in Washington CIA Deputy Director Jack Ryan is putting everything into his own plan, a plan that could finally bring peace to a Middle East still suffering from the ravages of war.

But too many groups have invested too much blood to allow the plan to succeed – the terrorists have one final, desperate card to play. With one terrible act the world is plunged into nuclear crisis.

His dreams of peace shattered, Jack Ryan is confronted with a situation he has never dared to imagine: with the world standing on the brink of war, what do you do if the President of the USA is incompetent to deal with the greatest crisis of all?

'Another classic Clancy . . . accurate and chilling, his most successful book . . . assures his place at the forefront of modern thriller writers.'   *Sunday Times*

'Clancy's best book since *The Hunt for Red October*. A treasure trove of geopolitical terrors . . . bulges with technological verisimilitude . . . a whiz-bang page-turner.'
                                                    New York Times Book Review

'I was quite entranced . . . Clancy is a brilliant describer of events. I read his lucid exposition with delight.'
                                          PATRICK O'BRIAN, *Washington Post*

ISBN 0 00 647116 1

Without Remorse
Tom Clancy

THE *SUNDAY TIMES* NO. 1 BESTSELLER

It is 1970. Back in the US after serving as a Navy SEAL in
Vietnam, John Kelly meets a woman who will change his
life forever. She has recently escaped from a nightmare
world of unimaginable suffering, yet before they can plan a
future together, the horrors of her past reach out to snatch
her from him. Kelly vows to gain revenge – but finds there
are others who have need of his deadly skills.

In Washington a high-risk operation is being planned to
rescue a key group of prisoners from a POW camp deep
within North Vietnam. Kelly has his own mission; the
Pentagon want him for theirs. As he attempts to juggle the
two, he must step into a netherworld as perilous as any he
has ever known – from which he may never return. . .

'Clancy's latest action thriller is certain to join his unbroken
string of bestsellers . . . a master storyteller.'

New York Times

'Sure to thrill . . . outstanding suspense. Satisfying,
engrossing, chock-full of meticulous knowledge of the
military, war heroics and nail-biting action.'

Boston Herald

'The reader becomes enthralled . . . politically fascinating.
Great fun.'   *Observer*

'Heart-stopping . . . the product of a master.'

Washington Post

ISBN 0 00 647641 4

Debt of Honour
Tom Clancy

It begins with the murder of an American woman in the back streets of Tokyo. It ends in war . . . Tom Clancy's record-breaking international #1 bestseller.

Called out of retirement to serve as the new President's National Security Adviser, Jack Ryan quickly realizes that the problems of peace are fully as complex as those of war. Enemies have become friends, friends enemies, and even the form of conflict has changed. When one of those new enemies readies a strike not only at America's territory, but at the heart of her economy, it is Ryan who must somehow prepare an untested President to meet the challenge. For there is a debt of honour to be paid – and the price will be terrifyingly high . . .

'Spectacular, scary and very thrilling. His sense of cliff-hanging is state of the art . . . breathtaking.'
Los Angeles Times

'Tom Clancy's mammoth new thriller is a convoluted cracker.'
Daily Mail

'With the grip of a born storyteller, Clancy casts a potent spell.'
Guardian

'Another blockbuster.'
The Times

ISBN 0 00 647974 X